Date with the Executioner

By Edward Marston

Date with the Executioner

EDWARD MARSTON

Allison & Busby Limited
12 Fitzroy Mews
London W1T 6DW
allisonandbusby.com

First published in Great Britain by Allison & Busby in 2017.

A CIP catalogue record for this book is available from
the British Library.

First Edition

ISBN 978-0-7490-2110-8

Typeset in 11/16.25 pt Adobe Garamond Pro by
Allison & Busby Ltd.

The paper used for this Allison & Busby publication
has been produced from trees that have been legally sourced
from well-managed and credibly certified forests.

Printed and bound by
CPI Group (UK) Ltd, Croydon, CR0 4YY

CHAPTER ONE

1816

Putney Heath was the chosen location for a death. At that time of the morning, it was deserted. A breeze was making the grass ripple gently. The two coaches arrived at dawn, emerging out of the shadows into the first light of day. They rolled to a halt on either side of the clearing, hidden from sight by the encircling foliage. There was a sense of secrecy vital to the enterprise. Duels were illegal. Those involved were risking punishment. That was why they'd come so far out of the city. Like Leicester Fields, Chalk Farm and Wimbledon Common, the place was a popular choice. Swords had clashed there many times and pistols had often been discharged in anger. Blood had irrigated the Heath. Deaths had occurred in the questionable name of honour.

Paul Skillen had had misgivings from the start about the issuing of the challenge. He was acting as second to Mark Bowerman, who was so incompetent with a pistol in his hand that he'd come to Paul for lessons in how to shoot straight. Bowerman was a fleshy man in his early forties, blessed with wealth enough to live in comparative luxury for the rest of his days. Yet he was prepared to take part in a duel against an adversary who, even at first glance, held many advantages. Paul had urged his friend to extricate himself somehow from the situation but Bowerman would not hear of it. That would not only smack of cowardice, it would lose him the love and respect of the woman he adored. The duel, he insisted, was over an affair of the heart. Having once fought in a similar contest, Paul understood how he must be feeling. The difference was that Paul was an expert with any weapon, whereas Bowerman was clumsy and inexperienced. What drove the latter on was a passion that blinded him to doubt and danger.

'I'll die sooner than yield her up to *him*,' he vowed.

'That would be a poor advertisement for my skill as an instructor,' said Paul, wryly. 'My chief aim is to keep you alive.'

'You've nothing with which to reproach yourself. Nobody could have taught me so much in so short a period of time.'

'Follow my orders to the letter and you may yet survive.'

'I'll do more than that,' said Bowerman with a surge of bravado. 'I mean to kill him for his insolence.'

He glared across at his opponent. Stephen Hamer was a tall, lithe, handsome man of thirty with impeccable attire and an air of supreme confidence. Paul could see that he was extremely fit. The man was at once relaxed yet eager for action. After glancing at Bowerman, he whispered something to his second then sent him across to his opponent.

'He's coming to ruffle your feathers,' warned Paul.

'Then he's wasting his time,' said Bowerman.

'Hold your tongue and let me give him his answer.'

'I'll do my own talking, if you don't mind, Mr Skillen.'

When the second reached them, he gave a polite nod of greeting. He was a thickset man in his late thirties, well dressed and well spoken.

'Good morning to you both,' he said, politely. 'We had not expected you to turn up, Mr Bowerman, so you deserve congratulations, if only for that. We all know that this is an unequal contest. During his time in the army, Captain Hamer won several shooting contests and more than one duel. He bade me tell you that he has no wish to kill you and offers you the opportunity to withdraw before your fate is sealed.'

'Never!' cried Bowerman.

'You would, of course, have to render an abject apology and give your word as a gentleman that you'll cease to bother the lady forthwith.'

'Miss Somerville is *mine*. I'm here to defend her from that vile rogue.'

'Is that the message I am to carry back with me?'

'It is,' said Paul, stepping in to get rid of the man before Bowerman lost the remains of his self-control. 'Away with you, sir, and take your insults with you.'

With a gracious smile, the man turned on his heel and went quickly away.

'Ignore him, Mr Bowerman,' said Paul. 'He was sent to vex you.'

'Hamer will be made to pay for that.'

'It's essential that you remain calm and collected.'

But there was no chance of that. Bowerman was throbbing with fury. Hamer, by contrast, was laughing happily with his second. It was as if the whole event was a joke to them. Paul feared the worst. The information that Hamer was an army man was unsettling. Both of the duellists had taken the precaution of bringing a surgeon with them but it was clear to Paul that it was Bowerman's who would be called upon.

When the light had improved enough, the preliminaries began. The referee, a short, squat man with a rasping voice, called the combatants to order. It was too late to turn back now. Bowerman seemed to realise at last the scale of his task.

'If, so be it, there *is* a mishap,' he said, grabbing Paul by the wrist, 'I beg of you to tell the lady that I showed courage.'

'You have my word, sir, though I hope such tidings will be unnecessary. In your own interests, I urge you to put Miss

Somerville out of your mind. The only person who matters to you at this moment is the one intending to shoot you.'

The advice helped to steel Bowerman. Pulling himself to his full height, he marched bravely towards the referee. The rules of the contest were recited, the box opened and the duelling pistols revealed. Hamer indicated that his opponent should have first choice of weapon. After dithering for a moment, Bowerman snatched up a pistol. Paul watched helplessly from the sidelines. Beside him, his valise already wide open, the surgeon was poised to run to Bowerman's assistance. Neither of them gave him an earthly chance of winning the duel because he was up against a proven marksman. They were being forced to witness an execution.

At the referee's command, the two men stood back to back then walked the requisite number of paces before turning and raising their pistols. Paul closed his eyes and waited for the gunfire. Instead, he heard loud, warning yells and the sound of many feet. Over a dozen men had suddenly materialised out of the bushes to interrupt the duel and to arrest everyone present. Paul recognised the man in command of them instantly. It was Micah Yeomans, a big, hulking man with unsightly features and gesticulating hands. The Bow Street Runner was in his element, enforcing the law by stopping the duel at the crucial moment and relishing the fact that he'd caught one of his sworn enemies. As the duellists were relieved of their pistols, Yeoman ambled across to Paul and grinned malevolently.

'Good morning,' he said, gloating. 'I've got you at long last. Am I talking to Mr Peter Skillen or to Mr Paul Skillen?'

Paul beamed at him. 'Why not hazard a guess?'

CHAPTER TWO

When the news came, they were in the shooting gallery. Gully Ackford, the big, broad-shouldered former soldier who owned the place, had just finished teaching someone the rudiments of boxing. Peter Skillen, as tall, lean and well-favoured as his twin brother, had spent two hours giving fencing lessons. Both men were glad of a respite. It was, however, short-lived. Their leisure was interrupted by Jem Huckvale, who flung open the door and darted into the room.

'You'll never guess what's happened,' he said, breathlessly.

'I'm afraid that I will,' said Peter with a sigh. 'My brother took his impulsive client to Putney Heath and is bringing his corpse back to the city.'

'You're quite wrong.'

'Are you telling me that Mr Bowerman actually *won* the duel?'

'It never took place,' said Huckvale.

'Why not?' asked Ackford. 'Bowerman would not have run away from the contest. There was far too much at stake for that. Did his opponent fail to appear?'

'They both turned up and, according to Paul, the duel was about to start when they were interrupted by Micah Yeomans and his men. Everyone was arrested and taken off to face the chief magistrate.'

Peter and Ackford were startled by the information. The

diminutive Huckvale enjoyed his brief moment as the bearer of important tidings. As a young assistant at the gallery, his life consisted largely of doing chores and running errands. It was good to be the centre of attention for once.

'How did you come by this news, Jem?' asked Peter.

'I chanced to meet one of the Runners, Chevy Ruddock. He was there when they jumped out of the bushes on Putney Heath. Ruddock was crowing about the fact that Paul was dragged back in handcuffs. So I ran straight to Bow Street to find out the details.'

'What did you learn?'

'All that there was to learn,' replied Huckvale. 'The parties involved in the duel were bound over in the sum of four hundred pounds each and a figure of half that amount has been set on those in attendance – including Paul.'

'I'll get over there and bail my brother,' decided Peter. 'He'll have moaned about the handcuffs but this might be the best possible outcome. Intervention by the Runners has saved Mr Bowerman's life. In Paul's opinion, the poor fellow was about to commit suicide.'

'Then he's been very lucky,' said Ackford. 'He's been given the chance to repent of his folly in issuing such a bold challenge.'

'I just hope that he'll seize that chance, Gully, but I harbour grave doubts. Mr Bowerman is in the grip of an obsessive love that shields him from any acquaintance with reality. So deep is his devotion to the person in question that he'll take on any rivals for her affections.'

'Only a remarkable creature could inspire such feelings.'

'Mr Bowerman described her as a jewel among women.'

'Is he an authority on the fairer sex?'

'Far from it,' said Peter. 'The only member of it he's really known is the wife to whom he was happily married. Her untimely death devastated him. He was still mourning her when Miss Laetitia Somerville came on the scene. Mr Bowerman told Paul that she'd resuscitated him.'

'Is the lady aware that he was about to fight a duel?'

'Oh, no – she'd have been horrified.'

'I don't blame her,' said Huckvale.

'What's the point of being given a new life if he's ready to throw it away so recklessly? Some women,' Peter went on, 'might be excited at the thought of two men fighting over them but, I suspect, Miss Somerville is not one of them. That is why Mr Bowerman and his adversary went to some lengths to conceal the truth from her.' He moved to the door. 'But I must be off. Paul will be chafing at the bit.'

After a flurry of farewells, Peter let himself out. Ackford turned to Huckvale.

'There's something you didn't tell us, Jem.'

'Is there?'

'The duel was a closely guarded secret. Only a handful of us knew of it.'

'That's true.'

'Then, how on earth did the Runners catch wind of the event?'

Huckvale gulped. 'I forgot to ask that.'

It was a question that still vexed Paul Skillen and Mark Bowerman. Awaiting their release, they were alone in a private room at the Bow Street Magistrates' Court. The handcuffs had been removed and Paul was rubbing his sore wrists.

'This is Hamer's work,' said Bowerman, sourly.

'I think not.'

'Fearing that I'd kill or wound him, he made sure the duel was stopped.'

'Whatever else you can accuse him of,' argued Paul, 'it is not cowardice. When you issued your challenge, it was promptly accepted and Captain Hamer made no attempt to withdraw. He was incensed when the Runners appeared out of nowhere this morning.'

'So was I, Mr Skillen.'

'It was not in his interests to halt the duel.'

'Yes, it was. His nerve failed him at the last moment.'

'That was patently not the case. The Runners were in hiding before we even got there. They had advance notice of time and place. Hamer must be absolved of complicity. He was not responsible in any way.'

'Why are you taking *his* part?' protested Bowerman. 'You are *my* second.'

'I am, indeed, and my prime commitment is to you. That is why I view the interruption – annoying as it was in some respects – as an unexpected bonus.'

'Bonus!'

'You are still alive, sir. For that, I am eternally grateful.'

'I was prepared to surrender my life.'

'You've been spared that unwise gesture,' said Paul. 'The sensible thing is for you and Captain Hamer to settle your differences with a handshake, then each of you can go his separate way.'

'Am I hearing you aright?' asked Bowerman, spluttering. 'You're counselling me to forget that Stephen Hamer has designs on the woman I love? That's shameful advice, Mr Skillen, and I reject it forthwith. The issue is quite simple. One duel has been prevented. Another must be arranged.' His eyes blazed. 'You'll understand why I'll employ a different second next time.'

'That's your privilege, sir.'

'I need someone who knows what it is to risk *everything* for a woman.'

'Oh, I've been in that position, I do assure you, and I found true happiness as a result. But that's an irrelevance. Consider this, Mr Bowerman,' he added, solemnly. 'What will Miss Somerville think when she hears that you came perilously close to sacrificing yourself on her behalf?'

'I hope that she will think well of me.'

'The lady would prefer you to be alive. You're no use whatsoever to her when you're dead.'

Bowerman smiled fondly. 'That is where you are mistaken.'

'What do you mean?'

'It's none of your business, Mr Skillen.'

Before Paul could question him, there was a tap on the door and it opened to admit his brother. Bowerman had met Peter at the gallery but he still marvelled at the uncanny likeness between the twins. He kept looking from one to the other.

'Good day to you, sir,' said Peter. 'I'm sorry to find you in such unhappy circumstances.'

'They are only temporary, Mr Skillen,' said Bowerman, airily. 'I will be out of here in no time at all.'

'My brother can leave immediately. I've arranged for his bail.'

'Thank you,' said Paul.

'This whole affair can now be forgotten, I hope.'

'Then you hope in vain, I fear.'

'You do, indeed,' said Bowerman, thrusting out a defiant chin. 'I will never let the matter rest until I have killed Stephen Hamer and rescued a dear lady from his unwanted attentions. Mark my words, gentlemen, I am resolved to see this dispute through to the bitter end. It can only be terminated by a death.'

After what they saw as a minor triumph, the Runners adjourned to the Peacock Inn, their unofficial headquarters. Micah Yeomans was soon quaffing a celebratory pint with Alfred Hale, his closest friend. After years of humiliation at the hands of the Skillen brothers, they were delighted to have got their revenge on one of them.

'He didn't like being handcuffed,' said Hale. 'Nobody else was.'

'I reserved that treat for Paul Skillen.'

'He was only the second.'

'I don't care if he was a casual bystander, Alfred. I wasn't going to miss the chance to make him suffer. He was at the site of an illegal duel.'

'I'd have been inclined to let it go ahead.'

'We have to enforce the law, Alfred.'

'We haven't always done so,' Hale reminded him, 'especially where we've been paid to look the other way. Everyone knows that duelling is a tradition among the nobs. It wasn't all that long ago that Viscount Castlereagh, our esteemed foreign secretary, fought a duel against Mr Canning, who is now in the same Cabinet. Would you have dared to interrupt that?'

'No,' admitted Yeomans, 'I'd have had more sense than to interfere. I fancy that Mr Canning still rues the day it happened. All that the foreign secretary lost was a button from his coat whereas Mr Canning was wounded in the thigh.'

'So why do we ignore *some* duels and prevent others from taking place?'

'The chief magistrate had a letter imploring him to take action. That's why we were dispatched to Putney Heath before dawn. And the effort was well worth it,' said Yeomans, chuckling. 'Paul Skillen fell into our hands.'

They clinked their tankards then drank deep.

A solid individual of medium height, Hale was dwarfed by his companion. Yeomans was not only a man of daunting bulk, he'd acquired strong muscles during his years as a blacksmith. The few criminals brave enough to tackle him were still licking their wounds. As the leading Bow Street Runners, they had built up a fearsome reputation in the capital. What irked them more than anything else was that it was overshadowed all too often by the achievements of Peter and Paul Skillen.

'It's a pity we didn't catch the *two* of them today,' said Yeomans, punching his chest with a fist before releasing a belch. 'I'd have found an excuse to keep them behind bars for a whole night. That would have brought them to heel.'

'It might have done the opposite,' said Hale.

'*We* are charged with policing London, not them. We have the legal right and the proper experience. The Skillen brothers have neither of those things.'

'Yet they do have an amazing record of success, Micah.'

'They've been lucky, that's all.'

'And clever, let's be honest.'

'Paul Skillen won't be feeling very clever after being arrested today. We taught him a lesson,' said Yeomans, complacently. 'As a result, he and that odious brother of his will steer well clear of us. From now on, we won't even get a glimpse of them.'

When the gardener arrived early that morning, he sensed that something was wrong. Though nothing was visible to the naked eye, his curiosity was aroused. He began a systematic search of the whole area, looking at flower beds, shrubs, bushes and trees, and even peering behind the statuary. His instinct was finally rewarded when he reached the arbour. Seated on the wooden bench was a stranger, a gentleman of middle years, apparently asleep. His hat lay on the ground as if tossed there uncaringly. The gardener cleared his throat noisily but it produced no reaction at all. Trying to wake him up, he shook the man vigorously but all that he succeeded in doing was to make him roll off the bench completely. Only then did the dagger embedded in his back come into view. It was surrounded by a large bloodstain.

Mark Bowerman had warned that the dispute could only be resolved by a death. His words had been prophetic.

CHAPTER THREE

Eldon Kirkwood was a small man who wielded a large amount of power. As the chief magistrate at Bow Street, he was an expert on the nature and extent of crime in London. Those who cowered before him in court braced themselves for the tartness of his strictures and the severity of his punishments. He could be neither bribed nor deceived. Anyone who tried to intimidate him got especially short shrift; Kirkwood used the extremity of the law to pound them into submission. Yet it was not only the criminal fraternity who feared him. The Runners were equally afraid of the peppery magistrate. When his summons reached Micah Yeomans, therefore, he responded at once and took Alfred Hale speedily along to Bow Street. Still panting from the race to get there, the two men stood before his desk to await orders.

'Foul murder has been committed,' he told them.

'That's nothing new,' muttered Hale.

'Be quiet!'

'Yes, sir.'

'Don't speak until you have something worthwhile to say.'

'No, sir.'

'And the same goes for you,' said Kirkwood, flicking his gaze to Yeomans. 'I have important details to impart. Listen to them very carefully.'

'We will, sir,' said Yeomans.

The chief magistrate was crisp and concise. He explained that the murder victim had been found in the garden of someone else's house. A dagger had pierced his heart. The name of the dead man was Mark Bowerman.

'We arrested him only yesterday,' said Hale.

'You also arrested the person he was about to face in a duel, one Stephen Hamer. He must be your prime suspect. Unable to kill his enemy on Putney Heath, he obviously resorted to another method of attack. Captain Hamer needs to be arrested and interrogated.' He held out a sheet of paper. 'Thanks to the fact that he came before me yesterday, we have his address. Hunt him down.'

'We'll do so immediately,' said Yeomans, taking the paper from him.

'What if it's not him, sir?' asked Hale.

'Then it will be someone set on by him,' insisted Kirkwood, 'and that makes him culpable of homicide. It's as plain as the nose on your face, Hale. By some means or other, Hamer was determined to murder Bowerman. Instead of being shot in the chest, the victim was stabbed in the back.'

'I agree with your deductions, sir,' said Yeomans, obsequiously. 'It has to be Hamer. He was furious when we robbed him of the chance to shoot Mr Bowerman in that duel. It took two men to hold him.'

'I was one of them,' said Hale. 'He's a strong man.'

Yeomans straightened his back. 'I'm stronger.'

'There's no question about that, Micah.'

'Use that strength of yours to overpower the fellow and bring him to justice,' said Kirkwood. 'We must act swiftly before he has the chance to go to ground.'

'Leave it to us, sir,' said Yeomans, leading Hale out.

'I'm right behind you, Micah,' said the other, trotting after him.

As soon as they got outside, they paused to exchange a few unflattering remarks about Kirkwood. Much as they loathed him, they had to respect his authority. They were grateful to be given the opportunity to impress him for once. No difficulties could be foreseen by Yeomans. The main suspect in a murder case had just been served up to them on a plate.

'I wish that all crimes were so easily solved,' he said, airily. 'It would make our job a lot less problematical. The beauty of this one is that we won't have the Skillen brothers getting under our feet.'

'That's true.'

'They'll see what *real* policing can achieve.'

'Suppose they get to hear what's afoot?'

Yeomans was dismissive. 'There's no chance of that happening,' he said, curling a lip. 'We'll have Captain Hamer in custody before word even reaches them that Mr Bowerman is dead.'

It was a hollow boast. Peter and Paul Skillen had already been told of the murder and were hearing the salient details. Seated in the back room at the shooting gallery, they listened intently to Silas Roe, the victim's butler. Deeply upset by the fate of his master, Roe was on the verge of tears throughout. He was a gaunt, grey-haired old man who'd been with Bowerman for many years and been fiercely loyal to him and to his late wife. Holding his hat in both hands, Roe bent his head and accepted what he saw as his share of the guilt.

'I should have insisted,' he said, apologetically. 'When the message came yesterday evening, Mr Bowerman was so pleased that he left the house at once. It wouldn't have taken long to send for a carriage but he was too eager to be off. He didn't tell me where he was going but I could guess who'd sent the letter.'

'Was it Miss Somerville, by any chance?' asked Paul.

'It was, sir. The paper had her fragrance. He was at her beck and call.'

'You sound as if you were very unhappy about that.'

'It's not my place to be happy or unhappy, sir. I was there to do anything I was asked and to . . . keep a watchful eye on my master.'

'How did you first hear of the murder?' said Peter.

'The gardener who discovered the body came knocking on our door. He'd found Mr Bowerman's visiting card in his pocket so he ran straight to the house to break the terrible news. It hit me like a thunderbolt, sirs, I don't mind admitting it.'

'What was your master doing in that garden in the first place?'

'That's the mystery, sir. To my knowledge, he'd never been anywhere near that house. As it happens, the property was empty, awaiting the arrival of new tenants. The gardener had been asked to carry out his duties as usual.'

'We'll need to speak to him,' decided Paul.

'I thought you might,' said Roe. 'I got his name and address for you.'

'Who reported the crime?'

'I did, sir. I went to Bow Street in person. That was after I'd been to the garden to verify what had happened, of course. I wouldn't believe that the master was dead until I'd seen proof with my own eyes.'

'Did you search him?' asked Peter.

Roe became defensive. 'I felt it was my duty.'

'That wasn't a criticism. I just wondered if you found the letter that had summoned him there in the first place.'

'It's exactly what I was looking for, sir, but it wasn't there. That was the strange thing. I knew he took it with him because I saw him put it in his pocket. The killer must have removed it.'

'Why would he do that?'

'I don't know.'

'Was anything else missing from Mr Bowerman's pockets?' said Paul.

'No, sir, there wasn't. Nothing else had been touched – including his purse.'

'Theft was not the motive, then.'

'Something else impelled the killer to strike,' said Peter. 'He could have been exacting revenge, for instance, or settling an old score.' He turned to Roe. 'It was very sensible of you to come to us.'

'Mr Bowerman spoke so highly of you,' said the old man, addressing Paul, 'that I felt obliged to come here. He had great faith in you, sir.'

Paul shrugged. 'I'm sorry I wasn't there to protect him.'

'I feel the same. I'll never forgive myself.'

'The obvious suspect is his opponent in the duel,' suggested Peter.

'I agree, sir.'

'I fancy that you're both mistaken there,' said Paul.

'Are we?' said Peter.

'Stephen Hamer had his faults, I daresay, but he's no back-stabber. He was an army man. He'd want the satisfaction of looking Mr Bowerman in the eyes before shooting him.'

'You met the fellow, Paul. I didn't. I accept your judgement.'

'My master said he was a fiend in human form,' said Roe, bitterly.

'That would be going too far,' said Paul. 'What I saw during my brief acquaintance with him was an arrogant dandy who'd brush people brutally aside if they stood between him and his ambitions. Hamer would have welcomed a second duel and ensured that it was decisive.'

'Did you ever meet the man, Mr Roe?' asked Peter.

'No, sir, and I had no wish to do so. What he did to my master was nothing short of torture. It was painful to watch.'

Peter had heard most of the details from his brother. In the wake of his wife's death, Mark Bowerman had largely withdrawn from society. The couple had been childless so he had no other family members living in the house. Fearing that he might turn into a hermit, a friend had invited him to a dinner at which he'd first met a young woman named Laetitia Somerville. In spite of the age gap, there'd been an instant attraction between them. It was not long before Bowerman formed a real attachment to her. He'd confided to Paul that he intended to propose marriage and that she'd already given him indications that she'd willingly accept the offer. Before the relationship could develop to that point, however, another admirer suddenly appeared and – with no encouragement at all from Miss Somerville – began to make overtures towards her. It was too much for Bowerman to bear. Haunted by the prospect that his happiness would be snatched away from him, he'd challenged the interloper to a duel. It was a matter of honour.

Silas Roe added some information that was new to the brothers.

'There were things I kept from Mr Bowerman,' he confided. 'He had enough preying on his mind as it was. So I dealt with the other matters and told the rest of the staff to say nothing to the master.'

'What sort of things are you talking about?' asked Paul.

'It started with trespass. I heard someone walking in the garden at night. I frightened him away but he was back after a few days.

21

This time he pushed a bench into the pond. I kept vigil after that and there was no trouble for a week. Then a trellis was pushed over and flower beds were trampled. I must have dozed off,' said Roe, 'because I didn't hear a sound.'

'They sound like acts of provocation,' said Peter.

'Yes, sir, they were, and Captain Hamer was behind them.'

'Do you have any proof of that?'

'No,' admitted the other, 'but I'll wager anything that it was his doing.'

'It was kind of you to protect your master like that.'

'As it was,' said Paul, 'he didn't need any more provocation. Hamer's arrival was sufficiently aggravating in itself. When he saw how distressed Miss Somerville was by the man's pursuit of her, Mr Bowerman confronted him.'

The brothers were grateful that Roe had come to the gallery. Sad to hear of his master's death, they were at the same time intrigued by the mystery surrounding it. Having been so closely involved with the man, Paul felt that he had a responsibility to look more closely into the circumstances of his murder. He thanked the old man for coming and assured him that he'd take on the investigation. Relieved to hear it, Roe gave him the name of the gardener who had found Bowerman's corpse and the address of the house where he stumbled upon it. The butler then took his leave.

Something puzzled Peter. He scratched his head.

'You never actually met Miss Somerville, did you?'

'No,' replied Paul, 'but I saw her clearly through Mr Bowerman's eyes.'

'They were somewhat blinkered by desire, I suspect.'

'She is, reportedly, a very beautiful woman.'

'That's what interests me,' said Peter, thoughtfully. 'On one side, we have a jaded widower of middle years with – according to you – little physical appeal; on the other, there is a handsome former soldier who could cut a dash in any hostess's ballroom. In every way, the two men are unequal. Why did this fabled beauty favour Mr Bowerman when a much younger suitor was at hand?'

Bond Street was a fashionable promenade for the beau monde, a long strip of exclusive shops known for the quality of their stock and the steepness of their prices. The Runners had no time to stare in the windows or to mingle with the throng. Their destination was a neat double-fronted house in a side street off the main thoroughfare. Stephen Hamer's house suggested money and good taste. Having come with the prospect of arresting a murderer, Yeomans and Hale were dismayed to discover that Hamer was not only absent but that, according to the servant who answered the door, he had spent the night in St Albans. Since he was due back later that morning, the Runners decided to wait. They were conducted into the butler's pantry and asked to make themselves comfortable.

Hale was worried. 'If he's been away from London all night,' he said, 'he couldn't possibly have carried out the murder.'

'Yes, he could,' said Yeomans. 'To begin with, we only have the word of his servant that he went to St Albans. That could well be an alibi devised by Hamer to throw us off the scent. And even if he *did* go there last night, he could have stabbed Mr Bowerman before he left. I think we're sitting in the home of a killer, Alfred.'

'That's only supposition.'

'It's common sense. He wanted the man dead.'

'Then why bother to go to all the trouble of a duel?'

'It was a more formal way of committing murder.'

'I'm not convinced, Micah.'

'Well, I am and – more to the point – so is the chief magistrate.'

'It won't be the first time we've arrested the wrong man.'

'Rely on my instinct. Has it ever let us down before?'

The truthful answer was that it had but Hale lacked the courage to say so. Yeomans had a scorching temper when roused. It was safer to pretend to agree with him. The other Runner therefore kept his doubts to himself.

'What about the lady in the case?' he asked.

'What about her?'

'She may well be unaware of the murder of Mr Bowerman. I think that she has a right to be told at the earliest opportunity.'

'We'll call on her when we have Captain Hamer in custody.'

'Suppose that he resists arrest?'

Yeomans smirked. 'One punch will take all the fight out of him.'

The wait gave them time to slip out of the pantry and take a peep at the drawing room. It was high-ceilinged, well proportioned and filled with exquisite furniture. What commanded their attention was the portrait of Hamer above the fireplace. Dressed in the uniform of the Royal Horse Guards, he looked proud, haughty and resolute. When they eventually heard the clatter of hooves outside the window, they went quickly back to the pantry. It was not long before Hamer was admitted to the house by his servant. Dressed in his riding attire, he sailed into the room, whip in hand. It was clear that he'd ridden some distance. There was thick dust on his boots and coat, and perspiration on his face. He looked from one to the other with contempt.

'There's no duel to prevent this time,' he said, pointedly.

'We're here on a related matter,' explained Yeomans. 'Sometime yesterday evening, Mr Bowerman was murdered. We have reason to believe that you were responsible for his death.'

'That's a monstrous allegation!'

24

'We must ask you to accompany us, sir.'

'The pair of you can go to the Devil!'

'Now, now,' cautioned Hale, 'respect our position. As Runners, we have a legal right to make an arrest.'

'On what possible evidence are you making it?'

'You had good reason to kill Mr Bowerman,' said Yeomans.

'I had an excellent reason but I would only have considered taking his life in the course of a duel. I'd never shoot him otherwise.'

'He was stabbed to death, sir.'

'There you are, then. Isn't that irrefutable proof that I'm innocent of the charge? I didn't even know *how* he died. Can you really imagine someone like me resorting to a dagger? It's unthinkable. When he challenged me to a duel,' said Hamer, 'I gave him the choice of weapons – pistols or swords. Those are the weapons of a gentleman. Since neither of you will ever aspire to that status in society, you won't understand the rules by which we operate.'

'*Our* rules are much simpler,' said Yeomans, stung by the insult. 'When a crime is committed, we arrest the culprit.'

'Then go off and find him, you oaf.'

'We already *have*, Captain Hamer.'

The Runner glared meaningfully at him. His companion, however, was already wavering. Hamer's indignant denial had the ring of truth. Having arrested many villains in the course of his work, Alfred Hale had seen how they usually reacted. Most of them protested their innocence but few had ever done so with such blazing sincerity. He remembered the portrait above the fireplace. Could such a heroic individual stoop to a callous act of murder? It seemed impossible.

After a long, bruised silence, Hamer mounted his defence. He spoke slowly, as if talking to people of limited intelligence.

'When I left Bow Street yesterday morning,' he explained, 'I came straight back here and made arrangements for my trip to St Albans. I set off just after noon. The person whom I visited will tell you the time of my arrival and the length of my stay with him. I'll happily furnish you with his name and address. Since his family was there at the time, you'll have five other witnesses who will swear that I've been telling you the truth. At what time was Bowerman killed?'

'It was . . . sometime in the evening,' said Yeomans, uncomfortably.

'I have a very long reach,' said Hamer, 'but even my arm is not able to touch London from St Albans. *Where* did the murder take place?'

'It was in the garden of a house near Cavendish Square.'

'I have neither friends nor acquaintances in that part of the city and, hence, no reason whatsoever to visit it. How am I supposed to have gained access to the place?'

'A resourceful man like you would have found a way in.'

'We are now in the realms of complete fantasy,' said Hamer with a sneer. 'Do what you foolishly assume to be your duty, if you must, but remember this: there is such a thing as wrongful arrest. Consequences will follow.'

Yeomans hesitated. Increasingly edgy, Hale turned to his friend.

'What are we going to do now, Micah?' he whispered.

CHAPTER FOUR

As he set off to find the lady in question, Paul Skillen had no clear idea of what to expect. Laetitia Somerville was patently a striking young woman. If she could arouse the affections of men as diverse as Mark Bowerman and Stephen Hamer, he reasoned, she had to be a person of rare qualities. During their time together at the shooting gallery, Bowerman had rhapsodised about her and, crucially, provided Paul with her address in case he was shot to death in the duel against his rival. Judged by its nondescript exterior, the house in Green Street was unremarkable. When he was invited in by a servant, however, he found himself in a dwelling of overwhelming charm and with a pervading air of prosperity. The place was so bright, well appointed and filled with delicate colours that Paul felt embarrassed at being the bearer of bad news. He would be besmirching a miniature paradise.

Shown into the library, he was struck by its faint whiff of perfume and by the number of poetry books on the shelves. He was not alone for long. Laetitia appeared magically in the doorway. Paul was momentarily dumbfounded. Since he lived with Hannah Granville, the most talented actress in London, he was accustomed to being alone with a gorgeous woman, but Laetitia's beauty was of a totally different order than that of his beloved. While Hannah's arresting good looks could enchant a whole audience for hours on end, Paul was now within feet of an altogether more subdued, almost shy, private beauty. Laetitia was small, slim and graceful with a face of elfin loveliness framed by fair hair that hung in ringlets. She had a demure quality entirely lacking in the actress. She was followed into the room by a maidservant acting as a chaperone.

After an exchange of greetings, she waved him to a chair and perched on one directly opposite. Her sweet smile was evidence to Paul of her complete ignorance of the duel and the fate of one of those involved. He chose his words with care.

'I come as a friend of Mr Bowerman,' he began. 'He held you in the highest regard, Miss Somerville.'

'His devotion to me is very flattering.'

'He was distressed to learn that he had a rival suitor.'

'If you are referring to Captain Hamer,' she said, softly, 'then you should know that I would never accept him as a suitor. We were friends in the past but those days are . . . long gone.'

'Yet he boasted to Mr Bowerman that the two of you were intimates.'

Her eyes flashed. 'That was unworthy of him and wholly untrue.'

'It caused great upset.'

'I shall apologise to Mr Bowerman on the captain's behalf.'

'That . . . won't be possible, I fear,' said Paul.

'Why not?' There was a long pause. Her voice now had a tremor. 'I repeat my question, Mr Skillen,' she went on, '*why* will it not be possible?'

'It's . . . difficult to explain.'

'Answer my question, please.'

'Miss Somerville—'

28

'Come, sir. Say what you have to say and don't prevaricate.'

Paul took a deep breath before speaking. 'It's my painful duty to pass on sad tidings,' he said. 'They concern Mr Bowerman.'

She was on her feet at once. 'Has something happened to him?'

'I'm afraid that it has.'

'Then please let me hear what it is. Don't keep me in suspense.'

Paul got up slowly from the chair. 'Yesterday morning,' he said, gently, 'Mr Bowerman took part in a duel with his rival.'

'Heavens!' she exclaimed. 'What madness has seized him? He'd be no match for Captain Hamer.'

'Fortunately, the duel was interrupted by Bow Street Runners.'

'Thank goodness for that! He was rescued from certain death.'

'He met it elsewhere,' said Paul, moving closer to her. 'Sometime during yesterday evening, Mr Bowerman was, it appears, in receipt of a letter ostensibly sent from you.'

'But I never wrote any letter to him. I swear it.'

'Someone did, Miss Somerville, and its contents were such that he left the house at once in his haste to reach you. His body was found early this morning in the garden of a house near Cavendish Square. Mr Bowerman, I regret to tell you, had been stabbed to death.'

'No, no,' she cried, grabbing him by the coat. 'Tell me it's not true.'

'I wish that I could.'

'Mr Bowerman and I were about to be . . .' She shook her head in disbelief. 'He was *murdered*? That dear, kind, considerate man was killed?' Paul nodded. 'Who could *do* such a dreadful thing? The very thought is unbearable.'

Her face had crumpled and her whole body was trembling. After putting a hand to her throat, she swooned. The maidservant cried out in alarm. Paul was quick enough to catch Laetitia before she hit the floor.

* * *

Jack Linnane, the gardener, was a short, stout, round-shouldered man in his fifties with a ragged beard and eyes that were half obscured by bushy eyebrows. He was pulling out weeds when Peter Skillen arrived at the house and let himself in through the unlocked garden gate. Linnane straightened.

'This is private property, sir,' he warned.

'I've not come to trespass. I simply want information.'

Peter introduced himself and explained that he'd been given details of what had happened by Silas Roe, servant to the murder victim. Linnane brightened at once. He was ready to talk to anyone who was determined to solve the crime. The story he told was virtually the same as the one passed on by Roe but there were some new details as well. He'd been gardener there for years. Most of the houses nearby were owned by families who lived there on a permanent basis. This one, Linnane told him, had been occupied by a series of short-term tenants. Whether or not anyone was in residence, he was paid to keep the garden in good condition. After looking around, Peter praised him for his thoroughness.

'Show me where you found the body,' he asked.

'I told you, sir,' said Linnane, pointing a finger, 'it was over there.'

'Show me *exactly* where it was.'

'Why?'

'It may be of help to me.'

Linnane did as he was told, even sitting down on the spot on the bench where he'd found Bowerman. Shielded from the rest of the garden by trellises covered with trailing plants, the arbour was a natural suntrap. Immediately behind the bench was a low privet hedge. When Peter stood behind the seated gardener, he realised how easy it would have been for the killer to put an arm around the victim's neck before thrusting a dagger between the wooden uprights. In the struggle, Bowerman's hat would have been knocked off and landed on the ground where the gardener found it.

'This is a nice spot,' observed Peter.

'Best part of the garden, sir,' said Linnane. 'When I've finished my work for the day, I always sit here and smoke a pipe.' He chuckled. 'It does no harm if I have ten minutes thinking I own the house.'

'Who *does* own it?'

'I don't know, sir. I just do what the agent tells me.'

'You have a key to the garden, obviously.'

'It's all I have. I've never been in the house itself. Everything I need is out here. I can draw water from the well. I keep my tools locked in the outhouse.'

'It's a stout door in a high wall,' said Peter, looking at the gate. 'It would be difficult to get in here without a key. I'll need to speak to the agent to find out how many keyholders there are.'

'Nobody ever touches *my* key,' affirmed Linnane. 'I look after it carefully.'

'And so you should.' Peter glanced up at the house. 'Before I let myself into the garden, I went to the front door. It was securely locked and there was no sign of a broken window. Nobody forced their way into the property.' He turned to the gardener. 'Has anyone else been here to question you?'

'No, sir, they haven't.'

'They will. The Runners will certainly call at some point. When they do, will you pass on a message to them, please?'

'Yes, sir, I'll do so gladly.'

'Tell them that my brother and I are delighted to be working with them again.'

'Is that all, sir?'

'Oh,' said Peter, smiling, 'that will be more than enough.'

* * *

31

After weighing up the possibilities, Yeomans decided that he'd rather face the wrath of the chief magistrate than worry about the threat made by Stephen Hamer. Since he was at least flirting with the possibility that the man might not, after all, be guilty of the murder, he refrained from actually handcuffing him. He simply arrested Hamer and, after delivering a lacerating tirade, the latter agreed to go with them. They rode to Bow Street in the same jolting carriage. Not a word was spoken during the journey. The atmosphere was tense and Hale writhed in discomfort. Accustomed to manhandling dangerous villains, he was virtually paralysed while seated opposite the fuming Stephen Hamer. All three of them went into the chief magistrate's office. In less than ten minutes, one of them came out alone. Those who remained were given a verbal whipping.

'The pair of you are complete idiots!' snarled Kirkwood. 'What on earth possessed you to arrest Captain Hamer?'

'We were only obeying your orders, sir,' said Yeomans.

'The fellow was obviously innocent of the charge.'

'*You* were the one who said that he was guilty, sir,' recalled Hale. 'You told us it was as plain as the nose on my face.'

'I merely said that there was a faint likelihood that he *might* be involved. I was assuming – foolishly, as it transpired – that you and Yeomans would exercise discretion. Clearly, that was beyond your meagre capacities.'

'We're sorry, sir.'

'Didn't you *listen*? Didn't you hear what Hamer said? He has reliable witnesses who place him in St Albans at the time when the victim was murdered.'

'He could still have instigated the crime, sir,' said Yeomans. 'It was a point that *you* made when you sent us off to apprehend him.'

'I was mistaken,' said Kirkwood, 'and I knew it the moment he stepped into this office. He was enraged and rightly so. Didn't you stop to wonder why?'

'Nobody likes to be arrested, sir.'

'We didn't make a forcible arrest, Micah,' Hale reminded him.

'He behaved as if we had.'

'That was not the reason for his fury,' said Kirkwood. 'What upset him was not so much the fact that he was under suspicion. It was because he'd been robbed of the opportunity to kill Bowerman in a second duel. The real target of his ire was the man who wielded that dagger. Captain Hamer's rival may have been removed but *he* was not responsible for his death. That rankles with him.'

'Why didn't he tell us that?' asked Hale.

'You shouldn't have *needed* telling. It was writ large all over him.'

'All *I* saw was a very angry man.'

'Now you mention it, sir,' said Yeomans, hoping to curry favour, 'there was a strange tone to his protests. He behaved as if something very precious had been stolen from him. It was clever of you to identify it.'

'I prefer action to congratulation,' said Kirwood with vehemence. 'I want proof that you have one functioning brain between the two of you. Hamer can be eliminated from the investigation. Find the *real* killer.'

'Yes, sir.'

'Have you visited the scene of the crime?'

'No, sir.'

'Do so immediately.'

'Yes, sir.'

'Question the gardener who found the body.'

'We will, sir.'

'Have you been to Mr Bowerman's house?'

'Not yet, sir.'

'Seek out Roe, the butler. When he reported the crime, he left only the bare details. Ask if his master had any enemies.'

'Yes, sir.'

'What of the lady at the eye of this little hurricane?'

'Are you referring to Miss Somerville, sir?'

'Who else, man? It was she who unwittingly caused the duel to take place.'

'We ought to speak to her, Micah,' said Hale. 'She might not even know that one of her suitors has met a gruesome end.'

'There's one more thing,' Kirkwood told them.

'Yes, sir. We need to have handbills printed.'

'I will take on that task, if only to ensure that it's done properly. You must do something that should already have been done and that's to examine the corpse. Search for clues. That dagger is one of them. It may be distinctive enough to be recognised. If so, a description of the murder weapon could be included in the handbill. Above all else,' said the chief magistrate, raising his voice, 'act with more celerity.'

'We already did that, sir,' confessed Yeomans, 'and we are rightly chastised for doing so. We apprehended Captain Hamer too hastily.'

'That's not why I'm advocating urgency.'

'Isn't it?'

'Mr Bowerman was a wealthy man. There'll be a large reward offered for information leading to the arrest and conviction of his assassin. You both know what happens when money is at stake.'

'Peter and Paul Skillen will come sniffing, sir,' said Hale.

'We'll not be deprived of our lawful prize this time,' vowed Yeomans.

'Then get out there and vindicate your reputations,' said

Kirkwood, opening the door wide. 'Don't come back until you have redeemed yourselves by solving this crime promptly and leaving the Skillen brothers trailing impotently in your wake.'

'Yes, sir,' they said in unison before scuttling through the open door.

Paul Skillen was caught in an awkward situation. As he was lowering Laetitia Somerville gently to the floor, a manservant, alerted by the chaperone's cry of alarm, burst into the room. What he saw was a stranger bending over his employer as if about to molest her. In his eyes, it was a picture that told its story all too clearly. Without hesitation, the servant grabbed Paul and tried to drag him away. Since he was a strong young man, there was a fierce struggle. Paul's explanation of what had happened went unheard. All that the servant wanted to do was to defend Laetitia and overpower a man he thought was her assailant. It took Paul a couple of minutes to shake him off then stun him with a blow to the jaw. By that time, Laetitia's eyelids were starting to flutter.

'What happened?' she murmured.

'I brought some dire news, I fear,' said Paul.

She saw the manservant. 'What are *you* doing here, Robin?'

'Misconstruing what occurred, he bravely came to your assistance. I'd be grateful if you'd tell him I did not assault you in any way.'

'No, no, of course you didn't. Stand off,' she told the man as he moved forward to grapple with Paul once more. 'Mr Skillen was no threat to me. He kindly brought me tidings he felt I had a right to know. That was why I collapsed. The shock was too much for me.' She tried to move. 'Could you help me up, please?'

Paul and the manservant lifted her carefully to her feet. Robin was anxious.

'Would you like me to call a doctor?' he asked.

'No, no, there's no need for that. Thank you, Robin,' she said, dismissively. 'You may go now. It's quite safe to leave me.'

'Call me, if you need me.'

Staring resentfully at Paul, he rubbed his chin as he backed out of the room.

'I remember it all now,' said Laetitia, sitting down. 'You told me that Mr Bowerman had been ready to fight a duel with Captain Hamer but that it was interrupted. Later that evening . . .'

Her eyes moistened and she bit her lip. When Paul tried to put a consoling arm around her, she raised her palms and he backed away. He could see the anguish distorting her features. Eventually, she regained her composure.

'What must you think of us?' she said, apologetically. 'You come here out of the goodness of your heart and what happens? I collapse at your feet and my servant starts beating you. By any standards, that's poor hospitality.'

'What happened is understandable, Miss Somerville.'

'I think you deserve an explanation.'

'Are you sure that I'm not intruding?'

'No, no, not at all – do sit down again, please.'

'Thank you,' he said, lowering himself onto a chair beside her.

Laetitia needed a few moments to gather her thoughts. Paul waited patiently until she was ready. Her voice was heavy with grief.

'Mr Bowerman and I had become close friends,' she said, measuring her words. 'I'm sure that he has told you what aroused his interest in me. It's only fair that you should look at the attachment from my side as well. Beauty is both a blessing and a curse, Mr Skillen. It is pleasing to look at in a mirror but it can excite the wrong feelings altogether in others. Suffice it to say that I have had far too many self-proclaimed admirers nursing improper thoughts about me. Such treatment makes one wary and not a little cynical.'

'I know someone in the identical predicament,' said Paul, thinking of Hannah. 'Being pursued by over-amorous gentlemen is a constant problem.'

'That is what set Mark . . . Mr Bowerman, that is, apart from the pack. He didn't try to harass, trick or entrap me. He offered me true love and devotion. It was wonderfully refreshing. I'd never met anyone so considerate and undemanding.'

'I formed the same view of Mr Bowerman.'

'The more I got to know him, the closer I was drawn to him. Yes, he was somewhat older than me but that meant he had wisdom and maturity. They are qualities I greatly appreciate. When he touched very lightly on the possibility of a betrothal, I was thrilled by the notion. It was only a matter of time before he'd have found the words and the courage to seek my hand.' Her body sagged. 'It will never happen now.'

'You meant everything to him, Miss Somerville.'

'I like to think so.'

'I am quoting his exact words.'

After nodding her thanks, she took out a handkerchief and dabbed at her eyes. Since she seemed to have got over the immediate shock of Bowerman's murder, Paul probed for information about his rival.

'You said earlier that Captain Hamer had been a friend in the past.'

'He was more of an acquaintance, really,' she said, evasively, 'but he did engage my interest at first, I must admit. He was handsome and daring and had fought in the Peninsular War. Any woman would be impressed by that.'

'You've no need to justify it.'

'He pursued me for some time, then he . . . disappeared. Soon after that, I was introduced to Mr Bowerman and the captain faded in my memory. Then, out of the blue, he appeared on my doorstep and declared his love. I did my best to send him on his way but he was very persistent.'

'That's why Mr Bowerman challenged him to a duel.'

'It's the *last* thing he should have done,' she wailed.

'What will happen if Captain Hamer comes calling again?'

She was decisive. 'He'll find my door slammed shut in his face.'

After plying her with more questions, Paul rose to leave.

'One last thing,' he said, casually. 'You mentioned that he fought in the Peninsular War.'

'That's right. Captain Hamer was in the Royal Horse Guards. He was immensely proud of the fact that he saw action at the battle of Fuentes de Oñoro. He boasted about it every time he gave me one of the souvenirs he'd brought back from the war.'

CHAPTER FIVE

The friendship between Charlotte Skillen and Hannah Granville was an example of the attraction of opposites. When she first saw the actress onstage, Charlotte had been dazzled by her histrionic skills. A career in the theatre was something she could never have aspired to herself because she had neither the talent nor the temperament. Nor could she ever have entered into the liaison outside marriage that Hannah enjoyed with Paul. Though she'd worried about it at first, Charlotte had come to accept that her brother-in-law had the right to live the kind of life he chose and, if it involved cohabitation with a famous actress, then he should be supported rather than condemned. Her husband, Peter, took the same view.

Though they had little in common, the two women got on extremely well together. Both were attractive, intelligent and in their late twenties but there the similarity ended. While Charlotte was reserved and thoroughly respectable, Hannah had the surface hardness necessary in such a competitive profession. She was loud, exhibitionist and volatile, having none of her friend's equanimity. Whenever she visited the house, she was struck by its atmosphere of calm.

'I love coming here, Charlotte,' she said with an extravagant gesture. 'It's a haven of peace in a war-torn world.'

'Thankfully, hostilities against the French have ceased.'

'I was speaking of the daily battles I have to fight to get my way.'

'Is the theatre quite such a contest of strength?'

'It is when rehearsals are going badly,' replied Hannah, 'and they reached their nadir today. That is why I flounced out and sought your company. You are so consoling, Charlotte. I love Paul to distraction but, when I most need his support, he becomes argumentative. Peter is an altogether more placid individual. Be grateful that you are not married to his brother.'

Charlotte suppressed a smile. There had, in fact, been a time when Peter and Paul had both sought her hand in marriage and she had been forced to choose between them. She had never for a moment regretted her decision. Even though he could never bring the same wild excitement as his brother, Peter offered a stability that was more suited to Charlotte's needs and personality. She was relieved that Paul had never told Hannah about his earlier pursuit of her. It might well have compromised the warm relationship she now shared with the actress.

'What is the problem with the play?' she asked.

Hannah groaned. 'If I gave you chapter and verse,' she said, 'we'd be here until Doomsday. It's all so lowering.'

'Are you rehearsing a tragedy or a comedy?'

'You may well ask, Charlotte.'

'What is its title?'

'*The Piccadilly Opera.*'

'There will be music and singing, then.'

'Very little of either,' said Hannah with disgust. 'It's an opera with no arias, a tragedy with no suffering and a comedy without the slightest hint of true wit.'

'Heavens!'

'It's exasperating.'

'Who wrote this perverse play?'

'Ah!' cried Hannah with a harsh laugh. 'There you have it. His accursed name is Abel Mundy and he shouldn't be allowed within a hundred miles of a public stage. The man is an abomination. He is the kind of playwright I detest most.'

'And what kind is that?'

'A *live* one.'

They were seated in the drawing room. While Charlotte remained in her chair, however, Hannah felt the need to rise to her feet from time to time in order to express herself with more force. Charlotte was happy for her to do so. She was relishing a performance for which most people would have to pay.

'Give me a dead author before all else,' said Hannah, warming to her theme. 'His plays will have survived the test of time and have proven merit. Shakespeare is a case in point. An actor himself, he knew what actors needed. He gave them roles that stretched them to the limit of their art. And there are many others whose contribution to the annals of drama I value greatly. Their chief appeal, however, is that they are no longer alive to *interfere*. Abel Mundy, alas, does nothing else.'

'Why, then, did you agree to take part in *The Piccadilly Opera*?'

'It was the biggest mistake of my career.'

'Did you not see the play in advance?'

'I was merely given a description of it by the playwright and – since he was so pleasant and plausible at our first meeting – I placed my trust in him. There were, of course, temptations offered by the manager. One was financial but that was the least of my considerations. What persuaded me to accept the role was the promise that I could choose the next three plays in which I was to appear. Needless to say,' she went on, 'the first was *Macbeth*.'

'Your performance of Lady Macbeth was well received in Paris. What other English actress could play the part in French, as you did?'

'It's impossible to name one, Charlotte. But you see my dilemma. I go from the heights of *Macbeth* to the depths of *The Piccadilly Opera.*'

'Is there no way to withdraw from the play?'

'Not without a financial penalty and severe damage to my reputation. The truth of the matter is that I bought a pig in a poke.'

'What, then, is the solution?'

'I came here in the hope that *you* could tell me that. Your advice is always so sensible. I've come to a dangerous point in my career, Charlotte,' said Hannah, one hand on her heart. 'Do I revoke my contract altogether or do I grit my teeth and risk derision in this theatrical catastrophe?'

Peter Skillen moved to the window so that he could examine the dagger in the best light. It was a long, narrow-bladed weapon and, now that the blood had been wiped from it, it was glinting.

'It was made in Toledo,' he said.

'How do you know?' asked his companion.

'Toledo steel is the finest in the world. That was known as long ago as Roman times. Their armies chose Toledo blades above any other. As it happens,' Peter went on, 'I once had a rather memorable encounter with a dagger just like this.'

'Really?'

They were in the room in the morgue where the body of Mark Bowerman lay on a slab. Peter had only glanced at the corpse when the shroud was pulled back. He was less interested in the victim's wound than in the weapon used to kill him. He could feel its perfect balance. The stringy old man beside him was one of the coroner's assistants, charged with cleaning and preparing the cadavers for burial. Sensing a story, he pressed for details.

'Are you telling me that someone tried to kill you with a Toledo dagger?'

'He tried and he almost succeeded, my friend.'

'When was this?'

'It was during the war with France,' explained Peter. 'My work often took me to Paris and, on one occasion, someone decided to make it my last possible visit there. Fortunately, I'd been warned of his intentions. When he tried to strike, I was ready for him.'

'A weapon like that could cut you to shreds.'

'It most certainly could.'

'How did you escape, Mr Skillen?'

'I didn't elude the dagger completely,' admitted Peter, indicating his shoulder. 'I still carry a vivid memento of it. As to the circumstances, I'm not able to recount them. I'm just grateful to be alive.'

It had not been Peter's only brush with death. Because he spoke French fluently, he'd been employed as a spy during the war and made frequent trips to the French capital. It was a hazardous period of his life and, though it had been quite exhilarating, he was relieved when it was all over. At the same time, he liked to think that he'd made a small but useful contribution to the war effort. The scar on his shoulder was a stark reminder of the days when he'd been in almost continuous jeopardy. Conscious of the agonies Charlotte had endured while he was away, he had been even more attentive to her since his return.

After turning the dagger over in his hand, he handed it back to the assistant.

'The one consolation, I suppose, is that death would have been almost instantaneous,' he said. 'Mr Bowerman would not have suffered.'

'It's his wife and family who'll do the suffering, sir.'

'Mrs Bowerman died some years ago. They had no children.'

'There'll still be relatives to mourn him.'

'I'm sure there will be.' Peter looked at the dagger once more. 'It's curious, isn't it?'

'I've never seen a weapon quite like it, sir.'

'That's what puzzles me. It's so individual. You'd have thought the owner would prize it. Instead of that, he left it buried in someone's back. Most killers would have taken it away so that it could be used again,' said Peter. 'In this case, however, it was deliberately left behind. I'm intrigued to find out why.'

When she left the house in a hackney carriage, Hannah was grateful that she'd sought advice about the quandary in which she found herself. While she had not been able to solve the actress's problem, Charlotte had managed to soothe her and offer much-needed sympathy. Having arrived there in a state of outrage, Hannah departed in a far more tranquil frame of mind. Paul Skillen had brought many wonderful things into her life and his sister-in-law was amongst the best of them. Charlotte could do what Paul himself could not and that was to view a situation coolly and dispassionately. Unlike Hannah, she would never act on impulse. The actress was unable to emulate her because she was the slave of an ungovernable spontaneity. It was one of the qualities that had first attracted Paul to her.

Should she honour her contract or refuse to perform in a play she felt so unworthy of her? There was no simple answer. Taking part in *The Piccadilly Opera* might well be injurious to the reputation she'd so assiduously built up, yet turning her back on a commitment she'd undertaken would not endear her to any theatre manager. They'd hesitate to employ an actress who'd behaved in such a cavalier fashion. Since she'd signed a contract, there'd also be legal repercussions, not to mention the substantial loss of money that was involved. Either course of action was perilous. Hannah felt trapped.

She was still deep in thought when she reached the home she shared with Paul. As she stood on the doorstep, waiting for a servant to admit her, she was wholly unaware of the angry pair of eyes trained on her from the other side of the street. The door was opened and Hannah disappeared. Only then did someone emerge from their hiding place and glare at the house with undisguised hatred.

Jack Linnane was wheeling a barrow when the Runners came in through the garden gate. Because they strutted towards him with an air of importance, he took against them at once. Peter Skillen had been polite and friendly towards the gardener. The Runners, by contrast, were brusque and demanding. It was almost as if he was being treated as a suspect himself. After brief introductions, Yeomans told him that he wanted truthful answers and complete cooperation. Linnane provided both under duress. He showed them where the murder had taken place and responded, albeit reluctantly, to the questions fired at him in quick succession by both men. Yeomans was not satisfied. Because the gardener was slow of speech, he felt the man was misleading them. He grabbed Linnane by the scruff of his neck and shook him.

'Did you really *find* the dagger in the victim's back?' he yelled. 'Or did you put it there yourself?'

'No, no, sir,' protested the other. 'I'd never seen the man before.'

'I think you're lying.'

'It's not him, Micah,' said Hale.

'He's got such a villainous look about him.'

'That doesn't make him the killer. If he wanted to stab someone to death, he'd do it in a dark alley and relieve him of his purse. When the crime was reported to Bow Street, it was made clear that Mr Bowerman's purse and watch were still on the body. What could this man hope to *gain* from the murder?' He waved a hand. 'Let him go, Micah. He's innocent.'

'I still have doubts, Alfred.'

Nevertheless, he released the gardener who retreated a few steps. Hale contended that only a fool would invite Runners to investigate a crime that he'd just committed and the gardener was not that stupid. After a short argument, Yeomans finally accepted that Linnane had not been involved in any way. They gave him no apology for treating him so roughly. As he and Hale headed for the gate, the gardener called out to them.

'One moment . . .'

Yeomans turned. 'Yes?'

'I'm to give you a message,' he said.

'Who asked you to do that?'

'It was a gentleman, sir.'

'What was his name?'

'Mr Peter Skillen.'

Hale groaned. 'Has *he* been here?'

'Yes, sir.'

'What was the message?'

'I was to say how much he was looking forward to working with you again.'

The Runners froze, exchanged a look of horror then stalked out.

Linnane felt so pleased to have thoroughly upset them that he sat in the arbour and rewarded himself with a pipe of tobacco.

Back at the shooting gallery, the brothers met up to exchange information. Gully Ackford was fascinated by what they'd so far unearthed. He showed particular interest in the murder weapon.

'It has to be one of Hamer's souvenirs from the Peninsular War,' he said.

'Not necessarily,' warned Peter.

'You heard what Paul discovered. Hamer was in the habit of giving Miss Somerville gifts he'd brought back from Spain and Portugal. And what is a soldier most likely to bring back? I can tell you that from my own experience. I brought back things I picked up on the battlefield.'

'Captain Hamer is hardly likely to have given Miss Somerville a dagger.'

'I'm not suggesting that he did. He kept it and used it to kill Mr Bowerman.'

'I disagree,' said Paul.

'It's too big a coincidence.'

'Hundreds of soldiers must have brought back a dagger like that one. It's not unique, by any means. And I refuse to believe that Hamer would stab a man he could easily kill in a second duel.'

'One of us must go and see him,' said Peter.

'I'll take on that office. Miss Somerville furnished me with his address.'

'You told us that she never wanted to see him again.'

'I can reinforce that message for her,' said Paul, firmly. 'I'd like the opportunity to learn a little more about Hamer.'

'There's one easy way of doing that,' suggested Ackford.

'Is there?'

'Yes, Paul. We can ask a favour of your brother.'

Peter was surprised. 'I know nothing whatsoever of Hamer.'

'Perhaps not, but you have a means of gaining intelligence. After all the work you did for the Home Secretary, he's indebted to you. I'm not simply thinking of your work as a spy in France. It was not all that long ago that you solved a mystery at the Home Office itself. Call on Viscount Sidmouth. A man in his position will have ready access to the War Office. He simply has to tell one of his minions to look into the regimental history of the Royal Horse Guards with reference to the name of Captain Stephen Hamer.'

'That's a brilliant notion, Gully.'

Ackford grinned. 'I have them from time to time.'

'He clearly painted a self-portrait of a hero when he first courted Miss Somerville,' said Paul. 'How true a representation was that?'

'Between the pair of you, you should be able to find out.'

'Right,' said Peter to his brother. 'You tackle Hamer and I'll repair to the Home Office. I'm quite sure that Viscount Sidmouth will help us.'

Before they could leave, the door opened and Charlotte came in.

'I'm sorry that I'm late,' she said, 'but I had a visitor as I was about to leave the house. Paul can guess who it was.'

'Yes,' he said, 'it was Hannah. I told her to speak to you about the problem.'

'Thank you for having so much faith in me. I'm not sure I was altogether worthy of it. I know nothing at all about the way that the world of theatre operates.'

'You'd give her uncritical support, Charlotte. That's what she needed.'

'May we know what all this is about?' asked Peter.

'Hannah is grappling with a difficult problem,' explained Charlotte. 'She's reached a turning point in her career.'

'Put succinctly,' said Paul, 'she wants to murder a man by the name of Abel Mundy.'

Lemuel Fleet was known, paradoxically, for his slowness. Short, plump and in his fifties, he looked as if he carried the worries of the world on his shoulder, bearing down on him so hard that the fastest speed he could manage was a laboured trudge. Whenever he made the slightest physical effort, his flabby face would glisten with perspiration and the wig that covered his bald pate would shift to and fro from its mooring. While his body was sluggish, however, his mind could move like lightning and it was often required to do so. As manager of the Theatre Royal, Drury Lane, he had the immense responsibility of helping to entertain London and he knew only too well how fickle audiences could be. One mistake in the choice of a drama or the casting of a central character and they would howl the play off the stage, forgetting the endless delights he'd offered them in the past. A single failure could eclipse fifty successes.

When he called on Hannah Granville, he was carrying a sheaf of plays under his arm. The additional weight made him sweat more obviously than usual. Though she agreed to speak to him, Hannah laid down the rules at the outset.

'Do not *dare* to ask me to apologise to that man,' she declared.

'It would never occur to me to do so.'

'If an apology is in order, he should be making it to *me*.'

'You're being unkind to Mr Mundy,' he said, shuffling the plays. 'He came to us with the highest recommendation.'

'From whom, may I ask?'

'Theatre managers in different parts of the country.'

'It arose purely from their relief at having got rid of the fellow,' she said, acidly. 'Did any of them ever put *The Piccadilly Opera* on their stages?'

'Of course not, Miss Granville, that was new-minted for you. What they did present was *The Jealous Husband*, *The Provok'd Wife*, *Love's Dominion* and *The Fair Maid of Marylebone* – all of them triumphs written by Abel Mundy. And there are three others here from his talented pen.' He set the plays down on the table. 'I've brought copies of them for you to peruse.'

'I am grateful to you, sir. We are always in need of paper kindling for the fire.'

'Read them, I beg you. They are proof positive of his rare talent.'

'Oh, he does have a rare talent, I grant you that. Unfortunately it's for writing tedious drivel. His plot is ridiculous, his characters have no depth and the dialogue suggests that English is a foreign language to him. I am used to playing in the greatest dramas ever written, Mr Fleet. You are asking me to appear in one of the worst.'

'That's a harsh judgement, Miss Granville.'

'Whatever made you commission this dross?'

'I was inspired by the quality of his earlier plays,' he said, indicating the pile. 'And when he told me that *The Piccadilly Opera* would be his finest work, I was quick to seize on it for my theatre.'

'And *now?*' she asked, pointedly. 'Did he deliver what he promised?'

'Not exactly . . . but the work still has merit.'

'I've been unable to detect it.'

'Let's not argue over that,' said Fleet, attempting a benign smile that somehow degenerated into a leer. 'I come as a peacemaker. There must be a way out of the impasse.'

'Yes – you must release me from my contract.'

'That's out of the question. You are the toast of London, Miss Granville.'

'I was when I last trod the boards at your theatre,' she said, tossing her head. 'I had Mr William Shakespeare to thank for that. All that Mr Mundy will do is drag me down to his own banal level. I'll not bear such disgrace, sir.'

'We *need* you,' he cried.

'Then change the play.'

'Don't even suggest it, dear lady!'

'Bury this one before it buries both of us.'

'The piece does have *some* virtues.'

Sensing that she had the upper hand, Hannah delivered her ultimatum.

'Make your choice, sir. Either Mr Mundy goes – or I do.'

He was quivering with fear. 'You can't mean that.'

'I stand by what I say. Send that charlatan on his way or I'll quit the company forthwith. But let me warn you of one thing, Mr Fleet. Offer the leading role in *The Piccadilly Opera* to someone else and there's not an actress in the whole realm who will lower herself to accept it.' Grabbing the plays, she thrust them violently back into his hands. 'Take this offal away before its stink pervades the whole house!'

CHAPTER SIX

Peter Skillen was glad of an excuse to visit the Home Office. Apart from anything else, he knew that he'd receive a cordial welcome. He'd not only undertaken many assignments during the war at the Home Secretary's instigation. In its wake, Peter had also unravelled one plot to assassinate Viscount Sidmouth and another to kill the Duke of Wellington. As a result, both men had written effusive letters of thanks to him. As he approached the building, he remembered the hidden secrets he'd earlier found inside it. Peter was in search of another secret now.

Three people were waiting impatiently to see the Home Secretary and they were annoyed when Peter's name was enough in itself to move him to the front of the queue. Sidmouth even opened the door of his office in person, stepping out to shake the visitor's hand.

'Do come in,' he invited. 'You're most welcome.'

'Thank you, my lord,' said Peter, stepping into the room.

'It's always a pleasure to see you, Mr Skillen. Everyone else brings me problems. You alone trade in solutions.'

'I've come in search of one this time, my lord.'

'To what does it pertain?'

'It relates to a brutal murder.'

'Take a seat and tell me all.'

They settled down opposite each other and Peter told his tale. As usual, he was concise, articulate and free from pointless digression. Sidmouth listened intently. He was a tall, slim man in his fifties, visibly worn down by the cares of state but retaining a quiet dignity. Earlier in his career, he'd been prime minister but had not excelled in the role, acting, as he did, in the long shadow of Pitt the Younger to whom he was often compared unfavourably. Even when ridiculed mercilessly by word and by caricature, he'd somehow maintained his composure. Peter admired him for that.

'Well,' said Sidmouth, sitting back, 'it's a desperately sad story. I can't pretend that I believe a duel is the most civilised way to resolve an argument. If we all reached for a weapon every time someone irritated us, the population of this country would soon be halved.' He gave a dry laugh. 'Yet one has to be impressed by the unexpected bravery of this Mr Bowerman in challenging a man who's made a profession out of bearing arms.'

'It was an unfair contest from the start.'

'Did your brother make no effort to avert it?'

'Paul did everything in his power, my lord, but Mr Bowerman was adamant.'

'He seems to have been a decent, upstanding gentleman who was given a glimpse of happiness that helped him to shake off his erstwhile gloom. The lady herself must be in despair.'

'My brother said that she swooned on receipt of the news.'

'It's a blow from which she may never recover,' said Sidmouth, seriously, 'but I sense that you came in pursuit of something. This gruesome narrative was the preface to a request, was it not?'

'It was indeed, my lord. We seek more information about Captain Hamer. He arrived out of nowhere to interrupt the burgeoning romance between Miss Somerville and Mr Bowerman.

Where had he been until then? The War Office will have a record of his service to the regiment. In brief, what sort of soldier was he?'

'That's a very reasonable enquiry, Mr Skillen.'

'Will you be able to oblige me?'

'I'll do more than that,' said the other, reaching for his quill and dipping it in the inkwell. 'I'll draft a letter this very minute and you shall bear it to the War Office in person. Leave it there and await developments.'

'That's very kind of you, my lord.'

'You once saved my life, Mr Skillen. Writing a letter is the least I can do for you in recompense. As soon as I get a reply, I'll communicate the information at once. Will that content you?'

Peter got up. 'It will, indeed.'

'I can, however, forewarn you of one thing.'

'What's that?'

Sidmouth looked up at him. 'All that you will learn from the War Office,' he said, 'is that Captain Hamer was an exemplary soldier. We are talking about the Royal Horse Guards, remember. They expect the highest standards of their officers.'

A duel of another kind was troubling Lemuel Fleet. Though the enmity between his playwright and his leading lady had only sparked a war of words so far, he feared that in time they might resort to more dangerous weapons. After a lifetime in the theatre, he'd met many oversensitive authors and tempestuous actresses but none as determined to have their respective way as Abel Mundy and Hannah Granville. Neither of them showed the slightest inclination to compromise. The play had been advertised and substantial interest had been aroused. Fleet shuddered at the thought that *The Piccadilly Opera* might have to be cancelled.

Having tackled Hannah, he'd been shaken by her ultimatum.

To keep her, he had to get rid of the play altogether. That was unthinkable. In the vain hope that Mundy might be amenable to a suggestion or two, he called on the playwright at the house where he was staying throughout rehearsals. When the manager was shown into the room, Mundy leapt to his feet and ran across to him. He was a tall, angular man in his forties with a scholarly appearance.

'Have you seen that raving she-devil?' he demanded.

'I've not long left her.'

'Did you give her my stipulations?'

'Not exactly, Mr Mundy—'

'I'll not budge an inch. I hope you told her that.'

'Miss Granville understands your position.'

'I'm not sure that she does,' said Mundy. 'She needs to be reminded that without people of my profession, unlettered hoydens like her would have no work.'

Fleet adjusted his wig. 'That's grossly unfair, sir,' he said, trying to assert his authority. 'She is neither unlettered nor a hoyden. Miss Granville is an actress capable of the most taxing roles. During her season in Paris, she played Lady Macbeth in French.'

'It's a language more suited to her excitability.'

'As for having to rely on men who follow your calling, I have to correct you. If every living playwright were to die this instant, the theatre would still thrive because we would be able to call on its rich heritage. Given the choice, I might as well tell you, Miss Granville would be happy to spend her entire career performing plays written two hundred years ago by the Bard of Avon.'

'Then perhaps you should remind her that Shakespeare had an advantage that we who follow him do not. He wrote exclusively for *male* actors,' said Mundy, 'and did not have to put up with the tantrums of hysterical women.'

Feeling that he'd scored an important debating point, he sat down with his arms folded. Fleet was a tolerant and forgiving man, making him a rarity in a contentious profession, but even he could not bring himself to like Abel Mundy. While he was ready to boast about his own talent, Mundy showed scant respect for that of other people. As far as he was concerned, actors were like toy soldiers taken out of a box and told where to move and what to say. In short, they were totally in his control. He denied them any right of protest. Mundy believed that they should be so grateful to take part in one of his dramas that they would succumb willingly to any of his requirements. Someone like Hannah Granville, who challenged him outright, was anathema.

'I believe that she is susceptible to reason,' said Fleet, forcing the lie out between clenched teeth. 'I am hoping that you may feel able to meet her halfway, so to speak.'

'I have no wish to meet that screeching shrew *anywhere*.'

'Miss Granville has legitimate grievances with regard to your play.'

'Oh,' said Mundy, nastily, 'so you've taken *her* side, have you?'

'I am completely impartial, sir. My only concern is to put something on the stage that is at once entertaining and uplifting. *The Piccadilly Opera*, I believe, is both of those things, once a few minor modifications have been made.'

Mundy stiffened. '*Modifications*, Mr Fleet?'

'Let's call them refinements.'

'I don't care what you call them. They are wholly unnecessary.'

'Miss Granville disagrees.'

'The lady is disagreeable by nature.'

'She has a large following, Mr Mundy.'

'As do I,' retorted the other, nostrils flaring. 'My play, *The Provok'd Wife*, was the talk of Bristol.'

'Provincial success is no guarantee of general approbation here in the capital. London audiences are harsher critics. Many plays that have won plaudits in places like Bristol, Bath and Norwich have shrivelled into miserable failures when put to the test here. I am not saying that your work will suffer the same fate,' he went on, quickly. 'It has enormous promise. But you are unknown here, Mr Mundy. That is why I engaged Miss Granville. Her name adds lustre to any play.'

'Unhappily, that is *all* it adds. Her real gift is for subtraction. When she speaks my lines, she takes away their poetry and their pathos. She robs my work of all the elements that give it truth and vitality.'

'You exaggerate, sir.'

'And what about *her*?' demanded the other. 'She goes through life in a veritable cloud of hyperbole.'

'One must make allowances for Miss Granville.'

'Upon my word, I'll not make a single one!'

'Then we are surely doomed,' said Fleet, removing his wig to scratch his pate. 'You wish for her to be removed from your play and Miss Granville urges with equal passion for the summary withdrawal of *The Piccadilly Opera*.'

'That's a scandalous idea!'

'Your own solution is just as impractical.'

'Get rid of that damnable harpie and all will be well!'

'If only it were that simple. Consider my dilemma. I have undertaken to offer drama that will please the palates of the most discerning audience in the world. Together, you and Miss Granville might conjure up something magical. Apart, you will only create a disaster. Is that what you and she *really* want to do? Is it your joint endeavour to crucify me in public and bring my theatre to its knees?' He replaced his wig and struck a pose. 'Come to composition with the lady,' he urged. 'Find a means of working harmoniously together or *The Piccadilly Opera* will never leave the pages on which it was written.'

While Alfred Hale was still looking at the corpse with intense curiosity, Micah Yeomans was examining the murder weapon. The coroner's assistant took the opportunity to display his knowledge.

'It's a Toledo blade, sir.'

'How do you know?'

'I recognise it by its quality. Roman soldiers did the same. That's why they chose Toledo steel for their swords.'

'You seem well informed.'

'I am only passing on what the other gentleman told me.'

Yeomans glowered. '*Other* gentleman?'

'Yes, sir, he called here earlier – a Mr Skillen.'

'He's done it yet again,' complained Hale. 'Whether it's Peter or Paul, they always seem to know something that we don't.'

'Those confounded brothers should have been strangled at birth,' said Yeomans, vengefully.

'Why do they always hold the whip hand over us, Micah?'

'I'll snatch it from them and use it to flay them alive!'

'Then you've more courage than sense. I've seen them in action. It would be madness to take on either of the Skillen brothers. With sword, pistol or bare fists, they are invincible.'

'Then we'll have to choose some *other* weapons, Alfred.'

'What do you mean?'

'We are upholders of the law,' said Yeomans, grandiloquently. 'It's high time we let the two of them feel its full force.'

With a sudden downward jab, he left the dagger embedded in the table on which the body lay. It was still vibrating as they left the room.

* * *

'They *arrested* you?'

'Yes, they did, then the dolts accompanied me to Bow Street as if I was the lowest criminal.'

'This is insupportable, Stephen.'

'I made that point in the choicest language I could find.'

'Could they really imagine that you'd ever stab a man in the back?'

'Patently, they could.'

'Then they don't know the Stephen Hamer that I do.'

'Thank you.'

Rawdon Carr had been his second at the ill-fated duel, an old and trusted friend to whom he often turned for advice. They were in Hamer's house, looking back over recent events. Carr was furious that the Runners had dared to suspect Hamer of murder and urged him to institute legal action. They were still discussing its nature when a servant knocked on the door and opened it.

'You have a visitor, Captain Hamer,' he said.

'What's his name?'

'Mr Paul Skillen.'

'It's the fellow who acted as Bowerman's second,' said Hamer, puzzled. 'What can he possibly want with me?'

'At least he won't have come to arrest you,' said Carr. 'He discharged his duties well on Putney Heath. Have him admitted.'

Hamer gave a signal and the servant disappeared. Seconds later, he conducted Paul into the room then left all three men together. After formal introductions, Paul was invited to sit down.

'I'd prefer to remain standing, if you don't mind,' said Paul.

Carr smiled. 'That sounds ominous.'

'I came to deliver a message to the captain.'

'Then let's hear it,' said Hamer.

'Miss Somerville wishes you to know that she has no wish ever to see you again. She requests that you make no attempt to call on her because you will not be allowed inside her house under any circumstance.'

'And *this* is the message she asked you to communicate?'

'I may have paraphrased her words.'

'Why did she choose *you* as her intercessor? You don't even know her.'

'It fell to me to break the news of Mr Bowerman's death to her,' explained Paul. 'It caused her untold anguish. When I asked about you . . . Miss Somerville said that the door would be slammed in your face.'

'That doesn't sound like Laetitia,' said Hamer.

'Indeed, it doesn't,' agreed Carr. 'It's far too unladylike. You misheard her, Mr Skillen. Such sentiments could never be expressed by her.'

'I promise you that they were,' said Paul, stoutly. 'But that's not the only reason that brought me here. I wanted to speak to Captain Hamer about his time in the Peninsular War.'

Hamer became wary. 'Why the devil should you want to do that?'

'I've known many soldiers in my time and – to a man – they like to collect trophies from their victories. The souvenirs usually comprise uniforms, hats, flags or, more often, perhaps, enemy weapons.'

'Damn your effrontery, Mr Skillen!'

'Are you saying that you did *not* forage on the battlefield?'

'Oh, Captain Hamer came back with a whole arsenal of weapons,' said Carr, laughing, 'but, frankly, that's none of your business.'

'It might be if the collection included a dagger made of Toledo steel and having a decorative handle.'

'I think it's time that you left,' said Hamer, forcefully.

'Evidently, you've not seen the murder weapon that took Mr Bowerman's life. It was such a dagger as I've described. It crossed my mind to wonder if it had once belonged to you.'

Hamer took a menacing step forward. 'Mind what you say, Mr Skillen.'

'It's a simple question,' said Paul, holding his ground.

'Are you going to leave or must I throw you out bodily?'

'I wouldn't advise the latter course of action, sir. I'm no defenceless opponent like Mr Bowerman. Even with my tuition, he could never have won a duel. The odds were stacked too overwhelmingly in your favour.' He drew himself up. 'The situation is very different now.'

Hamer looked as if he was about to attack Paul but something held him back. His cheeks reddened and his jaw muscles tightened. There was sheer malice in his eyes but there was also a hint of respect as well. They stood there in silence for several minutes. When Hamer turned sharply away, Paul knew that he'd won the confrontation.

'Remember what Miss Somerville said,' Paul reminded him.

'Get out of my house!'

'Good day to you, sirs.'

'And to you,' said Carr, cheerfully.

Turning on his heel, Paul left the room and could soon be heard opening the front door of the house. Carr had viewed it all with mingled interest and amusement but the visit had left Hamer fuming.

'Do you *have* such a weapon, Stephen?' asked his friend.

'As a matter of fact, I do,' replied the other, 'but I was not going to tell that to him. I can't believe the infernal cheek of the man. He was lucky that I didn't knock him to the floor.'

'The luck may have been yours. Had you attacked him, I might now have been helping *you* up from the carpet. Mr Skillen is no mean adversary. He has the look of a fighting man to me.'

'I should have refused to see him, Rawdon.'

'But the fact is that you did and, as a consequence, I'm curious. If you have a dagger of the kind described, I'd be most interested to look at it.'

'You've seen my collection before.'

'Yes, but I did so without any particular weapon in mind – there are so many to choose from, after all. Things have changed now.'

'Oh, well,' said Hamer, reluctantly, 'if you must . . .'

'It's an odd coincidence if the murder weapon is identical to yours.'

'There won't be the slightest resemblance between them.'

He led his friend out and along a corridor to the rear of the house. Producing a key from his pocket, he opened the door of a room and stood back so that his friend could go in first. Carr entered what was, in effect, a small military museum. Filled with weapons of every description – from foreign as well as British armies – it also had an assortment of uniforms, hats, boots, gloves and medals. A large telescope interested Carr enough to make him handle it for a moment.

'It's French,' said Hamer.

'Nobody would have parted with this easily. It's an expensive instrument.'

'I had to kill its owner to get it.'

'What about the rest of these items?'

'Spoils of war.'

Carr replaced the telescope on a table. 'What about the dagger?'

'It's over here,' said Hamer, leading him to a glass-fronted cabinet. 'As you see, it's a large and varied collection. The one that Skillen referred to is right here at the front of the . . .'

Words ran dry and he simply gaped. Opening the cabinet, he took out the weapons one by one until they were all side by side on the table. Carr was concerned about his reaction.

'What's the trouble, dear fellow?'

'It's not here, Rawdon.'

'Are you quite certain that it *was* here?'

'Yes, of course.'

'One of the servants might have absent-mindedly moved it.'

'They wouldn't *dare*.'

'Then it's somewhere else,' said Carr, looking around.

'It's gone, I tell you. It's been *stolen*.'

'But that's impossible.'

'So I thought, Rawdon, but I was wrong. This room was not as secure as I intended. Since the dagger is not here . . .' He shook his head in disbelief. 'Then it might have been the murder weapon, after all.'

'Let's find out at once,' urged his friend. 'If Skillen can get access to Bowerman's corpse, then so can we. I'll bear you company. This is mystifying.'

Peter Skillen returned to the gallery to find his wife seated at the table, writing something in a large notebook. It contained a record of all the cases in which they'd been involved over the years. Kept scrupulously up to date, it had details of every criminal who had ever crossed their paths. In some cases – if Charlotte had actually seen the person – there would be a rough portrait of him or her. The record book was an invaluable source of information and it was only one of many initiatives that she'd introduced. She gave her husband a welcoming smile and he responded with a kiss.

'Did you manage to see the Home Secretary?' she asked.

'I did more than that, Charlotte. He was so eager to help me that he dashed off a letter there and then. I've just come from delivering it to the War Office.'

'It pays to have friends in high places.'

'I *earned* his friendship, my love – and you know how.' He sat opposite her. 'But what's all this fuss about Hannah's latest play? Can she really have murder on her mind?'

'It's becoming something of an obsession, Peter.'

'Who exactly is Abel Mundy?'

'If you listen to her, he's the most black-hearted villain Hannah has ever met. She called him a freakish monster germinated outside lawful procreation.' Peter laughed. 'It's not a cause for glee,' she said, reprovingly. 'I had to endure almost an hour of her diatribes. The situation is intractable.'

'There's always a way out of a dilemma.'

'Not if both parties are obdurate.'

'Give me the full details, my love.'

'That would take far too long. All you need is the essence.'

But there was not even time for Charlotte to reveal that. Before she could utter another word, the door was flung open and a dozen men charged into the room on the heels of Micah Yeomans. Peter and his wife jumped to their feet.

'This is very uncivil of you,' he protested.

'Civility has to go by the board when a crime has been committed,' said the Runner. 'We've had information that a wanted man is hiding here.'

'That's arrant nonsense.'

'Harbouring a fugitive is against the law.'

'And that's precisely why we'd never dream of doing it. Everybody in this building has a legal right to be here.'

'We'll need to make sure of that,' said Yeomans, turning to his men. 'Search every nook and cranny of the place. Flush him out of his lair.'

The members of the foot patrol who'd come in support charged off to begin their search, making as much noise as possible and causing as much disruption.

'I will complain to the chief magistrate,' said Peter, angrily. 'It's wholly unwarranted.'

'Complain, if you must, Mr Skillen, but I would have thought you'd like to keep well away from Mr Kirkwood. You were before him only yesterday.'

'That was my brother, Paul.'

'Really?' Yeomans gaped. 'I could have sworn that *you* were Paul.'

'That's not the only mistake you've made today.'

'We are acting on reliable information, sir.'

'I beg leave to doubt that.'

'If the rogue is here, my men will find him.'

'You should mention this incident the next time you talk to the Home Secretary,' said Charlotte to her husband. 'He can overrule the chief magistrate with ease.'

'Viscount Sidmouth is wedded to law and order,' said Yeomans, pompously, 'so do not think you can frighten me by waving his name in the air like a banner. We came to smoke out a villain and that's what we will do.'

The next moment, there was the sound of a fierce struggle as several feet clattered down the staircase. Loud protests were filling the air.

'That sounds like Jem,' said Charlotte, going through the open door.

Peter followed her and was horrified to see Jem Huckvale being manhandled down the stairs by Alfred Hale, Chevy Ruddock and two other men. Small but powerful, Huckvale was wriggling like an eel. They had difficulty holding him.

'We caught him, sir,' said Ruddock, breathlessly. 'This is the man we were after. I'd recognise him anywhere. He stole a leg of mutton in the market this very morning.'

'I haven't left the gallery,' cried Huckvale.

'It's true,' said Peter. 'Jem lives and works here. He's being arrested for a crime he couldn't possibly have committed.'

'Besides,' added Charlotte, 'he's the most law-abiding person. Release him at once, Mr Yeomans. You have the wrong man.'

'We'll see about that, Mrs Skillen.' He nodded to the others. 'Take him out.'

Still protesting his innocence, Huckvale was more or less carried out.

'I understand your game,' said Peter, coldly. 'Because we have more success at solving crimes than you do, you try to frighten us by raiding our premises. As you well know, Jem is no thief. You'll soon have to release him.'

'In that case,' said Yeomans, beaming, 'we'll have to raid the gallery again, won't we? And we'll keep on doing it until we catch the man we're after. He's here somewhere. I sense it.'

He walked jauntily out of the building.

CHAPTER SEVEN

On the journey to the morgue, Stephen Hamer sat in the carriage bristling with an irritation tempered by perplexity. He was utterly baffled. Someone appeared to have stolen an item from his collection of weapons. The discovery came only a day after the duel in which he'd been involved had been rudely interrupted. How could anyone enter his house so easily and walk away with a prized dagger? Who could have learnt of the duel and alerted the Runners? Were the two incidents the work of the same person? If so, had he also been the killer of Mark Bowerman? It seemed very likely.

One question dominated: where *was* the villain?

'I share your concern,' said Carr, patting his friend's knee. 'Somebody is one step ahead of us and that's vexatious. We need to track him down.'

'I agree, Rawdon, but how do we do that?'

'Let's start with the dagger. It may have gone missing but that doesn't mean it has to have been the murder weapon. You're not the only soldier to bring weapons back from the Peninsular War. London is probably awash with them.'

'There's only one that matters to me,' said Hamer, grimly.

'After we've established if it was or wasn't used to kill Mr Bowerman, I suggest that we pay a visit to the gentleman's house. We need to find out where the attack took place and what Bowerman was doing there in the first place. There will be an investigation into the murder but – from what you tell me of the Runners – it would be foolish to place any trust in them.'

'They're imbeciles. It's no wonder that crime is so rampant in the capital. If they are the only means of enforcing the law, then malefactors will continue to run riot. Look for no help from the Runners.'

'We'll act without them, Stephen. They may, of course, object.'

'A fig for their objections!' exclaimed Hamer with an obscene gesture.

The carriage rolled to a halt and they got out in turn. Once they'd identified themselves at the front door, they were taken to the room where Bowerman's corpse was kept. Herbs had been sprinkled to ward off the stink of death but it still invaded Carr's nostrils and he began to cough. More accustomed to the abiding reek of decay, Hamer was untroubled. During his days in uniform, he'd become habituated to endless casualties on the battlefield. After a brief examination of the cadaver, he asked to see the murder weapon. As he retrieved it from a drawer, the assistant passed on some information.

'It's made of Toledo steel,' he said, handing it over. 'That's the finest there is, sir. As a matter of fact—'

'Stop blathering,' snapped Hamer, interrupting him. He turned the dagger over to examine it from every angle. 'I know all about Toledo steel.'

'Well?' asked Carr. 'Is it yours?'

'It is,' confirmed the other.

'How can you tell?'

'I recognise one of my weapons when I see it, Rawdon.'

'Then how did it end up in Mr Bowerman's back?'

'That's what I intend to find out.'

'I'm afraid that you can't keep that dagger,' said the assistant, extending a hand. 'It's evidence in a case of murder. You can reclaim it when the crime is solved.'

Reluctant to give it back, Hamer eventually did so, warning the man to take good care of it. He then asked if the Runners had been there.

'Oh, yes, sir,' replied the other. 'I had a visit from Mr Yeomans and Mr Hale but they were not the first to come. A younger gentleman called before them. He was the one who told me about Toledo steel.'

'What was his name?' asked Hamer.

'Mr Skillen.'

'Why is *he* poking his nose into this affair?'

'He was Bowerman's friend,' said Carr, not realising that it was Peter Skillen who'd been there rather than his brother, 'and, like any decent man, he wishes to know who committed the murder. If *you'd* been the victim, I'd have done the same. In fact, I wouldn't have rested until I'd learnt the full truth.'

They left the building and paused outside the door. Hamer was rancorous.

'We don't want Skillen getting in our way,' he said.

'I concur.'

'He's not like those bumbling incompetents who decided that *I* was the killer. Skillen is more intelligent, for a start.'

'He's more intelligent and, I'd venture, more resolute.'

'We must find a way to frighten him off.'

'He won't be frightened easily,' said Carr, thoughtfully, 'so it might be better simply to divert his attention. I'm sure we can devise a means of doing that.'

* * *

The moment he stepped across the threshold, Paul knew that he was in a house of mourning. It was a palatial residence that reflected the character of its late owner. The well-stocked library, the plethora of fine artwork and the selection of musical instruments told of a cultured man. Shown into the drawing room, Paul was able to view the striking portrait above the mantelpiece.

'That was the *first* Mrs Bowerman,' explained Silas Roe in a voice hoarse with grief. 'A happier couple never existed. They were ideally suited.'

'And yet he was prepared to embark on a second marriage.'

'That's true.'

'How did that come about?'

'I can't give you precise details, Mr Skillen. It was not my place to pry. The master was an intensely private man. I respected his privacy.'

'Someone must have introduced him to Miss Somerville.'

'That would be Sir Geoffrey Melrose.'

'How did he come to know the lady?'

'I have no idea, sir.'

'Was he a close friend of Mr Bowerman's?'

'He called here occasionally,' said Roe, 'and very few people did that.'

'Your master confided to me that he first saw Miss Somerville at a dinner party. Presumably, Sir Geoffrey Melrose was the host.'

'That's my understanding.'

'And, I daresay, you noticed a change in Mr Bowerman.'

'Indeed, we did,' said the butler, failing to keep the disapproval out of his reply. 'We were all very much aware of it.'

Paul questioned him for some time and was disappointed to learn that Roe had no idea of Sir Geoffrey's London address. On another front, too, he was thwarted.

'You told me that, on the day of the murder, Mr Bowerman received a letter.'

'Yes, sir, it was from Miss Somerville.'

'How could you be certain of that?'

'Her correspondence always had a pleasing aroma.'

'Did you actually see the handwriting?'

'I saw it and recognised it, Mr Skillen.'

'So you'd seen examples of it before, obviously.'

'Yes, sir.'

'Given the strength of feeling he clearly had for the lady,' said Paul, carefully, 'he'd certainly have kept her billets-doux.' Roe nodded. 'Might I see them, please?'

'I'm afraid not, sir.'

'Do you know where they are?'

'Yes, I do.'

'All that I ask is to have a quick peep at them.'

'That will not be possible,' said Roe, firmly.

'But they may contain valuable clues helpful to my investigation.'

'It was private correspondence, sir. Nobody will ever see it.'

'I was hoping for more cooperation from you, Mr Roe.'

The butler straightened his back. 'I know where my duty lies, sir.' He regarded Paul quizzically. 'May I ask if you are married, sir?'

'As it happens, I am not.'

'But there is a lady in your life, I dare swear.'

'There's a very special lady,' confirmed Paul.

'Then ask yourself this, Mr Skillen. How would *you* feel if a stranger was allowed to read letters sent by her for your eyes only?'

'I'd feel very angry.'

'You'd have every right to be so, sir,' said Roe. 'I'm sorry to turn down your request but perhaps you'll understand why now.'

Paul accepted that the butler was protecting the privacy of his late master and he admired him for that. He was about to put more questions to him when the doorbell clanged. Voices came along the corridor and Paul identified one of them at once. As the Runners came into the room, he spread his arms in a mock welcome.

'Ah,' he said, grinning mischievously, 'you've got here at last. Speed was never your forte, Mr Yeomans, was it?'

'That's the third time in a row,' said Hale. 'Garden, morgue and here – he always gets there first.'

'Someone has to show you the way. Though I have to correct you with regard to the morgue – it was my brother, Peter, who went there.'

'You've no business being under this roof,' said Yeomans, features twisted into an ugly scowl. 'I must ask you to leave.'

'I'll go in my own good time.'

'You'll not tarry when you hear what happened at the shooting gallery.'

Paul tensed. 'Why – what have you been up to now?'

'We've been doing our duty and upholding the law,' said Hale. 'When we had reports of a fugitive at the gallery, we descended on the place and searched it.'

'There are no fugitives there, man!'

'Yes, there was. We found him skulking upstairs and arrested him. His name is Jem Huckvale and we've a witness who will depose that he saw the little wretch steal a leg of mutton.'

'Jem is no thief!' yelled Paul. 'He's as honest as the day is long.'

'He's cooling his heels in Bow Street,' said Yeomans, enjoying Paul's discomfort. 'It's not like you to consort with criminals, Mr Skillen.'

'This is an example of pure spite. It's an act of shameless retaliation.'

'Our job is to clean up the streets of London.'

'Then you might begin by rounding up all the villains who pay you to ignore the way they make their living. Everyone knows how corrupt you are. How dare you accuse Jem Huckvale of a crime when the pair of you flout the law every day.'

'Do you want to end up in the same cell as your friend?' taunted Yeomans.

'I want him released immediately.'

'You're in no position to make demands, Mr Skillen.'

'We have a very good lawyer,' said Paul, warningly.

'Then he's going to be extremely busy in the future.'

'Why do you say that, Mr Yeomans?'

'I have a strange feeling that we'll get other reports of fugitives going to ground in your gallery,' said the Runner, 'don't you, Alfred?'

'Oh, yes,' agreed Hale. 'You're going to be seeing a lot of us, Mr Skillen.'

As he left the room, their sniggers followed him all the way to the front door.

True to her profession, Hannah Granville was bereft when she had no audience. With only the servants in the house, she felt that any performance she gave was bound to be unappreciated. She therefore hired a carriage to take her to the gallery where she could be assured of a sympathetic hearing. On her way there, the driver obeyed her instruction to take her past the Theatre Royal, Drury Lane, so that she could feast her eyes on a place that had been instrumental in advancing her career in the past. It had become, to some extent, her spiritual home and she drew strength simply from looking at it. As the carriage drove on, however, other thoughts flooded into her mind. Having been an inspiration to her, the Theatre Royal might now become a scaffold on which her reputation could die. Thanks to Abel Mundy, her long years of toil and dedication would be meaningless. She was facing execution.

Arriving at the gallery, she told her friend how concerned she was.

'Why don't you talk to the manager again?' advised Charlotte.

'I've already done that. He called on me earlier.'

'Had he spoken to Mr Mundy?'

'I'm not sure if he had the opportunity to speak,' said Hannah. 'When he came to me, Mr Fleet was like a beaten dog. When he left me, he was going to confront Mundy once again. At their first meeting, that ogre made excessive demands.'

'Your own have not exactly been marked by restraint,' said the other, gently.

'They've been calm and sensible, Charlotte.'

'That's a matter of opinion.'

'All I ask is the removal of this hideous man and his hideous play.'

'And what is to replace them?'

Hannah tossed her head. 'Who cares?'

'*Everyone* cares,' said Charlotte, reasonably. 'The manager cares because his livelihood is threatened, you care because you require a play commensurate with your talent and the audience cares because it has been starved of the pleasure of seeing Hannah Granville onstage for a while and wants to welcome their favourite actress back. Then, of course,' she went on, 'there is the rest of the company to consider. What is *their* opinion of *The Piccadilly Opera?*'

'That's irrelevant. My opinion is the only one that matters.'

Charlotte was about to point out that her friend was being rather selfish when they heard feet running down the corridor. The

74

door opened and Paul came into the room. Hannah instinctively threw herself into his arms.

'Thank God you've come, Paul! I need you.'

'What are *you* doing here?' he asked.

'We've been discussing Hannah's latest play,' said Charlotte.

'Let's put that aside for a minute.'

Hannah stamped a foot. 'I won't have it put aside for a single second.'

'Something of more immediate importance has come up, my love,' he said, planting a consoling kiss on her forehead. 'I've just heard some disturbing news from Yeomans. Is it true that Jem has been arrested on a trumped-up charge?'

'Yes,' replied Charlotte.

'He must be set free at once.'

'Peter is already taking care of that.'

'Apparently, the Runners intend to raid the gallery again.'

'Gully is considering measures to prevent that. It may even be necessary to close the place for a few days.'

'I wish someone would raid the Theatre Royal,' said Hannah, petulantly, 'and arrest Abel Mundy for breaking all the laws of drama. *The Piccadilly Opera* is an act of criminality in itself.'

'With respect,' said Paul, gently squeezing her arm, 'Jem's situation is more critical than yours. If it were proved – by means of arrant lies – that Jem *did* steal a leg of mutton, it would be the end of him. At best, he'd face transportation; at worst, he'd be given a death sentence.'

Hannah was for once forced to think about someone else's plight.

'Is it really that serious, Paul?'

'It could be.'

*   *   *

As it happened, Peter Skillen did not have to invoke the name of the Home Secretary to secure the release of his friend. When Jem Huckvale was taken to Bow Street, the chief magistrate heard the details of the case in the privacy of his office. Since he was the supposed witness to the crime, Chevy Ruddock gave his testimony, saying that he'd seen Huckvale sneaking away from the market with the mutton tucked inside his coat. It did not take long for Eldon Kirkwood to dismiss the case on the grounds of insufficient evidence. Much as he regretted doing so, he ordered Huckvale's release. Peter had brought a spare horse to Bow Street. Riding side by side with his friend, he expressed his sympathy.

'I'm sorry that they picked on you, Jem,' he said. 'Paul and I were the real targets. We were lucky that the chief magistrate is so meticulous. He soon found holes in the witness's testimony.'

'I was scared,' admitted Huckvale. 'I thought I was done for. And I was shocked that Chevy Ruddock could tell such barefaced lies.'

'He was suborned. You could tell that.'

'I've always thought he was the best of the Runners. He's a decent man at heart. When he tried to keep watch on Paul, I pushed Ruddock in the Thames. There were times when I regretted that. Today, I wished I could do it all over again.'

'He'll think twice before he arrests you again.'

'How many times must it have happened before?' asked Huckvale.

'What – someone bearing false witness?'

'Yes, Peter.'

'It does happen occasionally, I fear.'

'If Mr Kirkwood had believed him, I might have . . .'

'You might have suffered the fate of other innocent victims,' said Peter, finishing the sentence for him. 'Fortunately, the chief magistrate is not easily fooled. Ruddock will get a roasting for what he did.'

'Mr Yeomans is the real culprit.'

'That fact won't go unnoticed.'

'Is he going to keep on raiding the gallery?'

Peter grinned. 'I have a feeling that he might be dissuaded from pursuing that particular line of attack on us,' said Peter. 'He'll get more than a rap on the knuckles from Mr Kirkwood.'

Heads bowed and cheeks red, Yeomans, Hale and Ruddock stood in front of his desk like three felons awaiting sentence in court. They were united by a collective sense of shame. The chief magistrate kept them waiting for a few minutes and let his fury simmer. When he suddenly rose to his feet, they took an involuntary pace backwards.

'Who was the author of this travesty of justice?' he demanded.

'I was, sir,' confessed Yeomans, 'but it was no travesty. We did have legitimate grounds for suspicion. Ruddock *did* actually witness the theft of that leg of mutton.'

'It's true,' said Ruddock. 'I'd swear it.'

'And the thief looked uncannily like Huckvale.'

'I'd swear to that as well.'

'It was Chevy who set us in motion,' said Hale, attempting to shift the blame to their younger colleague. 'If he hadn't reported what he'd seen, the arrest would never have taken place.'

'Be quiet, Hale,' ordered Kirkwood. 'In my view, you are all equally culpable. I have three observations to make. First, when you saw the crime taking place, why didn't you arrest the thief on the spot?'

'I tried to do so, sir,' said Ruddock, 'but he ran off. I gave chase and would certainly have caught him had not his accomplice, lurking outside the market, tripped me up. I still have the bruises from the fall.'

'Don't expect sympathy from me.'

'No, sir.'

'Second, all this happened a week ago.' He transferred his gaze to Yeomans. 'Why did it take you seven days to arrest the man Ruddock claims to have seen at the market?'

'We've been very busy, sir,' said Yeomans.

'A case like this should have taken priority.'

'We realise that now.'

'If Huckvale *had* been the thief, he'd have had a whole week to leave the city and hide somewhere well beyond your grasp. Strike while the iron is hot. That's my rule. When you suspect someone, arrest him immediately.'

'We usually do, sir.'

'Third – and this is a damning indictment of your behaviour – the butcher whose mutton was stolen reported the theft. I took the trouble to look at the record and read what he said. All that Ruddock saw of the man was his back as he fled the scene. The butcher, on the other hand, was face-to-face with him. Do you know how he described the malefactor?'

Yeomans ran his tongue over dried lips. 'No, sir.'

'He said that the man was tall, skinny and rat-faced.'

'Huckvale is skinny, sir.'

'And he's rat-faced as well,' added Hale.

'That's why I was convinced it was him, sir,' explained Ruddock.

Kirkwood narrowed his lids. 'How could you confuse a tall man with a very short one?' he asked. 'Or are you going to suggest that Huckvale has lost six or seven inches since the crime? Is this the effect that eating a leg of mutton has on a man? His body shrinks in size? Is that your claim, Ruddock?'

'No, sir,' said the other, meekly.

'What about you two?'

'No, sir,' said Yeomans.

'No, sir,' said Hale.

'At least we're all agreed on that,' said Kirkwood. 'I put it to you that you used this alleged sighting of a thief in the market as a pretext for raiding the shooting gallery where Huckvale works. While there, Mr Skillen assures me, you made an alarming amount of noise and caused actual damage to the property. And all of this was done in the search for a tall, skinny, rat-faced man who was not even on the premises. Is that an accurate account of today's farcical intervention?'

'We went there with the very best of intentions, sir,' said Yeomans.

'You went there to cause havoc and to upset the Skillen brothers.'

'That was not our primary purpose.'

'You also threatened further raids on the gallery.'

'It's the only way to keep them under control, sir. They are a nuisance and are already impeding the murder investigation.'

'Then the best way to establish your superiority is to solve the crime ahead of them. How can you do that when you waste time descending on their premises and seizing an innocent man? Mr Bowerman's killer must be caught but, I'll wager, the last place you're likely to find him is at the gallery.'

'We've made progress to that end, sir.'

'What end?'

'The hunt for the killer,' said Yeomans. 'We called at the victim's home.'

'Not before time, I may say!'

'His butler told us something of what lay behind the duel with

Captain Hamer. And we were given a much deeper insight into his master's character.'

'Did the butler have any idea who might have murdered him?'

'None, sir. Mr Bowerman was a man with no known enemies.'

'What about Captain Hamer? He qualified as an enemy.'

'That's precisely why we arrested him.'

'Yes,' said Kirkwood, cynically, 'it was another of your blunders. Try to arrest people who will actually *remain* in custody, not those we have to set free with abject apologies for your over-exuberance. I suppose that I should be thankful you didn't accuse the captain of stealing a leg of mutton as well.'

'It couldn't have been him, sir,' Ruddock put in, helpfully. 'He's too handsome to be called rat-faced.'

'Going back to the murder victim,' said Yeomans, 'we feel that we can see the path that the investigation must follow. As a next step, we must introduce ourselves to Miss Somerville.'

'You should already have done that. It's what I advised.'

'We'll go there at once, sir.'

'I must first extract a promise from you.'

'You shall have it, sir.'

'Whatever else you do,' said Kirkwood, scornfully, 'don't arrest the lady as well. In fact, don't arrest *anybody*. Your record in that regard has been lamentable. Gather evidence as patiently as you can and try, I beg of you, to be tactful for once. Mr Bowerman was on the brink of proposing marriage, you tell me. That being the case, Miss Somerville must be looked at as a grieving widow. Tread very carefully. She will be fragile.'

Seated on the ottoman in her boudoir, Laetitia Somerville untied the pink ribbon around the letters she'd received from Mark Bowerman and began to read them in chronological order. It had been a slow courtship at first but had soon picked up pace. The letters became longer and increasingly affectionate. They were infused with a tentative passion that matured into something far stronger. Written by a man who'd never expected to find love again, each one marvelled at his good fortune in meeting her. It was impossible not to be touched by the poignancy of it all. He was not simply dead, Bowerman had been cruelly murdered. What troubled Laetitia most was that a missive, allegedly written by her, had been used as the bait. Who had committed the forgery and how could they possibly have known it would entice him out of the safety of his house? Impelled by the hope of seeing her again, Bowerman had answered the summons and gone to a designated place where someone lay in wait for him.

Having read the correspondence in its entirety, Laetitia got up abruptly and took all but the final letter across to the little fireplace. Tossing them into the grate, she set them alight and watched the thwarted ambitions of Mark Bowerman going up in smoke. When she returned to the ottoman, she picked up his last communication to her and read it with a smile of satisfaction.

CHAPTER EIGHT

Hester Mallory arrived at the bank just before it was closing. The chief clerk tried to turn her away, suggesting that she might return on the following day, but the manager then caught sight of her. Leonard Impey had always had an eye for a pretty woman and he was momentarily startled. Hester was far more than pretty. Still in her early thirties, she had a beauty and sophistication that would turn heads anywhere. Acting as her chaperone was a young, pallid manservant. Dismissing his clerk, the manager introduced himself and shepherded the visitors into his room. When he closed the door behind them, he felt a thrill at the fact that they were in private together. Her companion was invisible. Hester's attire, bearing, graceful movement and soft voice made her thoroughly enchanting.

Offered a seat, Hester lowered herself into a chair. Impey hovered around her. He was a plump man in his fifties with a flabby face and overlarge lips. Gazing at her over the top of his spectacles, it was all he could do to stop himself dribbling with pleasure.

'How may I be of service to you, Miss . . . ?'

'It's Mrs Mallory,' she replied. 'Mrs Hester Mallory.'

'Welcome to our humble bank.'

'Thank you, Mr Impey. It was recommended to me as the most trusted institution of its kind in the whole of London.'

'That's praise indeed, Mrs Mallory. May I know who spoke of us in such fulsome terms?'

'I can do more than that,' she said, opening her bag. 'I have a letter of introduction from him. I'm sure that you remember Mr Jacob Picton?'

'How could I forget such a distinguished gentleman? We were fortunate to do business with him for many years. How is Mr Picton?'

'Read what he says and all will be explained.'

Taking out the letter, she handed it over to him. Impey retreated to his desk and sat down to peruse the missive. Picton had invested heavily in property in the capital and, when more houses came on to the market, he'd borrowed money from the bank to purchase them. His record of success was almost unrivalled. Rental income alone allowed him to live in luxury in Mayfair. It was only when his health began to fail that he sold off much of his property empire and moved to a country estate in Hampshire.

'Mr Picton speaks well of you,' said Impey, reading the letter and recognising his old friend's distinctive calligraphy. 'You and your husband are neighbours of his, I see. Is Mr Mallory travelling with you?'

'No, Mr Impey, my husband rarely stirs from the country, but I felt that it was time I stayed here for a while to rub off the rust a little, so to speak. I do have another purpose for the visit, as it happens.'

'Do you?'

'My husband will soon be celebrating his fiftieth birthday and I am going to give him a gift that he has sought ever since we met.'

'What might that be?'

'Why, it's a portrait of his dear wife, of course.'

He tittered. 'I should have guessed.'

'It's long overdue.'

'And is Mr Mallory aware of your plan?'

'That would spoil the surprise,' she said, laughing gaily. 'I've been in secret correspondence with an artist who has a reputation for portraiture. According to Mr Picton, he's without compare. Unfortunately,' she added, with a wry smile, 'artists of that kind tend to come at a high price.'

'I'd be surprised if he charged you a single penny,' he said, gallantly, 'for he'll realise what a privilege it will be to have you as a client.'

'It's kind of you to say so, Mr Impey!'

'He'll have the pleasure of looking at you for long periods.'

'I hope they're not too long, sir. I am very restive.'

Impey stood up to lean across the desk and return the letter. She gave him a smile of thanks before popping it into her bag. Having felt jaded after a long day's work, he was refreshed. He was also anxious to help a potential client.

'What exactly has brought you to us, Mrs Mallory?'

'I merely wanted to introduce myself,' she explained, 'and to establish trust between us. You need to know something of me before any transaction can take place and I, in turn, wanted to find out if Mr Picton's high opinion of this bank was justified.'

'That's a wise precaution.'

'It's one that I always take.'

'If you have any questions about the way that we operate, I'll be happy to answer them. I think you'll find that we've maintained the high standards noted by Mr Picton. Do please give him my regards when you're next in touch with him.'

'I'll certainly do so.'

Hester studied him carefully as if trying to weigh him up. Feeling a trifle uncomfortable under her scrutiny, Impey resumed his seat. When her appraisal was over, she gave him a reassuring smile.

'I can see that you're a man with financial acumen,' she said, approvingly.

'It's an essential quality for a bank manager.'

'You are far too experienced to take a new client at face value.'

'That's quite right.'

'Then let me ask you this, Mr Impey . . .'

Yeomans and Hale could still hear the chief magistrate's invective ringing in their ears. What they'd conceived of as a clever ruse to keep the Skillen brothers at bay had rebounded against them. Their prisoner had been released and they'd been roundly chastised. As they approached the house where Laetitia Somerville lived, they felt hurt and badly misunderstood.

'I still think it was a clever idea of yours, Micah,' said Hale.

'It gave them a fright and taught them we'll stand for no interference.'

'Mr Kirkwood doesn't appreciate us.'

'We must force him to do so, Alfred.'

'And how do we do that?'

'For a start,' said Yeomans, 'we must make the most of this visit. Leave me to do the talking to Miss Somerville. I have a way with distressed ladies. I know how to calm them. When we leave here, we must have a lot of new evidence to impress the chief magistrate. It's the only way to win back his good opinion of us.'

'But I don't think he ever *had* a good opinion of us.'

'He knows our true value.'

Yeomans pointed at the bell and Hale stepped forward to ring it.

When the door opened, a manservant looked at them enquiringly. Explaining who they were, Yeomans asked to see Miss Somerville.

'I'm afraid that won't be possible, sir,' said the man.

'Is the lady not at home?'

'Miss Somerville is here but she's taken to her bed. She's left orders that she wishes to see nobody – nobody at all. Good day to you.'

Before they could stop him, the servant shut the door. Hale was despondent.

'Everything is going wrong for us today.'

Yeomans bit back an expletive. 'We'll be back,' he vowed.

Gully Ackford was delighted that Jem Huckvale had returned to the gallery and greeted him with a warm embrace. He treated Huckvale like a son and had schooled him in all the disciplines that were taught there. Though he looked small and almost puny, Huckvale was a difficult opponent in a boxing ring and several clients preferred to seek tuition from him. Ackford took his young friend away to offer solace after the fright of his arrest. Peter and Paul were left alone. Conscious that Hannah would be in the way, Charlotte had accompanied her back to the house. The brothers were therefore able to talk in private at last. After exchanging their respective news, they discussed their strategy.

'One problem is solved,' said Peter. 'After today's little episode, we needn't fear another raid from the Runners. Gully can take down the barricades.'

'He was relieved to hear that.'

'What will you do next, Paul?'

'I'd like to track down Sir Geoffrey Melrose. As the person who invited Mr Bowerman to a dinner party at which he met Miss Somerville, he'll be able to tell us something valuable about both of them.'

'How will you go about finding him?'

'I have friends in high places,' said Paul.

Peter laughed. 'The only reason you know them is that they frequent *low* places. Your years of wild abandon have finally come in useful, Paul.'

'Half the nobility love to gamble. It may well be that Sir Geoffrey is among them. At all events, I'm certain that one of the acquaintances I made during my time at the gaming tables will be able to tell me how I can get in touch with him.'

'Won't he come forward of his own volition when he hears of Bowerman's death?'

'That depends on whether or not he lives in London, Peter. If he resides in the country, it may be some time before he finally hears the news. And it will not bring him to *our* doors. Sir Geoffrey is more likely to seek out the Runners.'

'There is a simpler way to locate him.'

'Is there?'

'Why not approach Miss Somerville? If he knew her well enough to invite her to a dinner party, Sir Geoffrey will be part of her circle. Ask her for his address.'

'I thought of that but decided against the idea. There's something about Miss Somerville I find slightly disquieting and the annoying thing is that I've no idea what it is. Besides, since she's now in mourning, she may be distressed to hear that we are looking into her past, as it were.'

'That's a valid point.'

'What will you be doing, Peter?'

'I've been thinking about the house where the murder occurred,' said his brother. 'Why was Mr Bowerman lured there and how did the killer know that it would be unoccupied? More to the point, how did he get into the garden in the first place? The house must be rented by an agent. I'll seek him out.'

'I'll be interested in your findings.'

'What I'll be interested in is what the War Office can tell me about Captain Hamer. We mustn't forget him, Paul.'

'He won't *let* us, I promise you.'

'You had your doubts about him and your judgement is always sound.'

'Hamer worries me. At the very time when Mr Bowerman was about to propose marriage to Miss Somerville, he came back into her life. It was almost as if he responded to a cue.'

'There's another reason to distrust the man,' said Peter, taking a letter from his pocket. 'This arrived earlier. It was sent by the man I met at the mortuary.'

'What does it say?'

'The dagger that killed Mr Bowerman *did* belong to Hamer, after all.'

Evening found the two of them at Rawdon Carr's club in Pall Mall. While Carr was relaxed, however, Stephen Hamer was tense and preoccupied. His friend nudged him.

'You haven't touched that excellent glass of port.'

'It must have been someone from my army days,' said Hamer.

'Are you still obsessed with that dagger?'

'Who else would know that I possessed it?'

'*I* did, your servants did and, I daresay, you showed your collection to the occasional visitors. Why look to the army for a culprit?'

'I made enemies, Rawdon.'

'We all do that, sometimes without even knowing it.'

'These enemies bear grudges. I wounded one of them badly in a duel and I seduced another one's mistress. They'd both have cause to strike at me.'

'Then why haven't they done so before now?'

'I don't know.'

'And how would they have been aware that Mr Bowerman even existed? You can discount your former comrades, Stephen. The person we're after, I fancy, is closer to home. Have you had to get rid of any servants recently?'

'I have, as a matter of fact. A man called Grainger had to be dismissed.'

'What was his offence?'

'He questioned a decision of mine. I had him out of the house in minutes.'

'Then he's a much more promising suspect.'

'Grainger wouldn't *dare* to steal anything from me.'

'He dared to challenge your authority.'

'That's true . . .'

'And since he lived under your roof,' said Carr, 'he'd know all about your collection of weapons and where to find the key to the room where it's kept. As for information about Bowerman, he could easily have gained that by listening outside a door. We discussed the duel at length.'

Hamer shook his head. 'Grainger was dismissed over a week before we knew that there would *be* a duel. He couldn't possibly have heard of Bowerman, still less planted a dagger in his back. No, it has to be someone else.'

'You've been brooding on it ever since we examined the body.'

'A shot between the eyes would have been a kinder death for him.'

Carr smirked. 'Since when have you discovered the concept of kindness?'

'Someone is trying to implicate me in a murder, Rawdon. I resent it.'

'I don't blame you.'

'I want to use that dagger of mine to slice off his balls and gouge out his—'

'Keep your voice down,' said Carr, cutting in. 'I don't need to know the gory details. The first step is to identify the man and any confederates who may have been involved. I was hoping we might learn something useful by calling at Bowerman's house earlier on but the visit was fruitless. All that the butler could tell us was where the murder took place.'

'He told us something else as well.'

'Did he?'

'Yes – Paul Skillen had been there.'

'He's an enterprising young man. We must be equally enterprising.'

'You said that we ought to divert his attention.'

'The matter is in hand. Shall I tell you what I've done?'

Smiling complacently, Carr drained his glass in one satisfying gulp.

There were two of them. It was well after midnight when they arrived. Each of them carried a sledgehammer. While one man attacked the front door of the shooting gallery, the other pounded away at the rear entrance to the premises. The locks soon burst apart. The men were not done yet. Each had brought a snarling dog on a thick leash. The animals were released into the gallery and went racing around the building, barking madly and searching for prey. There was pandemonium.

Huckvale was awakened by the first hammer blow. The second violent thud made him leap out of bed and rush to open the window but he could see nothing down below in the darkness.

Grabbing one of the swords he used for instruction, he came out on to the landing with the intention of descending the stairs to see what was causing the noise. The baying of the dogs and the sound of their paws on the wooden steps changed his mind instantly and he retreated to the safety of his bedroom, slamming the door behind him and bemused by what was happening.

Ackford, by contrast, assessed the situation quickly. They were under attack. Roused from his slumber, he took down the loaded musket that hung on his wall and left his room purposefully. Though he could only see blurred outlines of the animals, he knew that they had to be destroyed before they could sink their jaws into him. He shot the first one dead then used the stock of the weapon to knock the other one unconscious. Sword in hand, Huckvale emerged from his room to see the two carcases on the floor.

'Where did they come from?' he asked.

'Fetch a lantern. We'll have to make some repairs.'

'Someone must have knocked down the door.'

'Arm yourself with a pistol. It may be needed.'

When the lantern was alight, they went downstairs and examined the damage. Outside both broken doors was a dog leash. Once he was certain there was no danger, Ackford put his musket aside.

'Take the horse and ride to Peter's house.'

'He'll be fast asleep, Gully.'

'So were we until a few minutes ago. Peter needs to be told. He's used to being woken up at all hours.'

'What about Paul? Shall I rouse him as well?'

'My guess is that he's still awake. With a woman like Hannah beside me, I know that I would be. Paul can wait until morning. His brother is the one we need.'

* * *

Paul and Hannah were, in fact, still wide awake and had not even retired to bed. They had spent hours discussing a plea from Lemuel Fleet when he'd called at the house for the second time. The manager had implored Hannah to attend a rehearsal the following day, assuring her that the playwright would not be present so they could talk openly about the defects in his play. He stressed that there were other people in the company and that their views ought to be taken into account.

'I'm not going,' said Hannah, reaching her decision.

'I believe that you should.'

'You don't have to act in that dreadful play.'

'If I was contracted to do so,' said Paul, 'then I'd honour that contract.'

'Don't talk to me about honour,' she cried.

'You have a legal obligation, Hannah.'

'Where in the contract does it oblige me to speak atrocious lines and sing appalling ditties? *The Piccadilly Opera* is beneath me. I was beguiled into agreeing to act in it. Mr Fleet misled me completely.'

'The manager is a reasonable fellow. Discuss changes with him.'

'I demand to change the whole play.'

'That's no basis for a proper discussion.'

'Do you *want* me to be pilloried?' she howled, jumping to her feet. 'Are you pleased at the thought that I'll be jeered until the entire audience flees the theatre in disgust? Have you no pity on me?'

'I have the greatest pity,' said Paul, enfolding her in his arms, 'but I also have faith in your powers as an actress. You can make the most banal lines sound like the work of a Marlowe or a Shakespeare. And when you sing, the silliest of ditties become arias from Handel. There's no risk whatsoever of derision,

Hannah. You sprinkle magic on every play in which you appear.'

Hannah was sufficiently mollified to let him kiss her. She even agreed to sit down again. The manager's second visit had given her food for thought. She had no quarrel with Fleet himself and every reason to deal kindly with a man who'd given her so much help and support. Hannah felt sorry that she'd sent him off twice with a flea in his ear. He deserved better. At the same time, however, she resolved that she was not going to appear in what she considered to be a threadbare play written by an egregious playwright. Simply by letting her pour out her heart, Paul had been helpful. Hannah saw that it was unkind of her to keep him up any longer.

'Let's go to bed,' she suggested.

'I'm not sharing it with a third person,' he warned.

'What do you mean?'

'When I get between the sheets, I don't want to find that you've invited Abel Mundy to join us. Leave him downstairs, Hannah. We've talked about him enough. I'm not going to let him come between us. Is that agreed?'

She kissed him full on the lips. Paul had his answer.

Peter Skillen did not mind in the least that he'd been pulled from his bed in the dead of night. If there was a crisis at the gallery, he wanted to be there. After saddling his horse, he galloped off with Huckvale trying to keep up with him. By the time they got to their destination, Ackford had tied up the unconscious dog and already repaired the broken doors. They could offer stiffer resistance if attacked by a sledgehammer now. As a precaution, Ackford had also reloaded his musket and kept it within reach. Having heard Huckvale's account of what happened, Peter heard a more measured description of events from Ackford.

'Who was responsible for the attack?' asked Peter.

'Jem has a theory,' said the older man.

'Yes, I know. He thinks that the Runners are to blame.'

'It's their revenge,' argued Huckvale. 'They were livid that I couldn't even be held in custody for a while. I wouldn't be at all surprised if Yeomans and Hale were swinging those sledgehammers.'

'I would,' said Peter. 'They'd never stoop to anything like this.'

'I disagree.'

'Peter is right,' said Ackford. 'The Runners might ruffle our feathers but they'd stop well short of launching an assault on the gallery. It was lucky that I had my old Brown Bess musket when I met those dogs. It's the one I first fired at the Battle of Yorktown when I was a raw recruit in the British army and it probably saved my life. If I hadn't dealt with those ravening curs, they'd have torn me to bits. This is not simply a matter of damage to property. It was a case of attempted murder. Yeomans and Hale would never condone that.'

'So who would?' asked Huckvale.

'I wish I knew, Jem.'

'Is it someone we helped to put in gaol? Did one of them ask their friends to attack us out of spite? Is that what happened?'

'It's possible,' said Ackford, pensively.

'It's more than possible, Gully.'

'What's your opinion, Peter?'

'It *could* be connected to some villain we put behind bars,' conceded Peter. 'Most of them threaten to get even with us one day. But I incline to the view that that's not the case here. The key lies in the timing.'

'That's why I thought it was the Runners,' said Huckvale. 'They boasted about making our lives more difficult – and then *this* happens.'

'Something else has happened, Jem. A blameless man was stabbed to death because he had the misfortune to fall in love with a beautiful woman. She already had an admirer and he's the person we should start looking at.'

'Captain Hamer?'

'He resents the fact that Paul is investigating the murder. My brother had a frosty reception when he called on the man. The one thing Hamer knows about Paul is that he works here at the gallery and taught Mr Bowerman how to fire a pistol. It's a natural assumption on Hamer's part that my brother also lives here. I think that tonight's ugly business was a warning. It was telling my brother to stop trying to find Mr Bowerman's killer.'

'Nobody can stop Paul from doing what he thinks is right,' said Ackford. 'As for frightening him off, the attack will only make him more determined to press on. And the same goes for the rest of us.'

'Perhaps I should have brought Paul here as well,' said Huckvale.

'I told you it was unnecessary.'

'Let him have his sleep, Jem,' said Peter. 'I'll speak to my brother first thing.'

'He'll be very angry. He doesn't have your self-control, Peter. When he hears what happened here, he'll fly into action.'

'My feeling is that Paul will reach exactly the same conclusion as me. Captain Hamer is behind this attack. The burning question is this: how do we respond?'

After a night of heavy drinking at Carr's club, Stephen Hamer had reeled home and been put to bed by the servants. He lapsed into a deep sleep and might well have stayed in bed for hours had he not heard – or thought he'd heard – a persistent whining outside the front door of the house. As he occupied the front bedroom, he was closest to the noise. Hamer tried to ignore it but it was impossible.

There was a note of pain and pleading that eventually forced him to investigate. Pulling himself out of bed, he padded across the room and drew back the curtain. It was sometime after dawn and there was enough light for him to see clearly. What he saw directly below the window made him gasp.

Two dogs were on the ground. One was so motionless that it looked dead. The other had his legs tied together and wore a muzzle that restricted him to the piteous whine. Hamer remembered something that Rawdon Carr had boasted about the previous evening. It had involved two dogs.

Stomach heaving, he began to retch.

CHAPTER NINE

Leonard Impey always arrived early at the bank in the morning so that he could supervise its opening. Because he was anticipating the return of Hester Mallory, he turned up with a decided spring in his step. They'd had a most satisfying discussion on the previous day and he felt that he'd convinced her to do business with his bank. He had not relied entirely on the letter of introduction she'd brought from a friend. As with every new client, he'd asked a series of searching questions. All of them had been answered in a way that reassured him. He felt that it would be a pleasure to serve Mrs Mallory and tried to think of ways that would prolong her visit to his office. As each of his employees arrived, he took the opportunity to step outside the building and look up and down the street, even though the bank would not actually be open for almost an hour. His behaviour did not escape the notice of the others and they traded sly giggles. All of them had seen the woman when she'd first arrived and been struck both by her evident charm and by its effect on the manager.

When the last member of his staff came in, Impey seized the chance to slip once more out of the bank. The chief clerk appeared at his shoulder.

'Are you looking for someone, sir?' he asked.

'No, no,' replied the other. 'I just wanted some fresh air.'

'Does that mean you're not feeling well, Mr Impey?'

'I feel perfectly well.'

'I'm glad to hear it, sir. Do you have any specific orders for me today?'

'As a matter of fact, I do,' said Impey. 'You saw Mrs Mallory visit us yesterday. If she's decided to do business with us, she could be an important client. When she returns, have her shown into my office immediately.'

Paul Skillen had been horrified to hear of the attack on the gallery and, as his brother predicted, he singled out Stephen Hamer as the likely culprit. It was his idea to leave the two dogs outside the man's front door, giving him a shock and letting him know that he'd been identified as the culprit. When Peter called on him for the second time that day, his brother's fury had not subsided.

'We should have smashed down the doors of *his* house and let in a whole pack of wild dogs,' said Paul, vehemently. 'Gully and Jem might have been seriously hurt.'

'Luckily, they weren't.'

'We have to fight back somehow, Peter.'

'We did that when we left the dogs outside his home.'

'It's not enough. I'll go and confront him this morning.'

'You've a more pressing duty before you do that,' said his brother. 'Thanks to one of your acquaintances from that gambling hell you once patronised, you know where Sir Geoffrey Melrose may be found. Unfortunately, he's not here in London at the moment. Ride out to his estate and pass on the bad tidings about Mr Bowerman. It's likely that he's unaware of the murder. His reaction to the news will be interesting.'

'He'll be upset. He was a friend of Mr Bowerman.'

'We need to know the nature of that friendship.'

'Very well,' said Paul, 'but we mustn't let Hamer off the hook.'

'I couldn't agree more.'

'I'll call on him at once.'

'No, Paul, I can do that. While you visit Sir Geoffrey, I'll go to Hamer's house and take him to task for what occurred last night. As it happens, I have another reason for meeting the fellow.'

'Have you?'

'Yes,' said Peter, 'someone brought a letter from the Home Secretary earlier this morning. It contained the reply that he got from the War Office.'

'What did it say about Captain Hamer?'

'See for yourself.'

Taking a letter from his pocket, he passed it to Paul. He was amused to see his brother's eyes widen in amazement as he read the contents.

'I was as surprised as you are,' said Peter.

'I suppose that I shouldn't have been. This is typical of Hamer. I'd love to see his face when you wave this under his nose. It will take the swagger out of him.' After finishing the letter, he handed it back. 'Watch out for that friend of his, Rawdon Carr. He's the oily devil who acted as second at the duel and tried to make Mr Bowerman tender an apology in exchange for his life. Carr is one of Hamer's hangers-on.'

'I'll give the two of them your regards, Paul.'

'I'll still want to meet them face-to-face.'

'You can do that when you've spoken to Sir Geoffrey. Find out if he was deliberately playing the matchmaker when he invited Mr Bowerman and Miss Somerville to dinner.'

'I'll also ask him why he thought that two such different people would ever be attracted to each other.'

'There's no accounting for taste, Paul.'

'I learnt that when I first met Hannah. She seemed hopelessly beyond my reach. I was ensnared at once but it never crossed my mind for a second that I'd have the slightest appeal for someone like her. Miraculously, I did somehow.'

'I still can't understand it,' teased Peter. 'Being serious, there's something I must ask on Charlotte's behalf. She spent a fair amount of time yesterday listening to Hannah's woes about this play she's acting in. Charlotte wants to know if any decision has been made.'

Paul rolled his eyes. 'Thankfully, it has.'

'Has she pulled out?'

'No, she eventually agreed to attend a rehearsal this morning. It took me hours to persuade her to do that. The theatre is her lifeblood. When she meets the other actors again, she'll be among friends. It might help to soften her stance against Abel Mundy.'

'Is he really the fiend she describes?'

'Hannah calls him the Prince of Darkness.'

The rehearsal got off to a promising start. The moment that Hannah entered, the rest of the cast rose to their feet and gave her a spontaneous round of applause. She was touched and even permitted a few welcoming kisses on her cheek. Simply being back in the theatre was a tonic for her. It brought her fully alive. Lemuel Fleet was at her elbow immediately, thanking her profusely and promising her that alterations and additions would be made to *The Piccadilly Opera*.

'There *are* parts of the play that will pass muster,' he said.

She arched an eyebrow. 'I've never seen any of them.'

'You look upon it with a jaundiced eye, Miss Granville.'

'Not to mention a queasy stomach,' she added, raising a laugh from the others. 'But you may be right, Mr Fleet. Perhaps I am being too critical. No play is entirely beyond redemption. All that this one needs is a change of title, a change of plot, a new cast of characters and, above all else, a skilful playwright.'

'Mr Mundy may yet rise to that level.'

'He has a desperately long way to go.'

Fleet changed his tack. 'Let us at least rehearse the first scene.'

'It's too flat and leaden,' she claimed.

'That's why I've decided to open with a fanfare. It will secure the attention of the audience and prepare them for your entrance. There are several other points in the text where I've introduced additional music.'

'Will there be songs worth singing?'

'We will lose those in the play and replace them with ones that will meet your approval. I want more jollity and sprightliness in the performance. Do you hear that, everyone?' he went on, raising his voice. 'Let a sense of enjoyment fill the theatre.'

'It's to be a real comedy, then,' she observed. 'That will be an improvement.'

There was general agreement. Unlike Hannah, most of the cast were not in constant demand so they had to suppress any mutinous feelings about a play. If any of them were singled out as being in any way rebellious, they would be viewed askance by theatre managements. Forced to hold their tongues, they were delighted to have a mouthpiece in Hannah. She was able to point out the many shortcomings of the play that they'd all discerned. It turned her into their heroine.

The rehearsal began and there was a new feeling of optimism. Scenes that had hitherto been limp and tedious now became brighter and more entertaining. There was a laughter that had never existed before. In spite of her objections, Hannah found herself relishing the experience of being back onstage again. The new songs she was given to sing made her even happier. All of the changes enhanced the play beyond measure. There were moments when she actually forgot how much she hated *The Piccadilly Opera*. The amended version made it almost presentable.

The euphoria could not last. Without warning, the joyful mood was shattered. Unbeknownst to anyone, Abel Mundy had walked in. Transfixed by what he saw, it took him minutes to find his voice. He used it to emit a high-pitched scream of rage.

'Stop, stop, stop!' he demanded. 'What are you doing to my play?'

'We've made a few slight changes,' said Fleet, 'that's all, Mr Mundy.'

'You've savaged my work.'

'It's what it required,' said Hannah, boldly. 'We put some life into it.'

'This is all your doing, Miss Granville,' said the playwright. 'I write a serious drama and you turn it into an inconsequential little squib. You could never reach the heights that my work demands.'

'Now, now,' said Fleet, jumping in before Hannah could reply. 'Let's keep the debate on a friendly level. Hot words leave bad feelings in their wake.'

'So do incompetent plays like this one,' murmured Hannah.

'I'll brook no insults,' howled Mundy.

'Then you'll best leave while you may, sir, or I'll tell you what I really think of this dull, dreary, lifeless piece of theatrical mediocrity that dares to call itself a play.'

'This is insufferable!'

'The door is behind you, Mr Mundy.'

'There'll be repercussions from this.'

'Yes, we'll finally have something worth performing.'

'That's enough!' yelled Fleet, removing his wig and throwing it to the floor. 'This is disgraceful behaviour. Differences of opinion should be settled in private. A true compromise can only be reached if there is moderation on both sides.'

'Look for no moderation from me,' said Hannah, pointing at

Mundy. 'I only have to see that hideous visage and I begin to feel sick. Look at him, everyone! What you see before you is the death's head of British drama!'

It was her last jibe and it struck home. Before she could add even more abuse, the quivering playwright swung round and ran out as if something had just set fire to his coat-tails. There was an ominous silence.

Fleet retrieved his wig. 'The rehearsal is over,' he growled.

In response to the summons, Rawdon Carr rode quickly to his friend's house. The first thing he saw on arrival was the gardener, loading a dead dog into a barrow before wheeling it around to the rear of the property. A servant came out to take care of his mount. Carr went into the house and found Hamer in the dining room, seated at the table with a half-empty decanter of claret in front of him.

'I've just seen someone wheeling a dead dog into your garden,' said Carr.

'He's going to bury it.'

'Whose animal was it?'

'Yours, Rawdon.'

'Don't be absurd!'

'You hired those two men to release dogs into that shooting gallery. What you just saw was one of the animals. I had the other put down as well. Its whining was giving me a headache.'

'I'm not sure that I follow you, Stephen.'

'He *knows*.'

'Who are you talking about?'

'Skillen knows that we were responsible for last night's attack.'

'But that's impossible.'

'Is it?' asked Hamer. 'Then perhaps you'll explain how the two dogs were dumped outside my front door, one of them shot dead

103

and the other trussed up. They were left there by Paul Skillen. The message was unmistakable.'

'I see,' said Carr, wincing. 'That is unfortunate, I grant you. My intention was to give him such a fright that he'd stop getting in our way.'

'He's much more *likely* to get in our way now, Rawdon.'

'That's not necessarily the case. Besides, Skillen has no proof whatsoever that we were in any way involved. If he challenges us, we simply swear that we had no part in the business.'

'What if the men you hired were caught?'

'They weren't, I assure you. I paid half their fee in advance so that I'd have confirmation that the job was done before they had their money in full. They said that it all went as planned.'

'Finding two dogs outside my house this morning was not part of the plan,' said Hamer, sourly. 'The sight of them almost made me puke.'

'I'm sorry about that.'

'Now you can see why I sent for you.'

'I can, Stephen, but we have nothing to worry about. Skillen has made a wild guess that we arranged that attack. We simply deny the allegation. I'll say that we spent most of the night at my club before rolling back to my house. The notion of setting a pair of dogs on him would never occur to us.'

'It occurred to *you*, Rawdon.'

'They'll never know that.'

Carr took the wine glass proffered by a servant. He poured himself a generous amount from the decanter then had a first sip of it. Hamer remained anxious.

'Cheer up, man!' said Carr, patting his shoulder. 'Brace yourself. You've faced enemy soldiers in battle. Why are you so upset by a couple of mangy dogs?'

'How would *you* like to see them outside your front door?'

'Frankly, I wouldn't.'

'We've been found out,' stressed Hamer. 'That could be awkward.'

When the doorbell rang, he sat up with a start. Carr was unperturbed.

'It's probably not him, Stephen. It's just a tradesman calling.'

'Then why has he come to the *front* door?'

'Stay calm. There's no need for concern.'

'I sincerely hope that you're right.'

They drank their wine and Hamer relaxed slightly. Moments later, there was a tap on the door and it swung open to reveal a servant.

'A Mr Skillen is asking to see you, sir.'

'Tell him I'm not at home,' said Hamer, tensing.

'No, don't do that,' advised Carr. 'That will only strengthen his suspicions. Let's face him together and send him packing.' After thinking it over, Hamer gave an affirmative nod. Carr took over. 'Show the gentleman in.'

The servants withdrew and Carr moved to stand behind his friend. It was a matter of seconds before Peter was escorted into the room. When the servant left this time, he closed the door behind him. Peter looked from one to the other.

'You are Mr Carr, I presume,' he said, directing the question at him.

'Heavens!' exclaimed the other, 'you have a very short memory, Mr Skillen. We shook hands on Putney Heath but two days ago.'

'You are mistaken, sir.'

'Have you taken leave of your senses?'

'They are in excellent condition, Mr Carr. Let me introduce myself properly. My name is *Peter* Skillen. The person who acted as Mr Bowerman's second was my brother, Paul.'

'Your *twin* brother, I see,' said Hamer, staring at him.

'I'm here in Paul's stead.'

'Then you must meet Captain Hamer,' said Carr, indicating his friend.

Peter pretended to look around. 'I see nobody of that name in this room.'

'He sits before you.'

'That's not *Captain* Hamer,' said Peter, levelly. 'It's Lieutenant Hamer.'

'Confound you, man!' cried Hamer, getting to his feet. 'I'll have you know that I was a captain in the Royal Horse Guards. The Blues are one of the finest regiments in the whole world. We fought at Waterloo.'

'Your regiment distinguished itself at Waterloo and it has my admiration and gratitude for doing so. But you were no longer a member of the regiment at that point in time, were you, Lieutenant?'

'*Captain* Hamer, if you please.'

'Show my friend due respect,' insisted Carr.

'He doesn't deserve it. As you well know, Lieutenant Hamer was court-martialled for conduct unbecoming an officer. He was drummed out of the regiment before it got anywhere near Waterloo.'

'Where the devil have you got these disgraceful lies?' demanded Hamer.

'They came to me via the Home Secretary,' said Peter, easily. 'As a favour to me, he made contact with the War Office and enquired about your military career, such as it was. In claiming to have been a captain, you're acting fraudulently.'

'We don't have to endure this nonsense,' said Carr. 'Be off with you, sir.'

He moved forward to touch Peter but saw the look in his eye and pulled back.

'I'm staying until I've said my piece,' asserted Peter. 'My first question is this. Posing as a captain, you fought a duel ostensibly for the hand of Miss Somerville. Is the lady aware of the deception you practised?'

'Mind your own business,' snarled Hamer.

'Is the regiment itself aware of what you've been doing in its name?'

'Don't answer that,' counselled Carr. 'He's trying to goad you.'

'The former Lieutenant Hamer doesn't need any goading, if you ask me,' said Peter. 'He's almost straining at the leash. On the subject of leashes,' he continued, 'what's happened to the two dogs we left outside your front door?'

'They've been buried,' grunted Hamer.

'But one of them was still alive.'

'He was shot.'

'That's poor reward for what he did at your behest. He and his companion ran all over the gallery. If it hadn't been for the quick thinking of my friends, someone could have been seriously injured, perhaps even killed.' He leant forward. 'Being guilty of attempted murder is far worse than conduct unbecoming an officer.'

'Get out!'

'Or was it *you* who hired those men to batter down the doors?' asked Peter, turning on Carr. 'Your friend gives the orders and you run the errands.'

'Be quiet!' yelled Carr, shaking with righteous indignation. 'You know nothing about us. We were not party to any attack on the shooting gallery. If you want the real culprits, look elsewhere.'

'I don't need to,' said Peter, coolly. 'They stand before me.' He turned to Hamer. 'My brother learnt something very interesting yesterday. The dagger that killed Mr Bowerman belonged to you. Is that true?'

'It might be,' admitted the other, 'but I never put it there.'

'We're resolved to find out who did use it,' declared Carr, 'no matter how long it takes us.' After taking a deep breath, he resorted to an attempt at charm, smiling warmly and speaking softly. 'Come, sir, we should not be enemies. We want the same thing as you and your brother and that's to catch the killer. That is where our energies are directed. Someone stole that dagger from here in order to embarrass the captain . . . my good friend, Stephen Hamer, that is. We should be combining resources and working together. The Runners will never find the villain in a month of Sundays. It therefore falls to us to do so.'

'Then you must work on your own,' said Peter, with biting contempt. 'We don't make common cause with a blatant liar like former Lieutenant Hamer and his pet monkey.'

'I'm nobody's monkey!' cried Carr.

'I speak as I find, sir.'

'Take care, Mr Skillen, I warn you.'

'How many dogs do you intend to set on the gallery next time?'

'We haven't a clue what you're talking about,' said Hamer, dismissively, 'so we'll thank you to stop making unsubstantiated allegations.'

'I endorse what the captain says,' added Carr.

'Except that he never attained that rank,' Peter reminded him. 'Since you've issued a warning to us, I'll reply with one of our own. My brother and I will carry out an independent investigation and, if you try to hamper us in any way, Paul and I will come looking for you. Is that plain enough for you, gentlemen?'

He had the satisfaction of seeing both men shift their feet uneasily.

* * *

When a couple of hours had passed, Impey began to give up hope that she would come. Though Mrs Mallory had expressed a desire to transact business with his bank, she admitted that she intended to speak to other banks before she committed herself. Impey came to suspect that she'd been offered a more cordial welcome or better terms elsewhere and reproached himself for not impressing her the previous day with his eagerness to serve her. Another hour dragged by and he accepted defeat. Then, out of the blue, she turned up with her chaperone and was shown in by the chief clerk. Impey was on his feet at once, holding the chair until she sat in it and pouring out a veritable flood of niceties. Having sent the clerk out, he enjoyed once more the frisson of pleasure at being so close to Hester Mallory.

'I thought you had deserted us,' he said, hands fluttering.

'Not at all, Mr Impey – I had other bank managers to visit, that is all.'

'Yet you've come back to us.'

'Nobody was able to accommodate me with the same readiness as you.'

'Any friend of Jacob Picton's will get preferential treatment here. Now,' he continued, sitting behind his desk, 'you said that you were in need of money to engage the artist who is about to paint your portrait.'

'That's true and, of course, I will need expenses while I'm here in London.'

'What is the total amount that you require, Mrs Mallory?'

'I feel that a thousand pounds will cover all eventualities.'

'I can authorise a loan at a very reasonable rate of interest.'

'Your trust in me is heartening, sir, but I'd like to offer additional proof that I am a bona fide client. As well as the letter from Mr Picton,' she said, taking a document from her bag, 'I have a bond for £2500, in Mr Picton's name, to offer as security for the loan.' She got up to pass it to him. 'The important thing is that my husband must know nothing of the portrait I intend to give him as a birthday gift. When he receives it, of course, he will be overjoyed and will reimburse Mr Picton without delay. I am sorry that a certain amount of deceit is involved but Mr Mallory deserves a complete surprise. He has been the dearest of husbands.'

'As well as the most fortunate,' said Impey, venturing a compliment.

She smiled. 'Thank you, kind sir.'

'I can see that you and Mr Picton have been co-conspirators.'

'None of this would have been possible without his assistance and advice.' She stood up. 'But you'll need time to study the bond before you advance any funds. I'll come back this afternoon.'

'No, no,' he said, 'there's no need for that. Give me a moment to examine it then I will open the safe myself and take out the specified amount. My only concern is that you should be leaving here with such a large amount of money. This is a very dangerous city, Mrs Mallory.'

'I have a carriage waiting outside.'

'That's very sensible of you.'

'We are all too aware of possible jeopardy,' she said. 'It's the reason my husband will never allow me to travel with money or with jewellery. Highwaymen will have no rich pickings from me. All I brought of real value was the bond and that is useless to any gentlemen of the road.'

'You and Mr Mallory have behaved very sensibly.'

'We always look ahead. It is an article of faith with us.'

Charlotte Skillen had been alarmed when they'd been roused from their beds with the information that the gallery had been attacked.

Peter had gone to inspect the damage and returned to tell her that everything was now under control. Nevertheless, it was only when she went there later that morning that she was persuaded the building now had stouter defences. Ackford had mended the doors and Huckvale fixed large brackets to the jambs so that he could slot in some thick planks of wood.

'We've done everything but install a portcullis,' he said.

'You've done well, Jem,' said Charlotte. 'It must have given you a terrible shock, having two large dogs running up the stairs to attack you.'

'It did. They sounded as if they wanted to eat us alive.'

'This is very upsetting. First, we have the Runners bursting in and arresting you. Then we have last night's attack. What next?'

'Whatever it is,' promised Ackford, 'we'll be ready for it.'

'And where will the trouble come from?'

'It won't be from the Runners, I'll wager.'

'Gully is right,' said Huckvale. 'In raiding the gallery, they went too far. They'll have been given a stern reprimand by the chief magistrate. Chevy Ruddock may get more than a rebuke.'

'So I should hope, Jem.'

'Peter is still certain that Captain Hamer instigated last night's assault. That's why he and Paul took those dogs to his house. Oh,' she went on, 'I shouldn't be calling him a captain any more. The Home Secretary had word from the War Office and passed it on. It turns out that Hamer never rose to the rank of captain and he was dismissed from the regiment after a court martial.'

'That tells us a lot about his character.'

'If he's a disgraced soldier,' said Huckvale, 'he could have been Mr Bowerman's killer, after all.'

'I doubt that, Jem.'

'Why?'

'It looks as if he's joined the hunt for the killer. That's what prompted last night's crisis. Hamer wants Peter and Paul out of the way so that he can have a clear field. If he solves the crime, he can claim the reward. Bills have been printed and posted up everywhere. Whoever catches the assassin stands to make a lot of money.'

'We can use it to repair the gallery properly,' said Charlotte. 'Peter and Paul have set their minds on apprehending the man who murdered Mr Bowerman.'

'Hamer is going to have serious competition.'

'It won't only come from Peter and Paul,' Huckvale pointed out. 'You're forgetting the Runners.'

'They're too slow.'

'They do solve *some* crimes. Give them credit for that.'

'I will,' said Ackford, 'though some of their so-called successes come about because of all the informers they retain, most of them seasoned rogues. No, Micah Yeomans will do his best but he'll always be trying to catch up with Peter and Paul. Hamer is the problem. We can ignore the Runners.'

Having been turned away the previous day, Yeomans and Hale called at the house again that morning. Given the same message that Miss Somerville was not to be disturbed, they camped on her doorstep and vowed to wait there until she was ready to admit them. It was noon when Laetitia finally relented and had them shown in. Removing their hats, they entered the house respectfully. Wearing a black velvet dress and an expression of deep sadness, she was seated on the edge of a sofa. Yeomans introduced himself and his companion. Her only response was a slight movement of her head. Hale felt that they were intruding on her grief.

'Perhaps we should come back another time,' he whispered.

'We've waited long enough already,' said Yeomans.

'Miss Somerville may not be in a fit state to answer questions.'

'She's as eager as we are to see this murder solved.' He took a step towards her. 'Isn't that true?'

'Yes, it is,' said Laetitia. 'I want to see Mr Bowerman's killer hanged.'

'We'll find him for you,' said Yeomans.

'Thank you.'

'But we'll do so much quicker if we have a little help from you.'

'How can I possibly be of assistance?'

'You knew the gentleman – we did not.'

'That's true.'

'What manner of man was he, Miss Somerville?'

'He was the most wonderful friend I've ever had,' she said, dabbing at a tear with her handkerchief. 'I've lost a rare jewel among men in Mr Bowerman. He changed my life when he came into it. How I shall manage without him,' she added, voice cracking, 'I simply don't know.'

'You have our sympathy.'

'Yes,' said Hale, 'we're sorry to bother you in your bereavement.'

'It is, however, necessary,' said Yeomans. 'Tell us a little more about Mr Bowerman. Take your time and go at your own pace. There's no hurry,' He took out a notebook. 'When and where did you first meet? How close were you and he? How did you feel when Captain Hamer turned up as if he had a claim on your affections?'

After waving them to some chairs, Laetitia spoke slowly and with great emotion. She talked about the fateful dinner party at which she'd first encountered Bowerman and how there'd been an immediate affinity between them. The courtship, she hinted, had been gentle and unforced. At no point was there any threat to their happiness. She admitted to being startled by the sudden reappearance of Stephen Hamer and insisted that she no longer considered him to be a friend, still less a suitor. When Yeomans asked her if Hamer should be viewed as a suspect, she shook her head firmly. She had no doubt whatsoever of his innocence.

'Do you have any idea who did murder Mr Bowerman?'

'No, I don't, Mr Yeomans.'

'Did he ever talk about his enemies?'

'How could he when he had none? Nobody could dislike Mark . . . Mr Bowerman, I should say. He was such a thoroughly decent man in every way.'

'We've known other thoroughly decent men who've been murdered,' said Hale, darkly. 'On closer examination, they turn out to be less angelic than they're painted.'

'That's clearly not the situation here,' said Yeomans, nudging him into silence. 'If he had no enemies, we must search for a motive other than simple hatred. One look at you, Miss Somerville, and a motive suggests itself at once. Someone coveted you so much that he could not bear the thought of a rival.'

'Mr Bowerman had no rival,' she declared. 'I discouraged all other attentions offered to me. There is no jealous lover.'

'What about Captain Hamer?'

'He belonged to my past.'

'You might say that. He believed otherwise.'

'I left him in no doubt about my feelings,' she said with a touch of irritation. 'Of one thing you may be absolutely certain, Mr Yeomans. It is quite *impossible* for me even to consider a closer union with Captain Hamer.'

CHAPTER TEN

Paul Skillen had always scorned danger. Whatever circumstances arose, he never considered risk. He preferred to plunge straight in and get the best out of an experience. It was the same when he went on a journey. Travel outside London exposed everyone to untold hazards and – on the basis that there was safety in numbers – most people chose to ride by coach or be in convoy with others. True to character, Paul went alone even though the journey to Eltham took him through open countryside at several points. Were he to encounter trouble, he was relying on his skill with sword and pistol to carry him through. As he set off, the steady, unvarying canter of his horse gave him a feeling of invincibility.

On his way to the country residence of Sir Geoffrey Melrose, he was able to enjoy the changing landscape around him and let his mind play with the possibilities surrounding the murder. Were they in search of one man or a gang? Who was capable of forging a message from Laetitia Somerville so cleverly that it achieved its object? Having pored over her letters for hours like the devoted suitor he was, Mark Bowerman would have known every detail of her calligraphy. Yet he'd somehow been deceived. Paul was convinced that the letter was the work of a woman, someone who was familiar with Laetitia's hand. The forger, he concluded, either had to be someone in her circle or someone who had been close to her but was now estranged. He needed to speak to Laetitia again.

What had the killer gained from the murder? That's what puzzled him. Significantly, no money was stolen from the victim and Paul could still not see what had been gained by his death. In the course of their time together, he'd got to know Bowerman well. The man was honest, well educated, invariably pleasant and, by nature, remarkably inoffensive. Nothing about him invited dislike, let alone hatred. It was ironic that, having taken part in a duel where he could easily have been shot dead in the chest, he was instead stabbed in the back during what he believed to be a rendezvous with the woman he intended to marry. Why had that particular house been chosen and who selected the garden as the murder scene?

One possible explanation surfaced: Bowerman had not been the prime target at all. The killer was really intent on hurting Laetitia Somerville and the best way to do that was to snuff out her hopes of marriage. Her new suitor was seen as dispensable. He had to die in order that she would suffer or, in time, be available for the killer himself. It might be that Bowerman had no enemies but she certainly did. Laetitia had told him that beauty could be a curse at times. Many men must have sought her hand or lusted after her body. Was one of them ready to commit murder in order to remove an obstacle?

Having stopped at a village inn to take refreshment and rest his mount, Paul climbed into the saddle again. It was not long before he returned to his meditation. Preoccupied as he might be, however, he was still alert to danger. When he came over a hill and saw a copse ahead of him, he noticed a beggar sitting beside the road with his back against a tree. Though the man seemed to be alone, Paul sensed that he might have an accomplice or two. Vigilance was paramount. As he got closer, therefore, he studied the man and looked at the branches of the tree beneath which he sat. There was a moment when the beggar adjusted his position and glanced upwards. Paul was quick to interpret the situation. They – at least two of them – were waiting for a lone and unwary traveller. Giving no indication that he suspected a trap, he kept his horse going at the same pace.

The beggar rose to his feet and stood in the road. He cupped his hands to plead for money. Slowing to a trot, Paul pretended that he was going to stop. He knew what was coming next. The beggar would grab the bridle and the man in the tree would drop down on Paul. In the event, they were out of luck. When the beggar tried to stop the horse, Paul kicked him so hard under the chin that he broke the man's jaw. Before the accomplice could leap down from the tree, he was shot in the arm. Paul then used the butt of his pistol to knock down a third man who came running out of the copse. Kicking his mount into a canter, Paul went on his way, leaving the robbers to lick their wounds and rue their misfortune.

'All I require is the name.'

'I'm sorry, Mr Skillen, but I'm unable to help you.'

'Is it a state secret?'

'All details of our property are confidential.'

'That garden was the scene of a murder,' said Peter, angrily. 'Doesn't that make a difference?'

'No, sir, it doesn't. We have our rules. I'd lose my position if I broke them.'

'Can't you see how *important* this information is?'

'We must protect the anonymity of our clients.'

Peter had to control the urge to strike the man. They were in the office of the agent responsible for letting the house but he refused to say who actually owned it. He was a tall, lean, sallow man in his forties with a face so nondescript that Peter would never remember a single feature of it when he left the building.

The agent's manner shifted annoyingly between condescension and unctuousness. Expecting cooperation, Peter was frustrated by the man's attitude.

'Supposing that you owned the property, sir,' said the agent.

'I don't understand.'

'How would *you* like it if we released your name and address to anyone who walked in here and asked for it? Most of our clients use this agency because we have a reputation for keeping secrets. Wouldn't you be offended if we betrayed you?'

'The only thing that offends me is your attitude.'

'I can't help that, sir.'

'If I obtained a warrant, you'd have to surrender the details.'

'Do you have such a warrant?'

'At the moment, I don't.'

'Then you have no legal right to inspect our files.'

'I simply want one name.'

'It makes no difference.'

Peter looked around the room. It was neat, tidy and purely functional. Beside the large, long table were a series of locked cabinets. Inside one of them, he thought, was the information he needed. He looked at the window. It was small in size but a man could still squeeze in through it. There were two locks on the door and a grill that could be pulled down outside it. The agency was well protected.

'Is there anything else I can do for you, sir?' asked the man, rubbing his palms together as if trying to warm them. 'Are you interested in renting a property?'

'Yes,' said Peter, 'as a matter of fact, I am.'

'Which part of London do you favour?'

'The one we've just been talking about.'

'We have three available houses in that area.'

'I already know the property I'd like to rent.'

The agent opened a sheaf and took some pages out of it, laying them down on the table with a flourish. He let his finger trail across them.

'Take your pick, Mr Skillen.'

'I've already made my selection and it's not one of these. I want the house where someone was murdered.'

'I've told you before. You're too late. New tenants are due to move in next week. They have a year's lease.'

'That's a pity,' said Peter, bitterly. 'If I occupied the property, I might actually get to know who owns it.'

Known for her patience and tolerance, Charlotte Skillen was fast approaching the point where one or both would give way. Hannah Granville had come to the gallery straight from the abandoned rehearsal. As before, she listed all of the play's faults and all of the playwright's failings. In the exchange with Abel Mundy, she boasted, she had been the clear winner and been supported by the rest of the cast. There was no hint of sympathy for the doomed manager. Charlotte felt impelled to point that out.

'One is bound to feel sorry for Mr Fleet,' she said.

'He is to blame for this whole imbroglio.'

'The manager acted in what he conceived of as the best interests of his theatre, Hannah. That is why he chose you as his leading lady.'

'I have no quarrel at all with *that* choice,' said Hannah. 'It's his selection of the play that is the point at issue.'

'You insisted on the right to have three choices against the one exercised by Mr Fleet.'

'That was a fair exchange.'

'It may appear so to you,' said Charlotte, softly, 'but it looks different to the unbiased observer. That's not to say I don't support you in every way,' she went on, 'but many people would not. They'd argue that you gained far more than the manager. As for the dispute, their advice would be that you and Mr Mundy should look for an amicable compromise.'

'*Amicable!*' exclaimed Hannah. 'You are asking me to be amicable towards that excrescence?'

'You've often worked before with people you detest. You've told me about them many times.'

'That was in my younger days when I was forced to do what I was told. I've outgrown that phase of my career. Fame gives me privileges. One of those is to appear in roles that allow me to dazzle an audience.'

'Regardless of the play, you'll always do that.'

'Not if I am shackled to *The Piccadilly Opera*.'

'Let's go back to the start,' suggested Charlotte. 'When the manager first described the plot to you, what was it that aroused your interest? I know that you hate every word of the play now but that wasn't the case beforehand. Something must have pleased you. What was it?'

Hannah relented. Having poured out her woes to Charlotte once again, she felt that her friend had been forced to listen to the harangue long enough. It was time to be reasonable. Concessions had to be made.

'The plot did have some value,' she confessed. 'Though it had elements both of *The Beggar's Opera* and of *The Duenna*, it also had traces of originality. What it did not have was the genius of a Gay or a Sheridan to develop them. My role, as it was described to me, had a surface attraction. I was to be the only daughter of a wealthy man determined to marry me off to a repulsive old lecher with whom my father did business. What I yearned for instead as a husband was a handsome young artist with all the qualities a woman could desire but with little money and no real prospects of acquiring any.'

'So you had to choose between obedience to your father and love?'

'What would *you* have done, Charlotte?'

'I'd have eloped with the handsome young artist.'

'That's exactly what I do in the play. In fact, it's the best moment I have. Once we think we're safe, we sing a duet that will bring tears to the eyes. Unfortunately, we've been betrayed. I am dragged back home and my lover is wrongfully imprisoned as a punishment. Luckily, he finds a friend in the prison chaplain, the only other decent man in the play. The chaplain has an important role. As for me, Esmeralda, how do I escape from a lewd old man and rescue my beloved from the cell he shares with the dregs of London life?'

Hannah went on to describe the twists and turns of a plot that had a lot of comic scenes to add spice and humour to the play. Without realising it, she was actually talking with a degree of enthusiasm about it. In getting her to accept that *The Piccadilly Opera* had some appealing features, Charlotte had done what she intended. She'd calmed her friend down and made her assess her position anew.

'*That's* how I was hoodwinked,' said Hannah.

'A presentable plot is no trick. It's true that some of it is plundered from better playwrights but you've often said that plagiarism is rife in the theatre.'

'It's true. Shakespeare stole his plots without blushing.'

'Then Mr Mundy can't be blamed for doing the same.'

'Don't couple his name with that of a master dramatist. Shakespeare could spin straw into gold. Mundy can only do that in reverse.'

'What will happen next?'

'That's no longer my concern. I've washed my hands of the enterprise.'

'How will Mr Mundy feel about that?'

'He'll be distraught, Charlotte.' She struck a pose. 'Without me, there'll *be* no performance of his play.'

Marion Mundy was a chubby, plain woman with an abundance of curly red hair and an unswerving loyalty to her husband. She'd shared his recurring setbacks in finding a market for his plays and consoled him as the letters of rejection – some of them harsh to the point of studied cruelty – quickly piled up. During moments when even his steely confidence began to bend, she was there to praise him and stiffen his resolve to pursue a life in the theatre. When at last he was given his opportunity, she sat proudly beside him at the first performance of his first play. It had its obvious faults but it managed to please an audience in York. The applause validated Abel Mundy. In his view, and that of his wife, he'd joined the theatrical elite.

From that moment on, his progress was slow but steady. Each new play was met with unstinting praise from his wife and he drew great strength from that. As he achieved more success and his reputation spread, they knew that it was inevitable that his work would eventually move from the backwaters of the provinces to one of the great theatres of the capital, buildings where the finest playwrights and actors had left vivid memories still hanging in the air. Mundy longed to be mentioned in the same breath as the titans of his profession. Marion loved being mentioned as his wife.

Returning from the rehearsal, he had a face like thunder. She was on her feet at once to wrap her arms around him and ease him down onto the sofa. Sitting beside him, she removed his hat and saw the perspiration on his brow.

'You've been running, Abel,' she said.

'I could not get away from the accursed place quick enough.'

'What happened?'

'It's too painful to relate.'

'Did it involve that hateful woman again?'

'It *always* involves Miss Granville.'

'Why will she not recognise your talent as a playwright?'

'She is too busy admiring herself in a mirror.'

'Did she dare to abuse you again?'

'Yes, Marion,' he replied, 'and she did so in front of the whole company.'

'That's unforgivable. Miss Granville should be dismissed at once.'

'I've urged that solution on the manager time and again.'

'What's his reply?'

'He is bound hand and foot, contractually.'

'It's she who should be bound hand and foot,' she said with sudden intensity, 'and then thrown into the Thames with a ship's anchor attached. Miss Granville should be shunned by respectable society,' she continued. 'It's an established fact that she lives in sin with a man.'

Mundy was about to point out that most of the actresses of his acquaintance shared a bed with a man who was not their husband. He'd met two of them who were the discarded mistresses of the Prince Regent and one who'd enjoyed a brief flirtation with no less a person than the Duke of Wellington. Moral standards were more fluid in theatrical circles. While he told his wife many things about his dealings with the acting profession, he concealed far more.

'I won't let you be treated like this, Abel,' she declared.

'What can you possibly do, my love?'

Marion tightened her fists until her knuckles turned white.

'I don't know as yet but . . . I promise that I'll think of something.'

* * *

Sir Geoffrey Melrose was a big, broad-shouldered man in his sixties with ruddy cheeks that dimpled when he laughed. If he was staying at his country residence, he loved to go for a ride first thing in the morning before galloping back to the house. Only the most inclement weather could prevent him from taking his favourite exercise. When he returned after a stimulating hour in the saddle, one servant came out to take care of his horse and another to receive his hat and his riding crop. The second man had news for his master.

'You have a visitor, Sir Geoffrey,' he said.

'Splendid! Who is it?'

'The gentleman's name is Mr Paul Skillen.'

'It's not a name with which I'm familiar. What's his business with me?'

'He refused to divulge it, Sir Geoffrey.'

'A touch of mystery, eh? I like that.'

He walked into the hall, went along a corridor and swept into the drawing room with a smile of anticipation. Paul rose to his feet immediately and introduced himself. Sir Geoffrey was hospitable.

'Sit down, dear fellow, do sit down. Have you been offered refreshment?'

'No, Sir Geoffrey, I haven't.'

'Then you must let me repair the lapse immediately. If you've ridden here from the centre of London, you'll need something to revive you.'

'I require nothing, I do assure you.'

'Then perhaps you'll tell me what's brought you to my door?'

'I have sad tidings to pass on, I fear.'

Sir Geoffrey's dimples vanished. 'Whom do they concern?'

'It's Mr Bowerman.'

'Why, what's old Mark been up to? He has no cause for sadness.

The lucky devil is likely to marry one of the prettiest fillies you've ever seen. Had I been twenty years younger, I'd have been his jealous rival. Mark Bowerman must be bursting with joy. What's all this about sad tidings?'

'Mr Bowerman is dead, Sir Geoffrey.'

'*Dead?* But he was a picture of health when I last saw him.'

'He did not die by natural means,' said Paul, quietly. 'I regret to inform you that he was murdered.'

Sir Geoffrey was so shocked that he collapsed into an armchair. A look of sheer despair covered his face. The news had silenced him completely so Paul went on to explain what exactly had happened, starting with a description of the duel. The other man had great difficulty matching what he was hearing to a friend for whom he had a deep affection. He was torn between anguish and incredulity.

'Mark tried to fight a duel?' he asked with a mirthless laugh. 'The fellow didn't know how to hold a pistol, let alone fire one. It was madness for him to challenge anyone. No disrespect to your tuition, Mr Skillen, but it would take you six months at least to get him to a point where he was even competent. Poor, dear, kind, blameless Mark!' he sighed. 'What have you done to deserve this? Who could dislike you so strongly that he was moved to sink a dagger in your back? It's beyond belief.' After struggling with grief for a few minutes, he suddenly looked up. 'What about dear Miss Somerville?' he asked. 'Does she know about this?'

'I had to apprise her of the situation,' said Paul. 'The lady was stunned.'

'I don't blame her. Well, what a turn of events this is! Thank you so much for taking the trouble to bring the news to me.'

'I'm not simply here as a messenger, Sir Geoffrey. I intend to find the man who killed Mr Bowerman. To that end, I'd be grateful for some help from you.'

'I don't see what help I can possibly give you, Mr Skillen, but I'm at your service, nonetheless. Ask me whatever you wish.'

Long after she'd departed, Leonard Impey was still savouring the experience. Hester Mallory had not only returned to transact business with his bank, she'd stayed for half an hour to converse with him. A customer who had an appointment with him was forced to wait while the manager revelled in the privacy of his office. When she'd eventually departed, Impey escorted his new client all the way to the waiting carriage, opening the door for her and assisting her into the vehicle with a gentle hand under her elbow. The fleeting moment of contact was exhilarating.

Back in his office, he'd showered the other client with apologies for making him wait, then discussed the loan that was requested. Much later, when he was alone again, Impey had another visitor. The chief clerk knocked on the door and entered without waiting for an invitation. He was carrying something in his hand.

'I've been looking at this bond, sir,' he said, worriedly. 'You deposited it in the safe when you took out some money for Mrs Mallory.'

Impey was tetchy. 'You had no reason to look at it.'

'I was only following your advice, sir. You've always insisted that, where a major transaction is involved, a second pair of eyes is recommended.'

'Perhaps I did say that, but you should have asked my permission first.'

'I'm sorry that I didn't,' said the clerk, 'and even sorrier that you didn't let me examine the document before you advanced the cash. I might have saved you from a rather embarrassing situation.'

'What do you mean?'

'Given the faith you so clearly placed in Mrs Mallory, I hesitate to suggest this, sir . . .'

'Don't beat about the bush, man,' said the manager, irritably. 'I'm a busy man. Say what you have to say then leave me alone.'

'The bond is not genuine, Mr Impey.'

'Don't talk nonsense. I've been through every line with great care.'

'Then perhaps I should remind you that I dealt with Mr Picton for many years. I got to know him extremely well. There is no way that he would have sanctioned a bond of this kind. I'm surprised that you missed this blatant error, for instance,' he went on, putting the document in front of the manager and jabbing a finger at a particular point. 'Do you see what I mean, sir?'

Snatching up the bond, Impey looked at the wording indicated. Doubts began to form and swiftly turned into fears. He'd given a stranger one thousand pounds from the safe and helped her into the carriage so that she could take the money away. The colour drained from his face and the authority from his voice.

'It's a forgery,' he croaked.

Hester Mallory sailed into the room with a smile of triumph.

'How did you get on at the bank?' asked the man.

'That fool of a manager would have given me twice the amount.'

Opening her bag, she took out the banknotes and threw them high into the air so that she could stand in a veritable blizzard of paper. Hester laughed.

'I'll try that other bank tomorrow,' she decided.

Joining in the laughter, the man swept her up in his arms.

'This deserves a celebration,' he said and he carried her quickly upstairs.

* * *

Sir Geoffrey Melrose talked at length about his late friend with an affection edged with sorrow. All that Paul had to do was to listen and toss in the occasional question. At the root of the relationship with Mark Bowerman there was a family connection. Sir Geoffrey was uncle to Bowerman's wife. Belonging to the same club, the two men saw a lot of each other until the unexpected death of Lucy Bowerman. As a result, her husband had become something of a recluse and Sir Geoffrey was one of the few people who could tempt him out of his self-imposed exile from society.

'When you got to know him,' he recalled, 'Mark was a delightful companion. He was witty, intelligent and interested in politics. We talked for hours on end. I fancy that I was his only contact with real life.'

'How did he come to meet Miss Somerville?' asked Paul.

'It was completely by accident.'

'You didn't deliberately bring them together, then?'

'Dear Lord – no! That's not what happened at all.'

Sir Geoffrey went on to explain his own routine. Crippled with arthritis, his wife rarely left their country estate but she insisted that he went up to London on a regular basis to enjoy seeing his friends. Mark Bowerman was one of them. Though he didn't confide his plan to Lady Melrose, he hit on the idea of holding a dinner party at his London address for some male friends and a group of beautiful young women. With a disarming smile, Sir Geoffrey warned Paul not to misunderstand the situation. His female guests had not been professional sirens, hired for the occasion and prepared to be compliant. They were all eminently respectable and were simply there to adorn the room and lighten the conversation. The dinner party, Sir Geoffrey said, had been an unqualified success.

'Laetitia Somerville was a gorgeous creature but too serious-minded for my taste. To be candid, I preferred one of the others. A serious thought had never passed through her brain, God bless her.' He quickly wiped the broad grin from his face. 'Not that anything untoward happened between us, of course. She was far too young and I was far too married. In any case, it was not that kind of occasion.'

'Did Mr Bowerman and Miss Somerville have the opportunity to speak alone?' asked Paul.

'No, we all stayed together in the dining room. In fact, Mark hardly said a word to Laetitia. He was mesmerised by her. As soon as the guests departed, he demanded to know how he could get in touch with her.'

'Did you give him her address?'

'I'd have given him the address of anyone who cheered him up so much.'

'He told me that she had a resemblance to his first wife.'

'That's true. Lucy was a beauty as well.'

'Did you ever see him and Miss Somerville together again?'

'No,' said Sir Geoffrey, 'but I was hoping to do so at their wedding. That was an event that even Lady Melrose would insist on attending. Alas, it was not to be!'

'Thank you,' said Paul, getting to his feet. 'That was enlightening. You've been more helpful than you know.'

'I'm glad to hear you say that.'

'There is one favour I'd like to ask. Could you possibly provide me with the names of all the people who were at that dinner party you gave?'

As he considered the request, Sir Geoffrey's eyebrows formed a chevron.

'I'm not sure that I can,' he said at length.

Charlotte was still dazed by her latest visit from her friend. Hannah Granville had talked at her for the best part of an hour. When her husband returned to the gallery, Charlotte was grateful for his welcoming kiss.

'Thank you, Peter,' she said, 'I needed that.'

'Don't tell me that Hannah's been chewing your ear off again.'

'*Somebody* has to listen to her.'

'Why must it always be you?'

'There's yet another crisis, Peter. Suffice it to say that the chances of the play actually being performed are very slim. Still,' she continued. 'what's your news?'

'I was baulked.'

'Didn't they tell you who owns the property where the murder occurred?'

'The agent refused to do so.'

'Then he was withholding what might be valuable evidence.'

'I made the point very forcefully. That garden was no random choice. The killer selected the venue on purpose.'

'Is there no way of identifying the owner?'

'Oh, yes,' said Peter, blithely. 'I'll get the information tonight.'

'But you just told me that the agent refused to give it to you.'

'There's more than one way to skin a cat, Charlotte.'

'You don't mean . . . ?' He gave a nod. 'But that's illegal.'

'If it's the only way to get what we need, so be it.'

'I don't want you taking any risks, Peter.'

'It will be something of a squeeze to get into the building but I think that I can manage it. On the other hand,' he went on as an alternative popped into his mind, 'it would be even easier for my accomplice.'

'Who do you mean?' Peter looked up at the ceiling. 'Jem?'

'He'd be ideal. Jem is small enough and nimble enough.'

'Be careful, Peter. We don't want him to have another brush

with the law. The Runners would dearly love to have a legitimate reason to arrest Jem.'

'They won't get the chance, my love. He'll be in and out of there in a flash. Besides, the Runners have something far more important to worry about than a case of trespass. Micah Yeomans has a murder to solve.'

As they stood on the Thames embankment, the Runners discussed ways of trying to appease the chief magistrate. All their efforts had so far been frustrated and they were stung by the realisation that Peter and Paul Skillen were moving faster than them.

'How do they do it?' asked Hale. 'They're always ahead of us. I felt sure that we'd be the first to call on Miss Somerville but one of them had already been to the house. In fact, he broke the news of the murder to her. *We* should have done that, Micah.'

'Be quiet.'

'Why didn't we?'

'I'm thinking,' said Yeomans. 'We need to hobble the Skillens.'

'We tried that when we raided the gallery.'

'There has to be a subtler way.'

Hale pondered. 'We could always get Chevy to keep an eye on them,' he said after a short while. 'He could lurk outside the gallery.'

'No, he'd only give himself away. When we asked him to keep Paul Skillen under surveillance, the idiot finished up down there in the Thames.' He spat into the river. 'Besides, he can't tell the difference between the two brothers.'

'Neither can I, if I'm honest.'

'It's easy,' said Yeomans. 'One is right-handed and the other is left-handed.'

'Which is which?'

131

'Peter is right-handed.' He scratched his head. 'Or is that Paul?'

They began to stroll meditatively along the embankment, searching for a way to advance their own investigation at the expense of the one being pursued by their rivals. Hale offered a few suggestions but they were hastily dismissed by his colleague. It was Yeomans who finally believed that he'd espied a way to seize the advantage.

'The duel,' he said, coming to a halt. 'We're forgetting the duel, Alfred.'

'But it never took place.'

'Exactly.'

'I don't understand.'

'We are privy to information that the Skillen brothers don't have.'

'Are we?'

'How did we know when and where the duel was to take place?'

'An informer gave us the information.'

'That's our starting point,' argued Yeomans. 'We must find the informer. I'll wager that we'll get a lot more evidence that way. It's somebody who *knows* all the people involved and who had a motive for preventing that duel.'

'You're right, Micah. How do we find him?'

'We don't, Alfred.'

'But you just said that he might be the key we needed.'

'Try listening properly,' said Yeomans, giving him a shove. 'I didn't mention a man at all. The one thing we do know about our informer is this: it was a woman.'

CHAPTER ELEVEN

When Paul eventually arrived at the gallery, they were all keen to know what he'd found out in Eltham. Since Jem Huckvale was busy teaching someone the fundamentals of swordsmanship, only Peter, Charlotte and Gully Ackford were left to form an attentive audience. While the men were amused by his treatment of the robbers who'd lain in ambush, Charlotte was concerned.

'Supposing there were more of them? You might have been hurt.'

'As you see,' said Paul, stretching his arms, 'there's not a scratch on me.'

'Are you going to tell Hannah about this encounter?'

'No, Charlotte, I'm not.'

'What's the reason for that?'

'There are two reasons, actually. First, Hannah is not in a listening mode. All she wants to do is to talk about this latest play of hers. It's been a source of friction with the manager ever since she agreed to act in it.'

'The friction continues,' warned Charlotte. 'Hannah walked out of a rehearsal today after a fierce argument with the playwright.'

Paul grimaced. 'That means I'll hear all the gruesome details.'

'What's the second reason?'

'I don't wish to upset her. When she first realised what a hazardous life Peter and I lead, I almost lost her. It's far better if I keep the truth from Hannah. For instance, she knew nothing about the duel.'

'In your place, Peter would have told me everything.'

'That's because I can trust you not to try to stop me,' said Peter. 'Hannah is different. She'd be more fearful.'

'Go on with your story, Paul,' suggested Ackford. 'What sort of man was Sir Geoffrey Melrose and did you learn enough to make the journey worthwhile?'

'Oh, yes,' replied Paul, 'I did.'

He went on to describe Sir Geoffrey and the life that he led in the country. It was very different to the time he spent in the city. Freed from his disabled wife, the man was a bon viveur who spread his wings wide. Of his fondness for Bowerman, Paul had no doubt. It had been a deep and lasting friendship. He'd been interested to discover more about the man for whom he'd acted as a second. What Paul was less certain about was Sir Geoffrey's account of the fateful dinner party. The older man had claimed that he couldn't remember how the women came to be invited and he only provided the name of one male guest.

'What's he trying to hide?' asked Ackford.

'I don't know,' said Paul.

'Do you think he deliberately arranged for Mr Bowerman to meet Miss Somerville? Is that what happened? Was he playing Cupid?'

'He swears that he'd never met her before.'

'Yet he obviously knew the sort of woman who could attract Bowerman. It was one who reminded him of his first wife.'

'Sir Geoffrey said that that was an agreeable coincidence.'

'It doesn't sound as if he's been entirely truthful with you, Paul,' said his brother. 'He wanted to give the impression of helping you while holding some of the information back.'

'I got one name out of him, Peter. Before I track down the man, I want to pay a second visit to Miss Somerville. I've lots of questions for her. For a start, I'd like to see if her memories of the dinner party chime in with those of Sir Geoffrey.' He turned to his brother. 'What will you be doing, Peter?'

'Jem and I are going to break the law,' said the other.

'Then be very careful.'

'It won't take long, Paul.'

Before he could explain what he was planning to do, Peter was interrupted by a sharp knock on the door. He opened it to find a man standing there with a letter in his hand. He held it up.

'I'm to deliver this to a Mr Peter Skillen,' he said.

'Who sent it?'

'I've come from Mr Impey.'

'Then it's important,' said Peter, taking the missive from him. 'Come in a moment. When I've read this, you can take back my reply.'

He stood back to admit the man then walked to a corner of the room. Unfolding the letter, he read the single sentence that it contained.

'You won't need to give him my reply,' he said to the man. 'I'll deliver it in person.' He turned to the others. 'Mr Impey needs help. He wouldn't summon me unless it was very serious. I'll have to go to the bank immediately.'

Notwithstanding the setback following their first visit there, the Runners decided to call at Stephen Hamer's house for the second time. When they were invited in, they had to face some stinging invective both from Hamer and from Rawdon Carr. They withstood it with fortitude. As it eventually died away, Yeomans tried to mollify the two men with an apologetic shrug.

'You are right to criticise us, gentlemen,' he said. 'We acted too quickly and too unwisely. I'm hoping that we can put that mistake behind us.'

'Have you come to make another one in its place?' asked Hamer, cynically.

'We've come to ask for your help, sir.'

'First, you arrest me and now you have the gall to court me.'

'You want the killer as much as we do, Captain Hamer.'

'You're wrong. We want him far more. For you, he's simply one more villain out of the many you've pursued during your career. For me, this is a very personal matter.'

'It's true,' added Carr. 'That's why we don't want the Skillen brothers to be the first to unmask him. The killer is a prize we reserve for ourselves.'

'But it's our duty to arrest him,' said Hale. 'We're Runners.'

'You've barely learnt to *walk* properly, man, let alone run.'

'Insults will get us nowhere,' cautioned Yeomans. 'Mr Carr has just given us another reason for cooperation. We share a mutual dislike of Peter and Paul Skillen. They have been a nuisance to us for many years – nay, "nuisance" is too mild a word. The Skillens have been a positive menace.'

'I can see why,' agreed Hamer. 'We, too, have had our problems with them.'

'They need to be controlled, that's all,' said Carr.

'It's a question of working out how best to do that.'

'We tried and failed,' admitted Hale.

'The more obstacles you can strew in their path,' said Hamer, 'the better. But what's this talk of cooperation? How can you possibly help us, Yeomans?'

'We can help each other,' replied the Runner.

'How do we do that?'

'We go back to your dispute with Mr Bowerman. You and Mr Carr went to Putney Heath in the firm conviction that the duel would take place. Correct?'

'Yes, that's correct.'

'Everything was about to go as planned,' said Carr, 'when you and your cohorts suddenly jumped out of the bushes.'

'Do you know *why* we did that, sir?'

'Someone betrayed us.'

'We can't wait to get our hands on him,' said Hamer, malevolently. 'If you know his name, we demand that you release it.'

'The letter that reached us was unsigned,' Yeomans told them. 'One thing, however, was unmistakable. It was not written by a man at all. The hand was clearly that of a woman. Now, gentlemen,' he went on, 'can either of you suggest who that woman might be?'

Hamer and Carr stared at each other in surprise.

Peter Skillen was no stranger to the bank. He and Paul had had many commissions from Leonard Impey, most of them involving either the transfer of large sums from one place to another or the recovery of stolen money. Banks were natural targets for robbers. Runners like Yeomans and Hale derived a comfortable income from London banks, which retained them as guards at certain times every month. Country banks were especially vulnerable and Runners were often paid to pursue those who'd robbed them. Like many other bank managers, Impey had learnt that the Runners had severe limitations. Effective at frightening potential thieves away, they were less reliable when investigating more complex cases. Because of their superior rate of success, Peter and Paul were therefore often in demand. They were deemed to be more intelligent, resourceful and, crucially, more honest.

As he entered the bank, Peter saw a smile of gratitude light up the gloomy countenance of the chief clerk. Peter could see he was needed. Shown into the manager's office, he shook hands with Impey.

'Thank goodness you've come, Mr Skillen!'

'There was a faint whiff of desperation about your summons,' said Peter.

'We've had a minor calamity.'

'If it was an armed robbery, I trust that none of your employees was hurt.'

'It was not an *armed* robbery,' said Impey with bitterness. 'If anything, it was a case of theft by *disarming*. Take a seat and you shall hear what happened.'

When they'd both settled down, Impey gave a full account of the forgery. He didn't spare himself. He confessed that he'd been cunningly wooed by Mrs Mallory and that he'd been tortured by regret ever since. He heaped praise on his head clerk for exposing the fraud and wished that he'd had the sense to have the man present during the discussions with their new client. His narrative ended with an apology.

'I should have listened to your advice, Mr Skillen.'

'It's a simple precaution,' said Peter. 'As soon as a complete stranger, however attractive, presents you with a bond or comes in search of a substantial loan, it's sensible to check their credentials. If they claim to be newcomers to the capital, get someone to confirm that the address they've given you for their stay here is a correct one. I guarantee that you'll find the hotel whose name was given to you by this Mrs Mallory will have no record of her as one of their guests.'

'We've already established that fact.'

'But you did so *after* the event. The damage was already done.'

'You've no need to censure me,' said Impey. 'I've scourged myself soundly, I promise you. When I think how easily I was deceived, I ache all over. This will cast a dark shadow over my future here. Unless we can somehow recover the money, I will face demands for my resignation. You've saved me before,' he went on, extending his arms in a plea, 'do so again, I implore.'

'I'll do what I can, sir.'

'Is there a glimmer of hope that you will succeed?'

'Oh, yes,' said Peter. 'Mrs Mallory – or whatever her real name is – may have used her charms to obtain money by forgery but she's also left a firm imprint on your mind of what she looks like. You'll be able to give me a very accurate description of the lady and so, I fancy, will your chief clerk.'

'She was unforgettable, Mr Skillen.'

'It will be easier to trace someone who is so distinctive.' He took out a notebook. 'Paint a portrait of Mrs Mallory for me.'

Impey winced at the mention of a portrait. It had been one of the many lies that he'd accepted without question. Shamefaced and embarrassed, he gave a detailed picture of her, drawing attention to her voice and deportment. Peter noted everything down carefully.

'What is your first step?' asked the manager, anxiously.

'It's to issue a warning, sir. I am not free to devote all my time to this case because I am already involved in the pursuit of a man wanted for murder. But I will do my best to deal with both crimes in parallel. You will simply have to be patient.'

'I know that forgery is a lesser crime than murder but my future is at stake here. Yes, it was my own fault, I admit that freely. I just ask that you show some pity and understanding.'

'There is one thing I can do immediately,' said Peter, rising to his feet. 'I'll go to the Bevington Hotel.'

'But we already know that Mrs Mallory is not staying there.'

'She may well have done so in the past, sir. Why settle on that particular hotel if she was not familiar with it? If she *has* used it before, they will certainly recognise her from the description you've given to me.'

'That's true, Mr Skillen.'

'The other avenue open to us, of course, is Mr Picton. How could the lady have a letter purportedly written by him if she didn't have some contact with the man? Correspondence of some sort must have passed between them.'

'I never thought of that.'

'Out of courtesy,' Peter told him, 'Mr Picton ought to be made aware of the way that his name was misused. He'll be very annoyed.'

'He'll be very annoyed with *me*, I know that.'

'I'd suggest that he be allowed to see the forged bond.'

'Yes, yes,' said Impey, opening a drawer in his desk. 'I have it here.'

'Of equal interest to Mr Picton, of course, is the letter of introduction he is supposed to have drafted, but I daresay that Mrs Mallory was careful to retain that.'

'She was, Mr Skillen.' Coming around his desk, he handed over the bond. 'Thank you so much for responding to my call. You've already given me some comfort.'

'When you spoke of the lady,' remembered Peter, 'you spoke of her dainty feet. No matter how dainty, they'll have left large footprints for me to follow. And there may be another source of comfort for you, sir.'

'I'm in sore need of it.'

'You will not be the only victim of her guile.'

'What makes you think that?'

'We are dealing with a greedy woman,' said Peter. 'If the bond had been for a much smaller amount, your chief clerk would not have been quite so suspicious. Mrs Mallory's demand was excessive. And since she was given money so willingly by you, she'll go in search of other amenable bank managers.'

When she heard that Paul Skillen had called on her again, Laetitia Somerville was eager to see him and to hear if his investigation had borne fruit. She therefore had him shown into the drawing room where she was reclining on a sofa. Head bowed in grief, Laetitia was wearing her black dress.

'I'm sorry to intrude, Miss Somerville,' he said, gently. 'I know that you're not in the mood for visitors.'

'I'm not in the mood for anything at the moment, Mr Skillen.'

'I wish that I was able to bring you good news for a change. While I'm still bent on locating the man who killed Mr Bowerman, I have no real progress to report.'

'He *must* be caught and hanged,' she said.

'He will be. I give you my word.'

'Thank you, sir. I have every faith in you.'

'What I can tell you, however, is that the inquest will take place tomorrow. I was told of the arrangements just before I came here.'

She was flustered. 'Am I expected to be present?'

'That won't be necessary.'

'There's nothing I'd have to say.'

'Nobody will call upon you.'

'I'd find it too distressing to bear, Mr Skillen.'

'Then you must stay away. It will, perforce, be a relatively short event. The coroner's verdict is easy to predict. Mr Bowerman was killed by a person or persons unknown.'

'*Someone* must be called to account,' she insisted.

'They will be.'

He looked at her more closely. Sorrow had veiled her beauty, aged her visibly and left a rather unprepossessing visage in its place. Her eyes were dead, her cheeks hollowed and the corners of her mouth turned down. Paul compared her unfavourably with Hannah Granville. Whatever the situation, she never lost her essential loveliness. If she was angry or sad, excited or passive, her beauty continued to dominate. Indeed, when her temper flared and her eyes blazed, she was at her most alluring.

'May I ask if Captain Hamer has been in touch with you?' he said.

'I've not heard a word from him.'

'Not even a letter of condolence?'

'He knows that my door is barred to him.'

'We've been finding out curious details about him,' said Paul. 'It turns out that he never held a captaincy and, after a court martial, he was ejected from his regiment.'

She sat up in astonishment. 'Where did you learn this?'

'It came from the most reliable source – the War Office.'

'Well, well,' she said, 'that does come as a shock. Are you certain of this?'

'I am, Miss Somerville. Something about the fellow struck a jarring note.'

'Then I'm glad I've done with him.' She appraised him for a moment. 'You are a clever man, Mr Skillen. You are also very thorough.'

'It's a tool of my trade,' he explained. 'There's something else you should know about the former Lieutenant Hamer.'

'What is it?'

'He's trying to scare me away.'

Paul told her about the raid on the gallery and how he

was convinced it was the work of Hamer and Carr. Having confronted them, he was certain that they'd make another attempt to hamper his investigation. Listening carefully to every word, Laetitia was especially interested to hear that he had a twin brother.

'To whom am I speaking at the moment?' she asked.

'I'm Paul Skillen.'

'How can I be sure of that?'

'My brother had no dealings with Mr Bowerman. He was a client of mine who became a good friend. Peter never even met him.'

'Yet he's prepared to search for his killer.'

'In an emergency like this, we always help each other.'

'That's . . . reassuring to know,' she said, slowly.

'At the moment, of course, it's *your* assistance I seek.'

She drew back slightly. 'What can *I* possibly tell you?'

'You can explain how you came to meet Sir Geoffrey Melrose.' He saw the confusion in her eyes. 'You surely remember him, Miss Somerville. I met him myself this morning. Sir Geoffrey is a man who makes a lasting impression. It was at his dinner party that you first met Mr Bowerman.'

'Of course,' she said, recovering quickly. 'I did meet him but it was only on that one occasion. All I recall of that dinner is the fact that Mark came into my life. That blotted everything else out.'

'How did you come to be invited to Sir Geoffrey's house?'

'As it happens, I went there with a friend.'

'May I ask his name?'

'It was a woman friend,' she said.

'Could you provide me with her name and address?'

She was guarded. 'Why should you wish to speak to her?'

'I'd like to hear her memories of that dinner party as well.'

143

'That may be difficult,' said Laetitia. 'Some time ago, I heard that she'd moved to France and was seriously ill. She may not still be alive.'

Irritated at first that the Runners should dare to call on them, Hamer and Carr were glad that they'd spoken to them. They'd learnt that Yeomans and Hale were not the complete buffoons they'd imagined. They had a good record of arrests and – judging by the quality of their apparel – they contrived to make policing the city a lucrative task. Their antipathy towards the Skillen brothers had pleased Rawdon Carr. He wanted to know everything they could tell him about the way their rivals operated. In particular, he'd wanted to know what their weak points were. Hamer, on the other hand, was still trying to digest the information that a woman was responsible for the abandoned duel. As soon as their visitors had left, he rounded on Carr.

'Did you hear what they said? We were thwarted by a woman.'

'All that we know, Stephen, is that a woman wrote the letter. The most likely thing is that it was dictated to her by a man.'

'Why do you say that?'

'What better way to hide his identity?'

'A man could easily have scrawled the details in such a way as to disguise his hand completely. No, Rawdon, we made a startling discovery today. If for nothing else, I'm grateful to the Runners for that.' His brow wrinkled in thought. 'Who could it possibly have been?'

Carr smirked. 'There are rather too many suspects,' he said. 'You've seduced and cast aside any number of women since you came to live in London. One of them wanted to get even with you.'

'But how could she possibly know about the duel?'

'Vengeful women will go to any lengths, Stephen. You should

know that by now. The arrangements were secret but someone might have passed on the details if offered enough money. That would be my guess. One of your mistresses is behind this. She chose her moment with care.'

'But what did she stand to gain?'

'What women always crave. They want satisfaction.'

'I can't see that anyone would be satisfied with merely disrupting an event like that. The one explanation is that it was an admirer of Bowerman, desperate to stop me putting a bullet inside his stupid head.'

'Yes,' said Carr, 'that's a possibility as well. In fact, now that I think about it, that may be a more convincing answer.'

'What about the murder?'

'No woman was capable of that, Stephen. It was a task for a man.'

'Yet a woman was involved. Bowerman was tricked by a letter that seemed to come from Laetitia.'

'In that case,' decided Hamer, 'we are looking for *two* women – one who cared enough for Bowerman to save him and another who wanted him dead. How could such a dry and humourless fellow interest two passionate women? It's beyond my comprehension.' About to walk across the room, he came to a dead halt. 'There is *one* person capable of forging a letter, of course . . .'

'You can rule *her* out at once.'

'She's a malicious little bitch.'

'There's just one problem,' said Carr. 'Rumour has it that she's been struck down by a malady and is unlikely to recover. Besides, she moved to Paris months ago so we can definitely leave her out of our list of suspects.'

The Bevington Hotel was a relatively small but luxurious establishment in Park Lane. As soon as Peter laid eyes on it, his spirits rose. If he was visiting a large hotel with a multitude of guests moving in and out all the time, the woman he was tracking could have been lost in the crowd. There was no danger of that at the Bevington. When he spoke to the manager, he explained that he was acting on behalf of the bank.

'We've already had someone here on the same errand,' said the man.

'Not quite,' corrected Peter. 'He was asking if a Mrs Mallory was staying here. My question is somewhat different. I'd like to know if someone currently posing under that name ever stayed as a guest at your hotel.'

'When would this be, sir?'

'How good is your memory?'

'I flatter myself that it's extremely good.'

The manager was an unusually tall, thin, pale-faced man with an almost patrician air about him. Resenting his condescension, Peter nevertheless needed his help so he forbore to confront the man.

'Let's look back over the last year, shall we?' he said.

'A lot of people have stayed here during that time, Mr Skillen. I can't pretend to remember each and every one of them.'

'This lady would assuredly stay in the memory.'

'Under what name was she supposed to be a guest here?'

'That's what I'm endeavouring to find out.'

Peter went on to give him the description of her that he'd got from Impey. He emphasised the woman's unassailable buoyancy and the quality of her attire. Something of a dandy himself, the manager seized on the details of her appearance.

'I do believe I recall the lady in question,' he said.

'What was her name?'

'My memory is sound, sir, but it is not encyclopaedic. While her name escapes me, her reason for staying here does not. She was a guest for a few days before going on to Ascot.'

'That would mean she stayed here last June.'

'I can give you the exact date, if you wish.'

'I'd be most grateful.'

Peter followed him into the reception area and waited while the man went behind the counter and turned back the pages of a ledger. When he came to the relevant place, he ran his finger down the list of names.

'Here we are,' he said. 'I've found her for you.'

'Was she staying here as Mrs Mallory?'

'Oh, no,' replied the other.

'Then what name *was* she using?'

The manager looked up at him. 'Miss Arabella Kenyon.'

Unable to placate the playwright, Lemuel Fleet decided against another futile appeal to Hannah Granville. He employed a different tactic altogether and caught Charlotte by surprise. When he turned up unexpectedly at the gallery and introduced himself, she was taken aback.

'Have you come for lessons in fencing, boxing, archery or shooting?' she asked in wonderment.

'I'd love to be proficient in all of them,' he said, grimly, 'then I'd be able to kill the pair of them in four different ways. Let me explain, Mrs Skillen. That is your name, I believe?'

'It is, sir.'

'I've heard it often on Miss Granville's lips and, I gather, her beau is your brother-in-law. I need to speak to one or both of you.'

'Then you'll have to settle for me,' said Charlotte. 'Paul is not here and, in any case, is not able to prevail upon Miss Granville.'

'What about you?'

147

'I might have marginally more influence, Mr Fleet.'

'That's why I came. Talking to Mr Mundy is like banging my head against a brick wall. Talking to Miss Granville is akin to putting it inside the mouth of a lion.'

'You've no need to recount what happened today, sir. I already know.'

'What you heard was wildly prejudicial.'

Charlotte smiled. 'I allowed for that, sir.'

'In brief, the situation is this . . .'

Fleet spoke slowly and painfully. What Charlotte heard was a version of events that differed considerably from the one that her friend had given her. Entirely new facts emerged. Hannah, it transpired, had been a destructive force from the very start. She had two of the actors dismissed from the company – one man, who kissed her in the course of the play, had bad breath; the other, who tried to kiss her in the dressing room, had bad judgement. There was an endless litany of complaints. Hannah wanted this scene removed from the play and that song inserted in its place. She'd quarrelled with the costume designer. She'd insulted one of the stage hands. When he got on to Abel Mundy, the manager was able to reveal a catalogue of crimes. He accepted that he was at fault in putting actress and playwright together. They were archetypes of incompatibility.

When he paused for breath, Charlotte offered a comment.

'Miss Granville is my friend,' she began, 'but I can't defend some of the behaviour you've described. What I can suggest, Mr Fleet, is that her outbursts are symptoms of the fact that she is very unhappy.'

'Does that give her licence to make us all suffer?'

'No, it doesn't.'

'Then why has she turned into the company tyrant?'

'That may be overstating the case,' said Charlotte, reasonably. 'When she arrived at the rehearsal today, she was given a rapturous welcome.'

'The ovation was a sign of the sheer relief we all felt.'

'When did you first engage her, Mr Fleet?'

'I'm beginning to wish that I'd never done so, to be honest.'

'It was two years ago, wasn't it? Hannah was in *The School for Scandal*.'

'And she was magical,' he said.

'Did you have trouble from her in rehearsals?'

'We had none whatsoever.'

'Did she scatter insults wherever she went?'

'No, Mrs Skillen, she spread compliments far and wide.'

'What of the playwright? Did they come to blows?'

'Miss Granville adored Sheridan,' he said, 'and he worshipped her. It was a marriage of true minds in every sense. That's what made it a pleasure to employ her.'

'She is still that same talented actress,' Charlotte pointed out. 'Hannah has not lost one jot of that magic you noted. She's simply unable to bring it to *The Piccadilly Opera* because she thrives on enthusiasm and this play fails to enthuse her.'

Lemuel Fleet was struck dumb by her articulate comments. He'd come to appeal to Charlotte to intercede with Hannah on his behalf. Where he could only offer threats or concessions to the actress, a close female friend might be more persuasive. Charlotte's analysis of the problem was impressive. Though she understood little of the workings of the theatre, she sensed the emotional turmoil in which Hannah was caught up. Fleet dared to hope that he might have found an emissary.

'Could I ask a very special favour of you, Mrs Skillen?'

'I'm honoured that you deigned to approach me, sir.'

'I'd be prepared to offer you a fee.'

'It would only be returned,' she said, firmly. 'If I can help in any way, I'll be happy to do so but I'll not take a penny.'

'You're my one hope of salvation.'

'Then it's only fair to warn you I've so far failed to make Hannah view the situation in a more impartial way.'

'Would you try to do so again?'

'I'd try anything to bring peace and harmony, Mr Fleet.'

'Then you have my undying thanks. We *need* Miss Granville as a ship needs a mainsail. It may be that this vessel does not have the high quality to which she is accustomed but it is still seaworthy. Convince her of that and all will be well.'

'I can make no promises.'

'None will be demanded, Mrs Skillen. You spoke of peace and harmony. Having listened to you, I'm confident that both can be restored.'

Hannah Granville was more restless than ever. Nothing could divert her or hold her attention. She had tried resting on the bed, reading a novel, singing her favourite songs and accompanying herself on the piano. She soon lapsed back into a deep misery. What she wanted most was Paul's company because he was the only person who could raise her spirits. Unfortunately, he had commitments elsewhere. It might be hours before she saw him again. Bored, sulking and rudderless, she walked to the front window and stared out.

Seconds later, the glass was shattered by a stone.

CHAPTER TWELVE

Tiny shards of glass were scattered across the room. Several of them hit Hannah's body but it was the few that struck her face that threw her into a panic. As she felt blood trickling down her cheeks, she let out a hysterical scream. It brought the servants running to see what the trouble was. Hannah was quivering all over.

'I might have been *blinded*!' she cried. 'I could have been disfigured for life.'

'Come away from the window,' advised one of the women, leading her into the hall. 'It will be safer out here.'

'I can feel blood. Have I been scarred for life?'

'There are only a few scratches, Miss Granville.'

'It feels as if my whole face is on fire.'

'What happened?'

'Someone threw a stone at the window.'

'It might not have been aimed at you, Miss Granville. Whoever threw it might not even have known you were in the room.'

'They saw me,' insisted Hannah. 'When I stood in the window, it suddenly burst into smithereens. Someone was trying to kill me.' She shrank back. 'What if they're still there?'

'I don't think they will be.'

In fact, the manservant had already run out into the street in search of the assailant. He looked up and down but saw nobody at all. He came back into the house.

'They've gone,' he announced. 'It may have been children, having fun.'

'Fun!' exclaimed Hannah, dabbing at the wound. 'Is this their idea of fun? It's deplorable. A person can't even look out of a window with impunity.'

'I'll clear up the mess in the drawing room,' he volunteered.

'Thank you, Dirk,' said the servant who still had a supporting arm around Hannah. 'Why don't we go into the dining room, Miss Granville? You'll be perfectly safe in there.'

'I don't think I shall ever feel safe in this house again.'

She allowed herself to be led into the other room. Breaking away from the servant, she went straight to the mirror that hung over the mantelpiece to examine her face. Still in shock, she was horrified to see three red scratches on one cheek. Blood had only oozed from one of them but that was enough to alarm her.

'How do you feel now, Miss Granville?' asked the servant, solicitously.

'I feel dreadful,' she replied, dabbing at the blood with a handkerchief.

'I'll ask someone to go to the houses opposite and ask if there are any witnesses to what happened. It must have been horseplay of some kind. I can't believe that anyone would deliberately try to harm you.'

'Oh, yes, they would,' said Hannah, calming down sufficiently to make a considered judgement. 'I think I know who hurled that stone at me.'

'Who was it?'

'It's a nasty, vicious man named Abel Mundy.' Pulling a face, she put the handkerchief to her cheek again. 'It *stings* so much.'

'Would you like me to send for a doctor?'

'Yes, I would.'

'I'll get someone else to look after you.'

'No, no, I'm much better now. Fetch the doctor and don't worry about looking for witnesses. Mr Mundy hurled that stone. I'll wager anything on it.'

The servant headed for the door. 'I'll be as quick as I can.'

Left alone, Hannah inspected herself in the mirror yet again. One of the shards had grazed her cheekbone. When she saw how close it had been to her left eye, she shuddered. An actress lived by her looks. The partial loss of her sight and the ugliness of a damaged eye would spell ruin for her. That had been his intention, she believed. Mundy was not simply trying to frighten her, he wanted to drive her from the stage altogether and he might well have succeeded. Caught up in her plight, she didn't hear the sound of approaching hooves. Hannah was still staring into the mirror when the door opened and Paul rushed in to throw protective arms around her.

'I've just heard what happened,' he said.

'It was terrifying, Paul. The glass went everywhere.'

Holding her at arm's length, he scrutinised her. Dozens of shards had lodged in her dress but he didn't notice them. His gaze was fixed on the facial wounds and the specks of glass stuck in her hair.

'What happened?' he asked.

'Mr Mundy watched me standing in the window and threw a stone.'

'Did you actually see him?'

'No,' she admitted, 'but who else would do such a thing? He's so obsessed with getting his play on the stage that he's trying to force me out of the company for good. I could have been *killed*, Paul.'

153

'I don't think your life would have been in danger,' he said, 'but your career might have been. This is appalling, Hannah. If Mundy is responsible for this, he'll finish up behind bars and I'll be the one to put him there.'

'Don't leave me just yet,' she begged, clutching at him.

'I'll stay as long as you wish.'

'I've sent for a doctor but you're the best medicine. I feel better already.'

'Do you feel able to tell me in detail exactly what happened?'

'No,' said Hannah, nestling against his chest. 'To tell you the truth, I want to forget all about it. You've no idea how utterly defenceless I felt.'

They stood together in silence for several minutes. Paul could feel her heart still racing. Chiding himself for not being there to look after her, he realised that he had to balance her needs against the murder investigation that was taking up so much of his time. Paul was not entirely convinced that Mundy had been the culprit but he wasn't going to upset her by disagreeing with her claim. All he wanted was to comfort and reassure her.

When she came into the room, Charlotte Skillen dispensed with greetings.

'Your front window has been smashed,' she said, then noticed the tiny wounds, 'and what on earth have you done to your face, Hannah?'

On the principle that the bank manager was in dire need of some support, Peter Skillen returned to Impey's office and told him what he'd found out. The manager was gratified that he'd taken the time to make initial enquiries and was interested to hear that the woman who'd persuaded him to advance one thousand pounds against a bond worth over twice that amount had been in London before. She'd been calling herself Miss Arabella Kenyon on that occasion but was now operating under the guise of a new name. Peter made a suggestion.

'The lady can change her identity as easily as she can change her hat,' he said. 'It would be a kindness to your rivals if you warned them to be on guard against her. You may not wish to help people with whom you're in competition, of course. I'm not sure what the protocol is in your profession. But I feel sure that Mrs Mallory is not here to make one strike before fleeing the city. That warning would be appreciated by people in your position.'

'Quite so, Mr Skillen.'

'Does that mean you *will* spread the word?'

Impey sat back in his chair and breathed in deeply through his nose. There was a problem, he realised. In warning other bankers that there was a forger at work, he'd be admitting that he'd been taken in by her wiles. People might thank him for alerting them but they would also laugh up their sleeves at the thought that Leonard Impey, one of the most experienced bank managers in the city, had been swindled and humiliated by a scheming woman. In the banking community, he'd be ribbed about it for months afterwards. He reached his decision.

'I'll think about it,' he said, evasively.

'*You* would be glad of such a warning, sir.'

'That's true but there are other factors to consider here. Apart from anything else, it might be entirely in vain. Having made a killing here, Mrs Mallory may have left London altogether. In fact,' he continued, trying to persuade himself as well as Peter, 'that's her most likely course of action. If she was here last June, she might well have played the same trick on another bank before going on to Ascot to place some of her ill-gotten funds on the horses. That is the way she works, I believe. Her method is to hit and run.

Though the manager in question refused to make it public, she probably swindled another bank last year before disappearing. This year it was our turn. Thank you for your good counsel, Mr Skillen, but I'd prefer to keep our troubles to ourselves. No other bank is in danger. Mrs Mallory is too wily to take risks.'

Had he seen her at that moment, Impey might not have recognised her as the woman whose forged credentials had deceived him. A totally different dress and the careful application of cosmetics had changed her appearance markedly. The dark, curly wig and the wide-brimmed straw hat with its explosion of feathers completed the transformation. When she walked into the bank, even wearing a veil, she was the immediate cynosure. There was a sense of style and wholesomeness about her that was captivating. The manager noticed it at once. Emerging from his office, he first glanced then stared with unashamed curiosity. She glided across to him.

'Mr Oscott?' she enquired, sweetly.

'Yes, that's me.'

'I had a feeling you were the manager. You have an air of seniority. I've come for my appointment, Mr Oscott.'

'Then you must be . . .'

'That's right,' she said. 'My name is Kenyon – Miss Arabella Kenyon.'

He offered her a polite bow and inhaled her bewitching perfume.

'This way, please,' he said, indicating the door. 'Come into my office, Miss Kenyon. We have a lot to discuss.'

Charlotte's arrival was timely. While the incident had disturbed her, she was by no means persuaded that Abel Mundy was the person who'd thrown a stone at the window. At Hannah's instigation, Paul was ready to ride off at once to challenge Mundy but he had no idea where the man was lodging. Charlotte stepped in to suggest that he should first go to the manager. He could report what had happened and, if Fleet felt a visit to the playwright was justified, get the address from him.

'What if he refuses to give it?' asked Hannah.

'I think that's highly unlikely,' said Charlotte. 'He'll be as keen to know the truth about the incident as we are.'

'We already *know* the truth. It was Mundy's doing.'

'I still think there's some doubt about that,' said Paul.

Hannah shot him a look. 'Are you disagreeing with me?'

'I'm merely suggesting that we should get more evidence of his involvement before we accuse him. Don't worry, Hannah. If he's the culprit, he'll be made to pay handsomely for it. I can promise you that.'

'Challenge him to a duel.'

'This can be settled by lawful means.'

When Paul went out into the hall, Charlotte walked after him so that she could have a private word with her brother-in-law. She looked over her shoulder to make sure that Hannah was not listening.

'Be sure to tell Mr Fleet that I'm here.'

'Why should I do that?' asked Paul.

'It's exactly what he requested. Having failed to make any headway with the two warring parties, he came to the gallery and, as a last resort, sought my help. Mr Fleet thought that another woman might have more influence over Hannah.'

'That was a wise move.'

'We shall see.'

'You can talk to Hannah in a way that none of us can.'

'I can only do my best. As for the broken window, I'd absolve

Mr Mundy of the charge. He may be angry with her but he's not given to hasty action or he'd have taken it before. Were he caught committing such a crime, he'd be liable for arrest.'

'He'd get a beating from me beforehand,' said Paul. 'Like you, however, I don't think he'd be stupid enough to do anything so rash.' He kissed her on the cheek. 'Stay with Hannah and try to soothe her. Mr Fleet made the right choice when he came to you. *The Piccadilly Opera* may yet survive.'

Laetitia Somerville was inhospitable when she heard that the Runners had decided to call on her again. She asked for them to be turned away but they were too stubborn. Yeomans warned that they would stay outside the front door all night, if need be, because they had important information to pass on to her. At length, she capitulated and had the two of them let in.

'I was hoping that you'd show me more consideration,' she told them. 'You must have met many people who've suffered bereavement. It's a time when tact and forbearance are required. The last thing you should do is to call unbidden at people's houses.'

'You have our apologies,' said Yeomans.

'I said that we shouldn't bother you,' Hale put in.

'At least one of you has some sensitivity,' observed Laetitia. 'Now, what's this news you insist on passing on to me?'

'The inquest into Mr Bowerman's death is tomorrow.'

'Is that your pretext for coming here?'

'We thought it would interest you, Miss Somerville.'

'It does, sir, but it comes too late to be a surprise. Mr Skillen told me of it some hours ago. If that's all you have to say, I bid you farewell.'

'Paul Skillen was here *again*?' asked Hale in agony.

'He, too, has a good reason to catch the killer.'

'He may have a reason but he has no legal right. We *do*, Miss Somerville.'

'And how much evidence have you gathered?'

'Ah, well . . .'

'It's slow work,' said Yeomans, uneasily, 'but we have made some advances. We're expecting help from Captain Hamer and Mr Carr.'

'I'd rather you didn't mention his hateful name,' she said, turning her head away. 'If the captain hadn't chosen to make an unheralded reappearance, then Mr Bowerman and I would be making preparations for our wedding. Instead of that,' she said, wistfully, 'he will be visiting a church for his funeral.'

'We share your dismay.'

'Do you want the details of the inquest?' asked Hale.

'No, I do not,' she said, brusquely.

'But you could give your testimony.'

'There's nothing I can say that will have any bearing on the murder of someone who was precious to me. I'd rather remember Mr Bowerman as the person who gave my life a sense of purpose. An inquest would only distress me.'

'They always bore me,' admitted Hale.

'It's your choice, Miss Somerville,' said Yeomans. 'Have you had any further thoughts about who might be responsible for the murder?'

'No, I have not.'

'Is there anyone who would have resented the idea of you getting married?'

'I'm not going to discuss my private life with you,' she said, haughtily.

'But, without realising it, you may be able to give us some guidance.'

'The thing is this, Miss Somerville,' said Hale. 'You already know that a woman is involved because she sent Mr Bowerman a summons in your name. What you don't know, perhaps, is that the information we had about the duel was also in a woman's hand.'

'Can you suggest who she might be?' asked Yeomans.

'No,' she said, face impassive.

But her brain was whirring away.

Lemuel Fleet was surprised when Paul arrived at his house and disturbed when he heard about the injuries sustained by his leading lady.

'How badly was she hurt?' he asked. 'Will she have to withdraw?'

'By the grace of God, the wounds were superficial, but they could easily have caused permanent damage to Miss Granville's face.'

'It's an omen. This play is doomed.'

'Forgive me, Mr Fleet,' said Paul, forcefully, 'but my only concern is for Miss Granville's safety. That's more important than any play.'

'Bills have been printed, tickets have been sold.'

'That's not the point at issue.'

'It is in my opinion.'

'Then you have clearly not reached the same conclusion as Miss Granville. Had you done so, you'd realise that there was no prospect whatsoever of a single performance of the play taking place.'

Fleet gulped. 'The lady surely doesn't think that . . . ?'

'Oh, yes, she does.'

'But that's inconceivable, Mr Skillen.'

'There's been bad blood between her and Mr Mundy from the start.'

'Regrettably, that's true, but he'd never do anything like this.'

'He's already done it,' said Paul. 'According to Miss Granville, he's been throwing metaphorical stones at her since they first met. Today, she believes, he resorted to a real one.'

'That's fanciful. Mundy would be cutting his own throat. Without her, there'd *be* no play. I could never conjure an actress of her stature out of the air. Mundy knows that. He has to find a way to work with Miss Granville and vice versa.'

'That fantasy seems a long way off at the moment.'

Paul admitted that he, too, had doubts that the playwright was in any way culpable. He told Fleet that it was his sister-in-law's idea that he should first make contact with the manager in order to get Mundy's address.

'I'm indebted to the lady,' said Fleet, 'and I'd be grateful if you'd tell her that. Had you gone straight to confront Mr Mundy at his lodging, this whole business could have got dangerously out of hand. By coming here, you've at least had the time to review the situation with a degree of calm.'

'I may appear calm,' warned Paul, 'but I'm seething with anger. Miss Granville is very dear to me. If someone threatens her in any way, they'll have to answer to me. Mr Mundy may be innocent of the charge – that's yet to be proven, in my view – but somebody hurled that stone and I will hunt him down.'

'I'll gladly join you in that hunt, sir.'

'He's all *mine*, Mr Fleet.'

'I, too, have a score to settle with the villain. That stone may have been thrown at Miss Granville but it's an indirect attack on *me*. Without her, the play perishes.'

Paul chided him for taking such a selfish attitude, arguing that his major concern should be for Hannah rather than for the financial difficulties he might suffer as a result of cancellation.

Fleet was duly humbled. He had the sense to realise that Paul was a possible ally. Being so close to the actress, he could apply even more pressure on her than his sister-in-law. What he could not do, however, was to speak to her as another woman. That was why Charlotte's help was vital as well. In order to get a compromise, the manager needed both her and Paul.

'Let's first call on Mr Mundy together,' he said. 'There's no deceit in him. He's a man who wears his heart on his sleeve. When we tell him of this incident, we'll know immediately if he was behind it by his reaction.'

'It may even induce some sympathy in him for Miss Granville.'

Fleet was pessimistic. 'That's too much to ask.'

Back at the gallery, Peter was explaining to Jem Huckvale what they had to do. He'd even drawn a rough plan of the building and marked the window through which he believed the younger man could easily crawl. In the time he'd worked and lived at the gallery, Huckvale had done a wide variety of things but the overwhelming majority of them had been perfectly lawful activities. Having to commit a crime worried him.

'What if I'm caught?' he asked.

'There's no chance of that, Jem.'

'Being hauled off to Bow Street is not very nice. Last time, they had no reason to take me there. This time, they would.'

'Yeomans and Hale will be nowhere near the place we're going to,' said Peter, confidently, 'because it would never occur to them to ask why the murder took place where it did. While you're getting hold of a piece of crucial information, they will be chasing their own tails somewhere else.'

'I'm still not happy about it.'

'You've nothing to fear.'

With a consoling arm around his shoulders, Peter reminded him how many much more hazardous things he'd done in the past. Compared to those adventures, the burglary would be swift, silent and without danger. Though Huckvale was not entirely convinced, he would never turn down the opportunity to work alongside Peter and his brother. Theirs was a world of excitement and that was irresistible.

It was evening now and the gallery was closed. Peter promised that he'd return at midnight to collect Jem for their nocturnal outing. Waving goodbye, he let himself out of the building. A figure hurried up to him. Though light was fading, Peter was able to recognise Silas Roe at once. The butler was animated.

'I'm so glad to find you,' he said, grabbing Peter's arm. 'I was hoping against hope that you'd still be here.'

'Why is that, Mr Roe?'

'I've brought some news for you, sir. When you came to the house, the information was not then in my possession. It is now.'

'Before you go any further,' said Peter, raising a hand, 'I should tell you that I'm not *Paul* Skillen. I'm his brother, Peter. We did meet when you first came here.'

'I remember. I thought I was seeing double.'

'Paul is not here at the moment and I have no idea where he is.'

'Oh, that's disappointing.'

'Are you so anxious to make contact with him?' Roe nodded. 'Then perhaps you can tell me what this latest news is. If it has a bearing on our investigation, then I'm eager to hear it. I can pass it on to Paul when I see him.' Roe looked uncertain. 'Clearly, it's something of great importance. We don't want to be discussing it out here in the street. Why don't we step back inside the gallery? We can talk in relative comfort there.'

* * *

Fleet was glad that he'd be present when Paul and the playwright met so that he could act as a buffer between them. Determined to avenge the woman he loved, Paul was likely to take a more combative approach towards Abel Mundy. An argument might easily flare up. Even if Mundy had no connection with the smashing of the window, blows might be exchanged. Each one would be felt by the manager. When they reached the house, Fleet was on tenterhooks, appealing to Paul to hold his peace.

'Let me do the talking, Mr Skillen.'

'If he threw that stone, I'll say what I have to say with my fists.'

'No, no – anything but that, please!'

'Ring the bell,' ordered Paul. 'I want to meet the man who's caused Miss Granville so much pain and anguish.'

Fleet did as he was told. A servant answered the door and they were admitted to the hall. Marion Mundy received them in the drawing room. Having met the manager before, she gave him a guarded welcome. He introduced Paul as a friend of Hannah Granville. The woman's face darkened instantly.

'We need to speak to your husband, Mrs Mundy,' said Fleet.

'It's on a matter of the utmost urgency,' added Paul.

'I'm sorry, but he's not here,' she said.

'Where is he?'

'My husband is where he always goes at this time of the day, Mr Skillen. He's in church. In fact, he's been there for well over an hour.'

If Mundy had been in church that long, Paul reasoned, he couldn't possibly have thrown a stone through his front window. On the other hand, the wife was only telling them what she believed. The playwright might have cut short his devotions for once and slipped across to Paul's house to lurk outside it.

'We'll wait until he gets back,' said Paul.

* * *

The Peacock Inn was as busy as usual that evening but they had no difficulty finding a table. Yeomans had such physical bulk and such a daunting reputation that other patrons would always make way for him. Quaffing their pints, he and Hale sat in a corner and discussed what the day had brought them.

'I can see why Bowerman was attracted to her,' said Yeomans before releasing a sly belch. 'Miss Somerville would warm any man's bed.'

'She's well beyond our reach, Micah.'

'Thought is free.'

'Something about her worries me,' said Hale. 'Why is a woman like that not married already? And when she does finally choose a husband, why pick on someone like Mr Bowerman?'

'He's rich and respectable.'

'I think she'd set her sights a little higher than that.'

Yeomans beamed. 'On someone like me, you mean?'

'No – on a rich, respectable man with a title.'

They were still enjoying their beer when Chevy Ruddock walked into the pub.

He was a lanky young man with a willing heart and a face that seemed to sprout a new wart or pimple every month. Proud to work with the two leading Runners, he was ruthlessly exploited by them. He hurried across to their table.

'You sent for me, Mr Yeomans.'

'We have an assignment for you,' said the other.

'I'm ready, sir.'

'We had thought to give you the task of watching the Skillen brothers.'

'Oh no,' pleaded Ruddock, 'I've tried doing that before. Keeping an eye on Paul Skillen was like trying to hold an eel with a pair of soapy hands. It's not a job for one man but for twenty.'

165

'We can't spare that many from our foot patrol,' said Hale.

'So you'll be shadowing someone else,' explained Yeomans. 'You're to stick to him like a limpet even if it means staying up all night.'

'My wife won't like that, sir. She misses me.'

'We all have to make sacrifices.'

'Who do you want me to follow?'

'It's that man we arrested at the duel – Captain Hamer.'

'Then you must think he's still the main suspect.'

'No, you nincompoop – he's not the killer. I'm hoping that he'll lead us to the man so that we can apprehend him. Captain Hamer is set on revenge. It's not because of any love he had for the victim. If we hadn't stopped him, he'd have shot Bowerman dead on Putney Heath. Someone else killed him instead and that rankles with the captain. His pride was hurt badly.'

'I see,' said Ruddock. 'I'm to stay on his tail because you and Mr Hale have no means of tracking down the killer yourselves.'

'No!' yelled Yeomans. 'That's not the case at all.'

'We've picked up his scent already,' lied Hale, 'but the captain has advantages that we lack. The killer, we believe, is someone who is – or used to be – in his circle. Though he's refusing to admit it, he already has ideas of who it might be. Follow him and he'll lead us to the prize. We then jump in ahead of him and make the arrest.'

'I like the plan,' said Ruddock.

'While you're at it, look out for that friend of his, Mr Carr. They're often together. Between them, they'll soon identify the man we want.'

'There's just one thing, sir . . .'

'Yes?'

'What if Peter and Paul Skillen catch the man before us?'

'What if I hit your head with this tankard?' asked Yeomans, raising it high. 'Do as you're told, man, and stop trying to think on your own. It will addle your brain and make your prick turn blue.' He took a notebook from his pocket. 'I'll write down Captain Hamer's address for you,' he said. 'And while I'm doing that, you can order a pint apiece for the two us. Go on – do something useful for once.'

When he returned home and found his wife absent from the house, Peter knew exactly where to find her. He rode straight to Paul's house. Surprised to see no light in the front room, he was even more taken aback by the sight of the planks of wood in the window frame. Even in the poor light, he could see pieces of glass all over the ground. Let in by a servant, he found Charlotte in the dining room with Hannah. While the latter had largely recovered from the incident in the drawing room, she still bore the marks of it on her cheek. Grateful to see her husband, Charlotte gave him a brief account of what had happened. It was then embellished by Hannah who still held to the notion that the person who'd hurled the stone at her was Abel Mundy.

'Where's Paul?' asked Peter.

'He's gone to pound Mr Mundy into oblivion.'

'Yet he has no proof that the playwright is the culprit.'

'I don't need proof,' said Hannah. 'I feel it in my bones.'

'How long ago did Paul leave?'

'It was well over an hour or more,' replied Charlotte. 'Even though he went to see Mr Fleet first, I'd have expected him back by now.'

'I hope he's learnt who was behind this dreadful attack on Hannah.'

'It *has* to be Mundy,' asserted the actress. 'Who else has a reason to hate me?'

167

'Nobody – you are universally loved.'

She pointed at her face. 'Not when I look like this.'

The front door opened and they heard voices in the hall. All three of them rushed out of the room to greet Paul, asking what he'd found out. When he'd established a degree of calm, he took them all back into the dining room and made them sit down around the table. Hannah frothed with impatience.

'Has he been arrested and put in chains yet?' she demanded.

Paul shook his head. 'No, my darling, he has not.'

'But he committed a terrible crime.'

'*Someone* did but I'm satisfied that it was not Mr Mundy.'

'Don't believe a word he said.'

'It was his wife who did most of the talking,' explained Paul. 'What none of us knew is that Mundy is a deeply religious man. He attends church every day. His wife is the daughter of a country vicar and as devout as her husband. At a time when the window was broken, Mundy was in church. I know that for a fact because I took the trouble to go there. He was in conversation with a priest. They were discussing theological niceties.'

Hannah was deflated. 'And he'd been there a long time?'

'Yes,' said Paul. 'Mrs Mundy spent time with him in church as well.'

'That means it must have been . . . someone else.'

'Whoever it was, I'll catch him somehow. You have my promise. Meanwhile, I suggest that you keep away from the front window.'

Hannah was too distraught even to reply. Forced to accept that Mundy was not responsible, she had to accommodate the unsettling truth that someone else despised her enough to want to inflict injury. Seeing that the actress was in need of love and reassurance, Peter took his wife into the other room so that Paul was left alone with Hannah. They needed time together. Charlotte, meanwhile, told Peter about the plea from the theatre manager and how she'd done her best to talk Hannah round to the view that she had somehow to overcome her objections to the play and the playwright. It was well over a quarter of an hour before Paul joined them to say he'd persuaded Hannah to retire to bed. Peter seized his moment.

'Before you take her upstairs,' he said, 'I have important news for you.'

'What is it?'

'Mr Roe called to see you at the gallery. Disappointed that you weren't there, he instead passed on the information to me. It seems that he was rather more than a butler. He was the trusted friend and confidante of Mr Bowerman. He often dealt with his master's lawyer on his behalf.'

'Go on, Peter.'

'The lawyer came to visit the house today. He told Roe something that shook him. It appears that Mr Bowerman was so enchanted by Miss Somerville that he changed his will to make her the main beneficiary. In the event of his death,' said Peter, 'she was to inherit the bulk of his fortune. Don't you find that interesting?'

Along in her boudoir, Laetitia read his letter yet again then held it to her breast. It contained Bowerman's promise to amend his will in her favour. She knew that he would keep his word.

CHAPTER THIRTEEN

As he rode through the dark streets with Peter beside him, Jem Huckvale voiced his reservations. Having a great respect for the law, he was reluctant to break it.

'Is there no other way you can find out who owns that house?'

'No, Jem. The agent refused to tell me.'

'What about the neighbours? One of them might know.'

'All they know is that a succession of tenants have stayed there. The gardener said the same thing. He hasn't a clue who actually owns the property because he's never met the person. He takes his orders from the agent.'

'I'm still unhappy about breaking in there.'

'You'll be in and out in a flash. You're not really *stealing* anything. You're simply there to get hold of something that should be public knowledge. Why is the agent being so secretive?'

'Perhaps it's what the owner wants.'

'That's all the more reason to discover his name.'

Huckvale remained uneasy. Though he knew that Peter would never willingly endanger him, he still feared that something could go awry with the plan.

'I won't know where to look.'

'The details we want are locked away in one of the cabinets.'

Huckvale was fearful. 'That means I'll have to cause damage.'

'There may be a way of opening the lock with a knife. It's a very simple design. I took note of that.' He reached out a hand to touch his friend's shoulder. 'Calm down, Jem. You're going into an office, not into a bank vault.'

On their way there, they passed the garden in which Mark Bowerman had been murdered and Peter felt a pang of sympathy for him. In all probability, the victim had never been to the house before. Blinkered by love, it had never struck him as odd that he'd been asked to meet Laetitia there rather than at her home. He'd gone to his death with a pathetic eagerness.

When they reached their destination, Peter first carried out a close inspection of the area to make sure that nobody was about. He then tethered the horses at the rear of the property and led Huckvale to the window he'd picked out.

'I'd never get through that,' whispered the other.

'Yes, you would.'

'It's too high up even to reach.'

'You can stand on my shoulders, Jem. Go in head first.'

'But how do I open the window?'

'You're being very awkward,' said Peter. 'Ordinarily, you'd never ask a question like that. You'd simply work out a way to do something and get on with it.' He undid his saddlebag and took something out. 'This is a jemmy,' he went on, passing the tool over to him. 'It will get you in through the window and, if you can't open the cabinet with your knife, then you'll have to force it open with this.'

'When I get inside, how will I see?'

'I'll pass you the lantern by sitting astride my horse.' Huckvale was still unconvinced. 'If it were not important, I wouldn't ask you to do this. Yes, breaking and entering is a crime but it pales beside murder. Inside that office is a piece of information that may help us to identify the killer. We need your help to find it, Jem. Don't let us down.'

'No,' said the other, committing himself at last, 'I won't.'

'Then climb on my back and stand on my shoulders.'

'I will.'

'Once you're inside, you're quite safe. There's nobody else in the building.'

'What if somebody turns up out here?'

'I'll deal with that eventuality,' said Peter. 'Now let's get you in through that window. It will be child's play to someone as agile as you.'

Unable to sleep, Hannah lay propped up on the pillow. Paul was beside her but nothing he could say was able to take away her demons. She was afraid. Someone had tried to harm her, even to inflict permanent injury, and the most worrying feature of the situation was that it had not been Abel Mundy's doing. His proven innocence was like a physical blow to her and she searched for a means of involving him somehow in the attack on her. While he hadn't been responsible himself, she thought, he could easily have hired someone to loiter outside the house in the hope that she'd eventually appear in the window. That theory had a lot of appeal to her until she remembered that he'd been revealed as a man of Christian conviction. In response to her verbal assaults on him, he might revile her with words but that was all. Religion would hold him back from anything else.

Hannah had another enemy. The fact that he was unknown made him even more frightening. Would he strike again and, if so, where would he do it? It was unnerving. By virtue of her talents, she'd earned herself a vast number of admirers. Wherever she went, onstage or elsewhere, she was showered with praise. Hannah had been so accustomed to uncritical approval that she'd begun to take it for granted. It was one of the reasons for her feud with Mundy. He'd actually dared to criticise her performance. But the new development was a more sinister one. Someone reviled her as a person. He wanted blood.

'Try to get some sleep,' advised Paul.

'I daren't close my eyes.'

'You're in no danger when you're beside me, Hannah.'

'Then why do I feel so perturbed?'

'You have a vivid imagination, that's why.'

'Are these scratches imaginary?' she asked, pointing to her face. 'Did I dream up the pieces of glass in my clothes and hair? They were *real*, Paul.'

'I know, and I apologise.'

'Who is he?'

'I'll soon find out.'

'And why is he picking on me?'

'You're the most gorgeous woman in London,' he said, kissing her gently on the side of the head, 'and you have a legion of would-be suitors. It could be that one of them is unable to accept your rejection of him. In living with me, you exclude him from ever getting close to you. A rebuff like that would fester with some men.'

'That wouldn't make them turn on *me*,' she argued. 'You would surely be the target because you stand in the way of someone else's happiness. That stone would have been aimed at you, Paul.'

'There's merit in that argument,' he conceded. 'But I still refuse to believe that you could stir up real hatred in someone's heart. You're the kindest woman alive.'

'Abel Mundy hates me.'

'He dislikes you, Hannah, but he must respect your talent. And part of him must admire you as a woman.'

'Heaven forfend!'

'Under that crusty exterior, he's a normal human being. When he gazes at someone as dazzling as you, he's bound to look askance at that plain, homely, dull, unexciting wife of his. Anyway, enough of him,' he continued. 'Mundy was not to blame. That's certain. Is there anyone in the company who might wish to hurt you?'

'No, Paul, they've all been a delight to work with.'

'Then we must look elsewhere.'

'Where do I start?' she wailed. 'The very thought that he's still out there makes my stomach churn. To be honest, I'm terrified to leave these four walls.'

'But you must do so, Hannah. Don't let him see that he's frightened you. Be on your guard at all times, naturally, but don't let a stone through a window ruin your life. You're far too brave to do that, aren't you?'

'Yes,' she said with an attempt at firmness.

But, in the darkness, he could not see the naked fear in her eyes.

It was easier than Huckvale had imagined. Standing on Peter's shoulders, he jemmied open the window then went through it head first, curling up as he reached the floor and rolling forward like a ball. Peter lit the lantern and, by dint of mounting his horse, reached up to pass it through the window to his accomplice. Huckvale had another pleasant surprise. His knife unlocked the first cabinet without difficulty. Inside was a pile of ledgers. Holding one of them beside the lantern, he saw that it contained a list of the properties handled by the agency. He was about to search through them when he heard two sounds that made his blood run cold.

Peter reached up to tap on the window, a prearranged signal that somebody was coming. And Huckvale heard both horses moving away. Extinguishing the lantern, he crouched under the table in the dark and wished that he was still in bed back at the gallery.

Peter, meanwhile, was dealing with what might be an emergency. Hearing the approach of footsteps, he decided that the first thing he had to do was to lead the newcomer away from the building. He therefore took both horses around a corner and along a lane that ran between the houses. The footsteps behind him quickened and he was relieved that he'd only have to deal with one person. Finding a post to which he could tether the horses, he did so swiftly then dived into the doorway of a walled garden. Secure from sight, he waited.

The prowler was cautious. The footsteps slowed then stopped. Ears pricked, Peter listened for more sounds of movement. There were none. He came to believe that the stranger had backed off and gone on his way. It was only when he heard the sound of a leather strap being undone that he realised the man was very close to him, trying to open a saddlebag in search of booty. Peter came out of his hiding place at once, saw the hazy outline of the thief and flung himself at the man. While set on overpowering him, Peter was conscious that too much noise would only rouse people from their beds. He therefore clapped one hand over the man's mouth and used the other arm to drag him across to the wall.

The man responded by pounding away with both elbows and trying to shake Peter off but he was held too firmly. He was an older man in rough garb with a greasy cap that was knocked off in the struggle. Strong and determined, however, he bit Peter's fingers to make him pull his hand away from the mouth. A stream of expletives poured out, accompanied by the noisome stink of beer. Peter decided to end the brawl quickly. Grabbing the man by the hair, he smashed his head into the brick wall and sent blood cascading down his face. It took all the fight out of him. He was unable to do anything more than to flail wildly. When his head was banged against the wall a second time, he fell unconscious to the ground. Peter knew that they needed to complete their task and get away before the man woke up and started rousing the neighbours with a cry of rage. Valuable minutes had already been lost. There was no more time to waste.

He led the horses swiftly back in the direction from which they'd come, hoping that nobody else was abroad. A stray rider or pedestrian could ruin the whole enterprise.

Jem Huckvale was almost certain that he'd be caught. Someone had come. Peter might have been able to elude him but Huckvale was trapped. As soon as the open window was seen, his plight was settled. They'd know he'd entered the premises illegally. Being in the pitch-dark intensified his feeling of dread and vulnerability. He'd not only be caught, he'd have failed in his bid to get a telling piece of evidence. No magistrate would accept that he was committing one crime in order to solve a more heinous one. Huckvale had no legal right to be there.

When he heard knuckles banging on the window, his heart constricted. Someone had come in search of him. It was only when Peter hissed his name that he realised his friend was back. Huckvale leapt to his feet.

'Is everything all right?' he asked.

'It is now. Light the lantern again.'

'I haven't found what I'm after yet.'

'Keep trying,' said Peter. 'And please hurry up.'

Huckvale did as he was told. With a glow in the lantern once more, he went through the first ledger but found it unhelpful. He therefore pulled out the drawer again and saw that there were three others in there. Which was the one he needed? Or did he have to open one of the other drawers? Peter had assured him he'd be in and out in a matter of minutes. It already seemed like an hour.

He began to leaf through the pages as if his life depended on it.

Hannah Granville was too tired to stay awake yet too anguished to fall asleep. The only way that Paul could persuade her to drift off was to promise a search of the exterior house where, she feared, someone was waiting for a second opportunity to injure her. As soon as he got out of bed, her eyes closed and her breathing changed. By the time he eased the bedroom door gently open, she was already slumbering.

In his opinion, the search outside was a pointless exercise. The person who'd aimed the stone at Hannah had disappeared at once. Knowing that the whole house would now be on guard, he would not return. Paul nevertheless honoured his promise. He peeped out through windows in unoccupied rooms upstairs, then he went slowly down the steps. Expecting to find nothing at all threatening, he was alerted by the clip-clop of a horse. The noise took him quickly into the drawing room. Though most of the window was boarded up, some panes had been untouched by the stone. Paul was therefore able to see out. What he could discern in the gloom was a sturdy figure dismounting from the horse and creeping up the path towards the house.

Paul ran quickly into the hall and grabbed his sword from its scabbard. There was a slight rustling noise as something was pushed under the front door. Pulling back the bolt, he flung the door open, put a bare foot on the crouching man's chest and pushed him to the ground. Before the visitor could move, the sword was at his throat and Paul loomed over him.

'Who the devil are you?' demanded Paul.

'It's me,' said Peter, holding up both arms in surrender. 'It's your brother.'

Paul lowered the weapon. 'What are you doing here?'

'I was trying to leave a message without disturbing you. I had no idea that you were lurking behind the front door. You gave me a real fright.'

'*You* were the one who alarmed *me*,' said Paul, reaching out a hand to help him to his feet. 'Why on earth are you abroad in the small hours?'

'Jem and I have been at work.'

'Ah, yes, I'd forgotten. You wanted to break into that office.'

'That's exactly what happened.'

'Did everything go well?'

'The burglary was not without incident,' said Peter, retrieving his hat from the ground. 'Poor Jem reckons that his heart stopped at least four times.'

'And did you get what you were looking for?'

'I got rather more than that, Paul. My intention was simply to find out who owned the property and to see if he had any connection to the people with whom the murder has involved us.'

'What did you discover, Peter?'

'That house – or garden, to be more precise – was not chosen purely by accident. It was singled out.'

'Who actually owns the property?'

'Stephen Hamer.'

When his servant opened the bedroom curtains that morning, Hamer saw that light rain was falling out of a leaden sky. He ignored the weather. He was simply grateful that there were no dogs left outside his front door. It was an image printed indelibly on his brain. It reminded him that the Skillen brothers could not be intimidated. There'd always be reprisals. What he didn't notice from his bedroom was that someone was watching the house from a vantage point across the road.

An hour later, after he'd had his breakfast, Hamer had a welcome visitor. It was Rawdon Carr, the friend on whose advice he'd so often relied. When a servant had relieved the newcomer of his wet cloak and hat, Hamer conducted Carr into the drawing room.

'The Skillen brothers worry me,' he confessed.

'I'm still trying to find a way to get them off your back, Stephen.'

'Don't let it require dogs next time.'

'As it happens, it did cross my mind to use two terriers by the name of Yeomans and Hale but they'd never get the better of the brothers. They've tried before. The only use they have for us is as scavengers, gathering up evidence from that army of informers they keep. We can look for nothing more from the Runners.'

'They think they're in partnership with us, Rawdon.'

'Let them. When the time comes, we'll spurn them like mistresses who've outlived their usefulness and become tiresome.' He grinned. 'That's a situation we both know well.' He peered at the bags under his friend's eyes. 'You look as if you've hardly slept a wink.'

'I haven't.'

'Who was the lucky lady this time?'

'There isn't one.'

'It's not like you to take a vow of celibacy, Stephen.'

'I kept coming back to the same question. Who is doing this to *me*?'

'You do have a habit of making enemies,' said Carr, 'most of them female, I grant you, but there are probably men with long memories as well.'

'It has to be someone close to me, Rawdon.'

'Or someone who *was* close at one time. That brings us back to your spent mistresses. None of them went willingly. Didn't the last one assault you?'

Hamer laughed. 'She punched me hard,' he said, 'and I rather enjoyed that. A woman roused is always a joy to see. I took her back to bed for an hour then sent her on her way for good. Though she pretended to go quietly this time, the little baggage stole a silver salver from the dining room. I let her keep it as a souvenir.'

'Perhaps she stole a Spanish dagger as well,' suggested Carr.

Hamer's laughter died out at once. It was something he'd never considered. When he thought about his relationship with the woman, he realised how much she must have learnt about his life and circumstances. She'd been particularly keen to find out how wealthy he was. In fact, it was her wish to convert a fleeting romance into a marriage that convinced him to get rid of her.

'Did you ever confide in her?'

'No, Rawdon, that was not why the affair blossomed.'

'Was she ever in this house when you were absent?'

'As a matter of fact, she was.'

'There you are, then – she could have done some prying.'

'I expressly forbade it.'

'When the cat's away . . .'

'She wouldn't have *dared*.'

'A desperate woman would dare anything, especially if she has designs on becoming Mrs Hamer. She'd certainly find a means of getting into that collection of weapons you hold so dear. We know she had a thieving instinct because she filched your salver. *That's who got hold of the dagger, Stephen,'* said Carr, decisively. 'What's her name?'

'Miss Eleanor Gold.'

'Find her quickly and shake the truth out of her.'

'Not so fast,' said Hamer, 'you're leaping to conclusions like a master of hounds going over a five-barred gate. It was not a long attachment. She'd only have been left alone in this house two or three times.'

'Once was enough.'

'If she'd taken that dagger, she'd have tried to use it on me.'

'Miss Gold might have done something far more subtle,' Carr pointed out. 'She could've used it *against* you and left you to face the consequences.'

'I'm sorry, Rawdon, but there's a fatal flaw in your argument. Bowerman was not struck down anywhere. He was stabbed to death in a property that I own. Eleanor could never have known it belonged to me.'

'Her accomplice might have done so.'

'What accomplice?'

'I'm talking about the one who committed the murder, of course. A lot of forethought went into the plan. Bowerman was killed to throw suspicion on to you and a house you owned was chosen as the venue for the crime. Two enemies are in league against you,' said Carr, 'and only one of them wears a petticoat.'

'I refuse to believe it of Eleanor.'

'Soft-heartedness doesn't become you, Stephen.'

'She was fiery but not capable of plotting against me.'

'Then she was recruited by a man. He's the real villain.'

'I wonder . . .'

'Where is Miss Eleanor Gold now?'

Hamer was dismayed. 'I have no idea, Rawdon.'

'Then I suggest we find out – very quickly.'

When he called at the house, Lemuel Fleet did so with great trepidation. Hannah Granville needed to be handled with great tact at the best of times. In the wake of the attack on her, he suspected, she'd be in a state of constant turbulence. He was wrong. Much to his relief, he found her subdued and, for once, almost reasonable. Their discussion took place in a room at the rear of the house because she refused to enter the drawing room again.

'How are you, Miss Granville?' he asked.

'I'd rather not talk about the incident, if you don't mind.'

'Mr Skillen spoke of scratches to your cheek. I see no sign of them.'

'They are still there, Mr Fleet, but I choose to hide them.'

'And are you reconciled to the idea that Mr Mundy was not responsible for throwing that stone at the window?'

'I'm more than reconciled,' she said, quietly. 'I feel slightly abashed that I raged at an innocent man. That doesn't mean I'm ready to overlook all the insults he's directed at me,' she continued, 'but I no longer accuse him.'

'Is it permissible to pass on his best wishes to you?'

'I'd rather not hear his name at all, if you don't mind.'

'Then I might as well leave now,' he said, getting up.

'No, no, sit down again, please. There are things we must talk about.'

He resumed his seat. 'How can I do without mentioning his name?'

'You've spent your working life accommodating headstrong actresses, Mr Fleet. Accommodate *my* whims, please.'

'I've done rather a lot of that recently,' he murmured.

'What guarantees can you offer me?'

'I can offer you none with regard to . . . the gentleman who remains nameless.'

'That's not what I'm worried about,' she explained. 'In view of what happened, this house is my fortress. I'm afraid to stir outside it. What guarantees can you give me of my safety?'

'You shall have as many bodyguards as you wish. As well as looking after you during rehearsals, they'll convey you to and from the theatre.'

'Thank you. I needed that reassurance.'

'Does that mean you *will* return to the company?'

'It means that I will not rule it out, sir.'

Fleet smiled. 'I never hoped for the slightest concession from you.'

'Nor have you got one,' she said. 'If I'm to resume my painful acquaintance with *The Piccadilly Opera*, it is there that the concessions have to be made.'

'You have an unexpected ally, Miss Granville.'

'Is that really so?'

'Were I not forbidden to do so, I would tell you the lady's name.'

'Then I encourage you to do so,' said Hannah, curiosity taking over. 'You refer to Mrs Mundy, I take it. It's the husband I abominate. I feel nothing but sympathy for a wife who is yoked to such a burden for the rest of her life. What did Mrs Mundy say?'

'She was profoundly sorry to hear of your plight. The first thing she did was to offer up a prayer for your recovery. The lady is not so wedded to her husband that she is entirely blind to his failings. She has a vastly higher opinion of his play than you do, perhaps, but she's ready to admit its occasional inadequacies.'

'They are not *occasional*, Mr Fleet.'

'Please don't deliver another diatribe, Miss Granville.'

'I wasn't going to. Before I can think of returning to the fold, there is an urgent question to be answered.'

'What is it?'

'Since *he*, it transpires, is not bent on harming me, then who *is*?'

Now that she'd rallied visibly, Paul Skillen felt able to leave her alone at the house. He had enquiries to make elsewhere. When he'd called on Sir Geoffrey Melrose, the man's memory had been strangely uncertain regarding the dinner party he'd once given at his town house. While readily confirming that Mark Bowerman and Laetitia Somerville had been present, he could only supply Paul with one other name. It was that of Rollo Winters, described by Sir Geoffrey as a politician of sorts and a decent fellow to boot. Paul deduced that the two men were old cronies.

Having been told that Winters called at his club every morning at the same time, Paul made sure that he arrived there shortly after. There was no need for any introductions. Winters was already expecting him because he'd received notice of it. Paul could see that Sir Geoffrey had warned his friend not to be too forthcoming. Rollo Winters was an impressive man, tall, well proportioned and with more than a little of his earlier good looks. There was an almost noble quality about him. His long black locks were tinged with grey and his face deeply lined but he seemed far too sprightly to be the sixty-year-old proclaimed on his birth certificate.

'Good day to you, Mr Skillen,' he said with bogus jocularity. 'Sir Geoffrey has told me a little about you and your quest. I'm not sure that I can help you.'

'It depends on how retentive your memory is.'

'Oh, it's very retentive. That's essential in a politician. You have to remember an interminable number of names and be able to relate each one to the way they vote and the company they keep. You must never speak out of turn among fellow politicians. That could be fatal. Memory is your saviour.'

'Does it only operate in the House of Commons, Mr Winters?'

'I see what you're getting at. You refer to dinner parties.'

'I refer to one in particular, sir. It was at Sir Geoffrey's house.'

'Then a problem raises its head at once, Mr Skillen. When he is here, Sir Geoffrey often has dinner parties. You might say that it's a way of life for him. He's never happier than when entertaining friends. I've been to so many of the gatherings that I have difficulty separating them.'

'This one involved a gentleman named Mr Bowerman. After the death of his wife, he shunned society. Simply getting him to the table was an achievement in Sir Geoffrey's eyes. Since he only made that single appearance, your retentive mind *should* remember Mr Bowerman.'

'Indeed, I do. He was rather too shy and desiccated in my view. All that he did was to stare fixedly at the ladies present – one lady, actually – and contribute nothing whatsoever to the prevailing hilarity.'

'Let's talk about that one lady, if I may,' said Paul. 'Her name was Miss Laetitia Somerville.'

'Was it?' asked the other in mock surprise. 'I believe you're right. The truth is that I never remember the names of the fairer sex. Their faces, bodies and carriage are engraved on my mind for ever but, since they're of no political significance, I treat them as the pleasing and decorative objects that they are.'

'Had you met Miss Somerville before?'

'Unhappily, I had not.'

'Do you know how she came to be there?'

'Sir Geoffrey must have invited her.'

'I'm wondering if she came at *your* behest, Mr Winters.'

'That's very flattering,' said the other with a chuckle, 'but it's not true. When you reach my age, alas, beautiful young women don't flock to join your circle. A young man like you, however, is in a different position.' Closing one eye, he regarded Paul with the other. 'If you want to know who took her to the dinner party, why don't you approach the lady herself?'

'I've already done so, sir.'

'What was her explanation?'

'She went along at the invitation of a female friend.'

'Then that's your answer. Why bother me?'

'I was not entirely persuaded by her claim. Also, I thought you could tell me a little more about the occasion.'

'What is there to tell?' asked Winters with a grin. 'It was a typical dinner party thrown by Sir Geoffrey. The food was delicious, wine flowed freely, the ladies sparkled and the only thing that impaired the general gaiety was that gloomy individual, Bowerman. We just ignored him and revelled into the night.'

'Yet he was the one who gained the real prize,' said Paul. 'Having met Miss Somerville, he developed an interest in her that burgeoned until it reached the point where he wooed and won her over.'

'I'd never have thought him capable of it.'

'Appearances can be deceptive.'

'Oh, you don't need to tell me that,' said Winters, chuckling again. 'When I look at the benches opposite me in the Commons, I see rows of serious, upright and apparently respectable men. In reality, of course, many of them are rogues, charlatans, certifiable idiots and seasoned adulterers.' He put a hand to his chest. 'I am none of those things, by the way.'

But Paul had already made his appraisal of Rollo Winters. Beneath his affability was a calculating politician who'd learnt to keep intrusive questions at bay. It was evident that he remembered the dinner party extremely well and could, if he desired, have listed the names of everyone present. In doing that, however, he would have revealed the real nature of the event. It was not simply a gathering of like-minded friends. The women were expected to be more than merely decorative. Paul recalled that Bowerman had told him that Laetitia stood out from the other women because she didn't flirt or giggle drunkenly. Quiet and dignified, she'd never let her guard down. Bowerman had admired her for that.

'It's almost noon,' said Winters. 'Can I offer you refreshment of some sort?'

'No, thank you,' replied Paul.

'I only come fully awake with that first brandy. Don't you need something to brace yourself against the demands of the day?'

'I like to keep my head clear, Mr Winters.'

'Alcohol sharpens the brain, take my word for it.'

'Then why did it deprive you of the details of a dinner party you once attended? The wine may have flowed yet the memory was dulled.'

Winters scowled. 'You're not a member of this club, Mr Skillen,' he said, crisply. 'If you don't leave immediately, I'll ask the steward to throw you out.'

Paul smiled. 'I'll gladly take my leave of you.'

As he stood up, he caught sight of someone out of the corner of his eye. The man came in through the door, stopped and went straight out of the room again. When he turned around, Paul saw that there was nobody there.

CHAPTER FOURTEEN

In spite of his antagonism towards her, Abel Mundy had a vestigial sympathy for Hannah Granville. When he'd first heard what happened, he felt sorry for her and not a little relieved that she'd survived the attack more or less intact. Had she been seriously injured, she'd have been unable to appear in his play and the production would have had to be abandoned. Without her, it could not take place; even with her, unfortunately, its chances of being performed remained slim. Mundy had been shocked that a rehearsal should be held without his knowledge and that radical changes were made to his work. Fleet had done his best to soothe the irate playwright and to convince him that alterations were unavoidable. After staring into the abyss of possible cancellation, Mundy finally accepted that *The Piccadilly Opera* at least ought to include proper arias to justify its title. Without them, his play might vanish altogether without trace. Given the torment it had caused to everyone involved, no other London theatre would touch it. Lemuel Fleet was his only hope.

Since there had to be cooperation on his part, Mundy decided to go to the theatre and discuss the situation with the manager. Before he did so, he went into the drawing room to tell his wife what he was going to do. He found her on her knees in prayer in front of the small crucifix they'd put up on the mantelpiece. It was not unusual to see her in such a position. They said prayers together every night beside the bed before they got into it. What made a difference this time was the fact that she remained in an attitude of submission for much longer than usual. It was several minutes before she finished. Becoming aware of her husband, Marion rose to her feet immediately.

'I'm sorry,' she said. 'Were you waiting to tell me something?'

'Yes, my dear, I was. I'm going to see Mr Fleet to seek a compromise.'

'Then my prayers have been answered.'

'Yet you were the one who said that I shouldn't change a syllable of the play.'

'That was before Miss Granville was almost blinded. I've been tortured by the thought of what might have happened to her. You'd have lost the chance of seeing a play of yours at the Theatre Royal, perhaps, but you'll go on to write others that will grace the stage there. In her case,' she said, 'she'd have lost both her eyesight and her whole career. Miss Granville would never be able to act again.'

'God bless you, Marion. You have a tender heart.'

She thrust out her jaw. 'It can be a block of ice, if necessary.'

'This latest crisis has rightly melted it,' he said. 'As a gesture of compassion to Miss Granville, I'll allow more music in my play. Whether or not that concession will be enough to pacify her, only time will tell.'

'Would you like me to come with you, Abel?'

'No, I must deal with Mr Fleet man to man.'

'Don't give way too easily.'

'I won't, my dear. He'll have to beg me.'

They walked to the front door together and she opened it for him before she accepted a kiss on the cheek. Something had clearly touched her.

'I was too harsh on Miss Granville,' she admitted. 'When I

heard that she was cohabiting with a man, I was very scathing. I still condemn it strongly, of course. It's sinful behaviour. Yet somehow I found myself warming to Mr Skillen when he leapt so promptly to her defence.'

'It's no more than *I* would have done had *you* been in trouble, my dear.'

'That's my argument. He acted like a loving husband.'

'She's his paramour.'

'I'm not denying that, Abel.'

'That should tell you the sort of woman she is.'

'All that I wish to say is that Miss Granville is fortunate to have such a man at her side. Not that I'm condoning what they do,' she added, quickly. 'It's wrong before the eyes of God and anathema to both of us. But we mustn't sit in judgement on her private life. It behoves us to remember that *she* is the key to the future of your play.'

Peter felt that Jem's nocturnal antics had provided an intriguing clue to the crime. If a property owned by Stephen Hamer was specifically chosen as the murder scene, then he was either involved or someone was trying to put him in an awkward position. Should the Runners learn what Jem Huckvale had found out, they'd use it as another excuse to arrest Hamer. Because he was convinced that Hamer had not committed the crime, Peter would never inform Yeomans of their discovery in the agent's ledger. Paul agreed with his brother that the former soldier must have an enemy trying to wreak some sort of revenge. They could only guess what prompted it.

Having made a valuable contribution to the investigation, Peter felt able to take time off in order to render some assistance to the bank. He therefore rode in the direction of Epping Forest in search of Jacob Picton. A valued customer of the bank, the man would be aghast at the news that his name had been used to defraud the institution. Peter was hoping that he might be able to explain how a young woman was able to forge both a letter and a bond in his name. Like his brother, he set out alone on his horse. When he saw a coach going in the same direction, however, he was quick to ride behind it for safety.

Leonard Impey had told him that Picton was a prosperous man but Peter was unprepared for the size of his residence. Set in an estate of untold acres, it was imposing. Simply to maintain the extensive formal gardens, a large staff would have been needed. To run a house that large with its classical portico and its arresting symmetry, an even larger number of servants would be engaged. Picton shared his abode with a wife, four married sons and a confusing litter of grandchildren. Family friends were also staying there. Generous to a fault, Picton spread his bounty freely.

When Peter arrived, the butler did not immediately let him into the house. Stray callers were discouraged. Only when the name of the bank was mentioned was Peter allowed in. He was escorted along a wide corridor decorated with marble statuary and shown into the library. It was immense. A quick inventory of the shelves told him that Picton was a man of Catholic tastes. There were books on every subject under the sun with a special place reserved for tomes about architecture. He was just about to examine one of them when Jacob Picton came in.

'Mr Skillen?' he asked.

'Yes, sir – I'm very pleased to meet you.'

'I'm told that you're an employee of the bank.'

'I don't actually work there,' said Peter, 'but I've been retained by Mr Impey a number of times when there's been suspicious activity.'

'Is that what's brought you here – criminal behaviour?'

'Unhappily, it is.'

Picton was an old man bent almost double by age. Propped up by a walking stick, he shuffled across the room and lowered himself into a chair. Peter noticed the blue veins on the back of the man's skeletal hands. His long, snow-white beard was supplemented by wispy hair and by the tufts that grew in his ears. While his body was in decay, however, his faculties were undiminished.

'Why have you come to me, Mr Skillen?'

'First, let me show you this, sir,' said Peter, handing him the bond. 'We believe it to be a forgery and need you to endorse that view.'

Spectacles dangled on a ribbon around Picton's neck. He had some difficulty fitting them onto his nose. When he'd done so, he examined the document and emitted a growl of displeasure.

'Where did this come from?'

'They were presented to the manager by a Mrs Hester Mallory.'

'I know nobody of that name.'

'Is it a forgery?'

'It's a very clever forgery,' said Picton, squinting at it through his spectacles once again. 'I might almost have written this myself. The woman has copied my hand perfectly. What betrays her is a grammatical solecism of which I'd never be guilty. That's why I can say categorically that this is a fake bond.'

'Thank you for confirming it, sir.'

'Though I'm known for my generosity, I'd never advance an amount of that size to a total stranger.'

'I'm not sure that that's how she could be described, Mr Picton.'

'You think it was somebody I *know*?'

'It's certainly someone who knew you,' said Peter. 'At the very least, Mrs Mallory had access to correspondence of yours and an awareness of your dealings with the bank. Both letter and bond were sufficiently convincing to take in Mr Impey and he is not a gullible person.'

'How much money did he advance?'

'It was all of one thousand pounds.'

Picton clicked his tongue. 'That was uncharacteristically rash of him.'

'The lady seems to have been extremely plausible.'

'Feminine wiles are at play here, Mr Skillen. Had a man presented this bond to him, the manager would have needed more proof of his veracity before he handed over so much. I'm disappointed in him.'

'Mr Impey is very disappointed in himself, sir.'

'When you return to the bank, you can bear a letter to him from me. This time it *will* be genuine and not very pleasant to read.' He let the spectacles fall from his nose. 'I know what you're going to ask me. You want me to identify this lady posing under the name of Mrs Mallory. Describe her for me.'

Peter repeated what he'd been told by Impey, recalling the impression she made on first acquaintance. He also pointed out that she'd arrived just before the bank was about to close.

'That was deliberate,' he concluded. 'Mrs Mallory gave the manager very little time to question her. Having used your name as an endorsement, she promised to return on the following day.'

'Why didn't Mr Impey subject this bond to closer scrutiny?'

'He saw no reason to do so.'

'Impey should have done that as a matter of course.'

'Luckily, his chief clerk had doubts.'

'I'm glad that someone did. I find it very unsettling that my name was used.'

'That's why I wanted you to know what had happened.'

'What action have you taken on the bank's behalf?'

Peter told him of his visit to the hotel where Mrs Mallory claimed to be staying and how he'd learnt that, even though she was not a guest at the time, she had been in the past. On that occasion, she'd employed a different name. When he told

Picton what that name was, the old man's eyes kindled.

'Miss Kenyon, was it?' he said. 'I knew her as Edith Loveridge . . .'

When he heard the carriage draw up outside the house, he went to the window and saw her getting out and paying the driver. Moving quickly into the hall, he opened the front door and gave her a welcoming embrace before whisking her into the drawing room. He was eager to learn her news.

'How much did you get this time?'

'This manager is rather more careful than Mr Impey,' she said, 'and requires time to consider the transaction. No matter, I had him dangling like a fish on a line. In due course, I vow, we'll get every penny requested.'

Chevy Ruddock was unhappy. He hated surveillance work. When he'd had a similar assignment, he thought it would be a feather in his cap but that hope soon perished. Given the task of watching a brothel in Covent Garden, he'd spent interminable hours at his post and suffered all kinds of humiliation. It was the same on this occasion. On duty for the whole night, he'd been pestered by stray dogs, harassed by drunken oafs and soaked by the rain. The one consolation was that Yeomans had given him the use of a horse but it was never needed. Instead of passing the night with his wife in the comfort of their bed, he and the animal had stood together in mutual misery in the darkness. Ruddock was tired, bored and very wet.

Nothing of consequence had happened. Earlier that morning, Rawdon Carr had visited his friend then left. Though he made a note of the times of arrival and departure, Ruddock doubted that they would be of any significance. Hours rolled by. He was just about to drop off to sleep when there was some action at last. Stephen Hamer left the house and mounted the horse his servant brought out for him. He set off at a canter. Ruddock hauled himself into the saddle and went after him. His fear that he'd be noticed soon faded away. Hamer was riding with such urgency that he only had eyes for what lay ahead of him.

Eventually, he reached a fine house not far from Piccadilly and reined in his horse. A servant came out to take care of it and Hamer was admitted to the building. Ruddock dismounted, tethered his horse to a railing and studied the building. When someone emerged from a neighbouring house, he went quickly across to the man.

'Can you tell me who lives next door?' he asked, politely.

'Yes,' said the man, obligingly. 'It's a Miss Somerville.'

'Would that be Miss *Laetitia* Somerville?'

'Yes – do you know the lady?'

But Ruddock was already running back to his horse.

Paul called at the gallery at an ideal time. Gully Ackford and Jem Huckvale had just finished teaching their respective pupils and were having a rest. They were interested to hear Paul's latest theory. Having met both Sir Geoffrey Melrose and Rollo Winters, he had a clearer idea of what must have happened at the dinner party given by the former. It had not been an evening of intellectual debate. Sir Geoffrey and his friend were men of the world who took their pleasures where they found them or, in this case, where they set them up. Unencumbered by their wives, they wanted an evening of merriment that ended in the bedroom and they'd invited their guests accordingly. With the exception of Mark Bowerman, the men were of one accord; with the exception of Laetitia Somerville, the women were chosen because of their known readiness to acquiesce. Inevitably, Bowerman and Laetitia had been thrown together as the outsiders. That led Paul to one conclusion.

'Sir Geoffrey betrayed his friend,' he decided.

'Is that what he admitted?' asked Ackford.

'Oh, no, it was quite the reverse, Gully. He claimed to be acting in the spirit of true comradeship, rescuing Bowerman from his hermetic existence and introducing him to real life again. I fancy there was rather more to it than that.'

'I see what you mean, Paul.'

'He was invited for the sole purpose of meeting Miss Somerville.'

'Did the lady *know* it?' said Huckvale.

'I think she arranged it, Jem.'

'But she *wanted* to marry Mr Bowerman, didn't she?'

'She gave him reason to believe that she did,' said Paul, developing his theory as he went along, 'and she seemed genuinely distressed by his death when I first met her. Then we had the information that Bowerman's will had been changed recently in her favour. In one sense, therefore, his murder was actually good news for her.'

'Do you think she was involved in it?' asked Ackford.

'No, I don't. Miss Somerville was really shocked by it.'

'Then what exactly is going on?'

'I was going to ask the same question,' said Huckvale. 'It's all a bit confusing to me. From what you've told us, Mr Bowerman was a good man.'

'He was a person of great integrity,' said Paul. 'His one weakness was that he was somewhat unworldly and I certainly wouldn't have said that of Sir Geoffrey or Winters. What I'm coming to believe is this: Miss Somerville was looking for a wealthy man she could entrap and lead by the nose. I don't believe she ever intended to marry him. When he'd done what she really wanted and changed his will out of love for her, she was ready to dispose of him.'

'The duel,' said Ackford, smacking the table for effect. 'Another suitor turns up and lays claim to her, more or less forcing Bowerman into challenging him. Hamer didn't arrive out of the blue at all. He was waiting until he was called.'

'That's the way my mind is working, Gully. There could be a conspiracy here. Once he'd served his purpose, Mr Bowerman was in the way. Hamer was summoned to kill him in a duel. It's so cruel,' said Paul. 'In trying to make Miss Somerville his wife, Mr Bowerman was unwittingly setting a date for his own execution. Instead of using a noose, however, Hamer was planning to shoot him dead with a duelling pistol.'

'That's not only cruel,' said Huckvale, 'it's wicked.'

'Hamer and Miss Somerville have been working hand in glove all along.'

'Yet you said earlier that she was shocked by Mr Bowerman's murder.'

'What shocked her was that it didn't take place on Putney Heath. That was the execution she'd ordered. Someone chose a different way to kill him.'

'Who was that, Paul?'

'Your guess is as good as mine.'

'And why was he stabbed in the garden of Captain Hamer's house?'

'He was only a lieutenant, Jem.'

'Oh, yes. I was forgetting. Your brother told us about that.'

'In answer to your question,' said Paul, 'I don't know. What I suspect is that someone wanted to settle a score with Hamer and Miss Somerville. Both of them were stunned by the murder and she couldn't suggest who might possibly have been responsible for it. Now,' he went on, 'I must get back to Hannah. As you'll have heard, she's a trifle upset at the moment.'

'Yes,' said Ackford, 'Charlotte told us a stone smashed your window.'

'I've got a crime right on my doorstep.'

'It's no worse than being attacked by two dogs in the middle of the night.'

'Yes, that must have been a rude awakening, Gully.'

'I was really shaken.'

'And so was I,' admitted Huckvale. 'It was far worse than being arrested by the Runners. They can bark very loud but at least they don't bite.'

Troubled by hunger pains, Yeomans and Hale repaired to The Peacock to enjoy a meat pie apiece and to wash it down with a pint of beer. It was not long before they were joined by Chevy Ruddock, still sodden and so exhausted that he couldn't complete a single sentence without yawning dramatically. Yeomans grabbed him by the neck and shook him like a rag doll.

'Wake up, man!'

'I'm tired, Mr Yeomans.'

'We've told you before. Runners never sleep.'

'Well, I do,' said Ruddock, unable to suppress the biggest yawn yet.

'What have you found out, Chevy?' asked Hale.

Ruddock fingered his shoulder. 'I found out that there's a hole in this coat where the stitching's come undone. I'll have to ask my wife to sew it up again. The rain kept seeping in through the hole. My shirt is wet through.'

'Forget about your shirt. What did you learn?'

'Captain Hamer stayed in all night – unlike me.'

'Were there any visitors?'

'Not until this morning, sir. Then that friend of his arrived.'

'Mr Carr?'

'That's the one. He has a very sharp tongue. He called me all sorts of vile names when we interrupted that duel.' He pulled a notebook from his pocket and flipped through the pages. 'He arrived at nine o'clock and left exactly thirty-five minutes later. The captain came to the door to wave him off.'

Yeomans contributed his own yawn. 'Is that all you found out?'

'Oh, no, I haven't come to the best bit yet.'

'What is it?'

'Captain Hamer left his house at' – he consulted his notebook – 'it was three minutes after two o'clock and he was in a hurry.'

'Did you follow him?'

'Yes, Mr Yeomans.'

'Where did he go?'

'It was to this house in a street off Piccadilly. I'd love to live somewhere like that. Agnes, my wife, would be so happy there. But it will never happen unless we get taken on as servants. We know our place.' Yeomans shook him again. 'Don't do that, sir. I have a job standing up straight. If you shake me again, I'll finish up on the floor.'

'Give us some useful *information*, man!'

'I wondered who lived there so I asked a neighbour.'

'And?'

'It was Miss Somerville's house.'

The Runners gazed at him in surprise and then, when they were confronted by another monstrous yawn from Ruddock, they turned to look at each other.

'I thought she hated the captain,' said Hale.

'She did, Alfred. She didn't even want us to mention his name.'

'Then why did she let him go into her house?'

'Perhaps he forced his way in.'

'Is that what happened, Chevy?'

There was no reply to Hale's question because Ruddock had just nodded off to sleep. Eyes closed, he stood there immobile with a seraphic smile on his face. It was removed by a kick on the shin from Yeomans. Coming awake with a start, Ruddock hopped on one foot while he rubbed his other leg.

'That hurt!' he complained.

'Then tell us what we want to know,' said Yeomans. 'Did the captain have a struggle to get into the house?'

'No,' said Ruddock, barely managing to keep his balance. 'He was let straight in. A servant came out to stable his horse for him. It was almost as if he was expected.' He stood on both feet again. 'I thought you'd like to know.'

'We're delighted with the news,' said Hale.

'Well done, Ruddock!' said Yeomans.

'This deserves a reward. You look as if you're starving. Take my seat and help yourself to what's left of my pie.' Hale got up from the table. 'I'll fetch you a tankard of beer to help it down.'

In the face of such kind treatment, Ruddock glowed. He'd done something to gain their appreciation at last. He was still grinning when he fell asleep again.

Lemuel Fleet had come so close to falling into a crater of despair that he felt it was only a matter of time before he finally toppled. His profession acquainted him with possible danger every day. When trying to set up a performance of a new play, so many things could go wrong. All of them had happened to *The Piccadilly Opera*. There was no affliction from which the play had not suffered. As it stood, it was wholly unfit for public consumption. Were he to put it in front of an audience, it might ruin his reputation irreparably. He knew to his cost how wild theatregoers could be. They insisted on value for money. Fleet was aware just how many riots had been started by discontented patrons over the years. On one occasion, when higher prices were introduced, there had been continuous rioting for all of sixty-six days until the management relented.

Loving the fabric of his theatre as much as its traditions, he was terrified of wanton destruction. A bad play with a half-hearted actress as its central attraction would provoke anger and violence. He was staring into the crater yet again.

'I wonder if I might have a word, Mr Fleet.'

'What's that?' He came out of his reverie to see his visitor. 'Why are you here, Mr Mundy? No rehearsal is called for today.'

'I wish to speak to you.'

'Yes, yes, come on in, please do.'

'You said that your door was always open.'

Fleet was staggered less by the playwright's arrival than by the unusual tone of his voice. It was soft, low and almost apologetic. He got up to bring Mundy fully into the office and eased him into a chair, taking the one opposite for himself.

'I've been talking things over with my wife,' said Mundy.

'I do the same thing myself.' Fleet gave a nervous laugh. 'I don't mean that I talk to *your* dear spouse, of course. I converse with my own. It often helps me to see things in a new light somehow. Does it have the same effect on you?'

'As a rule, it doesn't.'

'I'm sorry to hear that.'

'My wife, Marion, is my mainstay. Whatever course of action I take, she will always endorse without ever questioning it.'

'There aren't enough women like that about,' said Fleet.

'That, I should add, was until today. She did think for herself this time.'

'Oh?'

'Indeed,' said Mundy, 'she resorted to prayer beforehand so that she had divine authority for it. She pointed out that we have both been too ready to abuse Miss Granville when all that she wants is for my play to be seen at its very best. The attack on her has made us take a more understanding view of her.'

'Am I actually *hearing* this?' asked Fleet, close to delirium. 'Are you telling me that you approve of Miss Granville's suggested improvements?'

'Oh, no, they are far too comprehensive. I stand by my right as the playwright to protect my work. I'll make changes after – and only after – reasonable discussion. In essence, I'm committing to finding a middle way between my own suggestions and Miss Granville's more savage approach to the text. Is that fair, Mr Fleet?'

'It's more than fair.'

'Will the lady herself take the same view?'

'We can but ask.'

'Then I urge *you* to do the asking. For some reason, I irritate the lady.'

'I simply can't understand why,' said Fleet, concealing the lie behind a broad smile. 'Once again, I am ready to act as a willing go-between.'

'Remember what the Bible says – "Blessed are the peacemakers". . . '

'I think that we should bless your dear wife as well. Mrs Mundy may have found the way to save all our skins.'

Slipping quietly into the church, Marion Mundy walked down the aisle then stepped into a pew. She knelt down and went through the prayers that she routinely said every day. Her mind then turned to her husband. Secure in the house of the Lord, she prayed in earnest for the success of his play and for the removal of the incessant bickering that it had so far produced. She remained on her knees until the pain eventually forced her to get up.

'I'm worried, Laetitia.'

'It's not like you to lose your nerve.'

'I *haven't* lost my nerve,' retorted Hamer. 'I'll face any kind of jeopardy without a shred of fear but I prefer it to be visible. That's what makes this situation so maddening. Things are happening out of sight.'

'We can deal with them.'

'You can't shoot at what you can't actually see.'

'I thought you might have worked out who is behind it all by now.'

'That's what I've been trying to do. Rawdon came up with the best suggestion. He wonders if it might be someone from whom I parted rather abruptly. The obvious name was Eleanor Gold.'

'Was she that pouting young woman with a high opinion of herself?'

'She was very appealing at first.'

'What happened?'

'I made the mistake of trusting her, Laetitia.'

'In what way?'

'Thinking it was safe to do so, I let her stay in the house when I wasn't there. Rawdon believes that she might have taken the liberty of reading your correspondence to me and of sneaking into my little museum. In other words,' said Hamer, 'Eleanor could have stolen that Spanish dagger of mine.'

'And if she read my letters to you,' said Laetitia with growing alarm, 'she'd have been aware of what we'd planned. She'd know, for instance, the exact time when the duel was taking place.'

'More importantly, she could have studied your hand carefully enough to forge a summons to that credulous fool, Bowerman. Yes,' he decided, 'I think we may be on the right track at last. Eleanor Gold and an accomplice are the villains.'

'Then it was stupid of you to let her get so close. Why didn't you just take what you wanted and throw her out?'

'She was very sweet, Laetitia.'

'She's sweet and murderous, by the sound of it.'

'Rawdon and I will find her,' he vowed. 'We just have to hope that someone else doesn't get to her first. If that happens, we're done for. Eleanor will be able to tell them how you tricked Bowerman into changing his will, then handed him over for me to kill in a duel. We must catch her *first*.'

'You'll have no competition from the Bow Street Runners.'

'I wasn't thinking of them.'

'Are you still concerned about the Skillen brothers?'

'They are the real problem,' he conceded. 'Rawdon tried to frighten them off but his plan was foiled. He's trying to devise another way of diverting them.'

'Then he needs to put it in place very soon.'

'I'd happily meet anyone in a duel but I'd think twice about it if the man with the other weapon in his hand was Paul Skillen. He's dangerous.'

'I agree with you, Stephen. He troubles me as well.'

'His brother is an equal threat to us.'

'Then we may have to get rid of both of them, permanently.'

'That won't be easy,' he said.

'Are you afraid of them?'

'No, of course I'm not, Laetitia. But I treat them with respect. When you signed the death warrant for Bowerman, you gave me an easy task. I'd have shot him dead before he'd even pulled the trigger.' He pursed his lips. 'Killing Peter and Paul Skillen is a much more daunting task but it's not one from which I'd flinch. In fact, I think I'd relish it.'

She was merciless. 'If it needs doing, you and Rawdon must do it.'

Laetitia heard the clang of the doorbell and moved to the

window. When she peered around the curtain, she saw Yeomans and Hale standing outside. She turned quickly back to Hamer.

'It's those damnable Runners again,' she said. 'They mustn't find you here.'

'I'll hide in there,' he said, moving towards the adjoining room. 'Don't come out until I call you.'

'Listen to what they want then send them quickly on their way.'

'Just go,' she urged, opening a door for him.

When Hamer had gone, Laetitia sat down again in a posture that suggested grief and remorse. She was still wearing the black dress and exuding a sense of irreplaceable loss. When the servant brought news of the visitors, she agreed to see them on the condition that they stayed only a short time. After passing on the message to the Runners, the servant ushered them into the room.

Yeomans came straight to the point. 'Where is Captain Hamer?'

'I beg your pardon,' she said.

'You told us that you detested the man.'

'And I do, Mr Yeomans. His name is abhorrent to me.'

'Then why did you let him into this house?'

'I'd never deign to do such a thing,' she said, hotly.

'Oh, yes, you would, Miss Somerville.'

'We had the captain's house watched,' said Hale, triumphantly. 'Earlier today, he was seen to leave his abode and ride straight here. One of your servants stabled his horse as if he was used to seeing Captain Hamer.'

'So I'll repeat my question,' said Yeomans, moving forward until he loomed over her like a huge, dark cloud. 'Where *is* he?'

CHAPTER FIFTEEN

Laetitia Somerville was rarely at a loss for words but she was groping in vain for them now. Their arrival and challenge was so unexpected that it took all the wind out of her. Maintaining her composure, she retreated into silence. It was soon broken. The door opened and Stephen Hamer charged angrily into the room.

'How dare you treat me like this!' he yelled. 'It's insulting. The chief magistrate will hear about it.'

'He will,' agreed Yeomans, 'and he'll praise us for exposing your lies.'

'Miss Somerville swore to us that she had no time for you,' said Hale, 'yet here you are, walking into this house as if you own it.'

'I have every right to a private life,' said Hamer with asperity, 'and so does Miss Somerville. What has this city come to when it condones the use of Peeping Toms on innocent people?'

'We're not sure that you *are* innocent, sir.'

'I take the same view as my colleague,' said Yeomans, heavily. 'When a person tells us one thing then does completely the opposite, we grow suspicious.'

'The captain was allowed in for only one reason,' said Laetitia, regaining her confidence, 'and for one reason only. He'd written to me, asking for permission to apologise in person. Because he expressed his heartfelt sympathy for the death of Mr Bowerman, I agreed to see him.'

'It's true,' said Hamer, catching her eye and reading its message.

'It does not mean that we are now on terms of friendship,' she went on. 'I've made that crystal clear. I've accepted the apology but that's all I've done. From today onwards, the captain is not welcome within these four walls.'

'It's no more than I deserve.'

'And that's all you have to say, is it?' taunted Yeomans.

'Yes,' said Hamer, 'so you can get out right now.'

'We haven't finished yet, sir. If – as you and Miss Somerville claim – this was a brief visit to say that you were sorry, two questions arise. Thanks to a colleague of ours, we know the exact time when you were admitted to the house. It was over an hour ago. Does it always take you that long to offer an apology?'

'Don't be impertinent!'

'The second question is the important one. If you had a good reason for being here, why were you hiding in another room so that we didn't see you?'

'If you are going to interrogate us like this,' said Laetitia, grandly, 'beware of the legal consequences. I retain one of the finest lawyers in the capital. If officers of the law step out of line, as both of you are now doing, he will have no compunction in having you dismissed.' She stood up to confront them. 'What did you do before you became a Bow Street Runner, Mr Yeomans?'

'I was a blacksmith,' he replied.

'It's an occupation more suited to a man of limited intelligence like yourself.' She turned to Hale. 'What about you?'

'I was a harness-maker,' said the other.

'So the pair of you worked exclusively with horses, did you?

That will explain your total lack of manners. Dumb animals have no need of etiquette.'

'We're used to people sneering at us, Miss Somerville,' said Yeomans. 'It's usually a sign of their guilt.'

'Of what are we supposed to be guilty?' demanded Hamer.

'We think you are in collusion with each other.'

'That's nonsense!'

'You can rant and rave all you wish, sir. We see what you see.'

'Then arrest me yet again, if you dare, and do the same to Miss Somerville this time. Take us before the chief magistrate and justify your mistake. I've been to Bow Street before, please remember, and I walked away as the innocent man I was. You would have been duly admonished for your mistake. On this occasion, I'll warrant, your fate will be much worse.'

'Not to worry,' said Laetitia, 'there's always a call for good blacksmiths.'

'Harness-makers are also in demand,' said Hamer.

'Do as the captain suggests and arrest us.'

They had reached an impasse. The certainty with which the Runners had entered the house had begun to crumble slightly. Had they placed the wrong construction on the fact that Hamer had called at a house where he was supposedly unwelcome? Ruddock had noted how familiarly he'd entered the building. Was that what had actually happened? If not, thought Yeomans, at least they'd have someone to blame. Ruddock would always be their whipping boy.

For their part, Laetitia and Hamer were hoping that their outraged denials were enough to put the visitors to flight. News that one of them was under surveillance had been a profound shock and a reminder that they needed to take the utmost care. Having derided the Runners, they now realised that Yeomans and Hale were not as inefficient as they'd assumed. When they saw grounds for suspicion, they acted accordingly. As a result, they'd caused Laetitia and Hamer acute embarrassment.

The two parties faced each other. Nobody moved and nobody spoke. Minutes steadily accumulated. Hamer looked for signs of weakness in the Runners while they, in turn, watched for an opening they could exploit. It never came. The impasse was eventually broken.

'To use an army term,' said Hamer, 'I'd advise a tactical retreat on your part.'

'We'd advise *you* to start telling the truth for once,' Yeomans retaliated.

'You have a warrant for our arrest?'

'No,' confessed Hale.

'Then it's time for you to withdraw.'

Though he was desperate to stay, Yeomans could find no reason to do so. Their mission had failed. He sought to win at least a token of gratitude from them.

'There was another reason why we came,' he said.

'Tell us what it is,' invited Laetitia, 'then get out of my house.'

'The inquest delivered its verdict.'

'It was exactly what we said it would be,' added Hale. 'It's recorded as a case of murder by a person or persons unknown.'

'Then get out there and catch them,' said Hamer. 'You won't find them here.'

'You heard Captain Hamer,' said Laetitia, reinforcing his command. 'He's given his word as a gentleman that he is innocent of the stabbing and I need hardly say that I, too, am wholly innocent of the crime. Your visit is therefore at an end. Please don't have the effrontery to come to this house again.'

After mumbling their apologies, the Runners crept out of the room.

* * *

When the letter arrived, Hannah read it with a mingled interest and distrust. Delivered by hand, it had been sent by Lemuel Fleet and told of the offer made by Abel Mundy. Hannah read it three times before she handed it over to Charlotte, who was seated at the rear of the house with her. Charlotte's response was more optimistic.

'This is good news, Hannah.'

'I wonder.'

'To some extent, it's an olive branch.'

'It's certainly not the surrender that I desire,' said Hannah. 'I am not only thinking of myself. I speak on behalf of the entire company.'

'I think they'd be cheered by the manager's letter. According to him, Mr Mundy is prepared to give ground.'

'Yes, but how much ground?'

'There's only one way to find out,' said Charlotte.

She was delighted that her friend had received encouragement at last. As well as reviving the hope that the play would be performed after all, it took Hannah's mind off the fear of another attempt to harm her. Dirk, the manservant, had been going out of the house regularly to make sure that nobody was watching for a chance to strike again. So far nothing remotely suspicious had been seen. While that had calmed Hannah, the letter had a less soothing effect on her altogether.

'His stipulation disturbs me, Charlotte.'

'Why is that?'

'Mundy insists that we discuss things together.'

'Isn't that the obvious thing to do?'

'Not when it forces me to look at that repulsive face of his.'

'Mrs Mundy doesn't find it repulsive.'

'That's neither here nor there,' said Hannah. 'If I'm honest, I'm afraid that the very sight of the man will make the hairs on the back of my neck stand up. I'll be in no state for the reasonable debate that Mr Fleet is suggesting.'

'The deadlock has to be broken somehow, Hannah.'

'Why must *I* make concessions?'

'All that the letter asks is that you recognise Mr Mundy's readiness to accept change and agree to search for a compromise acceptable to both of you. You're under no pressure to do anything that offends you.'

Hannah picked up the missive again but she had no time to read it again because Paul had just returned to the house. Coming into the room, he embraced Hannah then gave his sister-in-law a kiss.

'Dirk tells me that there's been nothing to report,' he said. 'It's as I thought. Nobody will dare to come back because they know we're on guard now.'

'Hannah's had a letter from Mr Fleet,' said Charlotte. 'He's calling a truce.'

'What does he say?'

'You can read it for yourself,' said Hannah, 'but only after you've told us where you've been and who you've seen. I'm not yet ready to make a decision about the play. In any case, it pales beside a murder investigation. What have you learnt?'

Paul told them more or less what he'd told Ackford and Huckvale at the gallery. He believed that the dinner party had been stage-managed in order to make possible a meeting between Bowerman and Laetitia Somerville. Who had actually devised the scheme, he was not sure, but Sir Geoffrey Melrose and Rollo Winters had been willing accomplices. Now that the relationship had ended with Bowerman's murder, both men had tried to distance themselves from any guilt. The two women listened open-mouthed to the revelations.

'Miss Somerville is *capable* of such villainy?' asked Charlotte.

'Oh, I think she could do much worse,' said Paul. 'What now seems clear is that she and the so-called Captain Hamer are working together.'

'Does that mean they're lovers?'

'I'm not sure about that, Charlotte, but their guilt is incontestable.'

'Then they should be in custody,' said Hannah. 'Why don't you and Peter arrest them and take them before a magistrate?'

'It's too early for that. Lock them away and we might never find out who killed Mr Bowerman because they are the only people who can lead us to the killer. Someone is venting his spleen on them by trying to incriminate them. Frankly,' said Paul, 'I'm more eager to catch the man who *did* murder Mr Bowerman rather than those who plotted to have him shot dead in a duel. Once that's done, Peter and I can round up Hamer and Miss Somerville.' He looked at Charlotte. 'By the way, where is my brother?'

'He rode off to see someone who lives near Epping Forest,' she said, glancing up at the clock on the mantelpiece, 'but he should be back by now.'

Leonard Impey had feared the reproaches of his old friend and client and he had good reason to do so. What Peter brought back from his visit to Jacob Picton was a letter of blistering criticism. It not only accused the manager of naivety and incompetence, it severed a relationship that had lasted for over thirty years. Impey collapsed into his chair and shrugged helplessly.

'It's all true, Mr Skillen. I deserve to be skinned alive like this.'

'Mr Picton did have *some* words of praise for you, sir.'

'Well, there's not one of them in his letter. What did he say?'

Peter told him of his visit to Epping Forest and how devastated the old man had been when he learnt what had happened. While he had never met a Mrs Mallory, he'd remembered an Edith

Loveridge only too well. She'd wormed her way into Picton's social circle by means of a friendship with one of his daughters-in-law. They'd shared an interest in painting and, between them, produced a number of landscapes of the surrounding countryside.

'So she didn't come to London in search of an artist, as she claimed,' said Impey, sourly. 'Edith Loveridge, alias Arabella Kenyon, actually *was* one. But how could she forge Mr Picton's calligraphy so convincingly?'

'I asked him that,' said Peter.

'What was his explanation?'

'He wrote her a letter of thanks when she gave him a watercolour of the house. The painting impressed him and used to be on a wall in his study. As a result of my visit, I expect that it's been destroyed.'

'And was he absolutely *sure* that she's now posing as Mrs Hester Mallory?'

'He was prepared to put his life savings on it, sir.'

'So before she deceived me, she insinuated herself into *his* affections.'

'Mr Picton never really liked the woman and, of course, he never advanced her any money. When I told him the name that she used in London, he was livid.'

'Why is that?'

'His wife's name is Hester.'

'It was very cruel of her to utilise it in such a way.'

'At least we know a lot more about her, sir.'

'But do you know enough to catch her yet?'

'I feel that I'm getting closer,' said Peter. 'That's all I can claim.'

Impey puffed his cheeks and went off into a world of his own. All that Peter could do was to wait. When the manager eventually came out of his daydream, he apologised profusely.

'I owe you profound thanks for finding out the truth, Mr Skillen.'

'I won't give up until I've caught up with the lady.'

'What about this murder enquiry in which you're entangled?'

'My brother has taken the lead there,' said Peter. 'I'll stay involved through him. As for the woman Mr Picton called "the fatal temptress", he had some advice.'

'It's in his letter. Since I'm such an easy prey to beauty, he urges me to retire.'

'That's a matter for you, sir. In the short term, there's something you could do that might be of help to me. Warn the other banks that there's a viper in town.'

'You know quite well that I can't do that,' said Impey. 'If one makes a huge error of judgement, one doesn't want to advertise the fact to one's competitors.'

'That's not what you'd be doing, Mr Impey.'

'Yes, it is.'

'There's no reason why anyone should know what really happened in this office,' explained Peter. 'I'm not going to tell them that you were fleeced. My intention is to warn them that you were approached by a forger but that you were clever enough to discern the forgery. They'll look on you favourably, sir. You'll become something of a hero in the banking world.'

'Will I?'

'You'll also be making it more likely for the woman to be caught. If I pass on the warning to other managers, it may well be that one of them has been approached by her to transact business. Miss Kenyon wants to make as much money as she can before disappearing from the city. Let's prevent her from doing that.'

'Yes, but in a sense we'll be telling them a lie. I *was* fleeced.'

'It's a necessary deception,' said Peter, 'in order to save others. Members of the banking fraternity will thank you for alerting them and know what to do if Miss Kenyon or Mrs Mallory knocks on their doors. I urge you to let me raise the alarm, sir. You will stand to gain for it,' he pointed out. 'If I can catch this woman, you may well get your money back.'

Impey laughed with relief. 'Then do it, Mr Skillen. Do it instantly.'

Rawdon Carr was troubled by the news that his friend's house had been spied upon. Calling on Hamer that afternoon, he was told about the confrontation with the Runners. The accusation that they were in league together had been a sobering moment for them.

'That would have ruined everything,' said Carr, uneasily. 'How did you extricate yourselves?'

'We browbeat them,' explained Hamer. 'Between us, Laetitia and I reduced them to snivelling wrecks. We forced them to apologise and away they went.'

'Don't ignore the warning, Stephen. They caught you together. That's what alarms me. What if it had been someone else? Had the Skillen brothers linked you and Laetitia, *they* wouldn't have been put to flight quite so easily.'

'We realise that.'

'I suggest that the two of you keep well apart for a while.'

'We've already agreed to do that, Rawdon.'

'That's a sound decision,' said Carr. 'Stand by it.' He changed tack. 'Have you had any more thoughts about Eleanor Gold?'

'Indeed, I have. I've been trawling through my memories of her. At the time, of course, I was swept away by her charms – and they were considerable. I always knew that someone like her would have a colourful past. Eleanor was very experienced.'

'Then she'd have sensed that you were tiring of her.'

'That's more than possible.'

'So she might well have plotted her revenge. It looks as if it might have involved stealing that dagger.'

'I'm inclined to agree.'

'If *she* stole it, who actually used it?'

'I don't know, Rawdon. It can only have been one of her former conquests, I suppose. Living as a courtesan, she will have had dozens of admirers.'

'Did she ever mention their names?'

'Oh, yes. She sometimes teased me that, if she were not with me, she could still be enjoying the perquisites of being Sir James Babington's mistress. She made it sound like a life of endless indulgence. I had to remind her that Sir James lost a leg in a riding accident.'

'What was her response to that?'

'Eleanor said that his income of forty thousand pounds a year was adequate consolation and that it helped her to overlook his physical shortcomings.'

'How did they part?'

'She always maintained that it was on the best of terms.'

'Then she could easily have gone back to him.'

'That's what I've been wondering,' said Hamer, running a hand across his chin, 'and there are a couple of other names that have popped into my mind.'

'Let's start with Sir James,' suggested Carr. 'I can make discreet enquiries about him. If he's recently acquired a new mistress, she might turn out to be Eleanor Gold. Ah, I see a problem,' he admitted. 'Would a one-legged man be capable of stabbing someone in the back?'

'Sir James is a politician. Back-stabbing comes naturally to him.' They traded a laugh. 'Seriously, he'd never do his own dirty work. He'd hire an assassin. But this is all conjecture. I can't be certain that he's in any way involved. Eleanor might have returned to someone else altogether. I can give you at least another four names.'

'We'll divide them up between us.'

'Thank you, Rawdon. You're always so helpful.'

'My motive is pure self-preservation,' said the other with a grin. 'I'm a partner in the enterprise. If you and Laetitia fall, then so do I.'

'Well, it won't be the Runners who bring us down. The people we must fear are these anonymous enemies who know far too much about us. That disturbs me. Then again,' he continued, 'we have Paul Skillen and his brother creeping up on us. I'd hoped you'd have dealt with them by now.'

'I promised to divert them,' said Carr, 'and I've kept my word.'

'What have you done?'

'You'll soon see, Stephen. The Skillens will no longer be a nuisance to us. They'll have an urgent problem to solve.'

Jem Huckvale was accustomed to dealing with a whole range of customers at the gallery, from nervous young men who wished to learn the noble art of self-defence to overconfident ones who felt they were expert swordsmen and who needed someone on whom to practise. Huckvale had even taught a woman how to handle a bow and arrow. When she was there, Charlotte handled all the bookings and recorded the names neatly in the ledger. Checking the list, Huckvale saw that his next task of the afternoon was an hour with one Mr Philip Needham, who wished for instruction in shooting. It was only when he actually arrived that it became clear that Needham was a man of the cloth. Of medium height, he was a solid individual in his thirties with a pleasant smile and a sense of other-worldliness about him. When he stepped into the shooting gallery, he answered the question burning its way into Huckvale's brain.

'Why am I here?' he said. 'That's what you wish to know. Why does a priest who abjures violence of any kind want to become proficient with a gun?'

'You wish to defend the church – is that it?'

'Metaphorically, I defend the church every day and I do so with a combination of faith and prayer. I was called, Mr Huckvale. Do you know what that means? I heard the voice of God one day and it drew me to labour unceasingly on His behalf.'

'Have you ever held a weapon before, Reverend?'

'I've held the Bible, the greatest weapon in the world against sin.'

'What about pistols?'

'They are foreign to me and I must learn to fire them. Every summer, you see, we hold a church fete and one of the events is a shooting match. It's won by the same obnoxious person time and again. My parishioners begged me to find someone to displace him as our champion.' He gave a bow. 'That honour falls to me.'

'Then I will do my best to turn you into a winner,' said Huckvale, 'though it may take several lessons to do so.'

'I'll come every day if necessary.'

Though he seemed an unlikely pupil, he was clearly dedicated. That would make the task much easier. Huckvale had taught far too many people who began with an enthusiasm that quickly diminished and made them half-hearted. Needham was acting out of commitment. The first thing he was taught was how to handle the weapon. Huckvale pointed out its constituent parts and warned him never to carry it with him if it was loaded. When Needham had memorised everything, his instructor turned to the target and explained how to hold the pistol straight. After loading the weapon, he fired it and hit the centre of the target.

Needham applauded him. 'That was magnificent.'

'I do it many times a day, Reverend. Practice makes perfect.'

'Then let me start practising at once. Please load it for me.'

Huckvale obeyed then handed him the pistol. Squinting at the target, his pupil planted his feet in the way he'd been told and extended an arm. On the point of pulling the trigger, he suddenly swung round and held the pistol against Huckvale's skull. His voice became harsher.

'May God forgive me for it,' he said, 'but I'm afraid that I've been lying to you. I can fire this as well as anybody, especially from close range. Please don't give me the opportunity to do it, Mr Huckvale.' He nudged his prisoner. 'Start moving.'

'Where are we going?'

'We're leaving by the backstairs. I have a friend waiting for us outside.'

'Who *are* you?'

'No more questions,' said the other, jabbing him in the ribs.

'But I work here. I have other people to instruct.'

'I'm the one giving the instruction now,' said Needham. 'If you dare to call for help, it will be the last time you ever utter a single word. Do you understand?'

'You're not a priest at all, are you?'

'Be quiet and do as you're told.'

A second jab in the ribs hurt even more and made Huckvale wince. He was helpless. As long as the weapon was held on him, he was at the mercy of someone who was strong, ruthless and armed. Huckvale was pushed unceremoniously down the backstairs and along the corridor to the rear door. After the attack by the two dogs, it had been reinforced but it offered no protection now. Compelled to open it, Huckvale drew back the thick bolts then turned the large key. The door swung back on its hinges. Waiting for him outside, Huckvale saw, was a short, thickset man with a sack in his hand. It was the last thing the prisoner remembered because his head was struck hard from behind by the butt of the pistol and he fell forward into oblivion. He didn't feel the sack being put over his head or realise that the man outside the door picked him up with ease and slung him over his shoulder.

The carriage was only yards away. Huckvale was bundled into it.

His visit to a third bank introduced Peter to Harold Oscott. The manager was a rotund man of middle years. Peter sensed that he was not entirely welcome. Whenever he'd called at the other banks to deliver his warning, he'd met with interest and gratitude. Oscott, however, had the look of someone who floated on a cloud of self-importance. The first thing he did when Peter was shown into his office was to consult his watch and shake his head.

'I can only give you two minutes, Mr Skillen,' he said.

'You might find that I require rather more than that.'

'I have appointments to honour. As it happens, there's a particularly important customer about to arrive.'

'He will be obliged to wait.'

Oscott spluttered. 'You can't come in here and tell me how to conduct business,' he protested. 'If you're from Mr Impey, as you claim, then you should confine your business to *his* bank.'

'I come in the spirit of fellowship, sir. Bankers should support each other.'

'We are rivals, sir. We thrive on competition.'

'Are you saying that you won't accept advice?'

'Not if it comes from Impey or any other manager. This bank maintains the very highest standards and has done so for many years. Our reputation speaks for itself. That is why we've been so successful under my aegis.'

'Mr Impey thwarted an attempt at fraud.'

'That's *his* concern.'

'It may also be yours, sir,' said Peter, annoyed by his peremptory manner. 'Other bank managers have been more receptive to what I have to say. That makes your attitude all the more surprising.'

'Good day to you, Mr Skillen,' said the other, looking at his watch again. 'Your time has run out. I need to speak to genuine customers.'

'One of them may try to defraud you.'

'Like others before them, all that they will do is to *try*. Nothing eludes me. I have a sixth sense where fraud and forgery are concerned. It's led to a number of arrests. I can do without your warning, sir. The door is behind you.'

'Then I bid you farewell,' said Peter, mastering his irritation.

He let himself out of the manager's office and walked to the main door. As Peter stepped out into the street, a carriage drew up outside. Glancing through the window, he could see the figure of a woman in a wide-brimmed hat. When she opened the door of the vehicle, however, he looked more closely. Everything about her suggested that she might be the very person about whom he'd attempted to talk to Oscott. She was young, shapely and excessively beautiful. There was a brimming confidence about her that alerted Peter. Oscott had spoken of a particularly important customer. Here, he surmised, she was.

Peter was in two minds. Part of him wanted to get out of her way in the hope that Hester Mallory or Arabella Kenyon would beguile the bank manager as skilfully as she'd enchanted Leonard Impey. Great satisfaction could then be drawn by Peter from the fact that Oscott had also been fleeced. Another part of him, however, urged him to strike while he had the opportunity. Left at liberty, she'd get away with the thousand pounds she'd extracted from Impey and whatever she conjured out of Oscott's safe. Peter decided to follow her into the bank so that he could challenge her there.

But the chance never came. The intense interest he'd shown in her had been noticed. The woman sensed danger at once. Instead of getting out of the carriage, therefore, she stepped straight back into it and a servant shut the door after her. She banged the roof of the vehicle and it set off down the street with the driver cracking his whip to demand more speed. Peter chased hard for some time but was unable to catch up with it. Cursing his luck, he stood on the pavement and panted from his exertions. When he got his breath back, he realised that he had one pleasurable duty to perform. He could return to the bank to inform Harold Oscott that the appointment with his important client had been abruptly cancelled and that the manager's fabled sixth sense had somehow detected nothing amiss about the lady.

Abel Mundy had learnt to rely on his wife over the years. Having no children, they'd been drawn ever closer together. What was remarkable about Marion Mundy was her ability to adapt to her husband's moods and needs. Most women brought up in a country vicarage would have looked askance at the whole business of theatrical presentation. In their opinion, it would have smacked of corruption and sexual licence. Those who flocked to watch plays, they believed, were as louche and venal as the people who actually appeared on the stage. It was a view supported by the stories of drunken brawls and riots that appeared in newspapers. Theatres were breeding grounds of danger.

When she'd first met Mundy, he'd been a devout young man of literary inclination. Poetry was his first love and she'd been wooed by his verses. While he'd made a living as a printer, he'd yearned for the status that came with being an author, wishing to write words himself instead of merely putting the work of others into print. Poetry had slowly given way to plays, initially of a strongly Christian character. His wife had been his only audience at first. In spite of her upbringing, she was slowly drawn towards the theatre and, when his first play was eventually performed in public, it was a moment of transfiguration for her.

'Miss Granville has at last agreed to meet me,' he told her.

'Thank heaven for that!'

'I'll need the patience of Job to contend with her.'

'Bear in mind what she's been through,' advised his wife. 'I think about it all the time. She was lucky not to be blinded. Deal gently with her, Abel.'

'I'll be gentle but firm, my dear.'

'Don't let her dictate. When all is said and done, it's your play.'

'What is left of it,' he said with a sigh. 'But all great works undergo a measure of rewriting. One must accept that. Even the Bard's plays have been amended over the years to suit the prevailing public taste. Nahum Tate's version of *King Lear*, for instance, has a happy ending.'

'I hope that the same can be said of your battle with Miss Granville.'

'She can be inspirational, there's no question about that.'

'Then she is privileged to work with an inspirational playwright.'

'Thank you, my dear.'

Mundy understood the significance of the meeting. It was a last chance to rescue his play. He therefore had to make the effort to bend a little. Whether or not the actress would do the same was an open question.

'You've come such a long way,' said Marion with pride. 'You're on the verge of fulfilling a life's ambition. Please don't fall at the final hurdle.'

'I won't,' he assured her. 'I feel that the storm is finally over.'

At the end of an hour of teaching someone how to fence with foil and rapier, Gully Ackford saw his pupil to the front door and waved him off. As one man left, another arrived for instruction in the boxing ring from Jem Huckvale. Inviting the newcomer in, Ackford called up the stairs for his colleague to come down. There was no reply. When he shouted even louder, the result was the same. It suddenly struck Ackford that, during the previous lesson, he'd heard very few shots being fired above his head. A lesson would normally be punctuated by gunfire. He ran quickly upstairs to the shooting gallery and found it empty. He made a quick search of the upper part of the building but saw no sign of Huckvale.

Ackford then heard a flapping sound. It seemed to come from the backstairs. Bounding down them two steps at a time, he saw that the rear door was ajar and was being blown to and fro by the wind. Since the invasion by the two dogs, they'd been very careful to keep the doors securely locked. Huckvale would never have dreamt of departing from the building that way without telling Ackford, and he would certainly never have left the door open. Huckvale had unaccountably disappeared. There was only one explanation.

He'd been kidnapped.

Bound, gagged and with a splitting headache, Huckvale lay in the dark and wondered where he could possibly be and how he could have got there.

CHAPTER SIXTEEN

After his adventures at one bank, Peter Skillen returned to the person who'd hired him so that he could deliver his report. Leonard Impey listened with an interest edged with disappointment. Hearing that the woman who'd comprehensively deceived him had made her escape, he sagged in his chair.

'So you missed your chance,' he groaned.

'I gave her an almighty fright, sir. That will slow her down. She knows that someone is on her tail now. I don't think she'll be unwise enough to venture into another bank for a while.'

'What about Oscott?'

'I had the pleasure of telling him that the woman had been ready to help herself to some of the bank's money with bogus documents. Since he'd already declared those documents to be legitimate,' said Peter, 'he was very embarrassed.'

'Then he'll know how *I* feel.'

'You actually *lost* money, sir. He didn't. When he realised just how close he'd come to doing so, he had the grace to thank me.'

'Did he apologise?'

'He mumbled a few words but that was all.'

'Oscott and I are two of a kind,' confessed Impey. 'We were

taken in by the woman's appearance and never thought to ask what lay behind it.'

'She's a very striking lady. Most men would have been similarly impressed.'

'I'm not paid to be impressed, Mr Skillen. I was given the task of running this bank because of my ability to read people's characters. I completely misread hers. My only solace is that she worked her spell on Oscott as well.'

'He begged me not to divulge that information.'

'His secret is safe with me.'

'So,' said Peter, 'I feel we've made progress. I now know exactly what Mrs Mallory, or Miss Kenyon, actually looks like and I've protected other banks from falling victim to her. She'll be more cautious from now on.'

'So will I, Mr Skillen.'

'I was very sorry that she got away and my other regret is that I didn't see who her companion was. All I caught was a glimpse of a man who stayed in the carriage. It must have been her accomplice. My instinct was to let her get inside the bank before I moved in. Having apprehended her,' explained Peter, 'I could then have gone outside to arrest the man as well.'

'The pair of them should hang.'

'Forgery is no longer a capital offence, sir.'

'It should be.'

'All victims of it must feel that.'

'What will you do now, Mr Skillen?'

'I'll continue my search for her,' replied Peter, 'though I can only devote limited time to it. The main thing is that Mr Picton is now aware of her forging documents in his name. As a consequence, he supplied valuable information about her. I was lucky enough to be on hand to encounter her but she interpreted my curiosity only too well.'

'That's a pity.'

'Knowing she's at risk, she'll stay hidden for a while.'

'You've done well,' said Impey, opening a desk and taking out a pile of banknotes. 'Let me know how much I owe you for the time you've already given me.'

'I won't take a penny until she and her accomplice are in custody.'

'When will that be?'

'The sooner, the better,' said Peter. 'This has been a fascinating case but, with respect, it lacks the importance of a brutal murder. I'm hoping that Mrs Mallory will be caught in the very near future, enabling me to concentrate all my energies on the search for a killer and his female confederate.'

'So there's a woman at the heart of both cases, is there?'

'Unhappily, there is. Crime has an attraction for both genders. Men *and* women can labour under the illusion that it will bring them a fortune and cost them no pain. By the time they realise they were misled, they feel the full weight of the law.'

'When was this, Gully?'

'It must have been well over an hour ago.'

'What was Jem doing?'

'He was teaching someone how to fire a pistol.'

'Do we know the man's name?'

'We know the one he gave to us. It was Philip Needham. In retrospect,' said Ackford, 'it's likely to have been false.'

The first thing he did when he discovered Huckvale's disappearance was to send word to Paul Skillen, who responded to the call for help instantly. Having ridden at a gallop to the gallery, Paul was now standing with his friend in the courtyard at the rear of the property.

'Have you searched for any witnesses?'

'That's what I did until you got here.'

'Did anyone *see* anything?'

'Two people watched a carriage leave here in a hurry but they had no idea who was inside it. It's ironic, Paul. Dozens of people were around at the time yet not one of them was aware what was happening right under their noses.'

'Did you actually meet this Philip Needham?'

'No,' said Ackford, 'but Charlotte did. She put his name in the book so she'll be able to give us a good description of him. But why pick on Jem? He has no family from whom a large ransom can be demanded.'

'Money is not at stake here.'

'Then what lies behind it?'

'This is another ruse from Hamer and that friend of his, I fancy. Having failed with their first attempt, they're set on diverting us another way. While we're spending all our time looking for Jem,' said Paul, 'they'll have the field clear.'

'Not entirely – there are the Runners.'

'Oh, they can be outwitted without too much difficulty. We can't, Gully, so we have to be removed from the chase. Hamer and Carr are determined to be the first to lay hands on the people behind the murder.'

'Do they covet the reward money?'

'No, they're wealthy men in their own right. They're driven by rage that someone robbed them of their prize. Mr Bowerman should have been shot dead on Putney Heath, not murdered in the garden of a house owned by Hamer.'

'Do you think that they'll hurt Jem?'

'There's no need for that. They simply want to hamper us.'

'So where do we start looking?'

'First of all, I'll tell Peter what's happened. Then the two of us will pay the counterfeit Captain Hamer a visit. He was warned of the danger of upsetting us.'

'What about me, Paul?'

'You must hold the fort here.'

'But I want to join in the search. Jem would expect it of me.'

'He'll know that we won't let him down, Gully. Wherever he is, Jem won't be downhearted. He can trust in us to rescue him.'

Though his eyes gradually grew accustomed to the dark, Huckvale could still see very little. What he did realise was that he was in a coal cellar. There was dust everywhere. He also had a nasty taste in his mouth and surmised that the sack put over his head had once contained rotten potatoes. Struggling to piece together what had happened, all that he could recall was that the Reverend Philip Needham had tricked his way into the gallery then put a pistol to Huckvale's skull. Unable to feel the large bump on his head, he knew that it was there because of its insistent throbbing. His attackers had tied him up securely and made it impossible for him to make any noise beyond a muffled cry. And who, in any case, was likely to hear him? He was underground in a cellar that served equally well as a dungeon.

Huckvale was helpless.

Lemuel Fleet was banking heavily on the success of the meeting between the two antagonists. The last time they'd come face-to-face, he reflected, was when Abel Mundy had interrupted the rehearsal of a revised version of his play and exchanged abuse with Hannah Granville before making a hasty exit. At that point, the situation had seemed irrecoverable. What had changed everything was a stone hurled through a window at Hannah. Terrifying her, it had opened a wellspring of compassion in the playwright that Fleet didn't suspect was there. Both parties were therefore coming in a different frame of mind.

Hannah had been chastened and Mundy was sympathetic towards her. It was a basis on which the manager felt that he could build.

There was a long table in his office. When the disputants arrived, he took care to seat them at either end and to put himself in the middle between them. Decanters and glasses had been set out. Hannah turned down the offer of a little wine but Mundy, unusually, accepted a glass of brandy to fortify him. Fleet talked in general terms about his plans for the rest of the season before turning to *The Piccadilly Opera*. He first invited each of them to make an opening statement.

Controlled and subdued, Hannah began with an apology for any hurt she'd caused the playwright by her unfair criticism of his work. She praised the aspects of it that she found most appealing and said that, in the interests of the whole company, she was prepared to be more tolerant of what she perceived as weaknesses. Mundy winced at the mention of weaknesses but he did not rush to the defence of the play. Instead he told her how sorry he and his wife had been to hear of the attack on her and he went on to say that it was a privilege to work with an actress who had no equal on the stage. He spoke with more caution than any real passion but he nevertheless managed to coax a slight smile onto her face.

So far, Fleet decided, it was going well. There was no hint of the pulsating hostility that had bedevilled their earlier conversations. Both were calm and respectful towards each other. It was the moment to reveal a bonus.

'I have been in communication with Benjamin Tregarne,' he said, pleased to see the looks of sudden joy on their faces. 'I took the liberty of showing the play to him and he was complimentary.' Mundy beamed. 'At the same time, he felt that it could be improved musically.'

'I accept that,' said the playwright.

'It's something I've advocated from the start,' added Hannah.

'At last,' said Fleet, 'we have something that unites us.'

Hannah did more than offer approval. Benjamin Tregarne had written some of the finest comic operas ever seen on the English stage. Now in his declining years, he didn't take on any more commissions for operatic work and confined himself to less taxing enterprises. To sing something specially composed for her by Tregarne was truly an honour in Hannah's eyes. By the same token, Mundy was thrilled to be associated with the renowned composer.

'Mr Tregarne feels that full-blown arias would be out of place,' Fleet told them, 'and he has suggested that, in their stead, he'd compose a series of ariettas to be placed throughout the play, mostly to be sung by Miss Granville. They would delight the ear and lift the whole performance immeasurably.' He looked from one to the other. 'Do we agree on that?'

'We do,' replied Hannah. 'Mr Mundy?'

'I couldn't be happier,' said the other.

'To secure Mr Tregarne's services is a coup on your behalf, Mr Fleet, but can he possibly compose the ariettas in time?'

'As it happens,' said Fleet, 'he has work in progress that he can adapt very easily to the demands of the play. It has everything we need. He played and sang one of the songs for me. It was exquisite. Needless to say, when his name appears on the new bills we'll have printed, there will be even more interest in the play.'

'That goes without saying,' said Mundy.

Hannah nodded. 'I've sung his songs before. They are magical.'

'I've made *my* attempt at improving the play,' said Fleet. 'Now it is your turn. Please state what you believe should be done in a polite and reasonable way.' He smiled at Hannah. 'Miss Granville.'

Opening her purse, she took out a sheet of paper and unfolded it.

'I have pared down my suggestions to a bare minimum,' she

said. 'In essence, the play is too long and too mawkish.' Mundy gulped. 'I believe that we should omit the last scene in Act One and the first in Act Two. The duet in Act Three is slightly awkward to sing but it may be that Mr Tregarne can rescue it from its inherent infelicities. The ending, of course, needs to be given more drama and deeper emotion. Apart from that,' she went on, refolding the paper, 'I have no comments to make.'

Mundy was already puce with anger but he managed to contain it somehow. A celebrated composer had liked his play enough to provide ariettas for it, yet its leading actress was tearing it to pieces. Benjamin Tregarne had lit a fire of hope inside the playwright. Hannah had just extinguished it. Mundy needed a few moments to recover his equilibrium.

'What's your reply?' asked Fleet.

'It's this,' said Mundy, straightening his back and staring at Hannah. 'I might consider some of Miss Granville's unjustified scorn if she would stop pulling faces during the duet, waving her arms about so wildly in the prison scene and grinning at the audience throughout as if they've paid their money for the sole purpose of admiring her teeth. In short, she should *act* the part properly instead of distorting it into a travesty of the original.'

Hannah leapt up truculently. 'I cannot believe I'm hearing this.'

'You may hear a lot more, if you wish,' he said.

'Silence, silence,' implored Fleet.

'Are you going to let him launch such a vicious attack on me?' she cried. 'It's worse than being hit by a shower of glass.'

'You insulted me,' roared Mundy.

'It's no more than you deserved.'

'Your behaviour has been reprehensible from the first rehearsal.'

'And yours has been boorish,' she retorted.

'You poison everything you touch.'

'Then please come closer so that I can touch *you*.'

'Miss Granville,' cried Fleet. 'We are all friends here.'

'I'd never befriend a man of no discernible talent.'

'When I agreed to work with you,' said Mundy with a sneer, 'I had to lower my standards considerably.'

'You don't *have* any standards,' snapped Hannah. 'I might have made the mistake of being in the wrong play, but you, sir, are in the wrong profession.'

'That's slander!'

'It's the truth.'

'I'll bring an action against you for defamation.'

'I'll bring one against you for brazenly impersonating a playwright.'

Once started, the argument quickly gathered pace and the insults became sharper and more personal. Perspiration glistening on his furrowed brow, Fleet begged them to stop but to no avail. All the bitterness that had been stored up on both sides now had an outlet. The manager was swept away by the surging torrent of abuse. When the two of them finally ran short of bile and of breath, Fleet spread his arms in supplication.

'What am I to tell Mr Tregarne?' he wailed.

Peter Skillen was outraged when he learnt that Huckvale had, apparently, been abducted. Back at the gallery, he found his brother and Ackford still trying to work out how it must have happened. Peter had dismissed all thought of the murder investigation and of his work for the bank. The priority now was to rescue Huckvale and call someone to account for the crime. Since Paul was convinced that the kidnap had been ordered by Stephen Hamer, the brothers rode straight to his house. They were in no mood for social niceties. When a servant answered the door, they pushed past the woman and went straight into the drawing room. Hamer and Carr were having a private conversation when the brothers burst in.

'What the devil are you doing?' yelled Hamer, getting to his feet.

'We've come to ask you the same thing,' said Paul. 'We believe that our close friend, Jem Huckvale, has been abducted from the shooting gallery. You gave the order for the kidnap.'

'I deny it wholeheartedly.'

'When the dogs were let loose, they failed to serve their purpose so you tried another way to frighten us off.'

'Why should I do that?'

'Because there are things you don't wish us to find out,' said Peter. 'You also want to catch the man who killed Mr Bowerman before we do.'

'That much is true,' conceded Hamer. 'The rest is sheer nonsense.'

'Before we go any further,' said Carr with a smile, 'it would be a great help if you could please identify yourselves. I can't tell one brother from the other.'

'This is Paul Skillen,' said Peter, indicating his brother, 'and I am Peter. We speak with one voice about Jem Huckvale. Have him released at once.'

'But we've no idea where he is, dear fellow.'

'Mr Carr is giving you an honest answer,' said Hamer, backing his friend up. 'We had no part either in the attack on the shooting gallery or in this supposed kidnap. Why are you so certain that your friend has been spirited away?'

'The gallery is his home and place of work,' said Paul. 'Jem would never leave it without giving a warning beforehand.'

'Perhaps he just wandered off.'

'You obviously don't know Jem. He's very conscientious.'

'What was he doing before he disappeared?' asked Carr.

'He was giving instruction to someone called Philip Needham.'

'Do either of you recognise that name?' asked Peter. The two men looked blank and shook their heads. 'You may, of course, know him under his real name.'

'And what's that, Mr Skillen?'

'We don't know.'

Carr raised an eyebrow. 'There seems to be a lot of things you don't know,' he observed, drily. 'You don't actually know if your friend was abducted or not. You assume that the man who came for instruction gave a false name but you have no proof of that. The search for a culprit has, mysteriously, brought you to this door yet there are no two people less likely to hatch a kidnap plot than Captain Hamer and I. Why single us out? It's the wildest kind of speculation.'

'It's based on my estimate of your characters,' said Paul, levelly. 'You and Lieutenant Hamer – I refuse to give him a rank to which he's not entitled – are palpably unworthy of any trust. You lied about having those dogs unleashed at the gallery and you're lying about this.'

'Get out of my house before I horsewhip you!' shouted Hamer.

'You'd regret trying to do that.'

'My brother will only beat you to a pulp,' said Peter, drawing a pistol. 'If you'd care to arm yourselves, we can step into the garden and settle our differences there.'

'Unlike the duel with Mr Bowerman,' said Paul, 'you'll have a more able adversary this time. Or are you too cowardly to accept the challenge?'

'Don't you dare accuse me of cowardice,' snarled Hamer.

'We've seen no signs of bravery in you.'

'Take that back, you rogue!'

Paul did not flinch. 'I take *nothing* back.'

Carr sounded a soothing note. 'Calm down, gentlemen,' he said. 'We are civilised human beings, not ruffians in a tavern who fight at the least excuse. Step apart from each other,' he urged, easing Hamer away from Paul. 'Something is missing here.'

'Yes,' said Paul, 'it's any semblance of honesty.'

'I was about to say that it was good manners, Mr Skillen. People don't usually enter someone else's house unless they are invited in. You came in by force. That was not only impolite, it was flirting with illegality.'

'We refuse to be fobbed off, Mr Carr.'

'Nobody is fobbing you off,' said the other. 'You have been allowed in to discuss the situation. We understand your anger. Your affection for your friend shines through and that's admirable. But before you hurl unjust accusations at us, there is something you should first have obtained – evidence.'

'We have the evidence of our own eyes,' said Peter.

'And of our own noses,' said Paul. 'This place reeks of deceit and treachery.'

'I told you to leave,' warned Hamer.

'Where is Jem Huckvale being held?'

'I don't give a damn where he is – now out you go!'

On the point of grabbing Paul, he was stopped dead by the pistol held at his throat by Peter. Everyone froze in position and there was a long silence. Hamer did not budge. He met Peter's gaze without fear.

'Kill me, if you wish,' he said, 'but it will be in defiance of true justice. I did not order the abduction of your friend and I have no inkling where he might be. As God's my witness, I am innocent of the charge.'

The weapon suddenly felt extremely heavy in Peter's hand.

Though he was relatively small, Huckvale was strong and lithe. Unable to break clear of his bonds, or to bite through the gag in his mouth, he instead conducted a brief search of the cellar by means of rolling over and over on the floor. He soon came into contact with lumps of coal fallen from the large pile that occupied much of the space. His head was still pounding and ropes were biting into his wrists and ankles yet he managed a smile of sorts. The best way to move coal was with a shovel. There had to be one somewhere in the cellar. Huckvale started to roll with even more urgency.

When she left the theatre, Hannah craved reassurance. Ideally, she wanted to go back to the house and fling herself into Paul's arms but she knew that he would not be there. The other person who'd offer her support and consolation was Charlotte, so she told the driver of the carriage to take her to the gallery. On the way there, she was smarting from what she felt was her maltreatment at the hands of Abel Mundy. Though his Christian beliefs held him back from using expletives, he'd nevertheless found words that could inflict deep wounds. As she recalled them, Hannah was affronted afresh. The carriage deposited her outside the gallery and she ran into the building. Flinging open the door, she dashed into the room used as an office, making Charlotte look up in surprise.

'What's happened?' she asked, getting to her feet.

'It was excruciating,' cried Hannah. 'I've just been through an unimaginable ordeal.'

Charlotte embraced her warmly then eased her gently into a chair. The tears came like a minor waterfall and all she could do was to wait for several minutes until Hannah had recovered enough to tell her friend what had befallen her. Nothing was left out of the narrative. She remembered each individual insult from the playwright. Reliving her ordeal brought on a fresh burst of tears at one point. Hannah then made an effort to sit up and regain her poise.

'He'll have to be dismissed,' she said.

'What about his play?'

'It ought to be destroyed, Charlotte.'

'Mr Fleet doesn't think so.'

'His judgement is abysmal.'

'Yet he thinks that you have no peer on the English stage.'

'In that instance, his opinion is sound,' said Hannah, 'but his assessment of Abel Mundy is woefully awry. That man is impossible to deal with.'

'The meeting was not entirely a disaster,' argued Charlotte. 'When you heard that no less a person than Benjamin Tregarne would compose some songs for the play, you were delighted.'

'It's true. I was.'

'Mr Mundy was also pleased.'

'We both were, Charlotte.'

'There must have been a wonderful feeling of goodwill as a result.'

'There was, there was,' said Hannah. 'I was floating on air.'

'That was before you made your demands.'

'But they weren't demands. They were sensible suggestions to improve the play and rescue it from its banality. I was trying to *help*.'

Much as she loved her friend, Charlotte had pangs of sympathy for Mundy. It was clear that he'd been cruelly provoked. Before they could discuss the meeting any further, Gully Ackford came into the room. He saw that Hannah had been crying.

'I shed tears myself when I realised that he'd gone.'

'Who had gone?' asked Hannah.

'Jem has been kidnapped. Isn't that why you've been crying?'

'No, it isn't.'

'Hannah was involved in an argument at the theatre,' explained Charlotte.

'What's this about a kidnap?'

'Jem disappeared earlier on. Gully is certain he was abducted.'

'But why – and by whom?'

'We don't know, Hannah.'

'Paul thinks he has the answer,' said Ackford. 'He believes that Hamer is behind it. Peter and Paul went off together to confront him.'

'This is terrible,' cried Hannah. 'Why did you let me ramble on about *my* problems when this has happened? Why didn't you tell me, Charlotte?'

'You needed comfort.'

'I feel so guilty. All that I had to endure was someone losing his temper. Jem Huckvale is the victim of a dreadful crime. Oh,' she went on, 'do forgive me for my selfishness. I should be thinking about Jem.'

'We'll find him somehow,' said Ackford.

'Why was he abducted?'

'Someone wants to take our minds off Mr Bowerman's murder. I suppose that that's a good sign in a way.'

'A *good* sign!' exclaimed Hannah. 'How can you possibly say that?'

'It shows that we've made more progress than we thought. Our rivals are scared, Miss Granville. They're trying to shackle us.'

'Poor Jem! My heart goes out to him.'

'If anyone can find him,' said Charlotte, 'it will be Peter and Paul.'

'I hope they can find the man who kidnapped him as well,' said Ackford, teeth gritted. 'I'd like a word with him.'

'What did you call yourself?'

'The Reverend Philip Needham.'

The other man guffawed. 'You've never been inside a church.'

'He didn't know that.'

'You fooled him good and proper.'

'My orders were to get him out of the way. That's what we did.'

'And we got well paid for it.'

He jingled the coins in his purse. The two of them were in a tavern, drinking ale and congratulating themselves on their success. Jem Huckvale had been easily deceived and just as easily overpowered.

'Where did you get that name from?' asked the shorter man.

'Philip Needham? He was a real person.'

'And was he a real priest?'

'No, Nathan, he was a butcher. My parents wouldn't get their meat from anyone else. He was a big, red-faced man with a huge belly on him.'

'Talking of names, what's his?'

'Who?'

He held up the purse. 'I mean the gentleman who gave us this.'

'People like him don't have names, Nathan.'

'How did you find him?'

'I didn't – he found *me*.'

'What happens to the lad we left in the coal cellar?'

'Nothing – he stays there.'

'I thought we'd have to let him go in the end.'

'That was the idea, Nathan, and that's what I agreed to do. I was to wait for the word then release him. But there's no point now, is there?' he said with a chuckle. 'We've been paid so we can forget all about Jem Huckvale. As far as I'm concerned, he can stay in that cellar and rot.'

He lifted his tankard and downed the remainder of his ale.

Fresh from another reprimand at the hands of the chief magistrate, Yeomans and Hale redoubled their efforts to solve the crime. Information came in from a variety of sources but it was difficult to link it into a coherent whole. One item did catch their attention. There was a report of unlawful entry into an agency dealing with rental property, much of it in the vicinity where the murder occurred. Though nothing appeared to have been stolen, they

240

felt that it was worth investigating. The agent gave the Runners a frosty reception.

'It's no good coming after the event,' he said, spikily. 'We expect you to prevent crime from happening in the first place.'

'How did the burglar get in?' asked Yeomans.

The agent pointed. 'He climbed through that window.'

'How do you know?'

'It was still open when I got here later on.'

'Yet nothing was stolen, I hear.'

'That's not the point. Somebody was trespassing. It's a crime.'

Hale studied the window. 'It's very small,' he said. 'I wouldn't have been able to climb through it and you couldn't even get your head in, Micah.' He recoiled from his companion's punch then turned to the agent. 'Has anyone been showing an unusual interest in this place recently?'

'Oddly enough,' said the agent, 'there was someone.'

'I don't suppose that you remember his name.'

'That's an offensive remark. I always remember names.'

'What was this man called?'

'Peter Skillen.' The Runners were astounded. 'I see that you know him.'

'We know him all too well,' said Yeomans. 'What did he want?'

'Mr Skillen was keen to know who owned the house where a murder took place a few days ago. I refused to give it to him. It's always been our policy to respect confidentiality.'

'How keen was he for the information?'

'He was extremely keen, not to say overeager.'

Turning slowly, Yeomans looked at the window. Hale read his mind.

'It wasn't him, Micah. Peter Skillen is agile but even he couldn't wriggle through a space like that.'

'I wasn't thinking about him, Alfred.'

'Then who *were* you thinking about?'

'Jem Huckvale.'

Hampered by the ropes and the darkness, he took a long time to find the shovel. In the course of the search, he created small clouds of coal dust, some of which got into his eyes. In the end, however, he rolled up against something hard and metallic. It was the shovel. Because his hands were tied behind his back, Huckvale had to wriggle into the most uncomfortable position in order to get close to the shovel. He felt the edges of the implement for the sharpest point. Then he put the rope against it and rubbed as hard as he could. It was slow, painful work and he could feel the circulation being cut off in his arms but he persisted until his strength was almost drained. Making one last effort, he exerted as much pressure as he could, then felt the strands burst apart at last. After tearing off the gag, he undid the ropes around his ankles. He rubbed his ankles and his wrists. Huckvale then felt the bump on his head gingerly.

With great difficulty, he hauled himself to his feet and rocked unsteadily for a few moments. When he was able to walk properly, he felt his way around the walls until he came to a door. Thrilled that he'd be able to escape, he turned the handle only to discover that the door was securely locked. His sense of triumph evaporated. His bonds might have been discarded, but he was still a prisoner. There was no way out.

CHAPTER SEVENTEEN

The brothers returned to the gallery to find that Hannah was still there with Charlotte. When Paul asked how the meeting with Abel Mundy had gone, the actress promised to tell him everything later on. Her predicament couldn't compare with the one in which Huckvale found himself. Hannah had been praying that no physical harm would come to him. Charlotte wondered about their visit to Hamer's home and, between them, they recounted in detail what had happened.

'They denied all knowledge of the kidnap,' continued Peter. 'For the first time since I had the misfortune to meet him, I actually believed Hamer when he said that he didn't know who'd seized Jem from here. There was a glimmer of sincerity in his eyes.'

'He's still involved somehow,' said Paul.

'We have to prove it.'

'Our main task is to find Jem quickly.'

'We can only do that if we track down his kidnapper.'

'I was hoping we could drag his name out of Hamer.'

'He wasn't the one who hired him, Paul,' said his brother. 'That's the kind of work Carr would have undertaken. He's the friend who runs errands for the captain.'

'Hamer's only a lieutenant.'

'Yet he did actually bear arms in battle. That's in his favour.

And he did bring back military souvenirs from Spain. One of them killed Mr Bowerman.' He turned to his wife. 'You're the only person who actually met this Philip Needham. What sort of person was he, Charlotte?'

'He was a well-built, well-dressed man in his thirties, a little above my height. In some ways he might have been accounted good-looking. He seemed polite and reasonably well educated,' she said. 'And he insisted on having Jem as his instructor. That struck me as odd, considering that Gully is the expert with any guns. When I told him that, Mr Needham said that it was Jem or nobody.'

'Did he explain why?'

'He claimed that a friend of his had recommended Jem.'

'Is that all you can tell us about him?' asked Paul.

'Well, no, as it happens, it isn't,' she said, recalling the meeting. 'Go on.'

'There was something vaguely familiar about him, Paul. I've been racking my brains trying to work out why that was.'

'Has he come to the gallery before?' asked Hannah.

'No, I don't think so.'

'How else can you have met him?'

'There's only one possibility,' said Charlotte, thinking hard. 'His was one of the countless faces I've seen at the magistrate's court. And the only reason I'd be there was that Peter or Paul must have arrested him at some time. Yes,' she went on with a growing certainty, '*that's* where it must have been. If so, we're in luck. I'll probably be able to tell you what Philip Needham's *real* name is.'

The unexpected visit of the two brothers had shaken him as much as it had annoyed him. Stephen Hamer needed two glasses of brandy before he calmed down. He turned angrily on Rawdon Carr.

'I asked you to get them out of my way,' he yelled, 'not set the pair of them on to me. Why did you have to arrange a kidnap?'

'It was the best way to distract them, Stephen. If they're spending all their time looking for their friend, they're not going to trouble you.'

'But that's exactly what they did. They forced their way in here.'

'Yes,' said Carr, easily, 'and you got rid of them by giving them an honest answer. You *didn't* contrive the abduction. You had no part in it. Until they rushed in here, you had no idea what I'd done.'

'I do now,' said Hamer, ruefully.

'I deliberately held back the details of what I'd arranged by way of protecting you. When they stopped hectoring you, Peter and Paul Skillen had to accept that your answers were patently truthful. The first time you even knew of the kidnap was when they accused you of organising it.'

'In future, I'd like to know exactly what you do, Rawdon.'

'So be it.'

'It was galling to be made to feel at a disadvantage in my own home. From now on, tell me what you've been up to at every point.'

'Then I will,' said Carr with an emollient smile. 'You already know about this man Huckvale now. His disappearance will keep them preoccupied for days. For the rest, I've set in motion a search for Miss Eleanor Gold and for the other two ladies whose names you gave me. I have minions looking for them right this moment.'

'I've done the same with regard to the other couple of women.'

'You shouldn't be so prodigal, Stephen. I can make a mistress last a year or more. I get full value out of my investment that way.'

'My appetite is stronger than yours. I wear ladies out.'

'You didn't wear Eleanor Gold out. She was eager to stay.'

245

'Her charms faded.'

'Throwing her out so roughly may have been a fatal error,' said Carr. 'You have to learn to be more considerate towards your conquests. If you treat them like mere whores, they nurse resentment.'

'Eleanor was certainly resentful. She's a real demon.'

'I look forward to meeting her when my men have found out where she is. Every new piece of information you give me about her makes me think she's the most likely person to be party to the persecution of you. We must locate her,' said Carr, 'and bewilder the Skillen brothers.'

'Paul Skillen is the worst of them. He's so tenacious.'

'Earlier today, I saw a good example of his tenacity. When I called into my club, I almost bumped into him.'

'Whatever was he doing there?'

'It was not difficult to descry his purpose,' said the other. 'He was talking to my old friend, Rollo Winters. I'm sure that you can guess what he was talking about.'

'It was that dinner party!'

'He's leaving no stone unturned, Stephen.'

'Laetitia told me that he's also been to see Sir Geoffrey Melrose.'

'Neither he nor Rollo will give anything away,' said Carr, confidently, 'but my point holds. Paul Skillen is obstinacy personified.'

'How do you know that it was Paul and not Peter?'

'You've seen them both together.'

'They're quite indistinguishable.'

'Not to my eye,' boasted his friend. 'Paul is the more flamboyant. That's how I identified him at the club. I was very careful not to let him spot me.'

'I'm glad of that, Rawdon. He knows too much about us already.'

'Well, he won't be in a position to gather any more information. I made sure of that. This friend of his, Jem Huckvale, is being hidden in a place that nobody would ever find. Skillen and his brother will spend *ages* looking for him.'

Newcomers to the gallery were always surprised to find a woman of Charlotte's appearance working there. Now in her thirties, she looked younger. She was intelligent, composed and beautiful. While she looked out of place, however, she fulfilled some important functions. In addition to helping to run the place, she had kept a record of every crime in which Peter and Paul had been involved as detectives. Most had been solved but there were occasional failures. If her husband and her brother-in-law were appearing in court to give evidence, she usually went along to watch the proceedings and to make notes about the defendant. Details of name, age, appearance and crime were duly entered in her record book and, if she had the time, she'd even include a rough sketch of the man or woman being convicted. It was through her sketches that she was now searching.

Two or three times, Charlotte stopped to scrutinise a particular face, trying to convert her deft lines into something of flesh and blood. While she pored over the table, the others waited expectantly. When she suddenly stood up, they thought that she'd found what she was after at last but it was a false hope. With a long sigh, she sat down and began to go through all the faces again.

'Have you found anyone remotely like him?' asked her husband.

'I've found at least two, Peter, perhaps more.'

'How recently did you actually see the man?'

'Oh, it must be two years ago, at least,' she said. 'I remember thinking that he looked too law-abiding to be a villain.'

'You could say that of a lot of them,' interjected Paul. 'They cultivate an appearance of innocence that sometimes fools a magistrate.'

'It would never fool the *chief* magistrate,' said Peter. 'Mr Kirkwood has eyes like a hawk. He can see through people.'

'Here he is,' said Charlotte, tapping a page. 'I think it is, anyway.'

They gathered round and looked over her shoulder at the sketch. Hastily drawn, it had nevertheless caught the salient details of the man's face.

'Who is he?' asked Hannah.

'His name is Luke Swait. He's a bootmaker by trade. He was charged with receiving stolen goods but the case was dismissed for lack of evidence.'

'I remember him,' said Peter. 'He was well spoken and very plausible.'

'Do you have an address, by any chance?'

'No,' said Charlotte, 'but I made a note of where you arrested him. It was in a tavern in Covent Garden called The Black Horse. It's probably one of his haunts.'

'Come on,' said Peter to his brother. 'Let's go there straight away.'

When they opened the door to leave, however, they found their way barred by Yeomans and Hale. The Runners stood there with folded arms.

'Where do you think *you're* going?' asked Yeomans.

'We're going to rescue a friend,' said Paul. 'He was kidnapped from here and we think we've identified the man involved.'

'We've come to speak to Jem Huckvale.'

'He's the person who's been abducted.'

'You're stopping us from catching the man responsible,' said Peter, irritably. 'In any case, why are you interested in Jem?'

'We've just come from an office that was burgled,' explained Yeomans. 'We were told that Peter Skillen – whichever one of you that is – went there to find out who owned the house where Mr Bowerman was murdered.'

'That's true. I did. I was turned away.'

'So you went back at night with Huckvale.'

'I did nothing of the kind.'

'He would have been small enough to climb through that little window,' said Hale. 'That was how the burglar must have got in.'

'London is full of people even smaller than Jem. Start questioning them. Our only concern at the moment is to rescue our friend. He could be in serious danger. Now, are you going to get out of our way or not?'

After a moment's token resistance, the Runners stood aside and the brothers ran out of the building. Yeomans and Hale went after them. If there was an arrest to be made, they intended to make it. And they were determined to accuse Huckvale of taking part in the burglary.

Huckvale tried his best to lever open the door with the help of the shovel but he could not get the edge of the tool into the tiny gap between door and jamb. All that he succeeded in doing was to expend a lot of energy and to bend the implement out of shape. After a brief respite, he sought to break the lock by smashing it with the shovel but it held firm. The real problem was that he couldn't actually see what he was doing so was unable to direct the blows accurately. He threw the shovel away in disgust and sat down on the dusty floor. Above him he could hear distant sounds of traffic as people moved freely about the street. Huckvale had shouted for help until his throat was hoarse. He was now aching badly and his hands were blistered.

Another idea then struck him. The coal must have been delivered from above through a hole. Somewhere in the dark ceiling would be a cast iron cover of some sort. All that he had to do was to find it. There was a problem. Even with the shovel fully extended, he could only just touch the ceiling. He prodded around until he heard a dull clang. While he'd located the cover, he couldn't push it with any force so it stayed firmly in place. The only way that he could get close enough to exert any force was to bring all the coal together in one pile. Ignoring the pain from his blisters, he therefore shovelled away for all he was worth, tossing the coal into the area directly below the cover. When he'd finished, he needed a few minutes to catch his breath.

Climbing onto the pile was hazardous. The first time he tried it, Huckvale slipped and fell, grazing his hands on the sharp pieces of coal and collecting a few bruises for good measure. But he was not deterred. He took more care as he picked his way up the pile for the second time. Coal shifted mutinously under his feet but he maintained his balance somehow. He also got the shovel fixed against the middle of the cover. With every ounce of his remaining strength, he pushed.

'Here we are,' said Swait, depositing two tankards on the table. 'Drink up.'

'It's my turn next,' said his friend.

'We can afford to drink for a week.'

Swait had a long, noisy sip of his ale then lowered himself onto his chair. Though the tavern was quite full, they managed to find a quiet corner where they could talk without being overheard. Swait was still enjoying the memory of how he'd tricked Huckvale at the gallery. His companion, however, was troubled by a twinge of compassion.

'I've been thinking, Luke . . .'

'What have you been thinking about?'

'It's that lad we locked in the coal cellar.'

'Best place for him, if you ask me.'

'Yes, but how will he get out?'

'I couldn't care less, Nathan.'

'It's dark down there and cold,' said the other. 'We ought to let him out at some point. He's tied up and can't move. If he's not released, he'll die of starvation, eventually.'

'Don't worry about that,' said Swait. 'We've finished with him.'

'But you were told to set him free when the word came.'

'Who's to know if we don't?'

'*I'll* know, Luke, and it'll be on my conscience.'

'If you work with me, you don't *have* a conscience.'

'I was ready to help you kidnap him but I'll not be a party to murder. That's what it'll be if we leave him down there.'

'Listen,' said Swait, pulling him close. 'This is the second time I've put work your way. When you knocked down the door of that shooting gallery and let the dogs in, you got paid more than you'd earn in months of selling vegetables in the market. You didn't have a conscience about that, did you?'

'No,' agreed his companion. 'I didn't.'

'Then why is this so different? You don't care if Huckvale is savaged by a dog yet you worry about him when he gets tied up in a dark cellar.'

'Nobody else knows he's down there, Luke.'

'Somebody will one day. When the weather changes and they need coal for a fire, somebody will find him. It's not our problem any more,' said Swait. 'Enjoy the money to the full. That's what I'm doing. What if he does die? Nobody will ever suspect us. We're in the clear.'

But even as he spoke, he saw a look of horror in the man's eyes as the latter noticed someone entering the tavern. Spinning round, Swait understood the reason for his friend's alarm. Yeomans and Hale, familiar figures to the criminal fraternity, were searching for someone and they had a third person with them.

It was Peter Skillen who spotted them first. He saw enough of Swait to recognise him from his wife's sketch and the man's reaction in any case gave him away. He and his companion leapt to their feet in a panic. Peter elbowed his way through the small crowd to get to them. While he tried to grab Swait, the Runners managed to intercept the other man before he could reach the back door. They quickly overpowered him. Peter, however, was having a struggle. He grappled with Swait until the latter shoved him hard and made him fall backwards over a stool, banging his head on the floor. In a flash, Swait ran to the rear exit and dashed out into a small courtyard, only to run straight into the arms of the waiting Paul Skillen.

'How did you get out *here?*' cried Swait in amazement. 'I just pushed you to the floor in the tavern.'

Paul grinned. 'Baffling, isn't it?'

Then he flung the man against a wall and felled him with a punch to the jaw.

On his way, Rawdon Carr made sure that he was not being followed. Having heard how Hamer's house had been watched, he was being even more cautious. Far too much information had already seeped out and that was disturbing. When he reached the house, he was admitted at once and taken into the drawing room. He whisked off his hat and gave Laetitia a token bow.

'Stephen sent me in his place,' he explained.

'It's good to see you, Rawdon. Do sit down.'

'Thank you.' He took the chair opposite her. 'I heard about the visit of the Runners. They're becoming a real nuisance.'

'They are indeed.'

'Stephen said that you browbeat them into making an apology.'

'It was the only thing we could do. We can't have them realising how close Stephen and I really are. That would spell danger for us all.'

'You're completely safe, Laetitia. Now that Bowerman is out of the way at last, you're a lady of leisure again. You don't have to pretend that you actually love that gullible fool now. After a decent interval, you can look for another likely victim to ensnare in the same way.'

'It was you who found Mark Bowerman for us, Rawdon.'

'I'm sorry that you had to put up with his tedious company for so long.'

'For all our sakes,' she said, 'I was prepared to do that. It was in the certain knowledge that he'd be shot dead by Stephen in a duel. That's what happened last time. You found the target, I brought him to the verge of a proposal of marriage and he kindly gave me proof of his devotion by amending his will in my favour. Just when he thought his happiness was about to be secured, I told him that I was being harassed by a former admirer. You know the rest.'

'Stephen killed him and we three shared the proceeds.'

'That's exactly what should have happened again.'

'I know it is.'

'Someone is toying with us, Rawdon. It makes me feel very uncomfortable.'

'We'll run them to earth, I promise you.'

'I keep coming back to the same name,' she told him.

'That's what I did at first, Laetitia,' he said, 'but it can't possibly have been her. Rumours of her illness were true, it seems. To put our minds at rest, I've made enquiries and learnt the truth. She died somewhere in France several weeks ago. We have to look at someone else.'

'Stephen mentioned a woman named Eleanor Gold.'

'She is now our main suspect. I've instituted a search for her. She's angry enough with Stephen to want to inflict real harm on him and, if she's the beauty he described to me, Miss Gold would have no trouble finding an accomplice. It has to be her,' he declared. 'She was left alone in his house with access to his correspondence from you and to the room where he kept his military souvenirs. She would not only have been aware of the time and place of the duel,' he went on, 'but, if she'd been through his papers, she'd have known about the other property that Stephen owned. That's why she had Bowerman murdered there – to give Stephen a fright.'

'It gave us all a fright, Rawdon.'

'We'll get her, I swear it.'

Laetitia was reassured. She looked at him with a fond smile.

'Where would we be without you?' she asked. 'You do so much for us.'

'Don't overestimate *my* contribution. You and Stephen do most of the work. I could never emulate your charms, nor could I be certain of killing a man in a duel. To be candid, I'd even have baulked at shooting as easy a target as Bowerman. I simply don't have Stephen's experience with a pistol in my hand.'

'You do more than your share, Rawdon, and we're deeply grateful.'

'Hearing you say that is enough reward in itself.'

They exchanged a look of mutual regard and he smiled sadly.

She became businesslike. 'There is another problem, of course. Paul Skillen must not be allowed to solve the murder before we do or he may learn some very sensitive secrets.'

'We'll get to the killer first,' he promised her, 'and shut his mouth for good. We'll deal with Eleanor Gold the same way. Being a woman won't save her life. As for Paul Skillen, he won't bother us again, Laetitia. I devised a plan to send him running around in circles. I arranged the kidnap of a close friend of his.'

It had taken him time and effort to shift the cover on the coal-hole. When he finally moved it enough to see daylight above, Huckvale was almost exhausted and dripping with sweat. Tossing the shovel aside, he was breathing stertorously. Though there was now an aperture through which he could escape, there was no way that he could climb up to it. What he could do, however, was to call for help. In the street above, he could hear hooves clacking, cartwheels turning and voices rising in argument. Gathering up his strength, he yelled at the top of his voice.

'Help! I'm down here!'

Nothing happened. Though he called out in despair a dozen times, nobody came to peer down into the cellar. So close to other human beings, he nevertheless began to feel that he would still be entombed indefinitely. He waited minutes before he was ready to shout again until his lungs and throat were on fire. This time, he accompanied his plea with a fusillade of coal, hurled piece by piece through the hole and into the street.

'Help!' he cried. 'I'm down here in the cellar.'

All of a sudden, he got a response that made him cry out with mingled joy and relief. The faces of Peter and Paul Skillen appeared above. Huckvale waved to them. When Peter saw his friend's dilemma, he lay face down on the ground and reached out his arm to its full extent. By standing on his toes, Huckvale was just able to grasp his hand. He was lifted slowly upwards and out of the cellar, emerging to find that Yeomans and Hale were there as well, each one holding a prisoner.

'Is that you, Jem?' asked Paul. 'You're covered in coal dust.'

'That's him,' said Huckvale, pointing to Swait. 'That's the Reverend Philip Needham, the barefaced liar who kidnapped me.'

'The other man is his accomplice. Both of them are under arrest for the kidnap and my guess is that they may have had something to do with those two mad dogs let loose at the gallery one night.'

'We'll get the truth out of them,' vowed Yeomans.

Swait gave a snort. 'We're saying nothing.'

'It was all Luke's fault,' said his accomplice. 'I wanted to have him released but Luke said we should leave him down there in the coal cellar to rot away. He's got no conscience but *I* have.'

'Your conscience didn't stop you from committing serious crimes,' said Peter. 'Who was your paymaster?'

'We don't know his name,' said Swait, sullenly.

'He's lying,' grunted Yeomans. 'But if he was planning to leave Huckvale trapped down there, then it's a case of attempted murder. Come on, Alfred. Let's take these villains where they belong.'

He and Hale marched the two prisoners off and left the brothers to console their friend. Huckvale shuttled between fear and delight.

'I thought I'd be left down there for ever.'

'You wouldn't have survived all that long without food,' said Peter. 'And if you were tied hand and foot, you'd have been in great pain.'

'I was, and my hands went all numb.'

'How did you get free of your bonds, Jem?'

'That was the easy bit,' replied the other. 'Getting the cover off was much harder. My arms are still aching.'

'Charlotte is the person to thank,' said Paul. 'When he came to arrange instruction, she met the man calling himself Philip Needham and fancied she'd come across him before. That gave us a vital clue.'

'How did the Runners get involved?'

'They came to the gallery to accuse you of burglary.'

Huckvale tensed. 'I *knew* I shouldn't have climbed into that place.'

'You committed no crime,' Peter assured him. 'On the contrary, you were helping to solve one by getting hold of an important piece of information. The Runners have suspicions but no evidence whatsoever to connect either of us with the burglary. If they challenge us again, deny their charge.'

'You need a bath,' said Paul, looking at his friend's black face. 'Let's get you back to Gully. He's been worried sick about you, Jem.'

Huckvale grimaced. 'I don't blame him,' he said. 'I was worried sick about myself.'

In all the time he'd been back in their accommodation, Abel Mundy had said no more than a few words. His wife didn't need to ask him what had happened. His expression and manner were eloquent. The attempted reconciliation had been a total failure. He and Hannah Granville were farther apart than ever. The only thing his wife could do was to put food and drink in front of him then stay discreetly out of his way. She was alone in the other room when he came in. Marion looked up from the Bible she'd been reading.

'I'm sorry,' he said, quietly.

'You don't have to say anything until you're quite ready, Abel.'

'I'm not sorry for what I said to her. Someone should have done it ages ago. Miss Granville is a tyrant. Give her full rein and she'll trample all over us. That's what she tried to do to me today and I refused to bow down before her.'

'I can see that tempers must have flared.'

'There was passion on both sides.'

'What about Mr Fleet?'

'He could do nothing, Marion. We were both out of control.'

'I'm so sad to hear that. Naturally, I take your side, Abel, but I did hope that you could moderate your demands and . . . take a step or two towards her.'

'If I'd done that, I'd have been tempted to strike her.'

She was shocked. 'You'd never raise your hand to a woman!'

'I came close to doing so today,' he confessed, 'and I'm ashamed of it.'

'Do you think that Miss Granville will be ashamed in any way?'

'She's not capable of it. Other people are always in the wrong. It's never *her*.'

Marion Mundy wanted to offer him comfort but she couldn't find the words even though she'd been searching for them in the scriptures. Bible stories were shot through with anguish and disaster but she'd never found one that related to the work of a playwright. Creating a drama of high quality had taken her husband almost a year and there'd been endless revisions after that as he strove to make it sufficiently appealing to win the interest of Lemuel Fleet. Having his play praised and accepted in London had been the pinnacle for Mundy. The ensuing period of time was one of constant disappointment and regret. All the joy had been squeezed out of him like a wet rag. The delicate hands doing the squeezing were, in his view, those belonging to Hannah Granville.

'What will you do now, Abel?'

'I don't know.'

'Would you like me to speak to Mr Fleet?'

'That would do no good.'

'Shall I try to reason with Miss Granville?'

'You'd only expose yourself to abuse and I won't allow that.'

'There must be *something* I can do, surely?'

'Just pray for me, Marion.'

'That's what I have been doing.'

'Pray for me and for my poor, dear, hapless play.'

Peter Skillen had decided to go to Bow Street to see what information he could glean from the two prisoners. It was left to Paul to take Huckvale safely back to the gallery. Both rode on the same horse. Jangled by the ordeal in the cellar, Huckvale was recovering quickly and blamed himself for being taken in so easily by someone masquerading as a priest.

'I should have known that he was an impostor.'

'You'll be more careful next time, Jem.'

'Working at the gallery used to be such a pleasure,' said Huckvale. 'Nothing ever went wrong. Yet in the last few days, it has. I've been charged with a crime I never committed, set on by a pair of angry dogs and kidnapped by two men who locked me up in a coal cellar. What's next?'

'Don't take it to heart,' said Paul. 'You suffered in a good cause. You're helping us to solve the murder of Mr Bowerman.'

'Am I?'

'That's why they abducted you. They know how much you mean to us. When *you're* in jeopardy, Peter and I won't rest until we've rescued you. While we're doing that, we can't be investigating the murder.'

They arrived back at the gallery to a cordial welcome. Though none of them was prepared to embrace him because of the filth on his clothing, Ackford, Charlotte and Hannah offered sympathy and kindness. They sat him down, brought him a glass of brandy and made much of him. It was rare for Huckvale to be the centre of attention and he savoured it. Charlotte produced her record book and showed him the sketch she'd once done of Luke Swait.

'That's him,' said Huckvale. 'That's the rogue who cozened me.'

'His days as a sham priest are over,' said Ackford. 'If he escapes the gallows, then he'll be transported for certain, and so will that friend of his.'

'Good riddance!'

'You, meanwhile, need a good bath and a long rest.'

'I'd be glad of the bath but I'm not going to rest. After what's happened, I'm eager to rejoin the search for the killer.' He indicated his apparel. '*He* did this to me. It was on his orders that I was knocked unconscious and thrown into that cellar. Whoever he is, he has a lot to answer for.' He took a sip of brandy and winced. 'I don't like the taste at all.'

'Drink it up,' advised Paul. 'It will do you good.'

'Then perhaps *I* should have a glass of it,' suggested Hannah. 'After my clash with Mundy, I'm in sore need of something to revive me.'

'Was the meeting with him a failure?'

'No, Paul, it was a catastrophe.'

'Whose fault was that, Hannah?'

'It was *his* fault, of course,' she said, annoyed that he should even ask the question. After a few moments of reflection, she made a slight concession. 'Well, he wasn't *entirely* to blame, perhaps, but he was the one who lit the fire in the first place. All that I did was to fan the flames a little.'

'I can imagine,' he said with a wry smile. 'But how do you feel now?'

'I feel desperately sad because the play will be abandoned.'

'I'm not thinking about that. I was wondering if you'd got over the shock of being hit by that shattered glass.'

'That's something I'll never forget until we find the culprit.'

'And we will, Hannah.'

'It's the one advantage of losing *The Piccadilly Opera*,' she said. 'I won't have to step onto a stage and be at the mercy of an unknown enemy in the audience. When I'm in the middle of a performance, I'm totally unguarded. He could do far more than throw a stone at me then. There,' she went on, turning to Huckvale, 'I'm doing it again. I'm going on about myself when I should be thinking about you, Jem. You've had far worse to bear than me. You must have thought you'd die down there in the dark.'

'I was afraid that nobody would ever find me,' said Huckvale.

'Well, we did,' added Paul. 'Not that we can actually recognise you. I've seen chimney sweeps with cleaner faces than you.'

'Time for that bath,' said Ackford, taking over. 'Off we go, Jem.'

Before they could leave the room, however, Peter returned. He looked grim and determined. They all gathered around to hear his news.

'Luke Swait couldn't give us a name,' he explained, 'because he was never told it. His paymaster was careful to give very little away. That said, I did eventually get a good description of the man out of Swait.'

'Did it sound like anyone we know?' asked Paul.

'Oh, yes, we've got to know him all too well.'

'What's his name, Peter?'

'It's the one I was expecting to hear,' said his brother. 'Mr Rawdon Carr.'

CHAPTER EIGHTEEN

As they marched into the chief magistrate's office, they did so without a shred of their usual apprehension because they had a triumph to report. Kirkwood looked up from his desk with weary cynicism.

'What setbacks have you come to relate?' he asked.

'We've brought nothing but good news, sir,' said Yeomans, brightly. 'To be honest, we feel that congratulations should be the order of the day.'

'That's right,' said Hale. 'We've made two important arrests.'

Yeomans nudged him. 'Let me explain, Alfred.'

'I'm sorry.'

'Remember your place.'

'I will, Micah.'

'I always take the lead.'

'When you two have finished arguing,' said Kirkwood, 'perhaps one of you would be kind enough to enlighten me. To what arrests do you refer?'

'We apprehended two men guilty of kidnap and other crimes,' said Yeomans, grandiloquently. 'Thanks to our quick thinking and prompt action, they were seized at The Black Horse in Covent Garden. Both men resisted arrest so we had to overpower them before dragging them back here.'

'What are their names?'

'One is Luke Swait, a bootmaker; the other is Nathan Cooper, a greengrocer.'

'And how did you find them?'

'It was by a combination of hard work and clever deduction, sir. We'd had our suspicions about them for some time. When we caught wind of the abduction, we knew that someone was in grave danger as a result so we moved swiftly to round up the malefactors.'

'That wasn't exactly what happened, Micah,' put in Hale.

'Keep out of this.'

'A certain amount of luck was involved.'

'Any good fortune we enjoyed was fully deserved,' said Yeomans, silencing him with a glance. 'Our experience at policing was the telling factor. That's why two villains are now languishing in custody and facing the prospect of transportation. In my view,' he added, voice deepening for effect, 'both of them should hang.'

'Oh,' said Kirkwood with light sarcasm, 'so you've promoted yourself to the magistracy now, have you?'

'No, no, sir, that would be presumptuous.'

'You'll need a far better knowledge of the law if you are to sit beside me.'

'I know my limitations.'

'We both do,' said Hale.

'In this instance, however, we feel that we surmounted them.'

'Let me recapitulate,' said Kirkwood. 'Suspecting these two individuals of various crimes, you heard of a kidnap and attributed it immediately to them. You therefore hastened to Covent Garden to make the arrests. Is that correct?'

'More or less,' said Yeomans.

'Do you have anything to add?'

'Only that we're proud to do our duty, sir.'

'What about you, Hale?'

'I agree with what Micah just told you, sir,' said Hale. 'It's an honour to uphold the law.'

'Then why can't you do it with at least a modicum of honesty?'

'We always do, Mr Kirkwood.'

'Honesty is our touchstone,' affirmed Yeomans.

'Yet your version of events is wildly at variance with the other one that I was given. Both accounts can't be right. What you clearly don't know,' said Kirkwood, 'is that Mr Peter Skillen gave me *his* report of what occurred.'

'Don't believe a word of it, sir.'

'He'll tell you anything,' warned Hale.

'*We* captured those two men.'

'Mr Skillen doesn't deny that you made the actual arrests,' said Kirkwood, 'but it was he who led you to the tavern where the two men were found. He, after all, had a personal interest in catching them because they'd abducted a close friend of his and left him trussed up in a coal cellar. It now transpires that Swait and Cooper were also responsible for knocking down doors and releasing two dogs at the shooting gallery in the middle of the night.'

'We were unaware of that, sir,' confessed Yeomans.

'You seem unaware of most things.'

'That's unfair. We made significant arrests.'

'Unfortunately,' said Kirkwood, 'you never got anywhere near their true significance because you never established who actually *paid* these ruffians. Mr Skillen clearly did. He was exuding quiet satisfaction. In essence,' he went on, 'this case has demonstrated why the Skillen brothers can out-think, outmanoeuvre and outrun you at every turn. Two prisoners are in custody and I applaud your role in putting them there. But you failed utterly to connect their activities with the murder of Mr Mark Bowerman. That is what Mr Skillen did and why he left here with such celerity.'

Yeomans gasped. 'He *knows* who hired those two rogues?'

'He's gone off to confront the man.'

'Who is he?' asked Hale. 'We must get to him first.'

'Yet again,' said Kirkwood, scornfully, 'you are far too slow. Instead of deserving the name of Runners, you should have another appellation altogether. You and Yeomans are Bow Street Snails. You can only crawl while the Skillen brothers do the actual running.' Yeomans and Hale were thunderstruck. 'Don't just stand there like a pair of marble statues. Get after them!'

Hannah Granville had improved markedly. On the journey between the gallery and the house, she showed no sign of fear and didn't once look out of the carriage window with trepidation. Seated beside her, Charlotte was pleased that her friend was no longer frightened of her own shadow. In place of her normal garrulity, Hannah was also remarkably quiet, not to say contemplative. The ride was conducted in silence for the most part. Charlotte waited until they were safely inside the house before she made any comment.

'I'm so pleased that you've regained your confidence,' she said.

Hannah looked bemused. 'Have I?'

'You're refusing to let anyone unsettle you.'

'That's because I'm unsettled enough as it is, Charlotte. The truth of it is that I behaved atrociously at the theatre. Mr Fleet was begging us to find a middle way and I stayed rooted to an extreme position.'

'According to you, Mr Mundy did likewise.'

'That was only in response to the stance I took,' admitted Hannah. 'If I'd been less demanding and more persuasive, we'd never have been in this mess. Yes, *he* was to blame as well. What he alleged about my performance was unpardonable. I despise him for it. But I offended him deeply. I hurt his pride so much that his only defence was to denigrate my talent.'

'It's beyond reproach,' said Charlotte. 'Everyone accepts that.'

There was another sign of improvement. Without even thinking, Hannah had led the way into the drawing room, the very place where the window had been smashed only feet away from her. It held no terrors for her now. Beside the prospect of the cancellation of the play, it was now a minor consideration.

Through a part of the window not boarded up, Charlotte saw a carriage draw up outside and wondered who the visitor might be. It was Hannah who identified him first. As the waddling figure of Lemuel Fleet alighted from the vehicle, she braced herself for the inevitable.

'It's the manager,' she said. 'He's come to tell me that *The Piccadilly Opera* has been replaced by another play and that I've been replaced in the company.'

'He can't do that. You have a contract.'

'In behaving the way I did, I effectively renounced it.'

'It would be madness to dispense with you, Hannah.'

'He might think it a greater lunacy to retain my services.'

Charlotte stood up. 'Would you like me to leave you alone with him?'

'No, no, I may need your support.'

'I don't wish to be in your way.'

'Without you, Charlotte, I'd be lost.'

She reached out to take her friend's hand and pull her back down onto the sofa. The doorbell rang and Lemuel Fleet was soon ushered into the room. In sweeping off his hat, he dislodged his wig, pushing it forward so that it covered one eye. He quickly readjusted it. After an exchange of greetings, he was offered a seat.

'How are you, Miss Granville?' he enquired.

'I am not at my best, sir.'

'Yet you seem considerably more serene now.'

'That's the serenity of exhaustion, Mr Fleet. I am *so* tired.'

'Then I won't keep you long from your slumber.'

There was an uncomfortable pause. Charlotte tried to lighten the atmosphere.

'Would you like some refreshment?' she asked.

'No, thank you.'

'I know that I'm intruding but only at Hannah's insistence.'

'I've no objection to your presence, Mrs Skillen,' he said. 'Miss Granville has oftentimes told me how staunch a friend you are. This is a time when we all need to lean on our friends.'

'Break it to me, Mr Fleet,' said Hannah, unable to stand the suspense. 'If I am to be dismissed, do it swiftly and without malice.'

The manager was shocked. 'How can you even suggest such a thing?'

'It would be no less than justice.'

'I'm not here to dismiss anybody,' he told her, reaching into his pocket to take out a scroll. 'I came to deliver this for your consideration.'

'What is it?'

'It's one of the songs that Mr Tregarne has composed for you. Strictly speaking, he did not have you in mind when he first worked on it but I think you'll find that it captures the mood perfectly in Act Five.' He handed her the scroll. 'Peruse it at your leisure. Do you have a piano here?'

'No, I don't.'

'There's one at our house,' volunteered Charlotte, 'and I'd be happy to accompany Miss Granville. But if this is a song for the play, are you saying that it might still be staged?'

'That's in the lap of the gods, Mrs Skillen. I say no more.'

He got up, bade them farewell and left the room. Hannah was motionless.

'Well, go on,' urged Charlotte. 'See what he brought for you. You have an opportunity to sing a new-minted song by no less a composer than Mr Tregarne. Every singer in the country will be green with envy.'

On his previous visit to the house, Peter Skillen and his brother had charged in without invitation. He was more patient this time. Arriving on his own, he asked the servant to tell her master that he'd called on a matter of urgency. After a long wait, he was allowed in. Stephen Hamer was alone in the room where he kept his souvenirs. Peter was shown in. There was a muted exchange of greetings.

'It seems that you've learnt some manners at last,' said Hamer.

'I've come with a simple request.'

'What is it?'

'I need the address of Mr Carr.'

'Why? What's your business with him?'

'I have to pass on some bad news,' said Peter. 'The two men he hired to abduct our friend are now in custody. As it happens, they were also behind the attack on the shooting gallery when the doors were battered down and dogs allowed in.'

'I've said before that I know nothing of that.'

'Mr Carr does. He paid them handsomely.'

'That's highly unlikely,' said the other, mustering some indignation. 'I've known Rawdon Carr for many years. He's a man of principle. If two villains are making allegations against him, I'd advise you to ignore them.'

'It may well be that Mr Carr is innocent of the charges. At all events, he deserves the right to defend himself against them. That's why I need his address. You are most welcome to accompany me, Lieutenant Hamer.'

Hamer winced. 'I was worthy of a captaincy,' he said.

'Your military career must bring you a lot of satisfaction,' said Peter, looking around the collection. 'It obviously meant a great deal to you. What a shame it is that you chose to throw it all away.'

'I fought for my country, Mr Skillen. It's more than *you* can claim.'

'That's debatable. For the record, I worked as an agent behind enemy lines for a number of years and was answerable directly to the Home Secretary. It was because of my relationship with him that I was able to obtain details of your service record from the War Office.' He indicated a weapon in a glass case. 'I carried a pistol just like that,' said Peter, 'and I had a dagger similar to those on display here secreted about my person in case of emergencies. They often cropped up. In our different ways, Lieutenant Hamer, we *both* fought for our country.'

Hamer studied him with a grudging respect. He and Carr were up against a more formidable opponent than they'd imagined. His immediate problem was how to buy time in order to warn his friend.

'You have come to the wrong place, Mr Skillen,' he said. 'The truth is that I don't know where Mr Carr lives. He never stays anywhere long. He will rent a house for a few months then move to another temporary abode. There's a touch of the nomad about Rawdon Carr.'

'Then all you have to do is to name the company from whom he rents his houses. Is it the same agency as the one looking after that house of yours where the murder of Mr Bowerman occurred?'

'It could be,' muttered the other.

'Then why didn't you give him free access to it? If Mr Carr is such a revered friend, why didn't you offer him the empty property that you own? That's what I'd have done in your position.'

'You're not *in* my position, Mr Skillen.'

'I'm sincerely grateful for that, sir.'

There was a moment of high tension. Hamer bristled and Peter got ready to repulse an attack. In a room full of weapons, it would have been easy to reach out and grab one. That was exactly what

Hamer seemed on the point of doing. What held him back was the discovery that Peter had worked as a British spy in France and must therefore have endured many hazards. Evidently, he would defend himself well.

'I'm afraid that I can't help you,' said Hamer at length.

'I had a feeling you'd say that.'

'As for these preposterous charges against my friend, I'd dismiss them out of hand. He would *never* be party to a kidnap.'

'You have a rather higher opinion of Mr Carr than I do.'

'He's stood by me through some very difficult times,' asserted Hamer, 'so I'm well aware of his strength of character. I'd trust him with my life.'

'Forgive me,' said Peter, 'but the only life that concerns me at the moment is that of our friend, Jem Huckvale, who was tied up in a coal cellar and could well have perished there – thanks to Mr Carr.'

'This is *nothing* to do with him.'

'We shall see.'

'You are relying on the word of two mendacious ruffians.'

'They're hoping to win favour by telling the truth for once,' said Peter. 'However, I can see that I'm wasting my time here. Since you seem strangely unaware of where your friend resides, we'll have to find his address by other means. Goodbye, Lieutenant.'

Turning on his heel, Peter walked to the front door and let himself out of the house. Hamer, meanwhile, was throbbing with anger. Going to the window, he watched his visitor mount his horse and ride away. Hamer rushed to the library, sat down at his desk and dashed off a letter before summoning a servant. He thrust the missive into the man's hands.

'Take this to Mr Carr immediately.'

* * *

As the man left the house at speed, he soon went past an alleyway without looking down it. The diminutive figure of Jem Huckvale stepped cautiously into view then set off in pursuit.

While his brother had gone to Stephen Hamer's house, Paul Skillen went in search of the same information at the home of Laetitia Somerville. Though he was admitted at once, he was kept waiting for a long time in the drawing room. He surmised that she was rehearsing her role as a bereaved widow. Even though she'd never married Mark Bowerman, she was behaving as if she'd been his loving wife. Paul wished that Hannah had been with him. In the presence of a real actress, Laetitia might wilt into the patent impostor she was.

When she eventually appeared, it was once again in mourning attire. She apologised for keeping him waiting but had a warning for him.

'State your business and leave,' she said, brusquely. 'Since Mr Bowerman's death, I have not slept a wink. A physician will be arriving shortly with a much-needed sleeping draught for me.'

'Oh, I'd wager you've been dozing happily enough,' said Paul.

'I find that remark insulting, Mr Skillen.'

'It will save time if you drop the pretence of being grief-stricken. We both know that Mr Bowerman was an unfortunate gull at the mercy of a clever plot. I've spoken to Sir Geoffrey Melrose and to Mr Winters, disreputable company for a putative lady like you to keep. You are a predator, Miss Somerville,' he said, 'but that's not why I'm here.'

'I've already heard enough,' she said, haughtily. 'Leave at once, sir, or I'll have you thrown out of this house.'

'Your manservant and I have tussled before. He'll need three or four others to help if he's to dislodge me. Threaten all you wish. It's pointless. I'll not move until you've answered the question that brought me here.'

'And what is that, pray?'

'Where is Mr Carr?'

She laughed. 'How on earth should I know?'

'You and he and Lieutenant Hamer are bosom friends.'

'I deny that.'

'Spare me your denials and furnish me with the address.'

'I cannot give you what I don't possess, Mr Skillen.'

'Are you claiming that you've never *been* to his house?'

'I've no reason whatsoever to do so.'

'Mr Carr strikes me as a hospitable man. He must have invited you there.'

'Rawdon Carr is no friend of mine,' she said with sudden force, 'and he never will be. I have no idea where he lives and no wish to do so. Really, Mr Skillen, you and your brother seem to have an alarming penchant for slander. If you persist in making groundless accusations, it will land both of you in court.'

'Litigation will certainly come in due course,' said Paul, blithely, 'and we'll welcome it. Mr Bowerman was my friend. To preserve his good name, I feel duty-bound to contest his will.' She paled visibly. 'I see that you understand my meaning.'

'Get out!' she yelled.

'I'm staying until you give me that address.'

Walking to a table, she picked up a small bell and rang it loudly. Within seconds, a manservant came into the room and levelled a pistol at Paul. The visitor gave a philosophical shrug.

'It seems that I may have to leave, after all,' he said.

Encouraged by the reception he'd received at her hands, Fleet left Hannah Granville to study the new song and went straight to the house where Abel Mundy was staying. He was dismayed to learn that the playwright was not available.

'My husband has taken to his bed,' explained Marion.

'Is he ill?'

'He's exhausted by all this spitefulness and uncertainty.'

'As, indeed, am I, Mrs Mundy.'

'Do you have a message for him?'

'I'd hoped to have a proper conversation,' said Fleet. 'Time is running out. A final decision must be made about the future of *The Piccadilly Opera*. The whole company is imploring me to save it from cancellation. Such a course of action would be a huge disappointment to the theatre-going public.'

'All that I care about is my husband's health.'

'He would surely recover if his play were to reach the stage at last.'

'That prospect seems less likely by the day. My husband has not given me the full details of the latest outburst by Miss Granville. Judging by the state in which it left him, I can only conclude that it was vile.'

'There were, alas, unkind epithets hurled on both sides.'

'I refuse to believe that Abel is capable of descending to outright abuse.'

Fleet thought better of disillusioning her. Marion Mundy had a vision of her husband that featured a reasonable voice and an angelic disposition. She didn't realise that, when provoked, he could lose his temper with violent effect.

'How *is* he, Mrs Mundy?' he asked, probing gently.

'He is in despair, sir. We spent some time praying together.'

'Then I wish the Lord had been more attentive to your pleas,' he said under his breath. 'If this play falters,' he added aloud, 'I stand to lose a lot of money and I'll sustain serious damage to my reputation as a manager.'

By way of a reply, she lowered her head. He accepted that it was no use asking her to intercede on his behalf. Concern for her husband's health took precedence over anything else. In her opinion, he was without fault. The problems all arose from the employment of Hannah Granville. Nothing would convince her otherwise. The manager was about to take his leave when the playwright came into the room.

'What are you doing here, Mr Fleet?' he asked.

'I was hoping to speak to you, sir.'

Mundy turned to his wife. 'You should have called me.'

'I didn't want to wake you up,' she said.

'I can't sleep at a time like this. Sit down, Mr Fleet.'

'Thank you,' said the manager, lowering himself into a chair.

'Do you wish me to stay, Abel?' asked his wife.

'Perhaps not, my dear,' said Mundy. Waiting until she'd left the room, he looked warily at Fleet. 'I hope that you've brought an apology.'

'I've showered both you and Miss Granville with a hundred apologies.'

'It's not *your* apology that I seek.'

'Let us not ask for the impossible. There are times, as you've now found out, when working in the theatre is like a descent into hell. It's a place of fire, fury and suffering. As a God-fearing man, you'll know all about the Devil's kingdom.'

'I've met the lady in person,' growled Mundy.

'Come, come, sir, let's not be vindictive.'

'You are right, Mr Fleet. Please forgive me.'

'I have just visited Miss Granville.'

'I knew that you'd go to her first,' complained Mundy, 'because you always do. She is always given priority over me.'

'I didn't go in order to spite you,' said Fleet. 'It just happens that the house where she is staying is on the way here. Had you lived closer to the theatre, my first call would have been to you.'

'What has Miss Granville said?'

'She simply thanked me for the gift I took.'

'Has she made any fresh demands?'

'No, Mr Mundy, I fancy that she regrets some of the ones she's already made. I didn't even raise the question of her attitude towards your play. I went there solely to give her a song written by Benjamin Tregarne.'

Mundy bridled. 'Why – was it destined for my play?'

'No, sir – as things stand, there *is* no play. You and she saw to that. Miss Granville has only had sight of one song. I'm bringing you something far more important.'

'What's that?'

'Mr Tregarne would like to meet you,' said Fleet. 'He finds your play both individual and interesting. If you accept, I'm to take you to his house.'

'What about Miss Granville?'

'She will not be there.'

'Won't she protest at being excluded?'

'Only if she gets to hear of the meeting and I'm certainly not going to tell her.' He gave him a confidential wink. 'Nor are you, I suspect.'

The brothers met outside a tavern as arranged and discussed what had happened. Both had met with the stout denials they expected and left without the address they sought. Stephen Hamer and Laetitia Somerville were trying to shield Rawdon Carr from them. It was a sign of how important he was in devising their machinations. Peter was amused that his brother had been expelled with a pistol at his back.

'At least I was able to leave of my own accord,' he said, 'though there was a moment when I thought I might have to fight for my life.'

'Leave part of him for me, Peter.'

'Your quarry is Miss Somerville.'

'I can see why she appealed to Mr Bowerman,' said Paul. 'He was enraptured by her because she curled up in his lap like a favourite cat. All that I was shown today were those vicious claws of hers.'

They were holding their horses as they talked. The sound of running feet made them look down the street and they saw Huckvale haring towards them at the kind of speed for which he was renowned. When he reached them, he was able to tell them where Carr lived. Mounting his horse, Peter offered his hand.

'Ride behind me, Jem,' he said.

Huckvale shook his head. 'Follow me – it's not far to run.'

They let him lead the way and trotted along behind him. Situated in a quiet side street, the house was smaller and less ostentatious than those occupied by Hamer and Laetitia. The brothers tethered their horses. Paul crept furtively around to the rear of the house to prevent an escape that way. Peter and Huckvale went to the front door and rang the bell. After a while, the summons was answered by a flat-faced servant with an unwelcoming scowl.

'We'd like to see Mr Carr, please,' said Peter.

'May I ask your name, sir?'

'I'm Peter Skillen and this is my good friend, Jem Huckvale.'

'Then I'm afraid that I can't help you,' said the man.

'In other words, you've been told to keep us at bay. Please take a message to your master: if he doesn't have the grace to invite us in, we'll enter by force.'

'That would be quite unnecessary.'

'Convey the message to him.'

'It's one thing I can't do,' said the man, standing back from the door. 'Come in, if you must, Mr Skillen. There's no need to use force. You'll find that your journey here was in vain.'

'Why is that?'

'Mr Carr has gone away for some time.'

'Has he left London?'

'He didn't tell me where his destination was, sir. My orders are to close the house up. Mr Carr's lease is due to expire. The one thing I can tell you is that he will not be coming back to this property.'

'Are you sure he's not skulking inside somewhere?'

'I'm absolutely certain,' replied the servant, opening the door to its fullest extent, 'but you don't have to take my word for it. I can see that you're very anxious to speak to Mr Carr. But I've told you the truth. He's no longer here.'

Laetitia was so rocked by the information that she flopped into a chair as if she'd been given a firm push. Hamer had called to tell her what his manservant had learnt at the erstwhile home of Rawdon Carr. Without warning either of them, Carr had quit London for some unspecified destination.

'He's run out on us,' gasped Laetitia.

'Rawdon would never do that. He must have heard of the arrests and made himself scarce before the Skillen brothers could catch up with him. I didn't sanction the kidnap of that friend of theirs,' said Hamer. 'It was his idea. Rawdon swore that he'd divert them somehow and that's what he did.'

'But it was only for a short length of time.'

'They must have found Huckvale.'

'Paul Skillen came to ask for Rawdon's address. I refused to give it to him. He knows far too much, Stephen,' she said, twisting her necklace with one hand. 'He even taunted me about being the beneficiary of Mark Bowerman's will.'

Hamer was taken aback. 'How, in the name of God, did he hear about that?'

'Mark must have told him.'

'But you swore him to silence, Laetitia.'

'It must have slipped out.'

'This is serious,' he said, pacing the room. 'It's one thing to use a decoy against those maddening twins, but it only creates a short space of time for us. If they know about the will, they may have to be removed altogether.'

She was hesitant. 'You'd kill *both* of them?'

'If it's the only way to protect our interests, I certainly will. As for Rawdon, I can't understand why he didn't warn me that he was about to fly the coop. We've been in constant touch until now.'

'That's what worries me, Stephen. He came to see me a while ago.'

'I know. I sent him. I didn't want to be caught here again.'

'He told me about the search he's instituted for that mistress of yours, Eleanor Gold. I've been thinking about her. Can she really be the scheming creature of report? Does she *hate* you that much, Stephen?'

'Oh, yes,' he said with feeling.

'What did you do to her?'

'I sent her packing, Laetitia. No woman likes to be discarded. Eleanor disliked it far more than I'd imagined. The others merely called me names and stormed out. Eleanor did much more than that. Of course,' he went on, 'that could be the other reason for Rawdon's sudden departure. He's discovered where she is. He told me that he had men looking for her. They must have picked up a trail.'

'Then why didn't he write to tell you that?'

'I don't know,' he admitted.

'And why did he leave orders to close the house up?'

'That was always in the offing. The lease was close to expiring and he'd been looking for accommodation elsewhere.'

She wrinkled her nose. 'Something is beginning to smell fishy, Stephen.'

'I refuse to believe that Rawdon has let us down in any way. He's been like an elder brother to me. In fact, there was a time when I'd hoped we might get even closer. I thought he might become my brother-in-law.'

'That was never a possibility,' she said, crisply. 'He understood that. It's ancient history. Please don't bring it up again.'

'I'm sorry, Laetitia. You shouldn't be so sensitive about it.'

'That period of my life is best forgotten.' She gave a sudden laugh. 'I've just remembered what I told the Bow Street Runners. I said that it was *impossible* for me to marry you. They didn't realise that any union between us would be a case of incest.' Hamer laughed as well. 'You make such a convincing former beau of mine, Stephen. Nobody would guess that we were brother and sister.' She became serious. 'But I'm still deeply upset about the latest turn of events. Vanishing like that without a word of explanation is so unlike Rawdon Carr.'

'I stand by my judgement of him,' he said, confidently. 'Look back on all the things he's done for us. We'd never have succeeded without his help and ability to organise everything. Rawdon is the most trustworthy man I know. Have faith in him.'

When the carriage drew up outside the hotel, she came out at once. She was followed by a man carrying her luggage. The door of the vehicle was opened from the inside and she clambered into it, falling into the arms of the other passenger.

'We did it,' said Carr, kissing her. 'We did it and we got away with it.'

CHAPTER NINETEEN

Charlotte Skillen was a competent pianist who could read a score and play it with feeling. The song given to Hannah Granville had never been played before by anyone but the composer. Since she was the first person after him to bring it to life, Charlotte was very nervous and she had to wipe away perspiration from her hands before she touched the keys. Hannah was equally in thrall to the achievements of Benjamin Tregarne, a man who could write plays and music with equal facility. What she'd been given by Lemuel Fleet was a haunting love song that would fit with ease into the last act of *The Piccadilly Opera*. Even when reading the lyrics, she was moved. When she actually sang them to Charlotte's accompaniment, they made her glow.

'I *must* sing this,' she declared.

'You just did, Hannah.'

'I got nowhere near the essence of the song. It will take days of rehearsal before I can do that. But it's a work of genius. Someday, and somewhere, I simply must sing it in public.'

'Why not delight the audience for Mr Mundy's play?'

'That's no longer a possibility.'

'The final decision has still not been made.'

'Yes, it has.'

'Only Mr Fleet can call it off, Hannah, and he seemed to be in no mood to do that when he came here earlier.'

'That's a matter of opinion.'

'I thought I detected a faint whiff of optimism in him.'

'Then you are deluding yourself. When you have a worthless play and a stubborn playwright who abuses the one actress who might actually redeem it, you have a recipe for abject failure. In its present form, *The Piccadilly Opera* doesn't deserve performance.'

'What about Mr Tregarne's song?'

'That does merit a wider audience.'

'Sing it for me again.'

'I daren't do so, Charlotte. It will grow on me.'

'Then I will sing it to you. I don't have a trained voice like you but I can sing in tune.' She played a few bars. 'It's such an evocative melody.'

After clearing her throat, Charlotte began to sing to her own accompaniment. Hannah stood behind her and looked at the music over her shoulder. Though she tried hard to resist the temptation to join in, she soon capitulated and sang in a beautiful soprano voice that gave the song more clarity and resonance. Indeed, she took it over so completely that Charlotte was able to lapse into silence and simply enjoy her friend's rendition. When it was all over, Hannah was exhilarated.

'It gets better each time I sing it.'

'It was a joy to hear you.'

'Mr Tregarne is such a clever man.'

'In his own way,' Charlotte thought, 'Mr Fleet is rather clever as well.'

After their setback at Rawdon Carr's house, they adjourned to a nearby tavern to discuss their next move. Peter and Paul were disappointed by the man's sudden departure but Huckvale felt cheated.

'I wanted to leave *him* tied up in that cellar,' he said, bitterly, 'so that he can see what it was like.'

'The law would have to take its course, Jem,' said Peter. 'We have no right to inflict punishment. I just wanted the pleasure of arresting Carr.'

'We should arrest Hamer and Miss Somerville instead,' suggested Paul. 'They must have condoned what happened to Jem.'

'I don't believe that Hamer did. When we told him of the kidnap, it was clearly news to him. I'm sure that he incited Carr to do something to mislead us but he had no knowledge of the details.'

'What about Miss Somerville?'

'She's too busy pretending to mourn Mr Bowerman's death.'

'All three of them are as guilty as hell, if you ask me,' said Huckvale.

'There's no doubt about that,' said Peter. 'The way that they planned to get rid of Mr Bowerman was despicable. Their plot worked so well at first that one is bound to wonder if it's the first time they've used it.'

'I'm certain it isn't,' decided Paul, 'and I'm even more convinced that the person who first devised it was Mr Carr. He has the guile that Hamer and Miss Somerville lack. Without him, they might never have dreamt up such a cunning way to acquire property and wealth.'

'Why has he run away?' asked Huckvale.

Paul chuckled. 'He heard that you were looking for him, Jem.'

'I'm serious, Paul.'

'Then the serious answer is that we don't rightly know. It may be that he was aware of the two arrests we helped to make or it may be that he decided to quit London for a holiday somewhere. There are all kinds of other reasons as well.'

'He's a deeper man than we thought,' said Peter. 'If he's bolted, we need to track him down, though I can't imagine how we'd do that.'

'Can I make a suggestion?' Huckvale piped up.

'Yes – go ahead, Jem.'

'Why not ask Hamer?'

'We've no guarantee that he'll know where Carr is. Didn't you say you watched his messenger arrive with that letter from Hamer?'

'Yes, he held it out but they wouldn't take it.'

'There you are, then,' concluded Paul. 'Hamer didn't know that his friend had left the house or he wouldn't have dispatched a letter to him. He may be as surprised as the rest of us by Carr's sudden departure.' He downed his drink. 'I'll go back to the house and question his servant more closely.'

'He doesn't know where his master went,' warned Peter.

'That's not what I was going to ask him.'

'What else can he tell you?'

'I'd like to know a little more about the kind of life that Carr has been leading. Clues are bound to emerge,' said Paul. 'Mr Bowerman's destiny was effectively settled at the dinner party where he met Miss Somerville. I'm sure that Rawdon Carr was involved in that somehow.'

Yeomans and Hale were sickened by the lack of appreciation shown for their work in making two arrests. It was true that they had to be led to The Black Horse by the Skillen brothers but they then came into their own. Their reward was to be berated by the chief magistrate yet again.

'He's always praising those twins at our expense,' said Hale.

'It annoys me, too, Alfred.'

'They only take an interest if a murder is committed and a large reward is on offer. We handle all sorts of crime.'

'We manage to make a profit out of them,' Yeomans reminded him. 'Some of it is spent on our informers but that's a cost we have to bear.'

'Our informers have been of no use in this case, Micah.'

'That's why I've been kicking their backsides.'

'What did Mr Kirkwood mean when he said that Peter Skillen was ahead of us in the race to catch the killer?'

'Forget about him and his brother. Concentrate on *our* investigation.'

Feeling that there was more intelligence to be gathered there, they were on their way to Laetitia Somerville's house. Their earlier call on her had resulted in an ignominious departure. Yeomans was determined that they would not be sent on their way so easily again. The Runners had a stroke of good fortune. When they reached the house, Stephen Hamer was about to leave and was holding Laetitia's hand. The newcomers moved in quickly.

'We've caught you,' said Yeomans, triumphantly. 'Last time we found you together, you swore that Captain Hamer had only come to apologise, yet here you are showing every sign of affection for each other.'

'Our private life is our own,' insisted Hamer. 'Miss Somerville and I have come to composition. That's all I'm prepared to say.'

'The captain has stated my position as well,' said Laetitia. 'May I ask what brought you to my door again?'

'You've aroused our suspicions,' replied Yeomans.

'We still think you're in league somehow,' added Hale.

'A moment ago, we had clear proof of it.'

'I'm more than entitled to kiss a dear friend,' said Hamer, defiantly.

'We feel that you know a lot more about Mr Bowerman's death than either of you are prepared to say.'

'The only thing we know is that it appalled us, Mr Yeomans. That's why we are so keen to catch the killer ourselves.'

'Why not leave that task to someone more suitable?'

'I don't regard either of you in that light.'

'We're not the only ones taking part in the search,' said Hale. 'Peter and Paul Skillen have taken an interest as well.'

'They always do,' moaned Yeomans.

'We've been pestered by them from the outset,' said Hamer, angrily. 'If you wish to help us, find a way to keep the pair of them tethered.'

'Someone else is trying to do that. We think it might be you.'

'That's an absurd accusation,' said Laetitia with a gesture of dismissal. 'Take your ugly suspicions elsewhere, Mr Yeomans.'

'The captain still hasn't explained why he's here.'

'Nor do I intend to do so,' retorted Hamer.

'We thought that we were visiting the home of a woman who is mourning the death of Mr Mark Bowerman, yet what we find is that she's receiving a kiss from the very person who tried to kill the gentleman in a duel.'

'He challenged me. I could hardly refuse.'

'You need never have incited the challenge in the first place.'

For the first time, Hamer looked unsettled and exchanged a glance with his sister. They'd been caught in what appeared to be a compromising situation. Realising that they could not browbeat the Runners as before, they adopted a different approach. Laetitia introduced a note of apology into her voice.

'I'm sorry if we've given you the wrong idea,' she said,

manufacturing a smile for their benefit. 'We should not be bickering out here on the doorsteps like fishwives. Why don't you step inside the house for a moment? The captain has to leave on business,' she went on, 'but I will answer any questions you put to me.'

'It's true,' said Hamer, taking his cue from her and softening his tone. 'I have an important meeting to attend. Miss Somerville will speak on my behalf. What you saw when you arrived was misleading. You will learn why.'

The Runners were not hoodwinked by the sudden change of attitude. They stepped into the house with their suspicions intact.

It was a revelation for Abel Mundy. During their long discussion of his play, not a single voice had been raised. Instead of being compelled to defend his work, he'd been given praise and encouragement. The gathering doubts about his future as a playwright were soon dispelled. He was given the validation for which he'd yearned. Benjamin Tregarne's comments were not without criticism but they were put to Mundy so politely and presented so persuasively that they didn't feel in the least like censure or disapproval. They were sensible suggestions for improving something that already had great value.

The three of them were in the room in Tregarne's house where he'd worked for so many years. It was in a state of chaos: books, newspapers and sheet music were scattered everywhere. The desk was awash with correspondence. Shelves groaned under the weight of dusty tomes. Only the two pianos and the harpsichord were free of clutter. Given the fact that his comic operas were events of continuous merriment that catered unapologetically for the coarser elements in the audience as well as for the more discerning, Mundy had expected Tregarne to be a man of Falstaffian girth and gross appetites. In fact, he was a small, skinny, wizened creature with a gleaming bald pate and an expressive face. He had a pleasing West Country burr.

'There you have it, Mr Mundy,' he said in conclusion. 'You've created something that will delight a London audience and live in its memory for many a day. Congratulations, my friend!'

'Coming from you, sir,' said Mundy, 'that's high praise, indeed.'

'We playwrights must stick together.'

'I find that writing is a profession that isolates me from everyone else.'

'That's a mistake,' warned Tregarne. 'The bustling streets of London gave me my material. All the characters I brought to life were based on people I'd actually met or seen walking past me. I'd had enough of isolation in Cornwall. Our cottage was ten miles from the nearest village. I couldn't wait to find an excuse to come here. It was a form of liberation.'

'I'd find a cottage in the country very appealing.'

'Stay close to human beings. You can't write plays about cows and sheep.'

'That's true,' said Fleet, chortling.

He got up to signal that it was time to leave. After effusive thanks to their host, the two men left the house with a sense of satisfaction. Mundy felt that he'd achieved most. His play had been applauded by a master of his craft and Tregarne had even been kind enough to suggest changes and refinements that the playwright accepted without a murmur. Incorporated into *The Piccadilly Opera* along with some new ariettas, they would add pace, definition and spirit.

For his part, Fleet was trying to conceal his excitement. Without realising it, Mundy had agreed to almost all the changes first mooted by Hannah Granville. Since they were voiced by a famous playwright, and couched in extravagant praise, Mundy didn't recognise them for what they were. The strategy was the last throw of the dice for the theatre manager. Tregarne might yet be his salvation.

Rollo Winters had an existence that suited him perfectly. Since the House of Commons was well endowed with supplies of alcohol, he was able to drift from one place to the other to exchange gossip and relish the latest scandal. When he was not in Parliament, he moved through a succession of favourite watering holes, always ending up at his club in Albemarle Street. It was there that Paul Skillen found him for the second time. Nursing a brandy, Winters had sunk into his favourite chair.

'Good day to you, sir,' said Paul, sitting beside him.

'Goodbye is more appropriate,' said the other, tartly. 'I've no wish to talk to you, sir.'

'But I bring you news of a friend of yours.'

'And who is that?'

'A gentleman named Rawdon Carr.'

'Yes,' admitted Winters. 'I know him well.'

'I've just come from his house,' explained Paul. 'One of the servants told me of his devotion to his club. When he'd celebrated rather too much, apparently, Mr Carr sometimes spent the night here.'

'We've all done that. It's a privilege of membership.'

'Then it's strange he should abandon it so lightly.'

'What do you mean?'

'Mr Carr has left London for good, it seems, and nobody has any idea where he went. Is that the kind of eccentric behaviour you expect from him?'

'No, it isn't. Rawdon is a sound man – intelligent, reliable and generous to a fault. I've spent many a happy evening at a dining table with him. Where can he possibly have gone?'

'I was hoping that *you* might have some idea of that, sir.'

Winters became cautious. 'What's your interest in him, Mr Skillen?'

'You might say that it was financial.'

'Rawdon owes you money?'

'Quite the reverse,' said Paul. 'I'm in a position to put some his way. Last time we met, we talked of Mr Bowerman's murder. I've been informed by his lawyer that his client named me as one of his executors. I therefore had the chance of an early peep at his last will and testament. Mr Carr is a beneficiary.'

'How much will he get?'

'It's a tidy amount, Mr Winters. I wanted to confide the good news to him but I can't do that if he's left the capital. The lawyer will be unable to get in touch with him as well. If the money is not claimed by a certain time, it will be forfeited.'

'We can't have that happening,' said Winters.

'I agree.'

'And it's a substantial amount, you say?'

'Mr Bowerman was a wealthy man.'

'Let me think for a moment . . .'

The politician had another drink to stimulate his brain, then began to pick his way through a veritable forest of memories. Having expected to be thrown out of the club, Paul had done better than he'd hoped. Winters had actually believed his story. After a lengthy period of meditation, the man sat up and jabbed a finger.

'He did once say something to me.'

'What was that, sir?'

'Well, we were talking about places to which we'd care to retire.

I cited this club because it fulfils all my needs except that of ready access to amenable women. Rawdon wanted to go much further afield. He told me that he was always drawn to Scotland.'

'Why was that?'

'Rawdon was born there. His parents brought him south when he was five and he's always nurtured a fondness for his birthplace.'

'Where exactly was it?'

'Edinburgh – he thinks it's the most beautiful city in the world.'

When the boat left the Thames Estuary, it came out into choppier water for a while. It hugged the coast as it sailed northwards. It was a relatively small vessel but large enough to carry its two passengers in comfort and complete safety. Relaxing in their cabin, Rawdon Carr and his companion were still heady with success.

'When will they realise what's happened?' she asked.

'Letters will reach them tomorrow. I gave orders that they should be delivered first thing. I want the information to bring them fully awake.'

'That was very naughty of you, Rawdon.'

'I've had a lot of time to plan this, my love.'

'Oh!' she cried, embracing him. 'Is there anything sweeter than revenge?'

'They both deserve it, Edith.'

'I'm just glad that I was able to do my share.'

Edith Loveridge was also glad that her real name had been restored to her. While she enjoyed posing as Hester Mallory or as Arabella Kenyon, she was happy that she was now with someone who knew and loved her as Edith Loveridge.

'Your contribution was unparalleled,' he told her. 'I was able to trick them into letting me invest all the money we got from the last time Laetitia used her charms on someone, leaving Stephen to kill the man in a duel. They trusted me completely. But only *you* could have forged their share certificates. Neither of them realises that they have worthless pieces of paper. I'd love to be there when they discover that their investment never actually existed.'

'That will wipe the arrogant sneer off Stephen's face.'

'Laetitia is the one I'll enjoy wounding most. There was a time when I adored that woman, Edith, and she gave me to believe that my attentions were welcome. When she turned on me so viciously,' he went on, 'I was mortified. From that moment on, I was thinking of getting even with her one day.'

'It was the same with Stephen. His treatment of me was not simply cruel. It was downright barbaric. He led me on with a promise of marriage then tossed me aside when he found someone else.'

'We should be grateful to them, really.'

'Never!' she decreed.

'Because they rejected you and me, they actually brought us together.'

He kissed and caressed her for several minutes and they forgot all about the lurching movements of the boat. Carr then told her that the most difficult part of the exercise was to convince them that she had died in France. He'd also had to replace Edith in their minds with another possible suspect.

'Her name was Eleanor Gold and Stephen cast her brutally aside.'

'That's exactly what he does.'

'I claimed that I had men out looking for her but that was a lie to deceive them. Because of the way I'd served them in the past, they believed me. For two intelligent people, they were so easy to manipulate.'

'What if they follow us to Scotland?'

'There isn't the slightest possibility of that, Edith.'

'Are you sure?'

'Yes, we've covered our tracks far too well.'

'Stephen might have heard you talking about Edinburgh.'

'I took great care never to mention my love of the city,' he said, 'and besides, neither he nor that venomous sister of his will be in a position to follow us. As well as sending letters to them, I've been writing to someone else.'

'Who is that?'

'I've sent word to the chief magistrate in Bow Street. Playing down my own part in the affair, I told him what Stephen and Laetitia had done between them to Mark Bowerman and to his predecessor. That should be enough to hang the both of them.'

'You've thought of *everything*, Rawdon.'

'I did it all for you, my love. As a result of hard work, I've accumulated a large amount of capital and your forays into the banking system in London and elsewhere have brought in even more. We'll be able to live in style, Edith.' He kissed her again. 'Meanwhile, Stephen and Laetitia will be dangling from the gallows.'

Charlotte had played the piano until her fingers began to ache. Though it was the same melody time and again, she didn't complain. The song never lost its appeal. Over her friend's shoulder, Hannah studied the notes once more and looked for ways to improve her rendition. She now knew the lyrics by heart.

'Let's try it again,' she said.

'You've already sung it fifteen or twenty times, Hannah.'

'I'm still feeling my way through it.'

'But it sounds wonderful to me.'

'Play it once more.'

'If this really is the last time, I will.'

The moment her fingertips touched the keys, however, Charlotte was forced to stop. After a tap on the door, one of the servants came in with a small parcel. She handed it over before going out again. Charlotte opened the parcel and marvelled at what she found inside.

'It's *another* song from Mr Tregarne,' she said, 'and it's dedicated to you.'

Back at the gallery, Peter Skillen explained what his brother had done. Ackford was quick to praise Paul for his enterprise but less than enthusiastic about the conclusion drawn by him. He wrinkled his brow before speaking.

'Just because he likes Edinburgh,' he said, 'it doesn't mean that Mr Carr has actually gone there. I've spent the last twenty years wanting to live on the north Devon coast but the closest I've ever got to it is here.'

'You don't have the same urgency to leave, Gully.'

'I agree,' said Huckvale. 'Mr Carr must know that those two men have been arrested. He'll realise we've guessed who hired them.'

'In that case, he might flee from London,' conceded Ackford, 'but why make for Scotland? It's too far and too uncivilised.'

Peter laughed. 'They're not all wild and hairy Highlanders.'

'I rubbed shoulders with a Scots regiment in America. They were very wild and very hairy, Peter, and they fought with real ferocity.'

'What about his friends?' asked Huckvale.

'What friends, Jem?'

'Mr Carr's friends – will they make a run for it themselves?'

'They won't see the need,' said Peter. 'As far as they're concerned, they're safe enough. Paul gave Miss Somerville a nasty shock by mentioning Mr Bowerman's will. What she doesn't know is that we've worked out the murderous game she and Hamer have been playing together. They'll stay where they are because they think they're safe. It's only Carr who has to get out quickly.'

'I still think he'd go to ground here,' said Ackford. 'That's what I'd do.'

'No, it isn't. You'd run off to the north Devon coast.'

They shared a laugh then continued to speculate on Carr's likely movements. Huckvale had the strongest motive to catch up with him. He could still feel the ropes eating into his wrists and ankles. He was about to recount his ordeal yet again when Paul arrived. They looked up hopefully at him.

'Well?' asked Huckvale. 'What did you find out?'

'I was right,' said Paul. 'He's gone to Scotland.'

'How do you know?'

'I first thought that, if he was making a permanent move, he'd have a lot of luggage and travel by coach. But there's another way to go such a distance. That's why I scoured the docks for details of any vessels sailing for Scotland. In the end, I found one.'

'Was Mr Carr aboard?' asked Ackford.

'The old salt I spoke to didn't know his name but he described a man who sounds very much like Carr. He gave me a more detailed description of the woman who accompanied him,' said Paul, 'because she was very striking.'

'Was it Miss Somerville?' asked Huckvale.

'No, but it was someone equally beautiful and well dressed. Like him, she was travelling with a fair amount of luggage. The two of them are sailing all the way up to Scotland. I'm sure they gave false names to the captain of the boat. I'm also sure that the man must have been Rawdon Carr.'

'What about the woman, Paul?'

'I haven't a clue who she might be.'

'I have,' said Peter, thinking about the forged letter that had lured Bowerman to his death. 'I'd never have connected them before but I can see now that they might be well suited. Carr is travelling with Mrs Hester Mallory or Miss Arabella Kenyon or, to be more exact, with both of them simultaneously.'

The pleasure of meeting Benjamin Tregarne had inspired Mundy. Throughout rehearsals, he'd had his talent called into question and it had sapped his strength and confidence. The time spent with Tregarne had restored both. When he returned to his lodging, he wanted to tell his wife all about the meeting but she was not there. Instead, therefore, he sat down at a table with his copy of the play and began to go through it line by line. There had already been a number of minor modifications. It was only when he went through each scene that he realised that what Tregarne had proposed was really quite radical. It involved cutting favourite passages and even losing some characters. The points where ariettas would be introduced were well chosen, he could not dispute that, but some of his beloved dialogue would have to be sacrificed in order to insert them.

The spirit of resistance was slowly awakened in Abel Mundy. Willing to make some changes, he had been lulled into the belief that his play needed structural alterations. While he refused to believe that it had been a deliberate trick on the part of Tregarne, he was not so ready to exonerate the theatre manager. It was Lemuel Fleet who'd contrived the visit, knowing that suggestions from an eminent dramatist and composer might be more acceptable than if they came from a strident actress.

Mundy closed the last page, picked up the whole play then slammed it down on the table. He would refuse to allow something that was tantamount to butchery of his work. His wife, he was certain, would endorse his decision. Together they would stand firm against the deviousness of the manager and the demands of Hannah Granville. Within minutes of reaching his decision, he was able to confide it to his wife. Returning to the house, she entered the room with great solemnity.

'Where have you been?' he asked.

'I went to church, Abel.'

'Do not waste time praying for the success of my play. It is beyond help.'

'I needed to talk to the vicar,' she explained. 'The load I've been carrying is too heavy to bear so I sought his advice.'

'There is no load now, Marion. It is all over. We can kick the dust of London from our feet and return to gentler pastures in the provinces. They like me there.'

'You don't understand.'

'What I understand,' he said, placing a gentle hand on her shoulder, 'is that I have a wonderful wife on whom I can depend in a crisis. Without you, I'd surely have crumbled by now. You have fought valiantly by my side.'

'I fear that I fought *too* valiantly, Abel.'

'In marrying you, I found myself a saint.'

'The vicar did not think me very saintly,' she said. 'He said that my secret would fester away inside me if I didn't tell the truth.'

'But you *have* no secrets from me, Marion.'

'Yes, I do.'

She looked him full in the face. Taking his hand from her shoulder, he stepped back a few paces. He opened his mouth in horror as he realised that the dear, devoted wife with her Christian virtues had struck back at the person who'd been plaguing him. It was Marion Mundy who'd hurled a stone through the window.

The second song composed by Tregarne was even better than the first. It left Hannah in a state of pure joy. Having sung it through several times, she took pity on Charlotte for spending so long at the piano and went back to her own house, singing both songs to herself alternately. Eager to tell Paul her good fortune, she was dismayed that he was not at home. In his place, waiting impatiently, was Lemuel Fleet.

'What did you think of the song?' he asked.

'Which one?' she replied. 'They are both delightful.'

'I'm so glad that you approve of them. I had a meeting with Mr Tregarne earlier on and he asked me to send you his kindest regards.'

'That was very kind of him.'

'He's looking forward to seeing you in *The Piccadilly Opera*.'

'How can he do that when it will never be performed?'

'There's been a change of mind on Mr Mundy's part.'

'What provoked that?'

'I've no idea, Miss Granville, but he sent me this missive a short while ago.'

He handed over the letter and Hannah unfolded it. What she read was at first unbelievable. Mundy was acceding to every demand she'd made. Written in a shaky hand, the letter was polite and respectful. It made a point of praising Hannah's talent and apologising to her for any aspersions cast upon it. There was no explanation of why the playwright had withdrawn all his objections. His surrender was complete.

'This is wondrous,' said Hannah, returning the letter.

'It is, indeed,' he said, chortling. 'It's truly miraculous.'

* * *

Having seen so little of her husband all day, Charlotte was delighted when he came home that evening. When he told her of his plans, her delight turned to dismay.

'You and Paul are going to *Scotland*?' she asked.

'We'd go much farther for the chance to catch Rawdon Carr.'

'But you've no guarantee that he's actually heading there.'

'We have enough evidence to convince us.'

'What if you don't find him?'

'We'll keep searching until we do, Charlotte.'

'He's an evil man and he deserves to be brought to justice,' she said, 'but you seem to be taking such a risk, Peter. If he *is* aboard that boat, he has already stolen a march on you.'

'Sailing can be hazardous at the best of times,' he told her, 'and boats can easily be blown off course. Paul and I will travel overland and reach Edinburgh well ahead of them. As the two of them get off the boat, we will be waiting to arrest them for their part in the murder of Mr Bowerman and for a number of other crimes. Seeing the look of surprise on their faces,' he went on, 'will be ample reward for the effort it will have cost us.'

CHAPTER TWENTY

When he got to Bow Street early that morning, Micah Yeomans was still trying to wipe the sleep out of his eyes. A long night drinking at The Peacock had taken its toll. Alfred Hale was in slightly better shape. The summons had got him out of bed instantly. To the mutual disgust of the Runners, the chief magistrate was bright and alert. He seemed to be able to work for twenty-four hours a day without any sign of strain. When he explained why he'd summoned them, Kirkwood emphasised the need for speed and decisiveness.

'Strike quickly and strike hard,' he said.

'What exactly is in Mr Carr's letter, sir?' asked Yeomans.

'It's a denunciation both of Captain Hamer – who never actually held that rank, apparently – and of Miss Somerville. In reality, he is her brother.'

Yeomans goggled. 'That's *immoral*. He can't marry his own sister.'

'He had no intention of doing so. He simply pretended to be her suitor in order to provoke someone into challenging him into a duel that he knew he could win.' He held the letter out to Yeomans. 'Read it for yourself. It's important for you to know the full details of their villainy before you arrest them.'

Standing side by side, the Runners read the letter simultaneously. It drew gasps of amazement from both of them. They were embarrassed to recall how easily Laetitia had allayed their suspicions on the previous day with a series of plausible explanations. When they'd left her house, they'd actually apologised. Yet, they now learned, their earlier assessment of her had been quite accurate. She and Hamer were heartless criminals. When the letter was handed back to him, Kirkwood was contrite.

'I need to offer you both an apology,' he began. 'When you interrupted that duel and prevented Mr Bowerman from being shot dead, you had your suspicions of Hamer. In the wake of Bowerman's murder, you arrested him.'

'He would not have come here of his own accord, sir,' said Yeomans.

'And you released him,' recalled Hale.

'You released him and you reprimanded us.'

'That's why I'm tendering an apology to both of you,' said Kirkwood, almost choking on the words. 'You were right and I was wrong. You smelt corruption and I did not. If everything in this letter is true, Hamer and Miss Somerville are monsters. They may not have killed Bowerman but that was their intention when they trapped him into challenging Hamer to a duel.'

'Why is Mr Carr telling us all this?' asked Hale.

'You've read what he said. He wants to salve his conscience.'

'But he collaborated with them, sir.'

'We'll deal with him in due course,' said Kirkwood. 'What we have here is a damning indictment of two individuals with perverse ambitions and a ruthlessness to achieve them. I writhe in disgust at the notion of Miss Somerville inheriting the bulk of Mr Bowerman's property and wealth. It's unseemly.'

'And it's criminal,' said Yeomans.

'Arrest them both at once.'

'Yes, sir.'

'And be on your guard. Hamer is likely to put up a fight.'

'We'll go armed, sir, and show no mercy.'

'To be on the safe side,' said Hale, 'we'll take plenty of men. Mr Yeomans and I have been rebuffed by the two of them time and again. The tables are now turned in our favour.'

'We know the shocking truth about them now,' said Yeomans.

'And we have a huge advantage, Micah.'

'Do we?'

'Of course,' said Hale, airily. 'We can take them completely by surprise.'

Laetitia was aghast when she read the letter from Rawdon Carr. Her maid took it up to the boudoir where she was reclining on the bed. The moment she saw the opening paragraph, she leapt to her feet. She couldn't believe that she and her brother had been so comprehensively taken in by a man they thought was a true friend. Laetitia was shocked to learn that she was being punished for her rejection of Carr's suit. More astounding, however, was the news that Carr was speaking on behalf of himself and of Edith Loveridge, a woman supposedly dead. Looking back, she saw how cleverly Carr had persuaded them that Edith, reeling from the blow of being spurned by Hamer, had gone abroad and contracted a fatal disease. All the time, in fact, she was Rawdon Carr's partner and an accessory to the murder of Mark Bowerman.

It was several minutes before her head cleared enough for her to make a decision. Running to the door, she opened it wide and called for her manservant. He dashed upstairs as fast as he could.

'Go to Captain Hamer's house and bring him here at once.'

'Yes, Miss Somerville.'

'If he's not yet awake, rouse him out of his bed.'

'What shall I say?'

'Tell him that it's a matter of life and death.'

Expecting far more resistance from Hamer, the Runners went to his house first and deployed their men around it, impressing upon them that the former soldier would try to fight his way out. Yeomans and Hale approached the house warily. It held some uncomfortable memories for them but they now had a chance to expunge them. The chief magistrate's apology had given both of them a fillip. Their pride had been restored. Whichever way it developed, they felt capable of handling the situation.

Yeomans gave his friend the honour of ringing the bell then let his hand slip to the pistol concealed under his cloak. The door was soon opened by a servant.

'We've come to see your master,' said Yeomans, pushing past her.

'But the captain is not here, sir,' she said.

'Don't lie to me, girl. Where is he?'

'He left the house not ten or fifteen minutes ago.'

'I don't believe you.'

He signalled to some of his men and four of them came running. They searched the house with noisy thoroughness from top to bottom but they found no trace of Hamer. Yeomans rounded on Hale.

'What happened to the advantage of surprise?'

The sudden departure of the two brothers had thrown Charlotte and Hannah together. So excited was the actress to pass on the good tidings that she called on her friend before breakfast. Charlotte was thrilled to hear that rehearsals of the play would resume and that it had been changed largely in accordance with Hannah's wishes.

'Did your arguments finally prevail?' asked Charlotte.

'Something happened to change his mind.'

'He was so adamant at first.'

'I think he recognised that I have the stronger will.'

'Does that mean he'll attend rehearsals?'

'No,' replied Hannah, 'that was the other concession. Mr Mundy promised to stay away until the latter stages so that he wouldn't be tempted to interfere.'

'What did Mr Fleet have to say?'

'Had he been able to do so, I fancy that he'd have turned somersaults. He told me that he'd met with Mr Tregarne yesterday.'

Charlotte smiled. 'I had a feeling that *he* might be involved.'

'It's marvellous news,' said Hannah, 'and it will help to console me during Paul's absence. I slept in a very cold bed last night.'

'So did I, Hannah.'

'He told me that it was all in a good cause.'

'Peter used the same phrase to me. I still think that they're putting themselves to a great deal of effort on the basis of a hopeful supposition.'

'Paul's suppositions are usually proved right.'

'Scotland is so ridiculously far away.'

'If I was in Mr Carr's shoes, that's exactly the sort of place I'd choose. He's betrayed his friends. They'll want his blood. He needs to put hundreds of miles between himself and them.'

'I'm worried about the dangers they might meet on their way there.'

'Peter and Paul love danger,' said Hannah. 'When I first discovered that, I demanded that Paul should find a gentler way of life.'

'That's like ordering the sun not to shine.'

'I soon learnt that.' She glanced towards the dining room. 'Have you had breakfast yet?'

'No,' said Charlotte, 'and I'm famished. Do please join me. Afterwards, I suppose, you'll want me to accompany you on the piano at my house.'

Hannah laughed. 'How did you guess?'

Placed side by side on the table, the letters looked identical. Hamer pointed out the crucial difference. At the bottom of his missive the letter 'e' was written so faintly as to be almost invisible.

'Edith is showing off,' he said, ruefully. 'Rawdon wrote your letter and she copied it for my benefit. She has an extraordinary gift.'

'It's more like a supernatural power, Stephen. How many other women can come back from the grave and exact their revenge on someone? It's your fault, really. You didn't handle Edith properly.'

'I had no complaints at the time.'

'You dallied shamelessly with her when what she expected was marriage.'

'Rawdon had the same fantasies about you, Laetitia.'

'They were foolishly unrealistic. That's why I had to shun him.'

Stephen studied his letter. 'Can those investments of ours really be bogus?'

'We won't get a penny.'

'What about Bowerman's property?'

'That, too, is beginning to recede before my eyes,' she said. 'Paul Skillen knows about the terms of the will. He talked of contesting it.'

'Then he'll fail. It was made in good faith by a man who loved you.'

'I thought that Rawdon Carr loved me once.'

Their anger was intensified by the searing pain they both felt at being cheated. Large amounts of money on which they'd depended no longer existed. The person they'd willingly allowed to control events had proved to be treacherous and, worse, was in league with a woman who'd turned forgery into an art. Their whole world suddenly began to rock.

'What are we going to do, Stephen?'

'My first task is to go after Rawdon and kill him,' he said. 'He's not only duped us, he's mocking us for our stupidity. Edith is probably sniggering beside him at this very moment.'

'You don't know where they've gone.'

'I'll find out somehow, Laetitia. They're bound to have left a trail.'

'Are we in danger?'

'I don't think so.'

'What if Rawdon decides to betray us to the authorities?'

'Even *he* wouldn't stoop to that level.'

There was a tap on the door and a servant entered nervously.

'Excuse me for interrupting,' she said, 'but people are surrounding the house.'

'Who are they?' cried Laetitia.

Hamer ran to the window and peered out. He saw Yeomans and Hale with a dozen or more men in support. They were closing in on the house.

'It's the Runners!' he yelled.

Having slept fitfully all night, Abel Mundy and his wife lay side by side in silence. Neither of them dared to speak or had the urge to move. Though they were within inches of each other, they seemed far apart. When a window was shattered within feet of

Hannah Granville, he'd been moved to sympathise with her. It never crossed his mind as even a remote possibility that the person who threw the stone was his wife. Now that the truth had finally come into the open, Mundy had weathered the immediate shock and sought for an explanation of why she acted as she did.

It was his fault. His bitter feud with a capricious actress had brought him such patent misery that Marion, a woman of great kindness and forbearance, had been driven to administer punishment on his behalf. He couldn't blame her because it was he who was really culpable. Instead of bringing his worries home, he should have kept them to himself. In sharing his anguish with his wife, he'd painted Hannah Granville in the garish colours of a destructive madwoman.

When Marion eventually found her voice, it was only a meek whisper.

'Do you think that I should confess?'

'You've already done that before God.'

'The vicar said that I should tell the truth to Miss Granville.'

'That would be humiliating to you and upsetting to her. The incident is over and is already fading into the past. Now that the play is back in rehearsal, she has got what she wanted. I hated having to cede victory but it was unavoidable. Because of what you told me,' he went on, 'I had to make amends.'

'But it's your play, Abel. You shouldn't have to surrender it.'

'Part of me has done so willingly, my dear. To tell you the truth, some of the demands she made were very reasonable. It was her hostile manner that made me so defensive. Mr Tregarne endorsed her views. Between them,' he said, philosophically, 'they added to the strength of my play. I should be grateful for that.'

She stretched out a tentative hand. 'Do you forgive me?'

'I can do that easily, Marion. But there's someone I can't forgive.'

'Miss Granville?'

'No, my dear,' he said, penitently. 'I can't forgive myself for turning you from the true Christian you are into a vengeful harridan. That's a terrible thing for any man to do to his wife.'

Yeomans waved an arm and the ring tightened around the house. He could catch both of them together now, he thought, and return to Bow Street to bask in the approbation of the chief magistrate. When everyone was in position, he and Hale walked slowly up to the front door. After ringing the bell, he stood back, one hand fingering the butt of his pistol. The door was opened by a manservant. Thrusting him aside, Yeomans charged into the drawing room with Hale. They came to a sudden halt. Laetitia was sitting calmly in a corner, reading a book. She looked up with interest.

'Good morning, gentlemen,' she said. 'Did you want something?'

'We've come on police business, Miss Somerville,' said Yeomans, gruffly. 'You are under arrest.'

She arched her back. 'On what possible grounds, I pray?'

'Mr Carr has given us several to choose from. We've received a deposition from him regarding you and your brother.' She was startled into jumping to her feet. 'Yes, we know who and what he is now. Mr Carr's letter told us everything.'

'Rawdon Carr is a notorious liar,' she said.

'You'll be able to make that point in court.'

He nodded to Hale and the latter moved to stand beside Laetitia, holding her arm. Though she tried to shake him off, his grasp was too firm. Yeomans took the pistol from his belt.

'Where is your brother, Miss Somerville?' he asked.

'Stephen is not here.'

'Yes, he is. We've been to his house. He received a summons from you and rode here at a gallop. Where are you hiding him?'

'He left before you arrived,' she snapped.

'Take her out to the carriage, Alfred. I'll lead the search.'

Struggling in vain to get away, she was almost carried out into the street then shoved into a waiting carriage. Hale got in after her. Yeomans, meanwhile, called in four of his men and began a systematic search of the house. If Hamer was there, he reasoned, he was likely to be armed so Yeomans kept his weapon at the ready. The search, however, was fruitless. Since they'd been over every inch of the property with excessive care, they had to accept that Hamer was not there. Going back out into the street, Yeomans climbed into the carriage and it set off.

Stephen Hamer watched it from his hiding place behind one of the chimneys. It was a precarious refuge but it had helped him to evade arrest. The Runners had gone and the members of the foot patrol went after them. It would soon be possible to descend. While he was waiting, he wondered how he could possibly rescue his sister.

Peter and Paul Skillen had put urgency before comfort and travelled in a bumpy coach for most of the night. The recent dry spell of weather had left the roads hard and rutted, making the vehicle rock from side to side and, every now and then, plunge into a deep pothole that jarred every bone. It was not until they stopped for refreshment at a wayside tavern that they could talk properly. During the journey, the presence of other passengers had made any meaningful conversation well-nigh impossible. The privacy they now enjoyed was a relief.

Peter harboured doubts. 'This could be a calamitous mistake, Paul.'

'They're going to Scotland. I'm convinced of it.'

'That may be so but are they going there *directly*? What if they stop off for a few days here and there? Scarborough, for instance, would be one of many agreeable places to stay at this time of year. They might not get to their ultimate destination for weeks.'

'In that case, we wait for weeks.'

'That won't make us popular back at home.'

'You were away for longer periods during the war, Peter, and so was I. Are you prepared to let Carr and his accomplice commit murder and remain unpunished?'

'No, I'm not.'

'There's a secondary reason why you should want to arrest his accomplice and take her back to London. She'll be carrying the money she swindled from the bank.'

'I'd forgotten that. Mr Impey will be overjoyed if I return it to him. She was using the name of Hester Mallory at the time. I daresay that she's passing herself off as Mrs Carr at the moment.'

'She's an interesting lady. I look forward to meeting her.'

'So am I,' said Peter, looking up at the clock on the wall. 'Well, I know what Charlotte is doing at the moment. She'll have had breakfast and will be setting off for the gallery very soon.' He looked at his brother. 'What about Hannah?'

'She's so pleased that the play has been rescued that she won't even notice that I'm not there. When I took my leave of her last night, all she could talk about was the fact that rehearsals would start in earnest this morning.'

'It looks as if we'll both have to miss the first performance.'

'Don't give up hope. Carr's boat may reach Edinburgh sooner than you think,' said Paul. '*The Piccadilly Opera* has caused so much turmoil that I despaired of it ever being performed. Now that it will, I promised Hannah that I'd be there on the opening night and I fully intend to honour that promise.'

The sense of relief was palpable. As she walked into the room, the rest of the company not only gave her a round of applause, they rushed across to thank her individually. In their eyes, she'd saved the play and ensured that they'd be paid for its duration. Fleet explained to them what changes would be made and how they needed to extend the length of rehearsals in order to make up for lost time. None of the actors had a complete copy of the play. All they were given were the pages containing their respective scenes. It was only when they watched the drama unfold before them that they realised how radical some of the alterations had been. The play began to flower for the first time. Freed from the glowering presence of Abel Mundy, the actors felt able to breathe properly at last and it showed in their improved performances.

During a brief pause, Fleet took the opportunity to speak to Hannah.

'What do you think of the play now, Miss Granville?'

'It's a work of genius,' she replied.

'That's what I said from the very start.'

'Its genius was too well hidden, then. We've brought it out and let it shine. I'm so gratified that Mr Mundy finally saw the wisdom behind my criticism.'

'That isn't quite what happened,' said Fleet.

'Oh?'

'But it's close enough to the truth. Mr Tregarne's intervention was a great help to us and his ariettas will provide an additional sparkle to the play. However, I bought the rights to stage *The Piccadilly Opera* with you in mind, Miss Granville. I have every confidence that, in its new form, it will even win unstinting applause from the man who first conceived it.'

Laetitia had had to suffer the indignity of being squashed between the Runners as the carriage rolled towards Bow Street. Having woken up in a fragrant boudoir and been surrounded by domestic luxury, she'd been arrested by men whose breath stank and whose clothing smelt of the beer carelessly spilt over it. At a stroke, she'd lost her wealth, her position in society and her prospects. She was fearful that her life would be forfeit as well. When they reached Bow Street, she was formally charged and locked in a small, dank, fetid cell with barely room to move. It was insufferable.

Rawdon Carr, their friend and mentor, had been responsible for her arrest but his wickedness was too appalling to contemplate. She therefore fixed her thoughts on her brother. Her one hope was that he would somehow come to her rescue. He would certainly not let her down. As long as he was at liberty, there was a chance of escape for her. Holding her nose to keep out the stench, she perched on the rough stool in her cell and closed her eyes.

It was the best part of an hour before they came to fetch her. The cell door was unlocked and she was hustled along a corridor and into the chief magistrate's office by Yeomans and Hale. They made her stand in front of the desk while Kirkwood read out the letter he'd received from Carr. It made her pulse with fury. The charges against her and Stephen Hamer were all there, laid out in chronological sequence.

'What have you to say for yourself, Miss Somerville?' asked Kirkwood.

'That letter is nothing but a farrago of spite, hatred and lies,' she said.

'Given what my officers have told me, I'm inclined to believe every last word written here.'

'And will Mr Carr be in court to justify his calumny?'

'I'm not sure that he has to be. Certain facts are irrefutable.'

He was about to deliver his standard homily to a person guilty of serious crimes when he was diverted by the sound of a commotion outside. Crossing to the door, Kirkwood opened it wide, only to be knocked back into the room by the solid frame of Chevy Ruddock.

'I'm sorry, sir,' said Ruddock. '*He* made me do that.'

Held by his collar, he had a pistol pointed at his skull by Stephen Hamer.

'If anyone so much as moves,' warned Hamer, 'I'll blow his head apart. My sister is leaving with me right now. Stand back, all of you!'

The Runners flattened themselves against the wall and Kirkwood squirmed his way into a corner. None of them doubted that the newcomer would shoot if necessary, and they were all too aware that he had a second pistol thrust into his belt. After killing Ruddock, he'd shoot one of them as well.

Thrilled by her brother's daring, Laetitia ran to his side. They began to back out of the room with Ruddock as their hostage. After finding their way to the main door, they went out quickly. A gig was waiting for them. Hamer helped his sister into the vehicle then clambered up beside her, snatching up the whip in order to crack it. The moment that Ruddock was released, however, he came to life. Instead of letting them ride off, he jumped on the gig from behind and got an arm around Hamer's neck. There was a fierce struggle and Yeomans and Hale came out to watch it. Ruddock was bravely trying to wrest the pistol off Hamer. For her part, Laetitia was screaming abuse and using both fists to pound away at Ruddock. The Runners moved in swiftly. Hale grabbed the bridle so that the horse could not bolt and Yeomans joined the fight with Hamer. As the three of them twisted and turned and threshed away, the pistol suddenly went off and Hamer let out a howl of pain. He'd shot himself in the leg. Yeomans relieved him of the other weapon and dragged him uncaringly from the gig. Ignoring her imprecations, Ruddock soon overpowered the hysterical Laetitia.

The attempted rescue had failed. They were doomed.

The rehearsals were not always conducted in a spirit of jollity. There were inevitable setbacks. Minor squabbles broke out between actors, the scenery did not at first conform to the original designs and there was further upset when costumes didn't fit. Lemuel Fleet presided over it all with avuncular tolerance. The main thing was that the play itself had acquired real quality in its new form and the contribution of Benjamin Tregarne added a wonderful operatic sheen. Words and music blended perfectly throughout. It was a pleasure to take part in it.

'It's very tiring,' said Hannah, 'but, at the same time, very refreshing.'

'Don't tell me too much about it,' warned her friend, 'or there'll be no surprises left for me. Are you happy with the ariettas?'

'Oh, yes. No disrespect to you and your piano, Charlotte, but the songs are so much better when sung in the auditorium for which they were written.'

'Have you seen any sign of Mr Mundy?'

'We've not had a peep out of him.'

'He's keeping to his promise, then.'

'He's finally realised that we work best when he's not there.'

It was almost a week since rehearsals had started again and

they were dining together at Charlotte's house. They'd heard of the arrests of Stephen Hamer and Laetitia Somerville and were shocked to discover that they were siblings. Charlotte had saved a newspaper that carried a full report of their arrests.

'Peter will be so interested to read it,' she said. 'I know that we ridicule the Runners sometimes, but they have their triumphs just as we do.'

'My triumph will be on the stage in ten days. Paul swore to me that he'd be there on the first night to support me but he could be marooned in Scotland for ages.' Hannah clicked her tongue. 'Why did he have to go all that way?'

'He wants to catch Mr Carr – and so does Peter.'

'But they have no idea if and when he'll actually go to Edinburgh.'

'Paul is certain of it.'

'What about Peter?'

'He's less certain, to be honest,' admitted Charlotte, 'but he knows that his brother's instincts are usually very reliable.'

'I don't like what I heard about this Mr Carr. Paul says that he's a cold and calculating man. He's the one who stabbed Mr Bowerman in the back.'

'That tells us everything about him.'

'He's going to be slippery.'

'Mr Carr will be off guard,' said Charlotte. 'When he sailed from London, he was confident that he and his accomplice had escaped justice. Who would bother to go such a long distance in pursuit of him? That's what he'll ask.'

'And he'll get his answer,' said Hannah.

The voyage had been relatively untroubled. As the boat sailed up the coast, they got a fascinating view of the geography of their

314

country. The captain put into port now and then to buy supplies and to give his passengers the opportunity to feel dry land beneath their feet for a while. Then the vessel was soon on its way again. Expecting some discomfort, Carr and Edith were surprised by how well they felt. Their appetites were unimpaired and they remained in good health.

'How much further is it, Rawdon?'

'The captain says that we should dock early in the morning.'

'Would that be Captain Hamer?' she asked with a teasing smile.

'No, it's the skipper of this boat, as you know only too well. In any case, Stephen was never really a captain, remember. The court martial disposed of that ambition. It meant that he was blackballed at his club so came as a guest to mine.'

'Where do you think he and Laetitia are?'

'They'll be awaiting sentence,' said Carr, complacently. 'The letter I sent to the chief magistrate was their death warrant. They're no threat to us now.'

'And what about those other men you told me about – the twins?'

'Their names are Peter and Paul Skillen and they were embarrassingly clever. I'm glad we've sailed away from their clutches. Their chances of catching us are non-existent because they don't have the slightest idea where we're going.'

Neither of them was temperamentally suited to a long, tedious wait but it had to be endured. For day after day, Peter and Paul had lurked in the harbour and watched vessels coming in or setting sail. Even at night they didn't relinquish their surveillance. Taking it in turns to stay on sentry duty, they checked each boat that docked in the darkness. As a new day dawned, they were seated beside the Firth of Forth once again. Peter was fretful.

'It's a crying shame,' he said. 'Carr was right to say that this is a beautiful city but we've had no time at all to appreciate it. All that we've seen is water lapping the wharves as the fishing boats bring in their catch.'

'It's only a matter of time, Peter.'

'You've been saying that for days.'

'I say it and I believe it. They'll come soon, mark my words.'

'Edinburgh's a fine place but some say that Glasgow will soon be bigger. What if Carr decides to go there instead?'

'*This* is where he was born,' said Paul, 'and this is where he'll come.'

Buoyed up yet again by his brother's certainty, Peter returned to his vigil. They'd come prepared. They'd brought a telescope with them. Since they'd been in Scotland, it had enabled them to study boat after boat as it approached.

The first gestures of day slowly gave way to a rising blanket of light. As their eyes scanned the water, they saw two vessels heading their way. The larger was clearly a fishing smack and, even from that distance, they could pick out members of the crew moving about the deck. The second boat was the one that interested them. By using the telescope, Paul could see a man standing on the deck with his arm around a woman. He handed the instrument to his brother.

'What can you see?'

Peter peered through the telescope. 'They're here at last!'

Legs braced against the swell, Rawdon Carr was pointing out some of the distinctive silhouettes of Edinburgh. He was thrilled to be back in his home town again. Edith listened to him patiently but there was far too much information to take in at once. What she was looking forward to was stepping off the boat for the last time.

The excitement of the early stages of the voyage had palled and she needed something more stable beneath her feet. Because the boat was moving at only a moderate speed, there was plenty of time to admire their new home. Carr had told her so much about Edinburgh that she couldn't wait to explore it. When the boat finally reached the wharf, it bounced against the timbers. While one of the crew tossed a rope, another jumped nimbly ashore to secure it to a bollard. When a second rope was in place, the vessel was safely moored. Carr and Edith thanked the captain and left a generous tip for him and his crew. They were then helped carefully off the boat.

A few carriages stood nearby. Two men in large hats and long capes stepped forward to pick up the luggage that was unloaded from the boat. They carried it up to the vehicle at the front of the queue. Opening the door and keeping his head down, one of the men helped Edith into the carriage then stood back so that Carr could climb in beside her. The couple looked weary but contented. Holding hands they sat back in their seats. As he barked an order, Carr was imperious.

'Take us to the Grand Hotel!'

'Oh, we'll take you much further than that,' said Paul, removing his hat and grinning at them through the open door. 'Welcome to Edinburgh, Mr Carr! I've been waiting for you.'

Carr was horror-struck. 'How the devil did *you* get here?'

'My brother came with *me*,' said Peter, opening the other door and doffing his hat. He smiled courteously at Edith. 'I'm pleased to meet you, Miss Loveridge,' he went on. 'I bring you greetings from Mr Impey, though he knew you as Mrs Mallory, of course. He'll be thrilled to attend your trial in London.'

'What's going on, Rawdon?' she cried. 'Who *are* these men?'

But Carr was unable to muster an answer. The plan he'd so

carefully drawn up had just vanished before his eyes. He offered a token resistance by trying to push Paul aside and get out of the vehicle but he was easily punched back into his seat. All that Carr would get was a fleeting glimpse of his birthplace before he was taken back to London to meet his death.

Fired by the promise of an exciting new play and the opportunity of hearing songs written by Benjamin Tregarne, people came in droves to watch the first performance. All seats had been sold and the auditorium was buzzing with anticipatory pleasure. Peter and Charlotte had the privilege of sitting with the composer and with Lemuel Fleet in the manager's box. Paul preferred to be in the pit so that he could be close to Hannah. Abel Mundy and his wife stayed at the rear, nursing their misgivings. When a fanfare sounded, the hubbub died down slightly and *The Piccadilly Opera* made its first appearance before an audience.

It was a sensation. The plot had been tightened, the characters defined more sharply and the humour scattered more freely throughout the play. Tregarne's ariettas were inspiring, each one greeted by an ovation. Costumes and scenery were superb, flooding the stage with colour and drawing gasps of wonder. The real surprise was Hannah Granville. Those who'd marvelled at her in tragic roles now realised that she had comedic talent of the highest order and a voice of operatic power. Following her lead, the cast surpassed themselves. A new play had been transformed from its earlier version into a brilliant piece of theatre. When it met thunderous acclaim at the end, nobody clapped louder than the playwright himself. Applause signalled acceptance. In the course of the evening, against all his earlier predictions, he'd become famous.

Back at Paul's house, celebrations went on long into the night.

He, Hannah, Peter and Charlotte toasted the success of the evening. It had obliterated all the problems that had bedevilled the play at the start. Everyone involved had been beneficiaries of an unqualified triumph.

'Before long,' said Paul, introducing a sombre note, 'another performance will take place and it's one that can never be repeated. There'll be no love story and no songs when Rawdon Carr and Edith Loveridge step onto the scaffold.'

'There will, however, be a baying mob,' said Peter.

Hannah grimaced. 'I think such a spectacle is grotesque.'

'I couldn't agree with you more,' said Charlotte, sadly. 'Both of them deserve to be executed for their crimes but it shouldn't take place in public.'

'Yes, it should,' argued Paul. 'It sends out a grim warning. I'm proud that Peter and I brought the pair of them back to London to answer for their crimes. They showed no pity for their victims and they deserve none themselves.'

'That sounds rather harsh.'

'It's meant to be, Charlotte. What we saw this evening was one of the finest entertainments ever put before a London audience and Hannah must be feted for what she did on that stage. It was pure magic. If I hadn't loved her already,' he went on, leaning across to kiss her, 'I'd have been bewitched by her. Yet the truth is that it was all make-believe in front of painted scenery. The execution will be an example of *real* drama. Peter and I are its co-authors. In a city as beset by crime as London, I'm afraid that it won't be the last time we have to take up our pens.'

THE
HONEY
GUIDE

RICHARD CROMPTON

Weidenfeld & Nicolson

LONDON

First published in Great Britain in 2013
by Weidenfeld & Nicolson
An imprint of the Orion Publishing Group
Orion House, 5 Upper St Martin's Lane,
London WC2H 9EA

An Hachette UK Company

1 3 5 7 9 10 8 6 4 2

The story 'The Origin of Death' is based on an excerpt from
Oral Literature of the Maasai by Naomi Kipury, reproduced with the
kind permission of East African Educational Publishers Limited, Nairobi.

All the characters in this book are fictitious,
and any resemblance to actual persons living
or dead is purely coincidental.

A CIP catalogue record for this book
is available from the British Library

978 0 297 86795 1 (cased)
978 0 297 86796 8 (trade paperback)

Typeset by Input Data Services Ltd, Bridgwater, Somerset

Printed and bound in Great Britain
by Clays Ltd, St Ives plc

The Orion Publishing Group's policy is to use papers that are
natural, renewable and recyclable products and made from wood
grown in sustainable forests. The logging and manufacturing
processes are expected to conform to the environmental
regulations of the country of origin.

www.orionbooks.co.uk

For Katya

Foreword

This novel is set in the run-up to, and the immediate aftermath of, the Kenyan election of 27 December 2007.

Amid claims of vote-rigging from both sides, the incumbent president, Mwai Kibaki, was sworn in on 30 December, sparking protests and violence across the whole country.

Some of the worst violence was seen amid the slums of the capital, where long-standing ethnic tensions rose to the surface.

This book is a work of fiction. The timeline is accurate, and most of the locations are real. But it is not intended to be a factual portrayal of events. Rather, it is an attempt to capture the spirit, energy and courage of this remarkable city, Nairobi, which I call my home.

It is thought that between 800 and 1,500 Kenyans lost their lives in the post-electoral violence. Countless others lost their homes and livelihoods, and experienced terror and deprivation. This book is a tribute to the memory of those who perished and to the resourcefulness of those who survived.

The Origin of Death

In the beginning there was no death. This is the story of how death came into the world.

There was once a man known as Leeyio, who was the first man that Naiteru-kop brought to earth. Naiteru-kop then called Leeyio and said to him: 'When a man dies and you dispose of the corpse, you must remember to say, "Man die and come back again, moon die, and remain away."'

Many months passed before anyone died. When, in the end, a neighbour's child did die, Leeyio was summoned to dispose of the body. When he took the corpse outside, he made a mistake and said: 'Moon die and come back again, man die and stay away.' So after that no man survived death.

A few more months elapsed, and Leeyio's own child died. So the father took the corpse outside and said: 'Moon die and remain away, man die and come back again.' On hearing this, Naiteru-kop said to Leeyio: 'You are too late now, for, through your own mistake, death was born the day when your neighbour's child died.' So that is how death came about, and that is why up to this day when a man dies he does not return, but when the moon dies, it always comes back again.

Traditional Maasai story

1

The sun is at the vertical, and shade is as scarce as charity on Biashara Street. Where it exists – in shopfronts and alleyways, like cave mouths and canyons – life clings: eyes blink; and patiently, they watch.

They see a man and a boy walking along the sidewalk, the boy adjusting his stride every third or fourth step to a skip to match his companion's rangy stride.

The man, in concession, has stooped slightly to maintain a conversational height. Their posture suggests that if either reached out a hand, the other would grasp it – but that for their own reasons, neither will offer. They are father and son.

—But where would you ride it? the father asks wearily. It's evidently a long-running conversation.

—Anywhere! says the boy. I could go to the shops for you.

—Adam, this is Nairobi. You go out on your own on a bike, you're going to get killed. Have you seen the drivers here?

—Then around the compound. Grandma's house. It's safe there. Michael's got a bike. And Imani, too, and she's only seven.

The tall man pauses in his stride and the boy runs into the back of his legs. Something has disturbed him: immediate, palpable, yet indefinable. The sense of trouble about to strike.

Just for once, thinks Mollel, just for *once*, I'd like to turn off this instinct. Be able to enjoy going shopping, enjoy spending

3

time with my son. Be a member of the public, instead of a policeman.

But he can't. He is what he is.

—That's the one I want! says Adam, pointing at the shop window.

Mollel is vaguely aware of a display of bicycles inside, but he is watching the reflection suspended upon the glass. A group of teenage girls, all gossip and gum, mobile phones wafting like fans, handbags slung over shoulders like bandoliers. And from the shadows, other eyes – hungry now – emerging. Watching without watching, getting closer without moving in, the men nonchalant yet purposeful, disparate yet unified, circling their prey: hunting dogs.

—Go inside the shop, Mollel tells Adam. Stay there till I come back for you.

—Can I choose a bike, Dad? Really?

—Just stay there, says Mollel, and he pushes the boy through the store's open door. He turns: it's happened already. The group of men are melting away: the girls are still oblivious to what has just taken place. He clocks one of the guys walking swiftly from the scene, stuffing a gold vinyl clutch bag – *so not his style* – under his shirt.

Mollel takes off, matching the hunting dog's pace but keeping his distance, eager not to spook him. No point in letting him bolt into a back street now. Pace up a beat, narrow the gap. Quit Biashara Street. Cross Muindi Mbingu. Weave through traffic – ignore the car horns. Busier here.

The hunting dog is in his late teens or early twenties, judges Mollel. Athletic. His shirt has the sleeves cut off at the shoulders, not to expose his well-developed arms, but to ease its removal. The buttons at the front will be fake, Mollel knows, replaced with a strip of Velcro or poppers to confound any attempt to grab the bag-snatcher's collar, leaving the pursuer holding nothing more than a raggedy shirt like a slipped snakeskin.

While he weighs his strategy – a dive to the legs rather than a clutch at the torso – Mollel realises the thief is heading for the city market. Got to close the gap now. Lose him in there, he's gone for good.

Taking up an entire city block, and with more ways in and out than a hyrax burrow, on a day like this the market's dark interior is thronged with shoppers escaping the sun. Mollel considers yelling *Stop, Mwezi!* or *Police!* – but calculates this would lose him precious time. The thief leaps up the steps and deftly vaults a pile of fish guts, pauses a moment to look back – showing, Mollel thinks, signs of tiring – and dives into the dark interior. Mollel's gaunt frame is just a few seconds behind, heart pounding, gulping lungfuls of air with relish, even as his stomach rebels at the powerful reek of fish. He hasn't done this for a while. And he is enjoying it.

It takes his eyes a moment to adjust. At first all he can see are tall windows high overhead, shafts of light like columns. Noise fills in what eyes cannot see: the hubbub of negotiation and exchange, the squawking of chickens, the multitudinous laughter and chatter and singing and hustle and bustle of life.

And amongst that hustle and bustle – a bustle, a hustle, that should not be there. He sees it now, as well as hears it, just a few stalls ahead. Figures tumbling, voices raised in protest. His quarry.

Through a gap in the crowd, Mollel sees the thief. He's scattering people and produce behind him in an attempt to obstruct his pursuer. No point going down that aisle. He looks left and right, plumps for right, rounds a stall and starts to run down a parallel row. Although he's keeping up with his prey, Mollel's not going to catch him this way. Ahead, he sees sacks of millet stacked loosely against one of the stalls. It's his chance. He bounds up, one, two, and is atop the stall, balancing on the boards which bound the grain.

A howl of protest rises from the woman behind the stall, swiping at his legs with her scoop. —Get down from there! But he is already gone, leaping to the next stall, hoping the rickety wood will take his weight – it does – and run, leap, again – it does.

A better view from here, and a clearer run – despite the efforts of stallholders to push him, grab him, drag him to earth. He rises above the hands, above the stalls, intent only on the pursuit.

The fresh, clean smell of peppers and onions cuts through the dusty dryness of millet. Easier to negotiate. He bounds across the stacked vegetables, skipping, skimming, recalling chasing goats across mountain scree when he was a child. Momentum is everything. Each footstep expects you to fall: cheat it. Be gone.

Outraged yells fill his ears but he feels as if the great hall has fallen silent: there is no one in it but him and the fleeing man. Distance between them measured in heartbeats: arm's reach; finger's grasp.

And then he is out of the door.

Mollel suddenly finds himself standing on the final stall, surrounded by furious faces. They barrack him and block him; hands reach for his ankles. He sees the back of the thief's head about to melt into the crowd outside the market. He sweeps his arm down; feels hair and hardness – coconuts – beneath his feet. Another goat-herding trick: if the animal is out of reach, throw something at it.

The coconut is out of his hand before he even thinks about it. It describes a shallow parabola, over the heads of the stallholders, through the square, bright doorway. He even hears the crack, and relaxes. He has time now to produce his card and clear the way to the doorway, where a circle has formed.

The crowd is now eager, anticipatory. The rear doorway of the city market is inhabited by butchers' stalls, and the metallic smell of blood is in the air.

They part before him, and Mollel steps into the ring. The thief is on his knees, gold handbag dropped to the ground, one hand dazedly rubbing the back of his head. The smashed coconut has already been snatched by a pair of children, front of the circle, who suck on the sweet flesh and grin at Mollel. Free food and a floor show. What more could you want?

—You're coming with me, says Mollel. The thief does not respond. But he staggers groggily to his feet.

—I said, says Mollel, you're coming with me. He steps forward and takes the thief by his upper arm. It is wider than Mollel can grasp and as hard as rock. He hopes the guy's going to remain concussed long enough to drag him downtown. If only he had cuffs—

—and then the arm wheels away from his, Mollel just having time to step back to take a little force out of the blow which lands on the side of his head. No concussion – the faintness feigned – the thief now alert and springing on his heels. A lunge – missed – at Mollel. The crowd cheers. He is strong but top-heavy, this fighter, and the policeman judges that a swift shoulder-ram would push him once more to the ground. Mollel seizes his chance, head down, body thrown at his opponent's chest, but he misjudges the timing, and the thief parries him easily. Mollel feels a sharp, agonising pain in his head – everywhere – stabbing and yanking, the pain of capture, and of submission.

His opponent laughs, and a roar of approval comes from the crowd. No partisans, these. Mollel feels his head jerked from side to side, up and down. There is nothing he can do.

—I have you now, Maasai, laughs the thief.

He has put his thumbs through Mollel's earlobes.

The bane of his life, those earlobes. Long and looped, the flesh stretched since childhood to now fall below his jawline, the *i-maroro* are a mark of pride and warriorhood within Maasai circles – but an object of ridicule and prejudice elsewhere. He knows many Maasai who have had the loops removed, but somehow the stumps sing of regret to him, and their ears seem just as conspicuous as his own.

One advantage, though: no one is going to grab them by the ears. The crowd are in near-hysterical laughter: he can expect no help from that quarter. They have never seen a policeman led by his ears before, like a bull with a ring through his nose. Even the

7

thief, his face now leering at arms' length, seems hardly able to believe his luck.

—All right, so this is what we're going to do, Maasai, he says. We're going to walk together, slowly, out on to K-Street. I'm not going to rip your pretty ears off. And you're not going to come after me. If you've got it, nod your head. Oh, I'm sorry, you can't, can you? Would you like me to nod it for you? Yeah, that's right!

Quite a comedian, this one, thinks Mollel, his head being tugged up and down. The thief enjoys the audience. He even swaggers somewhat as he holds the policeman captive – glancing at the crowd, enjoying his moment of fame. Let him, thinks Mollel. Means he won't be ready for what I'm about to do.

What he does – brutally, swiftly – evinces a sympathetic groan from all the men in the watching crowd. They have no illusions about what a size-ten police-issue steel-capped boot can achieve when brought into such intimate contact with its target.

Almost tenderly, the thief lets go of Mollel's ears. His eyes look into the policeman's with a look of heartbreak and agony. This time, Mollel knows he'll have no problems bringing him in.

2

—If this was *China*, the Chinese woman sobs, we not mess around. We get this sorted out!

—Well, it's not China, says the desk sergeant. This is Kenya. Here, we do things *properly*. He licks the tip of his ballpoint and starts writing in a large ledger. Work permit number?

—This not about me, this about my landlord! He take my money and change the locks! Who am I supposed to sleep with tonight, huh?

In the general merriment caused by this statement, Mollel catches the desk sergeant's eye over the heads of the throng. He is glad it is Keritch – no awkward questions. He just gets a quizzical look as the desk flap is lifted to allow him through. As Mollel leads his prisoner down the corridor to CID, he hears Keritch sighing once more: Work permit number? And has *anyone* got a pen that works?

Central Police Post. It's a long time since he's been here. Nothing's changed. The smell is of sweat and fresh paint – it's easier to paint the walls every couple of years than clean them daily. The single-storey building was once a homestead, and now sits dwarfed by the massive modern buildings around it. It's a sleepy, rustic image totally at odds with the constant activity within, presenting an aspiration of a Nairobi benignly overseen by one colonial-era bobby on a bicycle: which was probably the case when it was built. And it couldn't be farther from the truth, today.

—Well, well. Maasai. Brought a gift for us, I see?

Mollel directs the prisoner into the CID office. Decrepit office furniture and overflowing filing cabinets are squeezed into what was obviously once a bedroom. Mwangi sits at his same old desk, feet up, reading the *Daily Nation*. Grizzled, cynical, slightly greyer of moustache. Mollel approaches and flicks up the front page.

—What are you doing?

—Checking the date. It's the only way I can tell whether you've *moved* for two years.

—I wouldn't be so sure, says a younger man. Shirtsleeves, eating a *sambusa*, policeman's moustache on the way. He has it delivered to his desk these days.

—Mollel, meet Kiunga. My new partner, says Mwangi. And believe it or not, Kiunga, this Maasai used to be my partner, too.

—I've heard about you, says Kiunga, neutrally.

—*Everyone's* heard about him, says Mwangi. Question is, what is he doing back at Central? Last I heard, he'd been busted down to traffic duty in Loresho.

Kiunga laughs. —Is there any traffic in Loresho?

—There's a job to be done, replies Mollel. Overcrowded *matatus*, out-of-date tax discs. The occasional donkey-rage incident.

—And now you've brought us Oloo, says Mwangi, looking at the prisoner. The boss *will* be pleased.

—You know this guy?

—Oh, we know Oloo. Nice handbag, by the way, he says to the thief.

—What the hell is *he* doing here? thunders a voice from the back of the office. Mwangi casts Mollel a scathing glance and slowly lowers his feet to the ground. Oloo, the prisoner, visibly relaxes.

Otieno, the head of Central CID, has entered.

—I thought I told you I didn't want to see *him* in here again! he barks.

He is an imposing man, tall and massive, his round, blunt head retreating into his thick neck. His inky-dark skin is pocked and the colour bleeds into the whites of his eyes, which are stained like walnuts. Otieno, a Luo, in a profession dominated by Kikuyus, has developed a hide as thick as that of the ox he resembles, and a reputation for being just as stubborn.

—It wasn't us, boss, coughs Mwangi. It was our Maasai friend here.

Otieno turns to Mollel, seeing him for the first time. The wide face breaks into a dazzling grin – the last response Mollel had expected.

—There is an old Luo saying, says Otieno, slapping Mollel heartily on the back, that an unwelcome visitor brings good cheer. They mean, of course, when he leaves. But this time, this time, my unwelcome friend, you might just be able to help me out. Get rid of this nobody and I'll tell you all about it.

—I've got to charge him first, says Mollel. Robbery and resisting arrest.

Mwangi and Kiunga exchange a glance.

Otieno's grin disappears. He takes the gold handbag from Mollel and rifles through it.

—Mobile phone, purse, tampons, cigarettes ... he holds up an ID card. Amazing how careless some people can be with their valuables. Thank goodness there are good, honest citizens like Mr Oloo here, prepared to hand in lost property.

Now it is Oloo's turn to grin. —My pleasure, he says smugly. Now if you don't mind, Officers, I think I'll be on my way.

—But, boss! protests Mollel.

—But, nothing! Right now I'm running the best figures in Central Division since the nineties. Robbery is down eight per cent. You think I'm going to let a little *mavwi* like this mess up my statistics? Ask your buddies here.

Mwangi and Kiunga look at Mollel with resignation.

—Yeah, butts in Oloo. That's right. So, about this lost property, then. Where do I get my reward?

Otieno laughs a hearty, jovial laugh. Then, still smiling, he raises his fist like a shovel, and slams it into the thief's face.

—*There's* your reward.

Oloo is on the floor, blood gushing from his broken nose. Otieno turns to Mwangi and Kiunga.

—That was just to prove to you Kikuyus that there's no tribal favouritism going on. Mwangi, get him out of here. Kiunga, get the pool car. We're taking the Maasai on a little drive.

The police Land Rover weaves through the Nairobi traffic. Kiunga manages the jam with a young man's confidence, squeezing the vehicle into gaps with inches to spare, overtaking other cars on both sides, mounting the sidewalk when necessary.

—You never learned to drive, then, Mollel? Kiunga calls back, as he pushes the car into the narrowing canyon formed by two Citi Buses.

—No, replies Mollel. Did you?

Otieno, in the front passenger seat, gives a booming laugh.
—That's why you ended up in traffic division. It was *someone's* idea of a joke.

Yes, and Mollel knows whose. Still, if Otieno wants him along for the ride today, he must have something interesting in store.

They pull off the Uhuru Highway and on to Kenyatta Avenue, past the Serena Hotel, where Otieno barks some directions and Kiunga pulls an illegal U-turn on to the other carriageway. They push through the opposing traffic, Kiunga pointing a warning at an irate *matatu* driver, Otieno retaining his bulky composure. Then, up a kerb, and off the road: between two concrete bollards that Mollel thinks they couldn't possibly fit through – but they do – and into Uhuru Park.

Uhuru Park: Nairobi's playground. Named after freedom, but also granting it: a little freedom from the sprawl and the spread and the spleen of the city. Being Saturday, it is busy. People lying on the grass dotted in groups – families picnicking, lovers discreetly loving – or singly, people with nowhere else to go or a few hours to kill, sleeping on the ground. A larger group is stood in a circle, holding hands. They all wear the same red T-shirts: a prayer meeting. Vendors of sodas, nuts and ice cream push their wagons lazily down the paths – only to dive out of the way as the Land Rover bears down upon them.

They drive past the area known as Little Mombasa. In his forty-two years, Mollel has been to some extraordinary places, but he has never been to the Kenyan coast. He surmises, though, that the real Mombasa has a bit more going for it than a shallow boating lake and a paddling pool. The place is popular enough – but seems to be losing custom to a new attraction over towards the rear of the park, where the ground slopes steeply away from the city and eventually becomes Upper Hill.

The car draws to a halt by the mass of people, and the instant Kiunga cuts the engine, Mollel knows what they're going to find. The only time a group of Kenyans en masse is quiet like this, is when there's a body.

They descend from the car and push their way through the strangely reverent mob, towards the mess of chain-link fence and barbed wire which marks the boundary of the park. It seems far removed from the peaceful, green interior. As they draw to the front, Mollel sees a drainage culvert, some four feet deep, and a couple of uniformed city cops keeping a desultory eye on the crowd, who are all looking into the ditch.

Beyond them, standing in the concrete culvert but barely clearing the top, is Dr Achieng.

—Ah, Otieno. And you've brought your pet Maasai with you, I see. Good thinking. Been a long time, Mollel.

—You not retired yet? Mollel asks the old man.

—Can't afford to. I thought *you'd* disappeared.

Otieno butts in: —From your description of the body, I thought it would be useful to *re*appear him. What have we got, a termite?

Termite: Nairobi police vernacular for a body washed out of the storm drains after a heavy bout of rain, the way white ants are flushed from a flooded nest.

—Could be. Rain was probably heavy enough last night to bring her some distance. That could account for a lot of the impact wounds. Unless she was dead before she entered the drain.

Achieng beckons to Mollel. —Come, take a look. Tell me if our hunch was right.

Mollel takes the pathologist's small hand and steps down into the ditch. The steep concrete banks slope to a flat bottom about a metre wide, along which a further rill of just a few inches deep runs, to keep water flowing in dry times. There is barely a trickle now, despite the rains of some few hours earlier: such is Nairobi weather. Mollel places his feet either side of the body, which is laid on its side partially in the central rill, its spine curved into an impossible contortion: a non-recovery position.

She is wearing a flimsy dress, torn and blackened with mud, but expensive-looking nonetheless. It has ridden up above her waist. There is no underwear. Smears of blood and mud snake back across her thighs.

—You'll see that she has many wounds on the body, most of them consistent with a beating, says Achieng. But there appears to be considerable bleeding from between the legs. Have to turn her over in a moment to see more.

Mollel follows the line of the body's curvature; one arm unseen below the corpse, the other tossed upwards and above the head.

—Let me move this, says Achieng, lifting the arm. Are you ready to see the face?

Mollel nods. Achieng uses the arm to pull and pivot the corpse on to its back.

Mollel finds himself looking down at a young, oval face; the ashen greyness would have been a brilliant bluey dark in life. High cheekbones, high forehead. Noble. On either cheek, a small, low 'O' had been engraved, a long time since.

It is a familiar face. He does not recognise the person, but he knows the people: his own.

—Yes, she's Maasai, he says.

—Thought so. I'm not familiar with all tribal scars but those looked typically Maasai to me. Can you tell which clan?

—Not really. It's a commonplace enough marking. Could be from the west: Sikirari. Matapato. But I'm confused about the ears.

—The ears? I didn't see anything remarkable.

—Exactly. They should be looped, like mine. Probably pierced at the top, too. But look at her lobes. There's only a small hole, for fashion jewellery. She's got the cheek scars which are given at childhood, but not the ear loops, which Maasai girls get given at puberty. So it could be that she left her village before that time.

—Could be.

—No ID, I suppose?

—What you see, says Achieng, is what you get. Now, I want to move her, see if my suspicions are correct.

He beckons to a policeman near by, who joins them in the culvert. The pathologist motions for the policeman to grab the girl's ankles. Her lower body is still twisted, and with some difficulty, they straighten the legs.

A dismayed gasp goes up from the watching crowd.

—Oh, God, says Mollel.

He's seen plenty over the years. More dead bodies than he cares to think about. Blood, guts. But this is something else.

Achieng comes round to join him at the feet of the body.

—Vicious, he says. Looks like someone's taken a knife to her genitals. Brutally, too.

There is some commotion among the onlookers: someone has fainted.

—Get those people out of here! shouts Otieno. Even he, under his dark complexion, looks shocked. What do you think this is, a circus?

The uniformed policemen step forward and begin to disperse the crowd.

—Do you know anything about female circumcision, Mollel? asks Achieng, quietly.

—I know it's not like this, Mollel replies.

—Maybe not as brutal. But among Maasai, it means removal of the clitoris, doesn't it?

Mollel nods. —*E-muruata*. I've never seen it done, myself. Men are strictly forbidden from the ceremony. But yes, teenage girls have their clitoris removed, by a female elder. It's illegal now. But it still happens, of course.

—You say it's usually done at puberty? Like the ear loops?

—Yes.

—Maybe she never had it done as a girl, and someone was trying to put that right, mutters Otieno.

—I'll have to look more closely during the post-mortem examination. But it looks like that's what happened here. Certainly, no care was taken for the health of the patient. I'm pretty sure this is what killed her.

—Right, says Otieno. If you're done, Doctor, let's get this body taken to the City Mortuary. File it under *Unknown Maasai Prostitute*.

—What makes you think she was a prostitute? asks Mollel angrily.

—Be realistic, Mollel, replies Otieno. They always are.

3

—I'll get you a secondment back here to Central, Otieno says as the body is put into the back of the unmarked mortuary ambulance. A week or so should do it. Let's say ten days. I want this wrapped up quickly, Maasai. You can ask around. Talk to the hookers who work this patch. But also, follow this lead about it being a Maasai circumcision ceremony gone wrong.

—Gone wrong! I don't think we can put this down to accidental death. It's deliberate murder.

—Maybe. In the meantime, you can have Kiunga here to drive you around. Unless you want to borrow a bike.

A bike... the word nags at Mollel's memory. Something important, to do with a bike.

Adam!

His chest constricts. He'd slipped so easily back into the role of policeman that he'd forgotten about being a father. He grabs Kiunga's arm.

—I need you right now, he says. We have to go to Biashara Street.

—That's why I love you, Maasai, calls Otieno as Mollel pulls Kiunga towards the Land Rover. The case has just begun and you've got a lead already. See you back at the station.

As they pull on to Biashara Street, Mollel feels his pulse quickening and panic rising. It is gone one o'clock: on a Saturday, that means most stores are shutting up for lunch – many for the weekend. With the street emptied and the storefronts couched behind their blank steel shutters, Mollel has difficulty even locating the shop. When he does, he sees the shutter is left open a few inches, darkness within. He orders Kiunga to stop the car and he leaps out, rushes to the shutter and bangs on it furiously.

—Go away! We're closed! says a voice from within.

—My boy. I left my boy here. About an hour ago. I was only going to be a few minutes…

—There's no boy here.

—Are you sure he's not behind a display or something? Even asleep? I told him not to leave until I came back.

—Look – the shutter comes up a few more inches and the Indian storekeeper sticks his head out – there is no boy here. There *was* a small lad here who said he was waiting for his father, but I kicked him out. What do you think I am, a child-minding service?

—Which way did he go? But the shutter thunders down and Mollel hears the clanking of a lock within. He slams his fist against the steel.

—Dad!

It is Adam, and Mollel's breath catches with relief. Despite the heat, he shivers: he suddenly realises that he is drenched in sweat.

—I waited and waited, but you didn't come back!

—Good job he knows his grandmother's phone number, says Faith.

Adam has his hand firmly in Faith's. In the other hand he holds a rapidly melting ice cream.

Faith gives Mollel a look he's become familiar with over the years: a mixture of pity and contempt. Contempt seems to be winning out this time.

—The man in the shop wouldn't let me use his phone, continues Adam. But a lady in the shop next door did. Grandma came to collect me.

—Thanks, Faith, says Mollel sheepishly. It was police business.

—It's always police business, says Faith.

—Grandma says I can go home with her.

—I think that's for the best, says Faith. To Adam, she says: Give your father a hug.

The two of them look at each other awkwardly. It's not a natural gesture for either of them. Then Mollel bends to receive the hug, which makes him glow despite the cold ice cream to the neck.

—Thanks for the bike, Dad, whispers Adam in his ear. I know I wasn't supposed to find out about it until Christmas. But Grandma let slip.

Mollel stands. Faith casts him a challenging glance: he returns it, but softens. She is right. Better for the boy to have something to look forward to rather than dwell on being abandoned by his only parent. Mollel would never be able to say truthfully that he *liked* his mother-in-law. But she loves Adam, and for that reason alone, he is silent when she says:

—You have got to remember where your priorities lie, Mollel.

Kiunga is shaking hands with Adam now. The boy has taken an instant liking to his colleague, and is chatting freely about school.

—You've always had a powerful sense of justice, Faith continues. That's why Chiku loved you. I admired you for it, myself. But there's a difference, Mollel, between justice, and what's *right*.

She nods at Kiunga, who is showing Adam his police ID.

—Does he know about what you did to your colleagues?

—Everyone in the department knows, says Mollel.

—And he still wants to work with you?

—I don't think he has much choice, Mollel answers.

—Loyalty works both ways, Mollel. He seems like a good man. You may need him to be on your side.

—And I should be more loyal to Adam, too, isn't that what you're saying?

—He is your son, Mollel, replies Faith, her voice tinged with sadness. I don't see how your loyalty to him could ever be put in second place.

*

—Sweet kid, says Kiunga, after they've parted. And he's a red.

—A what?

—Supports Manchester United. Didn't you know?

—I don't really follow football. Have you got kids?

Kiunga laughs.—No way! The last thing I need is a dependant!

Dependant. Seems a curiously formal word to describe his son. But then, they have a curiously formal relationship.

When he was a child, back in the Kajiado foothills, his mother used to call him *ol-muraa*. Her little warrior. At fourteen, he became a *moran*. But she still called him *ol-muraa*.

You're not to call me little warrior any more, Mother. I'm a real warrior now. And you'll address me with respect.

How she had laughed! And then chased him out of the *boma* with a ladle. The injustice of it burned him – as did the eyes of his younger brother, Lendeva.

Lendeva had never known their father. Mollel, who had lived in fear of his beatings, felt that the younger boy was lucky.

He'd attempted, in his way, to become the father his brother never had: but Lendeva did not let him. Assertions of authority were met with amused contempt. And before long, Mollel gave up. And now – he paused to work it out – it was nearly twenty years since he had seen his brother. Just like his father, Mollel had no idea whether Lendeva was living or dead.

His father. Lendeva. His mother. His wife. All gone.

No wonder, thinks Mollel, he resists calling his son a dependant. If life had taught him one thing, it was that you could not be dependent upon anyone.

They're walking down Koinange Street – K-Street – Nairobi's notorious red-light zone. Not that there are any red lights here – apart from the ones studiously ignored by motorists. It's discreet at this time of day. Respectable, even. City folk walk the sidewalks unmolested, and the few girls who choose to ply their trade by day have retreated to the shadows rather than prowling the kerb.

Mollel walks directly up to three of them, sheltering from the sun under the canopy of a Chinese restaurant.

—Excuse me, he begins. The girls cast him and Kiunga a scornful, contemptuous look – Mollel compares the look, mischievously, to that which Faith gave him a few minutes before – and they melt away, all three in different directions, not bothering to even reply.

—You're not in any trouble! calls Mollel, but they are gone.

Kiunga is laughing. —We might as well be in uniform, he says. Look, I know how to deal with these girls. Watch, and learn.

They set off but have only gone a couple of metres before Kiunga grabs his colleague's arm.

—Steady up. They're always going to know we're police, there's no way around that. They smell it, or something. But there's no need to frighten them. Don't go storming up. Loosen. Relax your shoulders, walk with your palms out, like this. Yeah, I know it feels strange. But you're giving off a message: you have nothing to hide. Come on.

Sure enough, as they approach the next group of girls – Mollel hanging back, self-consciously aping Kiunga's ambling posture – they do not scatter, but regard the approaching policemen with a wry, sceptical attitude.

—Hello, ladies. Kiunga smiles. Pleasant afternoon.

—What do you want? one of them shoots to him, warily but without apparent hostility.

—Just to make conversation. Why, are you afraid we'll drive away trade?

—Get on with it.

Mollel admires the way Kiunga talks to the prostitutes: professional yet affable. He asks them whether they've heard about the girl found in the park; whether they know of anyone missing from her regular beat; whether the sound of a young Maasai hooker is familiar to them. The answers, all negative, strike Mollel as truthful and considered: these girls don't want a killer on the loose any more than the police do.

They move on. There's a girl on her own, not with any group. She's young, but her dishevelled appearance is in contrast to that of most of the others working this street. And despite the heat, she is standing in the full sun, wearing black leggings and a black cut-off top. She sways slightly as she turns and beats the same, tired loop on the sidewalk.

Mollel is ready to approach, but once more Kiunga steadies him with a touch to the arm.

—Don't bother. You won't get anything out of her.

—Why not?

—Look at the eyes.

As they walk past, Mollel looks at the girl's face. Her eyes are deep-set and sunken; they roll and slide under their lids.

—Hey, boys, she slurs. And in Kiswahili: *mnataka ngono?*

The straightforward proposition is completely different to the nod-and-wink approach of the other girls, and Mollel understands why this one will provide them with nothing. She's a drug addict. Well, so are most of the others. But she's also high right now, probably the only way she can cope with doing what she does.

The pair of them walk on, pounding K-Street for another hour or so, speaking to all the prostitutes they meet. Some gaze at them with the same blank, apathetic, junkies' eyes. Others are more willing to speak, especially to Kiunga. But the answers are always the same.

No, we haven't heard anything.

No, I don't know who she is.

The city heat begins to take its toll, and Mollel suggests a change of scene. They have walked the length of K-Street, anyway, and are back near Biashara Street, where the Land Rover is parked.

It's gone four o'clock. Mollel sees that the bike shop has opened its shutters once more, obviously banking on getting some last-minute Christmas trade. Mollel enters, Kiunga follows him.

—Welcome, sir. Are you looking for anything in particular, or just browsing?

—Remember the little boy who was here earlier?

—Oh, it's you, says the storekeeper, retreating behind the counter and switching instantly from obsequious to defensive. I told you before, other people's children are not my concern. I have got a business to run. And unless you want to buy something...

—Hold on, hold on, says Mollel. When he was here, did you notice him looking at any particular bike?

—Ah, I see. Well, now you come to mention it, I think it was this one that most occupied his attention, yes, yes, certainly.

The Indian storekeepers have a reputation for driving a hard bargain, and Mollel's heart sinks as he sees the man lead him towards what is obviously the most expensive child's bike in the shop. The man takes the handlebars and bounces the machine on its chunky tyres.

—Fifteen speed, front and rear suspension, alloy frame. You really can't get any better than this.

—How much does it cost?

—Might as well ask, how much will you *save*? Think of the constant repairs you'd have to make to a cheaper model. All those punctures from inadequate tyres, all the damage due to shoddy manufacture. Plus, think of the savings on fuel and *matatu* fares once the little man becomes independent.

—How much?

—Twenty. And that's the best price you'll find.

—Twenty thousand shillings? I can't afford that!

The storekeeper smiles. —It's a shame sir was not present when the young man was looking at this model, he continues. The way his face lit up. It made it seem all the more tragic, afterwards, when he realised – when he realised his daddy wasn't coming back to get him.

Kiunga steps forward. His face is blank, his arms folded, chest out. Neutrality never looked more threatening.

—I don't think you understood my colleague. He didn't say

he couldn't afford the *bike*. He said he couldn't afford the *price*.

—The price is non-negotiable, sirs, the shopkeeper persists, with a tremor in his voice. If you'd care to look at some of the cheaper ones – scarcely more than toys, really – but perhaps more fitting to your budget…

Kiunga places his hand on the bike's saddle. —I assume you have all the importation documents for this one? And the rest of your stock?

The storekeeper's mouth falls open, and Kiunga continues: Because we can either have a very *long* conversation about that – and about your business permits, and back taxes, and social security contributions – or we can have a very *short* conversation about your police discount.

—Police discount? Why didn't you tell me that you were officers of the law? Did I say twenty thousand shillings? I meant fifteen. And did I mention that I'd throw in a crash helmet for free?

4

Bike in the back of the car, they drive out of the city centre and back to Uhuru Park. Mollel wants to go over the crime scene again before it gets too dark. The sun is already low in the sky and they have to pull down the car's visors as they negotiate the Kenyatta Avenue roundabout. The park is less crowded, now: people are making their way back to their homes. With the heat less oppressive, those remaining in the park have a new-found vigour. Boys play football, children are flocked on the swings, lovers amble hand in hand.

At the scene, the removal of the body has dispersed the curious onlookers. A solitary uniformed officer is sitting on the low wall by the culvert, chatting on his mobile phone. He jumps to his feet and ends the call as the other policemen pull up.

—Oh, it's you, he says to Kiunga. I thought it was the boss.

—I *am* your boss, Kiunga responds. Three months' seniority and an extra five hundred shillings a week says so. You haven't met my new partner yet, have you? Mollel, this is John Wainaina. A disgrace to the service.

Wainaina grins broadly and shakes Mollel's hand. —Sorry you've been lumbered with this piece of wood, he says, indicating Kiunga. We were at school together. We always said he'd make detective – so long as he's tracking down food, or pussy.

—He's a *noma*, says Kiunga. Mollel does not know much *sheng* – the hybrid language of Swahili, English and Kikuyu

– but he infers that *noma* has a positive meaning. Someone who can be trusted.

The two *nomas* laugh heartily and for a fleeting moment Mollel wonders why he'd never managed to make any friends in the force like this. Probably for the same reason that he'd never sit around chatting on the phone when there was a crime scene to be investigated.

—Everything under control here?

Wainaina stretches. —Seems to be.

Mollel has brought a flashlight from the car. He descends into the concrete ditch – empty, now, but full of muddy footprints and smears where the body has been removed – and starts to track back along its length.

—Is this park part of your regular beat? he asks Wainaina.

—I suppose. I cover half of Central district one way or another.

—Do you come into the park at night?

—Not if I can help it. No reason to. It's officially closed – though, of course, there's no real way to stop people coming and going.

—And presumably they do? Mollel has reached the end of the ditch and is shining his flashlight up the large concrete pipe which feeds it.

—There's always activity. Some people sleep in the bushes. Others come here for sex. The K-Street hookers use it as a cheap alternative to hotel rooms.

—Right. So she could have been in the park with a client, killed some short distance from here, and thrown in the ditch?

—That'd be my take on it.

—I want you to come back later, round up some of the people who usually sleep or hang out near here at night. Find out if they saw anything.

Wainaina gives a loud sigh. Mollel pretends not to have heard it, and sticks his head into the pipe. It is wide enough to carry a person. With the flashlight, he can make out that it runs for a short distance more or less straight, then veers abruptly upwards. The smell is awful: a greasy slime coats the base of the pipe. He pulls out and gulps fresh air.

—Has anyone been up here?

—You must be joking.

Mollel takes off his shirt and hands it to Kiunga. No point getting too filthy. Wainaina and Kiunga watch with amusement as Mollel, bare chested, pushes his way steadily into the mouth of the pipe.

The sounds of the city fade behind him as he gets steadily farther in. The smell grows in intensity: there must have been an overflow from the sewage system in the heavy rains the previous night. He steps carefully on the surface below him, curved and slippery: a steadying arm pressed against the top of the pipe. He is bent nearly double, but has no intention of getting on to his hands and knees if he can help it.

At the junction with the inclined section, he takes the torch and looks up. The pipe disappears into darkness, following a steady ascent of about fifteen degrees. There is no sign of any grille or mesh: a body could easily be carried down here by fast-flowing water. That could be one explanation for the corpse's battered state. He circles the light around, looking for a telltale fragment of fabric or a murder weapon. But there is nothing.

—Where does this lead?

He has backed out to find Wainaina and Kiunga waiting patiently for him. They look at his smeared body with disgust.

—There's a tap over there, Wainaina says, pointing to a gardener's standpipe near by. Mollel goes over and starts washing.

In answer to his previous question, Kiunga says: —From the look of it, the drain goes straight up State House Avenue. Must bring water down from as far away as Kilimani and Lavington.

—OK. Let's try to trace it. To Wainaina: —You stay here.

The pair of them walk around the chain-link fence which bounds the park, and start trudging up Upper Hill. The road curves back round and they are standing some ten metres above Wainaina down at the pipe outflow.

—Here, says Mollel, pointing at an inspection hatch in the sidewalk. It is encrusted with mud and rust. He takes a penknife from his pocket and scrapes away enough to find an edge, which he prises up. Looking in, he sees a short drop to a pipe running along the contour of the hill.

Mollel hears a shout. —I can see you!

He stands up, and looking back down the hill, sees Wainaina leaning into the mouth of the pipe. They are still close enough for him to have seen the light from the lifted inspection hatch.

—It's the same pipe all right, says Kiunga.

—This hatch hasn't been disturbed for years, says Mollel. Come on.

They continue up the hill, spotting the hatches in the sidewalk or occasionally in the middle of the road, using them to track the course of the drainage pipe. All of them seem sealed by decades of neglect. But in a less salubrious part of town, they've been stolen for scrap metal long since.

They are on State House Avenue now, a quiet, leafy street which leads ultimately to the Presidential Palace.

—Please tell me, groans Kiunga, that we're not going to track this all the way back to State House. That would be one hassle I really don't need.

Mollel frowns. There should be another inspection hatch by now, yet he has scanned the road and the sidewalk for quite some distance, and failed to spot it. The others are spaced at pretty regular intervals. Why break the pattern?

—I think I found it, calls Kiunga. He is peering over a tall metal gate. Isn't that it, there?

Mollel retraces his steps and joins Kiunga at the gate. —Hard to tell, with the leaves. Could be. What is this place?

Over the gate, they can see an old-fashioned, colonial stone house. One storey high, not very large, windows dark. It has decidedly seen better days. The front courtyard – once, presumably, a garden – has been gravelled for parking, but is covered with a layer of leaves from the massive eucalyptus trees which shower the area with dappled shade.

A freshly painted metal sign towers above them. They both step back to take a better look.

—Orpheus House, says Kiunga, reading the sign.

Coming Soon, it proclaims, above a computer-generated image of a multi-storey building in creamy, fresh colours and white curving roofs. No sign of the dozens of stately trees which currently grace the site, though a foamy dot of green here and there on the picture's periphery suggest a sapling or two.

Orpheus House. A project of George Nalo Ministries, supported by international donors, and Equator Investments.

Mollel bangs on the gate. A small flock of mousebirds, disturbed by the noise, flee to the adjacent bushes. Otherwise, there is no sign that anyone has heard.

—Padlocked on the outside, says Kiunga, rattling the chain which secures the gate. Which suggests to me, there's no one here.

Kiunga cups his hands to offer Mollel a boost. A quick look up and down the street – all is quiet – and Mollel is up and over, landing softly on the leaves the other side.

—Keep a lookout.

—*Sawa sawa*, says Kiunga. Sure thing.

Despite Kiunga's confidence that the place is empty, Mollel can't shake the feeling that his progress towards the house is being observed. He scrutinises the windows: they are barred, dark. Cataracted with dust. No sign of life.

The farther he gets from the gate, the more the sounds of the city melt into the background, muffled by the trees, whose steady, gentle swishing has completely overwhelmed the noise of the traffic. Mollel is amazed that a place like this still exists so close to the centre of Nairobi, and he grieves a little for its imminent loss.

He walks around the house – gravel crackling under leaves – and takes a look through a ground-floor window. Nothing. An empty room. He continues walking and looks through the next window along: a larger window, but this time obscured by faded, heavy curtains on the other side. They're drawn tightly together. Not even a crack between them to get a clue about what lies within.

Moving on, Mollel sees that the plot extends far behind the house. Must be nearly two acres. Prime land. A small outbuilding lies at the far end, and this looks more promising. Mollel notices that a path seems to have been formed through the fallen leaves by the regular passage of feet. He approaches the brick outbuilding: a small house with two or three doors, each one a servant's quarter. One door is open, revealing a dark latrine. He smells charcoal burning, and as he rounds the small building, sees a glowing *jiko* with a fresh ear of maize roasting on top.

—Look out!

Mollel spins round on hearing Kiunga's cry, just in time to raise his arm against the metal bar which is brought down against him. He jumps back, ducking the second blow, seizing the moment when his assailant must raise the weapon again as his opportunity to grab it – he feels the cold metal in his palm and twists it, tugging it from the other man's grasp. He snatches it and now wields it high above his own head, ready to bring it down—

And nearly does so, on to Kiunga's head. He has come to Mollel's aid and has grasped the other man in both arms, holding him tight in a bear hug. The man is small and frail, and Kiunga towers over him.

—Watch it! says Kiunga. That's lethal. He could've put your skull in.

Mollel drops the iron bar with a clank. The old man looks up at him pitifully.

—Please, there is nothing to steal here. I'm just the day *askari*. The night guards will be here soon. And they've got dogs.

—Come off it, says Mollel. There's no sign of dogs here. They'd have padded a track round the perimeter. I'll bet there are no night guards, either. It's just you, isn't it? Why didn't you come to the gate when you heard us banging?

The old man points to his ear. —I'm very deaf, he says. Please, let me go. I'm not even a guard, properly. I used to be a caretaker here, and the owners let me stay on, to deter squatters. That's all.

—Don't worry, old man, says Kiunga, releasing him. We're not going to harm you. We're police officers.

The old man stumbles back, rubbing his arms. He doesn't appear overly reassured by that statement. Mollel shows him his card.

—What's your name?

—Githaka.

—Githaka, we want to take a look at the drain cover in the front yard. You don't have any objections, do you?

Githaka looks at them blankly. Mollel takes this as permission. The three of them walk around to the front of the house. Mollel and Kiunga kneel by the hatch.

Mollel takes his knife and uses it to lift some of the leaves away from the iron cover. He points out the rim to Kiunga: at the edges, someone has scraped the rust and mud aside, to lever it open. They've done it recently, too, and brushed the leaves back over to cover it up.

Kiunga lets out a low whistle.

—Get Wainaina on your phone, says Mollel. I want to try something out.

He lifts open the hatch and sets it gently to one side. Taking his torch, he flashes it around within. Nothing immediately apparent. He drops down and into the pipe. Crouching low, he sees it stretching before him up and down the hill; the same rank odour; the same blackness.

From above, Kiunga: —Wainaina's on the line.

—Tell him to get up the pipe, as far as he can, without losing the signal. Let me know when he's there.

Kiunga chuckles. —He'll be happy!

Mollel hears Kiunga explaining the task to his friend – and then, in response to an apparent protest, forcefully ordering him. They wait.

—OK, says Kiunga. He's there.

—Tell him to start shouting.

—Start shouting, says Kiunga into the telephone. I don't know what. Anything! Sing 'God Bless Kenya' for all I care. Use your imagination.

In the semi-darkness below, Mollel strains to hear. He flicks off his torch: somehow this heightens his hearing. Apart from the square of light above him, and Kiunga's feet, he can hardly see a thing. He hears rustling near by: scurrying. He tries not to think about rats.

And then he hears it: distant, echoing. A man's voice.

—Get me out of here, he says to Kiunga. I've heard enough. Kiunga reaches down and hauls his colleague out.

—Could you hear him?

—I could hear something. Shouting. I think he was speaking Kikuyu. The only word I could make out was *Maasai*.

Kiunga laughs. He holds the phone up to his ear.

—He's still shouting. He's saying that there's a terrible smell of goat shit in this tunnel. It must be because there's a Maasai at the other end of it.

Mollel takes the phone. The shouting stops and he hears the hoarse voice of Wainaina on the other end: *Kiunga, can I stop now?*

—Not yet, Mollel tells him. Just keep shouting.

He hands the phone back to Kiunga and bends down to replace the drain cover. —Are you just going to keep him shouting down there? asks Kiunga.

—Why not? Mollel chuckles. He can handle it. He's a *noma*.

5

They leave the old *askari* with a promise that they will return to look around inside the premises, and warn him not to tamper with the drain cover.

It is now dark. Time to go back to K-Street.

In the car on the way there, Mollel goes over what they have learned about Orpheus House. Old Githaka told them that it had been empty for a few months. For about twenty years previously, it was run as a women's shelter or refuge – a sort of safe house, for those wanting to escape from prostitution. A year ago, the charity had run into financial difficulties and it had been taken over by the church of George Nalo.

Nalo, Mollel has heard of. Kiunga tells him more: the pastor is something of a celebrity in town. Billboards proclaim his mission and you can hardly avoid him on the television. He has a mega-church out in Embakasi and is renowned for his social projects.

According to Githaka, the site is sitting idle while the funds are finalised for redevelopment. Mollel wonders what a site like that would be worth. He really does not have a clue. Millions of dollars, probably: hundreds of millions of shillings.

—Can we stop for a bite to eat, boss?

As usual, Mollel has forgotten to eat, and the realisation makes him feel a kind of queasy emptiness – not hunger. Time to take his pills, too.

They stop at Nelly's Country Inn on Koinange Street. The quaint name belies the bustling, functional interior: strip lights on the ceiling, worn linoleum on the floor, red plastic benches in the booths. The Country Inn is something of a Nairobi legend. It bears a sign above the counter which says: *Established 1970. Never closed.*

True enough. Mollel has been dropping in there for as long as he's been a policeman, even before, when he was a private *askari* on night shifts. There is something about their *chai masala* – spiced, milky tea – which no other café can replicate. Perhaps it is the patina of the ancient urn from which it is poured; surely a survivor, like the formidable ladies behind the counter, from the first day of business.

Kiunga grabs them two high stools at a bar across the front window: an ideal, if somewhat conspicuous, location for scoping the street. —I'll have a plate of *sambusas*, says Kiunga to the waitress. Make it ten, mixed. And a *tangawizi* to drink. Mollel?

—*Chai masala* and a bowl of *matoke*.

—Is that all you're having? No meat? I thought Maasais only ate meat.

Mollel shrugs. —It's all I feel like.

He does not mention that, lately, his medication has made him feel queasy after eating anything but the blandest food.

The clientele in Nelly's changes from hour to hour. During the day, it's almost respectable, making a good trade from office workers and shoppers looking for a snack. In the early evening, a student crowd tends to congregate, lining their stomachs with platters of greasy meat before an evening on the Tuskers. A high-spirited group of young men are spilling out from one of the booths now, making a lot of noise but not offending anyone. Later, the place will attract some of the street's more notorious residents: the call girls taking a break and having a gossip between clients. Somehow they know to stay away during the day, and Mollel wonders whether the management have warned them to steer clear, or whether mingling with respectable folk makes the girls feel uncomfortable.

—That was excellent, says Kiunga, wiping the remains of his last *sambusa* around the plate to pick up the end of the *pilipili* sauce. He pops it into his mouth and swallows with pleasure.

—You've not touched yours?

—I'll make it last, says Mollel. I want to stay here while you go talk to some of the girls.

—Smart thinking. No need to crowd them. I'll be back in a bit.

When Kiunga has left, Mollel removes a packet of pills from his pocket and carefully counts out his three for this evening: one of each of three different kinds. He places all three on his tongue and washes them down with his lukewarm *chai*. Then, without relish, he starts spooning back his grey *matoke*.

For half an hour or so he watches Kiunga approaching the girls on the street. At this time of the evening, they tend to be individuals rather than in groups. Soon Kiunga has moved out of sight. Mollel continues to watch the girls at work. They clearly have a relationship with the *askaris* who guard the shuttered-up shopfronts. Even in his own nightwatchman days, fifteen years ago, Mollel recalls that these spots on Koinange Street were well prized among the guards. It may seem boring, dangerous and cold to sit all night on a stool in front of a steel shutter, with little more than a truncheon and a transistor radio. But there is a lucrative sideline to be had. The *askaris* let the girls stash their belongings with them while they go off to stalk the sidewalks. Some turn up wearing long coats – presumably to avoid attention on the *matatu* – which they fold and leave beside an *askari*'s stool. It's discreet, but the *askaris* always charge something for this cloakroom service: often payment in kind. They offer other services, too. Protection. Pimping.

As for the johns, their uniformity is the only surprise: all middle aged, in their forties, fifties or sixties. Mostly paunchy. Mostly African, but a lot of Indians, too. They seem to share a relaxed, businesslike attitude to the whole transaction. They pull up in their cars, looking for someone they know or a face that takes their fancy. They chat a while with the girl leaning into the passenger-side window. Then she gets in, and they go. Where? wonders Mollel.

As ever, it's the details which fascinate Mollel. The Indian man who pulls up in a people-carrier, child seats in the back. The fat, bald African who seems to consider – then reject – at least ten girls before choosing two to disappear with. And the way in which the girls carry on their trade: the teamwork, the way they look out for each other; the surreptitious glances at licence plates and monitoring of suspicious activity, the scrutiny of the johns by the ones left behind.

Of a few basic truths Mollel is becoming convinced: one, only junkies work alone. All the other girls maintain a network of friendships and alliances for their own convenience and protection. Two, if his victim had been working this street, she'd have been known about, at least by someone. And three, if she is known here, it is likely that these girls know her killer too.

Kiunga comes back into sight. He's had enough time to cover the length of K-Street and is returning to speak to any girls he missed first time around. At the same moment Mollel notices another car pull up: a large silver Toyota Land Cruiser. Pretty new, slick without being ostentatious. He clocks the driver: a white man. No particular surprise there. He can't see much of the face, as he's wearing sunglasses, despite the darkness. A shock of white hair and flabby, pallid cheeks. The man is leaning over his steering wheel, scrutinising the girls on the sidewalk. There's something different in this man's approach. He seems nervous, cagey. Not so brazen as the other johns. He hasn't stopped the car, but continues to crawl slowly along the edge of the road. As some of the girls approach his passenger-side window, he waves them away, and keeps rolling. He's looking for a specific person. But he won't ask anyone where she is.

Mollel gets up and darts for the door. Kiunga is standing on the sidewalk on the other side of the street, about to be overtaken by the man in the silver car. Mollel calls to him: —Stop that car!

Kiunga looks over, then up at the car. He puts out his hand. The driver sees him; guns the accelerator. —Hey! Police! *Stop!* But Kiunga has to step away from the kerb as the car speeds past him. Mollel runs across the street to join him and together they watch the car hit the lights at the end of K-Street, jump the red, squeal left on to University Way and out of sight.

—I got the plate, says Kiunga. Shall we go after him?

—We'll never catch him. We'll have to follow it up later.

—I got a quick look at the driver. Looked like an old guy. A *mzungu*.

Mzungu: white man.

—I thought so, too, says Mollel. He takes out his notebook and gives it to Kiunga to write down the number, which Mollel checks tallies with his own reading.

—Now if this was a movie, says Kiunga, I'd pick up my radio, put out an APB, get the driver's name off the central computer, have him hand-delivered to Central for questioning.

—Yep, says Mollel. But this is Nairobi. And we don't have a radio, can't put out an APB, and getting his name means waiting until Monday morning, going down to the Motor Vehicle Licensing Office and hoping the clerk there will be in a good enough mood to fetch the card for you, rather than making you go through the files yourself.

—Another job for Wainaina?

—We'll see. I want to go back to the park and see who he's rounded up.

—You're enjoying this, aren't you? asks Kiunga.

Mollel is surprised by the statement. —I'm just doing my job, he mutters. But even as he says it, he realises how good it feels to be doing proper police work once more.

—Well, we're not ready to call it a day yet, says Kiunga. I got a lead from one of the girls. Looks like it's going to be a late night for us.

6

The lead is a rendezvous: according to Kiunga, one of the K-Street girls had seemed edgy and upset. She had broken away from the others and briefly told him to meet her at midnight in a more private location.

—Are you sure you want me there? Mollel laughs.

—Are you kidding me? replies Kiunga. I don't need to pay for it. Besides, she knows I'm not a john. And, the way I see it, there are two possible reasons she'd want to get me alone. And for either of them, I'd want company.

He's right. If she has information on the case, Mollel wants to hear it. And it's always possible that this is a trap: a scam to lure Kiunga into a secluded place and have him robbed – or worse.

They've rolled around to Uhuru Park once more, looking for Wainaina. The night is warm, but as they draw up near Little Mombasa he is rubbing his hands exaggeratedly.

—If I'd known I was going to end up on night shift, I'd have worn a coat, he says reproachfully. Oh, and thanks for leaving me hollering up that pipe. Must have been ten minutes before I realised you'd hung up the phone.

—I see you have someone for us, says Mollel. Beside Wainaina is a small, stooped figure wearing a floppy hat.

—Oh, yes. I got a terrific eyewitness. Saw everything.

As Mollel comes up to the two of them, he recognises the small man. Kiunga knows him too.

—Superglue Sammy, says Kiunga. Great. Shall we take him down for an ID parade? Maybe look at some photos? Hell, why don't we buy him a box of crayons, he can draw us a sketch.

—You're both very funny, says Sammy, removing his hat, and turning his sealed eyes towards them. But you don't need to see, to *see*.

Superglue Sammy is a well-known figure on the streets of Nairobi's downtown district. He is usually to be found outside one of the city's main banks or department stores, his brimmed hat in hand, eyes shut to the world.

Sammy is a young man, barely in his twenties – all of those years spent on the streets. Mollel thinks he can recall seeing him there as a baby or a toddler, his mother holding him up into the faces of passers-by, presenting his shuttered eyes as a plea for alms.

As the years passed, the mother-and-son begging team drew a measure of success: perhaps too much, because they attracted attention. First, there was a group of doctors from the Nairobi Hospital who wanted to send the boy for specialist treatment – an offer that the mother always refused. Then there were rumours, and following the rumours, the journalists. One day the *Daily Nation* had a big splash on the mother who super-glued her baby's eyes shut to increase his begging appeal. She denied it: the pots of discarded glue found all around her shack in Kibera were the result of her own addiction, she claimed. She was a loving mother, who had nothing else in her life but her little boy, whom she looked after impeccably. Certainly his portion of the tiny shack was clean and comfortable. There were even some toys. Jealousy, she said, motivated the allegations.

The child – then a boy of six – was taken away. The good doctors found the skin of his eyelids fused to his corneas: some said because of the glue; others suggested a prenatal infection. Either way, there was nothing to be done: the closed lids at least had the benefit of concealing the useless jelly beneath.

So they sent him back to Kibera, only his mother was not there any more. She'd become so lonely without Sammy that

39

she'd downed a bottle of the illegal local spirits, *chang'aa*, poured all her glue into a plastic bag, and stuck her head into it.

After that, Sammy went back to doing the only thing he knew – and has been on the streets ever since.

—So, Sammy, says Mollel. Tell us what you *heard* last night.

—OK. Follow me.

Sammy leads them away from Little Mombasa, into the park, parallel to the large, wide, open space at the rear of the gardens. During the day, this is a car park: at night, it is empty. At the far side is the drainage ditch where the girl's body was discovered. Wainaina and Mollel both turn on their flashlights, which they use to pick their way along a narrow path, winding through shrubs and hedges alongside the open ground.

—What do you notice about this place? asks Sammy.

—I don't notice a damn thing, replies Wainaina, inadvertently flicking a branch back into Mollel's midriff. It's pitch black!

—Exactly, says Sammy. And yet *I'm* leading *you*. See why I like to sleep here? It's safe, secluded, and I can hear anyone coming. *Karibu nyumbani*.

The phrase means *welcome home*, and Sammy has stopped before a large ornamental fan palm. He ducks behind it, and the three policemen follow. They find themselves in a small, sheltered spot. The ground is dry, it is perfectly secluded, even comfortable. Mollel, certainly, has slept in much worse places. In a hollow by the palm's base is a blanket and a small stash: some clothing, a radio.

Kiunga peers through the leaves.

—There's a clear line of sight to where the body was found, he says. Clear line of hearing, I should say.

—Ringside seat, Sammy grins.

—What did you hear?

—Let's get out into the open. I don't want your dirty police boots ruining my fine carpet.

Together, they go by a different route through some more bushes, and come out in the deserted car park.

—I stay there a couple of times a week, Sammy explains. Saves the *matatu* fare back to Kibera. Always Friday nights, as I need to be at my spot early on Saturdays, to get the shoppers, right? So I'm pretty familiar with the usual activity here. You get quite a few cars coming in, parking up. I hear the springs creaking, the moans. Even the money changing hands.

—No one here tonight, says Mollel.

—They're not going to bring their punters here now, are they? The place is cursed.

—What about last night?

—Last night. Now, *that* was out of the ordinary. Before I go on – he reaches out and touches Kiunga on the arm – Could I trouble you for a cigarette?

—What the…? Kiunga lifts his sleeve and sniffs it. Is it that obvious I'm a smoker?

Mollel and Wainaina laugh. Kiunga grudgingly takes a packet of Sportsman and a lighter from his pocket and hands a cigarette to Sammy, offering round the pack to the others too, but they refuse. He holds up the flame for Sammy to share.

Their faces glow and flicker in the light.

Sammy breathes the smoke deeply and exhales with satisfaction. —Where were we?

—Last night.

—Ah yes, last night. Well, last night was a strange one. About eleven, these buses start arriving. They woke me up. I counted them – four buses. They were here until three. I know that, because I listened to the radio afterwards, until it started raining.

—The K-Street girls are doing them by the busload now? jokes Wainaina, but the others ignore him.

—When they unloaded, they sounded like school buses. You know, all the feet? But these weren't kids. By the sound of the boots, I thought at first they were policemen.

—What makes you think they weren't?

—I know they weren't. First, because you lot are here asking about them. I reckon you'd know about it if it was your own boys. Second – no offence – they were too disciplined to be policemen. The buses were full, I reckon, but they all got off and lined up in just a few minutes, no talking, no joking, just a load of whispered orders. I heard them spread out, sounded like they were in teams. As if they were checking the place out. Then I heard them marching about. Back and forth, and around.

He takes another long drag from his cigarette.

—Four buses? asks Kiunga sceptically. That's two hundred men at least. Our night patrols would have seen them.

—I thought there were no night patrols in the park, Mollel remarks.

—They'd have seen that sort of activity from the street! says Wainaina.

Mollel looks around. Easily visible, above the trees, are the lights from the office blocks of the city. Closest is Nyayo House, the Home Ministry headquarters; but there was no chance of any civil servant being at his desk at that time of night to look down into the park. At ground level, though, the highway is not visible, except for the occasional flash of light through the foliage.

It reminds him of a name – one of many – that the Maasai have for this city. *Nakuso Intelon*. It means the Festooned Trees, and refers to the lights high on the skyline, visible from the plains for miles around.

—Nothing to see, continues Sammy. They were doing it in the dark.

—Oh, come on! protests Kiunga. We're supposed to believe that two hundred soldiers paraded around here for an hour in the middle of the night, in pitch darkness, and complete silence? And yet a *blind* man observed it all? Sammy, had you been at the *chang'aa* by any chance?

—I didn't say they were soldiers, says Sammy. But they did have weapons.

—Don't tell me they started taking potshots?

Sammy sighs.

—Tell us, says Mollel.

—I heard them doing drills: you know, a whispered order, then lots of clanking of wood against wood.

—They were fighting themselves, in the middle of the night, in the dark! Brilliant! says Wainana. Guys, can we go home now? It's so cold.

—How do you know they didn't have any lights? Mollel asks Sammy.

—The engines were silent. You don't leave the lights on for an hour without leaving the engine running. You get a flat battery on one of those old buses, you're going to need a tow truck.

—They might have had flashlights, says Kiunga.

—Possibly. But I don't think so. I heard a lot of whispering, a lot of orders given in low voices which I could not make out. But the only voice I heard out loud came from over here.

He beckons them to follow him to the edge of the open space. A low, shin-high hedge runs along the path at this point, the boundary between the gardens and the car park.

—I've walked into this myself a few times, admits Sammy. But then, as you keep reminding me, I am blind. You guys aren't going to walk into it with a flashlight, are you?

Mollel runs his flashlight along the low hedge. It's made from bougainvillea, with evenly spaced posts between which barbed wire has been stretched for the plants to grow over. No more than a foot from the ground – he certainly wouldn't want to blunder into it in the dark.

—So at one point, I heard the men marching this way. Then there's a yell of pain, and someone shouts *halt*! And then, some commotion. Now, even *policemen* aren't dumb enough to march into barbed wire if they have any way of seeing where they're going.

Mollel continues along the hedge, barbed wire glinting in his flashlight beam below the green-and-purple foliage of the bougainvillea. He stops: suddenly the hedge is disrupted, footprints in the earth before it. Large ones – a lot of them. He pushes the leaves away to look at the wire. After some searching, he finds a section with a shred of cloth on one of the barbs. He takes it off and examines it under his flashlight. It is thick, dark green material, with a dark black patch.

—Blood, says Kiunga, echoing Mollel's thoughts. Mollel shines the light on Sammy's trousers. They're grey. —Roll up your trouser legs, Sammy, he orders. The blind man does so: no sign of any injury.

—There were four buses, you say? Mollel asks Sammy. He walks away from the bushes and towards the centre of the car park. The others follow him, Kiunga leading Sammy by the arm.

—Let me guess, Sammy, says Mollel – he is now some distance ahead of them – it sounded to you like they were parked about here – he walks farther – and here – and he walks farther still – and here – and he's now got so distant that he has to shout: and here?

—Sounds about right, Sammy calls back.

Mollel casts his beam down upon the ground. He's standing above a patch of oil. He strides seven even paces back towards the others; shines the beam down; a patch of oil. Seven more paces; a patch of oil. Seven more paces and he's back with them. He shines the beam once more down at their feet. A patch of oil.

—They even *parked* in formation, he says. Sammy's right. Whoever these guys are, their transport may be clapped out, but they are *disciplined*.

7

SUNDAY, 23 DECEMBER 2007

It is just turning midnight as Kiunga coaxes the Land Rover into Banda Street. Away from K-Street – which never sleeps – the city centre has an eerie feel at this time. Cats, never evident during the day, stalk the emptiness, turning their moonbeam eyes towards the oncoming car before scurrying into the darkness. Humans are still present, occasionally sleeping cocooned in doorways or, rarer, swaying intoxicated along the sidewalk.

—She said she'd meet us up here, says Kiunga, drawing the car to a halt and getting out. Mollel descends too, and Kiunga locks up.

—This is the time for Night Runners, he says.

He's whispering: the silence around them seems to demand it. Together, their footsteps echo along Banda Street. A flash of movement at the far end – gone before Mollel can make out what it is.

Mollel has never seen a Night Runner, but he's heard enough credible reports not to dismiss the idea as pure fantasy. Indeed, every so often, one is caught and killed: usually in the villages. Of course, the Night Runner, once dead, returns to his or her form as a normal human, so there is no proving the stories of supernatural speed and strength. But what it does prove is that there are people who go about at night, usually naked: whether truly possessed by a witch, or merely mad, or simply up to no good, no one can say. What Mollel knows, though, is that there

45

are enough malignant spirits of the criminal variety on the streets of Nairobi at this time of night to make the undercurrent of fear he's feeling right now a perfectly healthy and rational response.

They've stopped by the mosque – the largest one in the centre of the city, and even more of a focal point by night than it is in the day. A series of floodlights from within the main dome and minaret pick out the high, arched windows in aqueous green: with no illumination, though, at ground level, the effect seems merely to increase the darkness in the street.

—Up here, says Kiunga, turning into a small alley which runs alongside the mosque – known with typical Nairobi economy, as Mosque Alley.

—She asked to meet here?

—She said it was safe.

Safe for her, Mollel does not doubt. It is near enough to K-Street for her to get here on foot without crossing too much of town alone. And if she fears being seen talking to the police, it is certainly a good spot to avoid prying eyes.

That's if she's genuine. Mollel's fear, though, is a trap. And with the long, high wall of the mosque bounding one side of the alley, and the facing wall equally blank and accessless, the two men would be easy prey if caught in the middle.

—She said midnight?

—It's only a few minutes past.

They get halfway down the alley, and stop. On any day of the week, this narrow lane is pretty busy. On a Friday afternoon it is thronged with the devout and the not-so-devout; the mosque-goers and the vendors of trinkets, Korans and *kufis*. If you want to buy a plastic replica of the *Ka'bah* at Mecca, which tells the time and date, and plays a series of tinny, yet rousing recordings of Koranic verse, this is the place to come. If you want to buy a DVD entitled *Al-Qaeda's Greatest Hits* from certain shady, bearded youths – before they are chased off by the mosque elders – this is the place to come. If you are penniless, homeless, hopeless – Muslim or *kaffir* – and want to tap some reliable sabbatarian charity – this is the place to come. But only on Friday afternoons.

These first few minutes of a Sunday morning, the alley is as silent as the grave. Perhaps it is the looming presence of the mosque itself which keeps away the street sleepers, the drug dealers, the junkies looking for a quiet place for a fix or the hookers looking for a quiet place to take their clients for a knee-trembler. Not even Night Runners would venture here. Or at least, Mollel hopes they won't.

A distant, regular tapping echoes through the streets now. It becomes a clack-clack: a confident, purposeful stride. High heels: female footsteps. Mollel strains, listening, trying to discover an undercurrent to this high note: a hidden bass, a quiet drumming male footbeat accompanying the more evident feminine percussion. But he does not hear any footsteps other than hers. It sounds as if she is alone.

She rounds the corner at the head of the alleyway, and in the undersea green light reflected from the mosque, she is a silhouette.

She walks towards them, never breaking her stride, feet falling determinedly one in front of the other, tapered ankles crossing each other's path. Her long legs are bare, the skirt high: the hips sway with the rhythm of her walk. Her shoulders are thrown back, and long, straight hair brushes her shoulders. Mollel is reminded of an impala, graceful, proud, powerful – and fragile.

She draws close, and finally is illuminated in the half-light before them. Unsmiling, challenging, she scrutinises the two men before her.

Mollel knows her.

And he does not know her.

And he *knows* her – or rather, he knows her face. It is the face of his mother and of his sisters, the face of the girls of his village and of his youth.

It is the face of the dead girl.

It is a Maasai face. And now the surprise has passed, and he has more of a chance to make out the girl's features, he sees that

47

beyond the high cheeks, the almond eyes, the typically Maasai straight nose, she is not a person he knows.

And yet, he *knows* her.

He might have anticipated this: the dead girl was Maasai, so she would naturally be friendly with another Maasai girl on the streets. They seem about the same age, too: early twenties, he guesses. This girl is taller, and she does not have any tribal scarring on her cheeks. Her ears, too, are pierced only in the regular, non-Maasai way, to allow her to wear a pair of glinting earrings.

—So, she says. You're a Maasai too. I saw you watching from Nelly's window. You looked like someone I could trust.

—You can trust me, and my colleague here, says Mollel. Whatever you say to us is confidential. It does not get back to K-Street. Or anywhere else.

—Do you think you might know the dead girl? asks Kiunga.

—I think so, she replies, quietly. I think she may be my friend.

There is never a good time to visit Nairobi City Mortuary, but superstition and sentiment aside, the early hours of Sunday morning may be better than most. The visitor is spared the grieving families, women wailing and ululating; the hard-luck stories from smartly dressed, credible-looking beggars who need just a hundred bob to help repatriate their uncle's body to Garissa (tomorrow it will be their grandmother, to Kisumu); the vendors of trinkets and charms, candles and rosaries; the coffin-makers, with their trays of small-scale replicas – or, hardly bigger, the real, ready-made baby and child coffins that they do a good trade in on the spot.

You are also spared the standing in queues, the standing in corridors, the standing around and about and wherever you can; squatting or sitting, and waiting and waiting, and waiting; and returning once and again to the counter to try to get hold of someone – anyone – who will deal with your request.

So, for all practical reasons, the mortuary is best visited at

night. Yet even Mollel – to whom this place is grimly familiar – needs to suppress a shiver as they crunch over the gravel
towards the main entrance.

It's a while before anyone answers the door. When he comes,
it's evident that the attendant has been sleeping. They watch
him through the glass as he fumbles with the lock. His eyes are
bleary and his cheeks creased. As he opens the door, the pungent, sour smell of home-brewed beer hits them. The attendant
rubs his hand across his bristled, grizzled chin.

—Visiting hours are over.

Mollel shows him his card. —We've got an ID to do.
Unknown female, found in Uhuru Park.

—Can't it wait until morning?

—It *is* morning, says Mollel. Point us in the right direction,
and you can go back to sleep.

—Third along, says the attendant, indicating a door with a
NO ENTRY sign before them.

—You sure about that? asks Kiunga. We don't want any
surprises.

—I'm sure.

—Surprises? asks Mollel as he pushes open the heavy door.
The immediate drop in temperature makes his skin prickle.

—I pulled back a sheet once, expecting to see a bank robber,
found half a dozen babies, says Kiunga in a low voice. All the
ones collected from the city that week. It was someone's idea of
a joke.

Mollel looks over at the girl. She has come in too, but stays in
reception, seemingly tuned out of their conversation.

—I'd better check it out first, before we show her.

He enters the morgue alone, finding a light switch and flicking it on. The fluorescent strips stutter and ping into life.

The room is the same as it was nine years ago, when he came
to find his wife. Except then it was overflowing, with the living
and the dead.

Days, he waited there. Nights, too. He used his policeman's

privilege to bypass the formalities, the crowd of desperate relatives forced to wait outside. He was among the first to see each new corpse as it was brought in from the rubble.

He looked like one himself. The thick, white concrete dust caked his clothes. His skin was a skin of ashes. Blood – some his own, most from others – streaked black against the white.

After a day or so, someone told him to go get cleaned up. They gave him some clothes.

He stood naked in the sluice room, rinsing the blood and dust from his body. That's where they cleaned the corpses, too: he had to dress hurriedly as another was brought in.

—It's not her, they said. We're still pulling out the ones from the upper storeys. If she was on the third floor, there's no saying when they'll find her. There's no saying they'll find her at all.

Now, there is an orderly line of gurneys, about fifteen or so, with the first six covered. He goes to the third – takes the sheet in his hand – and gently, slowly, lifts it.

It is the Maasai girl. She's been laid out, stripped and washed, but the post-mortem has not been performed yet. The body is battered. He sees that a gauze pad has been placed between the legs. He has no intention of removing it: he can wait for the results of the PM. Now, his concern is with making her presentable. He walks down the line of trolleys, and removes sheets from two of the empty ones. Then he turns the one covering the dead girl down to her neck. He takes one sheet, folds it to a strip a few inches wide, and drapes it over the head like a nun's wimple, framing the face. She looks placid now. Then he takes the third sheet and softly covers the face once more.

There was no such ceremony when Chiku was brought in. It was the fourth day: Mollel had been sleeping crouched against a wall. He had been dreaming of his baby son.

Someone had roused him. *We think this might be her.*

He'd known the body would be in a bad way. By that stage,

they were taking the corpses out of the embassy with diggers. But he wasn't prepared for what he saw.

That's why he wants no shocks this time. He says no prayer as he diligently shrouds the figure laid out before him. It is a purely practical measure. He is a detective, and he wants there to be no distraction, when the living girl meets the dead.

He returns to the door and indicates to Kiunga that the body is ready for viewing.

The girl crosses the boundary. She walks to Mollel, who leads her to the table. He looks at her to ask: ready? She nods.

The sheet is lifted. Kiunga's eyes inevitably drop to the body; Mollel's remain firmly on the girl. She winces in recognition.

—Yes, she says, almost inaudibly. Yes, it's Lucy.

8

—My name is Honey. Not my Maasai name, of course. That's En'cecoroi e-intoi Kipuri. It was Lucy who christened me Honey. She told me that if you washed your forehead when you took your new name, you washed away your past. That's what we were both trying to do. That's how we both ended up in Nairobi.

They're in the car, at the far end of the mortuary car park. Somehow, it seems the best place to do this. Neither the harsh white interior nor the cold night air beyond is conducive to talk. The car, now, lights off, is intimate and secluded. The girl seems to feel close enough – and private enough – to open up.

—My Maa is pretty rusty, Mollel admits. *En'cecoroi* – that's a bird, isn't it?

—In English, it's called Honey Guide. Lucy told me that.

Mollel recalls the bird: a drab little creature, but full of spirit. It does not fear humans, but leads them to bees' nests, in the hope of picking off the larvae for its chicks once the man has taken the honey.

There was a story his mother used to tell. The story of the Honey Guide: a story which would have been as old as the Maasai people themselves. He could not remember the details of the tale, but he knew that it always made him sad.

Honey would know the tale. She would have been told it every year, upon the anniversary of her *en-teipa* ceremony, when the baby is taken by its mother, fresh from her confinement, to the dwelling place of an animal whose spirit they hope will inhabit the newborn.

Often it's a lion's den – deserted, of course – to imbue the child with courage. Or a buffalo's scratching tree, for strength. The choice of the modest little bird signified a hope that the little girl would, in her turn, become a caring mother. And a resourceful one.

Mollel can't help wondering what her parents would think of her now.

But it's more important to find out about the victim.

—Do you know Lucy's Maasai name?

—No. She was just Lucy. She said, you need a street name that's easy enough for a drunk to remember. She was full of good advice like that, when I first started.

—So she's the one who got you into prostitution? asks Kiunga, leaning over from the driver's seat. Mollel, sitting next to her in the back, senses the girl bristle.

—She *helped* me, she says. Without her, I'd have starved.

—Do you know where she was from?

Honey shakes her head. —A village in the Loita Hills. She never told me its name.

—Well, this is helpful. Kiunga sighs.

Mollel has been impressed so far with his young partner, but – perhaps it's tiredness, perhaps it's something else – he seems edgy, irritable. He's certainly not helping the interview.

—Why don't you take a walk, Mollel suggests.

At least Kiunga's professional enough not to argue. He gets out and walks away from the car. They see a flash and a glow as he lights a cigarette, cradles it, and becomes nothing more than a red dot.

They sit in silence for a while. Then Mollel starts asking questions.

According to the stories, there are a few – a very select few – who see the world as it truly is: ravelling slowly back towards creation. They are the lucky ones. For them, death is not an end, it is the beginning of life. It is when the scavengers, the hyena, the birds, the worms, come together to put flesh on the bones so that the morning wind can breathe animation into them. Life, for them, is a joyful process of ever-increasing strength and virility, until the final, happy years, when one begins to shrink to perfection, safe in the arms of a mother.

Not for them this world of chaos and atrophy. No wonder some are envious, persecute them, call them idiots, cretins, *wazuzu*.

But Mollel remembers his mother telling him that these are the truly wise ones. That they have the ultimate gift, of starting with knowledge, and gradually unlearning it. What is left, is truth.

So this is how he interviews. Starting in the here and now, and steadily guiding the witness back. He finds the minutiae of recent memory unhelpful. He prefers the distillation granted by forgetting: what is left, is truth.

Honey has not seen Lucy for three months. She'd been keeping watch for her, hoping to see her, and hoping *not* to see her: because if she saw her, that meant Lucy was back on the streets.

She had told Honey that she'd met some people, some Christians. Lucy wasn't religious, but they'd not gone on too much about God, and all that. They'd offered her somewhere to stay. They'd talked about training, even getting her school certificate. It was the chance of a new life, said Lucy. She'd be mad not to take it.

Honey wasn't interested, herself. She'd seen people like this before. Their idea of salvation more often than not meant dull drudgery. And for the first time in her life, she was doing well, financially. Her plan involved saving enough to turn her back on the street on her own terms. But Lucy was different. She'd been having trouble lately with a certain client, and wanted out.

Though they were flatmates – they shared a small, one-room apartment in Kitengela – they did not see each other enough to share every intimacy. Both preferred not to discuss their clientele. It was one thing to do this job, quite another to talk about it. They overlapped rarely, Honey working nights and Lucy mostly days. But on one occasion, when they both found themselves at home and exhausted, and had curled up together on the narrow bed they usually shared in shifts, Lucy told Honey that she feared for her life.

She never told her the name. It was someone very powerful and influential, though, and Lucy had made the mistake of demanding too much from him.

Not more money – he wouldn't have had a problem with that. No, she'd been seeing him for a while, and she had found him kind, and charming, and very generous. Her mistake was thinking it was genuine. One evening, when she thought the time was right, she had told him that she wanted to quit the paid relationship, and suggested a girlfriend arrangement instead.

Turned out he didn't like that, one little bit. He already had plenty of girlfriends. Not to mention a wife. Why would he want to complicate matters?

He dropped her. When she tried to make contact again, to apologise, she was warned off. But she was foolish. She didn't take the advice. She couldn't afford to lose such a regular client, one who treated her so well. He'd been so kind to her. Surely they could go back to the way things were?

He didn't see it that way. Nor did whoever he sent. Lucy had showed Honey the bruises on her wrist. The offer from the Christians had come at just the right time. She didn't need to be asked twice.

—Your friend's on his second cigarette, says Honey. He must be getting cold.

—He'll be OK, says Mollel. He's a tough guy. Tell me how you met Lucy.

—It was three years ago. I'd been told there was money to be made on K-Street. I needed it: I hadn't eaten for days. But I didn't know what I was doing. Oh, I knew what to *do* – village life had prepared me for that. But I didn't know, for example, that you had to ask for the money up front. I learned that when I got thrown out of a moving car.

—It was Lucy who picked me up.

—She bought me egg and *chipsi*. And a soda: the first one I'd ever tasted. The bubbles made me laugh so hard, they came out of my nose.

—She was kind to me. She took me to her flat, cleaned me up, let me wear her clothes. She made me understand what this life meant: plenty of hassle, plenty of danger. But also money, freedom.

—We worked together for a while. There's always demand for two girls. But that's really a beginner's game: you do it for the safety, to learn new tricks. But you can't charge double, so in the long run it works out better to operate alone.

—How long had Lucy been working the street before you met her?

—She told me she came to Nairobi a year or so before I did.

—Do you know what she was running away from?

Honey gives a hollow laugh. Then she is silent. In the darkness, Mollel tries to make out her face. Is she crying? Angry?

Eventually she says: —I know what I ran away from. I always assumed it was the same for her.

—What was that, Honey?

Instead of answering, Honey says: I thought you'd understand, Mollel. Once, you were a Maasai. But the way you dress, the way you talk… you're a city man now. You've left it behind.

—Yes, I have.

—That's why you, of all people, should be *asipani*.

It takes him a moment to recall the meaning of the Maa word.

—I am trustworthy, he says.

—Prove it, she says. Promise me, whatever happens, you won't make me go back.

—No one can make you go back, Honey.

—I can't go back. I was betrothed the day I was born, and knew I'd be put to the knife the first day I bled. But I escaped – and you know the punishment for that.

—And you think Lucy was running from the same thing?

—Whatever she was running from, says Honey, they caught up with her in the end.

9

Mollel shaves by touch – a relic of village days, when he learned to shave his head years before the razor ever touched his face. This being Sunday, he takes the blade to his scalp once more. He does not need the mirror before him to know that he is going grey. The stubble falling in the sink tells him that story. He does not need to look to know that he is getting thinner. He knows it every time he puts on his clothes.

His wife used to say to him: if you get any thinner, you're going to disappear. He feels like he's been getting thinner for the last ten years, but he is still around.

He bends and washes cold water over his smooth head. It runs clear: no blood. He can hardly remember the last time he nicked himself.

He recalls the day he became an elder. He'd already moved from the village, then, but this was before he'd rejected that life completely. He had been working in the city as a guard, his dreadlocks as fearsome as any uniform. They were long, impeccably plaited, and stained red with henna. During the day, when the guards were off duty, the Maasai used to work on each other's locks, singing faintly and dreaming themselves out of the city.

The dreadlocks were Mollel's mark of being a *moran* – a warrior. Then, when he was in his mid-twenties, word reached him that the village elders had decided he was to join their number.

He felt grief – grief for his locks, grief for his youth. He felt resentment, too: many *morans* continued into their thirties. They were, in many ways, more powerful than the elders. They could have jobs, they could live in the city. He did not want to move back to the village, to marry, to have children to herd the goats the way he had done. Besides, there was a girl who lived in the compound he guarded in the city, a pretty Kikuyu girl, with an open smile, training to be a secretary, and who always took the time to talk to a Maasai when he came off duty.

Still, he went.

It was the mother's duty to shave her son's locks. They woke before dawn, his nose full of the strange, familiar smell of home, of smoke and dung and animals. He was led to the *boma*, the women ululating, the other *morans* chanting their deep, breathy, rhythmic song which rang in the ears. There he saw his mother. She had laid out a freshly tanned calfskin, specially prepared. He knelt before her, bowed his head in submission for a final time. She took a gourd, filled with milk and spirit, and poured it gently over his head. The milk ran down his cheeks. She commenced the cutting: tugging each lock as she applied the blade, taking it back to the skin. When she had a clear patch, she'd start to shave, and Mollel remembered the taste of milk changing to a taste of blood as she cut into his scalp: it was a sign of honour to bleed without flinching, and because his mother knew that this was expected, she had cut him gently where a small vein ran high on his temple, so that he bled profusely but without pain.

When he rose, and washed his head, he looked down at the small, bloody pile of locks in the centre of the calfskin. He rubbed his hand over his scalp, which had not been bare since boyhood, and felt the breeze on his skin. It was as though his past had been cleansed from him, that his future was his to determine. He knew, then, that he would not become an elder. He felt free.

*

This Sunday morning, Mollel finishes shaving. He takes his pills. Then he goes to his cupboard and takes out a suit: black. He pulls the plastic wrapper from it and sniffs for mustiness. It has been a long time in there, but the suit smells OK. He puts on one of his usual work shirts, a white one, and slips into the suit. The trousers are loose. He has to double up the waist an inch or two and tighten his belt. The jacket feels all right, so long as he wears it open. He takes a pair of shiny shoes from a box at the base of the cupboard, taps them instinctively to remove any scorpion which might have nested there, and puts them on his feet. Then he rises, finds his only tie – grey – hidden at the back of the sock drawer. He hangs it around his neck but does not tie it. Only then does he step into the hallway to look at himself in the tall mirror there.

And he smiles. He always feels slightly comical dressed like this. An impostor. He is much more comfortable in the slacks and shirt he wears most days – or even his police uniform. They are work clothes. No attempt to better himself. Yet this suit – even if the style is somewhat out of fashion these days – is a good suit. He wife chose it. It makes him look – her word – *distinguished*.

Not bad for a Kajiado goatherd, she would say on occasions like this. *Not bad at all.*

Kiunga raises his eyebrows when Mollel answers the door. — God, boss, you make me look shabby.

—You look fine, said Mollel. Kiunga is wearing jeans, a shirt and a lightweight jacket all made from the same denim material. The shirt is untucked and the trousers hang low on the hips – but deliberately, unlike Mollel's. Kiunga's ensemble has printed letters all over it, brand names, but despite the affected casualness, all of the items are crisply pressed and Mollel even gets a whiff of cologne. The young man has gone to even more trouble than he has.

—What time does the service begin? Mollel asks.

—Nine. We have to hit the road. Traffic shouldn't be too bad, but … where do you want this? Don't want you to get oil on your good suit.

Kiunga has brought the bike up with him.

—Leave it in the hallway. Adam's staying with his grandmother for a few days. That reminds me – Mollel takes the tie from around his neck. Knot this for me, would you? He normally ties my ties for me.

Calling George Nalo Ministries a church is a bit like calling the Maasai Mara a petting zoo. The *campus* – as the sign terms it – is sited just off the main Embakasi Road, down a specially laid section of gleaming, fresh tarmac with sidewalks and neatly clipped lawns and bushes alongside: smoother and cleaner than any stretch of public road in the whole city. Approaching from this driveway, a tower emerges from above the trees. It is modern and elegant: a twenty-first-century mission campanile.

Kiunga is directed by a warden in an official vest to an overflow car park, which leaves them some distance yet to walk. This suits Mollel: he wants to get a sense of the place. They park up and join the ever-increasing throng flocking to the sound of the bells.

Mollel is glad that he'd dug out his suit. There's quite a range of finery on display: here, a father and three young boys clad in identical designer outfits descending from a gold Range Rover; there, a family knocking the dust from their shoes, repairs visible on some of their clothing, but all neatly and respectfully presented none the less – the little girl in a pale yellow and gold chiffon with broad satin sash and lace around the hem, suitable for a fairy princess going to a ball.

Mollel notices that there are a lot of younger adults present. This church appears to be particularly popular among that generation. The girls are smartly dressed, modest without being conservative – a few knee-length skirts, plenty of patent leather high heels. The men are in sharp suits or, like Kiunga, the strange hybrid, baggy-chic, American style, all immaculately pressed.

They round a bend in the path and Mollel sees the church: a wide, low structure with a pair of massive doors standing open at the front. It makes him think of one of the aircraft hangars at Wilson aerodrome, and indeed, as he approaches, he realises the building is much larger than he first thought. It only looks low because it is so wide: drawing near to the doorway, which must stand four metres high, he feels as though he is being sucked into the mouth of a giant whale.

—Hi! says a young man, taking Mollel's hand and shaking it vigorously. I don't think I've seen you here before. Is this your first time?

Mollel looks at the space before him, slowly filling up. Inside, the building reminds him less of an aircraft hangar, and more of Nyayo Stadium.

—First time here, he confirms. How can you tell? You must have hundreds of people coming here.

—Thousands! The young man laughs. He is dressed all in black, black jacket, shirt and tie. Mollel sees twenty or so others identically dressed, greeting everyone as they come in. This usher, though, has one differentiating feature: the thick dreadlocks, pulled back and tied behind his head. For the second time that day, Mollel is reminded of his own youth. Such dreadlocks are not such a common sight these days, being mostly a preserve of Maasai, and reggae fans. And there is one other group which favours the style: the criminal sect, the dreaded Kikuyu gang-cum-mystery-cult whose very name inspires a unique terror in Nairobi. The *Mungiki*.

He looks around for Kiunga, who has effortlessly manoeuvred himself to be greeted by an attractive young woman.

—We have seats for six thousand here, the usher is continuing, and on a Sunday there are two thousand more standing. Plus the people who come during the week. But, you know, you get to spot the people who stand out. Like you, for example, with the ears.

Mollel impulsively raises his right had to touch his earlobe.

—We've got a few Maasai, not many, continues the young man. My name is Benjamin, by the way. You are?

—Mollel.

—As it's your first time, *Ole* Mollel, can I suggest that you and your friend sit near the front, on the bank of seats over there? You'll get a good view, and be able to follow the service more easily.

Mollel thanks him. He is impressed that the youngster has addressed him with a Maasai honorific: the greeters are obviously well trained. But, despite his use of the Maa word, that young man is no Maasai himself. His accent sounds Kikuyu. Which would tie in with the dreadlocks – unless they really are just a fashion statement.

Kiunga gives a low whistle as they make their way to their seats.

—Did you see the sweetie I was talking to? he asks. Wow. I gotta change churches. Where do you usually go?

—I don't, replies Mollel. Adam's grandmother takes him to the Catholic cathedral. Me, I've not been inside one of these for ten years.

They make their way through towards the front of the enormous hall, and along a bank of plastic seats, smiles of other congregants greeting them. The place is filling up. To one side of the large stage before them, a band is setting up: the guitarist picks out some notes on his electric guitar; the drummer checks his kit. In front of the stage, a man carrying a TV camera on his shoulder is chatting to a young woman with an earpiece and microphone. Looking around, Mollel sees another couple of TV cameras alongside the stage, and another high up behind him.

—They record this? he asks Kiunga.

—It's broadcast live. You haven't seen it?

—I don't have a TV, confesses Mollel.

—How do you watch football games? Do you go to a bar?

—I don't drink. And you know I don't like football. Adam watches it at his grandmother's.

—Man! says Kiunga, shaking his head. You're going to need to buy that kid more than a bike.

Before Mollel can ask what he means, a man takes to the stage. He picks up a microphone from a stand, taps it, prepares to speak. The hall is still filling up but the background buzz drops slightly.

—Is this Nalo? asks Mollel.

—No. This must be one of the junior pastors. He's kind of a warm-up man.

—*Are you here to praise JEE-SUS?* comes the call from the stage.

Around them, the churchgoers say: Yes.

The pastor cups his ear. —*I said are you here to puh-raise Juh-EEEE-SUS?*

—Yes!

—*I can't hear you, Nairobi. I am saying: Are. You. Here. To puh-RAISE the LORD?*

This time, even Kiunga shouts: Yes!

—*Amen!*

Whooping and clapping fill the hall. The place is now nearly full. The band have taken their positions and are providing an accompaniment to the preacher, punctuating his pauses with drum rolls, his questions with cymbal clashes; his exclamation marks with short bursts of rhythm.

—Praise the Lord. It is so good to see you all again, brothers and sisters, on this day. And what a blessed day this is. For this is the last Sunday of Advent, the last Sabbath day before we celebrate the birth of our Lord.

—*Amen!*

Mollel is familiar with the story: as someone who had actually been born in a stable – or something very similar – he has always felt a certain affinity. But he can't help feeling that, as far as miraculous babies are concerned, he prefers the Maasai story of Ntemelua, who was born with full faculties of speech. Ntemelua's mother and father were so frightened of the prodigy

– and tired of his nagging – that they sneaked away one night, leaving him in the custody of a cow, a donkey and a goat. When some *morans* tried to steal the animals, little Ntemelua hid himself up the cow's arse.

Now *that* is a trick Mollel would like to read about in the Gospels.

—I have to say I'm pleased to see so many brothers here today, the preacher continues. Particularly when there are so many important football matches being played.

Gentle laughter ripples through the audience. Kiunga groans.
—Don't remind me! he says in Mollel's ear.
—Yes, right now, Manchester United are playing Everton. Who wants to know the score? asks the preacher.

A few hands go up. Kiunga puts his fingers in his ears. — Don't say it, don't say it, he mutters.

—Don't worry, I won't ruin the suspense, booms the preacher. You can catch the highlights when you get home. You know, it's funny. When I'm watching a big match live, my hands get clammy, my heart starts racing...

He mimes leaning forward, watching a game. The audience laugh in recognition.

—I hate preachers like this, whispers Kiunga to Mollel. They want to be stand-up comedians.

—I feel that, even though I'm thousands of miles away, I can still affect the outcome. I *will* my team to score. I *will* the ball to go into the goal. It's never the same, watching a recording. And you know, that's a little bit what prayer is like.

—Here comes the scripture, murmurs Kiunga.

—James four, verse two, says the preacher, and there is a ruffle of Bible pages around the room. You desire what you do not have, so you kill. You covet but you cannot get what you want, so you quarrel and fight. You do not have because you do not ask God.

He pauses, letting the words sink in.

—Now I'm not saying you can pray for your team to win a

football match. It doesn't work like that. However much you'd like it to!

Some more polite laughter from the listeners.

—But you can change things in your own life. If you allow God to guide you. The only thing you can't change is what's already happened.

Mollel thinks of Chiku. She had had faith. She always tried to convince him, too. Whenever she had spoken about Jesus, her face lit up and her eyes shone with happiness. It was one of the things which had first attracted him to her. If she wanted him to worship her father-son God instead of the Maasai holy mountain of *Ol Doinyo Lengai*, fine. It did him no harm to attend sermons and pray to the man nailed to a cross. If doing so made Chiku happy, it made him happy. But he never believed it would change anything. And he never, not once, believed anything would bring her back.

He has stopped listening to the man on stage and has allowed his eyes to wander to the area to one side of it. The young woman wearing a headset is talking into her microphone; an expectant buzz of activity surrounds the dark curtain there. The warm-up preacher is doing his best to keep the audience's attention, but it is clear that their excitement is not for his theatrics – but for the main act.

—*Amen! Thank you! Halleluiah!* finishes the preacher, and the congregation join in, leaping to their feet. Mollel and Kiunga stand too. The band strike up a new tune, and, from the PA system, a voice starts to boom.

—Ladies and gentlemen. Brothers and sisters. From Nairobi, Kenya, direct to viewers all around the world. This is George Nalo Ministries. The word of God, from the heart of Africa. Now, will you please welcome the co-founder and director of George Nalo Ministries: Doctor Wanjiku Nalo.

The curtain opens and a large, middle-aged lady walks out. She is tall and well built, with a pleasant, youthful face despite her grey hair. Her determination and dynamism are palpable even at a distance. She waves to the audience, picks out a few individuals for a special smile of acknowledgement. Then she mounts the stage and takes a seat beside the large, gold lectern at its centre.

—And now, continues the announcer, here he is. Please give the most blessed Nairobi welcome to our founder, our shepherd, our guide. The one. The only. Reverend. George. Nalo!

The audience erupts, and the band burst into a frantic, uplifting, crashing melody. Suddenly Mollel becomes aware of a previously unseen choir, at least two hundred strong, in spotless crimson gowns, to the far side of the hall. It is immaculate stagecraft. Everyone seems to know what happens next, for as the choir begins its hymn, the congregation all around them join in with perfect unity. It is not a hymn that Mollel knows, but despite himself, he claps along to the rhythm. It is infectious. Even Kiunga's face has broken into a big, somewhat foolish grin. Just as the hymn reaches its chorus, a huge, suited man glides out from behind the curtain. He waves casually in acknowledgement of the frisson his presence causes, and he walks slowly across to the podium. He passes his wife, touching her briefly on the shoulder, and he gathers some notes at the lectern. He also produces a large white handkerchief from his pocket, and waits for the hymn to end.

—Halleluiah, he says.

He has a voice like a hundredweight of sharp sand. Deep, sonorous. And yet with a dry, treble note. Almost like several voices. And he begins quietly, taking the microphone but holding it nonchalantly away from his face. The effect is to silence the audience, focusing them on his words.

His quietness implies power withheld.

—Exodus chapter eighteen, verse twenty-one, he says, and Mollel sees many of those around him reach for their Bibles and flick through to the appropriate page.

—When Moses founded Israel, Nalo continues dryly, he knew that the country needed temporal law as well as spiritual.

He was told: look for able men from all the people, men who fear God, who are trustworthy and hate a bribe – here he turns his gaze directly to the audience for the first time, glaring outward – and place such men over the people as chiefs, and let them judge the people at all times.

—Now. We may not call them chiefs any more. We may call them politicians. But the commandment remains. Men who fear God. Men who are trustworthy. Men who hate a bribe. Does that sound like any politician you know?

A ripple of laughter reverberates around the hall.

—Those are the criteria. That is how we should select our chiefs, come the twenty-seventh day of this month. Men who fear God. Men who are trustworthy. Men who hate a bribe. And, in deference to my dear wife, I should point out that this applies to women, too.

Another polite laugh. Nalo takes his handkerchief and mops his massive brow. The act is a kind of punctuation point.

—And yet, he says. And yet I still have dear members of my flock – he waves his hand to encompass all those before him – my children, who come to me, and say, Pastor, who should I vote for? Perhaps, even now, you are hoping to hear me say a name, a party, even to drop a hint, a colour – orange, perhaps, or blue, or red… but my answer will always be the same. Who should you vote for?

—Those who fear God. Those who are trustworthy. Those who hate a bribe.

—Perhaps it is no wonder, when we look upon our politicians and find them so failing in every regard, that we turn to tribalism instead. If they are all corrupt, the logic goes, then I may as well vote for my kinsman. When he comes to disperse those government jobs, those constituency funds, those education grants, he'll remember his own. It may not be perfect, but life is not perfect. What more can we do?

—Fear God. Be trustworthy. Hate a bribe.

—Look around this great hall. Look around you.

The people in front of Mollel turn and look back at him and

Kiunga. He takes their lead and looks back up the row of seats. It's a dizzying experience. Everyone in the room is looking around them – and then, Mollel sees a flash of white hair, of pink skin, high up at the back of the stand.

—Turn to those around you and shake their hand. Go on.

Kiunga puts his hand out to Mollel, and Mollel shakes it distractedly. He is straining to see the white man. He feels a tap on his elbow, and the middle-aged lady in the seat beside him proffers her hand. He can't refuse it, so he shakes her hand, and then others: the hands of the couple in the row in front, and the family behind, even the little girl in her father's lap.

—Praise the Lord. Halleluiah.

The audience falls quiet again, a few keen stragglers still reaching for a final handshake. Mollel bobs his head to try to see the *mzungu* again, but can't make him out.

—We greet each other in the name of the Lord, because we have come together in defiance of ethnic division. When you shook your neighbours' hands just then, did you think: I am shaking hands with a Kikuyu, with a Luo, with a Kamba, with a Kisii? Did a Luhya shake hands with a Kalenjin, a Maasai with an Embu? I don't know. Because, from down here, I could not tell the difference. I just saw God-fearing, trustworthy Kenyans sharing in the love of the Lord. Amen.

—*Amen.*

Mollel leans over to Kiunga, and whispers: I'll see you at the main entrance at the end of the service. Then, delicately, trying not to attract attention, he stands and picks his way past the lady next to him and to the end of the row. Once there, he goes up the stairs, scanning each row as he does so. He reaches the top without seeing the *mzungu* again. At the back, there is a set of double doors and a stairwell. He slips through, and follows the stairs back down to ground level. He finds himself in some sort of service corridor, windowless and bare, with ducting and pipes running along the ceiling. He hears a sudden commotion and barely has time to leap aside before dozens of choristers race past him, pulling off their crimson gowns, revealing pure white ones underneath. Following them up is the woman with the headset: *Choir Two almost in position*, she shouts into her microphone. *Where on earth are those dancers?*

Mollel follows the choir along the corridor, which is curved. He passes a door and looks through the small window set into it: he's looking back up at the stage.

—Hey! What are you doing here? The voice is aggressive.

Mollel spins around. It is the young man who had greeted him at the entrance, Benjamin. He stands with his arms crossed. Unsmiling. He's not wearing the black jacket he wore earlier, just a T-shirt. Now Mollel can see the strength in his arms.

—This is not a public area.

—I was looking for someone, says Mollel. A *mzungu*. He must have just passed this way.

—You're a week too late, says the young man. Last Sunday we had two hundred *wazungu*, visitors from one of our sister churches in North Carolina. But this week… no. Now, please…

—Are you sure? White hair. Old guy.

—Sir, says Benjamin, in a quiet, threatening tone, you can go inside and worship the Lord, or step outside and enjoy his creation. But you can't stay here.

Mollel shows his police identity card.

—Now, let me ask again, says Mollel. Have you seen a white man here today, at all? An elderly man with white hair? Do you know anyone who fits that description?

The usher shakes his head, reluctantly compliant now he's seen the ID.

—Right. I need to speak with Reverend Nalo, when he comes off stage.

—You'd better come to the green room, says Benjamin.

It doesn't look very green to Mollel. In fact, the only green things in the wood-panelled room are the bottles of mineral water on the sideboard, glistening attractively with beads of condensation. Mollel ponders, waiting, then thinks what the hell, and pours himself a glassful.

He's been left alone here, but he's able to follow the show's progress, thanks to a huge TV screen on one wall. Nalo in full flow; the sandy tones filled out into a deep-throated, gravelly roar. Every time he shouts the name JESUS, he brings the microphone right next to his mouth. The TV is on mute: Mollel hears him, with a few seconds' delay, through the wall.

Along the bottom of the TV screen, a scrolling text bar urges donations and offers a telephone number and web address.

The water is cool and delicious. Mollel finishes his glass and replaces it alongside the others. He continues to inspect the room. There is no window. On the wall opposite the TV hangs a large oil painting of an eagle in full flight, a snake grasped between its talons. The inscription on a brass plaque below reads: *To our friends in George Nalo Ministries. From the United Tabernacle of Christ, Tashkent, Uzbekistan.*

Elsewhere the walls are dotted with pictures of George and Wanjiku Nalo. The Nalos shaking hands with former President Moi, President Kibaki. President Museveni of Uganda. Bill Clinton. George W. Bush. A lot of presidents.

Nalo has finished invoking Jesus, and is now visible on the screen, laying his hands upon congregants who have been brought to the stage. His mouth hangs open, his eyes are rolled back orgastically. As he touches the temple of each person presented to him, he shakes, and they fall back, caught in the arms of their supporters. With each new case, Nalo seems to weaken, his physicality shrinking, as though it is *his* strength which is being transferred. Through the wall, Mollel hears a massed wailing, howling.

Catholic church was never like *this*.

The noise level rises abruptly and, on the TV screen, Mollel sees Nalo preparing to leave the stage. At the same instant – there must be a few seconds' delay on the broadcast – the door of the green room bursts open and Nalo pushes in. He's even bigger than he seemed from a distance, though he is hunched and leaning wearily on the arm of the woman with the headset. She leads him to a leather sofa where he collapses. Then she darts to the sideboard and pours cold water into Mollel's used glass, and gives it to Nalo, who downs it in one. She produces a towel from a drawer and he wipes his face and neck, pulling open his collar.

Mollel makes to speak, but the stage manager holds up a warning finger. She leans over Nalo and removes a small black device from his pocket, and flicks a switch on it.

—The mic was live, she explains. You can talk now.

Nalo slumps back. His eyes seem shut, but he says: —Who are you?

—I'm Sergeant Mollel. Nairobi Central CID.

—Thanks, Esther. You can leave us.

—Back on in five, the woman reminds him as she leaves the room.

—That was quite a sermon, says Mollel, when the door is closed.

—Glad you enjoyed it, Sergeant.

—You're not endorsing a candidate? According to the papers, most of the major preachers have come out in favour of one party or another.

Nalo raises a weary finger skywards. —*His* is the only endorsement that matters.

—The papers say you may be a candidate yourself in five years. I suppose in that case, it's best to be neutral now.

—Neutral. Fearing God. Trustworthy. And hates a bribe. That's me, Sergeant. Does it describe you, too?

—Most of it.

—Only, it seems to me that whenever I have the pleasure of meeting one of our public custodians, there's usually a certain *tithe* to be extracted. What is it this time? Our singing has broken city noise regulations? You've found a fire door somewhere obstructed by a fallen leaf? Or perhaps the grass outside was growing a little too quickly, and you want to book it for speeding? Whatever it is, please talk to one of our church wardens. I never handle cash.

—Surely, replies Mollel, a bribe is equally hateful whether you're giving or receiving?

—There is a difference between bribery and extortion. If I pay a policeman to let me off a legitimate offence, that's a bribe. If he's fabricated the fine, that's extortion, backed up by the threat of force. Look around you. Look at what I've created. Do you think I could have made an organisation like this without attracting the worst sort of attention? Wherever there's an eagle, there are vultures. Let me tell you something. Back in the days when we were still running from a tin shack in Kibera, we were building a following. We'd started to put up awnings outside to give shade to all the people who could not fit in for the services. When we passed around the collection pots in those days, we didn't see notes, cheques. We saw fifty-cent, one-bob coins. We saw home-made trinkets and bags of *wimbi*. One day I saw a child's doll – a little girl had given her favourite toy. These people had nothing, Sergeant, nothing. And yet they gave. And it added up.

—Well, you can imagine what sort of effect that had in Kibera. Pretty soon we had the gangs come round. The *Mungiki*. Wanted to tithe our tithes. I said fine. You can have your payment. You know what would have happened if I'd said no?

—I can imagine.

—So I gave it to them. But I said, on the condition that you come to service. That way you can see what's going into the pot, and know I'm not cheating you. So they started coming to service. And you know what? Some of them stayed. They stopped taking their commission, and started helping out.

The door to the stage opens and Benjamin enters, followed by Wanjiku Nalo.

—In fact, continued Nalo, here is one of those young men now.

Benjamin glares at Mollel.

—I wondered if you were ex-*Mungiki*, Mollel says. The dreadlocks.

—Once, I believed that the only way to leave the *Mungiki* was with a police bullet in the head. Reverend Nalo gave me an alternative.

—Thank you, Benjamin, says Wanjiku Nalo. Tell Esther we'll be right out.

Benjamin leaves and Wanjiku takes a seat on the sofa next to her husband. —What's all this about? she asks.

—I was just wondering the same thing, says Nalo.

—I need to ask you some questions about Orpheus House, says Mollel. He has not been offered a seat, and is still standing.

—On a *Sunday*? says Wanjiku. Officer, this is the busiest day of our week. Can't you come by the office tomorrow?

—This is a murder inquiry.

That silences them.

—A young woman was found murdered in Uhuru Park on Saturday morning. We have reason to believe that her body may have been dumped in the storm drain at Orpheus House.

—How awful, says Wanjiku. But, Officer, the place is shut up. Awaiting renovation. If someone's illegally accessed the site, we can't be held responsible.

—There's a second line of enquiry, replies Mollel. The victim had recently come under the protection of a religious group, one which helps prostitutes get off the streets. That would be your organisation, wouldn't it?

—It could be, admits Wanjiku. There are a few charities doing similar work. Orpheus House is probably the best known. Can you tell us the poor girl's name?

—We only know her as Lucy, says Mollel. A Maasai.

George Nalo glances at his wife. He pulls the towel from around his neck and wipes his corpulent face with it.

—Lucy, says Wanjiku, quietly. Yes. She was one of our clients. So she's dead?

—You don't seem shocked at the idea.

—It's very sad. But no, I am not shocked. Officer, you know the sort of life these girls lead. That's what we're trying to save them from. If they insist upon returning to the streets, there's very little we can do for them.

—And that's what Lucy did? She returned to the streets?

—I suppose she must have. She just vanished one night. Upped and left. A while ago. Just before we shut down the old building.

The stage door opens again and the girl with the headset looks in. She holds a fresh shirt, tie and jacket on a hanger. — Reverend, you're on in two!

Nalo rises to his feet and takes the clothing.

—This is where I must bid you adieu, Officer, he says, pulling off his shirt. I hope you find whoever did this vile act. We'll pray for Lucy.

—I may need to speak to you again, says Mollel. And I need access to the building on Upper Hill.

—There's no point bothering my husband with this, interjects Wanjiku. He's just the spiritual guide. I'm the medical director of that project. I deal with the day-to-day side of things.

Nalo has hastily pulled on his new shirt and jacket. He stands still while Wanjiku ties his tie. She kisses him on the lips – tall as he is, she is almost the same height – and Nalo bursts through the door, and back on to stage, a wave of euphoric cheering greeting his return.

Then she turns to Mollel. —I have a meeting of the women's caucus after the service, but I can take you to the project quickly. We should be able to find Lucy's records. But I warn you: as far as patient confidentiality is concerned, I believe it applies just as much after death. You can have her contact information, but not her medical notes. If you want them, you'll need a court order. And for that matter, the Upper Hill house is half demolished inside, and dangerous. The only way you're getting in there is with a hard hat, and a warrant.

As Mollel follows her out of the door back into the service corridor, he glances back at Benjamin the usher.

—The Lord watches over his errant lambs, he says to Mollel. May you not stray too far from the path.

Mollel wonders whether that is a blessing, or a threat.

10

—This, says Wanjiku, is Orpheus House. At least, its present incarnation.

Mollel looks around the schoolroom. For there's no disguising what it is: posters of cartoonish biblical scenes adorn the walls; and the desks and chairs stacked up against the whiteboard are almost laughably child sized. The rest of the room is partitioned, sectioned off by green medical screens.

—We're conducting Sunday school in the open air, until the new building is ready. Right now, we don't have any residential clients. We're just offering a medical and counselling service.

Mollel thinks about the old, abandoned house on Upper Hill; the childish surroundings of this converted schoolroom; and the bright, white, architect's vision of the future Orpheus House. He remembers a snatch of catechism from his time with Chiku at the Catholic church: the Father, the Son and the Holy Ghost. He's never understood the concept – frankly, he doubts anyone really does – but perhaps this has something to do with it: the way the old becomes renewed, in pursuit of the ideal.

—Was Lucy a residential client? asks Mollel.

—Yes. Our last one, at the old place.

—How many others were there?

—Three or four at a time. They stayed between one week and six months. In total, we've had about three hundred women pass through.

—And your success rate?

—Pretty high. I can put you in touch with dozens of women who are now leading fulfilling lives in our community. You might even have seen some of them in church just now. Of course, there are always those, like Lucy, who fall by the wayside.

—How long was she with you?

—From memory, it was just a few weeks. But I'll have to find the records. Excuse me.

Wanjiku opens the door to a closet. The door jangles: on the inner surface, it is covered with cup hooks, on each hook a set of keys. A scrawl of marker pen above each hook seems to indicate each set of keys' purpose.

The floor and shelves of the closet are piled high with cardboard filing boxes, lids barely shut, overflowing with ledgers, files and stacks of paper.

—We haven't had a chance to sort out the paperwork yet. I think Lucy's records should be in this box.

Wanjiku reaches up to the topmost box. Despite the fact that she's probably an inch or two taller than he is – and, he guesses, just as strong – Mollel chivalrously steps forward. Wanjiku steps aside so that Mollel can get into the closet doorway. He takes the box. It's heavy – he turns on his axis and looks for somewhere to put it down.

—Here, she says, pushing aside one of the medical screens.

He sees an examination couch with steel stirrups spread wide; a trolley piled high with kidney dishes, clamps, swabs. He drops the box with a thump on to the couch.

—I'm a gynaecologist, says Wanjiku, sensing his surprise at the sudden appearance of this incongruous apparatus. The most important thing we can do for these women, even if we can't persuade them to give up the business, is to take care of their health. We give them a check-up, a blood test. Talk to them about STDs.

She lifts the lid off the box and starts to sift through its contents.

—Ever see any cases of female circumcision? Mollel asks.

She turns to him with a flash of anger. —Female genital mutilation, you mean! Don't soften it by suggesting it's merely ceremonial. Or some kind of cosmetic procedure. A clitoris is not a foreskin, you know. How'd you like to have the whole top of your penis cut off?

—I wouldn't! Mollel says defensively. And honestly.

—Statistically, it's on the decrease. The message seems to be getting through, especially among you Maasai. But it's still common practice in many tribes. The worst cases I've seen are from some of the northern nomads. They don't stop at a clitorectomy, you know. They can remove the whole labia. And there's nothing subtle about the way they do it.

With the image of Lucy's corpse in his mind, Mollel begins to feel queasy.

Wanjiku takes a set of stapled notes from the box. She glares at him with a fierce passion.

—You know *why* they do it, don't you?

She's drawn level with him, and Mollel is conscious of her physical presence: if a man squared up to him like this, Mollel would be preparing for a fight. But this is a woman. A grey-haired doctor. A pastor's wife.

He is utterly unnerved.

He answers, weakly: —Tradition?

—Tradition be damned! They do it for *power*. These pathetic men. *Old* men. You know full well, a Maasai can't wed until he's an elder. That's well into his thirties. Then, when he's rich, he can take another wife. He's getting on by then. A third, if he's successful enough. Probably in his sixties by now. These girls, they're child brides. But they grow up. The old man can't even satisfy one of them, let alone three. And all those young, virile, unmarried *morans* in the village. What to do? You cut off female sexuality, at source.

Mollel does not answer.

He knows it is true. It is all part of why he left. It is why Honey, and Lucy, and countless others left, and are leaving, and will leave.

79

But it's hard for him to hear these words in the mouth of a Kikuyu.

To a Maasai, a Kikuyu is the ultimate sell-out.

The two tribes once considered themselves cousins. The white man might class one Bantu, the other Nilotic – but the Kikuyu and the Maasai have always overlapped when it comes to territory: not to mention costume, mythology and vocabulary.

Sometimes they fought – minor skirmishes to full-scale wars – but it was a rivalry based on respect. Time was, the only outsider it was acceptable for a Maasai to marry was a Kikuyu, and vice versa.

When the Kikuyu rose up against the white man, it seemed to be a replay of the Maasai wars against the invaders of the previous century. But then they won, and renamed the country after their holy Kikuyu mountain. By this time, you never saw a Kikuyu in traditional dress. They seemed to prefer the ridiculous trousers and neckties of the foreigners.

Even though he married one – even though his son is half Kikuyu – even though he, himself, has long since rejected such tradition – it pains Mollel to hear a Kikuyu criticise the Maasai way of life. The Maasai might as well be invisible when it comes to government posts, civil servants or – as Mollel well knows – the police. They may not be the great industrialists, the celebrities, the movers and shakers. But, when the tourist board wants to attract visitors, who do they put on the billboards? If ever a picturesque African is needed, for a pop video or fashion shoot, whose image do they use?

Tradition, unfortunately, cuts both ways.

Wanjiku Nalo is glaring at him as though he, personally, is responsible for centuries of gender oppression. She rips the cover sheet from the stack of notes.

—This is all I can give you without a court order. Full name, age, the dates of her stay.

—That's enough to be going on with. One more thing. When Lucy came to you, had she been – was she already – mutilated?

—Medical confidentiality, Sergeant.

—And you're still insisting on a warrant before you let me into the old Orpheus House?

—We've gutted the place. It's not safe. I'm not prepared to take liability.

—Fine, concedes Mollel. Well, there's little chance of getting court time for a warrant until after Christmas, now. We'll just have to leave it until then, if it proves necessary at all. Thank you for your time, Doctor. I'd better find my colleague. I'm sure he's wondering where I've got to.

On the way out, Mollel feels the keys in his pocket. The ones he palmed when going to get the file box. The ones which had been hanging inside the closet door, on the hook marked *Orpheus House*.

11

There was a time – not so long ago – when Nairobi stopped on a Sunday. Apart from churches, the only places that opened their doors were some of the Muslim businesses in areas like Eastleigh. Now, Sunday is pretty much like a weekday, especially as far as the traffic down Mombasa Road is concerned.

Mollel rolls down the window of the Land Rover and sighs. They are stuck by Nyayo Stadium, the low roadside trees providing some relief from the overhead sun, but also a fresh danger: marabou storks. They love this stretch of highway and have colonised the trees here, feasting on the pickings dropped by the numerous hawkers who ply their trade through the stationary traffic. Four feet tall and with a long, sharp beak, they are totally fearless of humans, and teeter among the crowds of waiting *matatu* passengers, pouncing on titbits. When threatened, they spread their dirty grey wings and flap lazily into the trees above, whence their frequent and hefty bowel movements turn them into a menace for pedestrians and cars alike.

There is something about the marabou stork – *en-tialoo* in his own language – which reminds Mollel of an ancient Maasai: skinny legs propping up a hunched body wrapped in a shabby *shuka*; scrawny neck emerging to a bald, mottled head. Even the movements are those of an old, dying man.

He realises he's not thinking about marabou storks any more.

He's recalling the time, one long, dry season, when he had been moving the family herd from the dry Kajiado plains up into the lush pastures of the highlands. The sky was darkening, and he had promised his mother and Lendeva that he would return to their temporary *boma* in time to protect the animals from the creatures of the night.

But the dogs would not return his call, and investigating, he found them, whining anxiously, at the feet of an old man, huddled in his *shuka*, sitting against a rock, watching the sun descend in the sky.

The old man's hollow cheeks were covered with grey stubble and his eyes were pale blue and cataract-ridden. He seemed impossibly frail and feather light to the young Mollel, as though the slightest breath of wind would simply pick him up and carry him away.

He had come there to die.

It was the Maasai way, to die alone like this, and Mollel wondered whether he might deftly retrace his steps and escape without disturbing him. But the old man beckoned, and Mollel came closer. Neither spoke, but the old man raised a bony finger to the sheep and goats, and Mollel knew he must attend to them. He gathered them into a thicket, tied the largest ones there, and the youngsters huddled around for warmth. Then he cut a few thorn branches, placed them all around, and tied some of the goat's bells to them, as a warning, should a lion or leopard attempt to get close. Then he returned to the old man's side.

He was dead. But he had wanted Mollel beside him, so that the boy could guide his spirit into the night. So Mollel sat beside the stranger's corpse, guarding it and his flock until the first rays of gold gave shadows to the trees of the landscape before them.

Long ago, Mollel had begun to conflate the memory of the old man with his few memories of his father. His father had been a vigorous man the last time Mollel saw him. But had he lived, he would now be old and frail. If his time had already come, Mollel hoped that he had someone to sit vigil beside him.

He is shaken from his dreamlike state by the beeping of Kiunga's phone. Kiunga laughs: he had noticed that Mollel was dropping off.

—These police Land Rovers don't have air-con. Makes it hard to stay awake in jams.

—It's not that, says Mollel. I was just thinking.

—I do my best thinking in traffic, says Kiunga. Which I suppose, given that I live in Nairobi, ought to make me some kind of genius.

He slips the car into neutral and puts on the handbrake, so that he can rise up in his seat and reach into his trouser pocket for his cellphone. He slides back into place and looks at the phone's screen. Then he tut-tut-tuts.

—What is it?

—Take a look.

He hands Mollel the phone. Mollel looks at the message on the screen.

—My Kikuyu is too rusty. I can't read it.

—You're better off. It's another one of those hate messages doing the rounds. Says the Luos are massing. They're going to take Nairobi if their man loses the election, and kill any Kikuyu who stands in their way.

—Who's it from?

—I don't know. The number doesn't show. They have a way of bypassing the sender ID.

Some cars move up ahead, and Kiunga starts the engine. He edges the Land Rover forward less than one car's length and then stops, inches from the bumper of the vehicle in front. He kills the engine once more.

—You been getting a lot of these messages?

—That's the second today. Scroll through, you'll see more.

Mollel looks through the messages folder on Kiunga's phone. He opens one from someone called Mandy. He reads it aloud, trying to decipher the text shorthand.

—See you L-eight-R big boy I M gonna...

—Give it here! says Kiunga, snatching the phone back. Not that one! That's personal.

—Sorry, says Mollel. How come you've got all these messages, and I haven't?

—The ladies just find me irresistible, I guess.

—I meant the anonymous ones.

—You have an account, or use scratch cards?

—An account.

—Me too. I reckon whoever's sending these has someone at the phone company, checking off the names. Kiunga, Ngugi, Mungai, Mwangi, Wachira, Wambui. Not hard to tell the Kikuyus. It's even easier to spot the names of Luo subscribers. Otieno, Oketch, Odhiambo. You know Orengo, the desk sergeant? He's been getting messages in jaLuo, saying the Kikuyus are the ones going to attack first.

Although all the major political parties denied it, this election was firmly dividing along ethnic lines. President Kibaki's Party of National Unity was dominated by the Kikuyu. Raila Odinga's opposition, the Orange Democratic Movement, had the western Luo tribe at its core. Others among Kenya's forty or so tribal groups tended to gravitate to one or the other.

—I know you Maasai think there are only two tribes in Kenya, continues Kiunga: yourselves, and everyone else – but the way this election's shaping up, things are going to get nasty. And it looks like I'm not the only one who thinks so.

Kiunga gestures out of the window. —All this jam. It's people queuing for Nakumatt, look.

Mollel looks out of his window and notices for the first time that the jam they're stuck in is caused by cars backed up to get into the car park of the large supermarket whose entrance lies ahead. Now he's seen this, something else clicks too: the people passing by the car on both sides are not the usual traffic hawkers, selling newspapers, trinkets and fruit. They're ordinary people, carrying loads of shopping, laden in cardboard cartons and plastic bags. Bags of grain, flour or *wimbi*; bottles of water; canned goods. A lady strides purposefully past with a baby strapped to her back in a *khanga*; a similar shawl across her breast bulges with tin cans.

—Tell me this is just normal Christmas shopping, says Mollel.

Kiunga laughs. —Haven't you been stocking up, Mollel? You must be the only person in Nairobi who thinks this election is going to pass off with no trouble.

Mollel feels a hit of dismay. He has not stocked up: his meagre provisions would barely feed himself and Adam for a day. It's lucky the boy is with Faith.

He has been so caught up in this murder case that he has completely underestimated the looming situation. The threat of political violence has been a remote one for him, until now.

—The General Service Unit, he croaks, with realisation.

—What about them?

—It must have been the GSU that Superglue Sammy heard in Uhuru Park. If there's going to be trouble, they'd need to set up some sort of command post in the centre of the city. That's the ideal location: it's the closest open space to both Parliament, and the Central Business District.

—Why the secrecy, then? asks Kiunga.

—The GSU only take commands from State House, says Mollel. If word spread that they're already preparing a command post—

Kiunga finishes his thought. —It would be taken as a sign that the government is planning to steal this election.

—Would they kill someone to cover it up? asks Mollel.

—Who knows what those bastards are capable of? What I do know is that if Lucy got in their way...

He leaves the thought unfinished. He does not need to elaborate. Everyone knows that no woman is safe when the GSU are around.

The common perception of the General Service Unit is that they make the *Mungiki* look like girl scouts. Rumour has it, they are the direct descendants of the paid death squads the British used against the Mau Mau: when the former freedom fighters took over, they inherited the whole apparatus, and rather than disband them, employed them against their rivals.

In Moi's day, the GSU became a byword for repression, and the very presence of their dark green uniforms and crimson berets was enough to quell dissent. Those who were not intimidated tended to end up in the basements of the interior ministry building, where construction workers in the late nineties found an abandoned complex of hidden torture chambers.

Even though Moi has long since entered enforced retirement, the GSU retain their fearful reputation.

—Maybe they killed Lucy because she was a witness, says Mollel. She might have taken a client to Uhuru Park and stumbled across their manoeuvres. But what happened to the client? And why mutilate her like that?

—Perhaps the client's body has yet to turn up, says Kiunga, darkly. And as for the mutilation... some of those guys regard rape as an occupational benefit. Who knows how far they'd go when they're let off the leash?

—We need to warn Sammy. If they've eliminated one witness...

It's not easy to get off the static dual carriageway, and it's another twenty minutes before they get to a stretch where the central reservation is clear enough of trees, rocks and fencing for the Land Rover to get across. Although the traffic is still heavy in this direction, it is freer flowing and they reach Uhuru Park in another half-hour.

Car parked up, they head immediately back to Sammy's palm among the bushes, but the blankets and radio have gone. They cruise the streets for a couple of hours, checking all of Superglue Sammy's regular haunts, speaking to some of the other beggars who are known to hang out with him.

But he seems to have vanished off the face of the earth.

12

They're heading south again. They've left the snarl-up of city traffic behind them, and are back on Mombasa Road, but long past the stadium. They have taken a detour through the district known as South C and now the traffic is more free flowing. They pass the new office blocks being built either side of the highway. Construction work is taking place wherever Mollel looks. This part of town is barely recognisable from even a few months before. It seems at times as though the whole city is in a state of flux.

The road itself does not escape the constant churn of development. At Athi River they are forced to take a diversion where a new stretch of highway is being built, and they quit the tarmac and rumble and judder along a rutted, dusty track.

Progress sometimes means taking a step back.

Although the traffic is moving, it's still heavy, and numerous *matatus* and even the long-distance buses take advantage of the informal set-up to deviate from the track and plough across the open country on both sides, swerving round any obstacles, creating new paths and clouds of dust as they do so. It's a free-for-all, and Mollel is glad of the Land Rover's ground clearance when they are forced to swerve off the track by an intercity bus bearing down upon them, lights flashing and horn blaring out a ghastly tune. So what if they have right of way? Their two tons can't argue with his fifteen.

The road reconvenes at the cement works, and there's a bottle-neck as all the vehicles jockey to regain the tarmac. Mollel rolls up his window to block the choking dust which floods in any time they slow down. The only way to avoid it is to drive faster than it can blow in. Here, it has an acrid, alkaline taste from the off-spill from the factory and the waste ash which spills from the trucks bringing it to make cinder blocks. It is said that Athi River dwellers dare not go outside with their hair wet, for fear of their locks setting hard.

Mollel recalls his own circumcision ceremony. He and his brother, Lendeva, both in their early teens, grinning at each other with their faces whitened with ash – and he puts the thought from his mind.

They cross the bridge over the river – low at this time of year, despite the rains. If the girl's body had not been stopped in the park, this is where she would have washed up – or, ultimately, six hundred kilometres away in the Indian Ocean. This river also serves as sewer to most of Nairobi's informal settlements – in other words, the city's slums. Mollel notices a tanker truck parked down at the water's edge, a man holding a thick suction pipe mouth down in the six inches or so of river: the sign on the tanker's side reads *Clean Drinking Water*.

They roll into Kitengela, the last significant township this side of Nairobi, before the city gives way to the Kajiado plain. It's a busy, thriving area. Church is out, and Sunday night is a time for socialising, for seeing friends, and for being seen in one's finery. The *nyama choma* joints along the roadside are doing a brisk business, and the smell of roast meat makes Kiunga cast a longing glance at Mollel.

—I haven't eaten since lunchtime, boss, he pleads.

—It's only six!

—Exactly. I usually have something mid-afternoon. Just to keep me going.

—We're nearly there. Mollel takes out his notepad and looks at the address Honey wrote for them the previous night. *Paradise Towers, Prison Road, Kitengela. Next to the Happy Days Abattoir.*

—Take this left.

They turn down Prison Road. Paradise Towers is a four-storey apartment block – four and a half, to be accurate, as the fifth level is a concrete floor with reinforced piles sticking out of it, the owners presumably awaiting a time they can afford to build further. The ground floor is occupied by the usual array of enterprises – a mobile phone shop, a barber, a *nyama choma* joint.

—Remember, she asked us to park away from the building, says Mollel.

—*Sawa sawa*. Kiunga drives a few buildings further and stops the car outside a corrugated iron shack with a sign advertising *Video Games 10/- per go*. As they get out, Mollel sees a group within, young men and boys, clustered around a TV screen. A car racing game is being played, and the whole group leans from left to right as the player takes the corners of the race track.

A couple of youths are hanging around at the door. —You two, says Kiunga. Watch this car. Anything happens to it, you're paying for the damage.

—And if nothing happens? asks one of the boys.

—Ten bob.

They grin. —Each?

—*If* nothing happens.

—Don't worry, Officer. We'll take good care of your wheels.

The two detectives walk to Paradise Towers. There's enough foot traffic to for them to discreetly melt away from the police Land Rover. At the centre of the façade, between a shopfront and a noisy bar, there's a staircase, where they pause.

—Listen, Kiunga, says Mollel. With Sammy gone, Honey is our only witness. I don't want you to upset her.

—Upset her? Kiunga gives him a quizzical look.

—You know what I mean. Last time, you were pretty hard on her.

—She's a *poko*, Mollel. Prostitutes like her are used to worse than us.

—Maybe. But that's not the way I want to play it.

A frown crosses Kiunga's brow, but he seems to assent to his superior officer, and they make their way up to the fourth floor. Once there, the landing takes the form of a balcony which runs the length of the front of the building. There are no numbers on the doors: by the close spacing, Mollel reckons they're just single rooms. His suspicion is confirmed when he walks past an open door, and catches a glimpse of a family living in a space not much bigger than one of the holding cells at Central. Next, they pass a communal bathroom with the door open, a woman inside washing a seeming schoolful of children.

They come to the end of the balcony. —She said it was this one, says Mollel. He raps on the door with his knuckles. He wonders whether anyone inside could hear it, above the sound of traffic and screaming kids and passers-by, and music from the bar below. But after only a moment, he hears the scrape of a latch being pulled back and the door opens.

A woman answers, and Kiunga says: —Sorry. We were looking for someone else.

Mollel looks at her closely: smooth, shaved head; average height; Maasai features. It is Honey.

She laughs. —Come in, she says. Kiunga still looks non-plussed as they enter the cramped, bare space. He breathes an *oh* of realisation when he sees the long, glossy wig carefully placed upon a stand.

—The four-inch heels make a difference, too, she says with a smile. Sorry to disappoint you, boys. Not quite so attractive in the real world, eh?

Mollel surprises himself when he says: —You look lovely. Then, in his embarrassment, he looks at Kiunga, who raises an eyebrow at him.

Honey laughs again. —Kind of you to say so, Sergeant. But fellow Maasai aren't really my target market. You know? Now, I would offer you a seat, but…

She waves a hand around the small room. It is bare, except for a foam mattress covered by a *shuka* on the floor; a cooking ring attached directly to a gas cylinder, and a few utensils in a pot next to it; a dressing table and a row of clothes on hangers, dangling from a cane suspended from two pieces of string tied to two nails tacked to the ceiling. Another *shuka* covers the small window on the far wall.

—You both lived here? asks Kiunga.

—We shared, yes, says Honey. This is just somewhere to sleep. We both managed pretty well. This is not somewhere to bring clients, if that's what you're thinking.

—No, I'm sure it's not to their taste, says Kiunga, a note of sarcasm creeping into his voice. I expect you take them to the international hotels – the Balmoral, the Diplomat. Perhaps you slip the night manager a hundred bob to let you ply the bars. Or is the lunchtime trade more your thing? Bribing the housekeepers to give you an hour in a vacant room before the paying guest checks in?

Honey flashes Mollel a distressed look. —I thought we were going to be all right about… about what I do?

—What you do, says Kiunga, flatly, is what got your friend killed.

—That's one theory, said Mollel, shooting his colleague a glance of warning.

Honey turns to him, eyes glistening. —Can I speak to you, alone, please? she asks, in Maa.

Just as the night before, Mollel is stumped for a reply, so long has it been since he's conversed in his own language. Finally, he says to Kiunga in English: —Why don't you go get some food?

—With pleasure, says Kiunga. Then to Honey: We're only trying to help, you know.

She acknowledges him with a nod.

—Get you something? he asks Mollel.

—No, thanks. I'll see you downstairs.

—Give me a shout if you need anything, says Kiunga, and he meets Mollel's eye. Mollel just wants rid of him, and is cross that Kiunga has disregarded his advice. But Kiunga's look says: *Be careful.* Then he leaves.

—He's a good guy, really, says Mollel.

—I'm sure he is, says Honey. But you know, I can hear it in his voice. The contempt. The disgust. To him, I'm just another K-Street *poko*. Lucy's the same. Dead or alive, the job is all we are. That's why I came to you. I thought perhaps you'd have more sympathy for a poor little Maasai girl who went and got herself killed. That you'd see the person, not just the profession.

—I do.

—Yet you think it was the job that got her killed?

—We just go on the evidence. It is what it is. The location, what she was wearing, the time of night. We think that she may have gone there with a client. Perhaps he did it, perhaps she disturbed someone, saw something. If we could just find the client...

Honey throws her hands up in exasperation. Mollel continues: —Statistically, prostitute murders...

—Statistics! she wails. I'll show you statistics!

She flies to the door and to the balcony rail outside: for an instant, Mollel believes she is about to throw herself over. But she stops there, hands gripping the rail tightly, knuckles pale, elbows locked.

—Come! she shouts. Look for yourself!

Mollel joins her at the rail.

The sun is setting: the skyscrapers of the city centre are just visible as inky purple silhouettes on the horizon against the crimson sky. Between here and there is a panorama of houses and water towers; a landscape of corrugated iron, concrete and thatched *makuti* roofs. Every square inch seems populated. Television aerials sprout like seedlings; satellite dishes like fungi. Mobile phone masts and mosque minarets break the monotony, pushing up as if attempting to escape the humanity below. And where the sky darkens, away from the city, the cement works stand illuminated in halogen and phosphorus; steaming and suppurating dust; a white, powdery, moon city in contrast to the sun-soaked, blood-soaked Nairobi to the west.

The noise is constant: mechanical crashing from the cement works; the rumble of traffic on the highway; music; prayer; shouts; screams; laughter; life. Mollel can hear hundreds of human voices, but apart from the woman at his side, he cannot see a single human being until he looks down. Then, the street opens up before him with all its pulsing vitality. People course its length, moving like ants in a trail, each picking his own way but each a constituent part of the two-way flow. Mollel spots Kiunga leaning on the counter of a *nyama choma* joint over the street; he's chewing on a chicken leg and chatting up the serving girl. Farther down the street is their car, the two boys from the video shack lounging proprietorially against the wheel arch. Families, spruce in their Sunday best, little girls in puffy satin dresses and boys in replica lounge suits; a sausage vendor pushing his brazier; hawkers selling fruit and mosquito bats and magazines; *matatu* touts drumming up trade; goats and chickens nonchalantly grazing on trash whenever a spot of clear ground appears.

—You know, says Honey, this city didn't even exist a hundred years ago. It was our land then. *N'garan'airobi.* The place of cold springs. All these people – these Kikuyus, Luos, Merus, Embus, Kalenjin, Luhyas and whatever else – they're here because the white man came here one day and said, this is a nice, cool, fertile part of the country. I'll build my city here. Look down at that street. How many people do you reckon there are there?

—Five, six hundred? guesses Mollel.

—And that's one little side street. There are twenty, thirty streets like it in Kitengela. And Kitengela's just one district. There's Mlolongo, Athi, South B, South C, Embakasi, Donholm, Pipeline, Industrial Area. They all have streets like this, full of people. And we're only talking about the districts in this part of town. What's that, a quarter, an *eighth* of the city?

He shrugs. The scale of the place seems unknowable. Dizzying.

—There are all the rich areas, Karen, Hardy, Lavington, Westlands. The Indian districts. Then Somali-town, Eastleigh. And I've not even started on Mathare, Kibera, Kawangware,

Dagoretti – if you think it's crowded here, those areas make this place look like the *Mara*.

Mollel feels a slight tightening in his chest; a shallowness of breath. It's a physical memory of his first arrival in the city, a boy who'd grown up in a village of two dozen, whose only experience of crowds had been a herd of goats, or market day with two or three hundred people milling about. He'd found Nairobi overwhelming, terrifying, exciting, invigorating: he'd hated it and loved it and realised, with joy and fear, that *this* was the wilderness he'd been hoping to lose himself in.

—It's not our place any more, he says.

—No, she replies. Nairobi does not belong to the Maasai. It belongs to those people down there. People from all over Kenya. All over the world. Ten million of them. There's your statistic. Ten million people in this city. What's one *poko* less?

—That's not the way I feel, says Mollel.

—Really? And yet, that's the way you're conducting this investigation. She was killed, because she was a prostitute.

—It's the way the evidence points, protests Mollel.

The sky is dark: a light bulb flickers to life on the balcony. Honey turns to Mollel.

—What about Orpheus House? she demands. I told you, the last time I saw her, she was staying there. You admitted the drain leads to the spot where she was found.

—It's a stretch. If she wasn't dumped in the park, there are dozens of places farther up the drain where the body could have been washed from.

Honey is silent for a moment. Then she says: —So you don't believe me, that she'd quit the streets. You still think it's the fact that she was working as a prostitute which caused her death?

Mollel's answer is silence.

—What if I told you she could not have been working? What if I could prove that she had not been working for months?

—That might change things, says Mollel.

Honey fixes him with her dark eyes. Last time I saw her, she

95

says, Lucy was pregnant. She was going to have a baby. And it would have been born any time now.

Mollel reels. For a moment he doubts his ears. He casts his mind back to the body – there had been no sign of pregnancy. He hardly dares contemplate what that means. But he must.

—Why didn't you tell me this before?

—I'm only just beginning to trust you. There's a chance – a slim chance – this baby might still be alive. Lucy might have delivered it before she was murdered. In which case, that baby's in danger.

—From who?

—Don't you see? The father. Lucy's powerful, important client. He eliminated her. And to keep his secret, he'll probably want to eliminate the baby, too. From what she told me, he has contacts all the way through the police department. That's why I needed to know I could trust you.

—You're going to have to trust me now, says Mollel. You're going to have to tell me everything.

—But you won't tell anyone about the baby? Even...? She nods down to the street, where Kiunga is still eating.

—No.

—Then there is more I need to tell you. The last time I saw Lucy was not three months ago. It was last week. I was missing her. I wanted to track her down. I knew the place they'd taken her to, that old house on Upper Hill. I banged on the gate but the whole place looked closed up. Then – as I was about to leave – I saw her. At the window by the front door. Just for a second. Then the old man came, the guard, and chased me away. If you want to find out what happened to Lucy, that's where you need to go. Orpheus House.

13

Mollel does not believe in ghosts. But he believes that evil endures. And inside this empty house, he can feel it.

Getting in had been not been difficult. He'd asked Kiunga to drop him in town, told him he wanted to walk home.

—At this time of night? Are you crazy, boss?

Mollel shook the flashlight he'd taken from the car. The batteries were dead. He passes it back to Kiunga, who drops it into the glovebox. He fumbles in his pocket. —Here. Take this. Good job I'm trying to cut down, anyway.

He throws Mollel his cigarette lighter. —Not as good as a flashlight, but it might be some use to you.

—Thanks.

Mollel watches the Land Rover disappear, Kiunga off to his cosy bed. Then he swiftly changes direction and heads for Upper Hill.

Outside Orpheus House, he looks over the gate for any sign of the old man, Githaka. But the place is deserted.

In the light of a distant street lamp, he looks through the keys he'd swiped from Wanjiku Nalo's closet, selects one, and tries it in the padlock on the gate. It clicks open. Gingerly, he opens it just wide enough to slip through. Inside, he crouches and feels around in the leaf litter until he finds what he needs: a stick, just large enough to prop the gate shut while he is within.

Every footstep seems to crackle with explosive potential in that silent darkness. But he creeps over the gravel, past the storm drain hatch, into the greater, looming mass which is all he can distinguish of the house.

Here, he dares not flick the lighter into life, so he gropes his way forward until he feels the cold stone wall. Then, by memory, he works his way towards the door, concealed behind a heavy iron grille. Instinct tells him there should be another padlock there. There is: his fingertips find it eventually, and he fumbles with the keys, trying them at random until one slides into the barrel.

Then, one more door: a large iron latch-key, whose keyhole is mercifully easy to locate.

And now he stands within Orpheus House.

It has a dry, dusty, empty smell. The only light is a murky greyness which leaches in through the barred window next to the front door.

That must be the window at which Honey had seen Lucy. Mollel shivers, and reminds himself that he does not believe in ghosts. All the same, he is sorely tempted to spark up Kiunga's lighter for a moment, just to get a sense of the space around him.

He does not do it. He recalls from his daytime visit that the window to this room has no curtain. Can't risk Githaka or anyone else seeing a light within.

It's only natural to be afraid, he tells himself. If I'm caught here, trespassing, entering without a warrant, I'll be kicked off the force.

Yes, he decides. *That's* why I'm afraid. Perfectly natural caution.

He almost convinces himself, too, when he hears a scratching noise travel along the ceiling above him, right across the room, and beyond. It's all he can do to prevent himself from using the lighter, if only for the comfort the flame would bring. But he does not, and by the time the sound has gone, he is sure it was just a mouse in the attic. These old single-storey houses have just a layer of thin fibreboard as a ceiling, and it amplifies the tiniest noise on the other side.

He edges forward, heading towards the outline of a door. The next room he enters gives out on to the back of the property, where there are fewer trees to cover the sky. In the dribble of extra light he can make out slightly more of what is around him.

This is a kitchen: the worktops and units are still in place, though there are gaps where the oven and fridge would have been. The cupboard doors hang open. There's nothing significant here.

Back into the main corridor, and to the next door along. This opens on to a small room, which seems to have once been a bedroom. He feels the softness of carpet underfoot, rather than the peeling linoleum of the previous rooms. No furniture, but the dark shape of a crucifix is just discernible above where the bed must have stood.

He finds another couple of rooms which are much the same. He is beginning to wonder whether this is worth the risk, whether it wasn't merely Honey's overactive imagination which has sent him here, when he tries the door at the end of the corridor.

It is locked.

He produces the bunch of keys from his pocket, and feels his way through them. There is one left that he thinks he hasn't already used. He hopes it works.

He finds the keyhole. Inserts the key. It turns.

This room is different from the others. It's pitch black, for a start. No hope of seeing anything in here. But he senses it's bigger, too: and something about the way the sound of his footstep is deadened, rather than echoing, makes him think that there must be furniture or other objects in here.

He recalls how he tried to look into this window from the outside, when he came in the daytime. It had been obscured by heavy curtains, not even a gap between them.

Which means he can try a light.

He closes the door quietly behind him, produces Kiunga's lighter from his pocket, and sparks the flame alive.

The sudden light dazzles him at first, despite the blueness of the flame. He extinguishes it. In that first moment, though, he's taken in a chilling sight: an examination bench, just like the one in the Sunday school, steel stirrups pointed high in the air and spread wide. But this bench has something on it.

He lights the flame once more.

A crumpled, dark towel. One corner of it seems to have been bleached white. He looks closer and revises his opinion. It's a white towel, entirely stained deep, dark brown, except for one corner. It has dried, hard, encrusted.

Blood.

The blood smears show up glossy on the black plastic of the bench cover. They show up black on the lino floor, leading to a sink at one side of the room, where steel dishes and implements lie carelessly discarded, spattered, as is the sink itself, with blood.

A sudden burning pain causes him to drop the lighter. It clatters away from him on the floor in the darkness. He kneels and pats the floor around him. After a few frantic moments he finds it, stands, and presses the lighter's button once more.

He holds the flickering light and turns around the room with mounting horror. In one corner, a crumpled pile of green surgical scrubs. Stained with blood. More blood on the floor: here, a footprint in blood. A latex glove, fingers sucked in, palm covered in blood. A black garbage bag, swabs and gauze overflowing from the top. Covered in blood.

Everything is covered in blood.

14

Mollel's dreams are fractured, and tainted with blood. When he wakes, he picks up his phone to look at the time.

Nine forty a.m. Four missed calls. Honey.

—Mollel. Finally. I've been calling you.

—I was sleeping.

—Are you OK? You sound terrible.

—I'm fine. And then he remembers.

Orpheus House. The blood. The operating table. Something happened in that place. Something more than a simple murder.

—I think you're right. I think we're looking for a baby.

—And I know where to start, she says. Have you got any smart clothes?

—I have the suit I was wearing last night.

—That'll have to do. Can you meet me in town?

—Sure. I'll call Kiunga.

—No, says Honey. Not him. It has to be just you and me.

He meets her at the bus stage near the Ambassador Hotel. It's a busy interchange, serving all the *matatus* which run to the eastern half of the city, not to mention the numerous up-country buses. The touts accost him, as they do anyone standing still, assuming they're looking for a cheap fare. *Beba, beba* is the incessant cry: *all aboard*. Nearly full minivans blare their air horns in competition; passengers push for the final places rather than wait for another vehicle to fill. They throw their bags to the *kondos*, the conductors, to be lashed to the roof with lengths of inner-tube rubber. Others juggle their possessions in tied-up bundles, along with trussed chickens and swaddled children: whatever rides on your lap is free.

Many are returning home for Christmas. Still others, Mollel gathers from snatches of conversation all around him, are leaving the city for the election. Not with the intent of exercising their democratic right at home; but of keeping away from trouble.

The touts are aware of this new imperative, and are taking advantage. —Come on, *brazza*, one hisses at him, spitting a wad of *miraa* into the gutter. You can hold out all you like, but you won't get a better price. Everyone's leaving town. You wanna be left behind?

—I'm waiting for someone, replies Mollel. And I'm not your brother.

—Maybe I've seen them, says the tout, ever eager for a tip. Whatta they look like?

Mollel ignores him. What would he say? Tall, high heels, long hair, short dress? He can imagine the response. —*You're on the wrong street, brazza.*

Or would he say: shaved head, average height, young Maasai woman? —*Make your mind up, brazza!*

Someone touches his arm. He turns to see a smartly dressed businesswoman with a leather document case under her arm. Her hair is shoulder-length and as conservative as her suit. She smiles at him broadly.

—Honey!

She reaches up and gives him a peck on the cheek.

—It's all about looking the part, she says, in response to his surprise. Don't you have a tie, Mollel?

He pulls his tie out of his pocket and shows it to her sheepishly. Her bottom lip plumps with amused disdain. —That's the only one you've got? Come on, Mollel. Let's get you a new one.

—Now I see what you were waiting for, *brazza*. The tout leers. I've been waiting for a girl like that all my life.

They stop at a street stand which sells ties, socks and prophetic literature. The ties are rolled up neatly and arranged according to colour: the effect is of a rainbow of exotic fruit. Mollel's hand gravitates towards the browns and greys.

Honey reaches out and stops him.

—What is it about Nairobi men, she asks, that makes you all so afraid of colour? Everything's got to be drab. The West Africans aren't like that. You ever seen a Ghanaian or Nigerian man here on business? They're dressed finer and more colourfully than the women. But here, we seem to think we have to be like Europeans, all in black. It's you Maasai men I feel most sorry for. You're the finest of all, back in our homeland. Dyed dreadlocks. Necklaces and bangles. Red *shukas* you can see from miles away.

—In the bush, you want to be seen, says Mollel. In the city, it's more important to fit in. Especially in this profession.

—You can compromise, though, can't you? she says. She picks a deep red tie. Flame-tree red. Maasai red. Here. Try this.

She hands it to him. It's silky. Sheened. Its contours glimmer as she glides it over Mollel's hands.

—Good choice, sister, says the stallholder.

—Put it on, she says.

Mollel threads the tie under his collar, then stops, awkwardly.

—I don't know… he says, hesitantly.

—Oh, it suits you, she says. Don't you think?

The stallholder nods eagerly.

—I mean… He lowers his voice. He's ashamed to admit it. I mean, I don't know how to…

—Oh, you mean you can't tie it without a mirror? replies Honey, with a wink. Don't worry. Let me do it for you.

She reaches up, and knots the tie deftly, the silken material rustling against itself as she weaves it. The tie drops against his shirt, and she slides the knot up against his neck.

—There, she says. Very handsome. And not at all like a…

She mouths the word *policeman*.

—How much? asks Mollel.

—Three hundred, says the stallholder.

Honey reaches into her document holder and produces some notes. Mollel begins to protest.

—Don't even think about it, she insists. I chose it, I pay for it. You have to let me buy it for you, Mollel.

They take a taxi for the trip out of the city centre to Karen. Mollel doesn't know this part of town well: he knows it is named for a white woman who lived here, long ago. It seems as though, ever since, the whites – the *wazungu* – have wanted to create a suburb in the image of their own. Signs with crests and golden letters proclaim preparatory schools and country clubs, while high, immaculately clipped hedges and ornate wrought-iron gates hint at luxurious domesticity beyond.

And then, beside a sign for a shelter run by the Kenyan Society for the Prevention of Cruelty to Animals, is a smaller, hand-painted placard: *Divine Mercy Orphanage. A Project of George Nalo Ministries. By Appointment Only.*

—I phoned ahead, says Honey.

The orphanage is off the main road and down a dirt track, causing the taxi driver, in his low-slung saloon, to slow to a crawl and curse under his breath. But it's not far, and he visibly perks up when Honey says to him: —We won't be long.

Being paid to wait is every Nairobi taxi-driver's dream.

—We don't normally see people at such short notice, says the matron. But as it's so nearly Christmas…

She leaves the point unfinished, as though understood. Mollel and Honey nod.

—Do you have any children? the matron asks.

—I have a son, says Mollel. Nine years old.

The matron looks questioningly at him, then at Honey. Honey quickly adds:

—My husband's first wife died shortly after his son was born. We've been trying for several years. But the doctors say I can't.

Mollel looks at Honey, startled. She takes his hand in both of hers: he sees on her left ring finger a wedding band.

—I'm sorry, says the matron. But perhaps it is God's will that your misfortune will provide happiness for one of our children.

—I do hope so, says Honey.

—Will you excuse me a moment? asks Mollel.

—Of course.

Mollel gets up and walks to the open door. He steps outside. In the shade of a jacaranda tree, a group of children are playing with plastic cartons, happily scooping and piling mounds of dust. Others are chatting to the young woman who tends to them, while a couple of older boys mock-fight with twigs.

A girl approaches. She is about six years old, and twirls one foot beneath her in a mixture of boldness and bashfulness.

—*Jambo*, she greets him.

—*Jambo*, he replies. What's your name?

She runs away, giggling. Honey comes out and joins him.

—I told her that you get upset when you think about your first wife, she says.

—My *only* wife, he corrects her.

He recalls the look Kiunga gave him in Honey's flat: *Be careful*. He's angry at the thought that Honey might be manipulating him. And he's angry about the ring.

—I'm sorry, Mollel. But we have to pose as a couple. It's the only way we'll get information about what happens to the children who come through here.

—Where did you get the wedding ring? It sits loose on your finger. Stole it from one of your clients, I suppose.

Honey pulls him around to face her. She looks into his eyes imploringly.

—Don't be like that, she says. Please. Don't let her get suspicious. I don't think she's noticed anything yet. We can get away with a little bit of tension between us. We are supposed to be married, after all. Remember, we're trying to find a baby.

—A baby? The matron has appeared at the doorway. You're interested in a baby?

Honey links her arm with Mollel's. —Oh! You overheard us. Well, it's a point of difference between us. My husband thinks an older child would be better. But I can't help wanting a baby, you see.

The matron nods her head. —Everyone wants a baby, she agrees. But we try to encourage people to consider the older children. That's one of the reasons we put a premium on fees for adopting newborns.

Mollel feels Honey's arm tighten in his. —And how much are they, these fees?

—We consider a hundred thousand to be a suitable donation. The matron smiles.

—A hundred thousand! Honey laughs. Then her voice drops a tone. Bitterness tinges her words. So that's the price of a child.

Honey's abrupt change of manner causes the matron to look at her warily. This time, it is Mollel who hastily tries to put the conversation back on track.

—I suppose you don't have any newborns up for adoption at the moment? he asks.

—None at all. Our last was several months ago. And there's a considerable waiting list, as you might imagine. Now, perhaps you would like to talk to some of the older children? Get to know them a little? Some of them are very charming, I can assure you.

The little girl looks over at them and waves shyly at Mollel. He waves back.

—That's Felicity, says the matron. An adorable child. And we could let you have her in time for the new year, should all the arrangements work out.

—All the arrangements? asks Honey, now barely bothering to disguise her contempt. You mean, your *donation*. I presume she would cost less, being so much older?

—Well, yes, concedes the matron, uncertainly. We'd be keen

to get her into a good home. Perhaps… She turns to Mollel. Perhaps you need to talk about this. As a *couple.*

—Perhaps we do, agrees Mollel.

—Tell me, says Honey. What'll happen to that girl? Felicity? If she doesn't find someone to take her in?

The matron looks at them both. Her eyes are wary, now. —We do our best for all our children, she says. But you never know. It's tough being an orphan. Who knows where she might end up? Some of them, you know – she lowers her voice – get hooked into prostitution.

—Some people might prefer that to being bought and sold like slaves, says Honey, her voice full of challenge. After all, if you're going to be pimped out to the highest bidder, you might as well take a fair cut.

The matron stiffens. —I think you'd better come back when our director is here, she says. Doctor Nalo. She's the best one to deal with those kinds of questions.

—What's the matter? spits Honey. Her voice wavers with emotion. We're not good enough parents for you? I bet if we were a pair of rich *wazungu* looking for a little black baby, with a big fat cheque in our hands, you'd find one soon enough, wouldn't you?

—I think you'd better leave, says the matron.

As they walk to their taxi, Mollel casts a look back. Under the jacaranda tree, Felicity is standing, watching them leave. Her hand is raised.

He imagines it is still raised a long time after they have gone.

In the back of the cab, Honey buries her head in Mollel's shoulder. —I'm sorry, she says. Just the thought of those children in there. Lost. Without their mothers to look after them.

—Some of them will find homes, he says.

—Some of them *had* homes, she replies. While you were outside, that woman told me more about where the children come from. It's called an orphanage, but a lot of those children have parents, you know. Parents who can't afford them, or can't cope, or who have been told by the Church that they're unworthy. *Unworthy*, Mollel. Like Lucy. Or me.

She sits up, and looks out of the window. —Did you hear her, Mollel? *Everybody wants a newborn.* A hundred thousand shillings. I'd heard that was the going rate. It's not just older children they steal, you know. She'd never admit it, but I've heard the rumours. Some of these places take babies away from mothers in the delivery room. They lie to them. Tell them they had a stillborn. No. Lucy's baby's alive out there, somewhere. We've got to find it.

—Even if it is, concedes Mollel, we don't know whether Lucy's baby ever came through here. The matron denied having had a newborn recently.

—No, says Honey. But we can find out. The other thing I learned is that every adoption has to be registered. If Lucy's child was sold on, there'll be a record of it with the government.

—They took her baby away, Mollel, she says, with something like a sob, and he folds his arm around her. Can you even imagine that, Mollel? Can you even imagine what that's like?

15

—Where the hell have you been, boss? I've been trying to get hold of you.

—I got your messages. I was following another lead.

—I thought you might have got mugged, or killed, or something, after I left you last night.

—No. But I want to revisit Orpheus House. And I want to pull in any favours we've got, to try to get a forensic team down there.

—You're a bit behind the game, I'm afraid, boss. Where are you? I'll pick you up.

When they get to Orpheus House, one of the big, ancient city fire trucks is standing in the driveway. A crew of men are dousing the smouldering rafters, exposed like ribs. A rainbow plays in the spray as the afternoon sun pushes through the leaves, creating shafts in the lingering smoke.

—If it wasn't already scheduled for demolition, I'd call it an insurance job, one of the firemen is saying. The old man claims he saw no sign of any intruders. So I guess we'll just have to put it down to ghosts.

They laugh. Mollel and Kiunga walk past them, to where Wanjiku Nalo is standing, talking to the caretaker.

—Ah, Sergeant Mollel, she says, as she looks up and sees him.

Githaka was just telling me that we've had a vermin problem here for some time. I suppose one of them must have chewed through an electric cable. Nasty little creatures. You know, it was only last night I noticed that I'd somehow foolishly mislaid my keys for this place. But I guess I won't be needing them, now.

She casts him a triumphant smile. Mollel turns his back and walks away.

He rounds the back of the house. The damage is even worse here. The makeshift operating theatre had obviously been the seat of the fire. The glass in the large window has caved in, revealing the walls bare and black. The roof is open to the sky, and water drips down from the burnt rafters. The floor is covered with roof tiles and the remains of the ceiling; a pair of twisted stirrups gleam in the middle of the room.

There is an old tree stump farther down the plot, and Mollel sits on it, head in his hands.

—What's up, boss? asks Kiunga. If you don't mind me saying so, you seem a little… strange.

Mollel is scouring his memory. Could he have been seen last night? Had he left the door open on his way out? He can't even remember leaving. Whatever the reason, his most valuable evidence has been lost for ever.

For a moment, he even doubts whether he saw what he saw. But no: how else would he have known about the examination bench, whose remains can still just be made out under the rubble of the collapsed roof?

He gets like this when he misses his medication. He left the flat without taking his pills this morning. Well, he's skipped a dose before. He took it last night – didn't he?

But when he tries to recall whether he did take his pills last night, he can't remember that, either.

—Boss, we're partners, aren't we?

—What? Sure.

—If there was anything you weren't telling me, you'd tell me, wouldn't you? If you know what I mean.

—Yes, Kiunga.

—I got some good leads this morning, the young man continues. Want to hear about them?

—Go on, says Mollel, without enthusiasm.

—Well, I got hold of someone at vehicle licensing. That silver Land Cruiser we saw on K-Street, with the cagey *mzungu* behind the wheel? It's registered in the name of Equator Investments.

Mollel is hardly listening. Alternative lines of enquiry seem pointless. He's more concerned now with how he can make a case against Wanjiku Nalo, with no evidence. And no motive. He scours his mind for a possible reason for the doctor to have done what she did to Lucy. But he comes up blank.

—Well, Equator Investments sounded familiar to me. And then I remembered: here. This place.

Kiunga's words are starting to break through to Mollel.

—What about this place?

—It's on the sign, out front. Orpheus House. A project of George Nalo Ministries, with the support of international donors, and Equator Investments. So, I called a contact down at City Hall. She confirmed it. This land is owned by Equator Investments.

—Who are Equator Investments?

Kiunga laughs. —Boss, don't you read the papers? Equator Investments *is* David Kingori. The most powerful, influential businessman in Nairobi. He's the one…

But Mollel has leapt to his feet.

Powerful, influential. Those were the words that Honey had used about Lucy's client. The one she was scared of.

There might be life in this case yet.

Mollel strides excitedly through the business district. Equator House is just a short way from Upper Hill and Uhuru Park. Kiunga trots behind him, trying to keep up, and filling in Mollel with background on Kingori as they go.

III

The businessman has been subject to half a dozen official investigations, at least, that Kiunga knows about: everything from insider trading to gun-running. Yet the accusations always evaporate, key witnesses always retract their statements, evidence seems to miraculously disappear, and Kingori always emerges more bullish and brash than ever.

—It's a good job we decided to walk, says Kiunga. The traffic's here's completely backed up. I wonder what's going on?

A young man pushes past them. Something registers about him: his green T-shirt. Not in itself unusual. But Mollel notices for the first time that several people around them are wearing the same shirt. They are all headed the same way. It's a political rally – by the looks of things, one of the smaller opposition parties.

— Better go the other way, says Kiunga.

But Mollel continues on his path. More green T-shirts join them to left and right. He gets a kick out of watching their numbers grow. Soon, as they are making their way down Kenyatta Avenue, he and Kiunga become a minority. They are flanked by green. Banners are unfurled, and Mollel sees shopkeepers pulling down their shutters with a clatter.

—*What do we want?* calls out a shrill woman's voice, from some way ahead of them.

—*Justice!* comes the reply from all around them.

—*When do we want it?*

—*Now!*

A startled-looking businessman is stopped in the middle of the sidewalk, attempting to go against the green tide. As Mollel and Kiunga pass him, he says to them: —What should I do?

—Go home, says Kiunga.

—But I need to go that way, protests the businessman, pointing in the direction of the flow.

—Then ask her for a shirt, says Kiunga. A girl passes them, handing out green T-shirts from a large plastic bag. —Thank you, sweetie. Kiunga takes two, offers one to Mollel, who shakes his head, then throws one to the businessman.

112

—Congratulations! he shouts. You've just joined the opposition!

Kiunga stuffs the remaining T-shirt into his trouser pocket.

—That'll be good for the gym, he says with a grin. A few paces later, the two policemen draw to a stop. They have arrived.

Equator House. Today it sits anonymously in Nairobi's high-rise centre, but when it was built, in the heady optimism of a newly independent nation, its fourteen storeys earned it the title of *skyscraper*. Over the years, it has seen numerous name changes, as corporate clients came and went, none of them seeming to have made a profit on the site. Rumour had it that the building used to be secretly owned by Moi, the former president slashing or hiking the rent as he saw fit, according to favours deserving reward or slights requiring punishment. But today, the building belongs to Equator Investments, whose proprietor, David Kingori, also happens to be the sole residential occupant. On a Friday or Saturday night it is not unusual for the deserted streets to ring with the noise of a party drifting down from the penthouse above.

They walk into the building's shadow, push open the doors, and plunge into the cool, air-conditioned lobby. They both blink as their eyes become accustomed to the darkness. Everything is steel, marble and smoked glass. Even the chants of the demonstrators on the street outside disappear as the doors swing smoothly shut. A receptionist sits behind her desk, absorbed in her mobile phone. She raises her eyes to the visitors, but not her head.

Mollel shows his badge.

—What do you know about the company cars?

—Nothing to do with me. You want to see the head of security?

—Is Mr Kingori in?

—You have an appointment? she asks with a sceptical click of gum.

Kiunga slides over.

—Hi, he says, with a grin. So, they've got you working Christmas Eve? Must be kinda boring.

The girl raises her eyebrows as though to say, *no shit*.

—Us too. No let-up for the brave guardians of law and order.

Despite herself, she giggles. How does he do it? wonders Mollel.

—Look, my friend here is a bit embarrassed, continues Kiunga. The fact is, we're on an important investigation – nothing to do with this place. We're watching the place over the road.

—Over the road? Her curiosity is piqued. The dry cleaner's?

—Yeah, we think they might be money laundering.

The girl laughs, catches Kiunga's eye, looks back down.

—Anyway, my friend needs to use the bathroom. You know these Maasai, they think they can just *kojoe* anywhere, but I told him, you've got to go somewhere *respectable* ...

She giggles again, and puts down her phone. —I'll just be a minute, says Mollel, squeezing his knees together and making an agonised face.

—Go on, she says, hitting a buzzer beneath the desk. Next to her, the waist-high entry gate clicks. It's on the right.

Thanks, says Mollel, but the girl is already back to chatting with Kiunga. He pushes the gate and goes through. There is a pair of doors marked with toilet signs, and two lifts, but Mollel heads immediately to an unmarked door, which he delicately pushes open with his fingertips. It swings open just wide enough to slip through. He's in a stairwell. The steps lead up and down: down smells cooler, a slight edge of exhaust fumes. The car park. He creeps down the stairs and through another swing door.

Most of the spaces are vacant, but he's drawn to a row with several cars parked in it. A large notice on the wall proclaims *Parking for Equator Investments Only*.

One vehicle attracts his attention immediately. It was designed to do so: bright yellow, overspilling the parking lines painted on the floor. It's chunky and square. To Mollel, it looks more like one of Adam's toys than a real car. The chrome grille gleams and the windows are so black it's a wonder that anyone can see out.

But it is not the flashy Hummer which interests him. A couple of cars down is a silver Land Cruiser – the registration matches.

Glancing around for a guard, Mollel crosses the car park and goes to examine the Land Cruiser. He walks around it. Looks inside. No litter on the floor or personal possessions in the back – no sign of any personality or ownership. That indicates it's probably a pool car. He continues around, and reaching the front once more, notices a dent, and a scrape, on the front fender. He runs his finger along it, feeling minute, gritty particles. The damage is not from another car. More likely a wall or concrete post.

There is the sound of footsteps and talking, and Mollel ducks down. He recognises the booming, self-important voice from radio news reports. David Kingori. Like his car, he exists to be the centre of attention – even when there's nobody around. He's complaining loudly about something or other on his mobile phone. Mollel squeezes himself down behind the Land Cruiser. Kingori passes within inches of his face, but does not look down. He blips the Hummer and climbs inside. The car roars into life and Mollel is choked by a cloud of fumes. As soon as the Hummer turns the corner and mounts the ramp, Mollel darts back to the stairwell and runs to reception. Kiunga and the girl are chatting away.

—All done? says Kiunga.

—Let's go, says Mollel, dashing to the entrance.

—So, you'll call me? asks the receptionist. Kiunga turns back with a grin and makes a telephone sign with his fingers.

On the street, the green crowd is still massing, heading towards Parliament. The yellow Hummer is up ahead, slowly snaking its way through the throng. Mollel and Kiunga pace behind it, keeping a distance but watching intently, stalking.

—Can I give you some advice, boss? asks Kiunga, chattily. If it's not too personal. When you're dealing with women, you can't come out with what you want straight away. It's too direct. You got to sweet-talk them a bit, make them laugh, flatter them. Get them to open up. Then, maybe, you get what you want.

He hands Mollel a piece of paper. On it is written the name Estelle, and a mobile phone number.

—Not that side, says Kiunga. Mollel turns it over.

—James Lethebridge, he reads.

—These *wazungu* have some crazy names, huh?

—This is our Land Cruiser driver? Mollel slaps Kiunga on the back. In his way, the young man is proving a pretty good hunter.

Kiunga continues. —He's not a member of staff, apparently, but the girl sees him coming into the building every now and then. He comes, collects a pool car, or drops it off. That's the name he puts in the signing-in book. She says he's old – sixties probably – white hair, bit of a gut, and skin like an undercooked chapatti – you know, all pale, speckled and doughy.

Kiunga trails off as he notices that Mollel has stopped. The Hummer has drawn to a halt and the crowd has begun to cluster around it. The horn is blasting impatiently. Mollel and Kiunga draw closer.

The driver's-side window of the Hummer glides down and Kingori's head emerges. He waves his arm furiously. —You should watch where you're going!

A howl of protest rises up from around the car. —You watch where *you're* going! Another voice: —Learn how to drive, you stupid bastard!

As Mollel and Kiunga push their way round to the front of the car, they hear cries of pain. A young man is kneeling down, clutching his foot, while his friends hold his shoulders in concern.

Another blast of the horn. —Get out of the way!

Someone thumps the hood of the Hummer angrily. —You've run over his foot!

—I'll run you all down, you dogs, if you don't let me through!

Mollel and Kiunga exchange glances. The good-humoured mood of the crowd has turned. Things are in danger of getting ugly. Someone mutters: —Do you know who that is? David Kingori. And another, angrily: —Government puppet!

The driver's window draws silkily to a close and the engine revs loudly, but the crowd presses closer. The huge car begins, gently at first, to rock from side to side on its chassis. A placard – nothing more than a piece of cardboard tacked to a light wooden stick – bounces against the Hummer's windscreen. Mollel knows that a bottle or kerbstone could be next.

He has seen enough. He pushes himself forward to the side of the car and jumps on the running-board. He pulls himself up to full height, head and shoulders above the melee. Cheers go up at first, turning to jeers as he holds his police badge aloft, waving it in a slow, wide, arm's-length arc for all to see.

—Step away from the vehicle! he shouts. Despite the ill humour, the rocking of the car ceases. He scans the faces, gauging the mood. There is anger in the eyes, but it's an instant, hot anger, easily dissipated, unlike the cold, calculated fury he fears. This is not a crowd in search of trouble – at least, not today.

—Typical police! shouts one protester. Protect their own! The cry is greeted with calls of agreement.

—Now listen to me! shouts Mollel. There's been a small accident here, and a man's been hurt. We're going to deal with this properly. Now step back from the car.

There are some muted grumbles, and mutters about police bias, but the people at the front shuffle back slightly. Kiunga helps the injured man hobble to his feet. Mollel presses his badge against the driver's window and it whirrs down a reluctant inch. Mollel leans and speaks through the crack.

—Now, sir, he says softly, what you're going to do is you're going to lean back and unlock the rear door here. Don't use the central locking, just this door by me. I'm going to get in, with two other people. Don't do anything else until I say so, *sawa?*

The window snaps shut again and Mollel wonders for a moment whether Kingori is ignoring him. Then he hears the click of the rear passenger door being unlocked. He edges towards it along the running-board.

—Now, we're going to take this man to hospital, he shouts, for the benefit of the crowd. He beckons Kiunga, who has put the limping figure's arm around his shoulder, and the two of them come forward.

—Then, continues Mollel, we're going to the police station, and we're going to talk about compensation, and charges against the driver. OK?

—Yeah! call out a few members of the crowd. Charge him!

Mollel heaves open the Hummer's rear door – Kiunga bundles the protester in and follows suit – and then Mollel himself dives inside the darkened car and pulls it shut behind him, snapping the lock down.

—Right, carefully, slowly: drive!

Kingori edges the Hummer forward, the crowd shuffling out of the way, letting it pass, scowling at their own reflections in the blacked-out windows. There is a half-hearted thud of a fist, but nothing more sinister. The people melt back and, with a clear road ahead, Kingori guns the accelerator, speeding them away from the scene.

—Oh, it hurts, it hurts! You broke my foot!

—Let me take your shoe off, says Kiunga, but the young man keeps brushing him away.

—Oh, you're going to pay for this, he groans at Kingori. I'm going to sue you!

—Let me see, says Kiunga, finally succeeding in getting hold of the man's training shoe, and pulling it off. Why you … let me get this sock off. Your foot would be swollen like a melon if this car went over it. There's nothing wrong with you at all!

—There is, there is! He broke my foot! I need an X-ray! I need compensation!

—Pull over here, orders Mollel. As the car comes to a halt, he leans across and opens the door next to the young man.

—Get out.

—What? This isn't the hospital!

—Get out, or we'll push you out.

Reproachfully, the man gets out, feigning a whimper as he puts his shoeless foot on to the sidewalk.

—Here, says Kiunga. Take your shoe.

—You take it! says the young man, standing upright. He makes to fling it into the car but Kiunga pulls the door shut just in time, and it bounces pathetically off the window. Kingori accelerates and they leave the man behind them. Kiunga looks out of the back window.

—He's walking away normally, he chuckles. What a chancer!

From the driver's seat, Kingori roars with laughter. — Brilliant! Officers, thank you so much. Please allow me to show my appreciation.

Still driving, he fumbles in his pocket for a money clip, and rips out a couple of thousand-shilling bills. Now, is there anywhere I can drop you?

—Central Police Post, says Mollel.

—It's a bit out of my way. I have an important meeting in Westlands. Perhaps I could stop at a *matatu* stand?

—Central Police Post will be fine, says Mollel, measuredly. While we're there we can discuss a few matters. Like attempting to bribe a police officer.

16

—*I want a lawyer!*

Mollel and Kiunga are stood outside the filing room which gets used for interviews at Central Police Post. From within, they can hear a fist pounding on a desk. Then a chair falls over, and the fist pounds the door.

—*Get me a lawyer! Now!*

—This is decent *chai*, says Mollel, sipping from his mug.

—Mmm, we all chip in and get the good highland stuff, says Kiunga.

—You use *masala*?

—That's my special technique. Mix the spices in with the sugar.

—It's lovely.

—Thank you.

They drain their mugs, and each lets out a satisfied sigh.

—Shall we go in? asks Mollel.

—Delighted, says Kiunga.

Inside, Kingori is pacing furiously. He rushes to the door as it opens, but Mollel holds up a hand of warning.

—Take a seat, please, sir.

—I don't want a seat. I've been sitting here forty-five minutes!

—Please, be seated.

Kingori picks the chair off the floor and sits, crossing his arms. Mollel and Kiunga also sit.

—I demand to see a lawyer, immediately.

—Did you say you've been here forty-five minutes, sir? asks Mollel, innocently.

—At least!

—Well, that must make it... what time is it, Kiunga?

Kiunga looks at his watch. —Just gone five.

—Just gone five? And the duty lawyer finishes at five, doesn't he, Kiunga?

—Saw him leaving myself.

—Oh dear, says Mollel.

—Give me my phone! barks Kingori. I'll have my lawyer here in a shot.

—That's your right, sir. Mollel takes Kingori's cellphone – gold plated – from his pocket, and makes as if to hand it to him – then pauses. Of course, that would add a certain formality to proceedings. We'd need to charge you.

Kiunga nods. —Most definitely.

—And then you and your lawyer could discuss your situation with the magistrate – oh, but I'm forgetting, it's Christmas Eve, isn't it? They'll have gone home now, too. When will they sit again, Kiunga?

—Well, there's Christmas Day tomorrow, a public holiday on the twenty-sixth, then another holiday for the election, so it won't be until Friday, I'm afraid.

—Four days? Mollel tuts. And I hear the cells are fit to burst. But I'm sure we can squeeze you in somewhere, sir, if that's what you want.

He holds out the phone. Kingori takes it, and lays it on the desk.

—So, two thousand wasn't enough for you? You should have just said. I can buy and sell a couple of farmers like you a million times. What shall we say, ten thousand? Each? I can give it to you right now. Call it a Christmas bonus.

—It's not about money, says Kiunga.

—Tell us about James Lethebridge, says Mollel.

A slow grin speads over Kingori's face, and he leans back in his chair. His attitude says: now we're getting somewhere.

—Jimmy's in trouble, is he?

—So you know him?

—I know him. Firstly, you're saying it wrong. It's not Leather-bridge, it's *Leethie*-bridge. Like the river.

—What's the nature of your relationship with Mr *Leethie*-bridge?

Kingori laughs again.

—He's my fag. Oh, don't look so shocked, gentlemen. I'm aware of the contemporary understanding of the term. But in a British public school, the word is slang for *factotum*. Your do-everything person. Fetching, carrying, odd jobs. We were at school together, long before you were born. Long before this nation was born.

Mollel looks at him with surprise. From his brief glimpse of Lethebridge in the car – and the description provided by the receptionist – he's confident the man must be in his late sixties or seventies. That certainly tallies with being at school before Independence. But if Kingori is the same age, he's remarkably well preserved. A full head of hair, hardly a wrinkle, dazzling teeth. All too perfect. Mollel wonders whether anything about this guy would stand up to close scrutiny.

—So he is your employee? asks Kiunga.

—I keep him in work. Little tasks, here and there. He wouldn't be able to do anything else.

—Would one of these little tasks be procuring prostitutes from K-Street?

Kingori's smile disappears.

—I wouldn't know anything about that.

—He was seen kerb-crawling the other night.

—That's his concern.

—In a company car?

—Not my Hummer, I hope.

—A silver Toyota Land Cruiser.

—A lot of people use that car.

—Do you employ many *wazungu*, Mr Kingori?

—He's the only one. So he's been a naughty boy. I wouldn't have thought he had it in him, myself. But what has this got to do with me?

—What it has to do with you is that a K-Street hooker was found dead last Friday night. And she'd told her friend that she was scared of someone. Someone powerful. Now, from what I've heard, that doesn't match the description of Mr Lethebridge. But it could, pretty accurately, describe you. So how about it? Your movements, please, on Friday.

—This is ridiculous! You've got nothing on me!

—We can always resume this conversation after a visit to the cells, if you prefer.

Kingori scowls. —For what it's worth, from early morning until about seven in the evening, I was at State House, with the president, among about fifty others. We were discussing election strategy. Any number of people can place me there. In fact, I think it was even reported in *The Standard*. Is the head of state a good enough alibi for you?

—And afterwards?

—Well, I take it you'll be speaking to James. We were together all evening, at my flat. Demolishing some rather fine single malt and reminiscing about school.

Mollel takes an envelope out of the desk drawer and pushes it across to Kingori.

—Take a look.

It is a photo of Lucy, post-mortem. Somewhere under the Botox, Kingori's face flickers: with pity? Recognition? Guilt?

—This is the girl?

—Her name was Lucy e-intoi Sambu.

—A Maasai? Like you? I'm sorry she is dead. But I have never seen her before in my life. James will tell you all that.

Now it is Kiunga's turn to push something across the table: a notepad and pen.

—James Lethebridge's contact details, please. Address, phone number.

Kingori scrawls an address in Lavington, then picks up his phone, finds a number and copies it down.

—What do you know of George and Wanjiku Nalo? asks Mollel, taking the pad.

—The preacher? I know he's living proof that Bible school can be more profitable than an MBA.

—Meaning?

—Meaning, he is a sharp one. And his wife is even sharper.

—It sounds like you're speaking from experience.

—We've done business.

—What kind of business?

—Real estate. They're kind of tenants of mine.

—*Kind of* tenants?

Kingori shrugs. —They run a project out of some property I own. I'm allowing them to redevelop it rent free.

—Seems pretty generous, says Kiunga, pointedly. If that was my land, I'd put a bunch of apartment blocks on it.

—What can I say? That's the sort of guy I am.

After a moment's sceptical silence, Kingori adds: —OK, it's not pure philanthropy. Look, the Americans have a lot of money that their president says has to go to faith-based initiatives. Our government wants a prestige development in a visible location. Nalo makes all the right noises, I have the land, it's small beer for me. I let them use the property, I get help with some planning issues I have elsewhere.

—Have you been to Orpheus House?

Kingori laughs. —If I visited every property I owned, I'd never have time to get anything done.

—Has James Lethebridge?

—I don't know. Ask him.

Mollel replies: —We will. We're going to have him brought in right now.

—So be it. If you don't need me any more, I shall...

—No, says Mollel. You're going to stay here while we speak to Mr Lethebridge. You're not going to have any chance to compare alibis.

—Now look here! Kingori slams the table. I've been damn patient with you two and your stupid games. But be warned. If you don't let me go right now, it'll be more than your careers on the line. Do you understand?

The door opens and the massive presence of Otieno bursts into the room. Instinctively, Mollel and Kiunga stand. Kingori remains seated.

—David, says Otieno cordially.

—Otieno. They shake hands. Your clowns here have been treating me to a rather boring performance.

—Don't worry. I'll deal with them.

—I want them off the force.

—Oh, I have a far worse punishment in mind than that. I see your car's outside, please allow me to escort you there.

As Kingori passes, he turns to Mollel and hisses: —If I see you again, Maasai... He leaves the threat hanging in the air, shakes his head, and leaves.

17

—This case, says Otieno, is officially closed.

The two policemen stand before him like schoolboys in the principal's office. Mollel wishes he could take a seat. He is suddenly feeling an overwhelming sense of weariness.

—You can't do that! protests Kiunga.

—I can see you've learned some bad habits from our Maasai friend here. Tell me, Kiunga, did you happen to notice the sign on my door, as you came in? It says Superintendent. You know what that means? 'Super' – that means above. And 'intendent' – well, let's just say, that means you. Above. You. Which means that in my station, I can do what the hell I like.

—You can't shut down this case. We're getting somewhere. We just need a few more days.

—We don't *have* a few more days, Kiunga. Have you been paying attention to what's going on in this city? I need every available man for election duty – doing our job – trying to keep a lid on this cauldron.

—*That's* why you wanted me seconded here, Mollel says, suddenly understanding. It wasn't to solve the girl's death. It was just to boost your numbers during the election. Help keep the peace. Help you look good. You always intended to drop the case, once you had an excuse.

Mollel feels the blood thumping in his head. Uninvited, he

takes a chair from in front of Otieno's desk, and crashes down into it. Kiunga remains standing.

—How's this for an excuse? replies Otieno. A complaint from a member of the public. A *highly influential* member of the public. False arrest, intimidation…

—We never arrested him, Kiunga says.

The argument rings back and forth above him. He needs to get home. He needs to take his pills. But above all, what he needs is to solve this case.

Otieno's voice pounds remorselessly on. The words mean nothing, now. Just that sanctimonious, booming, bull-like bellow. Why can't he just stop talking, thinks Mollel. For just one second? Why can't he just shut the hell up, and *listen*?

The room falls silent.

They're both looking at him. Mollel realises he has spoken aloud.

He has the heady, blissful sensation of freedom. The same feeling he had when he decided to abandon his village, to turn his back on his tribe.

He does not care about the consequences. Instead, while Kiunga and Otieno listen to him in amazement, he tells them the truth.

He speaks with the bright, intense lucidity of anger. He tells them about stealing the keys, about his discovery of the operating theatre at Orpheus House. He tells them about his conviction that Wanjiku Nalo delivered a baby to Lucy. That somehow, the delivery was botched. Lucy either died during the procedure, or bled to death shortly afterwards. Wanjiku, helped by someone, dumped the body in the storm drain, having deliberately mutilated the body's genitals to try to disguise the fact that Lucy had recently given birth. She knew about female genital mutilation, and probably hoped that if the body was discovered, Maasai circumcision rites would get the blame.

Kiunga has slumped into the room's remaining chair. Otieno has tipped his own chair back, hands behind his head, big sweat patches under his arms. His expression has become totally neutral.

Mollel tells them about David Kingori. About the fact that he believes Kingori to be the father of the missing baby. That he was probably in league with Wanjiku Nalo, probably even ordered her to preside over the secretive birth – as the price he would exact for allowing the Nalos to build their new project on his site.

Mollel finishes his story. No one speaks. He feels the dramatic, shocked silence of the forest, in the moments after a tree has fallen. And then, his confidence drains. His anger evaporates. He senses, from the way that Kiunga refuses to meet his eye, that he has humiliated himself.

He's also betrayed his promise to Honey.

—Well, Maasai, Otieno says. I guess I have to thank you.

—For what?

—For giving me everything I need, to have you thrown out of the police force, and into prison. To Kiunga, he adds: Did you know anything about all this?

—No.

—Haven't you been listening to me? pleads Mollel. We're talking murder here. Including murder, or abduction, of a child. Not to mention arson, conspiracy…

—No, says Otieno slowly, deliberately. What you've told me – if I'm even to believe your ridiculous hypothesis – is accidental death.

—What about the child?

Otieno sighs. —Can't you see, Mollel, that this is not our problem? If the baby is alive, that means it's being cared for. And no doubt, much better than any cheap hooker could have cared for it. If it's dead, it's dead. We'd have no way of proving murder. We don't even have a body. All we have is unsubstantiated allegations against Nairobi's most powerful businessman, its most successful pastor, and its most respected gynaecologist.

—What about justice? croaks Mollel.

Otieno gives a sad smile. —Mollel, you're in the wrong

country. The wrong continent. Don't you know, there's something more valuable than justice here?

—What?

—Peace.

He leans forward. His eyes are fixed, glazed. He seems to be repeating a personal mantra.

—Justice is a luxury. Peace is a necessity. You want justice, move to some First World state with sophisticated crime labs, and DNA tests, and judges who can't be bought off. That's the only way you'd get to bring a case against people like this. Better still, become a judge yourself. They're the ones who are supposed to look after justice. We're only supposed to keep the peace.

Kiunga is saying nothing. Mollel feels drained.

—I feel sorry for you, says Otieno. You were a hero, once. No one can forget what you did when the bomb went off. You won a lot of admirers that day, Mollel, including me.

—But this rage of yours. You don't think about the consequences of your actions. Like when you were stationed here, before. You got so enraged about some petty little minor corruption, that you went running to the newspapers... I had to get rid of some good officers, because of that. And for what? Just doing what everyone else does, trying to get by.

—I ought to get rid of you. I've got every reason to. But I can't lose another officer right now. Besides, the press would crucify me. They'd see it as a sign that we were persecuting a whistle-blower. Did you know, Mollel, that the Commissioner himself has taken a personal interest in your career?

Mollel shakes his head.

—Oh yes. You're to be kept well away from anywhere you can cause trouble. I wish I'd taken his advice.

Mollel is silent, as he gradually deals with the realisation that he is not going to lose his job.

—Just to make it perfectly clear. You forget about this case. It's done. Closed. There's nothing we can do about it. I'm sorry, but that's the way it is. Understood?

They both reply: —Yes, sir.

—OK. It's late. Two days remaining until the election. Tomorrow will be the quiet before the storm. You've got Christmas day off. Go spend it with your families. Look to the living, not the dead.

18

—Come on, says Kiunga. Let's go for a drink.

—I don't drink, says Mollel.

—You can damn well sit next to me while I do, then, replies Kiunga. And I'm warning you, I intend to get completely *kutindi*.

They head off on foot across town. Mollel is expecting to be dragged to the Flamingo – the bar favoured by Nairobi's law enforcement community, where at any given time of day or night you're likely to find as many on-duty officers as off.

But they go straight past it, and head towards River Road. This part of the city is busy. Anyone still here has obviously decided to stay in town, and make the most of the Christmas holiday tomorrow: the bars are full, and many have decided to entice customers in by setting up their *nyama choma* barbeques on the sidewalk. The smell makes Mollel's stomach protest in a queasy mixture of hunger and agony.

—Here we are, says Kiunga. I thought I'd make you feel at home.

They are outside a bar with a large window giving straight on to the street. You can't see inside, though: the window is a closed display, a sort of cupboard, with a whole, flayed goat hanging inside, and various cuts of meat beside it. Despite the flies, it is obviously appetising enough to entice a regular flow of customers. Mollel and Kiunga have to wait at the door, where a man is giving detailed instructions to a member of staff about which exact cut he wants taken from the goat. When they get inside, it takes a moment for Mollel's eyes to adjust to the darkness.

—Mama Naitiku's, says Mollel. It's a long time since I've been here.

Its official name is the Hoteli Narok, but no one knows it as that. It is the first port of call for most Maasai in Nairobi, and a home from home for many who have migrated permanently to the city. For some, it has become a byword for the city itself: *going to Mama Naitiku's* is a familiar phrase in many villages, somehow more congenial, less daunting, less final, than saying *going to Nairobi.*

Groups of red-shawled Maasai men look up at them with suspicion. Kiunga strides purposefully to the bar. Mollel follows him.

—I'll have a Tusker. Cold. And my friend here…

—A Fanta, says Mollel.

The barman is a Maasai youth, his hair braided, *shuka* knotted over one shoulder. His bracelets jangle as he reaches down to a beer crate at his feet and pulls out a bottle.

—Cold enough for you? he asks Kiunga, challengingly.

—It'll do.

The barman pops the cap and slides the beer over. He does the same with a bottle of fluorescent soda for Mollel.

Kiunga pays. —Is Mama here? he asks.

—Where else would she be?

—Tell her we want to talk to her.

The two of them go over to a table and sit down. —Why are we here, Kiunga? Mollel asks.

Kiunga takes a long draught from the neck of his bottle and smacks his lips.

—We've looked into the fact that Lucy was a *poko*, he says. We've dug into Orpheus House. The Nalos. But the one thing we haven't dealt with yet is the biggest fact of all. She was a Maasai.

—I don't think it's relevant, says Mollel.

—Of course not. You're a Maasai yourself. But I think it is. So humour me a while, Mollel.

He looks up. An old woman is shuffling towards them, shaven head bent, long *shuka* brushing the floor. She wears a white, beaded necklace like a dinner plate around her neck, and it looks as though the weight – although it can't weigh anything at all – is dragging her down.

She pulls up a chair and sits beside them.

—What can I do for you, Officers?

Hardly surprising she recognised them as police. What's more surprising to Mollel is how little she's changed: she looked ancient even back when he first met her.

—Do you remember me, Mama? he asks.

She looks up at him through eyes which are watery but alert. He sees her processing the information: looped ears. Maasai face but Nairobi suit. He fingers Honey's tie nervously. The old woman reminds him of his own mother, and he can't help projecting a sense of disapproval, disappointment, into her expression.

—I see a lot of people, she says.

—I came here on my first night in Nairobi, Mollel says. I was with my brother, Lendeva. We were too poor to afford any meat, so you gave us both a bowl of *ugali*. We'd never seen *ugali* before. We didn't even know it was food. We sat out there, on the sidewalk, wondering what to do with it. When you came out to see how we were getting on, we'd made shapes out of it. Lendeva made a cow. I made a donkey.

Mama Naitiku smiles. She has fewer teeth, but the smile is the same.

—Are you a *Leliani*?

—That's right. Mollel.

—You were just boys.

—It was twenty years ago. You let us sleep on the floor, out back, while we looked for work.

—And you found it. With the police.

—That was much later.

133

—I do remember you, she says. And your brother. He was the bold one, as I recall. Dressed so fine, in all the warrior garb, with not a shilling in the world. He had great plans. I thought you would follow him everywhere. And what has become of him, now? Is he a policeman, too?

Mollel shakes his head. —I don't know where he is, he replies.

Kiunga shoots him a questioning glance. But Mollel has been thinking more about his brother in the last few days than he has for years. He does not want to continue the conversation.

—That's what happens when we turn our back on the village life, says the old woman, sadly.

—We need your help, says Kiunga. He brings out the photograph of Lucy that he had been using on K-Street. Do you know anything about this girl?

Mama Naitiku takes the photograph and looks at it. She turns to Mollel.

—*Shore lai kishoriki enapiak*, she says to him, in Maa.

He remembers the expression. *Old friends bring evil.*

—Do you know her?

—Is she dead? Mama Naitiku asks.

—Yes.

She shudders. —I knew her. She arrived, like you, penniless. A year or so ago. She was fleeing her village. I didn't ask why. I see so many girls like that. I assumed it was an arranged marriage that she didn't want to go through with.

—Did anyone come looking for her? asks Kiunga. Anyone try to take her back to her village?

She shakes her head. —Not that I know of.

—This is pretty unpleasant, says Kiunga. But please think about it. When we found this girl's body, she had been mutilated. Her genitals were slashed. Is there anything you know of – any ritual, any ceremony – that might involve that sort of thing?

—There's the circumcision ceremony, of course, she says. But that's done on much younger girls. I've heard of people dying from it. But much later, because of infection. No, done properly, they're no danger at all. It's not how you describe this poor girl's wounds. Not slashing. It has to be done precisely. Delicately.

She pauses for a moment. Discretion and professional pride seem to battle for an instant in her breast, before she says: —I should know. I do it myself.

—It's illegal! says Mollel.

The old woman's posture changes. She draws herself up. —You've chosen the new laws, she says. I choose the old ones.

Kiunga shifts uneasily. Some of the men at the tables around them have begun watching them with hostility. He picks up his bottle and drains it. —I think we should be going, he says. Mollel?

—Just a moment, says Mama Naitiku. What about the other girl? Have you spoken to her?

—The other girl? asks Mollel.

—Yes. I haven't seen this girl, the dead one, for over a year. But last time she was here, she left with another Maasai girl. Well dressed. Pretty obvious where her money came from. I chased her out. I don't allow that sort in my bar. But this poor girl followed her. If you ask me, that's the reason she ended up killed. Not because she was a Maasai.

Outside, on the street, Kiunga says: —OK, Mollel. It looks like you were right. But we had to look into the Maasai angle.

But Mollel is silent.

—What is it, boss? Is it what she said about the circumcisions? Look, we all know it still goes on. There's nothing we can do about it.

—It's not that, says Mollel. It's about what Honey said. About how she met Lucy. She told us that Lucy approached her, when she had just started working the streets. That Lucy was the one who showed her the ropes, taught her how to do it properly. That doesn't fit with what Mama Naitiku says.

—If you ask me, boss, replies Kiunga, you ought to be careful about getting too close to Honey. She's a *poko*, remember? And sleeping with men is only part of what they do for a living. The rest of it is lying. And to a good *poko*, that's second nature.

—What's your problem? asks Mollel, stopping on the sidewalk. Can't you see this attitude is what stops people like Honey coming to the police in the first place? We're all outsiders in one way or another, Kiunga. Why can't you see her as another human being? Besides, *you're* hardly one to lecture others on morality.

Kiunga turns and squares up to him. For a moment, Mollel thinks he's going to get hit. Then Kiunga gives a grim smile.

—I love sex, he says. I've never disguised it. But I love *love*, too. And all the girls I go with, whether it leads to anything or not, I love them. At least while we're doing it. I'm sorry, but once money comes into it, I don't want to know.

—You're a hypocrite, says Mollel.

—No. Like the old woman says, I choose the rules I live by. They may not be yours, Mollel, but at least I'm consistent. Now, if you'll excuse me, I'm going to find a *cold* beer. And I don't think they serve Fanta where I'm headed. Goodnight, Mollel.

19

He took his medication before he went to sleep, and perhaps because of it, Mollel was untroubled by dreams of blood – or of anything. But he still feels an uncharacteristic jumpiness when the doorbell to his flat rings.

—Hi, says Kiunga. Happy Christmas. Can I come in?

They stand in Mollel's bare galley kitchen, drinking instant coffee with no milk.

—I'm sorry for what I said last night, says Mollel.

—That's OK. Plenty of people have said worse.

After a while, Kiunga continues: —You know, you're the first partner I ever had who actually believes in proper detective work. Down at the station, there's old Mwangi, who doesn't give a shit. And Otieno, with his politics, and his pragmatism. Then you come along, and you're standing up for justice. You remind me of why I wanted to become a policeman in the first place. And you know, don't you, that just because I'm suspicious of *pokos*, doesn't mean I don't want justice for Lucy.

—I know that.

—OK, says Kiunga. So, I dropped by James Lethebridge's place on the way here. His *askari* told me he's gone up-country. Doesn't know where. But if you ask me, he wasn't telling the truth.

—No, agrees Mollel. So you've decided to stick with the case?

137

Kiunga shrugs. —It's Christmas Day. My family's all up-country. Why the hell not? I've got nothing better to do.

Mollel smiles. Then he says: —You know what the consequences might be, don't you?

—Of course.

—Even after what Otieno said? You realise you could lose your job. I'm quite happy to go it alone. It seems like I've got some degree of protection. You haven't.

—You didn't know that, when you admitted breaking into Orpheus House.

He takes a sip of his coffee. Then says: Listen, Mollel, if you want people to stop following your example, you need to take a page from Mwangi's book. Don't give a shit. For God's sake, he's never going to get people fired up about things like *justice*.

Kiunga grins. Mollel grins back.

—We've got a day to try to make headway in this case, before we both get dragged into election duty, says Mollel. Talking of which, where has he put you for the big day?

—*Kosovo.*

—Mathere? Mollel chuckles.

The slum got the nickname at the height of the Kosovo war, when images of shelled-out buildings were on the TV screens – and Mathere residents recognised the similarity.

—Where will you be? Kiunga asks.

—Kibera. Otieno's really got it in for us, hasn't he?

—Do you reckon he's on the take? asks Kiunga, his smile fading.

—I don't know.

—He certainly shut down the case pretty rapidly once Kingori came on the scene. And they obviously know each other.

—If you're suggesting Kingori might have bribed him, I don't think that's Otieno's style. For all his arrogance, I think he's more concerned about his career than his wallet. Who knows what pressure might have been brought in that department.

—Talking about little gifts, says Kiunga, don't we have a Christmas present to deliver?

Districts mean a lot in Nairobi. Take, for example, Lavington: one of the most desirable neighbourhoods in the city. Most people would agree, Lavington ends at the James Gichuru Road. West of there, it's Kawangware.

Most people would agree, but not Faith. It's well known, she insists, that Lavington extends at least one block west of James Gichuru. And that's where her house is. Any attempt to persuade her otherwise is met with a stern look and the response: I've lived here twenty years and it's always been Lavington.

James Gichuru Road is more than a psychological barrier, however. As soon as you cross it, a change as sudden as the Great Rift's rain shadow comes over the environment. The genteel colonial bungalows with their clipped lawns and jacaranda confetti are replaced with breeze-blocked walls and hastily erected apartment blocks. Street hawkers, who seemingly feel discomforted over the road, sell their maize and *mitumba* openly, and in recent years, this also appears to have become the destination of choice to buy knocked-off DVDs. Even the *matatus* respect the apparent frontier, coasting peacefully along Gitanga Road as far as James Gichuru, then pushing their way across their rivals' paths, jockeying for space alongside – and on – what passes for sidewalk, blasting their horns at any pedestrians who fail to fly into the bushes at their approach.

—I thought Faith lived in Lavington? says Kiunga, as Mollel gives him directions to her house.

—If she mentions it, just accept that her house *is* in Lavington. It's a little piece of Lavington, in the middle of Kawangware. Think of it as an embassy.

Today, this part of Lavington-cum-Kawangware is quieter than usual. Mollel directs Kiunga to pull off the main road and they go a short way down a dirt track. It's a few weeks since Mollel has been to Faith's house, and the first thing he notices is a frothy, metallic swirl, gleaming along the top of the wall. For a moment he thinks it's a Christmas decoration. Then he realises it is razor wire.

Next, he notices the youths loitering outside the gate. Actually, *youths* is an inaccurate description. They have the shiftless, cagey manner of truant schoolboys, simultaneously nervous and challenging. But these five men are no adolescents.

Even so, they instinctively palm their cigarettes when the police Land Rover approaches. Kiunga's instincts have clicked in, just like Mollel's: instead of driving to the gate he pulls up opposite the house and stops the engine.

—Ho, says one of the men. Looks like the old Kikuyu woman has visitors for Christmas lunch.

Mollel and Kiunga get out.

—*Habari vijana*, Kiunga says. What's up, boys?

—Nothing.

They mutter some words that Mollel recognises as belonging to the Luo language, and laugh. Then Kiunga addresses them in the same tongue. They look at him in shock.

—Yes, I speak jaLuo, says Kiunga, switching now to English. My first posting, straight after basic training, was to Kisumu. So I've heard every slang term for Kikuyu, and policeman, you could possibly come up with. Now, what's all this tribalist nonsense?

—It's not us, says the man at the front of the group. Ask those thieving Kikuyus! He waves his hand at Faith's gate, and Mollel sees a glint of glass bottle.

—Us Luos always get a bad deal, complains another. These Kikuyus come here, pushing up the rent.

—She's probably been here longer than you! protests Kiunga.

—Doesn't give her the right to tell us where we can and can't go. This is a public highway, isn't it?

—So she's complained about you hanging out here?

There is muttered assent.

—I don't blame her! says Kiunga. Look at you!

The men shuffle, and eye each other. Kiunga laughs. Slowly, grudgingly, they smile too.

—You want to talk about grievances? continues Kiunga. He's on a roll. He points to Mollel. Look at this guy. A Maasai. His lot were fighting off the *wazungu* with bows and arrows while you were still dragging *dagaa* out of the lake!

They give a reluctant laugh.

—Come on, says Kiunga. It's Christmas. I know the old woman can be a bit of a *jike*, but give her a break, huh? Can't you find somewhere else to drink your *chang'aa*?

—Suppose so.

—And we're all Kenyans, aren't we? Let's hear no more of this tribalist crap.

The men swagger away. The policemen watch them until they have cleared the corner.

—You handled that well, says Mollel.

—You've got deal with it with humour, says Kiunga, otherwise you'll end up with a panga in your head. Christ, I can't stand all this tribalism. You know, I spent the happiest five years of my life in Kisumu. I like Luos. I love Lake Victoria. Imagine, a Kikuyu whose favourite food is fish. And Luo girls…

The blissful, distant look on his face completes the sentence.

—And I do believe, says Mollel, that you called my mother-in-law a bitch.

—Sorry about that.

—I didn't say you were wrong.

Faith's first words, once they've brought the car inside the compound: —You saw those no-good *wamera* outside, then?

Mollel glares at her. —I hope you don't use language like that in front of Adam.

—What's wrong with that? They're Luos, aren't they? So they must be uncircumcised. It's simply a statement of fact.

—I don't want him picking up tribalist terms.

Faith scoffs. —You think he doesn't hear them every time he goes through the gate? He used to play on the street, there, until it got too much. They're trying to drive us out, me and the other Kikuyus. They want to make this a Luo-only zone.

—That's what they said about the Kikuyus.

—Well, it will have to be one or the other, says Faith. She looks at Kiunga. I suppose I'm going to have to set an extra place for lunch?

—Happy Christmas, Faith, says Kiunga. Don't worry about me. I've just come to help drop off Adam's present.

—Actually, says Mollel, getting the bicycle out of the back of the Land Rover, I won't be staying for lunch either.

—It's Christmas Day, says Faith. I've killed a chicken.

—I know. There's nothing I can do about it. It's work. I'll be here for supper.

—Well, you can tell him yourself. I'm not going to break it to him. He's round the back.

Behind the house, in the laundry area, Adam is kicking a football against the wall. Mollel feels a pang of dismay at the small square of sky above; the whole space seems so curtailed. At the same age, he'd easily cover five, sometimes ten miles a day. Forest, ravine, mountain, plain.

And then he thinks of the smart shoes on Adam's feet, his clean clothes, his school, his opportunities.

The boy is well off, he decides.

—Hi, Adam.

—Dad! He rushes up and hugs him. Happy Christmas!

—Happy Christmas. What's this, a new football?

Adam looks embarrassed. —Yes, Grandma bought it for me.

Mollel picks up the football. He turns it in his hands. It light, springy. It's orange in colour. A fun gift for a boy.

—Sorry, he says. I should have bought you a football before now. I never thought of it, not having had one myself, as a child.

—Oh, no worries, Dad.

The football in his hand, Mollel has an idea forming in his mind.

—Can I borrow this, for a while?

—I suppose so, says Adam.

—Don't worry. I've got something else for you instead. Come and see what your dad has bought you for Christmas.

They stay an hour or so, Adam wobbling up and down the road, Kiunga holding on to his saddle, the new bike getting smiles from passing neighbours, and envious glances from their children. With the Luo boys gone, the atmosphere in the street is relaxed, friendly. Even the roar of traffic from the nearby main road fades into the background, and the place feels like a village.

—Look, Dad! I'm doing it on my own!

He pulls away from Kiunga, who stops running, and puts his hands on his knees, laughing. Adam speeds towards the main road.

—OK, Adam, stop now!

—I can't! Panic in his voice.

—Stop him! cries Faith. But Mollel, who has never ridden a bike, is unable to think what to do. He feels the rush of air past him as Kiunga sprints after Adam. He watches as Kiunga catches up with the bike, grabs the boy's shoulders, and pulls, bringing the bike crashing to the ground just a few feet short of the main road, as a lorry roars past.

He doesn't run to his father. It's Kiunga's shoulder the boy chooses to bury his tearful face into.

20

—I wish it was Christmas every day, says Kiunga. Then, getting no response from Mollel, he continues: Not that I'm a big fan of festivities. I just like the lack of traffic. It would take us, what, an hour to get here normally? And we've just done it in ten minutes.

They pull up at the entrance to Uhuru Park. Kiunga squeezes through the concrete bollards. There are a couple of other cars in the car park, but no other sign of life.

—Stop here, says Mollel.

Kiunga parks, and they get out. Mollel approaches the bollards. He examines one, then the other. At the right-hand one, he crouches, rubs it with his fingers.

—What is it? asks Kiunga. He bends over for a better look.

—See here? This bollard's been hit. Not hard. Just enough to chip the concrete, probably dent the fender of the car. And leave a few flecks of paint behind.

He holds up his fingernail.

—Silver paint, he says. The Land Cruiser owned by Equator Investments has a scrape on the fender.

—Could be a coincidence, says Kiunga.

—Could be. Or it could be that James Lethebridge, or someone else driving that car, was here before Lucy's body was discovered.

—It doesn't really fit in with your theory, though, does it?

I mean, according to you, Lucy was dumped up the hill, at Orpheus House. They didn't know she was going to wash out down here.

—True, says Mollel. And he tries to convince himself that there are plenty of silver cars in Nairobi, plenty of places where that Land Cruiser could have picked up a scrape. This is all a distraction. It's Wanjiku Nalo he's after, and he has a baby to find, alive or dead.

And then, he thinks: if the facts don't fit the theory, maybe the theory's wrong.

But no. He's convinced of Wanjiku Nalo's guilt. And he's come here today to try to prove it.

—Get me the football from the car, would you?

At the place where Lucy's body was found, all that remains is a lot of smeared mud, and footprints. A steady stream of water runs down the central rill of the drainage ditch. Mollel takes the orange plastic football from Kiunga, and drops it down, like flowers into a grave.

The ball bounces off the concrete and rolls into the water. The current bears it swiftly away, and they watch it skitter and bob until it disappears from sight, into the gloomy, round mouth of a pipe.

—Do you ever wish you'd gone to university, Mollel?

—Never thought about it.

—All those student girls, says Kiunga wistfully.

They've left the park, and are now crossing the main quadrangle of the adjacent Nairobi University. Casting their glances down, they try to divine the course of the underground pipe into which the ball had vanished. After their investigations upstream, spotting the inspection hatches has become second nature to them.

Usually, the neatly clipped grass here is dotted with youngsters reading, chatting or flirting. If it wasn't for their smart appearance and studious air, you might mistake them for pleasure-seekers overflowing from the park. But today, the place is empty.

They cross the lawn and turn a corner round a building called FACULTY OF SCIENCE. The genteel façade gives way to a standard industrial-type building. A row of skips overflow with yellow plastic bags, and a smell best described as biological fills the air.

—This is the place they do all the *experiments*, says Kiunga, in a low voice. You know, all the human heads on rat bodies, and the like.

As if on cue, a rat scurries from under one of the skips, along the narrow alleyway, and disappears into a low sewer grate built at the bottom of a high wall some distance up ahead.

—That's where we're going, says Mollel.

—Oh, Jesus.

The iron grate looks solidly concreted in place, but with a swift jerk up and out, Mollel lifts it and places it to one side.

—I chased a *chokora* down here once, he explains. He went round the corner. I thought it was a dead end, so I stopped running. By the time I got here, he was gone. Took me ages to figure out how he got away.

—These street boys have secret escape routes everywhere.

—Look at the wall above the grate. See it?

—Just looks like scratches to me.

—That's what I thought, too. But see, they're not just random. Three lines, in a row. Once I'd spotted it I started seeing this mark all over town. Under bridges, beside manhole covers, on loose planks in fences. It means *place of safety*.

—Doesn't look very safe to me.

—We should be OK, as long as you watch your step.

Mollel lowers himself through the grate and drops a few feet into ankle-deep water.

—Hold on, says Kiunga. I'll take off my shoes.

—You'll want to keep them on, replies Mollel from below.

Kiunga groans. —I only bought these a week ago.

—They'll wash.

He drops down and Mollel steadies him as he lands.

—Dark, isn't it?

—Yeah, well, I suppose they haven't got round to putting street lights down here yet. Oh, what a smell!

—Come on, says Mollel.

21

—Fresh batteries, says Kiunga, producing his flashlight from his pocket and turning it on. He passes it to Mollel, who has gone ahead.

. They pick their way through the muddy water. Even at this low level, there is a discernible push against their ankles.

—According to my reckoning, says Mollel, this is a direct continuation of the drainage ditch in Uhuru Park, and above that, Orpheus House.

—And a whole lot of other places, besides.

—Sure. But right now, it's downstream that interests us. Wherever that ball ends up, we should find anything that was dumped at the same time as Lucy's body.

Like a baby, he thinks.

Kiunga lets out a cry of disgust. Mollel follows the beam of his flashlight, down to their feet, where excrement and wads of paper wash around them.

—It's only *mavwi*, says Mollel.

—Human *mavwi*! Forget about washing these shoes. I'm going to burn them!

The drain narrows and they walk single file, Kiunga holding on to Mollel's belt. The sound of running water mingles with the occasional rumble of a heavy vehicle overhead. At fairly regular intervals, they pass under a grate, and a shaft of sunlight falls through the crack above.

—Look, says Mollel, pointing. Two large concrete pipes join the drain. Mollel shines his beam at the wall.

—There's your three lines, scratched next to one of the pipes, says Kiunga. And on the other one – a cross. What do you suppose that means?

—I don't know. But these are both inlets. We're headed downstream, remember.

They trudge onwards. Mollel senses a void before them, before it is even discernible by sight: there is a change in the sound of the water, splashing and echoing; and the dense, confined odour of the tunnel is replaced by an earthier, more open smell. Mollel puts his foot forward and feels nothing beneath it; just in time he extends a hand, and finds an iron bar set in the wall. The flashlight, however, falls into the darkness with a splash, and he sees its suffused beam for a second as it sinks greenly into deep water below.

—I'm OK, he gasps.

—Oh, I'm so glad, mutters Kiunga sarcastically. He has grasped Mollel tightly around the waist. Now, are you going to go down and get the light?

But it's already died. Gradually, they become aware of grey daylight up ahead: just enough to see by.

Mollel extends his hand along the rail, and his foot finds a narrow ledge running perpendicular to the tunnel exit. It's some inches above water level, and dry. He steps on to it, and edges along, entering a new space, where there is just enough light for them to see around them.

He lets out a low whistle.

The void, though not large, feels massive after the confines of the tunnel. It's at least twenty metres along, and ten across. The ledge on which they are standing is less than half a metre wide, and the centre of the room is a large cistern, which acts as a sediment trap. At the far end is another grille, and beyond it, a wide corrugated tube, along which the reflection of gloomy daylight is just visible.

—I know where this is! says Kiunga. That tube comes out in the river, just below the Globe roundabout. You can see it from the *matatu* stage.

At their feet, the water froths into black depths, but as it gets to the grille, it is clogged with floating material, most of which is indistinguishable.

—Well, this is where your orange football should've ended up, says Kiunga.

They look around the walls of the chamber: besides the tunnel they came from, there are four other inlets of varying sizes. Mollel wants to get a closer look at the flotsam caught in the grille, so he edges along the ledge. His foot touches something soft, and he instinctively recoils.

—Watch it! shouts Kiunga. You nearly landed us in it then!

—Look at this.

They both peer down at their feet. There, on the ledge, is what can only be described as a bed.

One of the most disgusting and precarious beds Mollel has ever seen: one which makes Superglue Sammy's hideout in the bushes look like the Nairobi Hilton; but a bed, nonetheless.

A strip of unfolded cardboard carton is topped with a pile of filthy blankets. A crumpled porn magazine completes the scene.

—And our friend Kingori thinks he's the only one with a luxury pad in the centre of town! says Kiunga.

A distant sound of cheering rises from beyond the grille. Mollel has no option but to walk over the bed; he shudders as he treads gingerly across it, reaching the other side near the grille. From here, bending down, he can just make out the end of the corrugated pipe, but the small circle of light is too dazzling, in contrast to the darkness down here, for him to see anything further. He seizes the grille and tries to raise it, but it does not shift.

He stands up and peers back.

—Look, that's the tunnel we came in from, he says.

Above the tunnel, just discernible, are three scratched lines. Above the next inlet: a cross. The next one, another cross. The same for the next two. Then, the final inlet pipe – barely wider than the ledge they're standing on, and at shoulder height – with three lines above it.

—And there's our way out.

Nairobi's *matatus* still run on Christmas Day, though less frequently – and with the fare predictably hiked up. That's why there are only a handful of people waiting at the stand to witness a manhole cover pop open, and Mollel emerge, coughing.

He bends down and extends his hand to Kiunga, who squelches to a low fence where some of the waiting passengers sit, and examines his clothes with dismay.

The people near him get up and move away.

—What? protests Kiunga. You're too good to sit next to an officer of the law?

He takes off one of his shoes and drains it on the ground. He groans.

Meanwhile, Mollel crosses the road and heads for the centre of the Globe roundabout. It is a large open patch, supposedly earmarked for development for as long as anyone can remember, but mostly used as an impromptu *matatu* depot. Today, it's uncannily quiet, apart from the sound Mollel and Kiunga had heard echoing up through the tunnel. A group of about twenty skinny, raggedy street boys – *chokora* – have taken the opportunity to grab some space for themselves, and they whoop and cheer, delirious with the opportunity to play.

Although all of the *chokora* playing here probably live and work the streets within a short radius of this spot, none of them has ever played in the public park just three blocks away. Once, street boys infested the park as they do the sewers. But they were an inconvenience, and everyone was happy when they stopped seeing them in Uhuru Park – and few people asked questions. Perhaps it's only among the *chokora* that memory persists of the clean-up – the GSU, the raid, the beatings – and the faces and street names of the boys who were never seen again.

So Mollel approaches them with caution, knowing that the sight of a policeman is usually enough to send them scattering. But today, they hardly pay him any attention. It could be because of his unusual appearance – battered and stained, trousers soaked from the knee down – or it could be because they are too absorbed in their own game, gleefully kicking around a football.

An orange, plastic football.

—What do you want, old man? The game's full!
—I just want a word with you.
—You stink of *mavwi*. Get lost.
—I want to buy that ball off you.
That gets their interest.
—You know, I think you guys have talent. I really do. With a proper football, and a bit of practice, you might make it on the team for Mathere United.
One of the older boys, almost the same height as Mollel, but skinny as a Samburu goat, approaches him warily.
—You've made a mistake, *mzee*. We're not the kind of boys you're looking for. You want them, you need to go to Mombasa.
They laugh raucously.
—Panya will let you touch him for fifty bob!
—I will not!
—Make it a hundred, then!
That gets an even bigger laugh.
—No, no, says Mollel. That's not what it's about. Come on, with the money I'll give you, you could buy a decent, leather ball. Much better than that cheap, plastic one.
He notices that one of the smaller boys, the one they called Panya, has picked up the orange ball and is hugging it to his chest. He is frowning, annoyed at Mollel's dismissal of his prize possession. How old is he? It's hard to tell. He's no bigger than Adam, who, at nine, is already up to Mollel's chest. But Adam is well nourished and healthy. Even Panya's childish features are no indication of age in a street boy. The only thing to go on

is the eyes: how wary are they, how cautious? From the way he hangs back now, glancing about him, Mollel reckons that despite his baby face, Panya is about fifteen.

—Hey, he says to Panya. Tell you what, I'll give you five hundred shillings.

Panya shakes his head.

—Six hundred. Think about it.

—Go on, Panya, urge the others. We need a *real* ball to play with.

He comes closer, eyes on Mollel, but still grasping his own ball to his chest.

—You can even keep that one, says Mollel. I'll give you the money anyway. All I want is some information…

As soon as he utters the word *information* a cry goes up: *Polisi!*

The boys scatter but Mollel lunges out and grabs Panya by the arm.

—I knew you were no good, he hisses, writhing and twisting in Mollel's grip. Damn *Polisi* and your *information*!

Kiunga hobbles up. —Sorry, Mollel. I tried to put my shoes back on and I just… *couldn't*. Did I miss anything important?

—I got the one that matters. His name is Panya.

—Oho. So you're the little rat whose nest we found in the sewers?

Panya makes to bite Mollel's arm but Kiunga grabs his head. For a moment, the three of them struggle, and Mollel is struck by the sad thought that two grown men can attempt to subdue a small boy in the middle of the day, in full view of dozens of passengers waiting for their bus, and no one – *no one* – does anything.

Welcome to Nairobi.

—Had enough? asks Kiunga, once they've got Panya back under control. The boy spits at him.

—Spit all you like, says Kiunga. I'm going to wash myself in bleach when I get home, anyway.

—Relax, urges Mollel. We don't want to hurt you, and you're not in trouble. *Sawa?*

He lets go and the boy snatches his wrist back and rubs it.

—I'm serious about the money. You can have it, if you tell us where you got that ball.

—I didn't steal it!

—I know. You found it, right?

Panya nods.

—In the drain? Where you sleep?

—Yeah. It got washed down there. About half an hour ago. I reckoned some kid had lost it in the park. That's where most of the drains come in from. I only took it so the others would let me hang out with them. They don't, usually.

—How long have you been living there?

—Few weeks.

—Have you ever found anything else down there? Anything unusual?

The boy mutters something.

—What's that? What are you saying?

Kiunga shakes him. He mutters again. Mollel still doesn't catch what he says.

—The dirty magazine, explains Kiunga.

—We don't care about that. Anything else?

He shakes his head.

—How about – don't be alarmed – a body? A *baby's* body?

The boy's eyes widen, and instinctively, he steps back. —No! Oh, no! Nothing like that!

Mollel tries to suppress his disappointment. He reminds himself that no body at least means that the baby might still be alive. But he can't help wishing for the breakthrough which would help him make this case.

—Any clothing? continues Kiunga. Women's clothes? Shoes?

Panya is starting to edge away from them. Kiunga puts his hand on his neck.

—What is it, Panya?

The boy puts his arm behind his back, as if struggling to free himself. But when he whips his hand back, something glints from his fist.

Kiunga releases him and steps away. The boy holds the knife forward. His hand is shaking. The blade is small: only two inches long. But it is cruel.

—What's that, Panya? Is that what you found?

—Stay back! You'd better leave me alone!

With a swift, fluid movement, Kiunga swirls his arm towards Panya's and grabs his wrist. At the same time, he clasps his other hand around the boy's fist and prises the knife from between his fingers.

—Not very clever, Panya, he says. He releases him, and the boy slumps to the ground.

Kiunga passes the knife to Mollel. It is leaf-shaped, razor sharp, cut from flat metal plate. The handle – no longer than the blade itself – is wrapped in a strip of greasy, worn leather.

Panya mutters: —I saw it, shining. Down at the bottom of the water. Thought it might be a ten-bob coin. I jumped in, picked it out. I thought it might be useful. You never know when you might need something like that. I didn't mean to do anything wrong.

—You've told us enough, says Mollel. Here. He takes a thousand-shilling note from his wallet. It's yours. Don't go spending it on *chang'aa*, or glue, or whatever.

—I won't.

Panya takes the money, then scurries after the orange ball, which is still on the ground. He lets out a childish laugh, as though he cannot believe his luck. As he runs away, Mollel shouts to him: —Happy Christmas!

—What's Christmas? the boy shouts back.

22

The *pilao*, at lunchtime, must have been delicious; steaming, fluffy, white rice, a few grains every handful dyed a festive red or green. Chicken flesh falling off the bone. Now, the rice is sticky and hard, blackened where it has caught the pan. The chicken is greasy and cold.

Mollel pushes it around his plate.

—No appetite? says Faith.

He shakes his head.

—I'm glad you came home before he went to bed. He was wondering if you'd make it at all.

—It took longer than I thought. Then I had to go back to the flat to change.

He wrinkles his nose. He can still smell the sewer inside his nostrils, like the smell of carrion.

—I want to talk to you, Mollel.

—Is it about the football? He pushes his plate away. I'm sorry about that. I know you'd just bought it. Tell me where you got it, and as soon as the shops are open again, I'll get a replacement.

—It's not about the football. Though how you could take away the boy's present on Christmas Day… some Christmas he's had!

Mollel has learned over the years to let his mother-in-law's chastisements wash over him. But tonight he feels a pang of remorse. True, Christmas meant nothing to him. But he recalled the boy's excitement at seeing him turn up, and the disappointment in his eyes when he left. It was like the moment when the bike got out of control. Mollel just didn't know what to do. When it came to his son, he never seemed to know what to do.

He looks over at the frail woman sitting opposite him. She isn't even old, but something about her manner always makes her seem so. For a moment, he feels an urge to reach his hand over the table to hers; it's a fleeting thought, rejected. In all the years he's known her, there has never been any physical contact between them, apart from a brush of his lips against her cheek on his wedding day. And he felt her shudder that time, however much she attempted to suppress it.

She is looking down, composing herself. Her lips move, as though recalling rehearsed lines. And now he feels unnerved, on guard. He senses an imminent attack, but the quarter is unfamiliar. He'd rather take on the *Mungiki* than this small woman.

—I want to talk about Chiku's father.

That was certainly unexpected.

—Did she ever tell you about him? Faith continues.

—Of course. Many times. She worshipped him.

—Yes. What did she tell you?

Mollel puffs out his cheeks. —Well, that he was a Mau Mau hero. Fought the English. Turned down a cabinet post from Kenyatta. She always said there could have been a Harry Ngugi Street in town if he'd wanted it.

—All true.

—And then he saw the way the wind was blowing. Corruption, dictatorship. Tribal politics. It wasn't what he fought for. After Tom Mboya was killed, he became disillusioned. He dropped out of politics, became a teacher. Died of a broken heart.

Faith sighs. —That is not so true.

Mollel looks at her with surprise. —She lied?

—No, she didn't, says Faith. I did.

*

—Frankly, our family had done well out of the English. My father had risen to foreman at the plantation. That meant we got our own front door, some space to rear some chickens, a vegetable patch. And I got sent to school.

—Then, a new teacher came. And the word was, he'd been Mau Mau. I was afraid. Convinced he'd come and slit our throats in the night.

—And yet, I couldn't take my eyes off him. I remember the day I had the revelation. I was shocked. I felt like I'd left my own body and had shot up to the ceiling and bobbed there like a cork. I knew then, that it wasn't terror I felt. He was simply the most beautiful man I'd ever seen in my life.

—You must realise, even though this was some years after *Uhuru*, we knew very little about how it had all come about. We only had one history book at school, and that was all English kings. What we heard about Mau Mau was mostly horror stories from the newspapers. It was in Kenyatta's interest to keep those stories going. He'd turned against Mau Mau by that time: too much of a threat to his interests.

—So when he sat there telling us his tales, we were spell-bound. He spoke so softly, sometimes we had to strain to hear him. But we never interrupted. It was as though he was speaking to himself, as much as us. His arrest, his escape. How he'd broken into the camp, and led his whole village to freedom.

—Massacres. Administration Police, mostly Luos and Luhyas, killing twenty, fifty prisoners a time. The truck would stop in the middle of the night and the back would drop down…

—Secret meetings. In the forest. In hotels. Kampala, Khartoum, Cairo. Suitcases full of dollars, trucks full of guns. It made me tingle, hearing about our nation being formed, being just inches away from someone who formed it.

—He was a gentleman. He didn't propose until I'd graduated school. I was hoping my father would be outraged, but he took the news well. He always loved the elites, and Harry Ngugi was the new elite.

—Except, Ngugi was already a long way from the elite. He knew how to handle a rifle, but not a committee. He was disgusted when he saw Kenyatta shaking hands with the English. He became an embarrassment. He drank.

—He kept holding out for a better offer, even as the offers got worse and worse. Schools Minister. Ambassador to Hungary. A professorship. A lecturing post. Headmaster. Schoolmaster. He took that one. Back to teaching, the job he'd qualified for ten years before. A small village school near Kiambu…

—Chiku came along. She adored her father from the first day. The first minute. They put her on my chest and she just scowled. Then he held her, whispered to her. And she opened her eyes. She just knew him. She just looked at him, drinking him in. As if saying, *So this is what you look like.*

—I'd never seen two people fall in love with each other at the same time before. I've never seen it since.

—He lost his job. Used to go to Nairobi, or Thika, looking for old friends to borrow money from. They were fond of him. Many had links with struggles elsewhere. He was offered work in Tanzania.

—Training rebels, Mollel says. Chiku told me about it. Fighters from the South. Rhodesia. She said he taught the leaders of the continent.

—After he'd been gone a month, Faith continues, I got word from the camp. They were still waiting for him to start. He'd never turned up. He rolled home half a year later, broke. Camp not paying on time, he said. Chinese money not coming through. I never told him I knew the truth.

—Chiku was ten. She organised a *harambee* to welcome her father home. A ten-year-old. The whole village came. Everyone put something in the hat – ten bob, a hundred bob. Money to liberate our African brothers.

—He couldn't even find the vein when he slaughtered the goat. He virtually hacked its head off. I had to step in, hold it down. He said it was emotion. But he was drunk.

—We didn't see him again for over a year. As far as Chiku

159

knew, as far as anyone in the village knew, he was fighting in some foreign country, leading the resistance. But I heard reports. Someone told me they'd seen him in Tigoni with a woman and kids. It wasn't even an hour away. I went. It was true.

—I told him, if you want to write Chiku a letter, you'd better do it now. His hand was shaking. He dated it *Somewhere outside Windhoek*, a month before. It was a nice touch: he was an accomplished liar.

—I think I still have that letter among her things.

—I told her, your daddy died fighting for what he believed in. Your daddy was a hero.

Mollel takes a drink of his water. His curiosity has not eliminated his sense of foreboding.

—And you never told her the truth?

—That her father was a polygamist, an alcoholic? That he abandoned her?

—Yes.

She shakes her head.

—Her imaginary father was better than the real one.

—Why are you telling me this now, Faith?

—I want custody of Adam, she says. I want you to sign him over to me.

—It's not like it will make much difference, she says, in response to Mollel's silence. He spends so much of his time here, anyway. You can still see him, of course. But look: he idolises you. Let him continue. Just, at a distance.

—I'm a policeman, Faith. I'm not like Harry.

—You are. You just don't know it.

—How?

—I called the station today. You're not supposed to be on duty. You should have been here with your son.

—I'm on a case!

—There will always be an excuse! When Chiku was killed, you got a payout you could have retired on. You had a safe, nine-to-five post in traffic division. But you got yourself switched back to CID. It's not about the money. You could raise chickens and grow beans for all I care. But you'd be there for your son.

—You don't understand.

—No. And neither will your son.

—It's not going to happen, Faith. I'm grateful for your looking after him, but that's as far as it goes.

—That's not what my lawyer says.

—Lawyer?

—I'm sorry, Mollel, she says. Adam can have everything he needs here. A stable home, school, attention. I'm not going to lose another child.

23

Look to the living, not the dead.

He'd woken before dawn with Otieno's words in his head. He had been supposed to be attending a pre-election briefing in Kibera today. But he had time to do some more digging first.

Honey had said that the orphanage had to lodge their adoptions with the government. So he had come to the city records office.

If the baby was living, whoever had taken it would want to legitimise it as soon as possible. They would not want questions asked about why the birth was not registered sooner.

A pile of documents lands with a thud on the desk before him, raising a cloud of dust.

—Birth records, last four weeks, says the clerk.

—I asked for the last three months! protests Mollel.

—Just start on those, says the clerk. Can't you see I'm the only one here? It is a holiday, you know.

Mollel props himself against the counter and begins to browse through the folder. It's fairly bulky, but does not contain as many entries as he thought, as most are duplicates: a white sheet, filled in by the parent, and a pink one, by the attending physician. There are probably three or four hundred births recorded here.

—Is this a usual amount for a month?

—About usual, calls the clerk from the back of the office. Of course, more will come in over the next few weeks. We won't close December's file until January fifteenth.

—What happens to births recorded late?

—There's a fine for that. They go into a separate file which gets consolidated at the end of the year.

—So this year's won't have been consolidated yet?

—I suppose you'll be wanting that one too, the clerk sighs.

There's nothing in the December file which stands out. Most of the entries are from the main hospital, Kenyatta. Several from the other big ones, the Nairobi, the Aga Khan, the Coptic. The rest from smaller clinics. All of the information between the two sheets, white and pink, seemed to match.

Mollel turns to the next bundle.

—When I started here, says the clerk, climbing a stepladder, they told me that this would all be on computer within twelve months.

—When did you start here?

—Nineteen ninety-two.

The November file is fuller, but equally unrevealing. As more files arrive, the story is the same. Nothing from Wanjiku Nalo. Nothing from Orpheus House.

—Thanks, he says to the clerk, after working his way back to January.

—Did you find what you were looking for?

—I found nothing, replies Mollel.

—Oh, great! moans the clerk in dismay. I suppose you want 2006 now.

But Mollel is already out of the door. Nothing is as good as something for him. It means that if there ever was a baby, it was delivered illegally.

Look to the living, not the dead.

—Let's go pick her up, says Kiunga over the phone.

—Not yet.

—Why not? We can use Honey's testimony and the disparity

in the birth records to squeeze her. Might be able to get a confession from her that way.

—We still don't have enough.

—The word of a *poko*, you mean, mulls Kiunga. No, we can't give Otieno any excuse to let Wanjiku off the hook.

—How's Kosovo? Mollel asks, changing the subject.

—Exquisite. Kiunga laughs. But I hear Kibera's even nicer this time of year. I'm almost envious of you.

Despite his levity, Mollel can hear the exasperation in Kiunga's voice. He'd rather be on the case than guarding a slum polling station. Tomorrow, Mollel would be in the same boat – but he hardly dares consider how much worse Kibera would be.

As if reading his thoughts, Kiunga says: —If I were you, I'd chill out tonight. Try to get some rest. You got your briefing this afternoon?

—I'm going there now. Mollel hangs up.

But he's not going there directly. He wants to see someone first.

He's at Honey's apartment block in Mlolongo. A gaggle of children playing around the entrance stop and gawp at him as he approaches. He thinks it strange: he usually manages to remain more or less anonymous. He brushes past them. A fat woman mopping the stairs glares angrily and splashes his feet with black water.

By the time he reaches Honey's landing, Mollel knows something is wrong. A group of women are there, falling silent as the new arrival rounds the corner from the staircase. There are too many people here: their eyes fall upon Mollel with cold hatred.

A low, contemptuous hiss accompanies him as he makes his way to Honey's door. It stands open: the lock hangs uselessly from the splintered jamb.

—Dirty bastard, hisses a bystander. Another: We got *children* here. Do your filthy business elsewhere.

He's accustomed to abuse as a police officer. But this is different. He pushes his way past them: they shrink from him as though he is infectious. On her mattress, face in her hands, sits Honey. All around her, Mollel sees her little nest destroyed: bed tipped over, cupboard face down, drawers ransacked. On the far wall, across the window, blotting out the view of the plains, red paint: *POKO*.

—Whore! they yell from behind him. You're not wanted here!

—And you should be ashamed of yourself, someone else hisses in Mollel's ear. A jab in the ribs rams the point home.

He goes forward and Honey flies into his arms, sobbing. He slips his hand protectively around her shoulder and takes her to the doorway.

As they step out on to the landing, Honey screams. Her hair is pulled from her head and waved triumphantly by one of the women, before its trajectory widens, and it arcs over the railing, floating like a crow to the street below.

Nails flash – Honey's hands are to her eyes – the women descend. Mollel pushes between them, parting them, pulling them apart, like the thorn gates of a *boma*, touching Honey, pulling her, taking her, sheltering her, crouched over her – to the staircase.

—And don't come back! ring out voices behind them.

The fat old woman mopping the steps is still there. Mollel now understands the dirty look she gave him as he went up. He grasps her T-shirt and pins her to the wall.

—Who did this?

—Don't hurt me! the old woman cries.

He pulls back his arm, open hand.

—Mollel! yells Honey.

He lowers his hand. —Who did it?

—I don't know.

—You know! You must have been mopping the same stair for hours. Worth the wait, was it? To see the expression on her face?

—I can't tell you.

—You'll tell me, says Mollel, or I'll take you in. I'll chuck you in prison and lose the paperwork. I'll see you inside for the rest of your life. You got a family?

—Mollel! Honey cries again. You're going too far!

The woman is shaking, blubbering. She says something he can't make out. Snot pours from her nose.

—Muh-muh-muh, she mutters.

—For God's sake, Mollel! Honey claws at his arm. Leave her! Don't be like this! Don't be like *them*!

—*Mungiki*, sobs the woman. It was *Mungiki*. *Mungiki* did this!

24

They manage to find a cab, eventually. On the way, Honey explains what happened. She'd gone out to get some groceries. She came back to find her apartment already trashed. She hadn't been there long when Mollel came in.

It is gone seven by the time the taxi drops them at Mollel's apartment block, and dark. Honey puts a hand on his arm to steady herself as her heels crunch over the gravel driveway.

—Thank you for this. I really don't have anywhere else to go. I'll call my landlord in the morning. See about getting a new lock put on. More security.

—No, says Mollel. You think your neighbours would have you back, now they've found out what you do? Besides, you can't risk the *Mungiki* returning, and finding you home.

But he does not believe it was *Mungiki*. The old woman said it was a couple of men with dreadlocks. And he knows at least one who fits that description.

—Look, he says, reaching into his jacket pocket. It's there: small and hard and cold. He takes it out and gives it to Honey.

—Lucy's knife, she gasps. Where did you find it?

—In the sewer. Don't worry about that. The thing is, you might as well have it, for the time being. It is no use as evidence, having been in the water for so long. And I don't have anything else to give you.

—Thank you, Mollel, says Honey, a catch in her voice. You don't know what this means to me.

—Just be careful, he says. It's for self-defence. Let's hope you don't need to use it.

She clasps his hands in hers as he takes back the knife. —You can trust me, Mollel.

He hesitates. —What is it? she asks, sensing his doubt.

—It's just something someone said. Honey… were you telling me the truth about how you and Lucy met?

Honey drops her eyes. —Mostly, she concedes. But you're right. It wasn't her who helped me get into the game. It was the other way round. Oh, Mollel – she clutches his hands tightly – you've got to understand. If she hadn't been on the streets, she wouldn't be dead. I blame myself. I didn't want you to blame me too. I needed you on my side. It takes a murder to get anyone's interest around here, and even then, it's only you who seems to care, Mollel. It's hard to tell someone the whole truth. And believe me, you wouldn't like it if I was completely open. But I promise, I won't lie to you again.

—I believe you, says Mollel. And he opens her hands and relinquishes the knife.

When they reach the top of the stairs to the first floor, Mollel sees the door to his own apartment open.

—Stay here.

He puts out the landing light, the better to see within, and so as not to present a silhouette.

Slowly, he edges to the door: no sign of forced entry.

Lights are on, inside. He hears movement.

He has no weapon, now he has given away the knife – not that it would have been much good in this situation – so, entering, he picks up an umbrella from beside the door. It's better than nothing.

The noise of drawers opening comes from Adam's room. He edges along the hallway, umbrella raised. As he passes the entrance to the sitting room—

—Dad!

—Adam!

—Is it raining? Grandma said we had to come and get some clothes for me. I told her I didn't mind wearing the same clothes.

—No, but I mind, says Faith, coming out of the boy's room with a pile of folded clothes in her hands. I'll not have the women at church thinking my grandson is a street boy. I let myself in, she says to Mollel. I didn't know when you'd be back.

—Can't I stay here, now you're home, Dad? Adam has flung his arms around Mollel's waist.

—Best not. I've got to leave early for election duty tomorrow, and God knows what time I'll be back. The next few days are going to be very difficult, Adam. Best you stay with your grandmother.

There is a cough, and the three of them turn.

—Oh, says Faith. I didn't realise you had company.

—This is… Honey, this is my son, Adam, and his grandmother, Faith. This is Honey. Her name is Honey.

—Hi! says Honey to Adam, approaching him and placing her palm on the top of his head, crowning him. It's a curiously Maasai gesture. Instinctively, Adam smiles.

—Well, really! says Faith. We must be going. Come along, Adam. Let's leave your father and his… friend.

—Faith!

—No, no. I can see you've got your priorities. Work indeed! And as she passes: We'll see what the lawyer has to say about *this*!

—Grandma!

—Not now, Adam.

—But Grandma! The lady – she's crying!

There is a creature – in Maa, called *en-kelesure*, in English, pangolin – a hard, scaly eater of ants. It has powerful arms and long, sharp claws, and when cornered, will rise on its hind legs and display. Jab it with your stick, or spear – and it rolls into a ball. Hard. Impenetrable. Boys love to taunt such a creature when they catch one. And when they do, it always ends the same way: on the fire, blackened in the embers, the scales roasting with the smell of burned hair, sweet flesh picked straight from the shell.

Irritable, defensive, but soft inside: sometimes, Faith reminds Mollel of a pangolin.

The three adults are around the kitchen table, nursing *chai*.

—I never would have thought it of the Nalos. They seem like such good Christians. I mean, I know they're not Catholic, but—

—We can't prove *anything*, yet, says Mollel, his sense of procedure demanding the caveat.

—Oh, come on! After all this poor girl has told us?

Faith through and through. Half an hour ago, she could barely look at Honey. Now she's *this poor girl*.

—Mollel's right. If they killed my friend, and sold her baby, who knows what else they've done. We have to make a strong case against them. We have to find out if there are other children – and where they are.

—Lord above, says Faith. What has this country come to? Selling our children!

—The buyers are guilty too, says Mollel. He pushes away his *chai*, undrunk.

The gesture is noticed by Faith, who says to Honey: —It's late. My dear, you are coming home with me.

—What? says Honey. No, I couldn't impose.

—It is no imposition. You don't even have any clothes with you, do you? You can borrow some of mine. And tomorrow, with the election, there's no point going out, anyway. What would you do, stay here on your own all day? No, it's much better you come with me.

—You're very kind.

—I think you're owed a bit of Christian charity, don't you, dear?

Faith calls to the sitting room. —Adam, we're leaving soon. Before we go, Honey would like to see your video game. Can you show her?

—Sure.

The little boy excitedly begins to explain his game to Honey and passes her one of the controllers. He clearly relishes having someone to play with: Mollel has never done so. It's the sort of thing Chiku would have done.

Faith closes the door on them, and says to Mollel:

—Did Chiku ever tell you about Koki?

—No. Don't think so. Who's Koki?

Faith gets up and looks out of the darkened window.

—It was rainy season. Chiku noticed a tiny puppy. Pure white. There were lots of stray dogs living near our house, but none of them seemed to be its mother. She pestered and pestered me about that dog. Mama, who's going to look after it? Mama, it will die.

—So, I took in the dog. Washed it, fed it. Got it treated for rabies, everything. I have to say, it was a cute little thing. And adored Chiku. She called it Koki.

—But?

—But? It was wild. Even though it was so tiny, those days on the streets left their mark. When it grew up, it never lost its jealousy, its temper. And if you ever came between her and Chiku…

She rolls up her sleeve, and runs her finger along a small crescent scar on her arm.

—You can bring who you like into your house, she says quietly. But if it affects the safety of those already there—

—She was only going to stay the night, Faith. I would've slept on the sofa.

—Well, now she can go in my spare room. Where I can keep an eye on her.

—Believe it or not, I'm grateful. I'm not really set up for guests.

—Just be warned. If necessary, I will do anything, *anything*, to protect my grandson.

—Even if that means taking him away from me?

They both look up at the same time: Honey is in the doorway.

—Adam wants to know if he can bring his video game with him.

—Sure, says Mollel. Honey turns and goes back to the sitting room.

Faith scoops her car keys from the table and rises.

—Aren't you going to ask me what happened to Koki? she says.

—I don't want to know, answers Mollel.

25

Kibera. He's heard that a million people live here, two million. No one knows. Least of all the government: they don't even officially acknowledge that the settlement exists.

The slum is so close to the city centre that the towers of the business district are glimpsed, now and then, from between the tin roofs. It seems like a different world. But the shit and trash underfoot – under everything – ends up flowing into the same river as the water from the tunnels Mollel crawled through two days before.

He arrives at the edge of the slum half an hour before his shift is due to start. Trying to make up for missing the briefing yesterday. He's also concerned about getting lost. He has only been into Kibera twice before, and it would take many more than two visits to learn his way around.

As it is, he need not have worried. From the Langata Road, there are only a handful of access points, and each one is steeled with lines of GSU. He even gets a salute, and stumbles over returning it – a strange feeling, being back in uniform.

—I need to report to Champions Primary School.

—If you wait a few minutes, we've got a group going in.

—Any trouble?

The GSU man's only response is a hearty chuckle.

Kibera might be an informal settlement, but Kiberans vote. The local MP is the leader of the opposition – the slum, his Luo power base in the capital. The threat – real, or imagined – of an uprising from this massed humanity has often won him a place at the bargaining table.

The government has long practised a policy of containment in all the country's major slums. Why else are police dormitories and army camps always found adjacent to such areas? But this time they're leaving nothing to chance. The GSU, in their green uniforms and crimson helmets, flow around the exterior like a troupe of forest ants. Mollel spies a water-cannon truck and dozens of Administration Police Land Rovers, their green bodies and crimson roofs mirroring the uniforms of their occupants.

—We have a group reporting to Champions Primary?

Mollel steps forward, as do a half-dozen other regular police officers, and a couple of nervous-looking officials, their breath steaming in the chilly morning air.

—Right. This polling station is in part of Kibera known as Half London.

There's a humourless laugh from some of the other officers. Half London is a common name for any district which is fancy, lively or exclusive. Nairobi's slum dwellers have a good line in irony. Sometimes, they can be almost literal, too: Mollel wonders how Kiunga is getting on in Mathare's slum Kosovo.

—The ballots and boxes are already on site, continues the GSU officer, as are plenty of your colleagues. There's quite a queue already, waiting to get in, but no reports of any problems, so far. Now, there is no vehicular access to this site. We have to walk in – and out. That's why we're going in groups. Do not step away from the group. Do not depart from our route. Do not enter any residence or building, other than the polling station. Do not accept or buy any food or drink from locals. There are refreshments on site, securely prepared. Watch your step – the ground is treacherous, even when dry. Take a tip: don't try to jump over things. The locals have a saying: the only thing worse than stepping in it is landing in it. And lastly, look out for flying toilets.

—Flying toilets? asks one of the election officials.

—Plastic bags, says the GSU man with a smile. Flung over the rooftops. I'll leave you to imagine the contents.

A whistle is blown and they move off.

The crimson helmets part and they enter the slum.

The first sight is a kiosk: a small hut selling Coca-Cola, *chai* and *mandazi*, clumps of *sukuma* and strips of chewing gum. It is doing good trade, even at this early hour. Despite the public holiday for the election, there are still a large number of people bottled up this side of the cordon, huddled against the cold, attempting to leave Kibera for work in the city. Many wear the clothing of domestic servants: blue overalls and gumboots for gardeners; green or pink pinafores on the maids. One man, incongruous in suit and tie, sees the oncoming party and shakes his fist.

—They're not letting us out! he cries. No one said they could arrest all of Kibera! What is this, intimidation? Well, it won't work!

—Shut up, growls the GSU man leading the way. You'll get out in due course. Then, in an aside to Mollel, he adds: That one'll be going nowhere today, if he carries on like that.

The street narrows swiftly, and Mollel finds himself straddling a trickle of water. The compacted trash underfoot has some give in it, spongy: the one-storey houses around them are made from sticks and rusting iron sheets, ragged curtains in doorways, everywhere the smell of food, of smoke, the sound of babies crying and music playing and laughter. Chickens and children compete for space among the legs of women standing around the doorways. The place feels alive; organic. Mollel has a vision of himself and his colleagues as antibodies, invaders in a larger organism. That makes Nairobi the body – so which organ is Kibera? Dark, dense, condensing. Kibera is the liver.

—Look up there, says one of the policemen. Mollel sees a group of five or six men, standing on top of a tin-roofed shack abreast a small rise. Against the dawning light, they are silhouetted: he clearly sees their long, matted dreadlocks.

—*Mungiki*, says the policeman.

As they see the oncoming party, one of the dreadlocked men produces a blue flag, with the ruling party's emblem, and waves it. They jeer and whoop as Mollel and the others pass.

—Is he mad? They'll get ripped to shreds! It was only a few days ago some kid got lynched for wearing a pro-government T-shirt here. He didn't even know what the logo meant.

—But the GSU weren't here a few days ago, says Mollel.

—What's that supposed to mean? demands the GSU man.

—Everyone knows there are no *Mungiki* in Kibera. They're Kikuyu. They must have got through your lines somehow. I'll bet that just the other side of that rooftop is a GSU snatch squad, ready to take anyone who rises to the bait.

—You be careful what accusations you make, brother, says the GSU man.

As if on cue, a rain of missiles – empty bottles, stones and detritus – flies over their heads, sending the dreadlocked men hopping off the rootop like vultures. Mollel and the others duck their heads and wait until the volley dies down. A sound of hooting and cheering greets the disappearance from the rooftop.

—I hope for their sake there *are* none of your men the other side of that house, says Mollel. I saw quite a few flying toilets among that lot.

The polling station is little more than a concrete-block shell with a tin roof. The windows and the doors are mere openings in the walls, and a black-painted wall serves as blackboard. There is no school furniture, books or anything else: probably easier than having them stolen, supposes Mollel. Out back, though, there is the staple of the Kenyan workplace: a charcoal stove and a pair of sturdy women stirring a massive *sufuria* of *chai*. The rest of the party head towards them eagerly. In the otherwise empty room, a set of cardboard polling booths have been erected, and some officials sit at a trestle table, with papers, ink and stamps.

There is a sizeable queue outside. Some of those waiting shuffle their feet and, as Mollel passes, he is asked the time anxiously:

he feels that the enquirer is almost disappointed when he hears it is not yet seven. He is sure that there are many present who would like nothing more than the chance to make accusations of irregularities.

Farther down the line, he sees a familiar face. Standing with one hand on the wall, the other holding a cane with a small plastic cup taped to the bottom.

—Where have you been, Sammy?

—Oh, hello, Sergeant. How are things? Guess I never expected to run in to you here. How do you like Half London?

—Never mind that. You disappeared. I've been looking for you.

—Well, now you've found me. Eh, sounds like something's happening. You wouldn't want me to miss my chance of exercising my democratic right, would you, Sergeant?

Seven o'clock has arrived. The guards have started letting people into the school hall.

—I need to talk to you.

—Not here, hisses Sammy through a grin. He's right: far too many curious eyes.

—Well, where? When?

—A few days' time. When the elections are over, and I can get back to the city centre. I'll see you then.

Mollel puts his arm around the blind man's shoulder and digs his fingers in. —If you think I'm going to let you vanish again …

Sammy grimaces, then attempts to disguise it with a smile.

—As a registered blind person, you know, I am allowed someone to assist me with my vote, he says, through gritted teeth. I usually rely on the officials. But perhaps you'd care to be my helper?

It is a good idea. After they've presented his ID and done some paperwork, Mollel escorts Sammy to a cardboard booth on the far side of the hall. He waits a moment for the booths either side to be free, then he stands facing outward, while Sammy goes into the box. Mollel shakes his head at the official who guides voters to the booths, a signal not to send anyone else to their section.

—What's it all about, Sammy?

—Nothing, Sergeant, nothing. I told you everything I could that night.

—So why did you go? I thought someone had got to you.

—No, no, nothing like that. I just wanted a change of scene, you know. It was getting kind of crowded round the park.

—And gave up your pitch in town too? We looked for you for hours. Come off it!

—I swear to God!

—Look. We're already taking too long about this. If you like, we can walk out of here, arm in arm, and I can announce to the world that you're kindly helping the police with our enquiries. How would that go down?

—Don't do that, for God's sake.

—Right. So let's talk.

—You never told me it was the GSU in the park that night, Sammy says. If they wanted to keep it secret, I didn't want to hang around waiting for them to hear from one of your guys that I was a witness.

—How did you find out it was GSU?

—Come on, Mollel, says Sammy. If it was police, you'd have known about it. Who does that leave? And if *you* worked out it was them, why shouldn't I?

—And that's it?

—Not quite, says Sammy. He shuffles uneasily. There is something else. Something I didn't tell you. I was going to tell you soon, honest. But I thought that if I held out a little longer, there might be…

He rubs his thumb and forefinger together.

—Oh, there'll be a reward all right, Sammy. The reward is, I don't shout from the rooftops of Kibera that you're nothing more than a police informant.

—OK, OK. The blind man frowns. It was probably nothing, anyway. But just before those buses turned up, I heard a row. A woman screaming. And another woman's voice. I couldn't hear what she was saying, or who she was arguing with.

—And the woman shouting was different to the one screaming? Are you sure?

Sammy nods. —I have a good ear, he says.

—Could you identify the shouting voice if you heard it again?

—I'm sure I could.

—And this was *before* the buses came into the park, you say?

—Right before. It was them coming in that shut her up. But look, there's nothing else. That's all I know. Honest.

—It had better be, Sammy, says Mollel.

As they leave the polling station, Sammy holds up his ink-blotted pinkie for all to see.

—Thanks for your assistance, Officer!

—Will you be all right from here? I can't really leave the polling station.

—Oh, yes. I know every inch of this place. Good thing about a slum: no cars to worry about. And if you put out your hand – he stretches out and places his fingers against a corrugated sheet – there's always a familiar wall within reach.

Mollel watches the blind man go, cane tapping, the fingers of his free hand dancing over iron, cardboard, sticks and plastic sheeting. So Sammy heard two woman at the park that night. The screams must have come from Lucy. If the woman shouting was Wanjiku – and if Sammy could ID her – it might be enough to pin the murder on her. If a court was not convinced by the testimony of a prostitute, perhaps they'd take the word of a blind beggar?

He becomes aware of someone else watching, too, and looking down the line of waiting voters, sees the black-clad figure of Benjamin, Nalo's supposedly ex-*Mungiki* right-hand man. Benjamin gives him a smile, and a sharp nod, then turns and walks away.

26

Three in the afternoon, and the time for Mollel and his shift colleagues to be relieved has come and gone.

—I don't mind how long they take, says one of the younger policemen, barely out of training. Just think of that lovely overtime!

Neither Mollel nor anyone else is minded to tell him that this will fall under *special provisions* – the catch-all clause that superiors always invoke to avoid paying out overtime.

—I don't like it, says another policeman.

—It's all gone peacefully so far.

It has. As the day warmed up, so did the attendance, and the police were required to start double-queuing, snaking the line back and forth. Queuing is not a habit which comes naturally to the *matatu*-faring Nairobian, but this time the practice was adopted with grace and even good humour. Mollel was struck by how the dominant mood of the morning was enthusiasm, even optimism. This was opposition heartland, and the absence of any pro-government voice on this territory created a sense of inevitability, invincibility.

Kibera felt it was going to be heard.

Around lunchtime the relaxed atmosphere had been shattered by a disturbance. A middle-aged man, reeking of sour *chang'aa*, had staggered to the front of the queue and demanded to be allowed to vote. Those at the head of the line, who had been waiting patiently for over an hour, objected. The young policeman intervened: he pushed the man away from the line; *chang'aa* and gravity did the rest. He went flying into the mud. Most of the people who saw it laughed, and thought nothing more of it.

But soon the drunk returned, with a handful of his buddies. He began to harangue the officials. He'd been prevented from voting, he said. It was because he was Luo, he insisted. The polls were rigged. There was no way this Kikuyu government was going to allow the other tribes to speak.

This time, the people in the queue did not laugh. They were no longer the same people who had seen the drunk try to break in line. His accusations were met with dark murmuring and hostile glances at the officials.

It was Benjamin who defused the situation. He had been hanging around all day, talking to people in the line and passers-by, always just out of Mollel's earshot. As ex-*Mungiki*, he was certainly a Kikuyu, and in that sense was either brave or foolhardy to be in a place like this on a day like today. But Nalo's church drew a considerable constituency from Kibera: it was evident from the way many people greeted him that they knew Benjamin from there. Mollel wondered whether they would be so forgiving if they knew about his past, and then reflected: probably, yes. He had learned many times, from his own experience, that the capacity for forgiveness is greater among the poor than the rich.

Benjamin had approached the man, and Mollel saw the drunk's anger dissipate as Benjamin first listened to his protest, then spoke quietly with him for a while.

Benjamin then came to Mollel, who was supervising the head of the voting queue. It was the first time they had spoken since meeting at Nalo's church on Sunday.

—I need you to do something, said Benjamin.

—*You* need *me* to do something? How about you tell me what you're even doing here today?

—I'm an official observer. Call it part of my pastoral duties.

Ministering to our flock. And heading off trouble before it begins.

—Trouble, like a trashed apartment in Kitengela?

—You want to talk to me, fine. Let's do that. But let's do this first. There's a lot more at stake here than you realise.

Mollel, against his will, found himself beginning to trust the man. There was something about his intensity which suggested he was genuine.

—What do you want?

—I want you to let our friend here – he pointed at the drunk – in at the front of the line. He's to go into the voting hall, wait a few minutes, then walk out, with his finger inked.

—What about voting?

Benjamin shook his head.

—Then why… Suddenly Mollel laughed. I get it. That was what your little chat was about. He's not even registered, is he?

Benjamin smiled. —He didn't know he had to be.

—All that fuss about being denied his vote, and he wasn't eligible anyway!

—True. But, the thing is, he's got a big mouth, and a lot of drinking buddies.

—So you want to give him a face-saver. Better he boasts about skipping the queues than mouths off about being turned away.

—Exactly.

Mollel found himself feeling unexpected respect for Nalo's young man.

That was a couple of hours ago. Mollel had done as Benjamin requested, and the situation had calmed. For the moment.

One of Mollel's colleagues takes over from him at the main entrance to the polling station, and Mollel seizes the opportunity to walk around. The line is longer than ever, but – blame the afternoon heat, or something else – the atmosphere is different.

There is a tension in the air. People lower their voices to talk to one another: laughter and chatter have been replaced by quick, concerned glances. And another thing: seems like everyone who has a phone is using it, looking at screens, tapping out replies.

—Something's wrong, he says, as much to himself as anyone else, but a voice replies: —Yes. It is Benjamin. Seems like word is reaching here of what's been going on at Old Kibera, the young man says.

Old Kibera is one of the other polling stations in the district, half a mile or so from here as the crow flies, but considerably farther through the narrow, maze-like passages. In the age of the mobile phone, however, even the crow seems sluggish compared to the spread of news by text message.

—What's happened?

—People being turned away all day, by all accounts. Irregularities on the register. A big blank page where most of the letter Os should be.

Old Kibera ward is more mixed than this one. If the vote is going to be gerrymandered, it would make more sense to do it there. But surely no one would be as blatant as to strike out all the names which begin with O – disenfranchising nearly all the Luos at one stroke?

—I'm just telling you what is being said, says Benjamin. The latest is, Raila himself turned up, half an hour ago, to cast his vote. He wasn't allowed in.

Raila Odinga. Leader of the opposition. True or not, if that story was doing the rounds…

—This place is going to explode, says Benjamin, finishing Mollel's thought for him.

The sound, when it comes, makes everyone stop. For a moment they hope it is something innocuous – gravel raining down on tin roofs, perhaps, or construction work somewhere. But even those unfamiliar with it – and in Kibera there are few – quickly recognise it as gunfire.

—It's some way off, yet, Mollel says. The two tea ladies, four policemen, four officials and one GSU officer are gathered in the entrance to the polling station. Voting is continuing, though the queue has dissipated.

Somehow, Benjamin has been accepted into their group. Mollel is glad of his presence. He does not altogether trust the ex-*Mungiki* man yet. But he recognises his usefulness.

—That pop-pop-pop, that's automatic fire. Probably intimidating fire, says Mollel. He's not the ranking officer here – technically, that's the GSU man – but his calm assurance has naturally made all eyes gravitate to him.

—Who's shooting? Us or them?

—I'm guessing them. Our guys would be firing off single rounds.

The two armed policemen tote their AKs nervously. They only have a handful of rounds between them. If the situation arises, they're going to have to make every bullet count.

—There's every chance the trouble won't reach us, says Benjamin. It's been calm here all day.

—Equally, there's every chance it will, says Mollel. If so, all we can do is hole up and wait for relief. This building is the closest thing to shelter we have. We'll have to make a call on closing the poll.

—As returning officer, I insist the ballots be preserved.

Mollel suppresses a smile. The small man's terrified face is at odds with his words. But Mollel is pleased to see someone taking their job seriously.

—We'll do our best, he promises. Now, this building is constructed from concrete blocks. I'm afraid that's poor defence against AK-47 rounds. Our best hope is to stay in this building, and stay low. Avoid presenting a target.

—You sound like a soldier. The young policeman laughs, nervously. No one else smiles.

—You two, Mollel continues, turning to the tea ladies, who are quivering, holding hands. Are you from here? Local?

They shake their heads.

—You're going to need some kind of white flag. Can you make one?

They look around them. —We have tea towels. We can find a stick.

—OK. That's for when assistance comes. As soon as you see the crimson helmets, you start waving that flag, and you keep waving. Understood?

They nod, but it's clear they've not fully understood the implications of what Mollel is saying. Probably none of them has, except Benjamin: his fixed jaw says it all. The policemen's uniforms, the officials' suits; even Benjamin's smart suit. By enabling them to be quickly recognised, their clothes should afford them some measure of protection in any GSU counter-assault. But two women, wearing common Kenyan *kangas* and T-shirts, will have no such status. They might be seen as a threat, by some trigger-happy cop. Or, in the confusion, they might end up getting the standard GSU treatment for any woman they find in their path. And that, Mollel reminds himself, is still a possible scenario for what happened to Lucy.

On reflection, he's not sure a white flag is going to be enough.

—You stay with these two, he says to the young policeman. The man nods.

—Now, we've got four hours until polls close. Then we're out of here. So let's do all we can to ensure that happens.

As they all return to their posts, Benjamin sidles up to Mollel.

—What's the betting these ballot boxes won't make it as far as the count?

It's the first time the thought has occurred to Mollel. He's been wary of vote stuffing, of irregularities at the count, but he never considered that the whole ballot might go astray. Of course, nearly every one of those papers inside the boxes must be an opposition vote. And they rely on the security services to get them out. Surely – *surely* – they would not be so brazen?

And the only outside observer here is Benjamin.

They have been in close proximity to each other all day, but this is the first opportunity Mollel has to speak to him properly.

—Whose side are you on? he asks, frankly.

—Weren't you listening to the sermon on Sunday? We don't take sides.

—Oh, sure. Nalo's a business partner of David Kingori, who's hand in glove with the government. Don't tell me your church is a disinterested onlooker. And as for the *Mungiki* – word is, they're taking their orders directly from State House these days.

—I wouldn't know.

—Because your *Mungiki* days are far behind you, right? Then who ordered your *Mungiki* brothers to destroy an innocent girl's apartment?

Benjamin sighs.

—That should not have happened.

—So you admit it?

—I admit nothing. But say – just say – someone's going round, making serious allegations. You'd want to find out more about them.

—You mean, the Nalos wanted to find out what she had on them?

—Put it this way, says Benjamin. Intimidation is not my style.

—So you were looking for evidence. You thought she might have something which could prove the case against them.

—If there was any so-called evidence, it would be fabricated. The allegations are false.

—Either way. You say your guys didn't trash Honey's place. What did they do, leave the door open?

Benjamin remains silent.

—And the neighbours did the rest, continues Mollel. They'd probably been waiting for a chance for some time.

—I think we're understanding each other, says Benjamin.

—It doesn't let you off the hook. If I manage to pin it on you, I'll get you for obstructing an official investigation.

—There is no official investigation, says Benjamin. The way I hear it, you continue like this, you'll be off the force.

—The way you hear it?

Suddenly it becomes clear to Mollel. Benjamin's presence here today is no coincidence.

—You knew I'd been stationed here. I thought you said intimidation is not your style?

—This is not intimidation, says Benjamin. We had to find out if you were pursuing these false allegations. The fact that you know about the break-in at the girl's flat tells me you are. In fact, I would not be surprised if you knew, very well, where she is right now. And that's information which I'm sure your superior would be very keen to hear.

But Mollel is no longer listening. He's tuned into something else; a sound of cries and panic, underscored by a distant, yet distinct, smell.

—You smell that?

—Just burning charcoal.

—No. It's too pungent.

They rush outside, greeted on the doorstep by the sight of the young policeman dealing with a group of wild-eyed youths.

—I'm telling you, we don't have a fire extinguisher, he's saying.

Mollel looks up. Black smoke is pounding into the air: the occasional flame leaping into the sky.

—What's burning?

—One house, says one of the youths. But it will spread.

—Where can we get water here?

—Down at the stream. It's nearly dry.

—Put a call in to the command post, Mollel orders the GSU man. Tell them to raise the fire brigade.

—There's no way they'd get a fire truck in here!

—No, but with some extinguishers and a bucket chain from the stream, we should be able to get this under control.

He and Benjamin run with the youth to the scene of the fire. It's about three rows back from the polling station. A woman stands in the alley, a few pitiful possessions around her, baby clutched tightly to her chest. She is crying.

—Anyone inside?

—No.

—All the neighbours out?

Mollel can see that the inhabitants of the neighbouring shacks are leaving little to chance, throwing mattresses, furniture and foodstuff out of their doorways. This has the undesirable effect of further obstructing the alleyway, already crowded with onlookers.

—It was *Mungiki*! cries one bystander. Mollel wheels round and grabs him by the shirt.

—Did you see them?

—No, but others did! They set the fire, then ran off over the rooftops!

—She was cooking indoors, shouted a woman. She always does it! We told her it was dangerous, but would she listen?

—It was *Mungiki*, I tell you!

Mollel delivers the man a powerful slap with his open hand, and he slumps to the ground. —Shut up! You think we need panic now, on top of everything else?

—I think you may be too late, says Benjamin.

They look up to see a gang of young men rounding the corner of the alley. They are carrying pangas and sticks.

—Ha! So the *polisi* are here! shouts the leader. Not in time to stop their friends the *Mungiki* from burning Kibera to the ground!

Mollel looks desperately behind him. The crowd is thick in that direction, too. They gasp as the second building begins to take fire. Benjamin has started frantically punching his mobile phone, but the leader of the gang steps forward and knocks it from his hand with a stick.

—I'm trying to get help to put this fire out, he cries.

—Get help for *this*! shouts the youth, and brings the stick down towards Benjamin's head. Benjamin parries it with his forearm, and Mollel hears the cracking of bone.

—Ask *her*! Mollel is amazed to hear his voice reaching a scream. Ask *her*! It's her house! She can tell you how the fire started!

He points to the woman with the baby, but she is still crying, and raises her face to him, dumbly, tears and mucus running down her chin.

By now, flames are leaping from the top of three shacks in this alleyway, and Mollel is sure that those behind must also be ablaze. The fire is out of control. Benjamin, cradling his shattered arm, is slumped to his knees, Mollel supporting him. They are less than twenty metres from the polling station, and his armed colleagues. He considers shouting for them. But even if they could hear his cries, they would not come for him. They would not be foolish enough to abandon their post. He wildly scans the faces around him, looking for someone who might speak up for them, might offer them some mercy. But finds no one. The faces stare back blankly at two men who are about to die.

—Enough!

The voice is familiar, but wholly unexpected. Mollel has only ever heard him speaking softly, meekly. But now, all eyes turn to the blind man. Superglue Sammy holds his cane aloft like a sword. His face is full of rage and spit flies from his lips as he shouts: —These are not our enemy! *They're trying to help!*

—They're in league with the *Mungiki*! And the government!

—This Maasai? I've known him fifteen years. Do you know who he is? He's the one who pulled a hundred people out of the American embassy, the day it was bombed!

A strange hush comes over the mob. Mollel's story – if not the man himself – is widely known, even in the depths of Kibera.

—Yes, he's the one. He's the one who kept going back, kept bringing out survivors, even though his own wife was among the dead. And how did the government reward him?

Sammy has tapped his way round to Mollel and Benjamin. —You know what they did? They *demoted* him, sent him away, for daring to speak the truth about what goes on in the police department! He's no government stooge! He's on our side!

Mollel looks up. The gang are lowering their weapons – but the fire is breathing down his neck. He can feel his skin singeing.

—If he is who you say he is, Sammy—

—He is!

—Come on, boys, the leader says grudgingly. It's getting hot round here.

The gang turn to leave.

—No, wait!

It is Benjamin.

—Don't go. We need you – and your pangas.

—He's right, says Mollel. There's no chance of putting out this fire now. We've got to create a firebreak.

Energised, he reels off commands – take down any structure within three metres of the fire. Pull out everything inside, take it away from the flames. What little water they have – stinking, brown, in pans and *sufurias* – should not be wasted on the flames, but instead used to douse the roofs and walls of the shacks the other side of the firebreak. Meanwhile, anyone left without a task should be on hand with a blanket or broom, to tamp sparks.

It's remarkable – even in this confusion, Mollel notices it – how biddable the gang has become. Their rage has evaporated, and they take their orders with relish. With a newly instilled sense of purpose, they dash off to their duties.

—We should not hang around, groans Benjamin.

Mollel agrees. The two of them stagger back to the polling station. The door is closed. They hammer on it, and call, and one of the armed policemen raises his muzzle over the sill of the unglazed window.

—It's you! We thought you were dead.

—Just let us in!

They go in. —They're not letting the fire brigade through, says the GSU man, once they're inside. To his credit, he seems embarrassed by the decision. But Mollel ignores him. He runs over to one of the officials' desks, pulls it to a window, and jumps up. From there, he can reach to the outside, where he is able to pull himself up on to the flat concrete roof.

—Wait for me!

Mollel lowers his hand and Benjamin offers him his good arm, wincing as Mollel pulls him up alongside him.

The roof of the school is concrete and baking in the sun, and the heat from the nearby blaze stings the skin on their cheeks and eyes. Mercifully, the thick smoke is trailing almost straight up on this windless day, affording them a clear view of nearly all Kibera.

For a moment, they turn from the fire, and take in the panorama before them.

The black smoke carves a deep groove in the blue sky, serving to highlight the crystalline clearness of the view. On the horizon, the city, the skyscrapers looking close enough to touch. Then lush green of trees abruptly cut along a geometric boundary, stopping against red, the earth-red, rust-red, iron-red roofs of the slum, rolling like furrowed fields, a corrugated carpet, down the valley and flipping up the other side; in the fold sits a fine mist like morning haze.

—Tear gas, says Mollel.

—That's Old Kibera, confirms Benjamin, his words accompanied by a renewed pop-pop-popping, and they hear a whizz of bullets over their heads.

They both drop.

—So much for not presenting a target, Benjamin laughs.

They crawl to the edge and look over. Below them, they can see the gang clearing the firebreak. Five of them have taken the tin roof off one shack, and are now pushing and rolling the thin wooden structure below, while an elderly woman – the occupant, no doubt – looks on, sobbing. With a crash and a cloud of dust the walls collapse.

—Look, says Benjamin.

Children are scampering into the flattened shack, weaving through the legs of the demolition team, picking up whatever they can find, all accompanied by the screams of the owner. The young men hardly heed the kids as they begin hurling everything they can lay their hands on out of the fire's path. They're just in time, too: flames are already beginning to encroach across the gap. The children dance away, laughing: the peril is nothing to them.

Meanwhile, Mollel sees that several other shacks have come

down. The gang are working well. A rough square is being formed around the blaze, and the roofs and walls disappear all around, while water hisses from buckets on to the sun-baked roofs of the houses beyond.

—They're doing a good job.

—Let's hope so. They don't have much time.

Suddenly Mollel sees something which makes him lurch with desperate fear. Emerging from the smoke in one of the newly created clearings, stumbling over debris:

—Sammy!

The blind man has his hand out, flapping futilely for a wall, seaching in vain for a navigation point.

Mollel leaps to his feet. Benjamin stands too. Together, they shout out desperately, trying to raise the attention of some of the gang below. But their cries are lost in the tumult of destruction.

—He doesn't know where he is!

—Oh God, oh God, cries Benjamin.

Sammy turns, trying to judge by sound a safe passage. He puts his hand up, to gauge the heat – and makes a decision on which way to go.

The wrong decision.

—No, Sammy! No!

A flaming shack collapses a few feet before him: debris scatters at his feet. He stumbles; drops his cane. He wheels around, helplessly.

He trips; sinks to his knees. The fire is almost upon him. He puts his hands up to his sightless eyes, skin crackling and peeling in the heat.

—I'm going, yells Mollel.

—No!

But Mollel is already over the ledge. As he leaps, he hears the whizzing of bullets: he is not even aware of landing. He runs to the fire. He runs so slowly, he seems to cover no ground at all. And yet, within an instant, he is among the choking smoke.

He hears Benjamin's voice, though he can't make out what

he's shouting. He looks back at the school roof: through the smoke, he can just see him standing on the edge, indifferent to bullets: he is pointing frantically ahead of Mollel.

He takes a breath.

He plunges into blackness.

27

THE HONEY GUIDE

Once, there was a girl who was sent by her mother to collect berries.
Before she even started to pick the berries, she was approached by a
little bird. The bird told her: These berries are sweet, but I know of
something sweeter still. It is my secret. I would like to share it with
you, but because I do not wish others to know of it, you must close
your eyes. Follow the sound of my voice.

The girl closed her eyes, and followed the sound of the little bird's
voice. She guided her well, patiently sitting on branches while she
rounded thickets and crossed streams.

The bird guided the girl like this for some distance, and she felt the
coolness of night approach. But she thought that her mother would be
pleased with her for finding the sweetness. So she kept her eyes closed
tightly, and followed the song of the little bird.

Finally she heard a loud buzzing which began to fill her ears with
noise and her heart with dread. She opened her eyes and said: This is
a place of danger. You have tricked me.

There is no danger, protested the little bird. Simply do as I say and
we shall both get what we desire.

So the little bird told the girl to gather a pile of stones. She did
so. Then the bird told her to build a fire, directly underneath where
the bee's nest hung, high on the branches of the whistling thorn tree.
Fearfully she gathered kindling, but the bees were too busy returning
home for nightfall to molest her.

She found a discarded Weaver Bird's nest, and struck sparks into it from her little knife. Then she placed it among the kindling, and lay on the earth, blowing into the pile of sticks until flames lapped their edges. Still the bees took no notice of her. Then the little bird told her: gather the moss from the stones by the stream, and lay it upon the fire. She did as she was bid.

Immediately, thick grey smoke began to rise. The moment it curled up to the branches, the bees retreated inside, and the little bird shrieked excitedly: Now! Throw the stones at the nest!

She was afraid, for she knew the insects would attack her. And she was angry, for she knew she had been tricked. But she knew that she could not find her way home without the little bird to guide her. And still she craved the sweetness that the little bird had promised.

So she threw the stones, and the third one struck the nest, and it tumbled. It tumbled on to the fire, thick with smoke, and the bees poured out, and she began to run; but even as they alighted upon her, they crawled distractedly and did not sting and she brushed them easily to the ground.

All around they crawled, confused and harmless. Amid the smoke, the little bird hopped and flapped gleefully, ripping away at the broken nest with her beak. As she widened the hole, rich, dark honey oozed from within. The girl approached and dipped a finger in, raising it to her mouth. She had never tasted such sweetness. Greedily she took more and sucked it, rolling it around her mouth, letting it slip warmly down her throat.

Though she could gorge like this for hours, time was against her. Soon it would be too dark to see. She had a calabash and she tipped its water on to the soil and began to gather the honey within. As she did so, she looked down at the little bird beside her. It was not honey the bird sought: the girl saw that deeper still the nest writhed with life. Tiny grey grubs teemed and pulsed blindly as the bird repeatedly plunged her beak into the mass, each time withdrawing it to pull her head back and pour more of the larvae down her throat. She gave a small cackle of joy before returning to the nest.

Repulsed, the girl drew away. Her calabash fell on to the

smouldering fire. She pushed her way through the smoke, crunching over bodies of stupefied bees and stumbling blindly into the thorn bushes all around.

28

He is woken by the storm: a proper Nairobi storm. The sort that comes in like a drunken husband, makes a lot of noise, wakes the kids, and throws the place around a bit, if only for form's sake.

This time the fury is real. The thunderclap sounded like it was directly overhead, the sky being ripped apart from the heavens all the way to the ground. Now, the atmosphere vibrates and crackles with tension. The rain has yet to come: it is awaiting its cue, holding back until the wind has played its part.

In his groggy state, Mollel can make out that he's in a tent of some kind. A fresh squall causes the fabric to bulge and rise, giving the queasy sensation of being in a falling elevator. There is commotion beyond, as voices fight to be heard against the storm. They're attempting to lash down the tent before it capsizes. The steel poles groan and creak with the strain. Mollel attempts to rise. But weakness overcomes him. His head falls back on to the cot.

As his eyes slide, he takes in the scene around him. There's a strip light hanging from the tent's central pole by a short chain. It sways to and fro, casting fluorescent shadows over the faces of the people rushing about. The tent's roof, a large expanse of white plasticised canvas, falls away from the ridge pole. Its height and shallow pitch suggest to Mollel that this is a large tent, of the type people might hire for a wedding or *harambee*.

With effort, he manages to raise himself on to his elbows. He's aware of a bulkiness around his hands, and looking down, sees that they're wrapped in thick mitts of gauze bandage. But he feels no pain.

He looks to his right, and sees a young man sleeping, or unconscious, in the cot next to him. He has a heavy bandage over his shaved head, an ominous dark patch insinuating through the weave. Two men rush up, and grasp handles at the head and feet of the cot. With a groan, they lift the young man.

A dazzling pinpoint of red light bursts into Mollel's face.

—Ah, you're awake, says a voice, from somewhere behind the light. Good. Do you think you can walk?

—I don't know.

—Let's try. We've got to get everyone out of here. Take this jacket. We're going to get pretty wet outside, but it's better than having the tent collapse on us.

Mollel takes the man's arm as he pulls himself to his feet. Then he squeezes his bandaged hands through the sleeves of the dark green jacket. He recognises the camouflage pattern and the insignia.

GSU.

—Bloody paranoia, the man mutters, as much to himself as to Mollel. Everyone knows, you can't start treating patients while the field hospital is being put up around you. But no, they said. They've recce'd the site, but we'd have to wait until voting was over to put up the tents. Well, this is what you get for it!

A stark white flash picks out the tent's canvas and is followed, in less than a heartbeat, by a stomach-churning clash of thunder.

The man – he's a medic, Mollel has decided – has put his arm around Mollel's waist, and the two of them stagger unsteadily toward the exit. They push through a heavy canvas flap and Mollel's breath is taken away by a sudden blast of stinging rain.

—Can you make it on your own now? yells the medic. I've got to get the other patients out. Mollel nods. —*Sawa sawa*, the medic shouts. Head for those buses over there.

Mollel raises a bandaged hand. Now the rain has started, it is remorseless: it runs down his face, distorting the blinding light of arc lamps and vehicle headlamps. Men in uniform run around him on all sides. Many of them carry the same red-filtered flashlight as the doctor used. Mollel bows his head and pushes towards the vehicle headlamps. His bare feet stumble on the rough gravel. The gravel kicks up a memory within him: in this dizzying, disorientating place he has an indefinable sense of location. But before he can pin it down, he feels a shove between the shoulders. A violent gust of wind sends him spinning, nearly toppling him from his feet.

The shouts and cries all around him intensify. Mollel has turned around, away from the lights, squinting into the wind and rain. Before him appears the ghostly white shape of the tent, illuminated in the arc lamps, rising lazily from the ground, a dozen or more GSU men struggling to hold it as it tips forward, crashes, crunches, and rolls to rest like a downed bird, flapping with futility against the side of a military truck.

The gust drops as suddenly as it arose, and the men scurry to detach the canvas from the frame before it picks up again. No longer blinded by the rain, Mollel sees other tents – still standing, these – trucks coming and going – another roars past him now, and he catches a glimpse of rows of grim-looking GSU men in their green fatigues and crimson helmets serried in the back before they disappear in a cloud of diesel smoke. There is some sort of communications truck, bristling with aerials, and the buses: four big, old, military buses, their windows steamed, parked in a neat row on the gravel ground.

—I know this place, Mollel says aloud, barely hearing his own words.

Everything beyond the lights is black. But back where the tent had been, he sees the raised ridge of a concrete drainage ditch. He lunges forward, almost breaking into a run, despite his weakness and his bare feet. He goes past the cursing GSU men, over the flapping, exposed groundsheet, the neat hospital cots now exposed and overturned, to where the water gushes and bubbles in the ditch below, the torrent bursting forth from the pipe which leads all the way to Upper Hill, running swiftly and blackly at his feet.

He is in Uhuru Park.

He is at the spot where Lucy's body had been found.

29

—Mollel? Are you Mollel?

He gasps with pain. He raises his hands: they feel like they're on fire.

He sits up, stiffly. The whole bus smells of sweat and old blankets. He uses his two bandaged hands to pull the damp blanket off himself. He's still wearing the GSU jacket.

Daylight. The sun is pouring through the windows of the bus. Beyond, the fresh, green foliage of Uhuru Park, plumped by the rain, seems to burst with colour and life under the brilliant clarity of a blue Nairobi morning sky.

—I'm Mollel.

—Someone's here looking for you. How are the hands this morning?

He recognises the voice as that of the doctor who helped him from the tent the previous night.

—Sore.

—We'll get you something for that. Your friend is outside.

The medic helps Mollel to his feet and they pick their way out of the bus, stepping over the limbs and boots of GSU men sleeping or lolling in the seats either side of the gangway.

Despite the pain in his hands, and the stiffness of his body, Mollel can't help smiling when he sees Kiunga's broad grin. Kiunga offers his hand and assists Mollel down the last step.

—You would not believe the *shida* I've had trying to find you, he says. They told me GSU had rescued you from a fire in Kibera. But no one would let me know where they'd taken you. I've been round all the hospitals in the city. Then, on the way back from Kenyatta, I drove past Uhuru Park. Saw the whole place cordoned off, crawling with GSU. I spent more than an hour trying to persuade them to let me in. Quite a change, huh, from a few days ago?

The medic – who Mollel sees now properly for the first time, an anxious-looking man in a GSU uniform, with a white arm-band with a red cross on it – hands Mollel a couple of pills and a paper cup of water.

—Are you on any other medication? he asks.

—No, says Mollel. Kiunga casts him a doubtful look, but Mollel ignores him.

As he lifts the cup to his lips, Mollel becomes aware for the first time of a thirst almost as intense as his pain – and he drinks greedily after downing the pills.

—Those are all you'll get from me, says the medic. You were only brought here by mistake in the first place. You'll have to make your own way to the police infirmary.

—What is this place? asks Mollel.

—Forward Command Post, replies the medic. GSU HQ in Ruaraka is too far away from town to be effective. So we've set up here. It's the closest open space to Parliament, and the Central Business District.

—You told me last night, says Mollel, that they didn't want to set up this command post until voting was over. That means that they were expecting trouble? Anticipating accusations that the vote had been rigged?

—I don't know anything about that, says the medic, shifting on his feet. You guys really need to get out of here now.

—Not until we've spoken to your OIC, says Kiunga.

—Be my guest. You'll find him in the communications truck.

He disappears into the activity all around them.

—I noticed last night that a lot of these GSU men have been

issued with flashlights with red filters over the lens, says Mollel.

—Army trick, replies Kiunga. Scatters the light, makes the beams less likely to be seen.

—And less effective, says Mollel. Remember the shred of fabric we found where someone had blundered into the barbed wire? The red filters covered the light well enough to ensure that the passing police patrol didn't see the GSU last Friday night. But that's probably also why they didn't spot Lucy's body.

—Now we know why they were here, says Kiunga. They were doing a recce for this camp. They had to do it under cover of darkness. The last thing the government wanted was to give the impression that they were pre-empting the protests. So it seems our little blind friend was right all along, eh, boss?

Mollel feels a wave of pain and dismay.

—Sammy!

—What, boss?

—Superglue Sammy. He was there, in Kibera. It was him I was trying to save. What happened to him?

Kiunga casts his eyes down.

—There was no one else brought out of the fire, boss. Only you.

In daylight, it's easy to find Sammy's den once more, now he knows where it is. Mollel is just a few feet away from Kiunga – all he needs to do is hop over the low barbed-wire fence and duck between a fan palm and an ornamental papyrus – but it feels strangely sheltered, cocooned from the hubbub in the park beyond.

Sammy's blanket lies on the floor, and beside it, his treasured battery radio. Mollel picks it up. Awkwardly, with his bandaged hands, he manages to turn it on.

… with the worst violence reported in the Langata district of the capital. Meanwhile, the count continues at the Kenyatta International Conference Centre. The media have been ejected from the scene, but shortly before the ban, one official observer, the businessman David Kingori, categorically denied accusations of vote-rigging…

Mollel hears the familiar, condescending tones of David Kingori. Irresponsible forces, he is saying, were attempting to influence the outcome of the ballot, before all the results were even counted. The reporter asks him about discrepancies at the count: pro-government wins that appeared to be higher even than the number of registered voters. Mollel can hear the smile in Kingori's voice as he replies: *That's a matter for the electoral commissioner. All I can tell you is that I've been here at the count since the first boxes came in, and I've not seen anything suspicious.*

Mollel turns off the radio angrily. He thinks of Sammy, optimistically queuing up to cast his vote in Kibera, and he nearly casts the radio into the bushes in disgust. But instead, he folds the aerial, and puts it into the gym bag which Kiunga gave him. His colleague had raided his own wardrobe to bring Mollel a change of clothes, and Mollel's glad to see that, although somewhat big for him, they're sober and discreet: a white shirt and trousers, socks and shoes. And, crucially, a belt, which will be needed if he's going to be able to wear Kiunga's trousers without them falling down. He leaves the surgical gown and GSU jacket on the ground.

When he emerges from the bushes, Kiunga says: I was beginning to wonder if you were ever going to come out.

Mollel holds the belt between his bandaged hands.

—I need you to do this up for me.

With an embarrassed glance over his shoulder, Kiunga stands close to Mollel and hastily wraps the belt through the loops and pulls it tight. He stands back.

—Sorry about Sammy, boss, he says. But, you know, you mustn't feel guilty. You can't save everybody. There's not many people who would have even tried.

Mollel feels the young man's admiration like a burden. He feels the urge to confess: I didn't go in there to try to save Sammy's life. I was trying to save a witness. I was doing it for the case.

You can't save everybody.

If only he knew, thought Mollel. If only they all knew, that back then, in the rubble of the American embassy, he wasn't trying to save everybody. He was only trying to save one person. He only kept pulling the others out because they were getting in the way.

—You all right, boss?

—Sure. Come on, we have to speak to the guy in charge of this place.

—Only, you're looking pretty bad. Do you want to see the doctor again?

—I feel fine.

—Boss, I'm worried about you. When the doctor gave you those pills, you said you weren't on any other medication. Well, I know you are. You've tried to hide it, but I've noticed all the same. If you're feeling ill, boss, we can always go to the police infirmary, try to get what you need there.

—I feel fine, snaps Mollel. And we've got work to do. Unless you think the case doesn't matter any more? Perhaps you think we should give up on it, just like everyone else?

—No, boss, says Kiunga.

—We need to speak to whoever's in charge, says Mollel.

At the top of a set of aluminium steps, the rear door of the communications truck stands open. At the bottom of the steps, a GSU sergeant is sitting picking his teeth.

—We're police, adds Kiunga, showing his badge.

—I don't care, replies the GSU man. *Nenda huko.*

Which is about as close as you can get in Swahili to *fuck off.*

—OK, *rafiki*, keep cool, says Kiunga. We're on a murder investigation.

—It doesn't matter. The only people who get in here are GSU, and the president himself.

—I bet you boys are quite fond of this place by now, aren't you? It was you lot having a little midnight picnic party last Friday, wasn't it?

—What do you know about that?

—So it was you?

—You shut your mouth, *mtundu*.

—We need to speak to your boss, Mollel says. It won't take a minute.

—Lieutenant Kodhek hasn't got a minute, Maasai. In case you hadn't noticed, this country's heading for civil war. And what are you laughing at?

—Ashiruma Kodhek? asks Kiunga with a grin. Shitkicker Kodhek? They made him lieutenant, did they?

—Has been for some time now, says the GSU man, grudgingly.

—Tell him Collins Kiunga's here. We were at Embakasi together. Go on!

Somehow, the injunction works, and the sergeant flicks his toothpick, gets up, and lumbers into the back of the truck.

After a short while, a GSU officer comes over. Like the others, he's tall, over six feet, and wears the paramilitary dark green. Instead of a helmet, though, he wears a crimson beret. At the sight of Kiunga, he grimaces. He does not even bother to look at Mollel. The guard looms threateningly at his shoulder.

—So you're Lieutenant now, Shitkicker? says Kiunga.

—And you're still a constable? No surprise there.

—*Detective* constable.

—Great. So you get the same pay, but have to work in your own clothes. Well done.

—I wondered if this might be your regiment, says Kiunga. I notice your boys have all removed their unit insignia. Makes it kind of difficult working out who's who.

—What do you want, Kiunga?

—Well, much as I'd love to stand around and reminisce, says Kiunga, we've got a murder investigation to conduct. The body was found just inside the park here. We think the victim was killed, or dumped here, around the time your colleagues were conducting their little hush-hush night-time recce of the site. We'd like to ask a few questions, if you don't mind.

—I do mind. And what's this you've been saying about the other night?

—Just that we know you were here. We have witnesses. And it would be helpful to know whether you or any of your men saw anything that might help us with our investigation.

—We were not here. This is the first time that any GSU have been near this park. Isn't that right, Mwathi?

—That's right, Lieut, says the sergeant. Besides, they can't have a witness, 'cause no one saw us.

Kodhek rolls his eyes, and Kiunga and Mollel try to hide their smiles.

—Look, says Mollel. A girl was killed on Friday night. Her body was found there, in the drainage ditch. We're not accusing you lot of anything. We just want to verify a few things.

—Come back when the trouble's over.

—Oh yeah? When's that going to be? Do you know something we don't? Like the fact that there was always going to be trouble in the first place?

—Come on, Shitkicker, pleads Kiunga. How's that sweet little sister of yours? She must be about twenty, right?

—You leave my sister out of this, warns Kodhek. The guard at his side bristles, ready for the command to attack.

—I'm just saying, says Kiunga. I'm just saying, this girl. The one we found in the ditch. She was about twenty. Just like your sister.

—That girl, spits Kodhek, was nothing like my sister.

Then, realising he's said too much, he barks: —Mwathi! Get rid of these two. If they're not off this site in two minutes, chuck them in the happy wagon.

He turns on his heel and storms back into the truck, slamming the door behind him.

—You heard him. Get moving.

Mwathi has a pickaxe handle in his hand, and he swings it menacingly. He gestures to the park exit, which is guarded by a languid line of troops, many of them holding or leaning on the same standard-issue club.

—This way.

He leads them round the back of a canvas-covered truck, and looks over his shoulder. Kiunga readies his stance for a fight. But Mwathi puts down his club and leans it against the wheel of the truck.

—It's all right, I just want to talk to you. That girl was twenty years old, you say? I got a daughter that age myself.

—You don't look old enough, Kiunga grins.

—Save the flattery. We got to make this quick. If the lieut finds out I've been talking to you…

—*Sawa sawa*, says Mollel. What have you got to tell us?

—You were right, says Mwathi. We were here that night. I don't know if the bosses had prior warning of trouble, or not. All we were told was that we had to prepare in secret, otherwise it wouldn't look good. We got here around eleven.

Just as Sammy said, thinks Mollel.

—Anyway, just as we come in – four buses, lights off – we see a couple come out of the bushes, there.

—By the ditch? asks Mollel.

—Yes.

—Did you see them yourself? Can you describe them?

—Like I say, it was dark. But we knew what they'd been up to. The boys in the bus had a good laugh. They were pretty mismatched. She towered over him. We couldn't make out much of her, in the darkness. But him, though! That was the funny thing. White hair, white skin. Showed up, even in the darkness. A *mzungu*. The two of them were pretty startled, I reckon, 'cause they ran off to their car. A nice four-by-four, silver or white, I think. Drove off as fast as they could.

—Did they hit one of the bollards as they left? asks Mollel.

—Not that I noticed.

They're interrupted by the arrival of twenty or so GSU, fully rigged up in riot gear. They storm past Mwathi and the two policemen, and start plunging into the back of the truck.

—Where are you off to? shouts Mwathi.

—The KICC, one shouts back. They need reinforcements at the count.

—Any chance of a lift? yells Mollel.

The truck roars into life.

—The lieut told me to get you out of here. He didn't say how!

Mwathi gives Mollel and Kiunga a hand up to the back of the truck. They squeeze on to the bench, attracting quizzical looks from the riot troops.

The truck is already moving as Mwathi pushes up the tailgate and Kiunga locks it into place. Mwathi gives the two policemen a wave as the truck sweeps through the cordon and out of the park.

Kiunga leans over and says in Mollel's ear: —You know, sometimes you could mistake a GSU man for a human being.

Mollel looks at the blank, visored faces all around him.

—Only sometimes, he says.

30

The truck is too loud for conversation, but even if it hadn't been, the scene outside would have quelled any words.

Even the GSU men seem shocked by the city outside.

The truck bowls down Kenyatta Avenue – traffic lights are even more inconsequential than usual.

Outside the truck, there is not a human being in sight.

The shops are shut, shuttered. As they speed past Simmers, even that legendary Nairobi sleazepot is closed. No *Lingala* music drifts from behind the tables, tipped and hastily placed across the doorway as a makeshift barrier. A yellow dog trots down the sidewalk, her triangular teats flapping, ribs bare. She glances at a couple of white-shouldered crows going through a garbage bag, decides they would put up a better fight than she could, and slinks away. In the slipstream of the truck, pieces of paper and plastic whirl and eddy, then join the downdraught from the avenue's skyscrapers, floating upwards to where grey eagles, exuberant as the new masters of the city, gyre and scream.

The eye rises: above the steel-shuttered storefronts, signage proclaims barber shops, beauty salons, gymnasiums, even a marriage bureau – the first to third floors seem the preserve of the body and heart. Higher, more hand-painted signs: business colleges, stockbrokers, import-export agents. The upper floors are home to the speculative and aspirational. Perhaps they're the only ones who can manage the stairs.

These buildings speak of a different era: optimistic, but short sighted. The rate of growth of this city was never anticipated. Six, seven storeys was thought to be enough. Never intended for multiple tenants, the buildings bear the scar of each subsequent resident: windows boarded up like broken teeth; air-conditioning units hanging from them like cigarettes from a lip. Their roofs are ridged in slate or terracotta tiles, patched here and there with sheets of galvanised steel. So much for what Nairobi might have been.

But beyond, the glinting skyscrapers of the new Nairobi look down, impassively. The twin towers of the Nation Centre; the blue mirror-glass of the Standard building, reflecting its taller, stockier cousin, the Lonrho Tower, across the street. The glass elevators of the ICEA building hang static from the sides. There are no passengers today.

And over and above them all, the first sign of humanity that Mollel has seen since leaving Uhuru Park. On the lip of the helipad atop the KICC tower, a plump military helicopter wobbles into the air, wallows a moment, before pointing its head down purposefully and speeding away.

The Kenyatta International Conference Centre: its tower the most distinctive, if no longer the highest, in the whole city, crowned with its dinner-plate of a helipad. It's like the chimney of a termite mound: an expression of the energy and ambition of what lies beneath. The conference centre itself is a city within a city, a statement of Nairobi's intent to proclaim itself a world destination. A pin stuck in the map.

The truck dives off Kenyatta Avenue the wrong way up one-way street and into the administrative district: City Hall, Parliament. Life is back on the streets, even if the majority of it is crimson-helmeted. As they approach the gates of the KICC, the truck slows, and halts for a moment, while the GSU officers attempt to make way for it. A woman is there with a sheaf of papers.

—I'm an electoral official, she is shouting. You cannot deny me access to the count!

In her fury, she spills the papers and they scatter in the wind. The GSU men laugh. Nearby, a TV reporter is trying to shoot a piece to camera.

—Some moments ago, he is shouting into his microphone, all media outlets and observers were ejected from the KICC. Despite early exit polls predicting a landslide victory for the opposition, recent official results have shown the government edging ahead. It's unclear…

A GSU officer, baton in hand, interposes himself between the reporter and the cameraman, and thrusts his free hand into the lens. As the scene descends into a scuffle, the truck's engine roars into life again.

—We're going in, says Mollel.

Welcome to the Kenyatta International Conference Centre, proclaim the red letters on the massive LED screen. Below it, a barricade of GSU men, elbows interlocked, three deep and at least thirty wide, stand at the base of the stairs to the main entrance. The truck Mollel and Kiunga arrived in has driven off, having disgorged its occupants. Somehow, because they leapt out first, their presence is not questioned, and as their travelling companions race up the steps to join the picket, Mollel and Kiunga do the same. In the shuffling to accommodate the newcomers, the two policemen manage to slip through and find themselves at the glass doors of the main entrance. They are locked.

Kiunga pounds on the glass and cups his hands to look inside. The face of one of the KICC's private security guards appears. He looks terrified, little more than a teenager. Kiunga slams his police ID against the window.

—Let us in, he shouts.

The youth withdraws. Then there is the sound of a chain slipping and the door opens a crack.

—We're only supposed to let in army and GSU, he says.

—We're police, says Kiunga. We're all supposed to be on the same side.

—Until a couple of hours ago, says the youth, I didn't even know there *were* sides.

He opens the door wide enough for them to come in, then hurriedly closes it and replaces the chain.

Inside, twenty or more private security guards stand awkwardly. The arrival of the GSU has left them feeling usurped, redundant. Toy soldiers.

—We're looking for David Kingori, says Mollel. Anyone seen him?

The guards avoid eye contact and resist answering. They are used to obeying authority. Now they are unsure who the authority is. Eventually one says: —I think I saw him in the Plenary Hall.

—Which way is that? asks Mollel.

Relieved to have a question they can answer, the guards point in unison to a staircase.

—Thank you, says Kiunga, with a sarcastic bow. You've really earned your overtime today, boys.

On the staircase Kiunga says: —How did you know Kingori was here, boss?

Mollel thinks of the little battery radio he found in the park, the news report he heard on it.

—Sammy told me, he says.

Kiunga looks confused for an instant, but lets it pass.

—Our GSU witness has Lethebridge and Lucy walking *away* from where the body was found, he says.

—It might not have been Lucy, replies Mollel. He said it was a tall woman, remember? Lucy was not so tall. But Wanjiku Nalo is.

Kiunga puffs out his cheeks. —Seems a vague sort of identification.

It is. If only Sammy could have identified her voice – but that was no longer a possibility.

—But we have Lethebridge there, continues Mollel. He does nothing without Kingori's say-so. If we can get Kingori to connect Lucy with Wanjiku and Nalo, we'll have enough for an arrest.

—Yes, replies Kiunga, but *who*?

—Come on.

At the top of the staircase is a wide landing. The entrance to the Plenary Hall is crowded and there are more scuffles. Incongruously, the benches along the walls of this space are full of people either sleeping or sitting with their heads in their hands, as if in a waiting room. They seem either inured to the kerfuffle or to be studiously ignoring it.

—Let me in, booms a familiar voice. Don't you know who I am?

Mollel pulls Kiunga back behind a pillar. Otieno is arguing with a pair of plainclothes detectives, smart suits and sunglasses. One of them has his hand on Otieno's chest and, possibly for the first time ever, Otieno seems dwarfed by another man.

—I'm Otieno, head of Central CID, he shouts. *I'm part of this.*

—Go and catch some criminals, old man, scoffs one of the Special Branch officers. Better still, go home. Plenty of crooks in Luo land. Leave the politics to the big boys.

—You've not heard the last of this, thunders Otieno. He turns on his heel and Mollel and Kiunga duck back behind the pillar as he storms past them.

—That was close, says Kiunga. But if *he* can't get in, we haven't got a chance.

—But we don't need to get in, says Mollel. We just need to find Kingori. He points up to where the double-height foyer overlooks the upper windows of the Plenary Hall. There is a walkway there.

From here, the true expanse of the Plenary Hall can be appreciated. George Nalo's church could be dropped inside and still leave room for parking. But every inch of the space is packed. And despite the chaos outside, the activity has a diligent, harmonious quality to it, emphasised by the almost complete lack of sound getting through the glass. Steel ballot boxes are brought in and upturned beside large trestle tables. Several figures around each descend immediately upon the papers and start stacking and sorting them methodically, mechanically. Other figures are seated, inputting data on machines.

—There are hundreds of people there, says Kiunga. How are we going to spot Kingori?

—You start that side, says Mollel. I'll start this.

Kiunga runs to the far end of the walkway, jumping over the feet of a sleeping figure slumped against the wall halfway along. Mollel starts looking at the people below him. Foreshortening and the distance make it hard to distinguish individual features. He spends more than a minute scrutinising the back of one coiffured head which resembles Kingori's, only for the figure to turn and reveal that it is a woman. With all the movement in the hall, it is a futile task.

Besides, this place is not Kingori's scene. He's a commander, not a foot soldier. Mollel bangs the pane in frustration.

—Have you worked it out yet?

—What?

—Have you worked out how they're doing it?

The speaker is the slumped figure on the floor, who Mollel had assumed was asleep. His suit is crumpled, his tie pulled to one side. His cheeks are grizzled with stubble and his eyes are ringed with exhaustion, but also something else: defeat.

—How they're doing what?

—Rigging the election, of course. That's what you're looking for, isn't it?

—And you'd know all about it? asks Kiunga, who has returned to join them.

—Of course. I'm with the electoral commission. Or was. I suppose I've resigned. Just like all the others, downstairs. We walked out. Let me show you.

He begins to heave himself to his feet. Mollel and Kiunga help him up, and the three of them cross to the glass.

—You see the results coming in, in locked boxes. They're

being brought in by truck, from all over the city. They come in the service entrance, under police guard, accompanied by the returning officer and observers from the polling station. Then they're brought up here in the elevator. The boxes are opened, supervised by a scrutineer. The sorters – those are the ones at the end of each table – put them into piles for each candidate. The counters tally the result for each, discarding or returning any blanks or spoiled papers. Then the clerk enters the results on to the machine. A print-out is made, and attached to the file box you see there. Then the papers are put in, the box is sealed, and they move on to the next one.

—Who are the people walking around?

—Some are my lot, the ones who can't, or won't, see what's really happening. Others are independent observers. But only a chosen few. The *really* independent ones have all been kicked out.

—I still don't see it, says Kiunga. Is it the clerks? Are they putting false numbers in the machines?

The man laughs. —That would be picked up on a recount. Those boxes become evidence in any legal challenge.

—The sorters?

—You can look all day, says the man, and you won't find anything wrong in that room. It's all being done by the book.

—The ballot boxes, says Mollel quietly. They're being switched before they get here.

—That's right, says the man. Not all of them. Just a certain number from certain polling stations. Enough to tip the balance. We began to figure it out when the results made no sense. We were comparing an electoral roll from districts full of Luos and Luhyas with results of ninety, ninety-five per cent government. I mean, I know it's a secret ballot. But that's like chickens voting for a jackal.

—But where's the switch being done? asks Kiunga. You said the boxes arrive here under guard, and with observers.

—The elevator, gasps Mollel. The boxes go in the elevator. They'd take up all the floor space. The observers won't be able to

216

fit in. It's only a couple of floors. They wait for the next one, or walk. And that's where the switch is made.

He thinks about the helicopters, coming and going above them. The ones bringing in the ballots from distant rural polling stations. What if they are not only bringing – but taking away?

And suddenly Mollel knows where he will find David Kingori.

31

—It's thirty storeys, boss. You don't look fit to reach the mezzanine.

—Twenty-seven. We're three levels up already.

—Can we at least try to talk our way on to the elevator?

—You saw the guards. They'll never let us on.

—Let me go alone, then. I'll take the stairs, arrest Kingori, bring him back down. You have a rest. You look like you need one.

—We can't arrest him. I need to talk to him. In person.

—If he's even there.

—He's there.

A commander, not a foot soldier.

—Seriously, boss. Look at yourself. You'll never make it. The climb will kill you.

Mollel has to admit Kiunga may have a point. In his colleague's clothes, he looks even more gaunt than usual. And his bandaged hands are causing him pain again.

But he hasn't come this far to give up the hunt now. He leans over the banister and looks up at the levels disappearing above him.

—I'm not going to die today, he says.

—With respect, boss, says Kiunga, you don't know shit about dying.

The statement stops Mollel in his stride. He turns and looks at Kiunga, a couple of steps below him.

—What did you say?

—I said, you don't know shit about dying.

—Oh, really?

Kiunga's eyes remain steady against Mollel's glare.

—If you did, he says, coolly, you wouldn't push yourself like this.

—I've been surrounded by death, says Mollel, since I was a baby. I found my grandfather's corpse up on the mountain, when I was herding sheep. I was five years old. Thirty years later I pulled my wife's body out of the American embassy. You might remember that day. I certainly do.

—I didn't say you don't know *death*, Mollel. I said, you don't know *dying*.

—We don't have time for this.

Mollel starts up the stairs. He is halfway up the first flight before he pauses. His bandaged right hand is sliding on the banister, and in frustration, he bites at the gauze, loosens the end, and pulls the bandage off. He grimaces as the last layer peels away from his burned skin, and spits the bandage to the ground. Then, the skin on his knuckles splitting as he does so, he uses his free right hand to liberate the left.

The pain blazes through him but he manages to brush away Kiunga's concerned touch on his sleeve. The cold of the metal banister is like balm when he grabs it, but like fire when he hauls himself forward. Still, his grip is good. Blindly, he takes one step; two: then he reaches forward again. He grunts as his raw palm makes contact for a second time. He steels himself: squeezes, and pulls. Two steps; three. And he's reached the landing.

—Twenty-six floors to go, he gasps.

After that, it is all he can do to count off the storeys. Kiunga, though, keeps talking. It is as though he does not care whether Mollel is hearing him, or not. It is enough that his voice reverberates in this spiral.

—Death comes, says Kiunga. But dying takes effort.

Barely have his words ceased ringing from the walls before he calls: —I had a lot of people dying around me at that time. I know, you've known death too. But do you know dying?

Mollel is silent.

—If you live, you're dying. But that means you're still living. You know who told me that? A girlfriend. She was so beautiful, Mollel. The most beautiful woman you'd ever seen. And I mean it. You know, you could just see her, and you'd forget to take your next breath, man. Your heart would forget to beat. But by the time she died…

Keep trudging, Mollel tells himself. Keep lifting one foot, placing it in front of the other.

—Twenty-five floors to go.

—It was her husband who'd given it to her. The irony was, we were always so careful. Condoms every time. Extra strong. And I hate condoms, man. But I did it because I loved her. I really loved that girl.

—God knows where he'd picked it up. She said he was always a flop in bed, so maybe he was an *mbasha*. Who knows. Who cares. The thing was, he knew about it. He'd known about it a long time. He'd been on the ARVs for years. But *he* didn't use a condom, because, hey, he didn't want his wife to suspect anything. And she – well, she didn't suspect, did she? Didn't suspect a thing, until it was too late.

Twenty-four.

—It was too late to manage the HIV. The doctors said that the best they could do was give her time to get her affairs in order. That's how they put it. If she was admitted to hospital immediately, there were things they could do – drips, transfusions, things – to mitigate the worst effects. Buy her a few extra weeks, months. It was going to be costly. But he had a good job, didn't he? Nice benefits, company car – and a first-rate health insurance package.

—She went home, packed a bag. Never confronted her husband about the HIV. They both knew he was the one who gave it to her. But she figured, he's got his own price to pay. She didn't possess one trace of cruelty or malice, that girl. She told him she was going to the hospital, and that he wouldn't see her again. And she left.

Twenty-three.

—She called me. She told me. She had to. You never knew, however careful we'd been. It was all right, by the way. I was all clear. But, you know, I was pretty fucked up by the whole thing. I couldn't bring myself to go see her straight away. I needed to get my own head around it. What the hell, I wasn't as good as she was. I didn't deserve her. And when she needed me most – I wasn't there for her.

—After I got my results, I went out. Got trashed. Got myself beaten up – I mean, really. Somehow I found myself in a bar in Westlands. Picked the biggest, ugliest group of Asian guys and started telling them to leave our girls alone. Told them otherwise, I'd start sleeping with their daughters. You can imagine what happened next.

Twenty-two.

—So what was all that about? Self-loathing? Self-punishment? I didn't know at the time. I just knew that they felt good, those cuts and bruises. I stayed home and nursed them for a few days. Cherished them. Ran my hand over the lumps on my ribs and thought: I can still breathe. Counted the burst veins in my eye, and thought: I can still see.

—I think for the first time in my life, I was glad to be living. I'd had a close call, a near-miss. It was like, you have to nearly lose something, to appreciate what it's worth. What I can't believe now is that I knew that much, but still only thought about myself. I was a selfish bastard, Mollel. A shallow, selfish bastard.

Twenty-one.

—It took a long time for me to go and see her. At first, it was because my ribs were too sore for me to leave the flat. Then I told myself, I didn't want to upset her, my face all messed up like that. But my face healed. My ribs healed. And still I didn't go and see her.

—Work was a good excuse. You know I'm no slacker, Mollel. But I never worked so hard in my life. Extra shifts, double shifts. I was a one-man crime-fighting machine.

—I knew which hospital she'd checked in to and I always thought, next time I go past, I'll go in and see her. But I never went past. Somehow I'd always end up taking a different route, even if it meant zigzagging through back streets or circling through the suburbs.

Twenty.

—You know what made me go, in the end? It was Valentine's Day. Valentine's Day, Mollel. She always loved Valentine's Day. She never got anything romantic at home, and I played that game well. Knew what to buy her, where to take her, what to say to her.

—So there were all the office girls, in town, wearing red. Red blouses, red belts, red dresses. Man, you know how they love to play the game, too. Slushy music on the radio. I was getting a hard-on just thinking about it. And then I thought, with her insurance, she's probably got a private room. Sure, she might not feel up to it, but who knows? Certainly, a blow-job wasn't out of the question.

Nineteen.

—I bought some chocolates and a bunch of Naivasha roses off a street flower-seller. Three hundred shillings' worth of red roses, cost me nine hundred bob. But what the hell, it was Valentine's Day.

—I was feeling pretty pleased with myself as I went into the hospital. That's part of the charade of Valentine's Day, isn't it – walking round, flowers in hand, the gracious lover. I could see that the nurse on reception was impressed. I gave the name and she just stared at me. No such patient here, she said. There must be, I said.

Eighteen.

—The matron came over. Tight old *jike*, she was. Flowers meant nothing to her. In that job, she saw flowers every day, but I doubt she'd ever been given a bunch in her life.

—The patient you're asking for was discharged, she said. I'm like, discharged? I wonder why she never told me. But that's got to be good news, right? She's getting better?

—The matron told me they never even admitted her. She turned up, all right, letter of admission, all the paperwork in order – but these days, they always need pre-clearance from the insurance company. Just a formality. So they phoned – and the insurance had been cancelled. Her husband had removed her from his policy. The company wouldn't pay.

Seventeen.

—It was all about appearances, you understand, Mollel. A young woman like that – when she dies, you can call it malaria, you can call it cancer, but everyone knows what it is. Her husband didn't want people knowing she'd got it from him. He didn't want people knowing he had it at all. So, he made a big show of cutting her off. He played the betrayed husband really well. Even to

223

me. The big joke was, he didn't know about his wife and me at all. As far as he knew, she'd always been faithful. And that was the thanks she got.

Sixteen.

—I found her, eventually, at her sister's house. Her sister didn't want to admit she was there, at first. She didn't want the neighbours knowing she had someone dying of AIDS on the premises.

—I didn't know the sister was caring for their grandmother as well. There, on the couch, was an old woman, all hunched up, and bony. More like a skeleton than a living being. She could hardly move her head to look at me when I came in.

—She hasn't got long, the old woman, I thought. But I guess you know what I'm going to say. It wasn't the grandmother. It wasn't an old woman at all. That was my girlfriend, there. The woman I loved. My lover.

Kiunga is silent for the final few steps to the next landing. When he reaches it, Mollel pauses.

—Fifteen, Mollel pants. Fifteenth floor. We're halfway up.

—Not quite, replies Kiunga. We started on the fourth floor, remember?

Mollel leans on the rail. He looks down into the well. He turns, and looks up.

—It's still a good place for a rest, he says.

They sit on the steps. The sound of a helicopter outside seems to stretch and reverberate throughout this windowless tube, travelling down to the ground and back up again, until it fades into the walls, attenuates, and disappears.

Mollel wants to put his head in his hands, but they're too painful. He sits, instead, with the palms open before him like a book, and feels the air upon them.

—I let her down, says Kiunga. I didn't even have the courage to stick around and hold her hand, at the end. And I think about it every day of my life. I'm not thinking about her *death*, Mollel. I'm thinking about her *dying*.

—Come on, says Mollel. We've got a job to do.

—Do you see what I'm getting at, Mollel? You've got a son. People around who care about you. It doesn't have to be like this. So you're going to die. We're all going to die. But you've got a chance to manage your condition, keep it under control. Make the best of your time.

—Sorry, Kiunga, says Mollel. You've got it wrong.

—I don't think so. I've seen you popping the pills. You've tried to hide it, but I know you've got HIV. It's not just this case that's eating you up. It's the virus.

Mollel stands.

—Let's go, he says. It's my turn to do the talking.

32

—Fifteen more floors, says Mollel, rising to his feet. He contemplates the staircase immediately before him.

He counts fifteen steps. Take each flight at a time. He gasps as his hand grasps the banister: one foot forward, he hauls himself up.

—Fifteen storeys, he repeats. That's what my wife climbed every day. The secretarial college was on the fifteenth floor. She didn't like the elevator. It was always too full. She had to wait too long. The boys used to touch her. Pinch her.

Kiunga chuckles.

—Fifteen storeys, up and down. No place to buy food up there, of course. She'd take a packed lunch, or buy a *mandazi* on the way in. But that morning, she left her lunch on the table. I couldn't bear the thought of her getting hungry. I was on a late shift. So I thought, I'll take it to her.

Sixteenth floor.

—Ever think about what sixteen floors of reinforced concrete all around you is like, Kiunga? Ever think about the steel and pulverised stone that's holding us here?

—I try not to.

—Sure. That's what we all do. You think about anything too hard, it'll all just crumble to dust. You don't think about a landslide every time you climb a hill.

Mollel pauses for a moment. Catches his breath. Catches his thoughts.

—The *matatus* were jammed that morning, he continues. I was hoping I'd catch her in the foyer, but it was gone ten o'clock by the time I got through to Haile Selassie Avenue. I figured it would be quicker to get out and walk. There was some kind of hold-up ahead. There usually was. You know how the Americans were about security around their embassy. I remember hearing that squeal of tyres and thinking, *Kenyan driver*. But then, gunshots.

Seventeenth floor.

—You know that street, Kiunga. It's like a concrete trench. Buildings all sides. No one could tell where the gunshots were coming from. People tried to run, but they were all running in different directions. I wanted to go forward, someone pushed me back. The last thing I remember is, *Oh God, I've dropped her packed lunch*. Then it felt like the ground had dropped away beneath me. I slammed into a wall. And the wall kept pressing so hard against the side of my head, and I was thinking, *What's this wall?* But it wasn't a wall. It was the ground. I'd been thrown from my feet. And all the people who had been in front of me were on top of me. I managed to get up. I tried to look around, but I didn't even recognise where I was. There was a huge cloud of dust rolling down the street towards where I was standing. I just managed to turn my face away, as it hit. Dust, and grit, and ashes.

Mollel slaps the concrete wall beside him. —And whatever else goes into a building like this.

Eighteenth floor.

—I knew which way to walk, because I could feel the way things were flying towards me. They felt like birds or bats at first, the things flying into my face. I swiped them. Clawed them. Pushed them down. But it was paper. So much paper floating every-where. Then the cries started. It was as though everyone had been too shocked at first, but then found their voices. So many voices. But I knew I was going in the right direction. By that time I was having to climb. There was no road any more, no pavement. Nothing was stable or solid beneath my feet. Everything rolled. Shifted. Rocked. Slid. I kicked off my shoes, was on my hands and knees, my fingers and toes. The first time I felt hair and skin beneath my hands, I tried to help the person up. But whatever I grabbed was far too light. Too limp. It just came away.

Nineteenth floor.

—But then someone was speaking to me. The voice was so faint, I bent down and could just make out the woman. Her skin was white, as white as chalk, and I thought, a *mzungu?* But it was the dust. Like white ash. We were all like that. She was so small. So slight. It wasn't my Chiku. Where were you? I asked her. Are you from the secretarial college? But she couldn't reply. I tried to push her aside, Kiunga. I tried to push her down, but her hand kept grabbing my ankle. I kicked it away. I kept look-ing. But they just kept getting in the way, those people, those bodies, one after the other. Any time I found one I thought could be Chiku, I picked her up, carried her, as far as I could out of the rubble. There was a sort of flat area there, where I could put them down. Someone had water, or sometimes I used spit, to try to wipe their faces, but it was never Chiku. That's why I kept going back.

Twentieth floor.

—I didn't know it at the time. How could I? But the people I was pulling out weren't even from the same building the secre-tarial college was in. They weren't even from the US embassy. They were people who'd been hit by debris on the street. The girls from the college on the fifteenth floor weren't going to be reached until days later, when they sent in the diggers. Of course, it was a salvage operation by then, not a rescue. By that time, I'd become a permanent fixture at the morgue. Because of who I was, they let me stay, cleaned me up. I washed next to the corpses in the sluice room. Someone gave me some clothes. Every time they brought a new one in, if she fitted the description, they'd let me have a look. But it was getting to the point where descriptions didn't even matter. I still felt the need to look.

Twenty-first floor.

—A reporter from one of the international papers had heard about me. Tracked me down. Apparently the rescuers at the scene had described this Maasai who, despite his own injuries, kept going back into the rubble to bring more and more people out. The writer wanted a hero. He said not enough Americans had been killed to keep it on the front pages in his country any more. He needed to personalise the story. He said the people in his country didn't know the difference between the Arabs who did this and the African victims. He wanted an African hero to put on his front page. We spoke. Someone took pictures. To be honest, I don't even remember what was said.

Twenty-second floor.

—You know, a lot of things didn't matter to me after that. Even my son. Faith took over a lot of the work. He was a baby. I didn't know what to do with him. She did.

—And people wanted to talk to me. So I let them. The journalists came to speak to the hero of the embassy bombing. And I found they were interested in what I had to tell them. Not just about the bombing. About the police department, about how it worked. *Chai* money here, backhanders there. I suppose I must have told someone about how our division's new consignment of top-of-the-range patrol vehicles somehow turned into second-hand saloons with the chassis numbers ground off. Because it was the front page of the *East African* the following weekend.

Twenty-third floor.

—It would have been too obvious to sack me. So they sent me on sick leave. The psychiatrist was quite candid. He told me right at the start that he'd been instructed to find me unfit for duty. But after we spoke, he thanked me for not having to write a false report.

—I'd been having blackouts. Not thinking straight. He put me on the drugs. The drugs you've seen me take. That's what they're for, Kiunga. Not for HIV. But just like HIV, Kiunga, this illness can be managed. Never cured. But managed.

Twenty-fourth floor.

Mollel pauses to look back at Kiunga. He has a look on his face. A look of suspicion and distrust. A look which Mollel has seen before. Many times.

—I knew I shouldn't have told you, says Mollel. I should have kept it hidden. Just like the people kept hidden in every village. The ones locked away by their families, in case their madness infects others.

—I'm still the same person, Kiunga, says Mollel.

Twenty-fifth floor.

—But you're not, are you? says Kiunga. You're not the same person I thought you were. I've taken huge risks for you, Mollel. And you've hidden things from me. You never told me you were going into Orpheus House that night.

—I'm sorry, Kiunga.

—This whole investigation has been conducted your way. Cutting corners. Telling lies. I was prepared to go along with it when I thought there was a rational mind behind it. But now…

—We're nearly there. Let's put it to Kingori. He'll back my theory, I'm sure of it. I'm right about this. I can feel it.

Twenty-sixth floor.

Kiunga shakes his head. Mollel knows what he's thinking. What's the gut instinct of a madman worth?

—You can go back down now, says Mollel. Leave me to it. I didn't ask you to come along.

Kiunga stops on the stairs. Mollel continues.

Twenty-seventh floor.

—These blackouts, Mollel, Kiunga calls up from below. Do you still get them?

His voice echoes in the stairwell. Mollel heaves himself up a few more steps.

—Sometimes, he gasps. If I'm not taking my medication.

—And *are* you taking your medication, Mollel? *Are* you taking it?

Kiunga's voice becomes more distant as Mollel gets farther away. He can't bring himself to shout a reply, so he does not reply.

Kiunga's voice comes floating up again. —The night you broke into Orpheus House, Mollel. Did you black out then?

Twenty-eighth floor.

As he rounds the latest flight, Mollel leans over the banister and looks up. He's almost there. Just a few more steps to go. He turns and looks down. The staircases retreat below him in a foreshortened, polygonal spiral, illuminated in sickly fluorescent light. Far, far beneath is a small patch of grey. If he were to topple now, to tumble over the railing…

—What did you do with my lighter, Mollel?

Kiunga's voice drifts up to him.

—The night Orpheus House burned down, Mollel. You had my lighter. You never gave it back to me. What did you do with it, Mollel? What did you do?

Mollel turns back to the staircase and begins to mount once more.

Twenty-ninth floor.

What did he do? He has no recollection. Only the blood, the operating table. Surely, *surely*, the scene of the crime.

He takes the last few steps wearily. Kingori will tell me, he thinks, repeating it in his head like a mantra. Kingori will tell me everything.

The final paces feel like dragging himself through waist-high mud. He barely has the strength to take them. When, finally, he reaches the landing at the top, he sees a plain grey door, with the word HELIPAD painted on it. A single keyhole – locked. Apart from that, there is no handle. No way of opening it. It's a fire escape. It can only be accessed from the other side.

He lies down. Feels the cool concrete beneath him. Closes his eyes.

There is a crash, and a sudden blast of cold, crisp air. Revitalising. He opens his eyes, blinded for a moment by the crisp blue daylight which is flooding in upon him. Kiunga stands over him. The door flaps in the breeze, splintered lock hanging loose on its screws on the external side.

—I thought you'd left me, Mollel says.

—At least this way, says Kiunga, rubbing his shoulder, I've got a chance of taking the elevator back down.

33

The door gives out on to a gantry with a set of metal stairs leading up to a gap in the overhang above. At this height the air is icy, despite the midday sun reflected from the buildings and streets far below. The wide lip of the helipad which tops the building casts the gantry into complete shade. Mollel and Kiunga step out. Mollel tries not to look down, and instead focuses upon the small square of light up ahead.

The wind is powerful here. Not enough to disturb their climb, but enough to create the unsettling feeling that the next gust, or the one after that, might be the one that plucks you from the building and leaves you flying like a cinder on the air.

—Listen, calls Kiunga.

Mollel hadn't heard it at first, over the wind and the sounds of the city. But there it is approaching: that curious, syncopated throb of a helicopter, the roar of its engines, the beat of its blades. Louder now – the gantry itself buzzes under Mollel's agonised hands and his weary feet. Up – and out. As his head rises above the small parapet, the city opens before him, dazzling, clear. The sensation is akin to flying.

A group of men, mostly wearing military fatigues and orange ear-protectors, are clustered on the other side of the dish. They've not seen Mollel or Kiunga approach. There is a raised section where the elevator gives out. The doors are being held open, and a second group of men in business suits carrying heavy and laden steel boxes are coming out. Commanding them is David Kingori.

The army helicopter is now nearly upon them. As it finalises its approach, the downdraught causes all those present, Mollel and Kiunga included, to crouch instinctively and grab on to whatever they can. The aircraft's belly is suspended above them. It wobbles, turns, lines itself up. Mollel relinquishes his grip on the handrail to cover his ears. For a moment, the noise is deafening. A change in pitch tells him that the helicopter has touched down. And mercifully, the scream becomes less intense and the blades slow, from an invisible blur to a more leisurely pace, though they keep turning.

Mollel and Kiunga are on the far side of the landed helicopter now. A pilot, in sunglasses and civilian clothes, looks them over without curiosity. He casts Mollel a thumbs-up. Mollel returns it. He can see feet emerging on the other side, leaping out from the bowels of the machine. The men with boxes rush forward. Impossible, from here, to count how many are exchanged. Fifteen? Twenty?

Above the engines, a shout. Words indistinguishable. Then the helicopter roars again: a puff of diesel fumes heralding its imminent take-off. It rises at first unsteadily, like a baby gazelle finding its legs. Then pitches, teeters, hangs for a moment. Everyone is crouched once more. But as it departs, they righten themselves, and the men near the elevator hurry to put the new steel boxes – exactly the same as the others – back inside.

The elevator doors close. Kingori is left alone on the helipad. He looks exhausted. He cups his hand to his eyes, to watch the helicopter becoming a dot. Then he scans the horizon. He sees Mollel and Kiunga, standing on the far side. He does not move. Mollel and Kiunga walk towards him.

He gestures to the skyline like a man welcoming guests to his home.

—Great view, isn't it? Have you seen *Kirinyaga*? Mount Kenya? The Kikuyus' holy mountain. It's only visible a few days a year from Nairobi. Auspicious, don't you think?

—If I were you, I'd be more worried about the smoke, says Kiunga. Kibera, Mathare, Donholme, Eastleigh. The city's on fire.

—And yet, from up here, it all looks so peaceful, says Kingori, with a grin. Just breathe it in a moment, gentlemen.

—You're stealing the election! spits Kiunga.

—Come on, replies Kingori. You think those ballot boxes aren't already stuffed to the brim with opposition votes? All sides are playing the game, my friends. We just intend to play it better. Now, when that elevator returns in just a matter of seconds, my colleagues will take you into their custody. Whatever it is you came here for, you've seen things you shouldn't have seen, and I doubt very much we'll be seeing each other again.

—In that case, I'll get straight to the point, says Mollel. Lucy was carrying your baby.

There's a sudden grinding sound. The elevator doors open and a group of men step out. They stop, and look in surprise at Mollel and Kiunga. With them is an army officer, who hastily unholsters his handgun and points it at them.

—It's *sawa*, shouts Kingori. They're OK, they're with us. He starts to walk to the edge of the dish. Mollel and Kiunga follow. Kingori steps up to the railing. Looks down. There is a mesh net below. Through its wire grid, Mollel can see the crimson pinpoints of GSU helmets, pushing back a growing swarm of protesters at the gates.

—The autopsy came through, says Mollel. She was pregnant. We know the child was yours. You were the only person she was going with at that time.

Kingori shakes his head, not in denial, but in disbelief. —*Pregnant?*

—If you'd known it before you sent her away, you'd have forced her to have an abortion earlier. Still illegal, of course. But possible to do without risking the mother's health. She thought she was far gone enough to be safe. That's why she made contact again. She would have thought that no one could force her into a late-term abortion. It's practically murder. But she didn't count on how determined you were to keep your reputation. Or the fact that you had a hold over the one person in Nairobi desperate enough to conduct such an operation. Wanjiku Nalo.

—Boss, says Kiunga. His voice is low and urgent.

Mollel looks up, annoyed at his colleague's interruption. But Kiunga's glare is equally challenging. —I need a word with you, he says.

The two of them step away from the edge. Kingori remains there. He sinks his head into his hands.

When they're at a safe distance, Kiunga asks in low tones: —What are you doing?

—I'm trying to get the truth.

—By *lying*?

—I'm not lying. Honey told me about the baby, remember?

Kiunga stares at him in disbelief.

—*Honey?* He spits the name with contempt. You know there's not been any post-mortem, Mollel. You've just told him Lucy was carrying his baby. You've got no way of knowing whether that's true or not. You're staking the whole investigation on the word of a *prostitute*?

—Look at him, says Mollel.

Kingori is slumped. His swagger has evaporated.

—He looks broken, says Kiunga.

—Exactly. He's going to give us what we need to put the others away.

Kiunga shakes his head.

—It's not right.

—Trust me, says Mollel.

—Trust your *judgement*? replies Kiunga, grudgingly. How much are you keeping from me, Mollel? What reason have I got to trust your judgement at all?

Mollel looks up. Kiunga's raised voice has attracted the attention of the men in military fatigues. One of them approaches. —What's going on? he asks.

Mollel thumbs at Kingori. —He says you're to go back to the

count, he calls out to them. Don't worry, there's plenty of time before the next consignment.

The man calls out to Kingori: —Is that right, boss?

Kingori nods and waves them away.

The men look at each other, shrug, and get into the elevator. The doors close.

—We need to stay calm, says Mollel. If we attract too much attention now, we'll end up going where those boxes are going. Dumped in a lake somewhere, probably. Our only link to safety is Kingori. And if he begins to suspect we're bluffing him...

—You're not bluffing him, hisses Kiunga. You're *torturing* him. Is this how you get results, Mollel?

Mollel does not answer.

—We'll do it your way, says Kiunga. Then we're through.

The two of them walk back to the railings.

—Was it a boy? Kingori asks them. I always wanted a boy.

—I'm afraid it was, says Mollel. By now the lies seem to hardly matter.

—What do you want to know, asks Kingori.

—Everything, says Mollel.

Kingori sighs. He motions his hand around him. —This?

—We don't care about the vote-rigging. Who'd believe us, anyway? Just tell us about Lucy.

Kingori takes off his gold-rimmed glasses, folds them, and slips them into his breast pocket.

—James found her for me, he says. He was very good at that. He knew my tastes. She fitted the bill perfectly. I was very fond of her, really. She was shy. Damaged. She responded to tenderness the way most of those girls respond to diamond bracelets. I enjoyed her company. It was nice to be nice to someone for a change. But it wasn't going anywhere. A girl like that's all right for a little fun, but...

—When she started to get a little too needy, I told her, *It's over. We're calling it quits*. But I still felt sorry for her. So I put her in touch with some people I knew, some people who tried to get girls back on the straight and narrow.

—Orpheus House, says Mollel.

—My tenants, yes. I had no idea what it would lead to. It was quite some time later, George Nalo approached me with his plan. He said he could get funding from the Americans for a hospital. His wife would be director. But it had to be in a prominent location. The Americans like their generosity to be conspicuous. So, he said, he wanted me to sign over the land to him. I laughed in his face. *I could sell that land to developers and give you a donation that would run your hospital for five years*, I told him. *But you expect me to give it to you for free?*

—It wasn't about what the donors wanted, of course. It was all about him. Self-promotion. He needed to be more high profile, have everyone in Nairobi talking about what a great guy he was. Has he given you his talk yet about his lack of political ambitions? Don't believe a word of it. George Nalo is a politician through and through. I hadn't realised how much, until then.

—He told me about Lucy. She was a resident of Orpheus House now. Helped out with the other girls. A kind of outreach officer for them. She'd told him and Wanjiku all about our relationship. And he said Lucy was prepared to go public, if I didn't agree to his demands.

—I sent James to track her down. It wasn't easy. The Nalos had frightened her off. Told her that I was dangerous. That I would try to silence her.

He gives a hollow laugh.

—Turns out it was the other way round. *They* were the ones she should have been afraid of. I didn't know that, though. I just saw it as convenient. I mean, girls like that. They only work for two things. Money, and fear.

—So, once we found her, we let her believe the myth the Nalos had created. That we were the big bad guys. She'd better do what we say. James played the part particularly well. He can be quite menacing when he puts his mind to it.

—And it worked. She became our girl on the inside. Feeding us information about the Nalos.

—They were the ones who had started playing with fire. But they were going to get burned. It didn't take Lucy long to realise what was really going on at Orpheus House. Sure, they were doing all the outreach, the health services. But they were also doing abortions. Turns out Wanjiku, she's a fanatic. Early term, late term, it doesn't matter to her. She reckons she is saving the children from a world of pain.

—I could have destroyed the Nalos if I'd wanted to. If I'd had any idea Lucy was carrying my son... but she was too afraid to tell me.

—And besides, it suited me, this situation. It was important to keep my name clean, with the election looming. State House made it very clear that there were going to be a lot of contracts handed out after the success of this campaign. I wasn't going to be the one to throw it away in a tabloid scandal.

—So I had James pay them a little visit. Let them know that if they kept quiet about me and Lucy, I would keep quiet about their little abortion racket. The stakes were much higher for them than they were for me.

Kingori shakes his head. —But I didn't know about my baby. I'm nearly seventy. I've got three daughters. I never thought I'd have a chance of a son. And they killed him!

—It looks like your man James was part of it too, says Mollel. Seems he takes protecting your reputation very seriously. To the extent of arranging an abortion behind your back.

—That stupid bastard, mutters Kingori.

—They killed your child. And they killed Lucy, too.

—You think it was deliberate? asks Kingori, raising his face to Mollel. His eyes are puffy, his jaw slack. For the first time, he looks his age. —You don't just think they botched the abortion? It was very late, after all. That sort of thing has to be risky.

—I don't think they botched anything, says Mollel. Wanjiku Nalo is the best in her field. From the sound of it, she was doing late abortions all the time. No, maybe that's how they got Lucy on to the operating table in the first place. Persuaded her it was the right thing to do. Wanjiku can be very persuasive. But

Lucy's knowledge was a threat to them. They knew that after the election, their hold on you would be gone. So they needed to eliminate the threat. She let Lucy die, and together, she and Lethebridge got rid of the body.

—Jesus Christ!

Kingori thumps the railing. A crow, somewhere on the gantry below, is startled, and flaps cawing into the void.

—I'll do it, he says. I'll testify. I'll bring those murderers down.

34

—Here comes another helicopter.

Kiunga points to the pale horizon, where a black dot is suspended, soundless. Kingori pulls out his phone. Its gold plate glints in the afternoon sun.

—I'll call James, he says. He'll back up everything I say.

—Where is he? asks Mollel.

—At his home.

—I knew it, mutters Kiunga.

—Have him come to Central. Kiunga can meet him there. I'll go and deal with the Nalos.

The throb of the approaching helicopter fights for dominance for a moment or two with the sound of the city; then surpasses it. The elevator doors open and two men in fatigues come out. Between them, they are carrying a laden ballot box. They eye Mollel and Kiunga with suspicion as they pass, bound for Kingori, who is speaking on his phone.

—Let's go.

The two of them go to the elevator. Two more boxes are within, taped up with official seals.

—Help me shift these, says Mollel.

—I'm not touching them.

Mollel looks in surprise at Kiunga. —We've got other things to do.

—Those are real votes in there, Kiunga replies.

—They could be. Or, like Kingori says, they could be just as false as the ones they're switching them with. The opposition are just as likely to have tampered with these before they ever arrived here.

—We don't know that, mutters Kiunga. If I even touched one of those boxes I'd feel... tainted.

—We don't have time for this, mutters Mollel, as he grabs the handle of one of the steel boxes and drags it out of the elevator. With only one box remaining, there is enough space for them both to get in. Kiunga hits the button for the ground floor.

—That makes you part of it, he says, as the doors creak shut.

Mollel reaches over and presses the button for the third floor.

—We'll be part of it, all right, if we walk straight into their operation. Let's give ourselves a bit of breathing space.

As the elevator judders into life, Mollel says: —You're a principled man, Kiunga. You don't want to be involved in something that's wrong. I understand that.

The small screen above the door illuminates the floor numbers as they descend. The two of them count the figures down in silence until they hit 3, and the doors grind open. The lobby beyond is empty.

—Sometimes, though, says Mollel, doing nothing is not enough.

He steps out of the elevator, and pulls the remaining ballot box halfway through the door. Kiunga steps round and joins him just as the door begins to close. It hits the box and the elevator alarm sounds.

—It'll take them a while to work out why the elevator's jammed, says Mollel. Might get a few more honest votes counted in that time.

They head for the stairs.

—Just like this case, continues Mollel. You may think I'm doing it wrong. But it's better than doing nothing.

—You know who you sound like? says Kiunga. Otieno.

Mollel laughs.

—No, really, says Kiunga. You both think you can throw out

the rules if the end result's the right one. But where he does it out of caution, you do it out of recklessness. I used to admire you, Mollel. Until I realised that it's all just another symptom of your craziness.

Mollel walks over to the window. He can still hear the helicopter, a hundred metres above them. But here, near ground level, the sound of the crowd drifts over the gates, over the helmets of the GSU ranks, over the eerie calm of the empty grounds of the conference centre outside.

—Did you ever beat out a confession, Mollel?

—Of course not!

—Otieno does it all the time. Did you see the stains in the interview room? That's not spilled coffee, you know. What you did up there was just the same. Sure, you didn't grab Kingori by the arms and hold him over the edge of the building. But you might as well have done. You lied to him.

—I forced a confession.

—By tearing him apart! You broke him, Mollel. I thought you were a different sort of policeman. One I could admire. But you're just the same as all the rest.

—Look at that city, Mollel says, quietly. There will be plenty more Nairobians dead before this is over. But we've got the chance to get the people who killed one of them. Is that so mad?

Kiunga shakes his head.

—What did you really see in Orpheus House, Mollel? An operating table, blood? Or was that all a lie, too, to persuade Otieno to keep on with the case? To persuade *me*? You've had it in for the Nalos since we met them. You *wanted* them to be guilty. If there was no evidence at Orpheus House, would you burn the place down to cover that up?

—I know what I saw, says Mollel.

—You might have *seen* it, replies Kiunga. But was it *there*?

Getting out of the KICC proves easier than getting in. Immediately they pass through the GSU ranks, Kiunga turns to Mollel.

—I'm in this up to my neck. The best I can hope for is that James Lethebridge backs up Kingori's story. I'll go bring him in. You're going to get the Nalos?

—Yes.

—Good luck, says Kiunga coldly. I'd like to say it's been nice working with you, Mollel. But ... you know.

And he strikes off through the crowd of protesters, in the direction of Central Police Post, where he left the car.

Mollel finds himself alone on the streets just beyond the cordon, with no real idea of how he is going to get to Embakasi, and the Nalos' campus.

He wanders on to the Uhuru Highway. It's almost deserted. The only movement comes from GSU trucks, and one or two private cars. He flags a passing police car, but the driver ignores him. There are no *matatus* running. He wanders back towards the Intercontinental Hotel, in the hope of finding a taxi driver who might be willing or desperate enough to grab a fare on a day like this.

Outside the lobby he sees a khaki Land Rover, an elongated safari version, nine-seater, with enlarged windows for game viewing. Inside, like lobsters in a tank, are a group of elderly *wazungu* tourists. Their eyes are hollow with fatigue and fear. They all wear immaculate, pressed, khaki safari suits. Mollel guesses they've seen more of the wild than they anticipated on this trip. The Land Rover is idling, to keep the air conditioning running for the passengers. The driver is having a conversation with the hotel security guard. Mollel interrupts him, flashing his ID.

—Where are you taking them? he asks.

—To the airport, the driver replies nervously. They're being evacuated. Check-in closes in forty minutes. Do you reckon we'll get through?

—The highway's clear, says Mollel. But it takes you directly past South B, and there are reports of trouble there. If I were you, I'd take South C route via Embakasi. Could you do with an escort?

—Yes, please, says the driver, relief palpable in his voice.

—Let's go.

The tourists look up, startled, as Mollel jumps into the front passenger seat. They relax somewhat when their driver gets in.

—This is a policeman, he says. And the elderly *wazungu* smile and give Mollel a thumbs-up. The safari truck moves off, and Mollel starts to give directions. He gets a tap on the shoulder. One of the women in the group is pushing a small automatic camera at his face.

—Would you mind taking a photograph of us? she asks.

—Sure, says Mollel.

She explains how the camera works. The group pose. The fear and tension drain from their faces as they assume expressions of stoic good humour, already composing the caption in their minds: *This is us being evacuated from Kenya. Quite an adventure!*

Mollel takes the photograph, and passes the camera back to the tourist. She holds it up and looks at the screen with satisfaction. Outside the window, Mollel sees a kiosk overturned, people crawling in and running off with whatever pitiful supplies are within: sticks of laundry soap, razor blades, packets of flour. Now the other tourists are raising their cameras and snapping away.

The residential streets of South C flash by. The rows of houses run at right angles to the main road, guarded by high metal gates and barbed wire. Mollel catches the occasional glimpse of locals looking warily out from behind. There's no other traffic on the road, so they make good progress, but Mollel is aware of how quickly the situation could change. In Swahili he says to the driver: —Anyone steps in front of the car, or tries to stop us, just keep going. Understand?

—If you say so, says the driver, with barely concealed delight, and he puts his foot down on the accelerator, as though having been granted official sanction to drive the way he's always dreamed of.

Mollel becomes aware of the drone of conversation behind him.

—Of course, one of the tourists is drawling, you have to expect this sort of thing in Africa. However modern the place looks, tribal tensions are never very far from the surface.

The others murmur assent. —To think, chimes in a woman's voice, of all the money I've donated over the years. Well, I'll certainly be cancelling that subscription when I get home.

—Very wise, Louise, very wise, says the first speaker, warming to his theme. If you ask me, all the aid we give them is part of the problem. If you treat people like children, you can't be surprised when they throw their rattle out of the stroller.

—They *are* children, really, aren't they, chips in another of the women, brightly. I sometimes think they'd be better off if the modern world just left them alone, in their mud huts. I mean, they always look so happy, don't they? It's only wanting what they can't have that gets them all upset.

—Africa's a basket case. We should just cut them loose. See how they fare.

The sentiment seems to represent a consensus among the tourists, and with nothing left to add, their gaze returns to the windows.

—Do they always talk like this? Mollel asks the driver, in Swahili.

—Who?

—Tourists. Do they always talk as though you're not here?

—I don't know, the driver replies. I don't listen.

The sun is low, and flashes from between the houses. In the red dust of dusk, it's easy to imagine for a moment that the boys running away from a smashed-in car are simply playing with hoops; that the dogs pacing and jumping behind the chain-link are goats being herded for milking; that the woman sitting bleeding into her shawl on the kerbstone is simply winnowing maize.

An African sunset.

The Land Rover slows. The road is no longer clear: other

vehicles have joined the road, and are beginning to bunch up. Soon, the safari truck comes to a halt.

Mollel leans forward to try to make out what's happening. The jam extends some distance up ahead. He realises they're close to the Nalos' campus: the sight of a George Nalo Ministries bumper sticker confirms his suspicion. The cars are all headed for the church.

—I'll get out here, he says casually to the driver.

—Hey. What? calls one of the tourists. The others chime in with a chorus of: *What're we gonna do? We'll never make our flight! You can't just leave us like this! We need protection!*

—What the *hell*, says one of the men, in the authoritative, not-to-be-disobeyed voice of the white man abroad, do you think you're doing?

—I'm cutting you loose, says Mollel. Seeing how you fare.

And he gives them a jaunty wave as he hops out of the Land Rover and disappears into the throng of pedestrians streaming towards the dying red sun and the looming, glowering edifice of George Nalo Ministries.

35

Closer to the church, the cause of the jam becomes evident. Private cars have parked wherever they can, at the side of the road, tilted into the ditch. Some even seem to have been abandoned where they stood, leaving only the smallest gap through which to squeeze. Black-clad ushers at the gate, a panicky, frantic look on their faces, attempt to turn away the vehicles which have got that far: *No room, no room.* But still the people push in on foot.

Come nightfall, the Maasai men herd their cows into the *manyatta.* The boys follow with their goats, which leap and trip to try to get inside, as though they know that once the *il–timito*, the thick thorn branches, are pulled into place, they will be safe from darkness and the lions that hide beyond.

So it is with George Nalo Ministries. The place has become a sanctuary for those who hope that divine providence – or failing that, strength in numbers – will save them from the chaos which is engulfing their city.

Those around him couldn't present a greater contrast to the first time he came here. No Sunday best: people have come dressed in whatever they happened to be wearing when they decided to abandon their homes. Many of the children are in pyjamas: some, carried over their parents' shoulders, are still asleep.

Approaching the church building, Mollel feels he is being

swept along by the crowd. In the gloom, it is even more impressive than in daylight. The interior, illuminated, silhouettes the bobbing heads in front of him. It feels as if the building is sucking them into the light.

The crowd streams around an elderly woman pushing a handcart. In it is a husk of a man, his hair grizzled, eyes closed, sunken.

—Can you help me, brother? she asks as Mollel passes. He raises his raw, peeling hands in excuse. She looks at them, her face full of pity, even in her own predicament. God bless you, she says. Your suffering is almost at an end.

—Is it?

—Oh yes, she replies, and a smile breaks through her fatigue. The suffering of this world will soon be forgotten. These are the End Times.

He moves on, and begins to become aware of a noise. It is loud, and low. So low Mollel feels it in his teeth.

It is that of a swarm. When you first hear a swarm of bees, you can tell from the tone and the intensity how big it is and what mood the bees are in. But you can't place the sound. It's too low.

You can't tell what direction it's coming from, because it's coming from *everywhere*. All you know is, there are a lot of them, and they're dangerous.

Getting closer, the drone becomes more intense. The sound reverberates in his head and his chest and begins to pound and split and fracture into thousands of human voices.

The hall opens and splits before him as he passes through the doors, and is filled with the crying and the laughing and the clamour and the jabber and the babble of tongues. The aisles are packed, overflowing even into the lobby, where Mollel encounters the first ecstatic figures, hands held aloft, or clasped over their heart; heads tipped back, eyes closed. They sway as they cry, and speak; some have tears running down their cheeks.

The trance is transporting. Mollel is unnerved. His mind tries to tune in to each voice as he passes but it is successively drowned out by the next; he tries to grasp sounds, interpret meaning, but the sounds elide and evade meaning and it all collides and conflates into a primal, final cacophony.

But one voice begins to rise above the others. It is a gargle and a gurgle louder than all the others. It stands out, amplified. Word-sounds resound. The rapt stand limply, heads lolling: they are oblivious, and Mollel finds he can no longer push himself forward. He has reached an impasse.

Craning, he can see the distant stage up ahead. It is bright: the lights pick it up and place it on an ethereal level. Floating in the middle of the luminous disc is Nalo. Microphone dangles from his fingers, other hand aloft, head thrown back. Slivers of white visible below his eyelids. Flecks of spit visible, even at this distance, at the corners of his mouth. His mouth opens and shuts, his tongue probes and gropes around sound. His voice fills the auditorium.

No Wanjiku. No Benjamin.

Mollel turns, but the crush is as thick behind him now, as it is in front. He sees the woman with the cart. She has put it down, and she tenderly caresses the skeletal cheek of the prone man within.

The hubbub is ending.

—Praise the Lord, comes Nalo's voice.

The voice of another, unseen, speaker comes over the PA. —Healing is about to commence, it says. Those seeking healing, please make yourself known to an usher.

The rapture over, it is slightly easier for Mollel to weave his way back to the woman with the cart.

—I'll take him, he says.

—But your hands!

He grasps the handles. Winces. But to his relief, the man barely possesses weight, and he lifts the cart on its axis.

—A miracle! she gasps.

Those around them look on, and, as the word spreads, Mollel finds a way parting ahead of him. He pushes the cart forward, and black-clad ushers rush to meet him. They progress to the edge of the stage, where hands clamour to help him, and the old man is lifted and borne high and away. An usher takes Mollel's hands in his own, looks at them, and says: —This one too.

Mollel feels himself being impelled upwards. The usher clips something to his shirt collar, and slips a small, heavy box, about the size of a cigarette packet, into his pocket. —It's a microphone, he says into Mollel's ear. Don't speak until you're spoken to.

—Brothers and sisters, booms the unseen voice. The healing is about to commence.

The lights are blinding, and the heat of them brings a prickle of sweat to Mollel's skin. The usher who gave him the microphone moves away, and a stockier, more powerful figure takes his place at Mollel's side, grasping his shoulder forcefully.

—Just keep walking, a voice urges Mollel in his ear. Don't try anything.

It is Benjamin. He has now taken Mollel's arm, has his other arm around his waist. He holds him tightly. As they are brought up to Nalo, Mollel sees Wanjiku Nalo emerge from the shadows. She looks at him with a mixture of shock and anger.

The elderly man is the first brought up to the pastor. Nalo places both hands on the feeble shoulders. The sickly frame is being supported on all sides. His eyes are now open.

—What is your name, Father? says Nalo.

The microphone on his lapel picks up a crackling voice like dry leaves and spreads it throughout the auditorium. *Odolo*, it sounds like.

—Well, *mzee* Odolo, Nalo says, what is your problem?

—I'm sick, says the old man. I cannot walk. I cannot move. I do not have long left.

Because his words are barely picked up by the microphone, Nalo repeats for the audience:

—He's sick, he cannot walk. He says his time has come. Well, your time may be near old man, it is near for all of us, but it will not be today.

Then he takes one of his mighty hands and places it on the

old man's forehead, across his eyes. —Lord Jesus, Nalo implores, this is your servant. This is your son. This good man is in need of your divine mercy. Please will you assist him, O Lord.

The hall begins to reverberate again with voices. This time they aren't speaking in tongues: they are raised in prayer. Looking down, Mollel can see the figures nearest to the stage fervently reciting their prayers, fists clenched, or fingers clasped, entwined. He looks back at the elderly man. Nalo finishes his prayer, and powerfully, shockingly, with a plosive *Bam!*, he pushes the old man's head back.

It's obviously a practised move: the ushers tip him simultaneously. The old man swoons backward in their arms while one usher places his feet underneath him. They then pivot him back to a standing position, and with a flourish, theatrically, they all step aside, to reveal him there.

Standing.

The old man looks down at his legs in amazement. He looks up again, beaming. Tentatively, he lifts one foot, waves it, places it on the ground, does the same with the other leg. Then, in sheer joy, he shuffles, a little jig. The audience cheers in throes of ecstasy. The old man raises a hand to acknowledge them, but wobbles, as though he might fall, and the ushers swiftly run forward to steady him. He is then assisted – to Mollel it looks as though he is carried – off stage.

Now it is Mollel's turn to be brought forward. Benjamin grasps him tightly on one side. On the other he feels a new hand clutch his arm. It is Wanjiku. She looks into his eyes.

—I need to talk to you… he begins. His own words boom out across the hall. Wanjiku glares at him. Her finger flies to her lips and then points down at the microphone on his collar. She shakes her head. —*Not now*, she whispers. *After.*

She looks towards her husband. Nalo has come close. Mollel senses the ushers gathering behind him.

Nalo looks him in the eyes, and a flash of recognition passes across his face. He looks askance at Wanjiku. She nods. Nalo frowns, looks out at the darkness, where the massed audience now wait, filled with anticipation of the next miracle. He seems momentarily at a loss. Then he composes himself, and says to Mollel: —What is your name, my son?

—Mollel, says Mollel.

Nalo repeats: —Your name is Mollel. We welcome you, Mollel. What ails you, my brother?

Benjamin and Wanjiku, each holding one of Mollel's arms, thrust his hands forward, turning them upright. The heat of the spotlights makes his palms throb agonisingly, and Mollel grimaces.

—Aah, booms Nalo. Your hands are badly burned.

A sympathetic groan goes up from the audience.

Nalo places his palm on Mollel's forehead. Mollel tries to pull his head back and away but it is being thrust forward by one of the ushers behind him.

—But your hands are not your only ill, are they, my brother? continues Nalo. I sense... I sense a great disquiet in your mind. Allow us to help you, my brother. Allow the Lord Jesus Christ to assist you. Allow the Prince of Peace to bring you some respite from that which is torturing you.

The tumult in the hall is commencing again as the audience recognise the prompt for them to break into spontaneous prayer. Mollel can hear it all around him, but he cannot move, cannot shift. He sees nothing but Nalo's hand over his eyes.

—Oh, Jesus, cries Nalo. Please, assist this poor, deluded brother. Please, Jesus, bring an end to his suffering.

As before: *Bam!*

Mollel feels a sharp, jabbing pain in his arm.

Nalo's hand is removed from his eyes. Mollel looks down at his arm, just in time to see Wanjiku Nalo pressing the plunger of a hypodermic syringe. He feels the pressure of the liquid entering his muscle. Then feels the needle slide out as she removes it. He just has time to cast her a furious glance and open his mouth in protest before he is bundled forward.

And then Mollel is borne in a dozen pairs of arms and lifted upright: he is presented to the audience, spotlight shining in his face. He blinks and screws up his face like a newborn.

Absence of pain.

That's what he feels: and the deliverance is blissful.

He hadn't realised, until now, how much the pain had borne down upon him, constrained him. And now, held up by all these hands, he feels liberated.

—Are you healed? roars Nalo.

Mollel looks down at his hands. They are still raw. But now, instead of the heat from the spotlights searing him, his palms seem to merely glow and tingle as though warmed by the rising sun.

—Speak, Mollel. You have the microphone. Tell the audience. By the power of prayer, are you healed?

His eyes tell him his wounds are still livid. He knows that it is only the drug, whatever Wanjiku injected him with, which makes him feel this way. He looks at her, at Benjamin. They watch him anxiously. It would be the easiest thing in the world to denounce them now, to bring the whole edifice down around them.

The room is silent. Thousands of eyes are trained eagerly upon him. The fiction of the Nalos, their fraud, and their power, are now wholly in his command.

George Nalo's eyes probe his own. They burn into him like the spotlights. Mollel's mouth is dry. He croaks: —*Your wife...*

He hears his own voice, like a stir of leaves, reverberate around the hall. This is not the way he wants it. He puts his hand up to cover the bud of the microphone on his lapel. Nalo leans forward, his head inches from Mollel's mouth.

—Your wife, whispers Mollel. This time only he and Nalo hear his words. Your wife is a murderer. She killed Lucy.

36

The girl stumbled through the night. Her face and arms were scratched. She had lost her calabash and the honey, and her mother would be angry that she had not even picked the berries she was sent for. She did not care. She just wanted to get home.

But she did not know the way home. The little bird had guided her with her eyes closed, and the country was unknown to her here.

She sat down and started to cry. But even as she cried, she felt a tiny vibration in the folds of her shuka. *She sought it out, and in the pale moonlight saw that it was a bee. A solitary bee.*

It crawled out on to her arm and she was too tired to even flick it away. She expected it to sting her. But it did not sting her. And she asked it: Little bee, I destroyed your home. Why do you not sting me?

Why should I? replied the bee. My home is gone. My children are dead. Stinging you will not bring them back. But you have a mother, and she is missing you. I know this country well. I have gathered nectar from outside your door. Let me show you the way. Come.

And so the little bee flew off, and, tired and hungry, the girl followed its buzz as she had followed the song of the bird.

She followed the buzzing. Just as the bird had done before, the bee stopped and waited every time she stumbled or had to rest. The girl marvelled at the generosity and patience of this tiny insect which had lost everything.

After what seemed like an age, the bee said: We are here.

The girl looked about her. She did not see her boma, *or her hut. She could not smell her mother's cooking or hear the bleats of the flock.*

This is not my home, she said.

No, replied the bee. It was mine.

And then the girl saw the remains of the fire and the bee's nest upon it, broken and burned.

And the bees which had survived, no longer stupid from the smoke, rose from where they had fallen upon the ground, and throbbing with rage, they descended upon the girl.

Wait! she called out. It was not my fault! It was the bird!

But the bee which had brought her there replied: Do you think it matters to us? The bird has flown. But you are here!

And the girl's world went dark as the swarm clouded over the moon.

That was the point in the story when Mollel pulled the coarse blankets over his head. Lendeva would laugh and his mother would stroke him soothingly. He never understood, back then, why the story ended there.

But now, remembering the story for the first time in over three decades, he realised why. It felt as if the cover was being lifted from his head. The story wasn't about the girl. It was about the bees.

His thoughts are interrupted by crashing cymbals and voices raised in song. How long he has lain there, on the leather couch in the green room, he does not know. But he is roused just in time to see George and Wanjiku Nalo enter, all smiles. He hastily lets his eyes fall shut – almost as rapidly as their smiles fall from their faces.

—Don't worry about him, says Benjamin. He's out cold.

Nalo says: —I thought your magic shot was supposed to perk them up, not knock them out.

—It's a mixture of adrenalin and opiates, replies Wanjiku. His file says he's on antipsychotics. No way of predicting what effect that sort of mixture would have.

So they had his police medical records. No surprise, really. Nairobi's not a city to hold secrets long, especially in the face of people as rich as the Nalos and as resourceful as Benjamin.

Still, if they believe him to be no threat, let them. He feels too weak for any confrontation. He's content to let them think he's out cold for a while, and see what he can learn.

—That was damn foolish, what you did on stage, she says. Giving him the chance to speak like that. Whatever possessed you? He'd seen the syringe. He could have denounced us, in front of the whole congregation.

—I knew he wouldn't, says Nalo.

—How could you possibly know that?

Nalo gives a sigh. Mollel hears a chair being dragged from under the table, and creaking under his weight as he sits. — What a trial it is to have a wife of so little faith. You and your chemically enhanced miracles!

—Without my *enhancement* this church would still be in a tin shack in Kibera!

—And without me you'd still be performing back-street abortions! growls Nalo. Do you think they come here to see Wanjiku Nalo? No. They come here to see George Nalo. And your assistance is not always required. I knew this Maasai would not denounce us, because I wasn't healing his hands. I was seeing his *soul*.

Wanjiku lets out an contemptuous snort, but Nalo continues: —I saw what was within him. A real, profound yearning for peace. But that was not all. I saw a fire.

Wanjiku scoffs. —That's hardly a revelation, with two burned hands.

—I saw a fire, and someone lost within it.

—Benjamin told you about the blind man. The one who died in Kibera.

—No, says Benjamin. I didn't.

—It wasn't a man, anyway, says Nalo thoughtfully. It wasn't him. The sense of loss was much greater. It was a woman.

—That just proves you read the papers, retorts Wanjiku. His wife was lost in the bombing, remember? That's why he's crazy.

Nalo, quietly, says: —Maybe that's it. Maybe that's why I saw it. But I had the feeling I was seeing something else. Something not in the past. Something yet to come.

—Your trouble, says Wanjiku, bitterly, is that you believe your own hype. You're just a loudmouth with a knack for reeling off scripture. Without me you'd be nothing.

—Well, says Nalo, it looks like we're going to find out, aren't we?

—What do you mean?

—Why do you suppose he's here?

—He's still investigating Lucy's death, says Wanjiku.

—No, says Nalo. He's finished his investigations. He's come to make an arrest.

Eyes closed, Mollel can nevertheless feel the impact of Nalo's words. Beside him, Benjamin shifts uneasily. And Wanjiku spits: —What do you mean?

Softly, Nalo says: —I know where I was last Friday night, Wanjiku. I was in front of two thousand people at a group baptism ceremony, right here. But where were you?

Mollel hears movement and a sharp intake of breath: he raises his eyelids just enough to make out Nalo holding his wife's wrists. She must have tried to slap him.

—How dare you, she gasps. How could you?

Benjamin has sprung to his feet and pushes Nalo aside.

—Hurt her and I'll kill you.

—Relax, *Mungiki* man. Nalo laughs. She's the one trying to hit me.

He withdraws his hands and Benjamin tries to put his arms around Wanjiku, but she brushes him away.

—You'd like her out of the way, wouldn't you? says Benjamin. No more Orpheus House to get between you and the collection plate?

—I must admit, Orpheus House has been a burden to me.

258

Nalo sighs. Not financially, I don't care about that. But what you do there…

—You see? cries Benjamin to Wanjiku. He's trying to set you up. He'll turn against you, just like I always said he would.

—He won't do it, Benjamin. We've been married thirty years. He won't betray me.

—He betrays you every day, with his hookers and his hangers-on! How can you stand by him, after all you know? After he refused to stand by you?

—Because he will stand by me, replies Wanjiku. You can't understand it, Benjamin, and I don't expect you to. But that's the way it is.

—Will he still stand by you when I tell him where you were on Friday night? Mollel's going to wake up any minute, and he's convinced you murdered Lucy. Will your husband stand by you when I tell Mollel you were with me, all night?

The silence in the room is broken by a strange panting sound. For a moment Mollel is at a loss to identify where it is coming from. Then he realises it is George Nalo. He is laughing.

—Dear Benjamin, he wheezes. Did you think I didn't know about you two? It's part of our arrangement, you know. She turns a blind eye to my indiscretions, and I tolerate hers. It's not like you're the first.

—I'm so sorry, Benjamin, says Wanjiku, quietly.

There is the sudden clatter of a chair falling over and Mollel instinctively opens his eyes. He is afraid that Benjamin might attack Nalo, or Wanjiku – or both. But he sees the young man coming directly towards him.

—You're awake, says Benjamin. Good.

He bends over Mollel, and roughly pulls him into an upright position. He looks deeply into Mollel's eyes. As he does so, Mollel feels Benjamin's hand go into his pocket, as though he's being frisked. It's just for a moment, though, before Mollel is released once more.

—Now you're back with us, you can do what you came here

to do. You can talk to these two about the death of Lucy. Make sure they tell you everything. I can't say you'll get the whole story. But it will make interesting listening.

With that, he casts a final, contemptuous glare at George and Wanjiku Nalo, and storms out of the room.

Wanjiku looks solicitously into Mollel's eyes. —How are you feeling?

He's met the eyes of all three of them, now. He arrived convinced that they'd conspired to murder Lucy. He no longer believes it. But he senses he is close to the truth.

—I feel fine, he says. A bit weak.

—The drugs, she explains. You'll recover soon. How much of that did you hear?

—All of it.

—Then there's no point lying to you. Benjamin was right. He and I were together the night Lucy died. You can check at the hotel we were at. They – she casts her eyes down – they know us there.

Mollel puts his hands on the edge of the sofa to pull himself forward. He winces. The pain, so blissfully absent since the injection on stage, is starting to return.

—So much for your miracles, he says.

Wanjiku sighs. —Define *miracle*, Mollel, she says. In a city like Nairobi, it's a miracle that there's an organisation here that can get people to dig into their pockets to help others. You know how many people partake of our services one way or another? Education, health, welfare? The government's not looking after them, so someone has to. We've got children here who wouldn't be alive today if it wasn't for George Nalo Ministries. And the money doesn't come out of the air. A few miracles here and there are what keep the tithes rolling in. And besides, nobody's really tricking anyone else. The people we perform this on always feel better, even if it's only temporary.

—But it's a fraud, says Mollel.

—Is it? The Lord moves in mysterious ways.

There is a loud knock on the door, and the sound of some kind of scuffle. Mollel hears Benjamin's voice on the other side, and then the noise recedes.

—Tell me what happened at Orpheus House, he says.

—It wasn't the night of Lucy's death, says George Nalo, breaking his silence. There was going to be a baby. We didn't want it to be born in the hospital. Too public. We set up the delivery room in the abandoned house.

—Whose baby was it? asks Mollel.

Wanjiku looks up at him. Her eyes are clouded with tears.

—It was *our* baby, she says. Our miracle baby.

Mollel looks from her to her husband. Nalo has his head in his hands. Wanjiku must be well past childbearing age. But he senses that she does not mean that kind of miracle. Some words come back to him from the orphanage: something Honey had said. *Some of these places take babies away from mothers in the delivery room.*

—Where is the baby now? he asks.

—Dead.

—If, maybe, we'd been able to have our own children, sobs Wanjiku, neither of us would have turned to other people.

George Nalo has extended a hand to his wife. He gently caresses her shoulder. The love between these two is not straightforward. But it is profound.

—I always took it as a sign from God, she continues. A punishment. For what we do. For the babies that never made it. But I thought I was doing the right thing at the time.

—And then Lucy came to us, says Nalo. She told me there was going to be a baby. Unplanned. Unwanted. *My* baby.

—George's baby, repeats Wanjiku. She could give him the baby I never could. And she didn't even want it! Well, *I* did. We would deliver it secretly, at Orpheus House, then process the adoption through the agency. No one would have known any better. There'd be no scandal. George's secret would be safe. And finally, we'd have our baby.

—But the minute I saw it crown, I knew what the problem was. It's called *cyclopia*. Sometimes they're born with one eye, sometimes none. In cases like this, there isn't even a brain to speak of. I did the merciful thing. Even if it had the synapses, the nerve-endings in place, it wouldn't have felt a thing. I did not clamp the umbilical cord before I cut it. The little body drained of blood in a matter of seconds. We told the mother the baby was stillborn. But we never showed her the body. It would have been too distressing.

—So you didn't kill Lucy, says Mollel, quietly. But you did deliver her child.

—You still don't understand, do you, Mollel? says Nalo. *It wasn't Lucy.*

The door bursts open and a group of black-clad figures rush in: ushers. They're all wearing the headsets used to co-ordinate the show. One of them pushes Wanjiku aside and makes straight for Nalo's throat.

—You liar! he shouts. Another, a woman, slaps Wanjiku full in the face.

Mollel feels himself being hauled to his feet. Benjamin, who has come in behind the ushers, hisses in his ear: —We'd better get out of here.

He pulls Mollel past more oncoming figures. Behind them, Mollel can make out Nalo's defensive protestations, being shouted down by an increasingly angry mob.

And the swarm clouded over the moon.

37

Mollel stumbles through the darkness of the cold night air, led by the ex-*Mungiki* man. Above them, the stars swirl lustrously. An infinity of points of light.

Mollel's head reels with the last comment of Nalo's: *It wasn't Lucy.*

Benjamin leads him through the shadows of the church buildings around him. They pick their way through groups of people sitting on the lawns and against the walls, huddled against the chill. They are refugees, overflowing from the main church.

They approach a door. He recognises the building. It is the old schoolroom, the temporary home of Orpheus House.

—What's going on? Mollel asks Benjamin, but the young man puts a finger to his lips. Then he reaches into Mollel's jacket pocket and pulls out the transmitter. He yanks the wire, stripping the bud microphone from Mollel's lapel, and throws the device to the ground. It shatters, and batteries scatter.

Now Mollel understands the presence of the mob in the green room. When Benjamin had checked whether he was conscious, he had reached into Mollel's jacket to turn on the radio microphone.

—I know why you didn't denounce Nalo on stage, says Benjamin. There would have been a riot. And there's enough of that going on beyond these walls. But you gave me the idea. When I realised Wanjiku was using me – well, why shouldn't everyone know?

—But there was no riot, says Mollel.

—The service was over. It didn't go out over the PA. Just the internal system. I kept guard at the door long enough for plenty of the technical staff to hear just exactly the sort of people they're working for. We don't have long. I'm sure Nalo will be able to talk himself out of it, eventually. And I don't want to be here when he does.

Benjamin unlocks the door to the schoolroom and steps in. Mollel follows. Even though he knows it is there, it is a shock to see the gynaecological bench in the half-light. It brings back a chill memory of that blood-soaked night in the other Orpheus House. At least he knows now that he really saw what he saw and it was not, as Kiunga had suggested, the product of his fractured mind.

Benjamin heads away from the bench to the store cupboard. He opens it, its keys jangling on their hooks on the inside of the door.

—If you'd been less concerned with stealing our keys, he says, you might have seen this. It was right on the top of the pile.

He tosses him a slim cardboard folder. Mollel's damaged hands rise to meet it midair but he is unable to grasp it and the folder flaps to the floor, and the contents slide out.

He stoops to pick up a photograph.

—Take a good look, says Benjamin. Whatever you think of Wanjiku, she does not do what she does lightly. The law of this country says it would be more merciful to bring that child to full term, let it gasp for the few pitiful hours it can manage to survive in an incubator somewhere. Let me ask you, is that mercy? Is that God's love?

The photograph is of a baby. Its tiny body is wrinkled, pigmentless, caulked. The umbilical cord is still attached, but it's been cut at the placenta end. There is no clip, or knot on the cut.

The baby – foetus – would have bled to death in a matter of seconds. And above the baby's body, the head. Or what should be a head. There is a chin. An ear is visible. But moving up, there is a sucking, lipless cavity, where the mouth should be. No nose, no eyes. It is a stump. A smooth, rounded, unfinished, unmoulded lump.

—God made a mistake, says Benjamin. Wanjiku was just trying to put it right.

—And that was what you were trying to do when you burned down Orpheus House? Trying to put things right?

—Trying to protect her, says Benjamin.

A wave of relief floods through Mollel. More than the drug which took away his pain, the confirmation that he did not start the fire fills him with gratitude. Now only one uncertainty remains. If Lucy was not the mother of the baby…

He picks up the cardboard folder. In the gloom, Mollel cannot make out for a moment the characters written on the front of the file. Then they form into words.

Mother's name: En'cecoroi e-intoi Kipuri.

The first name, in Maa, means *Honey Guide*.

Honey.

The baby was Honey's.

And the blood all over the floor was the baby's. Wanjiku had probably lost control as she cut the cord. Its final few heartbeats would have sprayed its life fluids everywhere. No wonder it was a scene of horror. No wonder Benjamin returned to torch it.

The photograph of the faceless, headless creature remains in his hand. No wonder, too, that they chose to keep this from Honey.

They take children away from their mothers. They lie to them. Tell them they had a stillborn. Honey's words come back to him. First in disjointed bursts, then a torrent.

Everyone wants a newborn. Do you know what a fresh, healthy baby can fetch on the open market?

265

That baby's out there, alive, somewhere. We've got to find it.

It takes a murder to get anyone's interest around here, and even then, it's only you who seems to care, Mollel.

—Lucy brought her to us, says Benjamin. It was weeks before. Wanjiku knew the child was her husband's. She wanted it for herself. If there was no record of the birth, the adoption could be organised easily through the agency. So we set up the delivery room in Orpheus House. It was basic, but Wanjiku's an expert. If it had been a straightforward birth... But she couldn't do any prenatal scans. If she had, she would have known...

—What were you going to tell Honey? demands Mollel. You'd have taken the baby from her.

—We'd have told her what we did tell her. That it was stillborn. Only we didn't have to lie.

She knew it. No wonder she did not believe them.

—I wanted to bury it, says Benjamin. At least a little human dignity. But then we remembered that the whole site was going to be dug up for the new development. The body would have been found, questions would have been asked.

—That was when I remembered the storm drain. I'd heard it ring hollow under my foot a day or two before. We had to act quickly, in case Githaka, the caretaker, saw us. I scraped away the leaves, lifted the lid, dropped the bundle in. It had just started to rain. The flow was already quite heavy, from farther up the pipe. The bundle just disappeared, like that.

The room falls silent. They can distantly hear a helicopter and wailing voices, and the floating strains of a multitude of voices singing a hymn.

—You know she didn't believe you, says Mollel. She never believed you. She couldn't have. For nine months she'd carried that body inside her own. Felt its heartbeat. Even if it only twitched in reflex, it would have moved for her. She would never have accepted that it could have just died. You should have shown her.

So, this was her plan, thinks Mollel. She used the death of

her friend to guide him towards the Nalos. Towards the non-existent baby. Towards the adoption scam, and the baby she believed had been stolen from her. She hoped that in investigating the murder, Mollel would reunite her with her baby. Perhaps she did believe the Nalos killed her friend. More likely she didn't have a clue. He feels an overwhelming wave of pity for her.

And then he remembers Lucy. If she wasn't killed at Orpheus House, it must have been in the park after all. Killed where she was found. Where the GSU witness had seen a woman that night, with an elderly white man.

He reaches for his phone and turns it on. A message from Kiunga.

JL never showed.

So Lethebridge did not turn up at Central, as he had promised Kingori he would. Hardly surprising.

—James Lethebridge was supposed to wait at home to assist us with our enquiries. But he didn't.

—Lethebridge, says Benjamin quietly. He's the killer?

Mollel does not answer. Instead he asks: —What was he doing here at church, the day I first met you? I saw him.

Benjamin says: —He's the point of contact between us and Kingori. When it looked like Kingori was going to throw out Wanjiku's plans for Orpheus House, turn it into a residential development, we let James Lethebridge know that we had some information on his employer.

—His relationship with Lucy, says Mollel.

—Yes. But he had something on us too.

—The abortions.

Benjamin gives a faint smile. —Yes. Even with the evidence destroyed, he had Lucy to testify to that.

—So it was a stalemate, says Mollel. Until he got rid of Lucy.

He remembers Sammy's words: he heard *two* women's voices. That's how he would have ensured Honey's co-operation and got Lucy out of the way. By killing her friend in front of her, in the most ghastly way possible.

—We've got to find Lethebridge, says Mollel.

—We? asks Benjamin.

—You can't stay here, can you? Besides, I'm going to need you.

38

From up here, the city looks like a million points of light. But the power is off all over Nairobi and, apart from some security lights run from generators in the business district, most of the points are red and flickering.

The city is ablaze.

Benjamin pulls the car into a side street. The reflectors of the silver Toyota Land Cruiser glint in their headlight beams as they pull up. The Toyota is parked tight against a hedge, its front wheels twisted at an angle. A hurried, panicked park. It does not have the air of a car that someone intends to return to.

Benjamin parks next to the car and turns off the engine. He and Mollel step out.

—Kiunga? calls Mollel.

One of the red points of light rises up, glows, and descends. The movement is followed by a cough.

—Here.

Kiunga steps out of the shadow of a nearby tree, exhaling smoke.

—How long have you been waiting? asks Mollel.

—Two cigarettes. Maybe three. Who's your friend?

—This is Benjamin, says Mollel.

—Sorry for hiding in the bushes. But I wasn't expecting you in a car. And when I saw the dreadlocks... You know, the *Mungiki* are out in force tonight.

—That's why I brought him, says Mollel. Security in case we run into one of their roadblocks.

—And he was mine, adds Benjamin, in case we were stopped by the police. I stole plenty of vehicles in my bad old days. But I never had a serving officer ride shotgun with me before.

—It's a stolen car? Kiunga asks Mollel with surprise.

—George Nalo's, says Mollel with a shrug. Paid for by his congregation. How did you track Lethebridge's car down to here?

—After I tried to get Lethebridge at home, and he wouldn't answer the door, says Kiunga, I had a watch put on the place.

—A watch? But this is an unofficial investigation, how did you manage it?

—Strictly unofficially, Kiunga answers. Seems like the guy I chose has done a good job, though.

—No one gave me a second glance, says a boy's voice. A ragged, bare-footed figure appears from the darkness.

—Panya!

Mollel pats the boy on the back. It was a good idea of Kiunga's. A *chokora* is as good as invisible in Nairobi, even on the genteel streets of Lavington.

—He drove out of the house about an hour ago, Panya says. The only problem I had was persuading anyone to take me from the house. None of the taxi drivers wanted to take me, or believed I could pay them. The roads are all blocked, one way or another, anyway. Eventually I got a *boda-boda* who let me sit on the back. We had to do a lot of talking to get through. And a lot of riding around before we found this.

—Good work, says Mollel.

He goes to inspect the Toyota. He notes once more the scrape on the front fender. He opens the door. Looks inside. Nothing in the rear. Nothing on the seats. He climbs into the driver's seat, leans across, and opens the glove compartment. The car's instruction manual, nothing else. Typical company car. He folds down the sun visors, feels inside the seat pockets, opens the ashtrays. Nothing. Nothing. Nothing.

He slaps the steering wheel in frustration. It rattles. He looks closer. The central boss consists of a plastic shell, which is loose. He prises it off. Underneath, the car's airbag is loosely wedged in, crammed ineptly into its space. It's been deployed at some point and stuffed back into place.

Otherwise, there's nothing more to be learned from the car.

—He must have gone on from here on foot, says Mollel to Kiunga. What's near by?

—There's lots of office buildings, says Kiunga. Company headquarters, that type of thing. But none of them would be open now. More likely he's gone to one of the posh hotels. There's the Fairmont, the Panafric. It's easy enough to check those out. They're not your sleazy downtown fleapits. You have to show ID when you sign in. We'll just ask if they've had any British passport holders arrive in the last couple of hours.

British passport holders.

Mollel slaps the side of the Toyota.

—The British high commission, he says. He's gone to the British high commission.

—Of course, says Kiunga. That's why he's left his car. They won't allow anyone to leave a civilian vehicle *close* to that place. Not since … well, you know what.

Mollel knows what.

—I heard on the radio, they're evacuating British citizens, says Kiunga. Once he goes through those doors he'll be on British soil. We've lost him.

—We'll have to hope he's not got in yet. We'll get there quicker if we do what he did, and leave the car here. Benjamin, can you look after Panya? And the Toyota. We may need it for evidence. Cars like these won't stay unnoticed long.

—Don't worry, says Benjamin, with a grin. Chances are, anyone we meet from now on is going to be *Mungiki*. And I still hold some sway with my former brothers.

*

The two policemen take off on foot down a side street. There's a cut-through at the end which leads out on to the road where the British high commission is situated.

It's a wide, low fortress of a building. Built with the attack on the US embassy very much in mind. Concrete blast barriers divide the road. Signs at regular intervals exhort *No Stopping, No Dropping*. A phalanx of guards – a mixture of Kenyan police and private security – line the area in front of the high commission. But they're not preventing people from going through. A small crowd has gathered at a tiny reinforced glass window in the bare black slate wall. A sign above it reads *Enquiries*.

—My sister lives in Manchester, one woman is sobbing. You've got to let me in. The woman behind the bullet-proof glass is diligently avoiding eye contact with everyone on the outside. Instead, she points to a hastily handwritten notice which has been taped to the inside: *British Nationals Only Will be Admitted*.

—Have you had – Mollel pushes himself to the front – have you had a James Lethebridge come here?

—Wait your turn, please, sir, she replies, with barely disguised contempt.

—I'm police, he says, showing his ID card.

—You'll still have to wait your turn. She studiously turns away. An Indian-looking man grabs Mollel's shirt.

—You're police, he says. Can't you do something? I can't get back to my home. I can't get my passport to prove that I'm British. And these racists… I'm from Wembley. I'm only here visiting my cousins.

Other people seem to be latching on to the idea that Mollel is some kind of official. In their desperation they paw at him, implore him.

—Stand back, stand back! Kiunga comes to his assistance.

—I'm sorry, I'm sorry, says Mollel. There's nothing I can do. He and Kiunga walk away from the Enquiries window.

—We'll never be able to raise an arrest warrant before he leaves the country, says Kiunga, downcast. It'll be an extradition job, now, and what chance do you think we have of that?

—None, says Mollel.

They pass another entrance, darkened and locked. The sign says *Visa Office*, with a list of weekday opening hours. In front of it is a hard metal bench. A private security guard is rousing a huddled figure.

—Come on, you can't stay here, he is saying.

—Please! implores the man on a bench. I'm British! Can't you just let me stay here, even if you won't let me in?

—You've been told, sir. No passport, no entry.

The man stands.

—Just look at me! he says. He has a white face, white hair. He pulls up his sleeve to reveal pallid, white skin. Do I look Kenyan? Of course I'm British!

Mollel walks over and shows his ID to the security guard.

—I'll take care of this, he says.

—Just get him out of here, says the security guard. He says he's British, but his passport is Kenyan. That means he must have wanted to be Kenyan, once. I guess he reckons it's not such a privilege any more.

The security guard walks away.

—Hello, Mr Lethebridge, says Mollel.

James Lethebridge looks at him, takes him in. A slow, creeping realisation spreads over his face.

—You must be Mollel, Lethebridge says. David told me you were coming for me, Sergeant. But I didn't expect to see you here.

Kiunga nods. —You need to come with us. There's no point trying to resist.

—Thank God.

A rueful smile plays across Lethebridge's lips. —I can assure you, officers, I won't resist, he continues. I'd rather go with the sheepdogs than be cast to the wolves.

39

On their way back to the cars, the sound of gunfire makes them pick up their pace.

—That's pretty close, says Mollel.

—The opposition have called for a mass rally in Uhuru Park tomorrow, says Kiunga. I heard a rumour that some of them were planning to attack the GSU base there tonight. If they do, they'll have to come right through here.

—We'd better not stick around, then.

Panya and Benjamin are waiting for them beside Lethebridge's Toyota. George Nalo's car is gone.

—You guys took your time, Benjamin says. There was a gang of guys here a few minutes ago. Not *Mungiki*, but regular looters, out for what they could get. Some of them had pangas. They wanted to take both cars, but they were happy enough when I handed them the keys to Nalo's. I guess the Lord giveth, and the Lord taketh away.

A casual observer might consider the occupants of the silver Toyota Land Cruiser a strange assembly: two smart young men in front, the passenger dreadlocked; a gaunt, ashen Maasai and an elderly white man in the back seat, and, hunched on the jump seat in the rear, looking out through the glass, a ragged street boy taking his first ever ride in a car.

But there are no casual observers on the streets tonight:

no disinterested parties, no innocent bystanders.

They pass groups of men – and some boys – headed, it seems, for Uhuru Park. They walk purposefully, lithe limbs swinging. And something – sticks, or clubs, or *pangas* – bouncing at their sides.

As if to break the tension, Lethebridge chuckles.

—You know, he says, you really managed to wind up Kingori, after you interviewed him that first time. He told me to hide up at home, to say nothing to you. But he was genuine when he phoned me from the KICC and instructed me to co-operate. How did you get him to change his mind?

—More to the point, says Mollel, turning to face him, why did you decide to flee? I had the impression you always obeyed his instructions to the letter.

Lethebridge casts his eyes out of the window, into the darkness beyond. —I've never pretended to be a very brave man, he says, quietly. I had the feeling that whatever happened next, David wouldn't be able to protect me any more.

Kiunga drives them on a zigzag route through Upper Hill. He wants to avoid the main roads and ill-frequented ones alike, choosing a fine middle passage of routes which are unlikely to attract attention but wide enough to avoid an ambush.

—Let me tell you a bit about David Kingori, continues Lethebridge. He seems to be in the mood to chat, as a reaction to tension, or relief. Do you know we were at school together? In England. He was the first black African in the school. How the other boys used to mock him! They would steal his jumper, ask him how he liked the cold. But he just smiled and told them he was fine.

—I was the one who was homesick. I'd been told all my life that England was my home, yet when I turned up there, I pined for the African air. No wonder I clung to David. He was all I had.

—We were a strange pair. We'd been raised together. My father and his were in business together. It didn't start that way. Before I was born, my father owned a six-hundred-acre tea estate near Kericho. David's father was the farm manager. But when independence came, my father decided it would be politic to appoint a local partner. Somehow, every year, there were reasons why more and more of the business had to be signed over to Kingori. Eventually my father became the employee.

Lethebridge gives a hoarse laugh. —He thought it was so unfair. He never really stopped to question the policy of the old colonial administration which had given him the land in the first place.

They seem to have outstripped most of the gangs, and the sidewalks are mostly clear as they start to descend the hill which runs down to the park. There, in the darkness, is Orpheus House – or what is left of it. Mollel looks over his shoulder as they pass, but makes out nothing more than a glimpse of the *Coming Soon* sign. Behind him, in the jump seat, Panya is asleep.

—David took over the business after we finished school. He gave me a job. I think he enjoyed having a white man work for him. Gave him a certain kudos. But more importantly than that, he knew he could trust me.

—Part of my job, even from early on, was to find him girls. I didn't mind. I just enjoyed the fact that I was bringing him pleasure. I knew they never meant anything to him. I gave him the unquestioning devotion he needed. They gave him everything else.

—Lucy was different. She had something else that he needed. Information.

—The Nalos were pressing David for the lease of Orpheus House. He wanted the land for development, but with George Nalo's following and political clout, he did not dare evict them. She had been part of their operation. For a while, when she had wanted to get out of the game, she had gone there, been taken in. She knew what went on. She told me about the abortions. How Wanjiku was a fanatic. She thought she was saving the babies from a life of suffering, Lucy told us. Better off dead, than on the street.

*

Mollel looks at Benjamin. The back of his head betrays no emotion, no indication he's even listening. He's too astute to interrupt Lethebridge's flow now. The old man had shown no sign of recognising him from the church. Probably thought he was another police officer. Mollel can't help thinking he would have made a fine one.

—I didn't want to trouble David with the details, continues Lethebridge. I knew that this was what we needed to get the Nalos off our back. Their empire would have been ruined, if it was revealed. Once they were gone, it would also rid him of this troublesome girl, too. Get things back to how they were. But I needed more than one woman's hearsay. I needed evidence.

—Then, Lucy told me she had something on the Nalos which was dynamite. A friend of hers had got pregnant by George Nalo, and had been given an abortion by Wanjiku. Late-term, too. Testimony like that would ruin them. They'd have to do what we wanted.

—Lucy was offering her friend up on a plate. I'd give her enough money to disappear, once I had the girl. But Lucy didn't trust me, any more than I trusted her. She wouldn't give me her friend's name. Wouldn't tell me where to find her. We had to meet her together.

—She had a plan. I would pose as a punter. Her friend wasn't working at that time. It was still too soon after the operation. But she had agreed to help out Lucy. She could do with some money.

Descending Upper Hill, Kiunga drives through the red light at the junction with Haile Selassie Avenue. As they sweep around a curve, the black frontage of the gardens appears, lined with the imposing presence of GSU. Over their helmets and beyond their shields, Mollel can make out the tented field hospital and the command trucks. The car continues parallel to the picket, skimming the edge, somewhere behind that cordon, of the scene of the crime. Even at speed, the scraped concrete bollard is visible as the car which damaged it glides past.

—That's where you did it, says Mollel.

—That's where it happened, confirms Lethebridge. That's where they got me. They got me with the old twofer.

—Twofer?

—It's a classic hooker's trick. A good way of earning money if you don't want to go through with the act.

—I cruised down K-Street at a prearranged time. Lucy came to the window. I acted like we'd never met before. She played it by the book.

—We spoke. She looked over at her friend nervously. She was playing it great. *Look*, she said, *there have been some strange characters around here lately. Do you mind if my friend comes along?*

—I acted reluctant. *Oh, I don't know*, I said. Then she winked and said: *We'll give you a twofer. Two-for-one.* Well, I mean, who could have resisted? I played along. Lucy got in beside me, and her friend smiled as she got into the back.

—She was lovely. Tall, slender. My tastes don't run in that direction, Sergeant, as you might have guessed. But this girl. I might have made an exception, if I'd been a few years younger. She had a way about her. Her smile was seductive. It made you want to forget about everything, all the troubles of the world, and just give yourself up to her. Do you know what I mean?

Mollel knows what he means. —What happened next? he says. Honey got into the car, then what?

—Honey? says Lethebridge with surprise. Is that her name?

—That's her name.

—Honey, repeats Lethebridge, softly. Well, Lucy got into the front, next to me, and Honey slipped in behind. The plan was that I'd take them to the park. It was near by, it was private. Once there, Honey would not be able to run away. And hopefully, we'd be able to persuade her to speak.

—But as we went in through the park gate, I felt a sudden

278

pain. I didn't know what it was. I thought it was a heart attack. My time was up at last. I could not breathe.

Lethebridge fingers his neck thoughtfully.

—You see, the thing about the twofer was that it was all a ruse. The girls would get into the punter's car, get him to drive them somewhere secluded, then mug him. But Honey had obviously decided not to wait for the car to stop. She'd grabbed the seat belt and was pulling it as hard as she could. I was just aware of her knee in my back, pressing through the seat, the stabbing pain. Trying to reach for the buckle… Then we hit something. And I don't know what happened next.

—When I came to, my face was in the airbag, and the girls were gone. I thought at first they'd double-crossed me, but my wallet was still in my pocket. I got out. As my eyes grew used to the dark, I could just see them some distance away, up ahead. I could hear them too. It sounded like they were arguing.

—Honey was screaming. I could not make it out. Something about losing her baby. Lucy was saying *no, no*. I was groggy. I could hardly walk. By the time I got to them, I couldn't see Lucy any more. Just Honey, standing over the ditch.

Then she jumped in. I looked down. Lucy was in there, sprawled. And Honey was on top. I couldn't see what she was doing. I thought that Lucy had fallen, that Honey was trying to revive her. I was dizzy. So dizzy.

—I must have collapsed, because the next thing I knew, Honey was leading me back to the car. Her hands were wet on my arm. When I opened the car door and the light came on, I saw that she was covered in blood.

—*You say anything about this*, she told me, and I'll do to you what I did to her. *You understand?*

—I had no doubt she meant it, Sergeant. Her eyes were wild. When David phoned me and told me to co-operate with the police, I panicked. I knew she would come and get me. Do to me what she did to her friend. I just wanted to get away from here, get out of this country. As far away as possible.

—She told me to drop her somewhere. I can't remember

where. All the way she was muttering, *They took my baby away, they took my baby away.*

—*They took her baby away,* Mollel remembers Honey saying. *Can you even imagine what that's like, Mollel? Now Faith's trying to do the same to you. But don't worry. I'll never let that happen, Mollel. I'll never let that happen to you.*

He thinks of Kawangware, of Faith's house. Where Honey is. With Adam. And with Faith.

—Stop the car!

They're past the park now, on the deserted roundabout at the head of University Way. Barely half a kilometre from Central Police Post. But Mollel's tone of urgency compels Kiunga to come to a screeching halt halfway around the traffic circle.
Mollel opens the door and leaps out.
—Where are you going? cries Kiunga.
—Take him to Central, orders Mollel.
—You're going after Honey? Let me drive you!
—You heard what Panya said. The streets in that part of town are blocked off. No car's going to get through. I just about might.
—Leave her until morning, protests Kiunga, making to turn off the engine. But Benjamin steadies his hand.
—I've seen this man jump into fire, he says. You're not going to stop him.
And he turns to wish him well, but Mollel is already gone.

40

He runs.

Sometimes he passes a group headed in the opposite direction, towards the city centre. The boys – sometimes there are boys with them – cheer him as he passes, as though he is running a race. They wave their *pangas* aloft in support. But the men hardly cast him a glance. They pace on, determinedly. To them he is a Night Runner, and might as well be invisible. They have no concern with the otherworldly this night.

He runs through deserted suburban streets. Walls blank and windows barred. Hurlingham, Dagoretti, Lavington – church placards and business signs mark off the names of the neighbourhoods, but there is nothing neighbourly about them this night.

I won't let her take your child from you, Mollel.

He feels no pain, no fatigue. The urgency of his mission impels him: the act of running, too, recalls youthful days of trotting for hours behind the herd. Perhaps it's also the Nalos' miracle cure which gives him the heightened perception now, to see it all so clearly.

Honey wouldn't know, yet, that he had discovered she was the killer. She still needed him. She needed him because she believed her baby was alive, and had been farmed out to adoption by the Nalos. That was why she had led him to them, Mollel

281

understands now. She thought that if she exposed their racket, by blaming them for Lucy's death, the adoption agency would be investigated. She'd be able to track down her baby. Get it back.

So it is essential he does not alert her. When he gets to them, he must maintain the pretence. At least until Faith is safe.

As he nears Faith's house, where middle-class Lavington merges into Kawangware, he begins to hear the sound that's become so familiar in the last few days. It's the sound of breaking glass, of cries, of screams. Of women and children bawling in fear and men boiling with rage.

He hadn't expected the trouble to spread this far. Kibera and Mathare, sure. They were tinder just waiting for a match. It didn't take much to set those districts up in flames. But sleepy little Kawangware, with its up-and-coming pretensions?

Then he remembers the good-for-nothings who had been hanging round outside Faith's house on Christmas Day. They'd skulked off soon enough once Kiunga had sent them on their way. But he had no doubt that on a night like this, they'd be looking for scores to settle.

His heart pounds violently as he realises it's not just Faith in danger – but Adam. And Honey, too, for that matter. Anyone inside that property would be a Kikuyu, as far as an angry, drunken mob was concerned. And the Kikuyus have just stolen the election – haven't they?

People are heading past him in the other direction. Not the male gangs of before – these are nearly all women and children. He stops one woman – bent nearly double under the weight of a sleeping child strapped in a *khanga* on her back – and asks her: —What's going on?

—The GSU, she answers breathlessly. They've bottled up Kawangware.

He picks up his pace. He hopes that, somehow, the GSU might agree with Faith's silly snobbery, and decide that her house was in Lavington. Place their blockade a couple of streets to the west, with her on the safe side. But he knows they won't have. It would make no sense. The broad strip of James Gichuru Road was the natural defensive position to take. Rounding a corner, he sees with dread that he is right. A heavy line of riot officers, with trucks and armoured vehicles, is stationed at the junction of James Gichuru and Gitanga Road, completely cutting off Kawangware. The residents of Lavington might feel grateful for the barrier. But it means that inside Kawangware, anything could happen.

And it probably is happening right now, to judge by the constant arc of missiles which rain down upon the GSU troops. Mollel runs, zigzag, seeing a flash of flame whoosh past his eyes just an instant before a glass bottle explodes on the ground next to him. His legs are splashed with cold liquid and the oily stench of fuel oil fills his nostrils: he wipes his leg with his hand and rubs the viscous fluid between his fingers. The sting on his burned flesh makes him catch his breath. Then he steps on, and extinguishes, the already dying flame of the rag tied around the neck of the bottle. He counts himself lucky that whoever filled it didn't know the difference between diesel and petrol. But he might not be so lucky next time: he can already see blue flames spreading over the roof of one of the GSU trucks, the men near by scrambling to douse it with an extinguisher.

Mollel pushes himself towards the front but can't get through the line: the GSU men have interlocked their arms, shields forward. They are so intent on the mob facing them that they don't even appear to notice him trying to weave his way in.

He gives up, exasperated. He starts to look for an alternative way around, but the troops have blocked off the only way in and out. He can even see the green corrugated iron roof of Faith's house, just a few dozen metres away. At least it looks intact. He hopes that Faith would have had the common sense to snatch up Adam and make a dash for it while she still had the chance. But knowing Faith, he feels sure she would not have left her home. Which means that she, Honey and Adam are still in there.

—Hey! What the hell do you think you're doing? Grab him!

Mollel feels himself grasped on both sides and spun around. He is face to face with the pugnacious features of a GSU sergeant.

—Take him away, boys. Give him a good going over. I don't want to see his ugly face again.

Then his eyes screw up. He scrutinises Mollel more closely. —Hang on a moment, he says. Haven't I seen your ugly face before?

—You're Mwathi, says Mollel. I'm one of the police officers investigating the murder down in Uhuru Park. You said your daughter was the same age as the victim.

Mwathi's face breaks into a broad smile. —Let him go, boys, he says. He's one of us.

Mollel is roughly released. —That's the first time I've been called *one of us* by a GSU man, he says.

—We're all in this together now, says Mwathi. Unless, of course, you'd rather be in there, with *them*.

He nods his head towards the crowd beyond the line.

—Actually, says Mollel, I would.

Mwathi laughs incredulously. —Are you insane? They'd rip you apart.

—I don't think so. I'm not in uniform. And no one's going to think I'm a Kikuyu, with these ears. As far as I'm aware, no one's turned on the Maasai, yet.

—Give it time, says Mwathi. Give it time. So why do you want to throw yourself into that lion's den? Feeling suicidal?

—My family's in there.

Mwathi's eyes flicker with pity. —Where are they?

—In a house near the edge. If you could just push the cordon forward a block…

Mwathi shakes his head. —We can't do it. We're having enough difficulty holding the line as it is. Look, if they're inside a house, they'll probably be all right, if they just keep their heads down. Then, when it gets calmer…

Mollel squeezes the sergeant's arms tighter. Feels the agony in his hands. —I can't wait, he implores. They're in danger. The killer. The killer of the girl in the park. The killer's in there too. With my family.

He feels his knees begin to buckle. Mwathi looks down at him, sceptical at first. But his face changes as he realises that Mollel is telling the truth.

—The murderer's with your family? he asks.

—I didn't know. Mollel is gasping. I didn't know. I thought they would be safe.

—This is what we'll do, says Mwathi, pulling Mollel to his feet. I'll let you through. But you'll have to take your chances. If you make it to the house, you got to stay there. You understand? Don't try to get out. Not until all this is over.

—OK, says Mollel.

—And as for that murderer, says Mwathi, you do what you've got to do. Kill him, if you need to. No one's going to ask any questions about another body round here, come morning. Give me your ID.

—What? Why?

—You won't want it in there.

He's right: if Mollel gets robbed or searched, his police ID would be as good as a death sentence. But he feels denuded handing it over. His uniform, now this. It's as though he's been stripped of everything which marked him out as a policeman. Now he's just a man.

Mwathi rattles his stick against the helmets of two GSU men on the front line. —When I give the order, let this one through, he bellows. Close ranks immediately afterwards. Now!

The two men unlock their arms and Mwathi pushes Mollel through the gap. He immediately stumbles on a brick; Mwathi shouts: —Good luck. And sorry!

—For what?

—For this, cries Mwathi, as he brings his stick down on Mollel's shoulder. The pain courses through him. But he understands: Mwathi is giving him a chance with the mob. He takes his cue, and runs, head down, towards the opposing line.

41

The blow from the stick did the trick: welcoming arms greet him and pull him in. His dishevelled state is the perfect alibi. No one questions that he is anything other than a fellow rioter unlucky enough to have tasted summary GSU justice.

—Come, brother, says a voice with a thick Luo accent. You can't stay here.

He is helped, hobbling, through the throng of angry voices, to rest on a concrete kerbstone. His rescuer kneels beside him and glares into Mollel's face with angry eyes.

—What did they do to you, those bastards? he hisses.

—I was just trying to get home, mumbles Mollel, weakly.

The young man in front of him shakes his head. —They've been waiting a long time for this, he says. Those Kikuyu thieves shared out the country when the English left. They were happy to share with the Kalenjins when Moi was in power. But now it's time for the Luos! The Luos and the Luhyas, together we outnumber them. It's our turn! And yet, what do we get? This! Here, let me see your hands. You're injured, my brother.

Mollel is struck by the simple concern which the stranger shows him – in stark counterpoint to the visceral hatred in his words. Mwathi, too, on the other side, had shown him humanity. Was this always to be the way, that Kenyans would be capable of individual kindness, and group animosity?

He thinks about David Kingori on the roof of the KICC,

supervising the ballot-rigging. For all his vainglorious words about the Kikuyu homeland, Mollel never had the feeling that he was motivated by tribalism. Rather, that he was part of a deeply entrenched elite, and was desperate to dig himself in deeper.

But Mollel feels the point would be lost on his new-found saviour. Instead, he asks: —What's happening farther inside?

The young man shrugs. —Some of the shops have been looted. The Kikuyu-owned ones, mainly. Your family should be all right, if they're Maasai. You lot aren't part of this.

—I seem to recall an old Kikuyu woman who lives near here, says Mollel. Do you know what's happened to her?

—Her time will come, says the young man, bitterly. Her house is well protected. We've not had a chance to clear out all the cockroaches yet. But if the GSU keep us shut up here all night, there'll be plenty of opportunity.

—Thanks for your assistance, says Mollel, rising. As he does so, there is a flash of light and a cheer goes up: a petrol bomb has obviously hit an enemy target. The young man bends to lift the kerbstone Mollel had been sitting on. He prises it up, and the last Mollel sees of him, he is carrying it toward the chaos.

Mollel looks around him. The street lights are out, but in the glare of the fires he can see the familiar junction of the side street running to Faith's house. He walks past the point where Kiunga caught Adam on his bike. As he approaches, he sees, with relief, that the house seems to be unscathed, apart from some graffiti scrawled on the high metal gate.

He stretches and looks over, between the spiked bars which run along the top. The power is out in the whole neighbourhood, but the diffuse glow of a candle or kerosene lamp flickers somewhere behind the kitchen window. He bangs on the gate – nervously at first, afraid of attracting unwanted attention – then louder. A shadow falls across the window, but there is no other sign of movement from within. Why should there be? They're probably terrified.

He contemplates his options. Shouting would not be heard

above the general racket outside. Throw a stone – but that would only send them scurrying for refuge deeper inside the house. Scale the gate – but the spikes on top are cruel, and expressly designed to keep people out. Crueller still is the sparkling razor wire which Faith had recently installed: but her prescience had at least kept the family safe so far. The place was impenetrable.

—So you decided to join us after all?

It is his friend with the kerbstone. It's gone now, and in its place he carries a length of metal pipe. He's not alone. There's a mob of them, a breakaway group from the front line. Mollel thinks he recognises some of the lads whom Kiunga had warned off the place a few days previously. They're drunk: some of them are carrying what looks like *chang'aa* in plastic bottles. But they also carry pangas and other makeshift weapons. He does not doubt their ability to use them. He steps back slightly, casting his face into the shadows.

—There's no getting out of Kawangware tonight, the young man says. We might as well settle some scores while we're stuck here.

They're not drinking from their bottles, Mollel realises. That's not *chang'aa*. It's petrol.

—I've just been checking this place out, he blusters. It's not worth it. The security's pretty tight. Even if we did get in, one GSU push forward would see us trapped in there like rats.

This brings a laugh from the men. —They're not going to push forward, says one. Not if they know what's good for them.

—I heard that one of the old woman's relatives is a policeman, chimes in another.

—Exactly! says Mollel. That's the sort of trouble we don't need.

—All the more reason to torch the place, says one lad, pushing forward. He is in Mollel's face, and Mollel's suspicions are confirmed: he was one of those hanging around on Christmas Day.

—I know the policeman, too. I think he's the father of the little boy who lives here.

Mollel tries to quell the anger that is consuming him. A fight with these men now would leave him dead, and useless to those inside. Measuredly, quietly, he says: —Oh, yeah?

—Yeah, slurs the lad. I seen him teaching the kid how to ride his bike. Even spoke to him once. Cocky Kikuyu bastard. Thinks he knows how to speak jaLuo.

He means Kiunga, Mollel realises. Still the lad looks him up and down, as though trying to place the face. But he's too drunk to make the connection.

—I'll have that bike, when we're done with the people inside, shouts another one of the men. I bet she's got lots of other nice things in there, too.

He wants to fight them. He wants to grab a panga out of one of their hands and kill them all, slash them to pieces. This is what it takes, he thinks, even as his heart is pounding. This is what it takes to have the rage inside you to kill. To cut people up. When someone threatens your family, your child. Threatens to take away everything you have and destroy everything you love. And there's no recourse to law, no appeal to order. No one will protect you and no one will stand up for you and fight on your behalf. All you can do is kill.

This is what Honey felt.

This is what is destroying Kenya.

—Wait a minute, wait a minute, he says, hurriedly. You've got something there. The old woman, she's pretty well off, yeah? I bet she's even got money stuffed under her mattress. All Kikuyus do. Right. So the last thing we want to do is burn the place down. She's got stuff in there that we need.

He can sense the others taking in his argument. Greed and envy beginning to overcome even hatred. —So look, he continues. Let me get in there. Help me over the wall. I'll open up the gate, get access to the house. Then we can help ourselves. What do you say, boys?

The proposal is met with a cheer. But Mollel's sense of relief is short lived. He's bought himself some time. But even if he manages to get Adam, Faith and Honey out of there, he's still got to get them past the mob. And they won't be satisfied with looting the property. They're out for blood.

—You, says Mollel. The way I saw you pick up that kerbstone, you can definitely lift a skinny guy like me. Come on, give me a boost.

Now the decision's been made, he doesn't want to give anyone time to think about it. Hands are cupped, and Mollel steps into them. —Now on three, I need you all to push me over. OK?

He counts. On his count of three, he is impelled upwards, higher than he had expected, so he fails to grasp the smooth metal at the base of the spikes, but places his hands, raw flesh down, on the top of them. His impetus has given him just enough thrust to avoid bringing his hands down with force; instead, he pitches his palms down, against the rear of the spikes, and pushes himself forward. His trouser leg gets caught and rips, and he is thrown on to the gravel the other side of the gate head first. But at least, he thinks, as he staggers to his feet, he was not impaled.

There is a cheer from the other side. He makes a show of examining the inside of the gate. —It's padlocked, he calls. Wait here. I'll try to get into the house. Don't try to follow me. They may be armed.

—Get a move on, one of them urges him.

He runs to the kitchen window. Like all the windows of the house, it is barred. Inside, he can see a kerosene lamp burning on the table. But no one there. He bangs on the glass. —Faith? Honey? It's me, Mollel!

It's no good. He dare not shout too loudly for fear of the men outside the gate hearing him. And he can only imagine the fear that Adam, Faith and Honey must be feeling now, listening to someone banging on the windows and shouting.

Strange, he thinks, how he's still concerned about Honey. He knows that she killed Lucy – and he's convinced that she has the capacity to be a real threat to Faith. But somehow, thinking of the old woman and the young boy huddled in fear inside the house, he's glad that Honey is there, with them.

Then he thinks: *She's not Chiku.*

It comes as a shock to him, the realisation that he'd been carving out that role for her. But it had felt good at the time, the comfort she had provided him, the protection which he felt he was providing for her. He feels angry, foolish: she's suckered him. She is a professional. It is what she does.

All his assumptions about Honey have been wrong. He can't assume that Faith is safe, now: he hopes that Honey will be rational enough not to harm her while she still thinks he is on her side. But after what she's done to her friend…

He can't even assume Adam is safe.

He picks up a flowerpot and smashes the kitchen window. —Faith! He hisses through the gap. Damn these bars. Honey? Adam?

—What are you doing? comes a voice from over the gate. He looks back, sees a row of eyes watching him.

He knows where they will be. There's a store cupboard off the main hallway that has no windows, no external wall. It's the safest place in the house. If they haven't already taken shelter there, they will do now they've heard the breaking glass. They're unreachable.

He walks round the house, looking in the other windows, hoping for a glimpse of someone, a point of contact. But there is none.

—Come on, Maasai, booms a voice once more. Get a move on, or we'll storm the place.

The last time he prowled around a house like this, it was Orpheus House. Getting in there had been simple, once he had the key. He remembers the standing ruins, the roof caved in. It must have burned to the ground in minutes. Just as on this house, the roof was a flimsy corrugated metal construction, with only wooden joists and a thin layer of ceiling board below: fine for keeping the rain off, but deadly in a fire, when the whole structure would come crashing down. He desperately hopes none of the thugs outside are getting impatient to use their petrol.

The roof – of course. He runs back to the kitchen, where a water butt stands by the door, and hefts himself up on it. From there it is a fairly easy scramble up the downpipe, using the guttering as a handhold, to get on to the metal roof. He edges along – luckily the pitch is relatively shallow – until he feels a row of galvanised nails under his throbbing hands.

His theory is simple: rather than attempt to breach the seam between two sheets of metal, he'll start at the bottom edge, and pull. Hopefully, once the first set of nails gives way, he'll be able to use leverage to pull out enough to peel the sheet back.

He stands at the edge. Even this single-storey height gives him a dizzying feeling, with the fires and confusion just beyond the compound fence. The mob of men waiting at the gate holler and hoot at him. He casts them a wave of acknowledgement, then crouches and grasps the edge.

His hands flash with pain. But he defies it: feet spread, he heaves, the metal edge cutting into his raw, damaged flesh.

Nothing happens.

It's going to be harder than he had imagined. Looking down, he sees that the sheets lap each other, so that one side is pinned down by the next. With a crowbar it would be easy enough, but…

—Hey! he shouts to the men outside. I need a bar, or something.

The man who had picked up the kerbstone waves his metal pipe in the air. —How about this?

—Perfect, yells Mollel. The man raises the pipe and pitches it, spinning, over the wall. It sails in an arc towards Mollel, who ducks, and it crashes with a clatter on to the roof, and immediately begins to roll downward. Mollel dives and grasps it just as it teeters over the edge.

With the pipe in hand, he sets to work prising the edge of the metal sheet free. Raising one corner, he is now able to get a purchase on the sheet he wants to lift.

He strains again. It's slippery, this time: his blood runs along the edge. It's still not moving. A jeer rises up from the watching mob.

—Come on, Maasai, one of them yells. If you get in, you can have first go on the old woman!

He pulls again, gasping. Every muscle in his body is part of this effort. Pain burns through him. When he feels something give, just the minutest of shifts, he thinks at first it is his own body giving way. But it is not. It is the metal. Another heave, and it comes again, more definitely this time. He scrambles to realign his hands on the greasy sheet. And heaves.

With a creak, the sheet begins to come free. He pulls, and nails pop from their positions. One final effort, and he folds the sheet back, revealing a gap just wide enough for him to squeeze through. The mob cheer him, and he can't help casting them a grin and a triumphant wave, as he edges round, and down, and in.

42

He thinks of the mice, or rats, which had scuttled in the roof of Orpheus House. Now he is the one padding carefully across the rafters. He tries to recall where the hatch is, but can't even picture the layout of the rooms below.

—Faith? Honey? It's me. Mollel.

No sound. And nothing to see, either. The faintest glimmer of light leaks in from the hole he forced in the roof. He feels his way along the rafters with his feet, picking his path under crossbeams and over water pipes.

He pauses: against the sound of the clamour from outside, he thinks he hears a noise. He listens, trying to separate the strands of sound; that which is outside from that which is below.

It is prayer.

Unmistakably, directly beneath his feet, he hears prayer. Faith's voice: the Lord's Prayer. He bends his head down to be sure. Moves around so that he can bring his ear to lie flat against the board of the ceiling of the room below.

A blade thrusts up right in front of his eyes. It pulls down, leaving a hole, a sliver of streaming light. He cries out.

—No, no! It's me!

The blade appears again, between his legs. It's a *panga*, probably the one that Faith uses to cut plants in her garden. He recoils, feels himself toppling backwards from his perch on the rafter. He feels his back hitting the ceiling board, and it giving

294

below him, and with a sickening, split-second splintering, it breaks, and he free-falls, landing with a crash and a cloud of dust on the floor of the hallway of Faith's house.

He blinks. Dazed. Looks up. Honey is standing over him, the small, curved blade of Lucy's knife in her hand. Beyond her, through the doorway of the store cupboard, he can see Faith standing on a box, the panga raised. Adam is at her feet.

—Dad!

—Thank God it's you, cries Faith. We thought it was those *wamera* trying to get in. What have you done to my home, Mollel?

—Any closer with that panga, he says, and I'd have been circumcised a second time.

As he rises to his feet, he is almost knocked over once more by a sudden oncoming rush. He feels warm limbs around his neck and skin against his cheek. Adam is squeezing him with violent affection. Mollel puts his own arms around his son, and lifts him up with him as he stands.

For the first time, he realises what he could have lost. And he never wants to let the boy go.

Honey touches his shoulder and plants a gentle kiss on his cheek.

—I knew you wouldn't let us down, she says.

Reminded of her presence, Mollel reluctantly lowers Adam down and detaches himself once more.

—Where were you when we needed you, Mollel? demands Faith. We've been here all night with those yobs shouting threats and throwing stones. We thought… we thought they were going to kill us.

Faith sits down on the box and buries her face in her hands. Honey goes over to her and places her arm around the old woman's shoulders. The small, cruel knife is palmed in her hand.

—Shh, Faith, she says, comfortingly. Mollel got here as soon as he could. He was on his case. He had work to do. Did you find anything out, Mollel?

She raises her eyes to his. There is the faintest glimmer of challenge in her gaze.

—Not much, he says. The shape this city's in, I doubt one little murder's even going to count any more. I think I've hit a dead end. Have either of you got your phone? I can try to call for help.

—Don't you think we've tried? wails Faith. The network's down. Probably everyone in Nairobi's trying to call for help right now.

—What do you mean, a dead end? demands Honey. You're still going to investigate the Nalos, aren't you? Forget about the murder. What about finding Lucy's child?

She strokes Faith's neck, while she turns the knife in her hand.

—The priority right now, says Mollel, moving Adam behind him and edging forward, is to get out of here. Faith, what have you got in the house that we could defend ourselves with?

—I've got this panga, she says, looking up at him fearfully. There are some knives in the kitchen. And there's Ngugi's old walking stick around, somewhere.

—OK, says Mollel, that's a start. Honey, that little knife's not going to be any good to you. Better give it to me.

Honey looks up at him. —Why don't I hang on to it, just in case?

—It's evidence, remember? says Mollel. He is close, now. He holds his hand out, palm up. Burns and lacerations: a crippled hand. But a hand that's going to take the knife.

Honey gives a quiet laugh, and hugs Faith to her. The blade dances beside Faith's ear, her cheek, her neck.

—She's shaking, Mollel, sobs Faith. Can't you see she's terrified? We all are. Let her keep the knife if it makes her feel better.

Mollel's palm remains open, insistent.

—Give it to me, Honey.

She looks him in the eye. Her dark eyes shine with tears.

—You know, don't you? she says.

—Give me the knife, he repeats, softly.

—I'm sorry for lying to you, Mollel. I never thought anyone

296

would take a *poko* like me seriously. Most people would agree with Wanjiku, that the baby's better off elsewhere. But they don't know me, Mollel. I'd be a good mother. No one's got the right to take a baby away from its mother. No one had the right to take my baby away from me.

—From *you?* says Faith, jerking her head up. She gives a cry of pain.

—Careful, Honey! shouts Mollel.

—You're hurting me!

Honey tightens her arm around Faith's neck. The tip of the knife is pressed against her jugular.

—Mollel was the only person who ever listened to me, Honey cries into Faith's ear. The only one who really wanted to help me. And she told me, Mollel – she looks up – she told me how she was going to take Adam away from you. You were right. She thinks you're not a fit parent. Well, they did it to me. I'm not going to let her do it to you.

—Gran! shouts Adam.

Faith stares wildly in fear and astonishment. At that moment, there is a crashing sound. Metal collapsing. The gate to the compound has been forced.

—Take Adam and go, Mollel! shouts Honey. He doesn't need to see this! The two of you should be able to get out of here, if you go now!

Adam's arms grasp his waist. —Don't let her do it, Dad! Don't let her hurt Gran!

—What anyone else says or thinks means nothing to me any more, Mollel. But I want you to understand. I need you to understand.

—We can talk about it later, says Mollel. Please, Honey.

But even as he says it, he knows she won't leave this place.

She has a far-off look in her eyes. Her words begin to pour out, quietly, softly. As though she is speaking to herself as much as to them.

*

—I woke up in that little room. I was on the mattress. Lucy had curled up next to me. That was what we did, whenever we both needed to sleep at the same time. We were both used to it. Every Maasai is. I never really got used to sleeping alone, without the smell of hide and smoke and brothers and sisters all around.

—Her skin had the sweet, milky smell of a baby. And then, I remembered: my baby!

A rattle overhead signals another shower of missiles hitting the roof.

—Honey, whatever it is you've done… begins Faith. But Honey tightens her grip.

—You don't speak, she hisses. You're just the same as them.

—She's not, insists Mollel. She's not the same.

He advances towards Honey, but she casts him a look full of warning and danger.

—Hear me out, Mollel. You're going to hear me out.

He raises his hand, backs off a few steps.

— When I started to feel the pangs of labour, two months ahead of time, Lucy was the one who insisted I went to Orpheus House. She said I would get free treatment there, that it was the safest way to deliver my baby. I was nervous. The baby was *his*, after all. George Nalo's. How could I trust his wife to deliver it? But Lucy told me Wanjiku had no idea. She thought her husband practised what he preached. Lucy said I had nothing to worry about. That she'd be there with me.

—And yet – when I awoke, they told me that my baby had died. Just like that. No apology, no explanation. And no body. They told me that it was deformed, unhealthy. It couldn't have lived. But hadn't I felt it, every twist and turn and kick, inside of me?

—I knew that child. I knew it was healthy. I knew it was still alive. And it had been taken from me.

—*I'm sorry, Honey*, Lucy said. *But what sort of a life would the child have had, anyway?*

—She told me she had to leave. She'd taken a risk, bringing

me home. But she wanted to check that I was all right before she left Nairobi for good.

—She explained that she needed to get away from her boyfriend. She was going to go back to her village, back into Maasai life. She'd shave her head, put on the *shuka*, extend the holes in her ears. Someone would take her, even as a second wife. She would disappear.

—But she needed money. She had no family any more. No one to give cattle as a dowry. That was why, she said, she'd be in contact in a few days' time. She needed my help, to do one last job before she left Nairobi for ever.

—The job, she told me, was to rob a rich old *mzungu*. He was one of her clients. He always picked her up on Friday nights. It was a regular thing, apparently.

Recently, she'd been persuading him to go for a twofer. He'd been reluctant at first – imagine, she'd said to me. A K-Street regular, too conservative for a twofer. But she'd been working on him. My friend's really beautiful, she told him. She's young, but experienced. And if you don't want to join in – well, you can always watch.

—And then she said: you know, Honey – if it's nice, I *might* be open to persuasion, myself. And she smiled.

—She really wanted me along. She *needed* me along. She said she'd call me to confirm the meeting place, in a few days' time, when I was feeling better.

—She put a bottle of pills on the window ledge. A few hundred shillings underneath it, for food.

—It wasn't until after she'd gone that I realised I didn't even know if my baby had been a boy or a girl.

A horn blares outside. Mollel looks back nervously.

—I had a lot of time to think, those next few days, Honey says. Her eyes are glazed, trance-like. For the first time ever, I began to feel as though I could not trust Lucy. It was that wink that did it – that seductive wink. As though I was another client to be played with on the street.

—She needed money, she told me. Money for a dowry.

Yet how much money would we get from robbing a punter? Neither of us could drive, so it wasn't like we could take the car. Even an *mzungu* wouldn't carry enough cash to make it worth while. I should know – I've been through thousands of wallets in my time, when they're sleeping it off, or have gone for a piss. A few thousand shillings, maximum. And that's without splitting it.

—No, if she really intended to return to Maasai life – and this, at least, sounded true – she would need a pretty impressive dowry for any decent husband. He'd know, from her lack of family connections, that she'd run away. Anyone could see, just from looking at her, that she'd been in the city. And now she wanted to disappear into a village somewhere? It could only mean one thing. And to overlook that, her dowry would have to be large. Say – a hundred thousand shillings.

—A hundred thousand shillings, Mollel.—The price of a child.—It began to all come together for me.

—Lucy had told Wanjiku Nalo that my baby was her husband's. And knowing that the couple would not want any evidence of the pastor's infidelity, Lucy had suggested a solution. Sell the child into adoption. Get some desperate foreign couple to take it on. Take it away. As far away as possible.

—And all Lucy would have asked, for this little task – for offering up such a troublesome child, to be simply spirited away – all she would have asked was the going rate. The payment from the prospective parents. The facilitation fee. A modest sum, all things considered.

—A hundred thousand shillings.

—I still didn't know what Lucy's true plan was with the robbery. I didn't trust her any more. But I knew that it was my last chance to see her before she disappeared for ever. And my only chance to try to find out the truth, while there was a possibility my baby was still in the country. So, when she called me, I went to meet her, as arranged, on K-Street.

—It took some effort to get there. It took even more effort to look convincing. Being successful on K-Street is not just about the way you look, you know. It's about the way you walk, the way you hold yourself. That poise. The allure, the sexual promise, must be evident in every footstep, every sway of the waist. The way you crook one knee when standing, to emphasise your hip. The way you dip your belly to heighten your buttocks, when you lean in a car window. It's a performance, a dance. And just a few days before, I'd been in labour.

—It was painful. Painful physically, and even harder mentally. I hadn't been on the streets for months, and my body felt ravaged. The glances from the men told me I looked fine, though. I was fooling them. I just kept telling myself that whatever happened, this was not going to be a normal job. I wasn't going to have to go through with *that* – not for a long time.

—She met me, and we kissed – this time, she lingered a second longer than she needed to. Caught my bottom lip between hers as she pulled away, and then looked at me, and smiled. It was calculated. She played every trick on me that I played for the punters – her hand on my forearm, her eyes cast down, then flashing up, then looking away – every trick she had taught me.

—She thought she could seduce me. Foolish girl. She didn't realise that with every flutter of her eyelashes, she was confirming her treachery.

—The *mzungu* wasn't far behind. He came along in his four-by-four, pulled over so that we could get in. As we'd arranged, Lucy got into the front passenger seat. I slipped in behind.

—*You're right*, was the first thing he said to Lucy. *She is beautiful.* And he gave me a look in the rear-view mirror. There was no lust in that look. Not one hint of lust. Just pity.

—I knew for sure, then, that it was a set-up. This man was no punter. He wasn't even *straight*.

—The plan, as Lucy had explained it to me, was for him to drive us to a quiet place. No one around. Uhuru Park, she reckoned, would be safe enough, that time of night. Once we got there, and he'd stopped the car, she was going to pull a knife.

She always carried one when she was working the street, tucked into her dress, beside the curve of her back. We'd take the old man's wallet, phone, throw his keys into the bushes, and run off into the park.

—I could tell, though – from the look which passed between them – that it was *me* they wanted to get alone. Well, I wasn't going to give them the chance. We headed up K-Street, back on to Kenyatta Avenue. All the time I was thinking: what do they want from me? What are they going to do to me?

—By the time we reached the Uhuru Highway roundabout, I had it figured out. Whoever this guy was, Lucy had some hold over him. She'd managed to persuade him to assist her with her final task. When she left Nairobi, she didn't want any loose ends. I was the only one who knew where she'd come from. We'd talked so often about her home. I knew exactly where she could be found. And anyone who wanted to find her, could find her through me.

And she would have known that if I ever found out about the adoption – or even suspected that I'd lost my baby because of her – I would have every reason to turn her in.

—I wasn't ready to let them do it. I wasn't going to give up that easily.

As the car slowed for the roundabout, I thought about jumping out. I could've done it, easily. But I remembered the baby. It would be a few weeks, yet, before any international adoption could be finalised. If she told me the truth now, I might be able to stop it. To get my baby back. If I didn't get the truth that night, I might still be able to track her to her village. But it would be too late.

—So as the old man turned the car into the park, I leaned forward, and grabbed his seat belt. I pulled it. As hard as I could.

—He swerved, and we bounced over the kerb. But I didn't let go. We hit something, flew forward. His airbag went off. But I still didn't let go. I didn't let go until I heard him gurgle. And he went limp.

—Lucy's nose was bleeding. She hadn't been wearing a seat

belt, either. But she'd had time to brace herself. She was a bit beaten up, nothing too bad. She opened the door and stumbled out.

—I watched her stagger off. And then she was gone from the headlight beam. The old man was not moving. I got out, went after her. Caught up with her at the drainage ditch.

—I suppose her injuries must have been worse than I thought. She was there, kneeling. She was acting vague, concussed. Her head was rolling on her shoulders like a weight. I took her face in my hands. They came away wet. Blood.

What did you do with my baby? I asked. *Where is it? Where has it gone?*

—But she just laughed. And started to cough. The blood bubbled up in her throat.

—I shook her. She was slipping away. She pitched forward, started sliding into the ditch. She was so heavy. I couldn't stop her. She took me with her, but I kept shouting, *Where is my baby?*

—I couldn't believe she had cheated me, at that final moment. She had stolen my baby, sold it.

—I kept shouting long after she was dead. I was still shouting it when I found the knife in my hand, the knife she kept ready in the small of her back. It was such a tiny thing. When I held it, it felt like I was punching her. Punching her dead body. Punching her, where she had wounded me. Had cut the life out of me.

—I heard the white man's voice. He was standing over us. Horrified. *What have you done?*

—I got up. I didn't bother explaining to him. Lights swept across his face, and in his eyes I could see terror. Even then, I could see that it might be useful for him to think I could have killed her.

—I took her *khanga* and put it where I'd been stabbing her. A little dignity, in that ditch.

—The lights were getting brighter. There were vehicles coming in, crackling across the gravel. I held the knife to the old man's ribs, and together, we walked out of there, as if nothing had happened. It was starting to rain when we left.

Mollel reaches into his pocket and pulls out a crumpled piece of paper. He holds it in his damaged hand, proffers it to Honey.

—Take a look.

It is a baby. A dead baby. An incomplete baby.

Her baby.

—It's a trick, she says, weakly.

—No, Honey, it's not. It's your baby. Yours, and George Nalo's. I've seen the records. It never could have survived.

—Oh, Honey, says Faith. What have you done?

There is a loud bang at the kitchen door. And another.

—It's not murder, says Mollel. If she died because of the car crash, you have nothing to feel guilty for. Come with me. Make a statement. There's nothing here we can't deal with.

There is a clatter as the knife drops to the floor. Honey's body is limp. She no longer holds Faith: now, it is Faith holding her.

She mutters a few, quiet words in Maa.

Faith stands up, tentatively, and walks over to Adam. She scoops up the boy in her arms. —We've got to go now, she says.

Mollel extends his hand. —Honey? Are you coming?

The sound of splintering wood crashes through from the kitchen. Mollel turns towards it. Light streams in, powerful, white light. From it, he sees a figure emerge.

—Sorry about the door, comes a shout. Mwathi is standing there. We've forced the line, but can only hold it a few minutes. Are you coming, or not?

Faith runs forward, Adam up in her arms. She runs towards the light, through the shattered kitchen door. In the compound, a GSU truck is parked on top of the fallen gate, its engine running, headlights blazing.

—Come on, Honey!

He grabs her wrist, and pulls her with him, towards the doorway. He runs out, ducking, as a hail of missiles flies over his head, bouncing off the roof of the house. Faith and Adam have already taken shelter in the cab. Mollel turns to help Honey in—

—and she is gone.

Mwathi scrambles in the other side, behind the wheel. He releases the brake and starts to back out.

—Wait! shouts Mollel, standing in the door. There's someone still in there!

—Your killer, I suppose? says Mwathi. Leave him. He's going to get what's coming to him!

Mollel looks back at the house. The broken doorway stands black and empty in the beam of the headlights. —Honey! he shouts.

—She won't come, says Faith. Not now. She's made her choice.

Mwathi resumes reversing out. A petrol bomb arcs overhead and bursts on the gravel in front of them in a curtain of blue flame.

Something crashes on the roof of the cab and Mollel slams the door shut just as liquid fire begins to pour down the side. The cab is filled with the stench of burning and the window at his side snaps with the sudden heat.

The truck lurches back and swings round the gatepost. Mwathi grinds it into first and puts his foot down. GSU men either side of them scatter as the vehicle roars past; they lift their shields above their heads and run in its wake. As the flames pour away from the side window, Mollel has a fleeting glimpse of faces contorted in hate, baying at the truck as it passes. And then, they bump and rumble towards the GSU line, which parts, and the truck is suddenly surrounded by silence and the blackness of night.

—Honey, breathes Mwathi, turning off the engine. Funny name for a murderer.

43

—You sure you want to do this? asks Kiunga.

—I'm sure, says Mollel.

The City Mortuary is overflowing with bodies, but here at Central CID, a lone corpse occupies a cell all of its own.

Mollel bends over the bench. He takes a corner of the sheet and gently folds it back.

He flinches at the sight of the familiar face. Despite the round hole in the forehead, it looks peaceful. The dreadlocked skull behind it, however, is gaping and open.

—I'm sorry, says Kiunga. It's tough to lose someone you trust.

Mollel replaces the shroud.

—He saved our lives, continues Kiunga. It was just after you left us. If we'd kept going, we'd probably have been all right. But they were all around the car before I even noticed.

—We were only a few hundred metres from here. I couldn't raise them on the phone, so I blasted my horn, hoping to get their attention. The back window shattered. Panya scrambled forward but they had him by the ankles. They dragged him out. Lethebridge was screaming at me to drive, to just plough down those in front of me. I would've done, too, if it wasn't for Panya.

—Then Benjamin got out of the car. Someone swung a panga. It took off the wing mirror but he didn't even flinch.

He spoke to them, Mollel. I didn't catch it all. It was Kikuyu,

306

but it was that strange dialect the *Mungiki* speak. He spoke to them, and he told them we were going. He picked up Panya and I helped Lethebridge out of the car. The old man's face was pretty cut up from the glass. We were walking towards Central. I could see some of the other officers had come out. They were armed. They'd heard the horn. We were just steps away from safety.

—When I heard the explosion, at first I thought the gang had torched the car, that the petrol tank had gone up. I turned to look. The gang were scattered, but the car was intact. And then I saw Benjamin crumple to his knees. The last thing he did, you know, Mollel, was lay Panya down on the ground. So gently.

—The guys at the station had shot him. They saw the dread-locks, you see. It was all about the dreadlocks.

In the CID office, Panya is playing with a baton. Someone has found him an old uniform, and he flounders about in the over-sized shirt tucked into trousers belted with cord. He seems to be lecturing Mwangi about putting his feet on the desk.

—Where's Lethebridge now? Mollel asks Kiunga.

—Kingori's taken him. We've not got enough to bring charges at the moment. Maybe when all this has settled, we'll persuade Otieno to look at an obstruction charge. But from what you've told me, we'd never make accessory to murder stick. Or black-mail. The Nalos aren't going to back that one up.

—He's going to walk, isn't he? says Mollel.

—Looks like it, boss. I guess I don't call you boss any more now, though. You'll be back to traffic. I'll be back to Mwangi. Solving crimes. Catching thieves. Letting them go, when they don't fit with Otieno's statistics. Dishing out beatings and taking backhanders.

—That's not you, Kiunga.

—No, it's not, says Kiunga. It might have been. It would have been, a few years from now, if you hadn't come along. You showed me police work doesn't have to be done that way.

He breaks into a grin.

—I'm not saying I'd do it *your* way, either, mind you. Jesus Christ!

Back at his flat, he finds Faith and Adam in the sitting room, in front of the TV.

—Have you heard? Kibaki has had himself sworn in at State House. The electoral commission's declared him the winner. They've not even finished counting the votes yet!

If it weren't so serious, Mollel would find Faith's outrage amusing. Just a few days ago she had been lamenting what might happen if President Kibaki were not returned for a second term. But then, a lot had happened in the last few days.

She stands and walks towards the kitchen. There's a big pan of *chai* on the stove: she ladles Mollel a cup. He wraps his hands around it gingerly. He's grateful that during a lull in the chaos that morning, he was able to get a few groceries – enough to last them out the next few days. This latest news is not going to do anything to calm tensions in the city.

—Any news on Honey? she asks.

He shakes his head.

—That poor girl's going to face a higher judgement that we can give her, says Faith, sadly.

—She refused to believe that her baby was dead, Mollel says. She constructed a fantasy in which it survived, and was adopted. Just to spare her the guilt.

—Guilt? asks Faith. It wasn't her fault.

—I've been thinking about what she said, replies Mollel. Those final words I heard her speak. She said something in Maa. She said: *I ate my baby.*

Faith looks at him with incredulity.

—It's an old Maasai expression, he says. When a woman has a miscarriage, or a stillbirth, she's said to have eaten her child. It's usually blamed on having had sex when pregnant. When you consider she probably didn't even know she was carrying the baby for a long time… and who she was…

—She wasn't a murderer, though, says Faith. If she had come

308

with you, as you suggested, she might have had another life.

Mollel fingers the red silken tie which is hanging over the back of one of the kitchen chairs.

—No, he says. She was a murderer. All those things she said about Lucy. The manipulation, the seduction. When she was talking about Lucy, she was talking about herself. Those were the tricks she used on me. Lucy didn't die because of her injuries in the crash. Honey murdered her. Premeditated, cold-blooded murder. The reason she didn't come out of the house was because she knew I knew that. I'm just not as good a liar as she was.

Faith crosses herself. Then she looks at the tie in Mollel's hands.

—That's nice, she says. Why don't you wear it more often?

Adam comes in from the sitting room.

—The news is boring, Dad, he says. When will they start showing cartoons again?

—I don't know, Adam, says Mollel. Maybe in the New Year.

W&N blog

For exclusive short stories, poems, extracts, essays, articles, interviews, trailers, competitions and much more visit the Weidenfeld & Nicolson blog at:

www.wnblog.co.uk

Follow us on

 and **twitter**

Or scan the code to access the website*

De Vuist van God

Frederick Forsyth

De Vuist van God

A.W. Bruna Uitgevers B.V. Utrecht

Oorspronkelijke titel
The Fist of God
© Transworld Publishers Ltd, 1994
This edition is published by arrangement with Transworld
Publishers Ltd, 61-63 Uxbridge Road, London W5 5SA
Vertaling
Jan Smit
© 1994 A.W. Bruna Uitgevers B.V., Utrecht

ISBN 90 229 8160 6
NUGI 331

Voor de weduwen en de wezen van het Special Air Service Regiment.
En voor Sandy, zonder wiens hulp het veel moeilijker geweest zou zijn.

Ik dank de mensen die weten wat er werkelijk in de Golfoorlog is gebeurd en daar met mij over wilden spreken. Jullie weten wie je bent. Laat dat voldoende zijn.

Lijst van belangrijkste personen

DE AMERIKANEN

George Bush	President
James Baker	Minister van Buitenlandse Zaken
Colin Powell	Voorzitter van de chefs-van-staven
Norman Schwarzkopf	Generaal, bevelhebber van de Coalitiestrijdkrachten in de Golf
Charles (Chuck) Horner	Luitenant-generaal, bevelhebber van de luchtstrijdkrachten van de Coalitie in de Golf
Buster Glosson	Brigadegeneraal, plaatsvervangend bevelhebber van de luchtstrijdkrachten
Bill Stewart	Adjunct-directeur Operaties CIA
Chip Barber	Hoofd divisie Midden-Oosten CIA
William Webster	Directeur CIA
Don Walker	Gevechtspiloot
Steve Turner	Commandant jager-squadron
Randy Roberts	Wingman van Don Walker
Jim Henry	Navigator van Randy Roberts
Harry Sinclair	Hoofd CIA-bureau in Londen
Saul Nathanson	Bankier en filantroop
'Daddy' Lomax	Kernfysicus in ruste

DE BRITTEN

Margaret Thatcher	Minister-president
John Major	Haar opvolger als minister-president
Sir Peter de la Billière	Luitenant-generaal, commandant Britse strijdkrachten in de Golf
Sir Colin McColl	Chef SIS
Sir Paul Spruce	Voorzitter Medusa Comité
J.P. Lovat	Brigadegeneraal, directeur Special Forces
Bruce Craig	Kolonel, commandant 22e SAS-regiment
Mike Martin	Majoor bij de SAS
'Sparky' Low	SAS-officier in Khafji
Dr. Terry Martin	Academicus en arabist

Steve Laing	Hoofd Operaties, divisie Midden-Oosten van de SIS
Simon Paxman	Hoofd sectie Irak van de SIS
Stuart Harris	Brits zakenman in Bagdad
Julian Gray	Hoofd SIS-bureau in Riyad
Dr. Bryant	Bacterioloog, Medusa Comité
Dr. Reinhart	Gifgasexpert, Medusa Comité
Dr. John Hipwell	Nucleair deskundige, Medusa Comité
Sean Plummer	Hoofd Arabische sectie GCHQ
Philip Curzon	Luitenant-kolonel, commandant 608e squadron
Lofty Williamson	Majoor, piloot bij het 608e squadron
Sid Blair	Kapitein, Williamsons navigator
Peter Johns	Kapitein, piloot bij het 608e squadron
Nicky Tyne	Kapitein, Johns' navigator
Peter Stephenson	Sergeant bij de SAS
Ben Eastman	Korporaal bij de SAS
Kevin North	Korporaal bij de SAS

DE ISRAELI'S

Yaakov 'Kobi' Dror	Hoofd van de Mossad
Sami Gershon	Hoofd Operaties van de Mossad
David Sharon	Hoofd sectie Irak van de Mossad
Benjamin Netanyahu	Onderminister van Buitenlandse Zaken
Itzhak Shamir	Minister-president
Gideon 'Gidi' Barzilai	Controleofficier operatie Joshua, Wenen
Moshe Hadari	Hoogleraar en arabist aan de universiteit van Tel Aviv
Avi Herzog (alias Karim Aziz)	Mossad-agent in Wenen

DE OOSTENRIJKERS

Wolfgang Gemütlich	Adjunct-directeur Winkler Bank
Edith Hardenberg	Zijn privé-secretaresse

DE KOEWEITI'S

Ahmed Al-Khalifa	Koeweits zakenman
Abu Fouad	Kolonel, leider van het Koeweits verzet
Asrar Qabandi	Heldin van het Koeweits verzet

DE IRAKEZEN

Saddam Hoessein	President
Izzat Ibrahim	Vice-president
Hoessein Kamil	Saddams schoonzoon, hoofd van het MIMI (ministerie van Industrie en Militaire Industrialisatie)
Taha Ramadam	Minister-president
Sadoun Hammadi	Vice-premier
Tariq Aziz	Minister van Buitenlandse Zaken
Ali Hassan Majid	Gouverneur bezet Koeweit
Saadi Tumah Abbas	Generaal, commandant Republikeinse Garde
Ali Musuli	Generaal, commandant genietroepen
Abdullah Kadiri	Generaal, commandant pantserkorps
Dr. Amer Saadi	Assistent van Hoessein Kamil
Hassan Rahmani	Brigadegeneraal, hoofd contraspionagedienst
Dr. Ismail Ubaidi	Hoofd buitenlandse inlichtingendienst
Omar Khatib	Brigadegeneraal, hoofd geheime politie (Amn-al-Amm)
Osman Badri	Kolonel bij de genie
Abdelkarim Badri	Kolonel en gevechtspiloot bij de Iraakse luchtmacht
Dr. Jaafar al-Jaafar	Hoofd nucleaire programma
Kolonel Sabaawi	Chef geheime politie in bezet Koeweit
Dr. Salah Siddiqui	Kernfysicus

De man die nog tien minuten te leven had zat te lachen.

Hij lachte om een verhaal dat hij zojuist had gehoord van zijn persoonlijke assistente Monique Jaminé, die hem op die kille, druilerige avond van de 22e maart 1990 van zijn kantoor naar huis reed.

Het ging over een wederzijdse collega op het kantoor van de Space Research Corporation in de Rue de Salle, een vrouw die iedereen beschouwde als een echte vamp, een mannenverslindster, maar die lesbisch bleek te zijn. Dat sprak het primitieve gevoel voor humor van de man wel aan.

Om tien voor zeven waren ze vertrokken van het kantoor in de Brusselse voorstad Ukkel. Monique zat achter het stuur van de Renault 21 estate. Een paar maanden eerder had ze de Volkswagen van haar baas verkocht, omdat hij zo'n slechte chauffeur was dat ze bang was dat hij brokken zou maken.

Het was maar een ritje van tien minuten naar zijn appartement in het middelste van de drie flatgebouwen van het Cheridreu-complex in de buurt van de Rue François Folie, maar onderweg stopten ze nog even bij een bakker, vlak bij de begraafplaats. Ze stapten allebei de winkel binnen, waar de man zijn favoriete *pain de campagne* kocht. Het waaide en regende. Ze liepen met gebogen hoofd en letten niet op de auto die hen volgde.

Waarom zouden ze? Ze waren geen getrainde agenten. De onopvallende auto met zijn twee donkere inzittenden schaduwde de wetenschapper al een paar weken, op veilige afstand, zonder iets te ondernemen. Hij had hem niet opgemerkt. Anderen wel, maar dat wist hij niet.

Ze kwamen weer naar buiten. De man gooide zijn brood op de achterbank en stapte in voor het laatste deel van de rit. Om tien over zeven stopte Monique voor de glazen deuren van het flatgebouw, dat vijftien meter van de stoeprand stond. Ze wist dat hij zijn vriendin Helène verwachtte en niet wilde dat zij haar zou zien. Hij wilde de illusie in stand houden dat Helène gewoon een goede vriendin was die hem gezelschap hield terwijl hij in Brussel was en zijn vrouw in Canada. Zijn vrouwelijke staf, die hem op handen droeg, speelde het spelletje braaf mee.

De man stapte uit de auto, met de kraag van zijn regenjas opgeslagen en zijn ceintuur dichtgeknoopt, en gooide de grote zwarte canvastas, die hij bijna altijd bij zich droeg, over zijn schouder. De tas woog vijftien kilo en zat propvol met wetenschappelijke verhandelingen, projecten, calculaties en gegevens. De wetenschapper had geen vertrouwen in brandkasten en dacht

– onlogisch genoeg – dat de details van zijn meest recente projecten veiliger waren in zijn schoudertas.

Het laatste wat Monique van haar baas zag, was dat hij voor de glazen deuren bleef staan, met zijn tas over zijn schouder en het brood onder zijn ene arm, zoekend naar zijn sleutels. Ze zag hem naar binnen gaan. De glazen deuren gleden automatisch achter hem dicht en Monique reed weg.

De academicus had een appartement op de zesde verdieping. Het gebouw telde in totaal acht etages. Ingeklemd tussen de trappen bevonden zich twee liften. Hij nam een van de liften en stapte uit op de zesde verdieping. De gedempte lichten van de lobby gingen automatisch aan. Rammelend met zijn sleutels, naar één kant overhellend vanwege het gewicht van zijn tas en met het brood nog steeds onder zijn arm sloeg hij twee keer linksaf over het roestbruine tapijt van de lobby en wilde zijn sleutel in het slot van de deur steken.

De moordenaar had staan wachten aan de andere kant van de liftschacht in de zwak verlichte lobby. Zachtjes stapte hij de hoek om. In zijn hand had hij een 7.65-mm Beretta met geluiddemper, die hij in een plastic zakje had gewikkeld om de lege hulzen op te vangen.

Vijf schoten van nog geen meter afstand, alle in het achterhoofd en de rug van het slachtoffer, waren meer dan genoeg. De grote, forse man viel voorover tegen zijn deur en zakte ineen op het tapijt. De moordenaar nam niet eens de moeite om te controleren of hij dood was. Hij had dit al vaker gedaan, had kunnen oefenen op gevangenen, en hij verstond zijn vak. Lichtvoetig rende hij de zes trappen af, verliet het gebouw aan de achterkant en liep langs de bomen van de tuin naar de gereedstaande auto. Nog geen uur later had hij de Brusselse ambassade van zijn land bereikt en binnen een dag was hij uit België verdwenen.

Helène arriveerde vijf minuten later. Eerst dacht ze dat haar minnaar een hartaanval had gekregen. In paniek opende ze de deur en belde een ambulance. Toen herinnerde ze zich dat de dokter van haar vriend in hetzelfde gebouw woonde en belde hem ook. De ambulance was er eerder.

Een van de ziekenbroeders probeerde het zware lichaam, dat nog steeds voorover lag, te verschuiven. Toen hij zijn hand terugtrok, zat die onder het bloed. Een paar minuten later verklaarde de arts dat het slachtoffer dood was. De enige andere bewoonster van de vier flats op die verdieping, een oude dame die achter haar zware houten deur naar een klassiek concert had zitten luisteren en niets bijzonders had gehoord, kwam de gang op. Cheridreu was zo'n soort flat – heel discreet.

Het slachtoffer op de grond was dr. Gerald Vincent Bull, een grillig genie, een man die wapens ontwierp voor de hele wereld, en de laatste tijd vooral voor Saddam Hoessein, de president van Irak.

Na de moord op dr. Gerry Bull gebeurden er in Europa enkele vreemde dingen. In Brussel gaf de Belgische contraspionagedienst toe dat Bull al enkele maanden bijna dagelijks werd geschaduwd door een reeks onopvallende auto's met twee donkere mannen met een zuidelijk uiterlijk.

Op 11 april nam de Britse douane in de haven van Middlesborough acht grote stalen buizen in beslag, vakkundig gesmeed en voorzien van reusachtige flenzen met grote schroefgaten, waarmee ze aan elkaar bevestigd konden worden. De triomfantelijke douaneofficieren verklaarden dat het geen buizen waren voor een petrochemische fabriek, zoals op de vrachtbrief en de uitvoervergunning stond aangegeven, maar onderdelen van een reusachtige kanonsloop, ontworpen door dr. Gerry Bull en bestemd voor Irak. Zo werd de farce van het superkanon geboren, met onthullingen over bedrog, heimelijke activiteiten van verschillende inlichtingendiensten, bureaucratische blunders en politieke koehandel.

Binnen enkele weken doken overal in Europa onderdelen van het superkanon op. Op 23 april meldden de Turken dat ze een Hongaarse vrachtwagen hadden aangehouden die een tien meter lange stalen buis voor Irak vervoerde die ook bij het kanon zou horen. Dezelfde dag hielden de Grieken een andere truck met stalen onderdelen aan. De ongelukkige Britse chauffeur werd nog een paar weken als medeplichtige vastgehouden.

In mei onderschepten de Italianen vijfenzeventig ton onderdelen van de Societa Della Fucine, terwijl op het fabrieksterrein van Fucine bij Rome nog eens vijftien ton materiaal in beslag werd genomen. Deze elementen waren vervaardigd uit een titanium-staallegering en bestemd voor een deel van de stootbodem van het kanon, evenals een andere partij onderdelen die in een pakhuis in het Noorditaliaanse Brescia werd ontdekt.

De Duitsers meldden zich met ontdekkingen in Frankfurt en Bremerhaven – produkten van Mannesmann AG, die ook als onderdelen van het inmiddels wereldberoemde superkanon werden geïdentificeerd.

Gerry Bull had de orders voor zijn geesteskind bijzonder handig verdeeld. De buizen voor de loop waren inderdaad in Engeland vervaardigd, door twee firma's, Walter Somers in Birmingham en Forgemasters in Sheffield. Maar de acht buizen die in april 1990 werden onderschept waren de laatste van in totaal tweeënvijftig segmenten, voldoende voor twee complete lopen van 156 meter lang, met een ongelooflijk kaliber van één meter, in staat om een projectiel af te vuren ter grootte van een cilindervormige telefooncel.

De tappen kwamen uit Griekenland, de pijpen, pompen en kleppen van het terugslagmechanisme uit Zwitserland en Italië, het sluitstuk uit Oostenrijk en Duitsland en de drijfstof uit België. In totaal waren er acht landen bij de produktie betrokken, zonder dat één van de acht precies wist waar ze aan werkten.

De boulevardpers maakte er veel drukte over, evenals de enthousiaste douane-officieren en de Britse justitie, die meteen allerlei onschuldige mensen aanklaagde. Niemand wees erop dat de vogel al gevlogen was. De onderschepte onderdelen waren bestemd geweest voor Superkanon Twee, Drie en Vier.

De moord op Gerry Bull leidde tot enkele buitenissige theorieën in de media. Uiteraard kreeg de CIA de schuld, zoals altijd. Onzin, natuurlijk. Hoewel Langley in het verleden en onder bepaalde omstandigheden wel-eens de eliminatie van bepaalde personen had overwogen, gold dat haast altijd dezelfde figuren: overgelopen agenten en dubbelspionnen. Maar de suggestie dat de hal van Langley vol zou liggen met de lijken van voormalige agenten die door hun eigen collega's zouden zijn vermoord op bevel van moordlustige directeuren op de bovenste verdieping is amusant maar volstrekt belachelijk.

Bovendien kwam Gerry Bull niet uit dat clandestiene wereldje. Hij was een bekende wetenschapper, een ontwerper en uitvoerder van conventionele – maar ook zeer onconventionele – artillerie, een Amerikaans burger die jarenlang voor Washington had gewerkt en uitvoerig met zijn vrienden binnen het Amerikaanse leger over zijn plannen had gesproken. Als iedereen binnen de wapenindustrie die voor een land werkte dat later een vijand van Amerika werd moest worden geëlimineerd, had de CIA wel vijfhonderd ontwerpers en producenten in Noord- en Zuid-Amerika en Europa uit de weg kunnen ruimen.

Daar komt bij dat Langley de afgelopen tien jaar steeds meer aan banden was gelegd door nieuwe ambtelijke voorschriften en controlecommissies. Geen enkele CIA-officier zal opdracht tot een moordaanslag geven zonder een schriftelijke, ondertekende order. En voor iemand als Gerry Bull had zo'n order rechtstreeks van de directeur zelf afkomstig moeten zijn.

Op dat moment werd de CIA geleid door William Webster, een zeer formele ex-rechter uit Kansas. Het was net zo eenvoudig om William Webster een bevel tot een moordaanslag te laten tekenen als met behulp van een stomp theelepeltje uit Alcatraz te ontsnappen.

Maar de beschuldigende vinger wees toch vooral naar de Israëlische Mossad. De pers en de vrienden en familie van Gerry Bull trokken allemaal dezelfde voorbarige conclusie. Bull werkte voor Irak, Irak was een vijand van Israël, dus twee plus twee was vier. Het probleem was dat zo'n rekensom in dit wereldje van schaduwen en lachspiegels soms een heel andere uitkomst te zien gaf.

De Mossad is de kleinste maar ook de meest meedogenloze en brutaalste

14

van de belangrijke inlichtingendiensten in de wereld. In het verleden heeft de Israëlische geheime dienst ongetwijfeld heel wat aanslagen laten uitvoeren door haar drie *kidon*-teams (*kidon* is het Hebreeuwse woord voor bajonet). De *kidonin* vormen de geheime Komemiute-divisie, de harde kern. Maar zelfs de Mossad heeft haar regels, ook al heeft zij die zelf opgesteld. Moordaanslagen worden onderverdeeld in twee categorieën. Om te beginnen is er de 'operationele noodzaak', een onvoorziene situatie waarin het leven van bevriende figuren op het spel staat en het gevaar snel en permanent uit de weg moet worden geruimd. In dat geval heeft de *katsa* of controleofficier het recht om meteen in te grijpen om de missie te redden. Achteraf kan hij dan rekenen op de steun van zijn bazen in Tel Aviv.

De andere categorie wordt gevormd door personen op de zwarte lijst. Die lijst bevindt zich op twee plaatsen: in de persoonlijke kluis van de minister-president en in de brandkast van de directeur van de Mossad. Iedere nieuwe premier is verplicht om deze lijst, die dertig tot tachtig namen bevat, in te zien. Hij kan de namen van zijn paraaf voorzien, waarmee hij de Mossad toestemming geeft om toe te slaan als de kans zich voordoet, of hij kan eisen dat hij bij elke nieuwe missie op de hoogte moet worden gebracht. In beide gevallen moet hij het executiebevel ondertekenen.

Globaal gesproken is deze lijst verdeeld in drie groepen. De eerste bevat de namen van de paar nazi-oorlogsmisdadigers die nog in leven zijn, maar dat lijstje wordt steeds korter. Toen de Israëli's jaren geleden een grote actie op touw zetten om Adolf Eichman te ontvoeren en te berechten om een voorbeeld te stellen, werden andere nazi's gewoon in het geheim vermoord. Tot de tweede groep behoren bijna uitsluitend hedendaagse terroristen, voornamelijk Arabieren die al Israëlisch of joods bloed hebben vergoten – zoals Ahmed Jibril, Abu Nidal – of die dat van plan zijn, plus een paar niet-Arabieren.

Categorie drie, waaronder ook de naam van Gerry Bull had kunnen vallen, omvat mensen die voor Israëls vijanden werken en met hun werk Israël en zijn burgers in gevaar zouden kunnen brengen als ze niet ingrepen.

De gemeenschappelijke factor is dat alle personen op deze lijst bloed aan hun handen moeten hebben of kunnen krijgen.

Als een aanslag noodzakelijk is, verwijst de premier de zaak naar een juridisch onderzoeker die strikt in het geheim zijn werk doet. Maar weinig Israëlische juristen en geen enkele burger hebben ooit van hem gehoord. Deze onderzoeker houdt een 'rechtszitting' met een aanklager en een verdediger. Daarbij wordt de aanklacht onderzocht. Als het verzoek van de Mossad wordt toegewezen, gaat de zaak weer terug naar de premier, die zijn handtekening zet. Het *kidon*-team doet de rest... als het lukt.

De theorie dat Gerry Bull door de Mossad zou zijn vermoord rammelde aan alle kanten. Bull werkte inderdaad voor Saddam Hoessein. Hij ontwierp nieuwe conventionele artillerie (die Israël niet kon bereiken), een raketprogramma (dat ooit een gevaar zou kunnen worden) en een reusachtig kanon (waar Israël zich totaal geen zorgen over maakte). Maar er waren nog honderden anderen zoals Bull. Een stuk of zes Duitse bedrijven waren betrokken bij Iraks afschuwelijke gifgasproduktie, waarmee Saddam de Israëli's al had bedreigd. Duitsers en Brazilianen werkten hard aan de raketten van Saad-16. En de Fransen hielpen de Irakezen bij de ontwikkeling van een kernbom.

Dat Israël grote belangstelling had voor Bull, zijn ideeën, zijn ontwerpen en zijn activiteiten stond wel vast. Na zijn dood werd veel aandacht besteed aan het feit dat hij zich de voorafgaande maanden ongerust had gemaakt over inbraken in zijn flat tijdens zijn afwezigheid. Er was nooit iets gestolen, maar er waren wel sporen achtergelaten. Glazen waren verplaatst, ramen waren opengezet, een videoband was teruggespoeld en uit de recorder gehaald. Was dat soms als een waarschuwing bedoeld, had hij zich afgevraagd, en zat de Mossad erachter? Dat was inderdaad het geval, maar om een andere reden dan hij dacht.

De donkere vreemdelingen met het scherpe accent, die hem door heel Brussel hadden geschaduwd, werden door de media aangezien voor Israëlische agenten, die het juiste moment voor de aanslag hadden voorbereid. Het is alleen jammer dat Mossad-agenten niet de gewoonte hebben om rond te rennen en eruit te zien als Pancho Villa. O, ze waren er wel, maar niemand zag hen. Niet Gerry Bull en zijn vrienden en familie, en ook de Belgische politie niet. Ze waren in Brussel met een team dat voor Europeanen kon doorgaan – voor Belgen of voor Amerikanen, wat ze maar wilden. En zíj hadden de Belgen de tip gegeven dat Bull door een *andere* groepering werd geschaduwd.

Bovendien was Gerry Bull een bijzonder indiscreet man. Hij kon gewoon geen weerstand bieden aan een uitdaging. Hij had ooit voor Israël gewerkt – hij hield van het land en van de mensen – hij had veel vrienden in het Israëlische leger en hij kon zijn mond niet houden. Als je Bull provoceerde met opmerkingen als: 'Gerry, wedden dat je die raketten van Saad-16 nooit aan de praat krijgt?' hield hij rustig een monoloog van drie uur, waarin hij precies beschreef waar hij mee bezig was, hoe ver het project was gevorderd, wat de problemen waren en hoe hij die dacht op te lossen... Het ideale slachtoffer voor een inlichtingendienst. De week voor zijn dood had hij nog twee Israëlische generaals bij zich op kantoor ontvangen en hun een volledig beeld geschetst, zonder te weten dat alles werd opgenomen door de recorders in hun koffertjes. Waarom zouden de Israëli's zo'n bron van informatie hebben geëlimineerd?

16

En er was nog een ander punt. Als de Mossad een wetenschapper of industrieel wilde uitschakelen, kreeg het slachtoffer altijd een eerlijke waarschuwing – geen bizarre inbraak met verplaatste glazen of teruggespoelde videobanden, maar een serieuze verbale waarschuwing. Zelfs in het geval van dr. Yahia El Meshad, de Egyptische kernfysicus die aan de eerste Iraakse kernreactor werkte en op 13 juni 1980 in zijn kamer in het Parijse Meridien Hotel werd vermoord, was hieraan de hand gehouden. Een Arabisch sprekende *katsa* ging naar zijn kamer en zei hem onomwonden wat er zou gebeuren als hij zijn werk niet zou neerleggen. De Egyptenaar gaf hem een grote bek, wat niet zo verstandig was. Verzekeringsmaatschappijen vinden het niet verstandig om agenten van een Mossad *kidon*-team te beledigen. Twee uur later was Meshad dood. Maar hij had een eerlijke kans gekregen. Het jaar daarop werd het door de Fransen geleverde nucleaire complex van Osirak Een en Twee door een Israëlische luchtaanval vernietigd.

Bull was een ander type – een Amerikaan van Canadese afkomst, vriendelijk, sociaal en een groot whiskydrinker. De Israëli's konden als vrienden met hem praten en dat deden ze ook. Herhaaldelijk. Het zou heel simpel zijn geweest om hem te waarschuwen dat hij met zijn werk moest stoppen omdat er anders een doodseskader op hem zou worden afgestuurd. Niets persoonlijks, Gerry, maar zo gaan die dingen nu eenmaal.

Bull was niet geïnteresseerd in een postume onderscheiding van het Congres. Bovendien had hij de Israëli's en zijn goede vriend George Wong al verteld dat hij weg wilde uit Irak – letterlijk en contractueel. Hij had er genoeg van.

Met dr. Gerry Bull was iets heel anders gebeurd.

Gerald Vincent Bull werd in 1928 geboren in North Bay, in het Canadese Ontario. Op school was hij een goede leerling die graag hoge cijfers haalde en bewondering oogstte. Toen hij zestien was, mocht hij gaan studeren, maar alleen de Technische Hogeschool van Toronto wilde zo'n jonge student inschrijven. Daar bewees hij dat hij niet alleen slim was, maar werkelijk briljant. Op zijn tweeëntwintigste haalde hij zijn graad, de jongste student uit de geschiedenis. Vooral de vliegtuigbouw had zijn belangstelling en met name de ballistiek: de studie van voorwerpen – projectielen of raketten – tijdens de vlucht. Daaruit ontstond zijn interesse in artillerie.

Na zijn studie kwam hij in dienst bij CARDE, het Canadian Armament and Research Establishment in Valcartier, toen nog een kleine stad niet ver van Quebec. In het begin van de jaren vijftig richtte de mens zijn blik niet alleen op het luchtruim maar ook op het heelal. En het toverwoord was 'raketten'. Opnieuw liet Bull blijken dat hij meer was dan alleen maar technisch briljant. Hij had fantasie, hij was creatief en onconventioneel. Bij CARDE ontwikkelde hij voor het eerst het idee dat de rest van zijn leven zijn grote droom zou blijven.

Zoals alle nieuwe ideeën leek het heel simpel. Toen hij zich in het arsenaal van Amerikaanse raketten uit het eind van de jaren vijftig verdiepte, viel het hem op dat de eerste trap zo'n negentig procent van het hele ding uitmaakte. De tweede en derde trap daarboven waren veel kleiner en de capsule was niet meer dan een fractie van het geheel.

De eerste trap moest de raket de eerste 150 km omhoog stuwen, door de dichte atmosfeer, tegen de zwaartekracht in. Daarna was er veel minder kracht nodig om de capsule in de ruimte te brengen, in een baan van zo'n 400 tot 500 km boven de aarde. Bij iedere lancering brandde die grote en kostbare eerste trap volledig op en stortte vervolgens als schroot in de oceaan.

Stel dat je de tweede en derde trap met de capsule uit een reusachtig kanon zou kunnen afschieten om die eerste 150 km te overbruggen, peinsde Bull. In theorie was dat eenvoudiger en goedkoper, hield hij de financiers voor, en bovendien kon je dat kanon steeds opnieuw gebruiken.

Het was zijn eerste echte krachtmeting met de politiek en de bureaucratie, en die verloor hij, grotendeels vanwege zijn persoonlijkheid. Hij had de pest aan bureaucraten, en zij aan hem. Maar in 1961 had hij geluk. De McGill Universiteit steunde zijn idee, voornamelijk om publiciteit te krijgen. Het Amerikaanse leger zag er ook wat in, maar om heel andere redenen. De landmacht, verantwoordelijk voor de artillerie, was namelijk in een prestigestrijd met de luchtmacht gewikkeld om het gezag over de raketten en projectielen die hoger kwamen dan 100 km. Met hun financiële steun kon Bull op het eiland Barbados een klein research-complex installeren. Van de Amerikaanse landmacht kreeg hij een overtollig 16-inch scheepskanon (het grootste kaliber ter wereld), met één reserveloop, een kleine volgradar, een kraan en een paar trucks. McGill richtte de werkplaats in. Het was alsof Bull een formule-1 racewagen wilde gaan ontwikkelen in een garage in een achterbuurt, maar het lukte hem. En daarmee had hij zijn naam als uitvinder gevestigd. Hij was pas drieëndertig; verlegen, bedeesd, slordig, creatief en nog steeds een buitenbeentje.

Zijn onderzoek op Barbados noemde hij HARP of High Altitude Research Project. Hij stelde het oude scheepskanon op en richtte zijn aandacht op de raketten. Die noemde hij 'Martlet' of 'gierzwaluw', naar de vogel in het wapen van de McGill Universiteit.

Het was Bulls doel om een capsule met instrumenten sneller en goedkoper in een baan om de aarde te brengen dan wie ook. Hij besefte heel goed dat een mens nooit de druk van een lancering uit een kanon zou kunnen weerstaan, maar hij ging er terecht vanuit dat in de toekomst negentig procent van het onderzoek en het werk in de ruimte door machines zou worden verricht, niet door mensen. Maar onder Kennedy richtte Amerika – uitgedaagd door de ruimtevlucht van de Rus Gagarin – al zijn inspanningen op het sensationele maar vrij zinloze doel om muizen, honden, apen en uiteindelijk mensen in de ruimte te brengen.

Op Barbados werkte Gerry Bull stug door aan zijn kanon en zijn Martletraketten. In 1964 schoot hij een Martlet 92 km de lucht in. Daarna verlengde hij de loop van zijn kanon met nog eens 16 meter (tegen een kostprijs van maar 41 000 dollar) tot een lengte van 36 meter, waarmee het de langste geschutsloop ter wereld werd. Met dit kanon bereikte hij de magische grens van 150 km, met een capsule van 180 kilo.

Eén voor één loste hij alle problemen op. Een groot obstakel was de drijfstof. In een klein kanon komt de lading binnen een microseconde tot explosie. Het vrijkomende gas, dat nergens naartoe kan, stuwt het projectiel met een harde stoot naar buiten. Maar bij zo'n lange geschutsloop was een speciale, trager brandende drijfstof nodig om te voorkomen dat de loop zelf uiteen zou spatten.

Bull zocht daarom naar een poeder dat zijn raket uit die reusachtige loop zou lanceren met een lange, in snelheid toenemende 'whoesj'. Dat poeder bestond niet, dus ontwierp hij het zelf.

Ook wist hij dat geen enkel instrument de druk van 10 000 G zou overleven waarmee zelfs de tragere drijfstof de raket uit de geschutsloop stuwde. Daarom ontwierp hij een schokabsorberend systeem dat de druk tot 200 G verminderde. Een derde probleem was de terugslag. Dit was geen speelgoedpistooltje. De kracht van de terugslag hield gelijke tred met de omvang van de loop, de kracht van de lading en het gewicht van de capsule. Bull ontwierp een stelsel van veren en kleppen om de terugslag binnen aanvaardbare grenzen te houden.

Bulls oude tegenstanders op het Canadese ministerie van Defensie wisten hem in 1966 een hak te zetten door hun minister ertoe te bewegen de geldkraan dicht te draaien. Bull wierp tegen dat hij een capsule met instrumenten in de ruimte kon brengen voor een fractie van het bedrag dat een lancering vanaf Cape Canaveral kostte, maar tevergeefs. Om haar investering veilig te stellen besloot de Amerikaanse landmacht Gerry Bull daarom van Barbados naar Yuma in Arizona over te brengen.

In november van dat jaar schoot hij een capsule 180 km omhoog, een record dat vijfentwintig jaar stand zou houden. Maar in 1967 trok Canada zich volledig uit het project terug – niet alleen de regering, maar ook de McGill Universiteit sloot de geldkraan. En ten slotte zette ook de Amerikaanse landmacht er een streep onder. Het HARP-project werd afgesloten. Gerry Bull kocht een landgoed op de grens van North Vermont en Canada en vestigde zich daar als consulent.

Bij het HARP-experiment kunnen twee kanttekeningen worden geplaatst. Omstreeks 1990 kostte elke kilo instrumenten die met de Space Shuttle vanaf Cape Canaveral in de ruimte werd gebracht 10 000 dollar. En in 1988 begon men in het Lawrence Livermore National Laboratory in Californië met een nieuw project. Daarbij ging het om de ontwikkeling van een groot kanon, met een loop van een kaliber van slechts tien centimeter en vijftig meter lang. Met een budget van enkele honderden miljoenen dollars hoopten de Amerikanen een nog veel groter kanon te ontwikkelen om raketten de ruimte in te sturen. De naam van het project was SHARP, of 'Super-High Altitude Research Project'.

Gerry Bull woonde tien jaar op zijn landgoed in Highwater aan de Canadese grens, waar hij doorging met zijn eigen project. Hij werkte niet langer aan een kanon om raketten te lanceren, maar richtte zich volledig op zijn andere interesse, het lucratieve terrein van de conventionele artillerie.

Hij begon met het belangrijkste probleem. Bijna alle legers ter wereld hebben hun artillerie gebaseerd op het universele 155-mm houwitser veldgeschut. Bij een beschieting is de partij met het grootste bereik altijd in het voordeel. Die kan de vijand onder vuur nemen zonder zelf geraakt te worden. Daarom besloot Bull het bereik van het 155-mm veldgeschut te vergroten en de nauwkeurigheid te verbeteren. Dat was al eerder geprobeerd, maar niemand was daar nog in geslaagd. Gerry Bull lukte het binnen vier jaar.

Hij begon met de munitie. De granaat die Bull ontwierp, kwam met hetzelfde 155-mm kanon anderhalve keer zo ver, was veel nauwkeuriger en explodeerde met dezelfde kracht in 4700 fragmenten, terwijl de standaard NAVO-granaat slechts in 1350 fragmenten explodeerde. Toch was de NAVO niet geïnteresseerd. De Russen ook niet, goddank.

Bull liet zich niet uit het veld slaan, ploeterde verder en produceerde een totaal nieuwe granaat met een sterk vergroot bereik. Nog steeds had de NAVO geen belangstelling. Zij bleven bij hun oude leveranciers en hun standaardgranaat.

Hoewel de grootmachten geen interesse toonden, was er wel belangstelling uit andere landen. Militaire delegaties kwamen naar Highwater om met Bull te spreken. Daar waren Israëli's onder (met wie hij de vriendschap voortzette die op Barbados was begonnen toen Israël waarnemers had gestuurd), maar ook afgezanten uit Egypte, Venezuela, Chili en Iran. Verder gaf hij artillerie-adviezen op ander gebied aan Engeland, Nederland, Italië, Canada en de Verenigde Staten. Militaire deskundigen (behalve die van het Pentagon) volgden met ontzag zijn experimenten.

In 1972 kreeg Gerry Bull heel discreet de Amerikaanse nationaliteit. Het jaar daarop begon hij met de aanpassing van het 155-mm veldgeschut. Binnen twee jaar kwam hij met de volgende doorbraak, toen hij ontdekte dat de ideale lengte voor een geschutsloop exact vijfenveertig keer het kaliber bedraagt. Hij perfectioneerde een nieuw ontwerp van het standaard 155-mm kanon en noemde het GC-45 (een afkorting van 'Gun Calibre'). Dit nieuwe kanon, met zijn verbeterde granaten, had een groter bereik en was nauwkeuriger dan alle artilleriewapens binnen het communistische arsenaal. Maar als hij op een contract had gehoopt, kwam hij bedrogen uit. Weer koos het Pentagon voor de wapenlobby, met hun nieuwe plannen voor raketgestuwde granaten en met vergelijkbare prestaties als Bulls projectielen, maar wel acht keer zo duur.

Bulls ondergang begon onschuldig genoeg, toen hij na intriges van de CIA werd gevraagd als artillerie-adviseur in Zuid-Afrika, dat toen de door Moskou gesteunde Cubanen in Angola bestreed.

In politiek opzicht was Bull vreselijk naïef. Hij ging naar Zuid-Afrika en hij kon goed met de Zuidafrikanen opschieten. Het feit dat het land wegens de apartheidspolitiek een internationale paria was, kon hem niet schelen. Hij hielp bij de verbetering van de artillerie volgens de lijnen van zijn GC-45 houwitser met lange loop, waar steeds meer vraag naar kwam. Later produceerden de Zuidafrikanen hun eigen versie, en het waren deze kanonnen die de Sovjet-artillerie vernietigden en de Russen en Cubanen terugdreven.

Terug in Amerika begon Bull zijn granaten te exporteren. Inmiddels was Jimmy Carter president geworden en stond alles in het teken van een fatsoenlijke politiek. Bull werd gearresteerd op beschuldiging van illegale export naar een verboden land. De CIA liet hem meteen vallen. Hij kreeg het advies zijn mond te houden en schuld te bekennen. Het was maar een formaliteit, zeiden ze hem. Een berisping voor een technisch vergrijp, meer niet.

Op 16 juni 1980 werd hij tot een jaar gevangenisstraf veroordeeld, met een aftrek van zes maanden, en een boete van 105 000 dollar. Hij zat vier maanden en zeventien dagen in de Allenwood-gevangenis in Pennsylvania. Maar dat vond Bull niet eens het ergste.

Wat hij niet kon verdragen waren de schande en het verraad. Hoe hadden ze hem zo'n streek kunnen leveren? Hij had Amerika geholpen wanneer hij maar kon, hij had de Amerikaanse nationaliteit aangenomen en in 1976 was hij op het verzoek van de CIA ingegaan. Terwijl hij in Allenwood zat, ging zijn bedrijf SRC failliet. Hij was geruïneerd.

Toen hij uit de gevangenis kwam, verliet hij Amerika en Canada voorgoed en emigreerde naar Brussel, waar hij helemaal overnieuw begon in een één-kamerflatje met een kitchenette. Vrienden zeiden later dat hij een ander mens was geworden. Hij zou het Amerika en de CIA nooit vergeven, hoewel hij nog jarenlang vocht voor een nieuw proces en rehabilitatie.

Hij vestigde zich weer als consulent en ging in op een aanbod, hem al vóór zijn arrestatie gedaan, om voor de Chinezen te gaan werken aan de verbetering van hun artillerie. Tot halverwege de jaren tachtig werkte Bull voornamelijk voor Peking. Hij reorganiseerde de Chinese artillerie volgens het ontwerp van zijn GC-45 kanon, dat nu wereldwijd onder licentie werd verkocht door de Oostenrijkse firma Voest-Alpine, die het patent had gekocht voor een eenmalig bedrag van twee miljoen dollar. Bull was een slecht zakenman, anders zou hij multimiljonair zijn geweest.

Tijdens zijn afwezigheid was er van alles gebeurd. De Zuidafrikanen hadden zijn ontwerp verbeterd. Hun getrokken houwitser, de G-5, was gebaseerd op Bulls GC-45. Daarnaast kwamen ze met een zelfrijdend kanon, de G-6. Met Bulls verbeterde granaten hadden de twee kanonnen een bereik van 40 km. Zuid-Afrika exporteerde het geschut over de hele wereld, maar omdat Bull geen goede afspraken had gemaakt, kreeg hij geen cent aan royalty's.

Onder de klanten voor dit geschut was een zekere Saddam Hoessein, de president van Irak. Het waren deze kanonnen die tijdens de acht jaar durende Iraaks-Iraanse oorlog de menselijke aanvalsgolven van Iraanse fanatici braken en hen uiteindelijk versloegen in de moerassen van Fao. Maar Saddam had een eigen variant bedacht, die vooral in de strijd rond Fao werd toegepast. Hij had de granaten met gifgas gevuld.

Bull werkte toen voor Spanje en Joegoslavië, om de oude Joegoslavische 130-mm artillerie van Russische makelij om te bouwen tot 155-mm geschut met verbeterde granaten. Hoewel hij dat niet meer zou meemaken, waren dit de kanonnen die bij het uiteenvallen van Joegoslavië door de Serven werden geërfd en waarmee ze in de burgeroorlog de steden van de Kroaten en de moslims in puin schoten. In 1987 hoorde hij dat de Verenigde Staten toch tot de ontwikkeling van een raketkanon hadden besloten, maar zonder Gerry Bull daarbij te betrekken.

Die winter kreeg hij een vreemd telefoontje van de Iraakse ambassade in Bonn. Of dr. Bull een bezoek aan Bagdad wilde brengen als gast van Irak?

Wat hij niet wist was dat Irak halverwege de jaren tachtig getuige was geweest van 'Operation Staunch', een Amerikaanse poging om alle wapenexporten naar Iran stop te zetten na het bloedbad onder de Amerikaanse mariniers in Beiroet, bij een door Iran gesteunde aanval van de fanatieke Hezbollah op hun kazerne.

Hoewel Irak de vruchten plukte van 'Operation Staunch' concludeerde Saddam dat Irak hetzelfde zou kunnen gebeuren. Vanaf dat moment besloot Irak om zoveel mogelijk wapens zelf te produceren en niet van import afhankelijk te zijn. Gerry Bull was in de eerste plaats een ontwerper, en daarom hadden ze belangstelling voor hem.

De opdracht om hem te rekruteren ging naar Amer Saadi, de tweede man op het ministerie van Industrie en Militaire Industrialisatie, het MIMI. Toen Bull in januari 1988 in Bagdad aankwam, werd hij handig bespeeld door Saadi, een gladde, kosmopolitische diplomaat/wetenschapper, die behalve Arabisch ook Engels, Frans en Duits sprak.

De Irakezen, zei hij, wilden Bulls hulp bij hun droom om satellieten de ruimte in te sturen voor vreedzame doeleinden. Maar daar hadden ze een geschikte raket voor nodig. Hun Egyptische en Braziliaanse wetenschappers hadden voorgesteld om vijf Scud-raketten (waarvan Irak er negenhonderd van de Sovjetunie had gekocht) aan elkaar te koppelen. Maar dat leverde nogal wat problemen op. Daarom moesten ze toegang krijgen tot een supercomputer. Kon Bull hen daarbij helpen?

Bull was dol op problemen. Die waren zijn reden van bestaan. Hij had geen toegang tot een supercomputer, maar hij was er zelf bijna een. En als Irak werkelijk het eerste Arabische land wilde zijn dat een satelliet in de ruimte bracht, was er ook een andere mogelijkheid... goedkoper, eenvoudiger en sneller dan het gebruik van een conventionele raket. Hoe dan? wilde de Arabier weten. En Bull vertelde het hem.

Voor maar drie miljoen dollar, zei hij, kon hij een reusachtig kanon produceren dat een raket zou kunnen lanceren. Het was een programma van vijf jaar, waarmee hij de Amerikanen in Livermore een stap vóór zou zijn. Een geweldige triomf voor de Arabische wereld! Dr. Saadi reageerde vol bewondering. Hij zou Bulls idee aan zijn regering voorleggen, met een positief advies. En wilde dr. Bull intussen zijn licht laten schijnen over de Iraakse artillerie?

Tegen het eind van die eerste week had Bull toegezegd dat hij zich zou verdiepen in het probleem om vijf Scuds aan elkaar te koppelen als eerste trap van een raket voor de lange afstand; om twee nieuwe kanonnen voor het leger te ontwerpen; en om een formeel plan in te dienen voor zijn superkanon.

Net als bij Zuid-Afrika dacht hij niet na over het politieke karakter van het regime waarvoor hij werkte. Vrienden hadden wel verteld dat Saddam Hoessein meer bloed aan zijn handen had dan enige andere leider in het Midden-Oosten, maar in 1988 waren er nog duizenden fatsoenlijke bedrijven en tientallen regeringen die zaken wilden doen met het rijke Irak.

Het lokaas voor Gerry Bull was het superkanon, zijn troetelkind. Eindelijk had hij nu een regering gevonden die bereid was er voldoende geld in te steken, zodat hij zijn droom zou kunnen verwezenlijken en in het walhalla van de wetenschap zou worden opgenomen.

In maart 1988 stuurde Amer Saadi een diplomaat naar Brussel om met Bull te spreken. Ja, verklaarde de wetenschapper, hij had al vorderingen gemaakt met de technische problemen van de eerste trap van de Iraakse raket. Daar

23

wilde hij graag meer over zeggen, zodra er een contract was getekend met zijn bedrijf, de uit de as herrezen SRC of 'Space Research Company'. Er werd een akkoord gesloten. Irak besefte dat een bedrag van drie miljoen dollar veel te weinig was. De Irakezen maakten er tien miljoen dollar van, maar drongen wel aan op haast.

Als Bull snel werkte, dan werkte hij ook heel erg snel. Binnen een maand stelde hij een team samen van de beste beschikbare freelancers die hij kon vinden. Leider van het superkanonprogramma in Irak werd Christopher Cowley, een Britse projectingenieur. Voor het raketprogramma van Saad-16 in het noorden van Irak bedacht Bull de codenaam 'Project Bird'. Het superkanonprogramma kreeg de naam 'Project Babylon'.

In mei waren de exacte specificaties van Babylon al bekend. Het zou een ongelooflijke machine worden, met een boring van één meter, een loop van 156 meter en 1665 ton zwaar – meer dan twee keer de hoogte van de zuil van Nelson in Londen, even hoog als het Washington-monument. De vier terugslagcilinders hadden elk een gewicht van 60 ton, de twee buffercilinders wogen 7 ton en de stootbodem 182 ton.

Het speciale staal moest een inwendige druk van 70 000 pond per vierkante inch kunnen weerstaan, en over een treksterkte van 1250 megapascal beschikken.

Bull had Bagdad al duidelijk gemaakt dat hij eerst een kleiner prototype wilde bouwen, een mini-Babylon, met een boring van 350 mm en een gewicht van maar 113 ton. Daarmee zou hij neuskegels kunnen testen die ook nuttig waren voor het raketproject. De Irakezen vonden het best. Die technologie konden ze goed gebruiken.

De betekenis van die Iraakse belangstelling voor neuskegeltechnologie scheen Gerry Bull op dat moment te ontgaan. Of misschien dacht hij er liever niet over na, nu hij eindelijk de kans had zijn droom te verwezenlijken. Geavanceerde neuskegels zijn nodig om te voorkomen dat de nuttige last verbrandt door de wrijvingshitte op het moment dat de raket in de atmosfeer terugkeert. Maar capsules met instrumenten die in een baan om de aarde worden gebracht, keren niet terug in de atmosfeer. Die blijven boven.

Eind mei 1988 plaatste Christopher Cowley zijn eerste orders bij Walter Somers in Birmingham voor de buizen waaruit de loop van de mini-Babylon zou worden samengesteld. De segmenten voor de grote Babylons Een, Twee, Drie en Vier zouden later volgen. De andere merkwaardige staalorders werden over heel Europa verspreid.

Bull werkte in een indrukwekkend tempo. Binnen twee maanden had hij al resultaten geboekt waarvoor een overheidsproject twee jaar nodig zou hebben gehad. Eind 1988 had hij voor Irak twee nieuwe kanonnen ontworpen – zelfrijdend geschut in plaats van de getrokken houwitsers uit Zuid-Afrika.

24

De twee kanonnen waren veel krachtiger dan het geschut van de buurlanden Iran, Turkije, Jordanië en Saoedi-Arabië, die hun artillerie van de NAVO en uit Amerika betrokken.

Bull loste ook het probleem op hoe de vijf Scuds aan elkaar moesten worden gekoppeld als eerste trap voor de Bird-raket, die *Al-Abeid* of de 'Gelovige' zou worden genoemd. Hij had ontdekt dat de Irakezen en Brazilianen die aan Saad-16 werkten zich baseerden op foutieve gegevens uit een windtunnel, die niet goed werkte. Toen hij klaar was met zijn nieuwe berekeningen liet hij het werk verder aan de Brazilianen over.

In mei 1989 werd in Bagdad een grote wapenexpositie gehouden waarbij het grootste deel van de internationale wapenindustrie, de pers en talloze waarnemers van regeringen en inlichtingendiensten kwamen kijken. Er was grote belangstelling voor de modellen van de twee grote kanonnen. In december, begeleid door veel trompetgeschal in de media, volgde de proeflancering van de *Al-Abeid*, die voor westerse analisten een grote verrassing was.

Op de voet gevolgd door de Iraakse tv-camera's verhief de grote drietrapsraket zich bulderend vanaf de ruimtebasis Al-Anbar en verdween uit het gezicht. Drie dagen later moest Washington toegeven dat de raket inderdaad in staat leek een satelliet in de ruimte te brengen.

Maar de analisten trokken nog een conclusie. Als dat zo was, kon de *Al-Abeid* ook als een intercontinentale ballistische raket worden gebruikt. Westerse inlichtingendiensten kwamen haastig terug op hun mening dat Saddam Hoessein de eerstkomende jaren nog geen reële bedreiging kon vormen.

De drie belangrijkste diensten, de Amerikaanse CIA, de Britse SIS en de Israëlische Mossad, kwamen tot het inzicht dat het Babylon-kanon een amusant speeltje was en de Bird-raket een serieus gevaar. Daar vergisten ze zich in. Het was de *Al-Abeid* die niet werkte.

Bull wist ook waarom en hij vertelde de Israëli's wat er was gebeurd. De raket was tot 12 000 meter hoogte gestegen en daar uit het gezicht verdwenen. De tweede trap had zich niet van de eerste afgescheiden en een derde trap was er niet. Dat was een dummy. Bull wist dat, omdat hij voor de Iraakse regering in februari naar Peking moest om de Chinezen over te halen de derde trap te leveren.

Hij vertrok inderdaad naar China, maar daar kreeg hij nul op het rekest. Tijdens zijn verblijf sprak hij uitvoerig met zijn oude vriend George Wong. Er was iets misgegaan met het Iraakse project, iets waarover Gerry zich grote zorgen maakte maar dat niets met de Israëli's te maken had. Een paar keer zei hij tegen Wong dat hij uit Irak weg wilde, en snel. Hij had zich iets gerealiseerd, en het werd tijd om te vertrekken. Daar had hij gelijk in, maar het was al te laat.

25

Op 15 februari 1990 belegde president Saddam Hoessein een voltallige vergadering van zijn adviesraad in zijn paleis in Sarseng, hoog in de Koerdische bergen.

Hij hield van Sarseng. Het lag op een heuveltop en door het driedubbele glas van de ramen had hij uitzicht op de omgeving, waar de Koerdische boeren in hun hutjes de bittere winter moesten trotseren. Het lag niet ver van de ontredderde stad Halabja, waar Saddam op 17 en 18 maart 1988 bevel had gegeven de 70 000 burgers te straffen voor hun vermeende collaboratie met de Iraniërs.

Toen zijn artillerie weer zweeg, waren vijfduizend van die Koerdische honden gedood en zevenduizend voor het leven verminkt. Persoonlijk was hij zeer onder de indruk geweest van de uitwerking van de waterstofcyanide die de artilleriegranaten hadden verspreid. De Duitse bedrijven die hem hadden geholpen met de technologie om dit gas – en de zenuwgassen Tabun en Sarin – te produceren, was hij bijzonder dankbaar. Hun gas vertoonde veel overeenkomsten met Zyklon-B, dat jaren geleden zo effectief tegen de joden was gebruikt en in de toekomst misschien weer nuttige diensten kon bewijzen.

Die ochtend stond hij voor het raam van zijn kleedkamer en tuurde naar buiten. Al zestien jaar had hij de onbetwiste macht in dit land, en in die tijd had hij veel mensen moeten straffen. Maar hij had ook veel bereikt.

Een nieuwe Sennaherib was uit Nineveh verrezen, en een nieuwe Nebukadnezar uit Babylon. Sommigen hadden dat snel begrepen en zich onderworpen. Anderen hadden het op de harde manier moeten leren. De meesten van hen waren nu dood. Anderen, vele anderen, zouden nog volgen.

Hij hoorde het konvooi helikopters vanuit het zuiden naderen, terwijl zijn bediende het groene sjaaltje schikte dat hij graag in de V-hals van zijn uniformjasje droeg om zijn onderkin te verbergen. Toen hij tevreden was, pakte hij zijn persoonlijke wapen, een vergulde Beretta van Iraaks fabrikaat, en stak het in de holster aan zijn riem. Hij had het ooit tegen een minister van zijn kabinet gebruikt, en misschien zou dat nog eens nodig zijn. Hij droeg het altijd bij zich.

Een adjudant klopte op de deur en meldde dat de gasten in de vergaderzaal op de president zaten te wachten.

Toen hij de lange zaal binnenkwam, met de grote spiegelruiten die over het besneeuwde landschap uitkeken, stond iedereen op. Alleen hier in Sarseng was hij niet bang voor aanslagen. Hij wist dat het paleis werd omringd door drie linies keurtroepen van zijn presidentiële lijfwacht, de Amn-al-Khass, onder bevel van zijn eigen zoon Kusaj, en dat niemand die grote ramen zou kunnen naderen. Op het dak stonden Franse Crotale luchtdoelraketten opgesteld en zijn jagers patrouilleerden in het luchtruim boven de bergen.

Hij ging zitten op de indrukwekkende stoel in het midden van de tafel die de dwarsbalk vormde van de T. Naast hem zaten vier van zijn meest vertrouwde assistenten, twee aan elke kant. In Saddams ogen was er bij zijn medewerkers maar één eigenschap die telde: absolute, onvoorwaardelijke, slaafse trouw.

Maar zelfs daarin bestonden nog gradaties, zoals de ervaring hem had geleerd. Boven aan de lijst kwam zijn familie, daarna de clan en ten slotte de stam. Een oud Arabisch spreekwoord luidde: 'Ik en mijn broer tegen onze neef; ik en mijn neef tegen de wereld.' Daar geloofde Saddam in. Het werkte.

Hij kwam uit de sloppen van het stadje Tikrit, uit de stam van de al-Tikriti. Veel leden van zijn familie en de al-Tikriti bekleedden hoge posities in Irak. Alle wreedheden, mislukkingen en excessen werden hun vergeven zolang ze maar trouw bleven aan Saddam. Had zijn tweede zoon, de psychopaat Udaj, niet een bediende doodgeslagen en gratie gekregen?

Rechts van hem zat Izzat Ibrahim, zijn eerste assistent, daarnaast zijn schoonzoon Hoessein Kamil, hoofd van het MIMI, de man die over de wapens ging. Links zaten Taha Ramadan, de minister-president, en naast hem Sadoun Hammadi, vice-premier en een vroom sji'itisch moslim. Saddam zelf was een soenniet, maar godsdienst was het enige terrein waarop hij ruime opvattingen had. Hij was niet erg gelovig (behalve als het hem uitkwam) en dus kon het hem niet schelen. Zijn minister van Buitenlandse Zaken, Tariq Aziz, was een christen. Nou en? De man deed wat hem gezegd werd.

Langs de bovenkant van de stok van de T zaten de militaire leiders: de generaals van de Republikeinse Garde, de infanterie, de pantsertroepen, de artillerie en de genie. Wat verder weg zaten de vier deskundigen die met hun rapporten de reden waren voor deze vergadering.

Twee van hen zaten aan de rechterkant van de tafel: dr. Amer Saadi, een technoloog en assistent van Saddams schoonzoon, met naast hem brigade-generaal Hassan Rahmani, hoofd van de contraspionagesectie van de Mukhabarat, de Iraakse geheime dienst. Tegenover hen zaten dr. Ismail Ubaidi, hoofd van de sectie buitenland van de Mukhabarat, en brigadegeneraal Omar Khatib, de leider van de gevreesde geheime politie, de Amn-al-Amm. De drie hoofden van de geheime dienst hadden een duidelijk omschreven taak. Dr. Ubaidi ging over de spionage in het buitenland, Rahmani bestreed de buitenlandse spionage binnen Irak en Khatib hield de Iraakse bevolking onder de duim en drukte elk binnenlands verzet de kop in met behulp van een uitgebreid netwerk van verklikkers en door het verspreiden van geruchten over wat er gebeurde met gevangenen die naar de Abu Khraib gevangenis ten westen van Bagdad of naar Khatibs persoonlijke ondervragingscen-

27

trum onder het AMAM-hoofdkwartier werden gebracht, dat spottend de 'Gymzaal' werd genoemd.

Saddam Hoessein had al zoveel protesten gehoord tegen de wreedheid van het hoofd van zijn geheime politie, maar hij had ze altijd grinnikend weggewuifd. Het verhaal ging dat hij zelf Khatib de bijnaam had gegeven van Al Mu'azib, de Beul. Khatib was natuurlijk een al-Tikriti en trouw aan Saddam tot in de dood.

Sommige dictators houden een vergadering graag beperkt als er gevoelige zaken aan de orde komen, maar Saddam dacht daar heel anders over. Als er vuil werk verricht moest worden, wilde hij iedereen erbij betrekken, zodat niemand achteraf zou kunnen zeggen dat hij van niets wist en schone handen had. De boodschap aan zijn naaste medewerkers was duidelijk: als ik ten onder ga, sleep ik jullie allemaal mee.

Toen iedereen weer was gaan zitten, knikte de president naar zijn schoonzoon Hoessein Kamil, die dr. Saadi vroeg om verslag uit te brengen. De technocraat las zijn rapport voor zonder één keer zijn ogen op te slaan. Niemand was zo dom om Saddam recht aan te kijken. De president beweerde dat hij iemand in zijn ziel kon kijken, en veel mensen geloofden dat. Zo'n blik kon op moedig gedrag wijzen, maar ook als uitdagend of disloyaal worden uitgelegd. En als de president ontrouw vermoedde, stierf het slachtoffer een afschuwelijke dood.

Toen dr. Saadi was uitgesproken, dacht Saddam een tijdje na. 'Deze man, die Canadees, hoeveel weet hij eigenlijk?'

'Niet alles, maar genoeg om zijn conclusies te trekken, *sajidi*.'

Saadi gebruikte de aanspreektitel die overeenkwam met het Westerse 'meneer', maar die meer eerbied uitdrukt. Men kon Saddam ook met *sajid Rais* aanspreken: 'meneer de president'.

'Hoeveel tijd zou hem dat kosten?'

'Niet veel, *sajidi*.'

'En hij heeft met de Israëli's gesproken?'

'Dat doet hij regelmatig, *sajid Rais*,' antwoordde dr. Ubaidi. 'Hij is al jaren met hen bevriend. Hij is in Tel Aviv geweest en hij heeft lezingen over ballistiek gehouden voor de stafofficieren van hun artillerie. Hij heeft daar veel contacten, mogelijk zelfs bij de Mossad, hoewel hij dat misschien zelf niet weet.'

'Kunnen we het project ook zonder hem voltooien?' vroeg Saddam Hoessein.

Zijn schoonzoon Hoessein Kamil mengde zich nu in het gesprek. 'Hij is een vreemde man. Hij staat erop zijn belangrijkste papieren met zich mee te zeulen in een grote canvas tas. Ik heb de mensen van onze contraspionagedienst gevraagd erin te kijken en de papieren te kopiëren.'

28

'En dat is gebeurd?' De president keek naar Hassan Rahmani, het hoofd van de contraspionage.

'Onmiddellijk, *sajid Rais*. Vorige maand, toen hij hier op bezoek was. Hij drinkt veel whisky. Daar hebben we een middeltje in gedaan, zodat hij lang en diep zou slapen. Daarna hebben we zijn tas meegenomen en alle papieren gekopieerd. Bovendien hebben we al zijn technische gesprekken op de band opgenomen. De kopieën en de transcripties zijn allemaal aan onze kameraad dr. Saadi doorgegeven.'

De blik van de president gleed weer naar de wetenschapper. 'Ik vraag u dus opnieuw: kunt u dit project ook zonder hem voltooien?'

'Ja, *sajid Rais*, dat denk ik wel. Sommige van zijn berekeningen begreep hij alleen zelf, maar onze beste mathematici hebben er een maand op gestudeerd en kunnen ze nu ook volgen. De ingenieurs doen de rest.'

Hoessein Kamil keek zijn ondergeschikte waarschuwend aan. Vergis je niet, beste vriend.

'En waar is hij nu?' vroeg de president.

'Hij is naar China vertrokken, *sajidi*,' antwoordde het hoofd van de buitenlandse inlichtingendienst, Ubaidi. 'Hij probeert bij de Chinezen een derde trap voor de *Al-Abeid* raket los te krijgen. Dat zal hem helaas niet lukken. Half maart wordt hij in Brussel terugverwacht.'

'En daar hebt u goede mensen?'

'Jawel, *sajidi*. Ik laat hem al tien maanden schaduwen in Brussel. Zo weten we dat hij Israëlische delegaties in zijn kantoor ontvangt. En we hebben de sleutels van zijn appartement.'

'Geef het bevel dan maar. Als hij terugkomt.'

'Goed, *sajid Rais*.' Ubaidi dacht aan zijn vier mannen in de Belgische hoofdstad. Een van hen, Abdelrahman Mojeddin, had dit al eerder gedaan. Hij zou de opdracht krijgen.

De drie inlichtingenofficieren en dr. Saadi werden weggestuurd. De rest bleef. Toen ze alleen waren, richtte Saddam Hoessein zich tot zijn schoonzoon. 'En die andere zaak? Wanneer kan ik daarop rekenen?'

'Tegen het eind van het jaar. Dat hebben ze me verzekerd, *Abu Kusaj*.' Omdat hij familie was, mocht Kamil de intiemere aanspreekvorm 'vader van Kusaj' gebruiken. Het herinnerde de anderen eraan dat er rangen en standen waren.

De president bromde wat. 'We zullen een nieuwe plaats nodig hebben, een vesting. Geen bestaande plek, hoe geheim ook. Een nieuwe, geheime plaats waar niemand iets van weet, behalve een kleine groep. Niet eens iedereen die hier aanwezig is. Geen civiel technisch project, maar een militaire installatie. Kunt u dat regelen?'

Generaal Ali Musuli van de genie trok zijn schouders recht en richtte zijn blik halverwege de borst van de president.

29

'Met trots, *sajid Rais*.'
'En aan het hoofd stelt u uw allerbeste man.'
'Ik weet wie we nodig hebben, *sajidi*. Een kolonel. Een genie in constructies en camouflagetechnieken. Volgens de Rus Stepanov was hij de beste leerling van de *maskirovka*.'
'Breng hem bij me. Niet hier, maar in Bagdad. Over twee dagen. Ik zal hem persoonlijk de opdracht geven. Is hij een goed lid van de Ba'ath-partij, deze kolonel? Trouw aan de partij en aan mij?'
'Absoluut, *sajidi*. Hij zou voor u sterven.'
'Net als iedereen hier, neem ik aan.' Hij wachtte even, voordat hij er zacht aan toevoegde: 'Laten we hopen dat het niet zover komt.'
Daar wist niemand iets op te zeggen. Gelukkig was de vergadering afgelopen.

Op 17 maart kwam dr. Gerry Bull in Brussel terug, uitgeput en gedeprimeerd. Omdat zijn reis naar China niets had opgeleverd, veronderstelden zijn collega's. Maar er was meer aan de hand.
Toen hij twee jaar geleden voor het eerst in Bagdad was geweest, had Bull zich laten overtuigen – omdat hij het wilde geloven – dat het raketprogramma en het Babylon-kanon bestemd waren voor de lancering van kleine, van instrumenten voorziene satellieten in een baan om de aarde. Hij begreep wat het voor het zelfrespect en de trots van de hele Arabische wereld zou betekenen als Irak daartoe in staat zou zijn. Bovendien zou het geld opleveren omdat Irak dan communicatie- en weersatellieten voor andere landen de ruimte in kon sturen.
Zoals hij het had begrepen zou het Babylon-kanon zijn raket naar het zuidoosten afvuren, over de hele lengte van Irak, via Saoedi-Arabië en de zuidelijke Indische Oceaan, de ruimte in. Zo had hij het berekend.
Maar hij moest zijn collega's gelijk geven toen ze zeiden dat geen enkele westerse natie dat zou geloven. Die zouden ervan uitgaan dat het een militair kanon was. Daarom hadden ze de orders voor de loopsegmenten, de stootbodem en het terugslagmechanisme zoveel mogelijk verspreid.
Alleen hij, Gerald Vincent Bull, kende de waarheid, die heel simpel was: het kanon kon niet worden gebruikt voor de lancering van conventionele granaten, hoe groot die ook mochten zijn.
Om te beginnen kon het Babylon-kanon met zijn 156 meter lange loop nooit lang genoeg overeind blijven zonder steunen. Het had één steun nodig voor elke twee van de zesentwintig segmenten, zelfs als de loop – zoals Bull verwachtte – langs een 45 graden steile berghelling zou worden gelegd. Zonder die steunen zou de loop als natte spaghetti ineenzakken en scheuren.
Het was dus onmogelijk de loop te richten, niet omlaag of omhoog, en niet

naar links of rechts. Daarvoor moest het kanon eerst worden ontmanteld, wat weken zou kosten. Zelfs voor het schoonmaken en herladen zouden een paar dagen nodig zijn.

Bovendien zou een 'salvo' grote slijtage veroorzaken in de kostbare loop. En in de laatste plaats was het onmogelijk het Babylon-kanon te verbergen voor een tegenaanval. Iedere keer dat het vuurde, zou er een steekvlam van 90 meter lang te zien zijn, die geen enkele satelliet of vliegtuig kon ontgaan. Binnen enkele seconden zouden de Amerikanen de coördinaten kunnen vaststellen. En de trillingen konden zelfs door seismografische instrumenten in Californië worden geregistreerd. Tegen iedereen die het maar horen wilde had Bull daarom gezegd: 'Het kan nooit als een wapen worden gebruikt.'

Alleen was hij na twee jaar in Irak tot de conclusie gekomen dat wetenschap voor Saddam Hoessein maar één enkele toepassing kende: als middel om wapens te produceren, met de bijbehorende macht. Nergens anders voor. Waarom zou hij dan het Babylon-kanon financieren? Het kon maar één keer vuren voordat het door een vijandelijke luchtaanval zou worden vernietigd, en de enige mogelijke lading was een satelliet of een conventionele granaat.

Pas in China, in het gezelschap van de begripvolle George Wong, drong het eindelijk tot hem door. Het was het laatste probleem dat hij zou oplossen.

De grote Ram Charger reed in hoog tempo over de hoofdweg van Qatar naar Abu Dhabi in de Verenigde Arabische Emiraten. De airco hield de wagen koel en de bestuurder had een bandje met zijn favoriete countrymuziek in de cassettespeler gestoken.

Na Ruweis kwamen ze in open gebied. Links van hen was zo nu en dan tussen de duinen door de zee te zien. Rechts strekte de grote woestijn zich honderden zanderige, troosteloze kilometers uit naar Dhofar en de Indische Oceaan.

Naast haar echtgenoot tuurde Maybelle Walker gespannen naar de okerbruine woestijn in de zinderende hitte van de middagzon. Haar man Ray hield zijn ogen op de weg gericht. Hij had al zijn hele leven in de olie gezeten en woestijnen waren niets nieuws voor hem. Als je er één hebt gezien, heb je ze allemaal gezien, was zijn commentaar toen zijn vrouw opgewonden kreetjes slaakte bij al het nieuwe dat ze zag en hoorde.

Voor Maybelle Walker was alles nog spannend. Hoewel ze voor hun vertrek uit Oklahoma genoeg medicijnen had ingepakt om zelf een drogist te kunnen beginnen, genoot ze met volle teugen van elke minuut van hun veertiendaagse reis door het Golfgebied.

Ze waren op weg gegaan vanuit Koeweit in het noorden, met een terreinwagen die ze van het bedrijf hadden geleend. Daarna waren ze in zuidelijke richting naar Saoedi-Arabië gereden, via Khafji en Al-Khobar. Ten slotte waren ze de dam overgestoken naar Bahrein en via Qatar weer teruggereden naar de Verenigde Arabische Emiraten. Bij elke halteplaats had Ray Walker plichtmatig het kantoor van zijn bedrijf 'geïnspecteerd' – de officiële reden voor de reis – terwijl zijn vrouw met een gids van kantoor de plaatselijke bezienswaardigheden had bekeken. Ze voelde zich heel dapper dat ze met maar één blanke man als gezelschap door die smalle straatjes durfde te lopen. Geen moment realiseerde ze zich dat ze in de Amerikaanse grote steden meer gevaar liep dan hier tussen de Golf-Arabieren.

Maar ze was heel geestdriftig over alles wat ze op haar eerste en misschien wel laatste reis buiten Amerika te zien kreeg. Ze bewonderde de paleizen en minaretten, verbaasde zich over al het ruwe goud in de *soukhs* en was onder de indruk van de zee van donkere gezichten en veelkleurige gewaden in de oude wijken.

Ze had foto's gemaakt van alles en iedereen, om thuis aan het damesclubje te laten zien waar ze was geweest en wat ze had gezien. En ze had zich keurig aan de waarschuwing van de manager in Qatar gehouden om geen foto's van woestijn-Arabieren te nemen zonder hun uitdrukkelijke toestemming, omdat sommigen nog steeds geloofden dat een foto een deel van je ziel kon wegnemen.

Maybelle was een gelukkige vrouw, zoals ze zichzelf steeds voorhield, en ze had veel om blij over te zijn. Na haar middelbare school was ze bijna meteen getrouwd met de jongen met wie ze al twee jaar verkering had. Hij was een goede, betrouwbare echtgenoot gebleken, die bij een plaatselijke oliemaatschappij ging werken en gestaag carrière had gemaakt toen het bedrijf zich uitbreidde. Nu was hij adjunct-directeur.

Ze hadden een mooi huis in de buurt van Tulsa en een strandhuis voor vakanties bij Hatteras, tussen de Atlantische kust en de Pamlico Sound in North Carolina. Ze kon terugzien op een geslaagd huwelijk van dertig jaar, dat was beloond met een leuke zoon. En nu was ze op een veertiendaagse vakantie op kosten van het bedrijf, en kon ze genieten van de exotische bezienswaardigheden, de geluiden, de geuren en de ervaringen van een totaal andere wereld – het Arabische Golfgebied.

'Het is wel een goede weg,' merkte ze op toen ze over de top van een heuvel reden en de strook asfalt in de verte glinsterend in de zon zag verdwijnen. In de auto was het nog draaglijk, maar buiten was het bloedheet.

'Dat mag ook wel,' bromde haar man. 'We hebben hem zelf aangelegd.'

'De zaak?'

'Nee, Amerika verdomme.'

Ray Walker liet al zijn informatie vergezeld gaan van 'verdomme'. Er viel een kameraadschappelijke stilte.

Ray Walker liep tegen de zestig en vond het tijd worden om ermee te stoppen. Hij had een goed pensioen en nog een paar aandelen, en zijn dankbare bedrijf had hem een betaalde, eersteklas vakantie van twee weken aangeboden, zogenaamd om de vestigingen langs de kust te 'inspecteren'. Hoewel hij hier nooit eerder was geweest, was hij minder enthousiast dan zijn vrouw, maar hij vond het leuk dat zij er zo van genoot.

Zelf verheugde hij zich op het moment dat ze uit Abu Dhabi en Dubai konden vertrekken en met een eersteklas-ticket naar Londen zouden vliegen, waar hij op zijn gemak een grote, koude pils kon bestellen zonder dat hij stiekem een kantoor in hoefde te duiken. De islam, allemaal goed en wel, dacht hij, maar zelfs de beste hotels in Koeweit, Saoedi-Arabië en Qatar stonden volledig droog. Wat voor godsdienst verbood een mens nu een koud biertje te drinken op een hete dag?

Hij droeg de kleding die hij passend vond voor een oliemagnaat in de woestijn: laarzen, jeans, een riem, een hemd en een Stetson. Een beetje overdreven voor een chemicus die met de kwaliteitscontrole was belast.

Hij keek op de kilometerteller. Nog 120 kilometer tot de afslag naar Abu Dhabi.

'Ik moet even plassen, schat,' mompelde hij.

'Wees maar voorzichtig,' waarschuwde Maybelle. 'Er zitten hier schorpioenen.'

'Maar die kunnen geen halve meter de lucht in springen,' zei hij, bulderend om zijn eigen grap. In je pik worden gestoken door een springende schorpioen – dat zouden de jongens thuis wel leuk vinden.

'Ray, je bent een vreselijke man,' antwoordde Maybelle, maar ze moest ook lachen. Walker draaide de Ram Charger de berm in, zette de motor af en opende het portier. De hitte sloeg hem tegemoet als uit een oven. Hij stapte uit en sloeg het portier achter zich dicht om de koelte in de auto gevangen te houden.

Maybelle bleef zitten, terwijl haar man naar het dichtstbijzijnde duin liep en zijn gulp openritste. Toen keek ze weer naar voren en mompelde: 'Mijn god, kijk nou eens!'

Ze greep haar Pentax, opende haar portier en glipte naar buiten.

'Ray, zou hij het goed vinden als ik een foto van hem maak?'

Ray keek de andere kant uit, verdiept in een van de prettiger geneugten die voor een man van zijn leeftijd nog waren weggelegd.

'Ik kom er zo aan, schat. Wie?'

De bedoeïen stond aan de overkant van de weg. Blijkbaar was hij tussen twee duinen vandaan gekomen. Het ene moment was hij nog nergens te bekennen, het volgende moment was hij er opeens. Maybelle Walker bleef aarzelend bij de voorbumper van de auto staan, met haar camera in haar hand. Haar man draaide zich om, ritste zijn gulp dicht en tuurde naar de Arabier aan de overkant.

'Ik weet het niet,' zei hij. 'Het mag wel, denk ik. Maar kom niet te dichtbij. Waarschijnlijk heeft hij vlooien. Ik zal vast starten. Neem maar snel een foto. Als hij lastig wordt, spring je meteen in de auto. Opschieten!'

Hij ging achter het stuur zitten en startte de motor. Daardoor ging de airco weer aan, wat een hele verbetering was.

Maybelle Walker deed een paar stappen naar voren en hield haar fototoestel omhoog. 'Mag ik een foto van u nemen?' vroeg ze. 'Camera? Plaatje? Klik-klik? Voor mijn album thuis?'

De man keek haar onbewogen aan. Zijn *djellaba*, die ooit wit was geweest, hing nu vuil en stoffig vanaf zijn schouders op de grond. De rood-witte *keffijeh* zat met een dubbel zwart koord om zijn hoofd bevestigd. Een van de punten was onder het koord tegen zijn andere slaap gestoken, zodat zijn gezicht vanaf de brug van zijn neus tot onder aan toe was bedekt. De huid van zijn voorhoofd en zijn oogkassen, voorzover Maybelle die kon zien, was bruinverbrand door de woestijnzon. Ze had al heel wat foto's gemaakt, maar nog niet één van een echte bedoeïen tegen de achtergrond van de uitgestrekte Saoedische woestijn.

Ze bracht haar toestel omhoog. De man bewoog zich niet. Ze tuurde door de zoeker en plaatste de gestalte in het midden van de rechthoek, terwijl ze zich afvroeg of ze nog op tijd de auto zou kunnen bereiken als de Arabier op haar af zou komen. Klik.

'Dank u vriendelijk,' zei ze. De man verroerde nog steeds geen vin. Maybelle lachte stralend en liep achterwaarts naar de auto toe. Altijd glimlachen, herinnerde ze zich een advies uit de *Reader's Digest* aan Amerikanen die werden geconfronteerd met mensen die geen Engels spraken.

'Schat, kom nou!' riep haar man.

'Het geeft niet. Ik geloof dat het wel in orde is,' zei ze, en ze opende het portier.

Terwijl ze haar foto had genomen was het cassettebandje afgelopen, waardoor automatisch de radio werd ingeschakeld. Ray Walker stak zijn hand uit, sleurde haar de auto in en stoof met piepende banden weg.

De Arabier keek hen na, haalde zijn schouders op en verdween weer achter het zandduin waar hij zijn eigen zandkleurige Landrover had geparkeerd. Even later vertrok hij ook in de richting van Abu Dhabi.

'Waarom heb je zo'n haast?' vroeg Maybelle Walker op klaaglijke toon. 'Hij wilde me heus niets doen.'

'Daar gaat het niet om, schat,' antwoordde Ray Walker met opeengeklemde kaken – de man die alles onder controle had en iedere internationale crisis het hoofd wist te bieden. 'We rijden naar Abu Dhabi en nemen het eerste vliegtuig naar huis. Ik hoor net dat Irak vanochtend Koeweit is binnengevallen, verdomme. Ze kunnen ieder moment hier zijn.'

Het was tien uur plaatselijke tijd, in de ochtend van de 2e augustus 1990.

Twaalf uur eerder had kolonel Osman Badri gespannen en opgewonden staan wachten naast de rupsbanden van een T-72 gevechtstank bij het kleine vliegveld Safwan. Hoewel hij dat toen nog niet kon weten, zou de strijd om Koeweit daar beginnen en eindigen. Bij Safwan.

Naast het vliegveldje, waarop geen enkel gebouw stond, liep de hoofdweg van noord naar zuid. Op de weg naar het noorden, waar hij drie dagen geleden overheen was gekomen, lag de afslag naar Basra in het oosten en naar Bagdad in het noordwesten.

In zuidelijke richting, op acht kilometer van het vliegveld, lag de grens met Koeweit. Vanwaar hij stond, met zijn gezicht naar het zuiden, zag hij de vage gloed van Jahra, met in het oosten, aan de overkant van de baai, de lichten van Koeweit Stad. Hij was opgewonden omdat het grote moment voor zijn land eindelijk was aangebroken. De tijd was gekomen om dat tuig in Koeweit te straffen voor wat ze zijn land hadden aangedaan – voor de economische oorlog, voor de financiële schade en voor hun arrogante houding.

Had Irak niet acht bloedige jaren de Perzische horden tegengehouden die het noordelijke Golfgebied onder de voet wilden lopen om een eind te maken aan het luxe leventje van de Koeweiti's? En moest Irak nu werkeloos toezien terwijl de Koeweiti's zich meer dan hun rechtmatige deel van het gezamenlijke Rumailah-olieveld toeëigenden? Moest Irak tot de bedelstaf worden gebracht omdat Koeweit te veel olie produceerde en de prijs steeds verder drukte? Moest Irak gedwee instemmen nu die honden van Al Sabah plotseling die luizige vijftien miljard dollar opeisten die ze tijdens de oorlog aan Irak hadden geleend?

Nee, de *Rais* had gelijk, zoals gewoonlijk. Historisch gezien was Koeweit de negentiende provincie van Irak. Dat was altijd zo geweest, totdat de Britten in 1913 die vervloekte streep in het zand hadden getrokken, waarmee het rijkste emiraat ter wereld was geboren. Maar nu, deze nacht, zou Koeweit worden heroverd. En hij, Osman Badri, zou erbij zijn.

Als genie-officier zou hij natuurlijk niet in de voorste linie strijden, maar hij zou er vlak achteraan komen met zijn bruggenbouwers, zijn graafploegen, zijn bulldozers en zijn sappeurs om de weg vrij te maken. Niet dat hij veel obstakels verwachtte. Bij de luchtverkenningen waren geen verdedigingswerken, geen anti-tankwallen en geen betonnen valkuilen ontdekt. Maar als het nodig was, zouden de genietroepen paraat zijn, onder het bevel van Osman Badri, om alle versperringen uit de weg te ruimen voor de tanks en de gemechaniseerde infanterie van de Republikeinse Garde.

Een paar meter verderop stond de commandotent waar het wemelde van de officieren, die nog een laatste blik op de kaart wierpen en hun aanvalsplannen bijschaafden terwijl de uren en minuten verstreken, in afwachting van de beslissende order van de president uit Bagdad.

Hij had al overlegd met zijn eigen generaal, Ali Musuli, die het bevel voerde over alle genie-eenheden van het Iraakse leger en die hij met hart en ziel was toegedaan sinds Musuli hem in februari voor zijn 'speciale taak' had aanbevolen. Natuurlijk had hij zijn chef verzekerd dat zijn mannen gereedstonden om hun plicht te doen.

Toen hij met Musuli stond te praten was er een andere generaal naar hen toe gekomen en was hij voorgesteld aan Abdullah Kadiri, de commandant van de tanktroepen. Uit de verte had hij ook generaal Saadi Tumah Abbas, de bevelhebber van de elitaire Republikeinse Garde, de tent zien binnengaan. 'Smerige hielenlikker,' had hij tankgeneraal Kadiri horen mompelen. Als loyaal partijlid en volgeling van Saddam Hoessein had Badri zijn oren nauwelijks kunnen geloven. Hoe durfde Kadiri! Tumah Abbas was een vertrouweling van Saddam en was onderscheiden voor zijn overwinning in de belangrijke veldslag om Fao, waarin de Iraniërs definitief waren verslagen. Kolonel Badri had nooit geloof gehecht aan de geruchten dat die strijd in feite was gewonnen door generaal Maher Rashid, van wie niemand later nog iets had vernomen.

De manschappen en officieren van de Tawakkulna- en Medina-divisies van de Republikeinse Garde zwermden door de duisternis. Badri's gedachten gingen terug naar die gedenkwaardige avond in februari toen generaal Musuli hem had ontboden. Badri had juist de laatste hand gelegd aan het complex van Al Qubai toen hij bevel kreeg om naar Bagdad te komen. Hij veronderstelde dat hij een nieuwe opdracht zou krijgen.

'De president wil je spreken,' had Musuli abrupt gezegd. 'Je hoort nog wel wanneer. Neem je intrek in het officierenverblijf en houd je dag en nacht beschikbaar.'

Badri beet op zijn lip. Wat had hij misdaan? Wat had hij gezegd? Niets verraderlijks. Dat zou ondenkbaar zijn. Had iemand hem soms valselijk beschuldigd? Nee, dan zou de president hem niet willen spreken. Dan had hij hem gewoon laten oppakken door een van die knokploegen van brigadegeneraal Khatib om hem een lesje te leren. Toen Musuli zijn gezicht zag, was hij in lachen uitgebarsten, met blikkerende tanden onder de dikke zwarte snor die zoveel hoge officieren droegen in navolging van hun president.

'Maak je niet ongerust. Hij heeft een opdracht voor je. Een speciale opdracht.'

En dat was ook zo. Binnen vierentwintig uur was Badri ontboden naar de hal van het officierenverblijf. Buiten stond een lange zwarte dienstauto op hem te wachten, met twee mannen van de Amn-al-Khass, de presidentiële lijfwacht, die hem naar het paleis brachten voor de spannendste en belangrijkste ontmoeting van zijn leven.

Het paleis lag toen nog op de hoek van de Kindi Straat en de 14e Juli Straat, bij de gelijknamige brug – allebei genoemd naar de datum van de eerste van de twee coups van juli 1968, die de Ba'ath-partij aan het bewind had gebracht en de macht van de generaals had gebroken.

Badri zat twee uur in een wachtkamer en werd twee keer grondig gefouilleerd voordat hij voor de Man mocht verschijnen.

Toen de twee lijfwachten naast hem bleven staan, volgde hij hun voorbeeld, salueerde nerveus, rukte zijn baret af, stak die onder zijn linkerarm en sprong in de houding.

'Dus u bent het genie van de *maskirovka*?'

Er was hem verteld dat hij de *Rais* niet recht mocht aankijken, maar hij deed het toch. Saddam Hoessein was in een goed humeur. De ogen van de jonge kolonel tegenover hem glinsterden van toewijding en bewondering. Mooi zo. Van hem had hij niets te vrezen. Op afgemeten toon vertelde hij de genie-officier wat er van hem werd verwacht. Badri voelde zijn borst zwellen van trots en dankbaarheid.

Vijf maanden lang had hij dag en nacht gewerkt om het onmogelijke tijd-schema te halen, maar het was hem gelukt, met nog een paar dagen respijt. Hij had alle faciliteiten gekregen die de president hem had beloofd. Alles en iedereen stond tot zijn beschikking. Als hij meer beton of staal nodig had, kon hij Kamil op zijn privé-nummer bellen. Prompt stuurde de schoonzoon van de president hem het materiaal waar hij om vroeg, uit de voorraden van het ministerie van Industrie. Als hij meer mankracht wilde, arriveerden er honderden Koreaanse en Vietnamese contractarbeiders, die het zware graaf-werk deden en de hele zomer in schamele barakken in het dal woonden, tot ze weer verdwenen – Badri had geen idee waarheen.

Afgezien van de koelies kwam er niemand over de weg. Het smalle zand-pad, dat ten slotte ook verdween, werd alleen gebruikt door de cementwa-gens en de trucks die het staal en de rest van de materialen brachten. Alle andere mensen, behalve de vrachtwagenchauffeurs, werden gebracht door Russische MIL-helikopters met geblindeerde ruiten. Dat gold voor iedereen, van hoog tot laag.

Badri zelf had de plaats gekozen, na een dagenlange verkenning per heli-kopter boven de bergen. Ten slotte had hij een plek gevonden hoog op de Jebal Hamreen, ten noorden van Kifri, waar de heuvels van de Hamreen-keten overgingen in de bergen langs de weg naar Sulajmanijam.

Hij had twintig uur per dag gewerkt, op het terrein geslapen en zijn mannen met dreigementen, vriendelijke woorden en steekpenningen tot een gewel-dige krachtsinspanning aangezet. En het werk was gereedgekomen, tegen het eind van juli. Daarna was het gebied grondig schoongemaakt. Alle spo-ren van het werk, al het beton, alle stenen en alle staalresten die het zonlicht konden weerspiegelen, waren weggehaald. Zelfs op de rotsen was geen krasje meer te zien.

Er waren drie dorpen voor het wachtgarnizoen ingericht, compleet met hut-jes, geiten en schapen. Ten slotte was de toegangsweg omgeploegd en door een bulldozer het dal in geschoven, zodat de drie valleien en de verkrachte berg weer in hun oude staat waren hersteld. Bijna.

Want hij, Osman Badri, kolonel van de genie, erfgenaam van de architecten die Nineveh en Tyrus hadden gebouwd, leerling van de grote Rus Stepanov, meester van de *maskirovka* – de kunst van camouflage en vermomming – had de Qa'ala, de Vesting, voor Saddam gebouwd. Niemand kon het fort meer terugvinden en niemand wist waar het lag.

Voordat het complex werd gecamoufleerd, had Badri gezien hoe de anderen, de wetenschappers en artilleristen, dat ontzagwekkende kanon hadden gebouwd waarvan de loop zich tot aan de sterren leek te verheffen.

Toen alles klaar was, vertrokken ze weer. Alleen het garnizoen bleef achter. Zij zouden daar blijven wonen. Niemand kon zomaar vertrekken. Wie erheen wilde of wie weg moest, werd per helikopter vervoerd. En zelfs de helikopters landden niet. Ze bleven boven een grasveldje hangen, aan de andere kant van de berg. En de schaarse bezoekers werden geblinddoekt. De piloten en de bemanning werden gestationeerd op één vliegbasis zonder telefoons, die verboden was voor bezoekers. Het laatste wilde graszaad werd uitgestrooid, de laatste struiken geplant en de Vesting bleef eenzaam en verlaten achter.

Badri wist niet dat de drieduizend Aziatische contractarbeiders waren afgevoerd in bussen met geblindeerde ruiten. Ver weg in een ravijn stopten de bussen en de bewakers sloegen op de vlucht. Toen de berghelling door een explosie instortte, werden de bussen bedolven en voorgoed begraven. Daarna werden de bewakers door anderen neergeschoten. Ze hadden immers de Qa'ala gezien.

Badri werd in zijn overpeinzingen gestoord door een paar kreten uit de commandotent. Snel deed het nieuws de ronde. Het sein tot de aanval was gegeven.

De genie-officier rende naar zijn truck en hees zich in de rechterstoel terwijl de chauffeur de motor startte. Ze wachtten tot de tankbemanningen van de twee Gardedivisies die de speerpunt van de invasie vormden hun voertuigen hadden gestart. Met denderend geraas zetten de Russische T-72's zich in beweging en reden vanaf het vliegveld de weg naar Koeweit op.

Het was prijsschieten, zoals hij later vertelde aan zijn broer Abdelkarim, die gevechtsvlieger en kolonel bij de luchtmacht was. De weerloze politiepost aan de grens werd volledig verwoest. Om twee uur 's nachts stak de colonne de grens over, op weg naar het zuiden. Als de Koeweiti's nog de illusie hadden dat dit leger – het op drie na grootste ter wereld – tot aan de Mutla-keten zou oprukken om daar met zijn wapens te kletteren totdat Koeweit op de eisen van de *Rais* zou ingaan, kwamen ze bedrogen uit. Als het Westen dacht dat ze alleen de eilanden Warbah en Bubijan zouden bezetten om eindelijk toegang tot de Golf te krijgen, had het zich schromelijk vergist. De orders uit Bagdad waren duidelijk: bezet het hele land.

Kort voor zonsopgang woedde er een korte tankslag bij de kleine Koeweitse oliestad Jahra, ten noorden van Koeweit Stad. De enige Koeweitse pantserbrigade was snel naar het noorden gestuurd, nadat de tanks een week lang in reserve waren gehouden om de Irakezen niet te provoceren.

Het was een eenzijdig gevecht. De Koeweiti's, die als kooplui en olieprofiteurs werden beschouwd, streden hard en dapper. Ze wisten de elitetroepen van de Republikeinse Garde een uur lang tegen te houden, zodat hun Skyray- en Mirage-jagers vanaf de vliegbasis Ahmadi in het zuiden konden opstijgen, maar uiteindelijk hadden ze geen enkele kans. De zware Russische T-72's maakten gehakt van de kleinere Chinese T-55's van het Koeweitse leger. De verdedigers verloren twintig tanks in even zovele minuten. Ten slotte waren de laatste tanks gedwongen zich terug te trekken.

Osman Badri, die van anderhalve kilometer afstand zag hoe de mastodonten zigzagden en vuurden in wolken van rook en stof, terwijl de lucht boven Iran zich langzaam roze kleurde, kon niet weten dat dezelfde T-72's van de Medina- en Tawakkulna-divisies een half jaar later aan flarden zouden worden geschoten door de Challengers en Abrams van de Britten en Amerikanen.

Tegen het ochtendgloren denderden de voorste Iraakse eenheden de noordwestelijke buitenwijken van Koeweit Stad binnen en verdeelden hun aandacht over de vier hoofdwegen die vanuit die richting de stad naderden: de kustweg naar Abu Dhabi, de weg naar Jahra tussen de voorsteden Granada en Andalus, en de Vijfde en Zesde Ringweg in het zuiden. Nadat ze zich hadden opgesplitst drongen de vier aanvalsgolven het centrum van Koeweit binnen.

Kolonel Badri en zijn mannen waren nauwelijks nodig. Zijn genietroepen hoefden geen greppels dicht te gooien, geen versperringen op te blazen en geen betonnen obstakels weg te schuiven. Maar één keer hoefde hij weg te duiken voor zijn leven. Toen hij door Sulajbikhat kwam, vlak bij de christelijke begraafplaats (hoewel hij dat niet wist), dook een eenzame Skyray langs de zon en bestookte de tank vóór hem met vier raketten. De tank schokte, verloor een rupsband en vloog in brand. In paniek kroop de bemanning uit de geschutskoepel. Daarna dook de Skyray op de vrachtwagens af. Zijn neus spuwde vuur. Badri zag het asfalt uiteenspatten en wierp zich naar buiten op het moment dat zijn gillende chauffeur de truck de berm in stuurde, waar hij in een greppel terechtkwam en over de kop sloeg.

Niemand raakte gewond, maar Badri was woedend. Die brutale hond! Hij vervolgde de opmars in een andere truck.

De hele dag werd er sporadisch geschoten terwijl de twee Iraakse divisies van pantsereenheden, artillerie en gemechaniseerde infanterie door Koeweit Stad denderden. Een groep Koeweitse officieren verschanste zich in het ministerie van Defensie en probeerde de aanvallers te bestrijden met wat kleine wapens die daar lagen opgeslagen.

Een van de Iraakse officieren was zo redelijk erop te wijzen dat ze het nooit zouden overleven als hij het vuur zou openen met zijn tank. Terwijl enkele Koeweitse militairen met hem onderhandelden voordat ze zich overgaven, trok de rest snel burgerkleding aan en ontsnapte via de achterkant van het gebouw. Een van hen zou zich later opwerpen als leider van het Koeweitse verzet.

De zwaarste tegenstand ontmoetten de Iraakse troepen bij de residentie van emir Al Sabah, hoewel hij en zijn familie allang naar het zuiden waren gevlucht om asiel te vragen in Saoedi-Arabië. Maar ook dit verzet werd gebroken.

Tegen zonsondergang stond kolonel Osman Badri met zijn rug naar de zee op de noordelijkste punt van Koeweit Stad, aan de Perzische Golf, en tuurde naar de gevel van die verzetshaard, het Dasman Paleis. Enkele Iraakse militairen waren het gebouw binnengedrongen en zo nu en dan kwamen ze naar buiten met kostbaarheden die van de muren waren gesloopt. Ze stapten over de lijken op het bordes en brachten hun buit naar een truck.

Badri kwam in de verleiding zelf ook wat mee te nemen – een mooi cadeau voor het huis van zijn oude vader in Qadisijah – maar iets hield hem tegen: de erfenis van die vervloekte Engelse school in Bagdad waar hij zoveel jaar geleden op had gezeten, vanwege de vriendschap van zijn vader met de Engelsman Martin en zijn bewondering voor alles wat Brits was.

'Plunderen is stelen, jongens. En stelen is verkeerd. De bijbel en de koran verbieden het. Doe het dus nooit.'

Zelfs nu nog herinnerde hij zich hoe meneer Hartley, de hoofdonderwijzer van de Foundation Preparatory School, onder toezicht van de British Council, de Engelse en Iraakse leerlingen in hun schoolbankjes had toegesproken. Osman was lid geworden van de Ba'ath-partij. Hoe vaak had hij niet geprobeerd zijn vader ervan te overtuigen dat de Britten imperialisten waren en de Arabieren twee eeuwen lang hadden onderdrukt, alleen om hun eigen zakken te vullen?

Maar zijn vader, die nu zeventig was (Osman en zijn broer waren zoons uit zijn tweede huwelijk), lachte dan altijd en zei: 'Het zijn dan wel buitenlanders en ongelovige honden, maar ze zijn ook hoffelijk en ze hebben normen, mijn zoon. Welke normen heeft die Saddam Hoessein van jou?'

De koppige oude man had niet willen begrijpen hoe belangrijk de Ba'ath-partij voor Irak was, en dat de nieuwe leider het land glorie en roem zou brengen. Ten slotte had Osman het onderwerp maar laten rusten, uit angst dat zijn vader tegen de buren iets over de *Rais* zou zeggen waardoor ze allemaal in problemen zouden komen. Maar dit was het enige punt waarop hij met zijn vader van mening verschilde, want hij hield erg veel van hem.

Dank zij een hoofdonderwijzer van vijfentwintig jaar geleden bleef Badri daarom op afstand en deed niet mee aan de plundering van het Dasman Paleis – hoewel dat de traditie van al zijn voorouders was, wat die dwaze Engelsen er ook van mochten denken.

In elk geval had hij op zijn oude school vloeiend Engels geleerd, wat hem goed van pas was gekomen, want dat was de enige taal waarin hij had kunnen communiceren met kolonel Stepanov, lange tijd de hoogste genie-officier van de Russische Militaire Adviesgroep in Irak, voordat er een eind kwam aan de koude oorlog en hij naar Moskou was teruggekeerd.

Osman Badri was vijfendertig en 1990 zou het mooiste jaar van zijn leven worden. Zoals hij later tegen zijn oudere broer zei: 'Ik stond daar, met mijn rug naar de Golf en uitzicht op het Dasman Paleis, en ik dacht: "Bij de profeet, het is ons gelukt! Eindelijk hebben we Koeweit ingenomen. En binnen één dag." Het was zo voorbij.'

Daar vergiste hij zich in. Het was pas het begin.

Terwijl Ray Walker als een wervelwind de vertrekhal van het vliegveld van Abu Dhabi binnenstormde en met zijn vuist op de balie sloeg om als Amerikaans staatsburger onmiddellijk een ticket te eisen, had een aantal van zijn landgenoten het eind van een slapeloze nacht bereikt.

Zeven tijdzones bij hem vandaan, in Washington, had de Nationale Veiligheidsraad de hele nacht vergaderd. Vroeger kwamen de leden nog lijfelijk bijeen in het crisiscentrum in het souterrain van het Witte Huis, maar dank zij de moderne technologie konden ze nu via beveiligde videokanalen vanaf diverse plaatsen met elkaar overleggen.

De vorige avond – in Washington nog de 1e augustus – waren er berichten binnengekomen over vuurgevechten langs de noordelijke grens van Koeweit. Dat was niet onverwacht. Al dagenlang hadden de KH-11 satellieten boven het noordelijke Golfgebied de opbouw van de Iraakse strijdkrachten gesignaleerd. De verkenningssatellieten vertelden de Amerikaanse regering meer dan haar ambassadeur in Koeweit wist. Maar wat waren de bedoelingen van Saddam Hoessein? Intimidatie of een inval?

De vorige dag waren er dringende verzoeken naar het CIA-hoofdkwartier in Langley gestuurd, maar ook de inlichtingendienst kwam niet verder dan gissingen, op grond van de satellietbeelden van het National Reconnaissance Office en politieke informatie die al bij Buitenlandse Zaken bekend was.

'Dat had ik zelf ook kunnen bedenken,' gromde Brent Scowcroft, de voorzitter van de Nationale Veiligheidsraad. 'Hebben we geen bronnen binnen de Iraakse regering?'

Het antwoord was een spijtig nee. Dat zou nog maandenlang een probleem blijven.

De klap op de vuurpijl kwam nog vóór tien uur 's avonds, toen president George Bush juist naar bed was gegaan en de telefoon niet meer opnam. In de Golf was het toen bijna ochtend. De Iraakse tanks waren inmiddels Jahra gepasseerd en drongen de noordwestelijke buitenwijken van Koeweit Stad binnen.

Het was me het nachtje wel, zoals de betrokkenen later vertelden. Er waren acht videokanalen in gebruik – de Nationale Veiligheidsraad, Financiën, Buitenlandse Zaken, de CIA, de chefs-van-staven en Defensie. Iedereen gaf orders die onmiddellijk werden uitgevoerd. Hetzelfde gebeurde in Engeland, waar haastig een COBRA-vergadering ('Cabinet Office Briefing Room Annexe') bijeen werd geroepen. Londen had vijf uur tijdsverschil met Washington en maar twee uur met het Golfgebied.

Alle Iraakse financiële tegoeden in het buitenland werden door de Britse en Amerikaanse regering geblokkeerd, evenals die van Koeweit (met instemming van de Koeweitse ambassadeurs in de beide hoofdsteden), zodat een eventuele marionettenregering die met Irak collaboreerde geen greep in de kas zou kunnen doen. Door dit besluit werden vele miljarden oliedollars bevroren.

President Bush werd in de ochtend van de 2e augustus om kwart voor vijf gewekt om de papieren te tekenen. In Londen had Margaret Thatcher – die allang op was en een geweldige heisa had geschopt – hetzelfde gedaan voordat ze op het vliegtuig naar de Verenigde Staten stapte.

Een andere belangrijke beslissing was het bijeenroepen van de Veiligheidsraad van de Verenigde Naties in New York om de invasie te veroordelen en Irak op te roepen zich onmiddellijk terug te trekken. Dit gebeurde via resolutie 660, die nog dezelfde ochtend om half vijf werd ondertekend.

Omstreeks het ochtendgloren kwam er een eind aan de videovergadering en hadden de deelnemers nog twee uur de tijd om naar huis te gaan, zich te wassen, te scheren en te verkleden voordat ze om acht uur op het Witte Huis werden verwacht voor een voltallige vergadering van de Nationale Veiligheidsraad onder voorzitterschap van president Bush zelf.

Tot de nieuwkomers bij deze voltallige vergadering behoorden Richard Cheney van Defensie, Nicholas Brady van Financiën en Richard Thornburgh van Justitie. Bob Kimmitt vertegenwoordigde Buitenlandse Zaken, omdat minister James Baker en onderminister Lawrence Eagleburger de stad uit waren.

Colin Powell, de voorzitter van de chefs-van-staven, was uit Florida teruggekomen in het gezelschap van de bevelhebber van het Centraal Commando, een forsgebouwde generaal van wie de wereld nog meer zou horen. Norman Schwarzkopf kwam samen met generaal Powell de vergaderzaal binnen.

George Bush verliet de vergadering om kwart over negen, toen Ray en Maybelle Walker al opgelucht in het vliegtuig boven Saoedi-Arabië zaten, op weg naar het noordwesten en de veiligheid. De president stapte op het zuidelijke grasveld in een helikopter en liet zich naar de luchtmachtbasis Andrews brengen, waar hij overstapte in de Air Force One, op weg naar

43

Aspen in Colorado. Daar zou hij een lezing houden over de Amerikaanse defensie. Dat leek een toepasselijk onderwerp, maar het zou een veel drukkere dag worden dan voorzien.

Onderweg voerde hij een lang telefoongesprek met koning Hoessein van Jordanië, het kleine buurland in de schaduw van Irak. De hasjemitische vorst was in Caïro, waar hij vergaderde met de Egyptische president Hosni Moebarak.

Koning Hoessein vroeg Amerika de Arabische staten een paar dagen te gunnen om zich te bezinnen voordat de oorlog zich zou uitbreiden. Zelf stelde hij een vier-statenconferentie voor, met president Moebarak, hijzelf en Saddam Hoessein, onder voorzitterschap van koning Fahd van Saoedi-Arabië. Hij was ervan overtuigd dat zo'n conferentie de Iraakse dictator zou kunnen bewegen zich vreedzaam uit Koeweit terug te trekken. Maar hij had drie tot vier dagen nodig om alles te organiseren, en in die tijd wilde hij geen openbare veroordeling van Irak door een van de deelnemende landen.

'Goed,' stemde president Bush toe. 'Dan laat ik dat aan u over.' De ongelukkige George had toen nog niet gesproken met de dame uit Londen die in Aspen op hem wachtte. Ze ontmoetten elkaar nog diezelfde avond.

De 'IJzeren Dame' kreeg al snel de indruk dat haar goede vriend aarzelde. Binnen twee uur had ze hem volledig klem.

'Dit kunnen we niet tolereren, George. Uitgesloten.'

Geconfronteerd met die fonkelende blauwe ogen en die kristalheldere stem die dwars door het zoemen van de airconditioning sneed, kon George Bush niet anders dan beamen dat Amerika dat ook niet van plan was. Zijn naaste medewerkers vertelden later dat hij minder bang was voor Saddam Hoessein met zijn artillerie en tanks dan voor die indrukwekkende handtas.

Op 3 augustus vond er discreet overleg plaats tussen Amerika en Egypte. President Moebarak werd er nog eens aan herinnerd hoezeer zijn strijdkrachten afhankelijk waren van Amerikaanse wapens, hoeveel schuld Egypte nog had bij de Wereldbank en het Internationale Monetaire Fonds, en hoeveel hulp er uit de Verenigde Staten kwam. De volgende dag gaf de Egyptische regering een verklaring uit waarin Saddams invasie krachtig werd veroordeeld.

Tot leedwezen van de Jordaanse koning – hoewel hij die reactie wel had verwacht – weigerde de Iraakse despoot meteen om naar de conferentie van Jeddah onder voorzitterschap van koning Fahd te komen en naast Hosni Moebarak te gaan zitten.

Voor de Saoedische vorst was dat een grove belediging, en dat in een cultuur die zichzelf liet voorstaan op haar hoffelijkheid. Koning Fahd, die achter zijn innemende persoonlijkheid een sluw politiek brein verborg, was zeer ontstemd.

Dat was een van de twee factoren waardoor de conferentie van Jeddah mislukte. De andere was het feit dat de Saoedische koning Amerikaanse satellietfoto's had gezien waaruit bleek dat het Iraakse leger zijn opmars niet had gestaakt maar nog steeds op volle sterkte doorstootte naar het zuiden, in de richting van de Saoedische grens.

Zou Saddam Hoessein ook Saoedi-Arabië durven binnenvallen? Hij had redenen genoeg. Saoedi-Arabië beschikt over de grootste oliereserves ter wereld, gevolgd door Koeweit, met voorraden voor meer dan honderd jaar bij het huidige produktiepeil. Het derde olieland was Irak zelf. Door Koeweit te bezetten had Saddam de balans in zijn voordeel laten doorslaan. Bovendien bevond negentig procent van de Saoedische oliebronnen en reserves zich in het uiterste noordoosten van het koninkrijk, rondom Dharran, Al-Khobar, Damman en Jubail, en in het achterland van die havensteden. Deze driehoek lag precies op de route van de oprukkende Republikeinse Garde, en de foto's toonden aan dat er nog meer Iraakse divisies Koeweit binnenstroomden.

Gelukkig wist Zijne Majesteit niet dat er met die foto's was geknoeid. De divisies aan de grens waren zich aan het ingraven, maar de bulldozers waren weggeretoucheerd.

Op 6 augustus verzocht het koninkrijk Saoedi-Arabië de Amerikaanse strijdkrachten formeel om zich binnen de grenzen te legeren en het land te verdedigen.

De eerste squadrons jachtbommenwerpers vertrokken nog dezelfde dag naar het Midden-Oosten. Operatie Desert Shield was begonnen.

De ochtend van de 4e augustus sprong brigadegeneraal Hassan Rahmani uit zijn dienstauto en beklom haastig de treden van het Hilton Hotel, waar de Iraakse veiligheidstroepen in Koeweit Stad hun hoofdkwartier hadden gevestigd. Hij vond het een amusante gedachte dat het Hilton naast de Amerikaanse ambassade lag, allebei aan de kust, met een prachtig uitzicht op het glinsterende blauwe water van de Perzische Golf.

Met dat uitzicht zou het personeel van de ambassade zich voorlopig tevreden moeten stellen, want op Rahmani's bevel was het gebouw onmiddellijk omsingeld door Republikeinse Gardisten, en dat zou zo blijven. Hij kon niet verhinderen dat de buitenlandse diplomaten vanaf hun soevereine gebied berichten aan hun regeringen verstuurden, en hij beschikte niet over de supercomputers die nodig waren om de ingewikkelde codes van de Britten en Amerikanen te ontcijferen. Maar als hoofd van de contraspionagedienst van de Mukhabarat zou hij er wel voor zorgen dat ze niets anders te melden hadden dan wat ze door hun ramen konden zien.

Natuurlijk zouden ze telefonische informatie kunnen krijgen van landgenoten die nog vrij rondliepen in Koeweit. Dat was zijn eerste taak: alle externe telefoonverbindingen afsluiten of afluisteren. Dat laatste had zijn voorkeur, maar zijn beste mensen waren nog druk in de weer in Bagdad zelf.

Hij stapte de suite binnen die voor de contraspionagedienst was ingericht, trok zijn uniformjasje uit, wierp het naar de zwetende adjudant die zijn twee koffers met documenten had meegezeuld en liep naar het raam met uitzicht op het zwembad van de jachthaven. Een goed idee om straks nog te gaan zwemmen, dacht hij. Toen zag hij dat twee soldaten hun veldflessen uit het zwembad vulden en twee anderen erin stonden te pissen. Hij zuchtte.

Rahmani was zevenendertig, een goed verzorgde, knappe, gladgeschoren man, die niet meedeed aan de mode om een Saddam-snor te dragen. Hij had zijn functie uitsluitend te danken aan zijn capaciteiten en niet aan zijn politieke connecties, zoals hij heel goed wist. Hij was een technocraat in een wereld van vriendjespolitiek en onbenul.

Buitenlandse vrienden hadden hem weleens gevraagd waarom hij voor dit regime werkte. Dat vroegen ze meestal als hij hen dronken had gevoerd in de bar van het Rashid Hotel of op een meer besloten plek. Hij mocht met hen omgaan omdat het bij zijn werk hoorde. Maar zelf bleef hij broodnuchter. Niet omdat hij religieuze bezwaren had tegen alcohol. Hij bestelde gewoon een gin-tonic en wist dat de barman hem alleen tonic zou geven.

Hij glimlachte altijd om die vraag, en antwoordde schouderophalend: 'Omdat ik een Irakees ben, en daar ben ik trots op. Voor welk regime zou ik anders moeten werken?'

Zelf wist hij heel goed waarom hij een regering diende waarvan hij de meeste leden verfoeide. Hij beweerde vaak dat hij geen emoties kende, maar toch koesterde hij een grote liefde voor zijn land en zijn volk – de gewone mensen, die allang niet meer door de Ba'ath-partij werden vertegenwoordigd.

Maar de belangrijkste reden was toch dat hij vooruit wilde komen in de wereld. Voor een Irakees van zijn generatie waren de mogelijkheden beperkt. Hij kon zich tegen het regime verzetten en ontslag nemen. In het buitenland zou hij een paar centen kunnen verdienen met vertalen, voortdurend op de vlucht voor de Iraakse doodseskaders. Of hij kon in Irak blijven.

Dan bleven er drie mogelijkheden over. Hij kon oppositie voeren tegen het bewind, om ten slotte terecht te komen in de martelkamers van dat beest Omar Khatib, een vent die hij hartgrondig minachtte – en die hem minachtte, zoals hij heel goed wist. Hij kon ook proberen zich te handhaven als zelfstandig zakenman in een economie waarmee het steeds slechter ging. Of hij kon blijven grijnzen tegen die idioten en carrière maken op grond van zijn talent en zijn goede verstand.

En daarin zag hij niets verkeerds. Hij was een schaker, net als Reinhard

46

Gehlen, die eerst voor Hitler, daarna voor de Amerikanen en ten slotte voor de Westduitsers had gewerkt – net als Marcus Wolf, die de Oostduitse communisten had gediend zonder een woord van hun theorieën te geloven. Hassan Rahmani leefde voor het spel, voor de sluwe zetten van spionage en contraspionage. Irak was zijn persoonlijke schaakbord. Hij wist dat zijn collega's, waar ook ter wereld, dat zouden begrijpen.

Hassan Rahmani draaide zich bij het raam vandaan, ging achter het bureau zitten en begon aantekeningen te maken. Er was nog heel wat te doen voordat Koeweit weer met enige zekerheid als de negentiende provincie van Irak kon worden beschouwd.

Zijn eerste probleem was dat hij niet wist hoelang Saddam Hoessein in Koeweit wilde blijven. Waarschijnlijk wist de man het zelf niet eens. Het had weinig zin een grootscheepse contraspionage-operatie op touw te zetten om alle lekken en gaten te dichten als Irak zich binnenkort weer zou terugtrekken.

In zijn hart geloofde hij dat het Saddam kon lukken. Maar dan zou hij het handig moeten spelen, de juiste zetten moeten doen en de juiste dingen moeten zeggen. Om te beginnen moest hij morgen naar die conferentie in Jeddah gaan en koning Fahd gunstig stemmen. Daar kon hij beweren dat Irak niets anders wilde dan een rechtvaardig verdrag over de olie, toegang tot de Golf en onderhandelen over de openstaande lening. Zo kon hij de hele zaak onder Arabische controle houden, zonder dat de Amerikanen en de Britten eraan te pas kwamen. De Arabische gewoonte om eindeloos over alles te blijven praten, werkte in zijn voordeel. Het ongeduldige Westen zou al snel zijn belangstelling verliezen en de kwestie aan de vier Arabieren – de twee vorsten en de twee presidenten – overlaten. Zolang de olie maar bleef stromen die hun atmosfeer tot stikkens toe vervuilde, waren de Angelsaksen allang tevreden. Als Koeweit fatsoenlijk werd behandeld, zouden de media het onderwerp laten vallen, zou het verbannen Al Sabah-regime in Saoedi-Arabië in de vergetelheid raken en konden de Koeweiti's de draad van hun bestaan weer oppakken onder een nieuwe regering. En de conferentie van Jeddah zou nog tien jaar voortsukkelen, totdat niemand er nog enig belang aan hechtte.

Het was mogelijk, maar alleen met de juiste strategie, Hitlers strategie: ik zoek alleen een vreedzame oplossing voor mijn rechtvaardige eisen – dit is absoluut mijn laatste territoriale aanspraak. Koning Fahd zou erin trappen. De Koeweiti's waren niet populair, en die lotuseters van Al Sabah al helemaal niet. Koning Fahd en koning Hoessein zouden hen meteen laten vallen, zoals Chamberlain in 1938 de Tsjechen had laten vallen.

Helaas. Saddam was sluw genoeg, anders zou hij het niet zo lang hebben uitgehouden, maar van strategie en diplomatie had hij geen kaas gegeten.

De *Rais* zou een beslissende fout maken, vreesde Hassan Rahmani. Hij zou zich niet terugtrekken maar ook niet doorstoten om het Saoedische olieveld te bezetten en het Westen voor een voldongen feit te stellen. Ze zouden dan niets anders kunnen doen dan de oliebronnen vernietigen en hun eigen welvaart de komende twintig jaar naar de knoppen helpen.

Het Westen betekende Amerika, met de Britten aan hun zij. Angelsaksische volkeren. Hij kende de Angelsaksen. Vijf jaar op de Britse school van meester Hartley hadden hem een uitstekende beheersing van het Engels bijgebracht, plus een goed inzicht in de Britse mentaliteit. Hij wist dat je moest oppassen met die Angelsaksen. Ze konden je zonder enige waarschuwing op je smoel slaan.

Hij wreef zich over zijn kin, waar hij lang geleden eens zo'n klap had gekregen, en lachte toen hardop. Zijn adjudant aan de andere kant van de kamer maakte een sprong van schrik. Die vervloekte Mike Martin! Waar zat hij nu?

Hassan Rahmani, slim, beschaafd, bereisd en goed opgeleid, het prototype van de Irakees uit de betere klasse, in dienst van een misdadig regime, boog zich weer over zijn werk. Het was een zware opgave. Onder de 1,8 miljoen inwoners van Koeweit waren maar 600 000 Koeweiti's. Dan waren er 600 000 Palestijnen, van wie sommigen loyaal zouden blijven aan Koeweit en anderen de kant van Irak zouden kiezen omdat de PLO dat had gedaan. Maar de meesten zouden zich rustig houden en proberen de bezetting te overleven. Dan woonden er nog 300 000 Egyptenaren, van wie sommigen natuurlijk voor Caïro – en dus indirect voor Washington en Londen – werkten, plus 250 000 Pakistani, Indiërs, Bangladesji's en Filippino's die als gastarbeiders en huisbedienden werkten. Als Irakees vond Rahmani dat de Koeweiti's nog niet aan een vlooiebeet op hun kont konden krabben zonder er een gastarbeider bij te halen.

En dan waren er nog zo'n 50 000 burgers uit de eerste wereld – Britten, Amerikanen, Fransen, Duitsers, Spanjaarden, Zweden, Denen, noem maar op. En híj moest de buitenlandse spionage bestrijden... Zuchtend dacht hij terug aan de tijd dat berichten nog via boodschappers of telefonisch werden doorgegeven. Als hoofd van de contraspionagedienst kon hij wel de grenzen verzegelen en de telefoonlijnen afsnijden. Maar elke idioot kon tegenwoordig een nummer op een draagbare telefoon of een computermodem intoetsen om via een satelliet verbinding te krijgen met Californië. En zulke apparatuur was nauwelijks op te sporen, behalve met de beste instrumenten, en die had hij niet.

Hij wist dat hij geen controle had over de stroom van informatie en de groepjes vluchtelingen die druppelsgewijs over de grens ontsnapten. Ook kon hij weinig ondernemen tegen de Amerikaanse verkenningssatellieten, waarvan hij vermoedde dat hun baan inmiddels was aangepast, zodat ze nu om de paar minuten over Koeweit en Irak cirkelden. (Daar had hij gelijk in.) Het had geen zin het onmogelijke te proberen, hoewel hij tegenover zijn hoge bazen wel de schijn moest ophouden. Zijn belangrijkste doel was het voorkomen van actieve sabotage, aanslagen op Irakezen, vernietiging van hun materieel en de vorming van een serieuze verzetsbeweging. Daarnaast moest hij hulp van buitenaf – in de vorm van manschappen, kennis en materiaal – proberen tegen te gaan.

Daarbij zou hij regelmatig in botsing komen met zijn rivalen van de AMAN, de geheime politie, die twee verdiepingen boven hem zat. Hij had die ochtend gehoord dat Khatib de schurk Sabaawi, even onnozel en wreed als hijzelf, als hoofd van de AMAN in Koeweit had geïnstalleerd. Als tegenstribbelende Koeweiti's in zíjn handen zouden vallen, zouden ze net zo hard leren gillen als de dissidenten thuis. Hij, Rahmani, zou zich tot de buitenlanders beperken. Dat was zijn opdracht.

Kort voor twaalf uur die middag beëindigde dr. Terry Martin zijn college aan de School voor Oosterse en Afrikaanse Studies, een faculteit van de universiteit van Londen in de buurt van Gowen Street. Op weg naar de docentenkamer kwam hij Mabel tegen, de secretaresse die hij deelde met twee andere docenten Arabische studies.

'O, doctor Martin, er is een boodschap voor u achtergelaten.'

Ze boog haar knie, steunde haar koffertje tegen haar tweedrok en haalde er een velletje papier uit.

'Deze meneer vroeg of u hem wilde terugbellen. Hij zei dat het dringend was.'

In de docentenkamer legde Martin zijn aantekeningen over het Abbasidenkalifaat op een tafel en liep naar de muntjestelefoon aan de muur. Bij de tweede zoemtoon werd opgenomen. Een heldere vrouwenstem noemde het nummer. Geen naam, alleen het nummer.

'Mag ik meneer Stephen Laing?' vroeg Martin.

'Met wie spreek ik?'

'Eh, doctor Martin. Hij had mij gebeld.'

'O ja, doctor Martin. Hebt u één moment?'

Martin fronste. Ze wist dus van het telefoontje en ze kende zijn naam. Hij kon zich met de beste wil geen Stephen Laing herinneren. Even later hoorde hij een mannenstem.

'Met Stephen Laing. Heel vriendelijk van u om meteen terug te bellen. Ik weet dat ik u overval, maar we hebben elkaar een tijdje terug ontmoet op het Instituut voor Strategische Studies, toen u die indrukwekkende lezing over de Iraakse bewapening hield. Hebt u al een afspraak voor de lunch?'

Laing, wie hij ook mocht zijn, was zo iemand tegen wie je moeilijk nee kon zeggen – schuchter maar toch overtuigend.

'Vanmiddag? Nu meteen?'

'Wat waren uw plannen?'

'Sandwiches in de kantine,' zei Martin.

'Mag ik u dan een sole meunière aanbieden bij Scott's? U kent het toch wel? In Mount Street?'

Een van de beste en duurste visrestaurants in Londen. Natuurlijk kende Martin het. Twintig minuten met de taxi. Het was half een, hij was dol op vis, en Scott's was veel te prijzig voor een academicus. Wist Laing dat soms ook?

'Werkt u bij het ISS?' vroeg hij.

'Ik zal het u bij de lunch uitleggen, doctor Martin. Zullen we zeggen om één uur? Ik verheug me erop.' En de verbinding werd verbroken.

Toen Martin het restaurant binnenstapte, kwam de gerant naar hem toe om hem persoonlijk te begroeten. 'Doctor Martin? Meneer Laing zit al aan zijn tafeltje. Wilt u mij maar volgen?'

Het was een rustige tafel in een discrete hoek, waar je ongestoord met elkaar kon praten. Stephen Laing – Martin wist nu zeker dat hij hem niet kende – kwam overeind. Hij was een magere, hoekige man met dun grijs haar. Hij droeg een donker pak. Toen hij zijn gast een stoel had aangeboden, keek hij vragend naar een fles uitstekende Meursault in een ijsemmertje. Martin knikte.

'U werkt dus niet op het Instituut, meneer Laing.'

Laing verblikte of verbloosde niet. Hij wachtte tot de ober het koele, pittige vocht had ingeschonken en weer was vertrokken, met achterlating van de menukaart. Toen hief hij zijn glas.

'Nee, ik werk op Century House. Hebt u daar problemen mee?'

De Britse Secret Intelligence Service of SIS is gehuisvest in Century House, een nogal haveloos gebouw ten zuiden van de Theems tussen Elephant & Castle en Old Kent Road. Het is oud, ongeschikt en zo verwarrend dat bezoekers eigenlijk geen pasje nodig hebben. Binnen enkele seconden zijn ze verdwaald en roepen ze om hulp.

'Nee. Maar ik ben wel geïnteresseerd,' zei Martin.

'Net als wij. Ik ben een groot bewonderaar van u, doctor Martin. Ik blijf graag op de hoogte, maar u schijnt ons altijd een stap voor te zijn.'

'Dat kan ik me nauwelijks voorstellen,' zei Martin, maar toch voelde hij zich gevleid. Een academicus vindt het altijd prettig als zijn werk wordt gewaardeerd.

'Toch is het zo,' hield Laing vol. 'Tong voor twee? Uitstekend. Ik geloof dat ik alle lezingen ken die u voor het Instituut, voor de United Services en voor

Chatham hebt gehouden. Plus natuurlijk die twee artikelen in *Survival*.'

De afgelopen vijf jaar was Terry Martin ondanks zijn jeugdige leeftijd van vijfendertig jaar steeds vaker gevraagd als spreker door zulke eerbiedwaardige instituten als het ISS, het United Services Institute en Chatham House, het centrum voor de studie van internationale betrekkingen. *Survival* is het tijdschrift van het ISS, en van elk nummer gaan vijfentwintig exemplaren naar het Bureau voor Buitenlandse en Gemenebestzaken in King Charles Street, waarvan er vijf bij Century House terechtkomen.

Terry Martins interesse voor deze mensen had niets te maken met zijn grote academische kennis van het middeleeuwse Mesopotamië, maar met de andere pet die hij droeg. Uit persoonlijke belangstelling was hij jaren geleden begonnen met een studie van de strijdkrachten in het Midden-Oosten. Hij had defensie-exposities bezocht, contacten gelegd met wapenfabrikanten en hun Arabische cliënten, waarbij zijn vloeiende beheersing van het Arabisch hem goed van pas was gekomen. Nu, tien jaar later, was hij een wandelende encyclopedie. Hoewel het zijn hobby was, werd hij toch met veel respect behandeld door de vakmensen op dit gebied, zoals de Amerikaanse romanschrijver Tom Clancy als expert wordt beschouwd op het terrein van de bewapening van de NAVO en het voormalige Warschau Pact.

De twee soles meunières arriveerden en ze begonnen met smaak te eten.

Acht weken eerder had Laing, op dat moment Hoofd Operaties van de sectie Midden-Oosten op Century House, een geschreven portret van Terry Martin uit het archief laten ophalen. Hij was onder de indruk geweest van wat hij las.

Martin was geboren in Bagdad, opgegroeid in Irak en daarna in Engeland naar de middelbare school gegaan. Bij zijn eindexamen aan Haileybury had hij uitstekende cijfers gehaald voor Engels, geschiedenis en Frans. Hij werd als een briljante leerling beschouwd, geschikt voor een studiebeurs voor Oxford of Cambridge.

Maar de jongen, die al vloeiend Arabisch sprak, had liever Arabisch willen studeren en had zich daarom aangemeld bij de SOAS in Londen. Hij was meteen toegelaten en in de herfst van 1973 begonnen met zijn studie geschiedenis van het Midden-Oosten.

Binnen drie jaar had hij zijn doctoraal gehaald en daarna nog eens drie jaar aan zijn promotie gewerkt. Hij had zich gespecialiseerd in het Irak van de 8e tot de 15e eeuw, met speciale nadruk op het Abbasiden-kalifaat van 750 tot 1258. Hij promoveerde in 1979, waarna hij één jaar verlof nam. In 1980 was hij in Irak toen dat land Iran binnenviel – het begin van een oorlog die acht jaar zou duren. Daardoor ontstond zijn belangstelling voor de strijdkrachten van het Midden-Oosten.

Na zijn terugkeer, zesentwintig jaar oud, kreeg hij een baan aangeboden als wetenschappelijk medewerker aan het SOAS, een van de beste en zwaarste opleidingen in Arabische studies ter wereld. Op grond van zijn oorspronkelijke onderzoek werd hij op vierendertigjarige leeftijd benoemd tot hoofddocent in de geschiedenis van het Midden-Oosten, met de verwachting dat hij op zijn veertigste professor zou kunnen zijn.

Dat alles had Laing in zijn biografie gelezen. Maar wat hem meer interesseerde was Martins kennis van de wapenarsenalen in het Midden-Oosten. Jarenlang was dat een randkwestie geweest, in de schaduw van de koude oorlog. Maar nu...

'Het gaat om Koeweit,' zei hij ten slotte. De borden waren afgeruimd en ze hadden geen dessert genomen. De Meursault was goed gevallen en Laing had er handig voor gezorgd dat Martin het meeste had gedronken. Als uit het niets verschenen nu twee glazen oude port.

'Zoals u zich kunt voorstellen, is er de afgelopen dagen heel wat te doen geweest.'

Dat was een understatement. De IJzeren Dame was uit Colorado teruggekeerd in haar Boadicea-stemming, zoals haar medewerkers het uitdrukten – verwijzend naar de legendarische Britse koningin die de Romeinen neermaaide met de zwaarden die aan de wielen van haar strijdwagen waren bevestigd. Douglas Hurd, de minister van Buitenlandse Zaken, scheen al te overwegen een stalen helm te gaan dragen, en de spionnen in Century House werden overspoeld met verzoeken om informatie.

'Het punt is dat we graag iemand naar Koeweit zouden sturen om te ontdekken wat er precies aan de hand is.'

'Onder de Iraakse bezetting?' vroeg Martin.

'Ik vrees van wel. De Irakezen zijn er nu de baas.'

'Maar waarom ik?'

'Ik zal open kaart spelen,' zei Laing, die dat absoluut niet van plan was. 'We moeten meer gegevens hebben. Hoe groot het Iraakse leger is, hoe goed hun soldaten zijn getraind, over welk materieel ze beschikken. Bovendien is er grote onzekerheid over onze eigen landgenoten. Kunnen ze zich redden, zijn ze in gevaar, kunnen we hen veilig het land uit krijgen? Dat is belangrijke informatie, en daarom hebben we iemand ter plaatse nodig. Iemand die vloeiend Arabisch spreekt. U hebt uw leven lang tussen Arabieren gezeten, veel langer dan ik, dus...'

'Maar er moeten op dit moment toch honderden Koeweiti's in Engeland zijn die u daarheen kunt sturen?' opperde Martin.

Laing zoog langzaam op een stukje tong dat tussen zijn kiezen was blijven steken. 'We hebben liever een van onze eigen mensen,' mompelde hij.

'Een Engelsman? Die voor een Arabier kan doorgaan zonder dat hij iemand opvalt?'

'Precies. Maar ik betwijfel of we zo iemand kunnen vinden.'

Het moest de wijn geweest zijn, of de port. Terry Martin was niet gewend aan Meursault en port bij de lunch. Achteraf had hij zijn tong wel willen afbijten als hij de klok een paar seconden had kunnen terugzetten. Maar toen hij zijn mond opendeed, was het al te laat.

'Ik weet wel iemand. Mijn broer Mike. Die is majoor bij de SAS. Hij kan voor een Arabier doorgaan.'

Laing wist zijn enthousiasme goed te verbergen. Rustig haalde hij de tandenstoker uit zijn mond waarmee hij het stukje tong had verwijderd.

'O ja?' mompelde hij. 'Meent u dat nou?'

Verbaasd maar verheugd reed Steve Laing in een taxi naar Century House terug. Hij had de arabist voor de lunch uitgenodigd in de hoop hem ergens anders voor te strikken – dat was hij nog steeds van plan – en hij had de kwestie Koeweit maar terloops willen noemen.

Jaren van ervaring hadden hem geleerd om te beginnen met een vraag waarop het slachtoffer geen antwoord wist, om dan pas tot de zaak zelf te komen. De expert, in zijn beroepseer aangetast, was dan eerder bereid met het tweede verzoek in te stemmen.

De verrassende ontboezeming van dr. Martin vormde misschien de oplossing van een probleem dat de vorige dag tijdens een topconferentie in Century House aan de orde was gesteld. Op dat moment had niemand er een gat in gezien. Maar als de jonge academicus gelijk had... een broer die nog beter Arabisch sprak dan hij en die bovendien bij het Special Air Service Regiment zat en dus gewend was aan geheime opdrachten... Heel interessant.

Terug op kantoor liep Laing meteen naar zijn directe baas, het hoofd van de divisie Midden-Oosten. Na een gesprek van een uur gingen ze samen naar boven om met een van de twee adjunct-chefs te overleggen.

Ook in deze tijd van 'openheid' was de Secret Intelligence Service, beter bekend onder de onjuiste benaming MI-6, nog steeds een schimmige organisatie die haar geheimen goed bewaakt. Het was nog niet zo lang geleden dat de Britse regering het bestaan van de SIS officieel had toegegeven, en pas in 1991 werd de naam van de hoogste baas genoemd – volgens ingewijden een dom en kortzichtig besluit, dat geen enkel doel diende en waardoor de man gedwongen werd zich te omringen met lijfwachten die uit de belastinggelden moesten worden betaald. Maar dat zijn de bijverschijnselen van een democratisch bestel.

De medewerkers van de SIS staan in geen enkele gids vermeld. Ze komen als gewone ambtenaren voor op de loonlijsten van verschillende ministeries, voornamelijk die van Buitenlandse Zaken, waaronder de dienst ressorteert. Ook de begroting wordt weggewerkt in het budget van tien verschillende departementen.

Zelfs de plek van het haveloze hoofdkwartier werd jarenlang als een staatsgeheim beschouwd, totdat iemand erop wees dat iedere willekeurige Londense taxichauffeur die een passagier naar Century House moest vervoeren reageerde met: 'O, u bedoelt het spionnennest?' En als de Londense *cabbies* het wisten, was het vermoedelijk ook bij de KGB bekend.

De 'Firma', veel minder beroemd dan de Amerikaanse CIA, veel kleiner en veel slechter gefinancierd, heeft bij vriend en vijand toch een goede reputatie opgebouwd met haar 'produkt' (clandestien verkregen inlichtingen). Van de belangrijkste inlichtingendiensten in de wereld is alleen de Israëlische Mossad nog kleiner en schimmiger.

Het hoofd van de SIS wordt officieel 'Chef' genoemd en *nooit* directeur-generaal – ondanks de halsstarrige fouten in de pers. De SIS is de zusterorganisatie van de veiligheidsdienst MI-5, die verantwoordelijk is voor de contraspionage in Groot-Brittannië zelf en wel wordt geleid door een directeur-generaal.

Binnen de dienst staat de Chef bekend als 'C'. Dat lijkt een afkorting van 'Chef', maar dat is het niet. De allereerste Chef was admiraal Sir Mansfield Cummings. De 'C' is de eerste letter van de achternaam van deze allang overleden pionier.

De Chef wordt bijgestaan door twee adjunct-chefs, die weer vijf assistent-chefs onder zich hebben. Zij leiden de vijf belangrijkste afdelingen: Operaties (voor het verzamelen van clandestiene informatie), Inlichtingen (voor het analyseren ervan), Techniek (voor het vervaardigen van valse papieren, mini-camera's, speciale inkt, ultra-compacte verbindingsapparatuur en andere hulpmiddelen om illegale operaties in het buitenland uit te voeren en te ontsnappen), Administratie (voor het salarisbeheer, de pensioenen, het personeelsbeleid, de begroting, het archief, de juridische kanten enzovoort) en Contraspionage (belast met het antecedentenonderzoek om de dienst te vrijwaren van vijandelijke infiltratie).

Onder Operaties ressorteren de controleofficieren, verantwoordelijk voor de diverse internationale divisies: Westelijk Halfrond, Sovjetblok, Afrika, Europa, Midden-Oosten en Australazië – plus de sectie Verbindingen, die de lastige taak heeft om de samenwerking met 'bevriende' diensten te regelen. In de praktijk verloopt het niet allemaal even glad (niets in Engeland verloopt ooit glad), maar het werkt.

Die augustusmaand van 1990 was alle aandacht op het Midden-Oosten gericht, met name op de sectie Irak, waar de hele politieke en bureaucratische wereld van Westminster en Whitehall zich als een luidruchtige en onwelkome fanclub bovenop had gestort.

De adjunct-chef luisterde aandachtig naar wat de controleofficier van de divisie Midden-Oosten en het hoofd Operaties van die afdeling te zeggen hadden en knikte een paar keer. Dat zou een interessante mogelijkheid kunnen zijn.

Niet dat er helemaal geen informatie uit Koeweit binnenkwam. De eerste achtenveertig uur, voordat de Irakezen de internationale telefoonverbindingen hadden verbroken, hadden alle Britse bedrijven met een vestiging in Koeweit hun plaatselijke man voortdurend met telefoontjes, telexen en faxen bestookt. De Koeweitse ambassade had zich onmiddellijk met de eerste gruwelverhalen bij Buitenlandse Zaken gemeld en op een snelle bevrijdingsactie aangedrongen.

Het probleem was dat er maar weinig echt betrouwbare inlichtingen bij waren die de Chef aan het kabinet kon voorleggen. Op dit moment, vlak na de invasie, was het in Koeweit 'één grote, onoverzichtelijke bende', zoals de minister van Buitenlandse Zaken het zes uur eerder treffend had uitgedrukt.

De staf van de Britse ambassade zat gevangen op haar terrein aan de rand van de Golf, bijna in de schaduw van de naalddunne Koeweit Towers, en probeerde telefonisch contact te krijgen met de Britse burgers die nog in het land waren. Ze hadden een lijst, maar die was natuurlijk niet volledig. Angstige zakenlui en technici meldden dat ze zo nu en dan schoten hoorden. 'Hoe bestaat het!' was de reactie in Century House op dit soort nieuws.

Iemand ter plaatse, een getrainde agent die voor een Arabier zou kunnen doorgaan.... dat klonk heel interessant. Nog afgezien van de concrete informatie die ze zouden kunnen krijgen over wat zich daar afspeelde, was het ook een mooie kans om de politici te tonen dat er werkelijk iets gebeurde – en om William Webster van de CIA een vlieg af te vangen. Hopelijk zou hij zich in zijn after-dinner mints verslikken als hij het hoorde.

De adjunct-chef twijfelde niet aan Margaret Thatchers bijna dweperige (en wederzijdse) bewondering voor de SAS, sinds die middag in mei 1980 toen de Special Air Service de terroristen in de Iraanse ambassade in Londen had uitgeschakeld. Die avond was ze bij het team op bezoek geweest in de kazerne in Albany Road om een glas whisky met hen te drinken en naar hun stoere verhalen te luisteren.

'Ik denk,' zei hij ten slotte, 'dat ik maar eens een praatje ga maken met de DSF.'

Officieel heeft het Special Air Service Regiment niets te maken met de SIS. De commandoketen is heel anders. Het reguliere 22e SAS-regiment (het 23e is alleen part-time actief) is gelegerd in een kazerne met de simpele naam 'Stirling Lines', vlak bij de provinciestad Hereford in het westen van Engeland. De commandant rapporteert aan de DSF, de directeur van de Special Forces, die zijn kantoor heeft op de bovenste verdieping van een groot gebouw in West-Londen. Ooit was het een sierlijk monument met een zuilengevel, maar tegenwoordig lijkt het constant in de steigers te staan. Binnen is het een doolhof van gangetjes en kamertjes, waarvan de eenvoud in schrille tegenspraak is met het belang van de operaties die er worden voorbereid.

De DSF is verantwoording schuldig aan de directeur Militaire Operaties (een generaal), die weer rapporteert aan de chef van de generale staf (een nog hogere generaal). De generale staf valt onder het ministerie van Defensie.

Er is een reden voor de aanduiding 'Special' in de naam van de SAS. Sinds het regiment in 1941 door David Stirling in de westelijke Sahara werd opgericht, heeft het altijd clandestien geopereerd. Tot de taken van de SAS behoren het infiltreren achter de linies om de vijand te bespioneren, sabotage en moordaanslagen, en het stichten van algehele verwarring. Verder is het regiment belast met het bevrijden van gijzelaars, de bewaking van hoge functionarissen en het opleiden van bevriende eenheden in het buitenland.

Zoals de leden van ieder elitekorps leven de mannen van de SAS rustig en onopvallend binnen hun eigen gemeenschap. Ze mogen niet met buitenstaanders over hun werk praten, ze laten zich niet fotograferen en ze komen zelden uit de schaduw.

Omdat de leefwijze van de mensen binnen beide organisaties zo sterk op elkaar lijkt, kennen de meeste leden van de SIS en de SAS elkaar van gezicht. In het verleden hebben ze vaak samengewerkt, tijdens gemeenschappelijke operaties of als de inlichtingendienst een specialist van het regiment 'leende' voor een bepaalde taak.

Iets dergelijks had de adjunct-chef in gedachten toen hij die avond (met toestemming van Sir Colin McColl) een glas moutwhisky kreeg aangereikt van brigadegeneraal J.P. Lovat in het geheime Londense hoofdkwartier van de SAS. Buiten ging de zon al onder.

Het onderwerp van hun gesprek en van gedachten in het hoofd van sommige mensen in Londen en Koeweit zat op dat moment vele kilometers ver weg in een andere kazerne, over een kaart gebogen. De afgelopen acht weken hadden hij en zijn team van twaalf instructeurs als lijfwacht opgetreden voor sjeik Zajed bin Sultan van Abu Dhabi.

Het was een taak die het regiment al vaak had vervuld. Langs de westkust van de Golf, vanaf het sultanaat Oman in het zuiden tot aan Bahrein in het noorden, ligt een rij sultanaten, emiraten en sjeikdommen waar de Britten al eeuwenlang een vinger in de pap hebben. De Verdragsstaten, tegenwoordig de Verenigde Arabische Emiraten, werden zo genoemd omdat de Britten ooit een verdrag met de plaatselijke vorsten hadden gesloten om hen met de Royal Navy tegen piraten te beschermen in ruil voor handelsrechten. Die relatie bestaat nog steeds en een groot aantal sultans beschikt over een lijfwacht die door SAS-teams de kneepjes van het vak is geleerd. Daar wordt natuurlijk voor betaald, en het geld gaat naar het ministerie van Defensie in Londen.

Majoor Mike Martin had een grote kaart van de Golf en een groot deel van het Midden-Oosten op de tafel in de mess uitgespreid en bestudeerde die samen met zijn mannen. Met zijn zevenendertig jaar was hij niet de oudste man in de kamer. Twee van zijn sergeants waren boven de veertig – taaie, pezige, fitte soldaten die het met gemak tegen kerels van twintig jaar jonger konden opnemen.

'Verandert het iets voor ons, chef?' vroeg een van de sergeants.

Zoals bij alle kleine, hechte eenheden spraken de meeste mannen van het regiment elkaar met de voornaam aan, maar de officieren werden meestal chef genoemd.

'Ik weet het niet,' zei Martin. 'Saddam Hoessein is Koeweit binnengevallen. De vraag is: zal hij zich uit eigen beweging weer terugtrekken? En zo niet, zullen de Verenigde Naties dan een troepenmacht sturen om hem te verdrijven? Als dat gebeurt, denk ik dat wij ook wel een rol krijgen.'

'Mooi zo,' zei de sergeant voldaan. De andere zes mannen rond de tafel knikten. Het was al te lang geleden dat ze aan een spannende, serieuze actie hadden deelgenomen.

Het regiment kent vier basisdisciplines waarvan iedere rekruut er één onder de knie moet krijgen. Er zijn de 'Freefallers', gespecialiseerd in parachutesprongen vanaf grote hoogte, de 'Mountainmen', die vooral op berghellingen en hoge toppen actief zijn, de 'Armoured Scouts', die met kale, verlengde, zwaarbepantserde Landrovers over open terrein razen, en de 'Amphibians', die getraind zijn in onderwateracties en het varen met kano's en opblaasboten.

Martins groep van twaalf man telde vier Freefallers, onder wie hijzelf, vier Armoured Scouts, die de Abu Dhabi's de beginselen van de snelle aanval en tegenaanval in de woestijn moesten bijbrengen, en vier Amphibians, die instructies gaven in onderwatertechnieken. Abu Dhabi ligt aan de Golf.

Naast hun eigen specialisme moeten de SAS-mensen ook de andere technieken redelijk beheersen, zodat ze elkaar kunnen vervangen als dat nodig is. Bovendien worden er nog andere vaardigheden vereist, zoals radiotechniek, eerste hulp en talenkennis.

De basiseenheid bestaat uit vier mensen. Als een van hen wordt uitgeschakeld, worden zijn taken onder de andere drie verdeeld, of het nu om medische hulp of om de bediening van de radio gaat.

De SAS gaat er prat op dat ze een veel hoger opleidingsniveau heeft dan enig ander legeronderdeel. Omdat de mannen overal ter wereld opereren, is talenkennis een voorwaarde. Iedere soldaat moet minstens één vreemde taal leren. Jarenlang was Russisch favoriet, maar dat is veranderd sinds het einde van de koude oorlog. Maleis is nuttig in het Verre Oosten, en het regiment had jarenlang in Borneo gevochten. De belangstelling voor Spaans neemt toe sinds de clandestiene operaties in Colombia tegen de drugsbaronnen van Medellin en Cali. Frans is altijd handig.

En omdat het regiment al zo lang sultan Qaboos van Oman heeft gesteund in zijn strijd tegen de communistische infiltratie vanuit Zuid-Jemen naar Dhofar, en er regelmatig cursussen worden gegeven in Saoedi-Arabië en andere Golfstaten, spreken veel SAS-leden ook redelijk Arabisch. De sergeant die om actie had gevraagd was een van hen, maar hij moest toegeven: 'De chef slaat alles. Ik heb nog nooit een buitenlander zo goed Arabisch horen spreken. En hij lijkt ook nog op een Arabier.'

Mike Martin richtte zich op en streek met zijn gebruinde hand door zijn pikzwarte haar.

'Bedtijd, mannen.'

Het was een paar minuten over tien. Bij het eerste ochtendlicht moesten ze alweer hun bed uit voor de gebruikelijke duurloop van vijftien kilometer, samen met hun leerlingen, voordat het te heet werd in de zon. De Abu Dhabi's hadden er de pest aan, maar ze moesten van hun sjeik. Als die vreemde soldaten uit Engeland zeiden dat het nuttig was, dan was dat zo. Bovendien betaalde hij ervoor, en hij wilde waar voor zijn geld.

Majoor Martin trok zich in zijn eigen kamer terug en viel meteen in een diepe slaap. De sergeant had gelijk. Hij zag er inderdaad uit als een Arabier. Zijn mannen vroegen zich vaak af of hij soms zuidelijke voorouders had, met zijn olijfkleurige huid, zijn donkere ogen en zijn ravezwarte haar. Hij had het hun nooit verteld, maar ze vergisten zich.

Zijn grootvader van moeders kant was een Britse theeplanter in Darjeeling in India geweest. Als jochies hadden Terry en Mike weleens foto's van hem gezien – een lange man met een roze gezicht, een blonde snor, een pijp in zijn mond en een geweer in zijn hand, zijn voet op een neergeschoten tijger. Op en top de *pukka sahib*, de Engelsman van de Indiase Raj.

Maar in 1928 deed Terrence Granger iets onvoorstelbaars: hij werd verliefd op een Indiaas meisje en trouwde met haar. Zoiets dééd je gewoon niet. Hoe mooi en lief ze ook was. Hij kreeg geen ontslag bij de theemaatschappij, want dan zou de zaak in de openbaarheid zijn gekomen. Maar hij werd 'verbannen' (dat was het woord dat ze gebruikten) naar een afgelegen plantage in Assam.

Maar de straf pakte heel anders uit. Granger en zijn jonge bruid, die van zichzelf Indira Bohse heette, hadden het er geweldig naar hun zin. Ze hielden van de woeste ravijnen met kleinwild en tijgers, van de diepgroene theehellingen, van het klimaat en van de mensen. In 1930 werd Susan geboren. En ze werd daar opgevoed, een Anglo-Indiaas meisje met Indiase kameraadjes.

In 1943 breidde de oorlog zich uit tot India, toen de Japanners via Burma oprukten naar de grens. Granger was oud genoeg om zich niet te hoeven melden, maar hij stond erop. Na een basistraining in Delhi werd hij als majoor bij de Assam Infanterie ingelijfd. Alle Britse cadetten werden meteen tot majoor bevorderd. Zo hoefden ze niet te dienen onder Indiase officieren, die geen hogere rang konden krijgen dan luitenant of kapitein.

In 1945 sneuvelde Granger bij de oversteek van de Irrawaddy. Zijn lichaam werd nooit gevonden. Het verdween gewoon in die kletsnatte Burmese jungle – een van de tienduizenden die de zwaarste lijf-aan-lijfgevechten uit de oorlog hadden meegemaakt.

Met haar kleine pensioentje trok zijn weduwe zich in haar eigen cultuur terug. Twee jaar later ontstonden er nog meer problemen. In 1947 werd India verdeeld. De Britten vertrokken. Ali Jinnah eiste zijn islamitische Pakistan in het noorden op, Pandit Nehru kreeg het voornamelijk hindoeïstische India in het zuiden. Grote groepen vluchtelingen van de twee religies trokken daarop naar het noorden of het zuiden en er braken zware gevechten uit. Meer dan een miljoen mensen verloren het leven. Indira Granger, bevreesd voor de veiligheid van haar dochter, stuurde haar naar de jongere broer van haar overleden man, een keurige architect in het Engelse Haslemere. Zes maanden later kwam Indira bij de rellen om.

Susan Granger kwam op zeventienjarige leeftijd naar Engeland, het land van haar voorvaders dat ze nog nooit had gezien. Ze zat een jaar op een meisjesschool bij Haslemere en volgde een tweejarige opleiding als verpleegster in het Farnham General Hospital. Daarna werkte ze een jaar als secretaresse bij een advocaat in Farnham.

Toen ze eenentwintig was, de jongst toegestane leeftijd, meldde ze zich aan als stewardess bij de British Overseas Airways Corporation. Samen met de andere meisjes werd ze opgeleid aan de BOAC-school, het vroegere St. Mary's Klooster in Heston, niet ver van Londen. Haar achtergrond als verpleegster sprak in haar voordeel, en haar uiterlijk en manieren waren een extra pluspunt.

Ze was een mooie jonge vrouw, met lang kastanjebruin haar, hazelnootbruine ogen en een huid als van een zongebruinde Europese vrouw. Na haar opleiding werd ze geplaatst op Lijn 1, de vlucht van Londen naar India – een voor de hand liggende keuze voor een meisje dat vloeiend Hindi sprak.

Het was in die dagen nog een heel lange reis met de vierprops Argonaut. Eerst de route Londen-Rome-Caïro-Basra-Bahrein-Karachi-Bombay. Dan verder naar Delhi, Calcutta, Colombo, Rangoon, Bangkok en ten slotte Singapore, Hong Kong en Tokio. Natuurlijk kon die vlucht niet door een en dezelfde bemanning worden uitgevoerd. In Basra, in het zuiden van Irak, werden de piloten en stewardessen afgelost.

Het was daar, in 1951, bij een drankje in de Port Club, dat ze een verlegen jonge accountant van de Iraakse Petroleummaatschappij ontmoette, die toen nog in Britse handen was. Zijn naam was Nigel Martin en hij vroeg of ze met hem uit eten wilde. Ze was gewaarschuwd tegen opdringerige heren onder de passagiers en de bemanning tijdens de tussenstops, maar Nigel leek een aardige man en ze nam zijn uitnodiging aan. Toen hij haar terugbracht naar het BOAC-kwartier waar de stewardessen waren gehuisvest, stak hij zijn arm uit. Verbaasd schudde ze zijn hand.

Daarna lag ze wakker in de drukkende hitte en vroeg zich af hoe het zou zijn om Nigel Martin te kussen.

Bij haar volgende tussenstop in Basra was hij er weer. Pas na hun huwelijk gaf hij toe dat hij zo verliefd was geweest dat hij aan Alex Reid, de plaatselijke BOAC-vertegenwoordiger, had gevraagd wanneer ze weer zou komen. De herfst van 1951 brachten ze door met tennissen, zwemmen in de Port Club en wandelingen door de bazars van Basra. Op zijn voorstel nam ze verlof op en reisde met hem naar Bagdad, waar hij zijn werk had.

Al snel wist ze dat ze zich daar thuis zou voelen. Al die mensen in hun veelkleurige gewaden, de drukte op straat, de geuren van het gebakken vlees aan de oevers van de Tigris, de honderden winkeltjes die kruiden, specerijen, goud en juwelen verkochten – het deed haar denken aan haar jeugd in India. Toen hij haar ten huwelijk vroeg, zei ze meteen ja.

Ze trouwden in 1952 in de St. George's kathedraal, de Anglicaanse kerk in de buurt van de Haifa Straat. Hoewel zij geen familie meebracht, kwamen er een heleboel mensen van de oliemaatschappij en de Britse ambassade.

Het was een mooie tijd om in Bagdad te wonen. Het leven was er rustig en ontspannen, de jonge koning Feisal zat op de troon terwijl Nuri as-Said het land regeerde, en overal was de Britse invloed merkbaar. Dat kwam gedeeltelijk door de bijdrage van de oliemaatschappij aan de economie, en omdat de meeste militairen een Britse opleiding hadden gehad, maar vooral omdat de hele maatschappelijke bovenklasse door strenge Engelse gouvernantes zindelijk was gemaakt – wat altijd een blijvende indruk achterlaat.

De Martins kregen twee zoons, in 1953 en 1955. Michael en Terry waren totaal verschillend. Michael had duidelijk de trekken van zijn grootmoeder Indira geërfd: zwart haar, donkere ogen en een olijfkleurige huid. Toen al werd in de Engelse gemeenschap gefluisterd dat hij meer weg had van een Arabier. Terry, die twee jaar jonger was, leek op zijn vader – klein, gedrongen, met een roze huid en rossig haar.

Om drie uur 's nachts werd majoor Martin door een bediende gewekt. 'Er is een boodschap voor u, *sajidi*.'

Het bericht was simpel genoeg, maar de code 'blitz' en de ondertekening betekenden dat het van de directeur zelf afkomstig was. Er werd geen antwoord verwacht. Martin moest op het eerste vliegtuig naar Londen stappen.

Hij droeg zijn taken over aan zijn tweede man, een SAS-kapitein die voor de eerste keer in het Midden-Oosten was. Toen trok hij zijn burgerkleren aan en reed zo snel mogelijk naar het vliegveld.

Het toestel van vijf voor drie 's nachts naar Londen had allang vertrokken moeten zijn. De meer dan honderd passagiers snurkten verder of mopperden wat toen de stewardess opgewekt verklaarde dat er een 'operationele reden' was voor de anderhalf uur vertraging, maar dat ze nu spoedig zouden vertrekken.

Toen de deur openging en een magere man in jeans, woestijnlaarzen, een overhemd en een vliegeniersjack binnenstapte met een tas over zijn schouder, wierpen een paar mensen hem een nijdige blik toe. De man werd naar een lege stoel in de economy-klasse gebracht, waar hij zich installeerde. Een paar minuten na het opstijgen klapte hij zijn stoel naar achteren en viel in slaap.

Een zakenman naast hem, die uitvoerig had gedineerd, compleet met verboden verfrissingen, en daarna twee uur op het vliegveld en twee uur in het toestel had moeten wachten, nam nog een maagtablet en staarde broeierig naar de ontspannen slapende figuur in de stoel naast hem.

'Vervloekte Arabier,' mompelde hij, terwijl hij vergeefs trachtte de slaap te vatten.

Twee uur later brak de ochtend aan boven de Golf. De Britse jet, op weg naar het noordwesten, probeerde de zon voor te blijven en kwam kort voor tien uur plaatselijke tijd op Heathrow aan. Mike Martin ging als een van de eersten door de douane, omdat hij geen koffers bij zich had. Hij werd niet afgehaald, maar dat had hij ook niet verwacht. Hij wist waar hij heen moest. Buiten de aankomsthal stapte hij in een taxi.

In Washington schemerde het nog, maar de eerste stralen van de opkomende zon kleurden de verre heuvels van Georges County roze, vlak bij de plaats waar de Patuxent zich bij de Chesapeake voegt. Op de zesde en bovenste verdieping van het grote, rechthoekige gebouw op het complex waar de CIA haar hoofdkwartier heeft gevestigd, beter bekend als Langley, brandden de lichten nog.

Rechter William Webster, de directeur van de Central Intelligence Agency, wreef met zijn vingertoppen over zijn vermoeide ogen. Toen stond hij op en liep naar het raam. Het bos met zilverberken dat hem het uitzicht op de Potomac ontnam als ze volledig in blad stonden – zoals nu – was nog in duisternis gehuld. Binnen een uur zouden de bomen in het licht van de opkomende zon lichtgroen kleuren. Het was weer een slapeloze nacht geweest. Sinds de Iraakse invasie in Koeweit had hij alleen tijd gehad voor een paar hazeslaapjes. Hij werd constant gebeld door de president, de Nationale Veiligheidsraad, Buitenlandse Zaken, en door iedereen die zijn telefoonnummer had, leek het wel.

Achter hem, net zo vermoeid als hijzelf, zaten Bill Stewart, zijn adjunct-directeur Operaties, en Chip Barber, het hoofd van zijn sectie Midden-Oosten.

'Dus dat is het zo'n beetje?' vroeg Webster, alsof het herhalen van de vraag een beter antwoord zou opleveren.

Dat was niet zo. De president, de Nationale Veiligheidsraad en Buitenlandse Zaken zaten te springen om betrouwbare, geheime informatie uit het kleine kringetje rondom Saddam Hoessein. Zou hij in Koeweit blijven? Of zou hij zich terugtrekken onder dreiging van de resoluties van de VN-Veiligheidsraad of de olie- en handelsboycot? Wat ging er in hem om? Wat was hij van plan? En waar zàt hij, overigens?

De CIA had geen idee. Natuurlijk hadden ze een bureau in Bagdad, maar het hoofd van dat bureau was bekend bij die klootzak Rahmani van de Iraakse contraspionagedienst en kon dus weinig uitrichten. De inlichtingen die hem de laatste weken waren toegespeeld bleken absoluut niet te kloppen. Zijn 'bronnen' werkten blijkbaar voor Rahmani en hadden hem systematisch voorgelogen.

Natuurlijk, ze hadden satellietfoto's. Stapels en stapels. De KH-11's en KH-12's cirkelden om de paar minuten over Irak en fotografeerden zowat het hele land. Analisten werkten dag en nacht om uit te vissen wat *misschien* een gifgasfabriek of een nucleair complex zou kunnen zijn – of gewoon een fietsenwerkplaats, zoals de Irakezen beweerden.

Ooit zouden de knappe koppen van het National Photographic Interpretation Centre en het National Reconnaissance Office, een gezamenlijke onderneming van de CIA en de luchtmacht, wel een compleet beeld kunnen samenstellen: dit is een belangrijke commandopost, dit een SAM-batterij, dit een vliegbasis, enzovoort. Goed. En ooit zouden ze die strategische doelen naar het Stenen Tijdperk kunnen bombarderen, maar wat wisten ze verder nog? Wat lag er bijvoorbeeld onder de grond verborgen?

Jarenlang hadden ze Irak verwaarloosd en nu zaten ze met de gevolgen. De mannen achter hem, onderuitgezakt in hun stoelen, waren spionnen van de oude stempel, die hun sporen hadden verdiend bij de Berlijnse muur, toen het cement nog niet eens droog was. Ze stamden nog uit de goeie ouwe tijd, voordat de spionagewereld door elektronische snufjes was overgenomen.

En zij vertelden hem dat de camera's van het NRO en de luisterposten van de NSA in Fort Meade geen plannen konden onthullen, geen bedoelingen konden raden en niet in het hoofd van een dictator konden doordringen.

Ondanks al die satellietfoto's en de geluidsopnamen van alle telefoongesprekken en radioberichten van en naar Irak waren ze nog geen steek wijzer.

Dezelfde regering en hetzelfde Congres die zo door elektronica waren geobsedeerd dat ze miljarden dollars hadden uitgegeven om de allermodernste apparatuur de lucht in te sturen, eisten nu antwoorden die niet met elektronische middelen te vinden waren.

De mannen in de stoelen achter hem zeiden dat ELINT of 'elektronische informatie' slechts een aanvulling was op HUMINT of 'menselijke informatie', en geen vervanging. Leuk om te weten, maar wat schoot hij daarmee op?

Het Witte Huis stelde vragen die alleen konden worden beantwoord door een bron, een informant, een spion, een verrader, wie of wat dan ook, binnen de Iraakse regering zelf. En die had hij niet.

'Heb je al overlegd met Century House?'

'Ja, meneer. Die zitten met hetzelfde probleem.'

'Over twee dagen ga ik naar Tel Aviv,' zei Chip Barber. 'Ik heb een gesprek met Yaakov Dror. Zal ik het hem vragen?'

De directeur knikte. Generaal Yaakov 'Kobi' Dror was het hoofd van de Mossad, de minst toegankelijke van alle 'bevriende' buitenlandse diensten. Webster had nog steeds de pest in over de kwestie Jonathan Pollard, een Israëlische agent die voor de Mossad in Amerika had gespioneerd. Mooie vrienden. Hij vroeg de Mossad liever niet om gunsten.

'Probeer hem onder druk te zetten, Chip. Dit is belangrijk. Als hij een bron in Bagdad heeft, willen wij die ook. Intussen ga ik maar weer naar het Witte Huis om Scowcroft te spreken.'

En in die weinig hoopgevende sfeer eindigde de bijeenkomst.

De vier mannen die de ochtend van de 5e augustus in het SAS-hoofdkwartier in Londen zaten te wachten hadden die nacht niet stilgezeten.

De directeur van de Special Forces, brigadegeneraal Lovat, had urenlang getelefoneerd. Alleen van twee tot vier had hij zitten slapen in zijn stoel. Zoals veel militairen had hij de eigenschap ontwikkeld om een paar uur te kunnen tukken als de situatie dat toestond. Je wist maar nooit wanneer de volgende gelegenheid zich zou voordoen. Voordat het licht werd, had hij zich gewassen en geschoren, klaar voor een volgende drukke dag.

Hij was het die om middernacht Britse tijd een hoge functionaris van British Airways had gebeld om het lijntoestel in Abu Dhabi aan de grond te houden. Als je in Engeland snel iets voor elkaar wilde krijgen, zonder papieren rompslomp, was het heel handig om de juiste mensen op de juiste plaatsen te kennen. De man van British Airways, die uit zijn bed werd gebeld, vroeg niet eens waaròm hij een lijntoestel op bijna vijfduizend kilometer afstand aan de grond moest houden tot er een extra passagier was ingestapt. Hij kende Lovat omdat ze allebei lid waren van de Special Forces Club in Herbert Crescent. Hij wist ongeveer wat Lovats functie was en hij voldeed aan zijn verzoek zonder lastige vragen te stellen.

Nog voor het ontbijt had de dienstdoende sergeant met Heathrow gebeld en te horen gekregen dat het toestel uit Abu Dhabi al eenderde van de vertraging van anderhalf uur had ingelopen en omstreeks tien uur zou landen. De majoor zou dus tegen elven op het hoofdkwartier kunnen zijn.

Een motorordonnans had snel een personeelsdossier uit de Browning Barracks, de basis van het luchtlandingsregiment in Aldershot, opgehaald. De adjudant van het regiment had het dossier kort na middernacht uit het archief gelicht. Het was een overzicht van Mike Martins loopbaan bij de para's vanaf de dag dat hij zich als achttienjarige schooljongen had aangemeld en beschreef zijn hele, negentienjarige staat van dienst, behalve de twee lange perioden dat hij aan het SAS-regiment was uitgeleend.

De commandant van het 22e SAS-regiment, kolonel Bruce Craig – ook een Schot – was nog dezelfde nacht vanuit Hereford naar Londen gereden met het dossier over die twee perioden. Vlak voordat het licht werd stapte hij het hoofdkwartier binnen.

'Morgen, J.P. Waar is al die drukte om?'

Ze kenden elkaar al heel lang. Lovat, altijd aangesproken als J.P. of Jaypee, had het commando gevoerd over het team dat tien jaar eerder de Iraanse ambassade op de terroristen had heroverd. Craig was toen een van zijn teamleiders geweest.

'Century House wil een man in Koeweit laten infiltreren,' zei hij. Daar hield hij het bij. Hij was geen man van veel woorden.

'Iemand van ons? Martin?' De kolonel wierp het dossier op het bureau.

'Kennelijk. Ik heb hem teruggeroepen uit Abu Dhabi.'

'Krijg nou wat. En ga je daarmee akkoord?'

Mike Martin was een van Craigs officieren. Ze kenden elkaar al lang. Het beviel Craig niets dat zijn mensen door Century House onder zijn neus vandaan werden 'gestolen'.

De DSF haalde zijn schouders op. 'Misschien zit er niets anders op, als hij de geschikte man is. Ze kunnen het hoog spelen.'

Craig bromde wat en kreeg een kop sterke zwarte koffie van de dienstdoende sergeant, die hij begroette als Sid. Ze hadden nog samen in Dhofar gevochten. Op politiek gebied had de kolonel weinig illusies. De SIS gedroeg zich wel heel bescheiden, maar als het nodig was konden ze tot de hoogste instantie gaan. De twee militairen kenden Margaret Thatcher goed en hadden veel bewondering voor haar. Ze wisten ook dat zij, net als Churchill, een voorstander was van directe actie. Century House had dus de beste papieren. Het regiment zou moeten meewerken en de SIS zou de leiding krijgen, onder het mom van een 'gezamenlijke' operatie.

De twee mannen van de SIS kwamen vlak na de kolonel binnen, en iedereen werd aan elkaar voorgesteld. De leider van de delegatie was Steve Laing. Hij was in het gezelschap van Simon Paxman, het hoofd van de sectie Irak.

65

Ze kregen een stoel in een wachtkamer aangeboden, met een kop koffie en de twee personeelsdossiers om door te lezen. Even later waren ze verdiept in de achtergronden van majoor Mike Martin. De vorige avond had Paxman vier uur met Martins jongere broer gesproken om wat meer te weten te komen over de familie en hun jeugd in Bagdad en op Haileybury School.

Tijdens zijn laatste schooljaar, in de zomer van 1971, had Mike Martin een persoonlijk briefje aan de para's geschreven. In september was hij uitgenodigd voor een gesprek op de basis in Aldershot, vlak bij een oude, geparkeerde Dakota waaruit Britse parachutisten ooit waren neergedaald in een poging de Rijnbrug bij Arnhem te veroveren.

Toen de para's navraag deden bij zijn school (dat was de vaste procedure), bleek hij een matige leerling maar een uitmuntend sportman te zijn. Dat kwam het regiment heel goed uit. De jongen werd aangenomen en kon nog dezelfde maand met zijn opleiding beginnen – twintig zware weken, tot aan april 1972.

Vier weken werden besteed aan exercities, fundamentele wapentraining, militaire technieken en conditietraining. Dat ging nog twee weken zo door, gecombineerd met eerste-hulp, seinen en voorzorgsmaatregelen tegen NBC (nucleaire, bacteriologische en chemische oorlogvoering).

De zevende, achtste en negende week werd de conditietraining geleidelijk verzwaard, compleet met duurlopen door de Brecon Range in Wales, waar sterke mannen van kou en uitputting zijn gestorven.

In de tiende week werd geoefend op de schietbaan van Hythe in Kent. Martin, net negentien geworden, ontpopte zich als een uitstekend schutter. De elfde en twaalfde week waren bestemd voor uithoudingsproeven in het open terrein bij Aldershot – zandheuvels op en af rennen en boomstammen door de modder zeulen, in de winterse regen en de ijskoude hagel.

'Uithoudingsproeven?' mompelde Paxman terwijl hij de pagina omsloeg. 'Wat was de rest dan?'

Na afloop hiervan kregen de jonge kerels hun felbegeerde rode baret en para-kleding, voordat ze opnieuw drie weken naar de Brecons werden gestuurd voor defensie-oefeningen, patrouilles en schietoefeningen met scherpe munitie. Tegen die tijd, eind januari 1972, was het bitter koud in de bergen. De mannen sliepen in de open lucht, zonder vuur.

De zestiende tot en met de negentiende week waren bestemd voor een cursus parachutespringen op de RAF-basis Abingdon, waar nog een paar rekruten afvielen. Aan het eind daarvan kwam de 'Wings Parade', waarbij de geslaagden hun para-wings kregen opgespeld. Hoewel dat er niet bij stond, werd er die nacht stevig bier gehesen in de oude 101 Club.

Na nog twee weken veldoefeningen en het bijschaven van de exercities, volgde in de tweeëntwintigste week de 'Pass-Out Parade'. Dat was de dag waarop de trotse ouders eindelijk de pukkelige zoons, die zes maanden eerder van huis waren vertrokken, terugzagen.

Soldaat Mike Martin was zijn instructeurs allang opgevallen, en in mei 1972 werd hij naar de officiersopleiding aan de Koninklijke Militaire Academie van Sandhurst gestuurd. Daar volgde hij de nieuwe eenjarige militaire standaardcursus die in de plaats was gekomen van de oude tweejarige opleiding.

Het gevolg was dat de parade van geslaagden in het voorjaar van 1973 de grootste was die ooit op Sandhurst was gehouden. De cadetten van de oude cursussen studeerden tegelijk af met de mannen van de nieuwe eenjarige cursus – in totaal waren er 490 cadetten. De parade werd afgenomen door generaal Sir Michael Carver, de latere veldmaarschalk Lord Carver, chef van de legerstaf.

De jonge luitenant Martin werd meteen naar Hythe gestuurd om een peloton over te nemen als voorbereiding op uitzending naar Noord-Ierland. Daar had hij twaalf ellendige weken het bevel over een peloton bij de observatiepost Flax Mill, in de ultra-republikeinse enclave Ardoyne in Belfast. Maar die zomer was het vrij rustig op Flax. Na Bloody Sunday, in januari 1972, werden de para's door de IRA gemeden als de pest.

Martin was ingedeeld bij het derde bataljon, bekend als Para-Drie. Na Belfast keerde hij terug naar de basis Aldershot om het bevel op zich te nemen over een peloton rekruten dat dezelfde zware training moest ondergaan als hijzelf had doorlopen. In de zomer van 1977 werd hij weer teruggeplaatst naar Para-Drie, dat sinds februari van dat jaar was gelegerd in Osnabrück, als onderdeel van het Britse Rijnleger.

Ook dat was geen gezellige tijd. Para-Drie was ondergebracht in Quebec Barracks, een haveloos voormalig vluchtelingenkamp. De para's waren op dat moment in 'pinguïn-modus', wat inhield dat ze drie van de negen jaar als gewone infanterie moesten dienen. Alle para's hadden de pest aan pinguïn-modus. Het moreel was slecht, er waren voortdurend vechtpartijen tussen para's en gewone infanteristen, en Martin moest mannen op appel slingeren met wie hij het in zijn hart volledig eens was. Hij hield het bijna een jaar vol, totdat hij in november 1977 overplaatsing naar de SAS aanvroeg.

Een groot deel van de SAS is afkomstig van de para's, misschien omdat de opleiding overeenkomt, hoewel de SAS beweert dat hun training zwaarder is. Martins staat van dienst werd beoordeeld in Hereford, waar zijn perfecte beheersing van het Arabisch als een pluspunt werd genoteerd. In de zomer van 1978 werd hij uitgenodigd voor de selectietraining.

De SAS zegt dat zij alleen heel fitte rekruten aanneemt en daarvan echte kerels maakt. Martin deed de standaard 'introductiecursus' van zes weken, samen met andere para's, mariniers en vrijwilligers uit de infanterie, de pantsertroepen, de artillerie en zelfs de genie. Het is een simpele training, gebaseerd op een simpel concept.

De eerste dag riep een grijnzende instructeur: 'Bij deze opleiding proberen we jullie niet te trainen. We proberen jullie kapot te maken!'

En dat deden ze. Maar tien procent van de SAS-rekruten komt door de eerste selectie heen. Dat scheelt later veel tijd. Martin behoorde tot die tien procent. Daarna kwam de vervolgopleiding, een jungletraining in Belize en nog een extra maand in Engeland om te leren een zware ondervraging te doorstaan – je mond houden terwijl je wordt gemarteld. Gelukkig had je bij de training het recht om er een eind aan te maken.

'Ze zijn geschift,' zei Paxman. Hij legde het dossier neer en nam nog een kop koffie. 'Volkomen gestoord.'

Laing bromde wat. Hij was verdiept in het andere dossier: Martins ervaringen in Arabië. Die waren vooral belangrijk voor de missie die hij in gedachten had.

Tijdens zijn eerste termijn had Martin drie jaar bij de SAS gezeten als teamleider, met de rang van kapitein. Hij had gekozen voor de A-compagnie, de Freefallers. De andere compagnies werden B, C en G genoemd. Martins keus lag voor de hand voor iemand die bij de Red Devils, het vrije-val demonstratieteam van de para's, had gezeten.

Bij de para's had hij niet veel aan zijn kennis van het Arabisch gehad, maar bij de SAS wel. Van 1979 tot en met 1981 was hij toegevoegd aan het leger van de sultan van Oman in westelijk Dhofar, had in twee Golfstaten lesgegeven in VIP-bescherming, de Saoedische Nationale Garde in Riyad getraind en de privé-lijfwacht van sjeik Isa van Bahrein opgeleid. In zijn SAS-dossier stonden daarover enkele opmerkingen – dat hij zijn oude banden met de Arabische cultuur had versterkt, dat hij de taal sprak als geen andere officier binnen het regiment en dat hij de gewoonte had om in zijn eentje lange wandelingen door de woestijn te maken als hij een probleem wilde overdenken, zonder zich iets van de hitte of de vliegen aan te trekken.

Uit het dossier bleek verder dat hij in de winter van 1981, na zijn driejarige dienstverband bij de SAS, weer naar de para's was teruggekeerd en tot zijn vreugde had gehoord dat ze in januari en februari 1982 zouden deelnemen aan Operatie Rocky Lance in... Oman. Dus reisde hij opnieuw naar de Jebel Akdar. In maart nam hij verlof, maar in april werd hij haastig teruggeroepen toen Argentinië de Falkland Eilanden had bezet.

Hoewel Para-Een in Engeland achterbleef, werden Twee en Drie naar Zuid-Amerika gestuurd. Ze vertrokken met het lijnschip *Canberra*, dat haastig geschikt was gemaakt voor troepentransport, en gingen aan land bij San Carlos Water. Terwijl Para-Twee de Argentijnen uit Goose Green verdreef, sleurde Para-Drie door de regen en de natte sneeuw over East Falkland naar Port Stanley.

'Sleuren? Heet dat niet oprukken?' vroeg Laing aan sergeant Sid, die hem nog een kop koffie inschonk. De sergeant kneep zijn lippen samen. Onnozele burgers.

'Ja, bij de landmacht. Wíj noemen het sleuren.'

In elk geval kwam het neer op een uitputtende mars in slecht weer, met een bepakking van vijftig kilo.

Para-Drie sloeg zijn kamp op bij Estancia House, een afgelegen boerderij, en bereidde zich voor op de definitieve aanval op Port Stanley. Eerst zouden ze de zwaar verdedigde Mount Longdon moeten bestormen. Het was in die grimmige nacht van de 11e op de 12e juni dat kapitein Mike Martin door een kogel werd getroffen.

De geruisloze nachtelijke aanval op de Argentijnse stellingen werd al snel een luidruchtige actie toen korporaal Millne op een mijn stapte die hem zijn voet kostte. De Argentijnse machinegeweren openden het vuur, fakkels verlichtten de berghelling alsof het klaarlichte dag was en Para-Drie zou dekking moeten zoeken of onmiddellijk in de tegenaanval gaan. Ze kozen voor het laatste en veroverden Mount Longdon, ten koste van drieëntwintig doden en meer dan veertig gewonden. Een van hen was Mike Martin, die een kogel in zijn been kreeg en een stroom van zware vloeken uitbraakte, gelukkig in het Arabisch.

Nadat hij het grootste deel van de dag op de berghelling had doorgebracht, terwijl hij acht huiverende Argentijnse krijgsgevangenen onder schot hield en moeite had om niet flauw te vallen, werd hij overgebracht naar de medische post bij Ajax Bay. Hij werd opgelapt en met een helikopter naar het hospitaalschip *Uganda* vervoerd. Daar kwam hij op een brits naast een Argentijnse luitenant terecht. Tijdens de reis naar Montevideo werden ze vrienden en ze bleven elkaar schrijven.

In de haven van de Uruguayaanse hoofdstad werden de Argentijnen aan land gezet. Martin was inmiddels voldoende hersteld om op een lijnvliegtuig te kunnen stappen, terug naar Brize Norton. Thuisgekomen kreeg hij nog drie weken om te herstellen op Headley Court in Leatherhead.

Daar ontmoette hij de verpleegster Susan, met wie hij na een korte verkering trouwde. Misschien viel ze voor de 'glamour' van het leger, maar daarin kwam ze bedrogen uit. Ze gingen wonen in een huisje bij Chobham, goed bereikbaar voor haar baan in Leatherhead en zijn werk op Aldershot. Maar na drie jaar, waarin ze hem maar vierenhalve maand had gezien, zette Susan hem terecht voor het blok. Je kunt kiezen, zei ze. De para's en die vervloekte woestijn, of mij. Hij dacht erover na en koos voor de woestijn.

Ze had gelijk om bij hem weg te gaan. In de herfst van 1982 begon hij aan een studie voor het Stafcollege, het opstapje naar een hogere rang en een goede bureaubaan, misschien op het ministerie. In februari 1983 zakte hij voor het examen.

'Dat was opzettelijk,' zei Paxman. 'Volgens zijn commandant had hij het op zijn sloffen kunnen halen als hij dat had gewild.'

'Ik weet het,' zei Laing. 'Ik heb het ook gelezen. De man is... anders dan anderen.'

In de zomer van 1983 werd Martin benoemd tot Brits stafofficier op het hoofdkwartier van de landmacht van de sultan van Oman in Maskat. Hij verlengde zijn termijn met nog eens twee jaar, als commandant van het noordelijke grensregiment in Maskat. In de zomer van 1986 werd hij in Oman tot majoor bevorderd. Officieel maakte hij nog altijd deel uit van de para's.

Officieren die één dienstverband bij de SAS hebben voltooid, kunnen opnieuw in dienst treden, maar alleen op uitnodiging. In de winter van 1987, Martin was net terug in Engeland en zijn echtscheiding was uitgesproken, kreeg hij een uitnodiging uit Hereford. In januari 1988 keerde hij daar terug als compagniescommandant bij de Northern Flank, die in Noorwegen was gelegerd. Daarna werd hij naar de sultan van Brunei gestuurd en zat hij een half jaar bij de interne beveiliging op het hoofdkwartier in Hereford. In juni 1990 werd hij met zijn team van instructeurs naar Abu Dhabi gezonden.

Sergeant Sid klopte en stak zijn hoofd om de deur. 'De brigadegeneraal vraagt of u binnenkomt. Majoor Martin komt eraan.'

Toen Martin binnenkwam, vielen zijn zwarte haar en zijn donkere gezicht en ogen onmiddellijk op. Laing keek snel naar Paxman. Punt één was dus opgelost. Hij kon voor een Arabier doorgaan. Nu de twee andere vragen nog. Sprak hij accentloos Arabisch en nam hij de opdracht aan?

J.P. stapte naar voren en nam Martins hand in een verpletterende greep. 'Blij je weer te zien, Mike.'

'Dank u, generaal.' Daarna gaf hij kolonel Craig een hand.

'Mag ik je voorstellen aan deze twee heren?' zei de DSF. 'Meneer Laing en meneer Paxman van Century House. Ze hebben een... eh... voorstel aan je. Heren, ga uw gang. Of wilt u de majoor misschien onder vier ogen spreken?'

'Nee, nee,' zei Laing haastig. 'De Chef hoopt dat dit een gezamenlijke operatie zal worden als deze bespreking iets oplevert.'

Heel handig, dacht J.P., die verwijzing naar Sir Colin. Om mij duidelijk te maken hoeveel druk deze klootzakken kunnen uitoefenen als het nodig mocht zijn.

De vijf mannen gingen zitten en Laing nam het woord. Hij beschreef de politieke achtergrond, en de onzekerheid of Saddam Hoessein zich snel, langzaam of helemaal niet uit Koeweit zou terugtrekken tenzij hij met geweld verdreven werd. De politiek ging er voorlopig vanuit dat Irak eerst alles van waarde uit Koeweit zou stelen en daarna allerlei concessies zou eisen van de Verenigde Naties, die bepaald niet in een toegeeflijke stemming waren. Het zou dus een slepende zaak kunnen worden.

Engeland wilde weten wat er in Koeweit gebeurde – geen gissingen en geruchten of de wilde verhalen die in de media de ronde deden, maar keiharde informatie over de Britse burgers in het land, de bezettingsmacht en de vraag of het Koeweitse verzet Saddams fronttroepen zou kunnen bezighouden als het op een oorlog aankwam.

Martin knikte en luisterde, stelde een paar vragen, maar hield verder zijn mond. De twee hoge officieren staarden uit het raam. Kort na twaalf uur was Laing uitgesproken.

'Dat was het ongeveer, majoor. Ik verwacht niet meteen een antwoord, maar de tijd begint te dringen.'

'Is het goed als wij even persoonlijk overleggen met onze collega?' vroeg J.P.

'Natuurlijk. Dan gaan Simon en ik terug naar kantoor. U hebt mijn nummer. Kunt u me in de loop van de middag uw beslissing laten weten?'

Sergeant Sid bracht de twee burgers naar buiten en wachtte tot ze een taxi hadden aangehouden. Toen klom hij weer de trap op naar zijn hoge post onder de hanebalken achter de steiger.

J.P. liep naar een kleine koelkast en haalde er drie koude biertjes uit. Toen ze open waren, namen de drie mannen een flinke slok.

'Hoor eens, Mike, we hoeven je niets wijs te maken. Je weet wat ze van je willen. Als je het een krankzinnig voorstel vindt, hebben we daar alle begrip voor.'

'Absoluut,' zei Craig. 'Je zou bij het regiment geen slechte aantekening krijgen als je nee zei. Dit is hun idee, niet het onze.'

'Maar als je het doet,' zei J.P., 'ben je in hun dienst – vanaf het moment dat je die deur uit stapt, bij wijze van spreken. Natuurlijk worden wij er ook bij betrokken, omdat ze het niet alleen afkunnen, maar zij houden de leiding. Na afloop kom je gewoon bij ons terug alsof je met verlof bent geweest.'

Martin wist hoe het werkte. Hij kende de verhalen van anderen die een klus voor Century House hadden opgeknapt. Voor het regiment hield je op te bestaan tot je weer terugkwam. Dan zeiden ze 'Leuk dat je er weer bent', en werd er met geen woord meer over gesproken.

'Ik doe het,' zei hij.

Kolonel Craig stond op. Hij moest terug naar Hereford. Hij stak zijn hand uit. 'Veel succes, Mike.'

'Tussen haakjes,' zei de brigadegeneraal, 'je hebt nog een lunchafspraak.

71

Hier om de hoek. Geregeld door Century House.'

Hij gaf Martin een papiertje en nam afscheid. De majoor liep de trap af en het gebouw uit. Het adres op het velletje papier was van een klein restaurant, vierhonderd meter van het hoofdkwartier. Zijn gastheer was een zekere Wafic al-Khouri.

Behalve MI-5 en MI-6 had de Britse inlichtingendienst nog een belangrijke afdeling, het Government Communications Headquarters of GCHQ, ondergebracht in een paar gebouwen niet ver van de rustige stad Cheltenham in Gloucestershire.

Het GCHQ is de Britse tegenhanger van de Amerikaanse National Security Agency of NSA, waarmee ze nauw samenwerken. Met hun luisterposten en antennes kunnen ze bijna ieder radiobericht en alle telefoongesprekken ter wereld afluisteren.

Dank zij de samenwerking met het GCHQ beschikt de NSA ook over een aantal posten in Groot-Brittannië, afgezien van haar luisterposten in de rest van de wereld. En het GCHQ heeft zijn eigen overzeese posten, met name in Akrotiri, een Brits soeverein gebied op Cyprus.

Het station in Akrotiri, dat het dichtst bij het Midden-Oosten ligt, registreert alle elektronische communicatie in die omgeving en stuurt alles terug naar Cheltenham. Daar werken ook enkele Arabieren als analisten, die door de Britten volledig worden vertrouwd. Een van hen was Wafic Al-Khouri, die al heel lang in Engeland woonde, de Britse nationaliteit had en met een Engelse vrouw was getrouwd.

De minzame ex-diplomaat uit Jordanië werkte nu als hoofdanalist bij de Arabische divisie van het GCHQ. Natuurlijk waren er ook Engelsen die uitstekend Arabisch spraken, maar de woorden van de Arabische leiders hadden vaak een dubbele bodem, die Al-Khouri beter kon doorgronden. Hij was het, die op verzoek van Century House in het restaurant op Mike Martin zat te wachten.

Het werd een gezellige lunch die twee uur duurde. Al die tijd spraken ze uitsluitend Arabisch. Toen ze afscheid namen, slenterde de majoor naar het SAS-gebouw terug. Hij zou nog urenlang over allerlei punten worden geïnstrueerd voordat hij naar Riyad kon vertrekken met een vals paspoort van de SIS, compleet met visum.

Voordat hij uit het restaurant vertrok, liep Al-Khouri naar de telefoon bij de herentoiletten en belde een nummer.

'Geen probleem, Steve. Hij is perfect. Ik geloof dat ik nog nooit een buitenlander ben tegengekomen die zo goed Arabisch sprak. Niet uit een schoolboekje, maar het gewone Arabisch van de straat. Dat is voor jullie doel nog beter. Hij kent alle uitdrukkingen, al het bargoens, zonder een spoor van een accent... Ja, hij kan zich overal vertonen, in iedere stad in het Midden-Oos-

72

ten. Geen dank, beste kerel. Blij dat ik van dienst kon zijn.'

Dertig minuten later zat hij weer in zijn auto en reed via de M4 naar Cheltenham terug.

Voordat hij het SAS-hoofdkwartier binnenstapte, belde Mike Martin ook een nummer, van een gebouw niet ver van Gower Street. De man die hij belde zat op zijn kantoor bij het SOAS, gebogen over zijn papieren. Hij hoefde die middag geen college te geven.

'Hallo, broertje. Met mij.'

Dat was voldoende. Al sinds hun jeugd in Bagdad noemde hij Terry 'broertje'. Er klonk een onderdrukte uitroep aan de andere kant van de lijn.

'Mike? Waar ben je verdomme?'

'In Londen, in een telefooncel.'

'Ik dacht dat je ergens in de Golf zat.'

'Ik ben vanochtend teruggekomen. Vanavond moet ik weer terug, denk ik.'

'Luister, Mike. Doe het niet. Het is allemaal mijn schuld. Ik had mijn mond moeten houden...'

De zware lach van zijn oudere broer galmde door de telefoon. 'Ik vroeg me al af waarom ze opeens zoveel belangstelling voor me hadden. Zijn ze met je gaan lunchen?'

'Ja. We hadden het ergens anders over. Dit kwam toevallig ter sprake. En ik praatte mijn mond voorbij. Hoor eens, je hóeft toch niet te gaan? Zeg maar dat ik me heb vergist en...'

'Het is nu te laat. Ik heb al ja gezegd.'

'O god...' De jongere broer, omringd door zijn wetenschappelijke werken over het middeleeuwse Mesopotamië, was bijna in tranen. 'Mike, pas goed op jezelf. Ik zal voor je bidden.'

Mike dacht even na. Ja, Terry had altijd al een gelovig trekje gehad. Waarschijnlijk meende hij het.

'Doe dat, broertje. We zien elkaar als ik terugkom.'

En hij hing op. De rossige wetenschapper, die zijn krijgshaftige broer adoreerde, hield zijn hoofd in zijn handen.

Toen het toestel naar Saoedi-Arabië die avond om kwart voor negen vanaf Heathrow vertrok, was Mike Martin aan boord, met een paspoort en een visum op een valse naam. Uren later, tegen het eerste ochtendlicht, werd hij van het vliegveld gehaald door de chef van het SIS-bureau op de Britse ambassade in Riyad.

Don Walker remde voorzichtig. De klassieke Corvette Stingray uit 1963 hield even in bij de poort van de luchtmachtbasis Seymour Johnson om een paar campers te laten passeren voordat hij de weg opdraaide.

Het was een hete dag. De augustuszon brandde meedogenloos boven het stadje Goldsboro in North Carolina. Het asfalt leek in de verte te golven en te glinsteren als water. Walker vond het lekker om met de kap omlaag te rijden en de warme wind door zijn korte blonde haar te laten waaien.

De klassieke sportwagen, die overal de aandacht trok, zoefde door het sluimerende stadje naar Highway 70 en nam toen Highway 13 naar het noordoosten.

Don Walker, negentwintig jaar oud in die hete zomer van 1990, was vrijgezel en gevechtspiloot. En hij had zojuist gehoord dat hij naar het oorlogsgebied zou worden gestuurd. Tenminste... Dat hing af van een of andere rare Arabier, een zekere Saddam Hoessein.

Diezelfde ochtend had kolonel (de latere generaal) Hal Hornburg de plannen bekendgemaakt. Over drie dagen, op 9 augustus, zou zijn squadron, het 336e 'Rocketeers' van het 9e Luchtmachtregiment van het Tactical Air Command, naar het Golfgebied worden overgebracht. De orders waren afkomstig van het TAC-commando op de luchtmachtbasis Langley in Hampton, Virginia. Het was dus serieus. De piloten hadden uitbundig gereageerd. Wat hadden al die jaren training voor zin als je nooit de kans kreeg je lessen in de praktijk te brengen?

Met nog drie dagen te gaan was er heel wat te doen. En Walker, als wapenofficier van het squadron, had het extra druk. Maar eerst had hij vierentwintig uur verlof gevraagd om afscheid te kunnen nemen van zijn familie. Dat verzoek was ingewilligd, maar zijn chef, luitenant-kolonel Steve Turner, had hem gewaarschuwd dat hij het zou bezuren als er maar één klein dingetje zou ontbreken bij het vertrek van de F-15E Eagles op 9 augustus. Maar daarna had hij grijnzend tegen Walker gezegd dat hij moest opschieten als hij de volgende dag nog voor zonsopgang terug wilde zijn.

Daarom gaf Walker nu vol gas. Om negen uur stoof hij door Snow Hill en Greenville, op weg naar de reeks eilandjes ten oosten van de Pamlico Sound. Hij had geluk dat zijn ouders niet thuis in Tulsa zaten, helemaal in Oklahoma, anders had hij het nooit gered. Maar omdat het augustus was, hielden ze vakantie in hun strandhuisje bij Hatteras, vijf uur rijden van de vliegbasis.

Don Walker wist dat hij een talentvolle piloot was en daar genoot hij van. Het is een heerlijk gevoel om negenentwintig te zijn en de leukste baan ter wereld te hebben. Hij hield van de basis, van zijn collega's en van de sensatie en de kracht van de McDonnell Douglas F-15 Strike Eagle, de grondaanvalsversie van de 15C luchtsuperioriteitsjager. In zijn ogen was het het beste toestel binnen de hele Amerikaanse luchtmacht – wat die kerels van de Fighting Falcons ook mochten beweren. Alleen de F-18 Hornet van de marine was vergelijkbaar, maar daar had hij nog nooit mee gevlogen en hij was heel tevreden met zijn Eagle.

Bij Bethel sloeg hij af naar het oosten, in de richting van Columbia en Whalebone, waar de hoofdweg de eilandjes bereikte. Langs Kitty Hawk en Nag's Head reed hij in zuidelijke richting naar Hatteras, waar de snelweg eindigde en hij aan alle kanten door de zee werd omringd. Als jongen had hij geweldige vakanties doorgebracht in Hatteras. Vroeg in de morgen ging hij altijd met zijn grootvader op baars vissen, totdat de oude man ziek werd en niet meer mee kon.

Nu zou zijn vader, die bij een oliemaatschappij in Tulsa werkte, binnenkort met pensioen gaan en zijn ouders zouden veel meer tijd in hun strandhuis kunnen doorbrengen. Dat betekende dat Don er ook vaker zou zijn. Hij was jong genoeg om geen moment te overwegen of hij eventueel zou sneuvelen – als het op een oorlog zou uitdraaien.

Op zijn achttiende had Don met goede cijfers eindexamen gedaan. Toen hij van school kwam, had hij maar één brandende ambitie: piloot worden. Dat was altijd zijn droom geweest, zolang als hij zich kon herinneren. Hij had vier jaar luchtvaarttechniek gestudeerd aan de universiteit van Oklahoma State. In juni 1983 had hij zijn studie afgerond. In de tussentijd had hij zich aangemeld bij het Reserve Officer Training Corps en die herfst maakte hij voor het eerst kennis met de luchtmacht.

Hij kreeg zijn vliegeniersopleiding op de luchtmachtbasis Williams bij Phoenix, Arizona, op een T-33 en een T-38. Na elf maanden was hij als vierde van de veertig leerlingen geëindigd. Tot zijn onuitsprekelijke vreugde waren de beste vijf rekruten geselecteerd voor de Fighter Lead-In School op de basis Holloman bij Alamagordo in New Mexico. De rest van de groep – dacht hij met de arrogantie van een jonge vent die wist dat hij jachtvlieger zou worden – zou zich moeten behelpen met bommenwerpers of transporttoestellen.

Bij de Replacement Training Unit in Homestead, Florida, mocht hij de T-38 eindelijk verruilen voor de F-4 Phantom – een groot, zwaar toestel, maar wel een echte jager.

Na negen maanden in Homestead werd hij bij zijn eerste squadron geplaatst, in Osan in Zuid-Korea, waar hij een jaar lang op Phantoms vloog.

75

Hij was goed en dat wist hij, en zijn chefs blijkbaar ook. Na Osan stuurden ze hem naar de Fighter Weapon School van de Amerikaanse luchtmacht op de vliegbasis McConnell bij Wichita, Kansas.

Fighter Weapons wordt als de zwaarste opleiding beschouwd. Daar worden de beste piloten afgeleverd. De technologie van de nieuwe wapens is ontzagwekkend. Leerlingen van McConnell moeten alle bouten en moertjes kennen, elke siliciumchip en elke schakeling van de verwarrende hoeveelheid wapens die een moderne jager op zijn tegenstanders en doelwitten – in de lucht of op de grond – kan afvuren. Opnieuw kwam Don Walker als een van de besten uit de bus, wat betekende dat ieder squadron van de Amerikaanse luchtmacht hem graag wilde hebben.

Het werd het 336e op Goldsboro, in de zomer van 1987. Daar vloog hij weer een jaar op Phantoms, gevolgd door vier maanden op de luchtmachtbasis Luke in Phoenix, Arizona, waarna hij op de Strike Eagle – het nieuwe toestel van de Rocketeers – werd overgeplaatst. Hij vloog al ruim een jaar op de Eagle toen Saddam Hoessein Koeweit binnenviel.

Vlak voor het middaguur bereikte de Stingray de eilandjes en reed langs het monument bij Kitty Hawk waar Orville en Wilbur Wright hun constructie van stangen en draadjes een paar meter van de grond hadden gekregen om te bewijzen dat de mens werkelijk met een motorisch vliegtuig kon opstijgen. Ze moesten eens weten...

Hij volgde de file van campers en caravans door Nag's Head tot het verkeer zich weer verspreidde en de weg wat leger werd voorbij Cape Hatteras en de punt van het eiland. Een paar minuten voor één parkeerde hij zijn Stingray op de oprit van het houten huis van zijn ouders. Ze zaten op de veranda, die uitkeek op de rustige blauwe zee.

Ray Walker zag zijn zoon het eerst en slaakte een kreet van vreugde. Maybelle kwam uit de keuken waar ze de lunch stond klaar te maken en rende op hem toe. Ze omhelsden elkaar. Zijn grootvader zat in zijn schommelstoel, starend naar de zee.

Don liep naar hem toe en zei: 'Hallo, opa. Ik ben het. Don.'

De oude man keek op en knikte met een glimlach. Toen tuurde hij weer over de oceaan.

'Het gaat niet zo goed met hem,' zei Ray. 'Soms kent hij je, soms niet. Maar ga zitten en vertel ons al het nieuws. Hé, Maybelle, kan er wat bier komen voor een paar dorstige kerels?'

Toen het bier was ingeschonken, vertelde Don zijn ouders dat hij over vijf dagen naar de Golf zou vertrekken. Maybelle sloeg haar hand voor haar mond. Zijn vader keek plechtig.

'Nou ja, dat is natuurlijk het doel van zo'n opleiding,' zei hij ten slotte.

Don nam een flinke slok bier en vroeg zich niet voor het eerst af waarom ouders zich altijd zo ongerust maakten. Zijn grootvader keek hem aan met iets van herkenning in zijn waterige ogen.

'Don gaat de oorlog in, opa,' riep Ray Walker tegen hem. Er kwam wat leven in de ogen van de oude man.

Zijn hele leven was hij marinier geweest. Toen hij van school kwam, had hij meteen dienst genomen bij het korps. In 1941 had hij zijn vrouw vaarwel gekust en haar achtergelaten bij haar familie in Tulsa, met hun pasgeboren dochtertje Maybelle, en was naar de Zuidzee vertrokken. Hij had onder MacArthur gevochten op Corregidor en had hem horen zeggen: 'Ik kom terug.' En hij had op twintig meter afstand van de generaal gestaan toen MacArthur inderdaad was teruggekomen.

In de tussentijd had hij zich een weg gevochten over minstens tien ellendige atols in de Marianen en de hel van Iwo Jima overleefd. Hij had zeventien littekens aan de oorlog overgehouden en hij mocht de lintjes dragen van een Zilveren Ster, twee Bronzen Sterren en zeven Purperen Harten.

Hij had nooit officier willen worden. Hij was tevreden met zijn rang van eerste sergeant, omdat hij wist dat daar de werkelijke macht lag. In Korea was hij bij Inchon aan land gegaan, en toen ze hem eindelijk als instructeur naar Parris Island hadden gestuurd ter afsluiting van zijn loopbaan, had hij meer onderscheidingen dan iemand anders op de basis. Na twee keer uitstel was hij ten slotte gepensioneerd in het bijzijn van vier generaals – meer dan er gewoonlijk komen opdraven voor het afscheid van een collega-generaal.

De oude man wenkte zijn kleinzoon. Don stond op en boog zich naar hem toe.

'Kijk uit voor die Jappen, jongen,' fluisterde de oude man, 'anders nemen ze je te grazen.'

Don legde een arm om de magere, reumatische schouders van de oude man. 'Maak je geen zorgen, opa, bij mij komen ze niet in de buurt.'

De oude man knikte gerustgesteld. Hij was tachtig. Het waren uiteindelijk niet de Japanners of de Koreanen die hem te pakken hadden gekregen, maar de oude heer Alzheimer. Hij leefde nu grotendeels in een aangename droomwereld met zijn dochter en zijn schoonzoon, die voor hem zorgden omdat hij nergens anders heen kon.

Na de lunch vertelden Dons ouders hem over hun reis door het Golfgebied, waarvan ze vier dagen geleden waren teruggekomen. Maybelle pakte haar foto's, die ze juist had afgehaald.

Don ging naast zijn moeder zitten terwijl ze hem de paleizen, moskeeën, stranden en markten van al die emiraten en sjeikdommen liet zien.

'Wees voorzichtig daar,' waarschuwde ze haar zoon. 'Dit is het soort mensen waar je mee te maken krijgt. Gevaarlijke kerels. Moet je die ogen zien!'

Don Walker keek naar de foto in haar hand. De bedoeïen stond tussen twee zandduinen tegen de achtergrond van de woestijn, zijn gezicht half verborgen achter zijn *keffijeh*. Alleen zijn donkere ogen staarden achterdochtig in de lens van de camera.

'Ik zal voor hem oppassen,' beloofde hij haar. Dat leek haar gerust te stellen.

Om vijf uur moest hij weer terug naar de basis. Zijn ouders liepen met hem mee naar zijn auto. Maybelle omhelsde haar zoon en drukte hem nog eens op het hart om voorzichtig te zijn. Ray klemde hem tegen zijn borst en zei dat ze trots op hem waren. Don stapte in en reed achteruit de weg op. Toen keek hij om.

Vanuit het huis stapte zijn grootvader, leunend op twee stokken, de veranda op. Langzaam legde hij de stokken neer en richtte zich met moeite op, tot zijn oude rug en schouders de reumatiek hadden overwonnen. Toen bracht hij zijn hand, met de handpalm naar voren, naar de klep van zijn honkbalpet, in een saluut van een oude soldaat aan zijn kleinzoon die op weg ging naar de volgende oorlog.

Don beantwoordde het saluut vanuit de auto. Toen trapte hij het gas in en stoof weg. Hij zou zijn grootvader niet meer terugzien. De oude man overleed eind oktober, in zijn slaap.

In Londen was het al donker. Terry Martin had nog laat zitten werken. De studenten waren met vakantie, maar toch had hij het druk omdat hij colleges moest voorbereiden voor de speciale zomercursussen die de school organiseerde. Maar die avond had hij bewust naar werk gezocht om zijn gedachten af te leiden.

Hij maakte zich zorgen. Hij wist waar zijn broer naartoe was en in gedachten liet hij alle gevaren de revue passeren die een geheim agent in het door Irak bezette Koeweit konden bedreigen.

Om tien uur, toen Don Walker uit Hatteras terugreed naar het noorden, verliet hij de school, zei beleefd goedenavond tegen de oude conciërge die achter hem afsloot en liep door Gower Street en St. Martin's Lane naar Trafalgar Square. Misschien zouden de kleurige lichtjes hem wat opvrolijken. Het was een zachte, zwoele avond.

Bij St. Martin-in-the-Fields stonden de deuren open. Uit de kerk klonk gezang. Martin stapte naar binnen, vond een plaatsje achterin en luisterde naar de repetities van het koor. Maar de heldere zangstemmen maakten hem nog somberder. Hij dacht terug aan zijn jeugd in Bagdad, samen met Mike.

Nigel en Susan Martin woonden in een mooi, ruim oud huis van twee verdiepingen in Saadun, een fraaie wijk van Risafa. Mike was geboren in 1953, Terry twee jaar later. Zijn vroegste jeugdherinnering was dat zijn donkerharige broer keurig aangekleed op weg ging naar zijn eerste schooldag op de kleuterschool van juf Saywell. Hij droeg een overhemd, een korte broek, met schoenen en sokken – het uniform van de Engelse schooljongen. Mike had verontwaardigd geprotesteerd, verknocht als hij was aan zijn witte katoenen *disj-dasj*, waarin je koel bleef en alle vrijheid had.

Het leven was ontspannen en comfortabel voor de Britse gemeenschap in het Bagdad van de jaren vijftig. Je was lid van de Mansour Club en de Alwiya Club met zijn zwembad, tennis- en squashbanen, waar de mensen van de Iraakse Petroleummaatschappij en de ambassade kwamen om te spelen, te zwemmen, te luieren of een koel drankje te drinken aan de bar.

Hij herinnerde zich Fatima, hun *dada* of kindermeisje, een mollige, lieve meid uit een dorpje op het platteland. Haar loon werd opgespaard als bruidsschat zodat ze een welvarende jongeman zou kunnen trouwen als ze weer terugging naar haar stam. Terry speelde altijd op het gras met Fatima, tot ze Mike gingen afhalen van juf Saywells school.

Al voor hun derde jaar waren ze allebei volledig tweetalig. Ze leerden Arabisch van Fatima, van de tuinman en de kokkin. Vooral Mike had een goed taalgevoel, en omdat hun vader grote bewondering had voor de Arabische cultuur, kwamen er vaak Iraakse vrienden op bezoek.

Arabieren houden van kleine kinderen en hebben veel meer geduld met hen dan Europeanen. Als Mike over het grasveld rende met zijn zwarte haar en zijn donkere ogen, in zijn witte *disj-dasj*, ratelend in het Arabisch, riepen de vrienden van zijn vader lachend: 'Maar Nigel, hij lijkt meer op een van ons!'

In de weekends gingen ze kijken naar de Royal Harithiya Hunt, een soort Engelse vossejacht, overgeplaatst naar het Midden-Oosten, waar op jakhalzen werd gejaagd onder leiding van de gemeentelijke architect, Philip Hirst, en die werd afgesloten door een maaltijd van kuzi en groenten voor iedereen. En er waren heerlijke picknicks aan de rivier op Pig Island in het midden van de traag stromende Tigris die de stad doormidden sneed.

Na twee jaar was Terry net als Mike naar de kleuterschool van juf Saywell gegaan maar omdat hij zo slim was, mochten ze in hetzelfde jaar naar de eerste klas van de lagere school van meester Hartley.

Terry was zes en zijn broer acht toen ze voor het eerst naar Tasisiya gingen, een school voor Engelse jongens maar ook voor de zonen van een aantal vooraanstaande Iraakse families.

Inmiddels had er al één staatsgreep plaatsgevonden. De jonge koning en Nuri as-Said waren vermoord en de neo-communistische generaal Kassem had alle macht aan zich getrokken. Hoewel het aan de twee Engelse jongetjes voorbijging, begonnen hun ouders en de Britse gemeenschap zich ongerust te maken. Kassem, een aanhanger van de Iraakse communistische partij, vervolgde de leden van de nationalistische Ba'ath-partij, die op hun

79

beurt probeerden de generaal te vermoorden. Eén groepje had met machine-geweren een mislukte aanslag op Kassem gepleegd. Tot dat groepje behoorde ook een jonge heethoofd genaamd Saddam Hoessein.

Op zijn eerste schooldag werd Terry Martin omringd door een stel Iraakse jongens.

'Hij is een bleekscheet,' zei een van hen.

Terry begon te huilen. 'Ik ben geen bleekscheet,' snikte hij.

'Jawel,' zei de langste jongen. 'Je bent dik en bleek, en je hebt raar haar. Je bent een bleekscheet. Bleekscheet! Bleekscheet!'

In koor begonnen ze hem uit te schelden. Mike dook achter Terry op. 'Hou op mijn broertje te pesten,' waarschuwde hij. Natuurlijk spraken ze allemaal Arabisch.

'Je broertje? Hij ziet er helemaal niet uit als je broertje. Hij ziet eruit als een bleekscheet.'

Het gebruik van de vuist behoort niet tot de Arabische cultuur. Het komt maar in weinig culturen voor, behalve in delen van het Verre Oosten. Zelfs ten zuiden van de Sahara is de gebalde vuist geen traditioneel wapen. Zwarte mannen uit Afrika en hun afstammelingen moesten eerst leren hoe hun vuisten te ballen om te slaan. Pas daarna werden ze de beste boksers ter wereld. De vuistslag is een typisch Europese en met name Angelsaksische traditie.

Mike Martins rechtse directe raakte Terry's voornaamste plaaggeest vol op zijn kaak en de jongen ging onderuit. Zijn verbazing was groter dan zijn pijn. Maar niemand noemde Terry nog ooit een bleekscheet.

Vreemd genoeg werden Mike en de lange Iraakse jongen dikke vrienden. Hun hele schooltijd waren ze onafscheidelijk. De Arabische jongen heette Hassan Rahmani. Het derde lid van Mikes vriendengroepje was Abdelkarim Badri, die een jonger broertje had, Osman, van dezelfde leeftijd als Terry. Terry en Osman raakten ook bevriend, en dat kwam goed uit, want Badri senior kwam vaak bij hun ouders op bezoek. Hij was arts, en de huisdokter van de familie Martin. Hij was het die Mike en Terry door de bekende kinderziekten – mazelen, de bof en waterpokken – heen hielp.

Abdelkarim Badri was dol op poëzie, herinnerde Terry zich. Hij zat altijd met zijn neus in Engelse dichtbundels en hij won prijzen met het declameren van gedichten, ondanks de competitie van Engelse jongens. Osman, zijn jongere broer, was goed in rekenen en wilde ooit ingenieur of architect worden om mooie dingen te bouwen.

Toen hij op die warme augustusavond van 1990 in zijn kerkbankje zat, vroeg Terry zich af wat er van hen geworden was. Terwijl zij in Tasisiya op school zaten, speelden zich in Irak grote veranderingen af. Vier jaar nadat hij aan de macht was gekomen door de koning te vermoorden, werd Kassem zelf ten val gebracht door het leger, dat zich zorgen maakte over zijn flirt met het communisme. Daarna volgden elf maanden van gezamenlijk bestuur door het leger en de Ba'ath-partij en namen de Ba'athisten wraak op hun voormalige vervolgers, de communisten.

Maar ten slotte werd ook de Ba'ath-partij aan de kant geschoven door het leger, dat tot 1968 het land regeerde.

In 1966, toen hij dertien was, werd Mike naar Engeland gestuurd om zijn schoolopleiding af te maken op de Britse kostschool Haileybury. Terry volgde in 1968. Die zomer, eind juni, brachten zijn ouders hem naar Engeland, zodat ze daar samen een lange vakantie konden doorbrengen voordat Terry met Mike naar Haileybury zou teruggaan. Daardoor misten ze bij toeval de twee coups van 14 en 30 juli, waarbij het leger werd afgezet en de Ba'ath-partij weer aan de macht kwam onder president Bakr, met een zekere Saddam Hoessein als vice-president.

Nigel Martin had al vermoed dat er iets zou gebeuren en had zijn maatregelen genomen. Hij vertrok bij de Iraakse Petroleummaatschappij en trad in dienst bij de Britse oliefirma Burmah Oil. Hij wikkelde zijn zaken in Bagdad af en de familie Martin ging in Hertford wonen, niet ver van Londen, van waaruit Nigel dagelijks naar zijn nieuwe baan heen en weer kon reizen.

Vader Martin werd een enthousiast golfer en in de weekends fungeerden zijn zoons vaak als caddies als hij een partijtje speelde tegen een collega bij Burmah Oil, meneer Denis Thatcher, wiens vrouw grote belangstelling had voor de politiek.

Terry had het goed naar zijn zin op Haileybury, toen nog onder leiding van rector Bill Stewart. De twee broers zaten in Melill House, met Richard Rhodes-James als huismeester. Zoals verwacht, ontwikkelde Terry zich tot een uitstekende leerling en werd Mike een echte sportman. Net als in Bagdad bleef Mike zijn jongere broer beschermen, en Terry adoreerde hem.

Mike had geen zin om te gaan studeren en maakte al snel duidelijk dat hij het liefst in het leger zou gaan – een besluit waarmee meneer Rhodes-James van harte instemde.

Terry Martin verliet de donkere kerk toen de koorrepetitie afgelopen was, stak Trafalgar Square over en nam de bus naar Bayswater, waar hij met Hilary een flat deelde. Toen hij langs Park Lane kwam, dacht hij terug aan die laatste rugbywedstrijd tegen Tonbridge, waarmee Mike zijn vijf jaar aan Haileybury had afgesloten.

Tonbridge was altijd de lastigste tegenstander, en dat jaar speelden ze een thuiswedstrijd op The Terrace. Mike was fullback, er waren nog vijf minuten te spelen en Haileybury stond twee punten achter. Terry stond langs de lijn, als een trouwe hond, om zijn broer aan te moedigen.

De fly-half van Haleybury kreeg na een scrum de eivormige bal te pakken, passeerde een tegenstander en gaf een pass aan zijn dichtstbijzijnde drie-kwarter. Achter hen begon Mike al te sprinten. Alleen Terry zag hem ver-trekken. Op volle snelheid passeerde hij de 25-yardslijn, onderschepte een pass die bedoeld was voor een winger, sneed dwars door de Tonbridge-defensie en stormde op de touch-line af. Terry stond te springen en te jui-chen. Hij zou al zijn hoge cijfers en zijn studiebeurs hebben opgegeven om daar over het veld te kunnen rennen met zijn broer. Maar met zijn korte bleke benen, waarop de rossige haartjes alle kanten op staken, zou hij al bin-nen tien meter door de Tonbridge-verdediging zijn uitgeschakeld.

Opeens viel er een stilte toen de fullback van Tonbridge een tackle inzette. De twee achttienjarige schooljongens klapten met volle kracht tegen elkaar aan. De Tonbridge-speler sloeg tegen de grond, snakkend naar adem, en Mike Martin dook over de lijn om de winnende drie punten te scoren.

Toen de twee ploegen van het veld kwamen, stond Terry grijnzend bij de touwen langs de uitgang. Mike stak een hand uit en woelde hem door zijn haar.

'We hebben gewonnen, broertje!'

En omdat híj nu zo stom zijn mond voorbij had gepraat, was zijn broer als spion naar bezet Koeweit gestuurd. Terry had moeite zijn tranen van angst en frustratie te bedwingen.

Hij stapte uit de bus en liep haastig door Chepstow Gardens. Hij hoopte dat Hilary, die voor zaken drie dagen de stad uit was geweest, weer terug zou zijn. Hij had troost nodig. Toen hij de flat binnenkwam, hoorde hij meteen de vertrouwde stem.

Terry liep naar de huiskamer en vertelde hoe stom hij was geweest. Het vol-gende moment vond hij troost in de omhelzing van de lieve, begripvolle effectenmakelaar met wie hij zijn leven deelde.

Mike Martin had twee dagen doorgebracht bij de chef van het SIS-bureau in Riyad, dat inmiddels was versterkt met twee andere mensen van Century House.

Het SIS-bureau opereerde normaal van uit de ambassade, maar omdat Saoedi-Arabië als een zeer bevriend land werd beschouwd, was Riyad geen 'zware' post met veel faciliteiten. Dat was de afgelopen tien dagen veran-derd.

De pasgevormde coalitie van Westerse en Arabische landen verzette zich krachtig tegen de Iraakse bezetting van Koeweit en had al twee opperbevel-hebbers benoemd, generaal Norman Schwarzkopf van de Verenigde Staten en prins Khaled bin Sultan bin Abdulaziz, een vierenveertigjarige beroeps-militair, opgeleid in Amerika en aan Sandhurst. Hij was een neef van de koning en de zoon van prins Sultan, de minister van Defensie.

De Britten hadden de hulp ingeroepen van prins Khaled, die snel en hoffelijk een grote vrijstaande villa aan de rand van de stad ter beschikking had gesteld die nu door de Britse ambassade werd gehuurd. Technici uit Londen waren bezig zenders, ontvangers en codeerapparatuur te installeren. Zolang de crisis duurde, zou de villa als hoofdkwartier van de Britse geheime dienst fungeren. Elders in de stad was de CIA, die ook een belangrijke rol wilde spelen, bezig met een soortgelijke operatie. Van de wrevel die later tussen de Amerikaanse legerleiding en de geheime dienst zou ontstaan, was nu nog geen sprake.

Voorlopig logeerde Mike Martin bij de chef van het SIS-bureau, Julian Gray. Martin liet zich liever niet op de ambassade zien. De charmante mevrouw Gray, die haar man volledig in zijn carrière steunde, ontving hem heel gastvrij, zonder één keer te vragen wie hij was of wat hij in Saoedi-Arabië kwam doen. Martin sprak bewust geen Arabisch tegen het Saoedische personeel. Als hij zijn koffie kreeg, glimlachte hij en zei 'dank je' in het Engels.

De avond van de tweede dag kreeg hij zijn laatste instructies van Gray. Daarmee hadden ze alles besproken wat er vanuit Riyad gedaan kon worden.

'Morgenochtend vlieg je naar Dhahran, met een gewone lijnvlucht van Saudia. Ze vliegen niet meer rechtstreeks op Khafji. Je wordt van het vliegveld gehaald. De Firma heeft een agent in Khafji, die je met de auto naar het noorden zal brengen. Hij is ook afkomstig van de SAS, geloof ik, Sparky Low. Ken je hem?'

'Ja,' zei Martin.

'Hij heeft alle spullen waarom je hebt gevraagd. En hij heeft een jonge Koeweitse piloot gevonden met wie je misschien wilt praten. Van ons krijgt hij de laatste Amerikaanse satellietfoto's van het grensgebied en de belangrijkste Iraakse troepenconcentraties, plus alle andere informatie die we hebben. Deze opnamen heb ik zojuist uit Londen gekregen.'

Hij spreidde een rij grote, glanzende foto's op de eettafel uit.

'Saddam heeft kennelijk nog geen Iraakse gouverneur-generaal voor Koeweit benoemd. Hij probeert nog steeds een Koeweitse marionettenregering samen te stellen, maar dat lukt niet erg. Zelfs de Koeweitse oppositie heeft er geen zin in. Maar de Iraakse geheime politie heeft er wel haar tenten opgeslagen. Dit is het plaatselijke hoofd van de AMAM, een zekere Sabaawi, een echte klootzak. Zijn chef in Bagdad, het hoofd van de Amn-al-Amm is Omar Khatib. Hier heb je hem. Misschien komt hij ook nog langs.'

Martin keek naar het gezicht op de foto – nors, nijdig, met een wrede blik en een trek van boerenslimheid om zijn mond.

'Hij heeft een bloederige reputatie, net als zijn makker in Koeweit,

Sabaawi. Khatib is een jaar of vijfenveertig. Hij komt uit Tikrit, behoort tot dezelfde stam als Saddam en is al heel lang zijn beulsknecht. Over Sabaawi weten we niet zoveel, maar dat zal nog wel veranderen.'

Gray pakte een andere foto.

'Afgezien van de AMAM heeft Bagdad ook een delegatie van de contraspionagedienst van de Mukhabarat gestuurd, vermoedelijk om buitenlandse pogingen tot spionage en sabotage tegen te gaan. De dienst wordt geleid door deze man hier – een slimme vos die niet met zich laat spotten. Hij is de man voor wie je vooral moet oppassen.'

Het was 8 augustus. Er denderde een C-5 Galaxy over hun hoofd, op weg naar het militaire vliegveld, als onderdeel van de reusachtige Amerikaanse machinerie, die een eindeloze stroom materieel naar het nerveuze, verwarde en uiterst conservatieve islamitische koninkrijk overbracht.

Mike Martin pakte de foto op en keek in het gezicht van Hassan Rahmani.

Steve Laing belde weer.

'Geen interesse,' zei Terry Martin.

'Toch moeten we nog eens praten, doctor Martin. U maakt zich toch ongerust over uw broer?'

'Ja.'

'Dat is helemaal niet nodig. Hij kan goed voor zichzelf zorgen. Hij heeft hier vrijwillig voor gekozen. We hebben hem alle kans gegeven om nee te zeggen.'

'Ik had mijn mond moeten houden.'

'Bekijk het eens zo. Als het helemaal misloopt, moeten we misschien heel veel broers, echtgenoten, zoons, ooms en geliefden naar de Golf sturen. In dat geval willen we het aantal slachtoffers zo laag mogelijk houden. Dat moeten we toch proberen?'

'Dat is zo. Wat wilt u van me?'

'Kunnen we nog eens samen lunchen? Dat praat wat gemakkelijker. Kent u het Montcalm Hotel? Eén uur, oké?'

'Ondanks al zijn verstand is het een emotioneel baasje,' had Laing die ochtend tegen Simon Paxman gezegd.

'Is dat zo?' vroeg Paxman, als een entomoloog die juist over de ontdekking van een nieuw insekt heeft gehoord.

De wetenschapper en de man van Century House kregen een tafeltje apart. Daar had meneer Costa voor gezorgd. Toen de gerookte zalm was gearriveerd, vertelde Laing wat hij in gedachten had.

'De kans is groot dat het werkelijk tot een oorlog komt in de Golf. Niet meteen, natuurlijk. Het kost tijd om voldoende troepen en materieel over te

84

brengen. Maar de Amerikanen zijn vastbesloten, met de steun van onze strijdlustige dame in Downing Street, om Saddam Hoessein en zijn trawanten uit Koeweit te verdrijven.'

'En als hij zich uit eigen beweging terugtrekt?' opperde Martin.

'Prima. Dan is er geen oorlog nodig,' antwoordde Laing, hoewel hij het in zijn hart niet zo prima vond. Er deden verontrustende geruchten de ronde, die de werkelijke aanleiding vormden voor zijn lunchafspraak met de arabist.

'Maar als hij blijft zitten, zullen we hem moeten aanvallen – onder de vlag van de Verenigde Naties.'

'Wij?'

'Voornamelijk de Amerikanen, maar wij zullen ook troepen, schepen en vliegtuigen sturen. We hebben nu al schepen in de Golf, en onze jager- en jachtbommenwerpersquadrons zijn al op weg naar het zuiden. Mevrouw Thatcher houdt niet van halve maatregelen. Op dit moment beperken we ons tot Desert Shield, om te voorkomen dat die klootzak ook Saoedi-Arabië binnenvalt, maar misschien moeten we verder gaan. U kent de term NBC?'

'Massavernietigingswapens – nucleaire, bacteriologische en chemische oorlogvoering.'

'Precies. Dat is het probleem. Century House heeft de politieke leiders al jaren geleden voor zo'n situatie gewaarschuwd. Vorig jaar heeft de Chef een lezing gehouden over "Inlichtingendiensten in de jaren negentig". Het grootste gevaar sinds het einde van de koude oorlog is de verspreiding van nucleaire en andere zware wapens. De kans wordt steeds groter dat allerlei dubieuze dictators de beschikking krijgen over high-tech wapens, die ze misschien nog zullen gebruiken ook. De politiek was zeer onder de indruk, maar niemand deed er iets aan. En nu staan ze doodsangsten uit.'

'Hij heeft nogal wat van dat spul. Saddam Hoessein, bedoel ik,' merkte Terry Martin op.

'Juist. Daar gaat het om. Volgens onze schattingen heeft Saddam de afgelopen tien jaar vijftig miljard dollar aan bewapening uitgegeven. Daarom is hij nu bankroet. Hij is de Koeweiti's vijftien miljard schuldig, en hetzelfde bedrag aan de Saoedi's – en dat alleen voor leningen die hij tijdens de oorlog met Iran heeft afgesloten. Hij is Koeweit binnengevallen omdat ze weigerden hem die schuld kwijt te schelden en hem nog eens dertig miljard te lenen om zijn economie uit het slop te helpen.

De kern van het probleem is dat eenderde van die vijftig miljard, niet minder dan zeventien miljard dollar, is besteed aan de aanschaf van massavernietigingswapens of de middelen om die te produceren.'

'En nu wordt het Westen eindelijk wakker?'

'Zeg dat wel. Er is een geweldige paniek uitgebroken. Langley heeft opdracht om contact op te nemen met alle regeringen ter wereld die ooit iets aan Irak hebben verkocht en de exportvergunningen te controleren. En wij doen hetzelfde.'

'Dat hoeft niet zoveel tijd te kosten als iedereen meewerkt. En dat zullen ze wel doen,' zei Martin toen zijn moot zalm was opgediend.

'Zo simpel ligt dat niet,' zei Laing. 'We weten nog niet alles, maar het is wel duidelijk dat Saddams schoonzoon Kamil een verdomd goede organisatie op poten heeft gezet. Bij allerlei fabriekjes in Europa en Amerika heeft hij losse onderdelen gekocht die op zichzelf geen achterdocht wekten. De Irakezen werkten met vervalste exportaanvragen, en ze logen over het produkt en de eindbestemming. Maar met al die spullen zou je een paar heel onaangename wapens kunnen fabriceren.'

'We weten dat hij gifgas heeft,' zei Martin. 'Dat heeft hij tegen de Koerden en de Iraniërs bij Fao gebruikt. Fosgeen, mosterdgas... maar ook zenuwgassen. Onzichtbaar, volkomen reukloos, zeer dodelijk en snel afbreekbaar.'

'Precies wat ik dacht. U bent een goudmijn van informatie.'

Laing was al op de hoogte van het zenuwgas, maar hij wist hoe je iemand moest vleien.

'En dan heb je nog miltvuur. Daar heeft hij mee geëxperimenteerd, en misschien ook met longpest. Maar je kunt dit soort wapens niet in elkaar flansen met een paar keukenhandschoenen. Daar heb je speciale chemische apparatuur voor nodig. En die moet op de exportvergunningen terug te vinden zijn,' merkte Martin op.

Laing knikte en zuchtte vermoeid. 'Ja, dat zou je denken. Maar er zijn twee problemen. Enkele bedrijven, met name in Duitsland, verschuilen zich achter een rookgordijn, en bovendien kun je sommige stoffen voor meer doeleinden gebruiken. Als Irak een schip met pesticiden bestelt, wil het gewoon zijn agrarische produktie vergroten. Niets aan de hand. Uit een ander land laten ze een ander bestrijdingsmiddel komen. Nog steeds niets aan de hand. Totdat een handige chemicus die spullen tot gifgas mengt. Maar de leveranciers roepen natuurlijk dat ze nergens iets van wisten.'

'Het gaat om de chemische mengapparatuur,' zei Martin. 'Dit is high-tech scheikunde. Je kunt die stoffen niet in een badkuip mengen. Je moet de mensen vinden die de sleutelfabrieken hebben geleverd en opgestart. Die weten wel degelijk waar ze mee bezig waren – wat ze ook mogen beweren.'

'Sleutelfabrieken?'

'Ja, complete fabrieken, van de grond af opgebouwd door speciale bedrijven. De nieuwe eigenaar krijgt de sleutel en kan zo naar binnen stappen. Maar dat is niet de reden voor deze lunch. Jullie kennen genoeg chemici en natuurkundigen. Ik weet er toevallig iets van omdat het me interesseert. Wat wilt u precies van me?'

Laing roerde peinzend in zijn koffie. Dit vroeg om een voorzichtige aanpak. 'Inderdaad, we kennen genoeg chemici. Knappe koppen, allemaal, die ongetwijfeld een aantal vragen kunnen beantwoorden. Daarna vertalen we die antwoorden in begrijpelijk Engels en vergelijken we onze uitkomsten met die van de Amerikanen, met wie we nauw samenwerken. Het probleem is dat we nooit àlle antwoorden te weten komen. U hebt iets meer te bieden. Vandaar deze lunch. U weet toch dat de meeste politici en militairen nog altijd denken dat de Arabieren zelf geen kinderfietsje in elkaar kunnen zetten – laat staan er een uitvinden?'

Daarmee had hij een gevoelige snaar geraakt, en dat wist hij. Het psychologische profiel dat hij van dr. Terry Martin had laten maken wierp zijn vruchten af. De academicus liep rood aan en wist zich met moeite te beheersen.

'Daar kan ik zo kwaad om worden,' zei hij, 'dat zelfs mijn eigen landgenoten de Arabieren nog steeds als een stelletje kamelendrijvers zien, met theedoeken om hun hoofd. Zo wordt het zelfs letterlijk gezegd. Maar in werkelijkheid bouwden de Arabieren al zeer complexe paleizen, moskeeën, havens, wegen en irrigatiewerken toen onze voorouders nog in berevellen liepen. Ze hadden al wijze vorsten en wetgevers toen wij nog in de donkere middeleeuwen leefden.'

Hij boog zich naar voren en priemde met zijn koffielepeltje naar de man van Century House. 'Ik zal u eens wat vertellen. Irak beschikt over briljante wetenschappers en de beste bouwmeesters ter wereld. In de wijde omgeving zijn er geen betere bouwkundige ingenieurs te vinden, zelfs niet in Israël. Een groot aantal heeft in Rusland of in het Westen gestudeerd, maar ze hebben onze kennis als sponzen opgezogen en verder ontwikkeld...'

Hij schepte even adem. Daarvan maakte Laing gebruik.

'Doctor Martin, ik ben het volkomen met u eens. Ik zit pas een jaar bij onze divisie Midden-Oosten, maar ik ben tot dezelfde conclusie gekomen als u. De Irakezen zijn een zeer begaafd volk. Helaas worden ze geregeerd door een man die zich als een massamoordenaar heeft ontpopt. Moet al dat geld en al dat talent werkelijk worden aangewend om tien- of misschien wel honderdduizenden mensen de dood in te jagen? Zal Saddam zijn volk werkelijk roem en eer brengen, of de Irakezen naar de slachtbank leiden?'

Martin zuchtte.

'U hebt gelijk. De man is een schandvlek. In het begin viel dat nog mee, maar hij heeft het nationalisme van de oude Ba'ath-partij verminkt tot een soort nazisme, geïnspireerd op Adolf Hitler. Wat wilt u van me?'

Laing dacht een tijdje na. Hij had de vis bijna op het droge. Hij mocht hem nu niet verspelen.

'George Bush en mevrouw Thatcher hebben afgesproken dat onze twee landen een commissie zullen samenstellen om Saddams arsenaal van massavernietigingswapens te inventariseren en te analyseren. De onderzoekers moeten de feiten aandragen, de wetenschappers moeten ons vertellen wat ze betekenen. Wat heeft hij precies in huis, en hoeveel? Hoe modern is het? Hoe kunnen we ons ertegen beschermen als het oorlog wordt? Met gasmaskers, ruimtepakken of injecties met tegengif? We weten gewoon niet genoeg over zijn wapenarsenaal en de maatregelen die we daartegen moeten nemen.'

'Maar ik ben helemaal geen expert,' onderbrak Martin hem.

'Nee, maar u hebt ervaring met de Arabische manier van denken. Wij niet. U kunt Saddam beter peilen. Zal hij zijn wapens gebruiken, zal hij zich in Koeweit verschansen of zich terugtrekken? Wat is er voor nodig om hem te verdrijven? Is hij bereid om tot het uiterste te gaan? Onze mensen hebben te weinig inzicht in de Arabische visie op het martelaarschap.'

Martin begon te lachen. 'President Bush,' zei hij, 'en iedereen om hem heen zal reageren volgens zijn eigen opvoeding. Die is gebaseerd op de joodschristelijke morele filosofie, ondersteund door het Grieks-Romeinse concept van logica. Saddam reageert uitsluitend op basis van zijn eigen beeld van zichzelf.'

'Als Arabier en als moslim?'

'Nee. De islam heeft er niets mee te maken. Saddam is niet geïnteresseerd in de *hadith*, de leer van de profeet. Hij bidt voor de televisie, als hem dat zo uitkomt. Nee, zijn filosofie gaat terug tot Nineveh en Assyrië. Het kan hem niet schelen hoeveel doden er vallen, zolang hij nog denkt dat hij kan winnen.'

'Maar hij kan nooit winnen. Niet tegen Amerika. Dat kan niemand.'

'Dat is een denkfout. U gebruikt het woord "winnen" in de Britse of Amerikaanse betekenis, zoals Bush en Scowcroft en al die anderen. Saddam ziet dat anders. Als hij Koeweit opgeeft omdat koning Fahd bereid is hem te betalen – wat had kunnen gebeuren als de conferentie van Jeddah was doorgegaan – had hij met eer "gewonnen". Toegeven in ruil voor geld, dat is acceptabel. Dan wint hij. Maar dat zou Amerika nooit toestaan.'

'Nee. Uitgesloten.'

'Maar als hij voor dreigementen zwicht, dan verliest hij. En dat weet heel Arabië. Dat zou waarschijnlijk zijn dood worden. Dus zal hij niet opgeven.'

'En als de Amerikaanse machinerie tegen hem wordt ingezet? Dan wordt hij verpletterd,' zei Laing.

'Dat maakt niet uit. Hij heeft zijn bunker. Zijn mensen zullen sterven, maar dat is niet belangrijk. Als hij Amerika maar een slag kan toebrengen. Hoe zwaarder die slag, des te groter zijn triomf. Dan heeft hij gewonnen, dood of levend.'

'Verdomme, het ligt wel ingewikkeld,' verzuchtte Laing.

'Niet echt. Het is een geweldige stap in morele filosofie als je de Jordaan oversteekt. Maar ik vraag het nog een keer: wat wilt u van me?'

'Wij zijn bezig een comité te vormen om de politiek te adviseren over deze massavernietigingswapens. Kanonnen, tanks, gevechtsvliegtuigen – daar houdt Defensie zich wel mee bezig. Die vormen geen probleem. Dat is een ijzerwinkel die we vanuit de lucht kunnen vernietigen.

In feite gaat het om twee comités, één in Washington en één in Londen, met Britse waarnemers aan hun kant en Amerikaanse waarnemers bij ons. De leden zijn afkomstig van Buitenlandse Zaken, Aldermaston, Porton Down. Century House heeft twee plaatsen. Ik stuur Simon Paxman en ik zou u graag met hem mee sturen om te controleren of we de Arabische invalshoek niet over het hoofd zien. Dat is uw specialiteit. Dat zou uw bijdrage zijn.'

'Goed. Als ik u daarmee kan helpen. Maar stel u er niet te veel van voor. Hoe heet dat comité en wanneer komt het bijeen?'

'Simon belt u nog over de datum en de plaats. Het comité heeft een toepasselijke naam: Medusa.'

Laat in de middag van de 10e augustus daalde de zwoele, warme schemering van Carolina over de vliegbasis Seymour Johnson neer. Het beloofde een avond te worden voor een rum-punch uit de ijsemmer en een biefstuk met maïs op de grill.

De mannen van het 334e Tactical Fighter Squadron die nog niet operationeel waren met hun F-15E's, en hun collega's van het 335e squadron – de 'Chiefs', die in december naar de Golf zouden vliegen – keken toe. Samen met het 336e squadron vormden ze de 4e Tactical Fighter Wing van het 9e luchtmachtregiment. Het 336e stond op het punt om te vertrekken.

Twee dagen lang was iedereen druk in de weer geweest om de toestellen gereed te maken, de route te plannen, het materiaal te selecteren en de geheime handboeken en de squadroncomputer met al zijn tactische gegevens in containers te laden die door vrachtvliegtuigen zouden worden vervoerd. De verhuizing van een squadron gevechtsvliegtuigen is geen eenvoudige operatie. Het lijkt wel of je een kleine stad verplaatst.

Op het asfalt stonden de vierentwintig Eagles – dreigende monsters, ontworpen door kleine mensjes – te wachten tot andere kleine mensjes aan boord zouden klimmen om met nietige vingertjes hun ontzagwekkende kracht te ontketenen.

Ze zouden de lange route naar het Arabisch schiereiland in één keer afleggen. Iedere Eagle was voorzien van een interne brandstoftank met 13 000 pond vliegtuigbenzine. Langs de zijkanten waren twee extra tanks aangebracht, zo plat mogelijk, om de luchtweerstand te verminderen. Deze tanks bevatten elk nog eens 5000 pond brandstof. Onder de romp hingen drie lange, torpedovormige externe tanks met 4000 pond. Alleen al de brandstof, in totaal 13,5 ton, was net zo zwaar als de bommenlast van vijf bommen-werpers uit de Tweede Wereldoorlog. En de Eagle is een jager.

De persoonlijke bagage van de bemanning was in de voormalige napalm-tanks onder de vleugels gestouwd, die nu voor een vreedzamer lading wer-den gebruikt: hemden, sokken, ondergoed, zeep, scheergerei, uniformen, mascottes en mannenbladen. Het zou weleens een flinke wandeling kunnen worden naar de dichtstbijzijnde vrijgezellenbar.

De grote KC-10 tankers die de jagers de hele reis zouden vergezellen – vier tankers voor iedere zes jagers – waren al opgestegen en vlogen nu boven de Atlantische Oceaan.

Later zou een karavaan van Starlifters en Galaxies de rest vervoeren – het kleine leger van onderhoudsmonteurs, elektronicaspecialisten en ander per-soneel, de munitie en de reserveonderdelen, de hydraulica en de demonta-bele werkplaatsen, het elektrische gereedschap en de werkbanken. Want in Saoedi-Arabië was niets te vinden. Alles wat nodig was om twee dozijn van de modernste jachtbommenwerpers paraat en in de lucht te houden moest per vliegtuig naar de andere kant van de wereld worden overgebracht.

Elk van de Strike Eagles vertegenwoordigde een waarde van 44 miljoen dol-lar aan zwarte dozen, aluminium, koolstofcomposiet, computers, hydraulica en slimme vondsten. Hoewel het ontwerp al dertig jaar oud was, was de Eagle een nieuwe jager. Zoveel tijd is er nodig voor onderzoek en ontwikkeling.

De civiele delegatie uit Goldsboro stond onder leiding van burgemeester Hal K. Plonk, een brave overheidsdienaar die van zijn twintigduizend dank-bare medeburgers de bijnaam 'Kerplunk' had gekregen omdat hij de poli-tieke delegaties uit Washington altijd zo kostelijk amuseerde met zijn zuide-lijke accent en zijn arsenaal van moppen. Na een uurtje in het gezelschap van de olijke burgemeester schenen sommige politici in allerijl te zijn terug-gereisd, op zoek naar therapie. Bij iedere volgende verkiezing wist burge-meester Plonk meer stemmen te verzamelen.

Samen met kolonel Hal Hornberg zagen de burgers trots hoe de Eagles door trekkers uit hun hangars werden gesleept. Daarna ging de bemanning aan boord. De piloot stapte in het voorste deel van de dubbele cockpit, zijn 'wizzo' of navigator in het achterste gedeelte. Het grondpersoneel zwermde om de toestellen heen voor een laatste controle.

'Kent u die mop van de generaal en het hoertje?' vroeg de burgemeester opgewekt aan de hoge luchtmachtofficier naast hem.

Gelukkig startte Don Walker op dat moment zijn motoren. Het gebulder van de twee Pratt & Whitney F100-PW-220 turbojets overstemde de wederwaar-digheden van het lichte meisje en de militair. De F100 kan heel wat lawaai en hitte en een stuwkracht van 24 000 pond aan zijn fossiele brandstof ontlokken, en stond op het punt dat te doen.

Eén voor één startten de vierentwintig Eagles van het 336e squadron hun motoren en taxieden naar het begin van de startbaan, zo'n anderhalve kilometer verderop. Kleine rode vlaggetjes onder de vleugels markeerden de borgpennen waarmee de Stinger- en Sidewinder-raketten waren verankerd. Die pennen zouden vlak voor het opstijgen worden verwijderd. De reis naar Arabië zou waarschijnlijk zonder problemen verlopen, maar het was ondenkbaar om een Eagle de lucht in te sturen zonder een mogelijkheid om zich te verdedigen.

Langs de taxibaan stonden groepjes gewapende wachtposten en luchtmacht-politie opgesteld. Sommigen zwaaiden, anderen salueerden. Vlak voor de startbaan hielden de Eagles weer halt voor een laatste inspectie. Er werden blokken voor de wielen geschoven en het grondpersoneel controleerde of er geen lekken of losse contacten en panelen – problemen die bij het taxiën aan het licht waren gekomen – te vinden waren. Ten slotte werden de borgpennen van de raketten verwijderd.

De Eagles stonden geduldig te wachten, ruim 20 meter lang, 6 meter hoog en 13 meter breed, met een 'schoon' gewicht van 40 000 pond en een startgewicht van 81 000. Het zou wel even duren voordat ze los van de grond kwamen.

Ten slotte reden de toestellen de startbaan op, draaiden tegen de lichte bries in en maakten snelheid. De nabranders werden ingeschakeld toen de piloten vol gas gaven. Vlammen van tien meter lang spoten uit de staartpijp. Het grondpersoneel naast de startbaan, met helmen tegen het oorverdovende lawaai, salueerde toen hun baby's naar het Midden-Oosten vertrokken. Ze zouden ze pas in Saoedi-Arabië terugzien.

Na een run van anderhalve kilometer, bij een snelheid van 185 knopen, maakten de wielen zich van het asfalt los en stegen de Eagles op. Ze trokken hun landingsgestel in, de nabranders werden uitgeschakeld en de snelheid werd teruggebracht tot militair vermogen. De vierentwintig Eagles draaiden hun neus omhoog in een klim van ruim 1500 meter per minuut en verdwenen in de schemering.

Op een hoogte van 8000 meter trokken de piloten hun toestellen weer recht. Een uur later zagen ze de positie- en navigatielichten van de eerste KC-10 tanker. Tijd om bij te tanken. De twee F100-motoren waren bijzonder dorstig. Met ingeschakelde nabrander verbruikten ze 40 000 pond brandstof per uur. Daarom werd de nabrander alleen gebruikt bij het opstijgen, tijdens luchtgevechten of in noodgevallen. Zelfs bij een normale snelheid moesten de tanks om de anderhalf uur worden bijgevuld. Zonder de KC-10's, hun 'vliegende benzinepompen', zouden ze Saoedi-Arabië nooit in één keer kunnen bereiken.

Het squadron vormde nu een brede formatie, waarbij iedere wingman op één lijn met zijn leader vloog, op ongeveer anderhalve kilometer afstand. Don Walker, met zijn wizzo Tim achter zich, keek opzij en zag zijn wingman in de juiste positie. Ze vlogen nu naar het oosten, boven de donkere oceaan, maar de radar gaf de posities van alle vliegtuigen aan en bovendien waren ze te herkennen aan hun navigatielichten.

In de staart van de KC-10 boven hem, schuin voor hen uit, opende de brandstofoperateur zijn paneel en tuurde naar de zee van lichtjes achter hem. De benzineleiding was uitgerold en wachtte op de eerste klant.

Iedere groep van zes Eagles had zijn tanker al geïdentificeerd. Toen Walker aan de beurt was, gaf hij wat gas en naderde de tanker, tot hij binnen bereik van de benzineleiding was. De operateur bewoog de slang naar de klep aan de voorrand van de linkervleugel van het gevechtsvliegtuig. Toen de verbinding tot stand was gebracht, pompte hij de JP4-brandstof in de tanks, in een tempo van 2000 pond per minuut. De Eagle dronk gulzig.

Toen de tank vol was, trok Walker zich weer terug, om plaats te maken voor zijn wingman. Verderop herhaalde dezelfde procedure zich met drie andere tankers en hun zes Eagles.

De nacht was kort, omdat ze de zon tegemoet vlogen met een snelheid van 350 knopen, ongeveer 800 km per uur. Na zes uur kwam de zon weer op en kruisten ze de Spaanse kust. Ze bleven ten noorden van Afrika om Libië te mijden. Toen ze Egypte – een lid van de Coalitie – naderden, draaide het 336e naar het zuidoosten, over de Rode Zee, en ving een eerste glimp op van die geelbruine zand- en steenvlakte die bekend staat als de Arabische woestijn.

Na vijftien uur in de lucht te zijn geweest landden de achtenveertig jonge Amerikanen stijf en vermoeid op het vliegveld van Dhahran in Saoedi-Arabië. Een paar uur later bereikten ze hun eindbestemming, de vliegbasis Thumrait in het sultanaat Maskat en Oman.

Hier zouden ze vier maanden blijven, tot half december, in omstandigheden waar ze later met heimwee aan zouden terugdenken, 1100 km van de Iraakse grens en de gevarenzone. Zodra de rest van het materieel was gearriveerd, voerden ze oefenvluchten uit boven het binnenland van Oman, zwommen in het blauwe water van de Indische Oceaan en wachtten op wat de Heer en Norman Schwarzkopf voor hen in petto hadden.

Pas in december zouden ze terugkeren naar Saoedi-Arabië, waar een van hen – zonder het te weten – het verloop van de oorlog beslissend zou beïnvloeden.

Het vliegveld Dhahran was tjokvol. Toen Mike Martin uit Riyad vertrok, had hij het gevoel dat het halve Midden-Oosten op het punt van vertrekken stond. Dhahran, in het hart van de grote keten van olievelden waaraan Saoedi-Arabië zijn fabelachtige rijkdom te danken had, was allang gewend aan Amerikanen en Europeanen – heel anders dan Taif, Riyad, Yenbo en de andere steden van het koninkrijk.

Zelfs voor de drukke havenstad Jeddah was het iets bijzonders om zoveel Angelsaksische gezichten op straat te zien. Maar in die tweede week van augustus stond Dhahran werkelijk op zijn kop.

Sommige mensen probeerden weg te komen. Een groot aantal was de dam naar Bahrein overgestoken om daar op het vliegtuig te stappen. Anderen, voornamelijk vrouwen en gezinnen van oliemensen, zaten op het vliegveld van Dhahran te wachten op een vliegtuig naar Riyad en een aansluitende vlucht naar huis.

Anderen waren net aangekomen – een stroom van Amerikanen met wapens en voorraden. Martins eigen lijnvlucht had juist kunnen landen tussen twee grote C-5 Galaxies in, die deel uitmaakten van de bijna ononderbroken luchtbrug vanuit Engeland, Duitsland en de Verenigde Staten om het materieel over te brengen dat het noordoosten van Saoedi-Arabië in één groot legerkamp zou veranderen.

Dit was niet Desert Storm, de campagne om Koeweit te bevrijden. Nee, dit was nog maar Desert Shield, de operatie die moest voorkomen dat het Iraakse leger – inmiddels veertien divisies verspreid over Koeweit en langs de grens – nog verder naar het zuiden zou oprukken.

Voor een buitenstaander leek het misschien een heel indrukwekkende actie, maar wie scherper keek zag dat de bescherming niet veel voorstelde. De Amerikaanse pantsereenheden en artillerie waren nog niet gearriveerd. De eerste transportschepen hadden de Amerikaanse havens nog maar net verlaten. En de voorraden van de Galaxies, Starlifters en Hercules-toestellen waren maar een fractie van wat een schip kon vervoeren.

De Eagles die in Dhahran waren gestationeerd en de Hornets van de mariniers in Bahrein, plus de Britse Tornado's die pas uit Duitsland in Dhahran waren aangekomen, hadden voldoende wapens bij zich om een stuk of zes missies uit te voeren, maar meer ook niet. En dat is niet voldoende om de vastberaden opmars van een pantserdivisie te stuiten. Ondanks het indrukwekkende vertoon van militair materieel op enkele vliegvelden lag het noordoosten van Saoedi-Arabië bijna weerloos onder de zon.

Martin wrong zich door de menigte in de aankomsthal, met zijn tas over zijn schouder. Bij het hek zag hij een bekend gezicht.

De selectieproeven voor de SAS, waar ze hem hadden gezegd dat ze hem niet wilden trainen maar kapotmaken, hadden hem bijna de das omgedaan. Op een dag had hij in de stromende, ijskoude regen vijftig kilometer door de Brecons – een van de ruigste gebieden in Groot-Brittannië – moeten lopen, met een bepakking van vijftig kilo. Net als de anderen was hij volslagen uitgeput geweest en had hij zich teruggetrokken in een eigen wereld waarin niets anders meer bestond dan pijn en wilskracht.

Toen, godzijdank, zag hij eindelijk de vrachtwagen die op hem stond te wachten. Het einde van de mars en het einde van zijn beproeving waren in zicht. Nog honderd meter, tachtig, vijftig... De verlossing voor zijn gepijnigde lichaam kwam nader en nader. Zijn gevoelloze benen sleepten hem en zijn rugzak de laatste paar meters naar de vrachtwagen toe.

Achter in de truck zat een man, die dat kletsnatte, verwrongen gezicht steeds dichterbij zag komen. Toen de laadklep nog maar twintig centimeter van de uitgestrekte vingers vandaan was, tikte de man tegen de achterkant van de cabine, en de truck reed door. Niet honderd meter, maar nog eens vijftien kilometer. Sparky Low was de man achter in die vrachtwagen geweest.

'Hallo Mike, blij je te zien...'

Zoiets vergeef je iemand niet snel.

'Hallo Sparky, hoe staat het leven?'

'Niet zo best, als je het echt wilt weten.'

Sparky haalde zijn onopvallende 4WD jeep van het parkeerterrein. Dertig minuten later hadden ze Dhahran achter zich gelaten en reden ze naar het noorden. Het was driehonderd kilometer naar Khafji. Drie uur rijden. Maar toen ze de havenstad Jubail links waren gepasseerd, werd het een stuk rustiger op de weg. Niemand had behoefte aan een ritje naar Khafji, een oliestadje aan de grens met Koeweit. Op dit moment had Khafji meer van een spookstad.

'Komen er nog steeds vluchtelingen de grens over?' vroeg Martin.

'Een paar,' knikte Sparky. 'Niet veel. De grootste stroom is voorbij. Over de hoofdweg komen bijna alleen nog vrouwen en kinderen met pasjes. De Irakezen laten hen gaan om van hen af te zijn. Logisch. Als ik Koeweit bezet hield, zou ik de buitenlanders ook kwijt willen. De Indiërs negeren ze grotendeels. Dat is niet zo slim, want die hebben goede informatie en ik heb er al een paar teruggestuurd met berichten voor onze mensen.'

'Heb je de spullen waar ik om had gevraagd?'

'Ja. Gray heeft wat druk uitgeoefend denk ik. Gisteren is alles aangekomen, in een truck met een Saoedisch opschrift. Ik heb het in de logeerkamer gelegd. Morgenavond eten we met die jonge Koeweitse luchtmachtpiloot over wie ik je heb verteld. Hij beweert dat hij betrouwbare contacten heeft die van nut kunnen zijn.'

Martin bromde wat. 'Mijn gezicht krijgt hij niet te zien. Stel dat hij uit de lucht geschoten wordt...'

Sparky dacht even na. 'Oké.'

Sparky Low had zich een leuke villa toegeëigend. Het huis was van een Amerikaanse olieman van Aramco, die door zijn bedrijf was teruggeroepen naar Dhahran.

Martin was zo verstandig om niet te vragen wat Sparky Low in deze uithoek te zoeken had. Blijkbaar was hij ook door Century House 'geleend' en moest hij vluchtelingen onderscheppen om hun te vragen wat ze hadden gezien en gehoord.

Khafji was praktisch verlaten, afgezien van de Saoedische Nationale Garde die zich in en om de stad had ingegraven. Er liepen een paar Saoedi's doelloos rond. Bij een marktkoopman, die niet kon geloven dat hij werkelijk een klant had, kocht Martin de kleren die hij nodig had.

De elektriciteit was nog aangesloten, zodat de airco, de waterpomp en de boiler werkten. Maar Martin nam geen bad. Hij had zich al drie dagen niet gewassen, geschoren of zijn tanden gepoetst. Hij begon al te stinken, maar mevrouw Gray, zijn gastvrouw in Riyad, had er geen woord over gezegd. Om zijn gebit schoon te houden peuterde Martin na het eten met een splinter tussen zijn tanden. Sparky Low zei er ook niets over, maar hij kende de reden.

De Koeweitse officier bleek een knappe jonge vent te zijn van zesentwintig, woedend over de inval in zijn land. Hij was duidelijk een aanhanger van de verdreven Al Sabah dynastie, die inmiddels was ondergebracht in een luxe hotel in Taif, als gasten van koning Fahd van Saoedi-Arabië.

Tot zijn verbazing zag de jonge piloot dat zijn gastheer was wie hij had verwacht – een Brits officier in vrijetijdskleding – maar dat de derde gast aan tafel een andere Arabier bleek te zijn, gekleed in een smerige *thob* met een gespikkelde *keffijeh* om zijn hoofd, waarvan de punt de onderste helft van zijn gezicht bedekte. Low stelde hen aan elkaar voor.

'Bent u echt een Engelsman?' vroeg de jongeman verbaasd. Low vertelde hem waarom Martin zo gekleed was en zijn gezicht verborgen hield. Kapitein Al-Khalifa knikte. 'Neemt u me niet kwalijk, majoor. Ik begrijp het.'

Zijn verhaal was helder en duidelijk. Op de avond van de 1e augustus was hij thuis gebeld met orders zich onmiddellijk te melden op de vliegbasis

Ahmadi, waar hij was gestationeerd. De hele nacht hadden hij en zijn collega's naar de radioberichten over de Iraakse invasie van hun land geluisterd. Tegen de ochtend werd zijn squadron van Skyray-jagers bijgetankt, bewapend en gereedgemaakt om op te stijgen. De Amerikaanse Skyray was geen modern toestel, maar wel geschikt voor aanvallen op gronddoelen. De Skyray was niet opgewassen tegen de Iraakse MiG-23, -25 of -29 of de door Frankrijk geleverde Mirages, maar gelukkig was Al-Khalifa die niet tegengekomen op zijn eerste en enige gevechtsmissie.

Kort na het ochtendgloren had hij zijn doelen gevonden in de noordelijke buitenwijken van de stad.

'Ik heb een van hun tanks met mijn raketten uitgeschakeld,' verklaarde hij trots. 'Ik zag hem exploderen. Toen had ik alleen nog mijn kanon. Daarmee heb ik een aanval gedaan op de vrachtwagens die erachteraan kwamen. De voorste heb ik te pakken gekregen. Hij kwam in de greppel terecht en sloeg over de kop. Toen moest ik terug omdat ik geen munitie meer had. Maar boven Ahmadi kregen we van de vluchtleiding bevel om naar de grens in het zuiden te vliegen en de toestellen te redden. Ik had nog net genoeg brandstof om Dhahran te bereiken. We hebben meer dan zestig van onze vliegtuigen het land uit gekregen. Skyhawks, Mirages en Britse Hawk-trainers. Plus een stel Gazelles, Puma's en Super-Puma helikopters. Nu kan ik de strijd van hieruit voortzetten tot we zijn bevrijd. Wanneer zal de aanval beginnen, denkt u?'

Sparky Low glimlachte voorzichtig. De jongen was zo zeker van zijn zaak.

'Nog niet, vrees ik. U moet nog even geduld hebben. Er moet nog heel wat worden voorbereid. Vertel ons eens over uw vader.'

De vader van de piloot bleek een zeer rijke zakenman te zijn, een vriend van de koninklijke familie en een invloedrijk man.

'Zal hij de bezetters steunen?' vroeg Low.

De jonge Al-Khalifa reageerde verontwaardigd. 'Nee, nooit! Hij zal alles doen om de bevrijding te bespoedigen.' Hij keek de donkere ogen boven de geruite hoofddoek aan. 'Wilt u met mijn vader spreken? U kunt hem vertrouwen.'

'Misschien,' zei Martin.

'Wilt u hem dan een boodschap van mij doorgeven?'

Hij schreef iets op een velletje papier dat hij aan Martin gaf.

Toen hij terug was in Khafji, verbrandde Martin het papiertje in een asbak. Hij mocht geen belastende bewijzen bij zich hebben als hij de grens overging.

De volgende morgen pakten hij en Low de spullen waarom hij had gevraagd achter in de jeep en reden weer naar het zuiden, tot aan Manifah. Daar sloegen ze af naar de Tapline Road, de weg die evenwijdig loopt aan de Saoedisch-Koeweitse grens. De naam 'Tapline' is afgeleid van TAP, een afkorting van de Trans Arabian Pipeline, die zoveel Saoedische olie naar het westen transporteert. De weg hoort bij de pijpleiding.

Later zou de Tapline Road de belangrijkste transportader worden voor de grootste militaire landarmada uit de geschiedenis. In totaal zouden 400 000 Amerikaanse, 70 000 Britse, 10 000 Franse en 200 000 Saoedische en andere Arabische militairen vanuit het zuiden langs deze weg oprukken voor de invasie van Irak en Koeweit. Maar nu was er nog niemand te zien.

Een paar kilometer verderop sloeg de jeep weer naar het noorden af, terug naar de Saoedisch-Koeweitse grens, maar op een andere plaats, ver landinwaarts. Vlak bij het winderige woestijndorp Hamatijat ligt de grens het dichtst bij Koeweit Stad.

Uit de satellietfoto's die Gray hem in Riyad had laten zien bleek bovendien dat het grootste deel van de Iraakse troepen zich wel vlak boven de grens maar dichter bij de kust had geconcentreerd. Hoe verder landinwaarts, des te minder Iraakse voorposten er waren. De Iraakse hoofdmacht lag tussen de grensovergang bij Nuwaisib aan de kust en Al-Wafra, 65 km het binnenland in.

Het dorpje Hamatijat lag ruim 150 km de woestijn in, in een inham van de grens.

De kamelen waarom Martin had gevraagd stonden te wachten bij een kleine boerderij buiten het dorp – een pezig wijfje in de kracht van haar leven, met haar jong, een crèmekleurig kalf met een fluwelen snuit en lieve ogen, dat nog bij haar moeder dronk. Later zou het net zo'n gemeen kreng worden als de rest van haar soort, maar nu was het nog een schatje.

'Waarom dat kalf?' vroeg Low, terwijl ze vanuit de jeep de twee dieren achter het hek gadesloegen.

'Als dekmantel. Als iemand ernaar vraagt, breng ik haar naar de kamelenfarms bij Sulaibaja voor de verkoop. Daar krijg je een betere prijs.'

Hij liet zich uit de jeep glijden en schuifelde op zijn sandalen naar de kamelendrijver die in de schaduw van zijn hutje zat te dommelen. De twee mannen zaten een halfuurtje in het zand gehurkt om over de prijs van de twee dieren te onderhandelen. Het kwam geen moment bij de drijver op dat de stinkende man tegenover hem, met zijn donkere gezicht, zijn vuile tanden, zijn stoppelbaard en zijn smerige boernoes, geen bedoeïen zou zijn die twee kamelen zocht.

Toen ze het eens waren, betaalde Martin de man met een rol Saoedische dinars die hij van Low had gekregen en een tijdje onder zijn oksel had gehouden om ze smerig te maken. Daarna nam hij de twee kamelen mee en bracht ze anderhalve kilometer verderop, waar ze door de zandduinen aan nieuwsgierige blikken werden onttrokken. Low kwam hem achterna met de jeep.

Hij had van een paar honderd meter afstand toegekeken. Hoewel hij het Arabisch schiereiland goed kende, had hij nog nooit met Martin samengewerkt en hij was onder de indruk. De man spéélde geen Arabier. Toen hij uit die jeep stapte was hij in alle opzichten een bedoeïen geweest.

Hoewel hij dat niet wist, hadden twee Britse ingenieurs de vorige dag geprobeerd uit hun appartement in Koeweit te ontsnappen, gekleed in een lange witte *thob* met een *ghutra* hoofddoek om hun hoofd. Ze waren nog niet halverwege hun auto, vijftien meter verderop, toen een kind naar hen riep: 'Jullie dragen wel Arabische kleren, maar jullie lopen nog als Engelsen.' De ingenieurs waren naar hun flat teruggegaan en daar gebleven.

Zwetend in de zon, maar buiten het gezicht van toevallige voorbijgangers die dergelijke zware arbeid in de hitte van de dag misschien verdacht zouden vinden, brachten de twee SAS-agenten de spullen uit de jeep naar de tassen van de kameel over. Het dier lag met opgetrokken poten, maar protesteerde toch tegen het extra gewicht en spuwde en blies tegen de twee mannen.

De 200 pond aan Semtex-H explosieven verdween in een van de tassen, verdeeld in blokken van vijf pond die in doeken waren gewikkeld. Ze legden er een paar jutezakken met koffiebonen bovenop, voor het geval een Iraakse militair de bagage zou doorzoeken. In de andere tas gingen de machinepistolen, de munitie, de ontstekers, de timers, de granaten en Martins kleine maar krachtige zender-ontvanger met zijn inklapbare satellietschotel en de extra cadmiumnikkelbatterijen. Ook daar kwamen een paar zakken koffiebonen bovenop.

Toen ze klaar waren, vroeg Low: 'Kan ik verder nog iets doen?'

'Nee, dat was het. Bedankt. Ik blijf hier tot zonsondergang. Jij hoeft niet te wachten.'

Low stak zijn hand uit. 'Het spijt me van dat geval op de Brecons.'

Martin gaf hem een hand. 'Geeft niet. Ik heb het overleefd.'

Low lachte kort en schor. 'Ja, zo zijn we. We overleven alles. Hou dat zo, Mike.'

En hij reed weg. De kameel rolde met een oog, boerde wat eten omhoog en begon te herkauwen. Het kalf probeerde te drinken. Toen dat niet lukte, ging het naast haar moeder liggen.

Martin leunde tegen het zadel, trok zijn *keffijeh* voor zijn gezicht en dacht aan wat hem te wachten stond. De woestijn was geen probleem, de drukte van het bezette Koeweit Stad misschien wel. Hoe scherp waren de controles, hoe effectief de wegversperringen en hoe alert de soldaten die ze bemanden? Century House had hem valse papieren willen meegeven, maar daar was hij niet op ingegaan. De Irakezen zouden de pasjes kunnen veranderen.

Hij was ervan overtuigd dat zijn dekmantel een van de beste in de Arabische wereld was. De bedoeïenen komen en gaan zoals ze willen. Ze verzetten zich niet tegen binnenvallende legers, want die hebben ze al zo vaak gezien – de Saracenen en de Turken, de kruisvaarders en de Tempelridders, de Duitsers en de Fransen, de Britten en de Egyptenaren, de Israëli's en de Irakezen. En ze hebben ze allemaal overleefd omdat ze zich nooit met politiek of militaire zaken bemoeien.

Veel regimes hebben geprobeerd hen te temmen, maar zonder succes. Koning Fahd van Saoedi-Arabië, die besloot dat al zijn onderdanen in een huis moesten wonen, bouwde een mooi dorp genaamd Escan, voorzien van alle moderne gemakken – een zwembad, wc's, baden, stromend water. Er werden een paar bedoeïenen opgepakt en naar het dorp gebracht.

Ze dronken uit het zwembad (het leek op een oase), ze scheten op de patio, ze speelden met de kranen en vertrokken toen weer. Beleefd legden ze de koning uit dat ze liever onder de sterren sliepen. Escan werd schoongemaakt en tijdens de Golfcrisis door de Amerikanen gebruikt.

Martin wist dat zijn lengte het grootste probleem vormde. Hij was bijna één meter tachtig en de meeste bedoeïenen zijn veel kleiner. Eeuwen van ziekte en ondervoeding hebben hun sporen nagelaten. Het water in de woestijn wordt alleen als drinkwater voor mens, geit of kameel gebruikt. Daarom had Martin zich niet gewassen. De romantiek van het woestijnleven is een Westerse fantasie.

Hij had geen papieren, maar dat was geen probleem. Verscheidene regeringen hebben geprobeerd de bedoeïenen papieren uit te reiken. Ze zijn er meestal blij mee, omdat wc-papier altijd welkom is – beter dan een handvol grind. Politiemensen en militairen weten dat het geen enkele zin heeft een bedoeïen naar zijn papieren te vragen. Het belangrijkste voor de autoriteiten is dat de bedoeïenen geen last veroorzaken. Ze zouden zich nooit bij het Koeweitse verzet aansluiten, wist Martin. Hopelijk wisten de Irakezen dat ook.

Hij zat te dommelen totdat de zon onderging en stond toen op. Op zijn 'hut, hut hut' kwam ook de kameel overeind. Haar jong, dat aan haar zadel was vastgebonden, dronk een tijdje en daarna vertrokken ze met die rustige, golvende tred die heel traag lijkt maar waarmee je grote afstanden kunt afleggen. De kameel had goed gegeten en gedronken en zou het dagen kunnen volhouden.

Hij was al een heel eind ten noordwesten van de politiepost van Ruqaifah, waar een pad de grens kruist, toen hij om een paar minuten voor acht de Koeweitse grens overstak. Het was aardedonker, afgezien van het zwakke schijnsel van de sterren. Rechts zag hij de gloed van het Manageesh-olieveld in Koeweit, dat waarschijnlijk door de Irakezen werd bewaakt, maar in de woestijn was niemand te zien.

Op de kaart was het een tocht van vijftig kilometer naar de kamelenfarms ten zuiden van Sulaibija, het buitendistrict van Koeweit Stad waar hij zijn beesten wilde achterlaten tot hij ze weer nodig had. Maar vóór die tijd moest hij zijn spullen in de woestijn begraven en de plaats markeren.

Dat wilde hij een uur voor zonsopgang doen, als hij niet werd aangehouden en vertraagd. Een uurtje later moest hij zijn reisdoel hebben bereikt.

Toen de Manageesh-olievelden achter hem verdwenen, oriënteerde hij zich op zijn kompas en reed in een rechte lijn naar Sulaibija. De Irakezen bewaakten misschien de wegen en zelfs de paden, maar niet de verlaten woestijn, zoals hij al had verwacht. Geen enkele vluchteling zou proberen langs die weg te ontsnappen en geen vijand zou daar binnenvallen.

Vanaf de kamelenfarms zou hij na zonsopgang een lift met een vrachtwagen kunnen krijgen naar de stad, zo'n dertig kilometer verderop.

Hoog boven hem, aan de stille nachthemel, draaide een KH-11 satelliet van het National Reconnaissance Office voorbij. Jaren geleden hadden vorige generaties Amerikaanse satellieten hun foto's nog in capsules naar de aarde moeten sturen, waar de filmpjes werden ontwikkeld – een tijdrovende procedure.

De KH-11's, 21 meter lang en met een gewicht van zo'n 12 000 kilo, zijn veel moderner. Zij coderen hun opnamen automatisch in een reeks elektronische pulsen die omhóóg worden gestraald naar een andere satelliet.

Die ontvangende satelliet maakt deel uit van een netwerk dat in een geosynchrone baan met de aarde meedraait, waardoor de satellieten altijd boven dezelfde plaats blijven. Ze 'hangen' als het ware op één plek.

Als de 'hangende' satelliet de beelden van de KH-11 heeft ontvangen, kan hij ze rechtstreeks naar het Amerikaanse grondstation doorseinen of – als de kromming van de aarde in de weg zit – de signalen via een andere hangende satelliet omlaag laten stuiteren. Zo kan het NRO de beelden bijna 'live' ontvangen, een paar seconden nadat ze zijn gemaakt.

Dat is een geweldig voordeel in een oorlog. Het betekent dat de KH-11 een vijandelijk konvooi kan zien naderen, nog ruim op tijd om een squadron jachtbommenwerpers te waarschuwen dat de trucks naar het hiernamaals kan blazen. De ongelukkige soldaten in de wagens zullen nooit weten hoe die vliegtuigen hen hebben ontdekt, want de KH-11's werken dag en nacht en 'kijken' ook door mist en bewolking heen.

Daarom worden ze wel 'alziend' genoemd. Maar dat zijn ze niet. Die nacht cirkelde er ook een KH-11 over Saoedi-Arabië en Koeweit heen, maar de eenzame bedoeïen die het verboden gebied betrad, zag hij niet. En anders zou hij er niet op hebben gelet. Hij bewoog zich over Koeweit naar Irak. Hij zag talloze gebouwen, industriële mini-steden rond Al-Hillah en Tarmija, bij Al-Atheer en Tuwaitha, maar hij zag niet wat zich in die gebouwen bevond – de vaten met gifgas of het uraniumhexafluoride, bestemd voor de gasdiffusie-centrifuges van de isotopenscheidingsfabriek.

De satelliet draaide verder naar het noorden, over de vliegvelden, de wegen en de bruggen. Hij zag zelfs de autosloperij van Al-Qubai, maar lette er niet op. Hij zag de industriële centra van Al-Quaim, Jazira en Al-Shirqat, ten westen en noorden van Bagdad, maar niet de massavernietigingswapens die daar werden vervaardigd. Hij draaide over de Jebel Al Hamreen, maar zonder de ondergrondse Vesting te ontdekken die daar door de genie-officier Osman Badri was gebouwd. Hij zag alleen maar een berg tussen andere bergen, en een paar dorpjes tussen andere dorpen. Daarna draaide hij over Koerdistan naar Turkije.

Mike Martin reed verder door de nacht, in de richting van Koeweit Stad, onzichtbaar in kleren die hij bijna twee weken geleden voor het laatst had gedragen. Glimlachend dacht hij terug aan het moment waarop hij, na een wandeling in de woestijn bij Abu Dhabi, naar zijn Landrover terugliep en werd verrast door een mollige Amerikaanse dame die een camera op hem had gericht en 'klik klik' tegen hem had geroepen.

Het Medusa Comité hield zijn eerste bespreking in een ruimte onder de vergaderzaal van het kabinet in Whitehall. De belangrijkste reden was dat het gebouw goed was beveiligd en regelmatig op afluisterapparatuur werd gecontroleerd, hoewel de Russen de laatste tijd zo *aardig* waren dat ze zich misschien niet meer met zulke vervelende praktijken bezighielden.

De kamer waar de acht deelnemers naartoe werden gebracht lag twee verdiepingen onder de grond. Terry Martin had weleens gehoord van het netwerk van schokbestendige, elektronisch beveiligde ruimten onder het onschuldig ogende gebouw tegenover de Cenotaph, waar de meest geheime staatszaken in alle beslotenheid konden worden besproken.

Sir Paul Spruce zou de vergadering voorzitten. Hij was een gladde, ervaren bureaucraat met de rang van tweede permanente secretaris van het kabinet. Hij stelde eerst zichzelf en toen de anderen voor.

De Amerikaanse ambassade en dus de Verenigde Staten werd vertegenwoordigd door de assistent-zaakgelastigde voor defensie en door Harry Sinclair, een scherpe, door de wol geverfde agent uit Langley, die al drie jaar de leiding had van het CIA-bureau in Londen. Sinclair was een lange, hoekige man die meestal tweedjasjes droeg, regelmatig naar de opera ging en uitstekend met zijn Britse collega's overweg kon.

De CIA-man knikte en knipoogde naar Simon Paxman, die hij al eens had ontmoet bij een vergadering van de Gezamenlijke Commissie voor de Inlichtingendiensten, waarin de CIA permanent vertegenwoordigd was. Sinclair moest de observaties van de Britse wetenschappers aan Washington doorgeven, waar de veel grotere Amerikaanse tegenhanger van het Medusa Comité nu ook vergaderde. Daarna zouden alle gegevens worden verzameld en vergeleken om te bepalen hoe gevaarlijk de Iraakse vernietigingswapens werkelijk waren.

Er waren twee experts van Aldermaston, het instituut voor wapenonderzoek in Berkshire – de term 'nucleair' wordt meestal niet genoemd, maar daar gaat het wel om. Uit informatie uit de Verenigde Staten, Europa en elders, en uit de luchtfoto's van mogelijke Iraakse nucleaire installaties moesten zij proberen af te leiden hoe ver Irak was met de technologie om zelf een kernbom te vervaardigen.

Ook waren er twee wetenschappers uit Porton Down, een chemicus en een bacterioloog.

Porton Down is er in de linkse pers vaak van beschuldigd onderzoek te doen naar chemische en bacteriologische wapens voor toepassing door het Britse leger. In werkelijkheid is de research al jaren gericht op het vinden van antistoffen tegen gassen en bacillen die tegen de Britse en geallieerde troepen kunnen worden gebruikt. Helaas is het onmogelijk een antistof te ontwikkelen zonder eerst de eigenschappen van het gif te kennen. De twee deskundigen uit Porton Down hadden daarom – onder zeer strenge veiligheidsmaatregelen – een paar heel onaangename stoffen onder hun beheer. Maar dat gold ook, op die 13e augustus, voor de heer Saddam Hoessein. Het verschil was dat Engeland niet van plan was die middelen tegen de Irakezen te gebruiken, terwijl meneer Hoessein misschien minder scrupules had.

Uit de lijst met chemische stoffen die Irak de afgelopen jaren had gekocht moesten de mannen van Porton Down proberen vast te stellen welke giftige wapens hij zou kunnen produceren, hoeveel, hoe gevaarlijk en hoe bruikbaar. Ook zouden ze de luchtfoto's van een aantal fabrieken en werkplaatsen in Irak uitvoerig bestuderen om te zien of ze ontsmettingseenheden, emissiedempers en andere karakteristieke onderdelen van een gifgasinstallatie konden ontdekken.

'Heren,' richtte Sir Paul zich tot de vier wetenschappers, 'de belangrijkste taak rust op uw schouders. Wij zullen u daarbij zoveel mogelijk van dienst zijn en ondersteunen. Ik heb hier twee dossiers met inlichtingen die door onze ambassade, onze handelsmissie en eh... bepaalde andere diensten zijn verzameld. Het is nog vroeg. Dit zijn de eerste gegevens over de exportvergunningen die door verschillende landen voor leveranties aan Irak zijn verstrekt. Uiteraard is die informatie afkomstig van regeringen die ons in alle opzichten ter wille zijn. We hebben het terrein zo breed mogelijk gehouden – chemicaliën, bouwmaterialen, laboratoriumapparatuur, technische onderdelen, noem maar op. Bijna alles, behalve paraplu's, breiwol en knuffelbeesten.

Het grootste deel bestaat waarschijnlijk uit onschuldige aankopen voor vreedzame doeleinden. Irak is immers een land in ontwikkeling. Het onderzoek naar die produkten zal achteraf tijdverspilling blijken te zijn. Mijn excuses daarvoor. Toch moeten we niet alleen aandacht besteden aan wapens en verwante aankopen, maar vooral aan elementen die meer toepassingen kennen dan op de exportvergunning staan vermeld. Inmiddels hebben onze Amerikaanse collega's ook niet stilgezeten.'

Sir Paul reikte de dossiers uit. De man van de CIA deed hetzelfde. Verbijsterd staarden de experts van Aldermaston en Porton Down naar de stapels papier die ze voor hun neus kregen.

'We hebben geprobeerd doublures te vermijden,' vervolgde Sir Paul, 'maar dat zal niet altijd zijn gelukt. Ook daarvoor mijn excuses. En dan geef ik nu het woord aan collega Sinclair.'

Het verhaal van de hoge ambtenaar was nogal slaapverwekkend geweest. De chef van het CIA-bureau hield het kort en krachtig.

'Het gaat erom dat we misschien in oorlog raken met die klootzakken.'

Dat klonk al beter. Sinclair sprak zoals Britten dat van Amerikanen verwachten: direct en zonder omwegen. De vier wetenschappers zaten opeens rechtop.

'Als het zover komt, beginnen we met luchtaanvallen. En net als de Britten willen we onze verliezen zoveel mogelijk beperken. Dus moeten we hun infanterie, hun geschut, hun tanks en hun vliegtuigen uitschakelen. Dat betekent een groot aantal bombardementen op hun SAM-batterijen, hun verbindingscentra en hun commandoposten. Maar als Saddam gebruik maakt van massavernietigingswapens kan hij ons zware klappen toebrengen. Daarom willen we twee dingen weten.

Punt één. Wat voor wapens heeft hij eigenlijk? Als we dat weten, kunnen we maatregelen nemen – gasmaskers, beschermende kleding, antistoffen. Punt twee. Waar heeft hij de spullen verstopt? Zodra we de fabrieken en opslagplaatsen kennen, kunnen we ze vernietigen voordat hij er gebruik van kan maken. Bestudeer die foto's dus zo goed mogelijk, tot in de kleinste details. Neem er maar een vergrootglas bij. Dan sporen wij de aannemers op die de fabrieken hebben gebouwd en de technici die ze hebben ingericht. We zullen een hartig woordje met hen spreken. Maar misschien hebben de Irakezen een vals spoor uitgezet. Uw analyse is dus doorslaggevend.

Met uw werk kunt u veel levens redden, dus doe uw uiterste best. Probeer die vernietigingswapens te vinden, dan zullen wij ze met wortel en tak uitroeien.'

De vier wetenschappers wisten waar ze aan toe waren. Sinclair had er geen doekjes om gewonden. Sir Paul keek lichtelijk geshockeerd.

'Eh, juist. We zijn collega Sinclair zeer erkentelijk voor zijn eh... uitleg. Ik stel voor dat we opnieuw bijeenkomen zodra Aldermaston en Porton Down iets te melden hebben.'

Simon Paxman en Terry Martin verlieten het gebouw en slenterden in de warme augustuszon naar Parliament Square. Zoals gewoonlijk stond er een rij bussen met toeristen. Ze vonden een bankje dicht bij het standbeeld van Winston Churchill, die fronsend neerkeek op de brutale stervelingen beneden hem.

'Heb je het laatste nieuws uit Bagdad al gehoord?' vroeg Paxman.

'Natuurlijk.'

Saddam Hoessein had juist aangeboden om uit Koeweit te verdwijnen als Israël zich uit de West Bank en Syrië zich uit Libanon zou terugtrekken. Een poging tot koppelverkoop. De Verenigde Naties hadden het voorstel meteen verworpen. De Veiligheidsraad nam de ene na de andere resolutie aan om Irak in economisch opzicht volledig te isoleren. Maar de systematische verwoesting van Koeweit door de bezettingsmacht ging nog steeds door.

'Is het van enig belang?'

'Nee. Loze woorden om steun te winnen. Heel voorspelbaar. De PLO vindt het prachtig, maar het heeft geen enkele waarde.'

'Heeft Saddam wel een strategie?' vroeg Paxman. 'Niemand kan er enige lijn in ontdekken. Volgens de Amerikanen is hij gewoon gestoord.'

'Dat weet ik. Ik heb Bush gisteravond op de televisie gezien.'

'Is hij echt geschift?'

'Misschien. Maar hij is ook een sluwe vos.'

'Waarom valt hij dan niet de Saoedische olievelden binnen nu hij de kans nog heeft? De Amerikanen zijn nog maar pas begonnen met hun militaire opbouw, en wij ook. Een paar squadrons en vliegkampschepen in de Golf maar de grondtroepen moeten nog komen. En vliegtuigen alleen zijn niet voldoende om hem tegen te houden. Die Amerikaanse generaal die ze zojuist hebben benoemd...'

'Schwarzkopf,' zei Martin. 'Norman Schwarzkopf.'

'Precies. Hij denkt dat hij nog zeker twee maanden nodig heeft om voldoende troepen op de been te brengen om een invasie in Saoedi-Arabië te kunnen tegenhouden. Dus waarom zou Saddam nog wachten?'

'Omdat hij niet een andere Arabische staat wil aanvallen waarmee hij geen conflict heeft. Dat zou verwerpelijk zijn. Daarmee zou hij alle Arabieren van zich vervreemden. Het druist tegen hun cultuur in. Saddam wil roem oogsten en de Arabische wereld aan zijn voeten krijgen, niet door iedereen worden uitgekotst.'

'Maar toch is hij Koeweit binnengevallen,' wierp Paxman tegen.

'Dat is iets anders. Daarmee wil hij alleen een imperialistisch onrecht herstellen, omdat Koeweit historisch gezien altijd een deel van Irak is geweest.

Zoals Nehru ooit Portugees Goa binnenviel.'

'Toen nou, Terry. Saddam heeft Koeweit bezet omdat hij bankroet is. Dat weet iedereen.'

'Natuurlijk, maar voor het oog van de wereld kan hij volhouden dat hij Iraaks grondgebied terugeist. Dat gebeurt toch overal? India heeft Goa ingenomen, China heeft Tibet bezet, Indonesië heeft Timor geannexeerd, Argentinië heeft geprobeerd de Falklands in te nemen. En allemaal beweren ze dat het hun rechtmatige grondgebied is. Zo'n verhaal doet het goed bij de eigen bevolking.'

'Waarom hebben de andere Arabieren zich dan tegen hem gekeerd?'

'Omdat ze denken dat hij het verliest,' zei Martin.

'Daar hebben ze gelijk in.'

'Dank zij Amerika. Niet dank zij de Arabische wereld. Als hij Arabische steun wil krijgen, moet hij Amerika vernederen, niet een Arabisch buurland. Ben je weleens in Bagdad geweest?'

'De laatste tijd niet,' zei Paxman.

'Het hangt daar vol met portretten van Saddam als de koene woestijnridder op een wit paard, met geheven zwaard. Flauwekul, natuurlijk. De man is een ordinaire boef. Maar zo ziet hij zichzelf.'

Paxman stond op.

'Het is allemaal erg theoretisch, Terry. Maar bedankt voor je visie. Helaas moet ik me tot de harde feiten beperken. Trouwens, hoe zou hij Amerika kunnen vernederen? De Yanks hebben alle macht en alle technologie. Als ze er klaar voor zijn, kunnen ze Saddams leger en luchtmacht totaal vernietigen.'

Terry Martin tuurde omhoog naar de zon.

'Verliezen, Simon. Doden en gewonden. Amerika kan zich heel wat veroorloven, maar geen zware verliezen. Saddam wel. Het maakt hem niets uit.'

'Maar er zijn nog nauwelijks Amerikanen in de Golf.'

'Precies.'

De Rolls-Royce met Ahmed Al-Khalifa reed naar de ingang van het kantoorgebouw dat zich in het Engels en Arabisch als het hoofdkantoor van de Al-Khalifa Trading Corporation afficheerde en kwam sissend tot stilstand.

De bestuurder, een forsgebouwde bediende, half-chauffeur, half-lijfwacht, stapte uit en opende het achterportier voor zijn baas.

Misschien was het dom om met de Rolls te komen maar de Koeweitse miljonair had geweigerd met de Volvo naar zijn werk te gaan uit angst om de Iraakse soldaten bij de wegversperringen te provoceren.

'Laat ze maar barsten,' had hij aan het ontbijt gemopperd. De rit van zijn luxe, ommuurde villa in de weelderige buitenwijk Andalus naar zijn kantoor in Shamija was zonder problemen verlopen.

105

Binnen tien dagen na de invasie waren de gedisciplineerde, professionele militairen van de Iraakse Republikeinse Garde uit Koeweit Stad verdwenen om plaats te maken voor het dienstplichtige gepeupel van het Volksleger. Al-Khalifa had de pest gehad aan de Gardisten, maar voor dit tuig kon hij alleen maar minachting opbrengen.

De eerste paar dagen hadden de Gardisten zijn stad geplunderd, maar wel systematisch en opzettelijk. Hij had gezien hoe ze de Nationale Bank waren binnengedrongen en de nationale goudreserve van vijf miljard dollar hadden meegenomen. Dat was geen persoonlijke actie geweest. Het goud was in containers verpakt, in trucks geladen en naar Bagdad overgebracht.

De Goud-soukh had nog eens een miljard dollar aan massief gouden voorwerpen opgeleverd, die dezelfde weg waren gegaan.

Bij de wegversperringen hadden de Gardisten, herkenbaar aan hun zwarte baretten en hun professionele houding, zich correct gedragen. Maar al gauw waren ze naar het zuiden gestuurd om stellingen in te nemen langs de grens met Saoedi-Arabië.

Hun plaats was ingenomen door het Volksleger – ongeschoren, ongeregelde troepen die onvoorspelbaar reageerden en daardoor veel gevaarlijker waren. Ze hadden al enkele Koeweiti's doodgeschoten omdat ze weigerden hun horloge of hun auto af te staan.

Half augustus was de hitte als een mokerhamer op Koeweit neergedaald. De Iraakse soldaten hadden de tegels uit de straten gesloopt om hutten tegen de zon te bouwen. Alleen in de koelte van de ochtend kwamen ze nog tevoorschijn, zogenaamd om auto's te controleren op smokkelwaar – een smoes om burgers lastig te vallen, eten te roven en kostbaarheden te stelen.

Ahmed Al-Khalifa begon zijn werkdag graag om zeven uur, maar hij wachtte nu tot tien uur voordat hij naar kantoor ging. Dan kon hij ongehinderd de stenen hutten van de Iraakse militairen passeren. Twee haveloze soldaten zonder baret hadden zelfs voor de Rolls-Royce gesalueerd omdat ze dachten dat er een hoge functionaris uit hun eigen land in zat.

Natuurlijk kon dat niet lang goed gaan. Vroeg of laat zou de Rolls door een van die bandieten worden gestolen. Nou en? Als de Irakezen waren verdreven – wat onvermijdelijk zou gebeuren, alleen wist Al-Khalifa nog niet hoe – zou hij wel een nieuwe kopen.

Hij stapte uit, in zijn smetteloos witte *thob*. Het lichte katoen van de *ghutra*, met twee zwarte koorden om zijn hoofd bevestigd, viel over zijn gezicht. De chauffeur deed het portier dicht en liep terug naar de andere kant van de auto om hem naar het parkeerterrein te brengen.

'Een aalmoes, *sajidi*. Alstublieft. Voor een man die al drie dagen niet heeft gegeten.'

Hij had nauwelijks oog voor de man die op de stoep zat gehurkt, ogenschijnlijk slapend in de zon – een heel gewoon beeld in het Midden-Oosten. De bedoeïen was overeind gekomen en stak nu zijn hand uit.

Ahmed Al-Khalifa was een praktizerend moslim en probeerde zich te houden aan de leer van de koran, die voorschrijft dat iedereen een aalmoes moet schenken wanneer dat mogelijk is.

'Zet de auto maar weg,' beval hij, terwijl hij zijn portefeuille uit de zijzak van zijn boernoes haalde en een briefje van tien dinar pakte. De bedoeïen nam het geld met twee handen aan, als teken dat het zo'n gulle gift was dat hij die met beide handen moest tillen.

'Shukran, sajidi, shukran.' Op dezelfde toon voegde hij eraan toe: 'Laat mij naar uw kantoor komen. Ik heb nieuws van uw zoon uit het zuiden.'

De zakenman dacht eerst dat hij het verkeerd had verstaan. De bedoeïen schuifelde alweer weg en stak het bankbiljet in zijn zak. Al-Khalifa stapte naar binnen, knikte naar de portier en nam fronsend de lift naar zijn kantoor op de bovenste verdieping. Hij ging achter zijn bureau zitten, dacht even na en drukte toen op een knop van zijn intercom.

'Buiten op de stoep zit een bedoeïen. Ik wil hem spreken. Laat hem boven komen.'

Als zijn secretaresse zich afvroeg wat haar baas bezielde, liet ze dat niet merken. Alleen haar opgetrokken neus verried haar afkeer van de vreemde bezoeker toen ze de bedoeïen vijf minuten later het koele kantoor binnenliet.

Zodra ze de deur had gesloten, wees de zakenman naar een stoel.

'U zei dat u mijn zoon had gesproken?' vroeg hij kort, half in de verwachting dat het de man om nog meer geld te doen was.

'Inderdaad, meneer Al-Khalifa. Twee dagen geleden, in Khafji.'

De Koeweiti voelde zijn hart sneller kloppen. Hij had al twee weken niets van zijn enige zoon vernomen. Via een omweg had hij gehoord dat Khaled die ochtend van de vliegbasis Ahmadi was opgestegen, maar dat was alles. Geen van zijn contacten wist wat er met hem was gebeurd. Die 2e augustus was een chaotische dag geweest.

'En u hebt een boodschap van hem?'

'Inderdaad, sajidi.'

Al-Khalifa stak zijn hand uit. 'Geef maar hier. Ik zal u rijkelijk belonen.'

'Ik ken de boodschap uit mijn hoofd. Ik mocht geen papier meenemen.'

'Goed. Vertel me dan wat hij heeft gezegd.'

Mike Martin herhaalde woordelijk wat de Skyhawk-piloot op het velletje papier had geschreven.

'Beste Vader, ondanks zijn uiterlijk is de man tegenover u een Brits officier.'

Al-Khalifa schoot overeind en staarde Martin ongelovig aan.

107

'Hij is in het geheim naar Koeweit gekomen. Nu u dat weet, houdt u zijn leven in uw hand. Ik smeek u hem te vertrouwen, zoals hij u moet vertrouwen, want hij heeft uw hulp nodig.

Ik ben veilig en ik bevind me bij de Saoedische luchtmacht op de basis Dhahran. Ik heb één missie tegen de Irakezen uitgevoerd, waarbij ik een tank en een truck heb vernietigd. Tot de bevrijding van ons land zal ik bij de Saoedische luchtmacht vliegen.

Iedere dag bid ik tot Allah dat de uren tot aan mijn terugkeer en ons weerzien snel voorbij zullen gaan. Uw trouwe zoon, Khaled.'

Martin zweeg. Ahmed Al-Khalifa stond op, liep naar het raam en staarde naar buiten. Hij haalde een paar keer lang en diep adem. Toen hij zich had hersteld, ging hij weer zitten.

'Dank u. Dank u. Wat kan ik voor u doen?'

'De bezetting van Koeweit zal niet een paar uur of een paar dagen duren, maar enkele maanden. Tenzij we Saddam Hoessein ertoe kunnen dwingen zich terug te trekken...'

'De Amerikanen komen dus voorlopig niet?'

'De Amerikanen, de Britten, de Fransen en de rest van de Coalitie hebben tijd nodig om hun troepenmacht op te bouwen. Saddam heeft het op drie na grootste reguliere leger ter wereld – meer dan een miljoen man. Een deel daarvan stelt niet veel voor, maar er zijn ook goede troepen bij. Deze bezettingsmacht kan niet door een handjevol soldaten worden verdreven.'

'Goed, dat begrijp ik.'

'Ondertussen gaan we ervan uit dat iedere Iraakse militair, iedere tank en ieder kanon dat voor de bezetting van Koeweit nodig is, niet aan de grens kan worden ingezet.'

'U hebt het over verzet, gewapend verzet. Strijd tegen de bezetter,' zei Al-Khalifa. 'Een paar wilde jongens hebben dat geprobeerd en op Iraakse patrouilles gevuurd. Ze zijn als honden neergeschoten.'

'Ja, dat wil ik wel geloven. Heel dapper, maar ook dwaas. Er zijn betere manieren. Het gaat niet om een strijd op leven en dood. Het gaat erom de Iraakse bezetters nerveus te maken, zo nerveus dat ze iedere officier moeten escorteren, waar hij ook gaat, zo nerveus dat ze geen nacht meer rustig kunnen slapen.'

'Hoor eens, meneer de Engelsman, ik weet dat u het goed bedoelt, maar u bent met dit soort zaken bekend. Ik niet. De Irakezen zijn een wreed en primitief volk. We kennen hen uit de geschiedenis. Als wij doen wat u zegt, zullen er wraakacties volgen.'

'Het is net als bij een verkrachting, meneer Al-Khalifa.'

'Een verkrachting?'

'Als een vrouw op het punt staat te worden verkracht, kan ze zich verzetten

108

of toegeven. Als ze niets doet, wordt ze verkracht, waarschijnlijk geslagen en misschien gedood. Als ze zich verzet, wordt ze verkracht, zeker geslagen en misschien gedood.'

'Koeweit is de vrouw, Irak de verkrachter. Dat wist ik al. Dus waarom zouden we ons verzetten?'

'Omdat er een nieuwe morgen komt. Morgen zal Koeweit in de spiegel kijken. En dan zal uw zoon het gezicht van een strijder zien.'

Ahmed Al-Khalifa keek de donkere, baardige Engelsman lange tijd aan en zei toen: 'Zijn vader ook. Allah zij mijn volk genadig. Wat wilt u van me? Geld?'

'Dank u, nee. Ik heb geld.'

Hij had tienduizend Koeweitse dinars, afkomstig van de ambassadeur in Londen, die het geld had opgenomen bij de Bank van Koeweit op de hoek van Baker Street en George Street.

'Ik heb huizen nodig om me te verschuilen. Zes in totaal...'

'Geen probleem. Duizenden appartementen zijn verlaten.'

'Geen appartementen, maar vrijstaande villa's. Appartementen hebben buren. Niemand zal belangstelling hebben voor een arme man die is ingehuurd om een leegstaande villa te bewaken.'

'Ik zal ze voor u vinden.'

'En identiteitspapieren. Echte Koeweitse papieren. Drie series. Een voor een Koeweitse dokter, een voor een Indiase accountant en een voor een tuinder van buiten de stad.'

'Goed. Ik heb vrienden bij het ministerie van Binnenlandse Zaken. Ik geloof dat ze nog steeds de persen in handen hebben waarop de pasjes worden gedrukt. En de foto's?'

'Voor de tuinder neemt u een oude man op straat. Betaal hem ervoor. Voor de dokter en de accountant kiest u twee mannen uit uw personeel die op mij lijken, maar zonder baard. Die foto's zijn toch heel slecht.

En dan de auto's. Ik heb er drie nodig. Een witte stationcar, een 4WD jeep en een oude, aftandse pick-up truck. Alledrie in afgesloten garages, alledrie met nieuwe nummerborden.'

'Goed, ik zal het regelen. En waar kan ik de pasjes en de sleutels van de garages en de huizen afleveren?'

'Weet u de christelijke begraafplaats?'

Al-Khalifa fronste. 'Ik heb ervan gehoord, maar ik ben er nog nooit geweest. Hoezo?'

'Hij ligt aan de Jahra Road in Sulajbikhat, vlak bij de grote islamitische begraafplaats. Er is een onopvallend hek met een klein bordje: "Voor christenen". De meeste grafstenen zijn van Libanezen en Syriërs, met een paar Filippino's en Chinezen. In de verste rechterhoek ligt een graf van een koopvaardijmatroos, Shepton. De marmeren plaat ligt los. Daaronder heb ik een kuil gegraven in het grind. Laat de pasjes en de sleutels daar achter. Als u een boodschap voor me hebt, kunt u die daar ook kwijt. En controleer het graf eens in de week om te zien of ik een bericht voor u heb achtergelaten.'

Al-Khalifa schudde verbijsterd zijn hoofd. 'Ik ben niet geschikt voor dit soort werk.'

Mike Martin verdween tussen de mensenmassa in de smalle straatjes en stegen van de wijk Bneid-al-Qar. Vijf dagen later vond hij onder de grafplaat van matroos Shepton drie pasjes, drie sets autosleuteltjes, drie garagesleutels en zes huissleutels met adressen.

Twee dagen later werd een Iraakse truck die vanaf het olieveld Umm Gudayr naar de stad terugkwam, opgeblazen door een mijn.

Chip Barber, het hoofd van de sectie Midden-Oosten van de CIA, was twee dagen in Tel Aviv toen de telefoon ging in het kantoortje dat hij op de ambassade had gekregen. Het was de chef van het CIA-bureau.

'Alles in orde, Chip. Hij is terug in de stad. Ik heb een afspraak geregeld voor vier uur. Dan kun je het laatste vliegtuig vanaf Ben Goerion naar huis nog halen. De jongens sturen een auto naar kantoor.'

De CIA-chef belde van buiten de ambassade en hield het gesprek algemeen, voor het geval de telefoon werd afgeluisterd. Dat gebeurde ook, maar door de Israëli's, die al op de hoogte waren.

De 'hij' was generaal Yaakov 'Kobi' Dror, het hoofd van de Mossad. Het kantoor was de ambassade zelf en de jongens waren twee mannen van Drors persoonlijke staf, die om tien over drie in een anonieme auto kwamen voorrijden.

Barber vond vijftig minuten wel erg veel tijd om van de ambassade naar het hoofdkwartier van de Mossad in het Hadar Dafna Gebouw – een torenflat aan de King Saul Boulevard – te rijden. Maar blijkbaar zou de ontmoeting ergens anders plaatsvinden. De auto reed snel naar het noorden, de stad uit, langs de vliegbasis Sde Dov, totdat ze op de kustweg naar Haifa kwamen.

Even buiten Herzlia ligt een groot hotel- en appartementencomplex met de eenvoudige naam The Country Club. Hier komen Israëli's, maar voornamelijk oudere joden uit het buitenland, genieten van de talloze kuur- en fitnessfaciliteiten. De gasten kijken maar zelden omhoog naar de heuvel boven het complex.

Als ze dat deden, zouden ze op de top van die heuvel een mooi gebouw zien staan, met een prachtig uitzicht op de omgeving en de zee. En als ze zouden vragen wat het was, zouden ze te horen krijgen dat de minister-president hier zijn zomerresidentie had.

De Israëlische premier mag er inderdaad komen, als een van de weinigen, maar in werkelijkheid is het de opleidingsschool van de Mossad, binnen de dienst beter bekend als de Midrasha.

Yaakov Dror ontving de twee Amerikanen in zijn kantoor op de bovenverdieping, een lichte, ruime kamer waar de airco op volle kracht werkte. Dror, een kleine, schonkige man, droeg het gebruikelijke Israëlische uniform – een overhemd met korte mouwen en een open kraag – en hij rookte de gebruikelijke zestig sigaretten per dag.

Barber was dankbaar voor de airconditioning. Van sigaretterook kreeg hij een loopneus.

Het hoofd van de Israëlische geheime dienst stond op van achter zijn bureau en kwam met dreunende passen naar hen toe.

'Chip, beste vriend, hoe gaat het?' Hij omhelsde de langste van de twee Amerikanen. Hij vond het leuk de rol van de vriendelijke, joviale beer te spelen, als een slechte joodse acteur. Maar meer dan een rol was het niet. In zijn tijd als actief agent of *katsa* had hij bewezen hoe sluw en gevaarlijk hij kon zijn.

Chris Barber begroette hem met een geforceerde grijns. Het was nog niet zó lang geleden dat een Amerikaans gerechtshof Jonathan Pollard van de marine-inlichtingendienst tot een lange gevangenisstraf had veroordeeld wegens spionage voor Israël, een operatie die ongetwijfeld was geleid door de joviale Kobi Dror.

Na tien minuten kwamen ze ter zake. Irak.

'Ik moet zeggen, Chip, dat jullie het handig spelen,' zei Dror, terwijl hij zijn gast een kop koffie inschonk die hem dagenlang uit zijn slaap zou houden. Hij drukte zijn derde sigaret uit in een grote glazen asbak. Barber probeerde niet te ademen, maar dat hield hij niet lang vol.

'Als het oorlog wordt,' zei Barber, 'als hij niet vrijwillig uit Koeweit vertrekt, beginnen we met luchtaanvallen.'

'Natuurlijk.'

'En ons eerste doelwit zijn hun massavernietigingswapens. Dat is ook in jullie belang, Kobi. Op dat punt moeten we samenwerken.'

'Chip, we houden die wapens al jaren in de gaten. Verdomme, we hebben er zelfs tegen gewaarschuwd. Voor wie denk je dat al dat gifgas en die bacteriologische bommen bestemd zijn? Voor ons! Maar niemand wilde luisteren. Toen we negen jaar geleden zijn kernreactoren bij Osirak vernietigden, waardoor zijn programma voor de ontwikkeling van een atoombom tien jaar werd teruggedraaid, kregen we de hele wereld over ons heen, met Amerika voorop...'

'Dat was voor de schijn. Dat weet je best.'

'Goed, Chip. Maar nu er Amerikaanse levens op het spel staan, is het niet langer voor de schijn. Stel je voor dat er Amerikanen zouden sneuvelen! Echte mensen!'

'Niet zo paranoïde, Kobi.'

'Klets niet. Luister, als jullie zijn gifgasfabrieken, zijn bacteriologische laboratoria en zijn nucleaire installaties willen vernietigen, mij best. We mogen ons er niet eens mee bemoeien omdat Uncle Sam nu Arabische bondgenoten heeft. Mij hoor je niet klagen. We hebben jullie alles verteld wat we weten over zijn geheime wapenprogramma's. We hebben niets achtergehouden.'

'Maar we weten nog niet genoeg, Kobi. Goed, we hebben Irak de laatste jaren wat verwaarloosd. We hadden het druk met de koude oorlog. Maar nu gaat het wel om Irak, en we hebben harde feiten nodig. Dus vraag ik je op de man af: hebben jullie bronnen binnen de Iraakse regering? Op het hoogste niveau? We hebben dringende vragen waarop we een antwoord willen. En dat hoeft niet voor niets. We kennen de regels.'

Het bleef een tijdje stil. Kobi Dror bestudeerde het puntje van zijn sigaret. De twee CIA-officieren staarden naar de tafel voor hen.

'Chip,' zei Dror langzaam, 'ik geef je mijn woord. Als wij een agent hadden binnen de regering in Bagdad zou ik het je zeggen. Dan mochten jullie hem gebruiken. Maar ik heb niemand. Je moet me geloven.'

Later zou generaal Dror tegenover zijn premier, een bijzonder nijdige Itzhak Shamir, verklaren dat hij strikt gesproken niet gelogen had. Maar hij had zijn mond gehouden over Jericho.

112

Mike Martin zag de jongen nog net op tijd, anders zou het joch zijn overmoedige daad niet hebben overleefd. Martin reed in zijn aftandse, vuile en roestige pick-up truck, geladen met watermeloenen die hij bij een van de tuinderijen buiten Jahra had gekocht, toen hij het in wit linnen gewikkelde hoofd zag opduiken achter een berg puin langs de weg. Hij ving ook een glimp op van een geweer, dat meteen weer achter het puin verdween.

De truck bewees goede diensten. Martin had bewust om een oud kreng gevraagd, omdat hij terecht veronderstelde dat de Irakezen vroeg of laat – eerder vroeg dan laat – alle goede auto's voor eigen gebruik zouden inpikken.

Hij keek in zijn spiegeltje, remde en draaide de berm in. Achter hem reed een vrachtwagen met soldaten van het Volksleger.

De Koeweitse jongen richtte zijn geweer op de truck en probeerde de wagen in zijn vizier te houden toen er opeens een hand tegen zijn mond werd gedrukt en een andere hand zijn geweer wegrukte.

'Je wilt toch niet dood?' gromde een stem in zijn oor. De legertruck denderde langs hen heen en het moment voor een schot was voorbij. De jongen was al nerveus genoeg geweest. Nu was hij doodsbang.

Toen de truck was verdwenen, liet de man hem los. De jongen liet zich op zijn rug vallen. Een lange, baardige, grimmige bedoeïen stond over hem heen gebogen.

'Wie bent u?' vroeg hij.

'Iemand die weet dat je geen Iraakse soldaat moet doodschieten als er nog twintig anderen in dezelfde wagen zitten. Hoe had je willen vluchten?'

De jongen, die een jaar of twintig was en probeerde een baard te laten staan, knikte naar een scooter die twintig meter verderop bij een paar bomen op zijn standaard stond. De bedoeïen zuchtte. Hij legde het geweer neer – een oude Lee Enfield .303 die de jongen bij een antiekzaak moest hebben gekocht – en trok de Koeweiti mee naar zijn pick-up truck.

Hij reed achteruit naar de berg puin, legde het geweer onder de watermeloenen, haalde de scooter en gooide die op het fruit. Een paar meloenen barstten.

'Instappen,' zei hij.

Ze reden naar een rustige plek bij Shuwaikh Port en stopten.

'Waar was je mee bezig?' vroeg de bedoeïen.

De jongen staarde door de met dode vliegen bevlekte voorruit. Zijn ogen waren vochtig en zijn lip trilde.

'Ze hebben mijn zuster verkracht. Ze is verpleegster... in het Al-Adan Ziekenhuis. Ze waren met z'n vieren. Ze hebben haar leven verwoest.'

De bedoeïen knikte.

'Dat zal wel meer voorkomen,' zei hij. 'En nu wilde je een paar Irakezen vermoorden?'

'Ja. Zoveel als ik kan. Voordat ik zelf moet sterven.'

'Je kunt beter blijven leven. Als je dat wilt, tenminste. Ik zal je wel trainen. Anders red je het nog geen dag.'

De jongen snoof. 'Bedoeïenen vechten niet.'

'Ooit gehoord van het Arabische Legioen?' De jongen zweeg. 'Of van prins Faisal en de Arabische Revolutie? Dat waren allemaal bedoeïenen. Heb je nog kameraden net als jij?'

De jongen bleek een student te zijn. Vóór de invasie had hij rechten gestudeerd aan de universiteit van Koeweit.

'We zijn met ons vijven. We willen allemaal hetzelfde. Ik was de eerste die het zou proberen.'

'Onthoud dit adres,' zei de bedoeïen. Hij noemde het nummer van een villa in een achterafstraat in Yarmuk. De jongen herhaalde het twee keer verkeerd, en toen goed. Martin liet het hem twintig keer herhalen.

'Vanavond om zeven uur. Dan is het donker. Maar de avondklok gaat pas om tien uur in. Jullie komen allemaal afzonderlijk. Parkeer op minstens tweehonderd meter afstand en loop het laatste stuk. Kom twee minuten na elkaar. Het hek en de deur staan open.'

Zuchtend keek hij de jongen na toen die wegreed op zijn scooter. Ruw materiaal, maar voorlopig had hij niets anders.

De studenten arriveerden op tijd. Martin lag op een plat dak aan de overkant van de straat en hield hen in de gaten. Ze waren zenuwachtig en onzeker, keken voortdurend over hun schouder en doken regelmatig een portiek in. Te veel Bogart-films gezien. Toen ze allemaal binnen waren, wachtte hij nog tien minuten, maar hij zag geen Iraakse veiligheidsagenten opduiken. Ten slotte liet hij zich van het dak glijden, stak de straat over en stapte door de achterdeur het huis binnen. De jongelui zaten in de huiskamer met de lichten aan en de gordijnen open. Vier jongens en een meisje, donker en heel gespannen.

Ze keken naar de gangdeur op het moment dat hij uit de keuken binnenkwam. Het ene moment was hij nog nergens te zien, het volgende moment was hij er opeens. Ze vingen niet meer dan een glimp van hem op voordat hij zijn arm uitstak en het licht uitdeed.

'Trek de gordijnen dicht,' zei hij zacht. Het meisje deed het. Vrouwenwerk.

Toen pas deed hij het licht weer aan.

'Ga nooit in een verlichte kamer zitten met de gordijnen open,' zei hij. 'Jullie mogen niet samen gezien worden.'

Hij had zijn zes villa's in twee groepen verdeeld. In vier ervan woonde hij. Hij wisselde op onregelmatige tijden, en overal liet hij kleine aanwijzingen achter – een blaadje tegen een deurpost, een blikje op de trap. Als die waren verdwenen, wist hij dat er bezoek was geweest. In elk van de andere twee huizen had hij de helft van zijn spullen opgeslagen, nadat hij ze uit de woestijn had opgegraven. Het huis waar hij de studenten ontving was de minst belangrijke van zijn villa's. Hij zou er nu nooit meer kunnen slapen.

Ze studeerden allemaal, behalve één jongen die op een bank werkte. Hij vroeg naar hun namen.

'Vanaf dit moment krijgen jullie nieuwe namen.' Hij noemde er vijf. 'Die vertel je aan niemand anders, niet aan je vrienden, je ouders, je broers, aan *niemand*. Als die namen worden gebruikt, weet je dat de boodschap van een van ons afkomstig is.'

'Hoe noemen we u?' vroeg het meisje dat nu 'Rana' heette.

'De Bedoeïen,' zei hij. 'Dat is voldoende. Jij daar, wat is dit adres ook alweer?'

De jongen die hij aanwees dacht na en haalde toen een papiertje uit zijn zak. Martin nam het weg.

'Geen papier. Je moet alles onthouden. Het Volksleger is misschien niet zo slim, maar de Geheime Politie wel. Als je was gefouilleerd, hoe had je dit dan willen verklaren?'

Hij wachtte tot de drie jongelui die het adres hadden genoteerd hun papiertjes hadden verbrand.

'Hoe goed kennen jullie de stad?'

'Vrij goed,' zei de oudste van het stel, de 25-jarige bankbediende.

'Niet goed genoeg. Koop morgen een plattegrond en bestudeer die alsof je voor een tentamen zit. Leer alle straten en stegen, alle pleinen en parken, alle lanen en boulevards, alle belangrijke openbare gebouwen, alle moskeeën en binnenplaatsen uit je hoofd. Jullie weten dat de straatnaambordjes worden weggehaald?'

Ze knikten. Binnen vijftien dagen na de invasie waren de Koeweiti's, bekomen van de eerste schrik, begonnen met tekenen van passief verzet en burgerlijke ongehoorzaamheid. Het was nog een spontane, ongecoördineerde beweging. Een van de onderdelen was het verwijderen van de straatnaamborden. Koeweit is al een ingewikkelde stad; zonder borden is er helemaal geen wijs uit te worden.

De Iraakse patrouilles verdwaalden voortdurend. Voor de Geheime Politie was het een nachtmerrie om het adres van een verdachte te vinden. 's Nachts

115

werden de borden op de belangrijkste kruispunten weggehaald of een andere kant op gedraaid.

Die eerste avond gaf hij hun twee uur les in de voornaamste veiligheidsregels. Bedenk altijd een sluitend verhaal om je aanwezigheid te verklaren. Neem nooit belastende papieren mee. Behandel de Iraakse soldaten altijd met respect, zo nodig met ontzag. Vertrouw niemand.

'Van nu af aan hebben jullie twee verschillende persoonlijkheden. De ene – die van de student of de bankbediende – kent iedereen. Dat is een beleefde, oppassende, gezagsgetrouwe, onschuldige, ongevaarlijke figuur. De Irakezen laten hem met rust omdat hij geen bedreiging vormt. Hij zal nooit hun land, hun vlag of hun leider beledigen. Hij vestigt nooit de aandacht van de AMAM op zich. Hij blijft vrij en ongedeerd. Alleen bij speciale gelegenheden, tijdens een missie, komt de andere persoonlijkheid naar boven. Die is handig en gevaarlijk en weet hoe hij in leven moet blijven.'

Hij onderwees hen over veiligheid, over de procedure bij een geheime afspraak: vroeg komen, niet in de buurt parkeren, in de schaduw blijven, twintig minuten wachten, de omringende huizen in het oog houden, bedacht zijn op een hinderlaag, op het geschuifel van soldatenschoenen op het grind, op het gloeiende puntje van een sigaret, op het rinkelen van metaal tegen metaal. Ruim op tijd voor de avondklok stuurde hij hen weg. Ze waren teleurgesteld.

'Maar de bezetters dan? Wanneer gaan we ze vermoorden?'

'Als jullie weten hoe het moet.'

'Kunnen we dan niets doen?'

'Hoe verplaatsen de Irakezen zich? Lopend?'

'Nee, met vrachtwagens, busjes, jeeps, gestolen auto's,' zei de rechtenstudent.

'En die hebben benzinedoppen,' zei de bedoeïen, 'die je snel kunt losdraaien. Suikerklontjes, twintig per tank. De suiker lost op in de benzine, stroomt door de carburateur en klontert tot harde caramel door de hitte van de motor. Dat is het einde van het motorblok. Zorg dat je niet gepakt wordt. Werk in paren, na het donker. De één houdt de wacht, de ander doet de suiker in de tank. Draai de dop er weer op. In tien seconden is het gebeurd.

Zaag stukjes triplex van tien bij tien centimeter en sla er vier scherpe stalen spijkers doorheen. Laat ze onder je *thob* op de grond vallen en schuif ze met je voet onder een van de voorwielen van een geparkeerde wagen.

Er zijn ratten in Koeweit, dus wordt er ook rattenkruit verkocht. Neem de witte soort, op basis van strychnine. Koop dan wat deeg bij een bakker. Meng het gif door het deeg. Draag rubber handschoenen, die je daarna vernietigt. Bak het brood in het fornuis in de keuken, als er niemand thuis is.'

De studenten staarden hem met open mond aan.

'Moeten we dat aan de Irakezen geven?'
'Nee. Je rijdt ermee rond, in open mandjes op je scooter of in de achterbak van je auto. De Irakezen stelen het als ze je bij een wegversperring aanhouden. Over zes dagen komen we hier weer bijeen.'

Vier dagen later kregen steeds meer Iraakse trucks met pech te kampen. Sommige werden weggesleept, andere achtergelaten – zes vrachtwagens en vier jeeps. De monteurs ontdekten waarom, maar ze wisten niet wanneer het was gebeurd of wie de daders waren. Andere wagens kregen lekke banden. De chauffeurs gaven de stukjes triplex aan de veiligheidstroepen, die woedend werden en een paar Koeweiti's in elkaar sloegen die ze van de straat hadden opgepikt.

In de ziekenhuizen werden soldaten binnengebracht die last hadden van misselijkheid en maagpijn. Omdat ze maar zelden eten kregen van hun eigen leger, waren ze gedwongen hun kostje bij elkaar te scharrelen in de buurt van hun wegversperringen en stenen hutjes. De artsen vermoedden dat ze vervuild water hadden gedronken.

Maar een Koeweitse laborant van het Amiri Ziekenhuis in Dasman besloot het braaksel van een van de Irakezen te onderzoeken. Verbijsterd meldde hij de uitslag aan zijn afdelingshoofd.

'Er zit rattenkruit in, professor. Maar de man beweert dat hij al drie dagen niets anders heeft gegeten dan brood en fruit.'

De professor begreep er niets van. 'Brood van het Iraakse leger?'

'Nee, die hebben al in geen dagen een rantsoen gestuurd. Hij heeft het brood gestolen van een Koeweitse bakkersknecht die voorbijkwam.'

'Waar heb je je monsters?'

'In het lab, op de tafel. Ik vond dat ik het u meteen moest vertellen.'

'Daar heb je gelijk in. Heel goed. Vernietig ze maar. Je hebt niets gezien en gehoord, begrepen?'

De professor liep hoofdschuddend terug naar zijn kantoor. Rattenkruit! Wie had dat nu weer bedacht?

Het Medusa Comité kwam weer bijeen op 30 augustus. De bacterioloog van Porton Down had alle beschikbare gegevens over de Iraakse bacteriologische wapens doorgewerkt.

'Ik vrees dat we niet veel verder komen,' verklaarde dr. Bryant. 'Het probleem is dat bacteriologische experimenten in ieder forensisch of veterinair laboratorium kunnen worden uitgevoerd met apparatuur die je in elk scheikundig lab aantreft en die je niet eens op de exportvergunningen terugvindt. Het grootste deel van dit soort onderzoek is heel nuttig – voor de bestrijding van ziekten, niet voor het verspreiden ervan. Het is dus heel normaal dat een ontwikkelingsland onderzoek wil doen naar bilharzia, beri-beri, gele koorts,

117

malaria, cholera, tyfus of hepatitis. En dan zijn er nog allerlei veterinaire ziekten die worden bestudeerd.'

'Dus eigenlijk is het onmogelijk vast te stellen of Irak nu wel of niet over een fabriek voor bacteriologische wapens beschikt?' vroeg Sinclair van de CIA.

'Ja,' antwoordde Bryant. 'Ik heb een document gevonden waaruit blijkt dat Irak in 1974, toen Saddam Hoessein nog niet op de troon zat, om het zo maar te zeggen...'

'Hij was toen vice-president, en de werkelijke macht achter de troon,' onderbrak Terry Martin hem.

Bryant was even van zijn stuk gebracht. 'Hoe dan ook... toen hebben de Irakezen een contract gesloten met het Institut Merieux in Parijs om een bacteriologisch laboratorium voor hen te bouwen. Officieel ging het om veterinair onderzoek naar ziekten bij dieren, en misschien was dat ook wel zo.'

'En die verhalen over miltvuurculturen die tegen mensen kunnen worden gebruikt?' vroeg de Amerikaan.

'Dat is niet onmogelijk. Miltvuur is een zeer gevaarlijke ziekte. Het treft vooral vee en andere dieren, maar ook mensen kunnen het slachtoffer worden als ze met besmette produkten omgaan of die eten. U weet misschien wel dat de Britse regering in de Tweede Wereldoorlog met miltvuur heeft geëxperimenteerd op het eiland Grinard in de Hebriden. Dat is nog steeds verboden gebied.'

'Is het zo gevaarlijk? En waar zou hij dat spul vandaan moeten krijgen?'

'Dat is het probleem, meneer Sinclair. Je kunt moeilijk naar een fatsoenlijk Europees of Amerikaans laboratorium stappen en vragen of ze een paar miltvuurculturen voor je hebben om tegen mensen te gebruiken. Maar dat is ook niet nodig. Overal in de derde wereld heb je vee dat met de ziekte is besmet. Zo gauw je over een epidemie hoort, koop je gewoon een paar kadavers op. En die vind je natuurlijk op geen enkele exportvergunning terug.'

'Dus misschien beschikt hij over die culturen om ze in bommen of granaten te verwerken, zonder dat wij het weten. Is dat juist?' vroeg Sir Paul Spruce, met zijn gouden pen in de aanslag boven zijn schrijfblok.

'Daar komt het wel op neer,' antwoordde Bryant. 'Maar er is ook goed nieuws. Ik betwijfel of het effectief zou zijn tegen een oprukkend leger. Stel dat hij inderdaad meedogenloos genoeg is om op die manier de vijand te willen tegenhouden...'

'Ga daar maar vanuit,' zei Sinclair.

'Dan heb je niet veel aan miltvuur. Als je de culturen met behulp van granaten op de vijand afvuurt, dringen de bacteriën in de grond. Alles wat daar groeit – gras, fruit, groenten – raakt dan besmet en alle beesten die ervan eten worden ziek. Wie het vlees van die dieren eet of hun huiden bewerkt, raakt ook besmet. Maar de woestijn is geen gunstige omgeving voor dit soort sporenculturen. Ik neem aan dat onze soldaten voorverpakte maaltijden en flessenwater krijgen?'

'Ja. Dat krijgen ze nu al,' zei Sinclair.

'Dan heeft het miltvuur niet veel effect, tenzij ze de sporen inademen. De ziekte slaat alleen toe via de longen of de spijsvertering. En gezien het risico van gifgas zullen ze wel gasmaskers dragen.'

'Dat is wel de bedoeling.'

'Onze mensen ook,' voegde Sir Paul eraan toe.

'Dan lijkt miltvuur me geen logische keuze,' zei Bryant. 'Het zal de soldaten niet tegenhouden, zoals gifgas, en mensen die toch besmet raken kunnen met antibiotica worden genezen. Bovendien is er een lange incubatietijd. De troepen zouden de oorlog allang gewonnen kunnen hebben voordat ze ziek worden. Het is meer een wapen voor terroristen dan voor militair gebruik. Als je de watervoorziening van een stad met miltvuur besmet, kun je een epidemie veroorzaken waar de medische voorzieningen niet tegen opgewassen zijn. Maar om een militaire opmars in een woestijn te stuiten, zou ik eerder zenuwgas gebruiken. Dat is onzichtbaar en het werkt snel.'

'Er zijn dus geen aanwijzingen dat Saddam over een laboratorium voor bacteriologische oorlogvoering zou beschikken?' vroeg Sir Paul.

'Ik zou alle veterinaire instituten in het Westen benaderen om te vragen of ze de afgelopen tien jaar mensen naar Irak hebben gestuurd en of die daar laboratoria hebben gezien die voor iedereen verboden waren en met strenge veiligheidsmaatregelen werden omgeven. Dat is de meest voor de hand liggende mogelijkheid,' zei Bryant.

Sinclair en Paxman maakten druk aantekeningen. Weer een nieuwe opdracht voor hun agenten.

'Als dat niets oplevert,' vervolgde Bryant, 'zou je op zoek moeten gaan naar een Iraakse wetenschapper op dit terrein die zijn land verlaten heeft en zich in het Westen heeft gevestigd. Bacteriologen vormen maar een kleine gemeenschap, een soort dorp. Meestal weten we van elkaar waar we mee bezig zijn, zelfs in dictaturen als Irak. Zo'n man weet misschien of Saddam een verdacht laboratorium heeft – en waar.'

'We zijn u zeer erkentelijk, doctor Bryant,' zei Sir Paul toen ze opstonden. 'Onze speurders weten weer wat hun te doen staat, nietwaar, meneer Sinclair? Ik heb gehoord dat onze andere collega van Porton Down, doctor Reinhart, over twee weken wat meer kan zeggen over de kwestie van het gifgas. We houden contact, heren. Dank u voor uw komst.'

Het groepje lag doodstil in de woestijn terwijl het eerste ochtendlicht over de zandduinen kroop. Toen ze de vorige avond naar het huis van de bedoeïen waren gekomen hadden de jongelui niet geweten dat er een nachtelijke actie op het programma stond. Ze hadden verwacht dat ze weer les zouden krijgen.

Ze hadden geen warme kleren bij zich, en de woestijnnacht kan bitter koud zijn, zelfs tegen het einde van augustus. Huiverend vroegen ze zich af hoe ze dit aan hun ongeruste ouders moesten uitleggen. Overvallen door de avondklok? Waarom hadden ze dan niet opgebeld? Omdat de telefoon niet werkte... of zoiets.

Drie van de vijf vroegen zich af of ze wel de juiste beslissing hadden genomen, maar het was nu te laat om nog terug te krabbelen. De bedoeïen had gezegd dat het tijd werd voor enige actie en had hen meegenomen naar een zware jeep die twee straten verderop stond geparkeerd. Nog voor het ingaan van de avondklok reden ze door de harde, vlakke woestijn. Daarna hadden ze niemand meer gezien.

Ze waren dertig kilometer over het zand naar het zuiden gereden, tot ze bij een smalle weg kwamen die van het Manageesh-olieveld in het westen naar de Outer Motorway in het oosten liep. Alle olievelden en doorgaande wegen werden bewaakt door de Irakezen. Ergens naar het zuiden hadden zestien divisies van het Iraakse leger en de Republikeinse Garde zich ingegraven, langs de grens met Saoedi-Arabië, waar steeds meer Amerikaanse troepen arriveerden. De jongelui waren zenuwachtig.

Drie leden van het groepje lagen in het zand naast de bedoeïen en tuurden in de ochtendschemering naar de weg voor hen. Het was nauwelijks meer dan een pad. Als twee auto's elkaar tegenkwamen, moesten ze de berm in om elkaar te kunnen passeren.

Over de helft van de weg lag een plank met spijkers. De bedoeïen had hem uit zijn jeep gehaald en hem over de weg gelegd met een paar jutezakken erop. Daarna hadden ze er zand overheen geschept, totdat het een heuveltje leek dat door de wind de weg op was gewaaid.

De andere twee, de bankbediende en de rechtenstudent, lagen op de uitkijk op twee zandduinen aan weerskanten van hun positie, om te waarschuwen wanneer er een auto aankwam. Als het een grote Iraakse truck was, of meer dan één, moesten ze op een bepaalde manier wuiven.

Een paar minuten over zes stak de rechtenstudent zijn arm op. Zijn signaal betekende: 'Te veel trucks.' De bedoeïen trok aan het vissnoer dat hij in zijn hand hield en de plank gleed van de weg af. Dertig seconden later reden twee vrachtwagens vol met Iraakse soldaten ongehinderd voorbij. De bedoeïen rende de weg op en legde de plank, de jutezakken en het zand weer terug.

Tien minuten later wuifde de bankbediende. Het goede signaal. Uit de richting van de snelweg naderde een dienstauto, op weg naar het olieveld.

De chauffeur vond het niet nodig om het heuveltje te ontwijken. Met één voorwiel raakte hij de spijkers, maar dat was genoeg. De band klapte, de jutezakken wikkelden zich om het wiel en de auto begon gevaarlijk te slingeren. De bestuurder herstelde zich op tijd en bracht de wagen half in de berm tot stilstand. De auto helde over naar de kant waar de lekke band zat.

De bestuurder sprong uit de wagen, gevolgd door twee officieren, een majoor en een luitenant. Ze schreeuwden iets naar de chauffeur, die zijn schouders ophaalde en mopperend naar het wiel wees. Daar kregen ze nooit een krik onder; de auto stond veel te schuin.

'Blijf hier,' mompelde de bedoeïen tegen zijn verbaasde leerlingen. Hij kwam overeind en daalde het duin af naar de weg. Over zijn rechterschouder droeg hij een kamelendeken die zijn rechterarm bedekte.

'*Salaam aleikhem, sajidi* majoor!' riep hij met een brede grijns. 'Ik zie dat u problemen hebt. Misschien kan ik u helpen. Mijn mensen zijn in de buurt.'

De majoor greep naar zijn pistool, maar haalde toen opgelucht adem. Hij wierp de man een vorsende blik toe en knikte.

'*Aleikhem salaam*, bedoeïen. Dit kamelejong heeft mijn wagen van de weg af gereden.'

'Ik zal hem weer de weg op trekken, majoor. Ik heb vele broeders.'

Martin was de Irakezen tot op tweeënhalve meter genaderd toen hij zijn arm omhoog bracht. Hij had de SIS om een Heckler & Koch MP5 machinepistool of een Mini-Uzi gevraagd. Het laatste type was Israëlisch en kon dus in Saoedi-Arabië niet worden gebruikt. En er waren ook geen H&K's beschikbaar. Daarom had hij genoegen genomen met de Kalasjnikov AK-47, de MS-versie met de inklapbare lade. Dit model was afkomstig van de Tsjechische fabriek Omnipol. Hij had de kolf erafgehaald en de neuzen van de 7.62 munitie stomp gevijld, zodat de kogels niet zouden uittreden.

Hij vuurde volgens de SAS-methode – twee kogels, pauze, twee kogels, pauze... De majoor werd vanaf tweeënhalve meter in het hart getroffen. Martin bewoog de AK iets naar rechts en raakte de luitenant in het borstbeen, waardoor hij tegen de chauffeur aan viel, die zich juist oprichtte bij de aan flarden gescheurde voorband. Op hetzelfde moment kreeg hij het derde paar kogels in zijn borst.

Het geluid van de schoten weergalmde tussen de zandheuvels, maar de woestijn en de weg waren verlaten. Martin wenkte de drie doodsbange studenten. Ze kwamen uit hun schuilplaats tevoorschijn.

'Leg de lichamen weer in de auto, de chauffeur achter het stuur en de officieren achterin,' zei hij tegen de twee jongens. Het meisje gaf hij een korte schroevedraaier, waarvan het blad tot een scherpe punt was gevijld.

'Steek drie gaten in de benzinetank.'

Hij keek naar zijn uitkijkposten, die gebaarden dat er nog steeds niemand naderde. Hij gaf het meisje opdracht haar zakdoek om een steen te binden en in de benzine te drenken. Toen de drie lijken in de auto lagen, stak hij de natte zakdoek aan en wierp de steen in de plas benzine die uit de tank was gelekt.

'Rennen!'

Ze hadden geen extra aansporing nodig. Zo hard als ze konden renden ze door het zand naar de jeep, die een eind verderop stond geparkeerd. Alleen Martin dacht eraan de plank mee te nemen. Toen hij zich omdraaide, vatte de benzinetank vlam en explodeerde. De auto verdween in een bol van vuur.

Zwijgend en onder de indruk reden ze terug naar Koeweit Stad. Twee van de vijf jongelui zaten naast de bedoeïen, de andere drie achterin.

'Hebben jullie goed gekeken?' vroeg Martin ten slotte.

'Ja, Bedoeïen.'

'En wat vonden jullie ervan?'

'Het ging zo... snel,' zei het meisje Rana eindelijk.

'Ik vond het juist lang duren,' zei de bankbediende.

'Het was snel en hard,' verklaarde Martin. 'Hoe lang denken jullie dat we op de weg hebben gestaan?'

'Een half uur?'

'Zes minuten. Waren jullie geschokt?'

'Ja, Bedoeïen.'

'Goed. Alleen psychopaten zijn niet geschokt als ze dit voor het eerst meemaken. Er was eens een Amerikaanse generaal, Patton. Ooit van gehoord?'

'Nee, Bedoeïen.'

'Hij zei dat het niet zijn taak was om zijn soldaten voor hun land te laten sneuvelen, maar om die andere klootzakken voor hùn land te laten sterven. Duidelijk?'

De filosofie van George Patton was niet eenvoudig in het Arabisch te vertalen, maar Martins leerlingen begrepen het.

'Als je oorlog voert, kun je je niet voortdurend verbergen. Op een gegeven moment moet je een keuze doen. Dan is het jij of hij. Die keus moeten jullie nu maken. Jullie kunnen weer gaan studeren, of de strijd aanbinden met de bezetters.'

Ze dachten een paar minuten na. Het was Rana die het eerst iets zei. 'Ik ga door, als u me wilt helpen, Bedoeïen.'

Daarna moesten de jongens wel volgen.

'Goed. Eerst zal ik jullie leren hoe je aanslagen moet plegen zonder zelf te worden gedood. Kom over twee dagen naar mijn huis, vroeg in de ochtend, als de avondklok is opgeheven. Neem studieboeken mee. Jij ook, meneer de bankier. Als jullie worden aangehouden, gedraag je dan heel normaal, alsof je op weg bent naar college. Dat is ook zo, maar een heel ander college. Ik zet jullie hier af, dan kunnen jullie naar de stad liften. Ga met verschillende trucks mee.'

Ze reden weer over een geplaveide weg, vlak bij de vijfde ringweg. Martin wees naar een garage waar veel vrachtwagens stopten. Daar zouden ze wel een lift kunnen krijgen.

Toen ze waren uitgestapt, reed hij terug naar de woestijn, groef zijn radio op, reed vijf kilometer verder, vouwde de satellietschotel open en verzond via zijn Motorola een paar codeberichten naar het huis in Riyad.

Een uur na de hinderlaag werd de verbrande auto gevonden door de volgende patrouille. De lijken werden naar het dichtstbijzijnde ziekenhuis gebracht – Al-Adan, bij Fintas aan de kust.

De patholoog die sectie verrichtte onder de nijdige blikken van een kolonel van de Iraakse Geheime Politie, ontdekte de kogelgaten, niet meer dan kleine prikjes in het verkoolde vlees. Hij had zelf kinderen en hij kende de verpleegster die was verkracht.

Hij trok het laken over het derde lijk en stroopte zijn handschoenen af. 'Ik vrees dat ze door verstikking zijn omgekomen toen de auto vlam vatte na het ongeluk,' zei hij. 'Allah zij hen genadig.'

De kolonel bromde wat en vertrok.

Bij zijn derde ontmoeting met de jonge verzetsstrijders bracht de bedoeïen hen ver de woestijn in, naar een plek ten westen van Koeweit Stad en ten zuiden van Jahra, waar niemand hen kon bespieden. Alsof het een picknick was gingen de vijf jongelui rondom hun leraar in het zand zitten. De bedoeïen pakte een jutezak en stalde een reeks vreemde voorwerpen uit. Eén voor één wees hij ze aan.

'Dit zijn kneedexplosieven. Heel stabiel en gemakkelijk te verwerken.'

De studenten verbleekten toen hij het spul in zijn hand nam en kneedde alsof het boetseerklei was. Een van de jongens, de zoon van een sigarenwinkelier, had op Martins verzoek een paar oude sigarenkistjes meegebracht.

'Dit,' zei de bedoeïen, 'is een ontsteker met een timer. Als je deze vleugelmoer aan de bovenkant aandraait, verbrijzel je een ampul met zuur. Het zuur brandt door een koperplaatje heen. Dat duurt zestig seconden. Daarna worden de explosieven tot ontsteking gebracht door het kwikfulminaat. Kijk maar.'

Hij had hun onverdeelde aandacht. Hij nam een stukje Semtex ter grootte van een pakje sigaretten, legde het in een sigarenkistje en drukte de ontsteker erin.

'Nu hoef je alleen maar aan die vleugelmoer te draaien, het kistje te sluiten en er een elastiekje omheen te doen om het dicht te houden... zo. Dat doe je pas op het laatste moment.'

Hij legde het kistje in het zand, in het midden van de kring.

'Maar zestig seconden is heel wat langer dan je denkt. Tijd genoeg om naar een Iraakse truck of een bunker of een rupsvoertuig te lopen, het kistje naar binnen te gooien en ervandoor te gaan. Rustig lopen, nooit rennen. Dan val je op. Neem genoeg tijd om om de wagen heen te lopen. Begin niet te rennen, ook niet na de explosie.'

Met een half oog hield hij zijn horloge in de gaten. Nog dertig seconden.

'Bedoeïen...' zei de bankbediende.

'Ja?'

'Dat is toch geen echte?'

'Wat?'

'Die bom die u net hebt gemaakt. Die is toch niet echt?'

Vijfenveertig seconden. Hij boog zich naar voren en pakte het kistje.

'Jawel, het is een echte bom. Ik wilde jullie alleen laten zien hoe lang zestig seconden duurt. Je moet nooit in paniek raken met deze dingen. Dat wordt je dood. Blijf altijd rustig.'

Met een snelle polsbeweging gooide hij het kistje weg. Het kwam aan de andere kant van de heuvel terecht en explodeerde. De studenten zaten te trillen door de klap. Fijn zand daalde op hen neer.

Hoog boven het noordelijke deel van de Golf registreerde een Amerikaans AWACS-vliegtuig de explosie met een van zijn hittesensoren. De technicus meldde het aan zijn chef, die naar het scherm tuurde. De gloed van de explosie begon al af te nemen.

'Intensiteit?'

'Ter grootte van een tankgranaat, zou ik zeggen.'

'Goed, noteer het maar. Geen verdere actie.'

'Aan het eind van de dag kunnen jullie die dingen zelf maken. De ontstekers en timers verbergen jullie hierin,' zei de bedoeïen. Hij gaf ieder van hen een aluminium sigarenkoker, wikkelde een ontsteker in watten, stak hem in de koker en schroefde de dop erop.

'De kneedexplosieven vervoer je zo.' Hij haalde een zeepwikkel tevoorschijn, kneedde vier ons explosieven in de vorm van een stuk zeep, deed de wikkel eromheen en maakte die met plakband vast.

'De sigarenkistjes moet je zelf maar zoeken. Niet van die grote kisten voor Havanna's, maar een kleiner model. Houd altijd twee sigaren in het kistje voor het geval je wordt aangehouden en gefouilleerd. Als een Irakees de sigaar, het kistje of de zeep wil afpakken, laat hem dan.'

Hij liet hen oefenen in de zon, totdat ze binnen dertig seconden de 'zeep' konden uitpakken, de sigaren uit het kistje halen, de bom gereedmaken en het elastiekje om het kistje wikkelen.

'Je kunt het overal doen, achter in een auto, op het toilet van een café, in een portiek of 's nachts achter een boom,' zei hij. 'Kies eerst je doelwit uit, kijk goed of er geen soldaten in de buurt zijn die de klap kunnen overleven, draai dan de moer aan, doe het kistje dicht, leg het elastiekje erom, gooi de bom in de wagen en loop weg. Vanaf het moment dat je de moer aandraait, tel je langzaam tot vijftig. Als je het kistje dan nog in je hand hebt, gooi je het zo ver mogelijk weg. Meestal moet alles in het donker gebeuren, daarom oefenen we het nu op een andere manier.'

Hij gaf hun opdracht elkaar te blinddoeken en keek toe hoe ze onhandig aan het werk gingen. Maar tegen het einde van de middag konden ze het op de tast. Toen de avond viel, gaf hij hun de rest van de inhoud van de jutezak, voldoende voor iedere student om zes stukken 'zeep' te maken met zes timers. De zoon van de sigarenhandelaar zou voor de kistjes en de sigarenkokers zorgen. De watten, de zeepwikkels en de elastiekjes kon iedereen zelf wel krijgen. Daarna bracht hij hen terug naar de stad.

In de loop van september kwamen bij het AMAM-hoofdkwartier in het Hilton Hotel steeds meer berichten binnen over aanvallen op Iraakse soldaten en militair materieel. Kolonel Sabaawi kon niet veel uitrichten en werd steeds kwader.

Dit ging niet zoals verwacht. Hij had altijd gehoord dat de Koeweiti's een stelletje lafaards waren die geen last zouden veroorzaken. Eén voorproefje van de methoden uit Bagdad en ze zouden braaf doen wat hun werd gezegd. Maar dat viel tegen.

Er bestonden nu al verschillende verzetsorganisaties, waarvan de meeste nog gebrekkig waren georganiseerd. In de sji'itische wijk Rumaithiya verdwenen Iraakse soldaten gewoon. De moslims daar hadden een speciale reden om de Irakezen te haten, omdat hun sji'itische geloofsgenoten in Iran tijdens de Iraans-Iraakse oorlog bij honderdduizenden waren afgeslacht. Iraakse soldaten die zich in het labyrint van Rumaithiya waagden werd de strot afgesneden, en hun lijken werden in de riolen gegooid waar niemand ze ooit terugvond.

Onder de soennieten concentreerde het verzet zich rond de moskeeën, waar de Iraakse soldaten zelden kwamen. Daar werden berichten doorgegeven, wapens uitgedeeld en aanslagen voorbereid.

Het best georganiseerde verzet werd geleid door de Koeweitse notabelen, mannen met geld en een goede opleiding. Het werd vooral gefinancierd door Ahmed Al-Khalifa, die ervoor zorgde dat de Koeweiti's te eten hadden. En met de voedseltransporten werden ook andere goederen de stad binnengesmokkeld.

De organisatie had zes doelstellingen, waarvan er vijf een vorm van passief verzet inhielden. Punt een waren de papieren. Iedere verzetsstrijder kreeg een valse pas van medewerkers op het ministerie van Binnenlandse Zaken. Punt twee was informatie verstrekken aan het Coalitiehoofdkwartier in Riyad – over de Iraakse troepenbewegingen, de mankracht, de wapens, de kustverdediging en de raketinstallaties. Punt drie was het instandhouden van de openbare voorzieningen, zoals water, elektriciteit, brandweer en medische zorg. En toen de Irakezen, nadat de nederlaag onafwendbaar was geworden, de oliekranen openzetten om de zee zelf te verwoesten, wezen Koeweitse olietechnici de Amerikaanse jachtbommenwerpers precies welke kleppen ze moesten bombarderen om de oliestroom te stoppen.

In alle wijken waren solidariteitscomités actief, die vaak contact hielden met Europeanen en andere mensen uit de eerste wereld, die nog steeds gevangen zaten in hun flats, om hen uit handen van de Irakezen te houden.

Vanuit Saoedi-Arabië werd een satelliettelefoonsysteem het land binnengesmokkeld in de lege benzinetank van een jeep. Het was geen codesysteem, zoals dat van Martin, maar door voortdurend van plaats te veranderen wist het Koeweitse verzet de Irakezen te ontlopen en contact te houden met Riyad als er iets belangrijks te melden was. Een zendamateur bleef tijdens de hele bezetting actief en stuurde in totaal zevenduizend berichten naar een andere zendamateur in Colorado, die ze aan Buitenlandse Zaken doorgaf.

En dan was er nog het actieve verzet, voornamelijk geleid door een Koeweitse luitenant-kolonel – een van degenen die de eerste dag uit het ministerie van Defensie was ontsnapt. Omdat hij een zoon had die Fouad heette, werkte hij onder de codenaam Abu Fouad, vader van Fouad.

Saddam Hoessein had eindelijk zijn pogingen opgegeven om een marionettenregering te installeren en zijn halfbroer Ali Hassan Majid als gouverneur-generaal benoemd.

Het verzet was zeker geen spelletje. Er ontstond een kleinschalige maar zeer gemene ondergrondse oorlog. De AMAM had ondervragingscentra ingericht in de sporthal van Kathma en het stadion Qadisijah. De methoden die AMAM-chef Omar Khatib in de gevangenis van Abu Khraib bij Bagdad gebruikte werden ook hier uitvoerig toegepast. Voor de bevrijding van hun land verloren vijfhonderd Koeweiti's het leven, van wie de helft werd geëxecuteerd, vaak na langdurige martelingen.

Hassan Rahmani, het hoofd van de contraspionagedienst, zat aan zijn bureau in het Hilton Hotel en las de rapporten van zijn agenten door. Op 15 september was hij even teruggekomen van zijn werk in Bagdad. Maar de rapporten maakten hem niet vrolijker.

De aanvallen op Iraakse voorposten, wachthuisjes, legertrucks en wegversperringen langs eenzame wegen namen gestaag toe. Dat was voornamelijk

126

een zaak voor de AMAM, en die achterlijke idioot van een Khatib ging weer als een beest tekeer.

Rahmani had weinig op met de martelingen waar zijn rivaal binnen de Iraakse inlichtingendienst zoveel heil van verwachtte. Hij had meer vertrouwen in slim en geduldig speurwerk, hoewel hij moest toegeven dat het niet anders dan een wrede terreur was die de *Rais* al die jaren in het zadel had gehouden. En ondanks zijn goede opleiding moest hij erkennen dat die psychopatische straatvechter uit de stegen van Tikrit hem óók angst inboezemde.

Hij had geprobeerd de president te overreden hem de leiding te geven over de binnenlandse inlichtingendienst in Koeweit, maar het antwoord was een duidelijk 'nee' geweest. Een kwestie van principe, had Tariq Aziz, de minister van Buitenlandse Zaken, hem uitgelegd. Hij, Rahmani, moest de staat beschermen tegen spionage en sabotage uit het buitenland. En Saddam weigerde Koeweit als het buitenland te beschouwen. Het was de negentiende provincie van Irak. Daarom was Omar Khatib verantwoordelijk voor de binnenlandse orde.

Eigenlijk was Rahmani daar wel blij om toen hij die ochtend de stapel rapporten doorlas. De situatie was een nachtmerrie en Saddam Hoessein speelde het helemaal verkeerd, zoals Rahmani al had verwacht.

De gedachte om Westerse gijzelaars als een menselijk schild tegen een militaire aanval te gebruiken bleek een rampzalige misrekening. Saddam had de kans gemist om naar de Saoedische olievelden door te stoten en koning Fahd naar de conferentietafel te dwingen, en nu stroomden de Amerikanen het oorlogsgebied binnen.

Alle pogingen om Koeweit te assimileren waren mislukt en binnen een maand – misschien zelfs eerder – zou Saoedi-Arabië een onneembare vesting zijn geworden met Amerikaanse troepen langs de hele noordgrens.

Saddam kon zich nu niet meer eervol uit Koeweit terugtrekken. Maar als hij bleef, was de kans groot dat hij een nog oneervollere nederlaag zou lijden. Toch heerste er in kringen rond de president nog steeds een opgewekte stemming, alsof Saddam nog een troef achter de hand hield. Waar hoopte hij in godsnaam op? Dat Allah zelf zijn vijanden vanuit de hemel zou treffen?

Rahmani stond op van achter zijn bureau en liep naar het raam. Hij ijsbeerde meestal als hij nadacht. Dan kon hij zijn gedachten beter ordenen. Hij tuurde omlaag. De ooit zo sprankelende jachthaven was veranderd in een vuilnisbelt.

Er was iets vreemds met die rapporten op zijn bureau. Hij liep weer terug en keek ze nog eens door. Ja, iets heel vreemds. Sommige aanslagen door het verzet werden uitgevoerd met pistolen en geweren, of met bommen vervaardigd uit industrieel TNT. Maar er was ook een groep die kneedexplosieven

127

gebruikte. Semtex-H. Waar haalden ze dat vandaan, binnen Koeweit? En wie zat erachter?

En dan was er nog die radiozender die gecodeerde berichten verzond, steeds op andere tijden en vanaf andere plaatsen in de woestijn – uitzendingen van tien tot vijftien minuten, waar geen woord van te volgen was.

Ook waren er meldingen over een geheimzinnige bedoeïen, die overal opdook en dan weer verdween, een spoor van vernielingen achter zich latend. Twee zwaargewonde soldaten hadden vlak voor hun dood verteld dat ze de man hadden gezien. Een lange, zelfverzekerde vent met een rood-wit geruite *keffijeh* voor zijn gezicht.

Twee Koeweiti's hadden na folteringen toegegeven dat ze van de myste-rieuze bedoeïen hadden gehoord maar ze hadden hem nog nooit gezien. Daarna hadden Sabaawi's mensen de gevangenen nog zwaarder gemarteld, om hen te laten bekennen dat ze de man wèl hadden gezien. De idioten. Natuurlijk hadden de Koeweiti's dat toegegeven, alleen om de pijn te laten ophouden.

Hoe langer Hassan Rahmani erover nadacht, des te meer raakte hij ervan overtuigd dat ze met een buitenlandse infiltrant te maken hadden. En dat was zíjn terrein. Hij kon zich nauwelijks voorstellen dat een bedoeïen iets van kneedexplosieven of codezenders wist. Als het tenminste om één en dezelfde man ging. Waarschijnlijk had hij een paar Koeweiti's getraind, maar zelf had hij ook aanslagen gepleegd.

Het was onmogelijk om alle bedoeïenen in de stad en de woestijn op te pak-ken. Zo zou de AMAM het doen, om daarna nog jarenlang bezig te blijven met het uitrukken van vingernagels zonder dat ze daar een steek mee opschoten.

Rahmani zag maar drie mogelijkheden. Ze konden de man op heterdaad betrappen, maar dat zou wel heel toevallig zijn. Ze konden een van zijn Koeweitse handlangers aanhouden, in de hoop dat die hen naar de man zou kunnen leiden. Of ze konden hem verrassen als hij in de woestijn over zijn zender gebogen zat.

Rahmani koos voor de laatste mogelijkheid. Hij zou twee of drie van zijn beste radiodetectorteams uit Irak laten overkomen en die op verschillende plaatsen opstellen zodat ze de zender konden opsporen. Verder had hij een helikopter nodig met een team van de Speciale Eenheden om meteen in actie te kunnen komen. Zodra hij terug was in Bagdad zou hij er werk van maken.

Hassan Rahmani was die dag niet de enige die belangstelling had voor de Bedoeïen. In een villa in de buitenwijken, kilometers bij het Hilton van-daan, luisterde een jonge, besnorde Koeweiti in een witte katoenen *thob* geïnteresseerd naar het verhaal dat een vriend hem vertelde.

'Ik stond met mijn auto voor de stoplichten toen ik een Iraakse legertruck aan de overkant van de kruising zag. Hij stond stil, met een groepje soldaten eromheen die stonden te eten en te roken. Opeens kwam er een jonge vent, een Koeweiti, uit een café met een kistje onder zijn arm. Niets bijzonders. Het viel me nauwelijks op, totdat ik zag dat hij het onder die vrachtwagen gooide. Toen liep hij de hoek om en verdween. Het stoplicht sprong op groen, maar ik bleef staan.

Vijf seconden later vloog de truck de lucht in. Er bleef niets van over. De lichamen van de soldaten lagen overal verspreid, met afgehakte benen. Ik heb nog nooit een klein kistje gezien dat zoveel schade kon aanrichten. Ik heb meteen rechtsomkeert gemaakt voordat de AMAM verscheen.'

'Kneedexplosieven,' zei de legerofficier peinzend. 'Daar zou ik heel wat voor over hebben. Het moeten de mannen van de Bedoeïen zijn geweest. Geen idee wie die klootzak is trouwens. Ik zou hem graag eens ontmoeten.'

'Het punt is dat ik de jongen herkende.'

'Wat?' De jonge kolonel boog zich naar voren, opeens hevig geïnteresseerd.

'Ik zou hier niet helemaal naartoe zijn gekomen om u iets te vertellen wat u al wist, Abu Faoud. Zoals gezegd, ik herkende die bommengooier. Ik koop mijn sigaretten al jaren bij zijn vader.'

Drie dagen later sprak dr. Reinhart in Londen het Medusa Comité toe en maakte een vermoeide indruk. Hoewel hij al zijn andere werk in Porton Down opzij had gelegd, was het een gigantische opgave geweest om alle stukken door te lezen die hij bij de eerste bespreking had gekregen, plus de aanvullende informatie die later nog was binnengekomen.

'Het onderzoek is waarschijnlijk nog niet compleet,' zei hij, 'maar ik heb nu een aardig beeld. Om te beginnen weten we natuurlijk dat Saddam Hoessein over een grote gifgasproduktie kan beschikken. Meer dan duizend ton per jaar, schat ik.

Iraanse soldaten die tijdens de Iraans-Iraakse oorlog met gifgas in aanraking waren gekomen zijn hier in Engeland behandeld en ik heb hen kunnen onderzoeken. Toen al vonden we de sporen van fosgeen en mosterdgas. Maar nog ernstiger is dat Irak inmiddels twee veel gevaarlijker gassen in huis heeft, Duitse produkten met de namen Sarin en Tabun. Als die in de Iraans-Iraakse oorlog zijn toegepast – en daar zijn sterke aanwijzingen voor – hadden we de slachtoffers nooit in Britse ziekenhuizen kunnen behandelen. Dan waren ze ter plaatse overleden.'

'Hoe dodelijk zijn die gassen, doctor Reinhart?' vroeg Sir Paul Spruce.

'Sir Paul, bent u getrouwd?'

De gepolijste ambtenaar leek van zijn stuk gebracht.

129

'Eh, ja, inderdaad.'
'En gebruikt Lady Spruce weleens parfum uit een verstuiver?'
'Dat heb ik wel eens gezien, ja.'
'Hebt u dan ook gezien hoe klein die druppeltjes uit zo'n verstuiver zijn?'
'Gelukkig wel, gezien de prijs van het parfum.'
Het was een goede grap, vond Sir Paul zelf.
'Twee van zulke druppeltjes Sarin of Tabun op je huid, en je bent dood,' zei de scheikundige uit Porton Down.
Niemand lachte.
'Het Iraakse onderzoek naar gifgas gaat terug tot 1976. In dat jaar hebben ze het Britse bedrijf ICI benaderd met het verhaal dat ze een pesticidenfabriek wilden bouwen om ongedierte te kunnen bestrijden. Maar toen ICI zag welke spullen ze wilden hebben, is het verzoek meteen geweigerd. De Irakezen vroegen om materiaal voor corrosie-resistente reactorvaten, buizen en pompen die volgens ICI alleen bedoeld konden zijn voor de produktie van gifgas. En dus ging de koop niet door.'
'Goddank,' zei Sir Paul en hij maakte een aantekening.
'Maar niet iedereen had zoveel scrupules,' vervolgde de voormalige vluchteling uit Wenen. 'Irak bleef volhouden dat ze bestrijdingsmiddelen voor de landbouw wilden produceren en daar is natuurlijk gif voor nodig.'
'Misschien spraken ze de waarheid,' opperde Paxman.
'Uitgesloten,' zei Reinhart. 'Een ervaren scheikundige kijkt naar de hoeveelheid en het type van de stoffen. In 1981 was een Duitse firma bereid een laboratorium voor Irak te bouwen met een zeer speciale, afwijkende indeling. Daar moest fosforpentachloride worden geproduceerd, de grondstof voor organische fosfor, een van de ingrediënten van zenuwgas. Geen enkel normaal universitair laboratorium zou zulke zwaar giftige stoffen gebruiken. Dat wisten de betrokken chemici ook.
Op de exportvergunningen komt ook thiodiglycol voor. Daarvan kan mosterdgas worden gemaakt als het met zoutzuur wordt gemengd. In kleine hoeveelheden wordt thiodiglycol ook gebruikt voor de produktie van inkt voor balpennen.'
'Hoeveel hebben ze gekocht?' vroeg Sinclair.
'Vijfhonderd ton.'
'Dat zijn heel wat balpennen,' mompelde Paxman.
'Dat was begin 1983,' zei Reinhart. 'In de zomer werd hun grote gifgasfabriek in Samarra in gebruik genomen, waar yperiet of mosterdgas werd geproduceerd. In december begonnen ze het gas tegen de Iraniërs te gebruiken.
Bij hun eerste aanvallen op het Iraanse voetvolk gebruikten de Irakezen een mengsel van gele regen, yperiet en Tabun. Omstreeks 1985 hadden ze het

produkt verbeterd. Het bestond nu uit waterstofcyanide, mosterdgas, Tabun en Sarin. Daarmee bereikten ze een sterftepercentage van zestig procent onder de Iraanse infanterie.'

'Kunnen we ons beperken tot de zenuwgassen, doctor Reinhart?' vroeg Sinclair. 'Die vormen het grootste gevaar.'

'Dat is zo,' beaamde Reinhart. 'Vanaf 1984 kochten ze vooral fosforoxy-chloride, een belangrijke grondstof voor Tabun en twee voorlopers van Sarin, trimethylfosfiet en kaliumfluoride. Van de eerste van die drie stoffen probeerden ze 250 ton bij een Nederlands bedrijf te bestellen, dat is voldoende om alle bomen, struiken en grassen in het Midden-Oosten te vernietigen. De Nederlanders weigerden, net als ICI, maar Irak kocht wel twee andere stoffen die op dat moment nog niet verboden waren: dimethylamine voor de produktie van Tabun, en isopropanol voor de vervaardiging van Sarin.'

'Als ze in Europa niet verboden waren, dan zijn ze misschien inderdaad als bestrijdingsmiddelen gebruikt,' opperde Sir Paul.

'Nee. Niet in die hoeveelheden,' antwoordde Reinhart. 'En niet met die chemische processen, die apparatuur en die fabrieksopbouw. Geen enkele ervaren chemicus of scheikundig ingenieur zou eraan twijfelen dat het spul voor de produktie van mosterdgas werd gekocht.'

'Weet u ook wie in de loop der jaren de belangrijkste leverancier is geweest?' vroeg Sir Paul.

'Zeker. In het begin hebben de Sovjetunie en Oost-Duitsland nog wat wetenschappelijke kennis aangedragen. En in die tijd zijn er kleine hoeveelheden toegestane stoffen in acht verschillende landen gekocht. Maar tachtig procent van de fabrieken, de inrichting, de apparatuur, de chemicaliën, de technologie en de know-how is afkomstig uit West-Duitsland.'

'Ja, we protesteren al jaren in Bonn,' teemde Sinclair. 'Maar ze hebben die bezwaren altijd weggewuifd. Doctor Reinhart, kunt u de gifgasfabrieken aanwijzen op de foto's die we u hebben gegeven?'

'Natuurlijk. De plaats van sommige fabrieken is in de stukken terug te vinden, andere kun je met een vergrootglas herkennen.'

De chemicus legde vijf grote luchtfoto's op tafel. 'Ik ken de Arabische namen niet, maar aan deze nummers kunt u zien om welke foto's het gaat?'

'Ja. Als u de fabrieken maar aanwijst,' zei Sinclair.

'Hier, dit hele complex van zeventien gebouwen... En deze ene, enkele fabriek... Ziet u de luchtzuiveringsinstallatie? En deze... En dit complex van acht gebouwen... En deze nog.'

Sinclair bestudeerde een lijst die hij uit zijn koffertje had gehaald en knikte grimmig.

'Zoals we al dachten. A-Quaim, Fallujah, Al-Hillah, Salman Pak en Samarra. Doctor Reinhart, ik ben u bijzonder dankbaar. Onze eigen mensen waren tot dezelfde conclusie gekomen. Al deze fabrieken zullen bij de eerste luchtacties worden aangevallen.'

Na afloop van de bespreking liepen Sinclair, Simon Paxman en Terry Martin naar Piccadilly Circus om een kop koffie te drinken bij Richoux.

'Ik weet niet wat jullie ervan denken,' zei Sinclair terwijl hij in zijn capuccino roerde, 'maar het gifgas is voor ons het belangrijkste probleem. Generaal Schwarzkopf spreekt al over een "nachtmerrie-scenario" van massale gasaanvallen op al onze troepen. Als ze de strijd in gaan, zullen ze gasmaskers en beschermende kleding moeten dragen, van top tot teen. Maar gelukkig blijft dit gas niet lang werkzaam als het eenmaal aan de lucht is blootgesteld. Zodra het op de grond neerdaalt, is het onschadelijk. Je lijkt niet erg overtuigd, Terry.'

'Die gasaanvallen...' zei Martin. 'Hoe moet Saddam die lanceren?'

Sinclair haalde zijn schouders op. 'Met artilleriegranaten, neem ik aan. Net als tegen de Iraniërs.'

'Kunnen jullie zijn artillerie niet vernietigen? Die heeft maar een bereik van dertig kilometer. De kanonnen staan daar ergens in de woestijn.'

'Natuurlijk,' zei de Amerikaan. 'We hebben de technologie om al zijn kanonnen en tanks op te sporen, hoe goed ze zich ook hebben ingegraven of gecamoufleerd.'

'Maar als hij geen artillerie meer heeft, hoe moet Saddam dat gifgas dan verspreiden?'

'Met jachtbommenwerpers, vermoed ik.'

'Maar die hebben jullie ook al vernietigd tegen de tijd dat de grondtroepen oprukken,' merkte Martin op. 'Dan is Saddam zijn luchtmacht kwijt.'

'Nou goed. Misschien wil hij Scud-raketten gebruiken. Zoiets zal hij wel proberen. En die schieten we dan achter elkaar uit de lucht. Sorry, kerels, maar ik moet ervandoor.'

'Wat zit je dwars, Terry?' vroeg Paxman, toen de CIA-officier was vertrokken.

Martin zuchtte. 'Ik weet het niet. Maar Saddam en zijn adviseurs weten ook wel wat er gaat gebeuren. Die zullen de Amerikaanse vernietigingskracht niet onderschatten. Simon, kun je alle toespraken van Saddam uit de afgelopen zes maanden voor me te pakken krijgen? In het Arabisch, natuurlijk.'

'Dat zal wel lukken, denk ik. Het GCHQ in Cheltenham heeft ze wel, of anders de Arabische sectie van de BBC Wereldomroep. Op de band of op schrift?'

'Het liefst op de band.'

Drie dagen lang luisterde Terry Martin naar de scherpe, agressieve stem uit Bagdad. Hij speelde de banden een paar keer af, en steeds opnieuw kreeg hij de indruk dat de Iraakse dictator de verkeerde toon aansloeg voor een man met zulke grote problemen. Of hij besefte niet in wat voor situatie hij verkeerde, of hij wist iets wat zijn vijanden niet wisten.

Op 21 september hield Saddam Hoessein een nieuwe toespraak – of eigenlijk gaf de Revolutionaire Commandoraad een verklaring uit die duidelijk Saddams woordkeus verried. Hij verklaarde dat Irak zich onder geen beding uit Koeweit zou terugtrekken en dat iedere poging om de Irakezen te verdrijven tot 'de moeder van alle oorlogen' zou leiden.

Zo werd het vertaald. De media vonden het prachtig en het werd een beroemde kreet.

Terry Martin bestudeerde de tekst en belde Simon Paxman. 'Ik heb me nog eens verdiept in het dialect van de Tigrisvallei,' zei hij.

'Lieve hemel, wat een hobby,' antwoordde Paxman.

'Het gaat om die opmerking over "de moeder van alle oorlogen".'

'Wat is daarmee?'

'Je kunt het vertalen als "oorlog", maar waar Saddam vandaan komt betekent het ook "slachtoffers" of "bloedbad".'

Het bleef even stil aan de andere kant van de lijn.

'Maak je geen zorgen,' zei Paxman toen.

Maar dat deed Terry Martin wel.

De zoon van de sigarenwinkelier was bang, en zijn vader ook.

'Alsjeblieft, vertel ze wat je weet, zoon,' smeekte hij de jongen.

De twee man sterke delegatie van het Koeweits Verzetscomité had zich heel beleefd aan de sigarenhandelaar voorgesteld, maar ze hadden zijn zoon dringend aangeraden om de waarheid te vertellen.

De winkelier wist ook wel dat de mannen niet hun ware naam hadden genoemd, maar hij besefte dat het twee machtige en invloedrijke Koeweiti's moesten zijn. En het was een complete verrassing voor hem dat zijn zoon bij het actieve verzet betrokken was.

Erger nog, hij had zojuist gehoord dat zijn jongen niet eens voor de officiële Koeweitse verzetsbeweging werkte, maar dat hij een bom onder een Iraakse truck had gegooid in opdracht van een of andere bandiet van wie hij nog nooit had gehoord. Het was bijna voldoende om hem een hartaanval te bezorgen.

Ze zaten met hun vieren in de woonkamer van het comfortabele huis van de sigarenwinkelier in Keifan. Een van de bezoekers verklaarde dat ze niets tegen de bedoeïen hadden, maar juist met hem in contact wilden komen zodat ze konden samenwerken.

Dus vertelde de jongen wat er was gebeurd vanaf het moment dat zijn vriend bij die berg puin was weggesleurd toen hij op een passerende Iraakse truck had willen schieten. De mannen luisterden zwijgend. Alleen zijn ondervrager wilde zo nu en dan iets weten. De man die niets zei, de man met de donkere zonnebril, was Abu Fouad.

De ondervrager was vooral geïnteresseerd in het huis waar de groep de bedoeïen ontmoette. De jongen gaf het adres maar zei erbij: 'Ik geloof niet dat het veel zin heeft om erheen te gaan. Hij is heel voorzichtig. Een van ons is er een keer geweest om met hem te praten, maar toen zat alles op slot. Hij woont er niet, maar hij wist wel dat er iemand was geweest. Dat mochten we nooit meer doen, zei hij. Als het nog eens gebeurde, zou hij het contact verbreken en zouden we hem niet meer terugzien.'

Abu Fouad, die zwijgend in zijn hoek zat, knikte waarderend. In tegenstelling tot de anderen was hij een getrainde militair en meende hij de hand van een collega te herkennen.

'Wanneer zie je hem weer?' vroeg hij rustig.

Misschien zou de jongen een boodschap kunnen overbrengen, een uitnodiging voor een gesprek.

'Tegenwoordig neemt hij contact op met een van ons. Die waarschuwt dan de rest. Het kan nog wel even duren.'

De twee Koeweiti's vertrokken. Ze hadden een beschrijving van twee wagens, de aftandse pick-up truck van de 'tuinder' die zijn fruit vanaf het platteland naar de stad bracht, en een zware terreinjeep voor ritten door de woestijn.

Abu Fouad gaf de kentekennummers aan een vriend bij het ministerie van Transport, maar het bleken valse nummerplaten te zijn. De enige andere aanwijzing waren de pasjes die de man moest bezitten om langs de Iraakse wegversperringen en controleposten te komen.

Via zijn comité benaderde hij een ambtenaar van Binnenlandse Zaken. Hij had geluk. De man herinnerde zich dat hij zes weken geleden een valse pas had gemaakt voor een tuinder uit Jahra, als vriendendienst voor de miljonair Ahmed Al-Khalifa.

Abu Fouad was opgetogen en nieuwsgierig. De zakenman was een man van aanzien, met grote invloed in de verzetsbeweging. Maar iedereen dacht dat hij zich alleen met de financiering bezighield. Wat voor rol speelde hij dan als beschermer van die mysterieuze en gevaarlijke bedoeïen?

Ten zuiden van de Koeweitse grens ging de aanvoer van Amerikaans militair materieel gestaag door. De laatste week van september constateerde generaal Norman Schwarzkopf, begraven in het labyrint van geheime kamers, twee verdiepingen onder het Saoedische ministerie van Defensie aan de Old Airport Road in Riyad, dat de Amerikaanse troepenmacht eindelijk groot genoeg was om Saoedi-Arabië effectief tegen een Iraakse aanval te kunnen beschermen.

In de lucht had generaal Charles (Chuck) Horner een paraplu van patrouillerend staal opgebouwd – een snelle, zwaarbewapende armada van jagers, jachtbommenwerpers, tankers, zware bommenwerpers en Thunderbolt antitankjagers, voldoende om de Irakezen zowel op de grond als in de lucht te vernietigen.

Vanuit de lucht werd met radarsystemen iedere vierkante centimeter van Irak bestreken. De elektronica was in staat alle troepenbewegingen en opstijgende vliegtuigen te volgen, alle warmtebronnen te lokaliseren en alle Iraakse gesprekken in de ether af te luisteren.

Op de grond beschikte Norman Schwarzkopf nu over genoeg gemechaniseerde eenheden, lichte en zware pantservoertuigen, artillerie en infanterie om iedere Iraakse colonne te kunnen tegenhouden, te omsingelen en te verslaan.

In het diepste geheim, zelfs zonder dat Amerika's bondgenoten er iets van wisten, werden die laatste week van september plannen gemaakt om van het defensief in het offensief over te gaan – een volledig aanvalsplan tegen Irak, hoewel het mandaat van de Verenigde Naties nog steeds beperkt bleef tot de bescherming van Saoedi-Arabië en de Golfstaten.

Maar Schwarzkopf had problemen. Zo was het aantal Iraakse tanks, troepen en kanonnen nu twee keer zo groot als toen hij zes weken eerder in Riyad was aangekomen. En voor de bevrijding van Koeweit zou hij twee keer zoveel Coalitietroepen nodig hebben als voor de bescherming van Saoedi-Arabië.

Norman Schwarzkopf was dezelfde overtuiging toegedaan als zijn voorganger George Patton: iedere gesneuvelde Amerikaan, Brit, Fransman of andere bondgenoot was er één te veel. Voordat hij in de aanval ging, moesten er twee dingen gebeuren – een verdubbeling van zijn huidige troepenmacht en een luchtaanval die de sterkte van de Iraakse troepenmacht ten noorden van de grens met minstens vijftig procent zou verminderen.

Dat betekende meer tijd, meer materieel, meer voorraden, meer geschut, meer tanks, meer troepen, meer vliegtuigen, meer brandstof, meer voedsel en heel wat meer geld. Als ze een overwinning wilden, zei hij tegen de verbijsterde leunstoel-Napoleons op Capitol Hill, zouden ze over de brug moeten komen.

In feite was het Colin Powell, de wat diplomatiekere voorzitter van de chefs-van-staven, die de boodschap doorgaf en de taal wat kuiste. Politici spelen graag militaire spelletjes, maar worden minder graag in soldatentaal toegesproken.

De planning in die laatste week in september bleef dus strikt geheim. En dat was maar beter ook. Het zou nog tot 29 november duren voordat de Verenigde Naties, die het ene vredesvoorstel na het andere lanceerden, eindelijk toestemming gaven om Irak met alle noodzakelijke middelen uit Koeweit te verdrijven als Saddam zich op 16 januari nog niet had teruggetrokken. Als de voorbereidingen voor de aanval dan pas waren begonnen, was het veel te laat geweest.

Ahmed Al-Khalifa voelde zich opgelaten. Natuurlijk kende hij Abu Fouad en wist hij wat Fouad deed. Bovendien had hij begrip voor zijn verzoek. Maar hij had zijn woord gegeven, legde hij uit, en daar moest hij zich aan houden.

Zelfs aan zijn landgenoot en mede-verzetsstrijder vertelde hij niet dat de bedoeïen in werkelijkheid een Britse officier was. Maar hij beloofde wel dat hij een bericht voor de bedoeïen zou achterlaten op een plaats waar de man het vroeg of laat zou vinden.

De volgende morgen liet hij op de christelijke begraafplaats onder de marmeren grafplaat van matroos Shepton een brief achter met een persoonlijk verzoek aan de bedoeïen om contact op te nemen met Abu Fouad.

De groep telde zes soldaten, onder bevel van een sergeant. Toen ze de bedoeïen de hoek om zagen komen, waren ze net zo verbaasd als hij.

Mike Martin had zijn kleine truck in een van de garages achtergelaten en liep naar de villa waar hij de nacht wilde doorbrengen. Hij was moe en daardoor wat minder op zijn hoede dan anders. Hij vloekte toen hij de Irakezen zag en hij wist dat ze hem ook hadden gezien. In zijn werk kon één zo'n foutje fataal zijn.

De avondklok was allang ingegaan en hoewel hij eraan gewend was om in het donker door de verlaten stad te zwerven, beperkte hij zich altijd tot slecht verlichte straten en donkere stegen terwijl de Iraakse patrouilles juist de hoofdwegen en de belangrijkste kruispunten bewaakten. Zo liepen ze elkaar nooit tegen het lijf.

Maar toen Hassan Rahmani weer naar Bagdad was vertrokken en een vernietigend rapport had geschreven over het optreden van het Volksleger, was er wat veranderd. Hier en daar doken weer de groene baretten van de Speciale Eenheden op.

Hoewel ze niet tot de elite van de Republikeinse Garde behoorden, vormden de Speciale Eenheden een veel beter korps dan het dienstplichtige gepeupel van het Volksleger. Zes Groene Baretten stonden rustig naast hun truck op een kruispunt waar normaal geen Irakezen te bekennen waren.

Martin had nog net de tijd om op zijn stok te leunen en de houding aan te nemen van een oude man. Het was een verstandige vermomming, want in de Arabische cultuur werden oudere mensen nog met respect of in elk geval met mededogen behandeld.

'Hé, jij daar!' riep de sergeant. 'Kom eens hier.'

Er werden vier geweren op de eenzame figuur met de geruite *keffijeh* gericht. De oude man bleef staan en hinkte toen naar hen toe.

'Wat doe je hier nog om deze tijd, bedoeïen?'

'Ik ben maar een oude man die naar huis wil voordat de avondklok ingaat, *sajidi*,' antwoordde de man op klaaglijke toon.

'Die is allang ingegaan, oude dwaas. Twee uur geleden.'

De oude man schudde ontsteld zijn hoofd. 'Dat wist ik niet, *sajidi*. Ik heb geen horloge.'

In het Midden-Oosten zijn horloges niet onmisbaar. Ze zijn een teken van rijkdom, meer niet. De Iraakse soldaten in Koeweit hadden er allemaal een. Gestolen. Maar het woord 'bedoeïen' is afgeleid van *bidoen* of 'zonder'.

De sergeant bromde wat. Het klonk plausibel.

'Papieren,' zei hij toen.

De oude man klopte met zijn vrije hand op zijn kaftan. 'Die ben ik kwijt,' zei hij onderdanig.

'Fouilleer hem,' beval de sergeant. Een van zijn soldaten deed een stap naar

137

voren. De handgranaat die Martin tegen de binnenkant van zijn linker dijbeen had gebonden voelde aan als een van de watermeloenen op zijn truck.
'Blijf van mijn ballen af!' zei de oude bedoeïen scherp. De soldaat ver-
stijfde. Een van de anderen grinnikte. De sergeant probeerde zijn gezicht in
de plooi te houden.
'Schiet op, Zuhair. Fouilleer die man.'
De jonge soldaat aarzelde. Hij wist dat hij voor paal stond.
'Alleen mijn vrouw mag aan mijn ballen komen,' zei de bedoeïen. Twee
van de soldaten schoten nu openlijk in de lach en lieten hun geweren zakken. De anderen deden hetzelfde. Zuhair aarzelde nog steeds.
'Maar ze schiet er niks mee op. Ik ben te oud voor die onzin,' verklaarde de
oude man.
Dat deed de deur dicht. De hele groep bulderde van het lachen. Zelfs de sergeant grijnsde nu.
'Goed, oude man. Wegwezen. En kom na het donker niet meer op straat.'
De bedoeïen hinkte naar het eind van de straat, zich krabbend onder zijn
kleren. Bij de hoek draaide hij zich om. De granaat, met de lepel naar één
kant, rolde over de keien en kwam tot stilstand tegen de schoen van Zuhair.
De soldaten staarden ernaar. De granaat explodeerde. Het was het einde van
zes Iraakse militairen. En het einde van september.

Die avond, ver weg in Tel Aviv, zat generaal Yaakov Kobi Dror van de
Mossad in zijn kantoor in het Hadar Dafna Gebouw en dronk een biertje
met zijn oude vriend en collega Shlomo Gershon, beter bekend als Sami.
Sami Gershon was het hoofd van de Komemiute, de operationele sectie die
verantwoordelijk was voor de 'illegale' agenten. Hij was erbij geweest toen
zijn chef tegen Chip Barber had gelogen.
'Hadden we het hem niet moeten vertellen?' vroeg hij, omdat het onderwerp weer ter sprake kwam. Dror liet het bier in zijn glas ronddraaien en
nam een flinke slok.
'Laat ze de pest maar krijgen,' gromde hij. 'Ze rekruteren hun eigen spionnen maar.'
Als piepjonge soldaat had hij ooit, in het voorjaar van 1967, dekking
gezocht onder zijn Patton-tank in de woestijn terwijl vier Arabische staten
probeerden Israël te vernietigen. Hij herinnerde zich nog goed dat de buitenwereld afkeurend had gemompeld, maar meer ook niet.
Met de rest van zijn bemanning, onder bevel van een jongen van twintig
jaar oud, had hij deel uitgemaakt van de troepen van Israël Tal, die bij de
Mitla-pas een bres in de vijandelijke linies hadden geslagen en de Egyptenaren tot aan het Suezkanaal hadden teruggedreven.
En toen Israël binnen zes dagen het leger en de luchtmacht van die vier lan-

den had verslagen, hadden dezelfde westerse media die in mei nog ach en wee hadden geroepen over de dreigende vernietiging van Israël, het land opeens van agressie beschuldigd omdat het de oorlog had gewonnen.

Dat was het moment waarop Kobi Dror zijn besluit had genomen. Ze konden allemaal doodvallen. Hij was een *sabra*, geboren en getogen in Israël, en hij moest niets hebben van de brede visie of de terughoudendheid van mensen zoals David Ben Goerion.

Zijn politieke sympathie lag bij de rechtse Likoedpartij van Menachem Begin, die bij de Irgoen had gezeten, en van Itzhak Shamir, een ex-lid van de Sternbende.

Ooit, toen hij achter in de klas naar een van zijn medewerkers zat te luisteren die nieuwe rekruten lesgaf, had hij de man horen spreken over 'bevriende inlichtingendiensten'. Dror was opgestaan en had de les overgenomen.

'Er bestaan geen vrienden van Israël,' had hij gezegd, 'behalve misschien de joden in de diaspora. Je kunt de wereld in twee groepen verdelen: onze vijanden en een groep neutralen. Met onze vijanden rekenen we wel af. Met die neutralen moet je voorzichtig zijn. Neem alles van ze, maar geef niets terug. Lach tegen ze, sla ze op hun schouder, drink een borrel met ze, probeer ze te vleien, bedank ze voor hun tips, maar vertel ze niets.'

'Nou ja, Kobi, laten we hopen dat ze er nooit achterkomen,' zei Gershon.

'Hoe zouden ze erachter moeten komen? Er zijn maar acht mensen die er iets van weten, en die werken allemaal op het Kantoor.'

Het kwam waarschijnlijk door het bier. Hij had er één over het hoofd gezien.

In het voorjaar van 1988 bezocht de Britse zakenman Stuart Harris een handelsbeurs in Bagdad. Hij was verkoopdirecteur van een bedrijf in Nottingham dat apparatuur voor de wegenbouw produceerde. De beurs werd gehouden onder auspiciën van het Iraakse ministerie van Transport. Zoals bijna alle Westerlingen had hij een kamer in het Rashid Hotel in de Yafastraat, dat voornamelijk voor buitenlanders was gebouwd en altijd werd bewaakt.

Toen Harris op de derde dag van de beurs in zijn hotelkamer terugkwam, vond hij een envelop onder zijn deur. Er stond geen naam op, alleen een kamernummer, en dat klopte.

In de envelop zaten een velletje papier en een onbeschreven luchtpostenvelop. Op het papier stond in hoofdletters in het Engels: 'Geef deze brief na uw terugkeer in Londen ongeopend bij de Israëlische ambassade af.'

Dat was alles. Stuart Harris schrok zich een ongeluk. Hij kende de reputatie van de gevreesde Geheime Politie van Irak. De inhoud van die envelop kon zijn arrestatie, martelingen en zelfs zijn dood betekenen.

Toch hield hij het hoofd koel en probeerde na te denken. Waarom hadden ze juist hem uitgekozen? Er waren zoveel Britse zakenmensen in Bagdad. Waarom dan Stuart Harris? Ze konden toch niet weten dat hij een jood was – dat zijn vader in 1935 als Duitse vluchteling naar Engeland was gekomen als Samuel Horowitz? Of wel?

Hoewel hij het niet wist hadden twee ambtenaren van het Iraakse ministerie van Transport twee dagen eerder in de kantine van het beursgebouw met elkaar zitten praten. Een van hen had iets verteld over zijn bezoek aan een fabriek in Nottingham, in de herfst van het vorige jaar. Harris was steeds zijn gastheer geweest, maar één dag had hij ontbroken. De Irakees had geïnformeerd of Harris ziek was, maar een collega had hem lachend gezegd dat Harris een vrije dag had vanwege Jom Kippoer.

De twee Iraakse ambtenaren vonden het niet van belang, maar iemand aan het aangrenzende tafeltje wel. Hij rapporteerde het gesprek aan zijn chef. Die deed ook alsof het niet belangrijk was, maar later kwam hij erop terug, stelde een onderzoek in naar Stuart Harris uit Nottingham en ging na waar hij logeerde.

Harris vroeg zich af wat hij nu moest doen. Misschien had de anonieme afzender van de brief ontdekt dat hij joods was, maar één ding kon hij toch niet weten. Door een buitengewoon toeval was Stuart Harris ook een *sajan*.

Het Israëlisch Instituut voor Inlichtingen en Speciale Operaties, in 1951 opgericht op bevel van Ben Goerion zelf, is in de buitenwereld uitsluitend bekend als de Mossad – Hebreeuws voor 'Instituut'. De werknemers zelf spreken altijd over 'het Kantoor'. Van de belangrijkste inlichtingendiensten ter wereld is de Mossad verreweg de kleinste. Het aantal mensen op de loonlijst is zelfs opvallend klein. Op het hoofdkwartier van de CIA in Langley, Virginia, werken ongeveer 25 000 mensen, en dan zijn er nog vestigingen in de rest van de wereld. In de hoogtijdagen van de KGB telde het Eerste Hoofddirectoraat, net als de CIA en de Mossad verantwoordelijk voor spionage in het buitenland, zo'n 15 000 agenten, verspreid over de hele wereld, met nog eens 3000 man op het hoofdkantoor in Jazenevo.

De Mossad heeft nooit meer dan 1200 tot 1500 medewerkers gehad, en nog geen veertig *katsa's* of controleofficieren.

Dat de Mossad met zo'n klein budget en zo weinig mensen nog zulke goede resultaten bereikt, komt door twee factoren. Een daarvan is de mogelijkheid om een beroep te doen op de Israëlische bevolking als geheel, een bevolking die nog steeds zeer kosmopolitisch is, over vele talenten beschikt, uit allerlei delen van de wereld komt en talloze verschillende talen spreekt.

De andere factor is het internationale netwerk van helpers of assistenten, in het Hebreeuws *sajanim* genoemd. Dat zijn diaspora-joden (ze moeten volledig joods zijn, zowel aan moeders- als aan vaderskant) die sympathiseren met de staat Israël, hoewel de meesten ook trouw zijn aan het land waarin ze wonen.

Alleen al in Londen wonen tweeduizend *sajanim*, in de rest van Engeland nog eens vijfduizend, en tien keer dat aantal in de Verenigde Staten. Ze worden nooit bij operaties betrokken maar wel om gunsten gevraagd. En ze moeten erop kunnen rekenen dat hun hulp nooit tegen hun eigen land zal worden aangewend.

Hierdoor kan de Mossad haar operationele kosten aanzienlijk verminderen, soms wel met duizend procent. Een voorbeeld. Een Mossad-team komt in Londen aan voor een actie tegen een geheim Palestijns commando. Ze hebben een auto nodig. Een *sajan* in de autobranche wordt gevraagd een legitieme tweedehands auto op een bepaalde plaats achter te laten, met de sleuteltjes onder de mat. Na de missie wordt de auto weer teruggebracht. De *sajan* weet niet waarvoor hij is gebruikt. In zijn boeken noteert hij dat de wagen op proef aan een potentiële klant is uitgeleend.

Hetzelfde team heeft een dekmantel nodig. Een *sajan* in onroerend goed leent hun een lege winkel, die door een *sajan* in de zoetwarenhandel wordt ingericht met snoep en chocola. En als ze een postadres nodig hebben, leent een andere *sajan* hun de sleutel van een leegstaand kantoor.

Stuart Harris was met vakantie in de Israëlische badplaats Eilat toen hij in de bar van de Red Rock in gesprek raakte met een vriendelijke jonge Israëli die uitstekend Engels sprak. Later kwamen ze elkaar opnieuw tegen. De Israëli had toen een vriend bij zich, een oudere man die Harris voorzichtig polste over zijn gevoelens voor Israël. Tegen het eind van de vakantie had Harris toegezegd dat hij altijd bereid was om te helpen...

Hij ging naar huis met het advies om gewoon te doen alsof er niets was gebeurd. Twee jaar wachtte hij op een telefoontje, dat nooit kwam. Maar een vriendelijke bezoeker hield contact. Een van de tijdrovende taken van *katsa's* in het buitenland is om contact te onderhouden met de *sajanim* op hun lijst.

En zo zat Stuart Harris nu zenuwachtig in een hotelkamer in Bagdad en vroeg zich af wat hij moest doen. De brief zou een valstrik kunnen zijn. Misschien zouden ze hem op het vliegveld aanhouden als hij zou proberen hem het land uit te smokkelen. Kon hij hem stiekem in de tas van iemand anders stoppen? Nee, dat ging niet. Bovendien, hoe kreeg hij hem in Londen dan weer terug?

Ten slotte kalmeerde hij wat, bedacht een plan en voerde dat nauwgezet uit. Hij verbrandde de buitenste envelop en het briefje in een asbak, verpulverde de as en spoelde die door het toilet. Daarna verborg hij de luchtpostenvelop onder de reservedeken op de plank boven de kleerkast, nadat hij zijn vingerafdrukken had weggeveegd.

141

Als zijn kamer werd doorzocht zou hij gewoon zweren dat hij de deken niet nodig had gehad, niet in de buurt van de bovenste plank was geweest en dat de brief door een vorige hotelgast moest zijn achtergelaten.

In een kantoorboekhandel kocht hij een stevige bruine envelop, zelfklevende etiketten en plakband. Bij het postkantoor haalde hij genoeg postzegels om een tijdschrift van Bagdad naar Londen te versturen. Van de beurs nam hij een Irakees reclameblad mee en hij liet zelfs de envelop afstempelen met het logo van de beurs.

Op de laatste dag, vlak voordat hij met zijn twee collega's naar het vliegveld vertrok, ging hij nog even naar zijn hotelkamer terug. Hij stak de brief in het tijdschrift en plakte de envelop dicht. Daarna adresseerde hij die aan een oom in Long Eaton en plakte het etiket en de postzegels erop. In de hal had hij een brievenbus gezien. De volgende lichting was over vier uur. Zelfs als de envelop door de Geheime Politie zou worden opengestoomd, zou híj al hoog en droog boven de Alpen zitten, in een Brits lijnvliegtuig.

Het gezegde wil dat het geluk met de dommen of de dapperen is – of met allebei. De hal werd inderdaad in de gaten gehouden door agenten van de AMAM, om te zien of vertrekkende buitenlanders werden benaderd door Irakezen die hun iets wilden meegeven. Harris hield zijn envelop onder zijn jasje, onder zijn linker oksel geklemd. Een man in de hoek volgde hem van achter zijn krant, maar juist op het moment dat Harris de envelop in de brievenbus deed reed er een bagagewagentje voorbij dat de AMAM-agent het uitzicht benam. Toen hij Harris weer zag, stond de Brit al bij de balie om zijn sleutel in te leveren.

Een week later kwam de brochure in Engeland aan. Harris wist dat zijn oom met vakantie was, want hij had een sleutel voor noodgevallen. Harris ging naar het huis van zijn oom om de envelop op te halen. Daarna reed hij naar de Israëlische ambassade en vroeg zijn contactman te spreken. Hij werd naar een kamer gebracht waar hij moest wachten.

Een man van middelbare leeftijd kwam binnen, vroeg naar zijn naam en informeerde waarom hij 'Norman' wilde spreken. Harris deed zijn verhaal, pakte de luchtpostenvelop en legde die op tafel. De Israëlische diplomaat verbleekte, vroeg hem nog eens om te wachten en vertrok.

De ambassade op Palace Green nummer 2 is een fraai gebouw, maar de klassieke lijnen verraden niets over de versterkingen en technologie waarachter het Mossad-bureau in de kelder zich verschuilt. Uit dit ondergrondse fort werd een jongeman opgeroepen.

Harris wachtte en wachtte.

Zonder dat hij het wist, werd hij via een doorkijkspiegel geobserveerd terwijl hij daar zat, met de envelop op de tafel voor hem. Ook werd hij gefotografeerd, terwijl iemand het archief raadpleegde om er zeker van te zijn dat hij werkelijk een *sajan* was en geen Palestijnse terrorist. Toen de foto van Stuart Harris uit Nottingham in het archief bleek te kloppen met de man achter de doorkijkspiegel, stapte de jonge *katsa* eindelijk de wachtkamer binnen.

Glimlachend stelde hij zich voor als Rafi en vroeg Harris zijn verhaal te vertellen, vanaf het allereerste begin in Eilat. Harris deed het. Die episode in Eilat kende Rafi al (hij had zojuist het hele dossier gelezen), maar hij wilde zekerheid. Toen Harris over Bagdad begon, raakte hij pas echt geïnteresseerd. In het begin stelde hij nog niet veel vragen en liet hij Harris rustig zijn verhaal vertellen. Maar daarna kwam hij op een aantal punten terug, totdat Harris de gebeurtenissen in Bagdad enkele malen had beschreven. Rafi maakte geen aantekeningen. Het gesprek werd opgenomen. Ten slotte liep hij naar een telefoon aan de muur en sprak, zachtjes in het Hebreeuws met een collega in de andere kamer.

Toen bedankte hij Harris uitvoerig, complimenteerde hem met zijn moed en zijn koelbloedigheid, vroeg hem hier nooit met *iemand* over te spreken en wenste hem een veilige thuisreis. Daarna bracht hij Harris naar de deur.

Een man met een zware helm, een kogelvrij vest en handschoenen nam de brief mee. De envelop werd gefotografeerd en met röntgenstralen onderzocht. De Israëlische ambassade, die al eens iemand was verloren door een bombrief, nam geen enkel risico.

Ten slotte werd de envelop geopend. Er zaten twee dunne, dichtbeschreven luchtpostvelletjes in. De tekst was in het Arabisch. Rafi sprak geen Arabisch, evenmin als zijn collega's – tenminste niet voldoende om het priegelige Arabische handschrift te kunnen lezen. Daarom stuurde Rafi een uitvoerig codebericht naar Tel Aviv en schreef een nog uitvoeriger rapport in het formele, uniforme NAKA-jargon van de Mossad. Een diplomatieke koerier reed met de brief en het rapport naar Heathrow en stapte nog dezelfde avond op een El Al-toestel naar het vliegveld Ben Goerion.

Een ordonnans met een gewapend escorte wachtte de koerier op het vliegveld op en bracht de canvas tas naar het grote gebouw aan de King Saul Boulevard waar hij kort na het ontbijt werd afgeleverd bij het hoofd van de sectie Irak – een zeer bekwame jonge *katsa*, David Sharon genaamd.

Sharon sprak wel Arabisch, en wat hij op die twee velletjes luchtpostpapier las, gaf hem hetzelfde gevoel als toen hij tijdens zijn training bij de para's voor het eerst boven de Negev-woestijn uit een vliegtuig was gesprongen.

Dit materiaal was te gevoelig voor zijn secretaresse, en zelfs voor zijn tekstverwerker. Op zijn eigen schrijfmachine typte hij een letterlijke vertaling van de brief in het Hebreeuws. Daarna bracht hij de brief, de vertaling en Rafi's rapport naar zijn directe chef, de directeur van de divisie Midden-Oosten.

De schrijver van de brief was een hoge functionaris binnen het Iraakse regime, die bereid was voor Israël te werken. Voor geld. Dat was zijn enige motief.

Er stond nog wat meer in, onder andere een postbusnummer op het hoofdpostkantoor van Bagdad, waar de Mossad een antwoord naartoe kon sturen, maar dit was het belangrijkste.

Die avond was er topoverleg in het kantoor van Kobi Dror. Aanwezig waren, behalve Dror zelf, Sami Gershon, het hoofd van de afdeling Operaties, en Eitan Hadar, Sharons directe chef als directeur van de divisie Midden-Oosten, aan wie Sharon die ochtend de brief had doorgegeven. Ook David Sharon was ontboden.

Gershon vertrouwde de zaak niet erg.

'Het is een valstrik,' zei hij. 'Een klunzige poging tot een valstrik. Kobi, ik stuur er geen man heen om dit uit te zoeken. Dat zou zijn dood worden. Ik ben zelfs niet van plan een *oter* te sturen om contact te leggen.'

Een *oter* is een Arabier die door de Mossad wordt gebruikt om het eerste contact met een mede-Arabier tot stand te brengen – een onbelangrijke boodschapper, die veel beter gemist kan worden dan een Israëlische *katsa*.

De anderen leken Gershons mening te delen. De brief was een krankzinnige poging om een hoge *katsa* naar Bagdad te lokken, waar hij kon worden aangehouden, gemarteld, publiekelijk berecht en in het openbaar geëxecuteerd.

Ten slotte wendde Dror zich tot David Sharon. 'David, ik heb jou nog niet gehoord. Wat denk je ervan?'

Sharon knikte spijtig. 'Ik vrees dat Sami gelijk heeft. Het zou waanzin zijn om er een goede vent naartoe te sturen.'

Eitan Hadar wierp hem een waarschuwende blik toe. Er bestond een zware concurrentie tussen de verschillende divisies. Het had geen zin om Gershon de overwinning op een presenteerblaadje aan te bieden.

'Het moet een valstrik zijn. Dat is voor negenennegentig procent zeker.'

'En die ene procent, jonge vriend?' vroeg Dror plagend.

'Een dwaze droom. Er is één procent kans dat ons een nieuwe Penkovsky in de schoot is geworpen.'

Er viel een doodse stilte. De naam bleef in de lucht hangen. Gershon slaakte een diepe zucht. Kobi Dror staarde zijn directe chef aan. Sharon bestudeerde zijn nagels.

In de spionagewereld bestaan maar vier manieren om een agent in hoge regeringskringen van een ander land te rekruteren.

De eerste methode is ook de simpelste. Stuur een van je eigen landgenoten erheen, zo goed opgeleid dat hij voor een inwoner van het andere land kan doorgaan. Dat lukt bijna nooit, tenzij de infiltrant in het andere land geboren is en een goede reden kan geven waarom hij een tijdje in het buitenland heeft gezeten. Maar zelfs dan kan het jaren duren voordat zo'n *sleeper* een hoge positie binnen de regering heeft bereikt en toegang krijgt tot belangrijke geheimen.

Toch was Israël ooit een meester in deze tactiek. Toen de staat Israël pas bestond, stroomden er joden uit alle delen van de wereld binnen. Er waren joden die konden doorgaan voor Marokkanen, Algerijnen, Libiërs, Egyptenaren, Syriërs, Irakezen en Jemenieten – nog afgezien van alle joden die uit Rusland, Polen, West-Europa en Noord- en Zuid-Amerika naar Israël waren gekomen.

Het meest geslaagde voorbeeld was Elie Cohen, geboren en getogen in Syrië. Hij werd naar Damascus teruggestuurd met een Syrische naam. Daar raakte hij bevriend met hoge politici, ambtenaren en generaals, die op de feestjes van hun gulle gastheer vrijuit over hun werk spraken. Alles wat ze hem vertelden, waaronder alle Syrische oorlogsplannen, werd aan Tel Aviv doorgegeven – nog net op tijd voor de Zesdaagse Oorlog. Maar Cohen werd aangehouden, gemarteld en publiekelijk opgehangen op het Plein van de Revolutie in Damascus. Zulke infiltraties zijn bijzonder gevaarlijk en heel zeldzaam.

In de loop der jaren werden de oorspronkelijke immigranten steeds ouder. Hun *sabra*-kinderen kenden geen Arabisch meer en waren dus niet geschikt als infiltranten. Omstreeks 1990 beschikte de Mossad over veel minder goede arabisten dan de buitenwereld weleens dacht.

Maar er was nog een reden. Arabische geheimen kunnen eenvoudiger worden gestolen via Europa of Amerika. Als een Arabische staat een Amerikaans gevechtsvliegtuig koopt, is de technische informatie veel gemakkelijker en met minder risico's in Amerika zelf te vinden. Als een hoge Arabier bereid lijkt tot het verkopen van inlichtingen, kan hij veel simpeler worden benaderd tijdens een bezoek aan de vleespotten van Europa. Daarom worden de meeste Mossad-operaties nu in Europa en Amerika uitgevoerd, waar de gevaren veel minder groot zijn dan in de Arabische landen.

De koning onder de infiltranten was Marcus Wolf, die jarenlang de Oostduitse inlichtingendienst leidde. Hij had één groot voordeel – een Oostduitser kon gemakkelijk voor een Westduitser doorgaan.

In zijn tijd stuurde 'Mischa' Wolf tientallen agenten naar West-Duitsland. Een van hen was de privé-secretaresse van kanselier Willi Brandt zelf. Wolfs specialiteit was de preutse, onopvallende oude vrijster die zich als secretaresse onmisbaar maakte voor haar Westduitse minister en die alle documenten die haar bureau passeerden kopieerde en aan Oost-Berlijn doorgaf.

De tweede methode van infiltratie is een eigen agent die zich voordoet als

145

iemand uit een derde land. Hij is dus bekend als buitenlander, maar wordt voor een vriend aangezien.

Ook daarvan is een briljant voorbeeld bij de Mossad bekend. Ze'ev Gur Arieh werd in 1921 in het Duitse Mannheim geboren als Wolfgang Lotz. Wolfgang was een meter tachtig lang, blond, onbesneden, met blauwe ogen – maar toch een jood. Als jongen kwam hij naar Israël, werd daar opgevoed, nam een Hebreeuwse naam aan, vocht bij de ondergrondse Haganah en werd majoor in het Israëlische leger. Daarna werd hij door de Mossad gerekruteerd.

Hij werd twee jaar teruggestuurd naar Duitsland om zijn Duits bij te schaven en met Mossad-geld een goedlopend bedrijf op te bouwen. Met zijn nieuwe Duitse vrouw emigreerde hij vervolgens naar Caïro waar hij een manege begon.

Het was een groot succes. Egyptische stafofficieren werden geregelde gasten en dronken graag een glas champagne met Wolfgang, een echte rechtse, anti-semitische Duitser die ze volledig vertrouwden. En dus vertelden ze hem hun geheimen. En alles werd aan Tel Aviv doorgegeven. Lotz werd uiteindelijk ontmaskerd, maar had het geluk dat hij niet meteen werd opgehangen. Na de Zesdaagse Oorlog werd hij voor Egyptische krijgsgevangenen geruild.

Een nog succesvollere infiltrant was een Duitser uit een vroegere generatie. Richard Sorge was voor de Tweede Wereldoorlog buitenlands correspondent in Tokio. Hij sprak Japans en had goede contacten bij de regering van Hideki Tojo. Die regering steunde Hitler en veronderstelde dat Sorge een loyale nazi was, zoals hij zelf beweerde.

Het kwam geen moment bij de Japanners op dat Sorge geen Duitse nazi was maar een Duitse communist die voor Moskou werkte. Jarenlang gaf hij de Japanse oorlogsplannen aan de Russen door. Zijn belangrijkste coup was ook zijn laatste. In 1941 stond Hitlers leger voor de poorten van Moskou. Stalin moest dringend weten of de Japanners van plan waren om vanuit hun bases in Mantsjoerije de Sovjetunie binnen te vallen. Sorge kwam met het antwoord: nee. Daarom kon Stalin een Mongoolse troepenmacht van 40 000 man vanuit het oosten naar Moskou overbrengen. Het Aziatische kanonnenvlees hield de Duitsers nog een paar weken op afstand tot de winter inviel en Moskou werd gered.

Sorge niet. Die werd ontmaskerd en opgehangen. Maar zijn informatie had waarschijnlijk de loop van de geschiedenis veranderd.

De derde methode om een agent in de regering van een ander land te laten infiltreren komt het meest voor: iemand rekruteren die al een hoge positie heeft. Dat kan heel langzaam gaan of juist heel snel. 'Talentenjagers' zijn voortdurend op zoek naar geschikte kandidaten – hoge functionarissen die ontevreden zijn, een wrok koesteren of om andere redenen in aanmerking komen.

Bezoekende buitenlandse delegaties worden onder de loep genomen om te zien of er iemand kan worden benaderd. Als er een potentiële rekruut is gevonden, wordt er door een agent contact gelegd – een oppervlakkige vriendschap, die steeds hechter wordt. Ten slotte vraagt de 'vriend' dan om een kleine gunst: een paar inlichtingen van weinig belang.

Als de val zich eenmaal heeft gesloten, is er geen weg terug meer. Hoe meedogenlozer het regime in het land van de nieuwe rekruut, des te kleiner de kans dat hij zijn misstap zal durven bekennen.

De motieven van de spionnen verschillen nogal. Ze hebben schulden, een slecht huwelijk, ze zijn over het hoofd gezien bij een promotie, ze hebben een hekel aan het eigen regime, of ze willen een nieuw leven beginnen met veel geld. Soms worden ze ook gechanteerd met hun zwakheden – hetero- of homoseksueel – of laten ze zich gewoon ompraten met vleierij en mooie woorden.

Heel wat Russen, zoals Penkovksy en Gordievsky, spioneerden op grond van een oprechte overtuiging, maar de meeste spionnen zijn ijdel en denken dat ze een belangrijke rol spelen op het wereldtoneel.

De merkwaardigste rekruut is de 'binnenloper'. Zoals de naam al aangeeft, gaat het hier om spionnen die zich zomaar aanmelden.

Een inlichtingendienst die door zo iemand wordt benaderd reageert altijd sceptisch en vreest een valstrik van de andere partij. Toen een lange Rus in 1960 de Amerikanen in Moskou benaderde, verklaarde dat hij kolonel was bij de GRU, de Russische militaire inlichtingendienst, en zijn diensten aan het Westen aanbood, was er niemand die hem geloofde.

Verbijsterd wendde de man zich tot de Britten, die het erop waagden. Oleg Penkovsky ontpopte zich als een van de belangrijkste agenten aller tijden. In zijn korte, dertig maanden lange carrière, gaf hij ruim 5500 documenten door, in een gecombineerde Brits-Amerikaanse operatie. Al die stukken vielen in de categorie 'geheim' of 'topgeheim'. Nooit heeft de wereld geweten dat president Kennedy tijdens de Cubaanse rakettencrisis alle troeven van de Russische leider Nikita Chroesjtsjev kende – als een pokerspeler met een spiegel achter de rug van zijn tegenstander. Die spiegel was Penkovsky.

De Rus nam krankzinnige risico's en weigerde naar het Westen over te lopen toen hij de kans had. Na de rakettencrisis werd hij ontmaskerd door de Russische contraspionagedienst, berecht en doodgeschoten.

De drie andere Israëli's in het kantoor van Kobi Dror die avond kenden natuurlijk de geschiedenis van Oleg Penkovsky. In hun wereld was hij een legende. Dromerig staarden ze voor zich uit toen Sharon de naam had genoemd. Een echte, authentieke, 24-karaats spion in Bagdad? Zou dat echt waar kunnen zijn?

Kobi Dror keek Sharon lang en doordringend aan.

'Waar dacht je aan, jongeman?'

'Ik dacht alleen...' antwoordde Sharon met voorgewende bedeesdheid, 'dat een brief weinig risico oplevert... Gewoon een brief met een paar vragen, lastige vragen, dingen die we graag willen weten... Dan zien we wel of hij met de antwoorden komt.'

Dror keek naar Gershon, die verantwoordelijk was voor de 'illegale' agenten. Gershon haalde zijn schouders op. 'Ik ga over mensen,' leek dat gebaar te zeggen. 'Brieven zijn mijn afdeling niet.'

'Goed, jonge vriend David. We zullen hem een brief terug schrijven. Met een paar vragen. En dan wachten we af. Eitan, regel jij het maar met David. En laat me die brief zien voordat hij de deur uitgaat.'

Eitan Hadar en David Sharon vertrokken samen.

'Ik hoop dat je weet wat je doet,' mompelde het hoofd van de divisie Midden-Oosten tegen zijn protégé.

De brief werd heel behoedzaam opgesteld. Een paar interne deskundigen bemoeiden zich ermee – met de Hebreeuwse versie, tenminste. De vertaling kwam later wel.

David Sharon stelde zich voor met zijn voornaam, bedankte de afzender voor zijn moeite en verzekerde hem dat de brief veilig op de bestemde plaats was aangekomen.

Natuurlijk kon de afzender zich voorstellen dat zijn brief tot verbaasde en achterdochtige reacties had geleid, zowel vanwege de herkomst als vanwege de methode van verzending.

De afzender was niet dom, veronderstelde David, en daarom zou hij begrijpen dat 'Davids mensen' een paar garanties nodig hadden.

Als die zouden komen, zou de afzender zich geen zorgen hoeven maken over de betaling, mits de informatie aan de verwachtingen voldeed, dat was duidelijk. Zou de afzender zo vriendelijk willen zijn antwoord te geven op de vragen die op het aangehechte vel werden gesteld?

De brief was wat langer en omslachtiger, maar daar kwam het op neer. Aan het eind gaf Sharon de afzender een postadres in Rome waar hij zijn reactie naartoe kon sturen – een onderduikadres dat niet langer werd gebruikt en dat door het Mossad-bureau in Rome ter beschikking was gesteld, op dringend verzoek van Tel Aviv. Vanaf dat moment zou Rome een oogje houden op het leegstaande huis. Als de Iraakse geheime dienst in de buurt zou opduiken, zouden ze de zaak afblazen.

Ook de lijst van twintig vragen had veel hoofdbrekens gekost. Op acht vragen kende de Mossad het antwoord al, hoewel niemand dat zou vermoeden.

Iedere poging om Tel Aviv te misleiden zou dus stranden. Acht andere vragen betroffen gebeurtenissen die op hun waarheidsgehalte konden worden getest nadat ze zich hadden voorgedaan. En dan waren er nog vier vragen waarop Tel Aviv werkelijk het antwoord wilde weten – met name de bedoelingen van Saddam Hoessein zelf.

'Ik ben benieuwd of die vent echt zo'n hoge positie heeft,' zei Kobi Dror toen hij de lijst gelezen had.

Ten slotte werd een professor aan de Arabische faculteit van de universiteit van Tel Aviv gevraagd de brief te vertalen in die bloemrijke stijl van het geschreven woord. Sharon ondertekende de brief met de Arabische versie van zijn eigen naam, Daoud.

De tekst bevatte nog één ander punt. David wilde de afzender graag een naam geven. Als de man uit Bagdad daar geen bezwaar tegen had, mochten ze hem dan Jericho noemen?

De brief werd verstuurd vanuit het enige Arabische land waar Israël een ambassade had: Egypte.

David Sharon ging weer verder met zijn dagelijkse werk en wachtte af. Hoe langer hij erover nadacht, des te krankzinniger de hele zaak hem toescheen. Een postbusnummer in een land waar de contraspionagedienst onder leiding stond van een sluwe vogel als Hassan Rahmani... Dat was wel erg gevaarlijk. En vermoedelijk zou hij de geheime informatie in gewoon schrift doorgeven, want er was geen enkele aanwijzing dat Jericho geheimschrift kende. Ook al zo riskant... Als het werkelijk tot iets leidde, zouden ze nooit de gewone post kunnen gebruiken. Maar waarschijnlijk zou de zaak op niets uitlopen, dacht Sharon.

Daar vergiste hij zich in. Vier weken later kwam Jericho's antwoord in Rome aan. De brief werd in een bombestendige kist naar Tel Aviv overgebracht. Alle noodzakelijke veiligheidsmaatregelen werden getroffen. De brief kon immers explosieven bevatten of met een dodelijk gif zijn ingesmeerd. Maar toen de wetenschappers niets bijzonders konden vinden, werd hij geopend.

Tot hun stomme verbazing had Jericho de hele lijst afgewerkt. De acht vragen waarop de Mossad de antwoorden al kende, klopten precies. Acht andere vragen, over troepenbewegingen, promoties, ontslagen en buitenlandse reizen van Iraakse leiders, zouden moeten wachten totdat die hadden plaatsgevonden, als dat ooit gebeurde. De laatste vier vragen kon Tel Aviv niet controleren, maar de antwoorden leken heel plausibel.

Snel schreef David Sharon een brief terug, in bewoordingen die geen argwaan zouden wekken als de envelop werd onderschept: 'Beste Oom, heel veel dank voor uw brief die ik heb ontvangen. Fijn te horen dat u het goed maakt. Op enkele van uw vragen kan ik nog geen antwoord geven, maar als alles goed gaat, schrijf ik u weer snel. Uw liefhebbende neef, Daoud.'

De mannen in het Hadar Dafna Gebouw raakten er steeds meer van overtuigd dat Jericho toch een serieuze spion zou kunnen zijn. Als dat zo was, moesten ze snel iets ondernemen. Een paar brieven sturen was één ding, een spion begeleiden in een dictatuur zoals Irak was iets heel anders. De informatie mocht niet langer in gewoon schrift worden gesteld, en postbussen en postbestellingen waren uit den boze. Veel te riskant.

Er zou een controleofficier naar Bagdad moeten reizen om het contact met Jericho te onderhouden via de gebruikelijke methoden – geheimschrift, codes, geheime plaatsen om informatie achter te laten, en een veilige manier om de inlichtingen vanuit Bagdad naar Israël te smokkelen.

'Vergeet het maar,' herhaalde Gershon. 'Ik stuur geen hoge *katsa* naar Bagdad voor een langdurige illegale missie. Als hij geen diplomatieke onschendbaarheid krijgt, gaat het niet door.'

'Goed dan, Sami,' zei Dror. 'Dan gaat hij als diplomaat. Eens kijken wat we kunnen regelen.'

'Illegale' agenten kunnen worden gearresteerd, gemarteld, opgehangen, wat dan ook. Een officiële diplomaat hoeft daar niet bang voor te zijn, zelfs niet in Irak. Wanneer hij als spion wordt ontmaskerd, wordt hij tot ongewenst persoon verklaard en het land uitgezet. Zo gaan die dingen.

Verschillende afdelingen van de Mossad hadden het die zomer erg druk, vooral de sectie Onderzoek. Gershon had gezegd dat hij geen enkele agent in Bagdad had, op welke ambassade dan ook, en dat vond hij al pijnlijk genoeg. En zo begon de speurtocht naar een geschikte diplomaat.

Alle buitenlandse ambassades in Bagdad werden onder de loep genomen. Uit alle hoofdsteden van de betreffende landen werd een lijst opgevraagd met het ambassadepersoneel in Bagdad. Maar het leverde niets op. Er was niemand bij die ooit voor de Mossad had gewerkt en opnieuw kon worden ingeschakeld. Er kwamen zelfs geen *sajanim* op de lijsten voor.

Toen kwam iemand met een ander idee: de Verenigde Naties. De volkerenorganisatie had in 1988 nog één vertegenwoordiging in Bagdad, de Economische Commissie voor West-Azië.

De Mossad heeft heel wat mensen bij de Verenigde Naties in New York, die meteen een lijst opstuurden. Eén naam bood mogelijkheden: een jonge joods-Chileense diplomaat, Alfonso Benz Moncada. Hij was geen getrainde agent, maar wel een *sajan* en dus vermoedelijk bereid om te helpen.

Eén voor één werden Jericho's antwoorden bevestigd. Bepaalde legerdivisies verplaatsten zich zoals hij had gezegd. De promoties die hij had voorspeld werden afgekondigd, en de mensen die hij had genoemd werden ontslagen.

'Of Saddam zelf zit achter deze komedie, of Jericho is bereid zijn land met huid en haar te verkopen,' was het commentaar van Kobi Dror.

David Sharon stuurde nog een derde brief, ook in onschuldige termen. Voor zijn tweede en derde brief had hij de professor niet meer nodig. De derde brief verwees naar een bestelling van een cliënt in Bagdad – een zending zeer breekbaar glaswerk en porselein. Er was nog wat geduld nodig, schreef David, om een goede manier van transport te vinden om de zending tegen ongelukken te beschermen.

Een Spaans sprekende *katsa* die zich al in Zuid-Amerika bevond werd spoorslags naar Santiago gestuurd en overreedde de ouders van señor Moncada om hun zoon onmiddellijk terug te roepen omdat zijn moeder ernstig ziek was. De vader zelf belde met Bagdad. De geschrokken zoon kreeg meteen drie weken verlof en vloog terug naar Chili.

Daar trof hij geen zieke moeder aan, maar een heel opleidingsteam van de Mossad dat hem smeekte om zijn hulp. Hij besprak de zaak met zijn ouders en stemde toe. De emotionele band met Israël, waar geen van hen ooit was geweest, bleek sterk genoeg.

Een andere *sajan* in Santiago leende hun zijn zomerhuis zonder dat hij wist waarvoor. Het was een vrijstaande villa met een ommuurde tuin, niet ver van de zee. Het opleidingsteam ging aan het werk.

Het kost minimaal twee jaar om een *katsa* te trainen voor de begeleiding van een spion op vijandelijk terrein. Het team had precies drie weken. Ze werkten zestien uur per dag. Ze leerden de dertigjarige Chileen alles over geheimschrift en eenvoudige codes, minifotografie en het verkleinen van foto's op microformaat. Ze namen hem mee de straat op om hem te leren hoe hij kon weten of hij werd geschaduwd. Ze waarschuwden hem dat hij een achtervolger nooit mocht afschudden, behalve in een noodgeval, als hij geheim en gevaarlijk materiaal bij zich had. Als hij alleen maar *vermoedde* dat hij werd gevolgd, moest hij de afspraak meteen annuleren en het een andere keer opnieuw proberen.

Ze lieten hem zien hoe hij brandbare chemicaliën in een speciale vulpen kon gebruiken om belastende bewijzen binnen enkele seconden te verbranden – op een wc of gewoon om een hoek.

Ze reden met hem rond in auto's om hem te demonstreren hoe hij achtervolgers kon ontdekken, waarbij één lid van het team als instructeur fungeerde en de anderen hen schaduwden. Ze gingen maar door, totdat zijn oren tuitten en zijn ogen traanden en hij smeekte om een paar uur slaap.

Daarna leerden ze hem over de juiste plaatsen om informatie op te pikken en achter te laten – achter losse stenen in een muur, onder een grafplaat, in een spleet van een oude boom of onder een tegel.

Drie weken later nam Alfonso Benz Moncada afscheid van zijn angstige ouders en vloog via Londen naar Bagdad terug. De leider van het instructieteam leunde achterover in zijn stoel in de villa, streek vermoeid over zijn voorhoofd en mompelde tegen de anderen: 'Als die arme kerel vrij en in leven blijft, ga ik op bedevaart naar Mekka.'

Zijn collega's lachten. Hun leider was een diepgelovige orthodoxe jood.

Al die tijd dat ze Moncada hådden lesgegeven, had niemand geweten wat hij in Bagdad moest doen. Dat was ook niet nodig. De Chileen wist het zelf niet eens. Tijdens de tussenstop in Londen werd Moncada naar het Heathrow Penta Hotel gebracht. Daar ontmoette hij Sami Gershon en David Sharon, die hem vertelden wat de bedoeling was.

'Probeer hem niet te identificeren,' waarschuwde Gershon de jongeman. 'Laat dat maar aan ons over. Geef berichten door en haal de informatie op. We zullen je een lijst geven met vragen waar we een antwoord op willen. Je zult ze niet begrijpen, want ze zijn in het Arabisch. Ik geloof niet dat Jericho veel Engels spreekt. Misschien wel helemaal niet. Probeer nooit te vertalen wat we je sturen. Laat de berichten op de afgeproken plaatsen achter en zet de juiste krijtstrepen, zodat hij weet dat we iets voor hem hebben. Als je zijn krijtstreep ziet, ga dan naar het andere punt om zijn antwoord op te halen.'

In de slaapkamer kreeg Alfonso Benz Moncada zijn nieuwe bagage. Er zat een camera bij die in niets van een gewone Pentax te onderscheiden was maar die een extra cassette bevatte voor meer dan honderd opnamen, plus een onschuldig statief om de camera op exact de juiste hoogte boven een vel papier te houden. De lens was al op die afstand ingesteld.

Bij zijn toiletspullen zaten de brandbare chemicaliën, vermomd als aftershave, en een paar soorten onzichtbare inkt. In zijn schrijfmap zat papier dat al was voorbewerkt voor het geheimschrift. Ten slotte vertelden ze hem de manier waarop hij contact met hen kon onderhouden, een route die ze hadden georganiseerd terwijl hij in Chili werd getraind.

Hij zou brieven schrijven over schaken – hij was een enthousiast schaker – aan zijn correspondentievriend Justin Bokomo uit Uganda, een medewerker van het algemene secretariaat van de Verenigde Naties in New York. Zijn brieven moesten *altijd* met de diplomatieke post vanuit Bagdad worden verstuurd. De antwoorden zouden ook via Bokomo uit New York komen.

Moncada wist dat niet, maar bij de VN in New York werkte inderdaad een Ugandees die Bokomo heette. En in de postkamer werkte een Mossad-agent die de brieven zou onderscheppen.

Op de achterkant van de brieven van Bokomo zouden met onzichtbare inkt de vragen van de Mossad worden genoteerd. Die moesten zichtbaar worden gemaakt, gefotokopieerd, en via de geheime plaatsen aan Jericho worden doorgegeven. Jericho zou de antwoorden waarschijnlijk noteren in zijn priegelige Arabische handschrift. Elke pagina moest tien keer worden gefotografeerd (met het oog op vlekken) en Moncada zou de film aan Bokomo sturen.

Terug in Bagdad selecteerde de jonge Chileen, trillend van de zenuwen, zes geheime plaatsen, voornamelijk achter losse stenen van oude muren of vervallen huizen, onder tegels in verlaten steegjes en één onder een stenen vensterbank van een leegstaande winkel.

Ieder moment verwachtte hij de agenten van de gevreesde AMAM te zien opduiken, maar de burgers van Bagdad waren hoffelijk als altijd en niemand lette op hem toen hij, zogenaamd als nieuwsgierige toerist, door de stegen en straatjes van de Oude Wijk, de Armeense Wijk, de fruit- en groentemarkt van Kasra en de oude begraafplaatsen zwierf – overal waar hij afbrokkelende oude muren en losse tegels kon vinden waar niemand ooit iets zou zoeken.

Hij noteerde de locaties van de zes plaatsen, drie voor boodschappen van hem aan Jericho en drie voor de antwoorden van Jericho aan hem. Ook bepaalde hij zes plekken – muren, hekken, luiken – waar een onschuldig krijtstreepje Jericho zou waarschuwen dat er een bericht voor hem lag, of andersom. Elk van de krijtstrepen hoorde bij een andere 'brievenbus'. Hij beschreef de plaatsen zo nauwkeurig dat Jericho ze zonder probleem moest kunnen vinden.

Hij lette voortdurend op of hij niet gevolgd werd, per auto of te voet. Eén keer werd hij inderdaad geschaduwd, maar nogal onhandig en onverschillig. Blijkbaar koos de AMAM willekeurige dagen om willekeurige diplomaten te volgen. De volgende dag was hij weer alleen en kon hij zijn gang gaan.

Toen alles klaar was, typte hij zijn instructies op een schrijfmachine, vernietigde het lint, fotografeerde de vellen papier, verbrandde die ook en stuurde de film naar Bokomo. Via de postkamer van het VN-gebouw aan de East River in New York werd het kleine pakje doorgezonden aan David Sharon in Tel Aviv.

Het was niet zonder risico om de informatie aan Jericho door te spelen. Dat betekende nog één laatste brief naar die vervloekte postbus in Bagdad. Sharon schreef aan 'zijn vriend' dat de papieren die hij nodig had over veertien dagen, op 18 augustus 1988, precies om twaalf uur 's middags zouden worden afgeleverd en binnen een uur moesten worden opgehaald.

De juiste instructies, in het Arabisch, waren op de 16e bij Moncada. Op 18 augustus om vijf voor twaalf stapte hij het postkantoor binnen, werd naar de postbus verwezen en liet het pakje daar achter. Niemand hield hem aan of arresteerde hem. Een uur later opende Jericho de postbus en nam het pakje mee. Ook hij werd niet aangehouden.

Nu er een veilig contact tot stand was gebracht, kwam de informatiestroom pas goed op gang. Jericho hing een prijskaartje aan iedere inlichting waar Tel Aviv om vroeg. De informatie zou pas worden doorgegeven als het geld was betaald. Hij noemde een zeer discrete bank in Wenen, de Winkler Bank in de Ballgasse, vlak bij de Franziskanerplatz, en gaf er een rekeningnummer bij.

Tel Aviv ging akkoord en stelde meteen een onderzoek in naar de bank. Het was een klein, zeer discreet en bijna ondoordringbaar bankiershuis. En kennelijk had Jericho er al een rekening geopend, want de eerste betaling van twintigduizend dollar door Tel Aviv werd niet teruggestort met een verzoek om inlichtingen.

De Mossad vroeg of Jericho zichzelf misschien bekend wilde maken, 'voor zijn eigen veiligheid', voor het geval er iets mis zou gaan en zijn vrienden in het Westen hem wilden helpen. Maar Jericho weigerde categorisch. Sterker nog, als iemand zou proberen hem te identificeren als hij berichten achterliet, of als het geld niet zou worden betaald, zou hij ieder contact verbreken.

De Mossad schikte zich en probeerde het op een andere manier. Er werd een psychologisch profiel opgesteld, Jericho's handschrift werd geanalyseerd, er werden lijsten van hoge Iraakse functionarissen aangelegd en bestudeerd. Maar het resultaat viel tegen. Jericho moest een man van middelbare leeftijd zijn, met een matige opleiding. Hij sprak weinig of geen Engels en had een militaire of para-militaire achtergrond.

'Dat geldt voor de helft van de Iraakse legertop, de belangrijkste vijftig mensen binnen de Ba'ath-partij, plus Jan, Piet en Klaas,' mopperde Kobi Dror.

Alfonso Benz Moncada onderhield twee jaar lang het contact met Jericho. De informatie van de spion bleek goud waard. Hij gaf inlichtingen door over politiek, conventionele wapens, militaire vorderingen, veranderingen in het commando, wapenaankopen, raketten, gas, bacteriologische oorlogvoering en twee mislukte aanslagen op Saddam Hoessein. Alleen over de Iraakse nucleaire mogelijkheden bleef hij nogal vaag. Natuurlijk werd hij daarnaar gevraagd. Maar het nucleaire programma was streng geheim en alleen volledig bekend bij de Iraakse tegenhanger van Robert Oppenheimer, de natuurkundige dr. Jaafar al-Jaafar. En als hij te sterk zou aandringen, zou dat argwaan wekken, verklaarde Jericho.

In de herfst van 1989 meldde hij aan Tel Aviv dat Gerry Bull onder verdenking stond en in Brussel werd geschaduwd door een team van de Iraakse Mukhabarat. De Mossad, die Bull ook als een bron van informatie over het Iraakse raketprogramma gebruikte, probeerde hem zo subtiel mogelijk te waarschuwen. Ze konden hem niet openlijk vertellen wat ze wisten – dan zouden ze toegeven dat ze een hoge spion in Bagdad hadden, en geen enkele inlichtingendienst zal ooit zo'n kostbare bron prijsgeven.

De *katsa* die de leiding had van het grote Mossad-bureau in Brussel gaf zijn mensen in de loop van de herfst en de winter een paar keer opdracht Bulls appartement binnen te dringen en verhulde boodschappen achter te laten

154

door een videoband terug te spoelen, een paar wijnglazen te verplaatsen, een raam open te laten en zelfs een lange lok vrouwenhaar op zijn kussen te leggen.

De artillerie-ontwerper maakte zich wel ongerust, maar niet voldoende. Toen Jericho's bericht binnenkwam dat de Mukhabarat van plan was Bull te vermoorden, was het al te laat en had de aanslag plaatsgevonden.

Jericho's informatie gaf de Mossad een bijna volledig beeld van de Iraakse voorbereidingen op de inval in Koeweit in 1990. Wat hij schreef over Saddams massavernietigingswapens bevestigde en versterkte het beeldmateriaal dat ze hadden gekregen van Jonathan Pollard, die inmiddels tot een levenslange gevangenisstraf was veroordeeld.

De Mossad, die veronderstelde dat Amerika ook op de hoogte was, wachtte tot de Verenigde Staten zouden reageren. Maar terwijl de chemische, nucleaire en bacteriologische opbouw in Irak gewoon doorging, bleef het Westen passief. En dus hield Tel Aviv zijn mond.

Omstreeks augustus 1990 was er in totaal zo'n twee miljoen dollar overgemaakt op Jericho's bankrekening in Wenen. Hij was duur, maar zijn informatie was het waard. Maar toen viel Irak Koeweit binnen en gebeurde er iets onverwachts. De Verenigde Naties, die op 2 augustus een resolutie hadden aangenomen waarin Irak werd gemaand zich onmiddellijk uit Koeweit terug te trekken, vonden dat ze Saddam niet konden blijven steunen door een vestiging in Bagdad in stand te houden. Op 7 augustus werd de Economische Commissie voor West-Azië abrupt opgeheven en moesten de diplomaten uit Irak vertrekken.

Benz Moncada liet inderhaast een boodschap voor Jericho achter met de mededeling dat het contact voorlopig was verbroken, maar dat hij misschien zou terugkomen. Hij vroeg Jericho om regelmatig de aanwijzingen op de bekende plaatsen in het oog te houden. Daarna vertrok de jonge Chileen. In Londen werd hij uitvoerig ondervraagd, totdat hij David Sharon alles had verteld wat hij wist.

Daarom had Kobi Dror niet echt tegen Chip Barber gelogen. Op dat moment had hij inderdaad geen spion meer in Bagdad. Het zou heel pijnlijk voor hem zijn geweest om toe te geven dat hij de naam van de verrader nooit had kunnen traceren en dat hij nu het contact verloren had. Maar zoals Sami Gershon al zei, als de Amerikanen er ooit achterkwamen... Achteraf gezien had hij hun misschien toch over Jericho moeten vertellen.

Op 1 oktober ging Mike Martin naar het graf van matroos Shepton op de begraafplaats van Sulajbikhat en vond het verzoek van Ahmed Al-Khalifa. Hij was niet echt verbaasd. Als Abu Fouad van hem had gehoord, was hij ook op de hoogte van de nieuwe verzetsbeweging, hun toenemende activiteiten en hun mysterieuze leider. Het was bijna onvermijdelijk dat ze elkaar een keer moesten ontmoeten.

In zes weken tijd was de situatie voor de Iraakse bezettingstroepen drastisch veranderd. De invasie was zo gemakkelijk gegaan dat ze zich totaal geen zorgen hadden gemaakt over het eventuele verzet. Zonder tegenstand hadden ze kunnen plunderen en verkrachten, zoals alle veroveraars uit de historie, tot aan de tijden van Babylon.

Koeweit was immers een vette kip, klaar om geplukt te worden. Maar in die zes weken was de kip steeds feller gaan pikken en krabben. Meer dan honderd soldaten en acht officieren waren vermoord of spoorloos verdwenen. En die verdwijningen konden niet allemaal als desertie worden verklaard. Voor het eerst begonnen de bezettingstroepen angstig te worden.

Officieren reden niet langer in hun eentje rond, maar lieten zich escorteren door trucks met soldaten. Het hoofdkwartier werd dag en nacht bewaakt – de officieren schoten zelfs over de hoofden van de slapende wachtposten om ze wakker te houden.

's Nachts durfden de Iraakse militairen alleen nog in grote konvooien over straat. De wachtposten bij de wegversperringen trokken zich in hun bunkers terug zodra de duisternis viel. Maar nog steeds explodeerden er mijnen, gingen er voertuigen in vlammen op, werden motoren gesaboteerd, vlogen er granaten door de lucht en werden soldaten in goten en op vuilnishopen teruggevonden met een afgesneden keel.

Het toenemende verzet had het Iraakse opperbevel gedwongen het Volksleger te vervangen door de Speciale Eenheden – goede troepen, die eigenlijk aan het front nodig waren als de Amerikanen zouden komen. Begin oktober was voor Koeweit niet, om Churchill te citeren, het begin van het einde, maar het einde van het begin.

Martin kon niet reageren op Al-Khalifa's boodschap toen hij die vond. Pas de volgende dag liet hij een antwoord achter.

Hij was bereid tot een ontmoeting, schreef hij, maar op zijn eigen voorwaarden. Om gebruik te maken van de duisternis maar de avondklok te vermijden, stelde hij voor dat ze om half acht zouden afspreken. Hij gaf nauwkeurige instructies waar Abu Fouad zijn auto moest parkeren en bij welk bosje ze elkaar zouden treffen. De plek die hij in gedachten had lag in het district Abrak Kheitan, dicht bij de hoofdweg naar het verwoeste en onbruikbare vliegveld.

Martin wist dat het een wijk was met traditionele stenen huizen met platte daken. Op een van die daken zou hij zich twee uur van tevoren installeren om te zien of de Koeweitse officier werd gevolgd en door wie – zijn eigen lijfwachten of de Irakezen. De SAS-officier was nog steeds op vrije voeten omdat hij geen enkel risico nam.

Hij wist niet hoe betrouwbaar Abu Fouads veiligheidsmaatregelen waren, maar voorlopig had hij er geen hoge verwachtingen van. Als datum voor de ontmoeting noemde hij de 7e oktober. Hij liet zijn antwoord onder de marmeren grafplaat achter, waar het op de 4e oktober door Ahmed Al-Khalifa werd gevonden.

Dr. John Hipwell was niet het type van een kernfysicus, laat staan van iemand die zijn dagen sleet in het streng beveiligde complex van het Atomic Weapons Establishment bij Aldermaston waar hij plutoniumkoppen voor Trident-raketten ontwierp.

Hij had meer van een rondborstige boer die peinzend over een hek op de veemarkt leunt dan van een ingenieur die toezicht houdt op het vergulden van dodelijke plutoniumschijven.

Hoewel het nog redelijk weer was, droeg hij – net als in augustus – een geruit overhemd, een wollen das en een tweedjasje. Zonder iets te vragen stopte hij met zijn grote rode knuisten een pijp voordat hij verslag uitbracht aan het Medusa Comité. Sir Paul Spruce trok zijn neus op en gaf een teken om de airconditioning hoger te zetten.

'Heren, het goede nieuws is dat onze vriend Saddam Hoessein nog niet over een atoombom beschikt. Nog lang niet,' verklaarde Hipwell, terwijl hij in een wolk van lichtblauwe rook verdween.

Het bleef even stil toen de wetenschapper nog eens stevig aan zijn pijp trok. Ach, dacht Terry Martin, als je iedere dag het risico van een dodelijke dosis plutoniumstraling loopt, kan een pijpje op zijn tijd misschien geen kwaad.

Dr. Hipwell raadpleegde zijn aantekeningen. 'Irak is al sinds de jaren zeventig, toen Saddam aan de macht kwam, bezig met de ontwikkeling van een eigen kernbom. Het lijkt wel een obsessie voor die man. In die jaren hebben de Irakezen een compleet kernreactorsysteem van Frankrijk gekocht, dat toen nog niet gebonden was aan het non-proliferatieverdrag van 1968.'

Hij zoog tevreden aan zijn pijp en stampte de rood opgloeiende tabak nog eens aan. Een paar vonkjes daalden op zijn aantekeningen neer.

157

'Eh...' zei Sir Paul, 'was die kernreactor bedoeld om elektriciteit op te wekken?'

'Officieel wel,' antwoordde Hipwell. 'Maar dat was natuurlijk onzin, zoals Frankrijk heel goed wist. Irak heeft de op twee na grootste oliereserves ter wereld. Voor een fractie van de prijs hadden ze een aardoliecentrale kunnen bouwen. Nee, het punt was dat ze die centrale met laagwaardig uranium – caramel of *yellowcake* – konden stoken, dat ze nu op een legitieme manier konden kopen. Na het gebruik in de reactor blijft er plutonium over.'

Rondom de tafel werd geknikt. Iedereen wist dat de Britse reactor van Sellafield elektriciteit voor het net leverde en plutonium dat dr. Hipwell voor zijn kernkoppen kon gebruiken.

'De Israëli's lieten het er niet bij zitten,' zei Hipwell. 'Nog voordat hij werd verscheept werd een van de grote turbines al in Toulon door een Israëlische commandogroep opgeblazen, waardoor het project twee jaar vertraging opliep. En in 1981, toen Saddam zijn kostbare fabrieken Een en Twee bij Osirak wilde opstarten, voerden Israëlische jachtbommenwerpers een aanval uit en bombardeerden de installaties naar het hiernamaals. Het is Saddam nooit meer gelukt een andere reactor te kopen. Na een tijdje gaf hij de moed op.'

'Waarom?' vroeg Sinclair vanaf zijn kant van de tafel.

'Omdat hij het over een andere boeg gooide,' antwoordde Hipwell met een brede glimlach, alsof hij binnen een halfuur de kruiswoordpuzzel in de *Times* had opgelost. 'Tot die tijd wilde hij via plutonium aan een kernbom komen. Daarna richtte hij al zijn aandacht op uranium. Met enig succes. Maar niet genoeg. En toch...'

'Ik begrijp het niet,' onderbrak Sir Paul Spruce hem. 'Wat is het verschil tussen kernbommen op basis van plutonium of uranium?'

'Uranium is simpeler,' zei de kernfysicus. 'Er bestaan verscheidene radioactieve stoffen die je voor een kettingreactie kunt gebruiken, maar voor een eenvoudige en effectieve kernbom is uranium de beste oplossing. Daarom heeft Saddam het sinds 1982 op die manier geprobeerd. Hij is er nog niet, maar hij geeft het niet op, en ooit zal hij erin slagen.'

Dr. Hipwell liet zich terugzakken met een brede grijns, alsof hij het antwoord op het mysterie van de Schepping had gevonden.

Sir Paul Spruce begreep het nog steeds niet erg, evenmin als de anderen rond de tafel. 'Maar als hij uranium heeft gekocht voor zijn verwoeste reactor, waarom kan hij er dan geen bom mee maken?'

Dr. Hipwell stortte zich op de vraag als een boer op een voordelig koopje. 'Omdat er verschillende soorten uranium bestaan, mijn beste. Vreemd spul, uranium. Heel zeldzaam. Van duizend ton erts houd je niet meer over dan een blokje ter grootte van een sigarenkistje. Dat noemen we *yellowcake* of natuurlijk uranium, met een isotoopgetal van 238. Daar kun je een indus-

triële reactor mee stoken, maar het is niet geschikt voor een bom. Niet zuiver genoeg. Voor een bom heb je een lichtere isotoop nodig – uranium-235.'
'En waar haal je die vandaan?' vroeg Paxman.
'Uit de *yellowcake*. In dat kleine blokje zit een beetje uranium-235, niet meer dan je onder een vingernagel kwijt kunt. Het probleem is het scheiden van die twee soorten. Dat heet isotopenscheiding. Heel lastig, heel technisch, heel duur en heel langzaam.'
'Maar u zei dat Irak vorderingen maakt,' merkte Sinclair op.
'Jawel, maar ze zijn er nog niet,' antwoordde Hipwell. 'Er is maar één bruikbare manier om de *yellowcake* tot 93 procent zuiver uranium te distilleren. Jaren geleden hebben jullie een paar methoden getest in het zogenaamde Manhattan Project. Ernest Lawrence ging van de ene aanpak uit, Robert Oppenheimer van een andere. Daarna hebben ze beide methoden gecombineerd en genoeg uranium-235 overgehouden voor de produktie van Little Boy. Na de oorlog werd de ultracentrifugetechniek ontwikkeld en geleidelijk geperfectioneerd. Dat is tegenwoordig de enige methode. Het komt erop neer dat je het materiaal in een soort centrifuge doet, die zo snel draait dat het hele proces zich in een vacuüm moet voltrekken omdat de lagers anders zouden smelten.
Heel langzaam worden de zwaardere isotopen, die je niet nodig hebt, naar de buitenwand van de centrifuge gedreven en afgevoerd. Het restant is zuiverder. Niet veel, maar een beetje. Je moet het steeds herhalen, duizenden uren lang, om een plaatje zuiver uranium ter grootte van een postzegel over te houden.'
'En daar is Irak nu mee bezig,' drong Sir Paul aan.
'Ja. Al ongeveer een jaar. Om tijd te winnen worden die centrifuges in series geschakeld die cascades worden genoemd. Maar je hebt duizenden centrifuges nodig voor een cascade.'
'Maar als ze daar al sinds 1982 aan werken, waarom duurt het dan zo lang?' wilde Terry Martin weten.
'Je kunt zo'n centrifuge niet bij een ijzerhandel kopen,' antwoordde Hipwell. 'Dat hebben ze wel geprobeerd, maar niemand wilde hun de apparatuur leveren. Dat blijkt uit de stukken. Sinds 1985 hebben ze onderdelen gekocht om zelf zo'n installatie te bouwen. Ze hebben nu ongeveer 500 ton uranium-*yellowcake*, de helft afkomstig uit Portugal. Het grootste deel van de centrifugetechnologie komt uit West-Duitsland...'
'Ik dacht dat Duitsland een hele reeks internationale verdragen had getekend om de verspreiding van kernbomtechnologie tegen te gaan,' merkte Paxman op.
'Dat kan wel zijn. Ik weet niets van de politieke kant,' zei de wetenschapper. 'Maar ze hebben overal onderdelen vandaan gehaald – je hebt speciale draai-

159

banken nodig, ultra-sterk staal, anti-corrosievaten, speciale kleppen, zeer hete ovens die "schedelovens" worden genoemd omdat ze er zo uitzien, plus vacuümpompen en balgen. Het is een heel ingewikkelde technologie. En een groot deel daarvan, plus de benodigde kennis, kwam uit Duitsland.'

'Begrijp ik het nou goed?' vroeg Sinclair. 'Heeft Saddam al een paar van die ultracentrifuges in bedrijf?'

'Ja, één cascade. Die werkt nu ongeveer een jaar. En een tweede wordt binnenkort opgestart.'

'Weet u ook waar die installatie staat?'

'De ultracentrifugefabriek staat bij Taji... hier.' Hipwell gaf de Amerikaan een grote luchtfoto en omcirkelde een paar bedrijfsgebouwen.

'De werkende cascade schijnt ergens onder de grond te liggen, niet ver van die oude verwoeste Franse Osirak-reactor bij Tuwaitha. Ik weet niet of je die met een bommenwerper zou kunnen opsporen. Hij ligt ondergronds en hij is goed gecamoufleerd.'

'En de nieuwe cascade?'

'Geen idee,' zei Hipwell. 'Die zou overal kunnen staan.'

'Waarschijnlijk ergens anders,' meende Terry Martin. 'De Irakezen hebben de gewoonte hun installaties te dupliceren en te verspreiden sinds die keer dat ze de hele zaak op één plek hebben geconcentreerd en de Israëli's alles platgooiden.'

Sinclair bromde wat.

'Hoe zeker bent u ervan dat Saddam zijn bom nog niet heeft?' vroeg Sir Paul.

'Het is een kwestie van tijd. Hij is nog niet lang genoeg bezig,' antwoordde de fysicus. 'Voor een simpele maar bruikbare atoombom heeft hij 30 tot 35 kilo zuiver uranium-235 nodig. Hij is pas een jaar geleden begonnen. Eén draaicyclus kost twaalf uur. Je hebt duizend draaicycli nodig om van nul procent zuiver tot de vereiste 93 procent zuiver uranium te komen. Dat is dus vijfhonderd draaidagen, aangenomen dat de werkende cascade vierentwintig uur per etmaal in bedrijf zou zijn – en dat lukt nooit. De machines moeten ook onderhouden worden, en zo nu en dan valt er een uit. Zelfs met een cascade van duizend centrifuges die het hele jaar door blijft draaien, heb je nog vijf jaar nodig. Als je een tweede cascade opstart, kun je dat tot drie jaar terugbrengen.'

'Dus het zal minstens tot 1993 duren voordat hij zijn 35 kilo heeft?' vroeg Sinclair.

'Precies.'

'Nog één vraag. Als hij dat uranium heeft, hoeveel tijd heeft hij dan nog nodig om een atoombom te produceren?'

'Niet lang. Een paar weken. Die technologie heeft hij natuurlijk gelijktijdig ontwikkeld. Kernbommen zijn niet zo ingewikkeld, als je maar weet wat je doet. En Jaafar al-Jaafar is geen domme jongen. Die kan wel een bom in elkaar knutselen. We hebben hem verdomme zelf opgeleid, op Harwell. Alleen al op grond van het tijdschema is het dus onmogelijk dat Saddam over voldoende zuiver uranium zou beschikken. Hooguit 10 kilo, meer niet. Hij heeft nog minstens drie jaar nodig.'

Dr. Hipwell werd bedankt voor al zijn werk en zijn conclusies, en de vergadering werd gesloten.

Sinclair ging terug naar zijn ambassade om zijn uitvoerige aantekeningen in een rapport te verwerken dat zwaar gecodeerd naar Amerika zou worden verstuurd. Daar zou het worden vergeleken met de analyses van de Amerikaanse experts – natuurkundigen van de laboratoria van Sandia, Los Alamos en vooral ook van Lawrence Livermore in Californië, waar al jarenlang een geheime afdeling met de naam 'Department Z' de gestage internationale verbreiding van nucleaire technologie in de gaten hield, in opdracht van Buitenlandse Zaken en het Pentagon.

Wat Sinclair nog niet wist was dat de conclusies van de Britse en Amerikaanse deskundigen volledig overeenkwamen.

Terry Martin en Simon Paxman wandelden na afloop van de vergadering door Whitehall in een aangenaam oktoberzonnetje.

'Een hele opluchting,' zei Paxman. 'Die oude Hipwell was heel zeker van zijn zaak. En blijkbaar zijn de Amerikanen het met hem eens. Voorlopig heeft die klootzak dus nog geen kernbom. Dat is één nachtmerrie minder.'

Ze namen afscheid bij de hoek. Paxman stak de Theems over naar Century House en Terry Martin liep over Trafalgar Square via St. Martin's Lane naar Gower Street.

Vaststellen waar Irak – vermoedelijk – over beschikte, was één ding. De plaats van de installaties opsporen was een andere zaak. Alles werd gefotografeerd. De KH-11 en KH-12 satellieten draaiden voortdurend hun rondjes en maakten hun opnamen boven Irak.

Omstreeks oktober was er nog een mogelijkheid bij gekomen, een nieuw Amerikaans verkenningsvliegtuig dat zo geheim was dat zelfs het Congres er niets van wist. Het toestel, met de codenaam Aurora, vloog aan de rand van de ruimte met snelheden van mach-8, bijna 8000 km per uur. Voortgestuwd door zijn eigen vuurbol, het ramjet-effect, bleef het verborgen voor de Iraakse radar en onderscheppingsraketten. Zelfs de technologie van de uiteengevallen Sovjetunie kon de Aurora – de vervanger van de legendarische SR-71 Blackbird – niet opsporen.

Toen de Blackbird die herfst uit produktie was genomen was zijn plaats boven het Iraakse luchtruim ironisch genoeg ingenomen door een nog oudere 'getrouwe', de U-2. Dit veertig jaar oude vliegtuig, bijgenaamd de 'Dragon Lady', vloog nog steeds en nam nog steeds zijn foto's. In 1960 was Gary Powers met een U-2 neergeschoten boven Sverdlovsk in Siberië, en het was ook een U-2 die in de zomer van 1962 de eerste Russische raketten op Cuba had gesignaleerd. Pas later meldde Oleg Penkovsky dat het offensieve en geen defensieve wapens waren, waarmee hij Chroesjtsjevs protesten ontzenuwde maar ook zijn eigen ontmaskering inluidde.

De U-2 uit 1990, met de nieuwe naam TR-1, was eerder een 'luisteraar' dan een 'verspieder', hoewel hij nog altijd foto's nam.

Met al deze informatie, van wetenschappers en deskundigen, analisten en technici, onderzoekers en ondervragers, kon in de herfst van 1990 een beeld van Irak worden opgebouwd. En dat was een verontrustend beeld.

De gegevens uit die duizenden bronnen kwamen uiteindelijk samen in een zeer geheim kantoor, twee verdiepingen beneden het Saoedische ministerie van Luchtmacht aan de Old Airport Road in Riyad. Dit kantoor, in dezelfde straat waar de legerleiding overlegde over de geheime plannen voor de invasie van Irak, werd simpelweg het 'Zwarte Gat' genoemd.

In het Zwarte Gat bepaalden Britse en Amerikaanse experts van verschillende krijgsmachtonderdelen en verschillende rangen, van soldaat tot generaal, welke doelwitten in Irak moesten worden vernietigd. Zo ontstond ten slotte de oorlogskaart van generaal Chuck Horner, een kaart die zevenhonderd doelwitten telde. Zeshonderd daarvan waren van militaire aard – commandocentra, bruggen, vliegvelden, wapenopslagplaatsen, munitiedepots, raketinstallaties en troepenconcentraties. De andere honderd hielden verband met massavernietigingswapens: onderzoekscentra, assemblagefabrieken, chemische laboratoria en opslagplaatsen.

De ultracentrifugefabriek van Taji stond op de kaart, evenals de vermoedelijke positie van de ondergrondse centrifugecascade ergens in de buurt van het Tuwaitha-complex.

Maar de mineraalwaterfabriek van Tarmiya werd nergens vermeld, evenmin als Al-Qubai. Omdat niemand daar van wist.

Een exemplaar van Harry Sinclairs uitvoerige rapport werd bij de andere rapporten uit verschillende Amerikaanse en buitenlandse bronnen gevoegd. Ten slotte werd er een synthese opgesteld, die zijn weg vond naar een kleine, zeer geheime denktank van Buitenlandse Zaken, bij insiders in Washington bekend als de 'Political Intelligence and Analysis Group'. De PIAG is een soort analytische broeikas voor buitenlandse problemen en produceert rapporten die zeker niet voor het grote publiek bestemd zijn. De groep is uitsluitend verantwoording schuldig aan de minister van Buitenlandse Zaken, op dat moment James Baker.

Twee dagen later lag Mike Martin plat op een dak met uitzicht op de plek in Abrak Kheitan waar hij Abu Fouad zou ontmoeten.

Bijna exact op de afgesproken tijd zag hij een auto van de King Faisal Motorway naar het vliegveld komen en een zijweg inslaan. Langzaam reed de auto de straat door en liet de heldere lichten en het schaarse verkeer op de autoweg achter zich.

In het donker zag hij de auto stoppen op de plaats die hij in zijn bericht aan Al-Khalifa had aangegeven. Twee mensen stapten uit, een man en een vrouw. Ze keken om zich heen om te zien of ze niet door een andere auto vanaf de hoofdweg waren gevolgd en liepen toen rustig naar een klein bosje op een braakliggend stuk grond.

Abu Fouad en de vrouw hadden instructie gekregen om maximaal een half-uur te wachten. Als de bedoeïen dan nog niet was verschenen, moesten ze naar huis gaan. Ze wachtten veertig minuten, liepen toen gefrustreerd naar hun auto terug en stapten in.

'Hij is waarschijnlijk opgehouden,' zei Abu Fouad tegen zijn metgezel. 'Door een Iraakse patrouille misschien. Wie zal het zeggen? Verdomme, nou kunnen we weer overnieuw beginnen.'

'Je bent gek dat je hem vertrouwt,' zei de vrouw. 'Je hebt geen idee wie hij is.'

Ze spraken zacht. De Koeweitse verzetsleider keek de straat door om te zien of er geen Iraakse soldaten waren opgedoken.

'Hij is slim, hij werkt professioneel en hij boekt resultaten. Meer hoef ik niet te weten. Ik zou graag met hem samenwerken als hij dat wil.'

'Daar heb ik geen enkel bezwaar tegen.'

De vrouw slaakte een onderdrukte kreet. Abu Fouad schoot overeind in zijn stoel.

'Draait u zich niet om. Ik wil met u praten,' zei de stem vanaf de achter-bank. In zijn spiegeltje zag de Koeweiti het vage silhouet van een bedoeïense *keffijeh* en hij snoof de lucht op van iemand die al een tijd geen bad meer had genomen. Langzaam ademde hij uit.

'U beweegt zich onhoorbaar, bedoeïen.'

'Geluiden lokken Irakezen aan, Abu Fouad. En daar hou ik niet van, tenzij ik ze verwacht.'

Abu Fouads tanden blikkerden onder zijn zwarte snor.

'Goed, we hebben elkaar gevonden. Laten we praten. Waarom hebt u zich trouwens in de auto verborgen?'

'Als deze ontmoeting een valstrik was geweest, zou u iets anders hebben gezegd zodra u in de auto stapte.'

'Dan had ik mezelf verraden...'

'Natuurlijk.'

163

'En dan?'

'Dan was u nu dood geweest.'

'Begrepen.'

'Wie is de dame? Ik zei dat u alleen moest komen.'

'U hebt de ontmoeting georganiseerd, maar ik moest u kunnen vertrouwen. Zij is een betrouwbare bondgenote. Asrar Qabandi.'

'Goedenavond, mevrouw Qabandi. Waar wilt u over praten?'

'Over wapens, bedoeïen. Kalasjnikov-machinegeweren, moderne handgranaten, Semtex-H. Daarmee zouden mijn mensen veel kunnen doen.'

'Uw mensen worden overvallen, Abu Fouad. Tien verzetsstrijders hebben zich in één huis laten omsingelen door een hele Iraakse compagnie van de AMAM. Allemaal jongelui. Allemaal doodgeschoten.'

Abu Fouad zweeg. Het was een ramp geweest.

'Negen,' zei hij ten slotte. 'De tiende hield zich dood en is later weggekropen. Hij is gewond, maar we verzorgen hem. Hij heeft ons verteld wat er is gebeurd.'

'En?'

'Ze waren verraden. Als hij was gestorven, hadden we dat nooit geweten.'

'Aha, verraad. Dat ligt altijd op de loer binnen iedere verzetsbeweging. En de verrader?'

'Die kennen we, natuurlijk. We dachten dat we hem konden vertrouwen.'

'U weet zeker dat hij schuldig is?'

'Daar ziet het wel naar uit.'

'Daar ziet het naar uit?'

Abu Fouad zuchtte. 'De jongen die het overleefde zweert dat alleen de elfde man van de samenkomst en het adres op de hoogte was. Maar misschien is er een ander lek geweest. Of misschien is iemand gevolgd...'

'Dan moet hij worden getest, die verdachte. En gestraft, als hij schuldig is. Mevrouw Qabandi, wilt ons even alleen laten, alstublieft?'

De jonge vrouw keek even naar Abu Fouad, die knikte. Ze stapte de auto uit en liep naar het bosje terug. De bedoeïen vertelde Abu Fouad langzaam en zorgvuldig wat hij moest doen.

'Ik zal het huis niet voor zeven uur verlaten,' besloot hij. 'U mag dus niet vóór half acht bellen. Begrepen?'

De bedoeïen glipte de auto uit en verdween tussen de donkere steegjes tussen de vrijstaande huizen. Abu Fouad reed een eindje door en pikte Asrar Qabandi op. Samen reden ze naar huis.

De bedoeïen zag de vrouw nooit meer terug. Nog voor de bevrijding van Koeweit werd ze door de AMAM gearresteerd, zwaar gemarteld, verkracht, neergeschoten en onthoofd. Maar ze zei geen woord.

Terry Martin belde met Simon Paxman, die het druk had en de interruptie niet op prijs stelde. Maar omdat hij de pietluttige hoogleraar Arabisch wel mocht, nam hij het telefoontje toch aan.

'Ik weet dat ik stoor, maar heb je ook contacten bij het GCHQ?'

'Ja, natuurlijk,' antwoordde Paxman. 'Voornamelijk bij de Arabische sectie. Ik ken zelfs de directeur.'

'Zou je een gesprek voor me kunnen regelen?'

'Ja, ik denk het wel. Waar gaat het om?'

'Om de berichten uit Irak. Ik ken alle toespraken van Saddam en ik heb de verklaringen over de gijzelaars, de menselijke schilden en hun pijnlijke pogingen tot public relations op de televisie gezien, maar ik vraag me af of jullie nog andere dingen te horen krijgen – informatie die niet is vrijgegeven door hun ministerie van Propaganda.'

'Dat is inderdaad het terrein van het GCHQ,' beaamde Paxman. 'Het zal wel lukken. Je bent lid van het Medusa Comité, dus je bent gescreend. Ik zal hem bellen.'

De afspraak werd gemaakt en nog dezelfde middag reed Terry Martin naar Gloucestershire en meldde zich bij de zwaarbewaakte poort van het gebouwencomplex met het woud van antennes dat de derde poot van de Britse inlichtingendienst vormt, naast MI-6 en MI-5.

Het hoofd van de Arabische sectie van het Government Communications Headquarters was Sean Plummer, de baas van Al-Khouri, die Mike Martin elf weken eerder in een restaurant in Chelsea op zijn kennis van het Arabisch had getest. Plummer noch Terry Martin wist daar iets van.

Plummer had het druk, maar hij had toegestemd in een gesprek omdat hij als mede-arabist de reputatie van de jonge geleerde van de SOAS kende en waardering had voor zijn oorspronkelijke onderzoek naar het Abbasiden-kalifaat.

'Wat kan ik voor u doen?' vroeg hij toen ze achter een glas pepermuntthee zaten, een luxe die Plummer zich permitteerde om aan de ondrinkbare koffie van het instituut te ontkomen. Martin legde uit dat hij zich verbaasde dat er zo weinig berichten kwamen uit Irak.

Plummers ogen lichtten op. 'U hebt gelijk. Onze Arabische vrienden kletsen wat af over de telefoon. Maar de laatste paar jaar wordt dat steeds minder. Dat betekent dat de hele cultuur is veranderd, of...'

'Of dat ze de kabels in de grond hebben begraven.'

'Precies. Blijkbaar hebben Saddam en zijn makkers meer dan 70 000 km glasvezelkabel in de grond gelegd. En die gebruiken ze nu. Heel lastig voor ons. Ik kan Century House niet veel anders vertellen dan het weerbericht voor Bagdad en de waslijst van moeder Hoessein.'

Dat was bij wijze van spreken, besefte Martin. Plummers afdeling produceerde heel wat meer dan dat.

'Ze praten natuurlijk nog wel, de ministers, de ambtenaren en de generaals, en we onderscheppen zelfs het gekeuvel tussen de tankcommandanten aan de Saoedische grens, maar echt geheime telefoongesprekken zitten er niet bij. Dat was vroeger wel anders. Wat wilt u zien?'

De volgende vier uur nam Terry Martin een groot aantal onderschepte berichten door. Radio-uitzendingen lagen te veel voor de hand. Hij zocht naar een toevallig telefoontje, een verspreking, een vergissing. Maar ten slotte sloeg hij de dossiers zuchtend weer dicht.

'Wilt u,' vroeg hij, 'vooral letten op vreemde opmerkingen – iets wat ogenschijnlijk nergens op slaat?'

Mike Martin nam zich voor ooit nog eens een toeristische gids te schrijven over de platte daken in Koeweit Stad. Hij had er al heel wat uurtjes bovenop gelegen om de omgeving te verkennen. Ze waren nu eenmaal ideaal.

Op dit dak lag hij nu al bijna twee dagen, om het adres in het oog te houden dat hij aan Abu Fouad had genoemd. Het was een van de zes huizen waarvan hij de sleutel van Ahmed Al-Khalifa had gekregen – een huis dat hij nu nooit meer kon gebruiken.

Het was 9 oktober. Hoewel het al twee dagen geleden was dat hij het adres aan Abu Fouad had gegeven en er tot vanavond niets zou mogen gebeuren, had hij toch al die tijd op het dak gelegen, dag en nacht, met wat brood en fruit als voedsel.

Als hij vóór vanavond half acht Iraakse soldaten zag verschijnen, zou hij weten wie hem verraden had: Abu Fouad zelf. Hij keek op zijn horloge. Half acht. De Koeweitse kolonel moest nu het opgegeven nummer bellen, zoals afgesproken.

Aan de andere kant van de stad pakte Abu Fouad inderdaad de telefoon en draaide een nummer. Er werd opgenomen toen het toestel voor de derde keer overging.

'Salah?'

'Ja. Met wie spreek ik?'

'We hebben elkaar nooit ontmoet, maar ik heb veel goede dingen over u gehoord – dat u loyaal en dapper bent, en een van ons. De mensen kennen mij als Abu Fouad.'

De man aan de andere kant van de lijn hield zijn adem in.

'Ik heb uw hulp nodig, Salah. Kunnen wij... de beweging... op u rekenen?'

'Natuurlijk, Abu Fouad. Zeg maar wat ik moet doen.'

'Het gaat niet om mij, maar om een vriend. Hij is gewond en ziek. Ik weet dat u drogist bent. Hij moet zo snel mogelijk medicijnen hebben – verband, antibiotica, pijnstillers. Hebt u ooit gehoord van de man die ze de Bedoeïen noemen?'

166

'Jazeker, Abu Fouad. Maar hoe kent u hem?'
'Dat doet er niet toe. We werken al een paar weken samen. Hij is heel belangrijk voor ons.'
'Ik zal meteen naar de winkel gaan om de dingen te halen die hij nodig heeft en ze naar hem toe brengen. Waar kan ik hem vinden?'
'In een huis in Shuwaikh. Hij kan daar niet weg. Pak een potlood en papier.' Abu Fouad dicteerde het adres dat hij had gekregen. Salah noteerde het.
'Ik rijd er onmiddellijk heen, Abu Fouad. U kunt me vertrouwen,' zei Salah de drogist.
'U bent een goed mens. Wij zullen u belonen.'
Abu Fouad hing op. De bedoeïen had gezegd dat hij de volgende ochtend vroeg zou bellen als er niets was gebeurd. Dan stond de drogist niet langer onder verdenking.
Een paar minuten voor half negen zag Mike Martin de eerste truck aankomen. De bestuurder had de motor afgezet. De wagen rolde geruisloos het kruispunt over voordat hij een paar meter verder tot stilstand kwam, vlak om de hoek. Martin knikte waarderend.
Even later naderde een tweede truck, op dezelfde manier. Geluidloos sprongen twintig mannen uit de twee wagens, Groene Baretten, die wisten wat ze deden. In colonne slopen ze de straat door, aangevoerd door een officier die een burger bij de arm hield. De witte *disj-dasj* van de man glinsterde in het halfduister. Omdat alle straatnaambordjes waren weggehaald, hadden de soldaten een gids nodig om het adres te vinden. Huisnummers waren er nog wel.
De burger bleef voor het huis staan, tuurde naar het nummer en wees. De kapitein overlegde fluisterend met zijn sergeant, die met vijftien man in een steegje verdween om de achterkant van het huis af te grendelen.
Gevolgd door de rest van de soldaten sloop de kapitein naar de stalen deur in de muur om de kleine tuin. De deur was open. De mannen glipten naar binnen.
Vanuit de tuin zag de kapitein dat er op de bovenverdieping van het huis licht brandde. De benedenverdieping werd grotendeels in beslag genomen door de garage, die leeg was. Bij de voordeur lieten de soldaten hun omzichtigheid varen. De kapitein probeerde de deurkruk, maar die gaf niet mee. Hij gaf een van de soldaten een teken. De man vuurde met zijn automatische geweer een kort salvo op het slot af en de houten deur vloog open.
Met de kapitein voorop stormden de Groene Baretten naar binnen. Een paar liepen naar de donkere kamers beneden, terwijl de kapitein en de rest van de mannen de trap naar de slaapkamer beklommen.
Vanaf de overloop wierp de kapitein een blik door de deuropening van de zwak verlichte slaapkamer. Hij zag een leunstoel, die met de rug naar de

167

deur toe stond. Een geruite *keffijeh* stak boven de rugleuning uit. Hij vuurde niet. Kolonel Sabawi van de AMAM had duidelijke instructies gegeven: de man moest levend worden aangehouden zodat hij kon worden verhoord. De jonge officier stormde naar voren. De nylon vislijn tegen zijn schenen voelde hij niet.

Hij hoorde zijn eigen mannen door de achterdeur naar binnen stormen. Anderen renden de trap op. Hij zag de ineengezakte gestalte in de smerige witte kaftan, opgevuld met kussens, en de grote watermeloen onder de *keffijeh*. Zijn gezicht vertrok van woede en hij snauwde een belediging tegen de drogist, die bevend in de deuropening stond.

Vijf pond Semtex-H lijkt niet zoveel. De huizen in de buurt waren opgetrokken uit steen en beton. Dat was de reden waarom de naburige villa's, waarvan sommige door Koeweiti's werden bewoond, voor grotere schade bleven gespaard. Maar het huis waar de soldaten waren binnengedrongen werd totaal weggevaagd. De dakpannen werden later op honderden meters afstand teruggevonden.

De bedoeïen had het resultaat van zijn handwerk niet afgewacht. Hij was al twee straten verderop, schuifelend over de stoep, verdiept in zijn eigen bezigheden, toen hij de gedempte knal hoorde, als van een deur die werd dichtgeslagen, daarna een seconde stilte, gevolgd door het geraas van neerstortend puin.

De volgende dag gebeurden er drie dingen, allemaal na het invallen van de duisternis. In Koeweit had de bedoeïen zijn tweede ontmoeting met Abu Fouad. Deze keer kwam de Koeweiti alleen. Ze hadden afgesproken in de schaduw van een diepe portiek op maar tweehonderd meter van het Sheraton Hotel, waar nu tientallen hoge Iraakse officieren hun intrek hadden genomen.

'Hebt u het gehoord, Abu Fouad?'

'Natuurlijk. De hele stad praat nergens anders over. Er zijn meer dan twintig man gedood en de rest is gewond.' Hij zuchtte. 'We kunnen weer een reeks willekeurige represailles verwachten.'

'Wilt u ermee stoppen?'

'Nee, dat kan niet. Maar hoe lang moeten we dit nog doorstaan?'

'De Amerikanen en de Britten komen. Vroeg of laat.'

'Ik bid tot Allah dat het snel zal zijn. Hadden ze Salah bij zich?'

'Hij was hun gids. De enige burger. Hebt u het adres aan niemand anders genoemd?'

'Nee, alleen aan hem. Dus hij moet de verrader zijn. Hij is schuldig aan de dood van negen jonge kerels. Hij zal het paradijs niet bereiken.'

'Goed. Wat wilt u verder nog van me?'

'Ik vraag niet wie u bent of waar u vandaan komt. Als getraind officier weet ik dat u geen eenvoudige kamelendrijver uit de woestijn kunt zijn. U hebt voorraden explosieven, geweren, munitie en granaten. Mijn mensen zouden die ook graag hebben.'

'Wat stelt u voor?'

'Dat u zich bij ons aansluit en uw wapens meeneemt. Of dat u zelfstandig blijft opereren maar uw voorraden met ons deelt. Dat is geen dreigement. Ik vraag het alleen. Maar als u ons verzet wilt steunen, is dat de juiste manier.'

Mike Martin dacht een tijdje na. Na acht weken had hij nog maar de helft van zijn voorraden over, begraven in de woestijn en verspreid over de twee villa's die hij als opslagplaats gebruikte. Van zijn andere vier huizen was er één verwoest en het andere, waar hij zijn leerlingen had ontvangen, besmet.

Hij zou zijn voorraden aan de Koeweiti's kunnen geven en om een nachtelijke dropping vragen – gevaarlijk maar niet onmogelijk zolang zijn berichten aan Riyad niet werden onderschept. En dat wist hij niet. Of hij zou weer per kameel de grens kunnen oversteken om nieuwe spullen te halen. Maar zelfs dat was niet eenvoudig. Er lagen nu zestien Iraakse divisies langs de grens, drie keer zoveel als toen hij het land was binnengekomen.

Het werd tijd om contact op te nemen met Riyad en om instructies te vragen. Ondertussen zou hij Abu Fouad bijna alles geven wat hij had. In Saoedi-Arabië waren voorraden genoeg; hij moest ze alleen de grens over krijgen.

'Waar moet ik de spullen afleveren?' vroeg hij.

'We hebben een pakhuis in Shuwaikh Port. Heel veilig. Er ligt vis opgeslagen. De eigenaar is een van ons.'

'Over zes dagen,' zei Martin.

Ze spraken een tijd en een plaats af waar een adjudant van Abu Fouad de bedoeïen zou ontmoeten om hem de weg te wijzen naar het pakhuis. Martin beschreef de wagen waarin hij zou rijden en de vermomming die hij zou gebruiken.

Diezelfde nacht, twee uur later vanwege het tijdverschil, zat Terry Martin in een rustig restaurant niet ver van zijn appartement te spelen met een glas wijn. De man op wie hij wachtte kwam een paar minuten later binnen – een oudere man met grijs haar, een bril en een gestippeld strikje. Hij keek zoekend rond.

Terry Martin stond op. 'Moshe, hier!'

Haastig kwam de Israëli naar hem toe en begroette hem omstandig. 'Terry, beste kerel, hoe gaat het met je?'

'Blij je te zien, Moshe. Ik kon je niet uit Londen laten vertrekken zonder een etentje en de kans om bij te praten.'

De Israëli was oud genoeg om Terry's vader te zijn, maar hun vriendschap was gebaseerd op een gezamenlijke interesse. Ze waren allebei wetenschappers, met een grote belangstelling voor de oude Arabische beschavingen in het Midden-Oosten, hun culturen, hun kunst en hun taal.

Professor Moshe Hadari had een lange staat van dienst. Als jongeman had hij een groot deel van het Heilige Land opgegraven, samen met Yigal Yadin, zelf hoogleraar en generaal van het Israëlische leger. Zijn verdriet was dat een groot deel van het Midden-Oosten voor hem als Israëli verboden gebied bleef, zelfs voor wetenschappelijk onderzoek. Maar op zijn terrein was hij een van de besten, en omdat dat terrein maar klein was, hadden de twee academici elkaar al tien jaar geleden op een congres ontmoet.

Het was een gezellig etentje. Ze praatten over het laatste onderzoek en de nieuwste visies op het leven in de koninkrijken van het Midden-Oosten, tien eeuwen geleden.

Terry Martin wist dat hij tot geheimhouding verplicht was en niets mocht zeggen over zijn werk als adviseur van Century House. Maar bij de koffie kwam het gesprek als vanzelf op de Golfcrisis en de kans op oorlog.

'Denk jij dat hij zich vrijwillig uit Koeweit zal terugtrekken, Terry?' vroeg de professor.

Martin schudde zijn hoofd. 'Nee, dat doet hij niet. Tenzij hij een paar concessies krijgt waarmee hij zijn gezicht kan redden. Als hij zonder slag of stoot vertrekt, betekent dat zijn einde.'

Hadari zuchtte.

'Wat een verspilling,' zei hij. 'Al zolang als ik me kan herinneren. Wat een verspilling... Al dat geld, genoeg om van het Midden-Oosten een paradijs op aarde te maken. Al dat talent, al die jonge levens... En waarvoor? Terry, als het oorlog wordt, zullen de Britten dan meevechten met de Amerikanen?'

'Natuurlijk. We hebben de 7e Pantserbrigade al gestuurd en ik geloof dat de 4e binnenkort vertrekt. Dat betekent een volledige divisie, nog afgezien van de gevechtsvliegtuigen en de marine. Maar maak je geen zorgen. Met deze oorlog hoeft Israël... nee, màg Israël zich niet eens bemoeien.'

'Dat weet ik,' zei de Israëli somber, 'maar er zullen weer zoveel jonge mensen sterven...'

Martin boog zich naar voren en klopte zijn vriend op de arm. 'Hoor eens, Moshe, die man moet worden gestopt. Vroeg of laat. Als één land weet hoeveel massavernietigingswapens hij al bezit, is het Israël wel. Eigenlijk beseffen we nu pas wat een gevaar hij werkelijk vormt.'

'Maar onze mensen hebben natuurlijk geholpen. Waarschijnlijk vormen wij zijn voornaamste doelwit.'

'Ja, dat ligt voor de hand,' zei Martin. 'Maar het probleem is dat we zo weinig concrete informatie hebben uit de eerste hand. Niemand heeft betrouwbare bronnen in Bagdad. De Amerikanen niet, wij niet en zelfs jullie niet.'

Twintig minuten later stonden ze op. Terry Martin nam afscheid van professor Hadari, die voor het restaurant in een taxi stapte en terugreed naar zijn hotel.

Op bevel van Hassan Rahmani in Bagdad werden omstreeks middernacht in Koeweit drie luisterposten geïnstalleerd voor het uitvoeren van driehoekspeilingen.

Het waren radioschotels die de coördinaten van een zender konden opsporen. Er was één vast station, op het dak van een hoog gebouw in het district Ardija in de zuidelijke buitenwijken van Koeweit Stad. De schotel stond op de woestijn gericht. De twee mobiele stations waren op vrachtwagens gemonteerd, de schotels op het dak, een ingebouwde generator voor de stroom en een batterij scanners in de verduisterde cabine. De radiotechnici was verteld dat de illegale zender zich ergens in de woestijn moest bevinden, tussen de stad en de Saoedische grens.

Een van de radiowagens stond in de buurt van Jahra, een heel eind ten westen van het vaste station. De andere truck had zich aan de kust opgesteld, op het terrein van het Al-Adan Ziekenhuis waar de zuster van de rechtenstudent kort na de invasie was verkracht. Op basis van de peilingen van de andere posten, verder naar het noorden, zou de wagen in Al-Adan de plaats van de zender tot op enkele honderden meters nauwkeurig kunnen bepalen.

Op de vliegbasis Ahmadi, waar Khaled Al-Khalifa ooit met zijn Skyhawk was opgestegen, stond een Russische Hind-helikopter gereed. Het had Rahmani heel wat moeite gekost om het toestel en de bemanning bij de luchtmachtgeneraal los te peuteren. De radiotechnici waren mensen van Rahmani's eigen contraspionagedienst uit Bagdad – de besten die hij had.

Professor Hadari kon de slaap niet vatten. Iets in het verhaal van zijn vriend bleef hem bezighouden. Hij beschouwde zichzelf als een volledig loyale Israëli, een nazaat van een oude sefardische familie die kort na de eeuwwisseling naar het beloofde land was geëmigreerd, samen met mannen als Ben Yehuda en David Ben Goerion. Zelf was hij geboren in de buurt van Jaffa toen dat nog een drukke Palestijnse haven was, en als kleine jongen had hij Arabisch geleerd.

Hij had twee zonen, van wie er een was gesneuveld bij een hinderlaag in Zuid-Libanon. Hij was nu grootvader van vijf kleine kinderen. Wie zou durven zeggen dat hij niet van zijn land hield?

Maar toch klopte er iets niet. Als het oorlog werd, zouden veel jonge mensen sterven, net als zijn eigen Ze'ev, ook al zouden het dan Britten, Amerikanen en Fransen zijn. Was dit het moment waarop Kobi Dror zich door zijn haatdragende chauvinisme moest laten leiden?

Hij stond vroeg op, betaalde zijn rekening, pakte zijn koffers en bestelde

171

een taxi om hem naar het vliegveld te brengen. Voordat hij vertrok, aarzelde hij nog even bij de telefooncellen in de lobby van het hotel, maar nam toen een besluit.

Halverwege de rit veranderde hij van gedachten. Hij vroeg de chauffeur van de M4 af te slaan en een telefooncel te zoeken. De chauffeur deed wat hem werd gevraagd, mopperend over de extra tijd en moeite, en vond ten slotte een cel op een straathoek in Chiswick. Hadari had geluk. Het was Hilary die de telefoon in de flat in Bayswater opnam.

'Wacht even,' zei hij. 'Hij staat op het punt om weg te gaan.'

Even later meldde Terry Martin zich.

'Met Moshe. Terry, ik heb niet veel tijd. Zeg maar tegen je mensen dat de Mossad wel degelijk een hoge bron in Bagdad heeft. Ze moeten maar eens vragen wat er met Jericho is gebeurd. Tot ziens, beste kerel.'

'Moshe, wacht even! Ben je daar zeker van? En hoe weet je dat?'

'Dat doet niet ter zake. Je hebt dit niet van mij gehoord. Tot ziens.'

En Hadari hing op. Hij stapte weer in de taxi en reed door naar Heathrow. De oude academicus beefde bij de gedachte aan wat hij had gedaan. Maar hij had Terry Martin niet kunnen vertellen dat hij het was, de hoogleraar Arabisch aan de universiteit van Tel Aviv, die de eerste brief van de Mossad aan Jericho had vertaald.

Een paar minuten over tien werd Simon Paxman gebeld door Terry Martin.

'Lunch? Sorry, dat lukt niet. Ik heb een vreselijk drukke dag. Morgen misschien?' vroeg hij.

'Te laat. Dit is dringend, Simon.'

Paxman zuchtte. Waarschijnlijk had de kamergeleerde een nieuwe interpretatie van een of andere Iraakse radio-uitzending bedacht, die volgens hem de hele situatie kon veranderen.

'Lunch is onmogelijk. Ik heb een belangrijke vergadering. Maar een borrel zal wel lukken. De Hole-in-the-Wall, een pub onder Waterloo Bridge, hier vlakbij. Twaalf uur? Ik heb een halfuurtje voor je, Terry.'

'Dat is meer dan genoeg. Tot straks,' zei Martin.

Even na twaalven zaten ze achter een biertje in het café, waarboven de treinen naar Kent, Sussex en Hampshire voorbij denderden. Martin vertelde wat hij die ochtend had gehoord, zonder de bron te noemen.

'Allemachtig,' fluisterde Paxman. Er zaten mensen aan het tafeltje naast hen. 'Van wie weet je dat?'

'Dat mag ik niet zeggen.'

'Dat zal toch moeten.'

'Hij heeft zijn nek uitgestoken. Ik heb hem mijn woord gegeven. Hij is een belangrijke academicus. Meer zeg ik niet.'

172

Paxman dacht na. Een academicus die bevriend was met Terry Martin... Ook een arabist, dus. Misschien een adviseur van de Mossad. In elk geval moest Century House onmiddellijk worden gewaarschuwd. Hij bedankte Martin, liet zijn bier staan en liep haastig terug naar zijn haveloze hoofdkwartier.

Vanwege de vergadering was Steve Laing nog in het gebouw. Paxman nam hem apart en vertelde hem het nieuws. Laing belde onmiddellijk de Chef persoonlijk.

Sir Colin, die niet van overdrijving hield, noemde generaal Kobi Dror 'een vervelende kerel', zegde zijn lunchafspraak af, liet broodjes brengen en trok zich terug op de bovenverdieping. Daar belde hij via de beveiligde lijn met rechter William Webster, de directeur van de CIA.

In Washington was het pas half negen, maar de rechter begon graag vroeg en zat al achter zijn bureau. Hij stelde zijn Britse collega een paar vragen over de herkomst van de informatie, bromde wat toen Sir Colin daar niets over kon zeggen, maar beaamde dat ze het niet konden negeren.

Webster belde zijn adjunct-directeur Operaties, Bill Stewart, die ontplofte van woede en een halfuur overlegde met Chip Barber, het hoofd Operaties van de sectie Midden-Oosten. Barber was nog kwader, want hij had tenslotte tegenover generaal Dror in die zonnige kamer boven op de heuvel bij Herzlia gezeten en zich laten voorliegen.

Ze bespraken wat ze moesten doen en legden de directeur hun voorstel voor. Later die middag had William Webster een gesprek met Brent Scowcroft, de voorzitter van de Nationale Veiligheidsraad, die de zaak opnam met president Bush. Webster kreeg toestemming om zijn plan uit te voeren.

Hij belde minister James Baker van Buitenlandse Zaken, die meteen zijn medewerking toezegde. Nog dezelfde avond stuurde Buitenlandse Zaken een dringend verzoek aan Tel Aviv, dat drie uur later – vanwege het tijdverschil – aankwam.

De Israëlische onderminister van Buitenlandse Zaken, Benjamin Netanyahu, was een knappe, elegante, grijsharige diplomaat, de broer van Jonathan Netanyahu die als enige Israëli was gesneuveld bij de aanval op het vliegveld van Entebbe in Uganda, toen Israëlische commando's de passagiers van een Frans lijnvliegtuig hadden bevrijd dat door Palestijnse en Duitse terroristen was gekaapt.

Benjamin Netanyahu was een *sabra* van de derde generatie. Hij had een tijdje in Amerika gestudeerd en vanwege zijn uitstekende Engels en zijn hartstochtelijke chauvinisme trad hij in gesprekken met de Westerse pers vaak als woordvoerder van Itzhak Shamirs Likoed-regering op.

Twee dagen later, op 14 oktober, kwam hij op het vliegveld Dulles bij Washington aan, enigszins verbijsterd door het dringende verzoek van de Amerikanen.

Hij was nog verbaasder toen het twee uur durende gesprek met onderminister Lawrence Eagleburger niets anders opleverde dan een overzicht van de gebeurtenissen in het Midden-Oosten sinds 2 augustus. Gefrustreerd nam hij afscheid en wilde naar het vliegveld vertrekken om de nachtvlucht naar Israël te halen.

Maar voordat hij het ministerie van Buitenlandse Zaken verliet, drukte een assistent hem een duur visitekaartje in zijn hand. Er stond een persoonlijk wapen op, en de afzender vroeg hem in sierlijk handschrift of hij naar zijn huis in Georgetown wilde komen voor een zaak van groot belang 'voor onze beide landen en ons hele volk'.

Netanyahu kende de handtekening, de man, zijn rijkdom en zijn invloed. Een limousine stond al klaar. De Israëlische minister nam een besluit, vroeg zijn secretaresse om zijn koffers bij de ambassade op te halen en twee uur later naar Georgetown te komen. Dan konden ze daarvandaan naar Dulles rijden. Toen stapte hij in de wagen.

Hij was nog nooit bij de man op bezoek geweest, maar het huis beantwoordde aan zijn verwachtingen: een prachtige villa aan de dure kant van M Street, nog geen driehonderd meter van de universiteit van Georgetown. Hij werd naar een fraai betimmerde bibliotheek gebracht, vol met smaakvolle, zeldzame schilderijen en boeken. Even later stapte zijn gastheer binnen en kwam met uitgestoken hand over het Kashan-tapijt naar hem toe.

'Mijn beste Bibi, wat fijn dat je even tijd voor me hebt.'

Saul Nathanson, bankier en financier, was een zeer rijk man, maar hij had zijn fortuin verdiend zonder de trucs die op Wall Street gebruikelijk waren toen Boesky en Milken daar nog de macht hadden. Niemand wist precies hoeveel geld hij bezat, en de man zelf was veel te beschaafd om daarop te zinspelen. Maar de Van Dykes en Breughels aan de muren waren geen reprodukties en zijn giften aan goede doelen, waaronder de staat Israël, waren legendarisch.

Net als de jongere Israëlische politicus was hij een elegante man met grijs haar, maar zijn pak kwam van Savile Row in Londen en zijn zijden overhemd van Sulka.

Hij bood zijn gast een van de twee leren leunstoelen bij het haardvuur aan, en een Engelse butler bracht een zilveren blad met een fles en twee glazen.

'Ik dacht dat je dit wel zou waarderen, beste kerel, terwijl we praten.'

De butler schonk twee Lalique-glazen met rode wijn in, en de Israëli nam een slok. Nathanson trok vragend een wenkbrauw op.

'Uitstekend, natuurlijk,' zei Netanyahu. Château Mouton Rothschild '61 is niet zo gemakkelijk te krijgen en moet met aandacht gedronken worden. De butler liet de fles onder handbereik staan en vertrok.

Saul Nathanson was zo subtiel om niet meteen met de deur in huis te vallen.

174

Eerst praatten ze over andere zaken, toen pas over het Midden-Oosten.

'Het wordt oorlog,' zei hij somber.

'Ja, dat staat wel vast,' beaamde Netanyahu.

'Een oorlog die veel jonge Amerikanen het leven zal kosten – jonge kerels die het niet verdienen om te sterven. We moeten alles in het werk stellen om de verliezen zo klein mogelijk te houden, vind je ook niet? Nog wat wijn?'

'Ik ben het helemaal met je eens.'

Waar wilde de man naartoe? De Israëlische onderminister van Buitenlandse Zaken had werkelijk geen idee.

'Saddam Hoessein,' zei Nathanson, starend in het vuur, 'is een gevaar. Hij moet worden tegengehouden. En voor Israël is hij nog gevaarlijker dan voor zijn buren.'

'Dat zeggen we al jaren. Maar toen wij zijn kernreactor bombardeerden, werden we door Amerika veroordeeld.'

Nathanson maakte een wegwerpgebaar met zijn hand. 'De regering Carter. Allemaal flauwekul. Theater voor de buitenwereld. Dat weten we allebei. Ik heb een zoon die als militair naar de Golf is gestuurd.'

'Dat wist ik niet. Ik hoop dat hij veilig terugkomt.'

Nathanson was oprecht geroerd. 'Dank je, Bibi. Dank je. Ik bid elke dag voor hem. Mijn oudste kind, mijn enige zoon. Op een moment als dit moeten onze twee landen zo goed mogelijk samenwerken... in alle opzichten.'

'Absoluut.' De Israëli had het onprettige gevoel dat er slecht nieuws op komst was.

'Om de verliezen te beperken. Daarom wil ik je hulp inroepen, Benjamin. We staan toch aan dezelfde kant? Ik ben Amerikaan, maar ook jood.'

De volgorde waarin hij die woorden gebruikte, was niet zonder betekenis.

'En ik ben Israëli, en jood,' mompelde Netanyahu. Ook die volgorde was belangrijk. Maar de financier liet zich niet van zijn stuk brengen.

'Precies. Maar dank zij jouw studie hier zul je begrijpen... hoe zal ik het zeggen... dat de Amerikanen soms heel emotioneel kunnen reageren. Ik zal open kaart met je spelen.'

Eindelijk, dacht de Israëli.

'Als jullie iets kunnen doen om het aantal slachtoffers te beperken, al is het maar met een handvol, dan zouden ik en mijn landgenoten jullie eeuwig dankbaar zijn.'

De andere implicatie van die opmerking bleef onuitgesproken, maar Netanyahu begreep de hint. Als Israël iets zou doen of nalaten waardoor de Amerikaanse verliezen groter werden, zouden de Verenigde Staten dat niet licht vergeten.

'Wat kan ik voor je doen?' vroeg hij.

Saul Nathanson nam een slok wijn en tuurde in de flikkerende vlammen.

'Er schijnt iemand te zijn in Bagdad... met de codenaam Jericho...'
Toen hij was uitgesproken, was het een zeer bedachtzame onderminister die naar het vliegveld Dulles reed om op het vliegtuig naar huis te stappen.

De wegversperring waar hij werd aangehouden was op de hoek tussen de Vierde Ringweg en de Mohammed-ibn-Kassemstraat. Toen hij de controlepost zag opdoemen, maakte Mike Martin bijna rechtsomkeert. Maar er stonden Iraakse soldaten langs de weg opgesteld in beide richtingen, juist om zo'n manoeuvre te voorkomen. Het zou waanzin zijn geweest om hun salvo's te riskeren bij de geringe snelheid die voor een scherpe bocht noodzakelijk was. Hij moest dus wel doorrijden en zich aansluiten bij de file die al voor de wegversperring stond.

Zoals gewoonlijk had hij geprobeerd de hoofdstraten van Koeweit Stad te mijden, maar de zes ringwegen die in concentrische cirkels om de stad liepen, konden alleen via grote kruispunten worden overgestoken.

Door pas halverwege de ochtend te vertrekken had hij gehoopt in het drukke verkeer onder te gaan, met de kans dat de Irakezen zich al in de schaduw hadden teruggetrokken vanwege de hitte.

Maar half oktober was het een stuk koeler geworden, en de Speciale Eenheden met hun groene baretten waren heel wat professioneler dan het waardeloze Volksleger. Dus bleef hij achter het stuur van zijn witte Volvo-stationcar zitten en wachtte af.

Het was nog diep in de nacht toen hij met de jeep naar het zuiden was gereden om de rest van zijn explosieven, geweren en munitie – de voorraden die hij Abu Fouad had beloofd – uit de woestijn op te graven. Vlak voor het ochtendgloren was hij weer teruggekomen bij de garage in een steegje van Firdous, om de jeep voor de stationcar te verwisselen.

Tussen dat moment en het tijdstip waarop de zon hoog genoeg aan de hemel stond om de Irakezen de schaduw in te jagen had hij zelfs nog twee uur kunnen slapen, achter het stuur van de auto in de afgesloten garage. Daarna had hij de Volvo naar buiten gereden en de jeep naar binnen. Zo'n nuttige wagen liep de kans om snel te worden ingepikt.

Ten slotte had hij de vuile kaftan van de bedoeïen verruild voor de schone witte *disj-dasj* van een Koeweitse arts.

De file verplaatste zich langzaam naar de groep Iraakse infanteristen rondom de met cement gevulde tonnen. Nu eens wierpen de soldaten een vluchtige blik op de papieren van een bestuurder en wuifden hem door, dan weer lieten ze een auto stoppen om hem grondig te doorzoeken. Meestal waren het wagens met enige laadcapaciteit die uit de rij werden gehaald.

Martin was zich pijnlijk bewust van de twee grote houten hutkoffers in de laadruimte van de Volvo, die genoeg spullen bevatten voor een enkele reis naar de martelkamers van de AMAM.

Eindelijk was de auto voor hem ook de versperring gepasseerd en stond hij voor de tonnen. De sergeant die het bevel voerde vroeg niet eens naar zijn papieren. Toen hij de grote kisten achter in de stationcar zag, gebaarde hij al naar de berm van de weg en riep iets tegen een collega die daar stond te wachten.

Een olijfgroen uniform verscheen naast het portierraampje dat Martin al naar beneden had gedraaid. Het uniform bukte zich en een stoppelbaard werd zichtbaar.

'Naar buiten,' beval de soldaat. Martin stapte uit, richtte zich op en glimlachte beleefd. Een sergeant met een hard, pokdalig gezicht kwam naar hem toe. De soldaat slenterde om de auto heen en tuurde naar de kisten.

'Papieren,' beval de sergeant. Hij bestudeerde Martins pasje en vergeleek de foto achter het plastic met het gezicht tegenover hem. Als hij enig verschil zag tussen de Britse officier en de boekhouder van de Al-Khalifa Trading Company op de foto, liet hij dat niet blijken. Het pasje was een jaar eerder gedateerd, en in een jaar kan iemand gemakkelijk een korte zwarte baard laten staan.

'U bent arts?'

'Jawel, sergeant. Ik werk in het ziekenhuis.'

'Waar?'

'Aan de Jahra Road.'

'En waar gaat u heen?'

'Naar het Amiri Ziekenhuis in Dasman.'

De sergeant was een simpele man en in zijn cultuur gold een arts nog als iemand met een grote kennis en status. Hij bromde wat en liep naar de auto.

'Openmaken,' zei hij.

Martin opende de achterklep, die omhoog zwaaide. De sergeant keek naar de twee hutkoffers.

'Wat zit daarin?'

'Monsters, sergeant. Voor onderzoek in het laboratorium van het Amiri.'

'Openmaken.'

Martin haalde een paar koperen sleuteltjes uit de zak van zijn *disj-dasj*. Elk van de hutkoffers had twee koperen sloten.

'U weet dat die kisten gekoeld zijn?' vroeg hij luchtig, terwijl hij met de sleutels rammelde.

'Gekoeld?' De sergeant begreep het niet helemaal.

'Ja, ze zijn koud. Om de culturen op een lage temperatuur te houden, zodat ze niet actief kunnen worden. Als ik die kisten openmaak, ontsnapt de

178

koude lucht en worden de culturen geactiveerd. U kunt beter een stap achteruit gaan.'

Bij die woorden verscheen er een nijdige uitdrukking op het gezicht van de sergeant en richtte hij zijn karabijn op Martin, in de veronderstelling dat de kisten een of ander wapen bevatten.

'Wat bedoelt u?' snauwde hij.

Martin haalde verontschuldigend zijn schouders op. 'Het spijt me, maar ik kan er niets aan doen. Als die kisten opengaan, ontsnappen de bacillen.'

'Bacillen? Wat voor bacillen?' vroeg de sergeant verward en kwaad, niet alleen vanwege de houding van de arts maar ook vanwege zijn eigen onwetendheid.

'Ik zei toch waar ik werkte?' vroeg Martin vriendelijk.

'Ja. In het ziekenhuis.'

'Inderdaad. Op de afdeling Quarantaine. In die kisten zitten culturen van pokken en cholera, om te worden geanalyseerd.'

Nu sprong de sergeant werkelijk achteruit, minstens een halve meter. De littekens op zijn gezicht waren geen toeval. Als kind was hij bijna aan pokken overleden.

'Weg met dat spul, verdomme.'

Martin excuseerde zich opnieuw, deed de klep dicht, schoof achter het stuur en reed weg. Een uur later werd hij naar het vispakhuis in Shuwaikh Port gebracht en kon hij de spullen aan Abu Fouad overdragen.

Ministerie van Buitenlandse Zaken,
Washington, DC 20520

MEMORANDUM AAN: James Baker, minister van Buitenlandse Zaken
VAN: Political Intelligence and Analysis Group
ONDERWERP: Vernietiging van de Iraakse oorlogsmachine
DATUM: 16 oktober 1990
CLASSIFICATIE: Strikt persoonlijk

In de tien weken sinds de invasie door Irak van het emiraat Koeweit is er uitvoerig onderzoek gedaan, zowel door onszelf als door onze Britse bondgenoten, naar de juiste omvang, aard en status van voorbereiding van de oorlogsmachinerie waarover president Saddam Hoessein op dit moment beschikt.

Critici zullen ongetwijfeld beweren – achteraf – dat zo'n analyse al eerder had moeten plaatsvinden. Het zij zo. Het resultaat van de verschillende onderzoeken ligt nu voor ons en levert een zeer verontrustend beeld op.

Alleen al de conventionele strijdkrachten van Irak, met een regulier leger van één en een kwart miljoen man, plus artillerie, tanks, raketbatterijen en een moderne luchtmacht, maken Irak tot de machtigste militaire factor in het Midden-Oosten.

Twee jaar geleden ging men er nog vanuit dat de oorlog met Iran de Iraakse oorlogsmachine had verzwakt tot het punt waarop die geen reële bedreiging meer vormde voor de buurlanden. Immers, met Iran was dat ook gebeurd.

Inmiddels is duidelijk dat de strenge handelsboycot tegen Iran, in het leven geroepen door onszelf en de Britten, iedere verbetering van de Iraanse situatie onmogelijk heeft gemaakt. Irak heeft de twee tussenliggende jaren echter gebruikt voor een herbewapeningsprogramma van verbijsterende omvang.

U zult zich herinneren, meneer de minister, dat de Westerse politiek in het Golfgebied en de rest van het Midden-Oosten al heel lang gebaseerd is op het principe van evenwicht – de gedachte dat de stabiliteit en dus de status-quo alleen kan worden gehandhaafd als geen enkel land in het gebied de kans krijgt zo machtig te worden dat het al zijn buren zou kunnen onderwerpen en zich daardoor een dominante positie kan verwerven.

Alleen al op het gebied van conventionele wapens heeft Irak deze macht verworven, en Bagdad streeft nu naar een overheersende rol.

Maar dit rapport houdt zich vooral bezig met een ander aspect van de Iraakse voorbereidingen: de opbouw van een ontzagwekkend arsenaal van massavernietigingswapens, gekoppeld aan de ontwikkeling van steeds meer internationale en mogelijk intercontinentale afvuursystemen. Tenzij deze wapens, de afvuursystemen en de onderzoekscentra volledig worden vernietigd, biedt de nabije toekomst een zeer grimmig beeld.

Volgens studies van het Britse Medusa Comité en Amerikaanse deskundigen zal Irak binnen drie jaar over een kernbom beschikken, met de mogelijkheid die binnen een straal van 2000 km rondom Bagdad te lanceren.

Daarbij komt nog een voorraad van duizenden tonnen dodelijk gifgas en bacteriologische wapens die onder meer miltvuur, tularemie en mogelijk ook longpest en builenpest kunnen veroorzaken.

Als Irak door een welwillend en redelijk regime werd geregeerd, zou dit al verontrustend genoeg zijn. Maar de absolute macht in Irak berust bij president Saddam Hoessein, die zich laat leiden door twee duidelijk herkenbare psychiatrische verschijnselen: grootheidswaan en paranoia.

180

*Als er geen preventieve maatregelen worden genomen, zal Irak bin-
nen drie jaar op grond van dreigementen het hele gebied vanaf de
noordkust van Turkije tot aan de Golf van Aden, en vanaf de kust van
Haifa tot aan de bergen van Kandahar, in zijn greep kunnen krijgen.
De conclusie van dit alles is dat de Westerse opstelling drastisch moet
worden bijgesteld. De vernietiging van de Iraakse oorlogsmachine,
en met name de Iraakse massavernietigingswapens, moet de eerste
prioriteit zijn van de Westerse politiek. De bevrijding van Koeweit is
een irrelevante bijzaak, niet meer dan een rechtvaardiging.
Het gewenste doel kan nog worden gefrustreerd door de vrijwillige
terugtrekking van Irak uit Koeweit. Dit moet tot elke prijs worden ver-
meden.
De Amerikaanse politiek, en die van onze Britse bondgenoten, dient
daarom uit te gaan van vier doelstellingen:
(a) Saddam Hoessein in bedekte termen zoveel mogelijk te provoceren, zodat hij zal weigeren uit Koeweit te vertrekken.
(b) Ieder compromis dat hij aanbiedt te verwerpen en voldoende
argumenten in stand te houden voor onze geplande invasie en de vernietiging van Saddams oorlogsmachine.
(c) De Verenigde Naties onder druk te zetten om de lang vertraagde
Veiligheidsraadsresolutie 678 eindelijk in werking te stellen, om de
Coalitie het recht te geven zo snel mogelijk een luchtoorlog te beginnen.
(d) Ogenschijnlijk ieder vredesplan welwillend te ontvangen maar in
werkelijkheid alle verzoeningspogingen te frustreren, zodat Irak niet
de kans krijgt zich zonder kleerscheuren uit Koeweit terug te trekken.
In dat opzicht vormen Parijs, Moskou en de secretaris-generaal van
de VN de lastigste obstakels. Zij kunnen ieder moment een naïef voorstel lanceren om te voorkomen dat wij doen wat gedaan moet worden.
Het grote publiek zal uiteraard van het tegendeel worden verzekerd.*

Met de meeste hoogachting,
PIAG

'Itzhak, we zullen op dit punt moeten toegeven.'
De minister-president van Israël leek nog kleiner in de grote draaistoel ach-
ter zijn bureau in zijn gepantserde kantoor onder de Knesset in Jeruzalem.
De twee met uzi's bewapende para's voor de zware, met staal versterkte
houten deur konden geen woord verstaan van wat er binnen werd gezegd.
Itzhak Shamir keek zijn onderminister van Buitenlandse Zaken nijdig aan.
Zijn korte benen bungelden los boven het tapijt, hoewel zijn stoel met een

speciaal voetenbankje was uitgerust. Met zijn gegroefde, strijdlustige gezicht onder het warrige grijze haar leek hij meer dan ooit op een Scandinavische trol.

De onderminister was in alle opzichten zijn tegendeel: lang, elegant en beheerst. Toch konden ze goed met elkaar opschieten, omdat ze dezelfde rechtlijnige visie hadden op hun land en op de Palestijnen. Vandaar dat de in Rusland geboren premier de kosmopolitische diplomaat zonder aarzelen in zijn kabinet had opgenomen.

Benjamin Netanyahu had zijn argumenten goed naar voren gebracht. Israël had Amerika nodig. De Amerikaanse steun, die ooit werd gegarandeerd door de macht van de joodse lobby, werd nu aangevochten door het Congres en de media. De Amerikaanse donaties en wapenleveranties en het Amerikaanse veto in de Veiligheidsraad stonden op het spel. Dat was niet gering, tegenover het lot van maar één onbekende Iraakse agent van de Mossad.

'Laat hun die Jericho maar gebruiken, wie hij ook is,' drong Netanyahu aan. 'Als hij hen helpt Saddam Hoessein te verslaan, wat zullen wij ons dan druk maken?'

De premier bromde wat, knikte en stak zijn hand uit naar zijn intercom.

'Bel generaal Dror en zeg dat ik hem wil spreken. Hier, op mijn kantoor,' zei hij tegen zijn privé-secretaresse. 'Nee, niet als hij tijd heeft. Nu meteen.'

Vier uur later vertrok Kobi Dror weer uit het kantoor van de minister-president – ziedend van woede. Hij kon zich niet herinneren dat hij ooit zo kwaad was geweest, dacht hij toen zijn auto de heuvel afreed uit Jeruzalem en de brede weg naar Tel Aviv op draaide.

Dat je eigen premier je vertelt dat je fout zit, is al erg genoeg. Dat hij je een stomme klootzak noemt, gaat alle perken te buiten.

Normaal genoot hij altijd van de naaldbossen langs de weg. Toen de snelweg nog een karrepad was, hadden zijn vader en anderen tijdens het beleg van Jeruzalem een bres in de Palestijnse linies geslagen en de stad bevrijd. Maar nu beleefde hij weinig plezier aan de omgeving.

Terug op kantoor ontbood hij Sami Gershon en vertelde hem wat er was gebeurd.

'Hoe konden die Yanks dat weten, verdomme?' riep hij. 'Wie heeft zijn mond voorbij gepraat?'

'Niemand van het Kantoor,' zei Gershon beslist. 'Misschien die professor? Hij is net terug uit Engeland.'

'Die vervloekte verrader!' snauwde Dror. 'Ik breek hem zijn poten!'

'De Britten hebben hem natuurlijk dronken gevoerd,' opperde Gershon. 'En toen werd hij wat loslippig. Laat maar zitten, Kobi. Het is nu toch te laat. Wat moeten we doen?'

'Hij wil dat we hun alles over Jericho vertellen,' antwoordde Dror bits.

'Maar ik ga niet zelf. Stuur Sharon maar. De bespreking is in Londen, waar de zaak is uitgelekt.'

Gershon dacht even na en grijnsde toen.

'Wat is er zo grappig?' vroeg Dror.

'Wíj kunnen geen contact meer krijgen met Jericho. Laten zij het maar proberen. We weten nog steeds niet wie die vent is. Misschien komen zij erachter. Of misschien maken ze er een puinhoop van.'

Dror dacht even na. Toen gleed er een sluw lachje over zijn gezicht. 'Laat Sharon vanavond maar vertrekken,' zei hij. 'Dan beginnen wij met een ander project. Dat had ik al een tijdje in gedachten. We noemen het Operatie Joshua.'

'Waarom?' vroeg Gershon verbaasd.

'Weet je niet meer wat Joshua met Jericho heeft gedaan?'

De bijeenkomst in Londen was zo belangrijk dat Bill Stewart, de adjunct-directeur Operaties van de CIA, persoonlijk uit Langley was overgekomen, in het gezelschap van Chip Barber van de divisie Midden-Oosten. Ze logeerden op een van de onderduikadressen van de CIA, een appartement in de buurt van de ambassade op Grosvenor Square. Die avond gingen ze uit eten met een adjunct-directeur van de SIS en Steve Laing. De adjunct-directeur was erbij vanwege het protocol, gezien Stewarts rang. Maar bij het gesprek met David Sharon zou hij worden vervangen door Simon Paxman, het hoofd van de sectie Irak.

David Sharon arriveerde onder een andere naam uit Tel Aviv en werd van het vliegveld gehaald door een *katsa* van de Israëlische ambassade in Palace Green. De Britse contraspionagedienst MI-5, die niet op de komst van buitenlandse agenten is gesteld – ook niet uit bevriende landen – was door de SIS gewaarschuwd en herkende de *katsa* van de ambassade. Zodra hij 'meneer Eliyahu' had begroet, dook een delegatie van MI-5 op, die meneer Sharon hartelijk welkom heette in Londen en hem alle medewerking toezegde om zijn verblijf zo aangenaam mogelijk te maken.

De twee nijdige Israëli's werden naar hun auto geëscorteerd. Toen ze bij de vertrekhal wegreden, werden ze de hele weg naar het centrum van Londen gevolgd. De erewacht van de Brigade of Guards had het niet beter kunnen doen.

Het gesprek met David Sharon begon de volgende morgen en duurde een hele dag en een halve nacht. De SIS had een van haar eigen schuiladressen gekozen, een goed beschermd en 'elektronisch ingericht' appartement in South Kensington.

Het was (en is nog altijd) een grote flat, waarvan de eetkamer als vergaderruimte dienst doet. In een van de slaapkamers stond een batterij bandrecorders, met twee technici die ieder woord registreerden. Een keurige jongedame van Century House voerde de scepter in de keuken en zorgde voor dienbladen met koffie en broodjes voor de zes mannen rond de eettafel.

Twee fitte kerels in de hal beneden waren zogenaamd de hele dag bezig met de reparatie van de perfect werkende lift. In werkelijkheid moesten ze ervoor zorgen dat niemand anders dan de bekende bewoners van de flat hoger kwamen dan de begane grond.

Aan de eettafel zaten David Sharon en de *katsa* van de Londense ambassade (die toch al bekend was als agent), de twee Amerikanen, Stewart en Barber van de CIA, en de twee SIS-officieren, Laing en Paxman.

Op verzoek van de Amerikanen begon Sharon bij het begin en vertelde het hele verhaal zoals het zich had afgespeeld.

'Een huurling? Een binnenloper?' vroeg Stewart op een gegeven moment. 'Belazer je me nou?'

'Ik heb instructies om de zuivere waarheid te vertellen,' antwoordde Sharon. 'Zo is het gegaan.'

De Amerikanen hadden geen enkel bezwaar tegen een huurling. Dat was zelfs een voordeel. Van alle motieven om je land te verraden is geld het eenvoudigst. Dan weet je waar je aan toe bent. Geen kans op gewetenswroeging of spijt, geen kwetsbaar ego dat moet worden ontzien, geen irritaties die moeten worden gesust. Een huurling is een hoer. Dineetjes en voorspel zijn niet nodig. Een handvol dollars op het nachtkastje is voldoende.

Sharon beschreef de koortsachtige speurtocht naar een diplomaat in Bagdad, de gedwongen keuze voor Alfonso Benz Moncada, zijn opleiding in Santiago en zijn terugkeer naar Irak, waar hij twee jaar lang het contact met Jericho had onderhouden.

'Wacht eens even,' zei Stewart. 'Dus die Moncada, die... *amateur*, heeft het twee jaar volgehouden? Hij heeft zeventig zendingen van Jericho doorgestuurd zonder te worden betrapt?'

'Ja. Ik zweer het je,' zei Sharon.

'Wat denk je, Steve?'

Laing haalde zijn schouders op. 'Beginnersgeluk. Dat zou ik niet graag in Oost-Berlijn of Moskou hebben geprobeerd.'

'Nee,' beaamde Stewart. 'En hij is nooit geschaduwd en nooit in moeilijkheden gekomen?'

'Nee,' zei Sharon. 'Hij is wel een paar keer gevolgd, maar heel willekeurig en onhandig. Als hij van huis naar zijn werk ging, of terug. En één keer toen hij op weg was naar een "brievenbus". Maar dat had hij in de gaten en dus is hij teruggegaan.'

'Laten we eens aannemen,' zei Laing, 'dat hij wèl is geschaduwd door een professioneel team. Dat Rahmani's contraspionagedienst hem heeft opgepakt en hem heeft gedwongen mee te werken...'

'Dan zou de kwaliteit van zijn informatie zijn teruggelopen,' zei Sharon. 'Jericho heeft heel gevoelig materiaal doorgegeven en veel schade aangericht. Dat had Rahmani nooit toegestaan. Als hij was betrapt, zou Jericho publiekelijk zijn berecht en geëxecuteerd, en Moncada zou het land uit zijn gezet – als hij geluk had.

Hij werd vermoedelijk geschaduwd door mensen van de AMAM, hoewel buitenlanders eigenlijk het terrein van Rahmani zijn. Maar zoals gewoonlijk gingen ze heel slordig te werk. Moncada had het meteen door. Jullie weten dat de AMAM steeds probeert zich met de contraspionage te bemoeien...'

De anderen knikten. Concurrentie tussen verschillende afdelingen was niets nieuws. Dat gebeurde in hun eigen landen ook.

Toen Sharon bij het punt kwam waarop Moncada uit Irak werd teruggeroepen, slaakte Bill Stewart een vloek. 'Bedoel je dat jullie geen enkel contact meer met hem hebben? Dat hij niemand meer heeft om zijn materiaal aan kwijt te raken?'

'Precies,' zei Sharon geduldig. Hij richtte zich tot Chip Barber. 'Toen generaal Dror zei dat hij geen hoge spion in Bagdad had, meende hij dat ook. De Mossad was ervan overtuigd dat operatie Jericho op zijn gat lag.'

Barber wierp de jonge *katsa* een blik toe die zoveel betekende als: maak dat de kat wijs, vriend.

'We zouden het contact graag herstellen,' zei Laing vriendelijk. 'Maar hoe?'

Sharon beschreef de plaatsen van de zes geheime 'brievenbussen'. In de loop van die twee jaar had Moncada er twee gewijzigd – de ene omdat het huis werd gesloopt voor nieuwbouw, de andere omdat de leegstaande winkel weer in gebruik was genomen. Maar deze zes plekken, plus de plaatsen waar de krijtstrepen moesten worden aangebracht om contact te leggen, waren het meest recent.

De anderen noteerden de locaties tot op de centimeter.

'Misschien kunnen we een bevriende diplomaat vragen hem persoonlijk te benaderen om hem te zeggen dat de zaak weer doorgaat. Voor nog meer geld,' opperde Barber. 'Dan kunnen we al dat gedoe met oude muren en tegels omzeilen.'

'Nee,' zei Sharon. 'Hij werkt alleen met brievenbussen.'

'Waarom?' vroeg Stewart.

'Jullie zullen het niet geloven, maar we hebben nog steeds geen idee wie hij is. Ik zweer het.'

De vier Westerse agenten staarden Sharon een paar minuten aan.

'Jullie hebben hem nooit geïdentificeerd?' vroeg Stewart eindelijk.

'Nee. We hebben het wel geprobeerd en we hebben hem gevraagd of hij zich bekend wilde maken voor zijn eigen veiligheid, maar hij dreigde het contact te verbreken als we aandrongen. We hebben zijn handschrift geanalyseerd en een psychologisch profiel van hem opgesteld. We hebben een selectie gemaakt op grond van de informatie waartoe hij toegang had. Uiteindelijk hielden we een lijst over van een man of dertig, veertig – allemaal naaste medewerkers van Saddam Hoessein, allemaal lid van de Revolutionaire Commandoraad, het militaire opperbevel of de leiding van de Ba'ath-partij. Maar verder kwamen we niet. Twee keer hebben we een Engelse technische term in onze vragen opgenomen. Twee keer kregen we een verzoek om uitleg terug. Blijkbaar spreekt hij geen Engels, of maar heel weinig. Of hij probeert ons zand in de ogen te strooien. Misschien spreekt hij het wel vloeiend. Maar als we dat wisten, zou dat de keus tot twee of drie mensen beperken. Daarom schrijft hij altijd in het Arabisch.'

Stewart bromde wat. Hij leek overtuigd.

'Het klinkt als Deep Throat.'

Ze dachten terug aan de geheime bron in de Watergate-affaire, die vertrouwelijke informatie had doorgegeven aan *The Washington Post*.

'Maar Woodward en Bernstein wisten toch wie Deep Throat was?' merkte Paxman op.

'Ze zeggen van wel, maar ik betwijfel het,' zei Stewart. 'Volgens mij heeft hij zich nooit bekendgemaakt, net als Jericho.'

Het was al donker toen de vier mannen David Sharon eindelijk de kans gaven naar zijn ambassade te vertrekken. Hij had hun alles verteld, daar was Steve Laing van overtuigd. De Mossad had niets achtergehouden. Bill Stewart had hem gezegd dat Amerika zware druk had uitgeoefend.

De twee Britse en Amerikaanse inlichtingenofficieren, die genoeg hadden van broodjes en koffie, zaten in een restaurant in de buurt van het appartement. Bill Stewart, die last had van een maagzweer die er na twaalf uur sandwiches en spanningen niet beter op was geworden, schoof de gerookte zalm op zijn bord heen en weer.

'Het is een lastige zaak, Steve. Verdomd lastig. Net als de Mossad zullen we een geschikte diplomaat moeten vinden die ervaring heeft met clandestiene operaties en die bereid is voor ons te werken. Desnoods voor geld. Langley wil er goed voor betalen. Jericho's informatie zou heel wat levens kunnen redden als de oorlog uitbreekt.'

'Maar wie zijn er nog over?' merkte Barber op. 'De helft van alle ambassades in Bagdad is al gesloten en de rest wordt zwaar bewaakt. De Ieren, de Zwitsers, de Zweden, de Finnen?'

'De neutrale landen kun je wel vergeten,' zei Laing. 'Trouwens, ik betwijfel of die getrainde agenten in Bagdad hebben. De ambassades van de derde-

wereldlanden vallen ook af... Dat betekent dat we van voren af aan moeten beginnen.'
'Daar hebben we geen tijd voor, Steve. Dit is dringend. We kunnen het niet op dezelfde manier aanpakken als de Israëli's hebben gedaan. Drie weken training is veel te weinig. Dat kon toen nog wel, maar Irak is nu een land in oorlog. De veiligheidsmaatregelen zijn veel scherper. Je hebt nu minstens drie maanden nodig om een diplomaat voor dit soort werk op te leiden.'
Stewart knikte instemmend.
'Of we moeten iemand anders vinden die het land nog in en uit kan. Een zakenman of zo. We zouden met een Duitser kunnen werken, of een Japanner. Die hebben nog officiële contacten.'
'Maar die blijven nooit lang. Ideaal gesproken moeten we iemand hebben die Jericho de komende... noem eens wat... vier maanden zou kunnen begeleiden. Wat dacht je van een journalist?' opperde Laing.
Paxman schudde zijn hoofd.
'Ik spreek ze allemaal als ze terugkomen. Ze worden dag en nacht bewaakt. Buitenlandse correspondenten kunnen niet door steegjes in achterbuurten zwerven. Ze hebben voortdurend iemand van de AMAM achter zich aan. En als we geen diplomaat kunnen vinden, wordt het een illegale operatie, vergeet dat niet. Wat denk je dat er gebeurt met een agent die in handen valt van Omar Khatib?'
De vier mannen aan de tafel kenden de reputatie van Khatib, het hoofd van de AMAM.
'Soms moet je risico's nemen,' vond Barber.
'Maar wie krijg je zo gek?' merkte Paxman op. 'Welke zakenman of journalist zou zo'n opdracht ooit aannemen als hij weet welk gevaar hij loopt? Ik zou nog liever door de KGB worden opgepakt dan door de AMAM.'
Bill Stewart legde gefrustreerd zijn vork neer en bestelde nog een glas melk.
'Goed. Meer mogelijkheden zijn er niet – behalve een getrainde agent die voor een Irakees kan doorgaan.'
Paxman keek snel naar Steve Laing, die even nadacht en toen langzaam knikte.
'Wij hebben zo'n vent,' zei Paxman.
'Een tamme Arabier? Ja, de Mossad ook. Wij ook,' zei Stewart. 'Maar niet van dit kaliber. Dat zijn boodschappenjongens, meer niet. Dit is een belangrijke en zeer riskante operatie.'
'Nee, geen Arabier. Een Engelsman. Een majoor van de SAS.'
Stewart keek op, met zijn melkglas halverwege zijn mond. Barber legde zijn mes en vork neer en hield op met kauwen.
'Misschien spreekt hij vloeiend Arabisch, maar dat is nog niet genoeg,' zei Stewart. 'Hij moet in Irak voor een Irakees kunnen doorgaan.'

'Hij is donker, hij heeft zwart haar en bruine ogen. Hij is geboren en getogen in Irak. Hij is niet van een Irakees te onderscheiden, maar toch is hij honderd procent Brits.'

'En hij is opgeleid voor clandestiene operaties?' vroeg Barber. 'Verdomme, waar zit die vent nu?'

'In Koeweit,' antwoordde Laing.

'Je bedoelt dat hij daar vastzit?'

'Nee. Hij beweegt zich nog vrij rond.'

'Als hij kan vluchten, wat doet hij daar dan nog?'

'Irakezen om zeep helpen.'

Stewart dacht even na en knikte toen langzaam.

'Allemachtig,' mompelde hij. 'Kunnen jullie hem daar vandaan krijgen? We zouden hem graag willen lenen.'

'Dat zal wel lukken, de volgende keer dat hij zich via de radio meldt. Maar hij blijft onder ons bevel en we willen toegang tot alle informatie.'

Stewart knikte weer. 'Ja, dat begrijp ik. Jullie hebben ons over Jericho ingelicht. Oké. Ik regel het wel met Webster.'

Paxman stond op en veegde zijn mond af. 'Ik zal maar eens contact opnemen met Riyad.'

Mike Martin was eraan gewend dat je het geluk moest afdwingen, maar die oktobermaand was het zuiver toeval dat zijn leven redde.

De avond van de 19e, dezelfde avond dat de vier hoge inlichtingenofficieren van de CIA en Century House in South Kensington zaten te eten, moest hij zijn radiobericht verzenden aan Riyad.

Als hij dat had gedaan, zou hij – wegens het tijdverschil van twee uur – al uit de lucht zijn geweest voordat Simon Paxman naar Century House was teruggekomen om Riyad te waarschuwen dat Martin ergens anders nodig was.

Erger nog, dan zou hij minstens vijf tot tien minuten met Riyad hebben gesproken over de dropping van een nieuwe voorraad wapens en explosieven.

Maar toen hij kort voor middernacht bij de garage van de jeep aankwam, ontdekte hij dat de wagen een lekke band had.

Vloekend worstelde hij een uur lang met de opgekrikte jeep. De wielbouten waren bijna niet los te krijgen en leken op hun plaats gemetseld met een mengsel van olie en woestijnzand. Om kwart voor één reed hij eindelijk de garage uit, maar na een kilometer bleek de reserveband ook langzaam leeg te lopen.

Hij kon niets anders doen dan naar de garage terugrijden en het radiobericht aan Riyad uitstellen.

188

Het kostte hem twee dagen om de twee banden te laten plakken, en pas op de avond van de 21e reed hij eindelijk de woestijn in, tot ver ten zuiden van de stad. Daar draaide hij zijn kleine satellietschotel in de richting van de Saoedische hoofdstad, honderderden kilometers verderop, en zond een reeks snelle pieptonen uit om zich te identificeren en een bericht aan te kondigen.

Zijn radio was een simpele tienkanaals-zender met een vast kristal. Voor iedere dag van de maand was een bepaald kanaal aangewezen, volgens een roterend schema. Op de 21e gebruikte hij kanaal 1. Toen hij zich had geïdentificeerd, schakelde hij over op ontvangst en wachtte. Een paar seconden later hoorde hij een zachte stem: 'Rocky Mountain aan Zwarte Beer. We ontvangen u sterkte vijf.'

De codes voor Riyad en Martin zelf klopten met de datum en het kanaal – een voorzorgsmaatregel voor het geval iemand anders zich in het gesprek zou willen mengen.

Martin schakelde naar zenden en begon zijn bericht.

In het noorden, aan de rand van Koeweit Stad, werd een jonge Iraakse radiotechnicus gewaarschuwd door een knipperend lampje op zijn console in een gevorderd appartement op de bovenverdieping van een flatgebouw. Een van zijn antennes had de uitzending gesignaleerd en opgepikt.

'Kapitein!' riep hij dringend. Een officier van de radiosectie van Hassan Rahmani's contraspionagedienst kwam naar de console. Het lampje knipperde nog en de technicus draaide aan een knop om de richting te peilen.

'Hij is net in de lucht gekomen.'

'Waar?'

'Ergens in de woestijn, kapitein.'

De technicus luisterde via zijn koptelefoon terwijl de richtingzoekers de positie van de zender bepaalden.

'Het is een elektronisch gecodeerd bericht.'

'Dat moet hem zijn. De chef had dus gelijk. Wat is zijn positie?'

De kapitein greep de telefoon om de twee andere peilstations te waarschuwen – de radiotrucks in Jahra en bij het Al-Adan Ziekenhuis aan de kust.

'Twee-nul-twee kompaskoers.'

Dat was tweeëntwintig graden westelijk van pal zuid, en in die richting lag niets anders dan de Koeweitse woestijn, die bij de grens in de Saoedische woestijn overging.

'Frequentie?' blafte de officier toen de truck in Jahra zich meldde.

Het was een ongebruikelijk kanaal met een zeer lage frequentie.

'Luitenant,' riep hij over zijn schouder, 'waarschuw de vliegbasis Ahmadi en zeg dat die helikopter zich gereedhoudt. We hebben een peiling.'

Ver weg in de woestijn beëindigde Martin zijn bericht en schakelde naar ontvangst om het antwoord uit Riyad te horen. Het was niet wat hij had verwacht. Zelf had hij maar vijftien seconden gesproken.

'Rocky Mountain aan Zwarte Beer. Terugkeren naar het hol. Ik herhaal: terugkeren naar het hol. Dringend. Over en sluiten.'

De Iraakse kapitein gaf de frequentie aan de twee andere peilstations door. In Jahra en op het ziekenhuisterrein bedienden de technici hun apparatuur. Boven hun hoofd draaiden de ruim één meter brede schotels van links naar rechts. Het station aan de kust bestreek het gebied vanaf de Koeweitse noordgrens met Irak tot aan de grens met Saoedi-Arabië. De radiowagen in Jahra controleerde de sector vanaf de zee in het oosten tot aan de Iraakse woestijn in het westen.

Samen konden de drie stations een driehoekspeiling uitvoeren die tot op een paar honderd meter nauwkeurig was. Die positie gaven ze door aan de Hind-helikopter met zijn bemanning van tien gewapende soldaten.

'Is hij nog in de lucht?' vroeg de kapitein.

De technicus tuurde naar het ronde scherm met de graden van het kompas eromheen. Het middelpunt van de cirkel was het punt waar hij zat. Een paar seconden eerder had er nog een glinsterende lijn over het beeld gelopen, naar twee-nul-twee. Nu was het scherm leeg. Het zou pas weer oplichten als de zender opnieuw in de lucht kwam.

'Nee, kapitein. Waarschijnlijk luistert hij naar het antwoord.'

'Dan komt hij zo wel weer,' zei de kapitein.

Maar hij vergiste zich. Zwarte Beer had fronsend naar de instructies uit Riyad geluisterd, de stroom uitgeschakeld, zijn zender dichtgeklapt en de antenne ingevouwen.

De Irakezen controleerden de frequentie tot aan het ochtendgloren, toen zette de Hind-helikopter op Al-Ahmadi zijn motor af en klom de bemanning met stijve benen uit het toestel.

Simon Paxman lag op een veldbed in zijn kantoor te slapen toen de telefoon ging. Het was een codetechnicus van de afdeling Verbindingen in de kelder.

'Ik kom eraan,' zei Paxman. Het was een heel kort bericht, zojuist ontcijferd, afkomstig uit Riyad. Martin had contact opgenomen en zijn orders ontvangen.

Terug in zijn kantoor belde Paxman met Chip Barber in zijn CIA-flat bij Grosvenor Square.

'Hij is op de terugweg,' zei hij. 'We weten niet wanneer hij de grens zal oversteken. Steve wil dat ik erheen ga. Kom je ook?'

'Oké,' zei Barber. 'Stewart vliegt morgenochtend terug naar Langley, maar ik ga met jou mee. Ik wil die vent zien.'

In de loop van de 22e vroegen de Amerikaanse ambassade en het Britse ministerie van Buitenlandse Zaken de Saoedische ambassade toestemming om een extra diplomaat naar Riyad te mogen sturen. Geen probleem. Er werden meteen visa afgegeven voor twee paspoorten, geen van beide op naam van Barber of Paxman. Die avond om kwart voor negen stapten de inlichtingenofficieren op het toestel van Heathrow naar het internationale vliegveld King Abdulaziz in Riyad, waar ze vlak voor het aanbreken van de dag arriveerden.

Een auto van de Amerikaanse ambassade bracht Chip Barber meteen naar de Amerikaanse missie, waar het sterk uitgebreide CIA-bureau was onderge-bracht, terwijl een kleinere, onopvallende sedan Simon Paxman naar de villa reed waar de Britse SIS haar tenten had opgeslagen. Het eerste wat Pax-man hoorde was dat Martin de grens nog niet was overgestoken en zich nog niet had gemeld.

Riyads instructie om onmiddellijk terug te komen was eenvoudiger gezegd dan gedaan. Mike Martin was ruim voor het eerste ochtendlicht van de 22e oktober in Koeweit Stad teruggekeerd en had de rest van de dag besteed aan het afwikkelen van zijn zaken.

Onder de grafplaat van matroos Shepton op de christelijke begraafplaats liet hij een bericht voor Ahmed Al-Khalifa achter met de mededeling dat hij helaas uit Koeweit moest vertrekken. In een briefje aan Abu Fouad legde hij uit waar en hoe hij het restant van de wapens en explosieven kon vinden die nog in twee van zijn zes villa's lagen opgeslagen.

Toen hij 's middags klaar was, reed hij in zijn aftandse pick-up truck naar de kamelenfarm voorbij Sulaibija, waar de laatste buitenwijken van Koeweit Stad eindigden en de woestijn begon.

Zijn kamelen waren er nog en verkeerden in goede conditie. Het kalf was gespeend en beloofde een waardevol dier te worden. Hij gebruikte het om zijn rekening voor de verzorging van de dieren te betalen.

Kort voor het donker zadelde hij op en reed naar het zuid-zuidwesten. Toen de avond viel en de kilte van de woestijn op hem neerdaalde, had hij de bewoonde wereld al een heel eind achter zich gelaten.

In plaats van een uurtje kostte het hem nu vier uur om de plek te bereiken waar hij zijn radio had begraven. Het herkenningspunt was het roestige wrak van een auto die daar ooit pech had gekregen en was achtergelaten.

Hij verborg de radio onder de lading dadels in de tassen van zijn kameel. Het dier had een veel minder zware last te dragen dan op de heenweg, negen weken eerder, toen de tassen waren volgestouwd met wapens en explosieven. Echt dankbaar was de kameel daar niet voor. Ze gromde en spuwde. Liever was ze op de comfortabele farm gebleven. Maar geen moment vertraagde ze haar deinende pas, en gestaag gleden de kilometers in de duisternis voorbij.

Toch was het een heel andere tocht dan in augustus. Op weg naar het zuiden zag Martin steeds meer sporen van het grote Iraakse leger dat nu het gebied ten zuiden van de stad bezette en zich steeds verder naar het westen uitbreidde, in de richting van de Iraakse grens.

Regelmatig zag hij het lichtschijnsel van de verschillende oliebronnen in de woestijn. Hij wist dat de Irakezen daar patrouilleerden en reed er met een boog omheen.

Soms snoof hij de rook van hun kampvuurtjes op en kon hij nog net op tijd een patrouille ontwijken. Eén keer stuitte hij bijna op een bataljon tanks, verborgen achter een hoefijzervormige zandwal, met hun neus naar de Amerikanen en de Saoedi's aan de andere kant van de grens gericht. Hij hoorde bijtijds het gerinkel van metaal op metaal, trok de leidsels scherp naar rechts en dook weg tussen een paar zandheuvels.

Toen hij het land was binnengekomen, hadden er nog maar twee divisies van de Iraakse Republikeinse Garde langs de grens gelegen, veel verder naar het oosten, pal ten zuiden van Koeweit Stad.

Nu had de Hammurabi-divisie zich bij de andere twee gevoegd, terwijl elf andere divisies, voornamelijk van het reguliere leger, door Saddam Hoessein naar Koeweit waren gestuurd om gelijke tred te houden met de opbouw van de Coalitietroepen aan de Saoedische kant.

Veertien divisies betekent heel wat manschappen, zelfs verspreid over zo'n groot gebied. Gelukkig voor Martin zetten ze blijkbaar geen wachtposten uit en lagen ze te slapen onder hun voertuigen. Maar alleen al door hun enorme aantal werd hij steeds verder naar het westen gedrongen.

De korte route van veertig kilometer vanaf het Saoedische dorp Hamatijat naar de Koeweitse kamelenfarm kwam nu niet in aanmerking. Martin maakte een omweg in de richting van de Iraakse grens, gemarkeerd door de diepe kloof van de Wadi-al-Batin, die hij liever niet overstak.

Bij het eerste ochtendlicht bevond hij zich ver ten westen van het Manageesh-olieveld en nog steeds ten noorden van de politiepost Al Mufrad, een van de grensposten van vóór de crisis.

Het terrein was wat heuvelachtiger geworden en Martin vond een groep rotsen waartussen hij de dag kon doorbrengen. Toen de zon opkwam, lijnde hij de kameel aan – die vol afgrijzen aan het zand en de kale rots snuffelde, waar zelfs geen smakelijke doornstruik groeide die als ontbijt kon dienen – rolde zich in de kamelendeken en viel in slaap.

Kort na het middaguur werd hij gewekt door het geratel van tanks en besefte hij dat hij te dicht bij de hoofdweg lag die van Jahra in Koeweit via de douanepost Al Salmi naar Saoedi-Arabië loopt. Na zonsondergang wachtte hij bijna tot middernacht voordat hij verderging. Hij wist dat de grens niet meer dan twintig kilometer naar het zuiden kon liggen.

Door zijn late start zou hij de laatste Iraakse patrouilles om een uur of drie passeren – het nachtelijke uur waarop de menselijke weerstand het laagst is en wachtposten vaak in slaap sukkelen.

Bij het licht van de maan kwam hij langs de politiepost Qaimat Subah, en drie kilometer verderop wist hij dat hij de grens achter zich had gelaten. Voor alle zekerheid reed hij nog even door, tot hij de zijweg bereikte die in oost-westelijke richting van Hamatijat naar Ar-Rugi loopt. Daar stopte hij om zijn zender te installeren.

Omdat de Irakezen in het noorden zich op enkele kilometers van de grens hadden verschanst en generaal Schwarzkopf zijn troepen ook op veilige afstand hield om er zeker van te zijn dat de Irakezen – als ze aanvielen – inderdaad Saoedi-Arabië waren binnengevallen, bevond Martin zich nu in een niemandsland. Ooit zou een stortvloed van Saoedische en Amerikaanse troepen door dit gebied naar Koeweit oprukken, maar in de ochtendschemer van die 24e oktober had Martin de woestijn nog voor zich alleen.

Simon Paxman werd gewekt door een assistent van het inlichtingenteam dat in de villa was ondergebracht. 'Zwarte Beer heeft zich gemeld, Simon. Hij is de grens over.'

Paxman sprong zijn bed uit en rende in zijn pyjama naar de radiokamer. Een radiotechnicus zat op een draaistoel achter een console die een hele wand besloeg van wat ooit een fraai ingerichte slaapkamer was geweest. Omdat het inmiddels de 24e was, waren de codes veranderd.

'Corpus Christi aan Texas Ranger. Waar zit u? Wat is uw positie?'

De stem klonk blikkerig door de luidspreker van de console, maar was uit-stekend te verstaan. 'Ten zuiden van Qaimat Subah, op de weg van Hama-tijat naar Ar-Rugi.'

De technicus keek Paxman aan. De SIS-officier drukte de zendknop in en zei: 'Ranger, blijf waar u bent. We komen u halen. Begrepen?'

'Begrepen,' antwoordde de stem. 'Ik wacht wel op de taxi.'

Het was geen taxi maar een Amerikaanse Blackhawk-helikopter die twee uur later boven de weg neerdaalde. Een sergeant hing in de deuropening naast de piloot en speurde met een verrekijker de stoffige weg af. Op twee-honderd meter afstand zag hij een man naast een kameel. Hij wilde al verder vliegen toen de man zijn hand opstak.

De Blackhawk bleef boven de bedoeïen hangen en de piloot nam hem ach-terdochtig op. Ze waren vlak bij de Koeweitse grens. Maar de coördinaten die hij van de inlichtingenofficier van zijn squadron had gekregen klopten en verder was er geen mens te zien.

Het was Chip Barber die het Amerikaanse squadron op de vliegbasis van Riyad had gevraagd een helikopter te sturen om een Brit op te pikken die over de Koeweitse grens gekomen was. De actieradius van de Blackhawk was groot genoeg. Maar niemand had de piloot iets gezegd over een bedoeïen met een kameel.

Terwijl de bemanning vanaf zestig meter hoogte op hem neerkeek, legde de man op de grond een rijtje stenen neer. Toen hij klaar was, deed hij een stap achteruit. De sergeant richtte zijn verrekijker. De stenen vormden twee woorden: *'Hi there.'*

'Dat moet hem zijn,' zei de sergeant in zijn microfoon. 'Laten we hem maar oppikken.'

De piloot knikte en de Blackhawk daalde nog verder, tot hij vlak boven de grond zweefde, twintig meter van de man met zijn lastdier.

Martin had de tassen en het zware zadel al van de kameel getild en langs de weg gegooid. De radio en zijn eigen wapen, de dertienschots automatische Browning 9-mm die de SAS meestal gebruikte, zaten in zijn schoudertas.

Toen de helikopter begon te dalen, was de kameel in paniek geraakt en ervandoor gegaan. Martin keek haar na. Ze had hem goed gediend, ondanks haar slechte humeur. Er zou haar niets gebeuren, alleen in de woestijn. Hier was ze immers thuis. Ze kon haar eigen voedsel en water zoeken, totdat een bedoeïen haar zou vinden, geen brandmerk zou ontdekken en haar verheugd met zich mee zou nemen.

Martin dook onder de rotorbladen door en sprintte naar de open deur. Boven het geloei van de rotor uit riep de sergeant: 'Wat is uw naam?'

'Majoor Martin.'

De sergeant stak zijn hand uit en trok Martin naar binnen. 'Welkom aan boord, majoor.'

Op dat punt maakte het gebrul van de motor ieder gesprek onmogelijk. De sergeant gaf Martin een paar oorbeschermers en ze installeerden zich voor de terugreis naar Riyad.

Toen ze de stad naderden, werd de piloot naar een vrijstaande villa in de buitenwijken gedirigeerd. Ernaast lag een open stuk grond waar iemand drie rijen fel oranje stoelkussens had neergelegd in de vorm van een H. De Blackhawk daalde tot vlak boven de grond. De man in de Arabische kaftan sprong uit het toestel, zwaaide nog even naar de bemanning en liep naar het huis toen de heli weer opsteeg. Twee bedienden verzamelden de kussentjes.

Martin stapte door de boogpoort in de muur en kwam op een betegelde binnenplaats uit.

Twee mannen kwamen uit het huis naar buiten. Een van hen herkende hij van het SAS-hoofdkwartier in Londen, weken geleden.

'Simon Paxman,' zei de jongste van de twee, en hij stak zijn hand uit. 'Blij u weer te zien. Dit is Chip Barber, een van onze neven uit Langley.'

Barber gaf hem een hand en nam de man scherp op: de gevlekte, vuilwitte kaftan die tot aan de grond reikte, de gestreepte deken die opgevouwen over

194

zijn ene schouder hing, de roodwit geruite *keffijeh* met de twee zwarte banden om hem op zijn plaats te houden, en daaronder het magere, harde gezicht met de donkere ogen en de zwarte stoppelbaard.

'Prettig u te ontmoeten, majoor. Ik heb veel over u gehoord.' Hij trok even zijn neus op. 'Een warm bad lijkt me geen overbodige luxe.'

'Ja, ik zal er meteen voor zorgen,' zei Paxman.

Martin knikte. 'Bedankt.' Hij stapte de koele villa binnen, die door prins Khaled bin Sultan aan de Britten ter beschikking was gesteld. Barber en Paxman kwamen achter hem aan. Barber had moeite zijn enthousiasme te verbergen. Hij begon te geloven dat ze de juiste man hadden gevonden.

Martin moest het bad twee keer opnieuw laten vollopen voordat hij al het vuil en het zweet van de afgelopen weken had weggewassen. Toen sloeg hij een handdoek om zich heen, liet zijn natte haar knippen door een kapper die daarvoor speciaal was besteld, en schoor zich met Simon Paxmans scheergerei.

De *keffijeh*, de deken, de kaftan en de sandalen waren naar de tuin gebracht waar een Saoedische bediende ze had verbrand. Twee uur later, in een hemd met korte mouwen en een katoenen broek die hij van Paxman had geleend, zat Mike Martin aan de eettafel, waar een lunch van vijf gangen werd opgediend.

'Zou u me willen vertellen,' vroeg hij, 'waarom ik zo plotseling moest terugkomen?'

Het was Chip Barber die antwoord gaf.

'Goede vraag, majoor. Een verdomd goede vraag zelfs, die een verdomd goed antwoord verdient. We zouden graag willen dat u naar Bagdad vertrekt. De volgende week. Salade of vis?'

De CIA en de SIS hadden haast. Hoewel er nauwelijks over werd gesproken, toen of later, had de CIA eind oktober al een omvangrijke organisatie in Riyad opgebouwd.

En binnen de kortste keren kreeg de inlichtingendienst het aan de stok met de legertop die zich anderhalve kilometer verderop in het labyrint onder het Saoedische ministerie van Defensie had teruggetrokken om haar plannen uit te werken. De militairen, zeker de luchtmachtgeneraals, waren ervan overtuigd dat ze met hun technische middelen alles konden ontdekken wat ze over de Iraakse verdediging en de Iraakse voorbereidingen moesten weten.

Natuurlijk beschikten ze over een indrukwekkende technologie. Behalve de satellieten en hun opnamen van Irak, behalve de Aurora en de U-2 die foto's maakten van nog geringere hoogte, waren er nog andere geavanceerde toestellen die vanuit de lucht de situatie in het oog hielden.

Speciale satellieten in een geosynchrone baan boven het Midden-Oosten luisterden naar alle Iraakse verbindingen in de ether. Maar de gesprekken via de 70 000 km ondergrondse glasvezelkabels konden ze niet volgen.

Het meest opvallende vliegtuig was het 'Airborne Warning and Control System', beter bekend als de AWACS – een omgebouwde Boeing 707 met een grote radarschotel op zijn rug, die langzaam rondjes draaide boven het noordelijke Golfgebied, dag en nacht, om alle bewegingen in het Iraakse luchtruim te registreren. Er kon bijna geen Iraaks vliegtuig opstijgen zonder dat Riyad het nummer, de koers, de snelheid en de hoogte kende.

De AWACS werd ondersteund door een andere omgebouwde Boeing 707, de E8-A of J-STARS, die alle bewegingen op de grond in de gaten hield. Zijn grote Norden-radar stond omlaag en opzij gericht en kon heel Irak bestrijken zonder het Iraakse luchtruim binnen te hoeven dringen. Bijna ieder stukje bewegend metaal werd door de J-STARS geregistreerd.

De combinatie van deze en andere technische wonderen waaraan Washington miljarden dollars had uitgegeven, gaf de generaals de overtuiging dat ze alles konden zien en horen – en dus ook alles konden vernietigen als dat nodig was. Duisternis, regen en mist vormden geen obstakels meer. Nooit zou een vijand zich meer onder het bladerdak van de jungle kunnen verschuilen. Niemand was veilig voor de alziende ogen aan de hemel.

De inlichtingenofficieren uit Langley waren daar niet zo zeker van en lieten hun twijfels duidelijk blijken, tot grote ergernis van de militairen. Twijfel was iets voor burgers. Het leger had een zware klus op te knappen, en aan kritiek was geen behoefte.

Bij de Britten lag de situatie anders. Het SIS-contingent in de Golf was lang niet zo groot als dat van de CIA, hoewel het voor Century House toch een omvangrijke operatie was. Maar de SIS werkte veel clandestiener dan de collega's uit Langley.

Bovendien was de commandant van alle Britse troepen in het Golfgebied – de onderbevelhebber van generaal Schwarzkopf – een merkwaardige militair met een ongebruikelijke achtergrond.

Norman Schwarzkopf was een grote, stoere vent met een geweldige militaire kennis. Een echte generaal. 'Stormin' Norman' of de 'Beer', zoals hij wel werd genoemd, was onderhevig aan wisselende stemmingen, van joviale hartelijkheid tot uitbarstingen van woede die zijn staf als 'ballistische explosies' omschreef en die altijd snel voorbij waren. Zijn Britse collega was zijn absolute tegenpool.

Luitenant-generaal Sir Peter de la Billière, die begin oktober was aangekomen om het bevel over de Britse eenheden op zich te nemen, was een bedrieglijk tengere, magere, pezige man met een rustige houding en een aarzelende manier van spreken. De extraverte, zwaargebouwde Amerikaan en de tengere Brit vormden een vreemd koppel, maar ze konden goed met elkaar overweg omdat ze door elkaars façade heen konden kijken.

Sir Peter, bij de troepen bekend als PB, was de meest onderscheiden militair in het Britse leger, iets waar hij zelf nooit iets over zei. Alleen de mensen die tijdens verschillende campagnes onder hem hadden gediend, vertelden bij een glas bier weleens iets over zijn koelbloedigheid in de strijd waaraan hij al dat 'blik' op zijn uniform te danken had. Bovendien was hij ooit commandant van de SAS geweest, een achtergrond waardoor hij heel wat over het Golfgebied, clandestiene operaties en de Arabieren wist.

En omdat hij ooit met de SIS had samengewerkt, vonden de bezwaren van de inlichtingendiensten bij hem een williger oor dan bij de Amerikaanse bevelhebbers.

De SAS was al goed vertegenwoordigd in Saoedi-Arabië. Ze hadden hun eigen, afgelegen kamp in een hoek van een grotere militaire basis buiten Riyad. Als voormalig SAS-commandant vond generaal PB dat ze hun speciale talenten niet moesten verspillen aan routinetaken die ook door de infanterie of de para's konden worden uitgevoerd. Deze mannen waren specialisten in infiltratie en het redden van gijzelaars.

Er was al gefluisterd dat de SAS kon worden ingezet om de Britse gijzelaars te bevrijden die Saddam Hoessein nu als 'menselijk schild' gebruikte maar dat plan werd opgegeven toen Saddam de gijzelaars over heel Irak verspreidde.

In de villa buiten Riyad bedachten de CIA en de SIS die laatste week van oktober een operatie die zeer goed bij de mogelijkheden van de SAS paste. Toen het gereed was, werd het plan aan de plaatselijke SAS-commandant voorgelegd en hij ging ermee aan de slag.

De eerste middag van Martins verblijf in de villa kreeg hij zoveel mogelijk te horen over de achtergrond van Operatie Jericho. Hij had nog steeds het recht te weigeren en zich weer bij zijn regiment aan te sluiten. 's Avonds dacht hij erover na en gaf toen zijn antwoord aan de officieren van de CIA en de SIS: 'Goed, ik zal het doen. Maar onder bepaalde voorwaarden.'

Het belangrijkste probleem was zijn dekmantel, zoals iedereen begreep. Dit was geen bliksemactie waarmee hij de contraspionagedienst te slim af kon zijn. Hij kon ook niet rekenen op de clandestiene steun van het verzet, zoals in Koeweit, of buiten Bagdad door de woestijn zwerven als een bedoeïen.

Heel Irak was één groot legerkamp. Zelfs in streken die op de kaart verlaten leken, werd druk gepatrouilleerd. In Bagdad zelf waren overal controleposten van het leger, de AMAM en de militaire politie, op zoek naar deserteurs en verdachte personen.

De angst voor de AMAM was bij iedereen bekend. Zakenmensen, journalisten en diplomaten die uit Irak terugkwamen vertelden verhalen over de alom aanwezige Geheime Politie, die met een waar schrikbewind de Iraakse bevolking onderdrukte.

Als Martin zou gaan, zou hij er moeten blijven. Het begeleiden van een agent als Jericho zou niet eenvoudig zijn. Eerst moest de man worden opgespoord via de geheime 'brievenbussen', die misschien al in de gaten werden gehouden als Jericho inmiddels was ontmaskerd en had bekend.

Daarnaast moest Martin een plek vinden om te wonen, een geschikte basis van waaruit hij berichten kon versturen en ontvangen. En als de informatiestroom weer op gang kwam, zou hij door de stad moeten zwerven om Jericho's berichten op te halen die nu bestemd waren voor zijn nieuwe opdrachtgevers.

Maar het grootste probleem was toch dat Martin geen diplomatieke onschendbaarheid bezat en dus vogelvrij was als hij zou worden opgepakt. Dan wachtten hem onherroepelijk de gruwelijke verhoorcellen van Abu Ghraid.

'Wat eh... wat zijn die voorwaarden precies?' vroeg Paxman.

'Als ik niet als diplomaat kan gaan, wil ik aan de huishouding van een diplomaat worden toegevoegd.'

'Dat is niet zo eenvoudig, beste kerel. Alle ambassades worden bewaakt.'

'Ik had het niet over een ambassade, maar over een huishouding.'

'Als chauffeur of zoiets?' vroeg Barber.

'Nee. Die valt te veel op. Hij moet achter het stuur blijven zitten. Hij rijdt

zijn baas rond en hij wordt net zo scherp in de gaten gehouden.'
'Wat dan?'
'Als de situatie niet drastisch is veranderd, wonen de meeste diplomaten nog buiten de ambassade, en als ze hoog genoeg zijn hebben ze een vrijstaande villa met een ommuurde tuin. Vroeger liep daar altijd een tuinman-annex-klusjesman rond.'
'Tuinman?' vroeg Barber. 'Verdomme, man, dat is een handarbeider. Dan word je meteen voor het leger opgeroepen.'
'Nee. De tuinman doet alle klusjes om het huis. Hij onderhoudt de tuin, hij gaat op de fiets naar de markt om vis, fruit, groente, brood en olie te kopen. En hij woont in een hutje achter in de tuin.'
'Ja, en?' vroeg Paxman.
'Hij is volkomen onzichtbaar. Hij is zo gewoon dat hij niemand opvalt. Als hij wordt aangehouden, is zijn pasje in orde. Bovendien heeft hij een brief van de ambassade bij zich, die verklaart dat hij voor een diplomaat werkt, dat hij niet in dienst hoeft en dat de autoriteiten hem met rust moeten laten. Zolang hij niets verkeerds doet, zal de politie hem zijn gang laten gaan omdat ze anders problemen krijgen met de ambassade.'
De inlichtingenofficieren dachten een tijdje na.
'Misschien zou het lukken,' gaf Barber toe. 'Een heel gewone man, die niet opvalt... Wat denk je, Simon?'
'Dan moet de diplomaat ook op de hoogte zijn,' zei Paxman.
'Gedeeltelijk,' zei Martin. 'Zijn regering hoeft hem alleen maar opdracht te geven de man in dienst te nemen en zich nergens mee te bemoeien. Wat hij daarvan denkt, is zijn eigen zaak. Maar als hij zijn baantje wil houden, zal hij er met niemand over spreken. Zeker niet als het bevel van de hoogste instantie komt.'
'De Britse ambassade is uitgesloten,' zei Paxman. 'Dan zouden de Irakezen bewust problemen zoeken.'
'Dat geldt ook voor ons,' zei Barber. 'Waar dacht je aan, Mike?'
Toen Martin het hun vertelde, staarden ze hem ongelovig aan.
'Dat meen je niet,' zei de Amerikaan.
'Jazeker,' zei Martin kalm.
'Verdomme, Mike, maar dat moeten we met de premier zelf opnemen.'
'En met de president,' zei Barber.
'We zijn tegenwoordig toch zo goed bevriend? Ik bedoel, als Jericho de geallieerde verliezen beperkt kan houden, lijkt een telefoontje me niet te veel gevraagd.'
Chip Barber keek op zijn horloge. In Washington was het zeven uur vroeger dan in de Golf. In Langley hadden ze net geluncht. In Londen was het maar twee uur vroeger, maar misschien zaten de hogere mensen nog op kantoor.

Barber ging haastig naar zijn ambassade terug en stuurde een spoedbericht in code aan zijn adjunct-directeur Operaties, Bill Stewart, die meteen met William Webster overlegde. Webster belde op zijn beurt met het Witte Huis en vroeg om een onderhoud met de president.

Simon Paxman had geluk. Zijn codebericht bereikte Steve Laing nog op kantoor. Hij sprak met het hoofd Operaties van de divisie Midden-Oosten, die de Chef thuis belde. Sir Colin dacht na en belde de secretaris van het kabinet, Sir Robin Butler.

Het is een ongeschreven wet dat de Chef van de Secret Intelligence Service in noodgevallen een persoonlijk gesprek met zijn minister-president kan aanvragen, en Margaret Thatcher was altijd beschikbaar voor de mannen van de inlichtingendiensten en de speciale eenheden. Ze vroeg de Chef de volgende morgen om acht uur naar haar privé-kantoor op Downing Street 10 te komen.

Zoals altijd was ze al voor dag en dauw aan het werk en had ze haar post bijna afgehandeld toen de Chef van de SIS binnenkwam. Fronsend en verbaasd luisterde ze naar zijn vreemde verzoek, stelde een paar vragen, dacht even na en nam toen een kordaat besluit, zoals haar gewoonte was.

'Ik zal het met president Bush opnemen zodra hij wakker is. We zullen zien wat we kunnen doen. Deze man... zou het hem werkelijk lukken?'

'Dat is wel de bedoeling, mevrouw de minister-president.'

'Een van uw eigen mensen, Sir Colin?'

'Nee. Een majoor van de SAS.'

Thatchers gezicht klaarde op. 'Een bijzondere kerel, dus.'

'Het schijnt zo, mevrouw.'

'Als dit achter de rug is, zou ik hem graag ontmoeten.'

'Daar zullen we voor zorgen.'

Toen de Chef was vertrokken, belde de staf van Downing Street met het Witte Huis – hoewel het in Washington nog midden in de nacht was – en regelde een beveiligde telefoonverbinding voor acht uur 's ochtends Amerikaanse tijd, als het in Londen één uur 's middags was. De lunch van de premier werd een halfuur verschoven.

Net als zijn voorganger Ronald Reagan vond president Bush het altijd lastig de Britse minister-president iets te weigeren waar ze echt haar zinnen op had gezet.

'Goed, Margaret,' zei de president na vijf minuten. 'Ik zal wel bellen.'

'Hij kan hooguit nee zeggen,' merkte Thatcher op. 'En dat lijkt me niet waarschijnlijk na alles wat we voor hem hebben gedaan.'

'Zeg dat wel,' beaamde de president.

De twee regeringsleiders belden binnen een uur na elkaar, en het antwoord van de verbaasde man aan de andere kant van de lijn was bevestigend. Hij zou hun afgezanten zo snel mogelijk onder vier ogen ontvangen.

Die avond vertrok Bill Stewart uit Washington en stapte Steve Laing op het laatste toestel vanaf Heathrow.

Als Mike Martin enig idee had van de commotie die hij met zijn verzoek had veroorzaakt, liet hij dat niet merken. De 26e en 27e oktober bracht hij door met rusten, eten en slapen. Maar hij schoor zich niet meer, en er vormde zich weer een donkere schaduw op zijn wangen. Intussen werd er op andere plaatsen in de wereld uit zijn naam veel werk verzet.

De chef van het SIS-bureau in Tel Aviv was met één laatste verzoek naar Kobi Dror gegaan. De directeur van de Mossad staarde de Engelsman verbaasd aan.

'Dus jullie gaan het echt proberen?' vroeg hij.

'Ik weet alleen wat ik jou moet vragen, Kobi.'

'Verdomme, een illegale operatie! Je beseft toch wel dat ze hem te grazen zullen nemen?'

'Kun je ons helpen, Kobi?'

'Natuurlijk.'

'Binnen vierentwintig uur?'

Kobi Dror verviel weer in zijn rol uit *Anatevka*. 'Ik zou je zelfs mijn rechterarm geven, jongen. Maar het is een krankzinnig voorstel.'

Hij stond op van achter zijn bureau en legde zijn arm om de schouders van de Engelsman. 'Weet je, we hadden onze eigen regels al met voeten getreden, maar we hebben geluk gehad. Normaal sturen we onze mensen nooit naar een "brievenbus" toe. Het kan altijd een valstrik zijn. Wij gebruiken die brievenbussen maar in één richting: van de *katsa* naar de spion. Voor Jericho hebben we een uitzondering gemaakt. Moncada pikte daar zijn informatie op omdat er geen andere mogelijkheid was. En hij heeft geluk gehad. Twee jaar lang. Maar in elk geval had hij politieke onschendbaarheid. En nu willen jullie... *dit*?'

Hij pakte een fotootje van een droevig ogende man met Arabische trekken, piekerig zwart haar en een stoppelbaard. De Engelsman had het fotootje zojuist ontvangen uit Riyad. Omdat er geen civiele luchtvaartverbinding tussen de twee hoofdsteden bestond, was het gebracht met een HS-125 twinjet, het verbindingstoestel van generaal De la Billière zelf. De HS-125 stond nog op het militaire vliegveld van Sde Dov, waar het uitvoerig was gefotografeerd.

Dror haalde zijn schouders op.

'Goed. Morgenochtend. Ik beloof het je.'

De Mossad beschikt zonder enige twijfel over een van de beste technische diensten ter wereld. Afgezien van de afdeling Inbraak en de centrale computer met bijna twee miljoen namen en bijbehorende gegevens, zijn er in de

201

kelder een paar kamers waar de temperatuur altijd constant wordt gehouden. Die kamers bevatten 'papier'. Geen gewoon papier, maar heel bijzonder papier: de originelen van bijna alle paspoorten ter wereld, met duizenden andere identiteitskaarten, rijbewijzen, sofi-kaarten en dergelijke.

En dan zijn er de blanco indentiteitskaarten waarop de specialisten iedere gewenste naam kunnen invullen, met de originelen als voorbeeld.

Maar legitimatiepapieren zijn niet de enige specialiteit van deze afdeling. Er wordt ook geld vervalst, in grote hoeveelheden, om de economie van vijandige buurlanden te verstoren of 'illegale' operaties van de Mossad te financieren waar noch de minister-president noch de Knesset iets van weet of wil weten.

Pas na rijp beraad hadden de CIA en de SIS besloten de Mossad om een dienst te vragen, omdat ze zelf niet in staat waren betrouwbare papieren te leveren voor een 45-jarige Iraakse arbeider. Niemand had ooit de moeite genomen de originelen te verzamelen.

Gelukkig had de Sajret Matcal, een infiltratie-eenheid die zo geheim is dat de naam in Israël niet eens mag worden gedrukt, twee jaar eerder een actie in Irak uitgevoerd om een Arabische *oter* te installeren die daar een bepaald contact tot stand moest brengen. In Irak waren ze op twee boerenarbeiders gestuit, die ze hadden vastgebonden en van hun papieren beroofd.

Zoals beloofd werkten Drors specialisten de hele nacht door, en tegen de ochtend kwamen ze met een Iraaks pasje – beduimeld en vies alsof het al lang in gebruik was – op naam van Mahmoud Al-Khouri, 45 jaar oud, uit een dorpje in de heuvels ten noorden van Bagdad, die in de hoofdstad als arbeider werkte.

De vervalsers wisten niet dat Martin de naam had aangenomen van de man die hem begin augustus in een restaurant in Chelsea op zijn kennis van het Arabisch had getest. En dat hij het geboortedorpje van de tuinman van zijn vader had gekozen, de oude man die het Engelse jongetje lang geleden onder een boom in Bagdad had verteld over de plek waar hij geboren was, met de moskee, het koffiehuis en de velden met alfalfa en meloenen eromheen. Maar er waren nog meer dingen die de vervalsers niet wisten.

's Ochtends vroeg gaf Kobi Dror het pasje aan de SIS-chef in Tel Aviv.

'Deze pas doorstaat iedere controle. Maar ik zeg je één ding...' Hij tikte met een stompe vinger op het fotootje. 'Die tamme Arabier van jullie zal jullie verraden of binnen een week worden opgepakt.'

De SIS-officier haalde zijn schouders op. Zelfs hij wist niet dat de man op de vlekkerige foto geen Arabier was. Dat hoefde hij niet te weten, dus was het hem niet verteld. Zoals hem was opgedragen, bracht hij het pasje naar de wachtende HS-125, die terugkeerde naar Riyad.

Er was ook voor kleren gezorgd – de eenvoudige *disj-dasj* van de Iraakse arbeider, een saaie bruine *keffijeh* en stevige canvasschoenen met touwzolen.

Een mandenvlechter was bezig een rieten mand van wilgetenen te vlechten volgens een zeer ongebruikelijk ontwerp. De arme Saoedische rietvlechter wist niet waarvoor de mand bedoeld was, maar de vreemde buitenlander wilde er goed voor betalen en dus werkte hij snel door.

Op een geheime legerbasis in de buurt van Riyad werden twee speciale wagens gereedgemaakt. Een Hercules-transportvliegtuig van de RAF had ze opgehaald bij het hoofdkwartier van de SAS, verderop langs het schiereiland in Oman. Ze werden nu volledig gestript en opnieuw uitgerust voor een lange, zware tocht.

Het belangrijkste voordeel van de twee omgebouwde Landrovers met hun lange wielbasis was niet hun bepantsering of hun vuurkracht, maar hun snelheid en actieradius. Ze boden plaats aan de standaardbezetting van vier SAS-mannen. Een van de auto's zou een extra passagier meenemen, de andere een crossmotorfiets met zware banden, die ook van extra tanks was voorzien.

Het Amerikaanse leger bood assistentie in de vorm van twee grote, dubbelrotor Chinook-helikopters, die klaarstonden om op te stijgen.

Mikhail Sergejewitsj Gorbatsjov zat zoals gewoonlijk achter zijn bureau op zijn kantoor op de zevende en hoogste verdieping van het Centrale Comité aan Novaja Plosha, geassisteerd door twee secretarissen, toen de intercom de komst van de twee afgezanten uit Londen en Washington aankondigde.

Het afgelopen etmaal had hij zich al een paar keer afgevraagd waarom de Amerikaanse president en de Britse premier hem ieder een persoonlijke afgezant hadden gestuurd. Geen politicus of een diplomaat, maar een boodschapper. Wat was er in deze moderne tijd zo belangrijk dat het niet via de gebruikelijke diplomatieke kanalen kon worden afgehandeld? Ze hadden zelfs een beveiligde hotline die door niemand kon worden afgeluisterd – behalve door de tolken en de technici.

En omdat nieuwsgierigheid een van zijn opvallendste eigenschappen was, wilde hij het raadsel graag oplossen.

Tien minuten later werden de twee bezoekers binnengelaten in het privékantoor van de secretaris-generaal van de Communistische Partij, de president van de Sovjetunie. Het was een lange, smalle kamer met maar één rij ramen die uitkeken op het Nieuwe Plein. De president zat aan het eind van een lange vergadertafel, met zijn rug naar de muur gekeerd.

De jongere Gorbatsjov hield niet van de sombere, zware stijl van zijn twee voorgangers Andropov en Tsjernenko. Hij gaf de voorkeur aan een lichte inrichting. Het bureau en de tafel waren van licht beukehout, met rechte maar comfortabele stoelen eromheen. Voor de ramen hing vitrage.

Toen de twee mannen binnenkwamen, gaf hij zijn secretarissen een teken om de kamer te verlaten. Toen stond hij op en liep op de bezoekers toe.

'Gegroet, heren,' zei hij in het Russisch. 'Spreekt u mijn taal?'

Een van de mannen, die hij voor de Engelsman hield, antwoordde in hakkelend Russisch: 'Een tolk zou wel gemakkelijk zijn, meneer de president.'

'Vitali,' riep Gorbatsjov een van de vertrekkende secretarissen na, 'vraag of Jevgeny even komt.'

In afwachting van de tolk glimlachte hij tegen de mannen en bood hun een stoel aan. Even later stapte zijn persoonlijke tolk de kamer binnen en ging naast het presidentiële bureau zitten.

'Mijn naam is William Stewart, meneer de president. Ik ben adjunct-directeur Operaties van de Central Intelligence Agency in Washington,' begon de Amerikaan.

Gorbatsjovs mond verstrakte en hij fronste zijn voorhoofd.

'En ik ben Stephen Laing, hoofd Operaties van de divisie Midden-Oosten van de Britse inlichtingendienst.'

Gorbatsjov begreep er nu niets meer van. Spionnen, *tsjekisti*... Waar ging dit in vredesnaam naartoe?

'Onze beide diensten,' vervolgde Stewart, 'hebben hun regering gevraagd of zij voor ons dit gesprek met u konden regelen. Meneer de president, het Midden-Oosten stevent op een oorlog af. Dat weten we allemaal. Als we dat willen voorkomen, moeten we weten wat zich in regeringskringen in Irak afspeelt. Wat er in het openbaar wordt verklaard is vermoedelijk heel iets anders dan wat er in besloten kring wordt gezegd.'

'Dat lijkt me niets nieuws,' merkte Gorbatsjov droog op.

'Nee, inderdaad. Maar dit is een zeer onstabiel regime. Gevaarlijk voor ons allemaal. Als we de werkelijke bedoelingen van Saddam Hoessein en zijn kabinet zouden kennen, zouden we misschien meer kans hebben een oorlog af te wenden,' zei Laing.

'Daar hebben we diplomaten voor,' wees Gorbatsjov hem terecht.

'Normaal gesproken wel, meneer de president. Maar er zijn momenten waarop zelfs de diplomatie nog te openlijk is – niet geschikt om onze diepste gedachten uit te dragen. Herinnert u zich Richard Sorge nog?'

Gorbatsjov knikte. Iedere Rus had van Sorge gehoord. Hij stond zelfs op postzegels afgebeeld. Hij was een postume Held van de Sovjetunie.

'Op dat moment,' ging Laing verder, 'was Sorges informatie dat Japan geen aanval op Siberië voorbereidde van vitaal belang voor uw land. Maar dat was u via de ambassade nooit te weten gekomen.

We hebben reden om aan te nemen dat er in Bagdad een bron bestaat, een zeer hooggeplaatste figuur, die bereid is ons op de hoogte te houden van de geheimste beraadslagingen van Saddam Hoessein. Die kennis zou het verschil kunnen betekenen tussen oorlog en het vrijwillige vertrek van Irak uit Koeweit.'

Mikhail Gorbatsjov knikte. Hij was ook geen vriend van Saddam. Irak, ooit een gehoorzame vazalstaat van de Sovjetunie, was een steeds onafhankelijker koers gaan varen, en de grillige Iraakse leider had de Sovjetunie al enkele malen nodeloos beledigd.

Bovendien wist de Russische president dat hij grote financiële en industriële hulp nodig had – en dus de goodwill van het Westen – om zijn hervormingen te kunnen doorvoeren. De koude oorlog was voorbij. Dat was de realiteit. Daarom had de Sovjetunie zich aangesloten bij de VN-resolutie waarin de Iraakse inval in Koeweit werd veroordeeld.

'Heren, dan moet u contact opnemen met die bron en ons de informatie leveren waarmee wij de angel uit deze situatie kunnen halen. Dan zullen wij u allemaal dankbaar zijn. De Sovjetunie wil ook geen oorlog in het Midden-Oosten.'

'We zouden graag contact leggen, meneer de president,' zei Stewart, 'maar dat kunnen we niet. Onze bron weigert zich bekend te maken, en dat kunnen we wel begrijpen. Hij loopt natuurlijk groot gevaar. De diplomatieke route is uitgesloten. Hij is alleen geïnteresseerd in heimelijke contacten.'

'En wat wilt u nu van mij?'

De twee Westerlingen haalden diep adem.

'We willen een man naar Bagdad sturen om als schakel tussen de bron en onszelf te fungeren,' zei Barber.

'Een agent?'

'Ja, meneer de president, een agent. Die zich voordoet als Irakees.'

Gorbatsjov keek hen scherp aan. 'Hebt u zo'n man?'

'Ja, die hebben we. Maar hij moet ergens wonen, heel onopvallend, onschuldig en discreet, terwijl hij onze vragen doorgeeft en de antwoorden in ontvangst neemt. Daarom willen we u vragen of hij in dienst kan treden van een hoge functionaris van de Sovjet-ambassade in Bagdad.'

Gorbatsjov steunde zijn kin op de vingertoppen van zijn samengevouwen handen. Hij had genoeg ervaring met clandestiene operaties. Zijn eigen KGB had er heel wat uitgevoerd. En nu werd hij gevraagd de oude rivaal van de KGB bij zo'n operatie te helpen en de Russische ambassade als dekmantel te laten gebruiken. Het was zo krankzinnig dat hij bijna in de lach schoot.

'Als die agent van u wordt opgepakt, is mijn ambassade gecompromitteerd.'

'Nee, meneer de president. Dan doen wij het voorkomen of uw ambassade het slachtoffer is geworden van een cynisch Westers komplot. Dat gelooft Saddam onmiddellijk,' zei Laing.

Gorbatsjov dacht nog even na. Hij herinnerde zich het persoonlijke beroep van een president en een premier in deze zaak. Zij vonden het blijkbaar heel belangrijk, en híj moest hun goodwill wel belangrijk vinden. En dus knikte hij.

'Goed, ik zal generaal Vladimir Krjoetsjkov opdracht geven om volledig met u mee te werken.'

Krjoetsjkov was op dat moment hoofd van de KGB. Tien maanden later, toen Gorbatsjov vakantie hield aan de Zwarte Zee, zou Krjoetsjkov – samen met Defensieminister Dmitri Yazov en anderen – een staatsgreep tegen zijn president uitvoeren.

De twee Westerlingen schoven onrustig in hun stoel.

'Met alle respect, meneer de president,' zei Laing, 'we zouden het op prijs stellen als u de zaak alleen bespreekt met uw minister van Buitenlandse Zaken.'

Eduard Sjervarnadze was een goede vriend van Mikhail Gorbatsjov.

'Alleen met Sjervarnadze?' vroeg de president.

'Ja. Als u het niet erg vindt.'

'Goed. Dan regelen we alles via Buitenlandse Zaken.'

Toen de twee Westerse inlichtingenofficieren waren vertrokken, staarde Mikhail Gorbatsjov een tijdje peinzend voor zich uit. Alleen hij en Eduard mochten hier dus iets van weten. Krjoetsjkov niet. Wisten ze soms iets wat hij, de president van de Sovjetunie, niet wist?

De groep bestond in totaal uit elf Mossad-agenten, verdeeld in twee teams van vijf, plus de teamleider, die Kobi Dror persoonlijk had uitgekozen. De man was juist bezig met een saaie klus als instructeur bij de rekruten aan het opleidingsinstituut in de buurt van Herzlia.

Een van de teams was afkomstig van de Yarid-sectie, een tak van de Mossad die zich bezighield met operationele veiligheid en surveillance. Het andere team behoorde tot de Neviot, de afdeling die gespecialiseerd was in inbraak en afluistertechnieken – kortom alles wat met levenloze of mechanische objecten te maken heeft.

Acht van de tien agenten spraken goed of redelijk Duits. De teamleider sprak het vloeiend. De andere twee waren technici. De voorhoede van Operatie Joshua kwam verspreid over drie dagen in Wenen aan, vanuit verschillende Europese steden, met onberispelijke papieren en een geloofwaardige dekmantel.

Net als bij Operatie Jericho had Kobi Dror een paar regels aan zijn laars gelapt, maar zijn ondergeschikten deden daar niet moeilijk over. Joshua had de kwalificatie *'ain efes'* of 'niet te missen'. Die aanduiding, afkomstig van de baas zelf, gaf de operatie de hoogste prioriteit.

Yarid- en Neviot-teams tellen in het algemeen zeven tot negen leden, maar omdat het een civiel, neutraal, niet-professioneel en nietsvermoedend doelwit betrof, was het aantal agenten beperkt gehouden.

De chef van het Mossad-bureau in Wenen had drie van zijn onderduikadressen ter beschikking gesteld, en drie *bodlim* voor de dagelijkse verzorging.

Een *bodel* (meervoud *bodlim*) is meestal een jonge Israëli, vaak een student, die na een grondig onderzoek naar zijn achtergrond als manusje-van-alles wordt aangenomen. Hij doet boodschappen en knapt klusjes op zonder vragen te stellen. In ruil daarvoor mag hij gratis op een onderduikadres van de Mossad wonen – een belangrijk voordeel voor een arme student in een buitenlandse hoofdstad. Als er Israëlische agenten arriveren, moet de student verkassen, maar hij blijft verantwoordelijk voor het huishouden, de was en de boodschappen.

Hoewel Wenen misschien geen belangrijke hoofdstad lijkt, heeft de stad in het spionagewereldje altijd een grote rol gespeeld. Dat gaat terug tot 1945, toen Wenen als de tweede hoofdstad van het Derde Rijk door de zegevierende geallieerden werd bezet en in een Franse, Britse, Amerikaanse en Russische sector werd verdeeld.

Anders dan Berlijn hield Wenen haar vrijheid. Zelfs de Russen trokken zich terug, maar alleen als heel Oostenrijk zich neutraal zou verklaren. Toen de koude oorlog begon, tijdens de Berlijnse blokkade van 1948, werd Wenen al snel een broeinest van spionage. Zo dicht bij de Hongaarse en Tsjechische grens, open voor het Westen, maar dichtbevolkt met Oosteuropeanen, vormde Wenen een ideale uitvalsbasis voor talloze buitenlandse diensten. Oostenrijk zelf beschikte nauwelijks over een contraspionagedienst.

Kort na de oprichting in 1951 besefte de Mossad ook de voordelen van de stad en vestigde er zo'n belangrijk bureau dat het hoofd daarvan zelfs hoger in rang was dan de ambassadeur.

Dat besluit werd meer dan gerechtvaardigd toen de elegante, vermoeide hoofdstad van het voormalige Habsburgse rijk zich ontwikkelde tot een discreet financieel centrum, de thuisbasis van drie aparte VN-instanties en een geliefd doorgangshuis voor Palestijnse en andere terroristen.

Oostenrijk, dat angstvallig zijn neutraliteit handhaafde, had al heel lang een binnenlandse veiligheidsdienst die zo simpel te misleiden was dat Mossadagenten deze goed bedoelende officieren betitelden als *fertsalach* of 'scheet'.

Kobi Drors teamleider was een onverzettelijke *katsa* met een jarenlange ervaring in Berlijn, Parijs en Brussel.

Gideon Barzilai had ook dienst gedaan bij een van de *kidon*-executieteams die de Arabische terroristen hadden uitgeschakeld die verantwoordelijk waren voor het bloedbad onder de Israëlische atleten tijdens de Olympische

Spelen van München in 1972. Gelukkig voor zijn eigen carrière was hij niet betrokken geweest bij een van de grootste fiasco's uit de geschiedenis van de Mossad, waarbij een *kidon*-team een onschuldige Marokkaanse ober in het Noorse Lillehammer had vermoord nadat ze de man abusievelijk hadden geïdentificeerd als Ali Hassan Salameh, het brein achter de aanslag in München.

Gideon 'Gidi' Barzilai was nu Ewald Strauss, vertegenwoordiger van een sanitairfirma uit Frankfurt. Niet alleen waren zijn papieren in orde, maar in zijn koffertje had hij ook de juiste folders, orderboeken en correspondentie op het briefpapier van het bedrijf.

Zelfs een telefoontje naar zijn hoofdkantoor in Frankfurt zou zijn dekmantel hebben bevestigd, want op het briefpapier stond het telefoonnummer van een kantoor in Frankfurt dat door Mossad-agenten werd bemand.

Gidi's papieren en die van zijn tien collega's waren het produkt van weer een andere sectie van de Mossad. In dezelfde kelder in Tel Aviv waar de afdeling vervalsingen is ondergebracht, is ook een kantoor waar de bijzonderheden van een reusachtig aantal – bestaande en niet-bestaande – bedrijven zijn opgeslagen. Balansen, boeken, registraties en briefpapier zijn ruim voorradig, zodat iedere *katsa* op een buitenlandse missie kan worden voorzien van een bijna waterdichte dekmantel.

Nadat hij zich had geïnstalleerd in zijn eigen appartement, had Barzilai een uitvoerig gesprek met de chef van het plaatselijke Mossad-bureau en begon toen zijn missie met een betrekkelijk eenvoudige opdracht: zoveel mogelijk te weten komen over de discrete en zeer traditionele Winkler Bank, niet ver van de Franziskanerplatz.

Hetzelfde weekend vertrokken twee Amerikaanse Chinook-helikopters van de vliegbasis bij Riyad. Ze zetten koers naar de Tapline Road in het noorden, die evenwijdig loopt aan de Saoedisch-Iraakse grens, van Khafji tot aan Jordanië.

Elk van de helikopters vervoerde een verlengde Landrover, volledig gestript en daarna voorzien van extra brandstoftanks. Met iedere wagen waren vier SAS-agenten meegekomen, die zich in de kleine ruimte achter de bemanning hadden gewrongen.

Hun reisdoel lag verder weg dan hun actieradius toestond, maar op de Tapline Road stonden twee grote tankwagens te wachten, afkomstig uit Damman aan de Golfkust.

Toen de dorstige Chinooks op de weg landden, werden ze onmiddellijk bijgetankt. Daarna stegen ze weer op en vlogen verder in de richting van Jordanië, zo laag mogelijk boven de grond om de Iraakse radar aan de andere kant van de grens te ontwijken.

Even voorbij de Saoedische stad Badanah, vlak voor het punt waar de grenzen van Saoedi-Arabië, Irak en Jordanië samenkomen, landden de Chinooks opnieuw. Ook hier stonden twee tankers klaar, maar nu werden ook de Landrovers en de passagiers uitgeladen.

Als de Amerikaanse bemanning wist waar de zwijgzame Engelsen naartoe gingen, zeiden ze daar geen woord over, en als ze het niet wisten, vroegen ze er niet naar. De zandkleurige wagens werden over het luik naar buiten gereden. De Amerikanen gaven de Britten een hand en wensten hun succes. Toen werden de heli's weer bijgetankt en vertrokken ze in de richting waaruit ze waren gekomen. Ook de tankers maakten rechtsomkeert.

De acht SAS-agenten keken hen na en reden toen de andere kant uit, in de richting van Jordanië. Tachtig kilometer ten noordwesten van Badanah hielden ze halt en wachtten.

De kapitein die het bevel had over de groep controleerde zijn positie. Ooit, in de westelijke woestijn van Libië, had kolonel David Stirling – de oprichter van de SAS – zijn positie nog moeten bepalen aan de hand van de zon, de maan en de sterren. De techniek was inmiddels voortgeschreden.

De kapitein had een apparaatje in zijn hand dat niet veel groter was dan een pocketboek. Het was een 'Global Positioning System', ook wel SATNAV of 'Magellan' genoemd. Ondanks de geringe afmetingen kon de GPS de positie van de gebruiker – waar ook ter wereld – tot op tien meter nauwkeurig bepalen.

De draagbare GPS van de kapitein kon in Q-Code of P-Code worden geschakeld. De P-Code ging tot tien meter, maar daarvoor moesten vier Amerikaanse NAVSTAR-satellieten tegelijkertijd boven de horizon staan. De Q-Code was nauwkeurig tot op honderd meter en had maar twee satellieten nodig.

Die dag waren er maar twee satellieten beschikbaar, maar dat moest voldoende zijn. In die woestenij van zand en leisteen, kilometers van Badanah en de Jordaanse grens, kon je zelfs binnen een straal van honderd meter onmogelijk iemand over het hoofd zien.

Toen hij zich ervan had overtuigd dat ze de juiste plek hadden gevonden, schakelde de kapitein zijn GPS weer uit en kroop onder de camouflagenetten die zijn mannen tussen de twee Landrovers hadden gespannen als beschutting tegen de zon. De temperatuur was inmiddels opgelopen tot zo'n 50 graden Celsius.

Een uur later naderde een Britse Gazelle-helikopter vanuit het zuiden. Majoor Mike Martin was met een Hercules van de RAF naar het Saoedische stadje Al Jawf gebracht, het vliegveld dat het dichtst bij de grens lag. Ook de Gazelle was met ingeklapte rotorbladen in het transportvliegtuig geladen, compleet met de piloot, het grondpersoneel en de extra brandstoftanks die

nodig waren voor de tocht vanaf Al Jawf naar de Tapline Road en terug.
Voor het geval de Iraakse radar deze verlaten uithoek in de gaten hield, bleef de Gazelle zo laag mogelijk boven de woestijn, maar de piloot ontdekte al gauw de vuurpijl die de SAS-kapitein had afgeschoten toen hij de helikopter hoorde naderen.

De Gazelle landde op de weg, vijftig meter van de Landrovers, en Martin stapte uit. Hij had een plunjezak over zijn schouder en een rieten mand in zijn linkerhand. Toen hij de inhoud zag, had de piloot van de Gazelle zich afgevraagd of Martin op weg was naar een conferentie van pluimveehouders. In de mand zaten twee levende kippen.

Verder was Martin net zo gekleed als de acht SAS-mannen die op hem wachtten: woestijnlaarzen, een wijde broek van stevig katoen, een overhemd, een sweater en een soldatenjack in camouflagekleuren. Om zijn hals had hij een geruite *keffijeh* geknoopt die hij voor zijn gezicht kon trekken tegen het stof, en op zijn hoofd droeg hij een wollen bivakmuts met een zware stofbril.

De piloot vroeg zich af hoe de mannen het uithielden in die hitte, maar hij wist niet hoe koud de woestijnnacht kon zijn.

De SAS-mannen haalden de plastic jerrycans uit de Gazelle die de kleine verkenningshelikopter tot aan zijn maximale gewicht hadden belast en vulden de tanks bij. Toen het toestel was bijgetankt, stak de piloot zijn hand op en vertrok naar het zuiden, terug naar Al Jawf en Riyad – weg bij die krankzinnige kerels in de woestijn.

Toen hij uit het gezicht verdwenen was, voelden de SAS-mannen zich pas echt op hun gemak. Hoewel zij tot de D-Compagnie behoorden – de 'Armoured Scouts' – en Martin een 'Freefaller' van de A-Compagnie was, kende hij hen allemaal, op twee na. Toen ze elkaar hadden begroet, deden ze wat alle Britse soldaten doen als ze even tijd hebben: een pot sterke thee zetten.

De kapitein had een onherbergzaam gebied gekozen om de grens met Irak over te steken. In ruig terrein liepen ze minder gevaar op een Iraakse patrouille te stuiten. Het was niet de bedoeling de Irakezen te snel af te zijn, maar om ongezien het land binnen te komen.

De andere reden was dat hij zijn vrachtje zo dicht mogelijk wilde afzetten bij de lange Iraakse hoofdweg die zich vanaf Bagdad in westelijke richting door de grote woestijn naar de Jordaanse grenspost bij Ruweishid slingert.

Die troosteloze buitenpost in de woestijn was inmiddels bekend bij tv-kijkers over de hele wereld, omdat daar de stroom buitenlandse vluchtelingen uit Koeweit – Filippino's, Bengali's, Palestijnen en anderen – de grens over was gekomen om aan de chaos te ontsnappen.

In deze uiterste noordwesthoek van Saoedi-Arabië was de afstand van de grens tot aan de hoofdweg zo kort mogelijk. Naar het oosten, van Bagdad tot aan de Saoedische grens, lag de uitgestrekte woestijn, grotendeels zo glad als een biljartlaken. Het terrein leende zich daar beter voor een snelle rit vanaf de grens naar de dichtstbijzijnde weg naar Bagdad, maar de kans op legerpatrouilles en ongewenste belangstelling was daar veel groter. Hier, in het westen van de Iraakse woestijn, was het landschap heuvelachtiger, doorsneden door ravijnen waar in de regentijd woeste rivieren stroomden en die ook in het droge seizoen nog heel voorzichtig moesten worden overgestoken. Maar er werd nauwelijks gepatrouilleerd.

Het punt waar ze de grens wilden oversteken lag vijftig kilometer ten noorden van de plaats waar ze nu stonden. Vandaar was het nog eens honderd kilometer naar de weg van Bagdad naar Ruweishid. Toch ging de kapitein ervan uit dat het hun een hele nacht zou kosten, daarna nog een dag waarin ze zich moesten schuilhouden, om pas de volgende avond bij de weg aan te komen.

Ze vertrokken om vier uur 's middags. De zon brandde nog fel en ze hadden het gevoel of ze door een oven reden. Om zes uur begon het te schemeren en daalde de temperatuur snel. Om zeven uur was het volledig donker – en koud. Het zweet droogde op hun huid en ze waren dankbaar voor de dikke sweaters waarover de Gazelle-piloot zich zo had verbaasd.

De navigator zat in de voorste wagen naast de chauffeur en controleerde voortdurend hun positie en koers. Op de basis had hij met de kapitein al een uur besteed aan het bestuderen van een serie scherpe, vergrote luchtfoto's, gemaakt door een Amerikaanse U-2 van de basis bij Taif, die een beter beeld gaven dan de kaart.

Ze reden zonder lichten, maar de navigator hield met een zaklantaarn de directe omgeving in het oog en corrigeerde hun koers als ze door een kloof of een heuvel tot een omweg werden gedwongen.

Ieder uur stopten ze om hun positie te bepalen met de Magellan. De navigator had de randen van zijn foto's al voorzien van lengte- en breedtegraden in minuten en seconden, zodat de cijfers op de digitale display van de Magellan hun precies vertelden waar ze zich op de foto's bevonden.

Ze schoten niet erg op, omdat er bij iedere richel iemand vooruit moest om te kijken of er aan de andere kant geen onprettige verrassing wachtte.

Een uur voordat het licht werd, vonden ze een wadi met steile wanden, reden erin en gooiden de netten over de auto's. Een van de mannen klom naar een hoger punt, keek omlaag en gaf nog wat aanwijzingen, tot hij er zeker van was dat een verkenningsvliegtuig bijna een noodlanding in de wadi zou moeten maken om hen te ontdekken.

De dag verstreek met eten, drinken en slapen. Steeds hielden twee mannen de wacht, met het oog op ronddwalende herders of andere onverwachte reizigers. Soms hoorden ze Iraakse jets overvliegen en op een naburige heuvel begonnen een paar schapen te blaten. Maar de dieren schenen geen herder te hebben en slenterden weer verder, de andere kant op. Toen de zon onderging, reden ze weer verder.

Midden in de nacht, een paar minuten voor vier, zagen ze de lichten van het Iraakse stadje Ar-Rutba, dat aan weerskanten van de autoweg ligt. De Magellan bevestigde dat ze goed zaten, even ten zuiden van de stad, ongeveer acht kilometer lopen van de weg.

Vier van de mannen verkenden de omgeving tot ze een wadi met een zachte, zanderige bodem vonden. Daar groeven ze zwijgend een gat, met behulp van het gereedschap dat aan de zijkanten van de Landrovers hing om hen uit zandstormen te bevrijden. Ze begroeven de crossmotor en de jerrycans met extra benzine om naar de grens te vluchten, als dat nodig mocht zijn. Alles zat in stevig plastic verpakt tegen het zand en het water, want de regen moest nog komen.

Om te voorkomen dat de bergplaats zou worden weggespoeld, legden ze een stapeltje stenen neer om het zand op zijn plaats te houden.

De navigator klom naar de heuvel boven de wadi en peilde de exacte afstand tot de radiomast boven Ar-Rutba, waarvan het rode waarschuwingslicht in de verte te zien was.

Terwijl de anderen bezig waren, kleedde Mike Martin zich uit en haalde de kaftan, de hoofddoek en de sandalen van Mahmoud Al-Khouri, de Iraakse tuinman, uit zijn plunjezak. Met een linnen tas met brood, olie, kaas en olijven voor het ontbijt, een beduimelde portefeuille met zijn pasje en foto's van Mahmouds bejaarde ouders, en een gedeukt blikje met wat geld en een pennemesje, was hij klaar om te vertrekken. De Landrovers hadden een uur nodig om bij de plek vandaan te komen voordat ze een schuilplaats voor de dag zouden zoeken.

'Sterkte,' zei de kapitein.

'Goede jacht, chef,' zei de navigator.

'In elk geval hebt u een vers eitje bij het ontbijt,' zei iemand anders, en er werd onderdrukt gegrinnikt. SAS-mensen wensten elkaar nooit 'veel succes'. Mike Martin stak zijn hand op en vertrok lopend in de richting van de autoweg. Een paar minuten later waren de Landrovers verdwenen en lag de wadi er weer verlaten bij.

Het hoofd van het Mossad-bureau in Wenen had het adres van een *sajan*, die zelf een hoge positie had bij een van de grootste banken van het land. Hij kreeg het verzoek om een rapport op te stellen van de Winkler Bank, zo uitvoerig als mogelijk was. Hij kreeg alleen te horen dat bepaalde Israëlische ondernemingen met de Winkler Bank in aanraking waren gekomen en zich wilden overtuigen van de betrouwbaarheid en de handelwijze van de bank. Er werd immers zoveel gefraudeerd, tegenwoordig.

De *sajan* slikte het verhaal en deed zijn best – geen geringe prestatie, want het eerste dat hij ontdekte was dat de Winkler Bank nooit mededelingen naar buiten deed.

De bank was bijna honderd jaar geleden opgericht door de vader van de huidige directeur en de enige eigenaar. De zoon was inmiddels eenennegentig en stond in Weense bankierskringen bekend als 'Der Alte'. Ondanks zijn leeftijd weigerde hij zijn functie neer te leggen of zijn aandelen te verkopen. Hij was een weduwnaar zonder kinderen en had dus geen natuurlijke opvolger. Wie de erfgenamen waren, zou pas bekend worden als zijn testament werd voorgelezen.

De dagelijkse leiding berustte bij drie adjunct-directeuren, die eens per maand verslag uitbrachten bij de oude Winkler thuis. Winklers belangrijkste zorg scheen te zijn dat zijn eigen strenge normen werden gehandhaafd.

De zakelijke beslissingen werden genomen door de adjunct-directeuren, Kessler, Gemütlich en Blei. Het was natuurlijk geen handelsbank. Er waren geen rekeninghouders en er werden geen chequeboeken uitgegeven. De bank hield zich bezig met beleggingen, in veilige fondsen, voornamelijk op de Europese markt.

Het dividend van die beleggingen zou misschien nooit sensationeel worden, maar daar ging het niet om. Winklers cliënten waren niet uit op snelle groei of torenhoge winsten. Ze zochten betrouwbaarheid en discretie. En daarvoor zorgde de Winkler Bank.

Tot de strenge normen waar de oude Winkler zoveel waarde aan hechtte, behoorde absolute geheimhouding van de identiteit van de cliënten, en een grote afkeer van wat Der Alte betitelde als 'moderne nonsens'.

Daarom waren er geen computers voor de boekhouding of de opslag van gevoelige gegevens. Faxapparaten waren uit den boze en zelfs de telefoon werd maar sporadisch gebruikt. De Winkler Bank accepteerde wel instructies en informatie per telefoon, maar deed nooit mededelingen. De voorkeur ging uit naar ouderwetse correspondentie op het dure, crèmekleurige briefpapier van de bank of persoonlijke gesprekken op het kantoor zelf.

Binnen Wenen werden alle afschriften en andere papieren door een eigen boodschapper van de bank rondgebracht, in met was verzegelde enveloppen. Alleen voor het nationale en internationale verkeer maakte de bank gebruik van de gewone posterijen.

Wat de nummerrekeningen van buitenlandse cliënten betrof – daar was de *sajan* ook naar gevraagd – niemand wist precies hoeveel het er waren, maar er gingen geruchten over honderden miljoenen dollars. Als dat zo was, en gezien het feit dat sommige klanten overleden zonder iemand anders over hun geheime nummerrekening in te lichten, deed de Winkler Bank goede zaken.

Toen Gidi Barzilai het rapport las, vloekte hij langdurig en luid. De oude Winkler wist misschien niets over de nieuwste methoden om telefoons af te luisteren en computers te kraken, maar aan zijn intuïtie mankeerde niets.

In de jaren dat Irak zijn gifgasindustrie ontwikkelde, waren alle aankopen in Duitsland via drie Zwitserse banken verlopen. De Mossad wist dat de CIA de computers van die banken had gekraakt, oorspronkelijk om witgewassen drugsgeld op te sporen. Dank zij die informatie had Washington bij Duitsland kunnen protesteren tegen de uitvoer van de technologie. Je kon het de CIA niet kwalijk nemen dat bondskanselier Kohl de protesten minachtend had verworpen. De informatie klopte precies.

Als Gidi Barzilai had gehoopt dat hij de computer van de Winkler Bank zou kunnen kraken, kwam hij bedrogen uit. De bank hàd geen computer. Dat beperkte de mogelijkheden tot het onderscheppen van de post en het afluisteren van de kantoren en de telefoons, maar dat zou vermoedelijk ook niets opleveren.

Veel bankrekeningen hadden een *Losungswort* of wachtwoord nodig om er geld vanaf te kunnen halen of overschrijvingen te kunnen doen. Meestal kan zo'n wachtwoord telefonisch, in een fax of in een brief worden gebruikt. Maar de Winkler Bank was zo voorzichtig dat bij belangrijke buitenlandse cliënten als Jericho waarschijnlijk een veel ingewikkelder procedure werd toegepast – een persoonlijk bezoek met voldoende legitimatie, of een schriftelijke opdracht volgens zeer specifieke instructies, met codewoorden en symbolen op afgesproken plaatsen.

Natuurlijk zou de bank iedere storting accepteren, wanneer en van wie dan ook. Dat wist de Mossad, omdat ze Jericho zijn bloedgeld hadden betaald door een overschrijving op een rekening bij de Winkler Bank waarvan alleen het nummer blijkbaar voldoende was. De Winkler Bank overreden om geld over te maken, dat was een heel andere zaak.

Gekleed in de ochtendjas waarin hij het grootste deel van zijn leven naar kerkmuziek zat te luisteren moest de oude Winkler hebben begrepen dat de illegale technologie alle technische veiligheidsmaatregelen altijd een stapje vóór zou blijven. Heel vervelend.

De enige andere conclusie die de *sajan* veilig kon trekken was dat alle belangrijke nummerrekeningen persoonlijk door een van de drie adjunct-directeuren werden beheerd. En Der Alte had zijn ondergeschikten met zorg gekozen. Ze hadden alledrie de reputatie van harde, goed betaalde zakenmensen zonder enig gevoel voor humor. Onberispelijk. Israël hoefde zich geen zorgen te maken, besloot de *sajan*. Hij had het verkeerd begrepen. Gidi Barzilai maakte zich die eerste week van november juist grote zorgen over de Winkler Bank.

Een uur na zonsopgang kwam er een bus langs die stopte voor de eenzame passagier die zijn hand opstak bij een rotsblok langs de weg, vijf kilometer voor Ar-Rutba. De man betaalde met twee vuile dinarbiljetten, zocht een plaatsje achterin, zette zijn mand met kippen op zijn schoot en viel in slaap.

In het centrum van een stadje kwam de bus schokkend tot stilstand voor een politiecontrole. Een paar mensen stapten uit om naar hun werk of naar de markt te gaan. Nieuwe passagiers stapten in. De politie controleerde de persoonsbewijzen van de reizigers die instapten, maar beperkte zich tot een blik door de stoffige ruiten van de bus om te zien wie er waren achtergebleven. Ze hadden geen belangstelling voor de boer met zijn kippen achterin. Ze zochten naar verdachte types met subversieve bedoelingen.

Na een uurtje wachten reed de bus weer verder naar het oosten, hobbelend op zijn oude veren. Zo nu en dan moest hij de berm in als er een colonne legertrucks voorbij denderde, met ongeschoren dienstplichtigen achterin, die somber naar de stofwolken achter de wagens staarden.

Met gesloten ogen luisterde Mike Martin naar de gesprekken om hem heen, gespitst op onbekende woorden of accenten die hij misschien was vergeten. Het Arabisch in dit deel van Irak verschilde sterk van de taal die in Koeweit werd gesproken. Als hij in Bagdad voor een slecht geschoolde, onschuldige *fellagha* wilde doorgaan, konden die provinciale accenten en zinswendingen hem nog van pas komen. Weinig dingen sussen een grote-stadssmeris zo snel in slaap als een plattelandsaccent.

Voor de kippen in hun mand was het een zware rit, ook al had hij ze wat voer gegeven en een beetje water uit zijn veldfles, die hij had achtergelaten in de Landrover die nu onder het camouflagenet in de woestijn stond te bakken. Bij iedere kuil kakelden de kippen uit protest of poepten in het zand op de bodem van de mand.

Er was een scherpe blik voor nodig om te zien dat die bodem aan de buitenkant tien centimeter hoger was dan aan de binnenkant. De laag zand rond de poten van de kippen maskeerde het verschil. Het zand was maar tweeënhalve centimeter diep. In die tien centimeter diepe holte onder de vijftig bij vijftig centimeter brede mand zat een aantal voorwerpen die de politie in Ar-Rutba heel merkwaardig maar ook heel interessant zou hebben gevonden.

Een ervan was een opvouwbare satellietschotel, ingeklapt tot een soort paraplu. Daarbij hoorde een kleine zender-ontvanger met een oplaadbare cadmiumzilverbatterij – veel krachtiger dan het zendertje dat Martin in Koeweit had gebruikt. In Irak zou hij niet vanuit de woestijn kunnen uitzenden. Lange berichten waren veel te gevaarlijk. Dat was de reden voor de aanwezigheid van het laatste voorwerp: een heel bijzondere cassetterecorder.

Nieuwe technische ontwikkelingen beginnen meestal met grote, logge, lastige apparaten. Daarna gebeuren er twee dingen. Het binnenwerk wordt kleiner maar ingewikkelder, en het apparaat wordt eenvoudiger in het gebruik.

De zenders waarmee de agenten van de Britse SOE in de Tweede Wereldoorlog in Frankrijk infiltreerden, waren naar moderne maatstaven een nachtmerrie. Ze waren zo groot als een koffer, ze hadden een antenne nodig die een paar meter langs een regenpijp omhoog moest worden geleid, ze hadden buizen ter grootte van gloeilampen en ze konden alleen morsesignalen uitzenden. De agent moest minutenlang op zijn morsesleutel zitten tikken, waardoor de Duitsers alle tijd hadden om zijn zender te peilen.

Martins cassetterecorder was heel eenvoudig te bedienen, maar beschikte over een paar handige snufjes. Een bericht van tien minuten kon heel rustig via de microfoon worden ingesproken. Voordat het op de band werd opgenomen, had een speciale chip het al omgezet in een soort koeterwaals dat de Irakezen waarschijnlijk niet konden ontcijferen als ze het zouden onderscheppen.

Door een druk op de knop kon hij het bandje terugspoelen. Met een andere knop werd het bericht opnieuw opgenomen, maar nu tweehonderd keer zo snel, waardoor een uitzending van tien minuten werd teruggebracht tot een explosie van drie seconden – bijna onmogelijk te traceren.

Het was deze ingedikte versie die de recorder doorgaf zodra hij met de zender, de satellietschotel en de batterij was verbonden. In Riyad zou het bericht worden opgenomen, vertraagd, gedecodeerd en afgespeeld.

Martin stapte uit in Ramadi, waar de bus stopte, en stapte over op een andere, die langs het Habbanijah Meer en de oude RAF-basis reed, die inmiddels was omgebouwd tot een moderne vliegbasis voor Iraakse jagers. Aan de rand van Bagdad werd de bus aangehouden en de passagiers moesten uitstappen om hun papieren te laten zien.

Martin wachtte gedwee, met zijn kippen onder zijn arm, terwijl de passagiers langs het tafeltje van de politiebrigadier schuifelden. Toen hij aan de beurt was, zette hij zijn mand op de grond en haalde zijn pasje tevoorschijn. De brigadier wierp er een blik op. Het was warm en hij had dorst. Het was een lange dag geweest. Hij wees naar de naam van het geboortedorp op het pasje.

'Waar is dat?'

'Een klein dorp ten noorden van Baji. Heel bekend om zijn meloenen, *bey*.'

De brigadier krulde zijn lippen. 'Bey' was een eerbiedige aanspreektitel die nog uit de tijd van het Turkse rijk dateerde. Alleen mensen uit afgelegen delen van het platteland gebruikten het woord nog. Hij wuifde met zijn hand. Martin pakte zijn mand op en liep terug naar de bus.

Een paar minuten voor zeven remde de bus af en stopte. Majoor Mike Martin stapte uit op het busstation van Kadhimija, in Bagdad.

216

Het was een heel eind lopen vanaf het busstation in het noorden van de stad naar het huis van de Russische eerste secretaris in de wijk Mansour, maar Martin vond het een welkome afwisseling.

Hij had twaalf uur in de bus gezeten voor de rit van vierhonderd kilometer van Ar-Rutba naar de hoofdstad, en het was bepaald geen gerieflijke reis geweest. Bovendien gaf de wandeling hem de kans om weer te wennen aan de stad die hij niet meer had gezien sinds hij als zenuwachtig schooljongetje van dertien op het vliegtuig naar Londen was gestapt, nu vierentwintig jaar geleden.

Er was veel veranderd. Hij herinnerde zich een typisch Arabische stad, veel kleiner, gegroepeerd rondom de centrale wijken Shaikh Omar en Saadun op de noordwestelijke oever van de Tigris in Risafa, en de wijk Aalam aan de overkant, in Karch. Het grootste deel van het leven had zich afgespeeld in deze binnenstad van smalle straatjes, markten en moskeeën die met hun minaretten het stadsbeeld domineerden en de mensen herinnerden aan hun dienstbaarheid aan Allah.

Twintig jaar olierijkdom had tot de komst van lange vierbaanswegen geleid. Rotondes, viaducten en klaverbladen verstikten nu de ruime stad. Het autoverkeer was snel toegenomen en wolkenkrabbers verhieven zich naar de avondhemel – Mammon die zijn oude tegenstander uitdaagde.

Toen hij door de lange Rabia Straat in Mansour liep, herkende hij de wijk nauwelijks meer. Hij dacht terug aan de grote open ruimtes rond de Mansour Club, waar zijn vader hen op weekendmiddagen mee naartoe had genomen. Mansour was nog steeds een van de betere buitenwijken, maar alle ruimte was nu opgevuld met straten en huizen voor mensen die zich een goed leven konden veroorloven.

Op een paar honderd meter afstand passeerde hij de oude lagere school van meester Hartley, waar hij zijn lessen had geleerd en in de pauze had gespeeld met zijn vrienden Hassan Rahmani en Abdelkarim Badri, maar in het donker herkende hij de straat niet eens.

Hij wist nu wat Hassan voor werk deed, maar van de twee zoons van dr. Badri had hij al bijna een kwart eeuw niets meer gehoord. Zou de jongste, Osman, met zijn aanleg voor rekenen, ooit ingenieur zijn geworden? En zou Abdelkarim, die prijzen won met het declameren van Engelse poëzie, zelf zijn gaan schrijven of dichten?

Als hij op de manier van de SAS had gelopen, met stevige pas en zwaaiende schouders om de beweging van zijn benen te ondersteunen, had hij de afstand in de helft van de tijd kunnen afleggen. Maar dan zou iemand ongetwijfeld tegen hem hebben geroepen dat hij 'zich wel kleedde als een Arabier maar nog altijd liep als een Engelsman'.

En zijn schoenen waren geen soldatenkistjes maar linnen slippers met touwzolen, het schoeisel van de arme Iraakse *fellagha*, en dus schuifelde hij met gebogen hoofd en kromme schouders door de straat.

In Riyad hadden ze hem een actuele plattegrond van Bagdad laten zien, en talloze luchtfoto's die zo sterk waren vergroot dat je met een loep de tuinen achter de muren kon zien, en de zwembaden en auto's van de rijken en machtigen.

Hij had ze goed in zijn geheugen geprent. Hij sloeg linksaf de Jordaanstraat in, en voorbij het Jarmukplein rechtsaf, naar de door bomen omzoomde laan waar de Russische diplomaat woonde.

In de jaren zestig, onder Kassem en de generaals die hem waren opgevolgd, had de Sovjetunie een bevoorrechte positie ingenomen in Bagdad. De Russen steunden het Arabische nationalisme omdat het als anti-Westers werd beschouwd, terwijl ze tegelijkertijd probeerden de Arabische wereld tot het communisme te bekeren. In die jaren had de Sovjet-missie een aantal grote huizen gekocht buiten het ambassadeterrein, dat te klein was geworden voor de groeiende staf. Als concessie hadden deze huizen en hun tuinen de status van Sovjet-grondgebied gekregen. Zelfs Saddam Hoessein had dat privilege nooit teruggedraaid, vooral niet omdat de Russen tot halverwege de jaren tachtig zijn voornaamste wapenleveranciers waren geweest en zesduizend Russische militaire adviseurs hadden gestuurd om zijn luchtmacht en tankkorps met hun Russische materieel te trainen.

Martin vond de villa en las op de kleine koperen naamplaat dat het een woning was die tot de ambassade van de Sovjetunie behoorde. Hij trok aan de ketting naast het hek en wachtte.

Na een paar minuten ging het hek open en verscheen er een forse Rus met stekeltjeshaar, in de witte tuniek van een huisbediende. '*Da?*'

Martin antwoordde in het Arabisch, op de bedeesde toon van een ondergeschikte. De Rus keek hem fronsend aan. Martin zocht onder zijn kleren en liet zijn pasje zien. Dat begreep de bediende. In zijn eigen land wisten ze alles van binnenlandse pasjes. Hij pakte de kaart aan. 'Wacht hier,' zei hij in het Arabisch en deed het hek weer dicht.

Vijf minuten later was hij terug en gebaarde de Irakees in zijn vuile *disj-dasj* om hem te volgen naar het huis. Hij bracht Martin naar het bordes van de villa. Een man kwam de voordeur uit.

'Je kunt gaan. Ik regel dit wel,' zei hij in het Russisch tegen de bediende,

218

die de Arabier nog een minachtende blik toewierp en in het huis verdween. Joeri Koelikov, de eerste secretaris van de Russische ambassade, was een carrièrediplomaat die niets begreep van zijn orders uit Moskou, maar geen andere keus had dan te gehoorzamen. Blijkbaar zat hij juist te eten, want hij had een servet in zijn hand waarmee hij zijn lippen afveegde toen hij de treden afdaalde.

'Daar ben je dus,' zei hij in het Russisch. 'Luister, ik ben bereid aan die flauwekul mee te doen, maar verder bemoei ik me er niet mee. *Panimajesh*?'

Martin, die geen Russisch sprak, haalde hulpeloos zijn schouders op en vroeg in het Arabisch: 'Wat zegt u, *bey*?'

Koelikov vatte dat als een bewuste belediging op. Met enig genoegen besefte Martin dat de Russische diplomaat dacht dat zijn ongewenste nieuwe personeelslid ook een Rus was die hem door die vervloekte spionnen van de Loebjanka in Moskou op zijn dak was gestuurd.

'Goed, dan praten we wel Arabisch, als het moet,' reageerde hij geïrriteerd. Hij had de taal ook leren spreken, ook al had hij een Russisch accent, en hij was niet van plan zich door deze KGB-agent voor schut te laten zetten.

Daarom vervolgde hij in het Arabisch: 'Hier is je pasje weer terug, met de brief die ik voor je moest schrijven. Je kunt je intrek nemen in het schuurtje achter in de tuin. Je houdt de tuin bij en je doet de boodschappen die de kokkin van je vraagt. Verder hou ik me er buiten. Als je wordt gepakt, weet ik van niets. Ik heb je in goed vertrouwen aangenomen. Ga maar aan het werk en zorg dat je die kippen kwijtraakt. Ik wil die vervloekte beesten niet in mijn tuin.'

Geweldig, dacht de diplomaat bitter, toen hij zich omdraaide en naar de eetkamer terugliep. Als die klootzak werd opgepakt, zou de AMAM meteen begrijpen dat hij een Rus was. En dat de eerste secretaris hem bij toeval zou hebben aangenomen, was net zo waarschijnlijk als een schaatswedstrijd op de Tigris. In gedachten vervloekte Joeri Koelikov zijn chefs in Moskou.

Mike Martin vond zijn onderkomen tegen de achtermuur van de grote tuin – een schuurtje met een brits, een tafel, twee stoelen, een rij haken aan een van de muren en een losse wasbak op een plank in de hoek.

Naast het schuurtje was nog een diepe kast, en aan de tuinmuur zat een koudwaterkraan. Het sanitair was heel eenvoudig, en zijn eten zou hij wel bij de keukendeur van de villa moeten halen. Martin zuchtte. Het huis aan de rand van Riyad leek heel ver weg.

Hij vond een paar kaarsen en lucifers. Bij het vage schijnsel hing hij de dekens voor de ramen en begon met zijn pennemes de vloertegels los te wrikken.

Na een uurtje bikken in het schimmelige cement had hij vier tegels losgewerkt. Met een troffel uit het tuinschuurtje groef hij een gat. Nog een uur later had hij een kuil die groot genoeg was om zijn zender, de batterijen, de cassetterecorder en de satellietschotel in te verbergen. Toen hij de tegels weer had teruggelegd, wreef hij een mengsel van aarde en speeksel in de voegen, zodat er niets bijzonders aan te zien was.

Kort voor middernacht sneed hij met zijn mes de valse bodem uit de kippenmand en vulde de opening met zand om de holte te verbergen. De kippen drentelden over de vloer en zochten hoopvol naar graantjes die er niet waren. Ze stelden zich tevreden met wat insekten.

Martin at de rest van zijn kaas en olijven op en deelde de restanten van zijn pittabrood met zijn reisgenoten, die ook een kom water kregen uit de kraan aan de muur.

De kippen gingen weer in hun mand. Ze beklaagden zich niet dat hun huis nu tien centimeter dieper was. Het was een lange dag geweest en ze gingen slapen.

Als een laatste gebaar piste Martin in het donker over Koelikovs rozen voordat hij de kaarsen uitblies, zich in zijn deken wikkelde en het voorbeeld van de kippen volgde.

Zijn biologische klok wekte hem om vier uur in de nacht. Hij haalde de zender en de rest van de apparatuur tevoorschijn, die goed in plastic zat verpakt. Toen nam hij een kort bericht aan Riyad op, liet het tweehonderd keer versnellen, verbond de cassetterecorder met de zender en stelde de satellietschotel op, die een groot deel van het schuurtje in beslag nam en door de open deur naar buiten stond gericht.

Om kwart voor vijf verzond hij een bericht via de frequentie van die dag, brak zijn installatie weer af en verborg de spullen onder de vloer.

De hemel was nog donker boven Riyad toen een soortgelijke schotel op het dak van het SIS-gebouw het één seconde lange signaal opving en aan het verbindingscentrum doorgaf. Martins uitzendtijd lag tussen half vijf en vijf uur, en de radiotechnici waren op hun post.

Twee draaiende spoelen registreerden de boodschap uit Bagdad en een knipperend lampje waarschuwde de technici. Ze vertraagden het signaal tweehonderd keer, tot ze het via hun koptelefoon konden volgen. Een van de mannen noteerde het bericht in steno, typte het uit en verliet de kamer.

Julian Gray, de chef van het SIS-bureau in Riyad, werd om kwart over vijf gewekt.

'Een bericht van Zwarte Beer, meneer. Hij is aangekomen.'

Met stijgende opwinding las Gray de transcriptie en maakte toen Simon Paxman wakker. Het hoofd van de sectie Irak was tijdelijk naar Riyad overgeplaatst. Zijn werk in Londen werd overgenomen door zijn tweede man. Hij kwam overeind, meteen klaarwakker, en las het velletje papier.

'Verdomme. Nou, voorlopig gaat alles goed.'

'De problemen beginnen pas als hij contact wil opnemen met Jericho,' zei Gray.

Dat was een ontnuchterende gedachte. Van de voormalige Mossad-spion in Bagdad was al drie maanden niets meer vernomen. Misschien was hij ontmaskerd of aangehouden, misschien had hij gewoon geen zin meer, of misschien was hij overgeplaatst – bijvoorbeeld als hij een generaal was die het bevel voerde over eenheden in Koeweit. Er kon van alles zijn gebeurd.

Paxman stond op. 'We zullen Londen inlichten. Is er al koffie?'

'Ik zal vragen of Mohammed een pot wil zetten,' zei Gray.

Om half zes was Mike Martin al bezig de bloemen water te geven toen het huis tot leven kwam. De kokkin, een rondborstige Russische vrouw, zag hem vanuit haar raam en riep hem toen het water kookte.

'Kak nazyvaetes?' vroeg ze. Toen dacht ze even na en vroeg in het Arabisch: 'Naam?'

'Mahmoud,' antwoordde Martin.

'Hier is een kop koffie voor je, Mahmoud.'

Martin knikte een paar keer verheugd, mompelde *'shukran'* en pakte de hete mok met twee handen aan. Hij meende het echt. Het was prima koffie en zijn eerste warme slok sinds de thee aan de Saoedische kant van de grens.

Om zeven uur kreeg hij zijn ontbijt, een kom linzen met pittabrood, dat hij met smaak naar binnen werkte. Het bleek dat de huisbediende van de vorige avond en zijn vrouw, de kokkin, de huishouding deden voor eerste secretaris Koelikov, die niet getrouwd scheen te zijn. Om acht uur ontmoette Martin de chauffeur, een Irakees die een beetje Russisch sprak en daarom nuttig was als tolk.

Martin besloot uit de buurt te blijven van de chauffeur. De man zou voor de Geheime Politie kunnen werken, of misschien wel voor Rahmani's contraspionagedienst. Dat was geen probleem. Agent of niet, de chauffeur was een snob en behandelde de nieuwe tuinman met grote minachting. Maar hij wilde wel tegen de kokkin zeggen dat Mahmoud even weg moest om de kippen te verkopen.

Terug op straat liep Martin naar het busstation. Onderweg liet hij de kippen vrij op een braakliggend stukje grond.

Zoals in veel Arabische steden was het busstation van Bagdad niet alleen een plek voor reizigers naar de provincie om in en uit te stappen, maar een kolkende maalstroom van kooplui en arbeiders die van alles kwamen kopen en verkopen. Bij de zuidmuur was een vlooienmarkt. Daar kocht Martin na het verplichte afdingen een gammele fiets die piepte bij het rijden. Maar dat kon verholpen worden met een drupje olie.

Hij wist dat hij geen auto kon gebruiken, en zelfs een motorfiets was te duur voor een eenvoudige tuinman. Hij herinnerde zich dat de huisbediende van zijn vader op de fiets alle inkopen op de markt had gedaan en zo te zien was de fiets nog altijd het standaard vervoermiddel voor de gewone man.

Met zijn pennemes zaagde hij de bovenkant van de kippenmand eruit en maakte er een open boodschappenmand van die hij op de bagagedrager bevestigde met twee stevige rubber banden – oude ventilatorriemen van een auto, die hij bij een garage in een steegje had gekocht.

Toen fietste hij terug naar het centrum en kocht vier krijtjes in verschillende kleuren bij een kantoorboekhandel in de Shurjastraat, tegenover de katholieke St. Jozefkerk waar de Chaldeeuwse christenen hun diensten hielden.

Hij herinnerde zich de buurt nog uit zijn jeugd – de Agid-al-Nasara, de 'Christenwijk', de Shurja- en de Bankstraat, nog altijd vol met verkeerd geparkeerde auto's en buitenlanders die langs de winkels met kruiden en specerijen slenterden.

Toen hij een jongen was, waren er maar drie bruggen over de Tigris geweest: de spoorbrug in het nooren, de Nieuwe Brug in het midden en de Koning Feisalbrug in het zuiden. Nu waren er al negen. Vier dagen na de luchtaanvallen zou er geen enkele brug meer over zijn. Ze stonden allemaal op de lijst met doelwitten die in het Zwarte Gat in Riyad was opgesteld, en dus werden ze vernietigd. Maar die eerste week van november stroomde het verkeer er nog ongehinderd overheen.

Iets anders wat hem opviel was de nadrukkelijke aanwezigheid van de AMAM, de Geheime Politie, hoewel de agenten bepaald geen moeite deden om geheim te blijven. Ze hielden de mensen in de gaten vanaf straathoeken en vanuit geparkeerde auto's. Twee keer zag Martin dat een buitenlander werd aangehouden en naar zijn pasje werd gevraagd, en twee keer gebeurde dat ook met Irakezen. De buitenlanders reageerden geïrriteerd maar gelaten, de Irakezen waren duidelijk bang.

Oppervlakkig gezien kabbelde het leven gewoon door en waren de mensen in Bagdad nog net zo goedgehumeurd als Martin zich herinnerde, maar zijn intuïtie zei hem dat onder die oppervlakte een grote angst schuilging – angst voor de tiran in het grote paleis aan de rivier bij de Tamuzbrug.

Maar één keer die ochtend merkte hij iets van de gevoelens die het leven van de Irakezen beheersten. Hij was naar de fruit- en groentenmarkt van Kasra gefietst, aan de overkant van de rivier, en stond met een oude koopman te onderhandelen over de prijs van wat fruit. Als de Russen hem alleen peulvruchten en brood voorzetten, kon hij zijn menu beter aanvullen met verse vruchten.

Niet ver bij hen vandaan werd een jongeman hardhandig door de AMAM gefouilleerd en weer weggestuurd. De oude fruitkoopman spuwde een fluim in het stof, vlak langs een kistje met zijn eigen aubergines.

222

'Ooit zullen de Beni Naji terugkomen om dat tuig te verjagen,' mompelde hij. 'Voorzichtig, oude man, dat zijn domme woorden,' fluisterde Martin, terwijl hij in een paar perziken kneep. De oude man keek hem scherp aan.

'Waar kom je vandaan, broeder?'

'Ver hier vandaan. Uit een dorpje in het noorden, voorbij Baji.'

'Neem dan een goede raad aan van een oude man en ga terug. Ik heb al veel gezien. De Beni Naji zullen uit de lucht komen. Ja, en ook de Beni el-Kalb.'

Weer spuwde hij, en deze keer hadden de aubergines minder geluk. Martin kocht een paar perziken en citroenen en fietste terug. Tegen een uur of twaalf kwam hij weer bij het huis van de Russische eerste secretaris. Koelikov was allang naar de ambassade vertrokken met zijn chauffeur. De kokkin schold Martin in het Russisch uit, maar dat verstond hij niet. Hij haalde zijn schouders op en ging weer verder met de tuin.

Maar de woorden van de oude man hielden hem bezig. Sommige Irakezen verwachtten dus een invasie en hadden daar niet eens bezwaar tegen. De opmerking over het verjagen van 'dat tuig' kon alleen betrekking hebben op de Geheime Politie en dus op Saddam Hoessein.

In Irak worden de Britten meestal de 'Beni Naji' genoemd. Wie Naji precies was, is verloren gegaan in de nevelen van de tijd, maar hij moet een wijze en heilige man zijn geweest. Jonge Britse officieren die in de tijd van het Britse imperium in dit gebied waren gelegerd, kwamen naar hem toe om aan zijn voeten te zitten en naar zijn wijsheden te luisteren. Hij behandelde hen als zonen, hoewel ze christenen – en dus ongelovigen – waren. Daarom noemden de mensen hen de 'zonen van Naji'.

De Amerikanen staan bekend als de 'Beni el-Kalb'. *Kalb* is Arabisch voor hond, en de hond staat helaas niet hoog aangeschreven in de Arabische cultuur.

Gideon Barzilai vond in elk geval één bruikbare aanwijzing in het rapport van de *sajan* over de Winkler Bank. Die wees hem de richting waarin hij moest zoeken.

Eerst moest hij te weten komen wie van de drie adjunct-directeuren, Kellner, Gemütlich of Blei, de rekening van de Iraakse spion Jericho beheerde.

De snelste methode leek een telefoontje, maar uit het rapport bleek wel dat de bank niet bereid was telefonische inlichtingen te verstrekken.

Daarom stuurde hij een codebericht naar Tel Aviv, vanuit het zwaar versterkte ondergrondse Mossad-kantoor onder de Weense ambassade. De reactie kwam zo snel mogelijk.

Het was een vervalste brief op authentiek postpapier van een van de oudste en meest eerbiedwaardige Britse banken – Coutts, op de Strand in Londen, bankiers van Hare Majesteit de Koningin.

Zelfs de ondertekening was een perfecte kopie van de handtekening van een van de directeuren van de afdeling buitenland van Coutts. Er stond geen naam op de envelop of boven aan de brief. De aanhef luidde simpel: 'Mijne heren...'

Ook de inhoud was simpel en zakelijk. Een belangrijke cliënt van Coutts moest binnenkort een groot bedrag overmaken op een nummerrekening van een cliënt van de Winkler Bank, nummer zus-en-zo. Coutts' cliënt had hen gewaarschuwd dat er om technische redenen een vertraging van enkele dagen was ontstaan. Mocht Winklers cliënt informeren waar het geld bleef, dan zou Coutts het op prijs stellen als zij hun cliënt wilden meedelen dat de betaling onderweg was. Ten slotte zou Coutts graag een bevestiging krijgen van de goede ontvangst van deze brief.

Barzilai ging ervan uit dat banken graag geld ontvangen – zeker de Winkler Bank – en dat de degelijke oude bank in de Ballgasse zo hoffelijk zou zijn de bankiers van het koningshuis Windsor een brief terug te sturen. En dat gebeurde.

Tel Aviv had een bijpassende envelop gestuurd, met afgestempelde Britse postzegels, alsof de brief twee dagen eerder vanaf het postkantoor op Trafalgar Square was verstuurd. De envelop was geadresseerd aan de 'Directeur buitenlandse rekeningen, Winkler Bank', met het adres. Natuurlijk bestond die functie niet bij de Winkler Bank, omdat het werk tussen drie mensen was verdeeld.

Midden in de nacht werd de brief in de brievenbus van de bank gegooid.

Het Yarid-surveillanceteam hield de Winkler Bank inmiddels al een week in de gaten, had foto's van de medewerkers genomen en de dagelijkse routine genoteerd – de openings- en sluitingstijden, de binnenkomst van de post, het vertrek van de boodschapper voor zijn vaste ronde, de plaats van de receptioniste achter haar bureau in de hal op de begane grond, en de positie van de bewaker achter een kleiner bureau tegenover haar.

Het was geen nieuw gebouw. De Ballgasse en de Franziskanerplatz liggen in de oude wijk, niet ver van de Singerstrasse. Het bankgebouw moest ooit de patriciërswoning van een rijke Weense koopmansfamilie zijn geweest, groot en solide, veilig achter een zware houten deur met een discrete koperen plaquette. Te oordelen aan de indeling van een soortgelijk huis aan het plein dat het Yarid-team had geïnspecteerd door zich voor te doen als cliënten van een accountantskantoor dat daar was gevestigd, telde het maar vijf verdiepingen, met ongeveer zes kantoren per etage.

Het Yarid-team had ook genoteerd dat de uitgaande post iedere avond vlak voor sluitingstijd naar een brievenbus op het plein werd gebracht. Dat was de taak van de bewaker/conciërge, die daarna terugkwam om de deur open te houden als het personeel vertrok. Ten slotte liet hij de nachtwaker binnen

voordat hij zelf naar huis ging. De nachtwaker sloot zichzelf in en schoof voldoende grendels voor de houten deur om een pantserwagen tegen te houden.
Voordat de brief van Coutts bij de bank in de bus was gedaan, had het hoofd van het technische Neviot-team de brievenbus op de Franziskanerplatz onderzocht en minachtend gesnoven. Een van zijn mensen had de bus binnen drie minuten geopend en weer gesloten. Daarna hadden ze een sleutel gemaakt. Na enig bijvijlen paste de sleutel even goed als die van de postbode. Nader onderzoek leerde dat de conciërge van de bank de brieven altijd twintig tot dertig minuten vóór de lichting van zes uur 's avonds op de bus deed.
De dag dat de brief naar Coutts werd verstuurd, werkten de twee Mossadteams goed samen. Toen de conciërge weer terugliep naar de bank, had de technicus de klep van de brievenbus al open. De tweeëntwintig brieven van de Winkler Bank lagen bovenop. Binnen dertig seconden hadden ze de brief aan Coutts gevonden, de rest teruggelegd en de bus weer gesloten.
De vijf leden van het Yarid-team hadden zich onopvallend op het plein geposteerd voor het geval iemand zich zou bemoeien met de 'postbode', wiens uniform – haastig in een tweedehandszaak gekocht – een opvallende gelijkenis vertoonde met het echte uniform van de Weense posterijen.
Maar de brave burgers van Wenen zijn niet gewend aan agenten uit het Midden-Oosten die de onschendbaarheid van een brievenbus aantasten. Er liepen op dat moment maar twee mensen over het plein, die geen enkele belangstelling hadden voor een 'postbode' die gewoon zijn werk deed. Twintig minuten later kwam de echte postbode. Maar toen waren de twee voorbijgangers alweer verdwenen en liepen er andere mensen rond.
Barzilai opende de brief van de Winkler Bank aan Coutts. Het was een korte, maar beleefde bevestiging van ontvangst, geschreven in redelijk Engels, en ondertekend door Wolfgang Gemütlich. De teamleider van de Mossad wist nu wie Jericho's rekening beheerde. Nu moesten ze hem nog inpalmen of onder druk zetten.
Barzilai wist niet dat de echte problemen nog moesten komen.

De avond was al gevallen toen Mike Martin bij het huis van de eerste secretaris vertrok. Hij zag geen reden om de Russen te storen door de hoofdingang te gebruiken. Er was nog een poortje in de achtermuur, met een roestig slot waarvan hij de sleutel had gekregen. Hij duwde zijn fiets het steegje in, deed de deur achter zich op slot en vertrok.
Het zou een lange nacht worden, wist hij. De Chileense diplomaat Moncada had de Mossad een uitvoerige beschrijving gegeven van de drie geheime 'brievenbussen' die hij had gebruikt om berichten aan Jericho door te geven, en de plaatsen waar hij krijtstrepen neerzette om de onzichtbare spion te waarschuwen dat er een boodschap voor hem was. Martin had geen

225

andere keus dan hetzelfde bericht op alle drie de plaatsen achter te laten.

Hij had de boodschappen in het Arabisch geschreven, op dun luchtpostpapier dat hij in een plastic zakje had gevouwen. De drie zakjes zaten tegen de binnenkant van zijn dijbeen geplakt. De kleurkrijtjes had hij in een zijzak.

Zijn eerste halte was de Alwazia-begraafplaats in Risafa aan de overkant van de rivier. Hij herinnerde zich de plek van lang geleden en in Riyad had hij de luchtfoto's uitvoerig bestudeerd. In het donker een losse steen opsporen was een andere zaak.

Het kostte hem tien minuten. Hij tastte met zijn vingers in het duister van het ommuurde kerkhof tot hij de juiste steen gevonden had. Hij trok hem naar voren, legde een plastic zakje met een briefje erachter en schoof de steen weer terug.

Zijn volgende reisdoel was een oude, afbrokkelende muur bij de vervallen citadel van Aadhamija, waar een stinkende vijver het enige overblijfsel van de oude slotgracht vormde. Niet ver van de citadel lag het Aladham-heiligdom, en ertussenin stond een muur, even oud en brokkelig als de citadel zelf. Martin vond de muur en de eenzame boom die ertegenaan groeide. Hij stak zijn hand achter de stam en telde tien rijen stenen vanaf de bovenkant. De tiende steen zat los als een oude tand. Martin legde het tweede zakje erachter en duwde de steen weer op zijn plaats. Hij keek of iemand hem in de gaten hield, maar er was geen mens te zien. Niemand kwam graag na het donker op deze verlaten plek.

De derde en laatste 'brievenbus' bevond zich op een andere begraafplaats, een verlaten Brits kerkhof in Waziraja bij de Turkse ambassade. Het was een graf, net als in Koeweit – niet een holte onder een marmeren grafplaat maar een kleine stenen vaas, vastgemetseld op de plaats waar de grafsteen moest hebben gestaan, in een hoek van het kerkhof die allang niet meer werd gebruikt.

'Geeft niet,' mompelde Martin tegen de onbekende soldaat van het Britse rijk die eronder lag. 'Ga door, ouwe jongen. Je doet het uitstekend.'

Moncada had in het gebouw van de Verenigde Naties gewerkt, aan het eind van de Matar Sadam Airport Road, maar hij had zijn krijtstrepen dichter bij Mansour gezet, waar de wegen wat verder uit elkaar lagen en de tekens vanuit een passerende auto konden worden gezien. De regel was dat Moncada en Jericho als ze een krijtstreep zagen, naar de bijbehorende brievenbus zouden gaan en daarna de streep met een vochtige doek zouden wegwissen. Als degene die de streep had gezet de volgende dag voorbij kwam en zag dat het teken verdwenen was, wist hij dat de oproep was gezien en dat het bericht (vermoedelijk) van achter de steen was weggehaald.

Op die manier hadden de twee agenten twee jaar samengewerkt zonder elkaar ooit te hebben gezien.

Martin had geen auto, zoals Moncada, en moest dus het hele eind fietsen. Zijn eerste teken, een Andreaskruis in de vorm van een X, zette hij met blauw krijt op de stenen post van een hek van een verlaten landhuis.

De tweede aanwijzing was een Lotharings kruis in wit krijt, op de roestige plaatijzeren deur van een garage aan de achterkant van een huis in Jarmuk.

Het derde teken, een islamitische halve maan in rood krijt met een horizontale streep in het midden, kwam op de muur van het gebouw van de Unie van Arabische Journalisten aan de rand van de wijk Mutanabi. Iraakse journalisten worden niet gestimuleerd in hun speurzin, en een krijttekening op hun muur zou zeker de krant niet halen.

Martin wist niet of Jericho ondanks Moncada's belofte dat hij misschien zou terugkeren, nog steeds vanuit zijn auto op eventuele tekens lette. Het enige dat hij nu kon doen was dagelijks controleren en afwachten.

Op 7 november zag hij dat het witte kruis was verdwenen. Had de eigenaar van de garage zelf de roestige deur schoongemaakt?

Martin fietste door. Het blauwe kruis op het hek was weg, evenals de rode halve maan op de muur van het journalistengebouw.

Die nacht reed hij langs de drie 'brievenbussen' waar Jericho zijn berichten aan zijn contactman moest achterlaten.

Een ervan was een losse steen aan de achterkant van een muur rondom de groentemarkt bij de Saadunstraat. Er lag een opgevouwen velletje luchtpostpapier voor hem. De tweede plek, onder een losse stenen vensterbank van een vervallen huis in een steegje van het armoedige labyrint van de *soukh* op de noordelijke rivieroever bij de Shuhadabrug, leverde ook een velletje op. Ook op de derde en laatste vindplaats, onder de losse tegel van een verlaten hofje bij Abu Nawas, lag een dun briefje.

Martin verborg ze onder het plakband om zijn linker dijbeen en fietste terug naar Mansour.

Bij het licht van een flakkerende kaars las hij ze allemaal. Het was drie keer dezelfde boodschap. Met Jericho ging alles goed. Hij was bereid om weer voor het Westen te werken en begreep dat zijn informatie nu naar de Britten en de Amerikanen zou gaan. Maar de risico's waren veel groter geworden en dus wilde hij meer geld. Hij wachtte op een toezegging en op nieuwe instructies.

Martin verbrandde de drie berichten en verpulverde de as. Hij kende het antwoord op de twee verzoeken al. Langley was bereid goed te betalen als de informatie bruikbaar was. En Martin had al een lijstje met vragen over Saddams stemming, zijn strategie en de plaatsen van de belangrijkste commandocentra en fabrieken van de Iraakse massavernietigingswapens.

Vlak voordat het licht werd verzond hij zijn bericht aan Riyad: Jericho is terug.

227

Toen dr. Terry Martin op 10 november zijn kleine, rommelige kantoor op de School voor Oosterse en Afrikaanse Studies binnenstapte vond hij een briefje dat zijn secretaresse opvallend op zijn vloeiblad had gelegd: 'Er heeft een meneer Plummer gebeld. Hij zei dat je zijn nummer had en wist waar het over ging.'

Uit de abrupte stijl bleek dat Miss Wordsworth zich enigszins in haar wiek geschoten voelde. Ze was een dame die haar academische bazen graag beschermde met de bezitterige zorg van een moederkloek. En dus wilde ze altijd precies weten wat er aan de hand was. Ze had niet veel op met mensen die haar niet wilden vertellen waarover ze opbelden.

Nu de colleges weer waren begonnen en een nieuwe groep studenten zijn opwachting had gemaakt, was Terry Martin zijn verzoek aan het hoofd van de Arabische sectie van het GCHQ bijna vergeten.

Toen hij belde, was Plummer lunchen. Daarna was Martin zelf bezig tot een uur of vier. Vlak voordat hij naar huis ging, probeerde hij het nog een keer, met meer succes.

'O ja,' zei Plummer. 'Je had me toch gevraagd om je te waarschuwen als we vreemde berichten opvingen die ogenschijnlijk nergens op sloegen? Gisteren heeft onze luisterpost op Cyprus een merkwaardig gesprek opgevangen. Je mag het horen, als je wilt.'

'Hier in Londen?' vroeg Martin.

'Eh... nee, dat gaat niet. We hebben het op de band, maar er is een speciale recorder voor nodig om het af te spelen. De kwaliteit is nogal slecht. Zelfs mijn Arabische staf kan het niet goed volgen.'

De rest van de week hadden ze het allebei te druk. Ze spraken af dat Martin op zondag naar Cheltenham zou komen en Plummer bood hem een lunch aan in een 'heel redelijke kleine pub niet ver van het kantoor'.

Niemand lette op de twee mannen in tweedjasjes onder de balken van de oude kroeg toen ze die zondag allebei de dagschotel bestelden – rundvlees en Yorkshire-pudding.

'We hebben geen idee wie dit gesprek voeren,' zei Plummer, 'maar het moeten hoge functionarissen zijn. Om de een of andere reden gebruikt de beller een open lijn. Hij schijnt te zijn teruggekomen van een bezoek aan het vooruitgeschoven hoofdkwartier in Koeweit. Misschien is het een autotelefoon. Het is geen militaire frequentie dus de man met wie hij spreekt is vermoedelijk geen militair. Misschien een hoge ambtenaar.'

Het eten kwam, en ze zwegen toen het vlees werd opgediend met gebakken aardappels en pastinaak. Zodra de dienster was verdwenen, vervolgde Plummer: 'De beller lijkt te verwijzen naar berichten van de Iraakse luchtmacht dat de Amerikaanse en Britse vliegtuigen steeds agressiever patrouilleren, tot aan de Iraakse grens, en pas op het laatste moment weer afbuigen.'

228

Martin knikte. Hij kende die tactiek. Zo dwongen de Amerikanen de Iraakse luchtverdediging tot een reactie. Ze moesten hun zoekradar en de radarin-stallaties van hun SAM-batterijen activeren, waardoor ze hun posities verrie-den aan de AWACS die boven de Golf cirkelde.

'De beller heeft het over de Beni el-Kalb, de zonen van de honden... de Amerikanen dus... en de andere man beweert lachend dat het dom is van de Irakezen om op die provocaties te reageren en hun posities prijs te geven.

Daarna zegt hij iets wat we niet goed kunnen volgen. Er is wat storing, sta-tisch geruis of zoiets. We kunnen de kwaliteit wel wat verbeteren, maar het blijft onduidelijk. De andere man, die volgens ons in Bagdad zit, raakt geïr-riteerd en zegt dat de beller moet ophangen. Bijna onmiddellijk daarna gooit hij zelf de telefoon neer. Het gaat om de laatste twee zinnen die hij zegt. Daar moet je eens naar luisteren.'

Na de lunch reed Plummer met Martin naar het terrein van het GCHQ, waar op zondag gewoon werd gewerkt. In een geluiddichte ruimte, die aan een opnamestudio deed denken, vroeg Plummer een van de technici de mysteri-euze tape af te spelen. Zwijgend luisterden de twee mannen naar de Arabi-sche keelklanken uit Irak.

Het gesprek begon zoals Plummer had beschreven. Tegen het eind werd de beller duidelijk emotioneel.

'Het zal niet lang meer duren, *rafik*. Want binnenkort hebben we de...'

Wat hij daarna zei, was door een storing niet te volgen, maar de man in Bag-dad reageerde nijdig. 'Hou je mond, *ibn-al-gahba*,' viel hij de ander in de rede.

Daarna gooide hij de hoorn erop, alsof hij zich er opeens pijnlijk van bewust was dat ze via een open lijn spraken.

De technicus speelde de tape drie keer af, op verschillende snelheden.

'Wat denk je?' vroeg Plummer.

'Ze zijn allebei lid van de partij,' zei Martin. 'Alleen hoge partijleden gebruiken nog de aanspreektitel *rafik* of "kameraad".'

'Goed. Dus het zijn twee partijbonzen die een gesprek hebben over de Ame-rikaanse militaire opbouw en de Amerikaanse provocaties aan de grens.'

'De beller maakt zich kwaad, maar dan raakt hij opgewonden als hij iets bedenkt... Hij gebruikt de term "binnenkort".'

'Zou er iets gaan veranderen?' vroeg Plummer.

'Zo klinkt het wel,' zei Martin.

'Daarna komt het gedeelte dat we niet kunnen verstaan. Maar de andere man reageert wel heel fel, Terry. Hij smijt de telefoon neer en noemt de beller een "hoerezoon". Dat is niet gering.'

'Nee. Alleen de hoogste van de twee mannen zou ongestraft zo'n belediging kunnen gebruiken,' beaamde Martin. 'Maar waarom wordt hij zo kwaad?'

'Om die ene zin die we niet kunnen verstaan. Laten we nog eens luisteren.'
De technicus speelde de bewuste zin opnieuw af.

'Iets over Allah?' opperde Plummer. 'Spoedig zullen we bij Allah zijn? In de handen van God?'

'Het klinkt mij in de oren als: "Spoedig hebben we iets... iets... van God".'

'Ja, dat zou kunnen, Terry. De hulp van God, misschien?'

'Waarom zou die andere vent dan zo kwaad worden?' vroeg Martin. 'De hulp van de Almachtige inroepen is niets nieuws. En zeker geen reden om boos te worden. Ik weet het niet. Mag ik een kopie van dat bandje meenemen?'

'Natuurlijk.'

'Heb je onze Amerikaanse neven er al naar gevraagd?'

Na een paar weken in dit bizarre wereldje begon Terry zich het jargon al eigen te maken. Bij de Britse inlichtingendienst werd over de eigen mensen gesproken als de 'vrienden' en over de Amerikaanse collega's als de 'neven'.

'Natuurlijk. Fort Meade heeft hetzelfde gesprek opgevangen, via een satelliet. Zij komen er ook niet uit. Maar ze vinden het ook niet belangrijk.'

Terry Martin reed naar huis met het kleine cassettebandje in zijn zak. Tot Hilary's grote ongenoegen speelde hij het voortdurend af op de cassetterecorder naast hun bed. Toen hij protesteerde, antwoordde Terry dat Hilary soms urenlang kon zeuren over een woord in de kruiswoordpuzzel van de *Times* dat hij niet kon vinden.

Die vergelijking vond Hilary absurd. 'Maar ik weet de volgende ochtend het antwoord,' snauwde hij, voordat hij zich op zijn zij draaide en in slaap viel.

Terry Martin wist de volgende ochtend, of de ochtend daarna, nog steeds het antwoord niet. Hij speelde het bandje tijdens de lunchpauze en op andere momenten als hij even vrij had. Hij noteerde een aantal mogelijkheden, maar nog steeds was hij niet tevreden. Waarom was die andere man zo kwaad geworden over een onschuldige verwijzing naar Allah?

Pas vijf dagen later hoorde hij opeens wat er gezegd werd.

Toen de betekenis tot Martin doordrong, belde hij Simon Paxman op Century House, maar kreeg te horen dat Paxman voorlopig onbereikbaar was. Hij vroeg naar Steve Laing, het hoofd Operaties van de divisie Midden-Oosten, maar die was er ook niet.

Martin kon niet weten dat Paxman naar het SIS-hoofdkwartier in Riyad was afgereisd en dat Laing naar dezelfde stad was vertrokken voor een belangrijke bespreking met Chip Barber van de CIA.

De man die ze de 'verspieder' noemden, was in Tel Aviv op het vliegtuig gestapt en via Londen en Frankfurt naar Wenen gereisd, waar niemand hem van het vliegveld haalde. Hij nam een taxi van de luchthaven Schwechat naar het Sheraton Hotel, waar hij een kamer had geboekt.

De verspieder was een rondborstige, joviale vent met de papieren van een Amerikaanse advocaat uit New York. Zijn Duits was redelijk en zijn Amerikaans vlekkeloos. Hij had jaren in de Verenigde Staten gewoond.

Een paar uur na zijn aankomst in Wenen had hij met behulp van de secretaresse-service van het Sheraton op het briefpapier van zijn advocatenkantoor een beleefde brief geschreven aan een zekere Wolfgang Gemütlich, adjunctdirecteur van de Winkler Bank.

Het briefpapier was volledig authentiek en iemand die telefonisch navraag zou doen, zou de bevestiging krijgen dat de afzender inderdaad een vennoot van het vooraanstaande Amerikaanse advocatenkantoor was. Maar de vennoot was op dat moment met vakantie (zoals de Mossad in New York had nagevraagd) en hij was zeker niet dezelfde man als de bezoeker aan Wenen.

De brief had een verontschuldigende toon en was bedoeld om de nieuwsgierigheid te prikkelen. De afzender vertegenwoordigde een bijzonder rijke en machtige cliënt die een groot deel van zijn fortuin in Europa wilde beleggen.

Na een advies van een vriend had de cliënt gevraagd of zijn advocaat contact wilde opnemen met de Winkler Bank, en meer in het bijzonder met de heer Gemütlich.

De advocaat had van tevoren een afspraak willen maken, maar zowel zijn cliënt als het advocatenkantoor stelde hoge prijs op discretie. Telefoon en fax waren dus niet geschikt. De advocaat moest toch in Europa zijn, en daarom had hij van de gelegenheid gebruik gemaakt om persoonlijk naar Wenen te komen.

Helaas kon hij maar drie dagen blijven, maar als Herr Gemütlich zo vriendelijk wilde zijn om hem te ontvangen, zou hij graag naar de bank komen.

De brief werd 's avonds door de Amerikaan persoonlijk bij de bank in de bus gedaan, en de volgende dag bracht de boodschapper van de bank het antwoord naar het hotel. Herr Gemütlich zou de Amerikaanse advocaat de volgende morgen om tien uur ontvangen.

Vanaf het moment dat de verspieder de bank binnenkwam, nam hij alle details in zich op. Hij maakte geen aantekeningen, maar er was niets wat hem ontging en niets wat hij vergat. De receptioniste controleerde zijn geloofsbrieven en belde naar de adjunct-directeur om zijn komst aan te kondigen. De conciërge nam hem mee naar boven en klopte op een zware houten deur. Hij verloor de bezoeker geen moment uit het oog.

'*Herein,*' klonk het uit de kamer. De conciërge opende de deur, sloot hem weer achter de rug van de advocaat en liep terug naar zijn bureau in de hal beneden.

Wolfgang Gemütlich kwam overeind, schudde zijn bezoeker de hand, bood hem een stoel tegenover zijn bureau aan en ging weer zitten.

'Gemütlich' betekent 'gezellig' in het Duits, maar zelden had iemand een minder toepasselijke naam gehad. Herr Gemütlich was broodmager, voor in de zestig, met dun haar en een smal gezicht. Hij droeg een grijs pak met een grijze das. Zijn hele uitstraling was grijs. Er blonk geen sprankje humor in de bleke ogen en de glimlach om zijn dunne lippen deed denken aan de grijns van een ontzield lichaam in een mortuarium.

Het kantoor ademde dezelfde strenge sfeer – een donkere betimmering, ingelijste bullen in plaats van foto's, en een groot, fraai bewerkt bureau dat een keurig opgeruimde indruk maakte.

Wolfgang Gemütlich deed zijn werk niet uit plezier, dat was duidelijk. Hij hield niet van plezier. Het bankwezen was een serieuze zaak, net als het leven zelf. Als er één ding was waar Gemütlich een grote hekel aan had, dan was het aan geld uitgeven. Geld was er om te beleggen, bij voorkeur bij de Winkler Bank. Cliënten die geld opnamen bezorgden hem maagzuur en een grote overboeking van de Winkler Bank naar een andere rekening kon zijn hele week bederven.

De verspieder hoefde alleen maar te observeren. Zijn belangrijkste werk had hij al gedaan: hij kon Herr Gemütlich identificeren voor het Yarid-team op straat. Ook zocht hij naar een kluis waarin mogelijk de bijzonderheden van Jericho's rekening te vinden waren. Verder moest hij letten op sloten, grendels en alarmsystemen – kortom, op alles wat een professionele inbreker wil weten om zijn slag te kunnen slaan.

Zonder een exact bedrag te noemen, liet hij doorschemeren dat zijn cliënt een aanzienlijk kapitaal naar Europa wilde overhevelen. Hij informeerde naar de veiligheidsvoorzieningen van de bank en de mate van discretie. Herr Gemütlich legde hem omstandig uit dat een nummerrekening bij de Winkler Bank streng geheim bleef en dat discretie hoog in het vaandel stond.

Ze werden maar één keer gestoord, toen er een zijdeur openging en een onopvallende, saaie vrouw naar binnen stapte die Gemütlich drie brieven gaf om te ondertekenen. De adjunct-directeur leek geïrriteerd door de interruptie.

'U zei dat ze belangrijk waren, Herr Gemütlich,' zei de vrouw. 'Anders...' Bij nadere beschouwing was ze niet zo oud als ze leek. Een jaar of veertig, misschien. Maar door het strak achterovergekamde haar, het knotje, het tweedpakje, de dikke kousen en de platte schoenen maakte ze een oudere indruk.

'Goed, goed,' zei Gemütlich en hij pakte de brieven aan. *'Entschuldiging...'* zei hij tegen zijn gast.

Het gesprek was in het Duits gevoerd, omdat de Oostenrijker alleen gebrekkig Engels sprak. De advocaat kwam nu overeind en maakte een lichte buiging voor de vrouw. *'Grüss Gott, Fräulein,'* zei hij.

Ze keek hem geschrokken aan. Gemütlichs gasten stonden meestal niet op voor een secretaresse. Gemütlich voelde zich gedwongen om te reageren. Hij schraapte zijn keel en mompelde: 'Eh... o ja, dit is mijn privé-secretaresse, juffrouw Hardenberg.'

De verspieder sloeg de informatie in zijn geheugen op en ging weer zitten. Toen hij wilde vertrekken, met de verzekering dat hij zijn cliënt een positief advies over de Winkler Bank zou geven, was de procedure hetzelfde als bij zijn binnenkomst. De conciërge werd opgetrommeld uit de hal en verscheen in de deuropening. De verspieder nam afscheid en liep met de man mee.

Samen stapten ze door het hek de kleine lift binnen, die rammelend afdaalde. De verspieder vroeg of hij nog even van het toilet gebruik kon maken voordat hij vertrok. De conciërge fronste, alsof zulke lichamelijke ongemakken niet gebruikelijk waren binnen de Winkler Bank. Maar toch liet hij de lift op een tussenverdieping stoppen en wees naar een onopvallende houten deur. De verspieder verdween.

Het was een herentoilet, met één wc-hokje, een wastafel, een handdoekrol en een kast tegen de muur. De verspieder draaide de kraan open om voor wat achtergrondgeruis te zorgen en inspecteerde toen de ruimte. Er zaten tralies voor het raampje, met de draden van een alarmsysteem – een mogelijkheid, maar niet eenvoudig. Een automatische ventilator. In de kast zag hij een paar bezems, stoffer en blik, schoonmaakmiddelen en een stofzuiger. Het gebouw werd dus schoongehouden. Maar wanneer? 's Avonds of in het weekend? Te oordelen naar zijn eigen ervaring zouden de werksters ook in de gaten worden gehouden. De conciërge of de nachtwaker konden natuurlijk zonder moeite worden uitgeschakeld, maar dat was geen oplossing. Kobi Dror had duidelijk gezegd dat er geen sporen mochten achterblijven.

Toen hij uit het toilet kwam, stond de conciërge nog op hem te wachten. De verspieder zag de brede marmeren trap naar de hal, een halve verdieping lager en wees glimlachend die kant uit, om aan te geven dat hij voor zo'n korte afstand liever de trap nam dan de lift.

De conciërge kwam achter hem aan, liep met hem mee de trap af en bracht hem naar de deur. Even later hoorde hij de zware deur achter zich in het slot vallen. Als de conciërge toevallig boven was, vroeg hij zich af, hoe zou de receptioniste dan een cliënt of een boodschapper binnenlaten?

Twee uur lang bracht hij verslag uit aan Gidi Barzilai. Zijn rapport over de veiligheidsmaatregelen van de bank, voorzover hij die had gezien, was niet hoopgevend. De leider van het Neviot-team, die ook aanwezig was, schudde zijn hoofd.

Ze konden wel binnenkomen, zei hij. Geen probleem. Het alarmsysteem kon worden omzeild. Maar het zou niet eenvoudig zijn om geen sporen na te laten. Waarschijnlijk deed de nachtwaker op gezette tijden zijn ronde.

Bovendien, waar moesten ze precies naar zoeken? Een kluis? Waar stond die dan, wat voor type was het, hoe oud, en met wat voor een slot? Het kon uren duren. Ze zouden de nachtwaker moeten uitschakelen, en dat kon niet ongemerkt gebeuren. En Drors instructies waren duidelijk geweest.

De verspieder vloog de volgende dag terug naar Tel Aviv, nadat hij Wolfgang Gemütlich en Fräulein Hardenberg op foto's had geïdentificeerd. Toen hij was vertrokken, beraadslaagden Barzilai en de leider van het Neviotteam opnieuw.

'Eerlijk gezegd heb ik nog meer gegevens nodig, Gidi. Ik weet nog te weinig. Die papieren die je zoekt liggen natuurlijk in een brandkast. Maar waar? Achter de lambrizering? In de vloer? In het kantoor van de secretaresse? In een kluis in de kelder? We moeten meer informatie hebben.'

Barzilai bromde wat. Lang geleden, tijdens zijn opleiding, had een van de instructeurs opgemerkt dat iedereen zijn zwakke punten heeft. Als je die vindt, kun je iemand dwingen om mee te werken. Hij besloot om Wolfgang Gemütlich vierentwintig uur per dag te laten schaduwen.

Maar de stijve Weense bankier zou het ongelijk van de instructeur bewijzen.

Steve Laing en Chip Barber hadden een groot probleem. Halverwege november had Jericho de eerste antwoorden doorgegeven op de vragen die hem via Mike Martin waren gesteld. Er hing een hoog prijskaartje aan, maar de Amerikaanse regering had zonder protesten het gevraagde bedrag op de rekening in Wenen overgemaakt.

Als Jericho's gegevens klopten – en er was geen reden om het tegendeel te veronderstellen – was het zeer nuttige informatie. Hij had niet alle vragen beantwoord, maar wel enkele feiten bevestigd die al door de Amerikanen en Britten werden vermoed.

Hij had zeventien plaatsen genoemd die verband hielden met de produktie van massavernietigingswapens. Acht van deze plaatsen stonden al op de lijst van de geallieerden. Twee locaties had hij gecorrigeerd. De andere negen waren nieuw. De belangrijkste ervan was de plek van het ondergrondse laboratorium met de ultracentrifuge-cascade voor de produktie van uranium-235 als grondstof voor een kernbom.

Het probleem was hoe ze de militairen moesten inlichten zonder te verraden dat Langley en Century House een hoge spion binnen het Iraakse regime hadden.

Niet dat de inlichtingendiensten het leger niet vertrouwden. Natuurlijk deden ze dat. De legertop bestond uit zeer betrouwbare officieren. Maar in het inlichtingenwereldje gold de oude en beproefde regel dat je iemand nooit iets mocht vertellen dat hij niet absoluut hoefde te weten. Een man die niets weet, kan ook niets verraden, hoe onbewust ook. En als de inlichtingendiensten met een lijst van nieuwe doelwitten kwamen, hoeveel generaals, brigadegeneraals en kolonels zouden dan niet vermoeden waar die lijst vandaan kwam?

De derde week van de maand hadden Barber en Laing in het souterrain van het Saoedische ministerie van Defensie een vertrouwelijk gesprek met generaal Buster Glosson, de assistent van generaal Chuck Horner, die het bevel had over de geallieerde luchtmacht in de Golf.

Niemand gebruikte de voornaam van brigadegeneraal Glosson; hij werd altijd 'Buster' genoemd. Glosson was de man die de plannen voor de uiteindelijke luchtaanval op Irak had uitgewerkt – de bombardementen die aan de grondoorlog vooraf moesten gaan.

Londen en Washington waren het er allang over eens dat het doel van die oorlog niet alleen de bevrijding van Koeweit kon zijn, maar dat ook Saddam Hoesseins oorlogsmachine moest worden vernietigd. En daartoe behoorden ook de installaties waar gifgas, bacteriologische wapens en kernbommen werden geproduceerd.

Nog voordat Desert Shield het gevaar van een Iraakse invasie in Saoedi-Arabië had bezworen, waren de plannen voor de luchtoorlog al in een vergevorderd stadium, onder de codenaam 'Instant Thunder'. De architect van deze operatie was Buster Glosson.

Op 16 november zochten de Verenigde Naties en andere diplomatieke instanties nog steeds naar een 'vredesplan' om de crisis tot een vreedzame oplossing te brengen, maar de drie mannen in het souterrain wisten dat die pogingen tevergeefs zouden zijn.

Barber hield het kort en bondig. Zoals Buster wel wist, waren de Amerikanen en Britten al maanden bezig om informatie over Saddams massavernietigingswapens te verzamelen. De Amerikaanse luchtmachtgeneraal knikte behoedzaam. Verderop in de gang hing een kaart met meer spelden dan een egel stekels had. Elk van die spelden vertegenwoordigde een doelwit. Wat nu weer?

We zijn begonnen, Buster, met de exportvergunningen van verschillende landen en de bedrijven die produkten aan Irak hebben geleverd. Daarna hebben we ons geconcentreerd op de wetenschappers die de Iraakse fabrieken hebben ingericht, maar die werden meestal in geblindeerde bussen naar het werkterrein gereden, woonden op een afgelegen basis en wisten niet waar de fabrieken precies stonden.

Ten slotte, Buster, hebben we gesprekken gevoerd met de aannemers die de meeste van Saddams gifgaspaleizen hebben gebouwd. Dat leverde eindelijk wat op. Bruikbare informatie.

Barber schoof de lijst met nieuwe doelwitten naar de generaal toe. Glosson las hem met belangstelling door. Er stonden nog geen kaartcoördinaten bij,

235

die voor de plaatsbepaling noodzakelijk waren, maar de beschrijvingen waren duidelijk genoeg om de locaties op de luchtfoto's te kunnen terugvinden.

Glosson bromde wat. Sommige doelwitten stonden al op de lijst. Bij andere had een vraagteken gestaan. Die waren dus nu bevestigd. Maar er waren ook nieuwe plaatsen bij. Hij trok zijn wenkbrauwen op.

'Is dit serieus?'

'Absoluut,' antwoordde de Engelsman. 'Die aannemers wisten heel goed wat ze deden en waar ze zich bevonden. En ze waren eerder bereid om te praten dan de bureaucraten.'

Glosson stond op. 'Goed. Komt er nog meer?'

'We zijn nog bezig in Europa, Buster,' zei Barber. 'Als we nog meer concrete doelwitten opsporen, laten we het je weten. Ze hebben heel wat spul begraven. Diep onder de woestijn. Belangrijke projecten.'

'Als jullie weten waar ze liggen, gooien wij ze plat,' verklaarde de generaal. Later liet Glosson de lijst aan Chuck Horner zien. De commandant van de Amerikaanse luchtmacht was kleiner dan Glosson – een somber ogende, verfomfaaide man met een hondekop en de subtiele aanpak van een neushoorn met aambeien. Maar hij adoreerde zijn piloten en zijn grondpersoneel en die waardering was wederzijds.

Zijn mannen wisten dat hij hun belangen verdedigde bij bouwers, bureaucraten en politici, tot aan het Witte Huis toe, en zonder ooit een blad voor de mond te nemen. Hij was volstrekt openhartig.

Bij zijn bezoeken aan de Golfstaten Bahrein, Abu Dhabi en Dubai, waar sommige van zijn squadrons waren gestationeerd, bleef hij uit de buurt van de vleespotten. Voor hem geen Sheraton of Hilton, waar het goede leven bruiste. Hij at met zijn mannen op de basis en hij sliep op een brits in de barak.

Mannen en vrouwen in het leger kijken overal dwars doorheen. Ze weten wat ze waarderen en wat niet. Voor Chuck Horner zouden de Amerikaanse piloten zelfs met wrakke dubbeldekkers de oorlog tegen Irak zijn ingegaan.

Horner bestudeerde de lijst van de inlichtingendiensten en bromde wat. Twee van de lokaties waren niets anders dan stukken kale woestijn.

'Waar hebben ze die informatie vandaan?' vroeg hij aan Glosson.

'Van de aannemers die de complexen hebben gebouwd, beweren ze,' antwoordde Glosson.

'Gelul,' zei de generaal. 'Die lui hebben een spion in Bagdad. Buster, geen woord hierover tegen wie dan ook. We zetten die doelwitten gewoon op de lijst.' Hij dacht even na en zei toen: 'Ik vraag me af wie die vent is.'

Steve Laing vloog op de 18e naar Londen terug. De Conservatieve regering

was in rep en roer omdat een kamerlid de partijregels probeerde te misbrui-
ken om Margaret Thatcher als premier te wippen.

Een vermoeide Laing vond de boodschap van Terry Martin op zijn bureau
en belde hem op zijn instituut. De wetenschapper was zo opgewonden dat
Laing toestemde in een borrel na het werk. Als het maar geen lang gesprek
werd. Hij wilde naar huis.

Toen ze aan een hoektafeltje in een rustige bar in het West End zaten, haalde
Martin een recorder en een cassettebandje uit zijn koffertje. Hij vertelde
Laing over zijn verzoek aan Plummer en hun ontmoeting van de vorige
week.

'Zal ik het je laten horen?' vroeg hij.

'Als die lui van het GCHQ het niet kunnen volgen, dan gaat het mij ook
boven de pet,' zei Laing. 'Sean Plummer heeft toch Arabieren bij zijn staf,
mensen als Al-Khouri? Als die er niet uitkomen...'

Maar toch luisterde hij beleefd naar het bandje.

'Hoor je?' vroeg Martin enthousiast. 'Die "k" achter "hebben"? Hij roept
niet de hulp van Allah in. Het is een naam. Daarom wordt die andere vent zo
kwaad. Blijkbaar is die naam alleen bekend bij een selecte groep en mag hij
niet openlijk worden genoemd.'

'Maar wat zegt hij precies?' vroeg Laing verbijsterd. Martin staarde hem
aan. Begreep die man het nu nog niet?

'Hij zegt dat de Amerikaanse militaire opbouw niet van belang is, "want
binnenkort hebben we de *Qubth-ut-Allah*".'

Laing keek nog steeds verbaasd.

'Het moet een wapen zijn,' vervolgde Martin. 'Iets waarmee ze de Amerikanen kunnen tegenhouden.'

'Mijn Arabisch is niet zo best,' zei Laing. 'Wat betekent *Qubth-ut-Allah*?'

'De Vuist van God,' zei Martin.

Nadat ze elf jaar aan de macht was geweest en drie verkiezingen had gewonnen, werd de Britse premier op 20 november ten val gebracht, hoewel ze haar beslissing om op te stappen pas twee dagen later bekendmaakte. Haar val werd ingeluid door een obscure regel van de Conservatieve partij die vereiste dat zij van tijd tot tijd officieel als partijleider werd herkozen. In november was dat moment weer aangebroken. Haar herverkiezing had een formaliteit moeten zijn maar een ontslagen minister wierp zich op als tegenkandidaat. Zich niet bewust van het gevaar nam ze die uitdaging nauwelijks serieus, voerde een lauwe campagne en was op de dag van de stemming niet eens aanwezig omdat ze in Parijs een conferentie bijwoonde.

Achter haar rug leidden oude grieven, gekwetste ego's en de angst dat Thatcher de volgende verkiezingen zou verliezen tot een coalitie tegen haar, waardoor ze bij de eerste stemming niet automatisch werd herkozen. Was dat wel gebeurd, dan zou niemand meer iets van de uitdager hebben gehoord.

Bij de stemming van 30 november had ze een tweederde meerderheid nodig. Ze kwam vier stemmen tekort, waardoor een tweede ronde noodzakelijk werd. De paar losse stenen onder het fundament van haar aanhang veranderden binnen enkele uren in een complete lawine. Na overleg met haar ministers, die haar vertelden dat ze ging verliezen, nam ze zelf ontslag.

Om de uitdager tegen te houden, stelde John Major, de minister van Financiën, zich kandidaat voor de hoogste functie en won.

Bij de militairen in de Golf, zowel bij de Britten als de Amerikanen, sloeg het nieuws in als een bom. De Amerikaanse gevechtspiloten in Oman, die nu dagelijks samenwerkten met de SAS van de naburige basis, vroegen de Britten wat er aan de hand was. Het enige antwoord was een schouderophalen.

De mannen van de 7e Pantserbrigade, bijgenaamd de 'Woestijnratten', die onder hun Challenger-tanks aan de Saoedisch-Iraakse grens waren gelegerd in de toenemende kou van de woestijnwinter, luisterden naar hun transistors en vloekten luid.

Mike Martin hoorde het nieuws toen de Iraakse chauffeur naar hem toe kwam slenteren en het hem vertelde. Martin dacht even na, haalde toen zijn schouders op en vroeg: 'Wie is dat?'

'Stomme kaffer,' snauwde de chauffeur. 'De leider van de Beni Naji. Nu winnen we zeker.'

Hij liep terug naar zijn auto om lusteloos verder te luisteren naar Radio Bagdad. Een paar minuten later kwam eerste secretaris Koelikov haastig naar buiten en reed terug naar zijn ambassade.

Die nacht verstuurde Martin een lang bericht aan Riyad met de laatste informatie van Jericho en een verzoek om nieuwe instructies. Gehurkt in de deuropening van zijn schuurtje, om ongewenste bezoekers op een afstand te houden – de satellietschotel stond achter de open deur, naar het zuiden gericht – wachtte Martin op het antwoord. Een zwak knipperlichtje op de console waarschuwde hem om half één dat er een bericht was binnengekomen.

Hij demonteerde de schotel, verborg hem weer onder de vloer met de zender en de batterijen, vertraagde het bericht en speelde het bandje af.

Het was een nieuwe lijst met vragen aan Jericho en de bevestiging dat het gevraagde bedrag op zijn rekening was gestort. In een maand tijd had de spion binnen de Revolutionaire Commandoraad meer dan een miljoen dollar verdiend.

Aan de lijst waren nog twee extra instructies toegevoegd. De eerste was een verzoek aan Jericho om – als dat mogelijk was – bij zijn collega's een bepaalde suggestie naar voren te brengen om de politieke strategie van Bagdad te beïnvloeden.

Die suggestie kwam erop neer dat het nieuws uit Londen betekende dat de Coalitie waarschijnlijk niet tot een oorlog zou besluiten als Saddam Hoessein voet bij stuk hield.

Het zou nooit bekend worden of deze gedachte inderdaad tot de hoogste kringen in Bagdad was doorgedrongen, maar binnen een week beweerde Saddam dat de val van mevrouw Thatcher te danken was aan het protest van het Britse volk tegen haar vijandige houding tegenover Irak.

De tweede instructie was de vraag of Jericho ooit had gehoord van een wapensysteem dat bekend stond als 'De Vuist van God'.

Bij het licht van een kaars vertaalde Martin de vragen in het Arabisch en noteerde ze op twee dunne velletjes luchtpostpapier. Twintig uur later legde hij ze achter de losse steen in de muur bij het heiligdom van de imam Aladham in Aadhamija.

Het duurde een week voordat er antwoord kwam. Martin las Jericho's priegelige Arabische handschrift door en vertaalde alles in het Engels. Van uit een militair standpunt was de informatie heel interessant.

De drie divisies van de Republikeinse Garde – de Tawakkulna-, Medina- en Hammurabi-divisie – die aan de andere kant van de grens tegenover de Britten en Amerikanen waren gelegerd, waren uitgerust met een combinatie van T-54/55, T-62 en T-72 gevechtstanks, allemaal van Russische makelij.

Maar tijdens een recente inspectie had generaal Abdullah Kadiri van het Pantserkorps tot zijn schrik ontdekt dat de meeste bemanningen de accu's uit hun tanks hadden gehaald om als stroombron voor hun ventilatoren, kooktoestellen, radio's en cassettespelers te dienen. Het was de vraag of de accu's nog voldoende vermogen hadden om de tanks te laten starten als de oorlog uitbrak. Enkele soldaten waren ter plekke geëxecuteerd en twee commandanten waren van hun post ontheven en naar huis gestuurd.

Saddams halfbroer Ali Hassan Majid, de nieuwe gouverneur van Koeweit, had gemeld dat de bezetting een nachtmerrie dreigde te worden. De aanslagen op Iraakse militairen namen nog toe en steeds meer soldaten deserteerden. Het verzet liet zich niet afschrikken, ondanks de gruwelijke verhoren en de talloze executies door kolonel Sabaawi van de AMAM en twee persoonlijke bezoeken van zijn baas, Omar Khatib.

Erger nog, het verzet had op de een of andere manier de beschikking gekregen over Semtex, kneedexplosieven die veel krachtiger waren dan industrieel dynamiet.

Jericho had twee belangrijke militaire commandoposten geïdentificeerd, ondergebracht in ondergrondse ruimten en onzichtbaar vanuit de lucht.

De kleine kring rondom Saddam Hoessein geloofde nu heilig dat Saddam een belangrijke rol had gespeeld in de val van Margaret Thatcher. Al twee keer had hij zijn absolute weigering uitgesproken om een vrijwillige aftocht uit Koeweit zelfs maar te overwegen.

Ten slotte meldde Jericho dat hij nog nooit had gehoord van een wapen met de codenaam De Vuist van God, maar dat hij zijn oor te luisteren zou leggen. Persoonlijk geloofde hij niet dat Irak beschikte over een wapen of een wapensysteem dat de Coalitie nog niet kende.

Martin sprak de tekst op de band in, versnelde de opname en verstuurde het bericht. In Riyad werd het gretig ontvangen. De radiotechnici noteerden het tijdstip van binnenkomst: 23.55 uur, 30 november 1990.

Leila Al-Hilla kwam langzaam de badkamer uit. Ze bleef in de deuropening staan, tegen het licht, legde haar handen tegen de deurposten en hield die pose even vol.

Het licht dat door haar negligé viel, benadrukte haar rijpe, goedgevormde figuur. Dat moest voldoende zijn. Het nachthemd was van zwart kant – geïmporteerd uit Parijs en gekocht bij een boetiek in Beiroet. Het had een klein fortuin gekost.

De grote man in het bed wierp haar een hongerige blik toe, likte met zijn tong langs zijn dikke onderlip en grijnsde.

Leila trok zich graag even in de badkamer terug voordat ze seks had. Daar waste ze zich, gebruikte wat zalf, maakte haar ogen op, stiftte haar lippen rood en besprenkelde zich met parfum – verschillende geurtjes op verschillende plaatsen.

Ze had een mooi lichaam voor een vrouw van dertig lentes, het soort lichaam waar haar klanten van hielden: niet dik, maar goed gevuld en gespierd, met stevige heupen en borsten.

Ze liet haar armen zakken en liep naar het zwak verlichte bed, zwaaiend met haar heupen. Haar hoge hakken maakten haar tien centimeter langer en versterkten de deining van haar heupen.

Maar de man op het bed, die naakt op zijn rug lag – van top tot teen bedekt met zwart haar, als een beer – had zijn ogen gesloten.

Niet in slaap vallen, eikel, dacht Leila. Niet vanavond, nu ik je nog nodig heb. Ze ging op de rand van het bed zitten, gleed met een scherpe rode vingernagel door het haar op de borst en de buik van de man, trok aan zijn tepels en streelde toen zijn kruis.

Ze boog zich voorover en kuste hem op de lippen met open mond en een zoekende tong. Maar de man reageerde lauw en Leila rook de sterke geur van arak.

Hij is weer dronken, dacht ze. Waarom kan die idioot niet nuchter blijven? Aan de andere kant had de alcohol ook voordelen. Goed, aan het werk.

Leila Al-Hilla was een goede call-girl en dat wist ze. De beste in het hele Midden-Oosten, volgens sommigen – in elk geval een van de duurste.

Ze was jaren geleden, als kind, opgeleid aan een zeer besloten academie in Libanon, waar de seksuele technieken en trucs van de *ouled-nails* uit Marokko, de *nautsh* uit India en de subtiele methoden van *Fukutomi-cho* door de oudere meisjes werden gedemonstreerd, terwijl de kinderen toekeken en leerden.

Na vijftien jaar ervaring wist ze dat negentig procent van het werk van een goede hoer niets te maken heeft met het probleem van een onverzadigbare viriliteit. Dat komt alleen voor in pornobladen en films.

Vleien, complimentjes geven, bewondering veinzen, daar ging het om. Maar nog belangrijker was het om al die geborneerde kerels met hun afnemende potentie nog tot een erectie te krijgen.

Ze streek met haar tastende hand naar zijn kruis en voelde zijn penis. Slap als een vaatdoek, dacht ze met een onhoorbare zucht. Generaal Abdullah Kadiri, commandant van het Pantserkorps van het Iraakse leger, had vanavond wat hulp nodig.

Onder het bed had ze een tas van zachte stof verborgen, die ze nu tevoorschijn haalde en leeggooide op het bed.

Ze spoot een dikke, romige crème op haar vingers, smeerde er een middelgrote vibrator mee in, tilde een van de dijen van de generaal op en stak het ding handig in zijn anus.

Generaal Kadiri bromde, opende zijn ogen, zag de naakte vrouw die bij zijn genitaliën zat geknield en grijnsde met blikkerende tanden onder zijn zwarte snor.

241

Leila drukte op de schijf aan de onderkant van de vibrator en een trillende sensatie trok door het onderlichaam van de generaal. Onder haar hand voelde Leila het slappe orgaan omhoog komen.

Uit een flesje met een tuit nam ze een hap smakeloze, reukloze vaseline, boog zich naar voren en nam de opzwellende penis in haar mond.

De combinatie van de gladde, zachte vaseline en de snelle bewegingen van haar ervaren tong had het gewenste effect. Tien minuten lang, totdat haar kaken er pijn van deden, zoog en liefkoosde ze de erectie van de generaal, tot hij zo stijf mogelijk was.

Voordat hij weer kon verslappen, tilde ze haar hoofd op, sloeg haar volle dijbeen over hem heen, bracht hem bij haar naar binnen en ging op zijn heupen zitten. Ze had weleens een grotere en betere gevoeld, maar het lukte – min of meer.

Ze leunde naar voren en zwaaide haar borsten over zijn gezicht. 'O, mijn grote, sterke, zwarte beer,' koerde ze. 'Wat ben je weer geweldig.'

Hij glimlachte tegen haar. Ze bewoog zich omhoog, niet te snel, totdat ze zijn eikel nog juist tussen haar schaamlippen hield, en toen weer omlaag, totdat ze hem helemaal omvatte. Daarbij kneep ze met de goed ontwikkelde en geoefende spieren van haar vagina, en liet hem weer los – knijpen en los, knijpen en los.

Ze kende het effect van die dubbele sensatie. Generaal Kadiri begon te grommen en toen te schreeuwen, korte heftige kreten die hem werden ontlokt door de trillingen in zijn anus en de bewegingen van de vrouw die in steeds sneller tempo zijn erectie bereed.

'Ja, ja, ja, o ja! Wat lekker! Ga door, schat!' hijgde ze in zijn gezicht totdat hij eindelijk een orgasme kreeg. Toen hij klaarkwam tussen haar dijen, richtte Leila zich op, kromde haar bovenlijf en begon te schokken en te gillen alsof ze een geweldig hoogtepunt bereikte.

Meteen verslapte hij weer. Leila klom van hem af, gooide de dildo opzij en kroop snel naast hem, uit angst dat hij meteen in slaap zou vallen. Dat was het laatste wat ze wilde na al haar inspanningen. Ze was nog niet met hem klaar.

Ze trok het laken over hem heen, steunde op een elleboog, drukte haar borst tegen zijn gezicht en streelde zijn haar en zijn wang met haar vrije rechterhand.

'Arme beer,' mompelde ze. 'Ben je zo moe? Je werkt veel te hard, fantastische minnaar van me. Ze beulen je af. Wat was het vandaag nu weer? Meer problemen in de Raad? En jij moet ze weer oplossen, hmmm? Vertel het maar aan Leila. Je weet dat je alles aan je kleine Leila kunt vertellen.'

En dat deed hij, voordat hij in slaap viel.

Later, toen generaal Kadiri snurkend zijn roes van arak en seks uitsliep, liep Leila weer naar de badkamer. Ze deed de deur op slot, ging op de wc zitten met een dienblad op haar schoot en noteerde alles wat ze had gehoord in een keurig Arabisch handschrift.

Straks, als het ochtend was, zou ze de dunne velletjes – verborgen in een uitgeholde tampon voor het geval ze werd aangehouden – aan de man geven die haar betaalde.

Het was gevaarlijk, dat wist ze, maar het leverde veel geld op. Een dubbele betaling voor hetzelfde werk. Ooit zou ze rijk zijn. Rijk genoeg om voorgoed uit Irak te vertrekken en haar eigen academie te beginnen, misschien in Tanger, met genoeg lieve meisjes om mee te slapen en jonge Marokkaanse bedienden om af te ranselen als ze daar zin in had.

De veiligheidsmaatregelen van de Winkler Bank waren al frustrerend genoeg voor Gidi Barzilai, en het schaduwen van Wolfgang Gemütlich had na twee weken nog helemaal niets opgeleverd. De man was een ramp.

Zodra de verspieder hem had geïdentificeerd, hadden ze Gemütlich gevolgd naar zijn huis voorbij het Prater. De volgende dag, toen hij naar zijn werk was, had het Yarid-team het huis in de gaten gehouden toen Frau Gemütlich vertrok om boodschappen te doen. Het vrouwelijke lid van het team ging haar achterna en hield via de radio contact met haar collega's om hen te waarschuwen zodra ze terugkwam. Maar de vrouw van de bankier bleef twee uur weg, en dat was lang genoeg.

Het Neviot-team had geen moeite om het huis binnen te komen. Ze verborgen hun microfoontjes in de zitkamer, de slaapkamer en de telefoon. Snel en vakkundig doorzochten ze het huis, zonder een spoor achter te laten, maar de inspectie leverde niets op. Ze vonden de gebruikelijke papieren: de koopakte van het huis, paspoorten, geboortebewijzen, een huwelijksboekje en zelfs een aantal bankafschriften. Alles werd gefotografeerd, maar aan zijn privé-rekening te oordelen had Gemütlich geen geld van de Winkler Bank verduisterd. Het leek erop dat de man volkomen eerlijk was. Heel verontrustend.

In de kleerkast en de ladekastjes op de slaapkamer waren geen bewijzen van bizarre voorkeuren te vinden – altijd een goede reden voor chantage onder de respectabele middenklasse. Niet dat de leider van het Neviot-team, toen hij Frau Gemütlich had gezien, iets anders had verwacht. Zijn secretaresse was al onbeduidend genoeg, maar zijn vrouw leek helemaal een muis. Zelden had de Israëli zo'n timide wijfje gezien.

Toen ze werden gewaarschuwd dat de vrouw van de bankier weer op de terugweg was, waren de Neviot-experts allang klaar met hun werk en gingen ervandoor. De man in het uniform van de telefoonmaatschappij trok de voordeur achter zich dicht nadat de rest via de achtertuin was vertrokken.

Vanaf dat moment werden alle gesprekken in huize Gemütlich afgeluisterd in een bestelbusje aan het einde van de straat.

243

Twee weken later meldde de wanhopige Neviot-leider dat ze nauwelijks één bandje vol hadden. De eerste avond hadden ze achttien woorden opgenomen: 'Hier is je eten, Wolfgang,' had de vrouw gezegd. Geen antwoord. Ze had om nieuwe gordijnen gevraagd. Geweigerd. 'Het is morgen weer vroeg dag,' had hij toen gezegd. 'Ik ga naar bed.'

'Dat zegt hij iedere avond, verdomme. Misschien al wel dertig jaar,' klaagde de Neviot-man.

'En de seks?' informeerde Barzilai.

'Klets toch niet, Gidi. Ze praten niet eens met elkaar, laat staan dat ze neuken.'

Alle pogingen om Wolfgang Gemütlich op slechte gewoonten te betrappen mislukten. Hij bezondigde zich niet aan gokken, kleine jongetjes, wilde feesten, nachtclubs, maîtresses of prostituées. Eén keer ging hij 's avonds van huis. Het Neviot-team leefde op.

Gekleed in een donkere jas en hoed liep Gemütlich na het avondeten door de donkere buitenwijk naar een huis op vijf straten afstand.

Hij klopte aan en wachtte. De deur ging open en hij stapte naar binnen. Even later ging het licht op de benedenverdieping aan, achter dikke gordijnen. Voordat de deur dichtging, had een van de Israëli's een glimp opgevangen van een grimmig ogende vrouw in een wit uniform.

Een besloten badhuis? Een sauna met twee strenge dames die de berketwijgjes hanteerden? Toen ze de volgende morgen navraag deden, bleek de vrouw in het uniform een oudere pedicure te zijn, met een kleine praktijk aan huis. Wolfgang Gemütlich had zijn likdoorns laten weghalen.

Op de eerste december ontving Gidi Barzilai een brandbrief van Kobi Dror uit Tel Aviv. De tijd begon te dringen. De Verenigde Naties hadden Irak tot 16 januari de tijd gegeven zich uit Koeweit terug te trekken. Zo niet, dan was het oorlog en kon er van alles gebeuren. Opschieten dus.

'Gidi, we kunnen die klootzak schaduwen tot we erbij neervallen,' zeiden de twee teamleiders tegen hun chef, 'maar het levert gewoon niets op. Hij heeft geen zonden. Onbegrijpelijk. Er is niets wat we tegen hem kunnen gebruiken.'

Barzilai stond in tweestrijd. Ze zouden de vrouw kunnen ontvoeren en haar man dreigen dat hij moest meewerken, of anders... Het probleem was dat de vent nog liever zijn vrouw zou verliezen dan een lunchcoupon te stelen. Erger nog, hij zou meteen de politie erbij halen.

Ze konden Gemütlich zelf kidnappen en hem onder druk zetten. Maar ze moesten hem toch naar de bank laten gaan om Jericho's rekening af te sluiten. En terug op de bank zou hij moord en brand schreeuwen. Geen mislukkingen, had Kobi Dror gezegd, en geen sporen.

'Laten we het met de secretaresse proberen,' zei hij ten slotte. Privé-secretaressen wisten vaak net zoveel als hun baas.

En dus richtten de twee teams hun aandacht op de saaie Fräulein Hardenberg.

Voor haar hadden ze nog minder tijd nodig. Tien dagen maar. Ze volgden haar naar haar huis, een klein appartement in een degelijk oud huis bij de Trautenauplatz in het 19e district, de noordwestelijke buitenwijk Grinzing. Ze woonde alleen. Geen minnaar, geen vriend, zelfs geen huisdier. Onderzoek van haar papieren leverde een bescheiden bankrekening op, een oude moeder in Salzburg – het appartement was ooit door de moeder gehuurd, zoals uit het huurboekje bleek, maar de dochter had het zeven jaar geleden overgenomen toen de moeder naar haar geboortestad was teruggegaan.

Edith Hardenberg reed in een kleine Seat die ze voor het huis parkeerde. Maar meestal ging ze met het openbaar vervoer naar haar werk, ongetwijfeld vanwege de parkeerproblemen in het centrum.

Uit haar bankafschriften bleek een armzalig salaris – 'Die gierige klootzakken!' gromde de Israëli die het bedrag zag – en volgens haar geboortebewijs was ze negenendertig. 'Maar ze lijkt wel vijftig,' merkte een ander lid van het Neviot-team op.

Er waren geen foto's van mannen in het appartement te vinden, alleen een van haar moeder, een kiekje van hen allebei, op vakantie aan een of ander meer, en een portret van haar kennelijk overleden vader in het uniform van de douane.

Als er een man in haar leven was, moest dat Mozart zijn.

'Ze houdt van opera, dat is alles,' meldde de Neviot-leider aan Barzilai toen ze de flat weer net zo hadden achtergelaten als ze hem hadden gevonden. 'Ze heeft een grote collectie lp's – nog geen compact-discs. Allemaal opera. Daar gaat al het geld heen dat ze overhoudt. Boeken over opera, componisten, zangers en dirigenten. Affiches van het winterseizoen van de Weense Opera, hoewel ze de kaartjes niet kan betalen...'

'Geen man in haar leven?' vroeg Barzilai peinzend.

'Misschien valt ze voor Pavarotti, als je die kunt krijgen. Verder kun je het wel vergeten.'

Maar Barzilai vergat het niet. Hij herinnerde zich een zaak in Londen, lang geleden. Een ambtenaar bij Defensie, een echte oude vrijster. Toen waren de Sovjets gekomen met een knappe jonge Joegoslaaf... Zelfs de rechter had medelijden gehad tijdens het proces.

Die avond stuurde Barzilai een lang codetelegram aan Tel Aviv.

Half december was de opbouw van het Coalitieleger ten zuiden van Koeweit aangezwollen tot één grote, onafzienbare vloedgolf van manschappen en staal.

Driehonderdduizend mannen en vrouwen uit dertig landen lagen in verschillende linies in de Saoedische woestijn, verspreid over een gebied van meer dan 150 km vanaf de kust naar het westen.

In de havens van Jubail, Damman, Bahrein, Doha, Abu Dhabi en Dubai losten vrachtschepen hun lading kanonnen en tanks, brandstof en voorraden, voedsel en beddegoed, munitie en reserveonderdelen. Er leek geen eind aan te komen.

Vanuit de havens rolden de konvooien naar het westen over de Tapline Road om de grote logistieke bases in te richten die ooit het invasieleger zouden moeten bevoorraden.

Een Tornado-piloot uit Tabuq, die naar het zuiden terugkeerde na een gesimuleerde aanval boven de Iraakse grens, vertelde zijn collega's dat hij over het konvooi was gevlogen vanaf de kop tot aan de staart van de file. Met een snelheid van 800 km per uur had hij er zes minuten over gedaan. De colonne was tachtig kilometer lang en de trucks reden bumper aan bumper.

Op de Logistieke Basis Alfa was een terrein waar de olievaten in rijen van drie boven op elkaar stonden gestapeld, op pallets van één meter tachtig bij één meter tachtig, met paden ertussen ter breedte van een vorkheftruck. Het terrein was veertig kilometer in het vierkant.

En dat was nog maar de brandstof. Op andere gedeelten van Log Alfa lagen granaten, raketten, mortieren, caissons met machinegeweermunitie, antitank gevechtskoppen en anti-pantser granaten. Ergens anders stonden de tankbatterijen en de mobiele werkplaatsen en waren het voedsel, het water, de machines en het reservemateriaal opgeslagen.

Op dat moment had generaal Schwarzkopf zijn Coalitietroepen nog beperkt tot de sector van de woestijn pal ten zuiden van Koeweit. Bagdad wist niet dat de Amerikaanse generaal, voordat de aanval zou beginnen, nog meer troepen over de Wadi el Batin wilde sturen, nog eens honderdvijftig kilometer verder de woestijn in, voor een invasie in Irak zelf. Met een snelle opmars, eerst naar het noorden en vervolgens naar het westen, zou de Republikeinse Garde in de flank worden aangevallen en vernietigd.

Op 13 december vertrokken de Rocketeers, het 336e squadron van het Tactical Air Command van de Amerikaanse luchtmacht, van hun basis bij Thumrait in Oman naar Al Kharz in Saoedi-Arabië. Dat besluit was al op 1 december genomen.

Al Kharz was een kaal vliegveld met een paar start- en taxibanen maar verder niets – geen verkeerstoren, geen hangars, geen werkplaatsen, geen accommodatie voor het personeel, helemaal niets. Een paar stroken beton in de woestijn, dat was alles.

Maar het wàs een vliegveld. Met een verrassend vooruitziende blik had de Saoedische regering in de loop van de tijd genoeg vliegbases laten aanleg-gen voor een luchtvloot die meer dan vijf keer zo groot was als de Saoedische luchtmacht zelf.

Na de eerste december kwamen de Amerikaanse constructeurs. Binnen dertig dagen werd een tentenkamp gebouwd dat onderdak bood aan vijfduizend mensen en vijf squadrons jagers.

De belangrijkste bouwers waren de mannen van de zware genie, de Red Horse-teams, gesteund door veertig grote elektrische generatoren van de luchtmacht. Een deel van de apparatuur werd met diepladers over de weg aangevoerd, maar het meeste kwam per vliegtuig. De genietroepen bouwden de 'schelp'-hangars, de werkplaatsen, de voorraaddepots, de munitieopslagplaatsen, de instructieruimten voor de vliegers, het operationele centrum, de verkeerstoren, de voorraadtenten en de garages.

Voor de bemanningen en het grondpersoneel richtten ze een tentenkamp op met straten, latrines, badhuizen, keukens, eetzalen en een watertoren die werd bevoorraad door trucks vanaf de dichtstbijzijnde waterbron.

Al Kharz ligt tachtig kilometer ten zuidoosten van Riyad, net vijf kilometer buiten het maximale bereik van de Iraakse Scud-raketten. Het zou drie maanden lang de thuisbasis zijn van vijf squadrons – twee squadrons F-15E Strike Eagles, de Rocketeers en de Chiefs, en het 335e van de basis Seymour Johnson, dat nu ook uit Amerika was overgekomen, één squadron F-15C aanvals-Eagles en twee F-16 Fighting Falcon onderscheppingsjagers.

Er was zelfs een speciale straat voor de tweehonderdvijftig vrouwen van de Wing, onder wie een advocaat, grondpersoneel, vrachtwagenchauffeurs, administratief personeel, verpleegsters en twee inlichtingenofficieren.

De bemanningen kwamen met hun eigen toestellen uit Thumrait. Het grondpersoneel en de andere onderdelen werden met vrachtvliegtuigen overgebracht. De hele verhuizing nam twee dagen in beslag. Toen ze arriveerden, was de genie nog steeds aan het werk, en dat zou nog tot Kerstmis duren.

Don Walker had een plezierige tijd gehad in Thumrait. Er waren goede, moderne voorzieningen en de soepele regels van Oman stonden toe dat er op de basis alcohol werd geschonken.

Voor het eerst had hij samengewerkt met de Britse SAS, die hier een permanente trainingsbasis had, en andere 'contractofficieren' die aan de Omaanse strijdkrachten van sultan Qaboos waren toegevoegd. Er waren een paar gedenkwaardige feesten gehouden, er was geen gebrek aan vrouwen om een afspraakje mee te maken, en Don Walker had genoten van de gesimuleerde aanvalsacties van de Eagles langs de Iraakse grens.

Na een rit door de woestijn met hun lichte verkenningswagens had Walker tegen zijn nieuwe squadroncommandant, luitenant-kolonel Steve Turner, opgemerkt: 'Die lui van de SAS zijn totaal gestoord.'

In Al Kharz was alles anders. Saoedi-Arabië, het thuisland van twee heilige plaatsen, Mekka en Medina, houdt een streng verbod op alcohol in stand, en vrouwen zijn verplicht om kleding te dragen die hun hele lichaam tot aan de kin bedekt, de handen en voeten uitgezonderd.

In zijn Algemene Order Nummer 1 had generaal Schwarzkopf een alcohol-verbod ingesteld voor alle Coalitietroepen onder zijn bevel. De Amerikanen hielden zich daar keurig aan, en ook in Al Kharz werd er strikt de hand aan gehouden.

Maar in de haven van Damman verbaasden de Amerikanen zich over de hoeveelheid shampoo die voor de Britse luchtmacht werd aangevoerd. Kisten vol met het spul werden met vrachtwagens of c-130 Hercules transport-vliegtuigen naar de RAF-squadrons vervoerd.

De Amerikaanse havenwerkers konden niet begrijpen hoe de Britten in een omgeving met zo weinig water zoveel tijd konden besteden aan het wassen van hun haar. Het was een mysterie dat tot het eind van de oorlog onopge-lost zou blijven.

Aan de andere kant van het schiereiland, op de woestijnbasis Tabuq, waar Britse Tornado's en Amerikaanse Falcons waren gestationeerd, keken de Amerikaanse piloten nog verbaasder toen ze de Britten tegen zonsonder-gang voor hun tenten zagen zitten met een glas shampoo in hun hand, aan-gelengd met flessewater.

In Al Kharz deed dat probleem zich niet voor. Daar was geen shampoo. En er was heel wat minder ruimte dan in Thumrait. Behalve de wing-comman-der, die een eigen tent had, moest iedereen met een rang lager dan die van kolonel met twee, vier, zes, acht of twaalf mensen een tent delen, afhanke-lijk van zijn rang.

Bovendien was het vrouwenkamp tot verboden gebied verklaard, en dat was een hard gelag, vooral omdat de Amerikaanse dames, geheel volgens hun eigen cultuur en niet bespied door de Saoedische Mutawa (de religieuze politie), heerlijk in bikini konden zonnebaden achter de lage hekken die rond hun tenten waren neergezet.

Dat leidde tot een run op alle hi-lux trucks op de basis, wagens waarvan het chassis hoog boven de wielen was geplaatst. Met deze trucks reden de ware patriotten via een lange omweg naar hun vliegtuigen toe. Als ze onderweg op hun tenen gingen staan, konden ze nog juist zien of de dames in goede vorm waren.

Afgezien van deze avonturen moesten de meesten zich behelpen met een krakende brits en handbediening.

Maar er was ook een andere reden voor de omslag in de stemming. De Ver-enigde Naties hadden Saddam Hoessein een ultimatum gesteld om zich uiterlijk 16 januari uit Koeweit terug te trekken. Maar Bagdad bleef hals-starrig weigeren. Voor het eerst beseften de Coalitietroepen dat een oorlog onvermijdelijk was. En daardoor kregen de oefeningen opeens een heel ander karakter.

Om de een of andere reden was het die 15e december in Wenen heel zacht. De zon scheen en de temperatuur liep op. Tussen de middag stapte Fräulein Hardenberg de bank uit voor een bescheiden lunch, zoals gewoonlijk. In een opwelling besloot ze deze keer een paar broodjes te kopen en ze op te eten in het Stadtpark, niet ver van de Ballgasse.

's Zomers en soms in de herfst deed ze dat ook, maar dan nam ze zelf boterhammen mee van huis. Nu had ze die niet bij zich.

Maar toen ze naar buiten kwam in haar nette tweedjas en naar de heldere blauwe lucht boven de Franziskanerplatz keek, zag ze dat de natuur – al was het maar voor één dag – een *Altweibersommer*, een 'oudewijvenzomer', voor Wenen in petto had. En dus besloot ze om weer eens een broodje in het park te eten.

Er was een speciale reden waarom ze zo gesteld was op het parkje aan de overkant van de Ring. Aan één kant staat de Hübner Kursalon, een restaurant met glazen wanden als een grote serre, waar tussen de middag een klein orkest de muziek van Strauss, de meest Weense van alle componisten, ten gehore brengt.

Wie zich geen lunch bij Hübner kan veroorloven, kan toch in de buurt gaan zitten om te genieten van de muziek. En in het midden van het park, onder zijn stenen boog, staat het standbeeld van de grote Johann zelf.

Edith Hardenberg kocht broodjes bij een lunch-bar, zocht een bankje in de zon en nam een paar happen terwijl ze naar de walsen luisterde.

'*Entschuldigung.*'

Ze schrok op toen ze de zachte stem hoorde.

Fräulein Hardenberg had er een gruwelijke hekel aan om door onbekenden te worden aangesproken. Ze keek opzij.

Hij was jong, met donker haar en zachte bruine ogen, en hij sprak met een buitenlands accent. Ze wilde hem haar rug toekeren toen ze zag dat de jongeman een folder in zijn hand had en naar een woord in de tekst wees. Onwillekeurig keek ze wat er stond. Het was het geïllustreerde programma van de opera *Die Zauberflöte*.

'Neemt u me niet kwalijk. Dit woord, dat is toch geen Duits?'

Met zijn wijsvinger wees hij de term 'libretto' aan.

Op dat moment had ze natuurlijk moeten opstaan en weglopen. Ze begon haar broodjes weer in te pakken.

'Nee,' zei ze kortaf. 'Het is Italiaans.'

'O,' zei de man verontschuldigend, 'ik leer Duits, maar ik spreek geen Italiaans. Betekent het "muziek"?'

'Nee,' zei ze. 'Het betekent de tekst, het verhaal.'
'Dank u,' zei hij oprecht. 'Het is zo moeilijk uw Weense opera's te verstaan, maar ik hou er zo van.'
Haar handen, bezig om de rest van de broodjes in het papier te wikkelen, aarzelden even.
'Het speelt in Egypte,' verklaarde de jongeman. Wat een brutaliteit om háár dat te vertellen, zij die ieder woord van *Die Zauberflöte* kende!
'Ja, dat is zo,' zei ze. Dit was al ver genoeg gegaan. Wie hij ook was, hij was een zeer vrijpostige jongeman. Ze waren al bijna in gesprek. Het idee!
'Net als *Aïda*,' vervolgde hij, weer verdiept in het programma. 'Ik hou van Verdi, maar nog meer van Mozart.'
Ze had haar broodjes ingepakt en wilde vertrekken. Ze hoefde alleen maar op te staan en weg te lopen. Ze draaide zich naar hem toe en juist op dat moment keek hij op en glimlachte tegen haar.
Het was een heel verlegen glimlach, bijna smekend. Hij had bruine ogen, als een spaniel, met lange wimpers waar een fotomodel een moord voor had willen doen.
'Dat is geen vergelijking,' zei ze. 'Mozart is de grootste van allemaal.'
Zijn glimlach werd breder, waardoor ze zijn gelijkmatige, witte tanden zag.
'Hij heeft hier ooit gewoond. Misschien heeft hij hier weleens gezeten, op dit bankje.'
'Natuurlijk niet,' zei ze. 'Toen was dit bankje er nog niet.'
Ze stond op en draaide zich om. De jongeman kwam ook overeind en maakte een kleine Weense buiging voor haar.
'Het spijt me dat ik u heb lastiggevallen, Fräulein. Dank u voor uw hulp.'
Ze liep het park uit om de rest van de broodjes aan haar bureau op te eten. Gesprekken met jongemannen in het park, dacht ze, woedend op zichzelf. Waar moest het met haar naartoe? Aan de andere kant, hij was maar een buitenlandse student die iets over de Weense opera wilde weten. Daar stak toch geen kwaad in? Maar genoeg was genoeg. Ze kwam langs een affiche. O ja, de Weense Opera zou over drie dagen *Die Zauberflöte* opvoeren. Misschien hoorde die wel bij het studieprogramma van de jongen.
Ondanks haar hartstocht was Edith Hardenberg nog nooit naar een voorstelling in het Opernhaus geweest. Ze had het gebouw weleens bezichtigd als het overdag open was, maar de kaartjes waren veel te duur voor haar.
Abonnementen voor de opera werden van generatie op generatie doorgegeven en kostten verschrikkelijk veel geld. Andere kaartjes waren alleen via connecties te krijgen, en die had Edith niet. Zelfs de gewone kaartjes gingen haar begroting ver te boven. Ze zuchtte en liep weer door naar de bank.
Die ene warme dag was ook de laatste. Daarna kwamen de kou en de grijze wolken terug. En Edith at tussen de middag weer in haar vaste café aan haar

vaste tafeltje. Ze was een keurige dame die van regelmaat hield. De derde dag na haar wandeling door het park kwam ze precies op tijd het café binnen, liep naar haar tafeltje en zag in het voorbijgaan dat het tafeltje naast haar bezet moest zijn. Er lagen een paar studieboeken – ze las de titels niet – met een halfleeg glas water ernaast.

Nauwelijks had ze de dagschotel besteld toen er een jongeman van het herentoilet kwam en aan het andere tafeltje ging zitten. Toen hij opkeek, herkende hij haar en reageerde verbaasd.

'O, Grüss Gott... opnieuw,' zei hij.

Edith perste afkeurend haar lippen samen. De dienster bracht het eten. Ze zat in de val. De jongeman liet zich niet afschepen.

'Ik heb het programma uitgelezen. Ik geloof dat ik het nu begrijp,' zei hij.

Ze knikte en begon voorzichtig te eten.

'Fijn zo. Studeert u hier?'

Waarom had ze dat gevraagd? Wat bezielde haar? Maar overal om haar heen werd geanimeerd gepraat. Waar maakte ze zich druk om? Een beschaafd gesprekje, zelfs met een buitenlandse student, kon toch geen kwaad? Ze vroeg zich af wat Herr Gemütlich ervan zou denken. Die zou het niet kunnen waarderen, natuurlijk.

De donkere jongeman grijnsde voldaan. 'Ja. Ik studeer aan de Technische Hogeschool. Als ik klaar ben, ga ik terug om mijn land te helpen opbouwen. Ik heet Karim.'

'Fräulein Hardenberg,' zei ze stijfjes. 'En waar komt u vandaan, Herr Karim?'

'Uit Jordanië.'

O, lieve hemel, een Arabier. Nou ja, er zouden er wel meer studeren aan de Technische Hogeschool, die twee straten voorbij de Kärntner Ring lag. De meeste Arabieren in Wenen waren straathandelaren, vreselijke types die tapijten en kranten verkochten bij de cafés. Je kon ze soms niet van je afschudden. Maar de jongeman naast haar maakte een fatsoenlijke indruk. Misschien kwam hij uit een betere familie. Maar toch... een Arabier? Ze at haar bord leeg en vroeg om de rekening. Tijd om afscheid te nemen van dit jongmens, hoe beleefd hij ook was. Voor een Arabier.

'Maar ik denk niet dat ik erheen durf,' zei hij spijtig.

De rekening kwam. Ze zocht naar een paar schillingbiljetten.

'Waarheen?'

'Naar de opera. Naar *Die Zauberflöte*. Niet in mijn eentje. Dat durf ik niet. Al die mensen. Ik zou niet weten waar ik heen moest of wanneer ik moest applaudisseren.'

Ze glimlachte toegeeflijk. 'Ik denk niet dat je kaartjes kunt krijgen.'

Hij keek verbaasd. 'Nee, dat is het niet.'

Hij stak zijn hand in zijn zak en legde twee kaartjes op tafel. Op háár tafel. Naast haar rekening. De tweede rij stalles. Vlak bij de zangers. In het midden van de zaal.

'Ik heb een vriend bij de Verenigde Naties. Die krijgen kaartjes toegewezen. Maar hij wilde ze niet, dus heeft hij ze aan mij gegeven.'

Gegeven. Niet verkocht, maar gegeven. Die kaartjes waren een kapitaal waard, en hij gaf ze weg!

'Zou ik met u mee mogen?' vroeg de jongeman dringend. 'Alstublieft?'

Het was prachtig geformuleerd, alsof zij hèm zou meenemen.

Ze stelde zich voor hoe het zou zijn om in dat grote, gewelfde, vergulde rococoparadijs te zitten, genietend van de klanken van de bassen, de baritons, de tenoren en de sopranen, weergalmend tegen het beschilderde plafond...

'Hoe komt u erbij?' zei ze bits.

'O, het spijt me, Fräulein. Nu heb ik u beledigd.'

Hij pakte de kaartjes in zijn sterke jonge hand en wilde ze verscheuren.

'Nee!' Ze sloot haar hand om de zijne voordat er meer dan een klein scheurtje in de kostbare kaartjes zat. 'Dat moet u niet doen.'

Ze liep rood aan van verwarring.

'Maar wat moet ik er dan mee?'

'Nou ja...'

Zijn gezicht klaarde op. 'Wilt u me dan het Opernhaus laten zien? Ja?'

Laten zien... Dat was iets anders. Geen afspraakje om samen uit te gaan... Meer een soort rondleiding. Een hoffelijk Weens gebaar om een buitenlandse student een van de wonderen van de Oostenrijkse hoofdstad te laten zien. Dat kon geen kwaad...

Ze troffen elkaar om kwart over zeven bij de ingang. Ze was met de auto uit Grinzing gekomen en had zonder problemen kunnen parkeren. Ze sloten zich aan bij de menigte, die vol verwachting naar binnen stroomde.

Als Edith Hardenberg, na twintig eenzame zomers, ooit het gevoel had gehad dat ze het paradijs betrad, dan was het die avond in 1990 toen ze een paar meter van het toneel zat en helemaal opging in de muziek. Als ze ooit de sensatie had gekend om dronken te zijn, dan was het die avond, toen ze zich liet bedwelmen door het timbre van de stemmen.

Voor de pauze, toen Papageno zong en danste voor haar ogen, voelde ze een droge jonge hand op de hare. Werktuiglijk trok ze haar hand terug. Na de pauze, toen het weer gebeurde, liet ze het zo en voelde met de muziek ook de warmte van een ander mens in haar stromen.

Na afloop leefde ze nog steeds in een droomwereld. Anders had ze het nooit goed gevonden dat hij haar meenam naar het oude stamcafé van Freud, het

Café Landtmann aan de overkant van het plein, dat in zijn oude glorie van 1890 was hersteld. Robert zelf, de unieke hoofdkelner, wees hun een tafeltje waar ze konden eten.

Daarna bracht hij haar terug naar haar auto. Ze stond nu weer met beide benen op de grond en haar bedenkingen waren terug.

'Ik zou het zo leuk vinden als je me het echte Wenen zou laten zien,' zei Karim rustig. 'Jouw Wenen, de stad van de mooie musea en concerten. Anders zal ik nooit de Oostenrijkse cultuur leren begrijpen, niet zoals jij die me kunt tonen.'

'Wat bedoel je, Karim?'

Ze stonden bij haar auto. Nee, ze was niet van plan hem een lift aan te bieden naar zijn appartement, waar dat ook was. En als hij zou voorstellen om met haar mee te gaan, zou ze hem zeggen waar het op stond.

'Dat ik je graag nog eens zou zien.'

'Waarom?'

Als hij zegt dat ik mooi ben, krijgt hij een klap, dacht ze.

'Omdat je aardig bent,' zei hij.

'O.'

Ze bloosde even in het donker. Zonder nog iets te zeggen boog hij zich naar voren en kuste haar op de wang. Toen draaide hij zich om en liep terug over het plein. Ze reed in haar eentje naar huis.

Die nacht droomde Edith Hardenberg onrustig. Het waren dromen over lang geleden. Ooit was er Horst geweest, die haar die lange hete zomer van 1970 vurig had bemind, toen ze nog negentien en maagd was geweest. Horst, die haar maagdelijkheid had genomen en van wie ze was gaan houden. Horst, die 's winters was verdwenen zonder zelfs een briefje of een woord van afscheid.

Eerst was ze bang dat hij een ongeluk had gekregen en had ze alle ziekenhuizen gebeld. Toen dacht ze dat hij voor zijn werk als vertegenwoordiger naar een andere stad was vertrokken en dat hij wel zou bellen.

Later hoorde ze dat hij was getrouwd met het meisje in Graz met wie hij ook had gevreeën als hij in de stad moest zijn.

Ze had gehuild tot aan de lente. Toen had ze alle herinneringen aan Horst uit haar leven verbannen. Zijn cadeautjes had ze verbrand, net als de foto's die ze hadden gemaakt toen ze in het park wandelden en op de vijvers van het Schlosspark van Laxenburg voeren – en vooral de foto van de boom waaronder hij haar voor het eerst echt had bemind.

Daarna waren er geen mannen meer geweest. Ze laten je allemaal in de steek, had haar moeder gezegd, en ze had gelijk. Nooit wilde ze meer iets met een man te maken hebben. Nooit.

Die nacht, een week voor Kerstmis, droomde ze tot aan de ochtend, met het programma van *Die Zauberflöte* tegen haar magere boezem geklemd. En in haar slaap leken sommige rimpels om haar mondhoeken en haar ogen te verdwijnen. Ze glimlachte. Daar stak toch geen kwaad in?

De grote grijze Mercedes had moeite met het verkeer. Luid claxonnerend probeerde de chauffeur zich een weg te banen langs de auto's, de bestelwagens, de marktkraampjes en de handkarren die het bruisende leven tussen de Khulafa- en Rashidstraat beheersten.

Dit was het oude Bagdad, waar kooplui en handelaren, verkopers van textiel, goud en specerijen, venters van alle denkbare koopwaar, al tien eeuwen lang zaken deden.

De Mercedes draaide de Bankstraat in, aan weerskanten geblokkeerd door geparkeerde auto's, en bereikte ten slotte de Shurjastraat. Verderop werd de doorgang volledig gestremd door de kruidenmarkt. De chauffeur draaide zich half om.

'Verder kan ik niet.'

Leila Al-Hilla knikte en wachtte tot het portier voor haar werd geopend. Naast de chauffeur zat Kemal, de forse lijfwacht van generaal Kadiri, een logge sergeant van het tankkorps, die al jarenlang deel uitmaakte van Kadiri's staf. Leila haatte hem.

Na een aarzeling stapte de sergeant uit, rekte zijn lange lichaam en opende het achterportier. Hij wist dat ze hem weer had vernederd. Het stond te lezen in zijn ogen. Zonder hem te bedanken of aan te kijken stapte ze uit.

Een van de redenen waarom ze zo'n hekel aan hem had was dat hij haar overal volgde. Dat was natuurlijk zijn werk, in opdracht van Kadiri, maar dat maakte Leila's afkeer niet minder. Als hij nuchter was, gedroeg Kadiri zich als een harde beroepsmilitair. En op seksueel gebied was hij vreselijk jaloers. Vandaar de regel dat ze nooit in haar eentje de stad in mocht.

De andere reden voor haar weerzin tegen de lijfwacht was zijn duidelijke verlangen naar haar. Ze was een vrouw van de wereld en kon best begrijpen dat mannen haar lichaam wilden. Als ze genoeg betaalden, wilde ze al hun lusten bevredigen, ook de meest bizarre. Maar Kemals belangstelling voor haar was beledigend, omdat hij geen geld had. Hoe durfde hij zulke gedachten te koesteren? En toch deed hij dat – met een mengeling van minachting en brute begeerte, die hij alleen liet blijken als de generaal niet in de buurt was.

Kemal wist dat ze hem verachtte en hij schepte er genoegen in om haar met zijn blikken te beledigen terwijl hij haar zo beleefd mogelijk toesprak.

Ze had al eens haar beklag gedaan bij Kadiri, maar die had erom gelachen.

Hij wantrouwde iedere andere man, maar Kemal had een streepje voor omdat de sergeant hem het leven had gered in de moerassen van Al Fao tegen de Iraniërs. Kemal was bereid voor hem te sterven.

De lijfwacht smeet het portier dicht en liep met haar mee door de Shurjastraat.

De wijk waar ze zich bevonden wordt Agid al Nasara genoemd, de 'christelijke wijk'. Behalve de kerk van St. George aan de overkant van de rivier, gebouwd door de Britten voor het Anglicaanse geloof, zijn er nog drie christelijke gemeenten in Irak, die samen zo'n zeven procent van de bevolking uitmaken.

De grootste is de Assyrische of Syrische kerk, met een kathedraal in Agid al Nasara, vlak bij de Shurjastraat. Anderhalve kilometer verderop staat de Armeense kerk, dicht bij een ander labyrint van straatjes en stegen, de Camp el Arman, de oude Armeense wijk waarvan de geschiedenis vele eeuwen teruggaat.

Vlak naast de Syrische kathedraal staat de H. Jozef, de kerk van de Chaldeeuwse christenen, de kleinste gemeente. Het Syrische geloof vertoont overeenkomsten met de Grieks-Orthodoxe kerk, terwijl de Chaldeeërs een afsplitsing vormen van het rooms-katholieke geloof.

De bekendste vertegenwoordiger van de Chaldeeuwse christenen was de Iraakse minister van Buitenlandse Zaken, Tariq Aziz, hoewel zijn hondentrouw aan Saddam Hoessein en zijn politiek van genocide deden vermoeden dat meneer Aziz wel heel ver van de leer van de Vredesvorst was afgedwaald. Leila Al-Hilla was ook als Chaldeeuws christen geboren, en dat kwam haar nu goed van pas.

Het vreemde koppel kwam bij het smeedijzeren hek van de met keitjes bestrate binnenplaats voor de boogdeur van de Chaldeeuwse kerk. Kemal bleef staan. Als moslim mocht hij geen stap verder doen. Leila knikte tegen hem en stapte door het hek naar binnen. Kemal keek toe terwijl ze een kleine kaars kocht bij een stalletje naast de deur, haar zware kanten sjaal over haar hoofd sloeg en in de donkere, met wierookgeuren bezwangerde kerk verdween.

De lijfwacht haalde zijn schouders op en slenterde weg om een blikje cola te kopen en een plekje te vinden van waaraf hij de kerkdeur in de gaten kon houden. Hij vroeg zich af waarom zijn chef deze onzin toestond. De vrouw was een hoer. Ooit zou de generaal genoeg van haar krijgen, en hij had Kemal al beloofd dat hij zijn gang met haar mocht gaan als het zover was. Hij glimlachte bij het vooruitzicht en een straaltje cola droop langs zijn kin.

In de kerk bleef Leila staan om haar kaars aan te steken met een van de honderden andere die naast de deur stonden te branden. Toen, met gebogen hoofd, liep ze naar de biechthokjes aan de andere kant van het schip. Een priester in een zwarte kazuifel liep haar voorbij maar schonk geen aandacht aan haar.

Het was altijd dezelfde biechtstoel. Ze was precies op tijd, net voor een vrouw in het zwart die ook een priester zocht om haar zonden aan te biechten – waarschijnlijk heel wat banalere zonden dan die van de jonge vrouw die haar opzij duwde en haar plaats innam.

Leila trok de deur achter zich dicht, draaide zich om en ging zitten. Rechts van haar was een bewerkt houten hekwerk. Erachter hoorde ze iets ritselen. Hij was er al. Hij was er altijd, op het afgesproken uur.

Ze vroeg zich af wie hij was en waarom hij haar zo goed betaalde voor de informatie die ze hem bracht. Geen buitenlander, want hij had geen accent. Hij sprak het Arabisch van iemand die in Bagdad geboren en getogen was. En zijn geld was goed. Heel goed.

'Leila?' mompelde hij zacht. Ze moest altijd later dan hij aankomen, en eerder vertrekken. Hij had haar gewaarschuwd dat ze niet buiten de kerk mocht blijven rondhangen om hem te kunnen zien. Maar hoe zou dat mogelijk zijn, met Kemal die voortdurend over haar schouder keek? Die gorilla zou meteen argwaan krijgen en het aan zijn baas rapporteren. Dat risico nam ze niet.

'Wil je je bekendmaken?'

'Eerwaarde, ik heb gezondigd in de zaken des vlezes en ik ben uw absolutie niet waardig.'

Hij had het zinnetje zelf bedacht. Niemand anders zei zoiets.

'Wat heb je voor me?'

Ze stak haar hand tussen haar benen, trok het kruis van haar broekje opzij en haalde de uitgeholde tampon tevoorschijn die hij haar weken geleden had gegeven. Ze schroefde de ene kant los en haalde er een velletje papier uit dat ze strak had opgerold. Ze stak het door het houten hekwerk.

'Wacht.'

Ze hoorde het ritselen van het dunne papier toen de man een geoefende blik wierp op de aantekeningen die ze had gemaakt – een rapport over de beraadslagingen en de besluiten die door de Raad waren genomen, onder leiding van Saddam zelf. Generaal Abdullah Kadiri was er ook bij geweest.

'Goed, Leila. Heel goed.'

Deze keer betaalde hij haar in Zwitserse franken, biljetten met een hoge waarde, die hij haar door het hekwerk toestak. Ze verborg ze op dezelfde plaats waar ze haar informatie had verstopt – een plaats die door de meeste moslim-mannen op bepaalde dagen van de maand als onrein werd beschouwd. Alleen een arts of de gevreesde AMAM zou ze daar ooit vinden.

'Hoe lang gaat dit nog door?' vroeg ze.

'Niet lang meer. De oorlog kan ieder moment uitbreken. En dat betekent het

257

einde van de *Rais*. Anderen zullen de macht overnemen. Ik ben een van hen. Dan pas zul je echt worden beloond, Leila. Blijf kalm, doe je werk en word niet ongeduldig.'

Ze glimlachte. Echt beloond... Geld, heel veel geld, genoeg om ver weg te gaan en de rest van haar leven rijk te zijn.

'Ga nu.'

Ze stond op en verliet het hokje. De oude vrouw in het zwart had een andere priester gevonden voor haar biecht. Leila liep de kerk weer door en stapte het zonlicht in. De gorilla Kemal stond achter het smeedijzeren hek en verfrommelde een blikje in zijn vuist, zwetend in de hitte. Mooi zo, dacht ze. Laat hem maar zweten. Hij zou nog meer zweten als hij wist...

Zonder hem een blik waardig te keuren sloeg ze de Shurjastraat in en liep de drukke markt over naar de wachtende auto. Kemal sjokte woedend maar machteloos achter haar aan. Ze nam geen notitie van een arme *fellagha* die een fiets met een rieten boodschappenmand voortduwde en hij had geen oog voor haar. Hij was naar de markt gestuurd door de kokkin van het huis waar hij werkte, om foelie, koriander en saffraan te kopen.

De man in de zwarte kazuifel van een Chaldeeuwse priester bleef nog even in het biechthokje zitten om er zeker van te zijn dat Leila was verdwenen. Het was heel onwaarschijnlijk dat ze hem zou herkennen, maar in dit spel waren zelfs kleine risico's nog te groot.

Hij had gemeend wat hij tegen haar zei. Er zou oorlog komen. Zelfs de val van de IJzeren Dame in Londen zou daar niets aan veranderen. De Amerikanen hadden het bit tussen hun tanden en zouden het niet meer loslaten.

Als die dwaas in zijn paleis aan de rivier bij de Tamuzbrug maar geen streep door de rekening zou halen door zich vrijwillig uit Koeweit terug te trekken. Gelukkig leek hij vastbesloten zijn eigen ondergang tegemoet te gaan. De Amerikanen zouden de oorlog winnen en daarna naar Bagdad oprukken om het karwei af te maken. Ze zouden zich toch niet tot Koeweit beperken? Nee. Zo dom kon zo'n machtig volk niet zijn.

En als de Amerikanen kwamen, zouden ze een nieuw regime willen. Natuurlijk zouden ze een voorkeur hebben voor iemand die vloeiend Engels sprak, hun leefwijze en denkbeelden kende, en die precies wist wat ze wilden horen. Zijn opvoeding en zijn kosmopolitische achtergrond, die nu in zijn nadeel werkten, zouden dan juist in zijn voordeel zijn. Nu had hij nog geen toegang tot het hoogste overleg en de geheimste besluiten van de *Rais*, omdat hij niet tot die stompzinnige al-Tikriti stam behoorde, of al zijn leven lang een fanatieke aanhanger was geweest van de Ba'ath-partij. En hij was ook geen generaal of een halfbroer van Saddam.

Maar Kadiri was wel een Tikriti en werd door de president vertrouwd. De middelmatige tankgeneraal met de smaak van een bronstige kameel had ooit in de stoffige stegen van Tikrit met Saddam en zijn makkers gespeeld, en dat was genoeg. Hij, Kadiri, was aanwezig bij alle belangrijke vergaderingen en kende alle geheimen. En de man in het biechthokje moest die geheimen weten om zijn maatregelen te kunnen nemen.

Toen hij zeker wist dat de kust veilig was, stond hij op en vertrok. In plaats van het schip over te steken, glipte hij door een zijdeur de sacristie binnen, knikte tegen een echte priester die zich verkleedde voor de dienst, en verliet de kerk door een achterdeur.

De man met de fiets stond maar zes meter bij hem vandaan. Toevallig keek hij op toen de priester in zijn zwarte kazuifel het zonlicht in stapte. Nog net op tijd draaide hij zich om. De man in het priestergewaad keek om zich heen, zag niemand behalve een *fellagha* die over zijn fiets gebogen stond om zijn ketting bij te stellen, en liep snel het steegje door naar een kleine, onopvallende auto.

De *fellagha* voelde het zweet over zijn gezicht stromen. Zijn hart bonsde in zijn keel. Dat had verdomd weinig gescheeld. Hij was bewust uit de buurt gebleven van het Mukhabarat-hoofdkwartier in Mansour om te voorkomen dat hij deze man bij toeval tegen het lijf zou lopen. Wat had hij hier in vredesnaam te zoeken, als priester verkleed in de christelijke wijk?

God, wat was het lang geleden dat ze samen op het gras van de school van meester Hartley hadden gespeeld. Hij herinnerde zich nog dat hij de jongen op zijn smoel had geslagen omdat hij zijn jongere broertje had uitgescholden. En daarna hadden ze samen gedichten voorgelezen in de klas, hoewel Abdelkarim Badri altijd beter was.

Ja, het was lang geleden dat hij zijn oude vriend Hassan Rahmani, de huidige chef van de Iraakse contraspionagedienst, voor het laatst had gezien.

Het liep tegen Kerstmis en in de noordelijke woestijn van Saoedi-Arabië dachten 300 000 Amerikanen en Europeanen aan thuis, in de wetenschap dat ze de feestdagen in een moslim-land zouden doorbrengen. Maar ondanks het naderende geboortefeest van Christus ging de opbouw van de grootste invasiemacht sinds de landing in Normandië gewoon door.

De Coalitietroepen lagen nog steeds pal ten zuiden van Koeweit gelegerd. En was geen enkele aanwijzing dat de helft van die troepen uiteindelijk naar het westen zou oprukken.

In de havensteden kwamen nog altijd nieuwe divisies aan. De Britse 4e Pantserbrigade had zich met de 7e brigade, de Woestijnratten, tot de 1e Pantserdivisie gecombineerd. De Fransen hadden hun contingent inmiddels aangevuld tot 10 000 man, inclusief het Vreemdelingenlegioen.

De Amerikanen waren bezig met het transport van de 1e Cavaleriedivisie, het 2e en 3e Pantsercavalerieregiment, de 1e Gemechaniseerde Infanteriedivisie, de 1e en 3e Pantserdivisie, twee divisies Mariniers en het 82e en 101e Luchtlandingsregiment.

Op eigen verzoek hadden de Saoedische Taakgroep en de Saoedische Speciale Eenheden zich vlak langs de grens gelegerd, met steun van Egyptische en Syrische divisies en andere eenheden uit verschillende kleinere Arabische staten.

De noordelijke wateren van de Perzische Golf waren bijna geplaveid met oorlogsschepen van de Coalitielanden. In de Golf en de Rode Zee aan de andere kant van Saoedi-Arabië hadden de Verenigde Staten vijf vliegkampeskaders gestationeerd, aangevoerd door de *Eisenhower*, de *Independence*, de *John F. Kennedy*, de *Midway* en de *Saratoga*. De *America*, de *Ranger* en de *Theodore Roosevelt* waren nog onderweg.

Alleen al de luchtmacht van deze eskaders, met hun Tomcats, Hornets, Intruders, Prowlers, Avengers en Hawkeyes, vormde een indrukwekkend schouwspel.

In de Golf lag het Amerikaanse slagschip *Wisconsin* in positie, in afwachting van de *Missouri*, die in januari zou komen.

In alle Golfstaten en in heel Saoedi-Arabië was ieder vliegveld volgestouwd met jagers, bommenwerpers, tankers, transportvliegtuigen en radarvliegtuigen, die allemaal voortdurend patrouilleerden, hoewel ze niet in het Iraakse luchtruim doordrongen. Dat deden alleen de spionagevliegtuigen, die zo hoog vlogen dat ze niet werden opgemerkt.

In enkele gevallen deelde de Amerikaanse luchtmacht een vliegbasis met squadrons van de Britse RAF. Omdat de bemanningen dezelfde taal spraken, waren de contacten eenvoudig, informeel en ontspannen. Maar soms waren er ook misverstanden. Een bekend voorbeeld daarvan was een geheime Britse locatie die alleen bekend was onder de afkorting MMFD.

Bij een van de eerste trainingsvluchten werd een Britse Tornado door de verkeersleider gevraagd of hij al een bepaald keerpunt had bereikt. Nee, antwoordde de piloot, hij vloog nog steeds boven MMFD.

Steeds meer Amerikaanse piloten kregen deze naam te horen en zochten op hun kaart naar de juiste plaats. Het was een groot mysterie, om twee redenen: de Britse piloten vlogen er nogal eens overheen en het stond op geen enkele Amerikaanse kaart.

Iemand opperde dat het misschien een foutieve weergave was van KKMC of 'King Khaled Military City', een grote Saoedische vliegbasis. Maar dat leek niet waarschijnlijk en de speurtocht ging door. Na een tijdje gaven de Amerikanen het op. Waar MMFD ook mocht liggen, het was niet te vinden op de kaarten die de Amerikaanse squadrons van de leiding in Riyad hadden gekregen.

Ten slotte losten de Tornado-piloten het mysterie op: MMFD was een afkorting van *'miles and miles of fucking desert'*.

Op de grond leefden de soldaten nu in het hartje van MMFD. Voor de meesten, die onder hun tanks, kanonnen of pantserwagens sliepen, was het leven hard en – erger nog – saai.

Maar er waren ook afleidingen. Een daarvan was het bezoek aan naburige eenheden. De Amerikanen hadden uitstekende britsen, waar de Britten een begerig oog op hadden laten vallen. Toevallig hadden de Amerikanen ook zeer onsmakelijke voorverpakte rantsoenen, vermoedelijk samengesteld door een ambtenaar van het Pentagon die de troep zelf nooit zou willen eten. Ze werden MRE's genoemd, *'Meals-Ready-to-Eat'* ('maaltijden klaar om te eten'), maar volgens de Amerikaanse militairen was het een afkorting van *'Meals-Rejected-by-Ethiopians'* ('maaltijden geweigerd door Ethiopiërs'). De Britten kregen veel beter eten, en naar goed kapitalistisch gebruik ontstond er al snel een levendige handel in Amerikaanse bedden en Britse rantsoenen.

Een ander nieuwtje uit de Britse linies dat de Amerikanen nogal verbaasde was de bestelling van het Britse ministerie van Defensie van een half miljoen condooms voor de soldaten in de Golf. In de verlaten Arabische woestijn kon die aankoop alleen betekenen dat de Britten iets wisten wat de Amerikanen ontging.

Het raadsel werd opgelost op de dag voordat de grondoorlog begon. De Amerikanen waren voortdurend bezig geweest hun geweren te reinigen van het zand, stof en gruis dat steeds in de loop werd geblazen. De Britten trokken de condooms eraf en gingen met glimmende, goed geoliede wapens de strijd in.

Een andere belangrijke ontwikkeling vlak voor Kerstmis was dat de Franse troepen weer bij de plannen werden betrokken.

In het begin hadden de Fransen een rampzalige minister van Defensie, Jean-Pierre Chevenement, die grote sympathie voor Irak scheen te hebben en de Franse commandant opdracht had gegeven alle geallieerde plannen aan Parijs door te geven.

Toen generaal Schwarzkopf dat hoorde, schoten hij en Sir Peter de la Billière bijna in de lach. Monsieur Chevenement was in die tijd ook voorzitter van het Frans-Iraakse Vriendschapsverbond. Hoewel het Franse contingent onder bevel stond van een uitstekende commandant, generaal Michel Roquejoffre, moest Frankrijk nu buiten alle belangrijke plannen worden gehouden.

Tegen het eind van het jaar kreeg Frankrijk een nieuwe minister van Defensie, Pierre Joxe, die de opdracht van zijn voorganger onmiddellijk introk. Vanaf dat moment konden de Amerikanen en de Britten generaal Roquejoffre weer in vertrouwen nemen.

Twee dagen voor de kerst ontving Mike Martin het antwoord van Jericho op een vraag die een week eerder was gesteld. Jericho verklaarde nadrukkelijk dat de kern van het Iraakse kabinet, de Revolutionaire Commandoraad en enkele generaals, de afgelopen dagen in spoedzitting bijeen waren gekomen. Tijdens die vergadering was het punt aan de orde gekomen of Irak zich vrijwillig uit Koeweit zou terugtrekken. Niemand had die vraag concreet gesteld – dat zou heel dom zijn. Iedereen herinnerde zich maar al te goed een eerdere gelegenheid, tijdens de Iraans-Iraakse oorlog, toen Iran had voorgesteld om vrede te sluiten op voorwaarde dat Saddam Hoessein zou terugtreden. Saddam had de meningen gepeild.

De minister van Volksgezondheid had geopperd dat zo'n stap misschien verstandig zou zijn, zuiver als tijdelijke maatregel. Saddam was met de minister naar een zijkamertje gelopen, had zijn pistool getrokken, de man doodgeschoten en daarna de kabinetszitting vervolgd.

De kwestie Koeweit werd op een andere manier naar voren gebracht. De Verenigde Naties werden veroordeeld omdat ze zoiets maar dùrfden voorstellen. Daarna wachtte iedereen op een reactie van Saddam. De president zat als een spiedende slang aan het hoofd van de tafel en nam iedereen scherp op om te zien of hij een teken van ontrouw kon bespeuren.

Omdat de *Rais* niet reageerde, verstomde het gesprek. Toen nam Saddam het woord, heel rustig – zijn gevaarlijkste stemming.

Iedereen, verklaarde hij, die zo'n vernedering van Irak tegenover de Amerikanen zelfs maar overwoog, was een man die zich de rest van zijn leven als voetveeg van de Amerikanen wilde laten gebruiken. Voor zo'n man was geen plaats aan deze tafel.

En dat was dat. Iedereen riep om het hardst dat hij nooit op zo'n gedachte zou zijn gekomen, onder welke omstandigheden ook.

Daarna had de Iraakse dictator er nog iets aan toegevoegd. Alleen als Irak de oorlog zou winnen, voor het oog van de wereld, zouden de Irakezen zich uit hun negentiende provincie kunnen terugtrekken, zei hij. Iedereen rond de tafel knikte wijs, hoewel niemand begreep wat hij bedoelde.

Het was een lang rapport en Mike Martin verstuurde het nog diezelfde nacht naar de villa bij Riyad.

Chris Barber en Simon Paxman zaten uren over de tekst gebogen. Ze hadden allebei besloten om even naar huis te vliegen en de begeleiding van Mike Martin en Jericho aan Julian Gray en de chef van het plaatselijke CIA-bureau over te laten. Ze hadden nog maar vierentwintig dagen voordat het ultimatum van de Verenigde Naties zou verstrijken en generaal Chuck Horner met zijn luchtaanvallen op Irak zou beginnen. Daarom wilden de twee mannen een paar dagen verlof nemen. Ze konden het bericht met zich mee nemen.

'Wat denk je dat hij bedoelt met "winnen, voor het oog van de wereld"?' vroeg Barber.

'Geen idee,' zei Paxman. 'Laten we het maar voorleggen aan experts.'
'Ja. Ik denk dat er de komende dagen niet veel mensen op kantoor zijn. Ik
zal het aan Bill Stewart doorgeven, dan kan hij een analyse laten maken
door een paar deskundigen, voordat het naar de directeur en naar Buitenlandse Zaken gaat.'
'Ik weet wel iemand die ernaar kan kijken,' zei Paxman, en daarmee vertrokken ze naar het vliegveld en stapten op een toestel naar huis.
Op kerstavond kreeg dr. Terry Martin de hele tekst van Jericho's boodschap
te lezen, met de vraag wat Saddam Hoessein zou kunnen bedoelen met een
overwinning op Amerika als prijs voor zijn aftocht uit Koeweit.
'Tussen haakjes,' zei Martin tegen Paxman, 'ik weet dat het tegen de regels
is, maar ik maak me ongerust. En voor wat, hoort wat. Hoe gaat het met
mijn broer in Koeweit? Is alles nog in orde?'
Paxman staarde de arabist een paar seconden aan. 'Ik kan je alleen vertellen
dat hij niet meer in Koeweit zit,' zei hij. 'Meer mag ik er niet over zeggen.'
Terry Martin bloosde van opluchting. 'Dat is het mooiste kerstcadeau dat ik
me kon wensen. Bedankt, Simon.' Hij keek op en zwaaide met zijn wijsvinger. 'Nog één ding. Haal het nooit in je hoofd om hem naar Bagdad te sturen.'
Paxman zat al vijftien jaar in het vak. Zijn gezicht bleef onbewogen, zijn
toon luchtig. De academicus maakte natuurlijk een grapje.
'O nee? Waarom niet?'
Martin dronk zijn glas wijn leeg. De plotselinge schrik in de ogen van de
inlichtingenofficier was hem ontgaan.
'Mijn beste Simon, Bagdad is de enige stad ter wereld waar hij vandaan
moet blijven. Herinner je je die banden van Iraakse gesprekken nog, die ik
van Sean Plummer heb gekregen? Enkele stemmen zijn geïdentificeerd. Ik
herkende een van de namen. Stom toeval, maar ik weet het zeker.'
'Ja?' vroeg Paxman nonchalant. 'Wie dan?'
'Het is natuurlijk lang geleden, maar het moet dezelfde man zijn. En raad
eens? Hij is nu hoofd van de contraspionagedienst in Bagdad. Saddams
belangrijkste spionnenjager.'
'Hassan Rahmani,' mompelde Paxman. Terry Martin moest niet zoveel
drinken, zelfs niet met de kerst. Hij wist niet meer wat hij zei.
'Precies. Ze hebben samen op school gezeten. Wij allemaal. Op die goeie
ouwe school van meester Hartley. Mike en Hassan waren de beste vrienden,
begrijp je? Daarom mag hij niet naar Bagdad.'
Toen ze vertrokken, keek Paxman de kleine, dikke arabist nog even na.
'O, verdomme,' zei hij. 'Godgloeiende...'
Iemand had zojuist zijn Kerstmis vergald, en hij stond op het punt om Steve
Laings feestdagen te verzieken.

Edith Hardenberg was naar Salzburg gegaan om Kerstmis bij haar moeder door te brengen, een traditie van vele jaren.

Karim, de jonge Jordaanse student, was op bezoek bij Gidi Barzilai op zijn onderduikadres, waar de leider van Operatie Joshua een borrel schonk voor de mensen van het Yarid- en Neviot-team die op dat moment geen dienst hadden. Maar één ongelukkige was naar Salzburg afgereisd om Fräulein Hardenberg in het oog te houden voor het geval ze onverwachts naar de hoofdstad zou terugkomen.

Karims werkelijke naam was Avi Herzog en hij was negenentwintig. Een paar jaar eerder was hij naar de Mossad overgeplaatst vanuit Eenheid-504, een afdeling van de militaire inlichtingendienst die zich specialiseerde in acties over de grens. Daarom sprak hij vloeiend Arabisch. Vanwege zijn knappe kop en zijn bedrieglijk verlegen charme die hij naar believen kon gebruiken, had de Mossad hem al twee keer gebruikt om vrouwen te verleiden.

'Hoe gaat het, Don Juan?' vroeg Gidi toen hij de glazen ronddeelde.

'Langzaam,' zei Avi.

'Schiet een beetje op. De chef wil resultaten zien.'

'Het is een behoorlijk gefrustreerde dame,' antwoordde Avi. 'Ze is alleen in een platonische relatie geïnteresseerd – voorlopig.'

Als 'Arabische student' woonde hij in een kleine flat met een 'mede-student', een telefoontechnicus van het Neviot-team die ook Arabisch sprak. Als Edith Hardenberg of iemand anders ooit zou nagaan waar hij woonde en met wie, zou zijn verhaal dus kloppen.

De flat kon iedere inspectie doorstaan. Overal lagen technische studieboeken en Jordaanse kranten en tijdschriften. En de twee mannen hadden zich aan de Technische Hogeschool ingeschreven, voor het geval iemand navraag zou doen.

Het was zijn flatgenoot die zei: 'Een platonische verhouding? Lik m'n reet.'

'Dat heb ik haar ook gevraagd,' zei Avi. 'Maar ze wil niet.'

Toen iedereen was uitgelachen, vervolgde hij: 'Trouwens, ik wil gevarentoeslag.'

'Waarom?' vroeg Gidi. 'Ben je bang dat ze hem eraf bijt als je je broek laat zakken?'

'Nee. Het zijn al die musea, concerten, opera's en recitals. Straks sterf ik nog van verveling.'

'Je doet je best maar, mooie jongen. Je bent hier alleen omdat je volgens het Kantoor iets hebt wat wij niet hebben.'

'Ja,' zei het enige meisje van het Yarid-team. 'Ongeveer tweeëntwintig centimeter.'

'Zo kan-ie wel weer, jongedame Yael. Als jij niet oppast, ben je zo weer

264

terug bij de uniformdienst in de Hajarkonstraat.'

Er werd nog een tijd gepraat, gelachen en gedronken. Later die avond ontdekte Yael dat ze gelijk had gehad. Het was een gezellige Kerstmis voor het Mossad-team in Wenen.

'Wat denk je, Terry?'

Steve Laing en Simon Paxman hadden Terry Martin gevraagd naar een van de appartementen van de Firma in Kensington te komen. Daar hadden ze meer privacy dan in een restaurant. Over twee dagen zou het oudjaar zijn.

'Heel boeiend,' zei dr. Martin. 'Fascinerend. Is dit echt? Heeft Saddam dat allemaal gezegd?'

'Waarom vraag je dat?'

'Nou, het lijkt me een vreemd telefoongesprek. Jullie hebben het toch afgeluisterd? Volgens mij is het een verslag van iemand anders over een vergadering waar hij bij is geweest... die vent aan de andere kant van de lijn zegt geen woord.'

De SIS was niet van plan om Terry Martin te vertellen hoe ze aan dit rapport kwamen.

'De andere man zei niets bijzonders. Zo nu en dan bromde hij wat of zei hij ja. Dat hebben we niet genoteerd.'

'Maar Saddam heeft dit letterlijk gezegd?'

'Het schijnt zo.'

'Fascinerend,' herhaalde Martin. 'Het is voor het eerst dat ik iets lees dat niet voor publikatie of voor een groter publiek is bestemd.'

Martin hield niet het handgeschreven bericht van Jericho in zijn hand, dat door zijn eigen broer in Bagdad was vernietigd zodra hij het in de recorder had ingesproken, maar een getypte Arabische transcriptie van de tekst die voor de kerst door Riyad was ontvangen. Century House had er een Engelse vertaling bij geleverd.

'Die laatste zin,' zei Paxman, die nog dezelfde avond naar Riyad terug zou vliegen. 'Waar hij het heeft over "winnen, voor het oog van de wereld". Zegt je dat iets?'

'Natuurlijk. Maar jullie gebruiken het woord "winnen" nog steeds in de Europese of Noordamerikaanse betekenis. "Slagen" zou een betere vertaling zijn.'

'Goed, Terry, maar hoe zou hij kunnen slagen tegen Amerika en de Coalitie?' vroeg Laing.

'Door hen te vernederen. Ik zei al eerder dat hij Amerika voor schut wil zetten.'

'Maar hij is niet van plan zich de komende twintig dagen uit Koeweit terug te trekken? Dat móeten we weten, Terry.'

265

'Luister eens, Saddam is Koeweit binnengevallen omdat zijn eisen niet werden ingewilligd,' zei Martin. 'Hij wilde vier dingen: de overdracht van de eilanden Warbah en Bubijan om toegang te krijgen tot de zee; compensatie voor de extra olie die Koeweit volgens hem uit hun gezamenlijke olieveld pompte; een eind aan de Koeweitse overproduktie; en kwijtschelding van zijn oorlogsschuld van vijftien miljard dollar. Als hem dat lukt, kan hij zich eervol terugtrekken en Amerika het nakijken geven. Dan heeft hij gewonnen.'

'En denkt hij dat die eisen zullen worden ingewilligd?'

Martin haalde zijn schouders op.

'Hij denkt dat de vredesduiven binnen de Verenigde Naties de Amerikanen beentje zullen lichten. Hij gokt erop dat de tijd in zijn voordeel werkt. Als hij de zaak zolang kan rekken dat de VN de moed verliest, krijgt hij misschien gelijk.'

'Ik begrijp niets van die man,' zei Laing bits. 'Hij kent het ultimatum, 16 januari, nog geen twintig dagen. Hij wordt verpletterd.'

'Tenzij een van de permanente leden van de Veiligheidsraad op het laatste moment met een nieuw vredesplan komt en het ultimatum weer wordt verlengd,' opperde Paxman.

Laing keek somber.

'Parijs, Moskou, of allebei,' voorspelde hij.

'Maar als het oorlog wordt, denkt hij dan nog steeds dat hij kan winnen – pardon, dat hij kan "slagen"?' vroeg Paxman.

'Ja,' zei Terry Martin. 'Zoals ik al eerder zei, hij wil de Amerikanen zware verliezen toebrengen. Vergeet niet dat hij een straatvechter uit de sloppen is. Hij heeft niets te maken met de politieke wandelgangen in Caïro of Riyad. Zijn achterban zijn de stegen en bazars waar Palestijnen en andere Arabieren wonen die de pest hebben aan de Amerikanen omdat ze Israël steunen. Iedereen die Amerika een tik kan uitdelen, hoe hoog de prijs voor zijn eigen land ook is, kan op de steun van die miljoenen rekenen.'

'Maar dat lukt hem niet,' hield Laing vol.

'Hij denkt van wel,' wierp Martin tegen. 'Hoor eens, hij is slim genoeg om te weten dat de Amerikanen zich geen nederlaag kunnen permitteren. Dat kan gewoon niet. Kijk maar naar Vietnam. De veteranen uit die oorlog werden met rotte tomaten bekogeld toen ze terugkwamen. Zware verliezen tegen een verachtelijke tegenstander staat voor de Amerikanen gelijk aan een nederlaag. Dat is niet aanvaardbaar. Saddam kan vijftigduizend man opofferen, waar en wanneer dan ook. Dat maakt hem niets uit. Uncle Sam wel. Als Amerika dergelijke verliezen zou lijden, is dat een ramp. Dan zullen er koppen rollen, carrières sneuvelen, regeringen vallen. De beschuldigingen en het zelfverwijt zullen een generatie lang doorwerken.'

'Maar dat lukt hem niet,' zei Laing nog eens.

'Hij denkt van wel,' herhaalde Martin.

'Gifgas,' mompelde Paxman.

'Misschien. Tussen haakjes, hebben jullie nog ontdekt wat die opmerking in dat telefoongesprek betekende?'

Laing keek naar Paxman. Jericho. Ze mochten niets zeggen over Jericho.

'Nee. Niemand had ooit van die naam gehoord. Geen idee.'

'Het kan belangrijk zijn, Steve. Iets anders... geen gifgas.'

'Terry,' zei Laing geduldig, 'over minder dan twintig dagen zullen wij, de Amerikanen, de Fransen, de Italianen, de Saoedi's en de anderen de grootste luchtmacht op Saddam afsturen die de wereld ooit heeft gezien, met genoeg capaciteit om binnen nog eens twintig dagen evenveel bommen af te werpen als in de hele Tweede Wereldoorlog. De generaals in Riyad hebben het druk. We kunnen moeilijk zeggen dat ze alles stil moeten leggen omdat wij in een telefoongesprek een zinnetje hebben gehoord dat we niet begrijpen. Laten we eerlijk zijn, het was gewoon iemand die in zijn enthousiasme riep dat God aan hun kant stond.'

'Ja, dat is niet zo vreemd, Terry,' beaamde Paxman. 'Volkeren die een oorlog beginnen hebben altijd beweerd dat ze God aan hun zijde hadden. En meer was het niet.'

'Die andere man zei dat hij zijn mond moest houden en ophangen,' wees Martin hen terecht.

'Hij had het druk en hij was geïrriteerd.'

'Hij noemde hem een hoerezoon.'

'Hij mocht hem zeker niet.'

'Misschien.'

'Terry, laat het nou rusten. Het was zomaar een opmerking. Waarschijnlijk ging het over gifgas. Daar rekenen ze op. Met de rest van je analyse zijn we het volledig eens.'

Martin vertrok als eerste, de twee inlichtingenofficieren twintig minuten later. Diep in hun jassen gedoken, met hun kraag omhoog, zochten ze naar een taxi.

'Weet je,' zei Laing, 'hij is een slimme vogel en ik mag hem wel. Maar hij kan vreselijk zeuren. Je kent zijn privé-leven?'

Een lege taxi reed voorbij, met gedoofde lichten. Theepauze. Laing vloekte.

'Ja, natuurlijk. De Box heeft een onderzoek gedaan.'

De Box, of Box 500, is jargon voor de veiligheidsdienst MI-5. Ooit, heel lang geleden, was het postadres van MI-5 inderdaad postbus 500 in Londen.

'Ik bedoel maar,' zei Laing.

'Steve, dat heeft er toch niets mee te maken?'

Laing bleef staan en keek zijn ondergeschikte aan. 'Simon, geloof me nou maar. Hij berijdt een stokpaardje en hij verspilt onze tijd. Neem een goede raad van mij aan en laat die professor vallen.'

'Het moet gifgas zijn, meneer de president.'
Drie dagen na nieuwjaar waren de feestelijkheden in het Witte Huis – voorzover daar tijd voor was geweest, want alles ging gewoon door – allang voorbij. De hele westelijke vleugel, het hart van de Amerikaanse regering, bruiste van activiteit.
In de rust van het Oval Office zat George Bush achter zijn grote bureau, met zijn rug naar de hoge ramen met het twaalf centimeter dikke, lichtgroene, kogelvrije glas, onder het wapen van de Verenigde Staten.
Tegenover hem zat generaal Brent Scowcroft, de nationale veiligheidsadviseur van de president.
De president wierp een blik op de samenvatting van de analyses die hij op zijn bureau had liggen.
'Is iedereen het daarover eens?' vroeg hij.
'Ja. Ook de mensen in Londen. Saddam Hoessein zal zich niet uit Koeweit terugtrekken tenzij hij zijn gezicht kan redden, en die kans zullen we hem niet geven. Verder vertrouwt hij op massale gasaanvallen op de grondtroepen van de Coalitie, voor of tijdens de invasie.'
George Bush was de eerste Amerikaanse president sinds John F. Kennedy die zelf ooit had gevochten. Hij had Amerikanen zien sneuvelen in de strijd. Maar de gedachte dat jonge soldaten moesten sterven, kronkelend van pijn terwijl het gas hun longweefsels verscheurde en hun zenuwstelsel vernietigde, was gruwelijk en smerig.
'En hoe wil hij dat gas lanceren?' vroeg hij.
'Volgens ons zijn er vier mogelijkheden. Hij kan het gas in capsules laten afwerpen door jagers en jachtbommenwerpers. Dat ligt het meest voor de hand. Colin Powell heeft zojuist gebeld met Chuck Horner in Riyad. Generaal Horner denkt dat hij vijfendertig dagen nodig heeft voor zijn luchtoorlog. Na de twintigste dag zullen de Iraakse vliegtuigen de grens niet meer kunnen bereiken. Na de dertigste dag zal geen enkel Iraaks toestel langer dan een minuut in de lucht kunnen blijven. Dat is een harde garantie. Daar zet hij zijn carrière voor op het spel.'
'En de andere mogelijkheden?'
'Saddam heeft een aantal raketbatterijen voor de middellange en lange afstand.'
De Iraakse raketsystemen waren van Russische makelij en gebaseerd op de oude Katjoesjka's die in de Tweede Wereldoorlog met zo'n verwoestend effect door het Russische leger waren gebruikt. De gemoderniseerde versie kon in hoog tempo vanaf een rechthoekige 'batterij' op de achterkant van

268

een truck of een vaste stelling worden afgevuurd en had een bereik van 100 km.

'Gezien hun actieradius moeten ze vanuit Koeweit of de westelijke Iraakse woestijn worden gelanceerd. De JSTARS moeten ze met hun radar kunnen vinden zodat we ze kunnen uitschakelen. Camouflage heeft geen zin, want het metaal blijft zichtbaar op de radar.

Verder heeft Irak nog een grote voorraad artilleriegranaten waarmee gifgas kan worden afgevuurd. Het bereik is niet groter dan 37 kilometer. We weten dat die granaten al ter plaatse zijn, maar met een dergelijke actieradius komen ze niet ver. De Irakezen moeten ze vanuit de woestijn afvuren, waar ze geen enkele dekking hebben. Onze luchtmacht is ervan overtuigd dat we ze kunnen vernietigen. En dan zijn er nog de Scuds. Daar wordt nu al aan gewerkt.'

'En de preventieve maatregelen?'

'Die zijn voltooid, meneer de president. Iedereen is tegen miltvuur ingeënt. De Britten ook. Ieder uur neemt de produktie van anti-miltvuur vaccin nog toe. Verder hebben alle mannen en vrouwen een gasmasker en beschermende kleding. Als hij het zou proberen...'

De president stond op, draaide zich om en keek naar het Amerikaanse wapen. De kale adelaar, met de pijlen in zijn klauwen, keek terug.

Twintig jaar geleden had hij die lugubere plastic zakken met de lijken van gesneuvelde Amerikanen uit Vietnam zien terugkeren. Hij wist dat veel meer van dergelijke zakken nu in discrete containers onder de Saoedische zon lagen te wachten.

Ondanks alle voorzorgsmaatregelen zouden delen van de huid toch onbedekt blijven en zouden er soldaten zijn die te laat hun gasmaskers opzetten.

Het volgend jaar waren er verkiezingen. Maar daar ging het hem niet om. Of hij die verkiezingen nu zou winnen of verliezen, hij wilde niet de geschiedenis ingaan als de president die tienduizenden soldaten de dood in had gejaagd, niet – zoals in Vietnam – in negen jaar tijd, maar binnen een paar weken of zelfs dagen.

'Brent...'

'Meneer de president?'

'James Baker heeft binnenkort een gesprek met Tariq Aziz.'

'Ja. Over zes dagen, in Genève.'

'Vraag of hij bij me langs komt.'

De eerste week van januari begon Edith Hardenberg weer echt van het leven te genieten, voor het eerst in jaren. Ze vond het heerlijk om haar gretige jonge vriend te laten kennismaken met de wonderen van de Weense cultuur. Het personeel van de Winkler Bank had omstreeks de jaarwisseling vier

269

dagen vakantie. Daarna zouden ze hun culturele uitstapjes tot de avonden moeten beperken. Maar dan konden ze naar het theater, naar concerten of recitals gaan. En in het weekend waren de musea en galeries ook open.

Ze brachten een halve dag door in het Jugendstil, om de art nouveau te bewonderen, en nog een halve dag in het Sezession, met de permanente expositie van het werk van Klimt.

De jonge Jordaniër was verrukt en vroeg honderduit. Zijn enthousiasme werkte aanstekelijk en Ediths ogen straalden toen ze hem vertelde dat er nog een prachtige tentoonstelling in het Künstlerhaus was, waar ze het volgende weekend absoluut naartoe moesten.

Na het bezoek aan de Klimt-expositie nam Karim haar mee uit eten in de Rotisserie Sirk. Ze vond het veel te duur, maar haar nieuwe vriend verzekerde haar dat zijn vader een rijke chirurg in Amman was en dat hij een ruime toelage kreeg.

Tot haar eigen verbazing stond ze hem toe een glas wijn voor haar in te schenken, en ze zag niet dat hij het steeds bijvulde. Ze praatte geanimeerd en er kwam een blosje op haar bleke wangen.

Bij de koffie boog Karim zich naar voren en legde zijn hand op de hare. Verward keek ze om zich heen of iemand het had gezien, maar niemand lette op hen. Ze trok haar hand wel terug, maar heel langzaam.

Tegen het eind van de week hadden ze vier van de culturele bezienswaardigheden bezocht die ze in gedachten had, en toen ze na een avond in de Musikverein door de kille duisternis terugliepen naar haar auto, nam hij haar gehandschoende hand in de zijne en hield hem vast. Ze protesteerde niet en voelde zijn warmte door de katoenen handschoen heen.

'Het is heel aardig van je om dit allemaal voor mij te doen,' zei hij ernstig. 'Ik weet zeker dat het heel saai voor je is.'

'Nee, helemaal niet,' zei ze ernstig. 'Ik hou zelf ook van al die mooie dingen. En ik ben blij dat jij ervan geniet. Nog even en je bent een expert in de Europese kunst en cultuur.'

Toen ze bij haar auto kwamen, keek hij met een glimlach op haar neer, nam haar koude gezicht in zijn blote maar opvallend warme handen en kuste haar zachtjes op haar lippen.

'Danke, Edith.'

Toen vertrok hij. Ze reed in haar eentje naar huis, zoals altijd, maar haar handen trilden en ze raakte bijna een tram.

Op 9 januari had de Amerikaanse minister van Buitenlandse Zaken, James Baker, in Genève een ontmoeting met zijn Iraakse collega Tariq Aziz. Het was een lang gesprek, en niet bepaald vriendschappelijk. Dat was ook niet de bedoeling. Er was een Engels-Arabische tolk aanwezig, hoewel Tariq

Aziz uitstekend Engels kende en geen enkele moeite had de Amerikaan, die langzaam en duidelijk sprak, te verstaan.

Zijn boodschap was heel simpel: als uw regering tijdens de vijandelijkheden die mogelijk tussen onze landen zullen uitbreken, besluit om gifgas te gebruiken – een wapen dat volgens de internationale verdragen verboden is – kan ik u en president Hoessein meedelen dat mijn land gebruik zal maken van nucleaire middelen. Met andere woorden, dan zullen we een kernbom op Bagdad gooien.

De kleine, dikke Irakees met het grijze haar kon het nauwelijks geloven. Om te beginnen zou niemand bij zijn volle verstand zo'n dreigement aan de *Rais* durven overbrengen. Net als de vroegere Babylonische vorsten had Saddam de gewoonte zijn ongenoegen op de boodschapper af te reageren.

Bovendien wist hij niet zeker of de Amerikaan het serieus meende. De fallout en de andere gevolgen van een kernaanval zouden niet tot Bagdad beperkt blijven. Het halve Midden-Oosten zou erdoor worden verwoest.

Tariq Aziz reisde ongerust naar Bagdad terug. Er waren drie dingen die hij niet wist.

Een van die dingen was dat de moderne, zogenaamde 'slagveld'-kernbommen totaal verschillen van de bom die in 1945 op Hirosjima was geworpen. De explosie en de hitte van de nieuwe 'schone' bommen hebben nog steeds dezelfde afschuwelijke uitwerking, maar de radioactiviteit lost veel sneller op.

Het tweede punt was dat het slagschip *Wisconsin*, dat in de Golf voer en spoedig gezelschap zou krijgen van de *Missouri*, drie zeer bijzondere kisten van staal en beton aan boord had, sterk genoeg om tienduizend jaar intact te blijven als het schip zou zinken. In deze kisten zaten drie Tomahawk-kruisraketten waarvan de Verenigde Staten hoopten dat ze die nooit zouden hoeven gebruiken.

Het derde punt was dat de Amerikaanse minister van Buitenlandse Zaken het zeer serieus had gemeend.

Generaal Sir Peter de la Billière wandelde in zijn eentje door de donkere woestijn, alleen vergezeld van het knerpen van het zand onder zijn voeten en zijn eigen bezorgde overpeinzingen.

De la Billière, een beroepsmilitair met een lange ervaring in de strijd, gaf de voorkeur aan een sobere levensstijl die goed bij zijn schrale gestalte paste. Hij hield niet van de luxe van de stad en voelde zich meer op zijn gemak in legerkampen, bivaks en het gezelschap van zijn medesoldaten. Net als anderen vóór hem genoot hij van de Arabische woestijn met de weidse horizonten, de brandende hitte, de felle kou en de indrukwekkende stilte.

Die avond, bij een bezoek aan het front, had hij zichzelf een wandeling

271

beloofd. Na de inspectie was hij vertrokken uit het St. Partick's Camp, waar de dreigende Challenger-tanks onder hun camouflagenetten stonden te wachten als roofdieren, klaar voor de aanval, terwijl de bemanningen onder hun voertuigen het avondeten klaarmaakten.

De la Billière, inmiddels goed bevriend met generaal Schwarzkopf en op de hoogte van alle geheime plannen, wist dat een oorlog onvermijdelijk was. Binnen een week zou het ultimatum van de Verenigde Naties aflopen en Saddam Hoessein had nog geen enkel teken gegeven dat hij zich uit Koeweit wilde terugtrekken.

Wat hem die avond onder de sterren boven de Saoedische woestijn de meeste zorgen baarde was dat hij geen idee had wat de Iraakse dictator in zijn schild voerde. Als militair had hij graag inzicht in de motieven, de tactiek en de strategie van zijn tegenstander. Persoonlijk had hij niets dan minachting voor de man in Bagdad. Hij gruwde van de bewijzen van genocide, martelingen en moord onder het Iraakse regime. Saddam Hoessein was geen militair, dat was hij ook nooit geweest en zijn schaarse militaire talenten had hij grotendeels verspild door zijn generaals te dwarsbomen en zijn beste bevelhebbers te laten executeren.

Maar daar ging het niet om. Het probleem was dat Saddam persoonlijk alle politieke en militaire beslissingen nam, zonder dat iemand begreep waar hij mee bezig was.

Hij was Koeweit binnengevallen op het verkeerde moment en om de verkeerde redenen. Daarna had hij de kans voorbij laten gaan om zijn mede-Arabieren te tonen dat hij openstond voor redelijke argumenten en dat de zaak binnen de Arabische wereld kon worden opgelost. Had hij dat gedaan, dan zou de oliestroom naar het Westen vermoedelijk in stand zijn gebleven en zou de buitenwereld haar belangstelling hebben verloren terwijl de Arabische conferenties zich jarenlang voort zouden slepen.

Door Saddams eigen onnozelheid was het Westen erbij betrokken geraakt. De bezetting van Koeweit, gepaard met verkrachtingen en andere wreedheden, en de pogingen om Westerse gijzelaars als menselijke schilden te gebruiken, hadden hem volledig geïsoleerd.

In het begin, toen hij de rijke olievelden in het noordwesten van Saoedi-Arabië had kunnen veroveren, had Saddam zich ingehouden. Als zijn leger en luchtmacht door goede generaals waren geleid, hadden de Irakezen zelfs tot Riyad kunnen doorstoten en had Saddam zijn eisen kunnen dicteren. Maar dat had hij niet gedaan, en daarna was operatie Desert Shield gevolgd en had Bagdad in publicitair opzicht de ene blunder na de andere begaan.

Hij was misschien een sluwe straatvechter, maar in alle andere opzichten was hij een strategische onbenul. Of...? Zou iemand echt zo stom kunnen zijn, vroeg de Britse generaal zich af.

Ondanks de gigantische luchtmacht die zich nu tegen hem had verenigd, maakte hij de ene politieke en militaire fout na de andere. Had hij geen idee welke vernietigende kracht binnenkort op Irak zou worden losgelaten? Besefte hij niet dat de dreigende oorlog zijn wapenarsenaal binnen vijf weken tot het niveau van tien jaar terug zou reduceren?

De generaal bleef staan en tuurde naar het noorden. Er was geen maan die nacht, maar de sterren boven de woestijn gaven voldoende licht. Het vlakke landschap strekte zich uit naar het labyrint van zandwallen, loopgraven, mijnenvelden, prikkeldraadversperringen en tankgreppels die de Iraakse verdedigingslinies vormden en waarin de Amerikaanse genietroepen van de Big Red One een bres moesten slaan om de Challengers vrij baan te geven.

Maar nog altijd had de tiran in Bagdad één troef achter de hand waar de Britse generaal zich ernstig bezorgd over maakte. Hij zou zich gewoon uit Koeweit kunnen terugtrekken.

De tijd werkte niet in het voordeel van de geallieerden maar van Irak. Op 15 maart begon de islamitische ramadan. Dan mochten de moslims een maandlang tussen zonsopgang en zonsondergang niets eten of drinken. Tijdens de ramadan kon een islamitisch leger dus nauwelijks functioneren.

Na 15 april zou de woestijn veranderen in een hel met temperaturen van meer dan 50 graden Celsius. De druk van het thuisfront om de jongens naar huis te laten komen zou snel toenemen. Tegen de zomer zou die druk, gekoppeld aan de barbaarse omstandigheden, de doorslag geven. De geallieerden zouden zich moeten terugtrekken en nooit meer op deze schaal kunnen terugkeren. De Coalitie was een eenmalig verschijnsel.

De uiterste datum was dus 15 maart. Voor de grondoorlog waren ongeveer twintig dagen uitgetrokken. Die zou dus uiterlijk op 23 februari moeten beginnen – àls het zover kwam. Maar eerst hadden Chuck Horner en zijn luchtmacht nog vijfendertig dagen nodig om de Iraakse wapens, troepen en verdedigingswerken te vernietigen. Dat betekende dat de aanval niet later dan 17 januari mocht beginnen.

Stel dat Saddam zich zou terugtrekken. Dan zouden een half miljoen geallieerden voor schut staan, verspreid over de woestijn, zonder dat ze ergens naartoe konden. Maar Saddam had categorisch verklaard dat hij Koeweit niet zou verlaten.

Wat was die gek van plan? Wachtte hij soms ergens op – een denkbeeldige goddelijke ingreep die zijn vijanden zou verpletteren en hem tot overwinnaar zou maken?

De la Billière hoorde een stem uit het tankkamp achter hem. De commandant van de Royal Irish Hussars, Arthur Denaro, riep dat het eten klaar was. De stoere, joviale Denaro zou ooit als eerste met zijn tank door de bres heen rijden.

De Britse bevelhebber glimlachte en liep terug. Hij verheugde zich erop om met de mannen in het zand te hurken, met een blikje witte bonen in tomatensaus, luisterend naar de stemmen – al die Engelse en Ierse accenten – bij het schijnsel van het vuur, lachend om de grappen en de plaagstoten, de ruwe taal van kerels die zeiden waar het op stond, onverbloemd maar met gevoel voor humor.

De generaal vervloekte de man in het noorden. Waar wachtte hij in godsnaam op?

Het antwoord op de vragen van de Britse generaal lag op een met kussens bekleed wagentje in het tl-licht van een ondergrondse fabriek, vijfentwintig meter onder de Iraakse woestijn.

Een ingenieur poetste het instrument nog even op en sprong haastig in de houding toen de deur van de ruimte openging. Vijf mannen stapten naar binnen voordat de twee gewapende wachtposten van de presidentiële lijfwacht, de Amn-al-Khass, de deur weer sloten.

Vier van de mannen hielden eerbiedig afstand tot de vijfde, die in het midden liep. Zoals gewoonlijk droeg hij een uniform, glanzend zwarte, halfhoge laarzen, een pistool aan zijn riem en een groen katoenen sjaaltje in de driehoek tussen zijn jasje en zijn kin.

Een van de andere vier mannen was zijn persoonlijke lijwacht, die zelfs hier, waar iedereen vijf keer op verborgen wapens was gefouilleerd, geen moment van zijn zijde week. Tussen de president en zijn lijfwacht stond zijn schoonzoon, Hoessein Kamil, het hoofd van het ministerie van Industrie en Militaire Industrialisatie, het MIMI. Zoals zo vaak had het MIMI de zaak overgenomen van het ministerie van Defensie.

Aan de andere kant van de *Rais* stond het brein van het Iraakse programma, dr. Jaafar al-Jaafar, het genie dat openlijk de Iraakse Robert Oppenheimer werd genoemd. Naast hem, wat verder naar achteren, stond dr. Salah Siddiqui. Jaafar was de natuurkundige, Siddiqui de technicus.

Het staal van hun geesteskind glansde dof in het witte licht. Het ding was ruim vier meter lang en bijna twee meter in doorsnee.

Van de achterkant werd ruim één meter in beslag genomen door een ingewikkeld schokabsorberend mechanisme, dat zou worden afgeworpen zodra het projectiel was gelanceerd. De rest van de drie meter lange huls was in feite een sabot, een mantel die in acht identieke secties was verdeeld. Kleine explosieve bouten zouden de mantel laten breken zodra het projectiel was vertrokken voor zijn missie. Het enige dat dan nog overbleef was de dunne, zestig centimeter brede kern. De sabot was alleen bedoeld om het projectiel wat dikker te maken, zodat het in de één meter brede loop van het kanon paste, en om de vier stijve staartvinnen te beschermen.

Irak beschikte niet over de telemetrie om vanaf de grond via radiosignalen de vinnen van een wapen te besturen, maar de stijve vinnen zouden het projectiel tijdens de vlucht stabiel houden.

De messcherpe neuskegel aan de voorkant was vervaardigd uit ultra-sterk staal. Maar ook die zou uiteindelijk worden afgeworpen.

Als een raket na zijn reis door de ruimte de atmosfeer van de aarde weer binnendringt, ontstaat er door de wrijving met de lucht zoveel hitte dat de neuskegel smelt. Daarom hebben astronauten bij hun terugkeer naar de aarde een hitteschild nodig om te voorkomen dat hun capsule in brand vliegt.

Het projectiel dat de vijf Irakezen die avond bekeken was volgens hetzelfde principe gebouwd. De stalen neuskegel was nuttig bij het opstijgen, maar zou de landing niet overleven. Als hij op zijn plaats zou blijven, zou het smeltende metaal vervormen, waardoor het dalende projectiel zou kantelen en verbranden.

De neuskegel was ontworpen om op het hoogste punt van de baan te exploderen. Eronder zat een kleinere, kortere, stompere kegel van koolstofvezel, die de hitte wel kon weerstaan.

Toen dr. Gerry Bull nog leefde, had hij geprobeerd uit naam van Bagdad een failliete luchtvaartfirma in Noord-Ierland op te kopen. Dit bedrijf, LearFan, had zich gespecialiseerd in de bouw van straaljagers met een groot aantal onderdelen uit koolstofvezels. Het ging dr. Bull en de Irakezen niet om de vliegtuigen, maar om de koolstofvezelmachines van de fabriek.

Koolstofvezel is zeer hittebestendig maar ook lastig te bewerken. De koolstof wordt eerst gereduceerd tot een soort 'wol', waaruit een draad of vezel wordt gesponnen. Deze vezel wordt vele malen over een mal gevlochten en daarna tot de gewenste vorm geperst.

Omdat koolstofvezels van belang zijn voor de rakettechnologie en die technologie geheim is, wordt de export van koolstofvezelmachines streng gecontroleerd. Toen de Britse inlichtingendiensten ontdekten waar de Lear-Fan-apparatuur naartoe ging, pleegden ze overleg met Washington en ketste de zaak af. Daarna ging iedereen ervan uit dat Irak niet aan de noodzakelijke koolstofvezeltechnologie zou kunnen komen.

Dat was een vergissing. Irak probeerde een andere route, die werkte. Een Amerikaanse groothandel in airconditioning- en isolatieprodukten bleek bereid aan een Iraaks mantelbedrijf de machines voor de produktie van steenwol te verkopen. In Irak werden deze machines door Iraakse ingenieurs omgebouwd voor het spinnen van koolstofvezels.

Tussen de neuskegel en de schokdemper aan de achterkant rustte het werk van dr. Siddiqui – een kleine, alledaagse maar perfect functionerende atoombom, met een ontsteking volgens het artillerieprincipe, en met lithium en polonium als katalysatoren om de neutronenstorm te veroorzaken die noodzakelijk was voor het opwekken van de kettingreactie.

In de bom van dr. Siddiqui zat de ware triomf, een ronde bol en een buisvormige plug met een gezamenlijk gewicht van 35 kilo, geproduceerd onder supervisie van dr. Jaafar. Ze bestonden allebei uit zuiver verrijkt uranium-235.

Langzaam verscheen er een voldane glimlach onder de dikke zwarte snor. De president liep ernaartoe en streek met zijn wijsvinger over het gladde staal.

'Zal het werken? Werkt het echt?' fluisterde hij.

'Ja, *sajidi Rais*,' antwoordde de natuurkundige.

Het hoofd met de zwarte baret knikte een paar keer. 'Mijn gelukwensen, broeders.'

Onder het projectiel, op een houten standaard, was een eenvoudige plaquette geschroefd met maar drie woorden: *Qubth-ut-Allah*.

Tariq Aziz had lang nagedacht hoe – en òf – hij het Amerikaanse dreigement aan zijn president moest overbrengen.

Ze kenden elkaar al twintig jaar. Al die tijd had de minister van Buitenlandse Zaken zijn baas trouw gediend. Altijd had hij Saddams kant gekozen in de beginjaren, toen er nog om de macht binnen de Ba'ath-partij gestreden werd. Altijd was hij ervan uitgegaan dat het nietsontziende karakter van de man uit Tikrit zou zegevieren, en steeds opnieuw had hij gelijk gekregen.

Samen hadden ze de gladde paal van de macht binnen de Iraakse dictatuur beklommen, de één altijd in de schaduw van de ander. De kleine, dikke Aziz had het nadeel van zijn hogere opleiding en zijn talenkennis gecompenseerd door blinde gehoorzaamheid.

Hij had het geweld aan anderen overgelaten. Met instemming – zoals iedereen aan het hof van Saddam Hoessein – had hij toegekeken hoe tientallen legerofficieren en partijleden die ooit in de gunst stonden bij talloze zuiveringen waren weggevoerd om te worden doodgeschoten, vaak na langdurige martelingen door de beulen van Abu Khraib.

Hij was er getuige van geweest hoe bekwame generaals waren geëxecuteerd omdat ze voor de belangen van hun mannen opkwamen, en hij wist dat werkelijke samenzweerders een nog gruwelijker dood waren gestorven.

Hij had meegemaakt hoe de Al-Juburi stam, ooit zo machtig binnen het leger dat niemand zich tegen hen durfde te verzetten, was vernederd en van zijn invloed beroofd, totdat de overlevenden zich gehoorzaam aan het nieuwe bewind hadden onderworpen. Hij had gezwegen toen Saddams halfbroer Ali Hassan Majid als minister van Binnenlandse Zaken de volkerenmoord op de Koerden had beraamd, niet alleen in Halabja, maar ook in vijftig andere steden en dorpen die met bommen, artilleriebeschietingen en gifgas waren verwoest.

Net als iedereen in het gevolg van de *Rais* wist Tariq Aziz dat hij nergens naartoe kon. Als zijn chef iets zou overkomen, was het ook met hem gedaan.

Maar anders dan sommigen van zijn collega's was hij te slim om te denken dat dit regime geliefd was bij de bevolking. Zijn grootste angst gold niet het buitenland, maar de verschrikkelijke wraak van het Iraakse volk als hij het ooit zonder Saddams bescherming zou moeten stellen.

Toen hij die 11e januari, na zijn reis naar Europa, op het onderhoud met de president zat te wachten, wist hij nog steeds niet hoe hij het Amerikaanse dreigement moest overbrengen zonder Saddams woede over zich af te roepen. De *Rais* was in staat te denken dat hij, de Iraakse minister, de Amerikanen zelf dit dreigement had ingefluisterd. Paranoia kent geen logica, alleen instinct, dat soms terecht is en soms niet. Heel wat onschuldige mannen en hun families hadden de dood gevonden dankzij een of andere verdenking van de president.

Maar toen hij twee uur later naar zijn auto terugliep, lag er een glimlach van opluchting en verbazing op zijn gezicht.

Die opluchting was verklaarbaar. De president was in een ontspannen en vriendelijke bui geweest. Met instemming had hij geluisterd naar Tariq Aziz' gloedvolle beschrijving van zijn missie naar Genève, de grote sympathie die hij overal voor de Iraakse positie had ontmoet en de toenemende anti-Amerikaanse gevoelens in het Westen.

Hij knikte begrijpend toen Tariq tegen de Amerikaanse oorlogshitsers tekeerging. En eindelijk, meegesleept door zijn eigen verontwaardiging, had hij verteld waarmee James Baker hem had gedreigd. Angstig wachtte hij op de uitbarsting van de *Rais*.

Terwijl de anderen rond de tafel nog kookten van woede, zat Saddam te glimlachen en te knikken.

De minister van Buitenlandse Zaken glimlachte toen hij vertrok, omdat de president hem had gefeliciteerd met zijn Europese missie. Het feit dat die missie naar normale diplomatieke maatstaven een ramp was geweest – hij had overal bakzeil moeten halen, was ijzig koel behandeld en had niets kunnen veranderen aan de vastberaden houding van de Coalitie – scheen van geen belang.

Zijn verbazing had een andere oorzaak. Iets wat Saddam tegen het einde van het gesprek had gezegd. Het was niet meer dan een terzijde, een gefluisterde opmerking die alleen voor de oren van de minister was bestemd, toen de president hem naar de deur bracht.

'*Rafik*, kameraad, maak je geen zorgen. Ik heb een verrassing voor de Amerikanen in petto. Nu nog niet. Maar als de Beni el-Kalb ooit ons land binnenvallen, zal ik niet reageren met gas, maar met De Vuist van God.'

Tariq Aziz knikte instemmend, hoewel hij niet wist waar de *Rais* het over had. Net als de anderen ontdekte hij dat pas vierentwintig uur later.

De ochtend van de 12e januari kwam de voltallige Revolutionaire Commandoraad voor het laatst bijeen in het presidentiële paleis op de hoek van de 14e Julistraat en de Kindistraat. Een week later werd het paleis platgegooid, maar toen was de vogel allang gevlogen.

Zoals gewoonlijk kwam de oproep voor de vergadering op het laatste moment. Hoe hoog iemand ook steeg binnen de hiërarchie en hoeveel vertrouwen hij ook genoot, slechts een handjevol familieleden, getrouwen en lijfwachten wist ooit precies waar de *Rais* zich op een bepaalde dag op een bepaald tijdstip zou bevinden.

Dat hij nog leefde na zeven serieuze moordaanslagen dankte hij aan zijn obsessie voor zijn persoonlijke veiligheid.

Die vertrouwde hij niet toe aan de contraspionagedienst, ook niet aan de Geheime Politie van Omar Khatib of de Republikeinse Garde en zeker niet aan het leger.

Die taak viel toe aan de Amn-al-Khass. Hoe jong zijn lijfwachten ook waren, de meesten nog maar nauwelijks twintig jaar, hun trouw aan de Iraakse leider was absoluut. En ze stonden onder bevel van Saddams eigen zoon Kusaj.

Geen enkele samenzweerder wist ooit welke route de *Rais* zou volgen of in wat voor een auto. Zijn bezoeken aan legerbases en fabrieken waren altijd een verrassing, niet alleen voor de gastheren maar ook voor de mensen rondom Saddam zelf.

Zelfs in Bagdad wisselde hij voortdurend van locatie. Nu eens woonde hij een paar dagen in het paleis, dan weer in zijn bunker, schuin onder het Rashid Hotel.

Alle maaltijden die hem werden voorgezet werden eerst voorgeproefd, en de voorproever moest de oudste zoon zijn van de kok. En alle drank kwam uit een fles met een ongebroken zegel.

Die ochtend werden de uitnodigingen voor de vergadering op het paleis door een speciale boodschapper aan de leden van de Raad rondgebracht, één uur voordat de bijeenkomst zou beginnen. Niemand had dus de tijd om een aanslag voor te bereiden.

De limousines draaiden het hek binnen, leverden hun passagiers af en vertrokken naar het speciale parkeerterrein. Alle leden van de Revolutionaire Commandoraad moesten langs een metaaldetector lopen en niemand mocht een wapen bij zich dragen.

Drieëndertig mannen verzamelden zich in de grote vergaderzaal met de T-vormige tafel. Acht van hen zaten aan de bovenkant van de T, aan weerskanten van de lege 'troon' in het midden. De rest zat tegenover elkaar langs de poot van de T.

Zeven van de aanwezigen waren familie van de *Rais*, drie waren aangetrouwd. Zij en nog acht anderen kwamen uit Tikrit of de directe omgeving. Allemaal waren ze al heel lang lid van de Ba'ath-partij.

Tien van de drieëndertig waren minister, negen waren generaal bij de landmacht of de luchtmacht. Saadi Tumah Abbas, de voormalige commandant van de Republikeinse Garde, was die ochtend tot minister van Defensie bevorderd en zat stralend aan de hoogste tafel. Hij was de opvolger van Abd al-Jabber Shenshall, de overgelopen Koerd die lange tijd de kant had gekozen van de slachter van zijn eigen volk.

Onder de landmachtgeneraals waren Mustafa Radi van de infanterie, Farouk Ridha van de artillerie, Ali Musuli van de genie en Abdullah Kadiri van het tankkorps.

Aan de voet van de tafel zaten de drie leiders van de inlichtingendiensten: dr. Ubaidi van de buitenlandse inlichtingendienst Mukhabarat, Hassan Rahmani van de contraspionagedienst en Omar Khatib van de Geheime Politie.

Toen de *Rais* binnenkwam, stond iedereen op en applaudisseerde. Hij glimlachte, liep naar zijn stoel, gebaarde dat de anderen weer konden gaan zitten en opende de vergadering. Ze waren hier niet om iets te bespreken. Ze waren hier omdat hij hun iets te vertellen had.

Alleen zijn schoonzoon Hoessein Kamil toonde geen enkele verbazing toen de president de clou van zijn betoog bereikte. Na een monoloog van veertig minuten, waarin hij een ononderbroken opsomming had gegeven van de successen van zijn leiderschap, kwam Saddam met het grote nieuws. Er viel een verbijsterde stilte.

Dat Irak al jarenlang bezig was een kernbom te ontwikkelen, wisten ze wel. Maar ze konden nauwelijks geloven dat het juist op dit moment – nu de oorlog op uitbreken stond – was gelukt om het enige wapen te produceren waar de hele wereld, zelfs het machtige Amerika, bang voor was. Dat duidde op goddelijke interventie. Maar de godheid woonde niet in de hemel boven hen; hij zat hier beneden en glimlachte kalm.

Hoessein Kamil, die al op de hoogte was, kwam overeind en gaf het sein tot een ovatie. De anderen stonden haastig op, bang om de laatste te zijn of niet luid genoeg te applaudisseren. En niemand wilde de eerste zijn om te stoppen.

Toen hij twee uur later naar zijn kantoor terugging, ruimde Hassan Rahmani, de beschaafde, kosmopolitische chef van de contraspionagedienst, zijn bureau op, gaf orders dat hij niet gestoord mocht worden en bleef met een kop zwarte koffie peinzend voor zich uit zitten staren. Hij moest nadenken, heel goed nadenken.

Net als de anderen was hij geschokt door het nieuws. Met één klap was het hele machtsevenwicht in het Midden-Oosten gewijzigd zonder dat iemand het wist. Nadat de president, met zijn handen bescheiden geheven als dank voor de ovatie, de vergadering had voortgezet, was iedereen tot geheimhouding gezworen.

Dat kon Rahmani wel begrijpen. Ondanks de uitgelaten stemming waarin ze de vergadering verlieten en waarbij hij zich braaf had aangesloten, zag hij grote problemen opdoemen.

Een machtig wapen heeft alleen nut als je vrienden – en nog belangrijker, je vijanden – weten dat je het hebt. Pas daarna komen potentiële vijanden je hun vriendschap aanbieden.

Sommige landen die over een kernbom beschikten hadden dat gewoon aangekondigd door een atoomproef te doen, zodat de buitenwereld haar conclusies kon trekken. Andere landen, zoals Israël en Zuid-Afrika, hadden alleen de suggestie gewekt waardoor de rest van de wereld en vooral hun buren in het duister tastten. Soms werkte dat nog beter. De fantasie is vaak machtiger dan de werkelijkheid.

Maar dat gold niet voor Irak, wist Rahmani. Als het waar was wat hij had gehoord – en misschien was het hele verhaal wel een truc, in de hoop dat het zou uitlekken, om tijd te winnen – zou niemand buiten Irak het willen geloven.

En dus zou Irak moeten bewijzen dat het over een kernwapen beschikte. Maar dat was Saddam kennelijk niet van plan. En dat was ook niet eenvoudig.

Een test op eigen grondgebied was uitgesloten. Dat zou waanzin zijn. Een schip de Indische Oceaan op sturen en daar de proef uitvoeren zou ooit mogelijk zijn geweest, maar nu niet meer. Alle havens waren geblokkeerd.

Irak zou een team van het Internationaal Atoomenergie Agentschap van de Verenigde Naties in Wenen kunnen uitnodigen om zich te overtuigen. Inspecteurs van het IAEA brachten immers al tien jaar lang bijna jaarlijks een bezoek en waren altijd met een kluitje in het riet gestuurd. Maar als ze met de feiten werden geconfronteerd, zouden ze nederig hun eigen onnozelheid moeten bekennen en de waarheid bevestigen.

Maar Saddam had dat uitdrukkelijk verboden. Waarom? Omdat het allemaal een leugen was? Omdat de *Rais* iets anders in de zin had? En belangrijker nog: wat kon dit voor consequenties hebben voor hemzelf, Hassan Rahmani?

Maandenlang had hij erop gerekend dat Saddam Hoessein zich tot een oorlog zou laten verleiden die hij onmogelijk kon winnen. Dat had hij inderdaad gedaan. Rahmani had erop gerekend dat de Amerikaanse overwinning de val van Saddam zou betekenen – waardoor hij met steun van de Amerikanen als nieuwe sterke man naar voren zou kunnen stappen. Maar opeens was alles anders. Hij had tijd nodig om na te denken, besefte hij. Hij moest de beste manier zien te vinden om deze verrassende nieuwe troefkaart uit te spelen.

Die avond, toen het donker was, verscheen er een krijtteken op een muur achter de Chaldeeuwse kerk van de H. Jozef in de christelijke wijk. Het leek op een acht, op zijn kant.

De burgers van Bagdad sidderden die nacht. Ondanks alle propaganda via de plaatselijke radio, waar veel mensen blind vertrouwen in hadden, waren er anderen die in het geheim naar de Arabische uitzendingen van de BBC World Service luisterden – in Londen opgenomen en vanuit Cyprus uitgezonden – en wisten dat de Beni Naji de waarheid vertelden. Het werd oorlog.

De meeste mensen dachten dat de Amerikanen zouden beginnen met een grootscheeps bombardement op Bagdad. Zelfs in het presidentiële paleis ging men daarvan uit. Het aantal slachtoffers onder de burgerbevolking zou gigantisch zijn.

Dat kon de Iraakse regering weinig schelen. Het regime hoopte dat zo'n slachting onder de burgerij over de hele wereld tot heftige protesten zou leiden die de Amerikanen tot de aftocht zouden dwingen. Daarom werden er nog zoveel buitenlandse journalisten getolereerd en zelfs verwelkomd. De pers had zich geconcentreerd in het Rashid Hotel en gidsen stonden al klaar om de buitenlandse tv-ploegen naar de plaatsen van de volkerenmoord te brengen.

De burgers van Bagdad waren niet zo blij met deze strategie. Veel mensen waren al gevlucht, de niet-Irakezen naar de Jordaanse grens, waar ze zich aansloten bij de stroom van Koeweitse vluchtelingen van de laatste vijf maanden, en de Irakezen zelf naar het platteland.

Niemand, ook de miljoenen Amerikanen en Europeanen die aan hun tv-schermen zaten gekluisterd, kon vermoeden over hoeveel vuurkracht de grimmige Chuck Horner in Riyad nu beschikte. En niemand wist dat de meeste doelwitten zouden worden geselecteerd op basis van satellietopnamen, om te worden vernietigd door lasergeleide bommen die zelden iets anders raakten dan dat waarop ze waren gericht.

Wat de inwoners van Bagdad wel begrepen, toen de berichten van de BBC zich over de markten en de bazars verspreidden, was dat het die 12e januari nog maar vier dagen zou duren voordat het ultimatum afliep en dat daarna de Amerikaanse oorlogsvliegtuigen zouden komen. En dus wachtte de stad rustig af.

Mike Martin fietste langzaam de Shurjastraat uit en reed langs de achterkant van de kerk. Hij zag het krijtteken op de muur maar fietste gewoon door. Aan het eind van het steegje bleef hij staan, stapte af en rommelde wat aan zijn ketting terwijl hij omkeek om te zien of iemand hem in de gaten hield.

Nee. Geen schuifelende voetstappen van de Geheime Politie in een portiek, geen hoofden die over een dakrand gluurden. Hij fietste terug, veegde met een vochtige doek het krijtteken weg en vertrok.

De gekantelde acht betekende dat er een boodschap voor hem lag achter een steen in een oude muur bij de Abu Nawasstraat, niet ver van de rivier, nauwelijks achthonderd meter fietsen.

Als jongen had hij daar wel gespeeld, rennend over de kaden met Hassan Rahmani en Abdelkarim Badri, als de venters hun heerlijke *masgouf* bakten boven een bed van brandende mannastruiktakken en malse moten Tigriskarper aan voorbijgangers verkochten.

De winkels waren dicht en de theehuizen gesloten. Er wandelden nu veel minder mensen langs de kaden dan vroeger. Maar die stilte kwam hem heel goed uit. Aan het begin van de Abu Nawasstraat zag hij een groepje AMAM-agenten in burger, maar ze namen geen notitie van de *fellagha* die voor zijn baas onderweg was. De aanwezigheid van de agenten gaf Martin moed. De AMAM waren een stelletje amateurs. Als ze een 'brievenbus' bewaakten, zouden ze niet zo stom zijn om een groepje agenten aan het begin van de straat te posteren, maar hoe ze het ook deden, ze vielen altijd op.

Martin vond de boodschap, schoof de steen weer op zijn plaats en stak het opgevouwen velletje papier in het kruis van zijn onderbroek. Een paar minuten later stak hij de Ahrarbrug over de Tigris over, reed van Kisafa naar Karch, en weer terug naar het huis van de diplomaat in Mansour.

De afgelopen negen weken had het leven in de ommuurde villa zijn gewone loop hernomen. De Russische kokkin en haar man behandelden hem netjes en hij had zelfs iets van hun taal geleerd. Iedere dag ging hij naar de markt om vers fruit en groente te kopen – een ideale gelegenheid om al zijn brievenbussen te bezoeken. Hij had veertien berichten aan de onzichtbare Jericho doorgegeven en er vijftien ontvangen.

Acht keer was hij aangehouden door de AMAM, maar zijn nederige houding, zijn fiets en zijn mand met groente, fruit, koffie, kruiden en andere boodschappen, plus zijn brief van de Russische diplomaat en zijn armoedige voorkomen hadden hem steeds gered.

Hij kon niet weten welke oorlogsplannen er in Riyad werden uitgebroed, maar hij moest alle vragen zelf in het Arabisch noteren als hij ze via de radio had ontvangen, en hij las alle antwoorden van Jericho om ze in versnelde vorm aan Simon Paxman te kunnen verzenden.

Als soldaat begreep hij natuurlijk dat Jericho's politieke en militaire informatie van onschatbare waarde moest zijn voor de geallieerde bevelhebbers die een aanval op Irak voorbereidden.

Hij had een oliekacheltje voor zijn schuur versierd en een petroleumlamp als verlichting. Jutezakken van de markt had hij als gordijnen voor de ramen gehangen, en iedereen die het schuurtje naderde moest over het grind lopen, zodat hij zich door zijn voetstappen zou verraden.

Die avond keerde hij dankbaar naar zijn warme onderkomen terug, schoof de grendel voor de deur, controleerde of alle ramen waren afgedekt, stak zijn lamp aan en las Jericho's laatste bericht door. Het was korter dan anders, maar dat maakte de inhoud niet minder schokkend. Martin las het twee keer, bang dat hij opeens geen Arabisch meer kende, maar hij vergiste zich niet. 'Jezus Christus,' mompelde hij, terwijl hij de tegels loswrikte en de cassetterecorder tevoorschijn haalde.

Om ieder misverstand uit te sluiten las hij het bericht langzaam en zorgvuldig voor, zowel in het Arabisch als in het Engels, voordat hij de tekst van vijf minuten tot een bericht van anderhalve seconde versnelde.

Tien voor half één 's nachts verzond hij de boodschap naar Riyad.

Omdat hij wist dat Martin zich tussen kwart over twaalf en half één kon melden, was Simon Paxman die avond niet naar bed gegaan. Hij zat te kaarten met een van de radiotechnici toen het bericht binnenkwam. De andere technicus kwam ermee uit de radiokamer.

'Kom maar even luisteren, Simon... nu meteen,' zei hij.

Hoewel de SIS-sectie in Riyad veel meer dan vier mensen telde, was Operatie Jericho zo geheim dat alleen Paxman, Julian Gray – de chef van het bureau – en de twee radiotechnici erbij betrokken waren. Hun drie kamers waren praktisch van de rest van de villa afgesloten.

Simon Paxman luisterde naar de stem op de grote spoelenrecorder in de 'radiohut', een omgebouwde slaapkamer. Eerst las Martin twee keer de letterlijke Arabische tekst van Jericho voor, daarna twee keer zijn eigen vertaling.

Paxman had het gevoel of een grote koude hand zich om zijn maag klemde. Er was iets mis. Ernstig mis. Wat hij hier hoorde kòn gewoon niet waar zijn. De andere twee mannen stonden zwijgend naast hem.

'Is het hem wel?' vroeg Paxman dringend zodra de stem was uitgesproken. Zijn eerste gedachte was dat Martin was opgepakt en dat het bericht een vervalsing moest zijn.

'Ja, hij is het. Ik heb de ossy gecontroleerd. Geen enkele twijfel.'

Spraakpatronen hebben een bepaalde toon en ritme, een cadans die door een oscilloscoop kan worden omgezet in een reeks lijnen op een scherm, net als bij een hartmonitor in het ziekenhuis.

Iedere menselijke stem heeft zijn eigen karakteristiek, die niet kan worden nagebootst. Voordat hij naar Bagdad vertrok, was Martins stem op zo'n machine vastgelegd. Ieder bericht uit Bagdad werd met het patroon van de 'ossy' vergeleken, voor het geval de versnelling, de vertraging en andere invloeden van de recorders of de satelliettransmissie een vervorming hadden veroorzaakt.

De stem die ze nu uit Bagdad hoorden, kwam overeen met het patroon.

284

Het was Martin die sprak, en niemand anders.

Het was natuurlijk mogelijk dat Martin was opgepakt en met geweld was gedwongen dit bericht in te spreken. Maar dat leek Paxman erg onwaarschijnlijk.

Ze hadden bepaalde woorden, pauzes, aarzelingen en kuchjes afgesproken om Riyad te waarschuwen wanneer hij niet vrijwillig uitzond. Bovendien was zijn vorige bericht pas drie dagen oud.

Hoe wreed de Iraakse Geheime Politie ook mocht zijn, erg snel waren ze niet. En Martin was een harde. Een man die binnen zo'n korte tijd was gebroken, moest in een compleet wrak zijn veranderd, en dat zou aan zijn stem te horen zijn.

Dat betekende dat het een serieuze boodschap was die Martin nog diezelfde avond van Jericho had ontvangen. En dat wierp nieuwe vragen op. Had Jericho gelijk? Vergiste hij zich? Of was het een leugen?

'Waarschuw Julian,' zei Paxman tegen een van de radiotechnici.

In afwachting van het hoofd van het plaatselijke SIS-bureau belde Paxman via een privé-lijn met zijn Amerikaanse collega Chip Barber.

'Chip, kom onmiddellijk hier naartoe,' zei hij.

De CIA-man was meteen klaarwakker. Iets in de toon van de Engelsman zei hem dat dit niet het moment was voor slaperige praatjes. 'Problemen, kerel?'

'Daar lijkt het wel op,' beaamde Paxman.

Binnen dertig minuten was Barber vanaf de andere kant van de stad gearriveerd, in een sweater en een broek die hij haastig over zijn pyjama had aangetrokken. Het was twee uur in de nacht.

Paxman had de band al op scherp staan, met een transcriptie in het Engels en het Arabisch. De twee radiotechnici, die al jaren in het Midden-Oosten werkten en vloeiend Arabisch spraken, bevestigden dat Martins vertaling klopte.

'Dat kan niet waar zijn,' hijgde Barber toen hij de band hoorde.

Paxman zei hem dat ze Martins stem al hadden gecontroleerd.

'Luister, Simon, het is alleen maar een rapport van Jericho over wat Saddam vanochtend – sorry, gisterochtend – *zou hebben gezegd*. De kans is groot dat Saddam liegt. Dat zou niet voor het eerst zijn, zoals we allemaal weten.'

Maar een leugen of niet, dit was geen zaak voor Riyad. De plaatselijke SIS- en CIA-bureaus gaven de generaals wel de tactische en zelfs strategische informatie van Jericho door, maar politieke zaken werden uitsluitend door Londen en Washington behandeld. Barber keek op zijn horloge. In Washington was het nu zeven uur 's avonds.

'Die zitten aan de cocktail,' verklaarde hij. 'Een dubbele, wil ik hopen. Ik zal het meteen aan Langley melden.'

285

'Chocola en koekjes in Londen,' zei Paxman. 'Ik neem wel contact op met Century House. Dan mogen zij het verder uitzoeken.'

Barber vertrok om zijn kopie van het bericht gecodeerd aan Bill Stewart te versturen, met de hoogste prioriteit. Waar hij ook was, de code-afdeling zou hem opsporen en hem vragen om via een veilige lijn terug te bellen.

Paxman stuurde dezelfde boodschap aan Steve Laing, die midden in nacht zijn warme bed uit moest om in de ijskoude nacht naar Londen te rijden.

Paxman kon nog één ding doen, en dat deed hij ook. Martin had een bepaalde tijd waarop hij alleen hoefde te luisteren. Dat was om vier uur 's nachts. Paxman bleef op en stuurde zijn man in Bagdad een kort maar zeer expliciet bericht. Tot nader order moest Martin uit de buurt van zijn zes brievenbussen blijven. Voor alle zekerheid.

Karim, de Jordaanse student, maakte langzaam vorderingen in zijn relatie met Fräulein Edith Hardenberg. Hij mocht haar hand al vasthouden als ze door de straten van het oude Wenen liepen, knerpend over de bevroren keitjes. Ze moest zelfs bekennen dat ze het wel prettig vond.

De tweede week van januari bestelde ze kaartjes voor het Burgtheater. Karim betaalde. Het was een opvoering van een stuk van Grillparzer, *Gygus und sein Ring*.

Voordat ze naar binnen stapten, vertelde ze enthousiast dat het over een oude koning ging die een paar zonen had. De zoon aan wie hij de ring naliet, zou hem opvolgen. Karim volgde het stuk geboeid en vroeg zo nu en dan om een uitleg van de tekst, die hij de hele avond op zijn schoot hield.

In de pauze vertelde Edith nog wat meer over het stuk. Later zou Avi Herzog zich bij Barzilai beklagen dat het net zo interessant was als het programma van een wasmachine.

'Je bent een cultuurbarbaar,' vond de Mossad-officier.

'Ik ben hier niet voor de cultuur,' zei Avi.

'Schiet dan eens op, jongen.'

Op zondag ging Edith, een vrome katholiek, naar de ochtendmis in de Votivkirche. Karim legde uit dat hij als moslim niet met haar mee kon gaan, maar dat hij op haar zou wachten in het café aan de overkant van het plein.

Daarna, bij een kop koffie waar hij bewust een *schnapps* in had gedaan waarvan ze een blos op haar wangen kreeg, sprak hij over de verschillen en overeenkomsten tussen het christendom en de islam – de aanbidding van de ene ware God, de lijn van aartsvaders en profeten, de leer van de heilige boeken en de morele wetten. Edith vond het een beetje eng, maar was ook gefascineerd. Ze vroeg zich af of ze haar onsterfelijke ziel in gevaar bracht door hiernaar te luisteren, maar tot haar verbazing vertelde Karim haar dat moslims helemaal geen afgoden vereerden.

'Zullen we samen eten?' vroeg Karim drie dagen later.

'Jawel, maar je geeft veel te veel geld aan me uit,' zei Edith. Ze merkte dat ze genoot van dat jonge gezicht en die zachte bruine ogen, en ze moest zichzelf er voortdurend aan herinneren dat het leeftijdsverschil van tien jaar iets anders dan een platonische vriendschap volstrekt belachelijk maakte. 'Niet in een restaurant.'

'Waar dan?'

'Wil je voor me koken, Edith? Je kunt toch koken? Een echte Weense maaltijd?'

Ze bloosde bij de gedachte. Iedere avond, tenzij ze in haar eentje naar een concert ging, maakte ze een bescheiden hapje klaar in het alkoofje van haar appartement dat als eethoek diende. Maar ze kòn koken, dat was waar. Het was al zo lang geleden...

Bovendien had hij haar al een paar keer mee uit eten genomen in dure restaurants. En hij was een keurig opgevoede en zeer hoffelijke jongeman. Daar stak toch geen kwaad in?

Dat het bericht van Jericho in de nacht van 12 op 13 januari voor nogal wat beroering zorgde in bepaalde kringen in Londen en Washington, is zeer voorzichtig uitgedrukt. Nauwelijks onderdrukte paniek is een betere beschrijving.

Een van de problemen was dat er maar heel weinig mensen op de hoogte waren van Jericho's bestaan, laat staan van de details. Al die geheimhouding lijkt pietluttig, maar er is een goede reden voor.

Alle inlichtingendiensten voelen zich verantwoordelijk voor hun spionnen, die grote risico's nemen, hoe verachtelijk ze misschien als mens ook zijn.

Het feit dat Jericho alleen voor geld werkte en niet uit overtuiging, deed niet ter zake. Het feit dat hij cynisch zijn eigen land en zijn regering verraadde, deed er niet toe. Bovendien deugde het Iraakse regime voor geen cent, dus het was een geval van de ene boef die de andere een loer draaide.

Gezien zijn grote waarde en de overweging dat zijn informatie de geallieerde verliezen op het slagveld kon beperken, was Jericho een belangrijke spion voor de twee inlichtingendiensten. Daarom hadden ze zijn bestaan maar aan een klein kringetje ingewijden bekend gemaakt. Geen enkele minister, politicus, ambtenaar of militair was formeel van de zaak op de hoogte.

Zijn informatie werd op verschillende manieren gecamoufleerd, om de bron niet te hoeven onthullen. Zijn militaire gegevens waren zogenaamd afkomstig van overgelopen Iraakse soldaten in Koeweit, onder wie een denkbeeldige majoor die op een geheime basis in het Midden-Oosten – maar buiten Saoedi-Arabië – zou zijn verhoord.

De wetenschappelijke en technische informatie over de Iraakse massavernietigingswapens kwam van een Iraakse student die naar de Britten was overgelopen nadat hij aan het Imperial College in Londen had gestudeerd en verliefd was geworden op een Engels meisje. Verder waren er zogenaamd nieuwe gesprekken gevoerd met Europese technici die tussen 1985 en 1990 in Irak hadden gewerkt.

De politieke inlichtingen zouden afkomstig zijn van Iraakse vluchtelingen, geheime radioberichten uit bezet Koeweit, geavanceerde 'sigint'- en 'elint'-apparatuur (*'signals intelligence'*- en *'electronic intelligence'*-apparatuur) waarmee gesprekken konden worden afgeluisterd, en andere opsporingstechnieken.

Maar hoe moest je een rechtstreekse weergave verklaren van Saddams eigen woorden, hoe bizar ook, die hij tijdens een besloten vergadering in zijn eigen paleis had uitgesproken zonder toe te geven dat je een spion in de hoogste kringen had?

De risico's van zo'n bekentenis waren veel te groot. Om te beginnen was er het gevaar van een lek. Geheimen lekken altijd uit – kabinetsstukken, ambtelijke memo's, interdepartementale brieven, noem maar op.

Vooral politici zijn niet te vertrouwen. De meeste inlichtingendiensten hebben nachtmerries over ministers die hun mond voorbij praten tegen hun vrouw, hun vriendin, hun vriend, hun kapper, hun chauffeur of hun barkeeper. Sommige politici kletsen zelfs door als er een ober bij hun tafeltje staat.

En dan zijn er nog de pers en andere media, die beschikken over speurneuzen waarbij Scotland Yard en de FBI verbleken. Dus hoe moest je Jericho's informatie verklaren zonder Jericho te noemen?

En ten slotte woonden en wonen er in Londen nog altijd honderden Iraakse studenten, onder wie ongetwijfeld enkele agenten van dr. Ismail Ubaidi's Mukhabarat, die alles overbriefden wat ze zagen en hoorden.

Niemand zou Jericho natuurlijk bij name noemen. Dat was onmogelijk. Maar één hint dat de informatie uit Bagdad zelf afkomstig was, en Rahmani's contraspionagedienst zou overuren maken om de bron op te sporen en te isoleren. In het gunstigste geval zou dat betekenen dat Jericho zich verder koest zou houden om zichzelf te beschermen, in het ergste geval kon het tot zijn arrestatie leiden.

Terwijl het begin van de luchtoorlog steeds dichterbij kwam, raadpleegden de twee inlichtingendiensten al hun nucleaire deskundigen voor een snelle opinie over de nieuwe situatie. Was het mogelijk dat Irak een sneller en groter ultracentrifugeproject had opgestart dan eerder werd aangenomen?

In Engeland werd opnieuw de hulp ingeroepen van de deskundigen van Harwell en Aldermaston. In Amerika werd een beroep gedaan op Sandia,

Lawrence Livermore en Los Alamos. Department-Z van Livermore, de mensen die voortdurend de proliferatie in de derde wereld volgden, werden nog eens extra onder druk gezet.

De wetenschappers reageerden geïrriteerd en herhaalden hun eerdere mening. Zelfs in het ergste geval, zeiden ze, zelfs als er niet één maar twee ultracentrifugecascades niet één maar twee jaar lang in bedrijf waren geweest, kon Irak onmogelijk over meer dan de helft van het uranium-235 beschikken dat nodig was voor een middelgrote kernbom.

Er bleven dus enkele mogelijkheden over. Saddam was door zijn eigen mensen voorgelogen. Conclusie: onwaarschijnlijk. Wetenschappers die dat deden, zouden daarvoor met hun leven moeten betalen.

Saddam loog zelf. Conclusie: heel goed mogelijk. Om het moreel van zijn angstige en aarzelende aanhang wat op te vijzelen. Maar waarom zou hij het nieuws dan beperken tot zijn eigen kleine kring, de fanatici die hem door dik en dun steunden? Dit soort propaganda is bedoeld voor het grote publiek en voor het buitenland. Vreemd.

Saddam had nooit zoiets beweerd. Conclusie: het rapport was een leugen. Volgende conclusie: Jericho had gelogen omdat hij nog meer geld wilde en dacht dat zijn tijd gekomen was nu de oorlog ieder moment kon uitbreken. Hij had een prijskaartje van een miljoen dollar aan deze informatie gehangen.

Of Jericho loog omdat hij was ontmaskerd en alles had bekend. Conclusie: heel goed mogelijk, met grote gevaren voor zijn contactman in Bagdad.

Op dat punt nam de CIA de teugels stevig in handen. Langley had daar ook het recht toe, omdat zij Jericho betaalden.

'Ik zal je zeggen waar het op staat, Steve,' zei Bill Stewart tegen Steve Laing via een beveiligde telefoonlijn van de CIA naar Century House op de avond van de 14e januari. 'Saddam vergist zich of hij liegt. Jericho vergist zich of hij liegt. Hoe het ook zij, Uncle Sam is niet van plan een miljoen dollar op een rekening in Wenen te storten voor dit soort onzin.'

'Het is dus uitgesloten dat hij gelijk heeft, Bill?'

'Wat?'

'Dat Saddam het inderdaad heeft gezegd en dat het klopt?'

'Nee. Het is een drie-kaarten truc. We trappen er niet in. Luister, Jericho is de afgelopen negen weken heel nuttig voor ons geweest, hoewel we een deel van zijn informatie opnieuw zullen moeten controleren. Maar de helft is al bevestigd en heel bruikbaar. Maar met zijn laatste rapport heeft hij zijn hand overspeeld. Wij stoppen ermee. We weten niet wat hem bezielt maar dat is de beslissing van hogerhand.'

'Dan zitten wij met een probleem, Bill.'

'Dat begrijp ik, kerel, en daarom bel ik je ook meteen. De vergadering met de directeur is net afgelopen. Misschien is Jericho opgepakt en heeft hij alles bekend, of misschien is hij er zelf vandoor gegaan. Maar als hij hoort dat wij hem die miljoen dollar niet betalen, kan hij weleens lastig worden. En dat is slecht nieuws voor jullie man in Bagdad. Een goede vent, heb ik begrepen?'

'Ja, uitstekend. En met veel lef.'

'Haal hem daar weg, Steve. Snel.'

'Er zit weinig anders op, Bill. Bedankt voor de tip. Jammer. Het was een mooie operatie.'

'Zeg dat wel. Zolang het duurde.'

Stewart hing op. Laing ging naar boven om te overleggen met Sir Colin. Binnen een uur hadden ze een besluit genomen.

De volgende morgen, de 15e januari, wisten alle mannen en vrouwen van de Amerikaanse, Britse, Franse, Italiaanse, Saoedische en Koeweitse lucht-macht al aan het ontbijt dat de aanval zou beginnen.

De politici en diplomaten hadden gefaald, vonden zij. De hele dag waren de squadrons bezig met hun voorbereidingen.

De zenuwcentra van de campagne bevonden zich op drie plaatsen in Riyad.

Aan de rand van de luchtmachtbasis van Riyad stond een verzameling grote, van airconditioning voorziene tenten, die bekend stond als de 'Schuur', vanwege het zachte schijnsel dat door het groene tentdoek heen drong. Dit was de eerste zeef voor de stroom van luchtfoto's die al wekenlang binnen-kwam en de komende weken nog zou verdubbelen en verdrievoudigen.

De selectie die in de Schuur uit al deze verkenningsfoto's werd gemaakt, ging naar het hoofdkwartier van de Koninklijke Saoedische Luchtmacht, anderhalve kilometer verderop – waar de Centrale Luchtmacht of CENTAF was ondergebracht.

Het was een reusachtig gebouw van honderdvijftig meter lang, opgetrokken uit grijs, vlekkerig beton en glas, en gebouwd op pijlers. Eronder lag een kelder over de hele lengte, en daar, één verdieping onder de grond, bevond zich het hoofdkwartier van de CENTAF.

Ondanks de afmetingen van de kelder was er nog niet genoeg ruimte; daarom stond het parkeerterrein vol met groene tenten en mobiele kantoren, waar ook aan de informatie werd gewerkt.

In de kelder bevond zich het brandpunt van de hele onderneming, het Joint Imagery Production Centre ('Gemeenschappelijk fotoproduktiecentrum'), een labyrint van kamertjes waar gedurende de hele oorlog tweehonderdvijf-tig Britse en Amerikaanse analisten van alle rangen, afkomstig uit de drie strijdmachtonderdelen, samenwerkten. Dit was het Zwarte Gat.

Officieel berustte de leiding bij generaal Chuck Horner, de bevelhebber van de gezamenlijke luchtmacht, maar omdat hij veel tijd doorbracht op het ministerie van Defensie verderop langs de weg, werd hij meestal vervangen door zijn tweede man, generaal Buster Glosson.

Iedere dag, soms zelfs ieder uur, raadpleegden de plannenmakers in het Zwarte Gat een document dat de Basic Target Graphic werd genoemd: een lijst met een kaart van alles in Irak dat als doelwit voor een bombardement in aanmerking kwam. Daarop baseerden ze de dagelijkse bijbel van alle luchtmachtcommandanten, squadron-inlichtingenofficieren, operaties-officieren en bemanningen in het Golfgebied: de Air Tasking Order.

De ATO was een zeer uitvoerig document van meer dan honderd pagina's getypte tekst, dat elke dag opnieuw werd bijgewerkt. De voorbereiding kostte drie dagen.

Eerst kwam de 'Apportionment', het besluit over het percentage doelwitten in Irak dat binnen één dag kon worden aangevallen en het type vliegtuigen dat daarvoor beschikbaar was.

De tweede dag volgde de 'Allocation', de vertaling van het percentage Iraakse doelen in concrete cijfers en locaties. De derde dag was bestemd voor de 'Distribution', de toewijzing aan de verschillende eenheden. Dit proces bepaalde welke doelwitten door Britse Tornado's moesten worden aangevallen, of door de Amerikaanse Strike Eagles, de Tomcats van de marine, de Phantoms of de B-52 Stratofortresses.

Pas daarna kreeg ieder squadron en iedere wing zijn opdrachten voor de volgende dag. Ze moesten zelf hun doelen opzoeken, de route uitstippelen, contact leggen met de tankers, de richting van de aanval bepalen, secundaire doelwitten vaststellen voor het geval er iets tussenkwam, en de terugtocht plannen.

De squadron-commandant koos zijn bemanningen (veel squadrons moesten op één dag verscheidene doelen aanvallen), zijn flight-leaders en hun wingmen.

De wapenofficieren van de squadrons, zoals Don Walker, kozen de bewapening, ongeleide of lasergeleide bommen, lasergeleide raketten, enzovoort.

Anderhalve kilometer verderop, aan de Old Airport Road, stond het derde gebouw. Het Saoedische ministerie van Defensie is een reusachtig complex van vijf onderling verbonden gebouwen van glinsterend wit cement, zeven verdiepingen hoog, met sierlijke zuilen tot aan de vierde.

Op de vierde verdieping had generaal Schwarzkopf een fraaie suite gekregen waar hij maar zelden was, omdat hij liever in een kleine zitslaapkamer in het souterrain zat, dichter bij zijn commandopost.

Het ministerie is vierhonderd meter lang en ruim dertig meter hoog, een ruimte die heel nuttig bleek tijdens de Golfoorlog, toen er zoveel buitenlanders moesten worden ondergebracht.

Ondergronds zijn nog twee verdiepingen over de hele lengte van het gebouw. Van die vierhonderd meter had het commando van de Coalitie zestig meter in bezit genomen. Hier vergaderden de generaals, met een reusachtige kaart van het oorlogsgebied waarop stafofficieren de ontwikkelingen bijhielden – welke doelen waren geraakt of gemist, wat ze hadden ontdekt, wat zich had verplaatst, hoe de Irakezen hadden gereageerd en wat hun situatie was.

Beschut tegen de hete zon stond een Britse squadron-leider die januaridag voor de grote wandkaart met de 700 doelwitten in Irak – waaronder 240 primaire doelen – en zei: 'Dat was het ongeveer.'

Helaas vergiste hij zich. De plannenmakers vertrouwden volledig op hun satellieten en hun technologie, zonder rekening te houden met de kunst van de *maskirovka* of camouflage.

Op honderden emplacementen in Irak en Koeweit stonden Iraakse tanks onder hun camouflagenetten, geregistreerd door de radarsystemen van de geallieerden. Maar in veel gevallen bestonden ze uit hardboard, triplex en blik, met vaten schroot erin om de juiste metaalreflecties naar de sensors terug te kaatsen.

Tientallen oude vrachtwagens waren door de Irakezen voorzien van namaak-lanceerbuizen voor Scud-raketten. Die 'lanceerinstallaties' zouden binnenkort door de Coalitie worden vernietigd.

Nog belangrijker was dat zeventig belangrijke locaties van massavernietigingswapens niet door de geallieerde technologie waren opgemerkt omdat ze zich diep onder de grond bevonden of heel handig als iets anders waren gecamoufleerd.

Pas veel later zouden de plannenmakers zich verbaasd afvragen hoe de Irakezen hun totaal vernietigde divisies zo snel weer op de been konden krijgen. En nog weer later zouden de inspectieteams van de Verenigde Naties al die fabrieken en depots ontdekken die aan hun aandacht waren ontsnapt, met het akelige gevoel dat er nog veel meer installaties onder de grond verborgen lagen.

Maar die hete dag in januari 1991 wist niemand daar nog iets van. Het enige dat de jonge kerels op de vliegbases van Tabuk in het westen en Bahrein in het oosten tot aan het streng geheime Khamis Mushait in het zuiden wisten, was dat ze binnen veertig uur de oorlog in zouden gaan en dat sommigen van hen nooit zouden terugkomen.

De laatste dag voordat ze hun instructies kregen, schreven de meesten een brief naar huis. Ze kauwden op hun potlood, zoekend naar woorden. Ze dachten aan hun vrouw en kinderen en huilden bij het schrijven. Met handen die gewend waren om duizenden kilo's dodelijk metaal te bedienen probeerden ze nu onhandig de juiste woorden te formuleren om hun gevoelens uit te drukken. Soldaten schreven aan hun vriendin wat ze al veel eerder hadden willen fluisteren. Vaders drukten hun zoons op het hart om voor hun moeder te zorgen als het verkeerd zou gaan.

Kapitein Don Walker hoorde het nieuws samen met alle andere piloten en bemanningen van de Rocketeers van het 336e Tactical Fighter Squadron. De wing-commander van Al Kharz legde een korte verklaring af. Het was een paar minuten voor negen in de ochtend en de hitte sloeg al neer op de woestijn als een moker op een aambeeld.

Zonder de gebruikelijke grappen en vrolijkheid verlieten de mannen de grote legertent, verdiept in hun eigen gedachten. Die verschilden niet veel. De laatste poging om een oorlog te voorkomen was mislukt. De politici en diplomaten hadden de ene conferentie na de andere belegd, verklaringen uitgegeven, gemanipuleerd, oproepen gedaan en dreigementen geuit om een oorlog te vermijden, maar het was allemaal tevergeefs geweest.

Dat geloofden ze tenminste, die jonge kerels die zojuist hadden gehoord dat de tijd om te praten nu voorbij was. Ze beseften niet dat deze uitkomst al maanden van tevoren had vastgestaan.

Walker zag zijn squadron-commandant Steve Turner naar zijn tent lopen om misschien wel zijn laatste brief aan Betty-Jane in Goldsboro, North Carolina, te schrijven. Randy Roberts wisselde een paar woorden met Boomer Henry. Samen liepen ze weg.

De jonge piloot uit Oklahoma keek naar de hoge, lichtblauwe lucht, waar hij altijd naar had verlangd, al sinds hij een kleine jongen was geweest in Tulsa – en waar hij nu, als volwassen man van dertig, misschien zou moeten sterven. Hij draaide zich om en liep naar de rand van de basis. Net als de anderen had hij de behoefte om alleen te zijn.

Er stond geen hek om de basis Al Kharz. Het vliegveld ging gewoon over in het okergele zand, de leisteen en het gruis, dat zich eindeloos uitstrekte tot aan de horizon, en de volgende horizon, en die daarachter. Hij liep langs de hangars rondom de betonvlakte waar het grondpersoneel al bezig was met de machines, onder bevel van de crew-chiefs die overal rondliepen om te overleggen en ervoor te zorgen dat de vliegtuigen in perfecte conditie de oorlog in zouden gaan.

Walker zag zijn eigen Eagle. Zoals altijd was hij onder de indruk van de ingehouden dreiging die er op afstand van de F-15 uitging. Het toestel stond zwijgend tussen de zwerm mannen en vrouwen die in overalls over het stoere frame klauterden – immuun voor liefde of lust, haat of angst – rustig wachtend op het moment waarop het eindelijk kon doen waarvoor het was ontworpen: dood en verderf zaaien onder een volk dat door de Amerikaanse president als de vijand was aangewezen. Walker benijdde zijn Eagle. Hoe complex het vliegtuig ook was, het zou nooit iets kunnen voelen, het zou nooit bang kunnen zijn.

293

Hij liet de tentenstad achter zich en wandelde over de stenen grond, zijn ogen beschut tegen de zon door zijn zonnebril en de klep van zijn honkbalpet. De hitte op zijn schouders voelde hij nauwelijks.

Acht jaar lang had hij vliegtuigen voor zijn land gevlogen, en met plezier. Maar nooit had hij serieus nagedacht over de mogelijkheid dat hij in een oorlog zou sneuvelen. Iedere piloot denkt na over de kans om zijn kennis, zijn behendigheid, zijn durf en de mogelijkheden van zijn toestel te meten met een andere piloot, niet tijdens een oefening, maar in een gevecht op leven en dood. Maar tegelijkertijd gaat iedere piloot ervan uit dat dat nooit zal gebeuren. Hij zal nooit de zoons van andere moeders hoeven doden of zelf worden gedood.

Die ochtend besefte hij eindelijk dat het moment nu was aangebroken. Dat al die jaren van studie en training tot deze dag en deze plaats hadden geleid. Dat hij over veertig uur weer met zijn Eagle zou opstijgen maar deze keer misschien niet terug zou komen.

Net als de anderen dacht hij aan thuis. Als enig kind en vrijgezel dacht hij voornamelijk aan zijn moeder en zijn vader. Hij herinnerde zich zijn jeugd in Tulsa, waar hij zo vaak in de achtertuin van zijn huis had gespeeld. En de dag waarop hij zijn eerste honkbalhandschoen had gekregen en hij zijn vader had laten werpen tot het donker werd.

Zijn gedachten gingen terug naar de vakanties die ze samen hadden doorgebracht voordat hij naar de universiteit en de luchtmacht was vertrokken. Hij herinnerde zich vooral die keer dat zijn vader hem, als jongetje van twaalf, in de zomer had meegenomen op een visvakantie, als mannen onder elkaar.

Ray Walker was toen nog twintig jaar jonger geweest, slanker en fitter, sterker dan zijn zoon, voordat die verhouding in de loop der jaren was omgedraaid. Samen met een stel anderen hadden ze een kajak gehuurd, met een gids. Daarmee waren ze het ijskoude water van de Glacier Bay opgegaan, waar de zwarte beren op de berghellingen hun bessen verzamelden, de zeehonden op de laatste ijsschotsen van augustus in het zonnetje zaten en de zon opkwam boven de Mendenhall Glacier achter Juneau. Samen hadden ze twee monsters van zeventig pond uit de Halibut Hole opgehaald en koningszalmen gevangen in de vaargeul bij Sitka.

En nu liep hij over een zee van brandend zand in een land ver van huis, met tranen op zijn wangen die droogden in de zon. Als hij sneuvelde, zou hij nooit trouwen en kinderen krijgen. Twee keer had hij bijna een meisje ten huwelijk gevraagd. Eén keer een vriendinnetje op de universiteit, toen hij nog heel jong was en vreselijk verliefd, de tweede keer een rijpere vrouw die hij bij de basis McConnell had ontmoet, maar die had gezegd dat ze nooit met een gevechtspiloot wilde trouwen.

Nu, meer dan ooit, wilde hij zelf kinderen hebben. Hij verlangde naar een vrouw om bij thuis te komen aan het einde van de dag, een dochtertje om 's avonds naar bed te brengen met een verhaaltje voor het slapen gaan, en een zoon om te leren voetballen, honkballen, bergbeklimmen en vissen, zoals hij dat van zijn vader had geleerd. Maar meer dan alles wilde hij terug naar Tulsa om zijn moeder te omhelzen, die zich altijd zo ongerust had gemaakt om alles wat hij deed, hoewel ze dat dapper had verborgen...

Ten slotte liep de jonge piloot weer naar de basis terug, ging in zijn tent aan een wankel tafeltje zitten en probeerde een brief naar huis te schrijven. Hij was geen echte briefschrijver. De woorden kwamen niet gemakkelijk. Meestal vertelde hij wat er in het squadron gebeurde, hoe hij met zijn collega's omging, hoe het weer was. Maar dit was anders.

Hij schreef twee velletjes aan zijn ouders, zoals zoveel zoons die dag. En hij probeerde hun uit te leggen wat er in zijn hoofd omging, maar dat viel niet mee.

Hij vertelde hun over het nieuws dat die ochtend bekend was gemaakt en wat het betekende, en hij vroeg hun zich niet ongerust te maken. Hij had de beste opleiding ter wereld en vloog met de beste jager voor de beste luchtmacht die er bestond.

Hij schreef dat het hem speet van al die keren dat hij lastig was geweest en bedankte hen voor alles wat ze voor hem hadden gedaan, vanaf het moment dat ze zijn billen hadden afgeveegd tot de dag waarop ze heel Amerika waren doorgereisd om erbij te zijn toen de generaal hem aan het eind van zijn opleiding de felbegeerde wings op zijn borst had gespeld.

Over veertig uur, vertelde hij, zou hij weer opstijgen met zijn Eagle, maar deze keer zou het anders zijn. Voor het eerst zou hij mensen moeten doden en zouden anderen hem naar het leven staan.

Hij kon hun gezichten niet zien en hun angst niet voelen, zoals zij hem niet konden zien. Want zo gaat het in een moderne oorlog. Maar als hij niet zou terugkeren, wilde hij hun laten weten hoeveel hij van hen had gehouden. Hij hoopte dat hij een goede zoon was geweest.

Toen hij klaar was, plakte hij de envelop dicht, zoals er die dag in Saoedi-Arabië zoveel enveloppen werden dichtgeplakt. Daarna werden ze door de militaire posterijen opgehaald en afgeleverd in Trenton, Tulsa, Londen, Rouen en Rome.

Die avond ontving Mike Martin een spoedbericht van zijn controleofficieren in Riyad. Toen hij het bandje afspeelde, hoorde hij de stem van Simon Paxman. Het was geen lange boodschap, maar helder en duidelijk.

Jericho had zich vergist met zijn vorige bericht. Totaal vergist. Geen enkele wetenschapper hield zoiets voor mogelijk.

Bewust of onbewust had hij hun valse informatie toegespeeld. In het eerste geval was hij waarschijnlijk overgelopen, misschien opnieuw voor geld, of opgepakt. In het tweede geval zou hij zich beledigd voelen omdat de CIA weigerde hem nog één dollar te betalen voor zulke nonsens.

In elk geval moesten ze nu aannemen dat de hele operatie, met Jericho's medewerking, bekend was bij de Iraakse contraspionagedienst, 'die nu wordt geleid door je vriend Hassan Rahmani', of dat dit ieder moment kon gebeuren als Jericho in zijn verontwaardiging Rahmani een anonieme tip zou geven.

Alle zes 'brievenbussen' waren dus besmet. Martin mocht er niet meer in de buurt komen. Hij moest zich gereedmaken om uit Irak te ontsnappen bij de eerste gelegenheid die zich voordeed, misschien onder dekking van de chaos die over vierentwintig uur zou uitbreken. Einde bericht.

Martin dacht er de rest van de nacht over na. Het verbaasde hem niet dat het Westen Jericho niet geloofde. Dat ze de spion niet meer wilden betalen, was een grote klap. De man had alleen maar gemeld wat Saddam tijdens een vergadering had gezegd. Dus Saddam had gelogen. Dat was niets nieuws. Maar wat moest Jericho dàn doen? Het verzwijgen? Dat hij om een miljoen dollar had gevraagd, dat deed de deur dicht. Dat vonden ze te brutaal.

Maar verder was hij het met Paxman eens. Binnen vier dagen, misschien vijf, zou Jericho zijn rekening controleren en merken dat het geld niet was overgemaakt. Natuurlijk zou hij kwaad worden. En als hij zelf niet was opgepakt en ondervraagd door Omar Khatib, de Beul, zou hij de Geheime Politie misschien een tip geven.

Maar dat zou heel dom zijn. Als Martin werd aangehouden en zou bekennen – en hij had geen idee hoeveel pijn hij zou kunnen verdragen als hij door Khatib en zijn mensen in de Gymzaal werd gemarteld – zou hij ook Jericho kunnen verraden, wie de man ook mocht zijn.

Aan de andere kant, mensen doen soms domme dingen. Paxman had gelijk. Misschien werden de 'brievenbussen' in de gaten gehouden.

Maar uit Bagdad ontsnappen? Dat was gemakkelijker gezegd dan gedaan. Op de markt had Martin al gehoord dat er langs de uitvalswegen druk werd gepatrouilleerd door de AMAM en de militaire politie, op zoek naar deserteurs en dienstplichtontduikers. Zijn brief van de Russische diplomaat Koelikov gaf hem alleen de vrijheid om als tuinman in Bagdad te werken. Hij kon moeilijk verklaren wat hij in het westen van het land te zoeken had, op weg naar de woestijn waar zijn motorfiets begraven lag.

Daarom leek het hem beter om nog een tijdje in de Russische villa te blijven. Dat was waarschijnlijk de veiligste plek in Bagdad.

Het ultimatum aan Saddam Hoessein om Koeweit te verlaten liep op 16 januari om middernacht af. In duizenden kamers, hutten, tenten en cabines in Saoedi-Arabië en op de Rode Zee en de Perzische Golf keken mannen op hun horloge en toen naar elkaar. Er viel niet veel te zeggen.

Twee verdiepingen onder het Saoedische ministerie van Defensie, achter stalen deuren die sterk genoeg waren om als kluis van een bank te dienen, kwam dit moment bijna als een anti-climax. Na al dat werk en alle voorbereidingen viel er niets meer te doen, voorlopig. Nu moesten ze het aan die jonge kerels overlaten. Zij hadden hun taak, in het pikkedonker, hoog boven de hoofden van de generaals.

Om kwart over twee in de ochtend stapte generaal Schwarzkopf het commandocentrum binnen. Iedereen stond op. Hij las hardop een verklaring aan de troepen voor, de aalmoezenier zei een gebed en de opperbevelhebber besloot met: 'Goed, aan het werk.'

In de woestijn werd al druk gewerkt. De eerste vliegtuigen die de grens overstaken waren geen jagers maar een groep van acht Apache-helikopters van de 101e Luchtlandingsdivisie van het leger. Ze hadden een beperkte maar zeer belangrijke taak.

Ten noorden van de grens, niet ver van Bagdad, lagen twee krachtige Iraakse radarbases die met hun schotels het hele luchtruim vanaf de Golf in het oosten tot aan de westelijke woestijn bestreken.

Ondanks hun geringere snelheid waren de helikopters boven de jagers verkozen om twee redenen. Door laag boven de woestijn te vliegen konden ze aan de vijandelijke radar ontsnappen en de bases ongezien naderen, en bovendien wilde de legerleiding dat de piloten met eigen ogen en van dichtbij zouden zien dat de bases inderdaad waren vernietigd. En dat was alleen mogelijk met helikopters. Het zou veel slachtoffers kosten als die bases intact bleven.

De Apaches deden wat er van ze werd verwacht. Ze waren nog niet opgemerkt toen ze het vuur openden. De bemanningen waren uitgerust met nachtvizieren, die als korte verrekijkertjes voor hun ogen uit staken. Daarmee konden ze in het pikkedonker net zo scherp zien als met het blote oog in een maanverlichte nacht.

Eerst vernietigden ze de elektrische generatoren die de radarsystemen van stroom voorzagen, daarna de radioverbindingen waarmee andere bases verder landinwaarts konden worden gewaarschuwd, en ten slotte de radarschotels zelf.

In nog geen twee minuten hadden ze zevenentwintig lasergeleide Hellfireraketten afgevuurd, honderd 70-mm granaten en vierduizend zware patronen. Van de twee radarbases bleef slechts een rokende puinhoop over.

De missie sloeg een gapend gat in de luchtverdediging van Irak, en door die bres vond de rest van de aanval plaats.

De mensen die de plannen van generaal Chuck Horner kenden, beweerden dat het een van de meest briljante acties was die ze ooit hadden gezien. Het was een zeer nauwgezette, stapsgewijs opgebouwde operatie, maar voldoende flexibel om op onverwachte omstandigheden in te spelen.

Fase Een had enkele duidelijke doelstellingen, die automatisch tot de drie volgende fasen leidden. De eerste stap was het uitschakelen van alle Iraakse luchtverdedigingssystemen om de kracht van de geallieerde luchtmacht onmiddellijk te vertalen in een absolute suprematie. Voor de andere drie fasen van het strakke schema – de luchtoorlog mocht niet langer dan 35 dagen duren – moesten de geallieerde vliegtuigen heer en meester in het Iraakse luchtruim zijn.

De sleutel tot het uitschakelen van de vijandelijke luchtafweer waren de Iraakse radarsystemen. In de moderne luchtoorlog is de radar nog steeds het belangrijkste en meest gebruikte hulpmiddel, ondanks alle andere geavanceerde technologie.

De radar ontdekt naderende vliegtuigen, de radar begeleidt de eigen onderscheppingsjagers, de radar stuurt de luchtdoelraketten en de radar richt het geschut.

Zonder radar is de vijand blind, als een zwaargewichtbokser die met nietsziende ogen door de ring wankelt. Hij is nog wel groot en sterk, hij kan nog wel een flinke klap uitdelen, maar zijn tegenstander kan de hulpeloze Samson van alle kanten bestoken tot het onvermijdelijke einde.

Zodra er een gat in de voorste radarlinie van Saddam Hoessein was geslagen, stormden de Tornado's, de Eagles, de F-111 Aardvarks en de F-4G Wild Weasels door de opening, op weg naar de radarsystemen in het binnenland, de raketbases die van deze systemen afhankelijk waren en de commandocentra van de Iraakse generaals. Onderweg vernietigden ze alle verbindingsposten waarmee die generaals contact probeerden te houden met het front.

Vanaf de slagschepen *Wisconsin* en *Missouri* en de kruiser *San Jacinto* in de Perzische Golf werden die nacht tweeënvijftig Tomahawk-kruisraketten gelanceerd. Geleid door een combinatie van computergeheugens en tv-camera's in de neus, zijn de Tomahawks in staat het landschap te herkennen en een vastgelegde koers naar hun doelwit te volgen. Als ze vlakbij zijn, 'zien' ze hun doel, vergelijken het met de gegevens in hun geheugen, identificeren het juiste gebouw en duiken erop af.

De Wild Weasel is een versie van de Phantom, maar gespecialiseerd in radarvernietiging. Hij is uitgerust met HARMS, 'Hi-speed Anti Radiation Missiles'. Als er een radarsysteem oplicht, zendt het elektromagnetische golven uit. Dat kan niet anders. De HARMS zoekt die golven met zijn sensors en stormt recht op het hart van de radar af voordat hij explodeert.

Maar de vreemdste van alle oorlogsvliegtuigen die die avond door het donkere luchtruim naar het noorden vlogen was misschien wel de F-117A, beter bekend als de 'stealth'-jager.

Dit toestel, helemaal zwart geschilderd en met een eigenaardige vorm waardoor bijna alle elektromagnetische golven langs de romp afglijden of worden geabsorbeerd, is voor de radar nauwelijks waarneembaar en dus onzichtbaar voor de vijand.

De Amerikaanse F-117A's passeerden ongezien de Iraakse radarposten en wierpen hun lasergeleide 200-ponds bommen exact op de vierendertig doelwitten van de vijandelijke luchtverdediging. Dertien van die doelen lagen in en om Bagdad.

Zodra de bommen neerkwamen, vuurden de Irakezen blindelings in de lucht, maar ze konden niets zien en misten. In het Arabisch werden de Stealths 'shabah' of 'spoken' genoemd.

Ze kwamen van de geheime basis Khamis Mushait in het verre zuiden van Saoedi-Arabië, waarheen ze waren overgebracht vanaf hun even geheime thuisbasis Tonopah in de Amerikaanse staat Nevada. De minder fortuinlijke Amerikaanse piloten waren in tenten ondergebracht. Khamis Mushait was mijlenver van de bewoonde wereld aangelegd, maar wel met massieve hangars en barakken met airconditioning. Daarom waren de kostbare Stealths daar gestationeerd.

Omdat de basis zo ver weg lag, moesten zij de grootste afstand afleggen. Soms waren ze wel zes uur onderweg, uit en thuis – en dat onder moeilijke omstandigheden. Ze zochten hun weg ongezien door enkele van de zwaarste luchtafweersystemen ter wereld, die van Bagdad, zonder dat maar één van de toestellen werd geraakt, die nacht of later in de oorlog.

Toen ze hun werk hadden gedaan, slopen ze weer weg als pijlroggen in een kalme zee, terug naar Khamis Mushait.

De gevaarlijkste opdracht ging naar de Britse Tornado's. Zij zouden zich een week lang bezighouden met de vernietiging van de vijandelijke vliegvelden door de startbanen te bombarderen met hun grote, zware JP-233 bommen.

Daarbij hadden ze twee problemen. De Irakezen hadden bijzonder uitgestrekte vliegbases. Tallil was vier keer zo groot als Heathrow, met zestien banen die voor opstijgen, landen en taxiën konden worden gebruikt. Het was gewoon onmogelijk om al die banen te vernietigen. Het tweede probleem was de hoogte en de snelheid. De JP-233's konden alleen worden afgeworpen door een Tornado die een rechte, horizontale koers vloog. Na het bombardement hadden de Tornado's geen andere keus dan recht over het doelwit te vliegen. Ook als de radar was uitgeschakeld, kon de vijand nog wel iets uitrichten. De luchtdoelartillerie, bekend als Triple-A, bestookte de vijandelijke vliegtuigen in golven. Een van de piloten vertelde later dat hij het gevoel had of hij 'door buizen van gesmolten staal heen vloog'.

De Amerikanen hadden de proeven met de JP-233 gestaakt omdat ze de bommen te gevaarlijk vonden voor hun eigen piloten. Daar hadden ze gelijk in, maar de RAF ging stug door en verloor heel wat toestellen en bemanningen voordat ze een andere taak kreeg toegewezen.

De bommenwerpers werden gevolgd door een heel konvooi andere toestellen.

Luchtgevechtsjagers gaven de bommenwerpers dekking. De verbindingen tussen de Iraakse piloten (voor zover die erin waren geslaagd om op te stijgen) en de verkeersleiding op de grond werden gestoord door Ravens van de Amerikaanse luchtmacht en de vergelijkbare Prowlers van de Amerikaanse marine. De Iraakse gevechtsvliegers kregen dus geen mondelinge instructies en geen radarbegeleiding. De meesten waren zo verstandig om meteen terug te keren.

Ten zuiden van de grens cirkelden zestig tankers rond: Amerikaanse KC-135's en KC-10's, KA-6D's van de Amerikaanse marine en Britse Victors en VC-10's. Zij moesten de gevechtsvliegtuigen vanuit Saoedi-Arabië opvangen, bijtanken voordat ze aan hun missie begonnen en op de terugweg opnieuw van brandstof voorzien. Dat klinkt simpel, maar in het donker was dat geen sinecure. 'Alsof je spaghetti in de kont van een wilde kat probeert te steken,' was het commentaar van een van de piloten.

Boven de Golf, waar ze al vijf maanden waren gestationeerd, cirkelden de E-2 Hawkeyes van de Amerikaanse marine en de E-3 Sentry AWACS van de Amerikaanse luchtmacht, die met hun radar alle bevriende en vijandelijke toestellen in de gaten hielden en zo nodig de piloten waarschuwden en adviseerden.

Tegen het ochtendgloren waren de meeste Iraakse radarinstallaties vernietigd, de raketbases 'verblind' en de belangrijkste commandocentra verwoest. Het zou nog vier dagen en nachten kosten om het karwei af te maken, maar de geallieerden waren al bijna oppermachtig in de lucht. Later zouden ze zich concentreren op de krachtcentrales, telecommunicatiemasten, telefooncentrales, steunzenders, vliegtuighangars, verkeerstorens en alle bekende fabrieken en opslagplaatsen van massavernietigingswapens. Daarna volgde de systematische 'reductie' van vijftig procent van de gevechtskracht van het Iraakse leger ten zuiden en zuidwesten van de Koeweitse grens, een van de voorwaarden die generaal Schwarzkopf had gesteld voordat hij aan zijn grondaanval wilde beginnen.

Twee toen nog onbekende factoren zouden later het verloop van de oorlog wijzigen. Een daarvan was het Iraakse besluit om SCUD-raketten op Israël af te vuren; de andere factor was een gefrustreerde reactie van kapitein Don Walker van het 336e Tactical Fighter Squadron.

De ochtend van de 17e januari was het in Bagdad een grote chaos.

De gewone burgers hadden na drie uur 's nachts geen oog meer dichtgedaan. Zodra het licht werd, namen de eerste mensen voorzichtig een kijkje bij de puinhopen, verspreid over de stad. Dat ze de nacht hadden overleefd, scheen de meesten een wonder, want het waren eenvoudige mensen die niet wisten dat die twintig rokende ruïnes zorgvuldig waren geselecteerd en zo nauwkeurig waren getroffen dat burgers geen gevaar hadden gelopen.

Voor de leiding van het land was de klap veel groter. Saddam Hoessein had het presidentiële paleis verlaten en zich teruggetrokken in zijn merkwaardige bunker van enkele verdiepingen, schuin onder het Rashid Hotel, dat nog steeds vol zat met Westerlingen, voornamelijk journalisten.

De bunker was jaren eerder gebouwd, hoofdzakelijk met Zweedse technologie, in een enorme krater die met bulldozers was uitgegraven. De veiligheidsmaatregelen waren zo verfijnd dat het in feite een kist binnen een kist was. Rondom de binnenste kist zaten veren die zo sterk waren dat ze de bewoners tegen een kernexplosie konden beschermen. De schokgolven die de stad zouden verpulveren zouden in de bunker als een lichte trilling worden waargenomen.

Hoewel de schuilkelder bereikbaar was via een hydraulisch bediend luik in het braakliggende terrein achter het hotel, lag het grootste deel van het complex onder het hotel zelf, dat speciaal was gebouwd als onderkomen voor Westerlingen in Bagdad.

Een vijand die de bunker wilde verwoesten zou eerst het Rashid Hotel met de grond gelijk moeten maken.

Hoe ze ook hun best deden, de kritiekloze volgelingen van de president hadden grote moeite iets positiefs te ontdekken in de catastrofe van de afgelopen nacht. Heel langzaam begon de omvang van de ramp tot hen door te dringen.

Ze hadden allemaal gerekend op een bommentapijt op de hoofdstad waarbij de woonwijken zouden zijn vernietigd en duizenden onschuldige burgers de dood zouden hebben gevonden. Dan hadden ze het bloedbad aan de media

301

kunnen tonen en waren de gruwelijke beelden de hele wereld over gegaan. De golf van weerzin tegen president Bush en de Amerikaanse politiek zou de Veiligheidsraad hebben gedwongen de VN-troepen terug te trekken, na een veto van Rusland en China tegen nog grotere slachtingen.

Maar tegen de middag werd duidelijk dat de Zonen van de Honden zich niet aan dit scenario hadden gehouden. Voorzover de Iraakse generaals wisten, hadden alle bommen min of meer hun doel getroffen, en daar was het bij gebleven. De belangrijkste militaire installaties in Bagdad waren met opzet in dichtbevolkte wijken gesitueerd. Het leek dus onmogelijk om ze te vernietigen zonder duizenden slachtoffers te maken onder de burgerij.

Maar een inspectie van de stad maakte duidelijk dat twintig commandoposten, raketbases, radarinstallaties en verbindingscentra in puin waren gegooid terwijl de huizen in de directe omgeving weinig meer schade hadden opgelopen dan gebroken ruiten. De bewoners staarden met open mond maar ongedeerd naar de ravage.

Het regime moest dus zijn toevlucht nemen tot een denkbeeldig aantal slachtoffers en de bewering dat de Amerikaanse vliegtuigen als herfstbladeren uit de lucht waren geschoten.

De meeste Irakezen, murw gebeukt door jarenlange propaganda, geloofden die berichten, in het begin.

De bevelhebbers van de luchtverdediging wisten wel beter. Tegen de middag beseften de generaals dat ze bijna al hun radarsystemen hadden verloren, dat hun SAM-batterijen waren verblind en dat de verbindingen met de buitenposten bijna volledig waren verbroken. Erger nog, de radaroperateurs die het bombardement hadden overleefd beweerden dat de schade was aangericht door vliegtuigen die ze niet eens op hun scherm hadden gezien. Die leugenaars werden onmiddellijk gearresteerd.

Natuurlijk waren er ook slachtoffers gevallen onder de bevolking. Minstens twee Tomahawk-raketten, waarvan de vinnen niet door SAM-raketten maar door conventioneel Triple-A geschut waren beschadigd, hadden hun 'verstand' verloren en waren op de verkeerde plaats terechtgekomen. Een ervan had twee huizen verwoest en de tegels van een moskee geblazen, een schanddaad die 's middags aan de verzamelde pers werd getoond.

De andere was op een braakliggend terrein neergekomen en had daar een grote krater geslagen. Tegen het eind van de middag werd in die krater het lichaam van een vrouw gevonden, zwaar verminkt door de inslag die haar ogenschijnlijk had gedood.

De bombardementen gingen de hele dag door, zodat de ambulanceteams niet veel anders konden doen dan het lichaam haastig in een deken wikkelen en het naar het mortuarium van het dichtstbijzijnde ziekenhuis brengen.

Het ziekenhuis lag toevallig dicht bij een belangrijk commandocentrum van

302

de luchtmacht, dat door de bombardementen was verwoest. Alle bedden werden bezet door luchtmachtpersoneel dat bij de aanval gewond was geraakt. Ook enkele tientallen lijken van slachtoffers werden naar het mortuarium overgebracht. De vrouw was een van hen.

De patholoog had het druk en deed zijn werk snel en oppervlakkig. De identificatie en de doodsoorzaak waren zijn voornaamste prioriteiten. Hij had geen tijd voor een uitvoerig onderzoek. Aan de andere kant van de stad waren de explosies van nog meer bommen en het gebulder van de luchtafweer te horen, en de arts twijfelde er niet aan dat de avond nog meer doden zou opleveren.

Wat hem verbaasde was dat alle slachtoffers militairen waren, behalve de vrouw. Ze leek een jaar of dertig en ze was ooit knap geweest. De arts zag het cementgruis in het geronnen bloed op haar verbrijzelde gezicht, en wist waar ze was gevonden. Hij concludeerde dat ze op de vlucht was geslagen vlak voordat de raket op het braakliggende terrein was neergekomen en haar had gedood. Dat hadden de broeders ook op het kaartje aan haar voet geschreven voordat ze haar in een laken hadden gewikkeld om te worden begraven.

Naast haar lichaam was een handtas gevonden met een poederdoos, een lippenstift en haar papieren. Ze heette Leila Al-Hilla, ze was ongetwijfeld omgekomen bij het bombardement en de overwerkte patholoog liet haar afvoeren voor een haastige begrafenis.

Een uitvoeriger sectie, waarvoor hij die 17e januari geen tijd had, zou hebben uitgewezen dat de vrouw verscheidene malen bruut was verkracht voordat ze was doodgeslagen. Pas enkele uren later was haar lichaam in de krater gegooid.

Twee dagen eerder had generaal Abdullah Kadiri zijn comfortabele kantoor op het ministerie van Defensie verlaten. Hij had geen zin om zich door de Amerikanen te laten bombarderen want hij was ervan overtuigd dat het ministerie zou worden platgegooid voordat de luchtoorlog een paar dagen oud was. Daar kreeg hij gelijk in.

Hij had zich teruggetrokken in zijn eigen villa, die hopelijk anoniem genoeg was – hoe luxueus ook – om niet op de Amerikaanse lijst te staan. Ook daarin had hij gelijk.

De villa was lang geleden uitgerust met verbindingsapparatuur, die nu werd bediend door personeel van het ministerie. Al zijn contacten met de verschillende commandoposten van het tankkorps rondom Bagdad verliepen via ondergrondse glasvezelkabels, die veilig waren voor de bombardementen. Alleen de afgelegen eenheden – en natuurlijk de troepen in Koeweit – moesten via de radio worden opgeroepen, met de kans dat de berichten werden onderschept.

Maar toen de duisternis die avond over Bagdad neerdaalde, had hij andere problemen dan het contact met de commandanten van zijn Pantserbrigade, of de orders die hij hun moest geven. Zij speelden toch geen rol in de luchtoorlog. Het enige wat ze konden doen was hun tanks zoveel mogelijk verspreiden tussen de rijen nepvoertuigen, of ze in hun ondergrondse bunkers parkeren en afwachten.

Nee, Kadiri maakte zich zorgen over zijn persoonlijke veiligheid, en die werd niet bedreigd door de Amerikanen.

Twee nachten daarvoor was hij met een volle blaas uit bed gekomen, half versuft door de drank, zoals gewoonlijk. Toen hij naar de badkamer wankelde, bleek de deur te klemmen. Dat dacht hij tenminste. Hij gooide zijn volle gewicht van tweehonderd pond ertegenaan, de grendel scheurde los en de deur vloog open.

Hoe slaperig hij ook was, Abdullah Kadiri had zich niet uit de sloppen van Tikrit opgewerkt tot commandant van alle tanks buiten de Republikeinse Garde, had niet de glibberige ladder van de Ba'ath-partij beklommen en niet een bevoorrechte plaats in de Revolutionaire Commandoraad bemachtigd zonder een ruime mate van dierlijke sluwheid.

Zwijgend staarde hij naar zijn maîtresse, die in een ochtendjas op de wc zat, met op haar schoot een omgekeerde doos Kleenex waarop een briefje lag. Ze keek hem geschrokken aan, met open mond en haar pen nog in de lucht. Hij had haar overeind gesleurd en haar een kaakslag verkocht.

Toen ze bijkwam, doordat hij een flinke plens water in haar gezicht had gegooid, had de generaal het briefje al gelezen en zijn trouwe lijfwacht Kemal ontboden. Het was Kemal die de hoer had meegenomen naar de kelder.

Kadiri las het briefje nog een paar keer door. Als het over zijn levenswandel en zijn seksuele voorkeuren was gegaan – om hem in de toekomst te kunnen chanteren – had hij haar gewoon laten vermoorden. Voor chantage was hij niet bang. Zijn verdorven pleziertjes waren niets vergeleken met de manier waarop sommige andere volgelingen van de *Rais* tekeergingen, wist hij. En het zou Saddam een zorg zijn.

Maar dit was erger. Blijkbaar had hij haar dingen over de regering en het leger verteld. Ze was een spionne, dat was duidelijk. En hij moest weten hoe lang ze dit al deed, welke informatie ze had doorgegeven, en vooral aan wie. Kemal beleefde eerst zijn lang uitgestelde genoegen met haar, met toestemming van zijn baas. Geen enkele man zou nog opgewonden raken van wat er na de ondervraging van haar over was. Het duurde een paar uur. Toen wist Kadiri zeker dat ze Kemal alles had verteld wat ze wist.

Daarna ging Kemal voor zijn eigen plezier nog even met haar door, tot ze dood was.

Kadiri was ervan overtuigd dat ze niet de ware identiteit kende van de man die haar als spionne had gerekruteerd, maar de beschrijving die ze van hem gaf kon alleen maar van toepassing zijn op... Hassan Rahmani.

De uitwisseling van informatie voor geld in de kerk van de H. Jozef bewees dat de man professioneel te werk ging, en dat deed Rahmani zeker.

Dat hij in de gaten werd gehouden vond Kadiri niet erg. Iedereen in het gevolg van de *Rais* werd bespied. Sterker nog, ze bespioneerden elkaar allemaal.

De regels van de president waren simpel en duidelijk. Iedereen met een hoge positie moest in de gaten worden gehouden door drie van zijn collega's. Een aanklacht wegens verraad betekende meestal het einde. De meeste samenzweringen kwamen dus niet ver. Er was altijd wel iemand die de zaak verraadde zodat Saddam ervan hoorde.

Om het nog ingewikkelder te maken, werden de belangrijkste mensen ook van tijd tot tijd op de proef gesteld om te zien hoe ze reageerden. Een collega die daartoe opdracht kreeg nam een vriend apart en deed hem een verraderlijk voorstel.

Als de vriend daarin toestemde, of als hij de ander niet onmiddellijk aangaf, was hij verloren. Ieder subversief voorstel kon dus een provocatie zijn. Dat was de veiligste veronderstelling. En daarom gaf iedereen alles aan.

Maar dit was iets anders. Rahmani was het hoofd van de contraspionagedienst. Had hij zelf het initiatief genomen? En zo ja, waarom? Was het een operatie met medeweten en instemming van de *Rais* zelf? En zo ja, waarom?

Wat had hij allemaal gezegd, vroeg hij zich af. Onverstandige dingen, dat stond wel vast. Maar verraderlijk?

Leila's lichaam bleef in de kelder totdat de raketten insloegen. Daarna had Kemal een bomkrater gevonden waar hij het lijk in had achtergelaten. Kadiri had hem opdracht gegeven de handtas ernaast te leggen, zodat die schoft van een Rahmani zou weten wat er met zijn hoer gebeurd was.

Na middernacht zat generaal Abdullah Kadiri nog steeds te zweten. Hij deed wat water in zijn tiende glas arak. Als het alleen Rahmani was, zou hij wel afrekenen met die klootzak. Maar tot hoe hoog op de ladder werd hij verdacht? Hij zou heel voorzichtig moeten zijn, veel voorzichtiger dan vroeger. Nachtelijke uitstapjes naar de stad waren er niet meer bij. Trouwens, nu de luchtoorlog was begonnen, moest hij daar toch mee stoppen.

Simon Paxman was weer naar Londen teruggevlogen. Het had geen zin nog langer in Riyad te blijven. Jericho was door de CIA aan de kant geschoven, hoewel de onzichtbare spion uit Bagdad dat nog niet wist. En Mike Martin moest op zijn stek blijven totdat hij de kans kreeg naar de woestijn te vluchten en de grens over te steken.

Later zou hij met zijn hand op zijn hart kunnen zweren dat die ontmoeting met dr. Terry Martin op de avond van de 18e januari zuiver toeval was geweest. Hij wist dat Martin in Bayswater woonde, net als hij, maar het is een grote wijk met veel winkels.

Omdat zijn vrouw voor haar zieke moeder zorgde en hijzelf onverwachts was teruggekomen, had Paxman een lege flat en een lege koelkast aangetroffen. Daarom was hij naar een avondwinkel in Westbourne Grove gegaan om boodschappen te doen.

Terry Martins wagentje botste bijna tegen het zijne op toen hij bij de spaghetti en het hondenvoer de hoek om kwam. De twee mannen keken elkaar geschrokken aan.

'Ken ik je wel? Officieel?' vroeg Martin met een verlegen grijns.

Er was niemand in de buurt.

'Waarom niet?' zei Paxman. 'Ik ben maar een gewone ambtenaar die boodschappen doet voor het avondeten.'

Ze kwamen samen de winkel uit en besloten bij een Indiaas restaurant te gaan eten in plaats van thuis, in hun eentje. Hilary scheen ook weg te zijn.

Natuurlijk had Paxman dat nooit mogen doen. Hij had zich er niets van aan moeten trekken dat Terry Martins oudere broer zich in een levensgevaarlijke situatie bevond en dat hij – samen met anderen – daar verantwoordelijk voor was. Het had geen probleem voor hem mogen zijn dat de goedgelovige kleine academicus nu dacht dat zijn geliefde broer veilig in Saoedi-Arabië zat. In zijn beroep hoorde je je daar niet schuldig over te voelen. Maar dat deed Paxman wel.

En er was nog een probleem. Steve Laing, zijn chef op Century House, was nog nooit in Irak geweest. Wel in Egypte en Jordanië, maar niet in Irak. Paxman kende het land. En hij sprak Arabisch. Niet zo goed als Martin, natuurlijk, maar voordat hij tot hoofd van de sectie Irak was benoemd was hij een paar keer in het land geweest. En hij had groot respect gekregen voor het werk van de Iraakse wetenschappers en technici. Het was geen geheim dat de meeste Britse technische scholen hun Iraakse studenten tot de besten in de Arabische wereld rekenden.

Sinds zijn hoogste bazen hem hadden gezegd dat het laatste bericht van Jericho grote onzin was, was hij steeds bang geweest dat Irak – hoe onwaarschijnlijk ook – toch verder kon zijn dan de Westerse wetenschappers wilden geloven.

Hij wachtte tot de borden waren gebracht, omringd door alle bakjes die nu eenmaal bij een Indiase maaltijd horen, en nam toen een besluit.

'Terry,' zei hij, 'wat ik nu ga doen, kost me mijn baan als het ooit zou uitlekken.'

Martin keek hem geschrokken aan. 'Dat klinkt nogal dramatisch. Wat is er aan de hand?'

'Officieel mag ik niet meer met je praten.'

De academicus wilde juist wat mango-chutney op zijn bord scheppen. Zijn hand met de lepel bleef in de lucht hangen.

'Vertrouwen ze me niet meer? Steve Laing is zelf naar me toe gekomen!'

'Dat is het punt niet. Ze vinden dat je... je te veel zorgen maakt.'

Paxman wilde het woord 'zeuren' niet gebruiken.

'Misschien is dat wel zo. Dat komt door mijn opleiding. Academici houden niet van raadsels zonder een antwoord. Wij zoeken verder totdat we die vreemde hiërogliefen eindelijk begrijpen. Ging het om die opmerking in dat telefoongesprek?'

'Ja, onder meer.'

Paxman had kip khorma besteld, Martin had het graag wat heter, vindaloo. Omdat hij ervaring had met oosters eten, dronk hij er hete zwarte thee bij en geen ijskoud bier, dat de hitte alleen maar erger maakt. Hij knipperde met zijn ogen en keek Paxman over de rand van zijn kopje aan.

'Goed, maar wat wilde je me vertellen?'

'Beloof je me dat het onder ons blijft?'

'Natuurlijk.'

'We hebben nog een bericht onderschept.'

Paxman was niet van plan iets over Jericho te zeggen. Het groepje dat iets wist over het bestaan van de spion was heel klein, en dat wilde hij zo houden.

'Kan ik ernaar luisteren?'

'Nee. Het is geheim. Je hoeft Sean Plummer niet te bellen, want hij zou het glashard ontkennen. Bovendien zou hij dan weten van wie je het hebt gehoord.'

Martin nam nog wat raita om de kerrie te blussen.

'Wat staat er in dat bericht?'

Paxman vertelde het hem. Martin legde zijn vork neer en veegde zijn gezicht af, dat een roze kleur had onder zijn rode haar.

'Zou het... heel misschien... waar kunnen zijn?' vroeg Paxman.

'Dat weet ik niet. Ik ben geen natuurkundige. De hoge bazen geloven het niet?'

'Nee. De kerngeleerden zijn het er allemaal over eens dat het niet waar kan zijn. En dus heeft Saddam gelogen.'

Heimelijk vond Martin het nogal een vreemd radiobericht. Het klonk meer als vertrouwelijke informatie van iemand die bij een besloten vergadering aanwezig was geweest.

'Saddam liegt voortdurend,' zei hij. 'Maar meestal in het openbaar. Dit was toch een verklaring tegenover zijn naaste medewerkers? Ik vraag me af waarom. Om het moreel op te vijzelen nu de grondoorlog ieder moment kan uitbreken?'

'Ja, dat denken de deskundigen,' zei Paxman.

'Zijn de generaals op de hoogte gesteld?'

'Nee. Die hebben het nu erg druk en mogen niet worden lastiggevallen met een onzinverhaal.'

'Wat wil je precies van mij, Simon?'

'Je mening over Saddam. Niemand weet wat er in hem omgaat. In Westerse ogen gedraagt hij zich onbegrijpelijk. Wat is hij nou eigenlijk? Zwaar gestoord of een sluwe vos?'

'In zijn wereld het laatste. In zijn wereld gedraagt hij zich wèl begrijpelijk. De terreur die wij zo verafschuwen heeft voor hem geen morele kanten, alleen maar praktisch nut. Al die stoere taal en dreigementen zijn voor hem heel normaal. Pas als hij ònze wereld probeert binnen te dringen, met die afgrijselijke propaganda-uitzendingen uit Bagdad... toen hij dat jochie door zijn haar streek en de goedmoedige oom speelde, dat soort dingen... dan staat hij volledig voor schut. Maar in zijn eigen wereld niet. Daar overleeft hij alles, blijft hij aan de macht, houdt hij Irak verenigd en vernedert en vernietigt hij zijn vijanden...'

'Terry, terwijl wij hier zitten, wordt zijn land verwoest!'

'Dat maakt niet uit, Simon. Alles is vervangbaar.'

'Maar waarom zou hij dat hebben gezegd – àls hij het heeft gezegd?'

'Wat denken je bazen?'

'Dat het een leugen is.'

'Nee,' zei Martin. 'Hij liegt alleen voor het grote publiek. In zijn eigen kringetje hoeft dat niet. Die mensen blijven hem toch wel trouw. Nee, er zijn maar twee mogelijkheden. De bron van dat bericht heeft gelogen en Saddam heeft het nooit gezegd, of hij denkt dat het echt zo is.'

'Dan heeft iemand dus tegen hèm gelogen?'

'Dat zou kunnen. Maar die zal er zwaar voor moeten boeten als het uitkomt. Aan de andere kant, misschien heeft Saddam dat bericht bewust laten uitlekken, om te bluffen.'

Paxman kon niet zeggen wat hij wist. Het was geen onderschept bericht. Het kwam van Jericho. En in de twee jaar die hij voor de Israëli's en de drie maanden die hij voor de Engelsen en Amerikanen had gewerkt, had de spion zich nog nooit vergist.

'Je gelooft me niet?' vroeg Martin.

'Nee, niet echt,' gaf Paxman toe.

Martin zuchtte. 'Strootjes in de wind, Simon. Een zinnetje uit een telefoongesprek, een man die zijn mond moet houden en een hoerezoon wordt genoemd, een opmerking van Saddam over "slagen voor het oog van de wereld", en nu dit. We hebben een touw nodig.'

'Een touw?'

'Stro wordt alleen een baal als je er een touw omheen bindt. Er moeten nog meer aanwijzingen zijn over wat hij werkelijk denkt. Anders hebben jouw bazen gelijk en zal hij naar gifgas grijpen. Want dat heeft hij.'

'Goed. Ik zal op zoek gaan naar het touw.'

'En ik heb jou vanavond niet gezien,' zei Martin, 'en we hebben hier nooit over gesproken.'

'Dank je,' zei Paxman.

Op 19 januari, twee dagen nadat het was gebeurd, hoorde Hassan Rahmani van de dood van zijn spionne. Ze was niet komen opdagen voor een ontmoeting in de kerk en Rahmani, die het ergste vreesde, had de lijsten van de mortuaria opgevraagd.

Het ziekenhuis in Mansour had haar naam genoteerd, maar het lichaam was al begraven, samen met de militaire slachtoffers, in een massagraf.

Hassan Rahmani geloofde geen moment dat ze was gedood door een raketinslag terwijl ze midden in de nacht een open veldje overstak. Dat klonk als een spookverhaal. En de enige spoken in het luchtruim boven Bagdad waren de onzichtbare Amerikaanse bommenwerpers waarover hij in de Westerse militaire tijdschriften had gelezen. Dat waren geen spoken, maar logisch ontworpen machines. Zoals de dood van Leila Al-Hilla ook een logische verklaring had.

Het enige dat hij kon bedenken was dat generaal Kadiri haar had betrapt en zijn maatregelen had genomen. En dus had ze gepraat voordat ze was gestorven.

Dat betekende voor hem dat Kadiri een machtige en gevaarlijke vijand was geworden. Erger nog, zijn belangrijkste bron bij de geheime beraadslagingen van het regime was hij nu kwijt.

Als hij had geweten dat Kadiri net zo ongerust was als hijzelf zou Rahmani verheugd zijn geweest. Maar dat wist hij niet. Hij wist alleen dat hij bijzonder voorzichtig moest zijn.

Op de tweede dag van de luchtoorlog lanceerde Irak zijn eerste batterij raketten tegen Israël. De media beschreven ze meteen als Scud-B's van Russische makelij, en zo werden ze de rest van de oorlog genoemd, maar in feite waren het helemaal geen Scuds.

Het motief voor de aanval was niet zo vreemd. Irak besefte heel goed dat Israël niet bereid was een groot aantal slachtoffers onder de burgerij te accepteren. Toen de eerste raket in Tel Aviv insloeg, ging Israël meteen op het oorlogspad. Dat was precies wat Bagdad wilde.

Tot de Coalitie van vijftig landen tegen Irak behoorden ook zeventien Arabische staten, en als die één ding gemeen hadden – afgezien van de islam – was het hun vijandschap jegens Israël. Irak ging er, waarschijnlijk terecht, vanuit dat de Arabische landen zich uit de Coalitie zouden terugtrekken als Israël tot een militaire actie kon worden geprovoceerd. Zelfs koning Fahd, de vorst van Saoedi-Arabië en de hoeder van de twee heilige plaatsen, zou zich dan in een onmogelijke positie bevinden.

De eerste angst toen de raketten op Israël neerdaalden was dat ze met gifgas of bacteriën waren geladen. Als dat zo was geweest, had Israël wel móeten reageren. Maar al snel bleek dat de wapens van conventionele koppen waren voorzien. Toch was het psychologische effect op de Israëlische bevolking enorm.

De Verenigde Staten oefenden meteen zware druk op Jeruzalem uit om zich te beheersen. De geallieerden zouden wel terugslaan, beloofden ze Itzhak Shamir. Israël lanceerde wel een tegenaanval in de vorm van een groep F-15 jachtbommenwerpers, maar riep ze terug toen ze nog in het Israëlische luchtruim waren.

De echte Scud was een onhandige, verouderde Russische raket waarvan Irak er een paar jaar eerder 900 had gekocht. Hij had een bereik van nog geen 300 km en was uitgerust met een gevechtskop van ongeveer 1000 pond. De raket had geen geleidingssysteem en in zijn oorspronkelijke vorm kon hij, op maximale afstand, binnen een straal van 800 meter van zijn doelwit terechtkomen.

Voor Irak was het eigenlijk een nutteloze aankoop. In de Iraans-Iraakse oorlog waren de Scuds niet in staat om Teheran te bereiken, en Israël al helemaal niet, zelfs niet als ze vanuit het uiterste westen van Irak werden gelanceerd.

In de tussentijd hadden de Irakezen, met Duitse technologie, een paar bizarre ingrepen uitgevoerd. Ze hadden de Scuds in stukken gehakt en uit drie van die stukken twee nieuwe raketten gebouwd. Kortom, de nieuwe Al-Hoessein raket was een rommeltje.

Door extra brandstoftanks in te bouwen had Irak de actieradius van de raketten tot 620 km vergroot, zodat ze Teheran en Israël nu wel konden bereiken, en dat deden ze ook. Maar de lading was daardoor beperkt tot een miezerige 160 pond. De gebrekkige besturing werkte nog slechter. Twee ervan, die op Israël waren gericht, misten niet alleen Tel Aviv maar de hele republiek en kwamen in Jordanië neer.

Maar als middel tot terreur hadden ze bijna succes. Hoewel het totale aantal Al-Hoesseins dat in Israël insloeg minder lading had dan één Amerikaanse 200-ponder op Irak, brachten ze de Israëlische bevolking behoorlijk in paniek.

Amerika reageerde op drie manieren. Maar liefst 1000 geallieerde gevechts-vliegtuigen werden van hun reguliere taken boven Irak ontheven en kregen opdracht de vaste en – veel lastiger – de mobiele lanceerinstallaties van de raketten op te sporen.

Binnen enkele uren werd een aantal batterijen Amerikaanse Patriots naar Israël overgebracht om de inkomende raketten uit de lucht te schieten, maar voornamelijk om Israël te bewegen zich buiten de oorlog te houden.

De SAS en later ook de Amerikaanse Groene Baretten werden naar de weste-lijke woestijn van Irak gestuurd om de mobiele lanceerinstallaties te vinden en ze met hun eigen Milan-raketten te vernietigen of via de radio om een luchtaanval te vragen.

Het succes van de Patriots, die als redders van de schepping werden binnen-gehaald, was vrij beperkt, maar dat was hun schuld niet. Raytheon had de Patriots ontworpen om vliegtuigen te onderscheppen, geen raketten, en daarom moesten ze nu haastig aan hun nieuwe rol worden aangepast. De reden waarom ze zo zelden een inkomende gevechtskop raakten, is nooit bekendgemaakt.

De Al-Hoesseins hadden niet alleen een grotere actieradius dan de oude Scuds, maar ook een hogere baan. De nieuwe raket drong in zijn parabool-baan zelfs tot in de ruimte door, en werd vervolgens gloeiendheet als hij weer in de dampkring kwam. Daar was de Scud niet op berekend. Zodra hij in de atmosfeer terugkeerde, viel hij in stukken uit elkaar. Wat op Israël neerdaalde was geen complete raket, maar een omlaag tuimelend vuilnis-vat.

De Patriot deed braaf zijn werk, maar zodra hij de Al-Hoessein wilde onder-scheppen, stuitte hij niet op één raket maar op twaalf brokstukken. Met zijn kleine brein koos hij daarom het grootste stuk, meestal de lege brandstof-tank, die stuurloos naar beneden kwam. De veel kleinere gevechtskop, die ook was losgeraakt, stortte neer. Een groot aantal explodeerde niet eens, en de gevolgen bleven in het algemeen beperkt tot schade aan gebouwen.

De zogenaamde Scud had dus voornamelijk een pyschologisch effect, maar dat gold ook voor de Patriots die hem bestreden. In dat opzicht waren de tegenmaatregelen effectief.

Een ander gevolg was een afspraak tussen Amerika en Israël, die uit drie onderdelen bestond. Deel een was het leveren van Patriots, gratis. Deel twee was de belofte dat Israël zou kunnen beschikken over de verbeterde Arrow-raket zodra die in 1994 klaar was. En als derde concessie mocht Israël zelf honderd extra doelwitten kiezen die door de geallieerde luchtmacht zouden worden vernietigd. De selectie werd gemaakt: voornamelijk doelen in weste-lijk Irak die voor Israël van belang waren, zoals wegen, bruggen, vliegvelden, alles wat naar het westen gericht was. Geen van deze doelwitten had iets te maken met de bevrijding van Koeweit aan de andere kant van het schiereiland.

De jachtbommenwerpers van de Amerikaanse en Britse luchtmacht die op Scud-jacht werden gestuurd, meldden talloze treffers, hoewel de CIA daar nogal sceptisch over was, tot grote woede van generaal Chuck Horner en generaal Schwarzkopf.

Pas twee jaar na de oorlog gaf Washington officieel toe dat er nooit een mobiele Scud-lanceerinstallatie vanuit de lucht was vernietigd, een verklaring waar de betrokken piloten nog altijd woedend over worden. Feit was dat zij grotendeels werden misleid door camouflagetechnieken.

De zuidelijke woestijn van Irak is zo glad als een biljartlaken, maar het westen en noordwesten zijn rotsachtig en heuvelachtig, doorsneden met duizenden wadi's en kloven. Dat was het gebied waar Mike Martin doorheen was gereden op weg naar Bagdad. Voordat de luchtaanvallen begonnen, had Irak tientallen mobiele Scud-lanceerinstallaties nagemaakt, die samen met de echte installaties overal in het landschap waren verborgen.

De gewoonte was om ze 's nachts tevoorschijn te halen. Ze bestonden uit een buis van plaatmetaal op een oude truck met een vlakke laadbak. Tegen de ochtend werd dan een vat met olie en proppen katoen in de buis in brand gestoken. Heel ver weg registreerden de sensors van de AWACS de hittebron, en het radarvliegtuig waarschuwde de piloten. De jagers doken op de aangegeven coördinaten af, voerden een aanval uit en meldden dat ze de installatie hadden vernietigd.

De SAS-mensen lieten zich daardoor niet misleiden. Hoewel ze niet groot in aantal waren, zwermden ze in hun Landrovers en op hun motoren door de woestijn, hielden zich schuil in de zinderende hitte overdag en de ijzige koude 's nachts, en verkenden de omgeving. Vanaf tweehonderd meter afstand konden ze al zien wat een echte lanceerinstallatie was en wat niet.

Als de lanceertrucks tevoorschijn kwamen uit duikers en van onder bruggen waar ze waren verborgen, keken de SAS-mannen vanuit hun schuilplaatsen zwijgend toe. Als er te veel Irakezen in de buurt waren, vroegen ze via de radio om een luchtaanval. Als ze de kans kregen, gebruikten ze hun eigen Milan anti-tankraketten, die een flinke knal veroorzaakten als ze de brandstoftank van een echte Al-Hoessein raakten.

Al snel werd duidelijk dat er een onzichtbare noord-zuidlijn door de woestijn liep. Alleen de raketten ten westen van die lijn konden Israël bereiken. De geallieerden probeerden de Iraakse raketteams zo bang te maken dat ze zich niet meer ten westen van de lijn durfden te wagen maar hun wapens ten oosten van de lijn afvuurden en daarover logen tegen hun chefs. Het kostte acht dagen maar daarna was het afgelopen met de raketaanvallen op Israël en werden ze niet meer hervat.

Later werd de weg van Bagdad naar Jordanië als scheidslijn gebruikt. Ten noorden daarvan lag 'Scud Alley North', het terrein van de Amerikaanse Speciale Eenheden, die er met lange-afstands helikopters naartoe werden gebracht. Ten zuiden lag 'Scud Alley South', het gebied van de Britse Special Air Service. Vier dappere kerels sneuvelden in die woestijn, maar ze deden hun werk, terwijl miljarden dollars aan technologie zich om de tuin liet leiden.

Het 336e Squadron van Al Kharz was nog niet naar de westelijke woestijn gestuurd. Op de vierde dag van de oorlog, op 20 januari, moesten ze een grote SAM-raketbasis ten noordwesten van Bagdad aanvallen. De SAM's werden gestuurd door twee grote radarschotels.

Volgens de plannen van generaal Horner verplaatsten de luchtaanvallen zich steeds verder naar het noorden. Nu bijna alle raketbases en radarinstallaties ten zuiden van de horizontale lijn door Bagdad waren weggevaagd, was het moment aangebroken om het luchtruim ten oosten, westen en noorden van de hoofdstad schoon te vegen.

Met vierentwintig Strike Eagles in het squadron zou er die 20e januari meer dan één missie worden gevlogen. De squadron-commandant, luitenant-kolonel Steve Turner, had twaalf toestellen aan de raketbasis toegewezen. Zo'n grote zwerm Eagles stond bekend als een 'gorilla'.

De gorilla werd aangevoerd door twee majoors. Vier van de twaalf toestellen waren bewapend met HARM's, anti-radarraketten die zich op de infraroodsignalen van een radarschotel richtten. De andere acht hadden elk twee lange, glanzende, roestvrijstalen lasergeleide bommen bij zich van het type GBU-10-1. Als de radar was uitgeschakeld en de raketten stuurloos, zouden de bommen de raketbatterijen moeten vernietigen.

Alles leek goed te gaan. De twaalf Eagles vertrokken in drie groepen van vier, vormden een losse formatie en klommen naar een hoogte van 25 000 voet. De lucht was helderblauw en de okergele woestijn goed zichtbaar.

De weersverwachting voor het doelgebied sprak over een sterkere wind dan boven Saoedi-Arabië, maar er werd niet gerept over een *shamal*, een van die snelle zandstormen die een doelwit binnen enkele seconden onzichtbaar kunnen maken.

Ten zuiden van de grens ontmoetten de twaalf Eagles hun tankers, twee KC-10's. Iedere tanker kon zes dorstige jagers helpen. Eén voor één kropen de Eagles naar hun positie achter de tanker en wachtten tot de operator, achter zijn plexiglasruit op enkele meters afstand, de slang met de brandstofopening had verbonden.

Toen ze waren bijgetankt zwenkten de twaalf Eagles naar het noorden en drongen het Iraakse luchtruim binnen. Een AWACS boven de Golf meldde dat er geen vijandelijke toestellen waren gesignaleerd. Was dat wel zo geweest,

313

dan hadden de Eagles, afgezien van hun bommen, nog twee typen aanvals-raketten aan boord: de Air-Interception Missile-7 en de AIM-9, beter bekend als de Sparrow en de Sidewinder.

De raketbasis was snel gevonden, maar de radar was niet actief. Als de radarschotels nog niet werkten toen de Eagles naderden, hadden ze de vijandelijke toestellen meteen moeten aanstralen om hun SAM's te kunnen afvuren. Op het moment dat de radar actief werd, zouden de vier Strike Eagles met de HARM's de installaties hebben vernietigd en 'hun hele dag hebben verpest', zoals de piloten het meestal uitdrukten.

Of de Iraakse commandant gewoon bang was of juist heel slim, zouden de Amerikanen nooit te weten komen. In elk geval weigerde hij zijn radar te gebruiken. De eerste vier Eagles, onder aanvoering van hun commandant, doken op de basis af om de Irakezen te provoceren, maar ze reageerden niet. Het zou heel onverstandig zijn geweest van de bommenwerpers om een aanval uit te voeren terwijl de vijandelijke radar nog intact was. Als de radar opeens was ingeschakeld, hadden de Iraakse SAM's de Eagles zonder probleem uit de lucht kunnen schieten.

Na twintig minuten werd de aanval afgeblazen en kregen de verschillende onderdelen van de gorilla een ander doelwit toegewezen.

Don Walker overlegde snel met Tim Nathanson, zijn wizzo die achter hem zat. Het secundaire doelwit voor die dag was een vaste Scud-installatie ten zuiden van Samarra, die ook door andere jachtbommenwerpers zou worden aangevallen omdat het een bekende gifgasfabriek was.

De AWACS meldde dat er geen vliegtuigen waren opgestegen vanaf de twee grote Iraakse luchtmachtbases Samarra Oost en Balad Zuidoost. Don Walker riep zijn wingman op en samen gingen de twee toestellen op weg naar de Scud-lanceerinstallatie.

Alle communicatie tussen de Amerikaanse vliegtuigen werd gecodeerd door het 'Have-quick' systeem, dat de gesprekken onverstaanbaar maakt voor iedereen die niet over dezelfde apparatuur beschikt. De codering kan dagelijks worden veranderd, maar was hetzelfde voor alle geallieerde toestellen.

Walker keek om zich heen. Het luchtruim was leeg. Zijn wingman Randy 'R-2' Roberts vloog achthonderd meter achter hem, iets hoger, met zijn wizzo Jim 'Boomer' Henry achterin.

Toen ze boven de Scud-installatie kwamen, dook Walker omlaag om het doelwit te identificeren. Maar tot zijn woede werd het aan het gezicht ontrokken door wolken woestijnzand. Er was een *shamal* opgestoken, aangewakkerd door de krachtige woestijnwind vlak boven de grond.

Zijn lasergeleide bommen hadden daar geen last van, zolang ze de laserstraal maar konden volgen die hij op het doelwit richtte. Maar daarvoor moest hij de Scud-installatie wel kunnen zíen.

Bovendien begon zijn brandstof op te raken. Nijdig keerde hij terug. Twee tegenvallers op één ochtend. Dat was een beetje te veel. Hij had er de pest aan om te landen met al zijn bommen nog aan het rek. Maar er zat niets anders op. De weg naar huis liep naar het zuiden.

Drie minuten later zag hij een uitgestrekt industrieel complex beneden zich. 'Wat is dat?' vroeg hij aan Tim.

De navigator raadpleegde zijn gegevens. 'Het heet Tarmija.'

'Jezus, het is wel groot.'

'Ja.'

Ze wisten niet dat het industrieterrein van Tarmija 381 gebouwen telde en vijftien bij vijftien kilometer groot was.

'Staat het op de lijst?'

'Nee.'

'Ik ga er toch op af. Randy, geef me dekking.'

'Begrepen,' antwoordde zijn wingman.

De Strike Eagle dook omlaag vanaf een hoogte van 10000 voet. Het industriecomplex strekte zich naar alle kanten uit. In het midden stond een reusachtig gebouw, zo groot als een overdekt stadion.

'Ik val aan.'

'Don, het is geen doelwit.'

Walker liet zich zakken tot 8000 voet, activeerde zijn lasergeleidingssysteem en richtte het op de grote fabriek schuin beneden hem. Op zijn headsup display zag hij de afstand snel kleiner worden. De seconden telden af. Zodra de meter op nul stond, wierp hij zijn bommen af, met de neus van de Eagle nog steeds op het naderende doelwit gericht.

De laserzoeker van de twee bommen was van het PAVEWAY-principe. Onder de romp van de Eagle hing de geleidingsmodule, die Lantirn werd genoemd. De Lantirn wierp een onzichtbare infrarode straal naar het doelwit, die weerkaatste en een soort elektronische trechter vormde die naar de bom was toegekeerd.

De PAVEWAY-neuskegel vond die trechter, dook erin en volgde hem omlaag tot hij op de juiste plaats uitkwam.

Beide bommen troffen doel. Ze explodeerden onder de dakrand van de fabriek. Meteen trok Don Walker de neus van de Eagle omhoog en klom naar 25000 voet. Een uurtje later, nadat ze weer in de lucht hadden bijgetankt, landden Walker en zijn wingman op Al Kharz.

Voordat hij de neus van zijn toestel omhoog had getrokken, had Walker nog de verblindende flits van de twee explosies gezien, en een grote zuil van rook en stof.

Hij zag niet dat de twee bommen een groot deel van het dak de lucht in hadden gesmeten als het zeil van een schip op zee. Bovendien was het hem ontgaan dat de harde woestijnwind – die ook verantwoordelijk was voor de zandstorm die de Scud-installatie aan het oog had onttrokken – de rest had gedaan. Het complete dak werd van de fabriek gescheurd, als het deksel van een sardineblikje, en de stalen platen vlogen als dodelijke projectielen alle kanten op.

Terug op de basis moest Don Walker, zoals iedere piloot, uitvoerig verslag uitbrengen. Dat kostte veel tijd, maar het was niet anders. Hij werd ondervraagd door de inlichtingenofficier van het squadron, majoor Beth Kroger.

Niemand beweerde dat de gorilla een succes was geweest, maar alle piloten hadden hun secundaire doelwit uitgeschakeld. Op één na. De zelfverzekerde wapenofficier van het squadron had ook zijn tweede doelwit moeten opgeven en daarom een willekeurig ander doel gezocht.

'Waarom deed je dat, verdomme?' vroeg Beth Kroger.

'Omdat het zo groot was en nogal belangrijk leek.'

'Maar het stond niet op de lijst,' wierp ze tegen. Ze noteerde het doelwit dat hij had vernietigd, met de exacte locatie en beschrijving, voegde zijn eigen schaderapport erbij en stuurde de hele zaak door naar het TACC, het Tactical Air Control Centre, dat samen met de analisten van het Zwarte Gat in de kelder van de CENTAF onder het hoofdkwartier van de Saoedische luchtmacht in Riyad was ondergebracht.

'Als het een fabriek van babyvoeding of mineraalwater blijkt te zijn, zul je er nog van lusten,' waarschuwde ze Walker.

'Weet je, Beth, je bent best mooi als je kwaad bent,' plaagde hij haar.

Beth Kroger vond haar carrière belangrijk. Als ze wilde flirten, dan het liefst met een kolonel of een hogere rang. En omdat de enige drie kolonels op de basis keurig waren getrouwd, viel Al Kharz in dat opzicht behoorlijk tegen.

'Let op uw woorden, *kapitein*,' voegde ze hem toe, voordat ze verdween om haar rapport in te dienen.

Walker liep zuchtend naar zijn brits om een tukje te doen. Ze had natuurlijk gelijk. Als hij zojuist het grootste weeshuis ter wereld had platgegooid, zou generaal Horner zijn kapiteinsstrepen straks persoonlijk als tandenstokers gebruiken. Niemand vertelde Don Walker ooit wat hij die ochtend had geraakt. Maar het was geen weeshuis.

Dezelfde avond kwam Karim naar de flat van Edith Hardenberg in Grinzing, waar ze voor hem zou koken. Hij nam het openbaar vervoer naar de
buitenwijk en had cadeautjes bij zich: twee geurkaarsen, die hij op de kleine
tafel in het alkoofje aanstak, en twee flessen goede wijn.

Toen ze hem binnenliet, bloosde Edith verlegen, zoals altijd. Daarna liep ze
weer terug naar de kleine keuken waar ze Wiener schnitzels braadde. Het
was twintig jaar geleden sinds ze voor het laatst voor een man had gekookt,
en ze vond het een hele opgave, maar ook spannend.

Karim had haar bij zijn binnenkomst een kuise kus op haar wang gegeven,
waardoor ze nog meer in verwarring raakte. Even later had hij een plaat van
Verdi's *Nabucco* in haar collectie gevonden en zette hem op.

Al snel zweefde de geur van de kaarsen, muskus en patchoeli, op het zachte
ritme van het Slavenkoor de kamer door.

Het appartement was precies zoals het Neviot-team, dat een paar weken
geleden had ingebroken, hem had beschreven: heel keurig en heel schoon.
De flat van een werkende vrouw die alleen woonde.

Toen het eten klaar was, zette Edith het met uitvoerige excuses op tafel.
Karim probeerde het vlees en verklaarde dat hij nog nooit zoiets lekkers had
gegeten, waardoor ze nog heftiger bloosde maar duidelijk gevleid was.

Onder het eten praatten ze over culturele dingen – hun voorgenomen bezoek
aan het paleis Schönbrunn en de beroemde Spaanse Rijschool, de Hofreit-
schule aan de Josefsplatz, met de Lippizaner paarden.

Edith at zoals ze alles deed, heel netjes, als een vogeltje dat aan een lekker
hapje pikt. Ze droeg haar haar nog altijd in een knotje in haar nek.

Karim had de felle lamp boven de tafel uitgedaan. Bij het licht van de kaarsen was hij donker, knap en hoffelijk als altijd. Hij vulde regelmatig haar
wijnglas bij, waardoor ze veel meer dronk dan het schaarse glaasje dat ze
zichzelf meestal toestond.

De uitwerking van het eten, de wijn, de kaarsen, de muziek en het gezelschap van haar jonge vriend holde langzaam haar weerstand uit.

Toen ze klaar waren met eten, boog Karim zich over de lege borden naar
voren en keek haar diep in de ogen.

'Edith?'

'Ja?'

'Mag ik je wat vragen?'

'Zeg het maar.'

'Waarom draag je je haar zo strak naar achteren?'

Dat was een onbeschaamde, persoonlijke vraag. Ze bloosde weer. 'Ik... zo draag ik het altijd.'

Nee, dat was niet waar. Er was een tijd geweest, herinnerde ze zich, met Horst, toen het in dichte bruine lokken op haar schouders had gehangen, in de zomer van 1970. Toen had ze het laten wapperen in de bries op de vijver van het Schlosspark van Laxenburg.

Zonder een woord stond Karim op en kwam achter haar staan. Edith raakte half in paniek. Dit was belachelijk. Met behendige vingers haalde hij de schildpadkam uit haar knotje. Dit moest ophouden. Ze voelde dat hij de haarspelden lostrok, zodat haar haar los over haar rug golfde. Ze bleef stokstijf zitten. Dezelfde vingers tilden haar bruine haar op en lieten het aan weerskanten van haar gezicht vallen.

Karim kwam naast haar staan. Ze keek op. Hij stak haar zijn handen toe en glimlachte.

'Dat is beter. Zo zie je er tien jaar jonger uit, en veel knapper. Laten we op de bank gaan zitten. Kies jij maar je favoriete muziek, dan zal ik koffie zetten. Goed?'

Zonder haar toestemming te vragen pakte hij haar kleine handen en trok haar overeind. Hij liet zijn ene hand langs zijn zij vallen en bracht haar van het alkoofje naar de zitkamer. Toen liet hij haar andere hand los en liep naar de keuken.

Goddank, dacht ze. Ze trilde van top tot teen. Hun vriendschap was toch platonisch? Maar hij had haar ook niet echt aangeraakt. Niet ècht. Dat zou ze natuurlijk nooit goedvinden.

Ze zag zichzelf in de spiegel aan de muur, blozend, met haar haar op haar schouders, over haar oren, als omlijsting van haar gezicht. Heel even ving ze een glimp op van het meisje dat ze twintig jaar geleden had gekend.

Maar ze vermande zich en zette een plaat op. Haar geliefde Strauss, de walsen waarvan ze iedere noot kende. Gelukkig was hij in de keuken en zag hij niet dat ze de plaat bijna liet vallen. Zonder moeite leek hij de koffie, het water, de filter en de suiker te kunnen vinden.

Ze bleef zo ver mogelijk op de hoek van de bank zitten toen hij terugkwam, met haar knieën bij elkaar en haar koffie op haar schoot. Ze wilde met hem praten over het nieuwe concert van de Musikverein de volgende week. Maar de woorden kwamen niet. Zwijgend nam ze een slok koffie.

'Edith, alsjeblieft, je moet niet bang voor me zijn,' mompelde hij. 'Ik ben toch je vriend?'

'Doe niet zo raar. Natuurlijk ben ik niet bang voor je.'

'Gelukkig, want ik zou je nooit pijn doen.'

318

Haar vriend... Natuurlijk waren ze vrienden, een vriendschap gebaseerd op hun gezamenlijke liefde voor muziek, kunst, opera en cultuur. Meer was het niet. Maar het was zo'n kleine sprong van vriend naar vríend. Ze wist dat de andere secretaressen op de bank een echtgenoot of een vriend hadden. Ze zag hoe ze zich op een afspraakje verheugden, hoe ze de volgende dag op de gang stonden te giechelen en medelijden met haar hadden omdat ze altijd alleen was.

'Dat is toch *Rosen aus dem Süden*?'

'Ja, natuurlijk.'

'Dat is mijn liefste wals.'

'De mijne ook.' Zo ging het beter. Terug naar de muziek.

Hij nam haar kopje van haar schoot en zette het naast zijn eigen kop op het tafeltje. Toen stond hij op, pakte haar handen en trok haar overeind.

'Wat...?'

Hij nam haar rechterhand in zijn linker, sloeg een sterke, zelfverzekerde arm om haar middel, en het volgende moment dansten ze een wals op het parket in de kleine ruimte tussen de meubels.

Meteen toeslaan, ouwe jongen, zou Gidi Barzilai hebben gezegd. *Geen tijd verspillen.* Wat wist hij ervan? Niets. Eerst moest je het vertrouwen winnen. De rest kwam vanzelf. Karim hield zijn rechterhand veilig op Ediths rug.

Onder het dansen, op keurige afstand van elkaar, bracht Karim hun ineenge-strengelde vingers naar zijn schouder toe en trok Edith met zijn rechterarm wat dichter tegen zich aan. Het ging bijna ongemerkt.

Edith raakte met haar hoofd zijn borst en draaide haar gezicht opzij. Haar kleine boezem drukte tegen hem aan en ze rook zijn mannelijke geur.

Ze deinsde terug. Hij hield haar niet tegen. Met zijn rechterhand liet hij haar los en met zijn linker tilde hij haar kin omhoog. Toen kuste hij haar, onder het dansen.

Het was geen brutale kus. Hij hield zijn lippen gesloten en probeerde de hare niet van elkaar te dwingen. Edith viel ten prooi aan een maalstroom van gevoelens en sensaties, als een onbestuurbaar vliegtuig. Ze wilde pro-testeren, maar ze kon het niet. De bank, Herr Gemütlich, haar reputatie, zijn jeugd, zijn buitenlandse afkomst, het leeftijdsverschil, de warmte, de wijn, de geuren, zijn kracht, zijn lippen. De muziek stopte.

Als hij verder was gegaan, zou ze hem de deur uit hebben gezet. Maar hij liet haar los en wachtte tot haar hoofd weer tegen zijn borst rustte. Zo ble-ven ze een paar seconden roerloos staan, in het stille appartement.

Het was Edith die zich terugtrok. Ze draaide zich om naar de bank en ging zitten, voor zich uit starend. Hij liet zich op zijn knieën voor haar zakken en nam haar handen in de zijne.

'Ben je nu boos, Edith?'

319

'Dat had je niet moeten doen,' zei ze.

'Ik wilde het ook niet. Dat zweer ik je. Ik kon er niets aan doen.'

'Je kunt beter gaan.'

'Edith, als je boos bent en me wilt straffen, is er maar één manier. Door te zeggen dat je me nooit meer wilt zien.'

'Dat weet ik niet.'

'Zeg alsjeblieft dat ik weer bij je mag komen.'

'Ach, dat zal wel.'

'Als je nee zegt, geef ik mijn studie op en ga ik terug naar huis. Ik zou niet meer in Wenen kunnen wonen als jij me niet wilt zien.'

'Doe niet zo raar. Natuurlijk moet je je studie afmaken.'

'Mag ik je dan weer zien?'

'Goed.'

Vijf minuten later was hij vertrokken. Ze deed de lichten uit, trok haar preutse katoenen nachthemd aan, waste haar gezicht, poetste haar tanden en ging naar bed.

In het donker lag ze met opgetrokken knieën. Na twee uur deed ze iets wat ze in jaren niet had gedaan. Ze glimlachte in de duisternis. Er ging een krankzinnige gedachte door haar hoofd, steeds opnieuw, maar ze vond het niet erg. Ik heb een vriend! Hij is tien jaar jonger, een student, een buitenlander, een Arabier en een moslim. Maar dat kan me niet schelen.

Kolonel Dick Beatty van de Amerikaanse luchtmacht had die avond de late dienst, in de kelder onder Old Airport Road in Riyad.

Het Zwarte Gat sliep nooit. En die eerste dagen van de oorlog werd er nog harder en sneller gewerkt dan anders.

Het meesterplan van generaal Chuck Horner was enigszins verstoord door de honderden vliegtuigen die nu jacht maakten op de Scud-installaties in plaats van hun lijst met doelwitten af te werken.

Hoe zorgvuldig je je plannen ook voorbereidt, in de praktijk loopt het altijd anders, dat zal iedere generaal beamen. De onverwachte crisis van de raketaanvallen op Israël leverde grote problemen op. Tel Aviv schreeuwde tegen Washington en Washington tegen Riyad. De aanvallen op de Scud-batterijen waren de prijs die de Amerikanen moesten betalen voor Israëls afzijdigheid. Daar viel niets aan te doen. Iedereen begreep dat het voor de kwetsbare Coalitie tegen Irak een ramp zou zijn als Israël zijn geduld zou verliezen en zich in de strijd zou mengen, maar dat maakte de situatie niet minder lastig.

De oorspronkelijke doelwitten van de derde dag werden nu opgeschort wegens gebrek aan vliegtuigen, en dat leidde tot een domino-effect. Een ander probleem was dat er nog steeds geen goed beeld kon worden gekregen van de aangebrachte schade. En dat was van vitaal belang, omdat de gevolgen anders fataal konden zijn.

Het Zwarte Gat moest weten in hoeverre de luchtaanvallen waren geslaagd. Als een belangrijk Iraaks commandocentrum, een radarinstallatie of een raketbatterij op de lijst stond, werd er een bombardement op uitgevoerd. Maar was het doelwit werkelijk vernietigd? En in welke mate? Tien procent, vijftig procent, of was het met de grond gelijk gemaakt?

Het was gevaarlijk om voetstoots aan te nemen dat de vijandelijke basis was platgegooid. De volgende dag konden er nietsvermoedende geallieerde toestellen overheen vliegen, op weg naar een volgende missie. Als de basis nog functioneerde, zou dat de piloten het leven kunnen kosten.

Iedere dag moesten de vermoeide gevechtsvliegers dus precies beschrijven wat ze hadden geraakt – of dàchten te hebben geraakt – en hoe. De volgende dag werden er andere vliegtuigen naartoe gestuurd om foto's van de verwoeste doelen te maken.

Daarom moest de lijst met doelwitten iedere dag worden aangevuld met een 'tweede bezoek', om doelen die nog niet volledig waren uitgeschakeld definitief te elimineren.

Op 20 januari, de vierde dag van de luchtoorlog, was de geallieerde luchtmacht nog niet toegekomen aan de vernietiging van de fabrieken waar massavernietigingswapens werden geproduceerd. Ze waren nog steeds bezig met het uitschakelen van de vijandelijke luchtafweer.

Die avond werkte kolonel Beatty aan de lijst voor de fotoverkenningsvluchten van de volgende dag, op basis van de rapporten die de inlichtingenofficieren van de squadrons hadden ingediend.

Tegen middernacht was hij bijna klaar en gingen de eerste orders al naar de verschillende squadrons die bij het eerste ochtendlicht de verkenningsvluchten moesten uitvoeren.

'En dan hebben we dit nog, kolonel.'

Een adjudant van de Amerikaanse marine schoof hem het volgende rapport onder zijn neus.

'Wat is dit... Tarmija?'

'Ja, zo heet het.'

'Maar waar ligt het?'

'Hier, kolonel.'

De kolonel keek op de kaart. De locatie zei hem niets. 'Een radarinstallatie? Raketten, een vliegbasis, een commandopost?'

'Nee, kolonel, een fabriekscomplex.'

De kolonel was moe. Het was een lange avond geweest, en het zou een nog langere nacht worden. 'Verdomme, daar zijn we nog helemaal niet aan toe. Maar laat me toch de industriële lijst maar zien.'

Hij wierp een blik op de lijst, die alle bekende fabrieken van massavernietigingswapens – granaten, explosieven, voertuigen en onderdelen van kanonnen en tanks – bevatte.

Onder de eerste categorie vielen namen als Al-Qaim, As-Sharqat, Tuwaitha, Fallujah, Hillah, Al-Atheer en Al-Furat. De kolonel wist niet dat Rasha-dia, waar de Irakezen hun tweede ultracentrifugecascade voor de produktie van zuiver uranium hadden geïnstalleerd, op de lijst ontbrak. Het was die tweede cascade waar de wetenschappers van het Medusa Comité geen rekening mee hadden gehouden. De fabriek was niet ondergronds gebouwd, maar vermomd als een mineraalwaterbottelarij, zoals de Verenigde Naties later ontdekten.

En kolonel Beatty wist evenmin dat Al-Furat de ondergrondse locatie was van de eerste uraniumcascade, ooit bezocht door de Duitse dr. Stemmler, 'ergens bij Tuwaitha' – of dat de exacte positie door Jericho was prijsgegeven.

'Ik zie geen Tarmija,' bromde hij.

'Nee, het staat er niet bij,' bevestigde de adjudant.

'Geef me de coördinaten eens.'

Niemand kon van de analisten verwachten dat ze al die honderden Arabische plaatsnamen uit hun hoofd kenden, zeker niet omdat dezelfde naam soms bij tien verschillende doelwitten hoorde. Daarom hadden ze allemaal een coördinatennummer gekregen volgens het Global Positioning System – twaalf cijfers die een vierkant van vijftig bij vijftig meter aanduidden.

Toen hij de grote fabriek bij Tarmija had gebombardeerd, had Don Walker dat nummer opgeschreven en bij zijn rapport gevoegd.

'Nee, ik zie het niet,' zei de kolonel. 'Het is goddomme niet eens een officieel doelwit. Wie heeft het platgegooid?'

'Een piloot van het 336e van Al Kharz. De aanval op zijn eerste twee doelen ging niet door, buiten zijn schuld. Hij wilde zijn bommen kwijt, neem ik aan.'

'Klootzak,' mompelde de kolonel. 'Goed, stuur er maar een verkenningsvliegtuig heen. Maar het is niet dringend. Je hoeft er geen film aan te verkwisten.'

Eerste luitenant Darren Cleary zat gefrustreerd achter de knoppen van zijn F-14 Tomcat.

Onder zijn wielen had het vliegkampschip USS *Ranger* de steven naar de lichte bries gekeerd en kliefde nu met een vaartje van zevenentwintig knopen door de golven. Het water van de noordelijke Golf was heel rustig in de ochtendschemering, en de lucht zou snel helderblauw zijn. Het had een prettige dag moeten zijn voor de jonge marinepiloot, die met een van de beste jagers ter wereld vloog.

De dubbelvinnige tweemans-Tomcat, bijgenaamd de 'Fleet Defender', had een grote fanclub gekregen sinds zijn hoofdrol in de film *Top Gun*. Zijn cockpit is waarschijnlijk de meest geliefde stoel van de hele Amerikaanse luchtvloot, zeker bij de marine. Het besturen van zo'n vliegtuig op zo'n mooie dag, een week nadat hij in de Golf was aangekomen, had Darren Cleary dus heel tevreden moeten stemmen. Maar toch had hij de pest in omdat hij geen gevechtsmissie mocht vliegen maar op verkenning was gestuurd om foto's te nemen van bomschade – kiekjes maken, zoals hij de vorige avond had geklaagd. Hij had de operaties-officier van zijn squadron gesmeekt of hij geen jacht op MiG's mocht maken, maar het had niets uitgehaald.

'Iemand moet het doen,' had de officier geantwoord. Net als alle geallieerde gevechtspiloten was Cleary bang dat de Iraakse jets na een paar dagen uit de lucht zouden verdwijnen, zodat de kans op een spannend gevecht verkeken zou zijn.

Tot zijn grote ergernis was hij dus op weg voor een verkenningsmissie.

Achter hem en zijn navigator kwamen de twee straalmotoren van General Electric bulderend op toeren toen de dekploeg hem aan de stoomkatapult op het schuine vliegdek haakte en zijn neus iets opzij van de middellijn van de *Ranger* richtte. Cleary wachtte, met het gas in zijn linkerhand, de knuppel in vrijstand in zijn rechter, terwijl de laatste voorbereidingen werden getroffen. Daarna de korte vraag, de bevestiging, en de enorme krachtsexplosie toen hij het gas naar voren drukte en de nabrander inschakelde. Het volgende moment wierp de katapult hem en zijn 68 000 pond zware toestel naar voren. Binnen drie seconden accelereerde hij van nul tot 150 knopen.

Het grijze staal van de *Ranger* verdween beneden hem. De donkere golven flitsten voorbij, de Tomcat vond houvast in de lucht en klom soepel naar de oplichtende hemel.

Het zou een tocht van vier uur worden, met twee keer bijtanken onderweg. Hij moest twaalf doelwitten fotograferen, en hij zou niet alleen zijn. Voor hem uit vloog al een A-6 Avenger, bewapend met lasergeleide bommen voor het geval ze op Triple-A geschut zouden stuiten. Als dat gebeurde, zou de Avenger de Irakezen wel een lesje leren.

Een EA-6B Prowler vloog mee op dezelfde missie, bewapend met HARM's, voor het geval ze een radargeleide SAM-batterij zouden tegenkomen. De Prowler kon met zijn HARM's de radar uitschakelen, waarna de Avenger met zijn lasergeleide bommen de raketten zou vernietigen.

Als de Iraakse luchtmacht zich zou laten zien, zouden ze te maken krijgen met twee escorterende Tomcats, aan weerskanten van het verkenningstoestel, die met hun krachtige AWG-9 luchtradar de binnenbeenmaat van de Iraakse piloten al wisten voordat ze hun bed uit waren.

Al dit metaal en al deze technologie waren bedoeld ter bescherming van het apparaat onder de voeten van Darren Cleary, een 'Tactical Air Reconnaissance Pod System'. Deze TARPS, rechts onder de middellijn van de Tomcat, leek nog het meest op een gestroomlijnde doodskist van bijna zes meter lang. Het was een camerasysteem, maar wat ingewikkelder dan de gemiddelde Pentax.

In de neus was een lichtsterke camera aangebracht met twee posities: recht omlaag en schuin omlaag naar voren. Daarachter zat een panoramische camera, die een totaalopname maakte. En dan was er nog een infraroodtoestel, dat warmtebeelden en de bron daarvan vastlegde. Op zijn heads-up display kon de piloot zelf zien wat de camera's fotografeerden.

Darren Cleary klom naar 15 000 voet, maakte contact met zijn escortevliegtuigen en samen vlogen ze in de richting van de KC-135 tanker, even ten zuiden van de Iraakse grens.

Zonder dat de Irakezen hem een strobreed in de weg legden fotografeerde hij de elf voornaamste doelen die hij op zijn lijst had staan en vloog toen terug over Tarmija voor het twaalfde doelwit, dat van secundair belang was.

Toen hij over het fabriekscomplex vloog, staarde hij verbaasd naar zijn display en mompelde: 'Jezus, wat is dàt?' op het moment waarop zijn camera's juist hun laatste film hadden verbruikt.

Na een tweede keer bijtanken landden de toestellen zonder problemen weer op de *Ranger*. De dekploeg haalde de films uit de camera's en bracht ze naar het fotolab om ze te laten ontwikkelen.

Cleary bracht rapport uit over zijn weinig sensationele missie en liep met de inlichtingenofficier naar de lichtbak waarop de negatieven lagen. Bij iedere opname gaf de piloot een toelichting. De inlichtingenofficier maakte aantekeningen voor zijn eigen rapport, dat met de foto's bij Cleary's verslag zou worden gevoegd.

Toen ze bij de laatste twintig opnamen waren aangeland, vroeg de officier: 'Wat is dat?'

'Vraag het me niet,' zei Cleary. 'Het zijn foto's van dat doelwit bij Tarmija. Je weet wel, dat door Riyad op het laatste moment aan de lijst is toegevoegd.'

'Ja. Maar wat zijn dat voor dingen in die fabriek?'

'Frisbees voor reuzen?' opperde Cleary.

Die beschrijving bleef hangen. De inlichtingenofficier gebruikte hem in zijn eigen rapport, met de bekentenis dat hij geen idee had wat het waren. Toen alles compleet was, werd een Lockheed S-3 Viking vanaf het dek van de *Ranger* gelanceerd om de map naar Riyad te brengen. Darren Cleary mocht eindelijk gevechtsmissies vliegen, kwam geen enkele MiG tegen en vertrok eind april 1991 weer uit de Golf aan boord van de USS *Ranger*.

In de loop van de ochtend begon Wolfgang Gemütlich zich steeds meer zorgen te maken over zijn secretaresse.

Ze was beleefd en formeel als altijd, en zo efficiënt als hij maar kon eisen – en Herr Gemütlich was een veeleisend man. Gevoelig was hij niet, en daarom had hij in het begin nog niets in de gaten, maar toen ze voor de derde keer bij hem binnenstapte om een brief op te nemen, zag hij toch iets ongewoons aan haar.

Niets luchthartigs, natuurlijk, en zeker niets frivools – dat zou hij nooit hebben getolereerd – maar ze straalde toch iets uit. Hij bekeek haar eens wat beter toen ze over haar schrijfblok gebogen zijn dictaat opnam.

Ze droeg nog steeds dat saaie, zakelijke pakje met die rok tot over de knie. En ze had haar haar nog steeds in een knotje in de nek... Maar toen ze voor de vierde keer binnenkwam, besefte hij tot zijn ontzetting dat Edith Hardenberg haar gezicht had gepoederd. Niet veel, een klein beetje hier en daar. Snel keek hij of ze lippenstift droeg. Gelukkig niet.

Misschien vergiste hij zich wel. Het was januari en ijzig koud. Het poeder bood natuurlijk bescherming tegen een schrale huid. Maar er was nog iets anders.

Haar ogen. Geen mascara, *um Gotteswillen*, geen mascara! Hij keek nog eens goed, maar hij kon niets ontdekken. Hij had zich vast vergist. Pas toen hij tussen de middag zijn linnen servet op zijn vloeiblad uitspreidde en de boterhammen opat die zijn vrouw iedere dag braaf voor hem klaarmaakte, drong het tot hem door.

Ze sprankelden! De ogen van Fräulein Hardenberg sprankelden! Dat had niets te maken met de kou. Ze was toen al vier uur binnen. De bankier legde zijn half opgegeten boterham neer en herinnerde zich dat hij diezelfde blik weleens bij de jongere secretaressen had gezien vlak voordat ze op vrijdagavond naar huis gingen.

Het was geluk. Edith Hardenberg was gelukkig. Dat was te zien, begreep hij nu, zoals ze liep, zoals ze praatte en zoals ze eruitzag. Zo was ze de hele ochtend al. En natuurlijk dat vleugje poeder. Het beviel Wolfgang Gemütich helemaal niet. Hij hoopte dat ze geen geld had uitgegeven.

De 'kiekjes' van eerste luitenant Darren Cleary arriveerden die middag in Riyad, met de stroom van nieuwe foto's die iedere dag op het CENTAF-hoofdkwartier binnenkwamen.

Sommige opnamen waren afkomstig van de KH-11 en KH-12 satellieten hoog boven de aarde, die het totaalbeeld gaven. Als daarop geen verschillen met de vorige dag waren te zien, werden ze opgeborgen.

Andere kwamen van de TR-1's, die wat lager patrouilleerden. Er waren foto's bij van nieuwe militaire en industriële activiteiten in Irak – troepenbewegingen, taxiënde gevechtsvliegtuigen op nieuwe plaatsen, raketbatterijen op andere locaties. Dat was werk voor de analisten die de doelwitten vaststelden.

De foto's van Cleary's Tomcat gingen naar de Schuur, de verzameling groene tenten aan de rand van de vliegbasis. Daar werden ze keurig geïdentificeerd en van gegevens voorzien, en vervolgens doorgegeven aan het Zwarte Gat, verderop langs de weg, waar ze werden beoordeeld door de afdeling bomschade.

Kolonel Beatty begon die avond om zeven uur met zijn dienst. Twee uur lang verdiepte hij zich in de opnamen van een raketbasis (gedeeltelijk vernietigd, maar twee batterijen leken nog intact), een verbindingscentrum (met de grond gelijk gemaakt) en een paar vliegtuighangars met Iraakse MiG's, Mirages en Soekhois (verwoest).

Toen hij de twaalf foto's van de fabriek bij Tarmija onder ogen kreeg, stond hij fronsend op en liep naar een bureau met een sergeant-majoor van de Britse RAF.

'Wat is dit, Charlie?'

'Tarmija, kolonel. Herinnert u zich nog die fabriek die gisteren door een Strike Eagle is gebombardeerd? Die niet op de lijst voorkwam?'

'O ja. Het was niet eens een officieel doelwit.'

'Precies. Een Tomcat van de *Ranger* heeft vanochtend deze opnamen gemaakt, een paar minuten over tien.'

Kolonel Beatty tikte op de foto's in zijn hand. 'Wat is dat eigenlijk voor een fabriek?'

'Geen idee, kolonel. Daarom heb ik ze op uw bureau gelegd. Niemand kan er iets van maken.'

'Nou, die Eagle-piloot heeft wel de knuppel in het hoenderhok gegooid. Wat moeten we hier nu mee?'

De Britse onderofficier en de Amerikaanse kolonel tuurden naar de foto's van Tarmija. Ze waren haarscherp. Er zaten een paar schuine opnamen bij van de camera in de neus van de TARPS, waarop de gebombardeerde fabriek te zien was vanaf een hoogte van 15 000 voet. Andere foto's waren genomen door de panoramische camera in het midden van de capsule. De mannen in de Schuur hadden de beste twaalf uitgekozen.

'Hoe groot is die fabriek?' vroeg de kolonel.

'Ongeveer honderd bij zestig meter.'

Het reusachtige dak was er bijna volledig afgerukt; nog maar een kwart zat op zijn plaats. De rest was open, waardoor de indeling van het gebouw goed te zien was. De ruimte was door scheidingswanden onderverdeeld, en in iedere sectie stond een grote donkere schijf.

'Metaal?'

'Ja, kolonel. Volgens de infraroodscanners wel. Een of andere staallegering.'

Merkwaardig. Maar nog vreemder was de Iraakse reactie op de aanval van Don Walker. Rond het gebouw, dat nu zijn dak kwijt was, stonden vijf enorme kranen opgesteld, met hun armen boven de fabriek, als ooievaars die in een vijver visten. Door alle schade die inmiddels in Irak was aangericht, waren zulke grote kranen schaars.

In en om de fabriek waren grote aantallen arbeiders bezig de schijven aan de takels van de kranen te bevestigen om ze weg te halen.

'Heb je die mensen geteld, Charlie?'

'Meer dan tweehonderd man, kolonel.'

'En die schijven...' Kolonel Beatty raadpleegde het rapport van de inlichtingenofficier van de *Ranger*. 'Frisbees voor reuzen...?'

'Geen idee, kolonel. Ik heb die dingen nooit eerder gezien.'

'In elk geval zijn ze verdomd belangrijk voor Saddam Hoessein. Staat Tarmija echt niet op de lijst met doelwitten?'

'Nee, kolonel. Maar kijkt u hier eens naar.'

De sergeant-majoor pakte een andere foto uit de dossiers. De kolonel volgde zijn wijzende vinger.

'Een hek van zware kettingen.'

'Dubbele kettingen. En hier?'

Kolonel Beatty pakte zijn vergrootglas en keek nog eens. 'Een mijnenveld... Triple-A batterijen... wachttorens... Waar heb je dit vandaan, Charlie?'

'Hier heb ik een overzichtsfoto.'

Kolonel Beatty tuurde naar de nieuwe foto, een opname van grote hoogte van het hele Tarmija-complex en de directe omgeving. Toen haalde hij diep adem.

'Jezus Christus, we moeten Tarmija opnieuw bekijken, dat is duidelijk. Hoe hebben we dat over het hoofd kunnen zien?'

Het hele industriecomplex van Tarmija, met al zijn 381 gebouwen, was in eerste instantie door de experts als een niet-militair gebied geclassificeerd om redenen die later tot de folklore gingen behoren van de menselijke mollen in het Zwarte Gat.

De analisten in het Zwarte Gat waren allemaal Britten en Amerikanen en ze werkten voor de NAVO. Ze waren opgeleid in het herkennen van Russische doelwitten en getraind om alles door een Russische bril te bekijken.

Daarom letten ze op bepaalde vaste aanwijzingen. Als het gebouw of het complex een belangrijke militaire functie had, was het verboden terrein. Dan werd het afgesloten voor bezoekers en beschermd tegen aanvallen.

Waren er wachttorens, zware hekken, Triple-A batterijen, raketten, mijnenvelden en barakken te zien? Waren er sporen van zwaar vrachtverkeer? Liepen er hoogspanningskabels over het terrein of stond er een generator? Zulke aanwijzingen betekenden een doelwit. In Tarmija was dat allemaal niet te vinden, op het eerste gezicht.

Maar in een opwelling had de RAF-sergeant een overzichtsfoto tevoorschijn gehaald, gemaakt van grote hoogte, waarop het hele gebied te zien was. En nu zagen ze het opeens... het hek, de batterijen, de barakken, de versterkte poorten, de raketten, het prikkeldraad en de mijnenvelden. Maar heel ver weg.

De Irakezen hadden gewoon een enorm gebied van honderd bij honderd kilometer genomen en de hele zaak afgesloten. Zo'n grondverspilling zou in West- en zelfs in Oost-Europa onmogelijk zijn geweest.

Het industriecomplex, waarvan 70 van de 381 gebouwen later bleken te worden gebruikt voor oorlogsproduktie, lag in het midden van het vierkant, ruim verspreid om bomschade te vermijden. Het nam slechts vijf procent van het totale beveiligde gebied in beslag.

'Lopen er ergens hoogspanningskabels? Deze draden zijn nauwelijks genoeg voor een elektrische tandenborstel.'

'Hier, kolonel. Vijfenveertig kilometer naar het westen. Die kabels lopen de andere kant uit, maar ik zet vijftig pond tegen een glas lauw bier in dat ze nep zijn. De echte kabels liggen onder de grond en lopen vanaf die kracht-centrale rechtstreeks naar het hart van Tarmija. Dat is een centrale van 150 megawatt, kolonel.'

'Verdomme,' mompelde Beatty. Toen richtte hij zich op en pakte de stapel foto's. 'Goed werk, Charlie. Ik neem deze spullen mee naar Buster Glosson. Maar laten we niet te lang wachten. Die fabriek is van belang voor de Ira-kezen, dus we gooien hem in puin.'

'Goed, kolonel. Ik zet hem op de lijst.'

'Niet over drie dagen, maar morgen. Wie hebben we nog?'

De sergeant-majoor raadpleegde zijn computer.

'Niemand, kolonel. Iedereen zit vol.'

'Kunnen we niet een squadron omleiden?'

'Niet echt. We lopen al achter vanwege die Scud-jacht. O, wacht even, we hebben nog het 4300e in Diego. Die hebben nog capaciteit.'

'Goed, laat het dan maar over aan de Buffs.'

'Neemt u me niet kwalijk,' zei de onderofficier op die beleefde toon die een meningsverschil moet maskeren, 'maar de Buffs zijn niet bepaald precisie-bommenwerpers.'

'Luister, Charlie. Over vierentwintig uur hebben de Irakezen alles daar weg-gehaald. We hebben geen keus. Stuur de Buffs er maar op af.'

'Jawel, kolonel.'

Mike Martin was te rusteloos om zich meer dan een paar dagen op het terrein van de Russische villa te kunnen opsluiten. De huisbediende en zijn vrouw waren van streek en konden 's nachts niet slapen door de onophoudelijke explosies van de inslaande bommen en raketten, beantwoord door de uitgebreide maar weinig doelmatige luchtafweer van Bagdad.

Ze brulden beledigingen uit de ramen naar de Amerikaanse en Britse piloten, maar ze kregen ook gebrek aan eten en de Russische maag is een strenge meester. Dus stuurden ze Mahmoud de tuinman er weer op uit om boodschappen te doen.

Martin had al drie dagen door de stad gefietst toen hij het krijtteken zag. Het stond op de muur aan de achterkant van een van de oude Khajat-huizen in Karadit-Mariam en het betekende dat Jericho een boodschap in de corresponderende 'brievenbus' had achtergelaten.

Ondanks de bombardementen begon het normale leven weer op gang te komen, want mensen wennen nu eenmaal aan alles. Zonder dat er veel werd gezegd, behalve op fluistertoon en dan alleen tegen familieleden die de spreker niet aan de AMAM zouden verraden, kreeg de bevolking van Bagdad in de gaten dat de Zonen van de Honden en de Zonen van Naji nauwkeurig konden raken wat ze wilden, zonder verdere schade aan te richten.

Na vijf dagen lag het presidentiële paleis in puin (dat was al op de tweede dag gebombardeerd) en waren het ministerie van Defensie, de telefooncentrale en de belangrijkste krachtcentrale van de aardbodem weggevaagd. Maar het lastigste was dat alle negen bruggen nu op de bodem van de Tigris lagen. Een paar kleine ondernemers hadden veerdiensten over de rivier georganiseerd. Sommige pontjes waren groot genoeg om vrachtwagens over te zetten, andere boden plaats aan tien passagiers met hun fietsen, en weer andere waren nauwelijks groter dan een roeiboot.

De meeste belangrijke gebouwen stonden nog overeind. Het Rashid Hotel in Karch zat nog vol buitenlandse journalisten, ook al had de *Rais* zich in de bunker onder het hotel verschanst. Helaas was ook het hoofdkwartier van de AMAM, een verzameling doorgebroken huizen met oude gevels en moderne interieurs in een afgegrendelde straat bij Qasr-el-Abyad in Risafa, nog altijd ongedeerd. Onder twee van die huizen lag de Gymzaal, de martelkamer van Omar Khatib waarover alleen fluisterend werd gesproken.

Ook het grote kantoorgebouw van de Mukhabarat aan de overkant van de rivier in Mansour, waar de buitenlandse inlichtingendienst en de contraspionagedienst waren ondergebracht, had nog geen schade opgelopen.

Mike Martin dacht over het krijtteken na toen hij terugfietste naar de Russische villa. Hij kende zijn orders – geen contact. Als hij een Chileense diplomaat was geweest zou hij die orders hebben gehoorzaamd, en terecht. Maar Moncada was er nooit in getraind om roerloos op een uitkijkpost te blijven liggen, desnoods dagenlang, om de omgeving in de gaten te houden totdat de vogeltjes nesten bouwden in zijn hoed.

Die avond, toen de luchtaanvallen weer begonnen, stak hij te voet de rivier over naar Risafa en liep naar de groentemarkt van Kasra. Hier en daar waren nog mensen op straat, haastig op weg naar huis, alsof ze daar veilig zouden zijn voor een Tomahawk-kruisraket. Martin viel niet op. En zijn vermoeden over de AMAM bleek juist. De Geheime Politie had weinig zin om op straat te patrouilleren met die Amerikaanse bommenwerpers boven hun hoofd.

Hij vond zijn uitkijkpost op het dak van een fruitpakhuis, waar hij de straat, de binnenplaats en de 'brievenbus' onder een losse tegel in het oog kon houden. Acht uur lang, van acht uur 's avonds tot vier uur in de ochtend, hield hij de wacht.

Als de plek in de gaten werd gehouden, zou de AMAM niet minder dan twintig mensen hebben gebruikt. In al die uren moest Martin daar iets van hebben gemerkt – voetstappen op de stenen, iemand die hoestte of zijn stijve spieren strekte, het aanstrijken van een lucifer, het schijnsel van een sigaret, de barse order om hem te doven, wat dan ook. Hij kon gewoon niet geloven dat Khatibs of Rahmani's mensen zich acht uur lang roerloos en doodstil konden houden.

Een paar minuten voor vier kwam er een eind aan de bombardementen. Op de markt beneden brandde nergens licht. Hij keek nog eens of hij ergens een camera achter een hoog raam kon ontdekken, maar er waren geen hoge ramen in de buurt. Om tien over vier liet hij zich van het dak glijden, stak het duistere steegje over in zijn donkergrijze *disj-dasj*, vond de tegel, haalde het bericht eronder vandaan en was verdwenen.

Tegen het ochtendgloren klom hij over de muur van de Russische villa en was al in zijn schuurtje voordat het huis wakker werd.

De boodschap van Jericho was simpel. Hij had al negen dagen niets gehoord en geen krijtstrepen gezien. Sinds zijn laatste bericht was er geen enkel contact geweest en was er geen geld meer op zijn rekening gestort. Toch was zijn boodschap weggehaald. Dat had hij gecontroleerd. Wat was er aan de hand?

Martin gaf het bericht niet door aan Riyad. Hij wist dat hij zich aan zijn orders had moeten houden, maar híj en niet Paxman was de man ter plekke en daarom mocht hij zelf ook beslissingen nemen. Het was een verantwoord risico geweest. Hij was een ervaren agent tegenover betrekkelijke amateurs. Als hij één teken had bespeurd dat het steegje in de gaten werd gehouden, zou hij meteen zijn vertrokken zonder dat iemand hem had gezien.

Misschien had Paxman gelijk en was Jericho opgepakt. Maar het was ook mogelijk dat Jericho gewoon had doorgegeven wat hij Saddam Hoessein

330

had horen zeggen. Het ging om die één miljoen dollar die de CIA niet wilde betalen. Martin stelde zelf een antwoord op.

Hij schreef dat er problemen waren geweest door het uitbreken van de oorlog, maar dat verder alles in orde was en dat Jericho geduld moest hebben. Jericho's laatste bericht was inderdaad doorgegeven, maar als man van de wereld zou Jericho ook beseffen dat een miljoen dollar heel veel geld was en dat de informatie moest worden geverifieerd. Dat zou nog wel even duren. Jericho moest het hoofd koel houden in deze roerige tijden en wachten op het volgende krijtteken om hun contact te hervatten.

In de loop van de dag verborg Martin het bericht achter de losse steen in de muur bij de slotgracht van de Oude Citadel in Aadhamija en in de schemering zette hij het krijtteken op de roestige rode garagedeur in Mansour.

Vierentwintig uur later was het teken uitgewist. Iedere nacht luisterde Martin naar Riyad, maar er kwamen geen berichten meer. Hij wist dat hij bevel had om te vluchten en dat de SIS-officieren waarschijnlijk zaten te wachten tot hij de grens over kwam. Maar hij besloot het nog even aan te zien.

Diego Garcia is niet een van de drukst bezochte plaatsen ter wereld. Het is een klein eiland, niet veel meer dan een koraalatol, aan de punt van de Chagos-archipel in het zuidelijke deel van de Indische Oceaan. Ooit was het Brits gebied, maar het wordt al jaren verhuurd aan de Verenigde Staten.

Ondanks de afgelegen ligging was het eiland tijdens de Golfoorlog de thuisbasis van de haastig gevormde Amerikaanse 4300e Bomb Wing, uitgerust met B-52 Stratofortresses.

De B-52 was het oudste toestel en had de meeste oorlogservaring. Het was al meer dan dertig jaar in gebruik en werd vaak beschouwd als de ruggegraat van het Strategic Air Command, met zijn hoofdkwartier in Omaha, Nebraska – de vliegende mastodont die dag en nacht rond de grenzen van het Sovjetrijk vloog, bewapend met thermonucleaire gevechtskoppen.

Hoe oud het toestel ook was, het bleef een geduchte bommenwerper. In de Golfoorlog werd de aangepaste 'G'-versie gebruikt, met verwoestende gevolgen voor het ingegraven 'elitekorps' van de Iraakse Republikeinse Garde in de woestijnen in het zuiden van Koeweit. Toen deze keurtroepen van het Iraakse leger tijdens het geallieerde grondoffensief met hun handen omhoog uit hun bunkers kwamen, was dat gedeeltelijk omdat hun zenuwen waren murw gebeukt en hun moreel gebroken door de onophoudelijke bombardementen van de B-52's.

Er waren maar tachtig van deze bommenwerpers bij de oorlog betrokken, maar ze zijn zo groot en ze hebben zoveel bommen bij zich dat ze in totaal 26 000 ton explosieven afwierpen – veertig procent van het volledige tonnage dat tijdens de oorlog op Irak werd losgelaten.

331

Ze zijn zo zwaar dat hun vleugels, met de acht Pratt & Whitney J-57 motoren in vier groepen van twee, zichtbaar doorbuigen als ze aan de grond staan. Als ze met een volledige lading vertrekken, vangen de vleugels de wind het eerst en lijken zich als de wieken van een zeemeeuw boven de grote romp van het toestel te verheffen. Alleen tijdens de vlucht steken ze recht opzij.

Een van de redenen waarom ze de Republikeinse Garde in de woestijn zo'n angst aanjoegen was dat ze niet te zien of te horen zijn. Ze vliegen zo hoog dat hun bommen zonder enige waarschuwing op het doelwit neerdalen en daardoor nog meer paniek zaaien. Maar hoewel de B-52's wel geschikt zijn voor het leggen van een bommentapijt zijn het geen precisie-bommenwerpers, zoals de Britse sergeant-majoor terecht had opgemerkt.

Bij het eerste ochtendlicht van de 22e januari stegen drie 'Buffs' van Diego Garcia op en zetten koers naar Saoedi-Arabië. Ze waren alle drie maximaal geladen, met eenenvijftig 750-ponds 'domme' (ongeleide) bommen, die vanaf bijna 12 000 meter hoogte zouden worden afgeworpen. Zevenentwintig van die bommen waren intern ondergebracht, de rest hing aan rekken onder de vleugels.

De drie bommenwerpers vormden de gebruikelijke 'cel' van een Buff-missie. De bemanningen hadden zich juist verheugd op een dagje vissen, zwemmen en snorkelen bij een rif van hun tropische thuisbasis. Gelaten zetten ze koers naar een verre fabriek die ze nog nooit hadden gezien en ook niet zóuden zien.

De B-52 Stratofortress wordt niet 'Buff' genoemd vanwege zijn geelbruine kleur of omdat hij iets te maken zou hebben met het voormalige Britse regiment uit East Kent in Engeland. Het woord is zelfs geen samentrekking van de eerste twee lettergrepen van de naam, *'Bee-Fifty Two'*. Het is een afkorting van *'Big Ugly Fat Fucker'*.

De Buffs vlogen naar het noorden, vonden Tarmija, registreerden het signalement van de fabriek en wierpen hun 153 bommen af. Daarna keerden ze weer terug naar de Chagos-archipel.

De ochtend van de 23e, omstreeks de tijd dat Londen en Washington begonnen te schreeuwen om meer foto's van die mysterieuze 'frisbees', werd er een verkenningsvliegtuig naar Tarmija gestuurd om de bomschade vast te stellen, deze keer een Phantom van de Alabama National Guard vanaf de basis Sjeik Isa in Bahrein, plaatselijk bekend als 'Shakey's Pizza'.

Geheel tegen hun gewoonte in hadden de B-52's hun doelwit exact geraakt. Waar ooit de frisbee-fabriek had gestaan, lag nu een gapende bomkrater. Londen en Washington zouden zich tevreden moeten stellen met de twaalf foto's van eerste luitenant Darren Cleary.

De beste analisten van het Zwarte Gat hadden de opnamen gezien, hun schouders opgehaald en ze naar hun bazen in de twee hoofdsteden gestuurd.

Kopieën van de opnamen gingen meteen naar het JARIC, het Britse foto-interpretatiecentrum, en naar het ENPIC in Washington.

Wie dit saaie, vierkante gebouw op een straathoek in een verlopen wijk in het centrum van Washington passeert, zal niet gauw vermoeden wat er daarbinnen gebeurt. De enige aanwijzing voor de aanwezigheid van het National Photographic Interpretation Center is de batterij ventilatoren van de airconditioning, die een aantal van de krachtigste computers in Amerika constant op dezelfde temperatuur moet houden. Maar met zijn stoffige, vuile ramen, zijn weinig imposante deur en het vuilnis dat over straat waait, doet het gebouw eerder denken aan een vervallen pakhuis.

Toch komen hier alle satellietfoto's terecht en werken hier de analisten die de mensen van het National Reconnaissance Office, het Pentagon en de CIA exact vertellen wat al die dure 'vogels' hebben gezien. Ze zijn goed, die analisten – jong, intelligent en inventief. En ze zijn op de hoogte van de nieuwste technologie. Maar de frisbees van Tarmija hadden ze nooit eerder gezien. En dat zeiden ze ook, voordat ze de foto's opborgen.

Experts van het ministerie van Defensie in Londen en het Pentagon in Washington, die bijna alle conventionele wapens sinds de kruisboog kenden, bestudeerden de foto's, schudden hun hoofd en gaven ze terug.

Voor het geval ze iets met massavernietigingswapens te maken hadden, werden ze ook voorgelegd aan de wetenschappers van Porton Down, Harwell en Aldermaston in Engeland, en aan de deskundigen van Sandia, Los Alamos en Lawrence Livermore in Amerika. Met hetzelfde resultaat.

De zinnigste suggestie was dat de schijven een onderdeel waren van grote elektrische transformatoren, bestemd voor een nieuwe Iraakse krachtcentrale. Dat was de voorlopige conclusie. Toen er om meer foto's werd gevraagd, meldde Riyad dat de fabriek van Tarmija inmiddels met de grond gelijk was gemaakt.

De officiële conclusie was niet slecht gevonden, maar gaf geen antwoord op één vraag: waarom de Iraakse autoriteiten zo wanhopig hadden getracht de schijven te bedekken of weg te halen.

Pas op de avond van de 24e stapte Simon Paxman een telefooncel in om dr. Terry Martin in zijn flat te bellen.

'Zullen we bij de Indiër gaan eten?' vroeg hij.

'Ik kan vanavond niet,' zei Martin. 'Ik moet mijn koffers pakken.'

Hij zei er niet bij dat Hilary weer terug was en dat hij de avond met zijn vriend wilde doorbrengen.

'Waar ga je heen?' vroeg Paxman.

'Naar Amerika,' zei Martin. 'Ik ben uitgenodigd om een lezing te houden

over het Abbasiden-kalifaat. Heel vleiend. Blijkbaar waren ze onder de indruk van mijn onderzoek naar het rechtsstelsel van de derde kalief. Sorry.'
'We hebben nog iets ontvangen uit het zuiden. Weer zo'n raadsel waar niemand het antwoord op weet. Het gaat nu niet om de nuances van de Arabische taal. Het is een technische kwestie. Maar...'
'Wat is het dan?'
'Een foto. Ik heb een kopie.'
Martin aarzelde. 'Weer een strootje in de wind?' vroeg hij. 'Goed. Hetzelfde restaurant. Acht uur.'
'Meer is het waarschijnlijk niet,' zei Paxman. 'Een strootje.'
Wat hij niet wist, in die ijskoude telefooncel, was dat hij een heel lang stuk touw in handen had.

De volgende dag, kort na drie uur 's middags plaatselijke tijd, landde dr. Terry Martin op het internationale vliegveld van San Francisco, waar hij werd afgehaald door zijn gastheer, professor Paul Maslowski, een joviale, hartelijke man in het uniform van de Amerikaanse wetenschapper – een tweedjasje met leren elleboogstukken. Meteen voelde hij zich opgenomen in een warme golf van Amerikaanse gastvrijheid.

'Betty en ik vonden een hotel veel te onpersoonlijk. Zou je bij ons willen logeren?' vroeg Maslowski, zodra hij zijn kleine auto vanaf het parkeerterrein de weg opdraaide.

'Heel graag. Dat vind ik leuk,' zei Martin en hij meende het.

'De studenten verheugen zich echt op je college, Terry. We zijn maar met weinig mensen, onze Arabische faculteit is lang niet zo groot als jullie SOAS, maar ze zijn heel enthousiast.'

'Geweldig. Ik heb er echt zin in.'

Ze praatten geestdriftig over hun gezamenlijke passie, het middeleeuwse Mesopotamië, tot ze bij Maslowski's houten huis in een buitenwijk van Menlo Park aankwamen.

Daar ontmoette hij Pauls vrouw Betty, die hem naar een warme, comfortabele logeerkamer bracht. Hij keek op zijn horloge. Kwart voor vijf.

'Mag ik even telefoneren?' vroeg hij toen hij beneden kwam.

'Natuurlijk,' zei Maslowski. 'Naar huis?'

'Nee, hier in de buurt. Heb je een gids?'

De professor gaf hem het telefoonboek en vertrok. Het nummer stond onder Livermore, Lawrence L., National Laboratory, in Alameda County. Hij was nog net op tijd.

'Mag ik Department-Z?' vroeg hij toen de telefoniste opnam. Hij sprak het uit als 'Zed'.

'Wat?' vroeg het meisje.

'Afdeling *Zie*,' herstelde Martin zich. 'Het kantoor van de directeur.'

'Eén moment graag.'

Een andere vrouwenstem meldde zich: 'Kan ik u helpen?'

Zijn Britse accent was waarschijnlijk een voordeel. Hij vertelde dat hij dr. Terry Martin was, een academicus die voor een kort bezoek uit Engeland was overgekomen, en dat hij graag de directeur wilde spreken. Hij werd doorverbonden.

'Doctor Martin?' vroeg een mannenstem.
'Inderdaad.'
'Ik ben Jim Jacobs, de adjunct-directeur. Wat kan ik voor u doen?'
'Ik weet dat ik u overval, maar ik ben heel kort in het land om een lezing te houden aan de Midden-Oosten Faculteit van de universiteit van Berkeley. Daarna vlieg ik weer terug. Ik zou graag naar Livermore komen om u te spreken.'
De verbazing was hoorbaar over de lijn.
'Kunt u me ook zeggen waarover, doctor Martin?'
'Dat is niet zo simpel. Ik ben lid van het Britse Medusa Comité. Zegt u dat iets?'
'Jazeker. Maar we gaan nu sluiten. Zou het ook morgen kunnen?'
'Natuurlijk. 's Middags geef ik college. Morgenochtend dan?'
'Tien uur?' vroeg dr. Jacobs.
De afspraak was gemaakt. Martin had handig verzwegen dat hij geen kernfysicus was maar arabist. Waarom zou je de zaak nodeloos ingewikkeld maken?

Die avond, in een heel ander deel van de wereld, ging Karim met Edith Hardenberg naar bed. Het was geen haastige, onhandige verleiding, maar het natuurlijke besluit van een avond met concertmuziek en een dineetje. Toen ze hem na het concert meenam naar haar flat in Grinzing, probeerde Edith zich nog wijs te maken dat het alleen om koffie en een nachtzoen ging. Maar diep in haar hart wist ze wel beter.
Toen hij haar in zijn armen nam en haar zachtjes maar met overtuiging kuste, verzette ze zich niet. Haar vaste voornemen om te protesteren leek weg te smelten, zonder dat ze er iets aan kon doen. En eigenlijk wilde ze dat ook niet.
Hij tilde haar op en droeg haar naar de kleine slaapkamer. Ze draaide haar gezicht naar zijn schouder en liet het gebeuren. Ze voelde het nauwelijks toen haar keurige jurkje op de vloer gleed. Zijn vingers waren veel behendiger dan die van Horst – geen getrek of geduw, geen ritsen en knopen die bleven haken.
Ze had haar slip nog aan toen hij onder de *bettkissen*, het grote zachte Weense dekbed, naast haar schoof. De warmte van zijn jonge lichaam was heerlijk in de koude winternacht.
Ze wist niet wat ze moest doen, dus sloot ze haar ogen en wachtte af. Vreemde, afschuwelijke, zondige sensaties trokken door haar onwennige zenuwen toen haar lichaam door zijn lippen en zijn zacht zoekende vingers werd beroerd. Met Horst was het heel anders geweest.
Ze raakte in paniek toen zijn lippen van haar mond en haar borsten naar

andere plaatsen gleden, verboden plaatsen – wat haar moeder altijd 'daar beneden' had genoemd.

Ze protesteerde zwakjes en probeerde hem weg te duwen, omdat ze wist dat de reacties van haar onderlichaam niet netjes en fatsoenlijk waren, maar hij was zo gretig als een spanielpup met een neergeschoten patrijs.

Hij trok zich niets aan van haar *'Nein, Karim, das sollst du nicht!'* De sensaties werden een vloedgolf en zij was als een verloren roeiboot op een kolkende oceaan tot de laatste grote golf over haar heen sloeg en ze verdronk in een maalstroom die ze in al die negenendertig jaren nog nooit aan de pastoor van de Votivkirche had hoeven biechten.

Daarna nam ze zijn hoofd in haar handen, drukte zijn gezicht tegen haar magere borstjes en wiegde hem zwijgend in haar armen.

Twee keer die nacht beminde hij haar, één keer kort na middernacht en opnieuw in de duisternis voor het ochtendgloren. Beide keren was hij zo teder en sterk dat al haar opgekropte liefde als een explosie een uitweg zocht, zo heftig als ze nooit voor mogelijk had gehouden. Pas na de tweede keer durfde ze zijn lichaam te strelen toen hij sliep, verwonderd over zijn gladde, vochtige huid en de liefde die ze voelde voor iedere centimeter ervan.

Hoewel hij geen idee had dat zijn logé nog andere interessen had dan zijn Arabische studies, stond dr. Maslowski erop om Terry Martin die ochtend naar Livermore te rijden, zodat hij geen taxi hoefde te nemen.

'Ik geloof dat mijn gast belangrijker is dan ik dacht,' zei hij onderweg. Maar hoewel Martin dat ontkende, had de Californische geleerde genoeg over het Lawrence Livermore Laboratory gehoord om te weten dat je daar niet zomaar een telefonische afspraak kon maken. Maar Maslowski was heel discreet en stelde geen vragen.

Bij de ingang moest Martin zijn pas laten zien. De wachtpost bij het hek belde naar het kantoor en wees hen naar een parkeerterrein.

'Ik wacht hier wel,' zei Maslowski.

Gezien het soort werk dat er wordt gedaan is het Laboratory een vreemde verzameling gebouwen aan Vasco Road, gedeeltelijk modern maar met oude kazernes die nog dateren uit de tijd dat het een militaire basis was. Het is een merkwaardige mengeling van stijlen. En overal staan nog 'tijdelijke' kantoren die op de een of andere manier nooit zijn verdwenen. Martin werd naar een groep gebouwen aan de kant van East Avenue gebracht.

Al is het geen indrukwekkend complex, toch wordt hier de verspreiding van nucleaire technologie in de derde wereld bijgehouden.

Jim Jacobs bleek wat ouder te zijn dan Terry Martin – tegen de veertig. De natuurkundige begroette Martin in zijn kantoor, dat vol lag met stapels papier.

337

'Het is fris vanochtend. U dacht zeker dat het in Californië altijd warm was? Dat denkt iedereen. Maar hier is het niet altijd zo heet. Koffie?'

'Graag.'

'Suiker en melk?'

'Nee, zwart.'

Dr. Jacobs drukte op een toets van de intercom. 'Sandy, wil je twee koffie brengen? Eén kop zwart, en voor mij het vaste recept.'

Van achter zijn bureau keek hij zijn bezoeker glimlachend aan. Hij vertelde hem niet dat hij met Washington had gebeld om de identiteit van de Engelsman en zijn medewerking aan het Medusa Comité te verifiëren. Iemand van de Amerikaanse tak van het comité had de lijst bekeken en hem gerustgesteld. Jacobs was onder de indruk. Zijn bezoeker leek nog jong, maar hij moest heel wat invloed hebben in Engeland. De Amerikaan wist alles over het Medusa Comité, omdat hij en zijn collega's wekenlang zelf over Irak waren ondervraagd en alles hadden verteld wat ze wisten, die hele domme historie van Westerse luchthartigheid waardoor Saddam Hoessein nu bijna over een atoombom beschikte.

'Wat kan ik voor u doen?' vroeg hij.

'Ik weet dat het maar een kleine kans is,' zei Martin, terwijl hij in zijn koffertje zocht. 'U hebt deze foto's al gezien, neem ik aan?'

Hij legde een van de twaalf foto's van de fabriek van Tarmija op het bureau, de kopie die Paxman hem clandestien gegeven had.

Jacobs keek ernaar en knikte. 'Ja. Drie, vier dagen geleden hebben we er een stuk of twaalf uit Washington gekregen. Ze zeiden me niets. Ik kan u niet meer vertellen dan ik Washington al heb verteld. Ik heb die dingen nooit eerder gezien.'

Sandy kwam binnen met een blad met koffie. Ze was een vrolijke, blonde meid uit Californië, blakend van zelfvertrouwen.

'Hé, hallo,' zei ze tegen Martin.

'O, eh... hallo. Heeft de directeur ze ook gezien?' vroeg hij aan Jacobs.

De natuurkundige fronste bij de suggestie dat hij zelf niet belangrijk genoeg zou zijn.

'De directeur is skiën in Colorado. Maar ik heb onze beste mensen geraadpleegd. En geloof me, die zijn heel goed.'

'Ja, natuurlijk,' zei Martin. Weer een blinde muur. Nou ja, het was maar een kleine kans, zoals hij zelf al had gezegd.

Sandy zette de kopjes op het bureau. Haar blik viel op de foto's. 'O, die weer,' zei ze.

'Ja, die weer,' zei Jacobs met een plagerige grijns. 'Doctor Martin vindt dat een wat... ouder iemand er eens naar moet kijken.'

'Laat ze aan Daddy Lomax zien,' opperde het meisje, en ze verdween.

338

'Wie is Daddy Lomax?' vroeg Martin.

'O, let er maar niet op. Die werkte hier vroeger. Hij is nu met pensioen en hij woont in zijn eentje ergens in de bergen. Soms komt hij nog wel eens langs om te kletsen. De meisjes zijn dol op hem. Hij neemt bergbloemen voor ze mee. Een rare oude man.'

Ze dronken hun koffie, maar er viel weinig meer te zeggen. Jacobs had het druk. Hij verontschuldigde zich nog eens omdat hij Martin niet had kunnen helpen. Daarna bracht hij hem naar de deur en trok zich weer terug in zijn heiligdom.

Martin wachtte een paar minuten op de gang en stak toen zijn hoofd om de deur.

'Waar kan ik Daddy Lomax vinden?' vroeg hij aan Sandy.

'Ik weet het niet. Hij woont in de bergen. Niemand is er ooit geweest.'

'Heeft hij telefoon?'

'Er gaan geen kabels naartoe, maar ik geloof dat hij een zaktelefoon heeft. Dat moest van de verzekering. Hij is al heel oud,' verklaarde ze met die bezorgde blik van de Californische jeugd als het over mensen van boven de zestig gaat. Ze zocht in haar kaartenbak en vond een nummer. Martin noteerde het, bedankte haar en vertrok.

Tien tijdzones verderop, in Bagdad, was de avond gevallen.

Mike Martin fietste door de Port Saidstraat naar het noordwesten. Hij kwam langs de oude Britse Club bij de vroegere Southgate. Omdat hij het zich herinnerde, keek hij om.

Daardoor veroorzaakte hij bijna een ongeluk. Hij was bij het Nafuraplein gekomen en reed zonder te kijken door. Van links kwam een grote limousine die officieel geen voorrang had, maar de twee escorterende motorrijders waren niet van plan te stoppen.

Een van hen week haastig uit om de onhandige *fellagha* met de groentemand op zijn bagagedrager te ontwijken, maar met zijn voorwiel raakte hij de fiets, die tegen het asfalt sloeg.

Martin viel en de groente rolde over straat. De limousine remde en reed in een bocht om hem heen voordat hij weer snelheid maakte.

Martin hees zich op zijn knieën en keek de auto na. Het gezicht van de passagier op de achterbank keek om naar de kluns die het lef had gehad om hem één seconde te vertragen.

Het was een kil gezicht boven het uniform van een brigadegeneraal, mager en zuur, met diepe rimpels aan weerskanten van de neus tot aan de bittere mond. Maar in die halve seconde waren het vooral de ogen die Martin opvielen. Geen koude, nijdige ogen, niet bloeddoorlopen, sluw of zelfs maar gemeen. Nee, ze hadden geen enkele uitdrukking, de ogen van iemand die al lang geleden was gestorven. Toen was de auto weer voorbij. Ook zonder het gefluisterde commentaar van de twee arbeiders die hem overeind hielpen en de groente weer verzamelden, wist hij wie de passagier van die auto was geweest. Hij had dat gezicht al eerder gezien, heel vaag, tijdens een bezoek aan een juichende legerbasis, op een foto op een tafel in Riyad, weken geleden. Hij was zojuist bijna geschept door de auto van de meest gevreesde man in Irak na de president, misschien zelfs nog meer gevreesd dan de president. Ze noemden hem Al Mu'azib, de Beul, de man die iedereen tot een bekentenis kon dwingen, het hoofd van de AMAM, Omar Khatib.

Tussen de middag had Terry Martin het nummer geprobeerd dat hij van Sandy had gekregen. Maar er werd niet opgenomen. Het enige dat hij hoorde was een zoetgevooisde stem die hem meedeelde dat de abonnee die hij belde niet beschikbaar of buiten bereik was. Belt u later opnieuw, als u wilt.

Paul Maslowski had hem uitgenodigd voor de lunch met zijn collega's van de universiteit. De gesprekken waren levendig en interessant. Na afloop, op weg naar Barrow Hall met Kathlene Keller, het hoofd van de afdeling Midden-Oosten, belde hij nog eens, maar met hetzelfde resultaat.

Het college ging uitstekend. Er waren zevenentwintig studenten, allemaal bezig met hun doctoraal, en Martin was onder de indruk van het niveau van de scripties die ze hadden geschreven over het kalifaat dat centraal-Mesopotamië regeerde in wat de Europeanen de middeleeuwen noemden.

Toen een van de studenten was opgestaan om hem te bedanken dat hij zo'n lange reis had gemaakt om voor hen een lezing te houden, begonnen de anderen te applaudisseren. Terry Martin bloosde, maakte een kleine buiging en nam afscheid. Buiten in de gang zag hij een telefoon hangen en hij probeerde het nog eens. Deze keer werd er opgenomen.

'Ja?'

'Spreek ik met doctor Lomax?'

'Daar is er maar één van, vriend, en dat ben ik.'

'Ik weet dat het krankzinnig klinkt, maar ik kom uit Engeland en ik zou u graag willen spreken. Mijn naam is Terry Martin.'

'Uit Engeland? Dat is een heel eind. Wat wilt u van een ouwe zak als ik, meneer Martin?'

'Een beroep doen op uw geheugen. De mensen van Livermore zeggen dat u meer ervaring hebt dan wie ook, en dat u alles hebt meegemaakt. Ik wil u iets laten zien. Ik kan het moeilijk uitleggen over de telefoon. Mag ik naar u toekomen?'

'Het is toch geen belastingbiljet?'

'Nee.'

'Of de centerfold van *Playboy*?'

'Ik ben bang van niet.'

'U maakt me nieuwsgierig. Kent u de weg?'

'Nee, maar ik heb pen en papier. Kunt u me zeggen hoe ik er moet komen?' Daddy Lomax gaf hem een routebeschrijving. Het duurde even voordat Martin alles had genoteerd.

'Morgenochtend,' zei de fysicus in ruste. 'Nu is het te laat. Dan zou u verdwalen in het donker. En u hebt een terreinwagen nodig.'

Het was een van de twee enige E-8A J-STARS in de Golfoorlog die het signaal de ochtend van de 27e januari opving. De J-STARS waren nog in een experimenteel stadium en hadden voornamelijk civiele technici aan boord toen ze begin januari in allerijl naar Arabië moesten vertrekken vanaf hun basis bij de Grumman Melbourne-fabriek in Florida.

Die ochtend bevond een van de toestellen, gestationeerd op de vliegbasis van Riyad, zich hoog boven de Iraakse grens maar nog binnen het Saoedische luchtruim. Met zijn Norden-groothoekradar verkende hij de Iraakse woestijn over een gebied van meer dan honderdvijftig kilometer.

Het signaal was zwak, maar het was een reflectie van metaal dat zich langzaam verplaatste, ver in Irak – een konvooi van hooguit twee tot drie trucks. Maar daar was de J-STARS voor. Dus waarschuwde de commandant een AWACS die boven het noordelijke deel van de Rode Zee cirkelde en gaf de exacte positie door van het kleine Iraakse konvooi.

De missiecommandant van de AWACS voerde de locatie in en zocht een vliegtuig dat in de buurt was, om de trucks een onwelkom bezoekje te brengen. Alle operaties boven de westelijke woestijn waren nog steeds gericht tegen de Scuds, afgezien van de aanvallen op twee grote Iraakse vliegbases, H2 en H3, die ook in de woestijn lagen. De J-STARS had misschien een mobiele Scud-lanceerinstallatie ontdekt, hoewel dat niet zo waarschijnlijk was bij daglicht.

De AWACS vond twee F-15E Strike Eagles die vanuit Scud Alley North op weg waren naar het zuiden.

Don Walker vloog op een hoogte van 20 000 voet na een missie aan de rand van Al Qaim, waar hij en zijn wingman Randy Roberts zojuist een vaste raketbasis hadden vernietigd die een van de gifgasfabrieken beschermde die ook op de lijst stond om te worden gebombardeerd.

Walker kreeg het bericht door en controleerde zijn brandstof. Niet veel meer. Bovendien was hij zijn lasergeleide bommen kwijt. Er hingen alleen nog twee Sidewinders en twee Sparrows onder zijn vleugels – bedoeld voor een luchtgevecht als ze Iraakse jets zouden tegenkomen.

Ergens ten zuiden van de grens cirkelde zijn tanker geduldig rond, en hij had iedere drup kerosine hard nodig om naar Al Kharz terug te vliegen. Aan de andere kant, hij hoefde maar een omweg van vijfentwintig kilometer te maken voor een aanval op het konvooi. In elk geval kon hij een kijkje nemen, ook al had hij geen bommen meer.

Zijn wingman had alles gehoord. Walker maakte een gebaar achter de ruit van zijn cockpit naar zijn collega, nog geen kilometer verderop in de heldere lucht. Even later doken de twee Eagles gezamenlijk naar rechts.

Op 8000 voet zag hij de bron van het signaal dat de J-STARS had opgevangen. Het was geen Scud-lanceertruck maar een groepje van twee vrachtwagens en twee BRDM-2's, lichte pantserwagens van Russische makelij, met wielen in plaats van rupsbanden.

Vanuit zijn toestel kon hij heel wat meer zien dan de J-STARS. Diep beneden hem in een wadi ontdekte hij een eenzame Landrover met vier Britse SAS-mannen eromheen, als kleine mieren op de bruine deken van de woestijn. Wat zij niet zagen, waren de vier Iraakse voertuigen die hen in een hoefijzerformatie omsingelden, en de soldaten die uit de twee trucks sprongen om de wadi af te sluiten.

Don Walker had in Oman met de SAS kennisgemaakt. Hij wist dat ze in de westelijke woestijn op jacht waren naar Scud-installaties. Een paar piloten van zijn squadron hadden weleens radiocontact gehad als de Britten met hun typische accent om assistentie vroegen omdat ze een doelwit hadden opgespoord dat ze zelf niet konden uitschakelen.

Vanaf 3000 voet zag hij de vier Engelsen nieuwsgierig omhoog kijken. Net als de Irakezen, nog geen kilometer verderop.

Walker drukte zijn zendknop in. 'Neem jij de trucks.'

'Begrepen.'

Hoewel hij geen bommen of gronddoelraketten meer over had, zat er in zijn rechtervleugel, aan de buitenkant van de grote luchtinlaat, wel een M-61-A1 Vulcan 20-mm kanon, met zes roterende lopen die met hoge snelheid hun totale magazijn van 450 granaten konden afvuren. Een 20-mm granaat is zo groot als een kleine banaan en explodeert als hij inslaat. Voor wie in een truck of in het open veld wordt geraakt, is meestal de lol eraf.

Walker zette het boordgeschut op scherp. Op zijn heads-up display zag hij de twee pantserwagens plus een richtkruis dat rekening hield met afwijkingen en andere invloeden.

De eerste BRDM werd door honderd granaten getroffen en explodeerde. Walker trok de neus van zijn Eagle wat omhoog, en bracht het richtkruis op zijn HUD-scherm in lijn met de achterkant van de tweede wagen. Hij zag de benzinetank in brand vliegen. Het volgende moment was hij eroverheen, klimmend en rollend tot hij de bruine woestijn boven zijn hoofd zag verschijnen. Met een volgende rol bracht hij de Eagle weer omlaag. De horizon van blauw en bruin draaide weer in zijn normale positie met de woestijn beneden en de hemel boven. De twee BRDM's stonden in brand, één vrachtwagen lag op zijn kant, de andere was aan flarden geschoten. Kleine figuurtjes renden naar de rotsen om dekking te zoeken.

De vier SAS-mannen in de wadi hadden de hint begrepen. Ze sprongen in hun Landrover en reden de droge waterloop uit, zo ver mogelijk bij de hinderlaag vandaan. Ze hadden geen idee wie hen had ontdekt en hun positie had verraden – waarschijnlijk een paar rondzwervende herders – maar ze wisten wel wie zojuist hun leven had gered.

De Eagles stegen weer op, wipten even met hun vleugels en klommen naar de grens en de wachtende tanker.

De onderofficier die het bevel had over de SAS-patrouille was een zekere sergeant Peter Stephenson. Hij stak zijn hand op naar de vertrekkende jagers en zei: 'Ik weet niet wie jullie zijn, kerels, maar jullie hebben er een van mij tegoed.'

Toevallig had Betty Maslowski een Suzuki-jeep als boodschappenauto, en hoewel ze de vierwielaandrijving nog nooit had geprobeerd, stond ze erop dat Terry hem leende. Hoewel hij pas 's middags om vijf uur op het vliegtuig naar Londen zou stappen, ging hij toch vroeg van start omdat hij niet wist hoe lang het ging duren. Hij zei dat hij uiterlijk om twee uur terug wilde zijn.

Dr. Maslowski moest weer naar de universiteit, maar hij gaf Martin een kaart, zodat hij niet kon verdwalen.

De weg naar het dal van de rivier de Mocho liep vlak langs Livermore, waar hij afsloeg naar de Mines Road uit Tesla.

Na een paar kilometer waren de laatste huizen van de buitenwijk van Livermore verdwenen en werd het terrein steeds heuvelachtiger. Hij had geluk met het weer. De winter in deze streken is nooit zo koud als in de rest van de Verenigde Staten, maar door de nabijheid van de zee is het vaak dichtbewolkt en kan er snel mist optreden. Maar die 27e januari was het een heldere, frisse dag met een blauwe lucht.

Voor zich uit zag hij de besneeuwde top van de Cedar Mountain. Vijftien kilometer na de afslag verliet hij de Mines Road en nam een pad dat zich langs een steile heuvel omhoog slingerde.

Ver beneden hem in het dal glinsterde de Mocho tussen de rotsen in de zon. Het gras aan weerskanten maakte plaats voor een mengeling van bijvoet en casuarina. Hoog in de lucht cirkelden twee wouwen tegen de blauwe lucht. Het pad liep verder langs de rand van de Cedar Mountain Ridge, de wildernis in.

Hij kwam langs een eenzame groene boerderij, maar Lomax had gezegd dat hij het pad tot het eind moest volgen. Vijf kilometer verderop vond hij de blokhut, met een kale stenen schoorsteen waaruit de blauwe rookpluim van een houtvuur omhoog kringelde.

Hij stopte bij de achterkant van het houten huis en stapte uit. Vanuit een schuur staarde een Jersey-koe hem met fluwelen ogen aan. Vanaf de andere kant van het huis klonken ritmische geluiden. Martin liep naar de voorkant en vond Daddy Lomax op een heuveltje met uitzicht over het dal en de rivier ver beneden.

Hij was vijfenzeventig, en ondanks Sandy's bezorgdheid zag hij eruit of hij nog met grizzlyberen vocht als hobby. De oude geleerde was ruim één meter tachtig. Hij droeg een vuile spijkerbroek en een geruit hemd en stond hout te hakken met een gemak alsof hij boterhammen sneed.

Zijn sneeuwwitte haar kwam tot op zijn schouders en een stoppelige witte baard sierde zijn kin. Uit de V-kraag van zijn hemd krulde nog meer wit haar en hij scheen niets te merken van de kou, hoewel Terry Martin blij was met zijn gevoerde anorak.

'Hebt u het gevonden? Ik hoorde u al aankomen,' zei Lomax, terwijl hij met een geweldige klap het laatste blok in tweeën spleet. Toen legde hij de bijl neer en kwam naar zijn bezoeker toe. Ze schudden elkaar de hand. Lomax wees naar een houtblok en ging zelf op een ander zitten.

'Doctor Martin, zei u toch?'

'Ja, dat klopt.'

'Uit Engeland?'

'Ja.'

Lomax stak zijn hand in zijn borstzakje, haalde er een pakje shag en een vloeitje uit en begon een sigaret te rollen.

'U zeurt toch niet?' vroeg hij.

'Nee, dat geloof ik niet.'

Lomax bromde goedkeurend.

'Mijn dokter wel. Hij riep maar steeds dat ik met roken moest stoppen.'

De verleden tijd ontging Martin niet. 'Dus u bent bij hem weg?'

'Nee, hij is bij mij weg. Overleden, vorige week. Zesenvijftig. Stress. Waar komt u voor?'

Martin zocht in zijn koffertje. 'Ik wil bij voorbaat mijn excuses maken. Waarschijnlijk verspil ik uw tijd. Maar wilt u hier eens naar kijken?'

Lomax nam de foto aan en bekeek hem. 'Komt u echt uit Engeland?'

'Ja.'

'Dat is een lange reis om me dit te laten zien.'

'Weet u wat het is?'

'Dat zou ik denken. Ik heb er vijf jaar gewerkt.'

Martins mond viel open van verbazing. 'Hebt u daar *gewerkt*?'

'Ja, ik heb er vijf jaar gewoond.'

'In Tarmija?'

'Waar is dat in godsnaam? Dit is Oak Ridge.'

Martin slikte een paar keer. 'Doctor Lomax, die foto is zes dagen geleden gemaakt door een gevechtsvliegtuig van de Amerikaanse marine tijdens een verkenningsvlucht boven een gebombardeerde fabriek in Irak.'

Lomax keek op, met helderblauwe ogen onder zijn borstelige witte wenkbrauwen. Toen keek hij weer naar de foto.

'Wel verdomme,' zei hij ten slotte. 'Daar heb ik die klootzakken voor gewaarschuwd. Drie jaar geleden al. Toen heb ik in een rapport geschreven dat dit de technologie was die de derde wereld waarschijnlijk zou gaan gebruiken.

'Wat is er met dat rapport gebeurd?'

'Dat hebben ze in een la gelegd.'

'Wie?'

'Ach, hogerhand natuurlijk. Achterlijke zakken.'

'Die schijven, die "frisbees" in de fabriek, weet u wat dat zijn?'

'Natuurlijk. Calutrons. Ze hebben gewoon de oude fabriek van Oak Ridge nagebouwd.'

'Calu... wat?'

Lomax keek weer op.

'U bent geen doctor in de natuurwetenschappen?'

'Nee. Ik ben arabist.'

Lomax bromde weer wat, alsof Martin het niet getroffen had in het leven.

'Calutrons. Californische cyclotrons, afgekort calutrons.'

'En wat doen die?'

'Elektromagnetische isotopenscheiding of EMIS. In gewoon Engels komt het erop neer dat ze ruw uranium-238 kunnen verrijken om er uranium-235 uit te filteren dat je voor een kernbom kunt gebruiken. En die fabriek ligt in Irak, zegt u?'

'Ja. Vorige week is hij bij toeval gebombardeerd. Deze foto is de volgende dag genomen. Niemand wist wat het was.'

Lomax tuurde over het dal, nam een trek van zijn saffie en blies een blauwe rookwolk uit.

'Verdomme,' zei hij weer. 'Ik woon hier omdat ik het prettig vind. Weg van de smog en het verkeer. Daar had ik al jaren geleden genoeg van. Ik heb geen televisie, maar wel radio. Het gaat zeker om die Saddam Hoessein?'

'Ja. Kunt u me wat meer vertellen over calutrons?'

De oude man drukte zijn peuk uit en staarde voor zich uit – niet naar het dal, maar naar een ver verleden.

'Het begon in 1943. Meer dan vijftig jaar geleden. Dat is een lange tijd,

345

niet? Nog voordat u geboren was, voordat de meeste mensen uit deze tijd geboren waren. We waren toen met een hele ploeg, en we probeerden het onmogelijke te bereiken. We waren jong, gretig en slim – en we wisten niet dat het onmogelijk was. Daarom lukte het ons. Fermi en Pontecorve uit Italië, Fuchs uit Duitsland, Nils Bohr uit Denemarken, Nunn May uit Engeland en anderen. En dan wij, de Amerikanen: Urey en Oppie en Ernest. Ik was nog maar een broekie. Net zevenentwintig.

Het grootste deel van de tijd volgden we onze intuïtie, deden we dingen die nog nooit waren geprobeerd en testten we theorieën die volgens iedereen onmogelijk waren. We hadden een budget waar je tegenwoordig geen flikker mee zou kunnen beginnen, daarom werkten we dag en nacht en zochten we naar noodoplossingen. Dat moest wel. De tijd was net zo krap als het geld. En op de een of andere manier kregen we het voor elkaar, binnen drie jaar. We ontcijferden de code en we produceerden de bommen, *Little Boy* en *Fat Man*.

Daarna gooide de luchtmacht ze op Hirosjima en Nagasaki en riep de hele wereld dat we die dingen nooit hadden moeten uitvinden. Maar dan had iemand anders het wel gedaan. Nazi-Duitsland, Stalins Rusland...'

'Calutrons...' drong Martin aan.

'O ja. U hebt weleens gehoord van het Manhattan Project, neem ik aan?'

'Natuurlijk.'

'Nou, we hadden heel wat genieën in Manhattan, met name twee: Robert J. Oppenheimer en Ernest O. Lawrence. Ooit van gehoord?'

'Ja.'

'U dacht zeker dat het collega's waren? Partners?'

'Ja, zoiets.'

'Mis. Het waren concurrenten. Kijk, we wisten allemaal dat uranium de sleutel was. Het zwaarste element ter wereld. En in 1941 was al duidelijk dat alleen de lichtere isotoop 235 de kettingreactie kon veroorzaken die we nodig hadden. De truc was om die 0,7 procent van het 235 te scheiden die ergens in de massa van het uranium-238 verborgen zat.

Toen Amerika bij de oorlog betrokken raakte, kregen we veel meer geld. Na jaren van verwaarlozing wilde hogerhand opeens resultaten. Het oude verhaal. Dus probeerden we op alle mogelijke manieren die isotopen te scheiden.

Oppenheimer koos voor gasdiffusie: het uranium tot een vloeistof reduceren en daarna tot een gas, uranium hexafluoride – giftig, corrosief en lastig om mee te werken. De centrifuge kwam later pas. Dat was een uitvinding van een Oostenrijker die door de Russen gevangen was genomen en te werk was gesteld in Soekhoemi. Maar voor de komst van de centrifuge werkten we dus met gasdiffusie. Dat ging moeilijk en traag.

Lawrence koos voor de andere aanpak, elektromagnetische scheiding door deeltjesversnelling. Weet u wat dat inhoudt?'

'Ik vrees van niet.'

'Het komt erop neer dat je de atomen tot een enorme snelheid aanjaagt en ze dan met reusachtige magneten in een curve gooit. Als twee racewagens, een lichte en een zware auto, met hoge snelheid een bocht in gaan, welke komt er dan in de buitenbaan terecht?'

'De zware,' zei Martin.

'Precies. Dat is het principe. De calutrons werken met enorme magneten van ongeveer zes meter doorsnee. Dit...' hij tikte op de 'frisbees' op de foto, 'zijn de magneten. En de indeling van de fabriek is een exacte kopie van mijn oude baby in Oak Ridge, Tennessee.'

'Maar als het werkte, waarom is niemand er dan mee doorgegaan?' vroeg Martin.

'Een kwestie van snelheid,' zei Lomax. 'Oppenheimer won. Zijn methode was sneller. De calutrons waren heel langzaam en heel duur. Na 1945, en zeker toen die Oostenrijker door de Russen werd vrijgelaten en naar ons toe kwam om zijn centrifuge te demonstreren, is de calutrontechnologie verlaten. En vrijgegeven. Alle plannen en details kun je gewoon bij de Library of Congres opvragen. En dat hebben de Irakezen vermoedelijk gedaan.'

De twee mannen bleven een paar minuten zwijgend zitten.

'Wat u zegt,' concludeerde Martin, 'is dat Irak voor de technologie van de T-Ford heeft gekozen, en omdat iedereen veronderstelde dat ze Formule-1 wagens wilden bouwen, heeft niemand daarop gelet.'

'Precies, kerel. De T-Ford is oud, *maar hij reed wel*. Dat vergeten de mensen weleens. Hij bracht je waar je wezen wilde. Hij reed van A naar B. En hij was redelijk betrouwbaar.'

'Doctor Lomax, de wetenschappers die uw regering en de mijne adviseren, weten dat Irak één cascade van gasdiffusiecentrifuges in bedrijf heeft. Die werkt nu een jaar. Een tweede wordt binnenkort opgestart, maar is vermoedelijk nog niet actief. Daarom gaan ze ervan uit dat Irak onmogelijk al voldoende zuiver uranium kan hebben... zo'n 35 kilo... om een kernbom te maken.'

Lomax knikte. 'Dat klopt. Met één cascade heb je vijf jaar nodig, misschien langer. Met twee cascades minimaal drie jaar.'

'Maar stel dat ze die calutrons parallel hebben geschakeld. Als u de leiding had over het Iraakse kernbomprogramma, hoe zou u het dan aanpakken?'

'Niet op die manier,' zei de oude fysicus en hij rolde nog een sigaret. 'Hebben ze u in Londen verteld dat je begint met *yellowcake*, splijtstof van nulprocent zuiver uranium, en dat je die tot drieënnegentig procent zuiver ura-

nium moet verfijnen om de kwaliteit te krijgen die nodig is voor een bom?'
Martin herinnerde zich dr. Hipwell met zijn sputterende pijp, die in een vergaderzaaltje onder Whitehall precies hetzelfde had gezegd.
'Ja, inderdaad.'
'Maar hebben ze er niet bij gezegd dat het verrijken van nul tot twintig pro-
cent de meeste tijd kost? Dat het proces steeds sneller verloopt naarmate het
spul zuiverder wordt?'
'Nee.'
'Nou, dat is zo. Als ik calutrons en centrifuges had, zou ik ze niet parallel
schakelen, maar in serie. Dan zou ik het basis-uranium met de calutrons
bewerken om het van nul tot twintig of vijfentwintig procent te zuiveren, en
dat materiaal als grondstof voor de nieuwe cascades gebruiken.'
'Waarom?'
'Omdat het de tijd die je voor de cascades nodig hebt met een factor tien zou
bekorten.'
Martin dacht erover na terwijl Daddy Lomax aan zijn sjekkie trok.
'Wanneer zou Irak dan over die 35 kilo zuiver uranium kunnen beschikken?'
'Dat hangt ervan af wanneer je met de calutrons bent begonnen.'
Martin dacht na. Toen de Israëlische jets de Iraakse reactor van Osirak had-
den vernietigd, besloot Bagdad volgens twee principes verder te gaan: ver-
spreiding en duplicatie. De laboratoria werden over het hele land verspreid
zodat ze nooit meer tegelijk konden worden platgegooid, en bij de aankopen
en de experimenten werd voor een zo breed mogelijke aanpak gekozen.
Osirak was in 1981 verwoest.
'Laten we zeggen dat ze de componenten in 1982 op de open markt hebben
gekocht en ze in 1983 in elkaar hebben gezet.'
Lomax raapte een tak op en maakte een paar berekeningen in het zand.
'Hadden ze problemen met de aanvoer van *yellowcake*, de eerste splijtstof?'
'Nee, dat was er voldoende.'
'Ja, dat zal wel,' bromde Lomax. 'Je kunt het tegenwoordig bij de super-
markt krijgen.'
Na een tijdje tikte hij met de stok op de foto. 'Hier zijn twintig calutrons te
zien. Was dat alles wat ze hadden?'
'Misschien zijn er wel meer. Dat weten we niet. Laten we aannemen dat het
alles was.'
'Sinds 1983?'
'Ja, als uitgangspunt.'
Lomax rekende verder in het zand.
'En heeft Hoessein gebrek aan stroom?'
Martin herinnerde zich de 150-megawatt centrale in de woestijn en de sug-

348

gestie uit het Zwarte Gat dat er ondergrondse kabels naar Tarmija liepen.
'Nee, hij heeft stroom genoeg.'
'Wij niet,' zei Lomax. 'Die calutrons vreten energie. Bij Oak Ridge hebben
we de grootste kolengestookte krachtcentrale gebouwd die ik ooit heb
gezien. En daarnaast moesten we nog van het gewone elektriciteitsnet
gebruikmaken. Steeds als we dat deden, viel de stroom in Tennessee gedeel-
telijk weg, slappe patat en flakkerende lampen. Zoveel hadden we nodig.'
Hij kraste zijn berekening in het zand weg en begon aan een volgende op
dezelfde plek.
'Hebben ze tekort aan koperdraad?'
'Nee, dat kunnen ze ook op de open markt kopen.'
'Die grote magneten moeten in duizenden kilometers koperdraad worden
gewikkeld,' verklaarde Lomax. 'In de oorlog konden we dat niet krijgen.
Het was nodig voor de oorlogsindustrie. Weet u wat Lawrence deed?'
'Geen idee.'
'Hij heeft alle zilverstaven uit Fort Knox geleend en die tot draden omge-
smolten. Dat werkte ook. Na de oorlog kreeg Fort Knox alles weer terug.'
Hij grinnikte. 'Met die man kon je wat beleven.'
Ten slotte was hij klaar en richtte zich op.
'Als ze in 1983 twintig calutrons hebben opgesteld en daar *yellowcake* mee
hebben verrijkt tot in 1989... hielden ze dertig procent zuiver uranium over.
Als ze dat één jaar lang in een centrifugecascade hebben bewerkt, hadden ze
35 kilo drieënnegentig procent zuiver uranium kunnen hebben in... novem-
ber.'
'November aanstaande,' zei Martin.
Lomax stond op, rekte zich uit en trok zijn bezoeker toen overeind.
'Nee, kerel. November vorig jaar.'

Martin reed de berg weer af en keek op zijn horloge. Twaalf uur. Acht uur
's avonds in Londen. Paxman was al naar huis, en Martin had zijn privé-
nummer niet.
Hij zou nog twaalf uur in San Francisco kunnen wachten of meteen naar
huis kunnen terugvliegen. Hij besloot op het vliegtuig te stappen.
De ochtend van de 28e januari landde hij in Londen. Om half één was hij bij
Paxman. Om twee uur voerde Steve Laing een dringend gesprek met Harry
Sinclair op de ambassade in Grosvenor Square en een uur later sprak de
Londense CIA-officier via een rechtstreekse en ultra-beveiligde lijn met de
adjunct-directeur Operaties in Langley, Bill Stewart.

Pas de ochtend van 30 januari kon Bill Stewart een volledig verslag uitbrengen aan de directeur van de CIA, William Webster.

'Het klopt,' zei hij tegen de voormalige rechter uit Kansas. 'Ik heb mensen naar die blokhut bij de Cedar Mountain gestuurd en die oude man, Lomax, heeft het allemaal bevestigd. We hebben zijn oorspronkelijke rapport gevonden. Het was in een bureaula verdwenen. Uit de archieven van Oak Ridge blijkt dat die schijven inderdaad calutrons zijn...'

'Hoe is dit in godsnaam mogelijk?' vroeg de directeur. 'Waarom hebben we dat niet ontdekt?'

'Het idee is waarschijnlijk afkomstig van Jaafar al-Jaafar, de Iraakse leider van het nucleaire programma. Hij is niet alleen opgeleid in Harwell in Engeland, maar ook aan het CERN bij Genève. Daar staat een reusachtige deeltjesversneller.'

'En?'

'Calutrons zijn deeltjesversnellers. En in 1949 is alle calutrontechnologie vrijgegeven. Iedereen kan er informatie over krijgen.'

'En waar hebben ze die calutrons gekocht?'

'Voornamelijk in Oostenrijk en Frankrijk, in onderdelen. Niemand kreeg argwaan, omdat het zo'n verouderde technologie is. De fabriek is onder contract door de Joegoslaven gebouwd. Ze zeiden dat ze plannen nodig hadden dus heeft Irak ze gewoon de plannen van Oak Ridge gegeven. Daarom is Tarmija een exacte kopie.'

'Wanneer was dat allemaal?' vroeg de directeur.

'In 1982.'

'Dus die agent... hoe heet hij ook weer?'

'Jericho.'

'Die heeft niet gelogen?'

'Jericho heeft alleen doorgegeven wat Saddam Hoessein tijdens een besloten bijeenkomst zou hebben gezegd. Ik vrees dat we niet langer kunnen uitsluiten dat hij inderdaad de waarheid sprak.'

'Maar we hebben Jericho aan de kant gezet?'

'Hij vroeg een miljoen dollar voor die informatie. Dat hebben we niet betaald, want op dat moment...'

'Allemachtig, Bill! Dat was een koopje.'

De directeur stond op en liep naar de grote ramen. De espen waren nu kaal, anders dan in augustus, en in het dal stroomde de Potomac voorbij, op weg naar de zee.

'Bill, stuur Chip Barber weer naar Riyad om te zien of we het contact met die Jericho kunnen herstellen...'

'Er is nog een mogelijkheid. We hadden een Britse agent in Bagdad. Hij kan voor een Arabier doorgaan. Maar we hebben Century House het advies gegeven om hem terug te roepen.'

'Hopelijk hebben ze dat niet gedaan, Bill. We hebben Jericho weer nodig.

Wat het ook mag kosten. We moeten die kernbom vinden en vernietigen voordat het te laat is.'

'Ja. En eh... wie vertelt het de generaals?'

De directeur zuchtte.

'Over twee uur heb ik een afspraak met Colin Powell en Brent Scowcroft.'

Liever jij dan ik, dacht Stewart toen hij vertrok.

De twee mannen van Century House waren eerder in Riyad dan Chip Barber, die uit Washington moest komen. Steve Laing en Simon Paxman landden in alle vroegte met de nachtvlucht vanaf Heathrow.

Julian Gray, het hoofd van het SIS-bureau in Riyad, haalde hen af in zijn onopvallende auto en bracht hen naar de villa waar hij al vijf maanden bijna onafgebroken bivakkeerde. Hij kwam alleen nog thuis om zijn vrouw te zien.

Hij begreep niets van de onverwachte komst van Simon Paxman, laat staan zijn chef Steve Laing, voor een operatie die in feite al was afgelopen.

In de villa, achter gesloten deuren, vertelde Laing hem waarom ze weer contact moesten leggen met Jericho.

'Jezus, dus die klootzak heeft werkelijk een bom?'

'Daar moeten we van uitgaan, ook al hebben we geen bewijzen,' zei Laing.

'Wanneer kun je een bericht aan Martin verzenden?'

'Tussen kwart over elf en kwart voor twaalf vanavond,' zei Gray. 'Maar vanwege het risico hebben we al vijf dagen niets van ons laten horen. We gaan ervan uit dat hij ieder moment over de grens kan komen.'

'Laten we hopen dat hij daar nog zit. Anders wordt het een ramp. Dan moeten we hem terugsturen, en dat kan weken duren. Het wemelt van de Iraakse patrouilles in de woestijn.'

'Hoeveel mensen weten hiervan?' vroeg Gray.

'Zo weinig mogelijk, en dat houden we zo,' antwoordde Laing.

Londen en Washington hadden een kleine overleggroep gevormd, maar nog altijd te groot naar de zin van de inlichtingendiensten. In Washington waren de president en vier leden van zijn kabinet op de hoogte, plus de voorzitter van de Nationale Veiligheidsraad en de voorzitter van de chefs-van-staven. Daarbij kwamen nog vier mensen in Langley, van wie er één, Chip Barber, naar Riyad onderweg was. De onfortuinlijke dr. Lomax had een ongewenste gast in zijn blokhut om ervoor te zorgen dat hij geen contact had met de buitenwereld.

In Londen bleef de kring beperkt tot de nieuwe premier, John Major, de kabinetssecretaris, twee ministers en drie mensen van Century House.

In Riyad waren er nu drie man in de SIS-villa die ervan wisten, en Barber kon ieder moment aankomen. Van de militairen waren vier generaals, drie Amerikanen en een Brit, op de hoogte gebracht.

Dr. Terry Martin had een diplomatieke aanval van griep gekregen en was naar een gerieflijk SIS-schuiladres op het platteland overgebracht, met een moederlijke huishoudster en drie niet zo moederlijke oppassers.

Vanaf dit moment zouden alle operaties tegen Irak die betrekking hadden op de speurtocht naar en de vernietiging van het wapen dat vermoedelijk *Qubth-ut-Allah* of 'De Vuist van God' werd genoemd, worden uitgevoerd onder de dekmantel van een plan om Saddam Hoessein te elimineren, of een ander aannemelijk doel.

Dat was trouwens al twee keer geprobeerd. Er waren twee plaatsen geïdentificeerd waar de Iraakse president zou zijn – tijdelijk, tenminste. Niemand wist precies wanneer, want de *Rais* trok van de ene schuilplaats naar de andere als hij niet in zijn bunker in Bagdad te vinden was.

De twee plaatsen werden vanuit de lucht in de gaten gehouden. Een ervan was een villa op het platteland, zestig kilometer buiten Bagdad, de andere een camper die als commandocentrum was ingericht.

Op een gegeven moment hadden de luchtverkenners een paar mobiele raketbatterijen en lichte pantserwagens rondom de villa gezien. Twee Strike Eagles hadden het huis platgegooid. Maar het was loos alarm. De vogel zat niet op het nest.

De volgende keer, twee dagen voor het einde van januari, was de camper naar een andere plaats gereden. Weer werd er een aanval uitgevoerd en weer bleek het doelwit niet thuis te zijn.

Beide keren namen de piloten geweldige risico's, want de Iraakse artillerie bood hevig verzet. De twee mislukte aanvallen brachten de geallieerden in een dilemma. Ze wisten gewoon niet waar Saddam zich bevond. En ze waren de enigen niet. Niemand was van zijn bewegingen op de hoogte, behalve een kleine groep van persoonlijke lijfwachten onder bevel van zijn eigen zoon Kusaj.

In werkelijkheid reisde hij voortdurend rond. Ondanks de veronderstelling dat Saddam het grootste deel van de luchtoorlog in zijn ondergrondse bunker had gezeten, was hij daar nog niet de helft van de tijd.

Maar zijn veiligheid werd beschermd door een heel scala van afleidingsmanoeuvres en valse sporen. Een paar keer was hij 'gezien' door zijn juichende troepen. Volgens cynici juichten ze alleen omdat zij niet naar het front werden gestuurd om zich door de Buffs te laten bombarderen. De man die de Iraakse soldaten bij die gelegenheden zagen, was een van zijn dubbelgangers.

Op andere momenten reed er een konvooi van soms wel twaalf limousines met geblindeerde ruiten in hoog tempo door Bagdad, zodat iedereen dacht dat de *Rais* in een van de auto's zat. Maar dat was niet zo. Als de president vertrok, reisde hij soms maar met één onopvallende auto.

Zelfs binnen zijn eigen kringetje werden allerlei maatregelen genomen. Ministers werden pas vijf minuten voor het begin van een vergadering gewaarschuwd. Ze moesten dan meteen vertrekken en werden door motoren naar een bepaalde plek geëscorteerd. Maar die plek was niet de plaats waar de bijeenkomst werd gehouden.

Ze moesten in een donkere bus met zwarte ramen stappen, met een scherm tussen de passagiers en de chauffeur. En de chauffeur volgde een motorrijder van de Amn-al-Khass naar de uiteindelijke bestemming.

Achter de bestuurder zaten de ministers, de generaals en de adviseurs als schooljongens op een spooktocht, zonder te weten waar ze heen gingen of waar ze – na afloop – waren geweest.

De meeste vergaderingen werden gehouden in grote, afgelegen villa's, die voor één dag waren gevorderd en 's avonds weer werden verlaten. Een speciale afdeling van de Amn-al-Khass had geen andere taak dan het vinden van zo'n villa als de *Rais* een vergadering wilde houden. Ze hielden de bewoners van de villa zolang gegijzeld en lieten hen pas vrij als de president vertrokken was.

Geen wonder dat de geallieerden hem niet konden vinden. Maar ze probeerden het wel, tot de eerste week van februari. Daarna werden alle pogingen tot een aanslag stopgezet, zonder dat de militairen ooit begrepen waarom.

De laatste dag van januari, kort na de middag, arriveerde Chip Barber bij de Britse villa in Riyad. De vier mannen begroetten elkaar en wachtten op het moment dat ze contact konden opnemen met Martin, als hij nog in Bagdad was.

'Ik neem aan dat we een tijdschema hebben?' vroeg Laing.

Barber knikte. 'Ja. We hebben de tijd tot 20 februari. Dan wil Stormin' Norman zijn troepen de grens over sturen.'

Paxman floot. 'Twintig dagen? Allemachtig. En Uncle Sam betaalt de rekening?'

'Ja. De directeur heeft al opdracht gegeven om die miljoen dollar nog vandaag op Jericho's rekening te storten. Voor aanwijzingen over de locatie van het wapen – aangenomen dat het er maar één is – zullen we die klootzak vijf miljoen dollar betalen.'

'Vijf miljoen dollar?' riep Laing. 'Jezus, niemand heeft een spion nog ooit zoveel betaald.'

Barber haalde zijn schouders op.

'Jericho, wie hij ook mag zijn, is een huurling. Hij wil geld, anders niets. Laat hij het maar verdienen. Er zit wel een addertje onder het gras. Arabieren dingen af, wij niet. Vijf dagen nadat we hem het bericht hebben

354

gestuurd, gaat er iedere dag een half miljoen vanaf tot hij ons de juiste locatie noemt. Dat moet hij goed beseffen.'

De drie Britten dachten na over zoveel geld – meer dan ze met hun drieën in hun hele leven zouden verdienen.

'Nou,' merkte Laing op, 'dat zal hem wel motiveren.'

In de loop van de middag en de avond werd het bericht opgesteld. Eerst moest er contact worden gelegd met Martin, die met van tevoren afgesproken codes moest bevestigen dat hij nog in Bagdad zat en in vrijheid was. Daarna zou Riyad hem het aanbod aan Jericho meedelen, met alle details en de nadruk op het krappe tijdschema.

De mannen aten niet veel. Ze speelden met het eten op hun bord. De spanning was te snijden. Om half elf liep Simon Paxman met de anderen naar de radiohut en sprak het bericht op de band in. Het werd tweehonderd keer versneld en ingekort tot twee seconden.

Tien seconden na kwart over elf verzond de hoofdtechnicus een kort signaal – de vraag 'Bent u daar?' Drie minuten later ving de satellietschotel wat statisch geruis op. Toen het werd vertraagd, bleek het de stem van Mike Martin te zijn: 'Zwarte Beer aan Rocky Mountain. Ik ontvang u. Over.'

Er klonk een zucht van opluchting in de radiokamer in Riyad. Vier volwassen kerels sloegen elkaar op de schouders als schooljongens die een voetbaltoernooi hebben gewonnen.

Wie het nooit heeft meegemaakt kan zich nauwelijks voorstellen hoe het is om te horen dat 'een van onze jongens' ver achter de vijandelijke linies nog in leven en in vrijheid is.

'Hij zit daar nu al veertien dagen, godverdomme,' mompelde Barber verwonderd. 'Waarom is hij niet teruggekomen toen hij het bevel kreeg?'

'Omdat hij een koppige idioot is,' zei Laing. 'Gelukkig maar.'

De technicus, die heel rustig was gebleven, verstuurde nog een bericht. Hij vroeg om vijf codewoorden als bevestiging, hoewel de oscillograaf hem vertelde dat het de stem van Mike Martin was en dat de SAS-majoor niet onder dwang sprak. Maar veertien dagen is lang genoeg om een man te breken.

Het antwoord uit Bagdad was kort en bondig: 'Van Nelson en het noorden. Ik herhaal: van Nelson en het noorden. Uit.'

Weer verstreken er drie minuten. Toen ving Martin, gehurkt op de vloer van zijn schuurtje in de tuin in Bagdad, de volgende boodschap op. Hij sprak zijn antwoord in, liet het versnellen tot eentiende van een seconde, en verzond het naar de Saoedische hoofdstad.

'Bezing de roem van de briljante dag,' hoorden de mannen in Riyad hem zeggen.

De technicus grinnikte. 'Het is hem,' zei hij. 'Springlevend en op vrije voeten.'

'Komt dat uit een gedicht?' vroeg Barber.

'Ja,' zei Laing. 'De tweede regel luidt eigenlijk: "Bezing de roem van de glorieuze dag." Als hij het juist had geciteerd, had hij een revolver tegen zijn slaap gehad. En in dat geval...' Hij haalde zijn schouders op.

De technicus verzond het laatste bericht, de werkelijke opdracht, en sloot af.

Barber zocht in zijn koffertje. 'Ik weet dat het tegen de plaatselijke regels is, maar het diplomatieke bestaan heeft zo zijn voordelen.'

'Toe maar,' mompelde Gray. 'Dom Perignon. Kan Langley dat wel betalen?'

'Langley,' antwoordde Barber, 'heeft zojuist vijf miljoen dollar op de pokertafel gelegd. Die fles prik kan er ook wel af.'

'Verdomd fideel van je,' zei Paxman.

Eén enkele week had van Edith Hardenberg een totaal andere vrouw gemaakt – één week, en de liefde.

Na een lichte aansporing van Karim was ze naar een kapper in Grinzing gegaan die haar haar in een lange coup had geknipt, zodat het nu aan weerskanten langs haar gezicht viel en haar magere wangen wat opvulde. Daardoor leek ze vrouwelijker en knapper.

Met haar aarzelende toestemming had haar minnaar ook make-up spullen voor haar gekocht. Niets bijzonders, wat eyeliner, een foundation-crème, poeder en een lippenstift.

Voor Wolfgang Gemütlich, haar baas, was het een hele schok toen hij haar zo door het kantoor zag lopen, een paar centimeter langer op haar hoge hakken. Het was niet eens zozeer dat de schoenen, het kapsel of de make-up hem niet bevielen (hoewel hij zoiets bij zijn eigen vrouw niet zou kunnen waarderen), maar vooral haar houding, die zelfbewuste uitstraling als ze dictaat opnam of hem zijn brieven bracht om te ondertekenen.

Natuurlijk wist hij wat er was gebeurd. Een van die domme meiden beneden had haar ertoe aangezet om geld uit te geven. Dat was de wortel van alle kwaad, geld uitgeven. Daar kwam naar zijn ervaring nooit iets goeds van, en hij vreesde het ergste.

Ediths aangeboren verlegenheid was niet helemaal verdwenen en op de bank zei ze nog steeds niet veel, ook al zag ze er anders uit, maar in het gezelschap van Karim, als ze alleen waren, stond ze voortdurend versteld van haar eigen stoutmoedigheid. Twintig jaar lang had ze een afkeer gehad van alle fysieke zaken, en nu was het alsof ze een ontdekkingsreis maakte, langzaam en verwonderd, half bedeesd en half huiverig, half nieuwsgierig en half opgewonden. In het begin was het vrijen nog éénrichtingsverkeer geweest, maar nu nam ze zelf ook initiatieven. De eerste keer dat ze hem 'daar beneden' aanraakte, was ze bang dat ze zou sterven van schrik en schaamte, maar tot haar verbazing overleefde ze de schok.

De avond van de 3e februari bracht hij een cadeautje mee naar haar flat, een platte doos in cadeaupapier met een lint erom.

'Karim, dat moet je niet doen. Je geeft veel te veel geld uit.'

Hij nam haar in zijn armen en streelde haar haar. Ze had geleerd dat prettig te vinden.

'Hoor eens, poesje van me, mijn vader is rijk genoeg. Ik krijg een vorstelijke toelage. Moet ik die dan in nachtclubs uitgeven?'

Ze vond het leuk als hij haar plaagde. Natuurlijk zou Karim nooit in zo'n akelige gelegenheid komen. Daarom had ze het parfum en de make-up spullen aangenomen, zaken die ze twee weken geleden nog met geen vinger zou hebben aangeraakt.

'Mag ik het openmaken?' vroeg ze.

'Dat is de bedoeling.'

Eerst zag ze niet eens wat het was. De doos bevatte een wirwar van kleurige zijde en kant. Toen ze het begreep, omdat ze weleens advertenties in tijdschriften had gezien... niet het soort bladen dat ze zelf las, natuurlijk... werd ze pioenrood.

'Karim, dat kan niet! Dat is niets voor mij.'

'O jawel,' zei hij grijnzend. 'Toe maar, poesje, trek het maar aan. In de slaapkamer. Doe de deur maar dicht. Ik zal niet kijken.'

Ze legde de lingerie op het bed en keek ernaar. Zij, Edith Hardenberg? Nooit! Kousen, jarretelgordeltjes, slipjes en beha's, korte nachthemdjes, in zwart, roze, rood, crème en beige, van kant of zijde, afgezet met kant... Ze streek met haar vingertoppen over de soepele stof, glad als ijs.

Ze was een uur alleen in de slaapkamer voordat ze in een ochtendjas de kamer weer binnenstapte. Karim zette zijn koffiekopje neer, stond op en kwam naar haar toe. Met een lieve glimlach keek hij op haar neer en maakte toen de ceintuur van haar ochtendjas los. Ze bloosde opnieuw en ontweek zijn blik. Hij liet de jas openvallen.

'O, poesje,' zei hij zacht, 'wat zie je er prachtig uit.'

Ze wist niet wat ze moest zeggen, daarom sloeg ze haar armen om zijn nek, niet langer bang of huiverig toen haar dijbeen de erectie onder zijn jeans raakte.

Toen ze hadden gevreeën, stond ze op en liep naar de badkamer. Daarna bleef ze bij het bed staan en keek op hem neer. Ze hield van hem, helemaal. Ze ging op de rand van het bed zitten en streelde het vage litteken op zijn kin. Hij was een keer door een glazen kas in de boomgaard van zijn vader bij Amman gevallen, had hij haar verteld.

Hij opende zijn ogen, glimlachte en strekte zijn armen uit naar haar gezicht. Ze pakte zijn hand, liefkoosde zijn vingers en streelde de zegelring aan zijn pink, de ring met de bleekroze ovaal die hij van zijn moeder had gekregen.

'Wat zullen we vanavond doen?' vroeg ze.
'Laten we gaan eten,' zei hij. 'Een steak in het Bristol.'
'Je houdt te veel van biefstuk.'
Hij kneedde haar magere billen onder de dunne stof. 'Dit is de lekkerste biefstuk die ik ken,' zei hij grijnzend.
'Hou op! Je bent onverbeterlijk, Karim,' zei ze. 'Ik moet me verkleden.'
Ze maakte zich van hem los en zag zichzelf in de spiegel. Hoe had ze zó kunnen veranderen, vroeg ze zich af. Ze droeg zelfs lingerie! Maar toen begreep ze waarom. Voor Karim, haar Karim van wie ze hield en die van haar hield, wilde ze alles wel doen. De liefde was misschien laat gekomen, maar met de kracht van een woeste bergbeek.

Ministerie van Buitenlandse Zaken,
Washington, DC 20520

MEMORANDUM AAN: James Baker, minister van Buitenlandse Zaken
VAN: Political Intelligence and Analysis Group
ONDERWERP: Eliminatie van Saddam Hoessein
DATUM: 5 februari 1991
CLASSIFICATIE: Strikt persoonlijk

Het zal zeker niet aan uw aandacht zijn ontsnapt dat sinds het begin van de vijandelijkheden tussen de luchtmacht van de republiek Irak en de Coalitie, gestationeerd in Saoedi-Arabië en de aangrenzende staten, minstens twee en mogelijk meer pogingen zijn gedaan om de dood van de Iraakse president Saddam Hoessein te bewerkstelligen.
Al deze pogingen zijn door middel van bombardementen uitgevoerd en uitsluitend door ons. Daarom willen wij hier de gevolgen uiteenzetten van een geslaagde aanslag op Saddam Hoessein.
De ideale uitkomst zou natuurlijk zijn dat het nieuwe regime – gevormd onder auspiciën van de triomferende Coalitietroepen na de val van de huidige Ba'ath-regering – een menselijk en democratisch gezicht zou krijgen.
Wij achten deze hoop echter een illusie.
Om te beginnen is Irak geen verenigd land en is het dat nooit geweest. Nauwelijks een generatie geleden was het nog een lappendeken van rivaliserende en vaak oorlogvoerende stammen. Twee potentieel vijandige islamitische stromingen, de sji'iten en de soennieten, zijn ongeveer even sterk, en dan zijn er nog drie christelijke minderheden

– plus de Koerden in het noorden, die krachtig naar onafhankelijk-heid streven.

In de tweede plaats kent Irak geen enkele democratische traditie. Het land is van een Turks en een Hasjemitisch bewind rechtstreeks in han-den van de Ba'ath-partij gekomen zonder een democratische over-gang zoals wij die kennen.

Als er door een moordaanslag een abrupt einde aan de huidige dicta-tuur zou komen, zijn er daarom maar twee realistische mogelijkheden. De eerste is een poging om van buitenaf een coalitieregering te vor-men die alle belangrijke stromingen omvat. Waarschijnlijk zou zo'n regime maar een kort leven beschoren zijn. De traditionele, eeuwen-oude tegenstellingen zouden het bewind letterlijk verscheuren.

De Koerden zouden zeker van die langverwachte kans gebruikmaken om zich af te scheiden en in het noorden hun eigen republiek te vesti-gen. Een zwakke centrale regering in Bagdad, gebaseerd op compro-missen, zou daartegen weinig kunnen ondernemen.

De Turken zouden natuurlijk woedend reageren, omdat hun eigen Koerdische minderheid langs de grens zich onmiddellijk bij haar Koerdische broeders zou aansluiten om haar verzet tegen de Turkse overheid nog te versterken.

In het zuidoosten zou de sji'itische meerderheid rondom Basra en de Shatt-al-Arab zich tot Teheran wenden, en Iran zou in de verleiding komen om de slachting onder zijn jongeren in de recente Iraans-Iraakse oorlog te wreken door een poging om Zuidoost-Irak te annexeren, gebruikmakend van de machteloosheid van Bagdad.

In de pro-Westerse Golfstaten en Saoedi-Arabië zou de paniek toe-slaan bij de gedachte dat Iran tot aan de grens van Koeweit zou oprukken.

Verder naar het noorden zouden de Arabieren van Iraans Arabistan gemene zaak maken met hun geloofsgenoten aan de Iraakse kant van de grens, waarop een harde reactie zou volgen van de ayatollahs in Teheran.

In het centrum van Irak zou ongetwijfeld een strijd ontstaan tussen de verschillende stammen om oude rekeningen te vereffenen en de heer-schappij te verwerven over het restant van de Iraakse natie.

Allemaal volgen we met grote ongerustheid de burgeroorlog tussen de Serven en Kroaten in het voormalige Joegoslavië. Tot nu toe heeft deze strijd zich niet uitgebreid tot Bosnië, waar een derde volk – de Bosnische moslims – een grote rol speelt. Als de gevechten wel naar Bosnië overslaan, en dat is onvermijdelijk, zal de slachting groter en moeilijker te beheersen zijn.

Toch menen wij dat de ellende in Joegoslavië zou verbleken bij wat er zich in Irak zou voltrekken als het land uiteenvalt. In dat geval kunnen we een bloedige burgeroorlog verwachten in het centrum, met vier oorlogen aan de grenzen en een volledige chaos in de Golf. Het aantal vluchtelingen zou in de miljoenen lopen.

Het enige alternatief is dat Saddam Hoessein zou worden opgevolgd door een andere generaal of hoge functionaris van de Ba'ath-partij. Maar omdat de hele partijtop bloed aan haar handen heeft, zien wij weinig heil in het vervangen van de ene despoot door een andere, die misschien zelfs intelligenter is.

De beste oplossing, al is het niet ideaal, is daarom het handhaven van de status quo in Irak, behalve dat alle massavernietigingswapens moeten worden geëlimineerd en de conventionele strijdkrachten moeten worden teruggebracht tot een niveau dat de komende tien jaar geen bedreiging voor de buurlanden meer kan vormen.

Het feit dat het huidige Iraakse regime, als het deze oorlog overleeft, nog steeds de mensenrechten met voeten zal treden, is een zorgwekkende zaak. Zeker. Maar het Westen is ook getuige geweest van afschuwelijke taferelen in China, Rusland, Vietnam, Tibet, Oost-Timor, Cambodja en vele andere delen van de wereld. De Verenigde Staten zijn nu eenmaal niet in staat de hele wereld een menselijk bewind op te leggen, tenzij wij permanent oorlog willen voeren.

De minst rampzalige uitkomst van de huidige oorlog in de Golf en de uiteindelijke invasie van Irak is dus de handhaving van Saddam Hoessein als heerser over een verenigd Irak, maar zonder de mogelijkheid tot militaire agressie tegen het buitenland.

Om al deze redenen adviseren wij dringend een eind te maken aan de pogingen Saddam Hoessein te elimineren of naar Bagdad op te rukken en Irak te bezetten.

Met de meeste hoogachting,
PIAG

Op 7 februari vond Mike Martin het krijtteken. Nog dezelfde avond haalde hij de dunne plastic envelop uit de 'brievenbus' op. Kort na middernacht installeerde hij zijn satellietschotel voor de open deur van zijn schuurtje en sprak de kriebelige Arabische tekst op het luchtpostpapier op het bandje in. Na het Arabisch volgde zijn Engelse vertaling. Om zestien minuten over twaalf, één minuut nadat zijn zendtijd was begonnen, verstuurde hij het bericht.

Toen het in Riyad werd ontvangen, riep de technicus: 'Daar is hij! Zwarte Beer heeft zich gemeld.'

De vier slaperige mannen in de aangrenzende kamer kwamen meteen aan-
rennen. De grote bandrecorder tegen de muur vertraagde en decodeerde het
bericht. Toen de technicus de band startte, hoorden ze eerst de Arabische
tekst. Paxman, die het best Arabisch sprak, luisterde tot halverwege en siste
toen:
'Hij weet het! Jericho zegt dat hij het weet.'
'Stil, Simon.'
Daarna las Martin de Engelse vertaling. Toen hij zweeg en het bericht
beëindigde, sloeg Barber opgewonden met zijn vuist tegen de palm van zijn
andere hand.
'Verdomme, het is hem gelukt! Jongens, kunnen jullie een transcriptie voor
me maken? Nu meteen?'
De technicus spoelde de band terug, zette een koptelefoon op, boog zich
naar zijn tekstverwerker en begon te typen.
Barber liep naar een telefoon in de huiskamer en belde het ondergrondse
hoofdkwartier van de CENTAF. Hij hoefde maar één man te spreken.
Generaal Chuck Horner had niet veel slaap nodig. Niemand van het opperbevel van de Coalitietroepen onder het Saoedische ministerie van Defensie
of de luchtmachtstaf onder het hoofdkwartier van de Saoedische luchtmacht
kreeg die weken veel slaap, maar generaal Horner sliep nog minder dan de
anderen.
Misschien kòn hij gewoon niet slapen als zijn bemanningen diep in vijandelijk gebied waren doorgedrongen. En omdat er vierentwintig uur per etmaal
werd gevlogen, bleef er niet veel tijd over voor een tukje.
Hij had de gewoonte om midden in de nacht door de kantoren van de CEN-
TAF te zwerven, van de analisten in het Zwarte Gat naar het Tactisch Contro-
lecentrum van de luchtmacht en weer terug. Als er een telefoon rinkelde op
een plaats waar niemand zat, nam hij zelf op. Sommige luchtmachtofficie-
ren in de woestijn, die opbelden met een vraag en verwachtten de dienstdoende majoor aan de lijn te krijgen, hoorden tot hun verbazing de stem van
de baas zelf.
Dat was erg democratisch, maar het leidde ook tot vreemde situaties. Zo
belde er een squadron-commandant, die naamloos zal blijven, met de klacht
dat zijn piloten iedere nacht op weg naar hun doelen werden bestookt door
Triple-A geschut. Kon de Iraakse luchtafweer niet worden platgegooid door
een paar zware bommenwerpers, de Buffs?
Nee, zei generaal Horner tegen de luitenant-kolonel, dat was niet mogelijk.
De Buffs hadden het veel te druk. De squadron-commandant in de woestijn
protesteerde, maar Horner liet zich niet vermurwen. Ach, val dood,
reageerde de luitenant-kolonel.
Maar weinig officieren kunnen zich dat permitteren tegenover een generaal.

Het zegt veel over Chuck Horners waardering voor zijn vliegers dat de heet-gebakerde squadron-commandant twee weken later tot kolonel werd bevorderd.

Toen Chip Barber die nacht belde, zwierf de generaal ook weer rond. Horner vroeg de CIA-man om naar zijn kantoor in het ondergrondse complex te komen, en veertig minuten later zaten ze tegenover elkaar.

De generaal las de transcriptie van het Engelse bericht uit Bagdad somber door. Barber had hier en daar nog wat veranderd, zodat het niet meer op een radioboodschap leek.

'Is dat weer zo'n verhaal dat jullie van een zakenman uit Europa hebben gehoord?' vroeg hij kritisch.

'Wij gaan ervan uit dat het klopt, generaal.'

Horner bromde wat. Zoals de meeste militairen had hij weinig op met die 'spionnenbende'. Dat was niets nieuws, en er was een simpele reden voor.

Militairen moeten optimistisch blijven, gematigd optimistisch misschien, maar toch optimistisch. Anders zou niemand ooit aan een oorlog beginnen. De inlichtingendiensten zijn geneigd tot pessimisme. Die twee visies staan lijnrecht tegenover elkaar, en in deze fase van de oorlog raakte de Amerikaanse luchtmacht steeds meer geïrriteerd door de voortdurende insinuaties van de CIA dat ze veel minder doelwitten vernietigden dan ze zelf beweerden.

'En heeft dit zogenaamde doelwit iets te maken met waar ik denk dat het mee te maken heeft?' vroeg de generaal.

'We denken dat het heel belangrijk is.'

'Dan zullen we het eerst eens goed bekijken, meneer Barber.'

Deze keer was het een TR-1 vanaf Taif die de honneurs waarnam. De TR-1, een gemoderniseerde versie van de oude U-2, werd ingezet als een algemeen verkenningsvliegtuig. Het toestel kon boven Irak vliegen, onzichtbaar en onhoorbaar, en met zijn radar- en afluisterapparatuur tot diep in de vijandelijke defensie doordringen. Maar de TR-1 had ook nog gewone camera's aan boord, die van tijd tot tijd niet voor een algemeen beeld maar voor één specifieke opdracht werden gebruikt. En het fotograferen van een plek die alleen bekendstond als Al-Qubai was wel heel specifiek.

Er was nog een andere reden waarom voor de TR-1 was gekozen. Het toestel kon zijn beelden rechtstreeks doorgeven. Het hoofdkwartier hoefde niet te wachten tot het toestel was geland, de TARPS was uitgeladen, de film was ontwikkeld en de opnamen naar Riyad waren gebracht. Op het moment dat het vliegtuig over de aangewezen plaats in de woestijn, ten westen van Bagdad en ten zuiden van de vliegbasis Al-Muhammadi vloog, werden de beelden meteen op een televisiescherm in de kelder onder het Saoedische ministerie van Luchtmacht geprojecteerd.

Er zaten vijf mannen in de kamer, onder wie de technicus die de console bediende en die op bevel van de andere vier de computermodem opdracht kon geven een beeld te 'bevriezen' en er een afdruk van te maken.

Chip Barber en Steve Laing mochten erbij zijn, ondanks hun burgerkleding tussen al die uniformen in dit mekka van militaire technologie. De andere twee waren kolonel Beatty van de Amerikaanse luchtmacht en majoor Peck van de Britse RAF, allebei gespecialiseerd in het analyseren van doelen.

De naam Al-Qubai was alleen gekozen omdat het dichtstbijzijnde dorp zo heette. Maar het plaatsje was te klein om op de kaart te staan. De analisten werkten uitsluitend met de coördinaten.

De TR-1 vond het dorp een paar kilometer van de plaats die Jericho had aan-gegeven. De beschrijving klopte precies en er waren geen andere locaties die eraan beantwoordden.

De vier mannen zagen het doelwit in beeld komen, lieten het scherpste beeld stilzetten en vroegen om een afdruk.

'Ligt het dááronder?' fluisterde Laing terwijl hij de foto bestudeerde.

'Dat moet wel,' zei Beatty. 'In de hele omgeving is er verder niets wat erop lijkt.'

'Handige klootzakken,' zei Peck.

Al-Qubai was de technische fabriek binnen het nucleaire programma van dr. Jaafar al-Jaafar. Een Britse nucleaire ingenieur had eens opgemerkt dat zijn werk 'tien procent inspiratie en negentig procent loodgieterswerk' was. Maar zo eenvoudig ligt het niet.

De fabriek is de plek waar de technici de theorieën van de fysici, de calcula-ties van de wiskundigen en de computers en de uitkomsten van de scheikun-digen verwerken tot het eindprodukt. Het zijn de nucleaire ingenieurs die het ontwerp in een bruikbaar stuk metaal omzetten.

De fabriek van Al-Qubai was volledig onder de woestijn begraven, bijna vijfentwintig meter diep, en dat was nog maar het dak. Onder het dak lagen nog drie verdiepingen met werkplaatsen. De opmerking van majoor Peck sloeg op de handigheid waarmee het complex verborgen was.

Het is niet zo moeilijk om een hele fabriek onder de grond te bouwen, maar het complex camoufleren is heel wat lastiger. Als de fabriek eenmaal in zijn krater staat, kan het zand weer met bulldozers over de ijzeren en betonnen constructie worden geschoven tot het gebouw is verborgen. Ondergrondse drainagepijpen kunnen het water afvoeren.

Maar er moet ook airconditioning zijn. Daarvoor is frisse lucht nodig, via een inlaat en een uitlaat, zichtbare pijpen die boven de woestijn uitsteken.

Ook is er elektriciteit, geleverd door een krachtige dieselgenerator die een luchtinlaat en een rookuitlaat nodig heeft. Weer twee pijpen.

Het personeel moet afdalen via een lift en goederen moeten omlaag worden getakeld. Dat vereist een bovengrondse schacht. De bevoorradingstrucks kunnen niet door het rulle zand rijden, dus moet er een asfaltweg worden aangelegd.

De fabriek geeft warmte af. Overdag, in de hitte, is daar niets van te zien, maar in de koude nachten wel.

Hoe verklaar je dus een stuk maagdelijke woestijn met een asfaltweg die nergens naartoe leidt, vier grote pijpen, een liftschacht, het komen en gaan van vrachtwagens en de afgifte van warmte in de nacht?

Het was kolonel Osman Badri, het jonge talent van de Iraakse genietroepen, die een oplossing had bedacht waardoor de geallieerden met al hun spionagevliegtuigen zich om de tuin hadden laten leiden.

Vanuit de lucht zag Al-Qubai eruit als een grote autosloperij. Hoewel de vier mannen in Riyad het zelfs met een vergrootglas niet konden zien, waren vier roestige bergen auto's in feite aan elkaar gelast tot koepels waaronder de pijpen van de fabriek verse lucht aanzogen en afgewerkte gassen afvoerden.

De belangrijkste werkplaats, de snijderij, met de stalen zuurstof- en acetyleentanks ernaast, maskeerde de ingang van de liftschachten. En omdat er in zo'n werkplaats ook werd gelast, was de warmteafgifte heel verklaarbaar.

Dat er een asfaltweg naartoe liep, lag voor de hand. Vrachtwagens moesten immers de wrakken aanvoeren en het schroot ophalen.

Het hele complex was wel opgemerkt door een AWACS die een grote hoeveelheid metaal midden in de woestijn registreerde. Een tankdivisie? Een munitiedepot? Maar toen een verkenningsvliegtuig vaststelde dat het een autokerkhof was, was niemand meer geïnteresseerd.

Ook konden de vier mannen in Riyad niet zien dat vier van de roestige autobergen door een hydraulische krik konden worden bediend. Twee ervan bevatten een krachtige luchtdoelbatterij, een multi-loops Russisch ZSU-23-4 kanon, de andere twee verborgen een SAM-installatie, model 6, 8 en 9, niet de radargeleide raket maar het kleinere hittezoekende type. Een radarschotel zou te opvallend zijn geweest.

'Dus daar is het,' mompelde Beatty.

Terwijl ze toekeken kwam een lange vrachtwagen met autowrakken het beeld binnenrijden. Hij leek zich schokkerig te bewegen omdat de TR-1 die 80 000 voet boven Al-Qubai vloog enkele 'stills' per seconde produceerde. Gefascineerd zagen de twee inlichtingenofficieren hoe de truck achterwaarts de laswerkplaats binnenreed.

'Ik durf te wedden dat er voedsel, water en voorraden onder die wrakken zijn verborgen,' zei Beatty. Hij leunde naar achteren. 'Het probleem is dat we die verdomde fabriek nooit kunnen platgooien. Zelfs de bommen van de Buffs dringen niet zo diep door.'

'We kunnen de zaak wel stilleggen,' zei Peck. 'Als we de liftschacht vernietigen, zitten ze opgesloten. En als ze een reddingsploeg sturen, bombarderen we die.'

'Klinkt goed,' beaamde Beatty. 'Hoeveel dagen hebben we nog voordat de invasie begint?'

'Twaalf,' zei Barber.

'Dat moet lukken,' zei Beatty. 'Van grote hoogte, lasergeleid, veel vliegtuigen, een gorilla.'

Laing wierp Barber een waarschuwende blik toe.

'Liever een beetje discreet,' zei de CIA-man. 'Een aanval van twee vliegtuigen, laag boven de grond, met een visuele bevestiging van de schade.'

Het bleef even stil.

'Proberen jullie ons iets te vertellen?' vroeg Beatty toen. 'Bijvoorbeeld dat Bagdad niet mag weten dat we geïnteresseerd zijn?'

'Zouden jullie het op die manier kunnen doen?' drong Laing aan. 'Zo te zien is er geen luchtafweer. De camouflage is hun enige beveiliging.'

Beatty zuchtte. Vervloekte spionnen, dacht hij. Ze proberen iemand te beschermen. Maar dat was zijn zaak niet.

'Wat denk je Joe?' vroeg hij aan de Britse majoor.

'De Tornado's lijken me wel geschikt,' zei Peck. 'Met de Buccaneers om het doelwit te markeren. Zes 100-ponds bommen dwars door de deur. Die ijzeren schuur zal binnen wel versterkt zijn met gewapend beton. Dat zal de klap aardig opvangen.'

Beatty knikte. 'Goed, afgesproken. Ik regel het wel met generaal Horner. Wie wil je erop afsturen, Joe?'

'Het 608e squadron op Maharraq. Ik ken de commandant, Phil Curzon. Zal ik hem bellen?'

Luitenant-kolonel Philip Curzon had het bevel over de twaalf Panavia Tornado's van het 608e squadron van de RAF op het eiland Bahrein, waar ze twee maanden eerder waren aangekomen vanaf hun basis bij Fallingbostel in Duitsland. Die 8e februari, kort na twaalf uur, kreeg hij bevel zich onmiddellijk te melden op het CENTAF-hoofdkwartier in Riyad. Het was zo dringend dat hij het bericht nauwelijks had ontvangen toen de dienstdoende sergeant al meldde dat er een Amerikaanse Huron van Shakey's Pizza aan de andere kant van het eiland was geland en naar hen toe taxiede om hem op te pikken. Haastig trok hij zijn uniformjasje aan, zette zijn pet op en klom aan boord van de UC-12B Huron, het toestel van generaal Horner zelf, zag hij tot zijn verbazing.

De luitenant-kolonel vroeg zich af wat er aan de hand was, en met reden.

Op de vliegbasis van Riyad stond een dienstauto te wachten om hem naar het Zwarte Gat aan Old Airport Road te brengen.

De vier mannen die 's ochtends de beelden van de TR-1 hadden bekeken waren er nog. Alleen de technicus was vertrokken. Ze hadden geen nieuwe foto's meer nodig. De rest lag over de tafel uitgespreid. Majoor Peck stelde iedereen aan elkaar voor.

Steve Laing legde uit wat de bedoeling was en Curzon bekeek de foto's.

Philip Curzon was niet gek, anders zou hij niet het bevel hebben gehad over een squadron zeer kostbare Britse gevechtsvliegtuigen. Bij de eerste bombardementen met de JP-233's laag boven de Iraakse vliegvelden had hij twee toestellen en vier goede kerels verloren. Twee ervan waren dood. De andere twee waren zojuist, aangeslagen en half verdoofd, voor de Iraakse tv-camera's getoond in een van Saddams meesterlijke propagandapogingen.

'Waarom staat dit doelwit niet op de officiële lijst, zoals de rest? En waarom is er zo'n haast bij?'

'Ik zal open kaart spelen,' zei Laing. 'Wij denken dat dit complex een dekmantel vormt voor Saddams belangrijkste en misschien wel enige depot van een zeer gevaarlijk type gifgasgranaat. Er zijn aanwijzingen dat de eerste voorraden ieder moment naar het front kunnen worden overgebracht. Vandaar de haast.'

Beatty en Peck spitsten hun oren. Nu wisten ze eindelijk waarom de inlichtingendiensten zoveel belangstelling hadden voor de ondergrondse fabriek.

'Waarom dan maar twee vliegtuigen?' wilde Curzon weten. 'Dat lijkt me nogal weinig voor zo'n belangrijke missie. Wat moet ik tegen mijn bemanningen zeggen? Ik ga niet tegen hen liegen, heren, dat zeg ik u bij voorbaat.'

'Dat hoeft ook niet en dat zouden wij niet willen,' zei Laing. 'Vertel hun de waarheid maar. Op luchtopnamen hebben we gezien dat er vrachtwagens af en aan rijden. Volgens de analisten zijn het militaire trucks. Daaruit hebben ze de conclusie getrokken dat het een opslagplaats voor wapens moet zijn. Vermoedelijk liggen ze in die grote schuur in het midden. Dat is dus het doelwit. En we hebben maar twee vliegtuigen nodig omdat er geen luchtafweer is. U kunt het zelf zien. Geen raketten, geen Triple-A geschut.'

'En dat is de waarheid?' vroeg de luitenant-kolonel.

'Ik zweer het.'

'U houdt mij niet voor de gek. Als mijn mensen worden neergeschoten en ondervraagd, mag Bagdad niet weten waar de informatie werkelijk vandaan komt. U gelooft dat verhaal over die militaire trucks net zomin als ik.'

Kolonel Beatty en majoor Peck gingen er recht voor zitten. Deze man pakte de inlichtingenofficieren stevig aan. Mooi zo.

'Zeg het maar, Chip,' antwoordde Laing gelaten.

'Goed, overste. Ik zal eerlijk zijn. Maar praat er met niemand over. Wat ik u nu vertel is de zuivere waarheid. We hebben een overloper. In Amerika. Voordat de oorlog uitbrak studeerde hij aan een van onze universiteiten. Hij

366

is verliefd geworden op een Amerikaans meisje en hij wil blijven. Tijdens de gesprekken met de immigratiedienst kwamen een paar interessante dingen aan het licht. Een slimme ambtenaar heeft hem naar ons doorverwezen.'

'Naar de CIA?' vroeg Curzon.

'Inderdaad. Wij hebben een deal met hem gesloten. Hij mag in Amerika blijven als hij ons helpt. In Irak zat hij bij de genietroepen en heeft hij aan enkele geheime projecten gewerkt. Daar heeft hij ons over verteld. Nu weet u het. Maar het moet strikt geheim blijven. Het heeft geen invloed op de missie en u hoeft niet tegen uw mensen te liegen. Maar dit detail mag u hun niet vertellen.'

'Nog één vraag,' zei Curzon. 'Als die man veilig in de Verenigde Staten zit, waarom mag Bagdad dan niets over hem weten?'

'Omdat hij ook informatie over andere doelwitten heeft. Het zal tijd kosten, maar waarschijnlijk kan hij ons twintig nieuwe doelen noemen. Als Bagdad dat te weten komt, zullen ze hun wapens ergens anders verbergen. Ze zijn niet achterlijk.'

Philip Curzon stond op en verzamelde de foto's. Aan de rand van iedere foto stonden de coördinaten vermeld.

'Goed. Morgenochtend vroeg. Dan bestaat die schuur niet meer.'

Hij vertrok. Op de terugweg dacht hij nog eens na. Er zat een luchtje aan. Maar de uitleg klonk logisch en hij had zijn orders. Hij hoefde niet te liegen, maar hij mocht niet alles vertellen. In elk geval werd het doelwit beschermd door camouflage, niet door luchtafweer. Dat was een hele geruststelling. Zijn mannen zouden ongedeerd terugkomen. Hij wist al aan wie hij de missie zou opdragen.

Majoor Lofty Williamson zat tevreden onderuitgezakt in de avondzon toen hij werd opgeroepen. Hij was juist verdiept in het laatste nummer van *World Air Power Journal*, de bijbel van de gevechtspiloot, waarin een uitstekend artikel stond over een van de Iraakse jagers die hij misschien zou tegenkomen. Geïrriteerd kwam hij overeind.

De commandant zat in zijn kantoor, met een stel foto's voor zich. Een uurlang gaf hij Williamson zijn instructies.

'Je krijgt twee Bucks om het doelwit te markeren, dus je kunt meteen weer klimmen en wegwezen voordat die klootzakken beseffen wat er is gebeurd.'

Williamson zocht zijn navigator, de man in de stoel achter hem, die door de Amerikanen de 'wizzo' wordt genoemd maar tegenwoordig heel wat meer doet dan navigeren. De wizzo (WSO of 'wapensysteemofficier') houdt zich ook bezig met alle elektronica en de wapensystemen. Kapitein Sid Blair had de reputatie dat hij zelfs een groenteblikje in de Sahara kon opsporen als het gebombardeerd moest worden.

Samen met de operaties-officier zetten ze de route uit. Aan de hand van de coördinaten vonden ze de exacte ligging van het doelwit op hun eigen kaarten, die een schaal hadden van 1:50000, ongeveer een centimeter per vijfhonderd meter.

De piloot wilde vanuit het oosten aanvallen, op het moment dat de zon opkwam, zodat de Iraakse schutters (als die er waren) tegen het licht in moesten kijken, terwijl Williamson het doelwit scherp afgetekend zou kunnen zien.

Blair wilde een duidelijk herkenningspunt in de buurt van het doelwit om de koers te kunnen bijstellen als dat nodig was. Ze vonden een radiomast, bijna twintig kilometer ten oosten van het doelwit, precies anderhalve kilometer naast de aanvliegroute.

Doordat ze 's ochtends aanvielen, hadden ze de mogelijkheid het tijdstip van de aanval exact te bepalen. Dat is belangrijk, omdat een goede timing het verschil kan betekenen tussen succes en een ramp. Als de eerste piloot maar een seconde te laat is, kan het tweede toestel in de bomexplosies van zijn voorganger terechtkomen. Erger nog, dan krijgt de voorste piloot een Tornado in zijn nek, met een snelheid van bijna vijftien kilometer per minuut – geen prettige situatie. En als de eerste piloot te vroeg is of de tweede te laat, heeft de vijandelijke luchtafweer de tijd om wakker te worden en goed te richten. Daarom moet het tweede toestel aanvallen op het moment dat de bomexplosies van het eerste vliegtuig juist zijn uitgewoed.

Williamson haalde zijn wingman en de andere navigator erbij, twee jonge kapiteins, Peter Johns en Nicky Tyne. Om precies 07.08 uur zou de zon boven de lage heuvels ten oosten van het doelwit uitkomen. Dat was het moment waarop ze zouden aanvallen, pal naar het westen, op een koers van 270 graden.

Twee Buccaneers van het 12e squadron, dat ook op Mararraq was gestationeerd, zouden als escorte meegaan. Williamson zou contact opnemen met de piloten. De Tornado's werden uitgerust met drie 1000-ponds bommen met een PAVEWAY-geleidesysteem in de neus. Die avond aten de vier bemanningen om acht uur en gingen daarna naar bed. Ze zouden om drie uur 's nachts worden gewekt.

Het was nog aardedonker toen een korporaal met een truck bij het bivak van het 608e squadron arriveerde om de vier vliegers naar het operationeel centrum te brengen.

De Amerikanen op Al Kharz hadden het niet gemakkelijk, maar in Bahrein waren de omstandigheden veel beter. Sommige militairen deelden zelfs met hun tweeën een kamer in het Sheraton Hotel. Anderen waren ondergebracht in vrijgezellenflats dichter bij de basis. Het eten was uitstekend, alcohol was toegestaan en de eenzaamheid van het soldatenleven werd gedeeltelijk ver-

dreven door de aanwezigheid van driehonderd stewardessen aan het nabijgelegen opleidingsinstituut van Middle East Airways.

De Buccaneers waren pas een week eerder in de Golf aangekomen. Aanvan-
kelijk leken ze niet nodig te zijn, maar sinds hun komst hadden ze hun nut
ruimschoots bewezen. De Bucks waren eigenlijk bedoeld voor de jacht op
onderzeeërs. Meestal scheerden ze laag over de golven van de Noordzee, op
zoek naar Russische onderzeeboten. Maar in de woestijn voelden ze zich
ook goed thuis.

Hun specialiteit was laag vliegen. Het ontwerp was al dertig jaar oud, maar
tijdens oefeningen van de Amerikaanse luchtmacht bij Miramar in Californië ontsnapten ze soms aan de veel snellere Amerikaanse jagers door 'zand
te happen' – zo laag te vliegen dat ze niet meer te volgen waren tussen de
heuveltjes van de woestijn door.

In het internationale vliegwereldje gaat het verhaal dat de Amerikanen niet
van laag vliegen houden en hun landingsgestel laten zakken zodra ze lager
dan honderdvijftig meter komen, terwijl de Britse RAF zich dan juist prettig
voelt en boven de dertig meter al last krijg van hoogtevrees. Dat is natuurlijk onzin, maar de Bucks, die niet supersonisch zijn maar wel bijzonder
wendbaar, beweren dat ze lager kunnen vliegen dan wie ook.

Ze waren toch naar de Golf gehaald vanwege de verliezen onder de Tornado's
bij hun eerste lage missies. Toen ze nog in hun eentje opereerden, moesten de
Tornado's hun bommen afwerpen en ze helemaal tot aan het doelwit volgen,
recht op het luchtdoelgeschut af. Dat ging beter toen ze met de Buccaneers
samenwerkten. De bommen van de Tornado's waren met laserzoekende
PAVEWAY-neuskegels uitgerust, en de Bucks namen nu de PAVESPIKE-laserzen-
ders aan boord. Door schuin achter en boven de Tornado's te vliegen, konden
de Bucks het doelwit markeren, waardoor de Tornado's zich na het afwerpen
van de bommen meteen uit de voeten konden maken.

De PAVESPIKE was in een gestabiliseerde gyroscoop in de buik van de Bucks
gemonteerd, waardoor ze de vrijheid hielden om te manoeuvreren terwijl de
laserstraal toch op het doelwit gericht bleef totdat de bom zijn doel had
getroffen.

In het operationeel centrum spraken Williamson en de twee Buck-piloten af
waar ze de aanval zouden inzetten – twintig kilometer ten oosten van het
doelwit. Daarna gingen ze zich verkleden. Zoals gebruikelijk waren ze in
burger gearriveerd. De autoriteiten van Bahrein zagen liever geen uniformen op straat, om de bevolking niet in paniek te brengen.

Toen iedereen zich had verkleed, gaf Williamson als commandant zijn laatste instructies. Ze zouden pas over twee uur vertrekken. De dagen dat piloten binnen dertig seconden in hun toestel sprongen, zoals in de Tweede
Wereldoorlog, zijn allang voorbij.

Er was nog tijd genoeg voor een kop koffie en de rest van de voorbereidingen. Ze pakten hun persoonlijke wapen, een kleine Walther-PP waar ze weinig vertrouwen in hadden. Als ze in de woestijn werden aangevallen, konden ze het ding beter naar het hoofd van een Irakees gooien in de hoop hem op die manier uit te schakelen.

Daarna kregen ze hun vijf gouden *sovereigns* ter waarde van duizend pond, en een *'goolie chit'*. Dit vreemde document wekte nogal wat verbazing bij de Amerikanen in de Golf. Maar de Britten, die al sinds de jaren twintig in deze streken vlogen, kenden de bedoeling.

De *'goolie chit'* is een brief in het Arabisch en zes verschillende bedoeïenendialecten. De tekst luidt ongeveer: 'Geachte meneer de bedoeïen, de man die u deze brief overhandigt is een Britse officier. Als u hem terugbrengt naar de dichtstbijzijnde Britse patrouille, met zijn testikels intact en op de juiste plaats – dus niet in zijn mond – krijgt u een beloning van vijfduizend pond in goud.' Soms werkte dat.

De vliegoveralls waren voorzien van reflecterende epauletten die met sensors konden worden opgespoord als een piloot in de woestijn terechtkwam. Er zaten geen wings boven het linker borstzakje, alleen een Engelse vlag die met klitteband was bevestigd.

Na de koffie volgde de 'sterilisatie', minder erg dan het klinkt. Alle ringen, sigaretten, aanstekers, brieven, familiekiekjes, kortom alles wat bij een verhoor iets over de piloot zou kunnen vertellen, werden verwijderd. De mannen werden gefouilleerd door een knappe LUVA. Sommige jonge piloten vonden dit het spannendste deel van de missie en verborgen hun kostbaarheden op de vreemdste plekken om te zien of Pamela ze zou vinden. Gelukkig was ze verpleegster geweest en reageerde ze goedmoedig op al die flauwekul.

Nog één uur voor het vertrek. Een paar mannen zaten te eten, anderen konden geen hap door hun keel krijgen en deden een dutje of dronken koffie, hopend dat ze onderweg niet zouden moeten pissen. Sommigen moesten kotsen.

De bus bracht de acht mannen naar hun vliegtuigen, waar het grondpersoneel al druk aan het werk was. De piloten liepen nog eens om hun toestel heen voor een laatste controle en klommen toen aan boord.

Hun eerste taak was het insnoeren en het inschakelen van de Have-quick radio, zodat ze met elkaar konden praten. Daarna werd de APU, de hulpgenerator, opgestart en begonnen alle wijzertjes te dansen.

Achterin kwam het inerte navigatiesysteem tot leven en kon de wizzo zijn koers en manoeuvres invoeren. Williamson startte zijn rechtermotor en de Rolls-Royce RB-199 begon te loeien. Daarna startte hij de linker.

Ten slotte sloot hij de cockpit en taxiede naar Nummer Een, het verzamel-punt. Na toestemming van de toren reed hij naar het startpunt. Williamson keek naar rechts. De Tornado van Peter Johns stond naast hem, iets naar achteren, met de twee Buccaneers daarachter. Hij stak zijn hand op. Drie wit gehandschoende handen beantwoordden het teken.

Met de voetrem erop schakelde hij naar maximaal 'droog' vermogen. De Tornado stond zachtjes te trillen. Toen de nabranders werden ingeschakeld, rukte het toestel aan de remmen. Williamson stak zijn duim op en wachtte op de reactie van de anderen. Toen liet hij de remmen los. De Tornado sprong naar voren, het asfalt schoot steeds sneller onder de vleugels door, en even later waren ze in lucht. In een formatie van vier zwenkten ze over de donkere zee, lieten de lichten van Manama achter zich en zetten koers naar het ontmoetingspunt met de tanker, een Victor van het 55e squadron, die ergens boven de Saoedisch-Iraakse grens op hen wachtte.

Williamson schakelde de nabranders uit en klom met een snelheid van 300 knopen naar een hoogte van 20 000 voet. De twee RB-199's waren gulzige drinkers en verbruikten bij maximale 'droge' snelheid elk zo'n 140 pond benzine per minuut. Met ingeschakelde nabranders liep dat op tot 600 kilo, en daarom werd de nabrander maar sporadisch gebruikt, alleen bij het opstijgen, in luchtgevechten en om te vluchten.

De radar vond de Victor in het donker. De vliegtuigen sloten aan en vulden hun tanks bij uit de slangen. Ze hadden al een derde van hun brandstof verbruikt. Toen de Tornado's waren bijgetankt, maakten ze plaats voor de Bucks. Daarna draaiden ze alle vier opzij en doken naar de woestijn.

Op 200 voet trok Williamson zijn toestel recht, met een maximale kruissnelheid van 480 knopen. Zo vlogen ze Irak binnen. De navigators namen het over en stelden de eerste van drie verschillende routes in, met twee keerpunten, op weg naar het aanvalspunt in het oosten. Vanaf grotere hoogte hadden ze de opkomende zon al gezien, maar vlak boven de woestijn was het nog donker.

Williamson vloog met behulp van de TIALD, de 'Thermal Imaging and Laser Designator', een infrarood-lasersysteem, afkomstig van een omgebouwde koekjesfabriek in een achterafstraat in Edinburgh. De TIALD is een combinatie van een kleine, zeer scherpe tv-camera en een thermische infraroodsensor. Hoewel ze laag over de grond scheerden, konden de piloten de rotsen en de heuvels goed zien, alsof ze oplichtten.

Vlak voordat de zon opkwam, bereikten ze de aanvliegroute voor het bombardement. Sid Blair zag de radiomast en vroeg Williamson zijn koers één graad bij te stellen.

Williamson zette zijn bommenschakelaars in de 'slave'-stand en keek op zijn heads-up display waarop de mijlen en seconden tot aan het doelwit werden afgeteld. Hij vloog nu op een hoogte van dertig meter, boven vlak terrein, op een vaste koers. Ergens onder hem deed zijn wingman hetzelfde. Ze lagen precies op schema. Zo nu en dan schakelde hij de nabrander even in om de aanvalssnelheid van 540 knopen aan te houden.

De zon kwam boven de heuvels uit. De eerste stralen gleden over de vlakte, en Williamson zag het doelwit, op nog geen tien kilometer. Het metaal van de autowrakken glinsterde in de zon. De grote grijze schuur stond met zijn dubbele deuren naar hem toe gericht.

De Bucks vlogen dertig meter hoger, anderhalve kilometer achter hem. Ze hielden nu voortdurend radiocontact. Tien kilometer... acht... enige beweging rondom het doelwit... zes kilometer...

'Ik markeer het doelwit... nu!' meldde de navigator van de voorste Buccaneer. De laserstraal van de Buck verscheen op de deur van de schuur. Op vijf kilometer afstand trok Williamson de neus van zijn Tornado omhoog, waardoor hij het doelwit niet meer kon zien. De techniek moest de rest doen. Op honderd meter vanaf het doelwit gaf zijn heads-up display het teken om zijn bommen af te werpen. Hij haalde de schakelaar over en de drie 100-ponds bommen vielen van het rek.

Omdat hij al begon te klimmen, klommen de bommen nog even met hem mee, voordat ze in de greep van de zwaartekracht kwamen en een sierlijke parabool naar de schuur beschreven.

Nu zijn toestel opeens anderhalve ton lichter was, steeg Williamson snel naar een hoogte van 300 meter, helde toen 135 graden scherp opzij en bleef met zijn volle gewicht aan de knuppel hangen. De Tornado draaide en dook terug naar de aarde, in de richting waaruit hij gekomen was. De Buccaneer flitste over zijn hoofd en draaide toen ook weg.

Met de tv-camera in de buik van zijn toestel zag de Buck-navigator de bommen door de deuren van de schuur slaan. Het hele terrein voor de schuur verdween in een zee van vlammen en rook, en een enorme stofwolk steeg omhoog op de plaats waar de schuur had gestaan. Toen het stof neersloeg, stormde Peter Johns met de tweede Tornado op het doelwit af, dertig seconden na zijn aanvoerder.

De Buck-navigator zag nog meer. De bewegingen rondom het doelwit hadden een bepaalde systematiek. Hij zag de glinstering van geschut.

'Ze hebben Triple-A!' riep hij. De tweede Tornado trok zijn neus omhoog. De achtervolgende Buccaneer zag het gebeuren. De schuur was uiteengereten door de explosies van de eerste drie bommen. De metalen constructie eronder was volledig vervormd. Maar tussen de bergen autowrakken waren opeens de vuurmonden van kanonnen verschenen.

'Bommen los!' riep Johns en trok zijn Tornado zo scherp mogelijk opzij. Zijn eigen Buccaneer draaide ook bij het doelwit vandaan, maar de PAVE-SPIKE in de buik hield zijn laserstraal op de restanten van de schuur gericht.

'Voltreffer!' schreeuwde de navigator van de Buck.

Er flikkerde iets tussen de autowrakken. Twee draagbare sam-installaties vuurden op de Tornado.

Williamson had zijn toestel weer rechtgetrokken, dertig meter boven de woestijn, maar nu de andere kant op, de opkomende zon tegemoet. 'We zijn geraakt!' hoorde hij Peter Johns roepen.

Sid Blair achter hem zei niets. Vloekend van woede beschreef Williamson weer een bocht, in de hoop de Iraakse schutters te kunnen uitschakelen met zijn boordkanon. Maar hij was te laat.

'Ze hebben raketten,' hoorde hij een van de Bucks zeggen. Het volgende moment zag hij de rookpluim achter Johns' vluchtende Tornado. De motor stond in brand. 'We storten neer... We springen,' meldde de 25-jarige piloot. Ze konden niets meer doen. Bij eerdere missies waren de Bucks samen met de Tornado's teruggevlogen. Inmiddels was besloten dat de Buccaneers wel op eigen gelegenheid konden terugkeren. Zwijgend deden de twee Bucks waar ze het beste in waren: in de ochtendzon doken ze omlaag en bleven zo dicht mogelijk boven de woestijn.

Lofty Williamson zag bleek van woede. Hij was ervan overtuigd dat iemand gelogen had. Dat was niet zo. Niemand wist van het bestaan van het Triple-A geschut en de verborgen raketten van Al-Qubai.

Hoog in de lucht zond een tr-1 rechtstreekse beelden van de verwoestingen naar Riyad. Een e-3 Sentry had alle gesprekken gevolgd en meldde Riyad dat ze een Tornado kwijt waren.

Lofty Williamson keerde in zijn eentje terug om verslag uit te brengen en zijn woede te luchten tegen de plannenmakers in Riyad.

Onder het centaf-hoofdkwartier aan Old Airport Road kregen Steve Laing en Chip Barber de berichten door. Hun vreugde dat De Vuist van God was vernietigd in de schoot waarin hij was geschapen, werd getemperd door het verlies van de twee vliegers.

De Buccaneers, die laag over de vlakke woestijn in het zuiden van Irak scheerden, op weg naar de grens, kwamen een groepje bedoeïenen met grazende kamelen tegen. Dat stelde de twee piloten voor een lastige keuze: eromheen of eronderdoor.

Hassan Rahmani zat in zijn privé-kantoor in het gebouw van de Mukhabarat in Mansour en dacht bijna wanhopig terug aan de gebeurtenissen van de afgelopen vierentwintig uur.

Dat de belangrijkste militaire installaties en fabrieken van zijn land systematisch door bommen en raketten werden verwoest vond hij geen probleem. Dat had hij al weken geleden voorspeld. De bombardementen brachten alleen de Amerikaanse invasie en de val van de dictator uit Tikrit dichterbij.

Dat was iets wat hij had voorbereid en waarnaar hij vol vertrouwen had uitgezien. Dat het niet zou gebeuren, kon hij die middag van de 11e februari nog niet weten. Rahmani was een zeer intelligent man maar hij had geen kristallen bol.

Waar hij zich zorgen over maakte was zijn eigen veiligheid, de vraag of hij Saddams ondergang nog zou meemaken.

Het bombardement op de nucleaire fabriek van Al-Qubai, de vorige ochtend in alle vroegte, was een zware slag geweest voor de machthebbers in Bagdad. Niemand had verwacht dat de handig gecamoufleerde fabriek ooit zou worden ontdekt.

Binnen enkele minuten na het vertrek van de twee Britse bommenwerpers hadden de overlevenden contact opgenomen met Bagdad om de aanval te rapporteren. Toen hij het nieuws hoorde, was dr. Jaafar al-Jaafar in zijn auto gesprongen en naar Al-Qubai gereden om te zien hoe zijn ondergrondse medewerkers eraan toe waren. De wetenschapper was buiten zichzelf van woede en 's middags had hij bitter zijn beklag gedaan bij Hoessein Kamil, de minister van Industrie en Militaire Industrialisatie, die verantwoordelijk was voor het hele atoomprogramma.

Het ging om een project, had de kleine geleerde tegen Saddams schoonzoon geroepen (volgens de geruchten zelfs *geschreeuwd*), dat in tien jaar tijd maar liefst acht miljard dollar had opgeslokt van een totale defensiebegroting van vijftig miljard, een project dat was vernietigd op het moment dat het einddoel was bereikt. Kon de staat zijn burgers dan niet beter beschermen? Enzovoort, enzovoort.

De Iraakse academicus was niet veel langer dan anderhalve meter en niet sterker dan een mug, maar hij had behoorlijk wat invloed en volgens de verhalen had hij het hele ministerie bij elkaar gevloekt.

Later had een geschrokken Hoessein Kamil zich gemeld bij zijn schoonvader, die ook een woedeaanval kreeg. En als dat gebeurde, sidderde heel Bagdad.

Het personeel van de ondergrondse fabriek had de aanval overleefd en was zelfs ontsnapt, want vanuit de fabriek liep een smalle tunnel achthonderd meter onder de woestijn door, naar een ronde schacht met een ladder naar boven. Zo hadden ze zich in veiligheid gebracht, maar het was onmogelijk om de zware machines door dezelfde tunnel en schacht naar buiten te brengen.

De lift en de takel waren volkomen vernietigd tot op een diepte van zes meter. Het zou weken duren om de zaak te repareren, weken die Irak niet waren gegund, vermoedde Hassan Rahmani.

Voor Rahmani had dat eigenlijk een opluchting moeten zijn, want sinds die vergadering vlak voor het begin van de luchtoorlog, toen Saddam het bestaan van 'zijn' wapen bekend had gemaakt, had het hoofd van de contraspionagedienst zich grote zorgen gemaakt.

Maar nu sidderde hij ook voor de woede van het staatshoofd. Vice-president Izzat Ibrahim had hem de vorige middag gebeld. Rahmani had Saddams belangrijkste vertrouweling nog nooit zo van streek meegemaakt.

Ibrahim had hem verteld dat de *Rais* buiten zichzelf van woede was en als dat gebeurde, moesten er meestal koppen rollen. Dat was de enige manier om de man uit Tikrit te kalmeren. De vice-president had hem te verstaan gegeven dat hij, Rahmani, met resultaten zou moeten komen, en snel. Welke resultaten? had hij Ibrahim gevraagd. Hoe ze het bestaan van die fabriek hadden ontdekt! had Ibrahim tegen hem geschreeuwd.

Rahmani had contact opgenomen met vrienden in het leger, die met de artilleristen van de luchtafweer van Al-Qubai hadden gesproken. Over één ding was iedereen het eens. De Britten hadden de fabriek met twee vliegtuigen gebombardeerd. Wat hoger vlogen nog twee andere toestellen, maar dat waren vermoedelijk escortejagers geweest. In elk geval hadden ze geen bommen afgeworpen.

Na het leger had Rahmani met de afdeling Operationele Planning van de luchtmacht gesproken. Naar hun mening – en enkelen van de officieren waren in het Westen opgeleid – zou geen enkel doelwit van enig belang ooit met zo weinig toestellen worden aangevallen. Uitgesloten.

Maar als de Britten hadden vermoed dat die autosloperij iets anders was, wat dàn? De bemanning van het neergeschoten vliegtuig wist vermoedelijk het antwoord op die vraag. Rahmani had de piloten graag willen verhoren, ervan overtuigd dat hij met bepaalde hallucinogene drugs de waarheid binnen een paar uur boven tafel zou krijgen.

Het leger had bevestigd dat ze de piloot en de navigator binnen drie uur na de aanval te pakken hadden gekregen, ergens in de woestijn. Een van de mannen had zijn enkel gebroken en liep te hinken. Helaas was er meteen een eenheid van de AMAM opgedoken die de vliegeniers had meegenomen. Niemand discussieerde met de AMAM. En dus waren de twee Britten nu in handen van Omar Khatib – Allah zij hen genadig.

Beroofd van de kans om goede sier te maken met de informatie van de twee Engelsen, moest Rahmani dus iets anders verzinnen. Maar wat? Iets wat de *Rais* tevreden zou stellen. En wat kon dat zijn? Natuurlijk, een samenzwering! Dat was het antwoord. En daarvoor had hij een zender nodig. Hij pakte zijn telefoon en belde majoor Mohsen Zajid, het hoofd van zijn SIGINT-afdeling, de mensen die radioberichten onderschepten. Tijd voor een goed gesprek.

Dertig kilometer ten westen van Bagdad ligt Abu Khraib, een onopvallend stadje maar een beruchte naam in Irak, die maar zelden wordt uitgesproken. Want in Khraib stond de grote gevangenis die bijna uitsluitend voor de detentie en het verhoor van politieke gevangenen werd gebruikt. En daarom viel hij niet onder het nationale gevangeniswezen maar onder de Geheime Politie, de AMAM.

Op het moment dat Rahmani met zijn radiotechnicus belde, naderde een lange zwarte Mercedes de dubbele houten deuren van de gevangenis. Twee wachtposten, die de inzittende van de auto herkenden, sprongen haastig naar voren om de poort te openen. Net op tijd. De man in de auto kon meedogenloos reageren als iemand hem door nalatigheid ook maar één seconde oponthoud bezorgde.

De auto reed door en de poort ging weer dicht. De man achterin gaf geen enkel teken dat hij de inspanningen van de wachtposten had opgemerkt. Ze waren volstrekt onbelangrijk.

De auto stopte bij de trap naar het kantoor en een andere bewaker opende haastig het achterportier.

Omar Khatib stapte uit, keurig gekleed in een goed gesneden kamgaren uniform en liep de trap op. Overal werden de deuren haastig voor hem geopend. Een assistent nam zijn koffertje mee.

Khatib nam de lift naar zijn kantoor op de vijfde en hoogste verdieping. Toen hij alleen was, liet hij Turkse koffie komen en verdiepte zich in zijn papieren: rapporten over de informatie die aan de gevangenen in de kelder was ontfutseld.

Ondanks zijn ijzige houding was Omar Khatib net zo ongerust als zijn collega aan de andere kant van Bagdad, een man aan wie hij een gruwelijke hekel had.

Anders dan Rahmani, die met zijn gedeeltelijk Britse opvoeding, zijn talen-

376

kennis en zijn kosmopolitische houding verdacht was, had Khatib het belangrijke voordeel van zijn afkomst. Hij kwam uit Tikrit. Zolang hij zijn werk deed, en goed, zolang hij voldoende bekentenissen afdwong om de paranoia van de president te sussen, kon hem niets gebeuren.

Maar de afgelopen vierentwintig uur waren niet eenvoudig geweest. Ook hij had de vorige dag een telefoontje gekregen, maar van Saddams schoonzoon, Hoessein Kamil. Net als Ibrahim bij zijn bezoek aan Rahmani, had hij Khatib meegedeeld dat de *Rais* woedend was over de aanval op Al-Qubai en dat hij resultaten wilde.

Het was Khatib gelukt de Britse vliegers in handen te krijgen. Dat kon een voordeel zijn, maar ook een nadeel. De *Rais* zou willen weten – en snel – wat de vliegers over de missie te horen hadden gekregen, hoeveel de geallieerden over Al-Qubai wisten en hoe ze aan die informatie waren gekomen. En hij, Khatib, zou antwoord moeten geven op die vragen. Zijn mannen hadden de Britten nu vijftien uur onder handen gehad, sinds de vorige avond zeven uur, toen ze in Abu Khraib waren aangekomen. Voorlopig hadden die idioten nog geen woord gezegd.

Vanaf de binnenplaats onder zijn raam klonk een sissend geluid, gevolgd door een klap en een zacht gejammer. Khatib fronste verbaasd zijn voorhoofd, maar toen klaarde zijn gezicht weer op.

Op de binnenplaats hing een Irakees aan zijn polsen aan een balk, met zijn gestrekte tenen tien centimeter boven het zand. Vlakbij stond een emmer met pekel, die ooit helder was geweest, maar nu donker roze.

Iedere bewaker en soldaat die over de binnenplaats liep had strikte orders om te blijven staan, een van de twee rotanstokken uit de emmer met pekel te pakken en de hangende man tegen zijn rug te slaan, tussen zijn nek en zijn knieën. Een korporaal onder een afdakje hield de telling bij.

De onnozele kerel was een marktkoopman die de president een hoerezoon had genoemd en nu – wat te laat – een lesje leerde in het respect dat de burgers behoorden te tonen tegenover de *Rais*.

Heel interessant dat hij er nog steeds hing. Sommigen van die arbeiders waren moeilijk te breken. De koopman had al meer dan vijfhonderd stokslagen gehad, een absoluut record. Vóór de duizendste zou hij dood zijn – niemand had ooit duizend stokslagen overleefd – maar toch was het opmerkelijk. Nog interessanter was dat de man was verraden door zijn tienjarige zoontje. Omar Khatib nam een slok van zijn koffie, schroefde zijn gouden vulpen open en boog zich over zijn papieren.

Een halfuur later werd er zachtjes op zijn deur geklopt.

'Binnen,' riep hij, en hij keek vol verwachting op. Hij had goed nieuws nodig en maar één man mocht aankloppen zonder te worden aangekondigd door de adjudant voor zijn kantoor.

377

De man die binnenkwam was forsgebouwd en zelfs zijn moeder zou hem niet knap hebben genoemd. Hij had een pokdalig gezicht met twee ronde, glimmende littekens waar ooit cysten hadden gezeten. Hij sloot de deur en wachtte tot hij werd toegesproken.

Hoewel hij maar een sergeant was en zijn vuile overall niet eens die rang aangaf, was hij een van de weinige mensen met wie het hoofd van de Geheime Politie zich enigszins verwant voelde. Sergeant Ali was de enige die in Khatibs gezelschap mocht gaan zitten.

Ook deze keer wees Khatib naar een stoel en bood de man zelfs een sigaret aan. De sergeant stak op en blies dankbaar een rookwolk uit. Zijn werk was zwaar en vermoeiend, en de sigaret een welkome onderbreking. De reden dat Khatib op zo'n familiaire voet stond met iemand van zo'n lage rang was dat hij een oprechte bewondering koesterde voor sergeant Ali.

Het hoofd van de AMAM stelde veel prijs op doelmatigheid, en zijn trouwe sergeant had hem nog nooit in de steek gelaten. Hij was rustig, systematisch, een goede echtgenoot en vader, kortom, Ali verstond zijn vak.

'En?' vroeg Khatib.

'De navigator houdt het niet lang meer vol, generaal. De piloot...' Hij haalde zijn schouders op. 'Nog minstens een uur.'

'We moeten ze breken, Ali. Ik wil alles weten. En hun verhalen moeten kloppen met elkaar. De *Rais* rekent op ons.'

'Misschien moet u zelf eens komen kijken, generaal. Volgens mij hebt u binnen tien minuten een antwoord. Eerst de navigator, en als de piloot dat hoort, volgt hij ook wel.'

'Goed.'

Khatib stond op en de sergeant hield de deur voor hem open. Samen namen ze de lift naar beneden, tot aan de hoogste kelderverdieping, waar ze uitstapten. Aan het eind van de gang was een trap naar de lagere gedeelten. Langs de gang waren stalen deuren. Daarachter, gehurkt in hun eigen vuil, zaten zeven Amerikaanse vliegers, vier Britten, één Italiaan en een Skyhawk-piloot uit Koeweit.

Op de volgende verdieping waren nog meer cellen, waarvan er twee waren bezet. Khatib loerde door het kijkgaatje in de eerste deur.

De cel werd verlicht door een kaal peertje en de muren waren besmeurd met aangekoekte uitwerpselen en bruine strepen geronnen bloed. In het midden, op een plastic kantoorstoel, zat een spiernaakte man met de sporen van braaksel, bloed en speeksel op zijn borst. Zijn handen waren op zijn rug gebonden en over zijn gezicht zat een zak zonder ooggaten.

Twee AMAM-agenten in dezelfde overall als sergeant Ali stonden naast hem. In hun handen hielden ze een lange plastic slang die was ingesmeerd met teer, dat het gewicht vergrootte zonder de buigzaamheid te belemmeren. Ze hadden een stap teruggedaan om even uit te rusten. Vóór de onderbreking hadden ze zich blijkbaar op de schenen en de knieschijven van de gevangene geconcentreerd, waarvan de huid rauw en geelblauw was opgezwollen.

Khatib knikte en liep naar de volgende deur. Door het kijkgaatje zag hij dat de tweede gevangene geen zak over zijn hoofd had. Zijn ene oog was dichtgeslagen. De kapotte huid kleefde aan elkaar met gestold bloed. Toen hij zijn mond opende, waren er gaten te zien waar twee tanden waren weggeslagen. Schuimend bloed borrelde tussen zijn kapotte lippen.

'Tyne,' fluisterde hij. 'Nicholas Tyne. Kapitein. Vijf-nul-één-nul-negen-zes-acht.'

'De navigator,' fluisterde de sergeant.

'Wie van onze mensen spreekt Engels?' fluisterde Khatib terug.

Ali wees; de man aan de linkerkant.

'Laat hem hier komen.'

Ali stapte de cel van de navigator binnen en kwam terug met een van de ondervragers. Khatib overlegde met de man in het Arabisch. De ondervrager knikte, ging de cel weer binnen en trok de navigator een zak over zijn hoofd. Toen pas gaf Khatib toestemming de twee celdeuren te openen.

De ondervrager boog zich naar Nicky Tyne en sprak door de stof heen: 'Goed, kapitein,' zei hij in het Engels, met een zwaar accent. 'Dit was het. Het is voorbij. Geen straf meer.'

De jonge navigator hoorde de woorden en zakte half onderuit van opluchting. 'Maar uw vriend heeft minder geluk gehad. Hij is stervende. We kunnen hem naar het ziekenhuis brengen, met schone lakens, dokters, alles wat hij nodig heeft. Of we kunnen hem nu afmaken. U zegt het maar. Als u antwoord geeft op onze vragen, brengen we hem meteen naar het ziekenhuis.'

Khatib knikte naar sergeant Ali aan het eind van de gang. Ali stapte de andere cel binnen. Uit de deuropening klonk het geluid van een plastic slang die met kracht op een blote borst neerkwam. De piloot schreeuwde.

'Oké, oké!' riep Nicky Tyne van onder zijn kap. 'Granaten. Hou op, stelletje schoften! Het was een munitiedepot van gifgasgranaten...'

De afranseling stopte. Hijgend kwam Ali uit de cel van de piloot.

'U bent een genie, *sajidi* generaal.'

Khatib haalde bescheiden zijn schouders op. 'Engelsen en Amerikanen zijn sentimenteel, vergeet dat nooit,' zei hij tegen zijn leerling. 'Haal de tolken maar. Vraag alle bijzonderheden en breng de transcriptie naar mijn kantoor.'

Terug in zijn heiligdom belde Khatib met Hoessein Kamil. Een uur later belde Kamil hem terug. Zijn schoonvader was opgetogen. Hij wilde een vergadering houden, waarschijnlijk dezelfde avond nog. Omar Khatib moest zich gereedhouden.

Karim plaagde Edith Hardenberg weer, goedmoedig en zonder venijn, deze keer over haar werk.

'Verveel je je nooit op die bank, liefje?'

'Nee, het is heel leuk werk. Hoezo?'

'O, ik weet het niet. Ik begrijp niet wat je er leuk aan vindt. Ik zou het stomvervelend vinden.'

'Maar dat is het niet.'

'Wat is er dan zo interessant aan?'

'Nou, de verwerking van de rekeningen, het beleggen van kapitaal, dat soort dingen. Het is belangrijk werk.'

'Onzin. Je zegt alleen maar "Goedemorgen, meneer", "Jawel, meneer", "Nee, meneer", "Natuurlijk, meneer" tegen een hele rij mensen die vijftig schilling komen opnemen. Daar is toch niets aan?'

Hij lag op zijn rug op haar bed. Ze kwam naar hem toe, ging naast hem liggen en trok een van zijn armen om haar schouders zodat ze konden knuffelen. Ze hield van knuffelen.

'Je bent niet wijs, Karim. Maar dat vind ik wel leuk. De Winkler Bank is geen handelsbank, maar een beleggingsbank.'

'Wat is het verschil?'

'We hebben geen gewone rekeninghouders, mensen die geld komen opnemen en overschrijvingen doen. Zo werkt het niet.'

'Geen rekeninghouders? Dan hebben jullie ook geen geld.'

'Natuurlijk wel, maar alleen op deposito-rekeningen.'

'Die heb ik nooit gehad,' gaf Karim toe. 'Alleen een gewone bankrekening. Ik heb liever contant geld.'

'Dat kan niet als het om miljoenen gaat. Dan wordt het gestolen. Daarom zet je het op een bank om het te beleggen.'

'Je bedoelt dat die ouwe Gemütlich met miljoenen omgaat? Miljoenen van andere mensen?'

'Ja. Heel veel miljoenen, zelfs.'

'Schillingen of dollars?'

'Dollars, ponden... miljoenen en miljoenen.'

'Nou, ik zou hem míjn geld niet toevertrouwen.'

Ze ging overeind zitten, oprecht geschokt.

'Herr Gemütlich is volkomen eerlijk. Hij zou nooit iets verkeerds doen.'

'Hij misschien niet, maar iemand anders wel. Laten we zeggen dat ik iemand ken die een rekening heeft bij de Winkler Bank. We noemen hem Schmitt. Op een dag stap ik naar binnen en zeg: "Goedemorgen, Herr Gemütlich, mijn naam is Schmitt en ik heb een rekening hier." Hij kijkt in zijn boeken en zegt: "Inderdaad, dat klopt." Dan zeg ik weer: "Ik zou het graag allemaal opnemen." En als de echte Schmitt komt opdagen, is al het geld weg. Nee, contant geld is veel veiliger.'

Ze lachte om zijn onnozelheid, trok hem naar zich toe en knabbelde aan zijn oor.

'Zo werkt dat niet. Herr Gemütlich zou jouw meneer Schmitt waarschijnlijk persoonlijk kennen. In elk geval moet hij zich identificeren.'

'Een paspoort kun je vervalsen. Die vervloekte Palestijnen doen dat steeds.'

'En hij zou een handtekening vragen, waarvan hij een voorbeeld heeft.'

'Nou, dan zou ik Schmitts handtekening oefenen.'

'Karim, straks word je nog een crimineel. Je denkt veel te slecht.'

Ze giechelden allebei bij het idee.

'Maar als je een buitenlander was en ergens anders woonde, zou je waarschijnlijk een nummerrekening hebben. Die zijn absoluut veilig.'

Hij steunde op een elleboog en keek fronsend op haar neer. 'Wat is dat?'

'Een nummerrekening?'

'Ja.'

Ze legde het uit.

'Maar dat is krankzinnig!' barstte hij uit toen ze uitgesproken was. 'Dan kan iederéén het geld opnemen. Als Gemütlich de cliënt nooit heeft gezien...'

'Er zijn legitimatieprocedures, idioot. Hele complexe codes, manieren om een brief te schrijven, speciale plaatsen waar je een handtekening moet zetten, allerlei methoden om vast te stellen of de persoon werkelijk de rekeninghouder is. En als er iets niet klopt, zal Herr Gemütlich niet meewerken. Dus het is onmogelijk om je voor iemand anders uit te geven.'

'Dan mag hij wel een goed geheugen hebben.'

'Karim, klets niet zo dom! Dat wordt toch allemaal genoteerd! Neem je me mee uit eten?'

'Heb je dat verdiend?'

'Dat weet je best.'

'Goed dan. Maar ik wil wel een hors d'oeuvre.'

Ze keek verbaasd. 'Dan bestel je die toch?'

'Ik bedoel jou.'

Hij stak zijn hand uit, greep haar bij de rand van haar kleine slip en trok haar weer naar het bed. Ze giechelde van plezier. Hij kwam op haar liggen en kuste haar. Opeens hield hij op. Ze keek hem geschrokken aan.

'Ik weet al wat ik zou doen!' mompelde hij. 'Ik zou een brandkastkraker huren om de kluis van die ouwe Gemütlich open te breken en de codes te bekijken. Dàn zou het me lukken!'

Ze lachte, opgelucht dat hij niet van gedachten was veranderd over het vrijen.

'Nee, dat lukt ook niet. Mmmmmm. Doe dat nog eens.'

'Welles.'

'Aaaah. Nietes.'

'Welles. Brandkasten worden steeds gekraakt. Lees de kranten maar.'

Ze tastte 'daar beneden' en sperde haar ogen wijdopen.

'Ooh, is dat allemaal voor mij? Je bent een heerlijke, grote, sterke man, Karim, en ik hou van je. Maar die ouwe Gemütlich, zoals jij hem noemt, is toch wat slimmer dan jij...'

Een minuut later kon het haar niets meer schelen hoe slim Gemütlich was.

Terwijl de Mossad-agent lag te vrijen in Wenen, stelde Mike Martin zijn schotel op. Het liep tegen middernacht, de 11e februari.

Irak had nog precies acht dagen tot de geplande invasie van 20 februari. Ten zuiden van de grens, in het noordelijke deel van de Saoedische woestijn, was de grootste concentratie manschappen, geschut, tanks en voorraden samengetrokken die zich sinds de Tweede Wereldoorlog ooit in zo'n klein gebied had verzameld.

De luchtaanvallen gingen nog steeds door, hoewel de meeste doelwitten op generaal Horners oorspronkelijke lijst al waren gebombardeerd, soms twee keer of meer. Ondanks de toevoeging van nieuwe doelen na de Scud-aanvallen op Israël lag het programma weer op schema. Alle *bekende* fabrieken voor de produktie van massavernietigingswapens waren met de grond gelijk gemaakt, ook de twaalf nieuwe locaties die Jericho had genoemd.

Als effectief wapen bestond de Iraakse luchtmacht in feite niet meer. De meeste Iraakse onderscheppingsjagers die de strijd hadden aangebonden met de Eagles, Hornets, Tomcats, Falcons, Phantoms en Jaguars waren niet naar hun bases teruggekeerd, en halverwege februari hadden ze de moed bijna opgegeven. Met opzet was de elite van de jager- en jachtbommenwer-per-squadrons gedeeltelijk naar Iran gestuurd, waar de toestellen meteen in beslag waren genomen. Andere waren vernietigd in hun hangars of kapot-geschoten als ze op open terrein waren verrast.

De geallieerde legertop kon niet begrijpen waarom Saddam zijn beste gevechtsvliegtuigen naar zijn oude vijand had gestuurd. Maar hij ver-wachtte dat ieder land in het gebied op een gegeven moment voor hem zou moeten zwichten. Dan zou hij zijn vliegtuigen weer terugkrijgen.

Inmiddels was er nauwelijks een brug of een krachtcentrale meer intact.

Half februari richtten de geallieerden zich vooral op het Iraakse leger in het zuiden van Koeweit en in Irak zelf, vlak over de grens.

Vanaf de Saoedische noordgrens tot aan de hoofdweg van Bagdad naar Basra bestookten de Buffs de Iraakse artillerie, tanks, raketbatterijen en infanteriestellingen. Amerikaanse A-10 Thunderbolts, bijgenaamd de 'vlie-gende wrattenzwijnen' vanwege hun gratie in de lucht, zwierven rond en hielden zich bezig met hun specialiteit: het vernietigen van tanks. Eagles en Tornado's waren ook 'op tankjacht'.

Wat de geallieerde generaals in Riyad niet wisten was dat er nog altijd veertig belangrijke centra voor de produktie van massavernietigingswapens onder de woestijn en de bergen verborgen lagen en dat de Sixco-vliegbases nog intact waren.

Sinds het bombardement op het complex van Al-Qubai heerste er een wat opgewektere stemming bij de vier generaals die wisten wat voor een fabriek het werkelijk was, en bij de agenten van de CIA en de SIS in Riyad.

Die stemming bleek ook uit het korte bericht dat Mike Martin die nacht ontving. Zijn controleofficieren in Riyad vertelden dat de Tornado-missie een succes was geweest, ondanks het verlies van één toestel. Daarna feliciteerden ze hem met zijn werk en met zijn besluit om in Bagdad te blijven toen hij al toestemming had gekregen om te vertrekken. Ten slotte vertelden ze hem dat er niet veel meer te doen was. Ze hadden nog één laatste bericht voor Jericho, dat de geallieerden hem dankbaar waren, dat al zijn geld was betaald en dat het contact na de oorlog zou worden hersteld. Daarna, drukten ze Martin op het hart, moest hij serieus proberen om naar Saoedi-Arabië te ontkomen voordat het niet meer kon.

Martin schakelde de ontvanger uit, borg hem op onder de vloer en strekte zich uit op zijn bed. Hij dacht nog even na voordat hij in slaap viel. Interessant dat de geallieerde legers niet naar Bagdad zouden komen. Maar Saddam Hoessein dan? Was hij niet het doelwit geweest van de hele operatie? Blijkbaar was er iets veranderd.

Als hij iets had geweten van het gesprek dat op hetzelfde moment plaatsvond in het hoofdkwartier van de Mukhabarat, nog geen kilometer bij hem vandaan, zou Mike Martin niet zo rustig hebben geslapen.

Wat technische kennis betreft zijn er vier niveaus: competent, heel goed, briljant en begaafd. De laatste categorie betreft mensen bij wie technische kennis hand in hand gaat met een soort zesde zintuig, een aangeboren affiniteit met het onderwerp en de apparatuur, die onmogelijk uit boeken kan worden geleerd.

Op radiogebied was majoor Mohsen Zajid begaafd. Hij was nog jong en droeg een sterke bril die hem een studentikoos uiterlijk gaf. Zajid stond met radio op en ging ermee naar bed. Zijn kamer lag vol met de nieuwste tijdschriften uit het Westen, en als hij een nieuw apparaat ontdekte dat zijn radiodetectie-afdeling nog efficiënter kon maken, vroeg hij erom. En omdat hij Zajids werk op prijs stelde, deed Hassan Rahmani zijn best om de spullen te krijgen.

Kort na middernacht zaten de twee mannen in Rahmani's kantoor.

'Schiet het al op?' vroeg Rahmani.

'Ik geloof het wel,' antwoordde Zajid. 'Hij is er. Dat is duidelijk. Maar hij zendt versnelde berichten uit die bijna niet te peilen zijn. Veel te snel. Maar met veel geduld en handigheid kun je soms wat opvangen, al duren de uitzendingen maar een paar seconden.'

'Hoe dicht ben je hem al genaderd?' vroeg Rahmani.

'Ik heb de frequenties teruggebracht tot een vrij smalle band in het ultrafrequente bereik, en dat maakt het wat eenvoudiger. Een paar dagen geleden had ik geluk. We zaten bij toeval een smalle band af te luisteren, en daar was hij. Luistert u maar.'

Zajid pakte een bandrecorder en drukte op 'play'. Een kakofonie van geluiden vulde het kantoor.

Rahmani keek verbaasd. 'Is dat het?'

'In code, natuurlijk.'

'Natuurlijk,' herhaalde Rahmani. 'Kun je het ontcijferen?'

'Ik denk het niet. Het bericht is gecodeerd door een silicium-chip met een complex circuit.'

'Dus je kunt het niet decoderen?' Rahmani begreep er niets van. Zajid leefde in zijn eigen wereldje en sprak zijn eigen taal. Hij had nu al de grootste moeite om het zijn baas uit te leggen.

'Het is geen code in de letterlijke betekenis. Om die chaos in begrijpelijke taal om te zetten heb je precies dezelfde chip nodig. En er zijn honderden miljoenen mogelijkheden.'

'Wat heeft het dan voor zin?'

'Je kunt wel de zender peilen, en dat heb ik gedaan.'

Hassan Rahmani boog zich gespannen naar hem toe. 'Je hebt hem gepeild?'

'Ja, voor de tweede keer. En raad eens? Dat bericht is midden in de nacht verstuurd, dertig uur voor het bombardement op Al-Qubai. Volgens mij ging dat over die nucleaire fabriek. En er is meer.'

'Ga door.'

'Hij zit hier.'

'Hier in Bagdad?'

Majoor Zajid glimlachte en schudde zijn hoofd. Hij had het beste nieuws tot het laatst bewaard. Hij oogstte graag waardering.

'Nee, generaal. Hier in Mansour. Vlakbij. Ik heb het teruggebracht tot een gebied van twee bij twee kilometer.'

Rahmani dacht bliksemsnel na. Dit werd spannend. Verdomd spannend. De telefoon ging. Hij luisterde even, hing op en kwam overeind.

'Ik moet weg. Nog één ding. Hoeveel berichten moet je nog opvangen voordat je precies weet waar hij zit? In welke straat of zelfs in welk huis?'

'Met een beetje geluk maar één. Ik weet niet of ik hem de volgende keer weer kan betrappen, maar zodra ik hem hoor, weet ik waar hij zit. Ik hoop dat het een lange boodschap is, van een paar seconden. Dan kan ik het beperken tot een gebied van honderd bij honderd meter.'

Rahmani ademde zwaar toen hij de lift naar beneden nam en in de gereedstaande auto stapte.

In twee geblindeerde bussen reden ze naar de vergadering. De zeven ministers zaten in de ene, de zes generaals en de drie chefs van de inlichtingendiensten in de andere. Niemand wist waar ze heen gingen en de chauffeur achter zijn scheidingswand volgde gewoon de motorrijder.

Pas toen de bus stopte op een ommuurde binnenplaats, mochten de negen mannen in de tweede bus uitstappen. Het was een rit van veertig minuten geweest, met veel omwegen. Rahmani vermoedde dat ze ergens op het platteland waren, zo'n vijftig kilometer van Bagdad. Er was geen verkeer te horen en bij het licht van de sterren zag hij de vage omtrekken van een grote villa met zwarte gordijnen voor de ramen.

De zeven ministers zaten al te wachten in de huiskamer. De generaals namen hun plaatsen in en bleven zwijgend zitten. Wachtposten brachten dr. Ubaidi van de buitenlandse inlichtingendienst, Rahmani van de contraspionagedienst en Omar Khatib van de Geheime Politie naar hun stoelen, tegenover de grote, beklede stoel die voor de *Rais* zelf was gereserveerd.

De man die hen had ontboden kwam even later zelf ook binnen. Iedereen stond op en ging weer zitten.

Voor sommigen was het al drie weken geleden dat ze de president voor het laatst hadden gezien. Hij maakte een gespannen indruk, hij had wallen onder zijn ogen en zijn onderkin viel meer op.

Zonder omwegen begon Saddam Hoessein met de belangrijkste kwestie. Er was een bombardement geweest. Iedereen wist ervan, zelfs de mensen die van tevoren niets over Al-Qubai hadden geweten.

Het was zo'n geheim complex dat niet meer dan twaalf mensen in Irak de exacte locatie kenden. Toch was het gebombardeerd. Alleen de hoogste bazen van het land en een paar toegewijde technici waren er ooit geweest zonder blinddoek voor of in een geblindeerde auto. Maar toch was het gebombardeerd.

Het was doodstil in de kamer, de stilte van de angst. De generaals, Radi van de infanterie, Kadiri van het tankkorps, Ridha van de artillerie, Musuli van de genie, de bevelhebber van de Republikeinse Garde en de chef-staf, staarden naar het tapijt op de grond.

Onze kameraad, Omar Khatib, had de twee Britse vliegers ondervraagd, vervolgde de *Rais*. Hij zou nu verslag uitbrengen.

Alle ogen richtten zich op de broodmagere gestalte van Omar Khatib.

De Beul keek in de richting van het staatshoofd, zijn blik ongeveer ter hoogte van Saddams borst.

De piloten hadden gesproken, zei hij toonloos. Ze hadden niets achtergehouden. Hun squadron-commandant had hun verteld dat geallieerde vliegtuigen legertrucks op en neer hadden zien rijden naar een autosloperij. Daaruit hadden de Zonen van de Honden de conclusie getrokken dat het een munitiedepot moest zijn, vermoedelijk een opslagplaats van gifgasgranaten. Het werd niet als een heel belangrijk doelwit beschouwd en ze dachten dat het geen luchtafweer had. Daarom waren er maar twee bommenwerpers op afgestuurd, met twee vliegtuigen die vanaf grotere hoogte het doelwit hadden gemarkeerd. Er waren geen escortevliegtuigen bij om het luchtdoelgeschut uit te schakelen, omdat daar geen rekening mee was gehouden. Dat was alles wat de piloot en de navigator wisten.

De president knikte naar generaal Farouk Ridha.

'Klopt dat, *rafik*?'

'Het is gebruikelijk, *sajid Rais*,' zei de man die het bevel had over de artillerie en de SAM-batterijen, 'dat ze eerst gevechtsvliegtuigen sturen om de luchtafweer te vernietigen en pas daarna de bommenwerpers. Zo gaat het altijd. Twee vliegtuigen, zonder enige steun, naar een belangrijk doelwit sturen? Dat is nog nooit gebeurd.'

Saddam dacht even na. Zijn donkere ogen verrieden niets over zijn gedachten. Dat was een deel van zijn macht over deze mannen. Ze wisten nooit hoe hij zou reageren.

'Is er enige kans, *rafik* Khatib, dat deze mannen iets voor u verborgen hebben gehouden? Dat ze meer wisten dan ze hebben gezegd?'

'Nee, *Rais*, ze zijn... overreed om volledig mee te werken.'

'Daarmee is de zaak dus afgedaan?' vroeg Saddam rustig. 'Het bombardement was gewoon een ongelukkig toeval?'

Overal werd geknikt.

Iedereen zat als verstijfd toen Saddam opeens schreeuwde: '*Fout!* Jullie hebben het allemaal fout!'

Hij ging weer verder op normale toon, maar de angst was gezaaid. Iedereen wist dat die zachte stem de gruwelijkste onthullingen kon doen en de zwaarste straffen kon afkondigen.

'Er reden daar geen vrachtwagens, geen legertrucks. Dat was maar een verhaal dat ze die piloten hebben verteld voor het geval ze gevangen zouden worden genomen. En dus is er meer, nietwaar?'

De meesten zaten nu te transpireren, ondanks de airconditioning. Zo ging het altijd, al sinds mensenheugenis, wanneer het opperhoofd van de stam de medicijnman opdroeg om het kwaad uit te drijven en alle anderen beefden uit angst dat de staf hùn kant op zou wijzen.

'Het is een samenzwering,' fluisterde de *Rais*. 'Er is een verrader, die een komplot tegen mij beraamt.'

Hij zweeg een paar minuten om zijn volgelingen te laten zweten. Toen hij weer het woord nam, richtte hij zich tot de drie mannen tegenover hem. 'Vind hem. Vind hem en breng hem bij me. Hij zal de straf voor zijn misdaden leren kennen. Hij en zijn hele familie.'

Daarna beende hij de kamer uit, gevolgd door zijn persoonlijke lijfwacht. De zestien mannen die achterbleven durfden elkaar niet aan te kijken. Iemand zou geofferd worden. Niemand wist nog wie. En allemaal waren ze bang voor hun hachje, voor een onvoorzichtige opmerking of nog minder dan dat.

Vijftien van de mannen bleven op veilige afstand van de zestiende, de medicijnman, degene die ze Al Mu'azib noemden, de Beul. Hij zou het offer aanwijzen.

Ook Hassan Rahmani zweeg. Dit was niet het moment om over onderschepte radioberichten te beginnen. Zijn operaties waren discreet, subtiel, gebaseerd op speurwerk en concrete feiten. Het laatste waar hij behoefte aan had waren de zware laarzen van de AMAM die alle sporen zouden uitwissen.

Doodsbang vertrokken de ministers en generaals in de donkere nacht, terug naar hun werk.

'Hij heeft ze niet in de kluis op zijn kantoor,' zei Avi Herzog, alias Karim, tegen zijn teamleider Gidi Barzilai, de volgende morgen tijdens een laat ontbijt.

Het was een veilige ontmoeting in Barzilais eigen flat. Herzog had hem vanuit een telefooncel gebeld toen Edith Hardenberg al naar haar werk was. Kort daarna was het Yarid-team gearriveerd om hun collega van alle kanten in het oog te houden en zich ervan te overtuigen dat hij niet werd geschaduwd. Als dat wel zo was, zouden ze het hebben gemerkt. Dat was hun specialiteit.

Gidi Barzilai boog zich over de volgeladen ontbijttafel. Zijn ogen glinsterden.

'Goed gedaan, kerel. Nu weet ik dus waar ik ze niet kan vinden. Enig idee waar wel?'

'In zijn bureau.'

'Zijn bureau? Ben je gek? Iedereen kan een bureau openmaken.'

'Heb je het gezien?'

'Gemütlichs bureau? Nee.'

'Blijkbaar is het heel groot, prachtig bewerkt en heel oud. Een antiek stuk. De oorspronkelijke schrijnwerker heeft er een geheime bergplaats in gemaakt, zo geheim dat Gemütlich het veiliger vindt dan een kluis. Hij denkt dat inbrekers hun aandacht op de kluis zullen richten en niet op het bureau zullen letten. En zelfs als iemand het hele bureau zou doorzoeken, zou hij die geheime bergplaats nooit vinden.'

'En zij weet ook niet waar die bergplaats zit?'

'Nee. Ze is er nog nooit bij geweest als Gemütlich hem opende. Hij sluit zich altijd in zijn kantoor op als hij er iets uit wil halen.'

Barzilai dacht na. 'Handige klootzak. Dat zou ik niet achter hem hebben gezocht. Waarschijnlijk heeft hij nog gelijk ook.'

'Kan ik er nu mee ophouden, met die affaire?'

'Nee, Avi, nog niet. Als het klopt, heb je uitstekend werk geleverd. Maar hou het nog even vol. Blijf toneelspelen. Als je nu verdwijnt, zal ze aan jullie laatste gesprek terugdenken, haar conclusies trekken en misschien berouw krijgen of wat dan ook. Blijf nog een tijdje bij haar en praat met haar, maar niet meer over de bank.'

Barzilai dacht na over het probleem. Niemand van zijn team in Wenen had het bureau ooit gezien, op één man na.

Barzilai stuurde een gecodeerd bericht naar Kobi Dror in Tel Aviv. De verspieder werd ontboden en in een kamertje gezet met een tekenaar.

De verspieder had niet veel talenten, maar wel één unieke eigenschap: een fotografisch geheugen. Meer dan vijf uur lang zag hij met zijn ogen dicht en dacht terug aan het gesprek dat hij met Gemütlich had gehad, zogenaamd als advocaat uit New York. Hij had toen vooral moeten letten op alarminstallaties bij ramen en deuren, een wandkluis, draden die met druksensors waren verbonden, op alle trucs om een ruimte te beveiligen. Daarover had hij verslag uitgebracht. Het bureau had hem nauwelijks geïnteresseerd. Maar nu hij weken later in een kamertje onder de King Saul Boulevard zat, kon hij alles weer in zijn herinnering terugroepen.

Lijn voor lijn beschreef hij het bureau aan de tekenaar. Soms controleerde hij de tekening, liet iets veranderen en ging dan weer verder. De tekenaar werkte met oostindische inkt en een dunne pen, en kleurde het bureau met waterverf in. Na vijf uur had hij een vel tekenpapier met een exacte weergave van het bureau van Herr Wolfgang Gemütlich in de Winkler Bank in de Ballgasse in Wenen.

De tekening werd met de diplomatieke post uit Tel Aviv naar de Israëlische ambassade in Oostenrijk gestuurd. Binnen twee dagen was hij in Barzilais bezit.

Inmiddels had de lijst van alle *sajanim* in Europa de naam opgeleverd van een monsieur Michel Levy, antiquair aan de Boulevard Raspail in Parijs, een van de grootste kenners van antiek meubilair.

Pas op de avond van de 14e februari, dezelfde dag dat Gidi Barzilai in Wenen zijn tekening ontving, riep Saddam Hoessein zijn ministers, gene-

388

raals en inlichtingenofficieren weer bijeen.

De vergadering werd gehouden op verzoek van AMAM-chef Omar Khatib, die het nieuws over zijn succes had doorgegeven via Saddams schoonzoon Hoessein Kamil. En opnieuw was het een nachtelijke bijeenkomst in een of andere villa.

De *Rais* kwam gewoon binnen en vroeg Khatib om verslag uit te brengen.

'Wat kan ik zeggen, *sajid Rais*?' Het hoofd van de Geheime Politie hief zijn handen op en liet ze in een hulpeloos gebaar weer zakken. Het was een meesterlijk staaltje van valse bescheidenheid.

'De *Rais* had gelijk, zoals altijd, en wij vergisten ons allemaal. Het bombardement op Al-Qubai was inderdaad geen toeval. Er wàs een verrader en hij is gevonden.'

Er steeg een gemompel van geveinsde bewondering op, en er werd geapplaudisseerd. De man in de rechte, beklede stoel met zijn rug naar de blinde muur begon te stralen en maakte bezwerende gebaren. Dat applaus was toch echt niet nodig? Het verstomde, maar niet te snel.

Heb ik geen gelijk? vroeg die glimlach. Heb ik niet altijd gelijk?

'Hoe hebt u dit ontdekt, *rafik*?' vroeg de president.

'Door een combinatie van geluk en goed detectivewerk,' antwoordde Khatib bescheiden. 'En geluk is een geschenk van Allah, die de *Rais* gunstig gezind is, zoals wij allemaal weten.'

Van alle kanten klonk instemming.

'Twee dagen voor het bombardement door de vliegtuigen van de Beni Naji, werd er in de buurt een routinecontrole gehouden. Mijn mannen speuren voortdurend naar deserteurs en verboden goederen... Bij die controle zijn alle nummerborden van de auto's genoteerd.

Ik ben die nummers nagegaan. De meeste auto's, bestelwagens en trucks kwamen uit de buurt. Maar er was één dure wagen bij, met een nummer uit Bagdad. We hebben de eigenaar opgespoord, die misschien een goede reden had voor een bezoek aan Al-Qubai. Maar uit een telefoontje bleek dat hij *niet* in de fabriek was geweest. Wat had hij er dan te zoeken, vroeg ik me af.'

Hassan Rahmani knikte. Dat klonk als goed speurwerk, als het waar was. Het was niets voor Khatib, die meestal op brute kracht vertrouwde.

'En waarom was hij daar?' vroeg de *Rais*.

Khatib wachtte even voor het dramatische effect.

'Om een exacte beschrijving te noteren van de autosloperij, met de afstand tot het dichtstbijzijnde herkenningspunt vanuit de lucht, en de juiste kompaskoers. Alles wat piloten nodig zouden hebben om het te vinden.'

Er ging een zucht van verbazing door de kamer.

'Maar dat ontdekten we pas later, *sajid Rais*. Eerst heb ik de man op het hoofdkwartier van de AMAM uitgenodigd voor een openhartig gesprek.'

Khatibs gedachten dwaalden terug naar dat gesprek in de kelder onder het AMAM-gebouw in Saadun, Bagdad, de kelder die bekend stond als de Gymzaal.

Meestal liet Omar Khatib de ondervragingen aan zijn ondergeschikten over. Zelf bepaalde hij alleen hoeveel druk er moest worden uitgeoefend. Alleen op het eind was hij zelf aanwezig. Maar dit was zo'n delicate zaak geweest dat hij de verdachte zelf had verhoord en iedereen naar buiten had gestuurd, achter de geluiddichte deur.

Aan het plafond van de cel zaten twee haken, een meter uit elkaar, waaraan met korte kettingen een houten balk was opgehangen. Khatib had de verdachte met zijn polsen aan de balk laten hangen, met zijn armen ver uiteen. Dat maakte die houding nog pijnlijker.

De voeten van de man bungelden tien centimeter boven de vloer en zijn enkels waren aan een andere balk gebonden, die ook een meter lang was. De verdachte hing nu in een soort X, in het midden van de cel, zodat alle delen van zijn lichaam bereikbaar waren.

Omar Khatib legde de rotanstok op een tafeltje en benaderde de man van voren. Schreeuwend had de verdachte vijftig stokslagen ondergaan, daarna was het geschreeuw overgegaan in gefluisterde smeekbeden. Khatib keek hem strak aan.

'Je bent een dwaas, beste vriend. Je kunt dit gemakkelijk laten ophouden. Je hebt de *Rais* verraden, maar hij is een genadig man. Hij wil alleen een bekentenis.'

'Nee, ik zweer het... *wa-Allah-el-Adheem*... bij Allah de Grote... ik heb niemand verraden.'

De man huilde nu als een kind. Tranen van pijn stroomden over zijn gezicht. Hij had geen ruggegraat, dacht Khatib. Dit zou niet lang duren.

'Jawel, je hebt verraad gepleegd. Qubth-ut-Allah, weet je wat dat betekent?'

'Natuurlijk,' jammerde de man.

'En weet je waar De Vuist van God verborgen ligt?'

'Ja.'

Met kracht bracht Khatib zijn knie omhoog tegen de blote testikels van de man. De verdachte wilde zich dubbelvouwen, maar dat ging niet. Hij begon te kotsen. Het braaksel droop over zijn naakte lichaam en druppelde van zijn penis af.

'Ja... wat?'

'Ja, *sajidi*.'

'Dat is beter. En onze vijanden wisten niet waar De Vuist van God was verborgen?'

'Nee, *sajidi*, dat is geheim.'

Khatibs hand schoot uit en raakte de hangende man vol in het gezicht.
'*Manjouk*, smerige *manjouk*, hoe is het dan mogelijk dat vijandelijke vliegtuigen vanochtend de fabriek en ons wapen hebben vernietigd?'
De verdachte sperde zijn ogen open. De schok was nog groter dan de belediging. *Manjouk* in het Arabisch is de man die de vrouwelijke rol speelt in een homoseksuele paring.
'Maar dat kan niet! Een paar mensen wisten maar iets over Al-Qubai...'
'De vijand wist het ook en heeft de plek gebombardeerd.'
'*Sajidi*, dat kan niet! Ik zweer het. Ze zouden het nooit kunnen vinden. De man die het heeft gebouwd, kolonel Badri, heeft het te goed verborgen...'
De ondervraging was nog een halfuur doorgegaan, tot aan het onvermijdelijke einde.
Khatib werd uit zijn overpeinzingen opgeschrikt door de president zelf.
'En wie is hij, onze verrader?'
'De ingenieur, dr. Salah Siddiqui, *sajid Rais*.'
Er klonken verbaasde reacties. Maar de president knikte, alsof hij de man al langer had verdacht.
'Mag ik vragen,' zei Hassan Rahmani, 'voor wie die ellendeling werkte?'
Khatib wierp Rahmani een giftige blik toe en nam de tijd voor zijn antwoord.
'Dat heeft hij niet gezegd.'
'Maar dat komt nog wel,' zei Saddam.
Sajid Rais,' mompelde Khatib, 'ik vrees dat de verrader op dat punt van zijn bekentenis de geest gaf.'
Rahmani sprong overeind, zonder zich iets aan te trekken van het protocol.
'Meneer de president, ik moet protesteren! Dit is een ongelooflijke blunder. De verrader moet contact met de vijand hebben gehad, een manier om zijn informatie door te geven. Nu zullen we dat nooit te weten komen.'
Khatib keek hem zo gemeen aan dat Rahmani, die op de school van meester Hartley de boeken van Kipling had gelezen, onwillekeurig moest denken aan Krait, de zandslang die siste: 'Pas op, want ik ben de dood!'
'Wat hebt u daarop te zeggen?' vroeg Saddam.
'Wat kan ik antwoorden, *sajid Rais*?' zei Khatib boetvaardig. 'Mijn mensen houden van u als van hun eigen vader, misschien nog meer. Ze zouden voor u sterven. Toen ze die verraderlijke taal hoorden... zijn ze in hun drift te ver gegaan.'
Gelul, dacht Rahmani, maar de *Rais* knikte langzaam. Dat soort taal hoorde hij graag.
'Dat is begrijpelijk,' zei hij. 'Zulke dingen gebeuren. En u generaal Rahmani, die kritiek hebt op uw collega, hebt u al resultaat geboekt?'
Rahmani merkte dat hij niet met *rafik* of 'kameraad' werd aangesproken.

Hij zou voorzichtig moeten zijn, heel voorzichtig.

'Er is een zender, *sajid Rais*. Ergens in Bagdad.'

En hij vertelde wat hij van majoor Zajid had gehoord. Nog één bericht en we hebben de zender te pakken, wilde hij erbij zeggen, maar hij bedacht zich.

'Omdat de verrader dood is,' zei de *Rais*, 'kan ik u zeggen wat ik twee dagen geleden niet kon vertellen. De Vuist van God is niet vernietigd, en zelfs niet begraven. Vierentwintig uur voor het bombardement heb ik hem naar een veiliger plaats laten overbrengen.'

Het duurde een paar seconden voordat het applaus was verstomd. Saddams volgelingen gaven luidruchtig uiting aan hun bewondering voor hun geniale leider.

Hij vertelde hun dat het wapen was overgebracht naar de Vesting, waarvan ze de plaats niet hoefden te weten. Vanuit de Qa'ala zou de bom worden gelanceerd om de loop van de geschiedenis te wijzigen, op de dag dat de eerste laars van een Amerikaanse soldaat de heilige grond van Irak zou betreden.

Het nieuws dat de Britse Tornado's hun werkelijke doel hadden gemist bij het bombardement op Al-Qubai, had de man met de codenaam Jericho diep geschokt. Het kostte hem de grootste moeite om op te staan en samen met de anderen voor Saddam Hoessein te applaudisseren.

Op de terugweg naar Bagdad in de geblindeerde bus, samen met de andere generaals, zat hij zwijgend achterin, in gedachten verzonken.

Het feit dat het gebruik van het wapen dat nu was verborgen in de Qa'ala, de Vesting – waarvan hij nog nooit had gehoord en waarvan hij de plaats niet kende – talloze slachtoffers zou maken, kon hem geen zier schelen.

Hij dacht uitsluitend aan zijn eigen positie. Drie jaar lang had hij alles geriskeerd... zijn ontmaskering, zijn ondergang en een gruwelijke dood... door het regime van zijn land te verraden. Daarbij was het hem niet alleen te doen geweest om veel geld op een buitenlandse bankrekening. Door afpersing en diefstal had hij in Irak zelf ook een kapitaal kunnen vergaren, hoewel dat ook niet zonder risico was.

Nee, hij had zich in het buitenland willen vestigen met een nieuwe identiteit en een nieuwe achtergrond, met de hulp van zijn buitenlandse opdrachtgevers, veilig voor de wraak van de Iraakse moordcommando's. Hij wist wat het lot was van mensen die stalen en er met de buit vandoorgingen. Ze leefden voortdurend in angst, tot ze ooit op een dag door de Iraakse wrekers werden opgespoord.

Hij, Jericho, wilde niet alleen geld maar ook zekerheid. Daarom was hij blij geweest dat hij nu voor de Amerikanen werkte en niet meer voor Iraël. Zij zouden wel voor hem zorgen, hun afspraken nakomen en een nieuwe identiteit voor hem regelen, zodat hij iemand anders kon worden, met een andere nationaliteit, veilig in een mooi strandhuis in Mexico, waar hij de rest van zijn dagen in luxe en rust zou kunnen slijten.

Maar nu was alles veranderd. Als hij bleef zwijgen en het wapen zou worden gebruikt, zouden ze denken dat hij gelogen had. Dat was niet zo, maar in hun woede zouden ze hem nooit geloven. De Amerikanen zouden zijn rekening blokkeren en dan was alles voor niets geweest. Dus moest hij hen op de een of andere manier waarschuwen dat er iets mis was gegaan. Nog een paar risico's, en dan was alles achter de rug – Irak verslagen, de *Rais* ten val gebracht en hij, Jericho, veilig en heel ver weg.

In de beslotenheid van zijn kantoor schreef hij zijn bericht, zoals altijd in het Arabisch, op het dunne papier dat zo weinig ruimte in beslag nam. Hij vertelde over de vergadering van die avond. Dat het wapen nog in de fabriek van Al-Qubai had gelegen toen hij zijn eerdere bericht had verstuurd, maar dat het achtenveertig uur later, toen de Tornado's aanvielen, naar een andere plaats was overgebracht. Daar kon hij niets aan doen.

Hij schreef alles wat hij wist. Dat er een geheime plaats bestond die de Vesting werd genoemd. Dat het wapen daar nu lag en dat het vanuit de Qa'ala zou worden afgevuurd zodra de eerste Amerikaan de Iraakse grens overstak. Kort na middernacht stapte hij in een onopvallende auto en verdween in de stegen van Bagdad. Niemand hield hem tegen. Niemand zou dat durven. Hij liet zijn boodschap achter in de 'brievenbus' bij de fruit- en groentemarkt van Kasra en zette een krijtteken op de muur achter de kerk van de H. Jozef in de christelijke wijk. Het teken was enigszins anders. Hij hoopte dat de onbekende man die zijn boodschappen ophaalde geen tijd verloren zou laten gaan.

Toevallig was Mike Martin de ochtend van de 15e februari al vroeg bij de Russische villa vertrokken. De kokkin had hem een lange lijst van verse produkten meegegeven, produkten die steeds moeilijker te krijgen waren. Er dreigden voedseltekorten. Dat lag niet aan de boeren, maar aan het transport. De meeste bruggen waren verwoest en het midden van Irak is een land van rivieren die de oogsten bevloeien waar Bagdad zich mee voedt. Nu ze geld moesten betalen om met veerponten de rivieren over te steken, bleven de meeste handelaren thuis.

Gelukkig begon Martin bij de kruidenmarkt in de Shurjastraat. Daarna fietste hij om de kerk van de H. Jozef heen, door het steegje erachter. Met een schok zag hij het krijtteken op de muur.

Het hoorde een gekantelde acht te zijn, met één korte horizontale streep door de verbinding tussen de twee cirkels. Maar in geval van nood zou Jericho die streep vervangen door twee kruisjes, in iedere cirkel één. Die kruisjes stonden er nu.

Martin fietste snel naar de groentemarkt van Kasra, wachtte tot de kust veilig was, bleef staan om zogenaamd zijn sandaal vast te maken, stak zijn hand onder de tegel en vond de dunne plastic envelop. Pas tegen de middag was hij weer terug in de villa. Tegen de boze kokkin zei hij dat hij zijn best had gedaan maar dat er niet genoeg groente op de markt was aangevoerd. Hij zou het in de loop van de middag nog eens proberen.

Toen hij Jericho's boodschap las, begreep hij maar al te goed waarom de man in paniek was. Hij stelde zelf een bericht op om Riyad uit te leggen waarom hij de zaak in eigen hand moest nemen. Er was geen tijd meer voor vergaderingen in Riyad en het uitwisselen van berichten. Het ergste, voor hem, was Jericho's waarschuwing dat de Iraakse contraspionagedienst op de hoogte was van een illegale zender die ingekorte berichten verstuurde. Hij wist niet hoe dicht ze hem op de hielen zaten, maar het leek hem veiliger om voorlopig niet meer uit te zenden. Daarom nam hij nu zijn eigen beslissingen.

Martin las eerst het bericht van Jericho in het Arabisch, daarna de vertaling en zijn eigen boodschap. Toen versnelde hij het bericht en maakte alles gereed voor de uitzending.

Hij kon pas laat in de avond in de lucht komen. Die tijd was met opzet gekozen omdat iedereen in de villa dan sliep. Maar net als Jericho had hij ook een noodprocedure.

Dat was de uitzending van één hoge fluittoon, op een totaal andere frequentie, ver van de gebruikelijke VHF-band.

Hij controleerde of de Iraakse chauffeur met eerste secretaris Koelikov naar de ambassade in het centrum was vertrokken en of de Russische huisbediende en zijn vrouw zaten te lunchen. Toen installeerde hij zijn satellietschotel bij de open deur, ondanks het risico van ontdekking, en verzond de fluittoon.

In de radiohut – een voormalige slaapkamer – in de SIS-villa in Riyad ging een lamp aan. Het was half twee in de middag. De dienstdoende radiotechnicus, bezig met het normale verkeer tussen de villa en Century House in Londen, gooide al zijn werk neer, riep door de deuropening om assistentie en schakelde naar Martins frequentie van die dag, klaar voor ontvangst.

De andere technicus stak zijn hoofd om de deur. 'Wat is er?'

'Waarschuw Steve en Simon. Zwarte Beer heeft zich gemeld op de noodfrequentie.'

De man vertrok.

Martin gaf Riyad vijftien minuten en verzond toen zijn bericht.

Riyad was niet het enige station dat de boodschap opving. Buiten Bagdad stond een satellietschotel die onophoudelijk de VHF-band afzocht en een deel van het bericht registreerde. Het was zo lang dat het, zelfs in versnelde vorm, nog vier seconden duurde. De Iraakse technici vingen de laatste twee seconden op en voerden een peiling uit.

Zodra hij zijn boodschap had doorgegeven, verborg Martin zijn apparatuur weer onder de vloer. Hij was nauwelijks klaar toen hij voetstappen op het grind hoorde. Het was de Russische huisbediende, die in een edelmoedige bui de tuin door was gelopen om hem een Balkansigaret aan te bieden. Martin nam hem met veel buigingen en Arabische dankbetuigingen aan. De Rus, voldaan over zijn nobele gebaar, liep terug naar het huis.

Arme klootzak, dacht hij. Wat een leven.

Toen hij weer alleen was, schreef de arme klootzak een boodschap in het Arabisch op een luchtpostblok dat hij onder zijn brits verborgen had.

Op hetzelfde moment zat majoor Zajid, de begaafde radiotechnicus, over een zeer grootschalige plattegrond van de stad gebogen, turend naar de wijk Mansour. Hij maakte een paar berekeningen, controleerde ze nog eens en belde toen Hassan Rahmani op het hoofdkwartier van de Mukhabarat, nauwelijks vijfhonderd meter van het ruitvormige gebied in Mansour dat hij met groene inkt op de kaart had getekend. Rahmani vroeg hem om om vier uur langs te komen.

In Riyad ijsbeerde Chip Barber door de huiskamer van de villa met een uitdraai in zijn hand en vloekte zoals hij niet meer had gevloekt sinds zijn tijd bij de mariniers, dertig jaar geleden.

'Wat heeft dit te betekenen, verdomme?' brieste hij tegen de twee Britse inlichtingenofficieren in de kamer.

'Kalm nou maar, Chip,' zei Laing. 'Hij heeft het heel lang volgehouden. Hij staat onder grote spanning. De Irakezen zijn hem op het spoor. Eigenlijk moeten we hem daar weghalen, nu meteen.'

'Ja, hij is een geweldige kerel, dat weet ik wel. Maar nu gaat hij toch zijn boekje te buiten. Wij moeten het betalen, vergeet dat niet.'

'Natuurlijk,' zei Paxman, 'maar hij is onze man en hij staat er helemaal alleen voor. Als hij wil blijven, is dat alleen om zijn werk af te maken – net zo goed voor jullie als voor ons.'

Barber kalmeerde wat.

'Drie miljoen dollar! Hoe moet ik Langley vertellen dat hij Jericho drie miljoen dollar heeft geboden als hij deze keer de juiste plaats noemt? Die Iraakse klootzak had de eerste keer al over de brug moeten komen. Voor hetzelfde geld worden we belazerd.'

'Chip,' zei Laing, 'we hebben het over een kernbom.'

'Misschien,' bromde Barber. '*Misschien* hebben we het over een kernbom. *Misschien* heeft Saddam genoeg uranium, *misschien* heeft hij een bom geproduceerd. Maar we hebben niets anders dan de berekeningen van een paar geleerden en de bewering van Saddam zelf, àls hij het heeft gezegd. Verdomme, Jericho is een huurling. Hij kan liegen dat hij scheel ziet. Die geleerden kunnen zich vergissen. En Saddam is een beruchte leugenaar. Ik bedoel, wat hebben we concreet gekregen voor al dat geld?'

'Wil je het risico nemen?' vroeg Laing.

Barber liet zich in een stoel vallen. 'Nee,' zei hij ten slotte. 'Dat niet. Goed, ik zal het met Washington regelen. Daarna vertellen we het de generaals. Maar onthoud één ding. Ooit zal ik oog in oog staan met die Jericho, en als hij ons heeft belazerd, ruk ik hem beide armen van zijn lijf en sla hem dood met de natte kant.'

Om vier uur die middag stapte majoor Zajid met zijn kaarten en berekeningen het kantoor van Hassan Rahmani binnen. Zorgvuldig legde hij uit dat hij die dag zijn derde driehoekspeiling had uitgevoerd en het gebied had beperkt tot de ruitvormige sector van Mansour die hij op de plattegrond had aangegeven. Rahmani keek er weifelend naar.

'Het is honderd bij honderd meter,' zei hij. 'Ik dacht dat die moderne technologie tot op één vierkante meter nauwkeurig was.'

'Als ik een langer bericht zou opvangen wel,' legde de jonge majoor geduldig uit. 'Ik kan de straal van de ontvanger op één meter instellen. Kruis je die straal met een tweede peiling vanaf een ander punt, dan houd je inderdaad een plek van één vierkante meter over. Maar deze uitzendingen zijn heel kort. Niet langer dan twee seconden. Het beste resultaat is een heel smalle kegel, met zijn punt naar de ontvanger gericht, die naar buiten toe steeds breder wordt. Misschien een hoek van één seconde van één graad van het kompas, maar een paar kilometer verder is dat al honderd meter. Maar we hebben nu toch een redelijk klein gebied overgehouden?'

Rahmani tuurde op de plattegrond. Er stonden vier gebouwen binnen de ruit.

'Laten we maar eens gaan kijken,' stelde hij voor.

De twee mannen liepen met de kaart in hun hand door Mansour, tot ze het bewuste gebied gevonden hadden. Het was een zeer welvarende woonwijk. De vier gebouwen waren vrijstaande villa's met ommuurde tuinen.

Het begon al donker te worden. 'Morgen doen we een overval,' zei Rahmani. 'Ik zal de wijk met troepen afgrendelen. Heel onopvallend, natuurlijk. Jij weet waar je naar zoekt. Neem je specialisten mee en doorzoek die vier huizen. Als je de apparatuur vindt, hebben we de spion.'

'Er is één probleem,' zei de majoor. 'Ziet u die koperen plaquette daar? Die villa is een deel van de Russische ambassade.'

Rahmani dacht even na. Niemand zou hem dankbaar zijn als hij een internationaal incident veroorzaakte.

'Begin maar met die andere drie,' zei hij. 'Als dat niets oplevert, regel ik wel wat met Buitenlandse Zaken.'

Terwijl ze stonden te praten, was een van de personeelsleden van die Russische villa vijf kilometer bij hen vandaan. De tuinman Mahmoud Al-Khouri bevond zich op de oude Britse begraafplaats, waar hij een dunne plastic envelop in een stenen vaas bij een verwaarloosd graf legde. Later zette hij een krijtteken op de muur van de Journalistenbond. Toen hij vlak voor middernacht nog eens door de wijk liep, zag hij dat het krijtteken was verdwenen.

Die avond werd er vergaderd in Riyad – een besloten vergadering in een afgesloten kantoor, twee verdiepingen onder het Saoedische ministerie van Defensie. Er waren vier generaals aanwezig en twee burgers, Barber en Laing. Toen de inlichtingenofficieren waren uitgesproken, vervielen de militairen in somber stilzwijgen.

'Is dit serieus?' vroeg een van de Amerikanen.

'We hebben geen honderd procent zekerheid,' zei Barber, 'maar de kans is groot dat die informatie klopt.'

'Waarom zijn jullie daar zo zeker van?' vroeg de generaal van de Amerikaanse luchtmacht.

'Zoals u waarschijnlijk al had vermoed, hebben we al enkele maanden een agent in Bagdad, iemand met een hoge positie binnen het Iraakse regime.'

Er werd instemmend gebromd.

'Ik dacht ook niet dat al die informatie over nieuwe doelwitten uit de kristallen bol van Langley kwam,' zei de luchtmachtgeneraal, die nog steeds de pest in had omdat de CIA beweerde dat zijn piloten niet genoeg voltreffers scoorden.

'Het punt is,' vervolgde Laing, 'dat de berichten van onze man altijd volledig kloppen. Als hij nu liegt, dan heeft hij ons behoorlijk te grazen genomen. Het tweede punt is: kunnen we dat risico nemen?'

Het bleef een paar minuten stil.

'Er is iets wat jullie over het hoofd zien,' zei de luchtmachtgeneraal. 'De lancering.'

'Hoezo de lancering?' vroeg Barber.

'Een wapen produceren is één ding, maar je moet het ook op de vijand kunnen afvuren. Luister, niemand zal beweren dat Irak verstand heeft van miniatuurtechnologie. Dat is veel te geavanceerd. Saddam kan dat wapen... àls hij het heeft... dus niet met een tankkanon lanceren. En ook niet met een artilleriekanon, hetzelfde kaliber. Of met een Katjoesjka-batterij. Of met een raket.'

'Waarom niet met een raket, generaal?'

'Vanwege de effectieve lading,' antwoordde de luchtmachtgeneraal sarcastisch. 'Aangenomen dat het een vrij primitieve bom is, praat je toch gauw over een halve ton. Laten we zeggen over 400 kilo. We weten dat de Al-Abeid en de Al-Tammuz raketten nog pas in ontwikkeling waren toen we dat complex bij Saad-16 vernietigden. Hetzelfde geldt voor de Al-Abbas en de Al-Badr. Die hebben ze dus niet meer, of ze zijn niet geschikt voor zo'n zware last.'

'En de Scud?' vroeg Laing.

'Zelfde probleem,' zei de generaal. 'Hun lange-afstandsraket, de Al-Hoessein, valt uit elkaar zodra hij in de atmosfeer terugkeert. En hij kan maar een effectieve lading van 160 kilo vervoeren. Zelfs de oorspronkelijke Russi-

398

sche Scud had een maximale capaciteit van niet meer dan 600 kilo. Die dingen zijn gewoon te klein.'

'Ze kunnen die bom toch afwerpen met een vliegtuig?' opperde Barber.

De luchtmachtgeneraal keek hem nijdig aan. 'Heren, ik wil u persoonlijk de garantie geven, hier en nu, dat er van nu af aan niet één Iraaks vliegtuig de grens zal bereiken. De meeste komen niet eens meer van de grond. Maar ieder toestel dat toch opstijgt en koers zet naar het zuiden, zal halverwege de grens worden neergeschoten. Ik heb genoeg AWACS-vliegtuigen en genoeg jagers. Ik geef u de garantie.'

'En die Vesting?' vroeg Laing. 'Hun lanceerinstallatie?'

'Een geheime hangar, waarschijnlijk ondergronds, met een startbaan voor de uitgang. Daar staat nu een Mirage, een MiG of een Soekhoi, volledig toegerust en klaar voor de start. Maar die krijgen we ook te pakken voordat hij de grens over is.'

De beslissing berustte bij de Amerikaanse generaal aan het hoofd van de tafel.

'Denken jullie dat je die zogenaamde Vesting kunt vinden?' vroeg hij rustig.

'Ja, generaal. Daar werken we al aan. Misschien over een paar dagen.'

'Als jullie de basis opsporen, zullen wij hem vernietigen.'

'En de invasie, over vier dagen?'

'Dat horen jullie nog wel.'

Die avond werd bekendgemaakt dat de invasie van Koeweit en Irak was uitgesteld en pas op 24 februari zou beginnen.

Later gaven de historici twee redenen voor dit uitstel. De ene was dat de Amerikaanse mariniers de belangrijkste speerpunt van hun aanval een paar kilometer naar het westen wilden verleggen, waardoor eerst de troepen en het materieel moesten worden verplaatst en nieuwe voorbereidingen moesten worden getroffen. Dat was ook zo.

Een andere verklaring, waar de pers achteraf mee kwam, was dat twee Britse computerkrakers in de computer van het ministerie van Defensie hadden ingebroken en de weersverwachtingen voor het oorlogsgebied hadden verstoord waardoor verwarring ontstond over de beste dag om met de grondaanval te beginnen.

In werkelijkheid was het tussen de 20e en de 24e prachtig weer, en werden de omstandigheden juist slechter toen de opmars begon.

Generaal Norman Schwarzkopf was een grote, sterke vent, niet alleen fysiek maar ook mentaal en moreel. Maar het zou onmenselijk zijn geweest als de spanning van de afgelopen dagen geen enkel spoor zou hebben nagelaten.

Al zes maanden werkte hij twintig uur per dag, zonder onderbrekingen. Hij had niet alleen de leiding over de grootste en snelste militaire opbouw in de geschiedenis van de mensheid – een opgave die voor een minder sterke figuur al te zwaar zou zijn geweest – maar hij moest ook nog rekening houden met de gevoeligheden van de Saoedische samenleving, de vrede bewaren als er weer eens een conflict tussen de leden van de Coalitie uitbrak, en de eindeloze, goedbedoelde maar zinloze en vermoeiende interrupties van het Congres verdragen.

Toch waren dat niet de dingen die zijn broodnodige slaap verstoorden. Hij had vooral nachtmerries over de verantwoordelijkheid voor al die jonge levens.

In die nachtmerries kwam een Driehoek voor. Altijd weer die Driehoek. Het was een rechthoekige driehoek op zijn kant. De basis was de kustlijn van Khafji via Jubail naar de drie verbonden steden Damman, Al Khobar en Dhahran.

De loodlijn van de driehoek was de grens die vanaf de kust naar het westen liep, eerst tussen Saoedi-Arabië en Koeweit, en daarna de woestijn in, waar hij overging in de grens met Irak.

De hypotenusa was de schuine lijn die de laatste westelijke buitenposten in de woestijn met de kust bij Dhahran verbond.

Binnen die driehoek wachtten bijna een half miljoen jonge mannen en enkele vrouwen op zijn bevel. Tachtig procent daarvan waren Amerikanen. In het oosten lagen de Saoedi's, andere Arabische contingenten en de mariniers. In het midden waren de grote Amerikaanse pantser- en gemechaniseerde infanterie-eenheden gelegerd, met de Britse 1e Pantserdivisie. Aan de uiterste flank lagen de Fransen.

Eén keer had hij in zijn nachtmerrie gezien hoe tienduizenden jonge mensen op de bres afstormden voor de aanval, om daar te worden getroffen door een regen van gifgas en te sterven tussen de zandwallen en het prikkeldraad. Maar nu was het nog erger.

Nog maar een week eerder, toen ze de driehoek op de stafkaart bekeken, had een inlichtingenofficier van het leger daadwerkelijk opgemerkt: 'Misschien wil Saddam er een kernbom op gooien.' De man dacht dat hij een grapje maakte.

Die nacht probeerde de opperbevelhebber weer in slaap te komen, maar het lukte niet. Altijd weer die Driehoek. Te veel soldaten in een te klein gebied.

In de SIS-villa deelden Laing, Paxman en de twee radiotechnici een krat bier dat heimelijk uit de Britse ambassade was aangevoerd. Zij zaten ook over de kaart gebogen en zagen de Driehoek. Zij voelden ook de spanning.

'Eén vervloekte bom, één primitief bommetje, nog kleiner dan op Hirosjima, boven de grond of op de grond...' zei Laing.

Ze hoefden geen wetenschappers te zijn om te beseffen dat de eerste explosie meer dan honderdduizend jonge soldaten zou doden. Binnen een paar uur zou de stralingswolk, met miljarden tonnen radioactief zand uit de woestijn, zich verspreiden en alles doden wat op zijn pad kwam.

De schepen op zee zouden nog de tijd hebben alle luiken te sluiten, maar de grondtroepen en de bevolking van de Saoedische steden niet. De wolk zou naar het oosten drijven, steeds breder wordend, over Bahrein en de geallieerde vliegbases. De straling zou de zee vergiftigen, de kust van Iran bereiken en daar een van de categorieën vernietigen die volgens Saddam Hoessein het leven niet waard waren: 'Perzen, joden en vliegen.'

'Hij kan hem niet lanceren, verdomme,' zei Paxman. 'Hij heeft geen raket en geen vliegtuig meer over.'

Ver naar het noorden, verborgen onder de Jebal al Hamreen, diep in het staartstuk van een kanon met een loop van 180 meter lang en een bereik van 1000 km, lag De Vuist Van God roerloos te wachten om te worden afgevuurd.

Het huis in Qadisijah was nog maar half wakker en totaal niet voorbereid op de bezoekers die zo vroeg in de ochtend arriveerden. Toen de eigenaar het had laten bouwen, vele jaren geleden, had het nog tussen de boomgaarden gelegen.

Het stond vijf kilometer van de vier villa's in Mansour die majoor Zajid van de contraspionagedienst op dat moment in het oog liet houden. De zuidwestelijke buitenwijken van Bagdad hadden het oude huis inmiddels ingesloten en de nieuwe snelweg naar Qadisijah liep nu dwars door de voormalige velden met perziken en abrikozen.

Toch was het nog steeds een mooi huis, eigendom van een man die allang met pensioen was. Het had een ommuurde tuin waar nog een paar fruitbomen stonden.

Twee truckladingen AMAM-soldaten onder bevel van een majoor kwamen op het huis af zonder zich iets van de fatsoensnormen aan te trekken. Ze schoten het slot kapot, trapten het hek open, trapten de voordeur in en sloegen de oude bediende die hen wilde tegenhouden half bewusteloos.

Ze stampten het huis door, rukten kasten open en scheurden gordijnen van de rails, terwijl de doodsbange, bejaarde eigenaar van het huis zijn vrouw probeerde te beschermen.

De soldaten sloopten bijna het hele interieur, maar ze vonden niets. Toen de oude man smekend vroeg waar ze naar zochten, antwoordde de majoor dat hij dat heel goed wist, en de speurtocht ging verder.

Na het huis richtten de soldaten hun aandacht op de tuin. Helemaal aan het eind, bij de muur, vonden ze verse aarde. Twee van hen hielden de oude man vast, terwijl de soldaten groeven. Hij riep dat hij niet wist waarom de aarde was omgewoeld. Hij had er niets begraven. Maar ze vonden het toch.

Het zat in een jutezak en iedereen kon zien dat het een zender was. De majoor wist niets van radio's, en het had hem weinig kunnen schelen als hij had geweten dat het een heel ander type was dan de ultramoderne satellietradio die Mike Martin gebruikte en die nog steeds onder de vloer van zijn schuurtje in de tuin van eerste secretaris Koelikov lag. Voor de AMAM-majoor waren zenders het gereedschap van spionnen, en daar ging het om.

De oude man begon te jammeren dat hij het ding nooit eerder had gezien, dat iemand 's nachts over de muur moest zijn geklommen om de radio te begraven, maar ze sloegen hem tegen de grond met hun geweerkolven. Toen zijn vrouw begon te gillen, kreeg ze ook een paar klappen.

De majoor bekeek zijn trofee. Zelfs hij zag dat de letters op de jutezak Hebreeuws waren.

De bediende en de oude vrouw hadden ze niet nodig, alleen de man. Hij was boven de zeventig maar ze droegen hem voorover het huis uit, met vier soldaten die hem ieder bij een voet of een enkel vasthielden, en smeten hem als een zak vijgen achter in een truck.

De majoor was in een goede bui. Ze hadden een anonieme tip gekregen en hij had zijn plicht gedaan. Zijn chefs zouden tevreden zijn. Dit was geen geval voor de gevangenis in Abu Khraib. Hij bracht de verdachte naar het AMAM-hoofdkwartier en de Gymzaal. Dat, zo redeneerde hij, was de enige plaats voor Israëlische spionnen.

Dezelfde dag, op 16 februari, was Gidi Barzilai in Parijs om de tekening aan Michel Levy te laten zien. De oude antiquair was hem graag van dienst. Hij was maar één keer eerder benaderd, door een *katsa* die wat meubels wilde lenen om zogenaamd als antiekhandelaar een bepaald huis te kunnen binnenkomen.

Michel Levy zag het als een leuke, opwindende afwisseling in het bestaan van een oude man, om de Mossad op de een of andere manier te kunnen helpen.

'Boulle,' zei hij.

'Pardon?' vroeg Barzilai, die dacht dat hij beledigd werd.

'Boulle,' herhaalde de oude man, 'ook gespeld Buhl. De grote Franse schrijnwerker. Zijn stijl, absoluut. Maar hij heeft het niet zelf gemaakt. Het is uit een latere periode.'

'Van wie is het dan wel?'

Monsieur Levy was boven de tachtig. Zijn dunne witte haar lag tegen een gerimpelde schedel geplakt. Maar hij had roze appelwangen en glinsterende ogen, die nog blij waren met het leven. Voor zoveel van zijn generatiegenoten had hij al *kaddish* gezegd.

'Toen Boulle stierf, liet hij zijn werkplaats na aan zijn protégé, de Duitser Oeben. Die gaf de traditie weer door aan een andere Duitser, Riesener. Ik denk dat dit uit de Riesener-periode is. In elk geval van een leerling, misschien van de meester zelf. Willen jullie het kopen?'

Het was een grapje. Hij wist ook wel dat de Mossad geen antiek kocht. Zijn ogen twinkelden van plezier.

'Laten we zeggen dat ik er interesse voor heb,' zei Barzilai.

Levy vond het prachtig. De Mossad was weer een of andere stunt van plan. Hij zou nooit weten wat, maar hij genoot.

'Hadden die bureaus...'

'Schrijftafels,' zei Levy. 'Het is een schrijftafel.'

'Goed. Hadden die schrijftafels ook geheime laden?'

Het werd steeds leuker. En spannender.

'Aha, je bedoelt een *cachette*. Maar natuurlijk. Weet je, jongeman, heel lang geleden, toen mannen soms nog om hun eer duelleerden, moest een dame die een affaire had héél discreet zijn. Er was toen nog geen telefoon, geen fax, geen video. Haar minnaar kon zijn stoute gedachten alleen aan het papier toevertrouwen. En waar moest ze die brieven voor haar echtgenoot verbergen?

Niet in een wandkluis, want die bestonden nog niet. Niet in een geldkistje, want dan zou haar man de sleutel vragen. Mensen uit de betere kringen bestelden dus meubels met *cachettes*. Niet altijd, natuurlijk, maar soms. En het moest goed vakwerk zijn, anders zag je het.'

'Als je... zo'n meubel zou willen kopen, hoe kun je dan weten of er een geheime bergplaats in zit?'

Het werd steeds mooier! De man van de Mossad wilde geen Riesenerschrijftafel kopen, maar erin inbreken!

'Wil je er soms een zien?' vroeg Levy.

Hij belde een paar contacten. Daarna stapten ze de winkel uit en namen een taxi. Het was een andere antiquair. Levy overlegde fluisterend, de man knikte even en liet hen alleen. Als het tot een koop kwam, had Levy gezegd, wilde hij een kleine commissie. Zijn collega vond het best. Zo ging het wel vaker in de antiekwereld.

Het bureau dat ze bekeken leek sterk op dat in Wenen.

'De *cachette* is natuurlijk niet groot,' zei Levy. 'Anders zou je zien dat de binnenmaten niet kloppen met de buitenmaten. Het is dus een horizontale of verticale ruimte, meestal niet meer dan twee centimeter diep, verborgen in

een ogenschijnlijk massief paneel van zo'n drie centimeter dik, dat in werkelijkheid bestaat uit twee dunne platen met daartussen de *cachette*. Het gaat om het mechaniek van de opening.'
Hij trok een van de bovenste laden open. 'Voel maar eens,' zei hij.
Barzilai stak zijn hand erin totdat zijn vingers de achterkant raakten.
'Goed voelen.'
'Ik voel niets,' zei de *katsa*.
'Omdat er niets te voelen is,' zei Levy. 'In deze la niet. Maar er had een knopje of een palletje in kunnen zitten. Een gladde knop, daar druk je op, een ruwe knop is om te draaien. Een palletje schuif je opzij. Dan zie je wel wat er gebeurt.'
'Wat moet er dan gebeuren?'
'Je hoort een zachte klik en er springt een houten deurtje open dat met een veer op zijn plaats wordt gehouden. Daarachter zit de *cachette*.'
Zelfs de vindingrijkheid van de schrijnwerkers uit de 18e eeuw had haar grenzen. Binnen een uur had monsieur Levy de *katsa* de meest voorkomende tien plaatsen getoond waar je naar een knop of een palletje moest zoeken om de veer van de geheime bergplaats te openen.
'Gebruik nooit geweld,' waarschuwde Levy hem. 'Dat helpt toch niet, en bovendien laat het sporen na.'
Hij stootte Barzilai aan en grinnikte. Barzilai trakteerde de oude man op een uitstekende lunch bij de Coupole, nam toen een taxi en stapte op het vliegtuig terug naar Wenen.

Vroeg in de morgen van diezelfde 16e februari verschenen majoor Zajid en zijn mensen bij de eerste van de drie villa's die ze moesten doorzoeken. De andere twee waren afgesloten. Er stonden wachtposten bij alle deuren en de verbijsterde bewoners moesten binnen blijven.
De majoor was heel beleefd, maar zijn gezag duldde geen tegenspraak. Anders dan het AMAM-team, drie kilometer verderop in Qadisijah, bestond Zajids groep uit deskundigen, die efficiënt te werk gingen en weinig schade aanrichtten.
Ze begonnen op de begane grond, op zoek naar een bergplaats onder de vloertegels. Daarna werkten ze het hele huis door, kamer voor kamer, kast voor kast, ruimte voor ruimte.
De tuin werd ook doorzocht, maar er was niets bijzonders te vinden. Tegen twaalf uur was de majoor overtuigd. Hij bood de bewoners zijn excuses aan en vertrok. Daarna begonnen ze met het buurhuis.

De oude man lag op zijn rug in de kelder onder het AMAM-hoofdkwartier in Saadun, aan zijn polsen en zijn middel op een houten tafel vastgebonden en omringd door de vier experts die hem een bekentenis moesten afdwingen. Verder was er nog een arts aanwezig, en generaal Omar Khatib zelf, die in een hoek met sergeant Ali overlegde.

Het hoofd van de AMAM bepaalde zelf welke methoden moesten worden toegepast. Sergeant Ali trok een wenkbrauw op. Vandaag zou hij zeker zijn overall nodig hebben. Omar Khatib knikte kort en vertrok naar zijn kantoor op de bovenverdieping. Hij moest zijn administratie nog bijwerken.

De oude man hield vol dat hij niets van de zender wist en dat hij al vijf dagen niet in de tuin was geweest vanwege het slechte weer... Maar de ondervragers waren niet geïnteresseerd. Ze bonden zijn enkels aan een bezemsteel die ze over zijn wreven legde. Twee van de vier trokken de voeten van de verdachte in de gewenste positie, met zijn voetzolen naar de kamer toe, terwijl Ali en zijn collega de zware elektriciteitskabels pakten die aan de muur hingen.

Toen de afranseling begon, schreeuwde de oude man, zoals iedereen. Totdat zijn stem brak en hij het bewustzijn verloor. Een emmer ijswater uit de hoek, waar een hele rij klaarstond, bracht hem weer bij.

Zo nu en dan hielden de ondervragers even pauze om hun vermoeide armspieren rust te gunnen. Tijdens die pauzes gooiden ze bekers pekel tegen de bloederige voetzolen van de gevangene. Daarna gingen ze uitgerust weer verder.

Steeds als hij bij bewustzijn kwam, riep de oude man dat hij niet eens een zender kon bedienen en dat er een vergissing was begaan.

Halverwege de ochtend waren de huid en het vlees van zijn voetzolen weggeslagen en glinsterden de witte botten door het bloed heen. Sergeant Ali zuchtte en gaf de anderen een teken om te stoppen. Hij stak een sigaret op en genoot van de rook terwijl zijn assistent met een korte ijzeren staaf de benen van de gevangene brak, vanaf de enkels tot de knieën.

De oude man deed een beroep op de dokter, van collega tot collega, maar de AMAM-arts staarde naar het plafond. Hij had orders om de gevangene in leven en bij bewustzijn te houden, meer niet.

Aan de andere kant van de stad had majoor Zajid om vier uur ook het tweede huis doorzocht, juist op het moment dat Gidi Barzilai en Michel Levy in Parijs van hun tafeltje opstonden. Ook hier vond hij niets. Nadat hij beleefd zijn verontschuldigingen had aangeboden aan het doodsbange echtpaar dat had moeten toezien hoe hun huis binnenstebuiten werd gekeerd, vertrok hij met zijn mensen naar de derde en laatste villa.

In Saadun viel de oude man steeds vaker flauw. De arts protesteerde bij de ondervragers dat hij tijd nodig had om te herstellen. Er werd een injectiespuit gevuld en in een ader van de gevangene gestoken. Het middel had bijna meteen effect. De oude man ontwaakte uit zijn halve coma, en kreeg het gevoel in zijn zenuwen weer terug.

Toen de naalden in de brander gloeiendheet waren, werden ze langzaam door het verschrompelde scrotum en de verdroogde testikels gestoken.

Kort na zes uur 's avonds raakte de oude man weer in coma, en deze keer was de arts te laat. Hij deed zijn uiterste best, het zweet stroomde van zijn gezicht, maar zijn stimulerende middelen hadden geen effect meer, ook niet toen ze rechtstreeks in het hart werden ingespoten.

Ali verliet de kamer en kwam vijf minuten later terug met Omar Khatib. Hij wierp een blik op het lichaam. Jaren van ervaring vertelden hem iets waar hij geen medische opleiding voor nodig had. Hij draaide zich om en sloeg de arts met zijn vlakke hand hard in het gezicht.

De kracht van de klap en de reputatie van de man die hem had geslagen wierpen de arts tegen de grond, tussen zijn ampullen en injectiespuiten.

'Idioot,' siste Khatib. 'Verdwijn.'

De dokter gooide haastig zijn spullen in zijn tas en kroop op handen en voeten de deur uit. De Beul bekeek Ali's handwerk. Er hing een weeë geur in de kamer die de twee mannen al heel lang kenden – de stank van zweet, angst, urine, uitwerpselen, bloed, braaksel en de vage lucht van verbrand vlees.

'Hij bleef volhouden tot het eind,' zei Ali. 'Ik zweer het. Als hij iets had geweten, hadden we het uit hem gekregen.'

'Doe hem maar in een zak,' snauwde Omar Khatib, 'en stuur hem naar zijn vrouw terug voor de begrafenis.'

Het was een sterke, witte canvaszak van één meter tachtig lang en zestig centimeter breed die om tien uur die avond voor de deur van het huis in Qadisijah werd neergegooid. Langzaam en met grote moeite, want ze waren allebei al oud, droegen de weduwe en de bediende de zak naar binnen en legden hem op de eettafel. De vrouw nam haar plaats aan het hoofd van de tafel in en begon te jammeren van verdriet.

De verbijsterde oude bediende, Talat, liep naar de telefoon, maar die was van de muur gerukt en werkte niet meer. Hij pakte de telefoongids van zijn mevrouw, die hij niet kon lezen, liep ermee naar het huis van een buurman die apotheker was en vroeg hem of hij de jongeheer wilde waarschuwen – een van beide jongeheren.

Op hetzelfde moment dat de apotheker probeerde een nummer te bellen via het gehavende telefoonnet van Irak, en Gidi Barzilai, terug in Wenen, een nieuw telegram opstelde aan Kobi Dror, bracht majoor Zajid verslag uit over zijn mislukte huiszoekingen.

'Er was niets te vinden,' meldde hij aan Hassan Rahmani, 'anders hadden

we het wel gevonden. Dus het moet de vierde villa zijn, het huis van de diplomaat.'
'Weet je het zeker?' vroeg het hoofd van de contraspionagedienst. 'Het zou geen ander huis kunnen zijn?'
'Nee, generaal. Het dichtstbijzijnde volgende huis ligt ver buiten het gebied dat we hebben gepeild. De zender moet binnen die ruit op de kaart liggen. Daar durf ik een eed op te doen.'
Rahmani weifelde. Het huis van een diplomaat doorzoeken was niet eenvoudig. Die rende meteen naar Buitenlandse Zaken om zijn beklag te doen. Om bij Koelikov binnen te komen, zou hij de steun moeten hebben van het allerhoogste gezag.
Toen de majoor vertrokken was, belde Rahmani het ministerie van Buitenlandse Zaken. Hij had geluk. De minister, die maandenlang bijna constant op reis was geweest, was in Bagdad. Sterker nog, hij zat achter zijn bureau. Rahmani maakte een afspraak voor de volgende morgen tien uur.

De apotheker was een vriendelijke man en hij bleef het proberen, de hele nacht. De oudste zoon kon hij niet bereiken, maar via een kennis in het leger wist hij wel een boodschap door te geven aan de jongste van de twee zoons van zijn dode vriend. Hij kreeg hem zelf niet te spreken, maar de kennis zou hem waarschuwen.
De jongste zoon kreeg het bericht in alle vroegte, op zijn basis ver van Bagdad. Zodra hij het hoorde, sprong de officier in zijn auto en ging op weg. Normaal zou hij er niet langer dan twee uur over hebben gedaan. Maar die dag, 17 februari, kostte het hem zes uur. Overal waren patrouilles en wegversperringen. Maar dankzij zijn rang kon hij voordringen, zijn pasje laten zien en doorrijden.
Bij de verwoeste bruggen hielp dat niet veel. Daar moest hij op de veerpontjes wachten. Het was al middag toen hij bij zijn ouderlijk huis in Qadisijah aankwam.
Zijn moeder wierp zich in zijn armen en huilde tegen zijn schouder. Hij vroeg haar wat er precies was gebeurd, maar ze was niet jong meer en ze werd hysterisch.
Ten slotte tilde hij haar op en droeg haar naar haar kamer. In de chaos van medicijnen die de soldaten op de grond hadden gesmeten vond hij een flesje slaappillen die zijn vader had gebruikt als hij 's winters last had van reumatiek. Hij gaf zijn moeder twee pillen en ze viel spoedig in slaap.
In de keuken vroeg hij de oude Talat om koffie voor hen beiden te zetten. Ze gingen aan de tafel zitten en de bediende beschreef wat er sinds de vorige ochtend was gebeurd. Toen hij was uitgesproken liet hij de zoon van zijn dode baas het gat in de tuin zien waar de soldaten de zak hadden gevonden.

De jongeman klom over de muur en vond de sporen van de indringer die 's nachts was gekomen om de zak in de tuin te begraven. Ten slotte ging hij weer naar binnen.

Hassan Rahmani moest wachten, wat hem niet beviel, maar tegen elven werd hij eindelijk toegelaten tot het kantoor van de minister van Buitenlandse Zaken, Tariq Aziz.

'Ik geloof dat ik het niet goed begrijp,' zei de man met het grijze haar, en hij keek Rahmani door zijn bril uilachtig aan. 'Ambassades mogen via de radio contact houden met hun hoofdsteden, en hun berichten worden altijd gecodeerd.'

'Jawel, en die berichten komen uit de kanselarij zelf. Dat hoort bij het normale diplomatieke verkeer. Maar dit is iets anders. We hebben het over een clandestiene zender, zoals spionnen die gebruiken, die versnelde berichten verstuurt naar een ontvanger die zeker niet in Moskou staat maar veel dichterbij.'

'Versnelde berichten?' vroeg Aziz.

Rahmani legde het uit.

'Toch begrijp ik het nog niet. Waarom zou een agent van de KGB – want dan moet het een KGB-operatie zijn – die berichten vanuit het huis van de eerste secretaris versturen terwijl ze het volste recht hebben om de veel sterkere zender op de ambassade te gebruiken?'

'Dat weet ik niet.'

'Kom dan maar met een betere verklaring, generaal. Hebt u enig idee wat zich buiten uw eigen kantoor afspeelt? Weet u niet dat ik gisteravond laat uit Moskou ben teruggekomen na een intensieve discussie met Gorbatsjov en zijn afgezant Jevgeny Primakov, die hier vorige week nog is geweest? Weet u niet dat ik een vredesvoorstel bij me heb dat, als de *Rais* ermee akkoord gaat – en ik zal het over twee uur aan hem voorleggen – voor de Sovjetunie voldoende reden is om de Veiligheidsraad bijeen te roepen en de Amerikanen te verbieden ons aan te vallen?

En tegen die achtergrond, juist op dit moment, vraagt u mij de Sovjetunie te vernederen door een inval te doen in het huis van hun eerste secretaris? Bent u niet goed bij uw hoofd?'

En daarmee was alles gezegd. Woedend maar machteloos vertrok Hassan Rahmani van het ministerie. Maar één ding had Tariq Aziz hem niet verboden. Binnen zijn eigen muren was Koelikov misschien onaantastbaar, en in zijn auto was hij veilig, maar de straat was van iedereen.

'Omsingel dat huis,' beval Rahmani zijn mensen toen hij terugkwam op kantoor. 'Heel discreet en onopvallend, maar ik wil dat die villa vierentwintig uur per etmaal in de gaten wordt gehouden. En alle bezoekers moeten worden geschaduwd.'

Tegen de ochtend hadden de teams hun posities ingenomen. Ze zaten in geparkeerde auto's onder de bomen, om alle hoeken van Koelikovs villa en beide kanten van de straat te kunnen zien. Andere agenten, wat verder weg, hielden via de radio contact en zouden eventuele bezoekers melden en iedereen schaduwen die het huis verliet.

De jongste zoon zat in de eetkamer van zijn ouderlijk huis en staarde naar de lange canvaszak met het lichaam van zijn vader. Hij liet de tranen over zijn gezicht stromen en natte plekken vormen op het jasje van zijn uniform. Hij dacht terug aan de goede tijden, lang geleden, toen zijn vader nog een welvarende arts was geweest, met een grote praktijk, en zelfs sommige gezinnen van de Britse gemeenschap als patiënten had gehad, nadat hij daar was geïntroduceerd door zijn vriend Nigel Martin.
Hij dacht aan de keren dat hij en zijn broer in de tuin van de Martins hadden gespeeld, met Mike en Terry, en hij vroeg zich af wat er van hen geworden was.
Na een uurtje zag hij dat sommige vlekken op het canvas groter leken te worden. Hij stond op en liep naar de deur.
'Talat?'
'Jongeheer?'
'Wil je een schaar en een keukenmes voor me pakken?'
In zijn eentje knipte kolonel Osman Badri de canvaszak open, van onderen en langs de zijkant. Toen trok hij de bovenkant van de zak los en vouwde die terug. Het lichaam van zijn vader was naakt.
Volgens de traditie was dit vrouwenwerk, maar dit was geen taak voor zijn moeder. Osman vroeg om water en verband, waste het verminkte lichaam, verbond de gebroken voeten, zwachtelde de verbrijzelde benen en bedekte de zwartgeblakerde genitaliën. Hij huilde onder het werk, en door het huilen werd hij een ander mens.
Toen de avond begon te vallen belde hij de imam van de Alwazia-begraafplaats in Risafa en regelde de begrafenis voor de volgende morgen.

Mike Martin was de zondagochtend van de 17e februari op zijn fiets de stad in geweest om groente te kopen en de drie muren op krijttekens te controleren. Even voor twaalf uur was hij weer bij de villa terug. 's Middags had hij het druk met de tuin. Koelikov, die geen christen of moslim was en dus niet de islamitische vrijdag of de christelijke zondag als rustdag vierde, was met een verkoudheid thuisgebleven en klaagde over de toestand van zijn rozen. Terwijl Martin met de bloembedden bezig was, namen de agenten van de Mukhabarat onopvallend hun plaatsen in aan de andere kant van de muur. Jericho, redeneerde hij, zou de komende twee dagen nog geen nieuws kunnen hebben. Hij zou pas de volgende avond opnieuw naar krijttekens gaan kijken.

De begrafenis van dr. Badri vond plaats op Alwazia, een paar minuten over negen. Het was een drukke tijd voor de begraafplaatsen van Bagdad en de imam had veel te doen. Een paar dagen eerder hadden de Amerikanen een openbare schuilkelder gebombardeerd, waarbij meer dan driehonderd doden waren gevallen. De emoties liepen hoog op. Enkele nabestaanden van een andere begrafenis vroegen de kolonel of zijn familielid bij een Amerikaans bombardement was gedood. Hij antwoordde kortaf dat zijn vader een natuurlijke dood was gestorven.

Volgens het islamitische gebruik worden de overledenen al kort na hun dood begraven. Er was geen houten kist zoals in de christelijke traditie. Het lichaam was in doeken gewikkeld. De apotheker was er, om mevrouw Badri te steunen, en na de korte ceremonie vertrokken ze allen.

Kolonel Badri had bijna het hek van de begraafplaats bereikt toen hij zijn naam hoorde roepen. Een paar meter verderop stond een limousine met donkere ruiten. Het raampje van het achterportier was half naar beneden gedraaid. De stem riep hem weer.

Kolonel Badri vroeg de apotheker om zijn moeder naar huis te brengen in Qadisijah. Hij zou hen achterna komen. Toen ze waren vertrokken, liep hij naar de auto.

'Stapt u even in, kolonel, wij moeten samen praten,' zei de stem.

Badri opende het portier en keek naar binnen. De enige passagier was opzij geschoven om plaats te maken. Badri had vaag het idee dat hij het gezicht van de man kende. Hij had hem weleens eerder gezien. Hij stapte in en sloot het portier. De man in het donkergrijze pak drukte op een knop en het raampje ging dicht. De geluiden van de straat verstomden.

'U hebt zojuist uw vader begraven.'

'Ja.' Wie was die man? Waarom kon hij dat gezicht niet plaatsen?

'Hij is een gruwelijke dood gestorven. Als ik het op tijd had geweten, had ik misschien nog kunnen ingrijpen. Maar ik hoorde het te laat.'

Osman Badri had het gevoel of hij een klap in zijn maag kreeg. Opeens wist hij met wie hij sprak, een man die hem twee jaar geleden was aangewezen op een militaire receptie.

'Ik zal u iets zeggen, kolonel, waardoor mij een nog gruwelijker dood dan uw vader zou wachten als u er ooit met iemand over zou spreken.'

Dat kon maar één ding betekenen, dacht Badri. Verraad.

'Ooit,' zei de man zacht, 'hield ik van de *Rais*.'

'Ik ook,' zei Badri.

'Maar dingen veranderen. Hij is krankzinnig geworden. In zijn waanzin stapelt hij de ene wreedheid op de andere. Hij moet worden tegengehouden. U hebt natuurlijk gehoord van de Qa'ala.'

Weer was Badri verbaasd, deze keer over de onverwachte wending van het gesprek.

'Natuurlijk. Ik heb het gebouwd.'

'Precies. En weet u ook wat daar nu verborgen ligt?'

'Nee.'

De hoge officier vertelde het hem.

'Dat kan hij niet menen,' zei Badri.

'Hij meent het serieus. Hij wil het tegen de Amerikanen gebruiken. Dat is misschien onze zaak niet. Maar Amerika zal op dezelfde manier terugslaan. Er zal hier geen steen op de andere blijven. Alleen de *Rais* zal overleven. Wilt u daar deel aan hebben?'

Kolonel Badri dacht aan het lichaam op de begraafplaats, dat de grafdelvers nu met droge aarde bedekten.

'Wat wilt u van me?'

'Vertel me over de Qa'ala.'

'Waarom?'

'Dan zullen de Amerikanen het vernietigen.'

'Kunt u die informatie aan hen doorgeven?'

'Er zijn manieren, gelooft u me. De Qa'ala...'

En dus vertelde kolonel Osman Badri, de jonge ingenieur die zo graag mooie gebouwen had willen ontwerpen die de eeuwen zouden doorstaan, zoals zijn voorouders hadden gedaan, alles wat hij wist aan de man met de codenaam Jericho.

'En de coördinaten?'

Die gaf Badri hem ook.

'Ga terug naar uw post, kolonel. Er zal u niets gebeuren.'

Kolonel Badri stapte uit de auto en vertrok. Hij voelde zijn maag omdraaien. Hij was geen honderd meter verder toen hij zich afvroeg wat hij in godsnaam had gedaan. Opeens wilde hij met zijn broer praten, zijn oudere broer die altijd zijn hoofd koel hield en altijd verstandiger was.

De man die het Mossad-team de verspieder noemde, kwam die maandag weer in Wenen aan, nadat hij uit Tel Aviv was ontboden. Weer arriveerde hij als een invloedrijk advocaat uit New York, met alle noodzakelijke papieren om dat te bewijzen.

De echte advocaat was inmiddels van vakantie terug, maar de kans dat Herr Gemütlich, die een hekel had aan de telefoon en de fax, in New York navraag zou doen, was heel kein. Dat risico durfde de Mossad wel te nemen.

411

De verspieder nam weer een kamer in het Sheraton en schreef een persoonlijke brief aan Herr Gemütlich. Hij verontschuldigde zich opnieuw voor zijn onaangekondigde komst naar de Weense hoofdstad, maar vertelde erbij dat hij in het gezelschap was van de accountant van de firma, en dat zij graag de eerste grote storting wilden doen uit naam van hun cliënt.

De brief werd die middag met de hand bezorgd en de volgende morgen arriveerde het antwoord bij het hotel. Gemütlich stelde voor elkaar om tien uur 's ochtends te ontmoeten.

De verspieder had inderdaad gezelschap. De man die hij bij zich had stond eenvoudig bekend als de Kraker, want dat was zijn specialiteit.

Niet alleen beschikt de Mossad in Tel Aviv over een bijna unieke verzameling namaakfirma's, valse paspoorten, briefpapier en alle andere middelen tot bedrog, maar het belangrijkst zijn nog altijd de brandkastkrakers en slotensmeden. De Mossad staat er in het inlichtingenwereldje om bekend dat ze overal kunnen inbreken. Op dat terrein kan niemand aan hen tippen. Als er een Neviot-team bij Watergate betrokken was geweest, had niemand er ooit iets van geweten.

Britse slotenfabrikanten hebben de gewoonte een nieuw produkt aan de SIS te laten zien voor commentaar. Century House gaf het produkt dan aan de Mossad door, die het terugstuurde met de opmerking dat het niet te kraken was. Na een tijdje ontdekte de SIS dat ze door de Mossad werden belazerd.

De volgende keer dat een Britse slotenfabrikant een briljante nieuwe ontdekking had gedaan, vroeg Century House om een iets simpeler exemplaar voor onderzoek. Dat stuurden ze naar Tel Aviv. Het slot werd door de Mossad gekraakt en teruggestuurd als 'absoluut veilig'. Maar het was het oorspronkelijke slot dat de fabrikant op de markt bracht.

Dat leidde een jaar later tot een pijnlijk incident toen een Mossad-specialist drie uur zwetend en vloekend bezig was met zo'n slot in de gang van een kantoorgebouw in een Europese hoofdstad, voordat hij ziedend van woede weer naar buiten kwam. Sindsdien testen de Britten hun eigen sloten en mag de Mossad het zelf uitzoeken.

De slotensmid die naar Wenen kwam was niet de allerbeste maar de op één na beste. Daar was een reden voor. Hij had iets wat de beste slotensmid niet had.

's Avonds kreeg de jongeman zes uur lang college van Gidi Barzilai over het 18e-eeuwse handwerk van de Duits-Franse schrijnwerker Riesener. Daarna gaf de verspieder hem een uitgebreide beschrijving van de indeling van de Winkler Bank. Ten slotte bracht het Neviot-team hem op de hoogte van de routine van de nachtwaker, afgeleid uit de momenten dat in de loop van de nacht op verschillende plaatsen in de bank het licht werd aan- en uitgedaan.

Diezelfde maandag wachtte Mike Martin tot vijf uur 's middags voordat hij met zijn rammelende fiets over het grind naar het tuinpoortje liep en vertrok.

Hij stapte op en wilde naar de dichtstbijzijnde veerpont over de rivier rijden, waar de Jumhurijabrug had gelegen voordat de Tornado's zich erover hadden ontfermd.

Hij sloeg de hoek om, buiten het zicht van de villa, en ontdekte de eerste auto. Toen de tweede, verderop. Toen er twee mannen uit de tweede auto kwamen en midden op de weg bleven staan, voelde hij zijn maag omdraaien. Hij waagde een blik over zijn schouder. De twee mannen uit de voorste auto hadden de terugweg geblokkeerd. In het besef dat het allemaal voorbij was, fietste hij door. Er zat niets anders op. Een van de mannen wees naar de rand van de straat.

'Hé, jij daar!' riep hij. 'Kom eens hier.'

Martin stopte onder de bomen. Er doken drie soldaten op die hun geweren op hem richtten. Langzaam stak hij zijn handen in de lucht.

Die middag in Riyad hadden de Britse en Amerikaanse ambassadeur een ontmoeting, ogenschijnlijk informeel, om naar goed Engels gebruik samen thee te drinken. Andere gasten op het gazon van de Britse ambassade waren Chip Barber, zogenaamd als medewerker van het Amerikaanse gezantschap, en Steve Laing, die voor de culturele afdeling werkte als iemand ernaar vroeg. Een derde aanwezige, heel even van zijn ondergrondse werk verlost, was generaal Norman Schwarzkopf.

Al snel hadden de vijf mannen zich in een hoek van het grasveld teruggetrokken met een kop thee. Het was zoveel eenvoudiger als iedereen van elkaar wist wat voor werk hij deed.

Alle gasten praatten uitsluitend over de naderende grondoorlog, maar deze mannen wisten veel meer dan de rest, zoals de details van het vredesplan dat Tariq Aziz die dag aan Saddam Hoessein zou voorleggen, het plan waarmee hij uit Moskou was teruggekomen na zijn gesprekken met Mikhail Gorbatsjov. Een zorgelijke zaak, om verschillende redenen.

Generaal Schwarzkopf had die ochtend al een suggestie uit Washington verworpen om eerder aan te vallen dan de bedoeling was. Het Russische vredesplan riep op tot een staakt-het-vuren en de Iraakse terugtocht uit Koeweit, met ingang van de volgende dag.

Washington had die bijzonderheden niet van Bagdad maar van Moskou gehoord. Het Witte Huis had meteen geantwoord dat het plan positieve punten bevatte maar de belangrijkste kwesties omzeilde. Er werd niet gezegd dat Irak zijn aanspraken op Koeweit definitief moest opgeven. Er werd geen rekening gehouden met de onvoorstelbare schade in Koeweit: de vijfhonderd oliebranden, de miljoenen tonnen ruwe olie die de Golf in stroomden en het water vergiftigden, de tweehonderd geëxecuteerde Koeweiti's, de plundering van Koeweit Stad.

'Ik hoor van Colin Powell,' zei de generaal, 'dat Buitenlandse Zaken een veel hardere opstelling wil. Zij eisen een onvoorwaardelijke overgave.'

'Dat is waar,' mompelde de Amerikaanse ambassadeur.

'Daarom heb ik gezegd dat ze een arabist moesten raadplegen,' vervolgde de generaal.

'Juist,' zei de Britse ambassadeur. 'En waarom, als ik vragen mag?'

De twee ambassadeurs waren ervaren diplomaten die al jaren in het Midden-Oosten werkten. Ze waren *allebei* arabist.

'Omdat zo'n ultimatum bij Arabieren niet werkt,' antwoordde de opperbevelhebber. 'Dan sterven ze nog liever.'

Er viel een stilte. De ambassadeurs keken of ze een spoor van ironie op het onschuldige gezicht van de generaal konden bespeuren.

De twee inlichtingenofficieren zeiden niets, maar ze dachten allebei hetzelfde. De spijker op de kop, generaal.

'Je komt van het huis van de Rus.'

Het was een constatering, geen vraag. De man van de contraspionagedienst was in burger, maar hij was duidelijk een officier.

'Ja, *bey.*'

'Je papieren.'

Martin zocht in de zakken van zijn *disj-dasj* en toonde zijn pasje en de vuile, verfomfaaide brief die hij van eerste secretaris Koelikov had gekregen. De officier bestudeerde het pasje, vergeleek de foto met het gezicht en las toen de brief.

De Israëlische vervalsers hadden hun werk goed gedaan. Het simpele, stoppelige gezicht van Mahmoud Al-Khouri keek de officier van achter het groezelige plastic aan.

'Fouilleer hem,' beval de officier.

De andere agent in burger liet zijn handen over Martins lichaam onder de *disj-dasj* glijden en schudde toen zijn hoofd. Geen wapens.

'En zijn zakken.'

Uit Martins zakken kwamen een paar dinarbiljetten, wat munten, een pennemes, enkele kleurkrijtjes en een plastic envelop. De officier hield hem omhoog.

'Wat is dat?'

'De ongelovige had hem weggegooid. Ik bewaar er mijn tabak in.'

'Er zit geen tabak in.'

'Nee, *bey,* ik heb niets meer. Ik wil op de markt wat kopen als het lukt.'

'En noem me geen *bey.* Dat doen we sinds de Turken al niet meer. Waar kom je vandaan?'

Martin noemde de naam van het kleine dorp in het noorden. 'Het is bekend om zijn meloenen,' voegde hij er behulpzaam aan toe.

'Hou je kop over die vervloekte meloenen,' snauwde de officier, die sterk de indruk had dat zijn soldaten onderdrukt stonden te grijnzen.

Een grote limousine verscheen aan het andere eind van de straat en bleef op tweehonderd meter afstand staan. De lagere officier stootte zijn chef aan en knikte. De andere man keek om en zei tegen Martin: 'Wacht hier.'

Hij liep naar de grote auto en boog zich naar het achterraampje toe.

'Wie heb je daar?' vroeg Hassan Rahmani.

'De tuinman, generaal. Hij werkt daar. Hij houdt de rozen bij, hij harkt het grind en hij doet boodschappen voor de kokkin.'

'Slim?'

'Nee, heel onnozel. Een boer uit een of ander meloenendorp in het noorden.'

Rahmani dacht na. Als hij de tuinman zou aanhouden, zouden de Russen zich afvragen waarom hij niet was teruggekomen. Dat zou argwaan wekken. Hij hoopte dat hij alsnog toestemming voor een inval zou krijgen als het Russische vredesplan was mislukt. Maar als hij de tuinman liet gaan, zou de man zijn werkgevers kunnen waarschuwen. In Rahmani's ervaring was er maar één taal die iedere arme Irakees goed begreep. Hij pakte zijn portefeuille en haalde er een biljet van honderd dinar uit.

'Geef hem die maar. Zeg dat hij zijn boodschappen doet en weer terugkomt. Daarna moet hij goed opletten of hij iemand met een grote zilveren paraplu ziet. Als hij ons niet verraadt en morgen komt vertellen wat hij heeft gezien, krijgt hij een beloning. Als hij de Russen waarschuwt, lever ik hem uit aan de AMAM.'

'Jawel, generaal.'

De officier pakte het geld aan, liep terug en vertelde de tuinman wat hij moest doen. De man keek hem verbaasd aan.

'Een paraplu, *sajidi*?'

'Ja, een grote zilveren paraplu, of misschien zwart, die naar de hemel wijst. Heb je die daar ooit gezien?'

'Nee, *sajidi*,' zei de man droevig. 'Als het regent, vluchten ze allemaal naar binnen.

'Bij Allah de Grote!' mompelde de officier. 'Het is niet tegen de regen, stuk onbenul, maar om berichten te verzenden.'

'Een paraplu die berichten verzendt,' herhaalde de tuinman langzaam. 'Ik zal erop letten, *sajidi*.'

'Ga nou maar,' zei de officier vermoeid, 'en vertel niemand wat je hier hebt gezien.'

Martin stapte weer op zijn fiets en reed langs de limousine. Rahmani liet zich onderuit zakken. Die boer hoefde het gezicht van de chef van de Iraakse contraspionagedienst niet te zien.

Om zeven uur zag Martin het krijtteken en om negen uur had hij het bericht opgehaald. Hij las het bij het licht dat door een raam van een café viel waar een petroleumlamp brandde, want er was geen stroom meer. Toen hij de tekst had gelezen, floot hij tussen zijn tanden, vouwde het briefje zo klein mogelijk op en verborg het in zijn onderbroek.

Hij peinsde er niet over om naar de villa terug te gaan. Ze hadden de zender

416

opgespoord en het was veel te gevaarlijk om nog een boodschap te versturen. Hij dacht aan het busstation, maar daar zwierven patrouilles van het leger en de AMAM rond, op zoek naar deserteurs.

Daarom reed hij naar de fruitmarkt van Kasra, waar hij een vrachtwagenchauffeur vond die naar het westen moest. De man ging niet veel verder dan Habbanijah en voor twintig dinar wilde hij wel een passagier meenemen.

Veel chauffeurs reden liever 's nachts, omdat ze dachten dat de Zonen van de Honden in hun vliegtuigen hen dan niet konden zien – zich er niet van bewust dat aftandse groentewagens niet generaal Horners eerste zorg waren, overdag of 's nachts.

Ze reden door de donkere nacht bij het licht van koplampen die niet meer licht verspreidden dan een kaars, en tegen de ochtend werd Martin afgezet langs de weg ten westen van het Habbanijahmeer, waar de chauffeur afsloeg naar de welvarende boerderijen in het bovendal van de Eufraat.

Twee keer waren ze onderweg aangehouden door patrouilles. Martin had zijn pasje laten zien en de Russische brief, en erbij gezegd dat hij als tuinman voor de ongelovige had gewerkt, maar dat ze nu naar huis gingen en hem hadden ontslagen. Hij hield een klaagzang over de manier waarop ze hem hadden behandeld, totdat de ongeduldige soldaten hem de mond snoerden en de vrachtwagen lieten gaan.

Die avond bevond Osman Badri zich dicht bij Mike Martin in de buurt. Hij reed voor hem uit, dezelfde kant uit, op weg naar de vliegbasis waar zijn oudere broer Abdelkarim squadron-commandant was.

In de jaren tachtig had het Belgische bedrijf Sixco acht zwaar beveiligde vliegbases in Irak aangelegd om de elite van de Iraakse jager-squadrons onder te brengen.

Bijna alles bevond zich ondergronds: de barakken, de hangars, de brandstofdepots, de munitievoorraden, de werkplaatsen, de instructieruimten, de bemanningsverblijven en de grote dieselgeneratoren die de stroom leverden.

Alleen de startbanen, in totaal zo'n 3000 meter lang, lagen boven de grond. Maar omdat er geen gebouwen of hangars te zien waren, hielden de geallieerden ze voor 'kale' vliegvelden, net als Al Kharz in Saoedi-Arabië, voordat de Amerikanen zich daar legerden.

Een nadere inspectie zou de één meter dikke betonnen deuren bij de afritten aan het eind van de startbanen aan het licht hebben gebracht. Ieder van deze bases was vijf kilometer in het vierkant en werd omringd door prikkeldraad. Maar net als Tarmijah leken de Sixco-bases inactief en werden dus met rust gelaten.

De piloten kregen ondergronds hun instructies, stapten dan in hun cockpit en startten hun motoren. Zware muren beschermden de rest van de basis tegen het gebulder, en de uitlaatgassen werden afgevoerd naar buiten, waar ze zich vermengden met de hete woestijnlucht.

Pas als de motoren op toeren waren, werden de deuren geopend, stormden de jagers op volle snelheid naar buiten en waren binnen enkele seconden in de lucht. Als de AWACS-toestellen ze in de gaten kregen, leken ze uit het niets opgedoken. De geallieerden veronderstelden dat ze heel laag hadden gevlogen en ergens anders vandaan kwamen.

Kolonel Abdelkarim Badri was gestationeerd op een van de Sixco-bases, alleen bekend als KM 160, omdat de basis aan de weg van Bagdad naar Ar Rutbah lag, 160 km ten westen van de hoofdstad.

Kort na zonsondergang meldde zijn jongere broer zich bij het wachthuisje in de prikkeldraadomheining. Vanwege zijn rang werd de squadron-commandant meteen gebeld, en even later verscheen een jeep in de verlaten woestijn, ogenschijnlijk uit het niets.

Een jonge luchtmachtluitenant nam de bezoeker mee. Via een smalle, verborgen afrit daalde de jeep naar het ondergrondse complex af.

De luitenant liet de wagen op een parkeerterrein achter en ging Badri voor door een paar lange stenen gangen, langs holle spelonken waar mecaniciens aan de MiG-29's sleutelden. De lucht was zuiver en gefilterd, en overal klonk het zoemen van generatoren.

Ten slotte bereikten ze de officiersverblijven. De luitenant klopte op een deur. Een stem riep 'Binnen!' en de luitenant opende de deur van het appartement van de commandant.

Abdelkarim stond op en de twee broers omhelsden elkaar. De oudste van de twee was zevenendertig, en ook kolonel. Hij was een donkere, knappe man met een dun snorretje. Hij was nog altijd vrijgezel, maar het ontbrak hem niet aan vrouwelijke belangstelling. Zijn knappe kop, zijn ironische houding, zijn mooie uniform en de piloten-wings zorgden daar wel voor. En het was geen schijn. Zijn generaals gaven toe dat hij de beste jagerpiloot in de luchtmacht was, en de Russen die hem hadden opgeleid in het beste toestel van de Sovjetvloot, de supersonische MiG-29 Fulcrum, waren het daarmee eens.

'Mijn broer! Wat brengt je hier?' vroeg hij.

Toen Osman ging zitten en een kop versgezette koffie had gekregen, nam hij zijn oudere broer aandachtig op. Abdelkarim had lijnen om zijn mond en een vermoeide blik in zijn ogen die Osman nog niet eerder had gezien.

Abdelkarim was geen dwaas en geen lafaard. Hij had acht missies tegen de Amerikanen en de Britten gevlogen. En hij was acht keer teruggekeerd – op het nippertje. Hij had van nabij meegemaakt dat zijn beste collega's neerstortten of door Sparrows en Sidewinders aan flarden werden geschoten, en hij had er zelf vier ontweken.

Al na zijn eerste poging om de Amerikaanse jachtbommenwerpers te onderscheppen had hij de zinloosheid daarvan ingezien. De Iraakse piloten hadden geen begeleiding en geen informatie waar de vijandelijke toestellen zich bevonden, hoeveel het er waren, van welk type, hoe hoog ze vlogen of waarheen ze onderweg waren. De Iraakse radar was vernietigd, de commandocentra verwoest en de piloten moesten zich zelf maar zien te redden.

Erger nog, met hun AWACS konden de Amerikanen de Iraakse vliegtuigen al signaleren voordat ze driehonderd meter van de grond waren. Zo konden ze hun piloten de beste aanvalsposities wijzen. Voor de Irakezen stond iedere missie bijna gelijk aan een zelfmoordactie.

Maar daar zei hij nu niets over. Met een geforceerd lachje vroeg hij wat zijn broer hem te vertellen had. Toen hij het hoorde, verdween ook dat lachje.

Osman beschreef de gebeurtenissen van de afgelopen zestig uur – de komst van de AMAM-troepen in de vroege ochtend, de huiszoeking, de vondst in de tuin, de klappen die hun moeder en Talat hadden gekregen en ten slotte de arrestatie van hun vader. Hij vertelde dat hun buurman, de apotheker, hem na veel moeite had bereikt en hoe hij na zijn thuiskomst het lichaam van hun vader op de eettafel had aangetroffen.

Abdelkarims mond verstrakte toen Osman beschreef wat hij had gevonden toen hij de zak opensneed. Hij besloot met de begrafenis van hun vader, diezelfde ochtend.

De oudere broer boog zich naar voren toen Osman vertelde dat hij bij het kerkhof was aangehouden en waarover hij had gesproken met de man in de limousine.

'Heb je hem dat allemaal verteld?' vroeg hij toen zijn broer was uitgesproken.

'Ja.'

'En is het waar? Heb jij echt die Qa'ala, die Vesting, gebouwd?'

'Ja.'

'En je hebt hem de plaats genoemd, zodat hij de Amerikanen kan inlichten?'

'Ja. Was dat verkeerd?'

Abdelkarim dacht een tijdje na.

'Hoeveel mensen in Irak zijn hiervan op de hoogte?'

'Zes,' zei Osman.

'Noem ze eens.'

'De *Rais* zelf, Hoessein Kamil, die voor het geld en de mankracht heeft gezorgd, Amer Saadi, die verantwoordelijk was voor de technische kennis, generaal Ridha, die de artillerie moest leveren en generaal Musuli van de genie, die mij voor het karwei heeft aanbevolen. En ikzelf. Ik heb het gebouwd.'

'En de helikopterpiloten die de bezoekers brengen?'

'Ze kennen wel de richting, anders kunnen ze er niet komen. Maar ze weten niet wat het precies is. En ze worden ergens op een basis apart gehouden. Ik weet niet waar.'

'Hoeveel bezoekers kennen de plaats?'

'Niemand. Ze worden allemaal geblinddoekt als ze opstijgen.'

'Als de Amerikanen de Qubth-ut-Allah zouden vernietigen, wie zal de AMAM dan verdenken? De *Rais*, de ministers, de generaals... of jou?'

Osman steunde zijn hoofd in zijn handen. 'Wat heb ik gedaan?' kreunde hij.

'Ik vrees, broertje, dat je ons allemaal in het verderf hebt gestort.'

De twee mannen kenden de regels. Voor verraad eiste de president niet één offer, maar het uitroeien van drie hele generaties: vaders en ooms, zodat er geen besmet zaad meer was, broers om dezelfde reden, en zoons en neven zodat er niemand kon opgroeien om een vete tegen hem te beginnen. Osman Badri begon zachtjes te huilen.

Abdelkarim stond op, trok Osman overeind en omhelsde hem.

'Je hebt het goed gedaan, broer. Het was de juiste beslissing. Maar nu moeten we proberen hier weg te komen.'

Hij keek op zijn horloge. Het was acht uur.

'Er zijn geen openbare telefoonlijnen meer van hier naar Bagdad,' zei hij. 'Alleen ondergrondse lijnen naar de mensen van Defensie, in hun bunkers. Maar dit bericht is niet voor hen. Hoeveel tijd heb je nodig om terug naar huis te rijden?'

'Drie, misschien vier uur,' zei Osman.

'Ik geef je acht uur, heen en terug. Zeg tegen moeder dat ze alles van waarde in vaders auto legt. Ze kan wel rijden, maar niet erg goed. Laat zij Talat maar meenemen en naar Talats dorp rijden. Daar kan ze zich schuilhouden bij zijn stam totdat wij contact met haar opnemen. Duidelijk?'

'Ja. Morgenochtend ben ik weer terug. Waarom?'

'Zorg dat je er vóór het ochtendgloren bent. Morgen moet ik een groep MiG's naar Iran brengen. Er zijn al andere toestellen vertrokken. Het is een plan van de *Rais* om zijn beste jachtvliegtuigen te redden. Krankzinnig natuurlijk, maar misschien kan het ons leven redden. Jij gaat met mij mee.'

'Ik dacht dat de MiG-29 een éénzitter was.'

'Ik heb een trainingstoestel met twee plaatsen. Het UB-model. Je krijgt het uniform van een luchtmachtofficier. Als het meezit, moet het lukken. Ga nu.'

Mike Martin liep dezelfde avond langs de weg van Ar Rutbah naar het westen toen de auto van Osman Badri hem met hoge snelheid passeerde, terug naar Bagdad. Ze namen geen notitie van elkaar. Martin was op weg naar de volgende veerpont, vijfentwintig kilometer verderop. Daar zouden de trucks moeten wachten en had hij meer kans om een chauffeur te vinden die hem voor geld wilde meenemen.

In de kleine uurtjes van de ochtend vond hij een vrachtwagen, maar die bracht hem niet verder dan een eindje voorbij Muhammadi. Daar moest hij weer wachten. Om drie uur kwam de auto van kolonel Badri weer langs, de andere kant op. Martin hield hem niet aan. De bestuurder had duidelijk haast. Tegen de ochtend kwam er een truck uit een zijweg, die voor hem stopte. Weer betaalde hij de chauffeur uit zijn slinkende voorraad dinars, degene dankbaar die hem in Mansour het geld gegeven had. Over een paar uur zou de Russische huishouding zich wel beklagen dat ze hun tuinman kwijt waren.

Als het schuurtje werd doorzocht, zouden ze het schrijfblok onder de matras ontdekken – nogal vreemd voor een analfabeet – en bij een grondig onderzoek zou ook de zender onder de tegels aan het licht komen. Tegen de middag zou de jacht in volle gang zijn, eerst in Bagdad maar later ook in de omgeving. Hij moest dus proberen om vannacht al de woestijn te bereiken, zo ver mogelijk in de richting van de grens.

De vrachtwagen die hem had meegenomen was KM 160 al gepasseerd toen de groep MiG-29's opsteeg.

Osman Badri was doodsbang. Hij hield niet van vliegen. In de ondergrondse spelonken van de basis had hij zich afzijdig gehouden toen zijn broer de vier jonge piloten van de andere toestellen hun instructies gaf. De meesten van Abdelkarims leeftijdgenoten waren gesneuveld en deze jochies, ruim tien jaar jonger dan hij, kwamen pas van de opleiding. Maar ze luisterden goed naar hun squadron-commandant en knikten begrijpend.

In de MiG, zelfs met de cockpit dicht, was het gebulder van de motoren oorverdovend toen de twee Russische RD-33 turbofans naar hun maximale 'droge' vermogen accelereerden. Ineengedoken op de stoel achter zijn broer zag Osman de grote deuren aan hun hydraulische stangen openzwaaien. Een vierkantje blauwe lucht verscheen aan het einde van de tunnel. Het lawaai nam nog toe toen de piloot gas gaf en zijn nabrander inschakelde. De dubbelvinnige Russische onderscheppingsjager rukte aan zijn remmen.

Toen Abdelkarim de remmen losliet, had Osman het gevoel of hij een trap van een muilezel tegen zijn rug kreeg. De MiG sprong naar voren, de betonnen muren flitsten voorbij, de straaljager raasde over de oprit en stormde naar buiten in het eerste ochtendlicht.

Osman sloot zijn ogen en zei een schietgebedje. Het gedender van de wielen verstomde, hij leek te zweven en hij deed zijn ogen weer open. Ze waren in de lucht. De voorste MiG cirkelde laag boven KM 160 terwijl de andere vier jagers met brullende motoren uit de tunnel tevoorschijn kwamen. Daarna gingen de deuren weer dicht en leek de vliegbasis van de aardbodem verdwenen.

De UB was een trainer, en overal om hem heen zag hij metertjes, klokjes, knoppen, schakelaars, schermen en hefbomen. Tussen zijn knieën zat een dubbele stuurknuppel. Zijn broer had hem gezegd dat hij nergens aan mocht komen en dat was hij ook niet van plan.

Op een hoogte van zo'n 300 meter vormden de vijf MiG's een getrapte formatie, met de vier jonge piloten achter hun commandant. Abdelkarim zette een zuidoostelijke koers in en bleef zo laag mogelijk om niet te worden opgemerkt. Door over de zuidelijke buitenwijken van Bagdad te vliegen hoopte hij dat zijn MiG's voor de spiedende ogen van de Amerikanen verborgen zouden blijven tegen de achtergrond van industrieterreinen en andere radarbeelden.

Het was een grote gok om de radar van de AWACS boven de Golf te snel af te zijn, maar hij had geen keus. Afgezien van zijn orders had Abdelkarim Badri nu nog een extra reden om heelhuids in Iran aan te komen.

Hij had die ochtend geluk, door een van die toevalligheden die in een oorlog niet mogen voorkomen maar toch gebeuren. Aan het eind van iedere lange 'dienst' boven de Golf keerde de AWACS naar zijn basis terug om door een andere te worden vervangen. 'Volgende taxi,' heette dat. Het kwam weleens voor dat de radarcontrole dan even haperde. De lage vlucht van de MiG's over het zuiden van Bagdad en Salman Pak viel juist samen met zo'n hapering.

Door niet hoger te vliegen dan 300 meter hoopte de Iraakse piloot dat hij onder de Amerikaanse toestellen kon blijven, die meestal op zo'n 20 000 voet of nog hoger opereerden. Hij wilde de Iraakse stad Al Kut aan de noordkant passeren en vandaar zo snel mogelijk de Iraanse grens oversteken.

Die ochtend, op hetzelfde moment, had kapitein Don Walker van het 336e Tactical Fighter Squadron van Al Kharz het bevel over een groep van vier Strike Eagles ten noorden van Al Kut, die een belangrijke brug over de Tigris moesten bombarderen waar een J-STARS een colonne tanks van de Republikeinse Garde had gesignaleerd die onderweg was naar Koeweit.

Het 336e had veel nachtmissies gevlogen, maar de brug ten noorden van Al Kut was een noodgeval. Ze moesten snel ingrijpen als de Iraakse tanks die route wilden gebruiken om naar het zuiden op te rukken. De missie van die ochtend had daarom de code *'Jeremiah directs'*, wat betekende dat generaal Chuck Horner er haast mee had.

De Eagles waren bewapend met lasergeleide 2000-ponds bommen en luchtluchtraketten. Vanwege de plaats van de ophangpunten onder de vleugels van de Eagles hing de lading asymmetrisch. De bommen aan de ene kant waren zwaarder dan de Sparrow-raketten aan de andere. Dat werd een 'bastaardlast' genoemd. De automatische trimcontrole compenseerde dit, maar de meeste piloten waren niet blij met zo'n situatie als ze in een luchtgevecht verzeild raakten.

Terwijl de MiG's, die nu op 150 meter hoogte vlogen, vlak boven de grond, vanuit het westen naderden, kwamen de Eagles uit het zuiden, op 120 km afstand.

Het eerste dat Abdelkarim Badri van hun aanwezigheid merkte was een zachte pieptoon in zijn koptelefoon. Zijn broer, achter hem, wist niet wat het was, maar de piloten wel. De MiG-trainer vloog voorop, de vier andere toestellen in een losse V-formatie achter hem. Iedereen hoorde het signaal.

De pieptoon was afkomstig van hun RWR, de 'Radar Warning Receiver' of waarschuwingsradar. Het betekende dat er andere radars in de lucht actief waren.

De vier Eagles hadden hun radar in zoekmodus staan, om te zien wat er voor hen uit gebeurde. De Russische RWR's vingen de radarstralen op en waarschuwden de piloten.

De MiG's konden niets anders doen dan doorgaan. Op die geringe hoogte vlogen ze een heel eind onder de Eagles, en bovendien haaks op de geprojecteerde koers van de Amerikanen.

Op 100 km afstand werd de pieptoon nog scheller. Dat betekende dat de vijandelijke radar hen inmiddels had gesignaleerd.

Achter Don Walker zag zijn wizzo Tim Nathanson de verandering in het radarpatroon. De straal bewoog zich niet langer rustig heen en weer maar had zich op één punt geconcentreerd.

'Vijf onbekende toestellen op tien uur, beneden,' mompelde de wizzo en schakelde de IFF in. De drie andere navigators deden hetzelfde.

De 'Identification Friend or Foe' is een transponder die allle gevechtsvliegtuigen aan boord hebben. Het apparaat zendt een puls uit op bepaalde frequenties die iedere dag worden gewijzigd. Vliegtuigen van dezelfde oorlogvoerende partij vangen dit signaal op en reageren met: 'Ik ben een vriend'. Vijandelijke toestellen zwijgen. De vijf radarstipjes voor de Eagles uit, laag boven de grond, hadden vijf bevriende toestellen kunnen zijn die terugkwamen van een missie. Dat lag voor de hand. Er vlogen veel meer geallieerde dan Iraakse vliegtuigen boven de woestijn.

Nathanson zond het signaal in de modes Een, Twee en Vier. Geen reactie.

'Vijandelijke vliegtuigen,' rapporteerde hij. Don Walker schakelde zijn wapensystemen in. 'Aanvallen,' mompelde hij tegen de andere drie piloten. Toen drukte hij zijn neus omlaag en dook naar de grond.

Abdelkarim Badri was in het nadeel. Dat wist hij al vanaf het moment dat de Amerikaanse radar hem had gesignaleerd. Hij had geen IFF nodig om hem te vertellen dat dit geen Iraakse toestellen waren. Hij wist dat hij door de vijand was opgemerkt en dat zijn jonge collega's niet tegen de geallieerde piloten waren opgewassen.

Zijn nadeel was het type MiG waarin hij vloog. Het was een trainer, het enige model met twee plaatsen. Het was nooit bedoeld geweest voor een luchtgevecht.

De MiG-éénzitters hadden een groothoekradar voor hun wapens, maar de trainer alleen een afstandsradar die geen enkel nut had in een gevecht en slechts een hoek van zestig graden voor het toestel uit bestreek. Iemand had hem in het vizier, maar hij wist niet wíe.

'Wat zie je?' blafte hij tegen zijn wingman.

'Vier vijandelijke toestellen op drie uur,' hijgde de andere piloot angstig. 'Ze duiken op ons neer.'

De gok was dus mislukt. De Amerikanen vielen aan vanuit het zuiden, vastbesloten om hen uit de lucht te schieten.

'Verspreiden en duiken! Schakel je nabranders in en probeer naar Iran te komen!' riep hij.

Dat hoefde hij de jonge piloten geen twee keer te zeggen. De straalpijpen van de MiG's produceerden een spoor van vlammen toen de vier toestellen hun nabranders gebruikten. Hun snelheid werd bijna verdubbeld en ze doorbraken de geluidsbarrière.

Hoewel het veel meer brandstof kostte, konden de éénzitters hun nabranders lang genoeg gebruiken om de Amerikanen te ontlopen en Iran te bereiken. Ze hadden een voorsprong op de Eagles, die hen nooit zouden kunnen inhalen, ook al vlogen ze nu zelf ook op de nabrander.

Behalve Abdelkarim Badri. De Russische MiG-trainer had niet alleen een veel simpeler radar, maar door het extra gewicht van de leerling en zijn cockpit was de brandstofcapaciteit aanmerkelijk kleiner.

De kolonel had wel een paar lange-afstandstanks onder zijn vleugels, maar die waren niet voldoende. Hij kon vier dingen doen. Het kostte hem maar twee seconden om een beslissing te nemen.

Hij kon zijn nabrander inschakelen, de Amerikanen ontwijken en naar een Iraakse basis terugkeren waar hij vroeg of laat zou worden gearresteerd en naar de martelkamers van de AMAM zou worden afgevoerd voor een zekere dood.

Hij kon de nabrander gebruiken en doorvliegen naar Iran, maar dan zou hij vlak na de grens zijn brandstof hebben verbruikt. Zelfs als hij en zijn broer veilig uit het toestel konden springen, zouden ze terechtkomen tussen Perzische stammen die in de Iraans-Iraakse oorlog voortdurend door Iraakse piloten waren aangevallen.

Hij kon de nabrander inschakelen om aan de Eagles te ontsnappen, naar het zuiden afbuigen en boven Saoedi-Arabië uit het toestel springen om daar gevangen te worden genomen. Het kwam geen moment bij hem op dat de geallieerden hem humaan zouden behandelen.

Hij herinnerde zich een paar regels van lang geleden, regels uit een gedicht dat hij op de school van meester Hartley in Bagdad had geleerd. Tennyson? Wordsworth? Nee, Macaulay... nog iets. Een gedicht over een man tijdens zijn laatste momenten, een vers dat hij voor de klas had voorgedragen:

> *To every man upon this earth,*
> *Death cometh soon or late.*
> *And how can man die better*
> *Than facing fearful odds,*
> *For the ashes of his father*
> *And the temples of his gods?*

Kolonel Abdelkarim Badri drukte de hendel naar de nabrander toe, trok de Fulcrum omhoog in een klimmende bocht en stormde op de naderende Amerikanen af.

Zodra hij de neus opzij draaide, kwamen de vier Eagles binnen zijn radarbereik. Twee ervan waren afgebogen om de vluchtende éénzitters te achtervolgen, allemaal met ingeschakelde nabranders, allemaal sneller dan het geluid.

Maar de leider van de Amerikaanse formatie kwam recht op hem af. Badri voelde de klap toen de Fulcrum de geluidsbarrière doorbrak, stelde de stuurknuppel bij en klom naar de duikende Eagle toe.

'Jezus, hij komt frontaal op ons af,' zei Tim vanaf de achterste plaats. Walker had het al gezien. Op zijn eigen radarscherm zag hij de blips van de vier Iraakse vliegtuigen die naar Iran vluchtten en het oplichtende puntje van de eenzame vijandelijke jager die hem met grote snelheid naderde. De afstandsmeter leek wel een dolgedraaide wekker. Op een afstand van 50 km stormden ze op elkaar toe met een gezamenlijke snelheid van bijna 3500 km per uur. Hij kon de Fulcrum nog niet met het blote oog onderscheiden, maar dat zou niet lang meer duren.

In de MiG voelde kolonel Osman Badri zich volledig ontredderd. Hij begreep niets van wat er gebeurde. De schok van de ingeschakelde nabrander had hem weer een klap tegen zijn rug bezorgd, en bij de bocht van zeven G werd het hem zwart voor de ogen.

'Wat gebeurt er?' riep hij in zijn masker. Maar hij had de 'mute'-knop ingedrukt, zodat zijn broer hem niet kon horen.

Don Walker hield zijn duim boven de knoppen van zijn wapensysteem. Hij had twee mogelijkheden: de lange-afstands AIM-7 Sparrow, radargeleid door de Eagle zelf, of de AIM-9 Sidewinder, die een korter bereik had en met een hittezoeker was uitgerust.

Op 25 km afstand zag hij het vijandelijke toestel naderen, als een zwart stipje dat naar hem toe klom. Aan de dubbele vinnen herkende hij de MiG-29 Fulcrum, een van de beste onderscheppingsjagers ter wereld, in handen van een goede piloot. Walker wist niet dat hij met een onbewapende UB-trainer te maken had. Hij wist alleen dat de MiG een Russische AA-10 raket aan boord kon hebben, met een even groot bereik als zijn eigen AIM-7's. Daarom koos hij voor de Sparrow.

Van 20 km afstand lanceerde hij twee Sparrows, recht vooruit. De raketten sprintten weg, pikten de radarreflecties van de MiG op en koersten op hun doelwit af.

Abdelkarim Badri zag de lichtflitsen toen de Sparrows werden afgevuurd en wist dat hij nog maar een paar seconden te leven had tenzij hij de Amerikaan kon afschrikken. Hij tastte omlaag en haalde een schakelaar over.

Don Walker had zich vaak afgevraagd hoe het zou zijn. Nu wist hij het. Onder de vleugels van de MiG was een lichtflits te zien. Hij had het gevoel of een ijzige hand zijn ingewanden samenkneep, de sensatie van pure, onverdunde angst. De andere man had twee raketten op hem afgevuurd en hij staarde de dood recht in het gezicht.

Twee seconden nadat hij de Sparrows had gelanceerd had hij al spijt dat hij de Sidewinders niet had gebruikt. De reden was simpel. De Sidewinders konden zelf hun doelwit vinden, ook zonder de Eagle. Maar de Sparrows hadden de Eagle nodig om ze naar hun doel te leiden. Als hij nu op de vlucht sloeg, zouden de Sparrows hun 'verstand' verliezen en doelloos verder zwerven of zich in de grond boren.

Op het moment dat hij wilde vluchten, zag hij de 'raketten' van de MiG naar beneden tuimelen. Ongelovig besefte hij dat het helemaal geen wapens waren. De Irakees had hem om de tuin willen leiden door de brandstoftanks onder zijn vleugels af te werpen. De aluminiumtanks hadden de stralen van de ochtendzon weerkaatst, een lichtflits die deed denken aan de vuurstoot van een gelanceerde raket. Het was een truc. En hij, Don Walker uit Tulsa, Oklahoma, was er bijna ingetrapt.

In de MiG zag Abdelkarim Badri dat de Amerikaan zich niet liet afschrikken. Hij had blufpoker gespeeld en verloren. Achterin had Osman eindelijk de zendknop gevonden. Toen hij over zijn schouder keek, zag hij dat ze steeds hoger klommen, kilometers boven de grond.

'Waar gaan we heen?' schreeuwde hij.

Het laatste dat hij hoorde was de stem van zijn broer Abdelkarim, heel kalm: 'Vrede, mijn broer. We gaan onze vader begroeten. *Allah-o-Akhbar.*'

Op dat moment zag Walker de twee Sparrows exploderen in grote pioenen van rode vlammen, vijf kilometer bij hem vandaan. De brokstukken van de Iraakse jager tuimelden naar het landschap beneden. Hij voelde het zweet in straaltjes over zijn borst lopen.

Zijn wingman, Randy Roberts, die schuin boven en achter hem was gebleven, verscheen nu boven zijn rechter vleugeltop en stak zijn wit gehandschoende hand op, met de duim omhoog. Walker beantwoordde het gebaar en de twee andere Eagles, die hun zinloze achtervolging van de vluchtende MiG's hadden gestaakt, sloten zich weer in formatie aan. Zo vlogen ze verder naar de brug bij Al Kut.

In een luchtgevecht volgen de gebeurtenissen elkaar zo snel op dat de hele actie, vanaf het eerste vaste radarcontact tot de vernietiging van de Fulcrum, maar achtendertig seconden had geduurd.

Precies om tien uur die ochtend stapte de verspieder de Winkler Bank binnen, vergezeld door zijn 'accountant'. De jongeman had een grote attachékoffer bij zich met een bedrag van honderdduizend Amerikaanse dollars in contanten.

Het geld was een tijdelijke lening van een *sajan* uit het bankwezen, die opgelucht was toen hij hoorde dat het een tijdje bij de Winkler Bank zou staan en daarna aan hem zou worden teruggegeven.

Herr Gemütlich reageerde opgetogen toen hij het geld zag. Hij zou minder blij zijn geweest als hij had geweten dat de dollars maar de helft van de diepe koffer in beslag namen – om nog maar te zwijgen van wat er onder de dubbele bodem lag.

Met het oog op de geheimhouding werd de accountant zolang naar het kantoortje van Fräulein Hardenberg verbannen terwijl de advocaat en de bankier de codes en procedures bespraken voor het beheer van de nieuwe rekening. Toen hij terugkwam, kreeg hij een kwitantie voor het geld en tegen elf uur was alles rond. Herr Gemütlich belde de conciërge om de bezoekers weer naar de deur te brengen.

Op weg naar beneden fluisterde de accountant iets tegen de Amerikaanse advocaat, die het vertaalde voor de conciërge. De man knikte kort en liet de lift op de tussenverdieping stoppen, waar de drie mannen naar buiten stapten. De advocaat wees naar de deur van het toilet en de accountant verdween. De twee mannen bleven staan wachten.

Op dat moment ontstond er enig tumult beneden, duidelijk hoorbaar omdat de hal maar zes meter en vijftien marmeren treden bij hen vandaan was.

De conciërge mompelde een excuus en liep naar het eind van de gang om te zien wat er aan de hand was. Meteen rende hij de marmeren trap af om de zaak te regelen.

Het was een hele toestand. Op de een of andere manier waren drie ruige types, duidelijk aangeschoten, de hal binnengekomen, waar ze de receptioniste lastigvielen om geld voor nog meer drank. Later verklaarde ze dat ze de deur voor hen had geopend omdat een van hen zich voor de postbode uitgaf.

Verontwaardigd probeerde de conciërge de dronkelappen de deur uit te werken. In het tumult was het niemand opgevallen dat een van de mannen bij zijn binnenkomst een sigarettendoosje tegen de deurpost had geschoven, zodat de zelfsluitende deur niet helemaal in het slot zou vallen.

Door al het gedoe merkte ook niemand dat een vierde man op handen en knieën de lobby binnenkwam. Toen hij opstond, kreeg hij meteen gezelschap van de advocaat uit New York, die met de conciërge mee was gekomen.

Ze keken van een afstandje toe terwijl de drie zuiplappen op straat werden gezet, waar ze thuishoorden. Toen de portier zich omdraaide, zag hij dat de advocaat en de accountant al beneden waren. Met uitvoerige excuses voor het pijnlijke incident bracht hij hen naar de deur.

Buiten gekomen slaakte de accountant een zucht van verlichting. 'Dat doe ik niet graag nog een keer,' zei hij.

'Geen zorg,' zei de advocaat. 'Je hebt het uitstekend gedaan.'

Ze spraken Hebreeuws, omdat de 'accountant' geen andere talen kende. In werkelijkheid was hij een bankbediende uit Bersjeba. De enige reden waarom hij naar Wenen was gekomen, voor zijn eerste en laatste missie als geheim agent, was dat hij de tweelingbroer was van de Kraker, die nu in de donkere bezemkast op de tussenverdieping stond. Daar zou hij twaalf uur roerloos blijven staan.

Mike Martin kwam halverwege de middag in Ar Rutbah aan. Het had hem twintig uur gekost om een afstand te overbruggen waar een auto normaal zes uur over deed.

Aan de rand van de stad vond hij een herder met een kudde geiten. Tot vreugde en verbazing van de man kocht Martin met zijn laatste geld vier van de dieren voor bijna twee keer de prijs die de herder er op de markt voor zou hebben gekregen.

De geiten lieten zich gewillig meevoeren naar de woestijn, hoewel ze nu halters van touw droegen. Ze konden niet weten dat ze alleen maar een excuus vormden voor Mike Martins aanwezigheid in de woestijn ten zuiden van de weg, in de middagzon.

Zijn probleem was dat hij geen kompas meer had. Dat lag nog bij de rest van zijn spullen onder de vloer van het schuurtje in Mansour. Met behulp van de zon en zijn goedkope horloge berekende hij zo goed mogelijk de juiste richting vanaf de radiomast in de stad naar de wadi waar zijn motorfiets was begraven.

Het was een wandeling van acht kilometer. De geiten vertraagden het tempo, maar toch was hij er blij mee, want twee keer zag hij soldaten die hem vanaf de weg in de gaten hielden tot hij uit het gezicht verdwenen was. Beide keren lieten ze hem met rust.

Kort voordat de zon onderging vond hij de wadi, herkende de tekens op de nabijgelegen rotsen en rustte wat uit tot het bijna donker was. Toen begon hij te graven. De geiten slenterden tevreden weg.

De motor lag er nog, in zijn plastic zak – een slanke 125-cc Yamaha crossmotor, pikzwart, met beugels voor de extra benzinetanks. Daarnaast lag het kompas met het pistool en de munitie.

Jarenlang had de SAS de voorkeur gegeven aan de Browning 13-schots, maar ze waren juist overgestapt op de Zwitserse Sig Sauer 9-mm. Martin stak het zwaardere Zwitserse pistool in de holster aan zijn rechterheup. Nu kon hij zijn rol niet meer volhouden. Geen enkele Iraakse boer in dat gebied reed op een motor. Als hij werd aangehouden, zou hij moeten vechten.

Hij vertrok door de nacht, veel sneller dan de Landrovers op de heenweg. Met de crossmotor kon hij op de vlakke gedeelten een hoog tempo aanhouden, en bij de rotsrichels van de wadi's hield hij zijn voeten aan de grond.

Tegen middernacht vulde hij zijn tank bij, dronk wat water en at een paar K-rantsoenen uit de pakketten die in de schuilplaats waren achtergelaten. Daarna reed hij pal naar het zuiden, in de richting van de Saoedische grens.

Hij wist niet precies wanneer hij de grens zou passeren. Het was een kaal landschap van rotsen en zand, grind en steenslag, en door de zigzagkoers die hij volgde had hij geen idee hoeveel kilometer hij al had afgelegd.

Hij ging ervan uit dat hij op een gegeven moment de Tapline Road zou bereiken, de enige hoofdweg in het gebied. Dan wist hij zeker dat hij in Saoedi-Arabië was. Het terrein werd wat beter begaanbaar en hij had een snelheid van zo'n dertig kilometer toen hij de vrachtwagen zag. Als hij niet zo moe was geweest, zou hij sneller hebben gereageerd. Maar hij was half versuft van uitputting en zijn reflexen waren te traag.

Het voorwiel van zijn motor raakte de struikeldraad en hij sloeg tegen de grond. Na een paar duikelingen bleef hij op zijn rug liggen. Toen hij zijn ogen opende, zag hij iemand over zich heen gebogen staan. Het licht van sterren spiegelde in metaal.

'Bouge pas, mec.'

Geen Arabisch. Hij pijnigde zijn vermoeide hersenen. Heel lang geleden...

O ja, op Haileybury, die arme leraar die hem de geheimen van de taal van Corneille, Racine en Molière had willen bijbrengen.

429

'*Ne tirez pas,*' zei hij langzaam. '*Je suis Anglais.*'
Er zaten maar drie Britse sergeants bij het Franse Vreemdelingenlegioen en
een van hen heette McCullin.
'Meen je dat nou?' vroeg hij in het Engels. 'Loop dan maar als de bliksem
naar die rupswagen. En geef mij dat pistool als je het niet erg vindt.'
De patrouille van het Vreemdelingenlegioen bevond zich een heel eind ten
westen van haar normale positie in de geallieerde linies. Ze hielden de
Tapline Road in de gaten, op zoek naar Iraakse deserteurs. Met sergeant
McCullin als tolk vertelde Martin aan de Franse luitenant dat hij een missie
had uitgevoerd in Irak.
Dat geloofde het Legioen meteen. Missies achter de vijandelijke linies
behoorden tot hun specialiteiten. En gelukkig hadden ze een radio.

De Kraker wachtte de hele dinsdag geduldig in de donkere bezemkast. In de
loop van de middag kwamen er verscheidene mannen naar het toilet die
deden waarvoor ze gekomen waren en dan weer vertrokken. Door de muur
hoorde hij zo nu en dan de lift op en neer gaan. Hij ging op zijn koffertje zitten, met zijn rug tegen de muur en keek regelmatig op zijn lichtgevende
horloge om de tijd bij te houden.
Tussen half zes en zes uur hoorde hij het personeel langskomen op weg naar
de hal en naar huis. Om zes uur zou de nachtwaker arriveren, binnengelaten
door de conciërge, die alle namen van de vertrekkende personeelsleden op
zijn lijst had afgestreept.
Als ook de conciërge kort na zes uur was vertrokken, zou de nachtwaker de
voordeur sluiten en de alarminstallatie inschakelen. Daarna installeerde hij
zich voor de draagbare tv die hij iedere avond meenam om naar spelshows
te kijken totdat het tijd was voor zijn eerste ronde.
Volgens het Yarid-team werden zelfs de schoonmakers in de gaten gehouden. Het gewone werk – de gangen, trappen en toiletten – deden ze op
maandag-, woensdag- en vrijdagavond. Op dinsdagavond had de nachtwaker het rijk alleen. Op zaterdag kwamen ze terug om de kantoren schoon te
maken onder toezicht van de conciërge, die hen geen moment uit het oog
verloor.
De routine van de nachtwaker was steeds dezelfde. Hij maakte drie rondes
door het gebouw, om tien uur, twee uur en vijf uur 's nachts, waarbij hij alle
deuren probeerde.
Tussen het moment dat hij arriveerde en zijn eerste ronde keek hij tv en at
hij zijn meegebrachte avondeten. In de langste tussenpauze, van tien tot
twee uur, zat hij te dutten. Een wekker waarschuwde hem wanneer het twee
uur was. De Kraker wilde in die periode zijn slag slaan.
Hij had Gemütlichs kantoor al gezien. De deur was van massief hout, maar

430

gelukkig niet voorzien van een alarminstallatie. Er zat wel een alarm op het raam en hij had de vage omtrekken van twee druksensors tussen het kleed en het parket opgemerkt.

Precies om tien uur hoorde hij de lift naar boven komen, met de nachtwaker die aan zijn eerste ronde begon. Hij begon op de bovenverdieping en daalde per etage af.

Een halfuur later was de bejaarde man klaar, stak zijn hoofd om de deur van de toiletten, deed het licht aan om het versterkte en beveiligde raam te controleren, deed de deur weer dicht en liep terug naar zijn bureau in de hal om nog naar een late spelshow op de televisie te kijken.

Om kwart voor elf kwam de Kraker in het pikkedonker de wc uit en sloop de trap op naar de vierde verdieping.

De deur van Herr Gemütlichs kantoor kostte hem vijftien minuten. Er zat een insteekslot op met vier niveaus. Toen de laatste pal was weggevallen stapte hij naar binnen.

Hoewel hij een band met een klein lampje om zijn hoofd had, pakte hij een grotere zaklantaarn om de kamer te verkennen. Zo kon hij de twee druksensors ontwijken en het bureau van de onbeschermde kant naderen. Daarna deed hij de zaklantaarn weer uit en werkte verder bij het licht van het kleine lampje.

De sloten van de bovenste drie laden vormden geen probleem – koperen mechaniekjes van meer dan honderd jaar oud. Toen hij de drie laden eruit had gehaald, stak hij zijn hand in de ruimte en zocht naar een knop, een hefboom of een palletje. Niets. Pas een uur later, aan de achterkant van de derde la aan de rechterkant, vond hij het. Het was een kleine koperen hefboom van zo'n twee centimeter lang. Toen hij erop drukte, hoorde hij een zachte klik en sprong een strook fineer aan de onderkant van de ladebodem een centimeter naar voren.

Het blad dat erin zat was heel ondiep, nog geen tweeënhalve centimeter, maar voldoende voor tweeëntwintig vellen papier. Het waren kopieën van de machtigingsbrieven waarin de procedure voor de rekeningen onder het beheer van Herr Gemütlich waren vastgelegd.

De Kraker pakte zijn camera en een opvouwbaar aluminium statief met een vaste hoogte. De lens van de camera was al op die afstand ingesteld, voor een haarscherpe opname.

De bovenste brief hoorde bij de rekening die de vorige ochtend door de verspieder was geopend uit naam van zijn denkbeeldige cliënt in Amerika. De brief die hij zocht was de zevende. Het rekeningnummer kende hij al, de Mossad had er tenslotte twee jaar geld op gestort voordat de Amerikanen het overnamen.

Voor alle zekerheid fotografeerde hij alle brieven. Toen hij de *cachette* weer had gesloten, schoof hij de laden dicht, deed ze op slot, verliet de kamer en trok de deur achter zich dicht. Om tien over een stond hij weer in de bezemkast.

Toen de bank de volgende morgen openging, wachtte de Kraker eerst tot de lift een half uurtje op en neer was gegaan. Hij wist dat de conciërge de staf nooit naar boven begeleidde. De eerste bezoeker arriveerde om tien voor tien. Toen de lift voorbij was gekomen, kwam de Kraker voorzichtig uit de wc tevoorschijn, liep op zijn tenen naar het eind van de gang en wierp een blik in de hal. Het bureau van de conciërge was verlaten. Hij was naar boven met een cliënt.

De Kraker pakte een pieper en drukte twee keer op de knop. Drie seconden later werd er gebeld. De receptioniste boog zich over de intercom die met een luidspreker naast de voordeur was verbonden. 'Ja?'

'Lieferung,' klonk een blikkerige stem. Ze drukte op de zoemer, de deur ging open en een forse, montere bezorger stapte de hal binnen. Hij had een groot olieverfschilderij bij zich, in bruin papier gewikkeld, met touwen eromheen.

'Alstublieft, dame. Helemaal schoongemaakt en weer klaar om op te hangen,' zei hij.

Achter hem viel de deur dicht. Maar op het laatste moment kwam er vlak boven de grond een hand om de hoek, die een propje papier tegen de deurpost legde. Daardoor viel de deur niet in het slot.

De bezorger zette het schilderij op de rand van het bureau van de receptioniste. Het was groot – anderhalve meter bij één meter twintig. Het benam haar volledig het uitzicht op de hal.

'Maar ik weet niets over...' begon ze. De bezorger stak zijn hoofd om het schilderij heen.

'Wilt u even tekenen voor ontvangst?' vroeg hij, en hij legde een klembord met een kwitantie voor haar neer. Ze las het formulier. Op dat moment kwam de Kraker de trap af en glipte door de deur naar buiten.

'Maar hier staat Harzmann Galerie,' wees ze.

'Dat klopt. Ballgasse nummer 14.'

'Dit is nummer 8. Dit is de Winkler Bank. De galerie is verderop.'

De bebaasde verzorger maakte zijn excuses en verdween. De conciërge kwam de trap weer af en de receptioniste vertelde wat er was gebeurd. Hij snoof, ging achter zijn bureau aan de overkant zitten en verdiepte zich weer in zijn ochtendkrant.

Toen de Blackhawk-helikopter met Mike Martin om twaalf uur 's middags op het militaire vliegveld van Riyad landde, stond er een klein ontvangstcomité gereed, in gespannen afwachting. Steve Laing was erbij, en Chip Barber. Maar de man die hij niet had verwacht was zijn commandant, kolonel Bruce Craig. Terwijl Martin in Bagdad zat, had het SAS-detachement in de westelijke woestijn van Irak zich uitgebreid tot twee van de vier volledige compagnies uit Hereford. Eén was in Hereford achtergebleven als reserve, de andere was in kleinere eenheden verdeeld, voor trainingsmissies verspreid over de hele wereld.

'Heb je het, Mike?' vroeg Laing.

'Ja. Jericho's laatste bericht. Ik kon het niet via de radio verzenden.'

Hij legde in het kort uit waarom, en gaf hun het vuile velletje papier met Jericho's boodschap.

'Man, wat maakten we ons ongerust toen we je de afgelopen achtenveertig uur niet te pakken konden krijgen,' zei Barber. 'U hebt uitstekend werk geleverd, majoor.'

'Nog één ding, heren,' zei kolonel Craig. 'Als u met hem klaar bent, krijg ik dan mijn officier weer terug?'

Laing bestudeerde het bericht en probeerde het Arabisch zo goed mogelijk te ontcijferen. Hij keek op. 'Ja, natuurlijk. Met onze oprechte dank.'

'Wacht eens even,' zei Barber. 'Wat gaat u nu met hem doen, kolonel?'

'O, een brits op onze basis aan de andere kant van het vliegveld. En een hapje eten...'

'Ik heb een beter idee,' zei Barber. 'Majoor, wat dacht u van een Kansas-steak met patat, een uurtje in een marmeren badkuip en daarna een groot, zacht bed?'

'Klinkt niet slecht,' zei Martin.

'Goed. Kolonel, uw man krijgt vierentwintig uur een suite in het Hyatt, verderop langs de weg. Op onze kosten. Akkoord?'

'Oké. Dan zie ik je morgen, Mike,' zei Craig.

Tijdens het korte ritje naar het hotel tegenover het CENTAF-hoofdkwartier vertaalde Martin het bericht van Jericho voor Laing en Barber. Laing noteerde alles.

'Mooi zo,' zei Barber. 'De luchtmacht zal het zaakje wel platgooien.'

Chip Barber moest zich er persoonlijk mee bemoeien om voor een smerige Iraakse boer de beste suite van het Hyatt te regelen. Toen Martin zich had geïnstalleerd, stak de CIA-man de weg over naar het Zwarte Gat.

Martin zat een uurtje te weken in een vol, stomend bad en gebruikte de hotelspullen op de wastafel om zich te scheren en zijn haar te wassen. Toen hij uit de badkamer kwam, stonden de steak en de patat al op hem te wachten op een blad in de zitkamer.

Halverwege de maaltijd kon hij zijn ogen niet meer openhouden. Hij wankelde naar het grote zachte bed in de andere kamer en viel als een blok in slaap.

433

Terwijl hij sliep, gebeurden er een paar dingen.

In de zitkamer werden schoon ondergoed, een geperste broek, sokken, schoenen en een overhemd klaargelegd.

In Wenen verstuurde Gidi Barzilai de details en procedures van Jericho's nummerrekening naar Tel Aviv, waar een identieke brief werd opgesteld in de juiste bewoordingen.

Karim ving Edith Hardenberg op toen ze van haar werk kwam, nam haar mee voor een kop koffie en vertelde haar dat hij een weekje naar Jordanië terug moest omdat zijn moeder ziek was. Ze accepteerde zijn verhaal, hield zijn hand vast en vroeg hem zo gauw mogelijk terug te komen.

Het Zwarte Gat gaf orders aan de luchtmachtbasis van Taif waar een TR-1A spionagevliegtuig zich juist gereedmaakte voor een missie naar het uiterste noorden van Irak om nog wat foto's te maken van een groot wapencomplex bij As-Sharqat.

De piloot kreeg nieuwe coördinaten en het bevel om opnamen te maken van een heuvelachtig gebied in het noordelijke deel van de Jebal al Hamreen. Toen de squadron-commandant protesteerde tegen de onverwachte wijzigingen, kreeg hij te horen dat de orders waren voorzien van de classificatie *'Jeremiah directs'*. Dat maakte een eind aan zijn protesten.

De TR-1A vertrok een paar minuten over twee en om vier uur verschenen de opnamen op de schermen in een apart vergaderzaaltje aan het eind van een gang in het Zwarte Gat.

Het regende en er hing lage bewolking boven de Jebal, maar met zijn thermische en infraroodradar – het ASARS-2 systeem dat zich niets van wolken, regen, hagel, sneeuw of duisternis aantrekt – leverde het spionagetoestel de gevraagde beelden.

Ze werden bestudeerd door kolonel Beatty van de Amerikaanse luchtmacht en majoor Peck van de Britse RAF, de belangrijkste fotoverkenningsanalisten van het Zwarte Gat.

De voorbereidende bespreking begon om zes uur. Er waren maar acht mensen bij aanwezig. De vergadering werd voorgezeten door generaal Horners tweede man, de doortastende en joviale Buster Glosson. De twee inlichtingenofficieren, Steve Laing en Chip Barber, waren erbij omdat zij het doelwit hadden aangedragen en de achtergronden kenden. De twee analisten Beatty en Peck gaven een toelichting op hun interpretatie van de opnamen van het gebied. En dan waren er nog drie stafofficieren, twee Amerikanen en een Brit, die noteerden wat er gedaan moest worden en ervoor zouden zorgen dat dat ook gebeurde.

Kolonel Beatty begon met het belangrijkste thema van het gesprek: 'We hebben een probleem.'

'Leg maar uit,' zei de generaal.

'We hebben de coördinaten van de juiste plaats, twaalf cijfers – zes voor de lengte- en zes voor de breedtegraad. Maar het is geen SATNAV-referentie die het doelwit tot een paar vierkante meter beperkt. We praten over één vierkante kilometer. Voor alle zekerheid hebben we het gebied zelfs uitgebreid tot een vierkante mijl.'

'En?'

'Dat is het.' Kolonel Beatty wees naar de muur. Bijna de hele wand werd in beslag genomen door een sterk vergrote, scherpe foto, die door de computer was bijgewerkt. De vergroting besloeg een oppervlak van bijna twee bij twee meter. Iedereen keek ernaar.

'Ik zie niets,' zei de generaal. 'Alleen maar bergen.'

'Precies. Dat is dus het probleem. Er is niets te vinden.'

Alle aandacht richtte zich nu op de inlichtingenofficieren. Het was tenslotte hùn informatie.

'Wat zou daar moeten liggen?' vroeg de generaal langzaam.

'Een kanon,' zei Laing.

'Een kanon?'

'Het zogenaamde Babylon-kanon.'

'Ik dacht dat jullie dat al in het produktiestadium hadden onderschept.'

'Dat dachten wij ook. Maar blijkbaar is er een exemplaar door de mazen geglipt.'

'We hebben het hier al eerder over gehad. Het zou een raketbatterij moeten zijn, of een geheime basis voor jachtbommenwerpers. Een kanon kan onmogelijk zo'n grote lading afvuren.'

'Dit kanon wel, generaal. Ik heb het met Londen opgenomen. Het heeft een loop van meer dan 180 meter lang en een boring van één meter. Het kan een lading van ruim een halve ton afvuren, met een bereik van maximaal 1000 kilometer, afhankelijk van de drijfstof.'

'En wat is de afstand tot de Driehoek?'

'Ongeveer 750 kilometer. Generaal, kunnen uw jagers een granaat onderscheppen?'

'Nee.'

'Patriot-raketten?'

'Misschien, als ze op het juiste moment op de juiste plaats staan en op tijd gewaarschuwd worden. Maar ik zou er niet op rekenen.'

'Het punt is,' onderbrak kolonel Beatty hen, 'of het nu een kanon of een raketinstallatie moet zijn, het ìs er gewoon niet.'

'Ook niet ondergronds, zoals dat complex van Al-Qubai?' vroeg Barber.

'Dat was gecamoufleerd als een autosloperij,' antwoordde majoor Peck. 'Hier is helemaal niets te zien. Geen weg, geen paden, geen electriciteitskabels, geen versterkingen, geen heli-platform, geen prikkeldraad, geen wachthuisjes, alleen maar een wildernis van heuvels en lage bergen met dalen ertussen.'

'Laten we aannemen,' zei Laing defensief, 'dat ze dezelfde truck hebben toegepast als bij Tarmija, dat de afrastering een heel eind verder ligt, buiten de randen van deze foto?'

'Dat hebben we al gecontroleerd,' zei Beatty. 'We hebben tot tachtig kilometer in de omtrek gekeken. Niets te zien.'

'Misschien is het alleen gecamoufleerd en wordt het niet verdedigd,' opperde Barber.

'Uitgesloten. De Irakezen verdedigen hun belangrijke installaties *altijd*. Al was het maar tegen hun eigen mensen. En kijk hier eens.' Kolonel Beatty liep naar de foto en wees een groep hutjes aan.

'Een boerendorp, pal ernaast. Rook van houtvuurtjes, een geitenweitje, geiten die in het dal lopen te grazen. En er liggen nog twee dorpjes vlakbij.'

'Misschien hebben ze de hele berg uitgehold,' zei Laing. 'Zoals jullie met de Cheyenne Mountain hebben gedaan.'

'Dat is een serie ruimtes, tunnels en kamers achter versterkte deuren,' zei Beatty. 'We hebben het nu over een kanon van 180 meter lang. Als je dat in een berg wilt onderbrengen, stort alles in. De stootbodem en het magazijn van het kanon kunnen wel ondergronds worden verborgen, net als de ruimtes voor het personeel, maar een deel van die loop moet toch naar buiten steken. Maar je ziet niets.'

Ze tuurden allemaal weer naar de foto. Ze zagen drie heuvels en een deel van een vierde. Op de grootste van de drie waren nergens versterkte deuren of een toegangsweg te zien.

'Als dat kanon daar ergens ligt begraven,' zei Peck, 'kunnen we toch het hele gebied bombarderen – die vierkante kilometer of die vierkante mijl?'

'Goed idee,' zei Beatty. 'We kunnen de Buffs gebruiken, generaal. Dan gooien we alles plat.'

'Mag ik iets zeggen?' vroeg Barber.

'Ga uw gang,' zei generaal Glosson.

'Als ik Saddam Hoessein was, met zijn paranoia, en ik had één zo'n krachtig wapen dan zou ik een bevelhebber aanwijzen die ik vertrouwde. En ik zou hem opdracht geven dat kanon af te vuren zodra het fort werd aangevallen. Als de eerste bommen zouden vallen – en een vierkante mijl is een groot gebied – zou de rest misschien net te laat zijn.'

Generaal Glosson boog zich naar voren. 'Wat wilt u daarmee zeggen, meneer Barber?'

'Generaal, als De Vuist van God werkelijk in die heuvels begraven ligt, is hij bijzonder handig verborgen. De enige manier om het wapen met zekerheid te kunnen vernietigen is met een gerichte operatie. Eén enkel vliegtuig,

436

dat uit het niets opduikt en in één keer het doelwit raakt, zonder enige waarschuwing vooraf.'

'Ik weet niet hoe vaak ik het nog moet zeggen,' zei kolonel Beatty vermoeid, 'maar we weten niet precies waar het doelwit ligt.'

'Mijn collega bedoelt vermoedelijk dat we het doelwit eerst moeten markeren.'

'Maar dan hebben we nog een vliegtuig nodig,' wierp Peck tegen. 'Zoals de Buccaneers het doelwit voor de Tornado's markeren. Maar dan moeten ze het wel kunnen vinden.'

'Met de Scuds werkte dat goed,' zei Laing.

'Ja. Omdat de SAS de raketinstallaties aanwees. Dan konden wij ze platgooien. Maar de SAS-mensen waren dicht in de buurt, op nog geen 1000 meter afstand. Ze konden die installaties met hun verrekijkers zien,' zei Peck.

'Precies.'

Het bleef een paar seconden stil.

'Dus u wilt mannen die bergen in sturen om ons de exacte positie te kunnen wijzen, op tien meter nauwkeurig,' concludeerde generaal Glosson.

De discussie ging nog twee uur door. Maar steeds kwamen ze weer terug bij de argumenten van Steve Laing.

Eerst moest je het doelwit opsporen, dan markeren en dan vernietigen, zonder dat de Irakezen het te vroeg in de gaten kregen.

Om middernacht ging een korporaal van de RAF naar het Hyatt Hotel. Er kwam geen reactie toen hij bij de kamer aanklopte. De nachtmanager liet hem met een loper binnen. De korporaal liep naar de slaapkamer en schudde de man in de badjas bij zijn schouder.

'Wakker worden, majoor. Ze vragen of u naar de overkant komt.'

'Daar moet het verborgen liggen,' zei Mike Martin twee uur later.
'Waar dan?' vroeg kolonel Beatty oprecht nieuwsgierig.
'Ergens in dat gebied.'
In het vergaderzaaltje van het Zwarte Gat stond Martin over een tafel gebogen waarop een foto lag van een nog grotere sectie van de Jebal al Hamreen – een vierkant van acht bij acht kilometer. Hij wees met zijn vinger.
'Kijk maar naar die dorpen. Hier, hier en hier.'
'Wat is daarmee?'
'Ze zijn nep. Het zijn prachtige kopieën van bergdorpjes, compleet met boeren en herders, maar ze zijn nep.'
Kolonel Beatty keek naar de drie dorpen. Een ervan lag in een dal op achthonderd meter van de middelste van de drie bergen in het centrum van de foto. De andere twee lagen op terrassen op de berghellingen, wat verder opzij. Het waren maar gehuchten, niet groot genoeg voor een moskee. Ze hadden allemaal een grote schuur voor de opslag van winterhooi en voer, en kleinere schuren voor de schapen en de geiten. Een stuk of twaalf schamele huisjes vormden de rest van de nederzetting – lemen hutten met rieten of ijzeren daken, zoals die overal in de bergen van het Midden-Oosten te zien zijn. In de zomer lagen er meestal een paar veldjes met gewassen in de buurt, 's winters was alles kaal.
Het leven in de Iraakse bergen is 's winters hard, met zware bewolking en striemende, koude regen. Dat het overal in het Midden-Oosten altijd warm zou zijn is een wijdverbreide misvatting.
'Goed, majoor, u kent Irak. Ik niet. Waarom zijn ze nep?'
'Vanwege de voedselsituatie,' zei Martin. 'Te veel dorpen, te veel boeren, te veel geiten en schapen in een te klein gebied. Niet genoeg eten. Ze zouden verhongeren.'
'Verdomme,' vloekte Beatty uit de grond van zijn hart. 'Zo simpel!'
'Misschien,' zei Martin, 'maar het bewijst wel dat Jericho niet heeft gelogen en zich niet opnieuw heeft vergist. Als ze zoveel moeite hebben gedaan, moeten ze iets verbergen.'
Kolonel Craig, de commandant van de SAS, was ook naar de kelder gekomen. Hij had zachtjes met Steve Laing zitten praten. Nu kwam hij naar hen toe.
'Wat denk je, Mike?'

'Het moet daar ergens liggen, Bruce. Waarschijnlijk kun je het zien, vanaf 1000 meter, met een goede verrekijker.'
'Hogerhand wil er een team naartoe sturen om het te markeren. Maar jij gaat niet mee.'
'Onzin, kolonel. Het wemelt daar natuurlijk van de patrouilles. Er zijn geen wegen.'
'En? Patrouilles kun je ontlopen.'
'Maar als je er toevallig toch een tegenkomt? Niemand spreekt zo goed Arabisch als ik, dat weet u ook wel. Bovendien moeten we van grote hoogte springen. Helikopters zijn uitgesloten.'
'Je hebt voorlopig wel genoeg gedaan, heb ik begrepen.'
'Dat is gelul. Ik heb alleen maar op mijn kont gezeten. Ik heb genoeg van spionage. Ik wil echte actie. De anderen zwerven al weken door de woestijn terwijl ik een paar rozenperkjes mocht aanharken.'
Kolonel Craig trok een wenkbrauw op. Hij had Laing niet gevraagd wat Martin precies had gedaan – dat zou Laing hem toch niet hebben verteld – maar hij was verbaasd dat een van zijn beste officieren voor tuinman had moeten spelen.
'Kom maar terug naar de basis. Daar kunnen we het beter voorbereiden. Als je een goed plan opstelt, mag je het zelf uitvoeren.'

Tegen de ochtend had generaal Schwarzkopf beaamd dat er geen alternatief was en zijn toestemming gegeven. In de afgegrendelde hoek van het militaire vliegveld van Riyad waar de SAS haar hoofdkwartier had opgeslagen, legde Martin zijn ideeën aan kolonel Craig voor. Hij kreeg groen licht.
Kolonel Craig zou de actie op de grond coördineren, generaal Glosson was verantwoordelijk voor de eventuele luchtaanval.
Buster Glosson dronk die ochtend koffie met zijn vriend en chef Chuck Horner.
'Enig idee aan wie we dit kunnen toevertrouwen?' vroeg hij.
Generaal Horner dacht terug aan een zekere officier die hem twee weken eerder een bijzonder onvriendelijke opmerking had toegevoegd.
'Ja,' zei hij. 'Stuur het 336e er maar op af.'

Mike Martin had zijn discussie met kolonel Craig gewonnen door hem er – terecht – op te wijzen dat de meeste SAS-soldaten in de Golf al binnen Irak actief waren en dat hij dus de hoogste beschikbare officier was. Bovendien was hij commandant van de B-Compagnie, die op dat moment een missie in de woestijn uitvoerde onder bevel van Martins tweede man, en dat hij de enige was die vloeiend Arabisch sprak.
Maar het was toch zijn ervaring met vrije-valparachutespringen die de door-

slag gaf. Bij het 3e Bataljon van de para's had hij de speciale para-opleiding op de RAF-basis Brize Norton gevolgd en met het oefenteam gesprongen. Later had hij nog de vrije-valcursus in Netheravon gedaan en was hij uitgenodigd voor het demonstratieteam van de para's, de Red Devils, in die kringen beter bekend als de Red Freds.

De enige manier om onopgemerkt in de Iraakse bergen te infiltreren was door een sprong van grote hoogte, een zogenaamde 'HALO-drop' ('High Altitude, Low Opening'). Dat betekende dat de parachutisten op een hoogte van ruim 8000 meter uit het vliegtuig sprongen, een vrije val maakten en pas op 1200 meter hun parachutes openden. Dat was niet iets voor beginners.

Een goede voorbereiding zou minstens een week kosten, maar zoveel tijd was er niet. De enige mogelijkheid was om alle onderdelen – de sprong, de mars door het terrein en de keuze van de uitkijkposten – gelijktijdig te plannen. Daarvoor had Martin iemand nodig die hij blindelings vertrouwde. Veel keus had hij trouwens niet.

Terug op de SAS-basis op het militaire vliegveld van Riyad was zijn eerste vraag aan kolonel Craig: 'Wie kan ik meenemen?'

De lijst was kort. Bijna iedereen zat in de woestijn.

Toen de adjudant hem het rooster liet zien, sprong één naam er onmiddellijk uit.

'Peter Stephenson. Dat staat vast.'

'Je hebt geluk,' zei Craig. 'Hij is een week geleden weer over de grens gekomen. Daarna heeft hij uitgerust. Hij is fit.'

Martin kende Stephenson uit de tijd dat de sergeant nog korporaal was geweest en hijzelf kapitein tijdens zijn eerste termijn als teamcommandant. Net als Martin zelf was Stephenson een 'Freefaller' en lid van de luchtbrigade van zijn eigen squadron.

'Dit is ook een goede vent,' zei Craig, wijzend op een andere naam. 'Een bergbeklimmer. Daar heb je er twee van nodig.'

De naam die hij aanwees was die van korporaal Ben Eastman.

'Ja, ik ken hem. U hebt gelijk. Die neem ik mee. Wie verder nog?'

De vierde kandidaat was korporaal Kevin North, van een ander squadron. Martin had nog nooit met hem gewerkt maar North was een bergspecialist en had een goede aanbeveling van zijn teamcommandant.

Er waren vijf onderdelen die tegelijkertijd moesten worden voorbereid. Martin verdeelde de taken over zijn mensen en hield zelf de algehele leiding.

Eerst kwam de selectie van het vliegtuig dat hen naar het doelwit moest brengen. Zonder aarzelen koos Martin voor de C-130 Hercules, het vaste toestel van de SAS-para's. Op dat moment vlogen er negen in het Golfgebied, allemaal gestationeerd op het nabijgelegen King Khaled International Airport. Bij het ontbijt kregen ze nog beter nieuws. Drie van de toestellen waren afkomstig van het 47e Squadron van Lyneham in Wiltshire, het squadron dat al jaren samenwerkte met de Freefallers van de SAS.

Tot de bemanning van een van de drie toestellen behoorde ook een kapitein Glyn Morris.

Tijdens de hele Golfoorlog vormden de Hercules-transportvliegtuigen de spil van de operatie. Ze vervoerden het materiaal dat in Riyad aankwam naar de buitenposten van de RAF in Tabuk, Muharraq, Dhahran en zelfs naar Seeb in Oman. Morris had gevlogen als loadmaster, maar zijn werkelijke taak op deze aarde was die van spronginstructeur, en Martin had al eens onder zijn leiding parachutegesprongen.

De para's en de SAS hebben geen eigen vliegtuigen voor het parachutespringen. Die worden beschikbaar gesteld door de RAF, die ook de eindverantwoordelijkheid heeft voor het afwerpen van parachutisten boven gevechtszones. De relatie is gebaseerd op het wederzijdse vertrouwen dat beide partijen precies weten wat ze doen.

Commodore Ian MacFadyen, de commandant van de RAF in de Golf, wees de Hercules meteen aan de SAS-missie toe zodra het toestel terugkwam van een transportvlucht naar Tabuk. Het grondpersoneel maakte het onmiddellijk gereed voor de HALO-sprong, die nog voor dezelfde avond op het programma stond.

De belangrijkste aanpassing was een zuurstofconsole op de vloer van het laadruim. De Hercules vloog voornamelijk op geringe hoogte en had tot dat moment nog geen zuurstof nodig gehad voor de passagiers. Kapitein Morris had geen extra training meer nodig. Samen met een spronginstructeur van een andere Hercules, kapitein Sammy Dawlish, werkten ze daarom de hele dag aan de aanpassing van het vliegtuig. Tegen zonsondergang was alles klaar.

Het tweede belangrijke punt waren de parachutes zelf. De SAS had nog niet boven Irak gesprongen. Ze waren met auto's de woestijn binnengedrongen, maar bij de voorbereidingen op de oorlog hadden ze er wel op getraind.

Op de luchtmachtbasis bevond zich een afgesloten sectie met een constante temperatuur, waar alle gevoelige apparatuur werd bewaard. Daar had de SAS haar parachutes opgeslagen. Martin vroeg om acht valschermen plus reserve-parachutes, hoewel hij en zijn mannen maar de helft nodig hadden. Sergeant Stephenson werd belast met de controle en het inpakken.

De parachutes waren niet langer van het ronde, kegelvormige type, maar rechthoekig, met twee lagen stof. Tijdens de val wordt de lucht tussen de lagen door geleid, waardoor een half starre 'vleugel' ontstaat die de parachutist meer mogelijkheden geeft om te manoeuvreren. Dit type parachute wordt meestal ook bij demonstraties gebruikt.

De twee korporaals moesten alle andere voorraden controleren, zoals vier stel kleren, vier grote Bergen-rugzakken, veldflessen, helmen, riemen, wapens, rantsoenen, munitie en eerste-hulpkisten. De lijst was eindeloos. De mannen zouden tachtig pond in hun Bergen-rugzak dragen en iedere gram daarvan kon noodzakelijk zijn.

Het grondpersoneel werkte in de hangar aan de Hercules zelf. De motoren en alle andere bewegende delen werden nog eens aan een grondige inspectie onderworpen.

De squadron-commandant wees zijn beste bemanning aan en de navigator vertrok samen met kolonel Craig naar het Zwarte Gat om een geschikte dropping-zone of DZ te kiezen.

Martin zelf werd onder handen genomen door zes technici, vier Amerikanen en twee Britten, om vertrouwd te raken met het 'speelgoed' dat ze nodig hadden om het doelwit op te sporen en de exacte locatie aan Riyad door te geven.

Toen hij klaar was, werden de verschillende apparaten goed verpakt en naar de hangar gebracht, waar de berg met materiaal voor de vier mannen hoger en hoger werd. Voor alle zekerheid werd er van ieder instrument ook een reserve-exemplaar ingepakt, waardoor het gewicht nog toenam.

Martin zelf vertrok naar de plannenmakers in het Zwarte Gat. Ze stonden over een grote tafel gebogen die bezaaid lag met nieuwe foto's die een andere TR-1 die ochtend bij het eerste daglicht had genomen. Het was helder weer en de opnamen toonden alle hoeken en gaten van de Jebal al Hamreen.

'We nemen aan,' zei kolonel Craig, 'dat dat vervloekte kanon naar het zuiden of zuidoosten wijst. Het beste observatiepunt lijkt me daarom hier.'

Hij wees op een serie richels in de berghelling ten zuiden van de vermeende Vesting, de heuvel in het midden van de groep, binnen de vierkante kilometer die door de dode kolonel Osman Badri was aangegeven.

'Wat de DZ betreft... er is een klein dal, ongeveer veertig kilometer naar het zuiden. Je kunt het water zien glinsteren van een stroompje dat er doorheen loopt.'

Martin keek. Het was een kleine holte in de heuvels, vijfhonderd meter lang en ongeveer honderd meter breed, met een winters beekje tussen grazige oevers, bezaaid met stenen.

'Is dat de beste plaats?' vroeg Martin.

Kolonel Craig haalde zijn schouders op. 'Veel keus hebben we niet. De volgende plek ligt zeventig kilometer van het doelwit. En als je dichterbij landt, loop je het risico dat ze jullie zien.'

Volgens de kaart moest het bij daglicht geen probleem zijn. Maar in het pikkedonker, als ze met een snelheid van bijna 200 km per uur door de ijzige lucht afdaalden, zouden ze de plek gemakkelijk kunnen missen. Er waren geen fakkels of andere lichten om de plaats aan te geven. Ze zouden vanuit het duister naar het duister springen.

'Vooruit dan maar,' zei hij.

De RAF-navigator kwam overeind. 'Goed. Dan ga ik maar eens aan het werk.'

Hij had nog een drukke middag voor de boeg. Hij zou zijn weg moeten vinden in de donkere nacht, zonder het licht van de maan, niet naar de dropping-zone, maar naar een punt in de lucht waar hij, rekening houdend met de wind, de vier parachutisten moest afwerpen om op de juiste plaats terecht te komen. Zelfs vallende lichamen drijven af. Hij moest berekenen hoe ver.

Pas toen de schemering viel, kwamen ze allemaal weer bijeen in de hangar die voor alle buitenstaanders verboden gebied was. De Hercules stond klaar, met volle tanks. Onder één vleugel lag de stapel spullen die de vier mannen nodig zouden hebben. Dawlish, de spronginstructeur van de RAF, had de acht 22 kilo zware parachutes ingepakt alsof hij ze zelf zou moeten gebruiken. Stephenson was tevreden.

In een hoek stond een grote tafel. Martin, die de vergrote foto's uit het Zwarte Gat had meegebracht, liep met Stephenson, Eastman en North naar de tafel om de route uit te zetten vanaf de DZ tot aan de richels waar ze zich wilden verbergen om de Vesting te bestuderen, hoe lang dat ook mocht duren. Het zou vermoedelijk een mars van twee nachten worden. Overdag moesten ze zich schuilhouden. Ze konden niet bij daglicht verdergaan en ze mochten geen rechtstreekse route volgen.

Ten slotte pakten de mannen hun rugzakken in. Bovenop ging de Belt Order, een zwaar net met veel zakken, dat ze na de landing om hun middel zouden dragen.

Toen het donker was, lieten ze Amerikaanse hamburgers uit de kantine komen en rustten wat uit. Om 21.45 uur zouden ze vertrekken. De sprong stond gepland voor 23.30 uur.

Aan het wachten had Martin altijd de grootste hekel. Na de koortsachtige drukte van de afgelopen dag was het een soort anti-climax. Je kon nergens anders aan denken dan aan de spanning, het knagende gevoel dat je ondanks alle controles misschien toch iets over het hoofd had gezien. De anderen zaten te eten, te lezen of te dutten, schreven een brief naar huis of gingen naar de wc.

Om negen uur sleepte een trekker de Hercules naar de startbaan. De piloot, de co-piloot, de navigator en de werktuigkundige voerden hun controles uit. Twintig minuten later reed een geblindeerde bus de hangar in om de mannen en hun materiaal naar het vliegtuig te brengen, dat klaarstond met de achterklep omlaag.

443

De twee instructeurs wachtten al op hen, met de loadmaster en de materiaalverzorger, die de parachutes had klaargelegd. Zeven mannen liepen over de klep het grote, donkere ruim van de Hercules binnen. De klep kwam omhoog en de deuren gingen dicht. De materiaalverzorger was teruggegaan. Hij zou niet meevliegen.

De vier soldaten, de twee instructeurs en de loadmaster gingen op bankjes langs de wanden zitten, maakten hun riemen vast en wachtten. Om 21.44 uur steeg de Hercules op van het vliegveld van Riyad en draaide zijn stompe neus naar het noorden.

Terwijl het RAF-toestel zich op de avond van de 21e februari in de lucht verhief, wachtte een Amerikaanse helikopter op enige afstand voordat hij op de Amerikaanse sector van de basis landde.

Hij was naar Al Kharz gestuurd om twee mannen op te halen. De commandant van het 336e Squadron Tactische Jagers was door generaal Buster Glosson naar Riyad ontboden. En hij had de piloot meegenomen die hij het meest geschikt vond voor aanvalsacties laag boven de grond.

Noch de commandant van de Rocketeers noch Don Walker had enig idee wat de bedoeling was. In een kleine kamer onder het CENTAF-hoofdkwartier kregen ze een uur later tekst en uitleg. En er werd hun te verstaan gegeven dat ze met niemand, behalve met Walkers navigator, de man in de stoel achter hem, over de bijzonderheden van deze missie mochten spreken.

Daarna bracht de helikopter hen weer naar hun basis terug.

Na het vertrek maakten de vier soldaten hun riemen los en konden ze zich vrij door het ruim bewegen, bij het zwakke licht van de rode lampen boven hun hoofd. Martin liep naar voren, beklom de ladder naar de cockpit en bleef een tijdje bij de bemanning zitten.

Ze vlogen op 10 000 voet in de richting van de Iraakse grens. Na een tijdje begonnen ze te klimmen. Op 25 000 voet trok de Hercules zijn neus weer recht en passeerde de grens, ogenschijnlijk moederziel alleen onder de sterren aan de hemel.

Maar dat was hij niet. Een AWACS boven de Golf had opdracht voortdurend de omgeving te verkennen. Als een Iraakse radarinstallatie die om onbekende redenen nog niet door de geallieerde luchtmacht was vernietigd de Hercules zou aanstralen, zou hij onmiddellijk worden aangevallen. Daarom vlogen twee groepen Wild Weasels, bewapend met anti-radar HARM-raketten, op veel geringere hoogte met het transportvliegtuig mee.

Voor het geval een Iraakse gevechtspiloot juist die avond op avontuur wilde gaan, vloog links een team Jaguars van de RAF boven de Hercules en rechts een team F-15C Eagles. Het transportvliegtuig werd dus aan alle kanten beschermd door de modernste, meest dodelijke technologie. Geen van de

444

geallieerde piloten wist waarom. Ze hadden hun orders. Dat was alles. Als iemand in Irak die avond de blip op het radarscherm had gezien, zou hij waarschijnlijk hebben gedacht dat het vrachtvliegtuig op weg was naar Turkije.

De loadmaster deed zijn best om het zijn gasten naar de zin te maken met thee, koffie, frisdrank en koekjes.

Veertig minuten voor het afspringpunt schakelde de navigator een knipperlichtje in en konden de laatste voorbereidingen beginnen.

De vier soldaten gespten hun parachute en de reserve-parachute om, de eerste om de volle breedte van hun schouders, de tweede wat lager op hun rug. Daarna volgden de rugzakken, omgekeerd tegen hun rug, onder de parachutes, met de punt tussen hun benen. De wapens – Heckler & Koch MP5 SD machinepistolen met geluiddempers – werden met een clip aan de linkerkant gehangen en de zuurstoftanks rechts, over de buik.

Ten slotte zetten ze hun helm en hun zuurstofmasker op en verbonden die met de middenconsole, een buizenconstructie zo groot als een forse eettafel, vol met zuurstofflessen. Toen alles goed zat en iedereen normaal kon ademen, waarschuwden ze de piloot, die langzaam de lucht liet wegstromen totdat de druk in het ruim gelijk was aan die van de buitenlucht.

Dat duurde bijna twintig minuten. Toen gingen ze weer zitten wachten. Een kwartier voor het afspringpunt kreeg de loadmaster weer een order uit de cockpit. Hij gaf een teken aan de instructeurs, die naar de soldaten gebaarden dat ze moesten overschakelen van de zuurstofconsole naar hun eigen kleine tanks. Die hadden een voorraad voor dertig minuten. De sprong zou drie tot vier minuten duren.

Op dat moment wist alleen de navigator in de cockpit precies waar ze zich bevonden. Het SAS-team vertrouwde erop dat ze op het juiste punt zouden worden afgeworpen.

De loadmaster hield inmiddels contact met de soldaten via een reeks handsignalen. Ten slotte wees hij met beide handen naar de lichtjes boven de console. Zelf kreeg hij via zijn koptelefoon instructies van de navigator.

De mannen stonden op en kwamen in beweging. Heel langzaam, als ruimtevaarders, wankelend onder het gewicht van hun bepakking, liepen ze naar de klep. De instructeurs, die ook via zuurstofflessen ademden, liepen met hen mee.

De SAS-mannen bleven voor het gesloten luik staan. Iedereen controleerde de parachute van de man vóór hem. Vier minuten voor het afspringpunt ging de klep omlaag en staarden ze in de voorbij razende duisternis die ruim 8000 meter diep was. Nog een handsignaal – twee opgestoken vingers van de instructeur – gaf aan dat ze twee minuten hadden. Ze schuifelden naar de klep en keken naar de gedoofde lichten aan weerszijden van de opening. De lampjes lichtten rood op en ze trokken hun bril voor hun ogen. De lampjes sprongen op groen...

De vier mannen draaiden zich op één hak om, met hun gezicht naar het ruim, en sprongen met gespreide armen naar achteren. Meteen draaiden ze zich met hun gezicht naar beneden. De rand van de klep schoot onder hen voorbij en de Hercules was verdwenen.

Sergeant Stephenson was de eerste.

De vier mannen stabiliseerden hun positie en lieten zich geluidloos 8 km door de donkere nacht naar beneden vallen. Op een hoogte van 1200 meter trokken ze aan hun koord, dat met een drukcapsule was verbonden. De parachutes openden zich. Voor Mike Martin, in tweede positie, leek het of de schaduw vijftien meter beneden hem opeens tot stilstand kwam. Op hetzelfde moment voelde hij de trilling van zijn eigen parachute. Het scherm nam de druk over en zijn snelheid liep terug van 200 tot 20 km. Speciale buffers vingen een deel van de schok op.

Op 300 meter hoogte maakten de mannen de haken los die de rugzakken op hun rug hielden, lieten ze tussen hun benen zakken en haakten ze aan hun voeten. Daar zouden ze blijven hangen tot dertig meter boven de grond, waarna ze aan een vijf meter lange lijn omlaag moesten worden gegooid.

De parachute van de sergeant dreef naar rechts. Martin volgde. De lucht was helder, de sterren waren goed te zien en de donkere omtrekken van de bergen kwamen snel op hen af. Toen zag hij wat Stephenson ook had gezien: het glinsterende beekje in het dal.

De sergeant landde precies in het midden van de dropping-zone, een paar meter van de oever van het stroompje, op het mos en het zachte gras. Martin gooide zijn rugzak aan de lijn omlaag, begon te slingeren, hield zich weer stil, wachtte tot de rugzak was neergekomen en landde toen zelf, op twee voeten.

Korporaal Eastman scheerde boven zijn hoofd voorbij, draaide zich om, kwam weer terug en landde vijftig meter verderop. Martin was al bezig zich van zijn parachute te ontdoen en zag Kevin North niet landen.

De bergbeklimmer was de vierde en laatste van de groep. Hij daalde honderd meter verder, niet boven het gras maar boven een helling. Toen hij zijn koers corrigeerde, raakte zijn rugzak de grond, werd vijf meter over de helling meegesleept en bleef toen steken tussen twee rotsen.

Door de onverwachte ruk aan de lijn werd North opzij en omlaag getrokken, zodat hij niet op zijn voeten maar op zijn zij neerkwam. Er lagen niet veel rotsen op de helling, maar één ervan brak zijn linker dijbeen op acht plaatsen.

De korporaal voelde het bot breken, maar de klap was zo hard dat het een paar seconde duurde voordat de pijn in volle hevigheid tot hem doordrong.

446

Hij rolde heen en weer en klemde zijn bovenbeen in zijn handen. 'O god, nee!' fluisterde hij steeds weer. 'O god!'

De meervoudige breuk veroorzaakte een inwendige bloeding. Een van de botscherven boorde zich dwars door de slagader in zijn dijbeen, waardoor zijn levensbloed in het weefsel wegstroomde.

De andere drie vonden hem een minuut later. Ze hadden zich van hun parachutes en hun rugzakken ontdaan en dachten dat hij daar ook mee bezig was. Toen hij niet kwam opdagen, gingen ze hem zoeken. Stephenson richtte zijn zaklantaarn op het been van de korporaal.

'O, verdomme!' fluisterde hij. Ze hadden een eerste-hulpkist bij zich, en zelfs noodverbanden, maar dit was een ander geval. De korporaal moest voor een shock worden behandeld en had plasma nodig. Als hij niet snel werd geopereerd, was hij verloren. Stephenson rende terug naar Norths rugzak, greep de EHBO-kist en maakte een morfine-injectie gereed. Dat was al niet meer nodig. Door het bloedverlies nam ook de pijn snel af.

North opende zijn ogen en zag het gezicht van Mike Martin boven zich. 'Het spijt me, chef,' fluisterde hij en sloot zijn ogen weer. Twee minuten later was hij dood.

Op een ander moment en op een andere plaats had Martin misschien uiting kunnen geven aan de pijn die hij voelde bij het verlies van een man als North, die onder zíjn bevel was omgekomen. Maar dit was niet de tijd of de plaats daarvoor. De twee andere onderofficieren beseften dat ook en deden grimmig wat noodzakelijk was. Het verdriet kwam later wel.

Martin had de parachutes ergens anders willen begraven, maar dat ging nu niet. Ze moesten zich over Norths lichaam ontfermen.

'Pete, leg alles bijeen wat we moeten begraven. Zoek ergens een holte of graaf een gat. Ben, verzamel zoveel mogelijk stenen.'

Martin boog zich over het lichaam, verwijderde de naamplaatjes, pakte het machinepistool en richtte zich weer op om Eastman te helpen. Met hun messen en hun handen groeven ze een ondiep gat in het veerkrachtige gras en legden het lijk erin. De rest ging erbovenop – de vier parachutes, de reserve-parachutes, de zuurstofflessen, de lijnen en het tuig.

Daarna legden ze de stenen erop, niet in een nette stapel die zou opvallen, maar zo slordig mogelijk, alsof ze zo langs de helling naar beneden waren gerold. Met water uit het beekje spoelden ze de rode bloedvlekken weg. Op de kale plekken waar ze de stenen vandaan hadden gehaald maakten ze het zand met hun voeten wat losser en gooiden er wat mos overheen. Er moesten zo weinig mogelijk sporen in het dal achterblijven.

Ze hadden die nacht nog vijf uur willen lopen, maar het begraven van Kevin North kostte al drie uur. Een deel van de inhoud van zijn rugzak verdween ook in het graf – zijn kleren, zijn rantsoenen en het water. Andere zaken

447

moesten ze onderling verdelen, waardoor hun eigen rugzakken nog zwaarder werden.

Een uur voordat het licht werd vertrokken ze uit het dal, in een vaste formatie. Sergeant Peter Stephenson nam de leiding als verkenner. Bij iedere heuvelrug liet hij zich vallen en tuurde er voorzichtig overheen om onprettige verrassingen te vermijden.

De weg liep omhoog en Stephenson hield een stevig tempo aan. Hij was een kleine, pezige man, vijf jaar ouder dan Martin, maar hij kon beter lopen dan de meeste jongeren, zelfs met een bepakking van veertig kilo.

De lucht begon te betrekken en dat kwam goed uit. Daardoor bleef het wat langer donker en hadden ze nog een extra uur. Na een straffe mars van negentig minuten hadden ze twaalf kilometer afgelegd en lag het dal al een paar heuvels achter hen. Ten slotte werden ze door de ochtendschemering gedwongen een schuilplaats te zoeken.

Martin koos een horizontale kloof onder een rotsrichel, vlak boven een droge wadi, afgeschermd door wild gras. Terwijl de dag aanbrak aten ze wat rantsoenen, dronken water, trokken hun netten over zich heen en probeerden te slapen. Martin nam de eerste wacht.

Om elf uur wekte hij Stephenson om zelf wat te slapen terwijl de sergeant de wacht hield. Om vier uur werd hij door Ben Eastman in zijn ribben gepord. Toen hij zijn ogen opende, zag hij dat Eastman zijn vinger tegen zijn lippen had gelegd. Martin luisterde. Vanuit de wadi, drie meter onder hun richel, waren Arabische keelklanken te horen.

Sergeant Stephenson werd wakker en trok een wenkbrauw op. Wat nu? Martin luisterde een tijdje. De Iraakse patrouille bestond uit vier man. Ze waren moe van hun saaie tocht door de bergen en ze wilden slapen. Na tien minuten wist Martin dat ze van plan waren hier hun kamp op te slaan.

De SAS-mannen hadden al genoeg tijd verloren. Om zes uur, als de zon achter de heuvels verdween, moesten ze weer op pad zijn. De tocht naar die heuvel tegenover de Vesting duurde al lang genoeg. En misschien zouden ze nog meer tijd nodig hebben om naar de sporen in het landschap te zoeken.

De Irakezen wilden hout verzamelen voor een kampvuur. Dat betekende dat ze zeker in de buurt zouden komen van de struiken waarachter de SAS-mannen zich schuilhielden. En zelfs als dat niet gebeurde, zou het nog uren duren voordat ze zo diep in slaap waren dat Martins patrouille veilig langs hen heen kon glippen.

Er zat dus niets anders op.

Op een teken van Martin pakten de andere twee hun plattte, dubbelzijdige mes. Met hun drieën lieten ze zich over de richel in de wadi zakken.

Toen het karwei was geklaard, bladerde Martin de soldijboekjes van de dode Irakezen door. Ze hadden allemaal dezelfde achternaam, zag hij: Al-

Ubaidi. Ze behoorden dus alle vier tot de Ubaidi's, een bergstam uit deze omgeving. Ze droegen de onderscheidingstekens van de Republikeinse Garde. Blijkbaar waren deze bergbewoners speciaal uit de gelederen van de Garde geselecteerd om de Vesting tegen indringers te beschermen. Het waren magere, gespierde kerels zonder een onsje vet, die het vermoedelijk lang konden volhouden in dit bergachtige terrein.

Het kostte hun een uur om de vier lijken achter de richel te slepen, hun camouflagetent aan stukken te snijden en het zeildoek over hen heen te leggen, met een laag takken, onkruid en gras erbovenop. Maar toen ze klaar waren, was er een heel geoefend oog voor nodig om de bergplaats onder de overstekende rots te vinden. Gelukkig hadden de Irakezen geen zender bij zich. Waarschijnlijk hoefden ze zich pas te melden als ze terugkwamen, wanneer dat ook mocht zijn. Met een beetje geluk zou het twee dagen duren voordat iemand hen miste.

Bij het invallen van de duisternis gingen de SAS-mannen weer verder. Met behulp van het kompas zochten ze de juiste richting en bij het licht van de sterren probeerden ze de silhouetten van de heuvels op de foto's te herkennen.

De kaart die Martin bij zich had was een waar kunststukje, getekend door een computer op basis van de luchtopnamen van de TR-1. De route van de dropping-zone naar hun uitkijkpost tegenover de Vesting stond er duidelijk op aangegeven. Zo nu en dan hield hij halt om met zijn draagbare SATNAV-zender zijn positie vast te stellen en bij het licht van de zaklantaarn de kaart te raadplegen. Alles klopte. Om middernacht hadden ze nog vijftien kilometer te gaan.

In de Brecons in Wales hadden Martin en zijn mannen een tempo van zes kilometer per uur kunnen volhouden in dit soort terrein – een stevig wandeltempo voor iemand die zonder een zware rugzak 's avonds in een vlakke straat zijn hondje uitlaat. Het was een heel normale snelheid voor de SAS-soldaten.

Maar in deze vijandige heuvels, met het gevaar van Iraakse patrouilles in de buurt, moesten ze het veel rustiger aan doen. Ze waren al één keer op Irakezen gestuit, en twee keer was te veel.

Ze waren wel in het voordeel door hun nachtvizieren, die ze als ogen op stokjes voor hun gezicht droegen. Met de nieuwe groothoekversie konden ze het hele gebied bestrijken, in een lichtgroen schijnsel. Al het natuurlijk aanwezige licht werd door de lenzen versterkt, geconcentreerd en op het netvlies van het oog gericht.

Twee uur voor het aanbreken van de dag zagen ze eindelijk de Vesting opdoemen en beklommen ze de helling aan hun linkerkant. De berg die ze als uitkijkpost hadden gekozen lag aan de zuidelijke rand van de vierkante

449

kilometer die Jericho had aangewezen. Vanaf de top, op ongeveer gelijke hoogte als de tegenoverliggende berg, moesten ze een goed uitzicht hebben op de zuidelijke wand van de Vesting, àls het inderdaad de Vesting was. Het was een zware klim van ongeveer een uur. Na een tijdje snakten ze naar adem. Sergeant Stephenson, die voorop liep, ontdekte een geitepaadje dat omhoog leidde, om de berg heen. Vlak voor de top vonden ze de richel die de TR-1 had gefotografeerd. De situatie was gunstiger dan Martin had durven hopen: een natuurlijke kloof in de rots van tweeënhalve meter lang, ruim een meter breed en zestig centimeter diep. De rand was ongeveer een halve meter breed zodat Martin er met zijn bovenlichaam op kon rusten terwijl zijn benen en zijn onderlichaam achter de richel verborgen bleven.

De mannen pakten hun netten en camoufleerden hun schuilplaats voor nieuwsgierige blikken.

Hun rantsoenen en veldflessen propten ze in de zakken van hun vest, Martin hield zijn instrumenten klaar, en ze legden hun wapens onder handbereik. Vlak voordat de zon opkwam, gebruikte Martin een van de apparaten.

Het was een zender, veel kleiner dan het type dat hij naar Bagdad had meegenomen, nauwelijks groter dan twee pakjes sigaretten. Er hoorde een nikkelcadmiumbatterij bij, met voldoende stroom voor een paar weken.

De frequentie was van tevoren ingesteld en aan de andere kant werd vierentwintig uur per dag geluisterd. Om zich te melden hoefde hij alleen maar volgens een vaste code op de zendknop te drukken en te wachten tot de ontvanger met een andere code reageerde.

Het derde onderdeel was een opklapbare schotelantenne, veel kleiner dan het model dat hij in Bagdad had gebruikt. Hoewel hij zich nu ten noorden van de Iraakse hoofdstad bevond, lag dit gebied veel hoger.

Martin installeerde de schotel, richtte hem naar het zuiden, verbond de zender met de batterij en drukte op de knop: een-twee-drie-vier-vijf, pauze, een-twee-drie, pauze, een, pauze, een.

Vijf seconden later begon de ontvanger zachtjes te piepen: vier tonen, vier tonen, twee.

Hij hield zijn duim op de zendknop en sprak in de luidspreker: 'Van Nineveh tot Tyrus. Ik herhaal: van Nineveh tot Tyrus.'

Hij liet de knop weer los en wachtte. De ontvanger piepte opgewonden: een-twee-drie, pauze, een, pauze, vier. Ontvangen en begrepen.

Martin borg de zender weer in zijn waterdichte hoes, pakte een sterke veldkijker waarvoor een vogelliefhebber zijn rechterarm zou hebben gegeven, en schoof over de richel naar voren. Achter hem lagen sergeant Stephenson en korporaal Eastman als embryo's tussen de rotsen geklemd, redelijk comfortabel. Twee takken hielden het net omhoog. Martin stak zijn kijker door een van de mazen.

Terwijl de zon die ochtend van de 23e februari boven de bergen van Hamreen uitkwam, bestudeerde majoor Martin het meesterwerk van zijn oude schoolmakker Osman Badri – de Qa'ala, die geen enkel mechanisch oog kon zien.

In Riyad lazen Steve Laing en Simon Paxman het bericht waarmee de technicus haastig uit de radiohut was gekomen.
'Wel verdomme,' vloekte Laing met overtuiging, 'het is ze gelukt! Ze zitten op die vervloekte berg!'
Generaal Glosson werd ingelicht en twintig minuten later had het nieuws ook Al Kharz bereikt.

Kapitein Don Walker was in de kleine uurtjes van de 22e op zijn basis teruggekeerd, had nog even geslapen en ging kort na het eerste ochtendlicht weer aan het werk, op het moment dat de piloten van de nachtmissies hun rapportage afsloten en slaperig naar hun bed wankelden.
Tegen de middag had hij een plan gereed dat hij aan zijn superieuren voorlegde. Het werd meteen naar Riyad gestuurd en goedgekeurd. In de loop van de middag werden de noodzakelijke toestellen, bemanningen en ondersteunende diensten geregeld.
Officieel ging het om een aanval met vier vliegtuigen op de Iraakse luchtmachtbasis Tikrit Oost, een heel eind ten noorden van Bagdad, niet ver van de geboorteplaats van Saddam Hoessein. Het moest een nachtelijke actie worden, met lasergeleide 2000-ponds bommen. Don Walker kreeg het bevel, met zijn vaste wingman en nog twee andere Eagles.
Als door een wonder stond de missie meteen op de lijst van doelwitten, hoewel hij pas twaalf uur eerder was gepland en niet drie dagen geleden.
De andere drie bemanningen werden onmiddellijk van hun gewone taken ontslagen en op het rooster gezet voor de aanval op Tikrit Oost, die (mogelijk) in de nacht van de 22e zou plaatsvinden, of op een later tijdstip als dat beter uitkwam. Tot die tijd moesten ze zich gereedhouden.
Op 22 februari, tegen het eind van de middag, stonden de vier Strike Eagles in de startblokken, maar om tien uur 's avonds werd de aanval afgeblazen. Er kwam geen andere missie voor in de plaats. De acht vliegers kregen opdracht rust te nemen terwijl de rest van het squadron 'op tankjacht' ging boven de troepen van de Republikeinse Garde ten noorden van Koeweit.
Toen ze tegen de ochtend van de 23e terugkwamen, kregen de acht luierende collega's heel wat commentaar te verduren.
Er werd een route uitgestippeld naar Tikrit Oost, die de vier Eagles naar de corridor tussen Bagdad en de Iraanse grens moest brengen en vandaar naar het oosten, met een bocht van 45 graden over het meer van As Sa'dijah, en

451

ten slotte in noordwestelijke richting naar Tikrit.

Don Walker zat te ontbijten en nam juist een slok koffie toen hij door zijn squadron-commandant naar buiten werd geroepen. 'Het doelwit is gemarkeerd,' kreeg hij te horen. 'Probeer nog wat te slapen. Het zal een zware nacht worden.'

Bij zonsopgang tuurde Mike Martin door zijn kijker naar de berg aan de overkant van het steile dal. Met de maximale vergrotingsfactor kon hij zelfs de afzonderlijke struiken onderscheiden. Als hij de ring wat terugdraaide, kreeg hij ieder overzicht dat hij wilde.

Het eerste uur zag hij nog niets bijzonders. Gewoon een berg. Er groeide gras, er stonden struiken en bosjes, hier en daar lagen wat rotsblokken. De berg had een onregelmatig silhouet, zoals alle heuvels in de omtrek. Hij viel totaal niet op.

Zo nu en dan sloot hij zijn ogen om ze rust te gunnen, legde zijn hoofd op zijn armen en begon na een tijdje opnieuw.

Halverwege de ochtend viel hem een patroon op. Op bepaalde delen van de berg leek het gras anders te groeien – te regelmatig, in rechte stukken. Maar hij kon geen deuren ontdekken, of ze moesten zich aan de andere kant bevinden. Er liep geen weg, er waren geen bandensporen te zien, nergens staken luchtpijpen uit de berg omhoog en de grond leek niet kort geleden omgeploegd.

Het was de beweging van de zon die hem de eerste aanwijzing gaf.

Kort na elven meende hij iets te zien glinsteren in het gras. Hij bewoog de kijker weer terug en stelde de maximale vergroting in. De zon verdween achter een wolk. Toen hij weer tevoorschijn kwam, zag Martin dezelfde glinstering – een stuk draad in het gras, ongeveer dertig centimeter lang.

Hij knipperde met zijn ogen en keek nog eens. Het was een deel van een langere draad, met groen plastic omwikkeld. Maar een gedeelte was weggeschuurd, waardoor het metaaldraad zichtbaar was geworden.

Martin ontdekte nu een heel netwerk van draden, half verborgen in het gras. Soms waren ze even te zien, als de wind de grasprieten opzij boog. Ze vormden een diagonaal patroon, plat tegen de grond.

Tegen de middag kon hij ze beter zien. Op een deel van de helling werd de aarde met een net van groene draden tegen een oppervlak onder de grond gedrukt. In de ruitvormige openingen waren gras en struiken geplant die de draden bedekten.

Toen zag hij ook de terrassen. Een gedeelte van de berghelling bestond uit betonblokken – hij nam tenminste aan dat het beton was – waarvan iedere rij tien centimeter verder naar voren stak. Op de horizontale terrassen die zo ontstonden was aarde gestort waarop onkruid groeide. Dat viel niet meteen

452

op, omdat de plantjes allemaal een verschillende hoogte hadden, maar toen hij de stengels bestudeerde, zag Martin dat ze allemaal op één lijn stonden. En de natuur groeit niet in lijnen.

Hij bewoog zijn kijker, maar het patroon hield op een gegeven moment op en ging ergens anders weer verder, links van hem. In het begin van de middag begreep hij opeens waarom.

De analisten in Riyad hadden gelijk gehad, tot op zekere hoogte. Als iemand een berg vanuit het middelpunt probeerde uit te graven, zou hij instorten. Blijkbaar waren het ooit drie heuvels geweest, waarvan de binnenste wanden waren weggehakt, waarna de openingen tussen de toppen waren opgevuld om een reusachtige krater te vormen.

Daarbij waren de contouren van de oorspronkelijke heuvels gevolgd, door de betonblokken achterwaarts op te bouwen. Zo waren de terrassen tot stand gekomen, waarna van bovenaf tienduizenden tonnen aarde omlaag waren gestort om de randen te bedekken.

De netten waren later aangebracht. Waarschijnlijk zaten de met groen plastic omwikkelde draden op de betonblokken geniet en hielden ze zo de aarde op zijn plaats. Daarna was het graszaad gestrooid, met struiken en bosjes die in diepere holten in het beton waren ingezaaid.

De vorige zomer was het gras gaan groeien en had met zijn wortels een eigen tapijt gevormd. De struiken waren door de openingen in het netwerk omhoog geschoten en hadden zich bij het struikgewas van de oorspronkelijke heuvels aangesloten.

Het dak van de Vesting, boven de krater, was een geodetische koepel, zodanig ontworpen dat hij ook een laag aarde kon dragen waarin gras kon groeien. Er lagen zelfs namaak-rotsblokken op, grijs geschilderd in de tinten van echte steen. Hier en daar was de verf al doorgelopen.

Martin concentreerde zich op het punt waar de rand van de krater moest hebben gelegen voordat de bouw begon.

Ongeveer vijftien meter onder de top van de koepel vond hij wat hij zocht. Hij had zijn kijker al vijftig keer langs de kleine uitstekende rand bewogen zonder iets op te merken.

Het was een kleine rotspartij, lichtgrijs, met twee zwarte, horizontale lijnen erop. Hoe meer hij die lijnen bestudeerde, des te meer hij zich afvroeg waarom iemand zo hoog was geklommen om twee strepen op een rotsblok te trekken.

Zijn camouflagenet wapperde in een briesje uit het noordoosten. Dezelfde bries bracht een van de strepen in beweging. Het waren dus geen lijnen, besefte Martin, maar stalen draden die om de rots heen liepen en in het gras verdwenen.

Rondom het grootste rotsblok lagen nog een paar stenen, als wachtposten in een cirkel. Waarom in een kring? En waarom die stalen draden? Stel dat iemand van beneden aan die draden kon trekken om de rots in beweging te brengen?

Om half vier drong het tot hem door dat het helemaal geen rotsblok was. Het was een stuk tentzeil, op zijn plaats gehouden door de cirkel van stenen. En het kon inderdaad worden weggetrokken als iemand beneden een ruk aan die draden gaf.

Onder het zeil begon hij geleidelijk een vorm te herkennen, een ronde vorm van anderhalve meter doorsnee. Hij staarde naar het zeil waaronder – onzichtbaar voor de buitenwereld – de loop van het Babylon-kanon omhoog stak, vanaf de stootbodem tweehonderd meter in de krater, tot bovenaan. Alleen de laatste meter kwam boven de helling uit, verborgen onder het grijze zeil. En de loop stond gericht op Dhahran, 750 km verder.

'Afstandszoeker,' mompelde hij tegen de mannen achter hem. Hij gaf de verrekijker door en pakte het instrument aan. Het was een soort telescoop. Toen hij hem voor zijn oog hield, zoals ze hem in Riyad hadden gedemonstreerd, zag hij de berg en het zeildoek boven het kanon, maar niet vergroot. Op het prisma waren vier V-vormige chevrons aangebracht, met de punten naar binnen. Langzaam draaide hij aan de gekartelde knop aan de zijkant, tot de vier punten elkaar raakten en een kruis vormden dat precies op het tentzeil rustte.

Martin haalde de zoeker voor zijn oog vandaan en keek naar de getallen op de draaiende ring. Precies 1080 meter.

'Kompas,' zei hij. Hij legde de zoeker achter zich en kreeg het elektronische kompas in zijn handen gedrukt. Het was niet langer een schijf die in een schaal met alcohol dreef, en zelfs geen wijzer op een gyroscoop. Hij bracht het kompas naar zijn oog, richtte het op het tentzeil aan de overkant van het dal en drukte op de knop. Het kompas deed de rest. Het zeildoek bevond zich op 348 graden, 10 minuten en 18 seconden ten opzichte van zijn positie.

De SATNAV-satellietontvanger gaf hem de laatste informatie die hij nodig had: zijn eigen exacte positie op aarde, tot op 15 meter nauwkeurig.

Het was niet eenvoudig om de schotelantenne in de kleine ruimte achter de richel te installeren. Het kostte hem tien minuten. Maar toen hij Riyad opriep, kreeg hij onmiddellijk antwoord.

Langzaam las Martin drie reeksen cijfers voor: zijn eigen positie, de kompaskoers vanaf zijn positie naar die van het doelwit, en de afstand. De luisteraars in de Saoedische hoofdstad konden nu de rest berekenen en de piloot zijn coördinaten geven.

Martin kroop terug in de holte achter de richel en ging pitten. Stephenson nam zijn plaats in om een oogje te houden op eventuele Iraakse patrouilles.

Om half negen, in het pikkedonker, testte Martin de infrarode doelwitmarkeerlantaarn. Het leek inderdaad op een grote zaklantaarn, met een pistoolgreep, maar de lens zat aan de achterkant.

Martin sloot hem aan op de batterij, richtte hem op de Vesting en keek. De hele berg werd zichtbaar, alsof hij werd verlicht door een grote groene maan. Hij draaide de loop van de beeldversterker naar het zeildoek over de vuurmond van het Babylon-kanon en haalde de trekker over.

Eén enkele, onzichtbare infrarode straal flitste over het dal. Op de berghelling verscheen een kleine rode punt. Martin verplaatste de stip naar het zeildoek en hield hem daar een halve minuut. Tevredengesteld schakelde hij het apparaat uit en kroop weer onder het camouflagenet.

Om 22.45 uur vertrokken de vier Strike Eagles van de basis Al Kharz en klommen naar 20 000 voet. Voor drie van de bemanningen was een aanval op een Iraakse vliegbasis inmiddels een routineklus. Elk van de Eagles was uitgerust met twee lasergeleide 2000-ponds bommen, plus hun normale raketten voor een eventueel luchtgevecht.

Zonder problemen werden ze bijgetankt door een KC-10, even ten zuiden van de Iraakse grens. Daarna draaide de groep, die de roepnaam Bluejay had gekregen, in een losse formatie naar het noorden. Om 23.14 uur passeerden ze de Iraakse stad As-Samawah.

Zoals gebruikelijk namen ze radiostilte in acht en vlogen ze zonder lichten. De wizzo's konden de drie andere toestellen toch wel op hun radar zien. Het was een heldere nacht en de AWACS boven de Golf had al gemeld dat er geen Iraakse jagers in de lucht waren.

Om 23.39 uur mompelde Don Walkers navigator: 'Keerpunt over vijf minuten.'

Ze hoorden het allemaal. Over vijf minuten zouden ze over het meer van As Sa'dijah vliegen.

Op het moment dat ze aan de bocht van vijfenveertig graden naar bakboord begonnen voor de nieuwe koers naar Tikrit Oost, hoorden de andere drie bemanningen Don Walker duidelijk zeggen:

'Bluejay Leader heeft... motorstoring. We moeten terug naar de basis. Bluejay Drie, neem het maar over.'

Bluejay Drie was die nacht Bull Baker, de aanvoerder van de andere twee Eagles. Vanaf die opmerking begon het langzaam verkeerd te gaan, en op een hele vreemde manier.

Walkers wingman, Randy 'R-2' Roberts, sloot zich bij Walker aan maar kon geen aanwijzingen voor motorpech ontdekken. Toch verloor Walker snelheid en begon hij te dalen. Als hij naar de basis wilde terugkeren, was het normaal dat zijn wingman bij hem bleef, tenzij de problemen weinig voor-stelden. Maar dat is zelden het geval bij motorpech boven vijandelijk gebied.

'Begrepen,' antwoordde Baker. Toen hoorden ze Walker zeggen:

'Bluejay Twee, sluit u aan bij Bluejay Drie. Ik herhaal: sluit u aan bij Bluejay Drie. Dit is een bevel. Doorvliegen naar Tikrit Oost.'

Walkers wingman begreep er niets meer van, maar hij deed wat hem werd gezegd en klom achter de rest van team Bluejay aan. Hun commandant verloor steeds meer hoogte boven het meer. Ze zagen hem op de radar.

Op hetzelfde moment beseften ze dat hij een afschuwelijke fout had gemaakt. Om de een of andere reden, misschien geschrokken door de motorstoring, had hij niet via de Have-quick coderadio gesproken, maar via het gewone kanaal. En daarbij had hij hun doelwit genoemd!

Een jonge sergeant van de Amerikaanse luchtmacht die in de AWACS boven de Golf achter een batterij consoles zat, waarschuwde stomverbaasd zijn missiecommandant.

'We hebben een probleem. Bluejay Leader heeft motorpech. Hij wil naar de basis terug.'

'Goed. Genoteerd,' zei de commandant. In de meeste vliegtuigen heeft de piloot het volledige gezag. In een AWACS is de piloot wel verantwoordelijk voor de veiligheid van het toestel, maar de missiecommandant geeft de operationele orders.

'Maar Bluejay Leader sprak over het open kanaal,' protesteerde de sergeant. 'Hij heeft zelfs het doelwit genoemd. Zal ik de hele groep maar terugsturen?'

'Nee, de missie gaat door,' beval de commandant. 'Zoals gepland.'

De sergeant boog zich verbijsterd over zijn console. Dit was krankzinnig. Als de Irakezen dit gesprek hadden onderschept, zou de luchtafweer van Tikrit Oost gewaarschuwd zijn.

Toen hoorde hij Walker weer.

'Bluejay Leader. Mayday, mayday. Beide motoren uitgevallen. We verlaten het toestel.'

Hij sprak nog steeds via het open kanaal. De Irakezen konden het allemaal volgen, als ze luisterden.

Dat deden ze inderdaad. De berichten waren opgevangen. Op Tikrit Oost rukten de artilleristen het zeildoek van hun Triple-A, zetten hun hittezoekende raketten op scherp en luisterden naar het geluid van naderende motoren. Andere eenheden werden opgetrommeld om meteen naar de twee neergekomen vliegers in de omgeving van het meer te gaan zoeken.

'Bluejay Leader is neergestort!' meldde de sergeant. 'Nu moeten we de rest wel terugsturen.'

'Genoteerd. Negatief,' zei de commandant. Hij keek op zijn horloge. Hij had zijn orders. Hij begreep ze niet, maar hij moest ze uitvoeren.

Inmiddels was team Bluejay nog maar negen minuten bij het doelwit vandaan. De Eagles wachtte een warme ontvangst. De drie piloten waren muisstil.

De sergeant in de AWACS zag de blip van Bluejay Leader nog op zijn radarscherm, laag boven het meer. De Eagle was kennelijk verlaten en kon ieder moment neerstorten.

Vier minuten later scheen de missiecommandant opeens van mening te veranderen.

'AWACS aan team Bluejay. AWACS aan team Bluejay. Terugkeren naar uw basis. Ik herhaal: terugkeren naar uw basis.'

De piloten van de drie Strike Eagles, zwaar geschokt door de gebeurtenissen van die avond, braken hun missie af en zetten koers naar huis. De Iraakse artilleristen van Tikrit Oost, die geen radar meer hadden, wachtten nog een uur tevergeefs op de vijandelijke vliegtuigen.

In de zuidelijke uitlopers van de Jebal al Hamreen had een andere Iraakse luisterpost de gesprekken ook opgevangen. De kolonel die de leiding had hoefde Tikrit Oost en geen enkele andere basis te waarschuwen. Dat was zijn werk niet. Hij hoefde er alleen maar voor te zorgen dat geen enkel vijandelijk vliegtuig tot het berggebied kon doordringen.

Toen team Bluejay een bocht had beschreven over het meer, had hij bevel gegeven tot alarmfase geel. De route vanaf het meer naar Tikrit zou de Eagles boven de zuidelijke uitlopers hebben gebracht. Toen er één neerstortte, reageerde hij verheugd. Gelukkig kregen ook de andere ten slotte het bevel om terug te keren. De alarmfase werd opgeheven.

Don Walker was in een spiraal naar het meer gedoken, had dertig meter boven het water de neus van zijn toestel rechtgetrokken en zijn SOS-signaal uitgezonden. Terwijl hij laag over het water van het As Sa'dijah scheerde, toetste hij zijn nieuwe coördinaten in en draaide naar het noorden, op weg naar de Jebal. Op hetzelfde moment schakelde hij over op LANTIRN.

LANTIRN of 'Low Altitude Navigation and Targeting, Infra-red for Night', is het Amerikaanse equivalent van het Britse TIALD-systeem. Door op LANTIRN over te schakelen kon Walker vanuit zijn cockpit de hele omgeving zien, verlicht door de infraroodbundel die vanonder zijn vleugel werd geprojecteerd. Rijen getallen op zijn heads-up display gaven nu zijn koers, zijn snelheid en zijn hoogte aan – en de tijd die hem nog restte tot aan het doelwit.

Hij had de automatische piloot kunnen inschakelen en de besturing overlaten aan de computer die de Eagles door de dalen en valleien zou loodsen, langs de bergen en de rotsen, terwijl de piloot zijn handen in zijn schoot hield. Maar Walker vloog liever zelf.

Met behulp van de luchtfoto's die hij uit het Zwarte Gat had gekregen had hij een koers door het berggebied uitgezet die hem geen moment boven de horizon bracht. Hij bleef zo laag mogelijk, in de dalen, van de ene pas naar de andere, in een soort achtbaan die hem uiteindelijk bij de Vesting moest brengen.

Toen hij zijn SOS-bericht uitzond, reageerde Mike Martins radio met een afgesproken reeks pieptonen. Martin was naar de richel gekropen, had de markeringslamp op het zeildoek 1000 meter tegenover hem gericht en hield de rode punt nu recht in het midden van het doelwit.

De pieptonen van de radio betekenden 'nog zeven minuten tot de aanval'. Vanaf dat moment mocht Martin de rode stip niet meer verplaatsen.

'Het zal tijd worden,' mompelde Eastman. 'Ik verrek hier van de kou.'

'Nog even,' zei Stephenson, die zijn laatste spullen in zijn rugzak pakte, 'dan mag je rennen voor je leven, Benny. Dan word je wel warm.'

Alleen de radio pakten ze nog niet in. Die moest nog worden gebruikt.

Achter in de Eagle kreeg Walkers wizzo Tim Nathanson dezelfde informatie als zijn piloot: vier minuten tot het doelwit... drieënhalve minuut... drie minuten... De afstandsmeter op de heads-up display telde af terwijl de Eagle tussen de heuvels door op de Vesting af stormde. Hij scheerde over de wadi waar Martin en zijn mannen waren geland en overbrugde in enkele seconden de afstand waarover zij, zwoegend met hun zware bepakking, twee nachten hadden gedaan.

'Negentig seconden tot aan het doelwit...'

De SAS-mannen hoorden het geluid van de motoren vanuit het zuiden toen de Eagle begon te klimmen.

Precies op het moment dat de teller op nul stond, kwam de jachtbommenwerper boven de laatste heuveltop uit. In het donker maakten de twee torpedovormige bommen zich van hun ophangpunten onder de vleugels los en klommen nog een paar seconden, overgeleverd aan hun eigen traagheid.

In de drie namaakdorpen hoorden de wachtposten van de Republikeinse Garde het gebulder van de straaljager die uit het niets leek opgedoken. Ze sprongen uit bed en renden naar hun wapens. Binnen enkele seconden werden de daken van de voorraadschuren hydraulisch opzij geschoven en kwamen de raketbatterijen tevoorschijn.

De twee bommen voelden de zuiging van de zwaartekracht en begonnen te vallen. De infraroodzoekers in hun neus zochten de juiste richting, de kegel van onzichtbare infraroodstralen afkomstig van de rode stip op het doelwit, die ze niet meer uit het oog zouden verliezen als ze hem eenmaal hadden gevonden.

Mike Martin lag op zijn buik te wachten. De grond trilde onder het geweld van de motoren, maar hij hield de infraroodstraal strak op het Babylonkanon gericht.

De bommen zag hij niet eens. Het ene moment tuurde hij nog door de zoeker naar een bleekgroene berg, het volgende moment moest hij zijn hoofd afwenden en zijn ogen beschermen toen de nacht opeens veranderde in een bloedrode dag.

De twee bommen explodeerden tegelijkertijd, drie seconden voordat de kolonel van de Garde, diep onder de holle berg, de lanceerknop wilde indrukken. Hij was te laat.

Toen hij met het blote oog het dal door keek, zag Martin de hele top van de Vesting in vlammen opgaan. Bij het licht van het vuur ving hij een glimp op van een reusachtige geschutsloop, die steigerde als een gewond dier, trillend en schokkend door de explosies, totdat hij brak en samen met de brokstukken van de koepel in de krater verdween.

'Hel en verdoemenis,' fluisterde sergeant Stephenson naast hem. Het was een passend commentaar. In de krater laaide een oranje vuurzee op toen de eerste explosies waren verstorven en de bergen weer half in de schemering lagen. Martin pakte zijn radio en riep Riyad op.

Na het afwerpen van de bommen had Don Walker een scherpe bocht van 135 graden beschreven en was het dal weer in gedoken, voor de terugtocht langs dezelfde weg als hij gekomen was. Maar omdat hij niet boven vlak land vloog en de bergen zich overal om hem heen verhieven, moest hij hoger klimmen dan normaal, om niet tegen een top te pletter te slaan.

Het dorp dat het verst bij de Vesting vandaan lag, kreeg de beste schietkans. Heel even vloog de Eagle er recht overheen, op één vleugeltop, draaiend naar het zuiden. Op dat moment vuurden de Irakezen twee raketten af – geen Russische SAM's maar de beste die Irak bezat: Frans-Duitse Rolands.

De eerste was te laag gericht en zette de achtervolging in toen de Eagle over de bergen uit het gezicht verdween. De raket kwam niet over de heuveltop. De tweede scheerde er op het nippertje overheen en haalde de Eagle in het volgende dal in. Walker voelde een geweldige klap toen de raket de romp van zijn vliegtuig raakte. De stuurboordmotor werd verwoest en bijna van de vleugel gescheurd.

De Eagle werd door de lucht gesmeten. De kwetsbare systemen sloegen op tilt, de brandstof vatte vlam en liet een vurige staart na. Walker testte de instrumenten die veel te traag reageerden. Het was voorbij. Zijn toestel was stervende. Alle waarschuwingslampjes knipperden. Dertig ton metaal kon ieder moment uit de lucht storten.

'We gaan springen...'

De cockpit verbrijzelde automatisch, een fractie van een seconde voordat de twee schietstoelen de donkere lucht in vlogen, draaiden en zich stabiliseerden. De sensors wisten meteen dat ze heel laag zaten en vernietigden de riemen waarmee de vliegers in hun stoelen zaten gegespt zodat ze vrij waren van het vallende metaal en hun parachutes konden openen.

Voor Walker was het de eerste keer. Een paar seconden was hij totaal verdoofd door de schok en kon hij niet meer helder denken. Gelukkig hadden de fabrikanten daar rekening mee gehouden. Toen de zware metalen stoel omlaag viel, ging de parachute vanzelf open. Versuft keek Walker om zich heen in de duisternis, bungelend aan zijn riemen boven een dal dat hij niet kon zien.

Het was geen lange val. Daarvoor waren ze veel te laag. Binnen enkele seconden zag hij de grond al op zich af komen. Met een klap kwam hij neer, tuimelde opzij en rolde om zijn as. Koortsachtig klauwde hij naar de clip om de riemen los te maken. Opeens was hij vrij. De parachute dwarrelde het dal in en hij kwam op zijn rug in het gras terecht. Moeizaam hees hij zich overeind.

'Tim!' riep hij. 'Tim! Alles in orde?'

Hij rende het dal door, speurend naar een andere parachute, ervan overtuigd dat ze vlak bij elkaar waren neergekomen.

Dat was ook zo. De twee vliegers waren twee dalen ten zuiden van hun doelwit geland. In het noorden was een vage rode gloed aan de hemel te zien.

Na drie minuten liep hij ergens tegenaan en stootte zijn knie. Hij dacht dat het een rots was, maar bij het zwakke licht herkende hij een schietstoel. De zijne, of die van Tim? Hij zocht verder.

Ten slotte vond hij zijn navigator. Nathanson was goed uit het vliegtuig gekomen maar de raketinslag had het mechanisme vernietigd dat hem van zijn stoel had moeten bevrijden. Hij was met stoel en al op de berghelling neergekomen, met zijn parachute nog onder zich. Door de klap was hij eindelijk van de stoel verlost, maar niemand overleefde zo'n val.

Tim Nathanson lag op zijn rug, met al zijn botten gebroken, zijn gezicht verborgen achter zijn helm en vizier. Walker trok het zuurstofmasker weg, verwijderde de naamplaatjes, wendde zich af van de rode gloed boven de bergen en begon te rennen. De tranen stroomden over zijn gezicht.

Hij rende tot hij niet meer kon. Toen vond hij een holte in de berg en kroop erin om uit te rusten.

Twee minuten na de explosies in de Vesting kreeg Martin contact met Riyad. Hij verzond eerst zijn code en toen zijn bericht.

Het was kort: 'Nu Barrabas. Ik herhaal: nu Barrabas.'

Hij pakte de radio in, de drie SAS-mannen hesen hun rugzakken over hun schouders en begonnen de berg af te dalen, zo snel als ze konden. Er zouden nu overal patrouilles zijn, niet op zoek naar hen – het kon nog wel even duren voordat de Irakezen beseften hoe die aanval zo nauwkeurig kon zijn uitgevoerd – maar wel naar de neergeschoten Amerikaanse bemanning. Sergeant Stephenson had de positie van het brandende vliegtuig gepeild toen het over hun hoofd scheerde, en de richting waarin het was neergekomen. Aangenomen dat het nog even in de lucht was gebleven nadat de bemanning met de schietstoel was ontsnapt, moesten ze de twee vliegers ergens langs die route kunnen vinden, àls ze het hadden overleefd. Ze liepen snel, vluchtend voor de horde Al-Ubaidi's van de Republikeinse Garde, die uit hun dorpjes waren gekomen en de dalen in stroomden.

Twintig minuten later vonden Mike Martin en de twee andere SAS-mannen het lichaam van de dode navigator. Ze konden niets meer voor hem doen, dus liepen ze verder.

Tien minuten daarna hoorden ze achter hen het geratel van geweervuur. Het ging een tijdje door. Blijkbaar hadden de Al-Ubaidi's het lichaam ook gevonden en reageerden ze zich nu af door hun magazijnen leeg te schieten. Zo verrieden ze wel hun positie. De SAS-mannen trokken verder.

Don Walker voelde het scherpe mes nauwelijks toen sergeant Stephenson het tegen zijn keel drukte. Het lemmet was zacht en licht als zijde. Toen hij opkeek, zag hij een gestalte over hem heen gebogen staan, een donkere, magere man. Hij had een machinepistool in zijn rechterhand, op Walkers borst gericht, en hij droeg het uniform van de bergdivisie van de Iraakse Republikeinse Garde.

De man opende zijn mond. 'Een verdomd rare tijd om op de thee te komen, kerel. Zullen we er maar als de bliksem vandoor gaan?'

Die nacht zat generaal Norman Schwarzkopf alleen in zijn suite op de vierde verdieping van het Saoedische ministerie van Defensie.

Hij was er de afgelopen zeven maanden niet vaak geweest. Meestal was hij op rondreis langs de troepen of zat hij in de kelder met zijn medewerkers en plannenmakers. Maar als hij alleen wilde zijn, trok hij zich terug in het grote, comfortabele kantoor.

Die nacht zat hij achter zijn bureau, met de rode telefoon die een streng beveiligde lijn met Washington had, en wachtte.

Om tien voor een in de ochtend van de 24e februari ging de andere telefoon.

'Generaal Schwarzkopf?' vroeg een stem met een Brits accent.

'Spreekt u mee.'

'Ik heb een boodschap voor u, generaal.'

'Zeg het maar.'

'De boodschap luidt: Nu Barrabas. Ik herhaal: nu Barrabas.'

'Bedankt,' zei de opperbevelhebber en hing op. Om 04.00 uur die nacht begon de invasie over land.

De rest van de nacht hielden de drie SAS-mannen een straf tempo vol. De tocht ging bergopwaarts. Don Walker, die geen rugzak droeg en dacht dat hij in goede conditie was, raakte volledig uitgeput en buiten adem. Soms liet hij zich op zijn knieën vallen omdat hij niet meer kon en liever dood wilde dan nog langer de pijn in zijn spieren te moeten verdragen. Maar dan voelde hij die twee ijzeren handen onder zijn oksels en hoorde hij die Cockney-stem van sergeant Stephenson weer in zijn oor: 'Kom op, makker. Nog maar een klein eindje. Zie je die heuveltop? Als we daar overheen zijn, kunnen we misschien even rusten.'

Maar dat gebeurde nooit. In plaats van naar het zuiden te trekken, door de uitlopers van de Jebal al Hamreen, waar ze vermoedelijk op een muur van Republikeinse Gardisten met vrachtwagens zouden stuiten, was Mike Martin naar het oosten gegaan, door de hoge heuvels die zich uitstrekten tot aan de Iraanse grens. Het was een tactiek die de patrouilles van de Al-Ubaidi's dwong achter hèn aan te komen.

Toen hij kort na het aanbreken van de dag omlaag en achter zich keek, zag Martin een groepje van zes Gardisten, fitter dan de rest, nog steeds achter hen aan klimmen. Ze wonnen zelfs terrein.

Op het moment dat de Irakezen de volgende heuveltop bereikten, zagen ze een van hun vijanden op de grond zitten, half ineengezakt, met zijn rug naar hen toe.

De Al-Ubaidi's lieten zich achter de rotsen vallen, openden het vuur en doorzeefden de man met kogels. Het lijk stortte voorover. De zes Gardisten verlieten hun schuilplaats en stormden naar voren.

Te laat zagen ze dat het lijk een Bergen-rugzak was, met een camouflagepak eromheen, bekroond door Walkers pilotenhelm. De drie Heckler & Kochs, voorzien van geluiddempers, maaiden de Irakezen neer toen ze om het 'lichaam' heen stonden.

Boven het stadje Khanaqin hield Martin eindelijk halt en zond een bericht aan Riyad. Stephenson en Eastman hielden de wacht en tuurden naar het westen, waar mogelijke achtervolgers vandaan moesten komen.

Martin had Riyad alleen verteld dat er nog drie SAS-mensen over waren en dat ze een Amerikaanse piloot bij zich hadden. Hun positie noemde hij niet voor het geval ze werden afgeluisterd. Daarna liepen ze weer verder.

Hoog in de bergen, dicht bij de grens, vonden ze een schuilplaats in een stenen hutje dat 's zomers door herders werd gebruikt als de kudden naar de hoge weiden kwamen. Ze stelden een wachtrooster op. En daar, in dat hutje, zaten ze de vier dagen van de grondoorlog uit, terwijl ver naar het zuiden de geallieerde tanks en vliegtuigen het Iraakse leger verpletterden in een blitzkrieg van negentig uur, voordat ze Koeweit binnentrokken.

Dezelfde dag, de eerste dag van de grondoorlog, kwam een eenzame soldaat vanuit het westen Irak binnen. Hij was een Israëli van de Sajaret Matkalcommando's, gekozen omdat hij vloeiend Arabisch sprak.
Een Israëlische helikopter, voorzien van lange-afstands tanks en in de kleuren van het Jordaanse leger, kwam vanuit de Negev en scheerde over de Jordaanse woestijn om de man vlak over de Iraakse grens af te zetten, ten zuiden van de grensovergang van Ruweishid.
Daarna keerde de helikopter en vloog via Jordanië terug naar Israël, zonder dat iemand hem had opgemerkt.
Net als Mike Martin had de soldaat een stevige maar lichte terreinmotor met speciale woestijnbanden. Hij leek oud, roestig en aftands, maar de motor was in uitstekende conditie en er zat extra benzine in twee tanks boven het achterwiel.
De soldaat nam de hoofdweg naar het oosten en reed tegen zonsondergang Bagdad binnen. De angst van zijn chefs voor zijn veiligheid was overdreven geweest.
Via die wonderlijke tam-tam die nog sneller is dan alle elektronica schenen de inwoners van Bagdad al te weten dat hun leger in de zuidelijke woestijnen van Irak en Koeweit werd vernietigd. Tegen de avond van de eerste dag had de AMAM zich in haar kazerne teruggetrokken en liet zich niet meer zien.
Nu de bombardementen waren gestopt omdat alle geallieerde vliegtuigen boven het slagveld nodig waren, slenterde de bevolking van Bagdad ongehinderd over straat en sprak openlijk over de komst van de Amerikanen en de Britten om Saddam Hoessein te verdrijven.
Het was een euforie die een week zou duren, totdat duidelijk werd dat de geallieerden niet naar Bagdad kwamen en de AMAM haar terreur weer vestigde.
Op het centrale busstation wemelde het van de soldaten, de meesten in ondergoed, omdat ze hun uniformen in de woestijn hadden weggegooid. Het waren deserteurs die aan de executiepelotons achter de frontlinie waren ontkomen. Ze verkochten hun Kalasjnikovs voor de prijs van een buskaartje naar huis. Aan het begin van de week leverden de geweren nog vijfendertig dinar op, vier dagen later was de prijs al gezakt tot zeventien.
De Israëlische infiltrant had maar één opdracht, die hij 's nachts uitvoerde.

De Mossad kende drie 'brievenbussen' die Alfonso Benz Moncada voor zijn contacten met Jericho had gebruikt voordat hij in augustus was vertrokken. Toevallig had Martin twee van de drie geschrapt om veiligheidsredenen, maar de derde was nog in gebruik.

De Israëli liet drie identieke boodschappen in de 'brievenbussen' achter, zette de bijbehorende krijttekens op de muren en reed op zijn motor naar het westen terug, in de file van vluchtelingen die dezelfde kant uit trokken.

Het kostte hem nog een dag om de grens te bereiken. Daar verliet hij de hoofdweg in zuidelijke richting, reed de verlaten woestijn in, stak de grens met Jordanië over, groef zijn verborgen richtingsbaken op en gebruikte het.

Het signaal werd meteen opgepikt door een Israëlisch vliegtuig dat boven de Negev cirkelde, en de helikopter keerde terug om de infiltrant op te halen.

Hij had vijftig uur niet geslapen en maar weinig gegeten, maar hij had zijn missie volbracht en was ongedeerd thuisgekomen.

Op de derde dag van de grondoorlog kwam Edith Hardenberg verbaasd en boos op kantoor. De vorige ochtend, toen ze juist naar de bank wilde vertrekken, was ze opgebeld.

De spreker had zich in vloeiend Duits met een Salzburger accent als een buurman van haar moeder voorgesteld. Hij vertelde haar dat Frau Hardenberg van de trap was gevallen toen het glad was, en dat het niet goed met haar ging.

Edith probeerde haar moeder te bellen, maar kreeg voortdurend de ingesprektoon. In paniek belde ze de centrale in Salzburg, die haar meedeelde dat de aansluiting buiten bedrijf moest zijn.

Ze belde de bank dat ze niet op haar werk zou komen en reed naar Salzburg in de regen en de natte sneeuw. Tegen het einde van de ochtend kwam ze aan. Haar moeder, die niets mankeerde, was verbaasd haar te zien. Ze was helemaal niet gevallen. Maar een of andere vandaal had wel haar telefoonlijn doorgesneden buiten de flat.

Tegen de tijd dat Edith in Wenen terugkwam, was het te laat om nog naar haar werk te gaan.

De volgende dag trof ze Wolfgang Gemütlich in een nog slechter humeur dan zijzelf. Hij maakte haar bittere verwijten over haar afwezigheid de vorige dag en luisterde nors naar haar verklaring.

De reden voor zijn eigen somberheid werd al snel duidelijk. De vorige ochtend was er een jongeman op de bank verschenen die hem wilde spreken.

De bezoeker zei dat hij Aziz heette en dat hij de zoon was van de eigenaar van een forse nummerrekening. Zijn vader, verklaarde de Arabier, kon zelf niet komen maar had zijn zoon gestuurd.

Daarop had Aziz junior papieren overlegd die hem een volledige machtiging gaven als afgezant van zijn vader, met toegang tot de nummerrekening. Herr Gemütlich had de papieren uitvoerig bestudeerd, maar ze waren in orde. Hij had geen andere keus gehad dan meewerken.

De ellendeling had beweerd dat zijn vader de rekening wilde opheffen en al het geld wilde laten overmaken. Ongehoord, Fräulein Hardenberg! En dat terwijl er pas twee dagen geleden nog drie miljoen dollar op de rekening was gestort, waarmee het totaal op ruim tien miljoen dollar was gekomen.

Edith Hardenberg hoorde het verhaal zwijgend aan en vroeg toen naar de bezoeker. Ja, antwoordde Herr Gemütlich, zijn voornaam was Karim. En nu ze het zei, hij droeg inderdaad een zegelring met een roze opaal aan de pink van zijn ene hand en hij had een litteken op zijn kin.

Als hij zich niet zo had vastgebeten in zijn eigen verontwaardiging, had de bankier zich misschien afgevraagd hoe zijn secretaresse zoveel wist van een man die ze nooit eerder had gezien.

Natuurlijk had hij geweten dat de rekeninghouder een of andere Arabier was geweest, gaf Gemütlich toe. Maar hij had geen idee dat de man uit Irak kwam en dat hij een zoon had.

Toen ze van haar werk thuiskwam, begon Edith Hardenberg haar kleine flat schoon te maken. Urenlang was ze aan het boenen en schrobben. Ze bracht twee kartonnen dozen naar de grote vuilniscontainer honderd meter verderop. In de ene zaten make-upspullen, parfum, lotions en badzout, in de andere een verzameling damesondergoed. Daarna ging ze weer verder met schoonmaken.

Buren zeiden later dat ze de hele avond tot laat in de nacht platen had gedraaid. Niet haar gebruikelijke Mozart en Strauss, maar Verdi, en speciaal iets uit *Nabucco*. Een zeer oplettende buurman had zelfs het Slavenkoor herkend, dat ze voortdurend had gespeeld.

In de kleine uurtjes stopte de muziek en vertrok ze in haar auto, met twee dingen uit haar keuken.

Een gepensioneerde accountant die de volgende morgen om zeven uur zijn hondje uitliet in het Prater, ontdekte haar. Hij was van de Hauptallee afgedwaald om zijn hond in de bosjes zijn behoeften te laten doen.

Ze droeg haar nette grijze tweedjas, met haar haar in een knotje in haar nek, dikke katoenen kousen en zakelijke platte schoenen. De waslijn die ze over de tak van een eik had geslingerd had haar niet in de steek gelaten. Het keukentrapje lag een meter verderop.

Ze was heel stil en stijf in de dood, met haar handen langs haar zij en haar tenen keurig omlaag. Ze was altijd een keurige dame geweest, Edith Hardenberg.

De 28e februari was de laatste dag van de grondoorlog. In de Iraakse woestijnen ten westen van Koeweit was het Iraakse leger omsingeld en verpletterd. De divisies van de Republikeinse Garde die op 2 augustus het land waren binnengevallen en zich ten zuiden van Koeweit Stad hadden gelegerd, bestonden niet meer. Op 28 februari hadden de bezettingstroepen alles in brand gestoken dat maar wilde branden, en de rest zoveel mogelijk vernietigd. Daarna waren ze naar het noorden vertrokken in een lange slang van rupsvoertuigen, trucks, kleine vrachtwagens, auto's en karren.

De colonne werd overvallen op het punt waar de hoofdweg naar het noorden de Matla-heuvelrug kruist. De Eagles en Jaguars, Tomcats en Hornets, Tornado's en Thunderbolts, Phantoms en Apaches doken op de weg af en veranderden de colonne in een verkoolde puinhoop. Toen de voorste wrakken de weg versperden, kon de rest geen kant meer uit, en de heuvels aan weerszijden maakten iedere ontsnapping onmogelijk. Veel soldaten stierven in die colonne. De rest gaf zich over. Tegen het ochtendgloren trokken de eerste Arabische troepen Koeweit binnen om de stad te bevrijden.

Die avond nam Mike Martin weer contact op met Riyad en hoorde het nieuws. Hij noemde zijn positie en die van een redelijk vlakke wei, dicht in de buurt.

De SAS-mannen en Don Walker hadden geen eten meer, smolten sneeuw als drinkwater, en hadden het bitter koud. Maar ze durfden geen vuur te maken uit angst zich te verraden. De oorlog was voorbij, maar de patrouilles van de bergdivisie wisten dat misschien niet of zouden zich er weinig van aantrekken.

Kort na het eerste ochtendlicht werden ze opgehaald door twee lange-afstands Blackhawk-helikopters die door de Amerikaanse 101e Luchtlandingsdivisie aan de SAS waren geleend. De afstand vanaf de Saoedische grens was zo groot dat ze waren vertrokken van het basiskamp dat de 101e divisie tachtig kilometer binnen Irak had ingericht na de grootste helikopteraanval uit de geschiedenis. Maar zelfs vanaf die basis aan de rivier de Eufraat was het nog een lange tocht naar de bergen in het grensgebied bij Khanaqin.

Daarom waren ze met z'n tweeën. De tweede had nog meer brandstof bij zich voor de terugreis.

Voor alle zekerheid cirkelden er acht Eagles hoog in de lucht, om voor dekking te zorgen toen de heli's op het weitje bijtankten. Don Walker tuurde naar boven.

'Hé, dat zijn mijn jongens!' riep hij. Toen de twee Blackhawks aan de terugtocht begonnen, werden ze door de Strike Eagles geëscorteerd tot ze ten zuiden van de grens waren.

Ze namen afscheid van elkaar op een winderige zandvlakte, tussen de wrakstukken van een verslagen leger bij de Saoedisch-Iraakse grens. De rotorbladen van een van de Blackhawks wierpen zand en steentjes omhoog voordat hij Don Walker terugbracht naar Dhahran, waar hij op een ander vliegtuig stapte naar Al Kharz. Wat verderop stond een Britse Puma die de SAS-mannen naar hun eigen geheime, afgegrendelde basis vervoerde.

Die avond, in een comfortabel landhuis in het glooiende Sussex, kreeg dr. Terry Martin te horen waar zijn broer in werkelijkheid sinds oktober was geweest en dat hij heelhuids uit Irak was teruggekeerd.

De academicus voelde zich bijna misselijk van opluchting. De SIS bracht hem terug naar Londen, waar hij zijn leven als docent aan de School voor Oosterse en Afrikaanse Studies weer opvatte.

Twee dagen later, op 3 maart, kwamen de bevelhebbers van de Coalitietroepen bijeen in een tent op een klein, kaal Iraaks vliegveldje genaamd Safwan, om met twee generaals uit Bagdad de overgave te bespreken.

De enige woordvoerders aan geallieerde kant waren generaal Norman Schwarzkopf en prins Khalid bin Sultan. Naast de Amerikaanse commandant zat de bevelhebber van de Britse strijdkrachten, generaal Sir Peter de la Billière.

De twee Westerse officieren denken nog altijd dat er die dag maar twee Iraakse generaals naar Safwan kwamen. Maar het waren er drie.

De Amerikanen hadden strenge veiligheidsmaatregelen getroffen om mogelijke aanslagen te voorkomen. Een hele Amerikaanse divisie lag rond het vliegveld, met de wapens naar buiten gericht.

In tegenstelling tot de geallieerde bevelhebbers, die met helikopters uit het zuiden waren gearriveerd, had de Iraakse afvaardiging bevel gekregen om naar een kruispunt ten noorden van het vliegveld te rijden. Daar moesten ze hun auto's achterlaten en overstappen in enkele Amerikaanse pantserjeeps, zogenaamde Humvees, die door Amerikaanse chauffeurs naar het vliegveld en de tenten werden gereden, drie kilometer verderop.

Tien minuten nadat de generaals met hun tolken in de onderhandelingstent waren verdwenen, kwam er nog een zwarte Mercedes-limousine uit de richting van Basra naar het kruispunt toe. De wachtposten bij de wegversperring stonden onder bevel van een kapitein van de Amerikaanse 7e Pantserbrigade. Alle hogere officieren waren naar het vliegveldje vertrokken. De onverwachte limousine werd meteen aangehouden.

Achterin zat een derde Iraakse generaal, of eigenlijk een brigadegeneraal, met een zwart koffertje op zijn schoot. Hij en zijn chauffeur spraken geen Engels en de kapitein zeker geen Arabisch. Hij wilde het vliegveld al via de radio om orders vragen toen er een jeep met een Amerikaanse kolonel achter het stuur en een tweede kolonel achterin kwam aanrijden. De bestuurder droeg het uniform van de Speciale Eenheden, de Groene Baretten, de man achterin had de onderscheidingstekens van de G2, de militaire inlichtingendienst.

De twee mannen toonden hun legitimatie aan de kapitein, die de pasjes bekeek, ze weer teruggaf en salueerde.

'Het is in orde, kapitein. We verwachtten deze vent al,' zei de kolonel van de Groene Baretten. 'Blijkbaar is hij vertraagd door een lekke band.'

'Daarin,' zei de G2-officier, wijzend op het koffertje van de Iraakse brigadegeneraal, die nu niet-begrijpend naast de auto stond, 'zitten de namen van al onze krijgsgevangenen, onder wie de vermiste vliegers. Stormin' Norman wil die namen. Nu meteen.'

Er waren geen Humvees meer. De kolonel van de Groene Baretten gaf de Irakees een harde duw in de richting van de jeep. De kapitein stond perplex. Hij wist niets over een derde Iraakse generaal. Maar hij wist wel dat zijn eenheid het kort geleden bij de Beer had verbruid door te beweren dat ze Safwan hadden ingenomen terwijl dat niet zo was. Het laatste wat hij wilde was de 7e Pantserdivisie nog meer problemen met generaal Schwarzkopf bezorgen door iemand met de lijst van vermiste Amerikaanse vliegers tegen te houden. De jeep vertrok in de richting van Safwan. De kapitein haalde zijn schouders op en gebaarde naar de Iraakse chauffeur dat hij zijn auto bij de andere kon zetten.

Op weg naar het vliegveld reed de jeep tussen rijen geparkeerde Amerikaanse tanks en pantserwagens door. Het kordon was wel anderhalve kilometer lang. Daarna volgde een verlaten gedeelte tot aan de ring van Apache-helikopters rondom de tenten waar de onderhandelingen werden gevoerd.

Toen ze de tanks voorbij waren, draaide de G2-kolonel zich om naar de Irakees en zei in goed Arabisch: 'Ze liggen onder uw bank. Niet uitstappen, maar trek ze aan.'

De Irakees droeg het donkergroene uniform van zijn land. De opgerolde kleren onder de bank hadden de geelbruine kleur van een kolonel van de Saoedische Speciale Eenheden. Snel trok hij het andere jasje en de broek aan, en zette de baret op.

Vlak voor de ring van Apaches sloeg de jeep af, de woestijn in, reed het vliegveld voorbij en verdween naar het zuiden. Aan de andere kant van Safwan kwam hij op de hoofdweg naar Koeweit Stad, dertig kilometer verderop.

Overal stonden Amerikaanse tanks, met hun loop naar buiten gericht, tegen eventuele aanvallers. De commandanten zagen een van hun eigen jeeps met twee Amerikaanse kolonels en een Saoedische officier vanaf het vliegveld wegrijden, de andere kant op. Dat was hun zaak niet.

Het kostte de jeep bijna een uur om het vliegveld van Koeweit te bereiken, dat door de Irakezen volledig was verwoest en schuilging onder de zwarte rookwolken van de oliebranden die overal in het emiraat woedden. Het duurde zo lang omdat de jeep, om de met wrakken bezaaide weg naar de Matla-heuvelrug te mijden, een omweg maakte door de woestijn ten westen van de stad.

Acht kilometer voor het vliegveld pakte de G2-kolonel een zendertje uit het dashboardkastje en zond een reeks pieptonen uit. Boven het vliegveld naderde een toestel.

De geïmproviseerde verkeerstoren was ondergebracht in een trailer bemand door Amerikanen. Het naderende vliegtuig was een HS-125 van British Aerospace. Dat niet alleen, maar het was ook het privé-vliegtuig van de Britse commandant, generaal De la Billière. Dat moest wel. Het had de juiste kleuren en het juiste roepsein. De verkeersleider gaf het toestemming om te landen.

De HS-125 taxiede niet naar de puinhopen van de aankomsthal maar naar een uithoek van het vliegveld, waar hij een Amerikaanse jeep ontmoette. De deur ging open, de trap werd neergelaten en drie mannen stapten aan boord van de twin-jet.

'Granby One, verzoek toestemming om op te stijgen,' hoorde de verkeersleider. Hij was juist bezig met het binnenloodsen van een Canadese Hercules met medicijnen voor het ziekenhuis.

'Wacht even, Granby One. Wat is uw vluchtplan?'

Hij bedoelde, en dat was een snelle reactie: waar ga je verdomme naartoe?

'Sorry, Koeweit Toren,' antwoordde een stem met een duidelijk Brits accent, honderd procent RAF. De verkeersleider kende die stemmen. Ze klonken allemaal hetzelfde. Heel zelfverzekerd.

'Koeweit Toren, we hebben zojuist een kolonel van de Saoedische Speciale Eenheden aan boord genomen. Hij is ernstig ziek. Een staflid van prins Khalid. Generaal Schwarzkopf heeft gevraagd of we hem onmiddellijk wilden evacueren, daarom heeft Sir Peter zijn eigen toestel aangeboden. We verzoeken toestemming om op te stijgen, beste kerel.'

In bijna dezelfde ademtocht had de Britse piloot één generaal, één prins en een hoge Britse officier genoemd. De verkeersleider was een eerste sergeant, en goed in zijn werk. Hij had een veelbelovende carrière bij de Amerikaanse luchtmacht. Als hij zou weigeren een zieke Saoedische kolonel van de staf van een prins op verzoek van een generaal met het vliegtuig van de Britse commandant te laten vertrekken, zou dat zijn carrière waarschijnlijk geen goed doen.

'Granby One, u kunt vertrekken,' zei hij.

De HS-125 steeg op van Koeweit. Het toestel vloog niet naar Riyad, dat een van de beste ziekenhuizen in het Midden-Oosten heeft, maar zette koers naar het westen, langs de noordgrens van het koninkrijk.

De altijd attente AWACS zag het en vroeg wat zijn bestemming was. Deze keer antwoordde de geaffecteerde Britse stem dat ze naar de Britse basis bij Akrotiri op Cyprus vlogen om een goede vriend en mede-officier van generaal De la Billière, die ernstig gewond was geraakt door een landmijn, naar huis te brengen. De missiecommandant aan boord van de AWACS wist nergens van, maar vroeg zich af wat hij eraan kon doen. Het toestel laten neerschieten?

Vijftien minuten later verliet de HS-125 het Saoedische luchtruim en stak de grens met Jordanië over.

De Irakees achter in de luxe jet wist daar allemaal niets van, maar hij was onder de indruk van de efficiëntie van de Britten en Amerikanen. Hij had zijn twijfels gehad bij het laatste bericht dat hij van zijn Westerse opdrachtgevers had ontvangen, maar had toch besloten om eieren voor zijn geld te kiezen en nu zijn land te ontvluchten in plaats van later, zonder hulp. En het plan dat in de boodschap uiteen was gezet, liep op rolletjes.

Een van de twee piloten in een RAF-tropenuniform kwam uit de cockpit naar achteren en mompelde iets tegen de Amerikaanse G2-kolonel, die grinnikte. 'Welkom in de vrije wereld, generaal,' zei hij in het Arabisch tegen zijn gast. 'We hebben het Saoedische luchtruim achter ons gelaten. Straks zetten we u op een vliegtuig naar Amerika. O ja, ik heb nog iets voor u.'

Hij haalde een velletje papier uit zijn borstzakje en liet het de Irakees zien, die het met groot genoegen las. Het was een simpel getal: zijn banksaldo in Wenen, nu meer dan tien miljoen dollar.

De Groene Baret haalde een paar glazen uit een kastje en wat mini-flesjes whisky. Hij schonk een flesje in ieder glas en deelde de glazen rond.

'Goed, mijn vriend, op een rijk en rustig leven.'

Hij proostte. De andere Amerikaan ook. De Irakees lachte en dronk.

'U kunt wel even slapen,' zei de G2-kolonel in het Arabisch. 'We zijn er binnen een uur.'

Daarna lieten ze hem met rust. Hij legde zijn hoofd tegen het kussen van zijn stoel en dacht terug aan de afgelopen twintig weken, die zijn fortuin hadden gemaakt.

Hij had grote risico's genomen, maar niet voor niets. Hij herinnerde zich nog de dag dat hij in die vergaderzaal in het presidentiële paleis had gezeten en de *Rais* had horen zeggen dat Irak eindelijk, nog net op tijd, zijn eigen atoombom had ontwikkeld. Dat was een echte schok voor hem geweest, net als het verbreken van het contact nadat hij het bericht aan de Amerikanen had doorgegeven.

Maar opeens hadden ze zich weer gemeld, dringender dan ooit, omdat ze wilden weten waar het wapen lag.

Hij had geen flauw idee, maar voor een bedrag van vijf miljoen dollar was hij tot veel bereid. En het was eenvoudiger gebleken dan hij had kunnen dromen.

Ze hadden die vervloekte nucleaire ingenieur, dr. Salah Siddiqui, gewoon in Bagdad van de straat opgepikt en hem er onder martelingen van beschuldigd dat hij de plaats van zijn eigen geesteskind had verraden. In zijn heftige protesten had hij Al-Qubai en de camouflage van de autosloperij genoemd. Hoe had de geleerde kunnen weten dat hij drie dagen vóór het bombardement was ondervraagd, en niet twee dagen erna?

De volgende schok voor Jericho was het bericht over het neerschieten van de twee Britse vliegers. Dat had hij niet voorzien. Hij móest erachter komen of ze wisten hoe de informatie op het geallieerde hoofdkwartier terecht was gekomen.

Het was een geweldige opluchting dat ze niets anders wisten dan het doel van hun missie, en dat Al-Qubai een munitiedepot zou kunnen zijn. Maar opeens had de *Rais* geroepen dat er een verrader in het spel was. En dus moest dr. Siddiqui, die in een cel onder de Gymzaal zat vastgeketend, uit de weg worden geruimd. Dat was gebeurd met een zware injectie van zuurstof in het hart, waardoor een embolie was ontstaan.

Het protocol over het tijdstip van zijn verhoor, van drie dagen vóór het bombardement tot twee dagen erna, was aangepast.

Maar de allergrootste schok was toen hij hoorde dat de geallieerden het wapen niet hadden vernietigd – dat de bom was overgebracht naar een verborgen plek die de Qa'ala, de Vesting, werd genoemd. Welke Vesting? Waar?

Een toevallige opmerking van de kerngeleerde voordat hij stierf had hem op het spoor gebracht van het grootste talent op het gebied van camouflage, kolonel Osman Badri van de genietroepen. Maar uit zijn staat van dienst bleek dat de jongeman een vurige aanhanger was van de president. Hoe had hij dat kunnen veranderen?

Het antwoord was de arrestatie van zijn geliefde vader wegens een verzonnen aanklacht en de gruwelijke moord op de oude man. Daarna was de gedesillusioneerde Badri als was in Jericho's handen geweest, tijdens hun gesprek achter in de auto, na de begrafenis.

De man met de codenaam Jericho, ook bekend als Mu'azib de Beul, had vrede met de wereld. Een slaperig gevoel maakte zich van hem meester, misschien het gevolg van de spanningen van de afgelopen dagen. Hij probeerde zich te bewegen, maar zijn armen en benen gehoorzaamden niet. De twee Amerikaanse kolonels keken naar hem en spraken in een taal die hij niet verstond maar die geen Engels was. Hij probeerde iets te zeggen, maar zijn mond wilde de woorden niet vormen.

De HS-125 was naar het zuidwesten gedraaid en daalde boven de Jordaanse kust naar een hoogte van 10 000 voet. Boven de Golf van Akkaba opende de Groene Baret de buitendeur van het vliegtuig. Een harde wind joeg door de cabine, hoewel het toestel zoveel snelheid had geminderd dat het bijna haperde.

De twee kolonels hesen hem overeind. Slap, zonder verzet en zonder protesten liet hij zich meesleuren. Hij kon niets zeggen. Boven de blauwe golven ten zuiden van Akkaba verliet brigadegeneraal Omar Khatib het vliegtuig en sloeg te pletter tegen het water. De haaien deden de rest.

De HS-125 draaide naar het noorden, vloog bij Eilat het Israëlische luchtruim binnen en landde ten slotte op Sde Dov, het militaire vliegveld ten noorden van Tel Aviv. Daar trokken de twee piloten hun Britse uniformen uit en de kolonels hun Amerikaanse kleding. Ze namen hun gewone Israëlische rang weer aan. De jet werd van zijn RAF-tekens ontdaan, in zijn oorspronkelijke kleuren overgeschilderd en teruggegeven aan de *sajan* van de chartermaatschappij in Cyprus, die het toestel had uitgeleend.

Het geld uit Wenen werd eerst naar de Kanoo Bank in Bahrein overgemaakt, en vandaar naar een andere bank in Amerika. Een deel werd teruggestort op de Hapoalim Bank in Tel Aviv en aan de Israëlische regering geretourneerd, het bedrag dat Israël aan Jericho had betaald tot het moment dat de CIA hem had overgenomen. Het restant, meer dan acht miljoen dollar, verdween in het 'feestpotje', zoals de Mossad het noemde.

Vijf dagen na het einde van de oorlog keerden nog twee lange-afstands helikopters naar de dalen van de Hamreen terug. Ze vroegen geen toestemming. Het lichaam van luitenant Tim Nathanson, de navigator van de Strike Eagle, werd nooit teruggevonden. De Republikeinse Gardisten hadden het aan flarden geschoten met hun machinegeweren en de jakhalzen, de fenneks, de kraaien en de wouwen hadden de rest gedaan. Tot op de huidige dag moeten zijn botten nog ergens in die kille dalen liggen, nog geen 150 km van de plek waar zijn voorouders ooit zwoegden en weenden bij de rivieren van Babylon.

Zijn vader hoorde het nieuws in Washington, hield *shiva* voor hem en zei *kaddish*, en was alleen met zijn verdriet, in het grote huis in Georgetown.

Het lichaam van korporaal Kevin North werd wel teruggevonden. Terwijl de Blackhawks stonden te wachten, trokken Britse handen de stenen opzij en groeven de korporaal op, die in een lijkzak werd geborgen en via Riyad met een Hercules-transportvliegtuig naar Engeland werd teruggebracht.

Half april werd er een korte ceremonie gehouden op het hoofdkwartier van de SAS, een verzameling lage roodstenen barakken aan de rand van Hereford.

Er bestaat geen SAS-begraafplaats, geen speciaal kerkhof. Veel gesneuvelde zonen liggen verspreid over vijftig buitenlandse slagvelden, waarvan de meeste mensen zelfs de namen niet kennen.

Sommigen liggen onder het zand van de Libische woestijn, waar ze zijn gevallen in de strijd tegen Rommel in 1941 en 1942. Anderen liggen op de Griekse eilanden, in het Abruzzi-gebergte, de Jura of de Vogezen. Ze liggen verspreid over Maleisië en Borneo, Jemen, Maskat en Oman, in jungles en ijskoude vlakten, en onder het koude water van de Atlantische Oceaan bij de Falkland-eilanden.

Als de lichamen werden gevonden, werden ze naar Engeland teruggebracht, maar altijd door de familie begraven. En zelfs dan stond er op de grafsteen nooit de naam van de SAS, maar die van het oorspronkelijke regiment: de Fuseliers, de Para's, de Guards of een ander onderdeel.

Er is maar één monument. In het midden van het kamp bij Hereford staat een korte, plompe toren, met hout betimmerd en chocoladebruin geschilderd. De klok bovenin houdt de uren bij, daarom wordt het gebouwtje gewoon de klokketoren genoemd.

Rond de voet zijn dofkoperen platen aangebracht, waarop de namen van alle doden zijn geëtst, met de plaatsen waar ze zijn gesneuveld.

Die aprilmaand moesten er vijf nieuwe namen worden bijgeschreven. Eén SAS-man was in gevangenschap door de Irakezen doodgeschoten, twee waren omgekomen bij een vuurgevecht toen ze ongezien probeerden terug te keren over de Saoedische grens. Een vierde was bezweken door de kou nadat hij dagenlang in kletsnatte kleren in de vrieskou had rondgezworven, en de vijfde was korporaal North.

Er waren enkele voormalige bevelhebbers van het regiment aanwezig op die regenachtige dag. John Simpson was er, en Earl Johnny Slim en Sir Peter. De directeur van de Speciale Eenheden, J.P. Lovat, kwam ook, evenals kolonel Bruce Craig, de toenmalige commandant. En dan waren er nog majoor Mike Martin en een paar anderen.

Omdat ze in eigen land waren, mochten de actieve leden de zelden getoonde zandkleurige baret dragen, met het embleem van de gevleugelde dolk en het motto 'Who Dares Wins'.

Het was geen lange ceremonie. De officieren en manschappen zagen het doek opzijglijden. De pas geëtste namen staken in trotse witte letters af tegen het brons. De militairen brachten een groet en vertrokken weer naar de verschillende messgebouwen.

Niet veel later liep Mike Martin naar zijn kleine hatchback op het parkeerterrein, draaide de bewaakte poort uit en reed naar het huisje dat hij nog steeds had aangehouden in een dorpje tussen de heuvels bij Hereford. Onderweg dacht hij aan alles wat er in de straten en woestijnen van Koeweit was gebeurd, en in het luchtruim erboven, en in de stegen en bazaars van Bagdad en de heuvels van de Hamreen. En omdat hij een gesloten mens was, was hij om één ding blij: dat niemand het ooit zou weten.

Een woord tot slot

Uit alle oorlogen moet een les worden getrokken. Anders zijn ze voor niets geweest en zijn de slachtoffers voor niets gestorven.

De Golfoorlog heeft ons twee duidelijke lessen geleerd, als de grootmachten ernaar willen luisteren.

Om te beginnen is het waanzin dat de dertig belangrijkste geïndustrialiseerde landen van de wereld – samen goed voor 95 procent van de verkoop en produktie van alle high-tech wapens – bereid zijn deze wapens en produktiemiddelen te leveren aan krankzinnige, agressieve en gevaarlijke regimes, alleen om een paar grijpstuivers te verdienen.

Tien jaar lang heeft de regering van de republiek Irak de kans gekregen zich tot de tanden te bewapenen, dank zij een onrustbarende combinatie van politieke domheid, bureaucratische blindheid en economische hebzucht. De uiteindelijke, gedeeltelijke vernietiging van die oorlogsmachine heeft veel meer gekost dan de leverantie ervan heeft opgebracht.

Een herhaling kan gemakkelijk worden voorkomen door de instelling van een centraal register van alle export naar bepaalde regimes, met flinke straffen op ontduiking. Aan de hand van het type en de hoeveelheden van de bestelde of geleverde materialen krijgen analisten dan een goed overzicht en kunnen zij al snel bepalen of er massavernietigingswapens worden geproduceerd.

Het alternatief is een verspreiding van high-tech wapens, een situatie waarbij de koude oorlog achteraf een periode van vrede en rust zal lijken.

De tweede les betreft het verzamelen van informatie. Tegen het einde van de koude oorlog hoopten veel mensen dat daaraan nu veel minder behoefte zou zijn. Het tegendeel blijkt het geval.

In de jaren zeventig en tachtig werden zulke indrukwekkende vorderingen gemaakt op het gebied van de elektronische en technische informatievergaring, dat de regeringen van de vrije wereld het idee kregen dat de wonderen van de wetenschap deze taak wel alleen aankonden. De rol van de 'humint', de menselijke inbreng bij het verzamelen van gegevens, werd steeds minder belangrijk gevonden.

In de Golfoorlog werd het volledige scala aan Westers technisch vernuft in de strijd geworpen, dat – deels vanwege de enorme kosten – als bijna onfeilbaar werd beschouwd.

Dat was het niet. Met een combinatie van kundigheid, vindingrijkheid, sluwheid en grote inspanningen waren grote delen van het Iraakse wapenarsenaal en de bijbehorende produktiemiddelen al zo goed verborgen of gecamoufleerd dat die machinerie ze niet ontdekte.

De piloten deden hun werk goed, maar ook zij werden vaak om de tuin geleid door de slimheid van de mensen die de replica's en de camouflagetechnieken hadden bedacht en uitgevoerd.

Dat er geen bacteriën, gifgas of kernwapens zijn gebruikt was, net als de afloop van de Slag bij Waterloo, 'een dubbeltje op zijn kant'.

Aan het eind van de Golfoorlog is wel duidelijk geworden dat er voor bepaalde taken in bepaalde gebieden nog altijd geen vervanging bestaat voor het oudste instrument om informatie te vergaren: het Menselijk Oog, Type Een.

Lees ook van A.W. Bruna Uitgevers B.V.

Frederick Forsyth

De verrader

Sam McCready is de pokerface van de Britse inlichtingen-dienst. Pas als alle andere geheim agenten hebben opgegeven of gefaald, speelt hij zijn kaarten uit. Door nooit zijn ware identiteit te tonen misleidt hij zijn tegenstander in situaties waarin iedereen de verrader kan zijn...

Als hoofd van de afdeling Misleiding, Desinformatie en Psychologische Operaties wordt McCready keer op keer geconfronteerd met wereldomvattende opdrachten. Of hij nu te maken heeft met de Sovjets, Arabische terroristen of corrupte politici in het Caribisch Gebied, altijd speelt McCready zijn psychologische spelletje perfect: onopvallend wacht hij af om op het moment dat de tegenstander zijn eerste fout maakt onverwacht toe te slaan...

In *De verrader* bewijst Forsyth zich opnieuw als de meester van de thrillerauteurs. Adembenemend snel voert hij de lezer van de ene spectaculaire scène naar de andere; geraffineerd bouwt hij de spanning op, niet zelden gevolgd door een verrassende wending. Sam McCready, een held van absolute topklasse, zal miljoenen in zijn ban houden.

ISBN 90 229 7979 2

Lees ook van A.W. Bruna Uitgevers B.V.

Tom Clancy

De meedogenlozen

Ex-marineman John Kelly wacht een mogelijk dodelijke, bijna
onuitvoerbare opdracht. In Vietnam stond hij bekend als 'de
Slang', de man wiens voetstappen nooit gehoord werden en
wiens spoor niet te achterhalen was.
Nu hij terug is in de Verenigde Staten, weet men hem maar al
te goed te vinden. Admiraal James Greer van de
inlichtingendienst heeft iets zeer speciaals met hem voor. Ook
Dutch Maxwell, sous-chef Operatiën Vliegtuigzaken, heeft zo
zijn bedoelingen met John. Maar pas echt sinister zijn de
plannen van de drugsmaffia, die Kelly snel en pijnlijk
duidelijk maakt dat mensen niet meedogenloos worden
geboren, maar gemaakt.
Maar Kelly vecht terug onder zijn nieuwe identiteit als John
Clark. Uit naam van alles waar hij voor staat, moet John om
zijn eigen leven te redden een grens overschrijden en betreedt
hij de zwartste diepten van de onderwereld, vanwaaruit
terugkeer zeer twijfelachtig is...

Met *De meedogenlozen* introduceert de wereldberoemde auteur
Tom Clancy, na CIA-agent Jack Ryan, de held uit bestsellers
als *De jacht op de Red October* (verfilmd met Sean Connery)
en *Ongelijke strijd* (verfilmd als *Patriot Games* met Harrison
Ford), een nieuwe hoofdpersoon: CIA-agent John Clark.
Ook in *De meedogenlozen* weet Tom Clancy messcherpe
spanning, bloedstollende actualiteit en complexe intrige te
combineren met opmerkelijke hoofdpersonen.

ISBN 90 229 8114 2

Lees ook van A.W. Bruna Uitgevers B.V.

Clive Cussler

Sahara

April 1865. De Amerikaanse burgeroorlog woedt in alle
hevigheid. De *Texas*, een oorlogsschip van de Confederatie,
vecht zich een weg door de blokkade van de Unie en verdwijnt
– met haar geheime lading – spoorloos op de Atlantische
Oceaan...

Oktober 1931. De beroemde Australische pilote Kitty
Mannock probeert een nieuw vliegrecord te vestigen. Maar
boven de Sahara wordt plotseling alle radiocontact verbroken.
Niemand vindt ooit een spoor van haar of haar vliegtuig...

Mei 1996. Op het strand van Alexandrië proberen onbekenden
de charmante biochemicus Eva Rojas te vermoorden.
Gelukkig is Dirk Pitt in de buurt... De grote vraag blijft echter:
wie wil Eva vermoorden en waarom?

Meesterverteller Clive Cussler weet deze ogenschijnlijk los
van elkaar staande gebeurtenissen op geniale wijze samen te
brengen in een nieuw, spectaculair avontuur van Dirk Pitt.
Dit keer stuurt Cussler zijn held met een vrijwel onmogelijke
missie naar de Sahara. Pitt raakt verzeild in een ingenieus maar
gruwelijk komplot van een meedogenloze Franse industrieel
en een Westafrikaanse militaire dictator.
Een mysterieuze epidemie en een onvoorstelbaar gifschandaal
vormen een directe bedreiging voor al het leven op aarde...

ISBN 90 229 8141 X

Lees ook van A.W. Bruna Uitgevers B.V.

Ron Handberg

De schreeuw om wraak

Aankomend televisiejournaliste Jessica Mitchell raakt
geïntrigeerd door de moord op Edward Hill, die terechtstond
voor verkrachting, maar werd vrijgesproken. Na zich in deze
zaak verdiept te hebben, ontdekt ze al snel dat elk jaar op
dezelfde dag een man op gewelddadige wijze om het leven
wordt gebracht. Niemand gelooft dat er een verband tussen de
moorden bestaat, maar Jessica gaat door met haar onderzoek,
waarbij zij als geen ander de principes van gedegen
journalistiek speurwerk weet toe te passen.
Jessica trekt gaandeweg niet alleen de aandacht van de politie,
maar ook van een fanatieke aanklaagster die er kennelijk
belang bij heeft dat Jessica haar onderzoek staakt.
Desondanks geeft zij niet op, zeker niet als ze op een groepje
vrouwen stuit dat onder het voorwendsel van een
handwerkclubje regelmatig bijeenkomt, maar waarvan de
eingelijke bedoeling heel wat minder onschuldig is...

ISBN 90 229 8148 7